EVERYMAN'S LIBRARY

EVERYMAN,
I WILL GO WITH THEE,
AND BE THY GUIDE,
IN THY MOST NEED
TO GO BY THY SIDE

PHILIP PULLMAN

HIS DARK MATERIALS

NORTHERN LIGHTS
THE SUBTLE KNIFE
THE AMBER SPYGLASS

WITH A PREFACE BY
THE AUTHOR
AND AN INTRODUCTION BY
LUCY HUGHES-HALLETT

EVERYMAN'S LIBRARY

342

First included in Everyman's Library, 2011
Northern Lights © Philip Pullman, 1995
The Subtle Knife © Philip Pullman, 1997
The Amber Spyglass © Philip Pullman, 2000
Lantern Slides © Philip Pullman, 2007
Reprinted by permission of Scholastic Ltd.
Preface © Philip Pullman, 2011
Introduction © Lucy Hughes-Hallett, 2011
Chronology © Everyman's Library, 2011
Typography by Peter B. Willberg

www.everymanslibrary.co.uk

978-1-84159-342-5

A CIP catalogue record for this book is available from the
British Library

Published by Everyman's Library,
Northburgh House, 10 Northburgh Street,
London EC1V 0AT

Distributed by Random House (UK) Ltd.,
20 Vauxhall Bridge Road, London SW1V 2SA

The lines from "The Third Duino Elegy" by Rainer Maria Rilke are
reproduced from *The Selected Poetry of Rainer Maria Rilke*, translated by
Stephen Mitchell. Copyright © 1982 by Stephen Mitchell. Reprinted
by permission of Random House, Inc.

The lines from "The Ecclesiast" by John Ashbery are reproduced
from *Rivers and Mountains* (Holt, Rinehart and Winston, New York,
1967). Copyright 1962, 1963, 1964, 1966 by John Ashbery. Reprinted
by permission of Georges Borchardt, Inc., for the author.

Book design by Barbara de Wilde and Carol Devine Carson
Typeset in the UK by AccComputing, North Barrow, Somerset
Printed and bound in Germany by GGP Media GmbH, Pössneck

CONTENTS

---

v

INTRODUCTION *

Night. Snow. A mountain cave. A makeshift forge. A smith at work with a hammer made of smashed rock. A fire fierce enough to fuse metal and to scorch the skin of the workers. The smells of flaring resin and singed hair and charred bone. The clangour of the work: the roar of the workman. A task requiring physical endurance, the skill of a master craftsman and the trance-like concentration of an artist. A magical knife is being repaired.

This is a pivotal episode in Philip Pullman's modern epic. Its literary ancestry is grand. Homer's Hephaestus, at work on Achilles' marvellous shield, haunts it. So do memories of Beowulf's sword Hrunting, which fails him (as this knife has failed Pullman's boy hero) in his fight with a monstrous mother. So – most insistently – does Wagner's Siegfried, re-forging the sword Nothung which will assist him in playing his part in the downfall of the old gods.

None of these antecedents, though, is mentioned. Like the Spectres, Pullman's horrid wraiths who feed on human consciousness, they are invisible to children, and adults unaware of the literary tradition within which he is working lose only one of the subsidiary pleasures Pullman's writing offers. Like many episodes in *His Dark Materials*, the scene thrums with the complex energy generated by the body of legend and myth and literary imagining on which it draws, but it lays hold of the reader by the simplest and surest of means – by swift, direct story-telling, by descriptions of sensual experience, and by presenting us at once with wonders (the smith is a polar-bear king who speaks English, and among the other people present is a six-inch-tall "chevalier" whose mount is an outsize dragonfly) and with human characters who have stepped through windows from other worlds, but who are, all the same, as funny and vulnerable and emotionally muddled as the boy and girl next door. Psychological realism of a particularly sympathetic kind, plus an imaginative vision large enough to overleap the

* Includes outline of plot and dénouement.

vii

heavens, plus a plot of such headlong urgency that the death of God can only be spared a paragraph or two before the main action resumes – all this adds up to make of Philip Pullman's tripartite story a prodigiously compelling piece of fiction.

Its two main characters are children, but *His Dark Materials* is no more exclusively a book for children than *Alice in Wonderland* is, or *David Copperfield*, or *Lord of the Flies*. The fact that all these other novels are regularly given to children to read has been a boon for the generations of people who therefore found themselves allowed to revel, sooner than might otherwise be thought good for them, in sophisticated thought and richly complex writing. Pullman's is a slightly different case. His story grows up along with its young protagonists (and with any equally young readers fortunate enough to grow up alongside them).

It is a single work, although it has until now generally been published, for commercial and practical reasons, as three separate books. Pullman himself calls it "all one story" – not a series, not even a trilogy, but one coherent piece of fiction. It does, though, fall into three parts, distinguished one from another not only by their content and narrative structure, but also by the different moral values and literary sensibilities that shape them.

The first has a single protagonist, Lyra. Its politics, its code of honour and its social hierarchies all derive from the tradition of the warrior epic. Its form is that of a quest. The world in which it is set, full of marvellous novelties though it is, is one whose conventions most readers will recognize. It is the world of folklore and romance, where animals talk and magical objects confer strange powers, where the seeker undergoes a sequence of trials, and is aided by elders – variously human and superhuman, benign and dangerous – and arrives at last at the long-sought destination only to find that not only has she/he been transformed by the journey, but that the sought-after thing has also mutated into something far richer, stranger and less easily satisfying than could ever have been anticipated.

The second part is tougher, less seductive, more morally equivocal and intellectually risky. Now there are two main characters, Lyra and Will, from different worlds, with conflicting values. Set partly in a realist version of modern Britain, this part of the story draws on modern narrative conventions – those of the thriller, of dystopian visions of environmental disaster, of science fiction. It is edgy and alarming. We are in the main characters' and the book's awkward age. The lovable lone ranger dies and there are no fatherly bears or kindly witches to help the children now – only a tired young scientist who has no superpowers but her own intelligence. In the third part story-lines, characters and moods from the previous two reappear, only to be gradually laid aside as childish things, and subsumed into Pullman's fantastically ambitious vision (inspired partly, as he acknowledges, by John Milton and by William Blake's Prophetic Books, partly by his own idiosyncratic invention), in which playfulness and high seriousness each have a place. Heaven and hell, life and death, energy and entropy, swirl around the two vulnerable young people. And amidst all the *sturm und drang*, the gaping abyss and skies full of torrents of uncanny light, Pullman finds space for joking. This is, by far, the most humorous part of the book. Confronting the Four Last Things, we are moved to awe, but we are also entertained by a comically sulky angel, and by the delightful vision of an Eden inhabited by gentle creatures with elephantine proboscises who like to hurtle around on other-worldly bicycles.

The house of fiction, wrote Henry James, has "not one window but a million", each one of those windows being a viewpoint from which an author might look out on a world. Most novelists chose just one of them. Pullman, whose hero Will can cut windows in the air and step into parallel universes, is as bold as his imaginary boy in claiming his right to more than one window, more than one genre. *His Dark Materials* is epic and fantasy, psychological realism and devotional text, incantatory poem and social comedy. And so compelling is Pullman's story-telling and so flexible his prose, it holds together. This book (not books) is a house with many windows but, as its author claims, only one story.

*

Most easily lovable of that story's three parts, the first (*Northern Lights*) is the bait that lures the reader in. It is set in a world like our own but grander, in a parallel present with the archaic glamour of an imaginary past. There are no cars, though there are electric ("anbaric") lights and zeppelins. Flocks of witches clad in tattered black silk ("ragged, elegant" in Pullman's Homerically formulaic epithet for them) wheel through the sky, not on homely broomsticks, but on pine branches more appropriate to their wild nature. It is a hierarchical world. Aristocrats are deferred to, and Pullman doesn't, at this stage in his narrative, appear to question the assumption that a leader – be it the master of an Oxford college, the chief of a troop of waterborne gypsies, a witch queen or a bear king – is innately superior to others. This – politically and philosophically questionable though it may be – is the world we know from fairy-tales, in which the lost prince may be disguised as the son of a woodcutter but will nonetheless have a noble nature. Lyra, our heroine, looks and speaks like a scruffy orphan but, child of great parents as she gradually discovers herself to be, a grand destiny has been prophesied for her.

In this world everyone has a "dæmon", a familiar in the form of an animal in which a part of his or her own self is externalized. Dæmons are partially autonomous. Lyra and her dæmon Pantalaimon converse as two separate voices – each knows things the other doesn't, they differ in their opinions – and yet they are parts of one whole, and to separate them is death to both. This device is a master-stroke. It infuses the narrative with the warmth of affection. Everyone has an ideal imaginary friend, a loving and beloved talking animal. It is also a narrative device of boundless usefulness. No one has to "think to herself". Soliloquies become conversations. Internal debates become arguments. Moments of anxiety or confusion are expressed by comical bickering. Processes of deduction become collaborations in which human and dæmon help each other along. The loneliness of the inhabitants of other – dæmon-less – worlds is rendered intensely poignant. The existential solitude, which is the normal human condition, has never looked as pitiful to those who live with it as it does to these people, who are never alone, accompanied as they are at all times by their dear companions, their kindred spirits, their other halves.

Children's dæmons are protean. Pantalaimon can be a moth, or a mouse, or a dolphin or a bird, or – most often – something sleek and furry like a mink or a pine marten to nestle around Lyra's neck as she sleeps. But adults' dæmons have fixed characters. So Pullman is able to give a clear indication of a minor character's personality in a word. A servant's dæmon is usually a dog, a villain's is a venomous snake, a heroic leader's is a snow leopard. And however smoothly duplicitous people may be, a glance at their dæmons will reveal their true states of mind. Emotionally satisfying and technically ingenious, the invention of the dæmons is also at the centre of the plot of this first volume, and of the larger development of the book as a whole and the questions it asks about consciousness. Pullman's fun is mortally serious.

So is his playing around with history. Lyra inhabits a parallel universe full of piquant variations on our own reality which remind us to take nothing for granted, in fact or in fiction. Western culture in Lyra's world is altogether less Mediterranean-facing than it is in ours. Connoisseurs drink, not French or Italian wine, but Tokay, and the collective imagination has been shaped, not by Græco-Roman myth but by shamanism and forms of magic evolved in the far north. An alternative history of the North American continent is suggested by the names of its different regions – New Denmark, New France.

Most importantly, in this imaginary world the outcome of the Reformation was quite different from the one we know. Critics who have complained of Pullman's "anti-Catholicism" have missed the point that here the religious struggles of the sixteenth century went a different way, leaving a "Pope John Calvin" and his successors presiding, not in Rome but Geneva, over a puritanical Protestant church whose authority has become so great that all secular powers are subordinate to it, and all intellectual endeavour must take place under its aegis. What we call science the people here call "experimental theology" and a device for measuring photons is placed, not in a laboratory, but in an oratory. The "Magisterium", the secular power of the church, will be a contender in the great war of the worlds Pullman is preparing.

Lyra's adventures lead her northward. Pullman's names are always meaningful, and hers conflates lyre (as in Orpheus, the first poet, whose songs were the instruments of his power) with liar (as in Odysseus, another epic voyager who never told the truth). Lyra is both a story-teller herself, and the kind of picar-esque protagonist whose progress leads her serially from one story to another. She converses with witches. She is rescued by a Texan lone ranger in a balloon who will die self-sacrifi-cingly at "Alamo Gulch" – Pullman's tacit acknowledgement that the modern Western is another form of epic. Empty land-scapes of sublime grandeur are ravaged by terrifying foes, some employing modern technology, others served by ancient magic or by wolves. Everyone – good or bad – is a fighter. Lyra has grown up brawling with gangs of children in her alternate Oxford; now she is befriended by a sequence of bellicose heroes. Here is the Gyptian (gypsy) chieftain John Faa, a kind father-figure to her, talking about his enemies: "We shall leave them ruined and waste, broken and shattered, torn in a thou-sand pieces and scattered to the four winds. My own hammer is thirsty for blood, friends." Her other protector, the bear king Iorek Byrnison, announces that "war is the sea I swim in" and his duel *à outrance* with a usurper is as violent, and as beautifully worded, as any from Malory's *Morte d'Arthur*, another work which celebrated the glamour of a blood-boultered warrior society while sorrowing over its downfall.

There are many voices, many kinds of language, in this book. Pullman, whose public persona is bluntly self-deprecating, tends to present himself, when talking to interviewers, as a very straightforward sort of story-teller. "You see, when you write for an audience that largely consists of children, you have got to put the story at the centre of what you're doing ... you can't be self-conscious and postmodern and tricksy and self-referential and all that sort of stuff that the literary types like." For all that, he varies his viewpoints and his narrative voices as adroitly as any "literary type" could. There is direct begin-at-the-beginning story-telling, but that's not Pullman's only mode. Much of the narrative is conveyed in dialogue, in interrogations, in flashbacks as long and circumstantial as that in which Aeneas told Dido the story of the fall of Troy. Pullman pulls back to give a god's-eye view of a whole country gripped by fear of the child-stealing gangs of the "Oblation Board" as they hunt for sacrificial victims. He speaks as a witch, in a refined high style, to lament the tragic brevity of human life (witches live for centuries). He speaks as a bear, grand and direct and without emotional inflection. He speaks as the Texan, Lee Scoresby – cool, laconic and witty as a gunman from *The Magnificent Seven* (another epic drama with echoes here). He speaks as the various Gyptians and professors and children who take up the story from time to time. He speaks as Lyra, finding a convincing voice for a clever, arrogant, frightened girl. Putting the story at the centre of a piece of fiction doesn't preclude employing a rich range of narrative devices with which to colour it and heighten its emotional charge, and get it told.

Until Lyra and her dæmon walk into the sky at the end of *Northern Lights*, though, we are always in a self-consistent world. Intellectually demanding as the games it plays with alternate history and parallel universes may be, that fictional world can be comfortably accommodated within the genre of fantasy written for the young. The opening of *The Subtle Knife*, though, with its abrupt shift back to the familiar ugliness of modern Britain, with its ring-roads and housing estates and helpful/intrusive social services, is a shock, a come-down and a stimulus. Readers lulled by the grandeur of Pullman's imagined icy land-scapes, and the seductive rhythms of his prose, into an accept-ance of the bloodthirsty honour-code of ancient epic are shaken back to full moral alertness as they confront the horror of an inadvertent killing in a drab suburban street. Lyra, the natural-born aristocrat who could always make herself ringleader of any street gang, is joined by Will, whose name announces his real strength, but who has been the school bullies' victim and who has for a parent, not the fearsome Lord Asriel with his angelic name and masterful ways, but a pathetic woman who panics in supermarkets and is in danger of being taken into care. As Lyra, reading her alethiometer, has to descend step by step through levels of meaning to the truth, so, throughout the rest of *His Dark Materials*, worlds will overlap and call each other's values into question. When Lyra discovers that Will is a murderer she is pleased. To her way of thinking killers are strong and trust-worthy: her father Lord Asriel is one, and so is her beloved bear-friend Iorek. But Will has a more civilized, less brutally heroic, world view. When he is required to kill he trembles and retches and passionately cries out against the necessity. From this point on, Pullman's story is full of hard decisions and incompatible imperatives, of apparently honourable courses rejected, of broken vows, and duties performed only by dint of betrayals.

Pullman's narrative is now operating across many worlds (and yes, it is sometimes confusing). There is much toing and froing between alternative realities and some Martian humour as Will has to introduce Lyra to motor traffic, and baked beans, and the cinema. There is rather too much exposition, as witches and angels and trans-worldly explorers update each other on the news of an impending cataclysm, but there is also some thrilling action. Will wins his knife, becoming in the process that archetypal figure, the wounded hero (he loses two fingers in the fight for it) who can only be healed by the accomplishment of a vow. The knife allows him to open windows into an infinite number of parallel universes. It's a marvellous implement, and, like the dæmons, a useful narrative device, but the joyous inventiveness of the work's first section is replaced in this one by anxiety. Lord Asriel, Lyra's father, has opened a great breach in the barriers between the worlds. The natural order has been disrupted. Undreamt-of perils have been let loose. There are parables here about the dangers of irresponsible scientific curiosity, about climate change and weapons of mass destruction. The knife was made in another world three centuries ago, at about the time that, in this one, Newton and his great contemporaries were laying the groundwork of modern physics. Enlightenment, clear-eyed enquiry, uncensored knowledge – all these things, as Pullman makes explicit through the mouths of his most trustworthy characters, are admirable and positive, but they can have dire ecological side-effects. In Lyra's world the ice-caps are melting and polar bears migrate to the Himalayas in search of snow. In the one where she meets Will, cities stand deserted because the splitting of atoms has released Spectres which inflict an awful slow death.

We have left epic and romance behind. The "crossroads" world in which the children meet is a lonely, discomforting one which recalls the unpeopled architectural ensembles painted by Giorgio de Chirico, or film-makers' post-nuclear visions. In Will's world we are in a Cold-War thriller, where men, whose official status is unclear, break into houses or appear unexpectedly in our young hero and heroine's paths, speaking chilly, impersonal language, and threatening violence. A villain from Lyra's world, the suave, sinister Lord Boreal, has crossed into this world as well, but the children's encounters with him are not like the great battles on the snow-fields of the story's earlier phases: they are suburban burglaries. And the children's latest adult helper, nun-turned-scientist Mary Malone has, not a fantastic ice-palace overhung by the Aurora Borealis like Iorek Byrnison's, but a cramped modern office; not a beautiful golden instrument, but a computer.

Through that computer, though, Lyra speaks to something which she calls Dust, which Mary calls Shadows or Dark Matter or anomalous elementary particles, and which someone other-wise inclined might well call God. In the book's third part the conflict, which has been preparing from the story's outset, between what Pullman calls "the Authority", and rebels intent on dethroning the supposed deity, finally begins.

Pullman has been lazily defined as an "anti-religious" writer. But though he has declared he is not a believer, his tripartite story is a profoundly religious work. As a child he lived for some time with a grandfather who was a clergyman and the splendid rolling cadences of the King James Bible sound throughout his writing. The classics of English Christian litera-ture inspire his vision of a war in heaven. From its title page onwards ("His Dark Materials" is a quotation from *Paradise Lost*), this work is steeped in the rhythms and the imagery of Milton's poetry. Its angels are like those William Blake described and drew. (Blake – mad and brilliant – first saw angels, a whole tree full of them, when he was nine years old, and kept on seeing them throughout his life.) *The Pilgrim's Progress* is a model for its narrative structure, at once that of a journey, and of a sequence of instructive tableaux. And as religious literature shapes it, so the world described in it is too vast to be envi-sioned in any artistic tradition other than that of religious painters. When Lyra and Will descend into the underworld, they pass from a war-devastated land of the living, which might have been painted by the elder Brueghel, into a land of the dead as sublimely sad as the visionary landscapes conjured up by John Martin and by the illustrators of Dante's *Inferno*, William Blake again, or Gustave Doré.

Will's angel guides, and the dragonfly-riding spies sent by Lyra's father Lord Asriel to bring her to him, all want the young pair to intervene in the great celestial war. The "Authority" is now so aged as to be a mere flicker of life (Pullman's vision of him alludes to the hymn in which he is described as "the ancient of days"). He has been deposed and lives in a crystal sphere where, like the Cumaean sibyl in her bottle, he yearns for death. The kingdom of heaven is ruled in his stead by a tyrannical regent, for whose antecedents Pullman has drawn on the apocryphal Book of Enoch. "His chariots of wrath the deep thunderclouds form", says the hymn. Pullman's "chariot" is a flying mountain, once the city of God, now a mighty engine of war, throbbing with the ghastly glow of "darkness visible". Lord Asriel opposes it from his tower of adamant, built over vast mines and foundries, the dark Satanic mills which will allow him, like Milton's Satan, to challenge the Almighty. All this is done with tremendous narrative energy – the mustering of forces from worlds beyond worlds, the preparation for Armageddon – but Pullman demonstrates the freedom of his imagination most impressively when, having set up the conflict, he chooses to ignore it. Lord Asriel is the great man of the first epic/heroic phase of this book. His challenge to an Authority who (as we know but he doesn't) is already all but dead, is too literally belligerent, too simplistically heroic to be the focus of a story which has become by this time more humane, more pacific, and more concerned, not with the big gestures of war but with the complicated creative efforts required to make peace. Lyra and Will find themselves briefly in the maelstrom of battle, but it doesn't concern them. They have more important things to think about, like death.

Their journey down into the underworld bears traces of all its literary antecedents. Homer, Virgil and Dante all provide details: the harpies, the surly ferryman, the dreary light that is not light. But Pullman makes his own imaginative contributions to the tradition: the personified deaths, so ominously polite and self-effacing, each one quietly waiting for their person's appointed hour; the humiliation of Lyra's dæmon Pantalaimon, transformed, as never before, into a pathetic little dog, a mere pet, as the greater part of Lyra's self crosses the terrible river without him; the particular form the harpies' torture of the dead spirits takes, reminding them perpetually of their failings, so that they are doomed to spend eternity in a condition of remorse and self-loathing; the dreariness of a world without any kind of brilliance, so that the flash of the dragonflies which have come along with the children is the only touch of vividness in all that great waste of featureless space and despondent spirits.

By this stage Pullman has thrown aside the mask of the simple fellow who just wants to tell a jolly good story. His chapters have epigraphs indicating the breadth of his range of references, from John Ashbery, from Emily Dickinson, from Marvell, Keats and Rilke. While Asriel and Metatron are fighting it out in the archaic way of warriors, elsewhere a woman, an intellectual, is seeking to oppose evil with good, obscurantism with wisdom, by observation and reflection, by the power of mind. Mary Malone, the scientist, is in a world where evolution has taken a different course (one might wonder how come, in all other worlds we have visited, the inhabitants are human, and English-speaking at that – but fantasy must be allowed its own conventions, however irrational). Mary is living with the "mulefa", intelligent quadrupeds of a sort Jonathan Swift might have invented had he been kinder. Lyra and Will find her there, and Pullman, himself an "experimental theologian", gives us his version – pro-knowledge, pro-sexual love – of the Fall of Mankind.

This fall – not into sin but into love and mature self-knowledge – is triggered by a story. However careful Pullman is to keep the "self-referential" out of his narrative, *His Dark Materials* is, among many other things, a story about story-telling. Lyra interpreting the symbols on her mind-powered alethiometer (truth-measurer), Will feeling with his knife for openings into alternative worlds, Mary Malone trying to make contact with an unknown consciousness by means of a computer programme responsive to electrical events in the brain, all need to enter a trance-like state like that Keats described as "negative capability" (this literary inspiration is, for once, made explicit). In that state, a mind can see beyond the mundane and immediate, into a sphere of infinite possibilities, the sphere of the imagination. And events in that sphere influence those in every other. In the realm of the dead, Lyra, whose gift for lying has been one of her greatest powers, finds that in the words of St John (the "anti-religious" Pullman is now approvingly quoting the gospel), "the truth shall make you free". But story-telling and truth-telling are not antithetical. An alert reader has been aware for some time that Will and Lyra, now on the verge of puberty, are in love but, innocent or ignorant as they are, they don't yet know it themselves. Mary, who has been told to "play the serpent", tells them the true story of her own first love. Prompted by her narrative, boy and girl kiss, and conscious life-forms in myriads of worlds are saved from extinction.

Whether the sexual awakening of a pair of pre-teens can carry the allegorical weight here loaded onto it is questionable. For me, this – its culmination – is the weakest moment in the whole, splendidly ambitious fictional project. But Pullman recovers himself for a properly heart-breaking ending in which the children return, as the logic of the story requires, to reality (two separate realities in fact), sadder and wiser for their adventures, and having learnt the lesson which this tale of a million worlds seems designed to carry: "We have to build the republic of heaven where we are, because for us there is no elsewhere."

It's a downbeat moral but, happily, for readers of fiction it's not entirely true. Imagine something rectangular, flat, so nearly insubstantial as to be all but invisible when viewed exactly sideways on, something one might pass by without even noticing it, but which gives access to an infinite number of other ways of existing. It could be the patch of oddly shimmering air Pullman's Will Parry finds on a suburban stretch of the Oxford ring-road and through which he steps, escaping the danger and drabness of his own life and finding instead transformative adventures. Or it could be a piece of printed paper – any page from a novel. While there are books of this calibre to read, there are worlds elsewhere.

Lucy Hughes-Hallett

CHRONOLOGY

DATE	LIFE AND WORKS	LITERARY INFLUENCES
		These are roughly in the order in which I first came across them, though they may have been published long before.
1946	19 October: born to Audrey Pullman, wife of Alfred Pullman, RAF.	
1947		
1948		
1949		
1950		
1951		
1952	Learned to read. Travelled by sea and rail to Southern Rhodesia (Zimbabwe), where father was posted. Caught exchanging certain forbidden information with little girl. Punished. Learned to smoke.	*Noddy Goes to Toytown* (Enid Blyton), *Just So Stories* (Rudyard Kipling).
1953	Returned to grandparents' home in Norfolk. Father died in plane crash. Sent to village school wearing absurd hat from Rhodesian school. Got into fight on account of it.	*The Eagle* (comic).
1954		
1955		
1956	Travelled by sea through Suez Canal to Southern Australia, where stepfather, also RAF officer, was posted. Encountered American comics (*Superman*, *Batman*) for the first time. Listened avidly to old radio thrillers (no TV yet where we lived).	*Hiawatha* (H. W. Longfellow), *Superman*, *Batman* (comics). *The Magic Pudding* (Norman Lindsay).
1957	Returned by sea (round Cape of Good Hope) to London. Went briefly to posh school in Belgravia. Joined local library in Battersea. Fell in love with Moomins.	*Finn Family Moomintroll* (Tove Jansson), *Swallows and Amazons* (Arthur Ransome), *The Jungle Books* (Kipling), *20,000 Leagues under the Sea* (film).

Nuremberg Trials. Churchill's "Iron Curtain" speech. Beginning of Cold War. Attlee's Labour government begins nationalization programme.

Independence and partition of India.
National Health Service founded. Marshall Plan: US aid for European post-war recovery. Berlin airlift in response to Soviet blockade. State of Israel established.
NATO founded. Orwell's *Nineteen Eighty-four* published.
Korean war (to 1953).
Churchill prime minister. Festival of Britain. Defection of Burgess and Maclean.
Death of George VI. Britain tests its first atomic bomb. Mau Mau conflict in Kenya.

Stalin dies. European Court of Human Rights set up in Strasbourg. Hillary and Tenzing reach summit of Everest. Watson and Crick publish their discovery of the structure of DNA. Coronation of Queen Elizabeth II televised.

Vietnam war (to 1975).
Warsaw Pact formed. First ITV broadcast.
Suez crisis. Hungarian uprising. Britian's first nuclear power station opens.
John Osborne's *Look Back in Anger* staged.

Common Market founded. Britons have "never had it so good", according to Conservative prime minister Harold Macmillan.

DATE	LIFE AND WORKS	LITERARY INFLUENCES
1958	Family moved to north Wales. Went to Ysgol Ardudwy, local secondary (bilateral) school. Fight on first day because of different accent. Next day changed accent for purposes of camouflage.	
1960	Miss Enid Jones became my English teacher. Under her care I learned to read properly, and took part in plays she produced. She became my first proper reader.	
1960–65		*The Magnificent Seven* (film). I have stolen profitably from it ever since. *The Pan Book of Horror Stories*, my first glimpse of the weird and gloomy world of H. P. Lovecraft. *The Golden Treasury* (poetry anthology). *Dr No* (Ian Fleming), rapidly followed by every other James Bond book then available. *The Outsider* (Colin Wilson). *The Journey of the Magi* and other poems by T. S. Eliot, and a great deal of other modern poetry. *The Alexandria Quartet* (Lawrence Durrell). *Tropic of Cancer* (Henry Miller). *The New American Poetry* (anthology), containing especially "Howl" (Allen Ginsberg). *On the Road* (Jack Kerouac). *The Marriage of Heaven and Hell, Songs of Innocence and of Experience* (William Blake).
1964		*Paradise Lost*, Books 1 and 2 (A Level text). *The Varieties of Religious Experience* (William James). *The Decline of the West* (Oswald Spengler). There was a copy in the school library, for some reason.

CHRONOLOGY

DATE	LIFE AND WORKS	LITERARY INFLUENCES
1965	Entered Exeter College, Oxford, to read English. Soon realized that was a mistake. Too idle to do anything about it. Made friends, played the guitar, drank, smoked, fooled around.	
1966		*Giordano Bruno and the Hermetic Tradition* (Frances Yates). Thrillers of every kind, up to the present day.
1967		*Wolf Solent* (John Cowper Powys). *Where the Wild Things Are* (Maurice Sendak).
1968	Left Oxford with poor degree. Began writing first novel. Moved to London. Entered period of working in offices, shops, library, etc. Finished first novel. No good. Began another.	
1969		*Pioneers of Modern Design* (Nikolaus Pevsner). *The Gnostic Religion* (Hans Jonas).
1970	Married Jude Speller. Decided to become teacher. Finished second novel. Not much better. Began third.	Jorge Luis Borges. Alejo Carpentier.
1971	First son, James, born.	The Letters of Bernard Shaw.
1972	Started work in Oxford middle school. No syllabus, no national curriculum, could teach what I wanted. Began telling pupils stories from Greek mythology.	*A Voyage to Arcturus* (David Lindsay).
1973		
1974		*The Master and Margarita* (Mikhail Bulgakov).
1975		
1976	Moved to another school. Continued to tell stories. Started writing plays for pupils to perform. First reasonably OK novel (*Galatea*) published.	*The Balloonist* (Macdonald Harris).

CHRONOLOGY

Death of Churchill. Ian Smith makes Rhodesian Declaration of Independence; Britain declares regime illegal; civil war (to 1979). First major demonstrations against the Vietnam war in London. Comprehensive schools introduced (to 1975).

Mao launches Cultural Revolution in China. England wins the football World Cup.

De Gaulle blocks British entry to Common Market. Conversion to North Sea gas begins. Abortion and homosexuality are legalized. Arab-Israeli Six-Day War.
Student unrest throughout Europe and US. Soviet invasion of Czechoslovakia. Enoch Powell's "Rivers of blood" speech against immigration. Assassination of Martin Luther King. Nixon US president.

Americans land first man on the moon. British troops sent to Northern Ireland. US bombing of Cambodia begins. Concorde's first supersonic flight.

Edward Heath forms Conservative government.

Decimalization of currency. Friends of the Earth mark UK launch by dumping 1,500 non-returnable bottles outside Schweppes headquarters. "Bloody Sunday" in Northern Ireland; direct rule imposed by Britain. President Amin expels Ugandan Asians. Strategic Arms Limitation Treaty (SALT 1) between USA and USSR. First e-mails.

Miners' strike; power cuts and imposition of three-day week. First IRA bombing campaign in London. Britain joins Common Market.
Harold Wilson returned to office. Watergate scandal; resignation of Nixon. Famine in Bangladesh.
End of Vietnam war. USSR and Western powers sign Helsinki agreement. Civil war in Lebanon. In the country's first ever national referendum, Britain votes to stay in the Common Market.
Soweto uprising in South Africa. Death of Chairman Mao.

DATE	LIFE AND WORKS	LITERARY INFLUENCES
1977		*Symbolic Images* (E. H. Gombrich).
1978		*The Shows of London* (Richard Altick).
1979		
1980		
1981	Second son, Thomas, born.	
1982	Discovered principle of recycling by turning school play into novel (*Count Karlstein*). Moved to third school. Continued to tell stories. Wrote more plays.	
1983		
1984		
1985	Recycled another play into the novel *The Ruby in the Smoke*, the first of a quartet of novels about the Victorian adventurer Sally Lockhart.	
1986	Left school-teaching for Westminster College, in Oxford, where I trained students to be teachers. Started thinking systematically about stories, and about how words and pictures work together. Fell in love with comics all over again.	*Bleak House* (Dickens), *Middlemarch* (George Eliot), *Vanity Fair* (W. M. Thackeray). I had to teach them all of a sudden, which was a better reason for reading them than I had found as an undergraduate. I certainly got more out of them.
1987		*Italian Folktales* (Italo Calvino).
1988	Published *The Shadow in the North,* the second Sally Lockhart novel.	*The Complete Poems* (Elizabeth Bishop).

CHRONOLOGY

First bottle banks.

"Winter of Discontent" in Britain (to 1979); strike of public sector workers.
Camp David agreement between Carter (USA), Begin (Israel) and Sadat
(Egypt). First test-tube baby.
Margaret Thatcher becomes first woman prime minister in Britain. Soviet
forces invade Afghanistan. SALT 2 signed. Iranian revolution: Ayatollah
Khomeini comes to power.
World recession. Shipyard worker Lech Walesa leads strikes in Gdansk,
Poland. British rule in Rhodesia (Zimbabwe) formally ends. Ronald Reagan
elected US president.
Race riots in London, Liverpool and other major cities. "Gang of Four"
found Social Democratic Party. Greenham Common Women's Peace Camp
set up (to 2000). Hunger strikes by Republican prisoners in Belfast. IBM's
first Personal Computer. First Space Shuttle mission. Wedding of Lady
Diana Spencer and Prince Charles.
Falklands war. Term "Yuppie" coined. Unemployment in Britain reaches
3 million.

Reagan proposes Strategic Defence Initiative ("Star Wars"). US troops
invade Grenada. Mobile phones first marketed.
Arthur Scargill, president of National Union of Miners, calls national strike.
Famine in Ethiopia. IRA bomb at Conservative Party conference in
Brighton.
Mikhail Gorbachev becomes General Secretary in USSR; period of reform
begins. Bob Geldof organizes Live Aid.

"Big Bang": deregulation of London Stock Exchange heralds economic
boom. British Gas is the first of many major industries to be privatized.
Gorbachev–Reagan summit at Reykjavik. Nuclear explosion at Chernobyl.

Mrs Thatcher wins her third successive general election. "Black Monday":
world stock market crash.
Gorbachev announces withdrawal of Soviet troops from Afghanistan.
Terrorist bomb destroys Pan Am flight 103 over Lockerbie, Scotland.

DATE	LIFE AND WORKS	LITERARY INFLUENCES
1989	Recycling again: *Spring-Heeled Jack*, from a school play, was turned into a book with comic-strip elements such as speech balloons. The pictures were by David Mostyn.	*Watchmen* (Alan Moore and Dave Gibbons). All the Tintin books (Hergé).
1990	Published *The Broken Bridge*, a contemporary novel about a girl in north Wales. Really a love-letter to the landscape of Ardudwy.	*The Principles of Psychology* (William James).
1991	Re-re-cycling: I made *Count Karlstein* into the same sort of comic-book-cum-novel as *Spring-Heeled Jack*. This time the pictures were by Patrice Aggs. Published *The Tiger in the Well*, the third Sally Lockhart novel.	*Collected Poems* (Wallace Stevens).
1992	Published *The White Mercedes*, a contemporary teenage love story. It was later republished as *The Butterfly Tattoo*, but the reason for the re-titling has long escaped me.	
1993		
1994	Published *Thunderbolt's Waxwork*, a short comic novel about a group of urchins in Lambeth in the 1890s, the New Cut Gang. Also published *The Tin Princess*, the fourth Sally Lockhart novel.	
1995	Published *Northern Lights*, the first part of *His Dark Materials*. It went on to share the Guardian Children's Book Award. Published *The Wonderful Story of Aladdin and the Enchanted Lamp*. Published *The Firework-Maker's Daughter*, the first of a series of four fairy tales. Left Westminster College to write full-time.	*From the Beast to the Blonde* (Marina Warner).

CHRONOLOGY

HISTORICAL BACKGROUND

Collapse of Communism in Eastern Europe. Fall of Berlin Wall. Tiananmen Square massacre in China. Fatwa against Salman Rushdie proclaimed. Tim Berners-Lee invents the World Wide Web.

President F. W. de Klerk announces end of apartheid in South Africa; Mandela released from prison. Iraq invades Kuwait. Mrs Thatcher ousted; John Major becomes prime minister. "Poll tax" riots in London.

Gulf war. Release of Terry Waite after four years' captivity in Beirut. Boris Yeltsin elected president of the Russian Republic. Gorbachev and Bush sign START arms reduction treaty. Disintegration of USSR.

Bosnian war (to 1995). Bill Clinton elected US president. "Black Wednesday": Britain withdraws from European Exchange Rate Mechanism.

Palestinian leader Yasser Arafat and Israeli prime minister Yitzhak Rabin sign peace agreement in US. Maastricht Treaty, creating European Union, ratified. John Major launches Ulster peace initiative.
Tony Blair hails advent of "New Labour". IRA ceasefire announced. Civil war in Rwanda. Mandela elected president of South Africa. Russian military action in Chechnya. Channel Tunnel opens. First women priests ordained by the Church of England.

NATO bombing campaign in Bosnia. Assassination of prime minister Rabin in Israel.

DATE	LIFE AND WORKS	LITERARY INFLUENCES
1996	Published *Clockwork, or All Wound Up*, the second fairy tale. *Northern Lights* won the Carnegie Medal. It was published in the USA as *The Golden Compass*.	*Landscape and Memory* (Simon Schama).
1997	Published *The Subtle Knife*, the second part of *His Dark Materials*.	
1998	Published *Mossycoat*, my version of the great English Cinderella story. Also published *The Gasfitters' Ball*, the second adventure of the New Cut Gang, a very good story.	
1999	Published *I Was A Rat!*, my third fairy tale.	*Duino Elegies* (Rainer Maria Rilke).
2000	Published *The Amber Spyglass*, the final part of *His Dark Materials*. Also published *Puss in Boots*, an improvement on the original, I think. The illustrations in that were by Ian Beck.	*The Literary Mind* (Mark Turner).
2001	*The Amber Spyglass* won the overall Whitbread Prize, the first time that had ever been won by a children's book.	*Exercices de Style* (Raymond Queneau).
2002		*Secret Knowledge: Rediscovering the Lost Techniques of the Old Masters* (David Hockney).
2003	Published *Lyra's Oxford*, a little dark red book with woodcut illustrations by John Lawrence. *His Dark Materials* presented at the National Theatre, with an excellent script by Nicholas Wright.	
2004	Published the fourth of my fairy tales, *The Scarecrow and His Servant*. The pictures in this, as in the other three, are by Peter Bailey.	
2005		*The Anatomy of Melancholy* (Robert Burton).

CHRONOLOGY

HISTORICAL BACKGROUND

Bomb in Docklands area signals end of IRA ceasefire.

Tony Blair leads first Labour government since 1979. IRA ceasefire restored. Princess Diana killed in a car crash in Paris. Britain returns Hong Kong to China. Scotland and Wales vote in favour of devolution. Referendum in Northern Ireland; Good Friday Agreement is accepted and an assembly elected. Lewinsky affair; President Clinton impeached (acquitted 1999).

Serbs attack ethnic Albanians in Kosovo; NATO bombing of Belgrade. Single European currency introduced; Britain does not join. Millennium celebrations; Millennium bug fails to materialize and Millennium Dome fails to impress. George W. Bush elected US president. Milosevic's regime in former Yugoslavia collapses.

Al-Qaeda terrorist attacks of 9/11. US and allied military action against the Taliban in Afghanistan.

President Bush names Iran, Iraq and North Korea as part of an "axis of evil" obstructing the war against terror. Iraq weapons crisis.

American and British troops invade Iraq; Saddam Hussein captured.

Beslan school siege. Madrid train bombings. Indian Ocean tsunami. Ten new states join the European Union.

Al-Qaeda terrorist bombings in London. IRA formally calls an end to its armed campaign. Earthquake in Pakistan. Hurricane Katrina in US. Kyoto Protocol on controlling climate change comes into force, but without support from the US.

DATE	LIFE AND WORKS	LITERARY INFLUENCES
2006	BBC TV production of *The Ruby in the Smoke* broadcast. Public unimpressed.	
2007	*Northern Lights* won the Carnegie of Carnegies, the public's choice of their favourite Carnegie Medal winner. Made Honorary Freeman of the City of Oxford. Film of *The Golden Compass*, directed by Chris Weitz, released. BBC TV production of *The Shadow in the North* broadcast. Public even more unimpressed.	
2008	Published *Once Upon a Time in the North*, a little dark blue book with more illustrations by John Lawrence.	
2009	Awarded D. Litt. (Hon.) by Oxford University.	
2010	Published *The Good Man Jesus and the Scoundrel Christ*, my attempt to persuade people to read the Bible.	
2011	Worked on film script of *John Blake*, a story first written in comic-strip form. Also worked on a version of some selected tales of the Brothers Grimm. Continued to think about how stories work.	*The Rule of Law* (Tom Bingham). *Ill Fares the Land* (Tony Judt).

CHRONOLOGY

Israeli military campaign against Hezbollah targets in Lebanon. Renewed fighting in Afghanistan. Iran joins the "nuclear club".

Blair resigns; Gordon Brown becomes prime minister. Benazir Bhutto assassinated in Pakistan. Deadliest year for Coalition casualties in Iraq.

Beginning of the worst global recession since the Thirties. Barack Obama becomes first African-American to be elected US president.

Swine flu pandemic.

David Cameron becomes prime minister, leading a Conservative-Liberal Democrat coalition. Withdrawal of last frontline troops from Iraq. Arab Spring: uprisings against autocratic rule in Tunisia, Egypt, Libya and other Arab countries. Haiti earthquake.
Western allies launch air strikes against military targets in Libya. Riots in London and other English cities. China supersedes the US as the world's leading manufacturing nation.

PREFACE

I BEGAN TO WRITE this novel with little sense of the plot, even less notion of the theme, and only the vaguest idea of the characters. I'm convinced that that's the way to do it. I tried to work out the plan of a novel once, when I was young, ahead of writing it. It was an excellent plan. It took me months and covered page after page, and in the end I was so fed up with the damn thing I threw it away and started a quite different novel with no preparation at all, which came out much better. I suppose these things are partly temperamental; I know that some excellent writers make a great thing of planning every book before they write it; but it doesn't work for me.

One thing such a technique prevents is what I think every long book must have if I'm not to go mad writing it, and that's the element of surprise. I had no idea what Iorek Byrnison, the armoured bear, would say when Lyra first came face to face with him. His vulnerability to strong drink was a huge surprise. I knew there was going to be a boy called Will, but his reason for running away and thus meeting Lyra was a complete mystery to me until it happened. As for Lee Scoresby, I was as ignorant of his existence as the gyptians themselves the sentence before he turned up. These surprises are pleasant and exciting; they feel like a kind of reward. If I knew they were coming I wouldn't enjoy them at all.

In the first sentence above, I mentioned something I called the theme. By that I mean what the book is *about*, in some fundamental sense. I've heard that some writers decide on a theme first, and then make up some characters and a plot to exemplify it. They seem to get on all right, but again, it wouldn't work for me. A book, especially a long book like *His Dark Materials*, has to have some sort of theme, or else you'll be working for a long time (this story took me seven years) in a moral vacuum. But that doesn't mean that you have to decide what that theme is. If you're working as seriously as you know how to, for a matter of years, then a theme will emerge whether you want it to or not. It'll be something you think very important. It might be the most important thing you know. Once you know what it is, you can shape the story more precisely to help it show up, but it's a mistake to rely on the theme to lead the story for you. I think I did that in a couple of places in this book, and it's the worse for it. But there we are, we're never too old to learn. Next time I shall remember: the story should lead, and the theme will emerge in its own time and its own way. Besides, if you want to write something perfect, write a haiku. Anything longer is bound to have a few passages that don't work as well as they might.

So here is a story that was the best I could do at the time, written with all the power and all the love I had, about the things I think most important in the world. I think it was worth writing. I hope you think it's worth reading.

Philip Pullman

HIS DARK
MATERIALS

His Dark Materials is a story in three volumes. The first volume is set in a universe just like ours, but different in many ways. The second volume, *The Subtle Knife*, moves between three universes: the universe of volume one; the universe we know; and a third universe, which differs from ours in many ways again. The final volume of the trilogy, *The Amber Spyglass*, moves between several universes.

Note: the word dæmon which appears throughout the book, is to be pronounced like the English word "demon".

NORTHERN
LIGHTS

Into this wild abyss,
The womb of nature and perhaps her grave,
Of neither sea, nor shore, nor air, nor fire,
But all these in their pregnant causes mixed
Confusedly, and which thus must ever fight,
Unless the almighty maker them ordain
His dark materials to create more worlds,
Into this wild abyss the wary fiend
Stood on the brink of hell and looked a while,
Pondering his voyage . . .

JOHN MILTON,
Paradise Lost, Book II

CONTENTS

PART ONE:
OXFORD

I

THE DECANTER OF TOKAY

LYRA AND HER dæmon moved through the darkening Hall, taking care to keep to one side, out of sight of the kitchen. The three great tables that ran the length of the Hall were laid already, the silver and the glass catching what little light there was, and the long benches were pulled out ready for the guests. Portraits of former Masters hung high up in the gloom along the walls. Lyra reached the dais and looked back at the open kitchen door and, seeing no one, stepped up beside the high table. The places here were laid with gold, not silver, and the fourteen seats were not oak benches but mahogany chairs with velvet cushions.

Lyra stopped beside the Master's chair and flicked the biggest glass gently with a fingernail. The sound rang clearly through the Hall.

"You're not taking this seriously," whispered her dæmon. "Behave yourself."

Her dæmon's name was Pantalaimon, and he was currently in the form of a moth, a dark brown one so as not to show up in the darkness of the Hall.

"They're making too much noise to hear from the kitchen," Lyra whispered back. "And the Steward doesn't come in till the first bell. Stop fussing."

But she put her palm over the ringing crystal anyway, and Pantalaimon fluttered ahead and through the slightly open door of the Retiring Room at the other end of the dais. After a moment he appeared again.

"There's no one there," he whispered. "But we must be quick."

Crouching behind the high table, Lyra darted along and through the door into the Retiring Room, where she stood up and looked around. The only light in here came from the fireplace, where a bright blaze of logs settled slightly as she looked, sending a fountain of sparks up into the chimney. She had lived most of her life in the College, but had never seen the Retiring Room before: only Scholars and their guests were allowed in here, and never females. Even the maidservants didn't clean in here. That was the Butler's job alone.

Pantalaimon settled on her shoulder.

"Happy now? Can we go?" he whispered.

"Don't be silly! I want to look around!"

It was a large room, with an oval table of polished rose-wood on which stood various decanters and glasses, and a silver smoking-mill with a rack of pipes. On a sideboard nearby there was a little chafing-dish and a basket of poppy-heads.

"They do themselves well, don't they, Pan?" she said under her breath.

She sat in one of the green leather armchairs. It was so deep she found herself nearly lying down, but she sat up again and tucked her legs under her to look at the portraits on the walls. More old Scholars, probably: robed, bearded and gloomy, they stared out of their frames in solemn disapproval.

"What d'you think they talk about?" Lyra said, or began to say, because before she'd finished the question she heard voices outside the door.

"Behind the chair – quick!" whispered Pantalaimon, and in a flash Lyra was out of the armchair and crouching behind it. It wasn't the best one for hiding behind: she'd chosen one in the very centre of the room, and unless she kept very quiet . . .

The door opened, and the light changed in the room: one of the incomers was carrying a lamp, which he put down on the sideboard. Lyra could see his legs, in their dark green trousers and shiny black shoes. It was a servant.

Then a deep voice said, "Has Lord Asriel arrived yet?"

It was the Master. As Lyra held her breath she saw the servant's dæmon (a dog, like almost all servants' dæmons) trot in and sit quietly at his feet, and then the Master's feet became visible too, in the shabby black shoes he always wore.

"No, Master," said the Butler. "No word from the Aërodock, either."

"I expect he'll be hungry when he arrives. Show him straight into Hall, will you?"

"Very good, Master."

"And you've decanted some of the special Tokay for him?"

"Yes, Master. The 1898, as you ordered. His Lordship is very partial to that, I remember."

"Good. Now leave me, please."

"Do you need the lamp, Master?"

"Yes, leave that too. Look in during dinner to trim it, will you?"

The Butler bowed slightly and turned to leave, his dæmon trotting obediently after him. From her not-much-of-a-hiding place Lyra watched as the Master went to a large oak wardrobe in the corner of the room, took his gown from a hanger, and pulled it laboriously on. The Master had been a powerful man, but he was well over seventy now, and his movements were stiff and slow. The Master's dæmon had the form of a raven, and as soon as his robe was on, she jumped down from the wardrobe and settled in her accustomed place on his right shoulder.

Lyra could feel Pantalaimon bristling with anxiety, though he made no sound. For herself, she was pleasantly excited. The visitor mentioned by the Master, Lord Asriel, was her uncle, a man whom she admired and feared greatly. He was said to be involved in high politics, in secret exploration, in distant warfare, and she never knew when he was going to appear. He was fierce: if he caught her in here she'd be severely punished, but she could put up with that.

What she saw next, however, changed things completely.

The Master took from his pocket a folded paper and laid it on the table. He took the stopper out of the mouth of a decanter containing a rich golden wine, unfolded the paper, and poured a thin stream of white powder into the decanter before crumpling the paper and throwing it into the fire. Then he took a pencil from his pocket and stirred the wine until the powder had dissolved, and replaced the stopper.

His dæmon gave a soft brief squawk. The Master replied in an undertone, and looked around with his hooded, clouded eyes before leaving through the door he'd come in by.

Lyra whispered, "Did you see that, Pan?"

"Of course I did! Now hurry out, before the Steward comes!"

But as he spoke, there came the sound of a bell ringing once from the far end of the Hall.

"That's the Steward's bell!" said Lyra. "I thought we had more time than that."

Pantalaimon fluttered swiftly to the Hall door, and swiftly back.

"The Steward's there already," he said. "And you can't get out of the other door . . ."

The other door, the one the Master had entered and left by, opened on to the busy corridor between the Library and the Scholars' Common Room. At this time of day it was thronged with men pulling on their gowns for dinner, or hurrying to leave papers or briefcases in the Common Room before moving into the Hall. Lyra had planned to leave the way she'd come, banking on another few minutes before the Steward's bell rang.

And if she hadn't seen the Master tipping that powder into the wine she might have risked the Steward's anger, or hoped to avoid being noticed in the busy corridor. But she was confused, and that made her hesitate.

Then she heard heavy footsteps on the dais. The Steward was coming to make sure the Retiring Room was ready for the Scholars' poppy and wine after dinner. Lyra darted to the oak wardrobe, opened it, and hid inside, pulling the door shut just as the Steward entered. She had no fear for Pantalaimon: the room was sombre-coloured, and he could always creep under a chair.

She heard the Steward's heavy wheezing, and through the crack where the door hadn't quite shut she saw him adjust the pipes in the rack by the smoking-mill and cast a glance over the decanters and glasses. Then he smoothed the hair over his ears with both palms and said something to his dæmon. He was a servant, so she was a dog; but a superior servant, so a superior dog. In fact, she had the form of a red setter. The dæmon seemed suspicious, and cast around as if she'd sensed an intruder, but didn't make for the wardrobe, to Lyra's intense relief. Lyra was afraid of the Steward, who had twice beaten her.

Lyra heard a tiny whisper; obviously Pantalaimon had squeezed in beside her.

"We're going to have to stay here now. Why don't you listen to me?"

She didn't reply until the Steward had left. It was his job to supervise the waiting at the high table; she could hear the Scholars coming into the Hall, the murmur of voices, the shuffle of feet.

"It's a good thing I didn't," she whispered back. "We wouldn't have seen the Master put poison in the wine otherwise. Pan, that was the Tokay he asked the Butler about! They're going to kill Lord Asriel!"

"You don't know it's poison."

"Oh, of course it is. Don't you remember, he made the Butler leave the room before he did it? If it was innocent it wouldn't have mattered the Butler seeing. And I *know* there's something going on – something political. The servants have been talking about it for days. Pan, we could prevent a murder!"

"I've never heard such nonsense," he said shortly. "How do you think you're going to keep still for four hours in this poky wardrobe? Let me go and look in the corridor. I'll tell you when it's clear."

He fluttered from her shoulder, and she saw his little shadow appear in the crack of light.

"It's no good, Pan, I'm staying," she said. "There's another robe or something here. I'll put that on the floor and make myself comfortable. I've just *got* to see what they do."

She had been crouching. She carefully stood up, feeling around for the clothes-hangers in order not to make a noise, and found that the wardrobe was bigger than she'd thought. There were several academic robes and hoods, some with fur around them, most faced with silk.

"I wonder if these are all the Master's?" she whispered. "When he gets honorary degrees from other places, perhaps they give him fancy robes and he keeps them here for dressing up . . . Pan, do you really think it's not poison in that wine?"

"No," he said. "I think it is, like you do. And I think it's none of our business. And I think it would be the silliest thing you've ever done in a lifetime of silly things to interfere. It's nothing to do with us."

"Don't be stupid," Lyra said. "I can't sit in here and watch them give him poison!"

"Come somewhere else, then."

"You're a coward, Pan."

"Certainly I am. May I ask what you intend to do? Are you going to leap out and snatch the glass from his trembling fingers? What did you have in mind?"

"I didn't have anything in mind, and well you know it," she snapped quietly. "But now I've seen what the Master did, I haven't got any choice. You're supposed to know about conscience, aren't you? How can I just go and sit in the Library or somewhere and twiddle my thumbs, knowing what's going to happen? I don't intend to do *that*, I promise you."

"This is what you wanted all the time," he said after a moment. "You wanted to hide in here and watch. Why didn't I realize that before?"

"All right, I do," she said. "Everyone knows they get up to something secret. They have a ritual or something. And I just wanted to know what it was."

"It's none of our business! If they want to enjoy their little secrets you should just feel superior and let them get on with it. Hiding and spying is for silly children."

"Exactly what I knew you'd say. Now stop nagging."

The two of them sat in silence for a while, Lyra uncomfortable on the hard floor of the wardrobe and Pantalaimon self-righteously twitching his temporary antennae on one of the robes. Lyra felt a mixture of thoughts contending in her head, and she would have liked nothing better than to share them with her dæmon, but she was proud too. Perhaps she should try to clear them up without his help.

Her main thought was anxiety, and it wasn't for herself. She'd been in trouble often enough to be used to it. This time she was anxious about Lord Asriel, and about what this all meant. It wasn't often that he visited the College, and the fact that this was a time of high political tension meant that he hadn't come simply to eat and drink and smoke with a few old friends. She knew that both Lord Asriel and the Master were members of the Cabinet Council, the Prime Minister's special advisory body, so it might have been something to do with that; but meetings of the Cabinet Council were held in the Palace, not in the Retiring Room of Jordan College.

Then there was the rumour that had been keeping the College servants whispering for days. It was said that the Tartars had invaded Muscovy, and were surging north to St Petersburg, from where they would be able to dominate the Baltic Sea and eventually overcome the entire west of Europe. And Lord Asriel had been in the far North: when she'd seen him last, he was preparing an expedition to Lapland . . .

"Pan," she whispered.

"Yes?"

"Do *you* think there'll be a war?"

"Not yet. Lord Asriel wouldn't be dining here if it was going to break out in the next week or so."

"That's what I thought. But later?"

"Sssh! Someone's coming."

She sat up and put her eye to the crack of the door. It was the Butler, coming to trim the lamp as the Master had ordered him to. The Common Room and the Library were lit by anbaric light, but the Scholars preferred the older, softer naphtha lamps in the Retiring Room. They wouldn't change that in the Master's lifetime.

The Butler trimmed the wick, and put another log on the fire as well, and then listened carefully at the Hall door before helping himself to a handful of leaf from the smoking-mill.

He had hardly replaced the lid when the handle of the other door turned, making him jump nervously. Lyra tried not to laugh. The Butler hastily stuffed the leaf into his pocket and turned to face the incomer.

"Lord Asriel!" he said, and a shiver of cold surprise ran down Lyra's back. She couldn't see him from where she was, and she tried to smother the urge to move and look.

"Good evening, Wren," said Lord Asriel. Lyra always heard that harsh voice with a mixture of pleasure and apprehension. "I arrived too late to dine. I'll wait in here."

The Butler looked uncomfortable. Guests entered the Retiring Room at the Master's invitation only, and Lord Asriel knew that; but the Butler also saw Lord Asriel looking pointedly at the bulge in his pocket, and decided not to protest.

"Shall I let the Master know you've arrived, my lord?"

"No harm in that. You might bring me some coffee."

"Very good, my lord."

The Butler bowed and hastened out, his dæmon trotting submissively at his heels. Lyra's uncle moved across to the fire and stretched his arms high above his head, yawning like a lion. He was wearing travelling clothes. Lyra was reminded, as she always was when she saw him again, of how much he frightened her. There was no question now of creeping out unnoticed: she'd have to sit tight and hope.

Lord Asriel's dæmon, a snow leopard, stood behind him.

"Are you going to show the projections in here?" she said quietly.

"Yes. It'll create less fuss than moving to the Lecture Theatre. They'll want to see the specimens, too; I'll send for the Porter in a minute. This is a bad time, Stelmaria."

"You should rest."

He stretched out in one of the armchairs, so that Lyra could no longer see his face.

"Yes, yes. I should also change my clothes. There's probably some ancient etiquette that allows them to fine me a dozen bottles for coming in here dressed improperly. I should sleep for three days. The fact remains that –"

There was a knock, and the Butler came in with a silver tray bearing a coffee-pot and a cup.

"Thank you, Wren," said Lord Asriel. "Is that the Tokay I can see on the table?"

"The Master ordered it decanted especially for you, my lord," said the Butler. "There are only three dozen bottles left of the '98."

"All good things pass away. Leave the tray here beside me. Oh, ask the Porter to send up the two cases I left in the Lodge, would you?"

"Here, my lord?"

"Yes, here, man. And I shall need a screen and a projecting lantern, also here, also now."

The Butler could hardly prevent himself from opening his mouth in surprise, but managed to suppress the question, or the protest.

"Wren, you're forgetting your place," said Lord Asriel. "Don't question me; just do as I tell you."

"Very good, my lord," said the Butler. "If I may suggest it, I should perhaps let Mr Cawson know what you're planning, my lord, or else he'll be somewhat taken aback, if you see what I mean."

"Yes. Tell him, then."

Mr Cawson was the Steward. There was an old and well-established rivalry between him and the Butler. The Steward was the superior, but the Butler had more opportunities to ingratiate himself with the Scholars, and made full use of them. He would be delighted to have this chance of showing the Steward that he knew more about what was going on in the Retiring Room.

He bowed and left. Lyra watched as her uncle poured a cup of coffee, drained it at once, and poured another before sipping more slowly. She was agog: cases of specimens? A projecting lantern? What did he have to show the Scholars that was so urgent and important?

Then Lord Asriel stood up and turned away from the fire. She saw him fully, and marvelled at the contrast he made with the plump Butler, the stooped and languid Scholars. Lord Asriel was a tall man with powerful shoulders, a fierce dark face, and eyes that seemed to flash and glitter with savage laughter. It was a face to be dominated by, or to fight: never a face to patronize or pity. All his movements were large and perfectly balanced, like those of a wild animal, and when he appeared in a room like this, he seemed a wild animal held in a cage too small for it.

At the moment his expression was distant and preoccupied. His dæmon came close and leant her head on his waist, and he looked down at her unfathomably before turning away and walking to the table. Lyra suddenly felt her stomach lurch, for Lord Asriel had taken the stopper from the decanter of Tokay, and was pouring a glass.

"No!"

The quiet cry came before she could hold it back. Lord Asriel heard and turned at once.

"Who's there?"

She couldn't help herself. She tumbled out of the wardrobe and scrambled up to snatch the glass from his hand. The wine flew out, splashing on the edge of the table and the carpet, and then the glass fell and smashed. He seized her wrist and twisted hard.

"Lyra! What the hell are you doing?"

"Let go of me and I'll tell you!"

"I'll break your arm first. How dare you come in here?"

"I've just saved your life!"

They were still for a moment, the girl twisted in pain but grimacing to prevent herself from crying out louder, the man bent over her frowning like thunder.

"What did you say?" he said more quietly.

"That wine is poisoned," she muttered between clenched teeth. "I saw the Master put some powder in it."

He let go. She sank to the floor, and Pantalaimon fluttered anxiously to her shoulder. Her uncle looked down with a restrained fury, and she didn't dare meet his eyes.

"I came in just to see what the room was like," she said. "I know I shouldn't have. But I was going to go out before anyone came in, except that I heard the Master coming and got trapped. The wardrobe was the only place to hide. And I saw him put the powder in the wine. If I hadn't —"

There was a knock on the door.

"That'll be the Porter," said Lord Asriel. "Back in the wardrobe. If I hear the slightest noise I'll make you wish you were dead."

She darted back there at once, and no sooner had she pulled the door shut than Lord Asriel called, "Come in."

As he'd said, it was the Porter.

"In here, my lord?"

Lyra saw the old man standing doubtfully in the doorway, and behind him, the corner of a large wooden box.

"That's right, Shuter," said Lord Asriel. "Bring them both in and put them down by the table."

Lyra relaxed a little, and allowed herself to feel the pain in her shoulder and wrist. It might have been enough to make her cry, if she was the sort of girl who cried. Instead she gritted her teeth and moved the arm gently until it felt looser.

Then came a crash of glass and the glug of spilled liquid.

"Damn you, Shuter, you careless old fool! Look what you've done!"

Lyra could see, just. Her uncle had managed to knock the decanter of Tokay off the table, and made it look as if the Porter had done it. The old man put the box down carefully and began to apologize.

"I'm truly sorry, my lord – I must have been closer than I thought –"

"Get something to clear this mess up. Go on, before it soaks into the carpet!"

The Porter and his young assistant hurried out. Lord Asriel moved closer to the wardrobe and spoke in an undertone.

"Since you're in there, you can make yourself useful. Watch the Master closely when he comes in. If you tell me something interesting about him, I'll keep you from getting further into the trouble you're already in. Understand?"

"Yes, Uncle."

"Make a noise in there and I won't help you. You're on your own."

He moved away and stood with his back to the fire again as the Porter came back with a brush and dustpan for the glass and a bowl and cloth.

"I can only say once again, my lord, I do most earnestly beg your pardon; I don't know what –"

"Just clear up the mess."

As the Porter began to mop the wine from the carpet, the Butler knocked and came in with Lord Asriel's manservant, a man called Thorold. They were carrying between them a heavy case of polished wood with brass handles. They saw what the Porter was doing and stopped dead.

"Yes, it was the Tokay," said Lord Asriel. "Too bad. Is that the lantern? Set it up by the wardrobe, Thorold, if you would. I'll have the screen up at the other end."

Lyra realized that she would be able to see the screen and whatever was on it through the crack in the door, and wondered
whether her uncle had arranged it like that for the purpose.
Under the noise the manservant made unrolling the stiff linen
and setting it up on its frame, she whispered:

"See? It was worth coming, wasn't it?"

"It might be," Pantalaimon said austerely, in his tiny moth-
voice. "And it might not."

Lord Asriel stood by the fire sipping the last of the coffee and
watching darkly as Thorold opened the case of the projecting
lantern and uncapped the lens before checking the oil-tank.

"There's plenty of oil, my lord," he said. "Shall I send for a
technician to operate it?"

"No. I'll do it myself. Thank you, Thorold. Have they finished
dinner yet, Wren?"

"Very nearly, I think, my lord," replied the Butler. "If I understand Mr Cawson aright, the Master and his guests won't be
disposed to linger once they know you're here. Shall I take the
coffee-tray?"

"Take it and go."

"Very good, my lord."

With a slight bow, the Butler took the tray and left, and
Thorold went with him. As soon as the door closed, Lord Asriel
looked across the room directly at the wardrobe, and Lyra felt the
force of his glance almost as if it had physical form, as if it were
an arrow or a spear. Then he looked away and spoke softly to his
dæmon.

She came to sit calmly at his side, alert and elegant and dangerous, her green eyes surveying the room before turning, like his
black ones, to the door from the Hall as the handle turned. Lyra
couldn't see the door, but she heard an intake of breath as the
first man came in.

"Master," said Lord Asriel. "Yes, I'm back. Do bring in your
guests; I've got something very interesting to show you."

2

THE IDEA OF NORTH

"LORD ASRIEL," said the Master heavily, and came forward to shake his hand. From her hiding-place Lyra watched the Master's eyes, and indeed, they flicked towards the table for a second, where the Tokay had been.

"Master," said Lord Asriel. "I came too late to disturb your dinner, so I made myself at home in here. Hello, Sub-Rector. Glad to see you looking so well. Excuse my rough appearance; I've only just landed. Yes, Master, the Tokay's gone. I think you're standing in it. The Porter knocked it off the table, but it was my fault. Hello, Chaplain. I read your latest paper with great interest . . ."

He moved away with the Chaplain, leaving Lyra with a clear view of the Master's face. It was impassive, but the dæmon on his shoulder was shuffling her feathers and moving restlessly from foot to foot. Lord Asriel was already dominating the room, and although he was careful to be courteous to the Master in the Master's own territory, it was clear where the power lay.

The Scholars greeted the visitor and moved into the room, some sitting around the table, some in the armchairs, and soon a buzz of conversation filled the air. Lyra could see that they were powerfully intrigued by the wooden case, the screen and the lantern. She knew the Scholars well: the Librarian, the Sub-Rector, the Enquirer and the rest; they were men who had been around her all her life, taught her, chastised her, consoled her, given her little presents, chased her away from the fruit trees in the Garden; they were all she had for a family. They might even have felt like a family if she knew what a family was, though if she did, she'd have been more likely to feel that about the College servants. The Scholars had more important things to do than attend to the affections of a half-wild, half-civilized girl, left among them by chance.

The Master lit the spirit-lamp under the little silver chafing-dish and heated some butter before cutting half a dozen poppy-heads open and tossing them in. Poppy was always served after a Feast: it clarified the mind and stimulated the tongue, and made for rich conversation. It was traditional for the Master to cook it himself.

Under the sizzle of the frying butter and the hum of talk, Lyra shifted around to find a more comfortable position for herself. With enormous care she took one of the robes – a full-length fur – off its hanger and laid it on the floor of the wardrobe.

"You should have used a scratchy old one," whispered Pantalaimon. "If you get too comfortable you'll go to sleep."

"If I do, it's your job to wake me up," she replied.

She sat and listened to the talk. Mighty dull talk it was, too; almost all of it politics, and London politics at that, nothing exciting about Tartars. The smells of frying poppy and smoke-leaf drifted pleasantly in through the wardrobe door, and more than once Lyra found herself nodding. But finally she heard someone rap the table. The voices fell silent, and then the Master spoke.

"Gentlemen," he said. "I feel sure I speak for all of us when I bid Lord Asriel welcome. His visits are rare but always immensely valuable, and I understand he has something of particular interest to show us tonight. This is a time of high political tension, as we are all aware; Lord Asriel's presence is required early tomorrow morning in White Hall, and a train is waiting with steam up ready to carry him to London as soon as we have finished our conversation here; so we must use our time wisely. When he has finished speaking to us, I imagine there will be some questions. Please keep them brief and to the point. Lord Asriel, would you like to begin?"

"Thank you, Master," said Lord Asriel. "To start with, I have a few slides to show you. Sub-Rector, you can see best from here, I think. Perhaps the Master would like to take the chair near the wardrobe?"

The old Sub-Rector was nearly blind, so it was courteous to make room for him nearer the screen, and his moving forward meant that the Master would be sitting next to the Librarian, only a matter of a yard or so from where Lyra was crouched in the wardrobe. As the Master settled in the armchair, Lyra heard him murmur:

"The devil! He *knew* about the wine, I'm sure of it."

The Librarian murmured back, "He's going to ask for funds. If he forces a vote –"

"If he does that, we must just argue against, with all the eloquence we have."

The lantern began to hiss as Lord Asriel pumped it hard. Lyra moved slightly so that she could see the screen, where a brilliant white circle had begun to glow. Lord Asriel called, "Could someone turn the lamp down?"

One of the Scholars got up to do that, and the room darkened.

Lord Asriel began:

"As some of you know, I set out for the North twelve months ago on a diplomatic mission to the King of Lapland. At least, that's what I pretended to be doing. In fact my real aim was to go further north still, right on to the ice, to try and discover what had happened to the Grumman expedition. One of Grumman's last messages to the Academy in Berlin spoke of a certain natural phenomenon only seen in the lands of the North. I was determined to investigate that as well as find out what I could about Grumman. But the first picture I'm going to show you isn't directly about either of those things."

And he put the first slide into the frame and slid it behind the lens. A circular photogram in sharp black and white appeared on the screen. It had been taken at night under a full moon, and it showed a wooden hut in the middle distance, its walls dark against the snow that surrounded it and lay thickly on the roof. Beside the hut stood an array of philosophical instruments, which looked to Lyra's eye like something from the Anbaric Park on the road to Yarnton: aerials, wires, porcelain insulators, all glittering in the moonlight and thickly covered in frost. A man in furs, his face hardly visible in the deep hood of his garment, stood in the foreground, with his hand raised as if in greeting. To one side of him stood a smaller figure. The moonlight bathed everything in the same pallid gleam.

"That photogram was taken with a standard silver nitrate

emulsion," Lord Asriel said. "I'd like you to look at another one, taken from the same spot only a minute later, with a new specially prepared emulsion."

He lifted out the first slide and dropped another into the frame. This was much darker; it was as if the moonlight had been filtered out. The horizon was still visible, with the dark shape of the hut and its light snow-covered roof standing out, but the complexity of the instruments was hidden in darkness. But the man had altogether changed: he was bathed in light, and a fountain of glowing particles seemed to be streaming from his upraised hand.

"That light," said the Chaplain, "is it going up or coming down?"

"It's coming down," said Lord Asriel, "but it isn't light. It's Dust."

Something in the way he said it made Lyra imagine *Dust* with a capital letter, as if this wasn't ordinary dust. The reaction of the Scholars confirmed her feeling, because Lord Asriel's words caused a sudden collective silence, followed by gasps of incredulity.

"But how –"

"Surely –"

"It can't –"

"Gentlemen!" came the voice of the Chaplain. "Let Lord Asriel explain."

"It's Dust," Lord Asriel repeated. "It registered as light on the plate because particles of Dust affect this emulsion as photons affect silver nitrate emulsion. It was partly to test it that my expedition went North in the first place. As you see, the figure of the man is perfectly visible. Now I'd like you to look at the shape to his left."

He indicated the blurred shape of the smaller figure.

"I thought that was the man's dæmon," said the Enquirer.

"No. His dæmon was at the time coiled around his neck in the form of a snake. That shape you can dimly see is a child."

"A severed child –?" said someone, and the way he stopped showed that he knew this was something that shouldn't have been voiced.

There was an intense silence.

Then Lord Asriel said calmly, "An entire child. Which, given the nature of Dust, is precisely the point, is it not?"

No one spoke for several seconds. Then came the voice of the Chaplain.

"Ah," he said, like a thirsty man who, having just drunk deeply, puts down the glass to let out the breath he has held while drinking. "And the streams of Dust . . ."

"– Come from the sky, and bathe him in what looks like light. You may examine this picture as closely as you wish: I'll leave it behind when I go. I'm showing it to you now to demonstrate the effect of this new emulsion. Now I'd like to show you another picture."

He changed the slide. The next picture was also taken at night, but this time without moonlight. It showed a small group of tents in the foreground, dimly outlined against the low horizon, and beside them an untidy heap of wooden boxes and a sledge. But the main interest of the picture lay in the sky. Streams and veils of light hung like curtains, looped and festooned on invisible hooks hundreds of miles high or blowing out sideways in the stream of some unimaginable wind.

"What is that?" said the voice of the Sub-Rector.

"It's a picture of the Aurora."

"It's a very fine photogram," said the Palmerian Professor. "One of the best I've seen."

"Forgive my ignorance," said the shaky voice of the old Precentor, "but if I ever knew what the Aurora was, I have forgotten. Is it what they call the Northern Lights?"

"Yes. It has many names. It's composed of storms of charged particles and solar rays of intense and extraordinary strength – invisible in themselves, but causing this luminous radiation when they interact with the atmosphere. If there'd been time I would have had this slide tinted to show you the colours; pale green and rose, for the most part, with a tinge of crimson along the lower edge of that curtain-like formation. This is taken with ordinary emulsion. Now I'd like you to look at a picture taken with the special emulsion."

He took out the slide. Lyra heard the Master say quietly, "If he forces a vote, we could try to invoke the residence clause.

He hasn't been resident in the College for thirty weeks out of the last fifty-two."

"He's already got the Chaplain on his side . . ." the Librarian murmured in reply.

Lord Asriel put a new slide in the lantern frame. It showed the same scene. As with the previous pair of pictures, many of the features visible by ordinary light were much dimmer in this one, and so were the curtains of radiance in the sky.

But in the middle of the Aurora, high above the bleak landscape, Lyra could see something solid. She pressed her face to the crack to see more clearly, and she could see Scholars near the screen leaning forward, too. As she gazed, her wonder grew, because there in the sky was the unmistakable outline of a city: towers, domes, walls . . . buildings and streets, suspended in the air! She nearly gasped with wonder.

The Cassington Scholar said, "That looks like . . . a city."

"Exactly so," said Lord Asriel.

"A city in another world, no doubt?" said the Dean, with contempt in his voice.

Lord Asriel ignored him. There was a stir of excitement among some of the Scholars, as if, having written treatises on the existence of the unicorn without ever having seen one, they'd been presented with a living example newly captured.

"Is this the Barnard-Stokes business?" said the Palmerian Professor. "It is, isn't it?"

"That's what I want to find out," said Lord Asriel.

He stood to one side of the illuminated screen. Lyra could see his dark eyes searching among the Scholars as they peered up at the slide of the Aurora, and the green glow of his dæmon's eyes beside him. All the venerable heads were craning forward, their spectacles glinting; only the Master and the Librarian leant back in their chairs, with their heads close together.

The Chaplain was saying, "You said you were searching for news of the Grumman expedition, Lord Asriel. Was Dr Grumman investigating this phenomenon too?"

"I believe he was, and I believe he had a good deal of information about it. But he won't be able to tell us what it was, because he's dead."

"No!" said the Chaplain.

"I'm afraid so, and I have the proof here."

A ripple of excited apprehension ran round the Retiring Room as, under Lord Asriel's direction, two or three of the younger Scholars carried the wooden box to the front of the room. Lord Asriel took out the last slide but left the lantern on, and in the dramatic glare of the circle of light he bent to lever open the box. Lyra heard the screech of nails coming out of damp wood. The Master stood up to look, blocking Lyra's view. Her uncle spoke again:

"If you remember, Grumman's expedition vanished eighteen months ago. The German Academy sent him up there to go as far north as the magnetic pole and make various celestial observations. It was in the course of that journey that he observed the curious phenomenon we've already seen. Shortly after that, he vanished. It's been assumed that he had an accident and that his body's been lying in a crevasse all this time. In fact there was no accident."

"What have you got there?" said the Dean. "Is that a vacuum container?"

Lord Asriel didn't answer at first. Lyra heard the snap of metal clips and a hiss as air rushed into a vessel, and then there was a silence. But the silence didn't last long. After a moment or two Lyra heard a confused babble break out: cries of horror, loud protests, voices raised in anger and fear.

"But what –"

"– hardly human –"

"– it's been –"

"– what's *happened* to it?"

The Master's voice cut through them all.

"Lord Asriel, what in God's name have you got there?"

"This is the head of Stanislaus Grumman," said Lord Asriel's voice.

Over the jumble of voices Lyra heard someone stumble to the door and out, making incoherent sounds of distress. She wished she could see what they were seeing.

Lord Asriel said, "I found his body preserved in the ice off Svalbard. The head was treated in this way by his killers. You'll notice the characteristic scalping pattern. I think you might be familiar with it, Sub-Rector."

The old man's voice was steady as he said, "I have seen the Tartars do this. It's a technique you find among the aboriginals of Siberia and the Tungusk. From there, of course, it spread into the lands of the Skraelings, though I understand that it is now banned in New Denmark. May I examine it more closely, Lord Asriel?"

After a short silence he spoke again.

"My eyes are not very clear, and the ice is dirty, but it seems to me that there is a hole in the top of the skull. Am I right?"

"You are."

"Trepanning?"

"Exactly."

That caused a murmur of excitement. The Master moved out of the way and Lyra could see again. The old Sub-Rector, in the circle of light thrown by the lantern, was holding a heavy block of ice up close to his eyes, and Lyra could see the object inside it: a bloody lump barely recognizable as a human head. Pantalaimon fluttered around Lyra, his distress affecting her.

"Hush," she whispered. "Listen."

"Dr Grumman was once a Scholar of this College," said the Dean hotly.

"To fall into the hands of the Tartars –"

"But that far north?"

"They must have penetrated further than anyone imagined!"

"Did I hear you say you found it near Svalbard?" said the Dean.

"That's right."

"Are we to understand that the *panserbjørne* had anything to do with this?"

Lyra didn't recognize that word, but clearly the Scholars did.

"Impossible," said the Cassington Scholar firmly. "They'd never behave in that manner."

"Then you don't know Iofur Raknison," said the Palmerian Professor, who had made several expeditions himself to the Arctic regions. "It wouldn't surprise me at all to learn that he had taken to scalping people in the Tartar fashion."

Lyra looked again at her uncle, who was watching the Scholars with a glitter of sardonic amusement, and saying nothing.

"Who is Iofur Raknison?" said someone.

"The king of Svalbard," said the Palmerian Professor. "Yes, that's right, one of the *panserbjørne*. He's a usurper, of sorts; tricked his way on to the throne, or so I understand; but a powerful figure, by no means a fool, in spite of his ludicrous affectations – having a palace built of imported marble – setting up what he calls a university –"

"For whom? For the *bears*?" said someone else, and everyone laughed.

But the Palmerian Professor went on, "For all that, I tell you that Iofur Raknison would be capable of doing this to Grumman. At the same time, he could be flattered into behaving quite differently, if the need arose."

"And you know how, do you, Trelawney?" said the Dean sneeringly.

"Indeed I do. Do you know what he wants above all else? Even more than an honorary degree? He wants a dæmon! Find a way to give him a dæmon, and he'd do anything for you."

The Scholars laughed heartily.

Lyra was following this with puzzlement: what the Palmerian Professor said made no sense at all. Besides, she was impatient to hear more about scalping and the Northern Lights and that mysterious Dust. But she was disappointed, for Lord Asriel had finished showing his relics and pictures, and the talk soon turned into a college wrangle about whether or not they should give him some money to fit out another expedition. Back and forth the arguments ranged, and Lyra felt her eyes closing. Soon she was fast asleep, with Pantalaimon curled around her neck in his favourite sleeping-form as an ermine.

She woke up with a start when someone shook her shoulder.

"Quiet," said her uncle. The wardrobe door was open, and he was crouched there against the light. "They've all gone, but there are still some servants around. Go to your bedroom now, and take care that you say nothing about this."

"Did they vote to give you the money?" she said sleepily.

"Yes."

"What's Dust?" she said, struggling to stand up after having been cramped for so long.

"Nothing to do with you."

"It *is* to do with me," she said. "If you wanted me to be a spy in the wardrobe you ought to tell me what I'm spying about. Can I see the man's head?"

Pantalaimon's white ermine-fur bristled: she felt it tickling her neck. Lord Asriel laughed shortly.

"Don't be disgusting," he said, and began to pack his slides and specimen-box. "Did you watch the Master?"

"Yes, and he looked for the wine before he did anything else."

"Good. But I've scotched him for now. Do as you're told and go to bed."

"But where are *you* going?"

"Back to the North. I'm leaving in ten minutes."

"Can I come?"

He stopped what he was doing, and looked at her as if for the first time. His dæmon turned her great green leopard-eyes on her too, and under the concentrated gaze of both of them, Lyra blushed. But she gazed back fiercely.

"Your place is here," said her uncle finally.

"But why? Why is my place here? Why can't I come to the North with you? I want to see the Northern Lights and bears and icebergs and everything. I want to know about Dust. And that city in the air. Is it another world?"

"You're not coming, child. Put it out of your head; the times are too dangerous. Do as you're told and go to bed, and if you're a good girl, I'll bring you back a walrus tusk with some Eskimo carving on it. Don't argue any more or I shall be angry."

And his dæmon growled with a deep savage rumble that made Lyra suddenly aware of what it would be like to have teeth meeting in her throat.

Lyra compressed her lips and frowned hard at her uncle. He was pumping the air from the vacuum flask, and took no notice; it was as if he'd already forgotten her. Without a word, but with lips tight and narrowed eyes, the girl and her dæmon left and went to bed.

* * *

The Master and the Librarian were old friends and allies, and it was their habit, after a difficult episode, to take a glass of brantwijn and console each other. So after they'd seen Lord Asriel away, they strolled to the Master's Lodging and settled in his study with the curtains drawn and the fire refreshed, their dæmons in their familiar places on knee or shoulder, and prepared to think through what had just happened.

"Do you really believe he knew about the wine?" said the Librarian.

"Of course he did. I have no idea how, but he knew, and he spilled the decanter himself. Of course he did."

"Forgive me, Master, but I can't help being relieved. I was never happy about the idea of . . ."

"Of poisoning him?"

"Yes. Of murder."

"Hardly anyone would be happy at that idea, Charles. The question was whether doing that would be worse than the consequences of not doing it. Well, some Providence has intervened, and it hasn't happened. I'm only sorry I burdened you with the knowledge of it."

"No, no," protested the Librarian. "But I wish you had told me more."

The Master was silent for a while before saying, "Yes, perhaps I should have done. The alethiometer warns of appalling consequences if Lord Asriel pursues this research. Apart from anything else, the child will be drawn in, and I want to keep her safe as long as possible."

"Is Lord Asriel's business anything to do with this new initiative of the Consistorial Court of Discipline? The what-do-they-call-it: the Oblation Board?"

"Lord Asriel – no, no. Quite the reverse. The Oblation Board isn't entirely answerable to the Consistorial Court, either. It's a semi-private initiative; it's being run by someone who has no love of Lord Asriel. Between them both, Charles, I tremble."

The Librarian was silent in his turn. Ever since Pope John Calvin had moved the seat of the Papacy to Geneva and set up the Consistorial Court of Discipline, the Church's power over every aspect of life had been absolute. The Papacy itself had been abolished after Calvin's death, and a tangle of courts, colleges, and councils, collectively known as the Magisterium, had grown up in its place. These agencies were not always united; sometimes a bitter rivalry grew up between them. For a large part of the previous century, the most powerful had been the College of Bishops, but in recent years the Consistorial Court of Discipline had taken its place as the most active and the most feared of all the Church's bodies.

But it was always possible for independent agencies to grow up under the protection of another part of the Magisterium, and the Oblation Board, which the Librarian had referred to, was one of these. The Librarian didn't know much about it, but he disliked and feared what he'd heard, and he completely understood the Master's anxiety.

"The Palmerian Professor mentioned a name," he said after a minute or so. "Barnard-Stokes? What is the Barnard-Stokes business?"

"Ah, it's not our field, Charles. As I understand it, the Holy Church teaches that there are two worlds: the world of everything we can see and hear and touch, and another world, the spiritual world of heaven and hell. Barnard and Stokes were two – how shall I put it – *renegade* theologians who postulated the existence of numerous other worlds like this one, neither heaven nor hell, but material and sinful. They are there, close by, but invisible and unreachable. The Holy Church naturally disapproved of this abominable heresy, and Barnard and Stokes were silenced.

"But unfortunately for the Magisterium there seem to be sound mathematical arguments for this other-world theory. I have never followed them myself, but the Cassington Scholar tells me that they are sound."

"And now Lord Asriel has taken a picture of one of these other worlds," the Librarian said. "And we have funded him to go and look for it. I see."

"Quite. It'll seem to the Oblation Board, and to its powerful protectors, that Jordan College is a hotbed of support for heresy. And between the Consistorial Court and the Oblation Board,

Charles, I have to keep a balance; and meanwhile the child is growing. They won't have forgotten her. Sooner or later she would have become involved, but she'll be drawn in now whether I want to protect her or not."

"But how do you know that, for God's sake? The alethiometer again?"

"Yes. Lyra has a part to play in all this, and a major one. The irony is that she must do it all without realizing what she's doing. She can be helped, though, and if my plan with the Tokay had succeeded, she would have been safe for a little longer. I would have liked to spare her a journey to the North. I wish above all things that I were able to explain it to her . . ."

"She wouldn't listen," the Librarian said. "I know her ways only too well. Try to tell her anything serious and she'll half-listen for five minutes and then start fidgeting. And quiz her about it next time and she'll have completely forgotten."

"If I talked to her about Dust? You don't think she'd listen to that?"

The Librarian made a noise to indicate how unlikely he thought that was.

"Why on earth should she?" he said. "Why should a distant theological riddle interest a healthy thoughtless child?"

"Because of what she must experience. Part of that includes a great betrayal . . ."

"Who's going to betray her?"

"No, no, that's the saddest thing: *she* will be the betrayer, and the experience will be terrible. She mustn't know that, of course, but there's no reason for her not to know about the problem of Dust. And you might be wrong, Charles; she might well take an interest in it, if it were explained in a simple way. And it might help her later on. It would certainly help me to be less anxious about her."

"That's the duty of the old," said the Librarian, "to be anxious on behalf of the young. And the duty of the young is to scorn the anxiety of the old."

They sat for a while longer, and then parted, for it was late, and they were old and anxious.

3
LYRA'S JORDAN

JORDAN COLLEGE WAS the grandest and richest of all the colleges in Oxford. It was probably the largest, too, though no one knew for certain. The buildings, which were grouped around three irregular quadrangles, dated from every period from the early Middle Ages to the mid-eighteenth century. It had never been planned; it had grown piecemeal, with past and present overlapping at every spot, and the final effect was one of jumbled and squalid grandeur. Some part was always about to fall down, and for five generations the same family, the Parslows, had been employed full-time by the College as masons and scaffolders. The present Mr Parslow was teaching his son the craft; the two of them and their three workmen would scramble like industrious termites over the scaffolding they'd erected at the corner of the Library, or over the roof of the Chapel, and haul up bright new blocks of stone or rolls of shiny lead or baulks of timber.

The College owned farms and estates all over Brytain. It was said that you could walk from Oxford to Bristol in one direction and to London in the other, and never leave Jordan land. In every part of the kingdom there were dye-works and brick-kilns, forests and atomcraft-works that paid rent to Jordan, and every Quarter-Day the Bursar and his clerks would tot it all up, announce the total to Concilium, and order a pair of swans for the Feast. Some of the money was put by for re-investment – Concilium had just approved the purchase of an office-block in Manchester – and the rest was used to pay the Scholars' modest stipends and the wages of the servants (and the Parslows, and the other dozen or so families of craftsmen and traders who served the College), to keep the wine-cellar richly filled, to buy books and anbarographs for the immense Library that filled one side of the Melrose Quadrangle and extended, burrow-like, for several

floors beneath the ground; and, not least, to buy the latest philosophical apparatus to equip the Chapel.

It was important to keep the Chapel up to date, because Jordan
College had no rival, either in Europe or in New France, as a
centre of experimental theology. Lyra knew that much, at least.
She was proud of her College's eminence, and liked to boast of
it to the various urchins and ragamuffins she played with by the
Canal or the Claybeds; and she regarded visiting scholars and
eminent professors from elsewhere with pitying scorn, because
they didn't belong to Jordan and so must know less, poor things,
than the humblest of Jordan's Under-Scholars.

As for what experimental theology was, Lyra had no more idea
than the urchins. She had formed the notion that it was concerned with magic, with the movements of the stars and planets,
with tiny particles of matter, but that was guesswork, really.
Probably the stars had dæmons just as humans did, and experimental theology involved talking to them. Lyra imagined the
Chaplain speaking loftily, listening to the star-dæmons' remarks,
and then nodding judiciously or shaking his head in regret. But
what might be passing between them, she couldn't conceive.

Nor was she particularly interested. In many ways Lyra was a
barbarian. What she liked best was clambering over the College
roofs with Roger, the Kitchen boy who was her particular
friend, to spit plum-stones on the heads of passing Scholars or
to hoot like owls outside a window where a tutorial was going
on; or racing through the narrow streets, or stealing apples from
the market, or waging war. Just as she was unaware of the hidden
currents of politics running below the surface of College affairs,
so the Scholars, for their part, would have been unable to see
the rich seething stew of alliances and enmities and feuds and
treaties which was a child's life in Oxford. Children playing
together: how pleasant to see! What could be more innocent
and charming?

In fact, of course, Lyra and her peers were engaged in deadly
warfare. First, the children (young servants, and the children of
servants, and Lyra) of one college waged war on those of another.
But this enmity was swept aside when the town children attacked
a colleger: then all the colleges banded together and went into

battle against the townies. This rivalry was hundreds of years old, and very deep and satisfying.

But even this was forgotten when the other enemies threatened. One enemy was perennial: the brick-burners' children, who lived by the Claybeds and were despised by collegers and townies alike. Last year Lyra and some townies had made a temporary truce and raided the Claybeds, pelting the brick-burners' children with lumps of heavy clay and tipping over the soggy castle they'd built, before rolling them over and over in the clinging substance they lived by until victors and vanquished alike resembled a flock of shrieking golems.

The other regular enemy was seasonal. The gyptian families, who lived in canal-boats, came and went with the spring and autumn fairs, and were always good for a fight. There was one family of gyptians in particular, who regularly returned to their mooring in that part of the city known as Jericho, with whom she'd been feuding ever since she could first throw a stone. When they were last in Oxford, she and Roger and some of the other kitchen-boys from Jordan and St Michael's College had laid an ambush for them, throwing mud at their brightly painted narrow-boat until the whole family came out to chase them away – at which point the reserve squad under Lyra raided the boat and cast it off from the bank, to float down the canal getting in the way of all the other water-traffic while Lyra's raiders searched the boat from end to end, looking for the bung. Lyra firmly believed in this bung. If they pulled it out, she assured her troop, the boat would sink at once; but they didn't find it, and had to abandon ship when the gyptians caught them up, to flee dripping and crowing with triumph through the narrow lanes of Jericho.

That was Lyra's world and her delight. She was a coarse and greedy little savage, for the most part. But she always had a dim sense that it wasn't her whole world; that part of her also belonged in the grandeur and ritual of Jordan College; and that somewhere in her life there was a connection with the high world of politics represented by Lord Asriel. All she did with that knowledge was to give herself airs and lord it over the other urchins. It had never occurred to her to find out more.

So she had passed her childhood, like a half-wild cat. The only variation in her days came on those irregular occasions when Lord Asriel visited the College. A rich and powerful uncle was all very well to boast about, but the price of boasting was having to be caught by the most agile Scholar and brought to the House-keeper to be washed and dressed in a clean frock, following which she was escorted (with many threats) to the Senior Com-mon Room to have tea with Lord Asriel. A group of senior Scholars would be invited as well. Lyra would slump mutinously in an armchair until the Master told her sharply to sit up, and then she'd glower at them all till even the Chaplain had to laugh.

What happened on those awkward, formal visits never varied. After the tea, the Master and the other few Scholars who'd been invited left Lyra and her uncle together, and he called her to stand in front of him and tell him what she'd learned since his last visit. And she would mutter whatever she could dredge up about geometry or Arabic or history or anbarology, and he would sit back with one ankle resting on the other knee and watch her inscrutably until her words failed.

Last year, before his expedition to the North, he'd gone on to say, "And how do you spend your time when you're not diligently studying?"

And she mumbled, "I just play. Sort of around the College. Just . . . play, really."

And he said, "Let me see your hands, child."

She held out her hands for inspection, and he took them and turned them over to look at her fingernails. Beside him, his dæmon lay Sphinx-like on the carpet, swishing her tail occasion-ally and gazing unblinkingly at Lyra.

"Dirty," said Lord Asriel, pushing her hands away. "Don't they make you wash in this place?"

"Yes," she said. "But the Chaplain's fingernails are always dirty. They're even dirtier than mine."

"He's a learned man. What's your excuse?"

"I must've got them dirty after I washed."

"Where do you play to get so dirty?"

She looked at him suspiciously. She had the feeling that being on the roof was forbidden, though no one had actually said so. "In some of the old rooms," she said finally.

"And where else?"

"In the Claybeds, sometimes."

"And?"

"Jericho and Port Meadow."

"Nowhere else?"

"No."

"You're a liar. I saw you on the roof only yesterday."

She bit her lip and said nothing. He was watching her sardonically.

"So, you play on the roof as well," he went on. "Do you ever go into the Library?"

"No. I found a rook on the Library roof, though," she went on.

"Did you? Did you catch it?"

"It had a hurt foot. I was going to kill it and roast it but Roger said we should help it get better. So we gave it scraps of food and some wine and then it got better and flew away."

"Who's Roger?"

"My friend. The Kitchen boy."

"I see. So you've been all over the roof—"

"Not all over. You can't get on to the Sheldon Building because you have to jump up from Pilgrim's Tower across a gap. There's a skylight that opens on to it, but I'm not tall enough to reach it."

"You've been all over the roof except the Sheldon Building. What about underground?"

"Underground?"

"There's as much College below ground as there is above it. I'm surprised you haven't found that out. Well, I'm going in a minute. You look healthy enough. Here."

He fished in his pocket and drew out a handful of coins, from which he gave her five gold dollars.

"Haven't they taught you to say thank you?" he said.

"Thank you," she mumbled.

"Do you obey the Master?"

"Oh, yes."

"And respect the Scholars?"

"Yes."

Lord Asriel's dæmon laughed softly. It was the first sound she'd made, and Lyra blushed.

"Go and play then," said Lord Asriel.

Lyra turned and darted to the door with relief, remembering to turn and blurt out a "Goodbye."

So Lyra's life had been, before the day when she decided to hide in the Retiring Room, and first heard about Dust.

And of course the Librarian was wrong in saying to the Master that she wouldn't have been interested. She would have listened eagerly now to anyone who could tell her about Dust. She was to hear a great deal more about it in the months to come, and eventually she would know more about Dust than anyone in the world; but in the meantime, there was all the rich life of Jordan still being lived around her.

And in any case there was something else to think about. A rumour had been filtering through the streets for some weeks: a rumour that made some people laugh and others grow silent, as some people scoff at ghosts and others fear them. For no reason that anyone could imagine, children were beginning to disappear.

It would happen like this.

East along the great highway of the River Isis, thronged with slow-moving brick-barges and asphalt-boats and corn-tankers, way down past Henley and Maidenhead to Teddington, where the tide from the German Ocean reaches, and further down still: to Mortlake, past the house of the great magician Dr Dee; past Falkeshall, where the pleasure-gardens spread out bright with fountains and banners by day, with tree-lamps and fireworks by night; past White Hall Palace, where the King holds his weekly Council of State; past the Shot Tower, dropping its endless drizzle of molten lead into vats of murky water; further down still, to where the river, wide and filthy now, swings in a great curve to the south.

This is Limehouse, and here is the child who is going to disappear.

He is called Tony Makarios. His mother thinks he's nine years old, but she has a poor memory that the drink has rotted; he might be eight, or ten. His surname is Greek, but like his age, that is a guess on his mother's part, because he looks more Chinese than Greek, and there's Irish and Skraeling and Lascar in him from his mother's side, too. Tony's not very bright, but he has a sort of clumsy tenderness that sometimes prompts him to give his mother a rough hug and plant a sticky kiss on her cheeks. The poor woman is usually too fuddled to start such a procedure herself; but she responds warmly enough, once she realizes what's happening.

At the moment Tony is hanging about the market in Pie Street. He's hungry. It's early evening, and he won't get fed at home. He's got a shilling in his pocket that a soldier gave him for taking a message to his best girl, but Tony's not going to waste that on food, when you can pick up so much for nothing.

So he wanders through the market, between the old-clothes stalls and the fortune-paper stalls, the fruit-mongers and the fried-fish seller, with his little dæmon on his shoulder, a sparrow, watching this way and that; and when a stall-holder and her dæmon are both looking elsewhere, a brisk chirp sounds, and Tony's hand shoots out and returns to his loose shirt with an apple or a couple of nuts, and finally with a hot pie.

The stall-holder sees that, and shouts, and her cat-dæmon leaps, but Tony's sparrow is aloft and Tony himself halfway down the street already. Curses and abuse go with him, but not far. He stops running at the steps of St Catherine's Oratory, where he sits down and takes out his steaming, battered prize, leaving a trail of gravy on his shirt.

And he's being watched. A lady in a long yellow-red fox-fur coat, a beautiful young lady whose dark hair falls shining delicately under the shadow of her fur-lined hood, is standing in the doorway of the Oratory, half a dozen steps above him. It might be that a service is finishing, for light comes from the doorway behind her, an organ is playing inside, and the lady is holding a jewelled breviary.

Tony knows nothing of this. His face contentedly deep in the pie, his toes curled inwards and his bare soles together, he sits and chews and swallows while his dæmon becomes a mouse and grooms her whiskers.

The young lady's dæmon is moving out from beside the fox-fur coat. He is in the form of a monkey, but no ordinary monkey: his fur is long and silky and of the most deep and lustrous gold. With sinuous movements he inches down the steps towards the boy, and sits a step above him.

Then the mouse senses something, and becomes a sparrow again, cocking her head a fraction sideways, and hops along the stone a step or two.

The monkey watches the sparrow; the sparrow watches the monkey.

The monkey reaches out slowly. His little hand is black, his nails perfect horny claws, his movements gentle and inviting. The sparrow can't resist. She hops further, and further, and then, with a little flutter, up on to the monkey's hand.

The monkey lifts her up, and gazes closely at her before standing and swinging back to his human, taking the sparrow-dæmon with him. The lady bends her scented head to whisper.

And then Tony turns. He can't help it.

"Ratter!" he says, half in alarm, his mouth full.

The sparrow chirps. It must be safe. Tony swallows his mouthful and stares.

"Hello," says the beautiful lady. "What's your name?"

"Tony."

"Where do you live, Tony?"

"Clarice Walk."

"What's in that pie?"

"Beefsteak."

"Do you like chocolatl?"

"Yeah!"

"As it happens, I've got more chocolatl than I can drink myself. Will you come and help me drink it?"

He's lost already. He was lost the moment his slow-witted dæmon hopped on to the monkey's hand. He follows the beautiful young lady and the golden monkey down Denmark Street and along to Hangman's Wharf, and down King George's Steps to a little green door in the side of a tall warehouse. She knocks, the door is opened; they go in, the door is closed. Tony will never come out — at least, by that entrance; and he'll never see his mother again. She, poor drunken thing, will think he's run away, and when she remembers him, she'll think it was her fault, and sob her sorry heart out.

Little Tony Makarios wasn't the only child to be caught by the lady with the golden monkey. He found a dozen others in the cellar of the warehouse, boys and girls, none older than twelve or so; though since all of them had histories like his, none could be sure of their age. What Tony didn't notice, of course, was the factor that they all had in common. None of the children in that warm and steamy cellar had reached the age of puberty.

The kind lady saw him settled on a bench against the wall, and provided by a silent serving-woman with a mug of chocolatl from the saucepan on the iron stove. Tony ate the rest of his pie and drank the sweet hot liquor without taking much notice of his surroundings, and the surroundings took little notice of him: he was too small to be a threat, and too stolid to promise much satisfaction as a victim.

It was another boy who asked the obvious question.

"Hey, lady! What you got us all here for?"

He was a tough-looking wretch with dark chocolatl on his top lip and a gaunt black rat for a dæmon. The lady was standing near the door, talking to a stout man with the air of a sea-captain, and as she turned to answer, she looked so angelic in the hissing naphtha light that all the children fell silent.

"We want your help," she said. "You don't mind helping us, do you?"

No one could say a word. They all gazed, suddenly shy. They had never seen a lady like this; she was so gracious and sweet and kind that they felt they hardly deserved their good luck, and whatever she asked, they'd give it gladly so as to stay in her presence a little longer.

She told them that they were going on a voyage. They would be well fed and warmly clothed, and those who wanted to could send messages back to their families to let them know they were safe. Captain Magnusson would take them on board his ship very soon, and then when the tide was right they'd sail out to sea and set a course for the North.

Soon those few who did want to send a message to whatever home they had were sitting around the beautiful lady, as she wrote a few lines at their dictation and, having let them scratch a clumsy X at the foot of the page, folded it into a scented envelope and wrote the address they told her. Tony would have liked to send something to his mother, but he had a realistic idea of her ability to read it. He plucked at the lady's fox-fur sleeve and whispered that he'd like her to tell his mum where he was going, and all, and she bent her gracious head close enough to his malodorous little body to hear, and stroked his head and promised to pass the message on.

Then the children clustered around to say goodbye. The golden monkey stroked all their dæmons, and they all touched the fox-fur for luck, or as if they were drawing some strength or hope or goodness out of the lady, and she bade them all farewell and saw them in the care of the bold captain on board a steam launch at the jetty. The sky was dark now, the river a mass of bobbing lights. The lady stood on the jetty and waved till she could see their faces no more.

Then she turned back inside, with the golden monkey nestled in her breast, and threw the little bundle of letters into the furnace before leaving the way she had come.

Children from the slums were easy enough to entice away, but eventually people noticed, and the police were stirred into reluctant action. For a while there were no more bewitchings. But a rumour had been born, and little by little it changed and grew and spread, and when after a while a few children disappeared in Norwich, and then Sheffield, and then Manchester, the people in those places who'd heard of the disappearances elsewhere added the new vanishings to the story and gave it new strength.

And so the legend grew of a mysterious group of enchanters who spirited children away. Some said their leader was a beautiful lady, others said a tall man with red eyes, while a third story told of a youth who laughed and sang to his victims so that they followed him like sheep.

As for where they took these lost children, no two stories agreed. Some said it was to Hell, under the ground, to Fairyland.

Others said to a farm where the children were kept and fattened for the table. Others said that the children were kept and sold as slaves to rich Tartars . . . And so on.

But one thing on which everyone agreed was the name of these invisible kidnappers. They had to have a name, or not be referred to at all, and talking about them – especially if you were safe and snug at home, or in Jordan College – was delicious. And the name that seemed to settle on them, without anyone's knowing why, was the Gobblers.

"Don't stay out late, or the Gobblers'll get you!"

"My cousin in Northampton, she knows a woman whose little boy was took by the Gobblers . . ."

"The Gobblers've been in Stratford. They say they're coming south!"

And, inevitably:

"Let's play kids and Gobblers!"

So said Lyra to Roger the Kitchen boy from Jordan College. He would have followed her to the ends of the earth.

"How d'you play that?"

"You hide and I find you and slice you open, right, like the Gobblers do."

"You don't know what they do. They might not do that at all."

"You're afraid of 'em," she said. "I can tell."

"I en't. I don't believe in 'em, anyway."

"I do," she said decisively. "But I en't afraid either. I'd just do what my uncle done last time he came to Jordan. I seen him. He was in the Retiring Room and there was this guest who weren't polite, and my uncle just give him a hard look and the man fell dead on the spot, with all foam and froth round his mouth."

"He never," said Roger doubtfully. "They never said anything about that in the Kitchen. Anyway, you en't allowed in the Retiring Room."

"Course not. They wouldn't tell servants about a thing like that. And I *have* been in the Retiring Room, so there. Anyway, my uncle's always doing that. He done it to some Tartars when they caught him once. They tied him up and they was going to cut his guts out, but when the first man come up with the knife my uncle just looked at him, and he fell dead, so another one come up and he done the same to him, and finally there was only one left. My uncle said he'd leave him alive if he untied him, so he did, and then my uncle killed him anyway just to teach him a lesson."

Roger was less sure about that than about Gobblers, but the story was too good to waste, so they took it in turns to be Lord Asriel and the expiring Tartars, using sherbet dip for the foam.

However, that was a distraction; Lyra was still intent on playing Gobblers, and she inveigled Roger down into the wine cellars, which they entered by means of the Butler's spare set of keys. Together they crept through the great vaults where the College's Tokay and Canary, its Burgundy and brantwijn were lying under the cobwebs of ages. Ancient stone arches rose above them supported by pillars as thick as ten trees, irregular flagstones lay underfoot, and on all sides were ranged rack upon rack, tier upon tier, of bottles and barrels. It was fascinating. With Gobblers forgotten again, the two children tiptoed from end to end holding a candle in trembling fingers, peering into every dark corner, with a single question growing more urgent in Lyra's mind every moment: what did the wine taste like?

There was an easy way of answering that. Lyra – over Roger's fervent protests – picked out the oldest, twistiest, greenest bottle she could find, and, not having anything to extract the cork with, broke it off at the neck. Huddled in the furthest corner, they sipped at the heady crimson liquor, wondering when they'd become drunk, and how they'd tell when they were. Lyra didn't like the taste much, but she had to admit how grand and complicated it was. The funniest thing was watching their two dæmons, who seemed to be getting more and more muddled: falling over, giggling senselessly, and changing shape to look like gargoyles, each trying to be uglier than the other.

Finally, and almost simultaneously, the children discovered what it was like to be drunk.

"Do they *like* doing this?" gasped Roger, after vomiting copiously.

"Yes," said Lyra, in the same condition. "And so do I," she added stubbornly.

* * *

Lyra learned nothing from that episode except that playing Gobblers led to interesting places. She remembered her uncle's words in their last interview, and began to explore underground, for what was above ground was only a small fraction of the whole. Like some enormous fungus whose root-system extended over acres, Jordan (finding itself jostling for space above ground with St Michael's College on one side, Gabriel College on the other, and the University Library behind) had begun, sometime in the Middle Age, to spread below the surface. Tunnels, shafts, vaults, cellars, staircases had so hollowed out the earth below Jordan and for several hundred yards around it that there was almost as much air below ground as above; Jordan College stood on a sort of froth of stone.

And now that Lyra had the taste for exploring it, she abandoned her usual haunt, the irregular Alps of the College roofs, and plunged with Roger into this netherworld. From playing at Gobblers she had turned to hunting them, for what could be more likely than that they were lurking out of sight below the ground?

So one day she and Roger made their way into the crypt below the Oratory. This was where generations of Masters had been buried, each in his lead-lined oak coffin in niches along the stone walls. A stone tablet below each space gave their names:

> *Simon Le Clerc, Master 1765–1789 Cerebaton*
> *Requiescant in pace*

"What's that mean?" said Roger.

"The first part's his name, and the last bit's Roman. And there's the dates in the middle when he was Master. And the other name must be his dæmon."

They moved along the silent vault, tracing the letters of more inscriptions:

> *Francis Lyall, Master 1748–1765 Zohariel*
> *Requiescant in pace*

> *Ignatius Cole, Master 1745–1748 Musca*
> *Requiescant in pace*

On each coffin, Lyra was interested to see, a brass plaque bore a picture of a different being: this one a basilisk, this a fair woman, this a serpent, this a monkey. She realized that they were images of the dead men's dæmons. As people became adult, their dæmons lost the power to change and assumed one shape, keeping it permanently.

"These coffins've got skeletons in 'em!" whispered Roger.

"Mouldering flesh," whispered Lyra. "And worms and maggots all twisting about in their eye sockets."

"Must be ghosts down here," said Roger, shivering pleasantly.

Beyond the first crypt they found a passage lined with stone shelves. Each shelf was partitioned off into square sections, and in each section rested a skull.

Roger's dæmon, tail tucked firmly between her legs, shivered against him and gave a little quiet howl.

"Hush," he said.

Lyra couldn't see Pantalaimon, but she knew his moth-form was resting on her shoulder and probably shivering too.

She reached up and lifted the nearest skull gently out of its resting place.

"What you doing?" said Roger. "You en't supposed to touch 'em!"

She turned it over and over, taking no notice. Something suddenly fell out of the hole at the base of the skull – fell through her fingers and rang as it hit the floor, and she nearly dropped the skull in alarm.

"It's a coin!" said Roger, feeling for it. "Might be treasure!"

He held it up to the candle and they both gazed wide-eyed. It was not a coin, but a little disc of bronze with a crudely engraved inscription showing a cat.

"It's like the ones on the coffins," said Lyra. "It's his dæmon. Must be."

"Better put it back," said Roger uneasily, and Lyra upturned the skull and dropped the disc back into its immemorial resting-place before returning the skull to the shelf. Each of the other skulls, they found, had its own dæmon-coin, showing its owner's lifetime companion still close to him in death.

"Who d'you think these were when they were alive?" said

Lyra. "Probably Scholars, I reckon. Only the Masters get coffins. There's probably been so many Scholars all down the centuries that there wouldn't be room to bury the whole of 'em, so they just cut their heads off and keep them. That's the most important part of 'em anyway."

They found no Gobblers, but the catacombs under the Oratory kept Lyra and Roger busy for days. Once she tried to play a trick on some of the dead Scholars, by switching around the coins in their skulls so they were with the wrong dæmons. Pantalaimon became so agitated at this that he changed into a bat and flew up and down uttering shrill cries and flapping his wings in her face, but she took no notice: it was too good a joke to waste. She paid for it later, though. In bed in her narrow room at the top of Staircase Twelve she was visited by a night-ghast, and woke up screaming at the three robed figures who stood at the bedside pointing their bony fingers before throwing back their cowls to show bleeding stumps where their heads should have been. Only when Pantalaimon became a lion and roared at them did they retreat, backing away into the substance of the wall until all that was visible was their arms, then their horny yellow-grey hands, then their twitching fingers, then nothing. First thing in the morning she hastened down to the catacombs and restored the dæmon-coins to their rightful places, and whispered "Sorry! Sorry!" to the skulls.

The catacombs were much larger than the wine-cellars, but they too had a limit. When Lyra and Roger had explored every corner of them and were sure there were no Gobblers to be found there, they turned their attention elsewhere – but not before they were spotted leaving the crypt by the Intercessor, who called them back into the Oratory.

The Intercessor was a plump, elderly man known as Father Heyst. It was his job to lead all the College services, to preach and pray and hear confessions. When Lyra was younger he had taken an interest in her spiritual welfare, only to be confounded by her sly indifference and insincere repentances. She was not spiritually promising, he had decided.

When they heard him call, Lyra and Roger turned reluctantly

and walked, dragging their feet, into the great musty-smelling dimness of the Oratory. Candles flickered here and there in front of images of the saints; a faint and distant clatter came from the organ-loft, where some repairs were going on; a servant was polishing the brass lectern. Father Heyst beckoned from the vestry door.

"Where have you been?" he said to them. "I've seen you come in here two or three times now. What are you up to?"

His tone was not accusatory. He sounded as if he were genuinely interested. His dæmon flicked a lizard-tongue at them from her perch on his shoulder.

Lyra said, "We wanted to look down in the crypt."

"Whatever for?"

"The . . . the coffins. We wanted to see all the coffins," she said.

"But why?"

She shrugged. It was her constant response when she was pressed.

"And you," he went on, turning to Roger. Roger's dæmon anxiously wagged her terrier-tail to propitiate him. "What's your name?"

"Roger, Father."

"If you're a servant, where do you work?"

"In the Kitchen, Father."

"Should you be there now?"

"Yes, Father."

"Then be off with you."

Roger turned and ran. Lyra dragged her foot from side to side on the floor.

"As for you, Lyra," said Father Heyst, "I'm pleased to see you taking an interest in what lies in the Oratory. You are a lucky child, to have all this history around you."

"Mm," said Lyra.

"But I wonder about your choice of companions. Are you a lonely child?"

"No," she said.

"Do you . . . Do you miss the society of other children?"

"No."

"I don't mean Roger the Kitchen boy. I mean children such as yourself. Nobly born children. Would you like to have some companions of that sort?"

"No."

"But other girls, perhaps . . ."

"No."

"You see, none of us would want you to miss all the usual childhood pleasures and pastimes. I sometimes think it must be a lonely life for you here among a company of elderly Scholars, Lyra. Do you feel that?"

"No."

He tapped his thumbs together over his interlaced fingers, unable to think of anything else to ask this stubborn child.

"If there is anything troubling you," he said finally, "you know you can come and tell me about it. I hope you feel you can always do that."

"Yes," she said.

"Do you say your prayers?"

"Yes."

"Good girl. Well, run along."

With a barely concealed sigh of relief, she turned and left. Having failed to find Gobblers below ground, Lyra took to the streets again. She was at home there.

Then, almost when she'd lost interest in them, the Gobblers appeared in Oxford.

The first Lyra heard of it was when a young boy went missing from a gyptian family she knew.

It was about the time of the Horse Fair, and the canal basin was crowded with narrow-boats and butty boats, with traders and travellers, and the wharves along the waterfront in Jericho were bright with gleaming harness and loud with the clop of hooves and the clamour of bargaining. Lyra always enjoyed the Horse Fair; as well as the chance of stealing a ride on a less-than-well-attended horse, there were endless opportunities for provoking warfare.

And this year she had a grand plan. Inspired by the capture of the narrow-boat the year before, she intended this time to make a proper voyage before being turned out. If she and her cronies from the college kitchens could get as far as Abingdon they could play havoc with the weir...

But this year there was to be no war. As she sauntered along the edge of the boatyard in Port Meadow in the morning sun with a couple of urchins, passing a stolen cigarette from one to another and blowing out the smoke ostentatiously, she heard a cry in a voice she recognized.

"Well, what have you *done* with him, you half-arsed pillock?"

It was a mighty voice, a woman's voice, but a woman with lungs of brass and leather. Lyra looked around for her at once, because this was Ma Costa, who had clouted Lyra dizzy on two occasions but given her hot gingerbread on three, and whose family was noted for the grandeur and sumptuousness of their boat. They were princes among gyptians, and Lyra admired Ma Costa greatly, but she intended to be wary of her for some time yet, for theirs was the boat she had hijacked.

One of Lyra's brat-companions picked up a stone automatically when he heard the commotion, but Lyra said, "Put it down. She's in a temper. She could snap your backbone like a twig."

In fact, Ma Costa looked more anxious than angry. The man she was addressing, a horse-trader, was shrugging and spreading his hands.

"Well, I dunno," he was saying. "He was here one minute and gone the next. I never saw where he went..."

"He was helping you! He was holding your bloody horses for you!"

"Well, he should've stayed there, shouldn't he? Runs off in the middle of a job –"

He got no further, because Ma Costa suddenly dealt him a mighty blow on the side of the head, and followed it up with such a volley of curses and slaps that he yelled and turned to flee. The other horse-traders nearby jeered, and a flighty colt reared up in alarm.

"What's going on?" said Lyra to a gyptian child who'd been watching open-mouthed. "What's she angry about?"

"It's her kid," said the child. "It's Billy. She prob'ly reckons the Gobblers got him. They might've done, too. I ain't seen him meself since – "

"The Gobblers? Has they come to Oxford, then?"

The gyptian boy turned away to call to his friends, who were all watching Ma Costa.

"She don't know what's going on! She don't know the Gobblers is here!"

Half a dozen brats turned with expressions of derision, and Lyra threw her cigarette down, recognizing the cue for a fight. Everyone's dæmon instantly became warlike: each child was accompanied by fangs, or claws, or bristling fur, and Pantalaimon, contemptuous of the limited imaginations of these gyptian dæmons, became a dragon the size of a deer-hound.

But before they could all join battle, Ma Costa herself waded in, smacking two of the gyptians aside and confronting Lyra like a prize-fighter.

"You seen him?" she demanded of Lyra. "You seen Billy?"

"No," Lyra said. "We just got here. I en't seen Billy for months."

Ma Costa's dæmon was wheeling in the bright air above her head, a hawk, fierce yellow eyes snapping this way and that, unblinking. Lyra was frightened. No one worried about a child gone missing for a few hours, certainly not a gyptian: in the tight-knit gyptian boat-world, all children were precious and extravagantly loved, and a mother knew that if a child was out of *her* sight, it wouldn't be far from someone else's who would protect it instinctively.

But here was Ma Costa, a queen among the gyptians, in a terror for a missing child. What was going on?

Ma Costa looked half-blindly over the little group of children and turned away to stumble through the crowd on the wharf, bellowing for her child. At once the children turned back to one another, their feud abandoned in the face of her grief.

"What *is* them Gobblers?" said Simon Parslow, one of Lyra's companions.

The first gyptian boy said, "*You* know. They been stealing kids all over the country. They're pirates – "

"They en't pirates," corrected another gyptian. "They're cannaboles. That's why they call 'em Gobblers."

"They *eat* kids?" said Lyra's other crony Hugh Lovat, a kitchen boy from St Michael's.

"No one knows," said the first gyptian. "They take 'em away and they en't never seen again."

"We all know that," said Lyra. "We been playing kids and Gobblers for months, before you were, I bet. But I bet no one's seen 'em."

"They have," said one boy.

"Who, then?" persisted Lyra. "Have *you* seen 'em? How d'you know it en't just one person?"

"Charlie seen 'em in Banbury," said a gyptian girl. "They come and talked to this lady while another man took her little boy out the garden."

"Yeah," piped up Charlie, a gyptian boy. "I seen 'em do it!"

"What did they look like?" said Lyra.

"Well . . . I never properly saw 'em," Charlie said. "I saw their truck, though," he added. "They come in a white truck. They put the little boy in the truck and drove off quick."

"But why do they call 'em Gobblers?" Lyra asked.

"'Cause they eat 'em," said the first gyptian boy. "Someone told us in Northampton. They been up there and all. This girl in Northampton, her brother was took, and she said the men as took him told her they was going to eat him. Everyone knows that. They gobble 'em up."

A gyptian girl standing nearby began to cry loudly.

"That's Billy's cousin," said Charlie.

Lyra said, "Who saw Billy last?"

"Me," said half a dozen voices. "I seen him holding Johnny Fiorelli's old horse – I seen him by the toffee-apple seller – I seen him swinging on the crane –"

When Lyra had sorted it out, she gathered that Billy had been seen for certain not less than two hours previously.

"So," she said, "some time in the last two hours there must've been Gobblers here . . ."

They all looked around, shivering in spite of the warm sun,

the crowded wharf, the familiar smells of tar and horses and smoking-leaf. The trouble was that because no one knew what these Gobblers looked like, anyone might be a Gobbler, as Lyra pointed out to the appalled gang, who were now all under her sway, collegers and gyptians alike.

"They're *bound* to look like ordinary people, else they'd be seen at once," she explained. "If they only came at night, they could look like anything. But if they come in the daylight they got to look ordinary. So any of these people might be Gobblers . . ."

"They en't," said a gyptian uncertainly. "I know 'em all."

"All right, not *these*, but anyone else," said Lyra. "Let's go and look for 'em! And their white truck!"

And that precipitated a swarm. Other searchers soon joined the first ones, and before long, thirty or more gyptian children were racing from end to end of the wharves, running in and out of stables, scrambling over the cranes and derricks in the boat-yard, leaping over the fence into the wide meadow, swinging fifteen at a time on the old swing bridge over the green water, and running full pelt through the narrow streets of Jericho, between the little brick terraced houses and into the great square-towered oratory of St Barnabas the Chymist. Half of them didn't know what they were looking for, and thought it was just a lark, but those closest to Lyra felt a real fear and apprehension every time they glimpsed a solitary figure down an alley or in the dimness of the Oratory: was it a Gobbler?

But of course they weren't. Eventually, with no success, and with the shadow of Billy's real disappearance hanging over them all, the fun faded away. As Lyra and the two college boys left Jericho when supper-time neared, they saw the gyptians gather-ing on the wharf next to where the Costas' boat was moored. Some of the women were crying loudly, and the men were stand-ing in angry groups, with all their dæmons agitated and rising in nervous flight or snarling at shadows.

"I bet them Gobblers wouldn't dare come in here," said Lyra to Simon Parslow, as the two of them stepped over the threshold into the great lodge of Jordan.

"No," he said uncertainly. "But I know there's a kid missing from the Market."

"Who?" Lyra said. She knew most of the Market children, but she hadn't heard of this.

"Jessie Reynolds, out the saddler's. She weren't there at shutting-up time yesterday, and she'd only gone for a bit of fish for her dad's tea. She never come back and no one'd seen her. They searched all through the Market and everywhere."

"I never heard about that!" said Lyra, indignant. She considered it a deplorable lapse on the part of her subjects not to tell her everything and at once.

"Well, it was only yesterday. She might've turned up now."

"I'm going to ask," said Lyra, and turned to leave the Lodge.

But she hadn't got out of the gate before the Porter called her.

"Here, Lyra! You're not to go out again this evening. Master's orders."

"Why not?"

"I told you, Master's orders. He says if you come in, you stay in."

"You catch me," she said, and darted out before the old man could leave his doorway.

She ran across the narrow street and down into the alley where the vans unloaded goods for the Covered Market. This being shutting-up time, there were few vans there now, but a knot of youths stood smoking and talking by the central gate opposite the high stone wall of St Michael's College. Lyra knew one of them, a sixteen-year-old she admired because he could spit further than anyone else she'd ever heard of, and she went and waited humbly for him to notice her.

"Yeah? What do you want?" he said finally.

"Is Jessie Reynolds disappeared?"

"Yeah. Why?"

"'Cause a gyptian kid disappeared today and all."

"They're always disappearing, gyptians. After every Horse Fair they disappear."

"So do horses," said one of his friends.

"This is different," said Lyra. "This is a kid. We was looking for him all afternoon and the other kids said the Gobblers got him."

"The what?"

"The Gobblers," she said. "En't you heard of the Gobblers?"

It was news to the other boys as well, and apart from a few coarse comments they listened closely to what she told them.

"Gobblers," said Lyra's acquaintance, whose name was Dick. "It's stupid. These gyptians, they pick up all kinds of stupid ideas."

"They said there was Gobblers in Banbury a couple of weeks ago," Lyra insisted, "and there was five kids taken. They probably come to Oxford now to get kids from us. It must've been them what got Jessie."

"There was a kid lost over Cowley way," said one of the other boys. "I remember now. My auntie, she was there yesterday, 'cause she sells fish and chips out a van, and she heard about it . . . Some little boy, that's it . . . I dunno about the Gobblers, though. They en't real, Gobblers. Just a story."

"They are!" Lyra said. "The gyptians seen 'em. They reckon they eat the kids they catch, and . . ."

She stopped in mid-sentence, because something had suddenly come into her mind. During that strange evening she'd spent hidden in the Retiring Room, Lord Asriel had shown a lantern slide of a man holding up a wand with streams of light pouring into it; and there'd been a small figure beside him, with less light around it; and he'd said it was a child; and someone had asked if it was a severed child, and her uncle had said no, that was the point. Lyra remembered that severed meant cut.

And then something else hit her heart: where was Roger?

She hadn't seen him since the morning . . .

Suddenly she felt afraid. Pantalaimon, as a miniature lion, sprang into her arms and growled. She said goodbye to the youths by the gate and walked quietly back into Turl Street, and then ran full pelt for Jordan Lodge, tumbling in through the door a second before the now cheetah-shaped dæmon.

The Porter was sanctimonious.

"I had to ring the Master and tell him," he said. "He en't pleased at all. I wouldn't be in your shoes, not for money I wouldn't."

"Where's Roger?" she demanded.

"I en't seen him. He'll be for it, too. Ooh, when Mr Cawston catches him —"

Lyra ran to the Kitchen and thrust her way into the hot, clangorous, steaming bustle.

"Where's Roger?" she shouted.

"Clear off, Lyra! We're busy here!"

"But where is he? Has he turned up or not?"

No one seemed interested.

"But where is he? You *must've* heard!" Lyra shouted at the chef, who boxed her ears and sent her storming away.

Bernie the pastrycook tried to calm her down, but she wouldn't be consoled.

"They got him! Them bloody Gobblers, they oughter catch 'em and bloody kill 'em! I hate 'em! You don't care about Roger –"

"Lyra, we all care about Roger –"

"You don't, else you'd all stop work and go and look for him right now! I hate you!"

"There could be a dozen reasons why Roger en't turned up. Listen to sense. We got dinner to prepare and serve in less than an hour; the Master's got guests in the Lodging, and he'll be eating over there, and that means Chef'll have to attend to getting the food there quick so it don't go cold; and what with one thing and another, Lyra, life's got to go on. I'm sure Roger'll turn up . . ."

Lyra turned and ran out of the Kitchen, knocking over a stack of silver dish-covers and ignoring the roar of anger that arose. She sped down the steps and across the quadrangle, between the Chapel and Palmer's Tower and into the Yaxley Quad, where the oldest buildings of the College stood.

Pantalaimon scampered before her like a miniature cheetah, flowing up the stairs to the very top, where Lyra's bedroom was. Lyra barged open the door, dragged her rickety chair to the window, flung wide the casement and scrambled out. There was a lead-lined stone gutter a foot wide just below the window, and once she was standing in that, she turned and clambered up over the rough tiles until she stood on the topmost ridge of the roof. There she opened her mouth and screamed. Pantalaimon, who always became a bird once on the roof, flew round and round shrieking rook-shrieks with her.

The evening sky was awash with peach, apricot, cream: tender little ice-cream clouds in a wide orange sky. The spires and towers of Oxford stood around them, level but no higher; the green woods of Château-Vert and White Ham rose on either side to the east and the west. Rooks were cawing somewhere, and bells were ringing, and from the Oxpens the steady beat of a gas engine announced the ascent of the evening Royal Mail zeppelin for London. Lyra watched it climb away beyond the spire of St Michael's Chapel, as big at first as the tip of her little finger when she held it at arm's length, and then steadily smaller until it was a dot in the pearly sky.

She turned and looked down into the shadowed quadrangle, where the black-gowned figures of the Scholars were already beginning to drift in ones and twos towards the Buttery, their dæmons strutting or fluttering alongside or perching calmly on their shoulders. The lights were going on in the Hall; she could see the stained-glass windows gradually beginning to glow as a servant moved up the tables lighting the naphtha lamps. The Steward's bell began to toll, announcing half an hour before dinner.

This was her world. She wanted it to stay the same for ever and ever, but it was changing around her, for someone out there was stealing children. She sat on the roof-ridge, chin in hands.

"We better rescue him, Pantalaimon," she said.

He answered in his rook-voice from the chimney.

"It'll be dangerous," he said.

"Course! I know that."

"Remember what they said in the Retiring Room."

"What?"

"Something about a child up in the Arctic. The one that wasn't attracting the Dust."

"They said it was an entire child ... What about it?"

"That might be what they're going to do to Roger and the gyptians and the other kids."

"What?"

"Well, what does *entire* mean?"

"Dunno. They cut 'em in half, probably. I reckon they make

slaves out of 'em. That'd be more use. They probably got mines up there. Uranium mines for atomcraft. I bet that's what it is. And if they sent grown-ups down the mine they'd be dead, so they use kids instead because they cost less. That's what they've done with him."

"I think —"

But what Pantalaimon thought had to wait, because someone began to shout from below.

"Lyra! Lyra! You come in this instant!"

There was a banging on the window-frame. Lyra knew the voice and the impatience: it was Mrs Lonsdale the Housekeeper. There was no hiding from her.

Tight-faced, Lyra slid down the roof and into the gutter, and then climbed in through the window again. Mrs Lonsdale was running some water into the little chipped basin, to the accom- paniment of a great groaning and hammering from the pipes.

"The number of times you been told about going out there ... Look at you! Just look at your skirt — it's filthy! Take it off at once and wash yourself while I look for something decent that en't torn. Why you can't keep yourself clean and tidy . . ."

Lyra was too sulky even to ask why she was having to wash and dress, and no grown-up ever gave reasons of their own accord. She dragged the dress over her head and dropped it on the narrow bed, and began to wash desultorily while Pantalaimon, a canary now, hopped closer and closer to Mrs Lonsdale's dæmon, a stolid retriever, trying in vain to annoy him.

"Look at the state of this wardrobe! You en't hung nothing up for weeks! Look at the creases in this —"

Look at this, look at that . . . Lyra didn't want to look. She shut her eyes as she rubbed at her face with the thin towel.

"You'll just have to wear it as it is. There en't time to take an iron to it. God bless me, girl, your *knees* — look at the state of them . . ."

"Don't want to look at nothing," Lyra muttered.

Mrs Lonsdale smacked her leg. "Wash," she said ferociously. "You get all that dirt off."

"Why?" Lyra said at last. "I never wash my knees usually. No one's going to look at my knees. What've I got to do all this for?

You don't care about Roger neither, any more than Chef does. I'm the only one that —"

Another smack, on the other leg.

"None of that nonsense. I'm a Parslow, same as Roger's father. He's my second cousin. I bet you didn't know that, 'cause I bet you never asked, Miss Lyra. I bet it never occurred to you. Don't you chide me with not caring about the boy. God knows, I even care about you, and you give me little enough reason and no thanks."

She seized the flannel and rubbed Lyra's knees so hard she left the skin bright pink and sore, but clean.

"The reason for this is you're going to have dinner with the Master and his guests. I hope to God you behave. Speak when you're spoken to, be quiet and polite, smile nicely and don't you ever say *Dunno* when someone asks you a question."

She dragged the best dress on to Lyra's skinny frame, tugged it straight, fished a bit of red ribbon out of the tangle in a drawer, and brushed Lyra's hair with a coarse brush.

"If they'd let me know earlier I could've given your hair a proper wash. Well, that's too bad. As long as they don't look too close ... There. Now stand up straight. Where's those best patent-leather shoes?"

Five minutes later Lyra was knocking on the door of the Master's Lodging, the grand and slightly gloomy house that opened into the Yaxley Quadrangle and backed on to the Library Garden. Pantalaimon, an ermine now for politeness, rubbed himself against her leg. The door was opened by the Master's manservant Cousins, an old enemy of Lyra's; but both knew that this was a state of truce.

"Mrs Lonsdale said I was to come," said Lyra.

"Yes," said Cousins, stepping aside. "The Master's in the Drawing Room."

He showed her into the large room that overlooked the Library Garden. The last of the sun shone into it, through the gap between the Library and Palmer's Tower, and lit up the heavy pictures and the glum silver the Master collected. It also lit up the guests, and Lyra realized why they weren't going to dine in Hall: three of the guests were women.

"Ah, Lyra," said the Master. "I'm so glad you could come. Cousins, could you find some sort of soft drink? Dame Hannah, I don't think you've met Lyra . . . Lord Asriel's niece, you know."

Dame Hannah Relf was the Head of one of the women's colleges, an elderly grey-haired lady whose dæmon was a marmoset. Lyra shook hands as politely as she could, and was then introduced to the other guests, who were, like Dame Hannah, scholars from other Colleges and quite uninteresting. Then the Master came to the final guest.

"Mrs Coulter," he said, "this is our Lyra. Lyra, come and say hello to Mrs Coulter."

"Hello, Lyra," said Mrs Coulter.

She was beautiful and young. Her sleek black hair framed her cheeks, and her dæmon was a golden monkey.

4
THE ALETHIOMETER

"I HOPE YOU'LL SIT next to me at dinner," said Mrs Coulter, making room for Lyra on the sofa. "I'm not used to the grandeur of a Master's Lodging. You'll have to show me which knife and fork to use."

"Are you a female Scholar?" said Lyra. She regarded female Scholars with a proper Jordan disdain: there *were* such people but, poor things, they could never be taken more seriously than animals dressed up and acting a play. Mrs Coulter, on the other hand, was not like any female Scholar Lyra had seen, and certainly not like the two serious elderly ladies who were the other female guests. Lyra had asked the question expecting the answer no, in fact, for Mrs Coulter had such an air of glamour that Lyra was entranced. She could hardly take her eyes off her.

"Not really," Mrs Coulter said. "I'm a member of Dame Hannah's college, but most of my work takes place outside Oxford . . . Tell me about yourself, Lyra. Have you always lived at Jordan College?"

Within five minutes Lyra had told her everything about her half-wild life: her favourite routes over the roof-tops, the battle of the Claybeds, the time she and Roger had caught and roasted a rook, her intention to capture a narrow-boat from the gyptians and sail it to Abingdon, and so on. She even (looking around and lowering her voice) told her about the trick she and Roger had played on the skulls in the crypt.

"And these ghosts came, right, they came to my bedroom without their heads! They couldn't talk except for making sort of gurgling noises, but I knew what they wanted all right. So I went down next day and put their coins back. They'd probably have killed me else."

"You're not afraid of danger, then?" said Mrs Coulter admiringly. They were at dinner by this time, and as Mrs Coulter had hoped, sitting next to each other. Lyra ignored completely the Librarian on her other side and spent the whole meal talking to Mrs Coulter.

When the ladies withdrew for coffee, Dame Hannah said, "Tell me, Lyra – are they going to send you to school?"

Lyra looked blank. "I dun – I don't know," she said. "Probably not," she added for safety. "I wouldn't want to put them to any trouble," she went on piously. "Or expense. It's probably better if I just go on living at Jordan and getting educated by the Scholars here when they've got a bit of spare time. Being as they're here already, they're probably free."

"And does your uncle Lord Asriel have any plans for you?" said the other lady, who was a Scholar at the other women's college.

"Yes," said Lyra. "I expect so. Not school, though. He's going to take me to the North next time he goes."

"I remember him telling me," said Mrs Coulter.

Lyra blinked. The two female Scholars sat up very slightly, though their dæmons, either well-behaved or torpid, did no more than flick their eyes at each other.

"I met him at the Royal Arctic Institute," Mrs Coulter went on. "As a matter of fact it's partly because of that meeting that I'm here today."

"Are you an explorer too?" said Lyra.

"In a kind of way. I've been to the North several times. Last year I spent three months in Greenland making observations of the Aurora."

That was it; nothing and no one else existed now for Lyra. She gazed at Mrs Coulter with awe, and listened rapt and silent to her tales of igloo-building, of seal-hunting, of negotiating with the Lapland witches. The two female Scholars had nothing so exciting to tell, and sat in silence until the men came in.

Later, when the guests were preparing to leave, the Master said, "Stay behind, Lyra. I'd like to talk to you for a minute or two. Go to my study, child; sit down there and wait for me."

Puzzled, tired, exhilarated, Lyra did as he told her. Cousins the manservant showed her in, and pointedly left the door open so that he could see what she was up to from the hall, where he was helping people on with their coats. Lyra watched for Mrs

Coulter, but she didn't see her, and then the Master came into the study and shut the door.

He sat down heavily in the armchair by the fireplace. His dæmon flapped up to the chair-back and sat by his head, her old hooded eyes on Lyra. The lamp hissed gently as the Master said:

"So, Lyra. You've been talking to Mrs Coulter. Did you enjoy hearing what she said?"

"Yes!"

"She is a remarkable lady."

"She's wonderful. She's the most wonderful person I've ever met."

The Master sighed. In his black suit and black tie he looked as much like his dæmon as anyone could, and suddenly Lyra thought that one day, quite soon, he would be buried in the crypt under the Oratory, and an artist would engrave a picture of his dæmon on the brass plate for his coffin, and her name would share the space with his.

"I should have made time before now for a talk with you, Lyra," he said after a few moments. "I was intending to do so in any case, but it seems that time is further on than I thought. You have been safe here in Jordan, my dear. I think you've been happy. You haven't found it easy to obey us, but we are very fond of you, and you've never been a bad child. There's a lot of goodness and sweetness in your nature, and a lot of determination. You're going to need all of that. Things are going on in the wide world I would have liked to protect you from – by keeping you here in Jordan, I mean – but that's no longer possible."

She merely stared. Were they going to send her away?

"You knew that sometime you'd have to go to school," the Master went on. "We have taught you some things here, but not well or systematically. Our knowledge is of a different kind. You need to know things that elderly men are not able to teach you, especially at the age you are now. You must have been aware of that. You're not a servant's child either; we couldn't put you out to be fostered by a town family. They might have cared for you in some ways, but your needs are different. You see, what I'm saying to you, Lyra, is that the part of your life that belongs to Jordan College is coming to an end."

"No," she said, "no, I don't want to leave Jordan. I like it here. I want to stay here for ever."

"When you're young, you do think that things last for ever. Unfortunately, they don't. Lyra, it won't be long – a couple of years at most – before you will be a young woman, and not a child any more. A young lady. And believe me, you'll find Jordan College a far from easy place to live in then."

"But it's my home!"

"It has been your home. But now you need something else."

"Not school. I'm not going to school."

"You need female company. Female guidance."

The word *female* only suggested female Scholars to Lyra, and she involuntarily made a face. To be exiled from the grandeur of Jordan, the splendour and fame of its scholarship, to a dingy brick-built boarding-house of a college at the northern end of Oxford, with dowdy female Scholars who smelt of cabbage and mothballs like those two at dinner!

The Master saw her expression, and saw Pantalaimon's polecat-eyes flash red.

He said, "But suppose it were Mrs Coulter?"

Instantly Pantalaimon's fur changed from coarse brown to downy white. Lyra's eyes widened.

"Really?"

"She is by way of being acquainted with Lord Asriel. Your uncle, of course, is very concerned with your welfare, and when Mrs Coulter heard about you, she offered at once to help. There is no Mr Coulter, by the way; she is a widow; her husband died very sadly in an accident some years ago; so you might bear that in mind before you ask."

Lyra nodded eagerly, and said, "And she's really going to . . . look after me?"

"Would you like that?"

"Yes!"

She could hardly sit still. The Master smiled. He smiled so rarely that he was out of practice, and anyone watching (Lyra wasn't in a state to notice) would have said it was a grimace of sadness.

"Well, we had better ask her in to talk about it," he said.

He left the room, and when he came back a minute later with Mrs Coulter, Lyra was on her feet, too excited to sit. Mrs Coulter smiled, and her dæmon bared his white teeth in a grin of imp-like pleasure. As she passed her on the way to the armchair, Mrs Coulter touched Lyra's hair briefly, and Lyra felt a current of warmth flow into her, and blushed.

When the Master had poured some brantwijn for her, Mrs Coulter said, "So, Lyra, I'm to have an assistant, am I?"

"Yes," said Lyra simply. She would have said yes to anything.

"There's a lot of work I need help with."

"I can work!"

"And we might have to travel."

"I don't mind. I'd go anywhere."

"But it might be dangerous. We might have to go to the North."

Lyra was speechless. Then she found her voice: "Soon?"

Mrs Coulter laughed, and said, "Possibly. But you know you'll have to work very hard. You'll have to learn mathematics, and navigation, and celestial geography."

"Will *you* teach me?"

"Yes. And you'll have to help me by making notes and putting my papers in order and doing various pieces of basic calculation, and so on. And because we'll be visiting some important people, we'll have to find you some pretty clothes. There's a lot to learn, Lyra."

"I don't mind. I want to learn it all."

"I'm sure you will. When you come back to Jordan College you'll be a famous traveller. Now we're going to leave very early in the morning, by the dawn zeppelin, so you'd better run along and go straight to bed. I'll see you at breakfast. Good night!"

"Good night," said Lyra and, remembering the few manners she had, turned at the door and said, "Good night, Master."

He nodded. "Sleep well," he said.

"And thanks," Lyra added to Mrs Coulter.

She did sleep, finally, though Pantalaimon wouldn't settle until she snapped at him, when he became a hedgehog out of pique. It was still dark when someone shook her awake.

"Lyra – hush – don't start – wake up, child."

It was Mrs Lonsdale. She was holding a candle, and she bent over and spoke quietly, holding Lyra still with her free hand.

"Listen. The Master wants to see you before you join Mrs Coulter for breakfast. Get up quickly and run across to the Lodging now. Go into the garden and tap at the French window of the study. You understand?"

Fully awake and on fire with puzzlement, Lyra nodded and slipped her bare feet into the shoes Mrs Lonsdale put down for her.

"Never mind washing – that'll do later. Go straight down and come straight back. I'll start your packing and have something for you to wear. Hurry now."

The dark quadrangle was still full of the chill night air. Overhead the last stars were still visible, but the light from the east was gradually soaking into the sky above the Hall. Lyra ran into the Library Garden, and stood for a moment in the immense hush, looking up at the stone pinnacles of the Chapel, the pearl-green cupola of the Sheldon Building, the white-painted lantern of the Library. Now she was going to leave these sights, she wondered how much she'd miss them.

Something stirred in the study window and a glow of light shone out for a moment. She remembered what she had to do and tapped on the glass door. It opened almost at once.

"Good girl. Come in quickly. We haven't got long," said the Master, and drew the curtain back across the door as soon as she had entered. He was fully dressed in his usual black.

"Aren't I going after all?" Lyra asked.

"Yes; I can't prevent it," said the Master, and Lyra didn't notice at the time what an odd thing that was to say. "Lyra, I'm going to give you something, and you must promise to keep it private. Will you swear to that?"

"Yes," Lyra said.

He crossed to the desk and took from a drawer a small package wrapped in black velvet. When he unfolded the cloth, Lyra saw something like a large watch or a small clock: a thick disc of brass and crystal. It might have been a compass or something of the sort.

"What is it?" she said.

"It's an alethiometer. It's one of only six that were ever made. Lyra, I urge you again: keep it private. It would be better if Mrs Coulter didn't know about it. Your uncle –"

"But what does it do?"

"It tells you the truth. As for how to read it, you'll have to learn by yourself. Now go – it's getting lighter – hurry back to your room before anyone sees you."

He folded the velvet over the instrument and thrust it into her hands. It was surprisingly heavy. Then he put his own hands on either side of her head and held her gently for a moment.

She tried to look up at him, and said, "What were you going to say about Uncle Asriel?"

"Your uncle presented it to Jordan College some years ago. He might –"

Before he could finish, there came a soft urgent knock on the door. She could feel his hands give an involuntary tremor.

"Quick now, child," he said quietly. "The powers of this world are very strong. Men and women are moved by tides much fiercer than you can imagine, and they sweep us all up into the current. Go well, Lyra; bless you, child; bless you. Keep your own counsel."

"Thank you, Master," she said dutifully.

Clutching the bundle to her breast, she left the study by the garden door, looking back briefly once to see the Master's dæmon watching her from the windowsill. The sky was lighter already; there was a faint fresh stir in the air.

"What's that you've got?" said Mrs Lonsdale, closing the battered little suitcase with a snap.

"The Master gave it me. Can't it go in the suitcase?"

"Too late. I'm not opening it now. It'll have to go in your coat pocket, whatever it is. Hurry on down to the Buttery; don't keep them waiting . . ."

It was only after she'd said goodbye to the few servants who were up, and to Mrs Lonsdale, that she remembered Roger; and then she felt guilty for not having thought of him once since meeting Mrs Coulter. How quickly it had all happened!

And now she was on her way to London: sitting next to the window in a zeppelin, no less, with Pantalaimon's sharp little ermine-paws digging into her thigh while his front paws rested against the glass he gazed through. On Lyra's other side Mrs Coulter sat working through some papers, but she soon put them away and talked. Such brilliant talk! Lyra was intoxicated; not about the North this time, but about London, and the restaurants and ballrooms, the soirées at Embassies or Ministries, the intrigues between White Hall and Westminster. Lyra was almost more fascinated by this than by the changing landscape below the airship. What Mrs Coulter was saying seemed to be accompanied by a scent of grown-upness, something disturbing but enticing at the same time: it was the smell of glamour.

The landing in Falkeshall Gardens, the boat ride across the wide brown river, the grand mansion-block on the Embankment where a stout commissionaire (a sort of porter with medals) saluted Mrs Coulter and winked at Lyra, who sized him up expressionlessly . . .

And then the flat . . .

Lyra could only gasp.

She had seen a great deal of beauty in her short life, but it was Jordan College beauty, Oxford beauty — grand and stony and masculine. In Jordan College, much was magnificent, but nothing was pretty. In Mrs Coulter's flat, everything was pretty. It was full of light, for the wide windows faced south, and the walls were covered in a delicate gold-and-white striped wallpaper. Charming pictures in gilt frames, an antique looking-glass, fanciful sconces bearing anbaric lamps with frilled shades; and frills on the cushions too, and flowery valances over the curtain-rail, and a soft green leaf-pattern carpet underfoot; and every surface was covered, it seemed to Lyra's innocent eye, with pretty little china boxes and shepherdesses and harlequins of porcelain.

Mrs Coulter smiled at her admiration.

"Yes, Lyra," she said, "there's such a lot to show you! Take your coat off and I'll take you to the bathroom. You can have a wash, and then we'll have some lunch and go shopping . . ."

The bathroom was another wonder. Lyra was used to washing

with hard yellow soap in a chipped basin, where the water that struggled out of the taps was warm at best, and often flecked with rust. But here the water was hot, the soap rose–pink and fragrant, the towels thick and cloudy-soft. And around the edge of the tinted mirror there were little pink lights, so that when Lyra looked into it she saw a softly illuminated figure quite unlike the Lyra she knew.

Pantalaimon, who was imitating the form of Mrs Coulter's dæmon, crouched on the edge of the basin making faces at her. She pushed him into the soapy water and suddenly remembered the alethiometer in her coat pocket. She'd left the coat on a chair in the other room. She'd promised the Master to keep it secret from Mrs Coulter . . .

Oh, this *was* confusing. Mrs Coulter was so kind and wise, whereas Lyra had actually seen the Master trying to poison Uncle Asriel. Which of them did she owe most obedience to?

She rubbed herself dry hastily and hurried back to the sitting room, where her coat still lay untouched, of course.

"Ready?" said Mrs Coulter. "I thought we'd go to the Royal Arctic Institute for lunch. I'm one of the very few female members, so I might as well use the privileges I have."

Twenty minutes' walk took them to a grand stone-fronted building where they sat in a wide dining-room with snowy cloths and bright silver on the tables, and ate calves' liver and bacon.

"Calves' liver is all right," Mrs Coulter told her, "and so is seal liver, but if you're stuck for food in the Arctic, you mustn't eat bear liver. That's full of a poison that'll kill you in minutes."

As they ate, Mrs Coulter pointed out some of the members at the other tables.

"D'you see the elderly gentleman with the red tie? That's Colonel Carborn. He made the first balloon flight over the North Pole. And the tall man by the window who's just got up is Dr Broken Arrow."

"Is he a Skraeling?"

"Yes. He was the man who mapped the ocean currents in the Great Northern Ocean . . ."

Lyra looked at them all, these great men, with curiosity and awe. They were scholars, no doubt about that, but they were explorers too. Dr Broken Arrow would know about bear livers; she doubted whether the Librarian of Jordan College would.

After lunch Mrs Coulter showed her some of the precious Arctic relics in the Institute Library – the harpoon with which the great whale Grimssdur had been killed; the stone carved with an inscription in an unknown language which was found in the hand of the explorer Lord Rukh, frozen to death in his lonely tent; a fire-striker used by Captain Hudson on his famous voyage to Van Tieren's Land. She told the story of each one, and Lyra felt her heart stir with admiration of these great, brave, distant heroes.

And then they went shopping. Everything on this extra-ordinary day was a new experience for Lyra, but shopping was the most dizzying. To go into a vast building full of beautiful clothes, where people let you try them on, where you looked at yourself in mirrors ... And the clothes were so *pretty* ... Lyra's clothes had come to her through Mrs Lonsdale, and a lot of them had been handed down and much mended. She had seldom had anything new, and when she had, it had been picked for wear and not for looks; and she had never chosen anything for herself. And now to find Mrs Coulter suggesting this, and praising that, and paying for it all, and more ...

By the time they'd finished, Lyra was flushed and bright-eyed with tiredness. Mrs Coulter ordered most of the clothes packed up and delivered, and took one or two things with her when she and Lyra walked back to the flat.

Then a bath, with thick scented foam. Mrs Coulter came into the bathroom to wash Lyra's hair, and she didn't rub and scrape like Mrs Lonsdale either. She was gentle. Pantalaimon watched with powerful curiosity until Mrs Coulter looked at him, and he knew what she meant and turned away, averting his eyes modestly from these feminine mysteries as the golden monkey was doing. He had never had to look away from Lyra before.

Then, after the bath, a warm drink with milk and herbs; and a new flannel nightdress with printed flowers and a scalloped hem, and sheep-skin slippers dyed soft blue; and then bed.

So soft, this bed! So gentle, the anbaric light on the bedside table! And the bedroom so cosy with little cupboards and a dressing-table and a chest of drawers where her new clothes would go, and a carpet from one wall to the other, and pretty curtains covered in stars and moons and planets! Lyra lay stiffly, too tired to sleep, too enchanted to question anything.

When Mrs Coulter had wished her a soft good night and gone out, Pantalaimon plucked at her hair. She brushed him away, but he whispered, "Where's the thing?"

She knew at once what he meant. Her old shabby overcoat hung in the wardrobe; a few seconds later, she was back in bed, sitting up cross-legged in the lamplight, with Pantalaimon watching closely as she unfolded the black velvet and looked at what it was the Master had given her.

"What did he call it?" she whispered.

"An alethiometer."

There was no point in asking what that meant. It lay heavily in her hands, the crystal face gleaming, the brass body exquisitely machined. It was very like a clock, or a compass, for there were hands pointing to places around the dial, but instead of the hours or the points of the compass there were several little pictures, each of them painted with extraordinary precision, as if on ivory with the finest and slenderest sable brush. She turned the dial around to look at them all. There was an anchor; an hourglass surmounted by a skull; a bull, a beehive . . . Thirty-six altogether, and she couldn't even guess what they meant.

"There's a wheel, look," said Pantalaimon. "See if you can wind it up."

There were three little knurled winding-wheels, in fact, and each of them turned one of the three shorter hands, which moved around the dial in a series of smooth satisfying clicks. You could arrange them to point at any of the pictures, and once they had clicked into position, pointing exactly at the centre of each one, they would not move.

The fourth hand was longer and more slender, and seemed to be made of a duller metal than the other three. Lyra couldn't control its movement at all; it swung where it wanted to, like a compass-needle, except that it didn't settle.

"Meter means measure," said Pantalaimon. "Like thermo-meter. The Chaplain told us that."

"Yes, but that's the easy bit," she whispered back. "What d'you think it's *for*?"

Neither of them could guess. Lyra spent a long time turning the hands to point at one symbol or another (angel, helmet, dolphin; globe, lute, compasses; candle, thunderbolt, horse) and watching the long needle swing on its never-ceasing errant way, and although she understood nothing, she was intrigued and delighted by the complexity and the detail. Pantalaimon became a mouse to get closer to it, and rested his tiny paws on the edge, his button eyes bright black with curiosity as he watched the needle swing.

"What do you think the Master meant about Uncle Asriel?" she said.

"Perhaps we've got to keep it safe and give it to him."

"But the Master was going to poison him! Perhaps it's the opposite. Perhaps he was going to say, don't give it to him."

"No," Pantalaimon said, "it was *her* we had to keep it safe from –"

There was a soft knock on the door.

Mrs Coulter said, "Lyra, I should put the light out if I were you. You're tired, and we'll be busy tomorrow."

Lyra had thrust the alethiometer swiftly under the blankets.

"All right, Mrs Coulter," she said.

"Good night now."

"Good night."

She snuggled down and switched off the light. Before she fell asleep, she tucked the alethiometer under the pillow, just in case.

5
THE COCKTAIL PARTY

IN THE DAYS that followed, Lyra went everywhere with Mrs Coulter, almost as if she were a dæmon herself. Mrs Coulter knew a great many people, and they met in all kinds of different places. In the morning there might be a meeting of geographers at the Royal Arctic Institute, and Lyra would sit by and listen; and then Mrs Coulter might meet a politician or a cleric for lunch in a smart restaurant, and they would be very taken with Lyra and order special dishes for her, and she would learn how to eat asparagus or what sweetbreads tasted like. And then in the afternoon there might be more shopping, for Mrs Coulter was preparing her expedition, and there were furs and oilskins and waterproof boots to buy, as well as sleeping-bags and knives and drawing instruments that delighted Lyra's heart. After that they might go to tea and meet some ladies, as well-dressed as Mrs Coulter if not so beautiful or accomplished: women so unlike female scholars or gyptian boat-mothers or college servants as almost to be a new sex altogether, one with dangerous powers and qualities such as elegance, charm, and grace. Lyra would be dressed up prettily for these occasions, and the ladies would pamper her and include her in their graceful delicate talk, which was all about people: this artist, or that politician, or those lovers.

And when the evening came, Mrs Coulter might take Lyra to the theatre, and again there would be lots of glamorous people to talk to and be admired by, for it seemed that Mrs Coulter knew everyone important in London.

In the intervals between all these other activities Mrs Coulter would teach her the rudiments of geography and mathematics. Lyra's knowledge had great gaps in it, like a map of the world largely eaten by mice, for at Jordan they had taught her in a piecemeal and disconnected way: a Junior Scholar would be detailed to catch her and instruct her in such-and-such, and the lessons would continue for a sullen week or so until she "forgot" to turn up, to the Scholar's relief. Or else a Scholar would forget what he was supposed to teach her, and drill her at great length about the subject of his current research, whatever that happened to be. It was no wonder her knowledge was patchy. She knew about atoms and elementary particles, and anbaromagnetic charges and the four fundamental forces and other bits and pieces of experimental theology, but nothing about the solar system. In fact, when Mrs Coulter realized this and explained how the earth and the other five planets revolved around the sun, Lyra laughed loudly at the joke.

However, she was keen to show that she did know some things, and when Mrs Coulter was telling her about electrons, she said expertly, "Yes, they're negatively charged particles. Sort of like Dust, except that Dust isn't charged."

As soon as she said that, Mrs Coulter's dæmon snapped his head up to look at her, and all the golden fur on his little body stood up, bristling, as if it were charged itself. Mrs Coulter laid a hand on his back.

"Dust?" she said.

"Yeah. You know, from space, that Dust."

"What do you know about Dust, Lyra?"

"Oh, that it comes out of space, and it lights people up, if you have a special sort of camera to see it by. Except not children. It doesn't affect children."

"Where did you learn that from?"

By now Lyra was aware that there was a powerful tension in the room, because Pantalaimon had crept ermine-like on to her lap and was trembling violently.

"Just someone in Jordan," Lyra said vaguely. "I forget who. I think it was one of the Scholars."

"Was it in one of your lessons?"

"Yes, it might have been. Or else it might've been just in passing. Yes. I think that was it. This Scholar, I think he was from New Denmark, he was talking to the Chaplain about Dust and I was just passing and it sounded interesting so I couldn't help stopping to listen. That's what it was."

"I see," said Mrs Coulter.

"Is it right, what he told me? Did I get it wrong?"

"Well, I don't know. I'm sure you know much more than I do. Let's get back to those electrons . . ."

Later, Pantalaimon said, "You know when all the fur stood up on her dæmon? Well, I was behind him, and she grabbed his fur so tight her knuckles went white. You couldn't see. It was a long time till his fur went down. I thought he was going to leap at you."

That was strange, no doubt; but neither of them knew what to make of it.

And finally, there were other kinds of lesson so gently and subtly given that they didn't feel like lessons at all. How to wash one's own hair; how to judge which colours suited one; how to say no in such a charming way that no offence was given; how to put on lipstick, powder, scent. To be sure, Mrs Coulter didn't teach Lyra the latter arts directly, but she knew Lyra was watching when she made herself up, and she took care to let Lyra see where she kept the cosmetics, and to allow her time on her own to explore and try them out for herself.

Time passed, and autumn began to change into winter. From time to time Lyra thought of Jordan College, but it seemed small and quiet compared to the busy life she led now. Every so often she thought of Roger, too, and felt uneasy, but there was an opera to go to, or a new dress to wear, or the Royal Arctic Institute to visit, and then she forgot him again.

When Lyra had been living there for six weeks or so, Mrs Coulter decided to hold a cocktail party. Lyra had the impression that there was something to celebrate, though Mrs Coulter never said what it was. She ordered flowers, she discussed canapés and drinks with the caterer, and she spent a whole evening with Lyra deciding whom to invite.

"We must have the Archbishop. I couldn't afford to leave him out, though he's the most hateful old snob. Lord Boreal is in town: he'll be fun. And the Princess Postnikova. Do you think it would be right to invite Erik Andersson? I wonder if it's about time to take him up . . ."

Erik Andersson was the latest fashionable dancer. Lyra had

no idea what "take him up" meant, but she enjoyed giving her opinion none the less. She dutifully wrote down all the names Mrs Coulter suggested, spelling them atrociously and then crossing them out when Mrs Coulter decided against them after all.

When Lyra went to bed, Pantalaimon whispered from the pillow:

"She's never going to the North! She's going to keep us here for ever. When are we going to run away?"

"She is," Lyra whispered back. "You just don't like her. Well, that's hard luck. I like her. And why would she be teaching us navigation and all that if she wasn't going to take us North?"

"To stop you getting impatient, that's why. You don't really want to stand around at the cocktail party being all sweet and pretty. She's just making a pet out of you."

Lyra turned her back and closed her eyes. But what Pantalaimon said was true. She had been feeling confined and cramped by this polite life, however luxurious it was. She would have given anything for a day with her Oxford ragamuffin friends, with a battle in the Claybeds and a race along the canal. The one thing that kept her polite and attentive to Mrs Coulter was that tantalizing hope of going North. Perhaps they would meet Lord Asriel. Perhaps he and Mrs Coulter would fall in love, and they would get married and adopt Lyra, and go and rescue Roger from the Gobblers.

On the afternoon of the cocktail party Mrs Coulter took Lyra to a fashionable hairdresser's, where her stiff dark blonde hair was softened and waved, and her nails were filed and polished, and where they even applied a little make-up to her eyes and lips to show her how to do it. Then they went to collect the new dress Mrs Coulter had ordered for her, and to buy some patent-leather shoes, and then it was time to go back to the flat and check the flowers and get dressed.

"Not the shoulder-bag, dear," said Mrs Coulter as Lyra came out of her bedroom, glowing with a sense of her own prettiness.

Lyra had taken to wearing a little white leather shoulder-bag everywhere, so as to keep the alethiometer close at hand. Mrs Coulter, loosening the cramped way some roses had been bunched into a vase, saw that Lyra wasn't moving and glanced pointedly at the door.

"Oh, please, Mrs Coulter, I do love this bag!"

"Not indoors, Lyra. It looks absurd to be carrying a shoulder-bag in your own home. Take it off at once, and come and help check these glasses . . ."

It wasn't so much her snappish tone as the words "in your own home" that made Lyra resist stubbornly. Pantalaimon flew to the floor and instantly became a polecat, arching his back against her little white ankle-socks. Encouraged by this, Lyra said:

"But it won't be in the way. And it's the only thing I really like wearing. I think it really suits −"

She didn't finish the sentence, because Mrs Coulter's dæmon sprang off the sofa in a blur of golden fur and pinned Pantalaimon to the carpet before he could move. Lyra cried out in alarm, and then in fear and pain, as Pantalaimon twisted this way and that, shrieking and snarling, unable to loosen the golden monkey's grip. Only a few seconds, and the monkey had overmastered him: with one fierce black paw around his throat and his back paws gripping the polecat's lower limbs, he took one of Pantalaimon's ears in his other paw and pulled as if he intended to tear it off. Not angrily, either, but with a cold curious force that was horrifying to see and even worse to feel.

Lyra sobbed in terror.

"Don't! Please! Stop hurting us!"

Mrs Coulter looked up from her flowers.

"Do as I tell you, then," she said.

"I promise!"

The golden monkey stepped away from Pantalaimon as if he were suddenly bored. Pantalaimon fled to Lyra at once, and she scooped him up to her face to kiss and gentle.

"Now, Lyra," said Mrs Coulter.

Lyra turned her back abruptly and slammed into her bedroom, but no sooner had she banged the door shut behind her than it opened again. Mrs Coulter was standing there only a foot or two away.

"Lyra, if you behave in this coarse and vulgar way we shall have a confrontation, which I will win. Take off that bag this instant.

Control that unpleasant frown. Never slam a door again in my hearing or out of it. Now the first guests will be arriving in a few minutes, and they are going to find you perfectly behaved, sweet, charming, innocent, attentive, delightful in every way. I particularly wish for that, Lyra, do you understand me?"

"Yes, Mrs Coulter."

"Then kiss me."

She bent a little and offered her cheek. Lyra had to stand on tiptoe to kiss it. She noticed how smooth it was, and the slight perplexing smell of Mrs Coulter's flesh: scented, but somehow metallic. She drew away and laid the shoulder-bag on her dressing-table before following Mrs Coulter back to the drawing-room.

"What do you think of the flowers, dear?" said Mrs Coulter as sweetly as if nothing had happened. "I suppose one can't go wrong with roses, but you can have too much of a good thing . . . Have the caterers brought enough ice? Be a dear and go and ask. Warm drinks are *horrid* . . ."

Lyra found it was quite easy to pretend to be light-hearted and charming, though she was conscious every second of Pantalaimon's disgust, and of his hatred for the golden monkey. Presently the doorbell rang, and soon the room was filling up with fashionably-dressed ladies and handsome or distinguished men. Lyra moved among them offering canapés or smiling sweetly and making pretty answers when they spoke to her. She felt like a universal pet, and the second she voiced that thought to herself, Pantalaimon stretched his goldfinch-wings and chirruped loudly.

She sensed his glee at having been proved right, and became a little more retiring.

"And where do you go to school, my dear?" said an elderly lady, inspecting Lyra through a lorgnette.

"I don't go to school," Lyra told her.

"Really? I thought your mother would have sent you to her old school. A *very* good place . . ."

Lyra was mystified until she realized the old lady's mistake.

"Oh! She's not my mother! I'm just here helping her. I'm her personal assistant," she said importantly.

"I see. And who *are* your people?"

Again Lyra had to wonder what she meant before replying.

"They were a count and countess," she said. "They both died in an aeronautical accident in the North."

"Which count?"

"Count Belacqua. He was Lord Asriel's brother."

The old lady's dæmon, a scarlet macaw, shifted as if in irritation from one foot to another. The old lady was beginning to frown with curiosity, so Lyra smiled sweetly and moved on.

She was going past a group of men and one young woman near the large sofa when she heard the word *Dust*. She had seen enough of society now to understand when men and women were flirting, and she watched the process with fascination, though she was more fascinated by the mention of Dust, and she hung back to listen. The men seemed to be scholars; from the way the young woman was questioning them, Lyra took her to be a student of some kind.

"It was discovered by a Muscovite – stop me if you know this already –" a middle-aged man was saying, as the young woman gazed at him in admiration – "a man called Rusakov, and they're usually called Rusakov Particles after him. Elementary particles that don't interact in any way with others – very hard to detect, but the extraordinary thing is that they seem to be attracted to human beings."

"Really?" said the young woman, wide-eyed.

"And even more extraordinary," he went on, "some human beings more than others. Adults attract them, but not children. At least, not much, and not until adolescence. In fact, that's the very reason –" his voice dropped, and he moved closer to the young woman, putting his hand confidentially on her shoulder – "that's the very reason the Oblation Board was set up. As our good hostess here could tell you."

"Really? Is she involved with the Oblation Board?"

"My dear, she *is* the Oblation Board. It's entirely her own project –"

The man was about to tell her more when he caught sight of Lyra. She stared back at him unblinkingly, and perhaps he had had a little too much to drink, or perhaps he was keen to impress the young woman, for he said:

"This little lady knows all about it, I'll be bound. You're safe from the Oblation Board, aren't you, my dear?"

"Oh, yes," said Lyra. "I'm safe from everyone here. Where I used to live, in Oxford, there was all kinds of dangerous things. There was gyptians – they take kids and sell 'em to the Turks for slaves. And on Port Meadow at the full moon there's a werewolf that comes out from the old nunnery at Godstow. I heard him howling once. And there's the Gobblers . . ."

"That's what I mean," the man said. "That's what they call the Oblation Board, don't they?"

Lyra felt Pantalaimon tremble suddenly, but he was on his best behaviour. The dæmons of the two grown-ups, a cat and a butterfly, didn't seem to notice.

"Gobblers?" said the young woman. "What a peculiar name! Why do they call them Gobblers?"

Lyra was about to tell her one of the blood-curdling stories she'd made up to frighten the Oxford kids with, but the man was already speaking.

"From the initials, d'you see? General Oblation Board. Very old idea, as a matter of fact. In the Middle Ages, parents would give their children to the church to be monks or nuns. And the unfortunate brats were known as oblates. Means a sacrifice, an offering, something of that sort. So the same idea was taken up when they were looking into the Dust business . . . As our little friend probably knows. Why don't you go and talk to Lord Boreal?" he added to Lyra directly. "I'm sure he'd like to meet Mrs Coulter's protégée . . . That's him, the man with grey hair and the serpent-dæmon."

He wanted to get rid of Lyra so that he could talk more privately with the young woman; Lyra could tell that easily. But the young woman, it seemed, was still interested in Lyra, and slipped away from the man to talk to her.

"Stop a minute . . . What's your name?"

"Lyra."

"I'm Adèle Starminster. I'm a journalist. Could I have a quiet word?"

Thinking it only natural that people should wish to talk to her, Lyra said simply, "Yes."

The woman's butterfly-dæmon rose into the air, casting about to left and right, and fluttered down to whisper something, at which Adèle Starminster said, "Come to the window-seat."

This was a favourite spot of Lyra's; it overlooked the river, and at this time of night, the lights across on the south bank were glittering brilliantly over their reflections in the black water of the high tide. A line of barges hauled by a tug moved upriver. Adèle Starminster sat down and moved along the cushioned seat to make room.

"Did Professor Docker say that you had some connection with Mrs Coulter?"

"Yes."

"What is it? You're not her daughter, or something? I suppose I should know —"

"No!" said Lyra. "Course not. I'm her personal assistant."

"Her personal assistant? You're a bit young, aren't you? I thought you were related to her or something. What's she like?"

"She's very clever," said Lyra. Before this evening she would have said much more, but things were changing.

"Yes, but personally," Adèle Starminster insisted. "I mean, is she friendly or impatient or what? Do you live here with her? What's she like in private?"

"She's very nice," said Lyra stolidly.

"What sort of things do you do? How do you help her?"

"I do calculations and all that. Like for navigation."

"Ah, I see . . . And where do you come from? What was your name again?"

"Lyra. I come from Oxford."

"Why did Mrs Coulter pick you to —"

She stopped very suddenly, because Mrs Coulter herself had appeared close by. From the way Adèle Starminster looked up at her, and the agitated way her dæmon was fluttering around her head, Lyra could tell that the young woman wasn't supposed to be at the party at all.

"I don't know your name," said Mrs Coulter very quietly, "but I shall find it out within five minutes, and then you will never work as a journalist again. Now get up very quietly, without making a fuss, and leave. I might add that whoever brought you here will also suffer."

Mrs Coulter seemed to be charged with some kind of anbaric force. She even smelled different: a hot smell, like heated metal, came off her body. Lyra had felt something of it earlier, but now she was seeing it directed at someone else, and poor Adèle Starminster had no force to resist. Her dæmon fell limp on her shoulder and flapped his gorgeous wings once or twice before fainting, and the woman herself seemed to be unable to stand fully upright. Moving in a slight awkward crouch, she made her way through the press of loudly talking guests and out of the drawing-room door. She had one hand clutched to her shoulder, holding the swooning dæmon in place.

"Well?" said Mrs Coulter to Lyra.

"I never told her anything important," Lyra said.

"What was she asking?"

"Just about what I was doing and who I was, and stuff like that."

As she said that, Lyra noticed that Mrs Coulter was alone, without her dæmon. How could that be? But a moment later the golden monkey appeared at her side, and, reaching down, she took his hand and swung him up lightly to her shoulder. At once she seemed at ease again.

"If you come across anyone else who obviously hasn't been invited, dear, do come and find me, won't you?"

The hot metallic smell was vanishing. Perhaps Lyra had only imagined it. She could smell Mrs Coulter's scent again, and the roses, and the cigarillo-smoke, and the scent of other women. Mrs Coulter smiled at Lyra in a way that seemed to say, "You and I understand these things, don't we?" and moved on to greet some other guests.

Pantalaimon was whispering in Lyra's ear.

"While she was here, her dæmon was coming out of our bedroom. He's been spying. He knows about the alethiometer!"

Lyra felt that that was probably true, but there was nothing she could do about it. What had that Professor been saying about the Gobblers? She looked around to find him again, but no sooner had she seen him than the commissionaire (in servant's dress for the evening) and another man tapped the Professor on the shoulder and spoke quietly to him, at which he turned pale and followed them out. That took no more than a couple of seconds, and it was so discreetly done that hardly anyone noticed. But it left Lyra feeling anxious and exposed.

She wandered through the two big rooms where the party was taking place, half-listening to the conversations around her, half-interested in the taste of the cocktails she wasn't allowed to try, and increasingly fretful. She wasn't aware that anyone was watching her until the commissionaire appeared at her side and bent to say:

"Miss Lyra, the gentleman by the fireplace would like to speak to you. He's Lord Boreal, if you didn't know."

Lyra looked up across the room. The powerful-looking grey-haired man was looking directly at her, and as their eyes met he nodded and beckoned.

Unwilling, but more interested now, she went across.

"Good evening, child," he said. His voice was smooth and commanding. His serpent-dæmon's mailed head and emerald eyes glittered in the light from the cut-glass lamp on the wall nearby.

"Good evening," said Lyra.

"How is my old friend the Master of Jordan?"

"Very well, thank you."

"I expect they were all sorry to say goodbye to you."

"Yes, they were."

"And is Mrs Coulter keeping you busy? What is she teaching you?"

Because Lyra was feeling rebellious and uneasy, she didn't answer this patronizing question with the truth, or with one of her usual flights of fancy. Instead she said, "I'm learning about Rusakov Particles, and about the Oblation Board."

He seemed to become focused at once, in the same way that you could focus the beam of an anbaric lantern. All his attention streamed at her fiercely.

"Suppose you tell me what you know," he said.

"They're doing experiments in the North," Lyra said. She was feeling reckless now. "Like Dr Grumman."

"Go on."

"They've got this special kind of photogram where you can see Dust, and when you see a man there's like all light coming to him, and there's none on a child. At least not so much."

"Did Mrs Coulter show you a picture like that?"

Lyra hesitated, for this was not lying but something else, and she wasn't practised at it.

"No," she said after a moment. "I saw that one at Jordan College."

"Who showed it to you?"

"He wasn't really showing it to *me*," Lyra admitted. "I was just passing and I saw it. And then my friend Roger was taken by the Oblation Board. But –"

"Who showed you that picture?"

"My Uncle Asriel."

"When?"

"When he was in Jordan College last time."

"I see. And what else have you been learning about? Did I hear you mention the Oblation Board?"

"Yes. But I didn't hear about that from him, I heard it here."

Which was exactly true, she thought.

He was looking at her narrowly. She gazed back with all the innocence she had. Finally he nodded.

"Then Mrs Coulter must have decided you were ready to help her in that work. Interesting. Have you taken part yet?"

"No," said Lyra. What was he talking about? Pantalaimon was cleverly in his most inexpressive shape, a moth, and couldn't betray her feelings; and she was sure she could keep her own face innocent.

"And has she told you what happens to the children?"

"No, she hasn't told me that. I only just know that it's about Dust, and they're like a kind of sacrifice."

Again, that wasn't exactly a lie, she thought; she had never said that Mrs Coulter herself had told her.

"*Sacrifice* is rather a dramatic way of putting it. What's done is for their good as well as ours. And of course they all come to Mrs Coulter willingly. That's why she's so valuable. They must want to take part, and what child could resist her? And if she's going to use you as well to bring them in, so much the better. I'm very pleased."

He smiled at her in the way Mrs Coulter had: as if they were both in on a secret. She smiled politely back and he turned away to talk to someone else.

She and Pantalaimon could sense each other's horror. She wanted to go away by herself and talk to him; she wanted to leave the flat; she wanted to go back to Jordan College and her little shabby bedroom on Staircase Twelve; she wanted to find Lord Asriel –

And as if in answer to that last wish, she heard his name mentioned, and wandered closer to the group talking nearby with the pretext of helping herself to a canapé from the plate on the table. A man in a bishop's purple was saying:

". . . No, I don't think Lord Asriel will be troubling us for quite some time."

"And where did you say he was being held?"

"In the fortress of Svalbard, I'm told. Guarded by *panserbjørne*, you know, armoured bears. Formidable creatures! He won't escape from them if he lives to be a thousand. The fact is that I really think the way is clear, very nearly clear –"

"The last experiments have confirmed what I always believed – that Dust is an emanation from the dark principle itself, and –"

"Do I detect the Zoroastrian heresy?"

"What *used* to be a heresy –"

"And if we could isolate the dark principle –"

"Svalbard, did you say?"

"Armoured bears –"

"The Oblation Board –"

"The children don't suffer, I'm sure of it –"

"Lord Asriel imprisoned –"

Lyra had heard enough. She turned away, and moving as quietly as the moth-Pantalaimon, she went into her bedroom and closed the door. The noise of the party was muffled at once.

"Well?" she whispered, and he became a goldfinch on her shoulder.

"Are we going to run away?" he whispered back.

"Course. If we do it now with all these people about she might not notice for a while."

"*He* will."

Pantalaimon meant Mrs Coulter's dæmon. When Lyra thought of his lithe golden shape she felt ill with fear.

"I'll fight him this time," Pantalaimon said boldly. "I can change and he can't. I'll change so quickly he won't be able to keep hold. This time I'll win, you'll see."

Lyra nodded distractedly. What should she wear? How could she get out without being seen?

"You'll have to go and spy," she whispered. "As soon as it's clear we'll have to run. Be a moth," she added. "Remember, the *second* there's no one looking . . ."

She opened the door a crack and he crawled out, dark against the warm pink light in the corridor.

Meanwhile, she hastily flung on the warmest clothes she had and stuffed some more into one of the coal-silk bags from the fashionable shop they'd visited that very afternoon. Mrs Coulter had given her money like sweets, and although she had spent it lavishly, there were still several sovereigns left, which she put in the pocket of the dark wolfskin coat.

Last of all she packed the alethiometer in its black velvet cloth. Had that abominable monkey found it? He must have done; he must have told her; oh, if she'd only hidden it better!

She tiptoed to the door. Her room opened into the end of the corridor nearest the hall, luckily, and most of the guests were in the two big rooms further along. There was the sound of voices talking loudly, laughter, the quiet flushing of a lavatory, the tinkle of glasses; and then a tiny moth-voice at her ear said:

"Now! Quick!"

She slipped through the door and into the hall, and in less than three seconds she was opening the front door of the flat. A moment after that she was through and pulling it quietly shut, and with Pantalaimon a goldfinch again, she ran for the stairs and fled.

6

THE THROWING-NETS

SHE WALKED QUICKLY away from the river, because the Embankment was wide and well-lit. There was a tangle of narrow streets between there and the Royal Arctic Institute, which was the only place Lyra was sure of being able to find, and into that dark maze she hurried now.

If only she knew London as well as she knew Oxford! Then she would have known which streets to avoid; or where she could scrounge some food; or, best of all, which doors to knock on and find shelter. In that cold night, the dark alleys all around were alive with movement and secret life, and she knew none of it.

Pantalaimon became a wildcat and scanned the dark all around with his night-piercing eyes. Every so often he'd stop, bristling, and she would turn aside from the entrance she'd been about to go down. The night was full of noises: bursts of drunken laughter, two raucous voices raised in song, the clatter and whine of some badly-oiled machine in a basement. Lyra walked delicately through it all, her senses magnified and mingled with Pantalaimon's, keeping to the shadows and the narrow alleys.

From time to time she had to cross a wider, well-lit street, where the tramcars hummed and sparked under their anbaric wires. There were rules for crossing London streets, but she took no notice, and when anyone shouted, she fled.

It was a fine thing to be free again. She knew that Pantalaimon, padding on wildcat-paws beside her, felt the same joy as she did to be in the open air, even if it was murky London air laden with fumes and soot and clangorous with noise. Some time soon they'd have to think over the meaning of what they'd heard in Mrs Coulter's flat, but not yet. And some time eventually they'd have to find a place to sleep.

At a crossroads near the corner of a big department store, whose windows shone brilliantly over the wet pavement, there was a coffee stall: a little hut on wheels with a counter under the wooden flap that swung up like an awning. Yellow light glowed inside, and the fragrance of coffee drifted out. The white-coated owner was leaning on the counter talking to the two or three customers.

It was tempting. Lyra had been walking for an hour now, and it was cold and damp. With Pantalaimon a sparrow, she went up to the counter and reached up to gain the owner's attention.

"Cup of coffee and a ham sandwich, please," she said.

"You're out late, my dear," said a gentleman in a top hat and white silk muffler.

"Yeah," she said, turning away from him to scan the busy intersection. A theatre nearby was just emptying, and crowds milled around the lighted foyer, calling for cabs, wrapping coats around their shoulders. In the other direction was the entrance of a Chthonic Railway Station, with more crowds pouring up and down the steps.

"Here you are, love," said the coffee-stall man. "Two shillings."

"Let me pay for this," said the man in the top hat.

Lyra thought, why not? I can run faster than him, and I might need all my money later. The top-hatted man dropped a coin on the counter and smiled down at her. His dæmon was a lemur. It clung to his lapel, staring round-eyed at Lyra.

She bit into her sandwich and kept her eyes on the busy street. She had no idea where she was, because she had never seen a map of London, and she didn't even know how big it was or how far she'd have to walk to find the country.

"What's your name?" said the man.

"Alice."

"That's a pretty name. Let me put a drop of this into your coffee . . . warm you up . . ."

He was unscrewing the top of a silver flask.

"I don't like that," said Lyra. "I just like coffee."

"I bet you've never had brandy like this before."

"I have. I was sick all over the place. I had a whole bottle, or nearly."

"Just as you like," said the man, tilting the flask into his own cup. "Where are you going, all alone like this?"

"Going to meet my father."

"And who's he?"

"He's a murderer."

"He's what?"

"I told you, he's a murderer. It's his profession. He's doing a job tonight. I got his clean clothes in here, 'cause he's usually all covered in blood when he's finished a job."

"Ah! You're joking."

"I en't."

The lemur uttered a soft mewing sound and clambered slowly up behind the man's head, to peer out at her. She drank her coffee stolidly and ate the last of her sandwich.

"Good night," she said. "I can see my father coming now. He looks a bit angry."

The top-hat man glanced around, and Lyra set off towards the theatre crowd. Much as she would have liked to see the Chthonic Railway (Mrs Coulter had said it was not really intended for people of their class) she was wary of being trapped under-ground; better to be out in the open, where she could run, if she had to.

On and on she walked, and the streets became darker and emp-tier. It was drizzling, but even if there'd been no clouds the city sky was too tainted with light to show the stars. Pantalaimon thought they were going north, but who could tell?

Endless streets of little identical brick houses, with gardens only big enough for a dustbin; great gaunt factories behind wire fences, with one anbaric light glowing bleakly high up on a wall and a night-watchman snoozing by his brazier; occasionally a dismal oratory, only distinguished from a warehouse by the crucifix outside. Once she tried the door of one of these places, only to hear a groan from the bench a foot away in the darkness. She realized that the porch was full of sleeping figures, and fled.

"Where we going to sleep, Pan?" she said as they trudged down a street of closed and shuttered shops.

"A doorway somewhere."

"Don't want to be seen, though. They're all so open."

"There's a canal down there . . ."

He was looking down a side-road to the left. Sure enough, a

patch of dark glimmer showed open water, and when they cautiously went to look, they found a canal basin where a dozen or so barges were tied up at the wharves, some high in the water, some low and laden under the gallows-like cranes. A dim light shone in one window of a wooden hut, and a thread of smoke rose from the metal chimney; otherwise the only lights were high up on the wall of the warehouse or the gantry of a crane, leaving the ground in gloom. The wharves were piled with barrels of coal-spirit, with stacks of great round logs, with rolls of cahuchuc-covered cable.

Lyra tiptoed up to the hut and peeped in at the window. An old man was laboriously reading a picture-story paper and smoking a pipe, with his spaniel-dæmon curled up asleep on the table. As she looked, the man got up and brought a blackened kettle from the iron stove and poured some hot water into a cracked mug before settling back with his paper.

"Should we ask him to let us in, Pan?" she whispered, but he was distracted; he was a bat, an owl, a wildcat again; she looked all round, catching his panic, and then saw them at the same time as he did: two men running at her, one from each side, the nearer holding a throwing-net.

Pantalaimon uttered a harsh scream and launched himself as a leopard at the closer man's dæmon, a savage-looking fox, bowling her backwards so that she tangled with the man's legs. The man cursed and dodged aside, and Lyra darted past him towards the open spaces of the wharf. What she mustn't do was get boxed in a corner.

Pantalaimon, an eagle now, swooped at her and cried, "Left! Left!"

She swerved that way and saw a gap between the coal-spirit barrels and the end of a corrugated iron shed, and darted for it like a bullet.

But those throwing-nets!

She heard a hiss in the air, and past her cheek something lashed and sharply stung, and loathsome tarred strings across her face, her arms, her hands tangled and held her, and she fell, snarling and tearing and struggling in vain.

"Pan! Pan!"

But the fox-dæmon tore at the cat-Pantalaimon, and Lyra felt the pain in her own flesh, and sobbed a great cry as he fell. One man was swiftly lashing cords around her, around her limbs, her throat, body, head, bundling her over and over on the wet ground. She was helpless, exactly like a fly being trussed by a spider. Poor hurt Pan was dragging himself towards her, with the fox-dæmon worrying his back, and he had no strength left to change, even; and the other man was lying in a puddle, with an arrow through his neck –

The whole world grew still as the man tying the net saw it too.

Pantalaimon sat up and blinked, and then there was a soft thud, and the net-man fell choking and gasping right across Lyra, who cried out in horror: that was *blood* gushing out of him!

Running feet, and someone hauled the man away and bent over him; then other hands lifted Lyra, a knife snicked and pulled and the net-strings fell away one by one, and she tore them off, spitting, and hurled herself down to cuddle Pantalaimon.

Kneeling, she twisted to look up at the newcomers. Three dark men, one armed with a bow, the others with knives; and as she turned, the bowman caught his breath.

"That en't Lyra?"

A familiar voice, but she couldn't place it till he stepped forward and the nearest light fell on his face and the hawk-dæmon on his shoulder. Then she had it. A gyptian! A real Oxford gyptian!

"Tony Costa," he said. "Remember? You used to play with my little brother Billy off the boats in Jericho, afore the Gobblers got him."

"Oh, God, Pan, we're safe!" she sobbed, but then a thought rushed into her mind: it was the Costas' boat she'd hijacked that day. Suppose he remembered?

"Better come along with us," he said. "You alone?"

"Yeah. I was running away . . ."

"All right, don't talk now. Just keep quiet. Jaxer, move them bodies into the shadow. Kerim, look around."

Lyra stood up shakily, holding the wildcat-Pantalaimon to her breast. He was twisting to look at something, and she followed his gaze, understanding and suddenly curious too: what had happened to the dead men's dæmons? They were fading, that was the answer; fading and drifting away like atoms of smoke, for all that they tried to cling to their men. Pantalaimon hid his eyes, and Lyra hurried blindly after Tony Costa.

"What are you doing here?" she said.

"Quiet, gal. There's enough trouble awake without stirring more. We'll talk on the boat."

He led her over a little wooden bridge into the heart of the canal basin. The other two men were padding silently after them. Tony turned along the waterfront and out on to a wooden jetty, from which he stepped on board a narrow-boat and swung open the door to the cabin.

"Get in," he said. "Quick now."

Lyra did so, patting her bag (which she had never let go, even in the net) to make sure the alethiometer was still there. In the long narrow cabin, by the light of a lantern on a hook, she saw a stout powerful woman with grey hair, sitting at a table with a paper. Lyra recognized her as Billy's mother.

"Who's this?" the woman said. "That's never Lyra?"

"That's right. Ma, we got to move. We killed two men out in the basin. We thought they was Gobblers, but I reckon they were Turk traders. They'd caught Lyra. Never mind talk – we'll do that on the move."

"Come here, child," said Ma Costa.

Lyra obeyed, half happy, half apprehensive, for Ma Costa had hands like bludgeons, and now she was sure: it *was* their boat she had captured with Roger and the other collegers. But the boat-mother set her hands on either side of Lyra's face, and her dæmon, the yellow-eyed hawk, crooned a quick welcome to Pantalaimon. Then Ma Costa folded her great arms around Lyra and pressed her to her breast.

"I dunno what you're a-doing here, but you look wore out. You can have Billy's crib, soon's I've got a hot drink in you. Set you down there, child."

It looked as if her piracy was forgiven, or at least forgotten. Lyra slid on to the cushioned bench behind a well-scrubbed pine table-top as the low rumble of the gas-engine shook the boat.

"Where we going?" Lyra asked.

Ma Costa was setting a saucepan of milk on the iron stove and riddling the grate to stir the fire up.

"Away from here. No talking now. We'll talk in the morning."

And she said no more, handing Lyra a cup of milk when it was ready, swinging herself up on deck when the boat began to move, exchanging occasional whispers with the men. Lyra sipped the milk and lifted a corner of the blind to watch the dark wharves move past. A minute or two later she was sound asleep.

She awoke in a narrow bed, with that comforting engine-rumble deep below. She sat up, banged her head, cursed, felt around, and got up more carefully. A thin grey light showed her three other bunks, each empty and neatly made, one below hers and the other two across the tiny cabin. She swung over the side to find herself in her underclothes, and saw the dress and the wolfskin coat folded at the end of her bunk together with her shopping bag. The alethiometer was still there.

She dressed quickly and went through the door at the end to find herself in the cabin with the stove, where it was warm. There was no one there. Through the windows she saw a grey swirl of fog on each side, with occasional dark shapes that might have been buildings or trees.

Before she could go out on deck, the outer door opened and Ma Costa came down, swathed in an old tweed coat on which the damp had settled like a thousand tiny pearls.

"Sleep well?" she said, reaching for a frying-pan. "Now sit down out the way and I'll make ye some breakfast. Don't stand about; there en't room."

"Where are we?" said Lyra.

"On the Grand Junction Canal. You keep out of sight, child. I don't want to see you topside. There's trouble."

She sliced a couple of rashers of bacon into the frying-pan, and cracked an egg to go with them.

"What sort of trouble?"

"Nothing we can't cope with, if you stay out the way."

And she wouldn't say any more till Lyra had eaten. The boat slowed at one point, and something banged against the side, and she heard men's voices raised in anger; but then someone's joke made them laugh, and the voices drew away and the boat moved on.

Presently Tony Costa swung down into the cabin. Like his mother, he was pearled with damp, and he shook his woollen hat over the stove to make the drops jump and spit.

"What we going to tell her, Ma?"

"Ask first, tell after."

He poured some coffee into a tin cup and sat down. He was a powerful, dark-faced man, and now she could see him in daylight, Lyra saw a sad grimness in his expression.

"Right," he said. "Now you tell us what you was doing in London, Lyra. We had you down as being took by the Gobblers."

"I was living with this lady, right . . ."

Lyra clumsily collected her story and shook it into order as if she were settling a pack of cards ready for dealing. She told them everything, except about the alethiometer.

"And then last night at this cocktail party I found out what they were really doing. Mrs Coulter was one of the Gobblers herself, and she was going to use me to help her catch more kids. And what they do is —"

Ma Costa left the cabin and went out to the cockpit. Tony waited till the door was shut, and went on:

"We know what they do. Least, we know part of it. We know they don't come back. Them kids is taken up North, far out the way, and they do experiments on 'em. At first we reckoned they tried out different diseases and medicines, but there'd be no reason to start that all of a sudden two or three years back. Then we thought about the Tartars, maybe there's some secret deal they're making up Siberia way; because the Tartars want to move North just as much as the rest, for the coal-spirit and the fire-mines, and there's been rumours of war for even longer than the Gobblers been going. And we reckoned the Gobblers were buying off the Tartar chiefs by giving 'em kids, cause the Tartars eat 'em, don't they? They bake children and eat 'em."

"They never!" said Lyra.

"They do. There's plenty of other things to be told, and all. You ever heard of the Nälkäinens?"

Lyra said, "No. Not even with Mrs Coulter. What are they?"

"That's a kind of ghost they have up there in those forests. Same size as a child, and they got no heads. They feel their way about at night and if you're a-sleeping out in the forest they get ahold of you and won't nothing make 'em let go. Nälkäinens, that's a Northern word. And the Windsuckers, they're dangerous too. They drift about in the air. You come across clumps of 'em floated together sometimes, or caught snagged on a bramble. As soon as they touch you, all the strength goes out of you. You can't see 'em except as a kind of shimmer in the air. And the Breathless Ones . . ."

"Who are they?"

"Warriors half-killed. Being alive is one thing, and being dead's another, but being half-killed is worse than either. They just can't die, and living is altogether beyond 'em. They wander about for ever. They're called the Breathless Ones because of what's been done to 'em."

"And what's that?" said Lyra, wide-eyed.

"The North Tartars snap open their ribs and pull out their lungs. There's an art to it. They do it without killing 'em, but their lungs can't work any more without their dæmons pumping 'em by hand, so the result is they're halfway between breath and no breath, life and death, half-killed, you see. And their dæmons got to pump and pump all day and night, or else perish with 'em. You come across a whole platoon of Breathless Ones in the forest sometimes, I've heard. And then there's the *panserbjørne* – you heard of them? That means armoured bears. They're like a kind of Polar bear, except –"

"Yes! I have heard of them! One of the men last night, he said that my uncle, Lord Asriel, he's being imprisoned in a fortress guarded by the armoured bears."

"Is he, now? And what was he doing up there?"

"Exploring. But the way the man was talking I don't think my uncle's on the same side as the Gobblers. I think they were glad he was in prison."

"Well, he won't get out if the armoured bears are guarding him. They're like mercenaries, you know what I mean by that? They sell their strength to whoever pays. They got hands like men, and they learned the trick of working iron way back, meteoric iron mostly, and they make great sheets and plates of it to cover theirselves with. They been raiding the Skraelings for centuries. They're vicious killers, absolutely pitiless. But they keep their word. If you make a bargain with a *panserbjørne*, you can rely on it."

Lyra considered these horrors with awe.

"Ma don't like to hear about the North," Tony said after a few moments, "because of what might've happened to Billy. We know they took him up North, see."

"How d'you know that?"

"We caught one of the Gobblers, and made him talk. That's how we know a little about what they're doing. Them two last night weren't Gobblers; they were too clumsy. If they'd been Gobblers we'd've took 'em alive. See, the gyptian people, we been hit worse than most by these Gobblers, and we're a-coming together to decide what to do about it. That's what we was doing in the basin last night, taking on stores, 'cause we're going to a big muster up in the Fens, what we call a Roping. And what I reckon is we're a-going to send out a rescue party, when we heard what all the other gyptians know, when we put our know-ledge together. That's what I'd do, if I was John Faa."

"Who's John Faa?"

"The king of the gyptians."

"And you're really going to rescue the kids? What about Roger?"

"Who's Roger?"

"The Jordan College Kitchen boy. He was took same as Billy the day before I come away with Mrs Coulter. I bet if I was took he'd come and rescue me. If you're going to rescue Billy, I want to come too and rescue Roger."

And Uncle Asriel, she thought; but she didn't mention that.

7
JOHN FAA

NOW THAT LYRA had a task in mind, she felt much better. Helping Mrs Coulter had been all very well, but Pantalaimon was right: she wasn't really doing any work there, she was just a pretty pet. On the gyptian boat, there was real work to do, and Ma Costa made sure she did it. She cleaned and swept, she peeled potatoes and made tea, she greased the propellor-shaft bearings, she kept the weed-trap clear over the propellor, she washed dishes, she opened lock gates, she tied the boat up at mooring-posts, and within a couple of days she was as much at home with this new life as if she'd been born gyptian.

What she didn't notice was that the Costas were alert every second for unusual signs of interest in Lyra from the waterside people. If she hadn't realized it, she was important, and Mrs Coulter and the Oblation Board were bound to be searching everywhere for her. Indeed, Tony heard from gossip in pubs along the way that the police were making raids on houses and farms and building yards and factories without any explanation, though there was a rumour that they were searching for a missing girl. And that in itself was odd, considering all the kids that had gone missing without being looked for. Gyptians and land folk alike were getting jumpy and nervous.

And there was another reason for the Costas' interest in Lyra; but she wasn't to learn that for a few days yet.

So they took to keeping her below decks when they passed a lock-keeper's cottage or a canal basin, or anywhere there were likely to be idlers hanging about. Once they passed through a town where the police were searching all the boats that came along the waterway, and holding up the traffic in both directions. The Costas were equal to that, though. There was a secret compartment beneath Ma's bunk, where Lyra lay cramped for two hours while the police banged up and down the length of the boat unsuccessfully.

"Why didn't their dæmons find me, though?" she asked afterwards, and Ma showed her the lining of the secret space: cedarwood, which had a soporific effect on dæmons; and it was true that Pantalaimon had spent the whole time happily asleep by Lyra's head.

Slowly, with many halts and detours, the Costas' boat drew nearer the Fens, that wide and never fully mapped wilderness of huge skies and endless marshland in eastern Anglia. The furthest fringe of it mingled indistinguishably with the creeks and tidal inlets of the shallow sea, and the other side of the sea mingled indistinguishably with Holland; and parts of the Fens had been drained and dyked by Hollanders, some of whom had settled there; so the language of the Fens was thick with Dutch. But parts had never been drained or planted or settled at all, and in the wildest central regions, where eels slithered and waterbirds flocked, where eerie marsh-fires flickered and waylurkers tempted careless travellers to their doom in the swamps and bogs, the gyptian people had always found it safe to muster.

And now by a thousand winding channels and creeks and watercourses, gyptian boats were moving in towards the Byanplats, the only patch of slightly higher ground in the hundreds of square miles of marsh and bog. There was an ancient wooden meeting hall there with a huddle of permanent dwellings around it, and wharves and jetties and an Eelmarket. When a Byanroping was called, a summons or muster of gyptians, so many boats filled the waterways that you could walk for a mile in any direction over their decks; or so it was said. The gyptians ruled in the Fens. No one else dared enter, and while the gyptians kept the peace and traded fairly, the landlopers turned a blind eye to the incessant smuggling and the occasional feuds. If a gyptian body floated ashore down the coast, or got snagged in a fish-net, well – it was only a gyptian.

Lyra listened enthralled to tales of the Fen-dwellers, of the great ghost dog Black Shuck, of the marsh-fires arising from bubbles of witch-oil, and began to think of herself as gyptian even before they reached the Fens. She had soon slipped back into her Oxford voice, and now she was acquiring a gyptian one, complete with Fen-Dutch words. Ma Costa had to remind her of a few things.

"You en't gyptian, Lyra. You might pass for gyptian with practice, but there's more to us than gyptian language. There's deeps in us and strong currents. We're water people all through, and you en't, you're a fire person. What you're most like is marsh-fire, that's the place you have in the gyptian scheme; you got witch-oil in your soul. Deceptive, that's what you are, child."

Lyra was hurt.

"I en't never deceived anyone! You ask . . ."

There was no one to ask, of course, and Ma Costa laughed, but kindly.

"Can't you see I'm a-paying you a compliment, you gosling?" she said, and Lyra was pacified, though she didn't understand.

When they reached the Byanplats it was evening, and the sun was about to set in a splash of bloody sky. The low island and the Zaal were humped blackly against the light, like the clustered buildings around; threads of smoke rose into the still air, and from the press of boats all around came the smells of frying fish, of smokeleaf, of jenniver-spirit.

They tied up close to the Zaal itself, at a mooring Tony said had been used by their family for generations. Presently Ma Costa had the frying-pan going, with a couple of fat eels hissing and sputtering and the kettle on for potato-powder. Tony and Kerim oiled their hair, put on their finest leather jackets and blue spotted neckerchiefs, loaded their fingers with silver rings, and went to greet some old friends in the neighbouring boats and drink a glass or two in the nearest bar. They came back with important news.

"We got here just in time. The Roping's this very night. And they're a-saying in the town – what d'you think of this? – they're saying that the missing child's on a gyptian boat, and she's a-going to appear tonight at the Roping!"

He laughed loudly and ruffled Lyra's hair. Ever since they'd entered the Fens he had been more and more good-tempered, as if the savage gloom his face showed outside were only a disguise.

And Lyra felt an excitement growing in her breast as she ate quickly and washed the dishes before combing her hair, tucking the alethiometer into the wolfskin coat pocket, and jumping ashore with all the other families making their way up the slope to the Zaal.

She had thought Tony was joking. She soon found that he wasn't, or else that she looked less like a gyptian than she'd thought, for many people stared, and children pointed, and by the time they reached the great doors of the Zaal they were walking alone between a crowd on either side, who had fallen back to stare and give them room.

And then Lyra began to feel truly nervous. She kept close to Ma Costa, and Pantalaimon became as big as he could and took his panther-shape to reassure her. Ma Costa trudged up the steps as if nothing in the world could possibly either stop her or make her go more quickly, and Tony and Kerim walked proudly on either side like princes.

The hall was lit by naphtha lamps, which shone brightly enough on the faces and bodies of the audience, but left the lofty rafters hidden in darkness. The people coming in had to struggle to find room on the floor, where the benches were already crowded; but families squeezed up to make space, children occupying laps and dæmons curling up underfoot or perching out of the way on the rough wooden walls.

At the front of the Zaal there was a platform with eight carved wooden chairs set out. As Lyra and the Costas found space to stand along the edge of the hall (there was nowhere left to sit), eight men appeared from the shadows at the rear of the platform and stood in front of the chairs. A ripple of excitement swept over the audience as they hushed one another and shoved themselves into spaces on the nearest bench. Finally there was silence and seven of the men on the platform sat down.

The one who remained was in his seventies, but tall and bull-necked and powerful. He wore a plain canvas jacket and a checked shirt, like many gyptian men; there was nothing to mark him out but the air of strength and authority he had. Lyra recognized it: Uncle Asriel had it, and so did the Master of Jordan. This man's dæmon was a crow; very like the Master's raven.

"That's John Faa, the lord of the western gyptians," Tony whispered.

John Faa began to speak, in a deep slow voice.

"Gyptians! Welcome to the Roping. We've come to listen and come to decide. You all know why. There are many families here who've lost a child. Some have lost two. Someone is taking them. To be sure, landlopers are losing children too. We have no quarrel with landlopers over this.

"Now there's been talk about a child and a reward. Here's the truth to stop all gossip. The child's name is Lyra Belacqua, and she's being sought by the landloper police. There is a reward of one thousand sovereigns for giving her up to them. She's a land-loper child, and she's in our care, and there she's going to stay. Anyone tempted by those thousand sovereigns had better find a place neither on land nor on water. We en't giving her up."

Lyra felt a blush from the roots of her hair to the soles of her feet; Pantalaimon became a brown moth to hide. Eyes all around were turning to them, and she could only look up at Ma Costa for reassurance.

But John Faa was speaking again:

"Talk all we may, we won't change owt. We must act if we want to change things. Here's another fact for you: the Gobblers, these child-thieves, are a-taking their prisoners to a town in the far North, way up in the land of dark. I don't know what they do with 'em there. Some folk say they kill 'em, other folk say different. We don't know.

"What we do know is that they do it with the help of the land-loper police and the clergy. Every power on land is helping 'em. Remember that. They know what's going on and they'll help it whenever they can.

"So what I'm proposing en't easy. And I need your agreement. I'm proposing that we send a band of fighters up North to rescue them kids and bring 'em back alive. I'm proposing that we put our gold into this, and all the craft and courage we can muster. Yes, Raymond van Gerrit?"

A man in the audience had raised his hand, and John Faa sat down to let him speak.

"Beg pardon, Lord Faa. There's landloper kids as well as

gyptians been taken captive. Are you saying we should rescue them as well?"

John Faa stood up to answer.

"Raymond, are you saying we should fight our way through every kind of danger to a little group of frightened children, and then say to some of them that they can come home, and to the rest that they have to stay? No, you're a better man than that. Well, do I have your approval, my friends?"

The question caught them by surprise, for there was a moment's hesitation; but then a full-throated roar filled the hall, and hands were clapped in the air, fists shaken, voices raised in excited clamour. The rafters of the Zaal shook, and from their perches up in the dark a score of sleeping birds woke up in fear and flapped their wings, and little showers of dust drifted down.

John Faa let the noise continue for a minute, and then raised his hand for silence again.

"This'll take a while to organize. I want the heads of the families to raise a tax and muster a levy. We'll meet again here in three days' time. In between now and then I'm a-going to talk with the child I mentioned before, and with Farder Coram, and form a plan to put before you when we meet. Good night to ye all."

His massive, plain, blunt presence was enough to calm them. As the audience began to move out of the great doors into the chilly evening, to go to their boats or to the crowded bars of the little settlement, Lyra said to Ma Costa:

"Who are the other men on the platform?"

"The heads of the six families, and the other man is Farder Coram."

It was easy to see who she meant by the other man, because he was the oldest one there. He walked with a stick and all the time he'd been sitting behind John Faa he'd been trembling as if with an ague.

"Come on," said Tony. "I'd best take you up to pay your respects to John Faa. You call him Lord Faa. I don't know what you'll be asked, but mind you tell the truth."

Pantalaimon was a sparrow now, and sat curiously on Lyra's shoulder, his claws deep in the wolfskin coat, as she followed Tony through the crowd up to the platform.

He lifted her up. Knowing that everyone still in the hall was staring at her, and conscious of those thousand sovereigns she was suddenly worth, she blushed and hesitated. Pantalaimon darted to her breast and became a wildcat, sitting up in her arms and hissing softly as he looked around.

Lyra felt a push, and stepped forward to John Faa. He was stern and massive and expressionless, more like a pillar of rock than a man, but he stooped and held out his hand to shake. When she put hers in, it nearly vanished.

"Welcome, Lyra," he said.

Close to, she felt his voice rumbling like the earth itself. She would have been nervous but for Pantalaimon, and the fact that John Faa's stony expression had warmed a little. He was treating her very gently.

"Thank you, Lord Faa," she said.

"Now you come in the parley room and we'll have a talk," said John Faa. "Have they been feeding you proper, the Costas?"

"Oh, yes. We had eels for supper."

"Proper Fen eels, I expect."

The parley room was a comfortable place with a big fire, sideboards laden with silver and porcelain, and a heavy table darkly polished by the years, at which twelve chairs were drawn up.

The other men from the platform had gone elsewhere, but the old shaking man was still with them. John Faa helped him to a seat at the table.

"Now you sit here on my right," John Faa said to Lyra, and took the chair at the head of the table himself. Lyra found herself opposite Farder Coram. She was a little frightened by his skull-like face and his continual trembling. His dæmon was a beautiful autumn-coloured cat, massive in size, who stalked along the table with upraised tail and elegantly inspected Pantalaimon, touching noses briefly before settling on Farder Coram's lap, half-closing her eyes and purring softly.

A woman whom Lyra hadn't noticed came out of the shadows with a tray of glasses, set it down by John Faa, curtseyed and left. John Faa poured little glasses of jenniver from a stone crock for himself and Farder Coram, and wine for Lyra.

"So," John Faa said. "You run away, Lyra."

"Yes."

"And who was the lady you run away from?"

"She was called Mrs Coulter. And I thought she was nice but I found out she was one of the Gobblers. I heard someone say what the Gobblers were, they were called the General Oblation Board, and she was in charge of it, it was all her idea. And they was all working on some plan, I dunno what it was, only they was going to make me help her get kids for 'em. But they never knew . . ."

"They never knew what?"

"Well, first they never knew that I knew some kids what had been took. My friend Roger the Kitchen boy from Jordan College, and Billy Costa, and a girl out the Covered Market in Oxford. And another thing . . . My uncle, right, Lord Asriel. I heard them talking about his journeys to the North, and I don't reckon he's got anything to do with the Gobblers. Because I spied on the Master and the Scholars of Jordan, right, I hid in the Retiring Room where no one's supposed to go except them, and I heard him tell them all about his expedition up North, and the Dust he saw, and he brought back the head of Stanislaus Grumman, what the Tartars had made a hole in. And now the Gobblers've got him locked up somewhere. The armoured bears are guarding him. And I want to rescue him."

She looked fierce and stubborn as she sat there, small against the high carved back of the chair. The two old men couldn't help smiling, but whereas Farder Coram's smile was a hesitant, rich, complicated expression that trembled across his face like sunlight chasing shadows on a windy March day, John Faa's smile was slow, warm, plain and kindly.

"You better tell us what you did hear your uncle say that evening," said John Faa. "Don't leave anything out, mind. Tell us everything."

Lyra did, more slowly than she'd told the Costas but more honestly, too. She was afraid of John Faa, and what she was most afraid of was his kindness. When she'd finished, Farder Coram spoke for the first time. His voice was rich and musical, with as many tones in it as there were colours in his dæmon's fur.

"This Dust," he said. "Did they ever call it anything else, Lyra?"

"No. Just Dust. Mrs Coulter told me what it was, elementary particles, but that's all she called it."

"And they think that by doing something to children, they can find out more about it?"

"Yes. But I don't know what. Except my uncle ... There's something I forgot to tell you. When he was showing them lantern slides, there was another one he had. It was the Roarer –"

"The what?" said John Faa.

"The Aurora," said Farder Coram. "Is that right, Lyra?"

"Yeah, that's it. And in the lights of the Roarer there was like a city. All towers and churches and domes and that. It was a bit like Oxford, that's what I thought, anyway. And Uncle Asriel, he was more interested in that, I think, but the Master and the other Scholars were more interested in Dust, like Mrs Coulter and Lord Boreal and them."

"I see," said Farder Coram. "That's very interesting."

"Now, Lyra," said John Faa, "I'm a-going to tell you something. Farder Coram here, he's a wise man. He's a see-er. He's been a-follering all what's been going on with Dust and the Gobblers and Lord Asriel and everything else, and he's been a-follering *you*. Every time the Costas went to Oxford, or half a dozen other families come to that, they brought back a bit of news. About you, child. Did you know that?"

Lyra shook her head. She was beginning to be frightened. Pantalaimon was growling too deep for anyone to hear, but she could feel it in her fingertips down inside his fur.

"Oh, yes," said John Faa, "all your doings, they all get back to Farder Coram here."

Lyra couldn't hold it in.

"We didn't *damage* it! Honest! It was only a bit of mud! And we never got very far –"

"What are you talking about, child?" said John Faa.

Farder Coram laughed. When he did that, his shaking stopped and his face became bright and young.

But Lyra wasn't laughing. With trembling lips she said, "And even if we had found the bung, we'd never've took it out! It was just a joke. We wouldn't've sunk it, never!"

Then John Faa began to laugh too. He slapped a broad hand on the table so hard the glasses rang, and his massive shoulders shook, and he had to wipe away the tears from his eyes. Lyra had never seen such a sight, never heard such a bellow; it was like a mountain laughing.

"Oh, yes," he said when he could speak again, "we heard about that too, little girl! I don't suppose the Costas have set foot anywhere since then without being reminded of it. You better leave a guard on your boat, Tony, people say. Fierce little girls round here! Oh, that story went all over the Fens, child. But we en't going to punish you for it. No, no! Ease your mind."

He looked at Farder Coram, and the two old men laughed again, but more gently. And Lyra felt contented, and safe.

Finally John Faa shook his head and became serious again.

"I were saying, Lyra, as we knew about you from a child. From a baby. You oughter know what we know. I can't guess what they told you at Jordan College about where you came from, but they don't know the whole truth of it. Did they ever tell you who your parents were?"

Now Lyra was completely dazed.

"Yes," she said. "They said I was – they said they – they said Lord Asriel put me there because my mother and father died in an airship accident. That's what they told me."

"Ah, did they? Well now, child, I'm a-going to tell you a story, a true story. I know it's true, because a gyptian woman told me, and they all tell the truth to John Faa and Farder Coram. So this is the truth about yourself, Lyra. Your father never perished in no airship accident, because your father is Lord Asriel."

Lyra could only sit in wonder.

"Here's how it came about," John Faa went on. "When he was a young man, Lord Asriel went exploring all over the North, and came back with a great fortune. And he was a high-spirited man, quick to anger, a passionate man.

"And your mother, she was passionate too. Not so well-born as him, but a clever woman. A scholar, even, and those who saw her said she was very beautiful. She and your father, they fell in love as soon's they met.

"The trouble was, your mother was already married. She'd

married a politician. He was a member of the King's party, one of his closest advisers. A rising man.

"Now when your mother found herself with child, she feared to tell her husband the child wasn't his. And when the baby was born – that's you, girl – it was clear from the look of you that you didn't favour her husband, but your true father, and she thought it best to hide you away and give out that you'd died.

"So you was took to Oxfordshire, where your father had estates, and put in the care of a gyptian woman to nurse. But someone whispered to your mother's husband what had happened, and he came a-flying down and ransacked the cottage where the gyptian woman had been, only she'd fled to the great house; and the husband followed after, in a murderous passion.

"Your father was out a-hunting, but they got word to him and he came riding back in time to find your mother's husband at the foot of the great staircase. Another moment and he'd have forced open the closet where the gyptian woman was hiding with you, but Lord Asriel challenged him, and they fought there and then, and Lord Asriel killed him.

"The gyptian woman heard and saw it all, Lyra, and that's how we know.

"The consequence was a great lawsuit. Your father en't the kind of man to deny or conceal the truth, and it left the judges with a problem. He'd killed all right, he'd shed blood, but he was defending his home and his child against an intruder. On t'other hand, the law allows any man to avenge the violation of his wife, and the dead man's lawyers argued that he were doing just that.

"The case lasted for weeks, with volumes of argument back and forth. In the end the judges punished Lord Asriel by confiscating all his property and all his land, and left him a poor man; and he had been richer than a king.

"As for your mother, she wanted nothing to do with it, nor with you. She turned her back. The gyptian nurse told me she'd often been afeared of how your mother would treat you, because she was a proud and scornful woman. So much for her.

"Then there was you. If things had fallen out different, Lyra, you might have been brought up a gyptian, because the nurse begged the court to let her have you; but we gyptians got little standing in the law. The court decided you was to be placed in a Priory, and so you were, with the Sisters of Obedience at Watlington. You won't remember.

"But Lord Asriel wouldn't stand for that. He had a hatred of priors and monks and nuns, and being a high-handed man he just rode in one day and carried you off. Not to look after himself, nor to give to the gyptians; he took you to Jordan College, and dared the law to undo it.

"Well, the law let things be. Lord Asriel went back to his explorations, and you grew up at Jordan College. The one thing he said, your father, the one condition he made, was that your mother shouldn't be let see you. If she ever tried to do that, she was to be prevented, and he was to be told, because all the anger in his nature had turned against her now. The Master promised faithfully to do that; and so time passed.

"Then come all this anxiety about Dust. And all over the country, all over the world, wise men and women too began a-worrying about it. It weren't of any account to us gyptians, until they started taking our kids. That's when we got interested. And we got connections in all sorts of places you wouldn't imagine, including Jordan College. You wouldn't know, but there's been someone a-watching over you and reporting to us ever since you been there. 'Cause we got an interest in you, and that gyptian woman who nursed you, she never stopped being anxious on your behalf."

"Who was it watching over me?" said Lyra. She felt immensely important and strange, that all her doings should be an object of concern so far away.

"It was a Kitchen servant. It was Bernie Johansen, the pastry cook. He's half-gyptian; you never knew that, I'll be bound."

Bernie was a kindly, solitary man, one of those rare people whose dæmon was the same sex as himself. It was Bernie she'd shouted at in her despair when Roger was taken. And Bernie had been telling the gyptians everything! She marvelled.

"So anyway," John Faa went on, "we heard about you going away from Jordan College, and how it came about at a time when Lord Asriel was imprisoned and couldn't prevent it. And we remembered what he'd said to the Master that he must never do, and we remembered that the man your mother had married, the politician Lord Asriel killed, was called Edward Coulter."

"Mrs Coulter?" said Lyra, quite stupefied. "*She* en't my mother?"

"She is. And if your father had been free she wouldn't never have dared to defy him, and you'd still be at Jordan, not knowing a thing. But what the Master was a-doing letting you go is a mystery I can't explain. He was charged with your care. All I can guess is that she had some power over him."

Lyra suddenly understood the Master's curious behaviour on the morning she'd left.

"But he didn't want to . . ." she said, trying to remember it exactly. "He . . . I had to go and see him first thing that morning, and I mustn't tell Mrs Coulter . . . It was like he wanted to protect me from Mrs Coulter . . ." She stopped, and looked at the two men carefully, and then decided to tell them the whole truth about the Retiring Room. "See, there was something else. That evening I hid in the Retiring Room, I saw the Master try to poison Lord Asriel. I saw him put some powder in the wine and I told my uncle and he knocked the decanter off the table and spilled it. So I saved his life. I could never understand why the Master would want to poison him, because he was always so kind. Then on the morning I left he called me in early to his study, and I had to go secretly so no one would know, and he said . . ." Lyra racked her brains to try and remember exactly what it was the Master had said. No good; she shook her head. "The only thing I could understand was that he gave me something and I had to keep it secret from her, from Mrs Coulter. I suppose it's all right if I tell you . . ."

She felt in the pocket of the wolfskin coat and took out the velvet package. She laid it on the table, and she sensed John Faa's massive simple curiosity and Farder Coram's bright flickering intelligence both trained on it like searchlights.

When she laid the alethiometer bare, it was Farder Coram who spoke first.

"I never thought I'd ever set eyes on one of them again. That's a symbol-reader. Did he tell you anything about it, child?"

"No. Only that I'd have to work out how to read it by myself. And he called it an alethiometer."

"What's that mean?" said John Faa, turning to his companion.

"That's a Greek word. I reckon it's from *aletheia*, which means truth. It's a truth-measure. And have you worked out how to use it?" he said to her.

"No. Least, I can make the three short hands point to different pictures, but I can't do anything with the long one. It goes all over. Except sometimes, right, sometimes when I'm sort of concentrating, I can make the long needle go this way or that just by thinking it."

"What's it do, Farder Coram?" said John Faa. "And how do you read it?"

"All these pictures round the rim," said Farder Coram, holding it delicately towards John Faa's blunt strong gaze, "they're symbols, and each one stands for a whole series of things. Take the anchor, there. The first meaning of that is hope, because hope holds you fast like an anchor so you don't give way. The second meaning is steadfastness. The third meaning is snag, or prevention. The fourth meaning is the sea. And so on, down to ten, twelve, maybe a never-ending series of meanings."

"And do you know them all?"

"I know some, but to read it fully I'd need the book. I seen the book and I know where it is, but I en't got it."

"We'll come back to that," said John Faa. "Go on with how you read it."

"You got three hands you can control," Farder Coram explained, "and you use them to ask a question. By pointing to three symbols you can ask any question you can imagine, because you've got so many levels of each one. Once you got your question framed, the other needle swings round and points to more symbols that give you the answer."

"But how does it know what level you're a-thinking of when you set the question?" said John Faa.

"Ah, by itself it don't. It only works if the questioner holds the levels in their mind. You got to know all the meanings, first, and there must be a thousand or more. Then you got to be able to hold 'em in your mind without fretting at it or pushing for an answer, and just watch while the needle wanders. When it's gone round its full range you'll know what the answer is. I know how it works because I seen it done once by a wise man in Uppsala, and that's the only time I ever saw one before. Do you know how rare these are?''

"The Master told me there was only six made," Lyra said.

"Whatever the number, it en't large."

"And you kept this secret from Mrs Coulter, like the Master told you?" said John Faa.

"Yes. But her dæmon, right, he used to go in my room. And I'm sure he found it."

"I see. Well, Lyra, I don't know as we'll ever understand the full truth, but this is my guess, as good as I can make it. The Master was given a charge by Lord Asriel to look after you and keep you safe from your mother. And that was what he did, for ten years or more. Then Mrs Coulter's friends in the Church helped her set up this Oblation Board, for what purpose we don't know, and there she was, as powerful in her way as Lord Asriel was in his. Your parents, both strong in the world, both ambitious, and the Master of Jordan holding you in the balance between them.

"Now the Master's got a hundred things to look after. His first concern is his college and the scholarship there. So if he sees a threat to that, he has to move agin it. And the Church in recent times, Lyra, it's been a-getting more commanding. There's councils for this and councils for that; there's talk of reviving the Office of Inquisition, God forbid. And the Master has to tread warily between all these powers. He has to keep Jordan College on the right side of the Church, or it won't survive.

"And another concern of the Master is you, child. Bernie Johansen was always clear about that. The Master of Jordan and the other Scholars, they loved you like their own child. They'd do anything to keep you safe, not just because they'd promised to Lord Asriel that they would, but for your own sake. So if the Master gave you up to Mrs Coulter when he'd promised Lord Asriel he wouldn't, he must have thought you'd be safer with her than in Jordan College, in spite of all appearances. And when he set out to poison Lord Asriel, he must have thought that what

Lord Asriel was a-doing would place all of them in danger, and maybe all of us, too; maybe all the world. I see the Master as a man having terrible choices to make; whatever he chooses will do harm; but maybe if he does the right thing, a little less harm will come about than if he chooses wrong. God preserve me from having to make that sort of choice.

"And when it come to the point where he had to let you go, he gave you the symbol-reader and bade you keep it safe. I wonder what he had in mind for you to do with it; as you couldn't read it, I'm foxed as to what he was a-thinking."

"He said Uncle Asriel presented the alethiometer to Jordan College years before," Lyra said, struggling to remember. "He was going to say something else, and then someone knocked at the door and he had to stop. What I thought was, he might have wanted me to keep it away from Lord Asriel too."

"Or even the opposite," said John Faa.

"What d'you mean, John?" said Farder Coram.

"He might have had it in mind to ask Lyra to return it to Lord Asriel, as a kind of recompense for trying to poison him. He might have thought the danger from Lord Asriel had passed. Or that Lord Asriel could read some wisdom from this instrument and hold back from his purpose. If Lord Asriel's held captive now, it might help set him free. Well, Lyra, you better take this symbol-reader and keep it safe. If you kept it safe so far I en't worried about leaving it with you. But there might come a time when we need to consult it, and I reckon we'll ask for it then."

He folded the velvet over it and slid it back across the table. Lyra wanted to ask all kinds of questions, but suddenly she felt shy of this massive man, with his little eyes so sharp and kindly among their folds and wrinkles.

One thing she had to ask, though.

"Who was the gyptian woman who nursed me?"

"Why, it was Billy Costa's mother, of course. She won't have told you, because I en't let her, but she knows what we're a-talking of here, so it's all out in the open.

"Now you best be getting back to her. You got plenty to be a-thinking of, child. When three days is gone past we'll have another Roping and discuss all there is to do. You be a good girl. Good night, Lyra."

"Good night, Lord Faa. Good night, Farder Coram," she said politely, clutching the alethiometer to her breast with one hand and scooping up Pantalaimon with the other.

Both old men smiled kindly at her. Outside the door of the parley room Ma Costa was waiting and, as if nothing had happened since Lyra was born, the boat-mother gathered her into her great arms and kissed her before bearing her off to bed.

8

FRUSTRATION

LYRA HAD TO adjust to her new sense of her own story, and that couldn't be done in a day. To see Lord Asriel as her father was one thing, but to accept Mrs Coulter as her mother was nowhere near so easy. A couple of months ago she would have rejoiced, of course, and she knew that too, and felt confused.

But, being Lyra, she didn't fret about it for long, for there was the Fen town to explore and many gyptian children to amaze. Before the three days were up she was an expert with a punt (in her eyes, at least) and she'd gathered a gang of urchins about her with tales of her mighty father, so unjustly made captive.

"And then one evening the Turkish Ambassador was a guest at Jordan for dinner. And he was under orders from the Sultan hisself to kill my father, right, and he had a ring on his finger with a hollow stone full of poison. And when the wine come round he made as if to reach across my father's glass, and he sprinkled the poison in. It was done so quick that no one else saw him, but –"

"What sort of poison?" demanded a thin-faced girl.

"Poison out of a special Turkish serpent," Lyra invented, "what they catch by playing a pipe to lure out and then they throw it a sponge soaked in honey and the serpent bites it and can't get his fangs free, and they catch it and milk the venom out of it. Anyway, my father seen what the Turk done, and he says Gentlemen, I want to propose a toast of friendship between Jordan College and the College of Izmir, which was the college the Turkish Ambassador belonged to. And to show our willingness to be friends, he says, we'll swap glasses and drink each other's wine.

"And the Ambassador was in a fix then, 'cause he couldn't refuse to drink without giving deadly insult, and he couldn't drink it because he knew it was poisoned. He went pale and he fainted right away at the table. And when he come round they was all still sitting there, waiting and looking at him. And then he had to either drink the poison or own up."

"So what did he do?"

"He drunk it. It took him five whole minutes to die, and he was in torment all the time."

"Did you see it happen?"

"No, 'cause girls en't allowed at the High Table. But I seen his body afterwards when they laid him out. His skin was all withered like an old apple, and his eyes were starting from his head. In fact they had to push 'em back in the sockets . . ."

And so on.

Meanwhile, around the edges of the Fen country, the police were knocking at doors, searching attics and outhouses, inspecting papers and interrogating everyone who claimed to have seen a blonde little girl; and in Oxford the search was even fiercer. Jordan College was scoured from the dustiest boxroom to the darkest cellar, and so were Gabriel and St Michael's, till the heads of all the colleges issued a joint protest asserting their ancient rights. The only notion Lyra had of the search for her was the incessant drone of the gas engines of airships crisscrossing the skies. They weren't visible, because the clouds were low and by statute airships had to keep a certain height above Fen country, but who knew what cunning spy-devices they might carry? Best to keep under cover when she heard them, or wear the oilskin sou'wester over her bright distinctive hair.

And she questioned Ma Costa about every detail of the story of her birth. She wove the details into a mental tapestry even clearer and sharper than the stories she made up, and lived over and over again the flight from the cottage, the concealment in the closet, the harsh-voiced challenge, the clash of swords –

"Swords? Great God, girl, you dreaming?" Ma Costa said. "Mr Coulter had a gun, and Lord Asriel knocked it out his hand and struck him down with one blow. Then there was two shots. I wonder you don't remember; you ought to, little as you were. The first shot was Edward Coulter, who reached his gun and fired, and the second was Lord Asriel, who tore it out his grasp a second time and turned it on him. Shot him right between the eyes and dashed his brains out. Then he says, cool as paint, 'Come out, Mrs Costa, and bring the baby,' because you were setting up such a howl, you and that dæmon both; and he took you up and dandled you and sat you on his shoulders, walking up and down in high good humour with the dead man at his feet, and called for wine and bade me swab the floor."

By the end of the fourth repetition of the story Lyra was perfectly convinced she did remember it, and even volunteered details of the colour of Mr Coulter's coat and the cloaks and furs hanging in the closet. Ma Costa laughed.

And whenever she was alone, Lyra took out the alethiometer and pored over it like a lover with a picture of the beloved. So each image had several meanings, did it? Why shouldn't she work them out? Wasn't she Lord Asriel's daughter?

Remembering what Farder Coram had said, she tried to focus her mind on three symbols taken at random, and clicked the hands round to point at them. She found that if she held the alethiometer just so in her palms and gazed at it in a particular lazy way, as she thought of it, the long needle would begin to move more purposefully. Instead of its wayward divagations around the dial it swung smoothly from one picture to another. Sometimes it would pause at three, sometimes two, sometimes five or more, and although she understood nothing of it, she gained a deep calm enjoyment from it, unlike anything she'd known. Pantalaimon would crouch over the dial, sometimes as a cat, sometimes as a mouse, swinging his head round after the needle; and once or twice the two of them shared a glimpse of meaning that felt as if a shaft of sunlight had struck through clouds to light up a majestic line of great hills in the distance – something far beyond, and never suspected. And Lyra thrilled at those times with the same deep thrill she'd felt all her life on hearing the word North.

So the three days passed, with much coming and going between the multitude of boats and the Zaal. And then came the evening of the second Roping. The hall was more crowded than before, if that was possible. Lyra and the Costas got there in time to sit at the front, and as soon as the flickering lights showed that the place was crammed, John Faa and Farder Coram came out on the platform and sat behind the table. John Faa didn't have to make a sign for silence; he just put his great hands flat on the table and looked at the people below, and the hubbub died.

"Well," he said, "you done what I asked. And better than I hoped. I'm a-going to call on the heads of the six families now to come up here and give over their gold and recount their promises. Nicholas Rokeby, you come first."

A stout black-bearded man climbed on to the platform and laid a heavy leather bag on the table.

"That's our gold," he said. "And we offer thirty-eight men."

"Thank you, Nicholas," said John Faa. Farder Coram was making a note. The first man stood at the back of the platform as John Faa called for the next, and the next; and each came up, laid a bag on the table and announced the number of men he could muster. The Costas were part of the Stefanski family, and naturally Tony had been one of the first to volunteer. Lyra noticed his hawk-dæmon shifting from foot to foot and spreading her wings as the Stefanski money and the promise of twenty-three men were laid before John Faa.

When the six family heads had all come up, Farder Coram showed his piece of paper to John Faa, who stood up to address the audience again.

"Friends, that's a muster of one hundred and seventy men. I thank you proudly. As for the gold, I make no doubt from the weight of it that you've all dug deep in your coffers, and my warm thanks go out for that as well.

"What we're a-going to do next is this. We're a-going to charter a ship and sail North, and find them kids and set 'em free. From what we know, there might be some fighting to do. It won't be the first time, nor it won't be the last, but we never had to fight yet with people who kidnap children, and we shall have to be uncommon cunning. But we en't going to come back without our kids. Yes, Dirk Vries?"

A man stood up and said, "Lord Faa, do you know why they captured them kids?"

"We heard it's a theological matter. They're making an experiment, but what nature it is we don't know. To tell you all the truth, we don't even know whether any harm is a-coming to 'em. But whatever it is, good or bad, they got no right to reach out by night and pluck little children out the hearts of their families. Yes, Raymond van Gerrit?"

The man who'd spoken at the first meeting stood up and said, "That child, Lord Faa, the one you spoke of as being sought, the one as is sitting in the front row now. I heard as all the folk living around the edge of the Fens is having their houses turned upside down on her account. I heard there's a move in Parliament this very day to rescind our ancient privileges on account of this child. Yes, friends," he said, over the babble of shocked whispers, "they're a-going to pass a law doing away with our right to free movement in and out the Fens. Now, Lord Faa, what we want to know is this: who is this child on account of which we might come to such a pass? She en't a gyptian child, not as I heard. How comes it that a landloper child can put us all in danger?"

Lyra looked up at John Faa's massive frame. Her heart was thumping so much she could hardly hear the first words of his reply.

"Now spell it out, Raymond, don't be shy," he said. "You want us to give this child up to them she's a-fleeing from, is that right?"

The man stood obstinately frowning, but said nothing.

"Well, perhaps you would, and perhaps you wouldn't," John Faa continued. "But if any man or woman needs a reason for doing good, ponder on this. That little girl is the daughter of Lord Asriel, no less. For them as has forgotten, it were Lord Asriel who interceded with the Turk for the life of Sam Broekman. It were Lord Asriel who allowed gyptian boats free passage on the canals through his property. It were Lord Asriel who defeated the Watercourse Bill in Parliament, to our great and lasting benefit. And it were Lord Asriel who fought day and night in the floods of '53, and plunged headlong in the water twice to pull out young Ruud and Nellie Koopman. You forgotten that? Shame, shame on you, shame.

"And now that same Lord Asriel is held in the farthest coldest darkest regions of the wild, captive, in the fortress of Svalbard. Do I need to tell you the kind of creatures a-guarding him there? And this is his little daughter in our care, and Raymond van Gerrit would hand her over to the authorities for a bit of peace and quiet. Is that right, Raymond? Stand up and answer, man."

But Raymond van Gerrit had sunk to his seat, and nothing would make him stand. A low hiss of disapproval sounded through the great hall, and Lyra felt the shame he must be feeling, as well as a deep glow of pride in her brave father.

John Faa turned away, and looked at the other men on the platform.

"Nicholas Rokeby, I'm a-putting you in charge of finding a vessel, and commanding her once we sail. Adam Stefanski, I want you to take charge of the arms and munitions, and command the fighting. Roger van Poppel, you look to all the other stores, from food to cold-weather clothing. Simon Hartmann, you be treasurer, and account to us all for a proper apportionment of our gold. Benjamin de Ruyter, I want you to take charge of spying. There's a great deal we ought to find out, and I'm a-giving you the charge of that, and you'll report to Farder Coram. Michael Canzona, you're going to be responsible for co-ordinating the first four leaders' work, and you'll report to me, and if I die, you're my second in command and you'll take over.

"Now I've made my dispositions according to custom, and if any man or woman seeks to disagree, they may do so freely."

After a moment a woman stood up.

"Lord Faa, en't you a-taking any women on this expedition to look after them kids once you found 'em?"

"No, Nell. We shall have little space as it is. Any kids we free will be better off in our care than where they've been."

"But supposing you find out that you can't rescue 'em without some women in disguise as guards or nurses or whatever?"

"Well, I hadn't thought of that," John Faa admitted. "We'll consider that most carefully when we retire into the parley room, you have my promise."

She sat down and a man stood up.

"Lord Faa, I heard you say that Lord Asriel is in captivity. Is it part of your plan to rescue him? Because if it is, and if he's in the power of them bears as I think you said, that's going to need more than a hundred and seventy men. And good friend as Lord Asriel is to us, I don't know as there's any call on us to go as far as that."

"Adriaan Braks, you're not wrong. What I had it in my mind to do was to keep our eyes and ears open and see what knowledge we can glean while we're in the North. It may be that we can do something to help him, and it may not, but you can trust me not to use what you've provided, man and gold, for any purpose outside the stated one of finding our children and bringing 'em home."

Another woman stood up.

"Lord Faa, we don't know what them Gobblers might've been doing to our children. We all heard rumours and stories of fearful things. We hear about children with no heads, or about children cut in half and sewn together, or about things too awful to mention. I'm truly sorry to distress anyone, but we all heard this kind of thing, and I want to get it out in the open. Now in case you find anything of that awful kind, Lord Faa, I hope you're a-going to take powerful revenge. I hope you en't going to let thoughts of mercy and gentleness hold your hand back from striking and striking hard, and delivering a mighty blow to the heart of that infernal wickedness. And I'm sure I speak for any mother as has lost a child to the Gobblers."

There was a loud murmur of agreement as she sat down. Heads were nodding all over the Zaal.

John Faa waited for silence, and said:

"Nothing will hold my hand, Margaret, save only judgement. If I stay my hand in the North, it will only be to strike the harder in the South. To strike a day too soon is as bad as striking a hundred miles off. To be sure, there's a warm passion behind what you say. But if you give in to that passion, friends, you're a-doing what I always warned you agin: you're a-placing the satisfaction of your own feelings above the work you have to do. Our work here is first rescue, then punishment. It en't gratification for upset feelings. Our feelings don't matter. If we rescue the kids but we can't punish the Gobblers, we've done the main task. But if we aim to punish the Gobblers first and by doing so lose the chance of rescuing the kids, we've failed.

"But be assured of this, Margaret. When the time comes to punish, we shall strike such a blow as'll make their hearts faint and fearful. We shall strike the strength out of 'em. We shall leave

them ruined and waste, broken and shattered, torn in a thousand
pieces and scattered to the four winds. My own hammer is thirsty
for blood, friends. She en't tasted blood since I slew the Tartar
champion on the steppes of Kazakhstan; she's been a-hanging in
my boat and dreaming; but she can smell blood in the wind from
the North. She spoke to me last night and told me of her thirst,
and I said soon, gal, soon. Margaret, you can worry about a hundred things, but don't you worry that John Faa's heart is too soft
to strike a blow when the time comes. And the time will come
under judgement. Not under passion.

"Is there anyone else who wants to speak? Speak if you will."

But no one did, and presently John Faa reached for the closing
bell and rang it hard and loud, swinging it high and shaking the
peals out of it so that they filled the hall and rang the rafters.

John Faa and the other men left the platform for the parley
room. Lyra was a little disappointed. Didn't they want her there
too? But Tony laughed.

"They got plans to make," he said. "You done your part, Lyra.
Now it's for John Faa and the council."

"But I en't done nothing yet!" Lyra protested, as she followed
the others reluctantly out of the Hall and down the cobbled road
towards the jetty. "All I done was run away from Mrs Coulter!
That's just a beginning. I want to go North!"

"Tell you what," said Tony, "I'll bring you back a walrus
tooth, that's what I'll do."

Lyra scowled. For his part, Pantalaimon occupied himself by
making monkey-faces at Tony's dæmon, who closed her tawny
eyes in disdain. Lyra drifted to the jetty and hung about with
her new companions, dangling lanterns on strings over the black
water to attract the goggle-eyed fishes who swam slowly up to
be lunged at with sharp sticks and missed.

But her mind was on John Faa and the parley room, and before
long she slipped away up the cobbles again to the Zaal. There
was a light in the parley room window. It was too high to look
through, but she could hear a low rumble of voices inside.

So she walked up to the door and knocked on it firmly five
times. The voices stopped, a chair scraped across the floor, and the
door opened, spilling warm naphtha light out on the damp step.

"Yes?" said the man who'd opened it.

Beyond him Lyra could see the other men around the table, with bags of gold stacked neatly, and papers and pens, and glasses and a crock of jenniver.

"I want to come North," Lyra said so they could all hear it. "I want to come and help rescue the kids. That's what I set out to do when I run away from Mrs Coulter. And before that, even, I meant to rescue my friend Roger the Kitchen boy from Jordan who was took. I want to come and help. I can do navigation and I can take anbaromagnetic readings off the Aurora, and I know what parts of a bear you can eat, and all kinds of useful things. You'd be sorry if you got up there and then found you needed me and found you'd left me behind. And like that woman said, you might need women to play a part – well, you might need kids too. You don't know. So you oughter take me, Lord Faa, excuse me for interrupting your talk."

She was inside the room now, and all the men and their dæmons were watching her, some with amusement and some with irritation, but she had eyes only for John Faa. Pantalaimon sat up in her arms, his wildcat eyes blazing green.

John Faa said, "Lyra, there en't no question of taking you into danger, so don't delude yourself, child. Stay here and help Ma Costa and keep safe. That's what you got to do."

"But I'm learning how to read the alethiometer, too. It's coming clearer every day! You're bound to need that – bound to!"

He shook his head.

"No," he said. "I know your heart was set on going North, but it's my belief not even Mrs Coulter was going to take you. If you want to see the North you'll have to wait till all this trouble's over. Now off you go."

Pantalaimon hissed quietly, but John Faa's dæmon took off from the back of his chair and flew at them with black wings, not threateningly, but like a reminder of good manners; and Lyra turned on her heel as the crow glided over her head and wheeled back to John Faa. The door shut behind her with a decisive click.

"We *will* go," she said to Pantalaimon. "Let 'em try to stop us. We *will*!"

9

THE SPIES

OVER THE NEXT few days, Lyra concocted a dozen plans and dismissed them impatiently; for they all boiled down to stowing away, and how could you stow away on a narrow-boat? To be sure, the real voyage would involve a proper ship, and she knew enough stories to expect all kinds of hiding-places on a full-sized vessel: the lifeboats, the hold, the bilges, whatever they were; but she'd have to get to the ship first, and leaving the Fens meant travelling the gyptian way.

And even if she got to the coast on her own, she might stow away on the wrong ship. It would be a fine thing to hide in a lifeboat and wake up on the way to High Brazil.

Meanwhile, all around her the tantalizing work of assembling the expedition was going on day and night. She hung around Adam Stefanski, watching as he made his choice of the volunteers for the fighting force. She pestered Roger van Poppel with suggestions about the stores they needed to take: had he remembered snow-goggles? Did he know the best place to get Arctic maps?

The man she most wanted to help was Benjamin de Ruyter, the spy. But he had slipped away in the early hours of the morning after the second Roping, and naturally no one could say where he'd gone or when he'd return. So in default, Lyra attached herself to Farder Coram.

"I think it'd be best if I helped you, Farder Coram," she said, "because I probably know more about the Gobblers than anyone else, being as I was nearly one of them. Probably you'll need me to help you understand Mr de Ruyter's messages."

He took pity on the fierce, desperate little girl and didn't send her away. Instead he talked to her, and listened to her memories of Oxford and of Mrs Coulter, and watched as she read the alethiometer.

"Where's that book with all the symbols in?" she asked him one day.

"In Heidelberg," he said.

"And is there just the one?"

"There may be others, but that's the one I've seen."

"I bet there's one in Bodley's Library in Oxford," she said.

She could hardly take her eyes off Farder Coram's dæmon, who was the most beautiful dæmon she'd ever seen. When Pantalaimon was a cat he was lean and ragged and harsh, but Sophonax, for that was her name, was golden-eyed and elegant beyond measure, fully twice as large as a real cat and richly furred. When the sunlight touched her, it lit up more shades of tawny-brown-leaf-hazel-corn-gold-autumn-mahogany than Lyra could name. She longed to touch that fur, to rub her cheeks against it, but of course she never did; for it was the grossest breach of etiquette imaginable to touch another person's dæmon. Dæmons might touch each other, of course, or fight; but the prohibition against human − dæmon contact went so deep that even in battle no warrior would touch an enemy's dæmon. It was utterly forbidden. Lyra couldn't remember having to be told that: she just knew it, as instinctively as she felt that nausea was bad and comfort good. So although she admired the fur of Sophonax and even speculated on what it might feel like, she never made the slightest move to touch her, and never would.

Sophonax was as sleek and healthy and beautiful as Farder Coram was ravaged and weak. He might have been ill, or he might have suffered a crippling blow, but the result was that he could not walk without leaning on two sticks, and he trembled constantly like an aspen leaf. His mind was sharp and clear and powerful, though, and soon Lyra came to love him for his knowledge and for the firm way he directed her.

"What's that hourglass mean, Farder Coram?" she asked, over the alethiometer, one sunny morning in his boat. "It keeps coming back to that."

"There's often a clue there if you look more close. What's that little old thing on top of it?"

She screwed up her eyes and peered.

"That's a skull!"

"So what d'you think that might mean?"

"Death . . . Is that death?"

"That's right. So in the hourglass range of meanings you get death. In fact after time, which is the first one, death is the second one."

"D'you know what I noticed, Farder Coram? The needle stops there on the second go round! On the first round it kind of twitches, and on the second it stops. Is that saying it's the second meaning, then?"

"Probably. What are you asking it, Lyra?"

"I'm a-thinking . . ." She stopped, surprised to find that she'd actually been asking a question without realizing it. "I just put three pictures together because . . . I was thinking about Mr de Ruyter, see . . . And I put together the serpent and the crucible and the beehive, to ask how he's a-getting on with his spying, and –"

"Why them three symbols?"

"Because I thought the serpent was cunning, like a spy ought to be, and the crucible could mean like knowledge, what you kind of distil, and the beehive was hard work, like bees are always working hard; so out of the hard work and the cunning comes the knowledge, see, and that's the spy's job; and I pointed to them and I thought the question in my mind, and the needle stopped at death . . . D'you think that could be really working, Farder Coram?"

"It's working all right, Lyra. What we don't know is whether we're reading it right. That's a subtle art. I wonder if –"

Before he could finish his sentence, there was an urgent knock at the door, and a young gyptian man came in.

"Beg pardon, Farder Coram, there's Jacob Huismans just come back, and he's sore wounded."

"He was with Benjamin de Ruyter," said Farder Coram. "What's happened?"

"He won't speak," said the young man. "You better come, Farder Coram, cause he won't last long, he's a-bleeding inside."

Farder Coram and Lyra exchanged a look of alarm and wonderment, but only for a second, and then Farder Coram was hobbling out on his sticks as fast as he could manage, with his dæmon padding ahead of him. Lyra came too, hopping with impatience.

The young man led them to a boat tied up at the sugar-beet jetty, where a woman in a red flannel apron held open the door for them. Seeing her suspicious glance at Lyra, Farder Coram said, "It's important the girl hears what Jacob's got to say, mistress."

So the woman let them in and stood back, with her squirrel-dæmon perched silent on the wooden clock. On a bunk under a patchwork coverlet lay a man whose white face was damp with sweat and whose eyes were glazed.

"I've sent for the physician, Farder Coram," said the woman shakily. "Please don't agitate him. He's in an agony of pain. He come in off Peter Hawker's boat just a few minutes ago."

"Where's Peter now?"

"He's a-tying up. It was him said I had to send for you."

"Quite right. Now, Jacob, can ye hear me?"

Jacob's eyes rolled to look at Farder Coram sitting on the opposite bunk, a foot or two away.

"Hello, Farder Coram," he murmured.

Lyra looked at his dæmon. She was a ferret, and she lay very still beside his head, curled up but not asleep, for her eyes were open and glazed like his.

"What happened?" said Farder Coram.

"Benjamin's dead," came the answer. "He's dead, and Gerard's captured."

His voice was hoarse and his breath was shallow. When he stopped speaking his dæmon uncurled painfully and licked his cheek, and taking strength from that he went on:

"We was breaking into the Ministry of Theology, because Benjamin had heard from one of the Gobblers we caught that the headquarters was there, that's where all the orders was coming from . . ."

He stopped again.

"You captured some Gobblers?" said Farder Coram.

Jacob nodded, and cast his eyes at his dæmon. It was unusual for dæmons to speak to other humans than their own, but it happened sometimes, and she spoke now.

"We caught three Gobblers in Clerkenwell and made them

tell us who they were working for and where the orders came from and so on. They didn't know where the kids were being taken, except it was North to Lapland . . ."

She had to stop and pant briefly, her little chest fluttering, before she could go on.

"And so them Gobblers told us about the Ministry of Theology and Lord Boreal. Benjamin said him and Gerard Hook should break into the Ministry and Frans Broekman and Tom Mendham should go and find out about Lord Boreal."

"Did they do that?"

"We don't know. They never came back. Farder Coram, it were like everything we did, they knew about before we did it, and for all we know Frans and Tom were swallowed alive as soon as they got near Lord Boreal."

"Come back to Benjamin," said Farder Coram, hearing Jacob's breathing getting harsher and seeing his eyes close in pain.

Jacob's dæmon gave a little mew of anxiety and love, and the woman took a step or two closer, her hands to her mouth; but she didn't speak, and the dæmon went on faintly:

"Benjamin and Gerard and us went to the Ministry at White Hall and found a little side door, it not being fiercely guarded, and we stayed on watch outside while they unfastened the lock and went in. They hadn't been in but a minute when we heard a cry of fear, and Benjamin's dæmon came a-flying out and beckoned to us for help and flew in again, and we took our knife and ran in after her; only the place was dark, and full of wild forms and sounds that were confusing in their frightful movements; and we cast about, but there was a commotion above, and a fearful cry, and Benjamin and his dæmon fell from a high staircase above us, his dæmon a-tugging and a-fluttering to hold him up, but all in vain, for they crashed on the stone floor and both perished in a moment.

"And we couldn't see anything of Gerard, but there was a howl from above in his voice and we were too terrified and stunned to move, and then an arrow shot down at our shoulder and pierced deep down within . . ."

The dæmon's voice was fainter, and a groan came from the wounded man. Farder Coram leaned forward and gently pulled back the counterpane, and there protruding from his shoulder was the feathered end of an arrow in a mass of clotted blood. The shaft and the head were so deep in the poor man's chest that only six inches or so remained above the skin. Lyra felt faint.

There was the sound of feet and voices outside on the jetty.

Farder Coram sat up and said, "Here's the physician, Jacob. We'll leave you now. We'll have a longer talk when you're feeling better."

He clasped the woman's shoulder on the way out. Lyra stuck close to him on the jetty, because there was a crowd gathering already, whispering and pointing. Farder Coram gave orders for Peter Hawker to go at once to John Faa, and then said:

"Lyra, as soon as we know whether Jacob's going to live or die, we must have another talk about that alethiometer. You go and occupy yourself elsewhere, child; we'll send for you."

Lyra wandered away on her own, and went to the reedy bank to sit and throw mud into the water. She knew one thing: she was not pleased or proud to be able to read the alethiometer – she was afraid. Whatever power was making that needle swing and stop, it knew things like an intelligent being.

"I reckon it's a spirit," Lyra said, and for a moment she was tempted to throw the little thing into the middle of the fen.

"I'd see a spirit if there was one in there," said Pantalaimon. "Like that old ghost in Godstow. I saw that when you didn't."

"There's more than one kind of spirit," said Lyra reprovingly. "You can't see all of 'em. Anyway, what about those old dead Scholars without their heads? I saw them, remember."

"That was only a night-ghast."

"It was not. They were proper spirits all right, and you know it. But whatever spirit's moving this blooming needle en't that sort of spirit."

"It might not be a spirit," said Pantalaimon stubbornly.

"Well what else could it be?"

"It might be . . . It might be elementary particles."

She scoffed.

"It could be!" he insisted. "You remember that photo-mill they got at Gabriel? Well then."

At Gabriel College there was a very holy object kept on the

high altar of the Oratory, covered (now Lyra thought about it) with a black velvet cloth, like the one around the alethiometer. She had seen it when she accompanied the Librarian of Jordan to a service there. At the height of the invocation the Intercessor lifted the cloth to reveal in the dimness a glass dome inside which there was something too distant to see, until he pulled a string attached to a shutter above, letting a ray of sunlight through to strike the dome exactly. Then it became clear: a little thing like a weathervane, with four sails black on one side and white on the other, that began to whirl around as the light struck it. It illustrated a moral lesson, the Intercessor explained, for the black of ignorance fled from the light, whereas the wisdom of white rushed to embrace it. Lyra took his word for that, but the little whirling vanes were delightful whatever they meant, and all done by the power of photons, said the Librarian as they walked home to Jordan.

So perhaps Pantalaimon was right. If elementary particles could push a photo-mill around, no doubt they could make light work of a needle; but it still troubled her.

"Lyra! Lyra!"

It was Tony Costa, waving to her from the jetty.

"Come over here," he called. "You got to go and see John Faa at the Zaal. Run, gal, it's urgent."

She found John Faa with Farder Coram and the other leaders, looking troubled.

John Faa spoke:

"Lyra, child, Farder Coram has told me about your reading of that instrument. And I'm sorry to say that poor Jacob has just died. I think we're going to have to take you with us after all, against my inclinations. I'm troubled in my mind about it, but there don't seem to be any alternative. As soon as Jacob's buried according to custom we'll take our way. You understand me, Lyra: you're a-coming too, but it en't an occasion for joy or jubilation. There's trouble and danger ahead for all on us.

"I'm a-putting you under Farder Coram's wing. Don't you be a trouble or a hazard to him, or you'll be a-feeling the force of my wrath. Now cut along and explain to Ma Costa, and hold yourself in readiness to leave."

* * *

The next two weeks passed more busily than any time of Lyra's life so far. Busily, but not quickly, for there were tedious stretches of waiting, of hiding in damp crabbed closets, of watching a dismal rain-soaked autumn landscape roll past the window, of hiding again, of sleeping near the gas-fumes of the engine and waking with a sick headache, and worst of all, of never once being allowed out into the air to run along the bank or clamber over the deck or haul at the lock gates or catch a mooring-rope thrown from the lockside.

Because of course she had to remain hidden. Tony Costa told her of the gossip in the waterside pubs: that there was a hunt the length of the kingdom for a little fair-haired girl, with a big reward for her discovery and severe punishment for anyone concealing her. There were strange rumours, too: people said she was the only child to have escaped from the Gobblers, and she had terrible secrets in her possession. Another rumour said she wasn't a human child at all but a pair of spirits in the form of child and dæmon, sent to this world by the infernal powers in order to work great ruin; and yet another rumour said it was no child but a fully grown human, shrunk by magic and in the pay of the Tartars, come to spy on good English people and prepare the way for a Tartar invasion.

Lyra heard these tales at first with glee and later with despondency. All those people hating and fearing her! And she longed to be out of this narrow boxy cabin. She longed to be North already, in the wide snows under the blazing Aurora. And sometimes she longed to be back at Jordan College, scrambling over the roofs with Roger with the Steward's Bell tolling half an hour to dinner time and the clatter and sizzle and shouting of the Kitchen . . . Then she wished passionately that nothing had changed, nothing would ever change, that she could be Lyra of Jordan College for ever and ever.

The one thing that drew her out of her boredom and irritation was the alethiometer. She read it every day, sometimes with Farder Coram and sometimes on her own, and she found that she could sink more and more readily into the calm state in which the symbol-meanings clarified themselves, and those great mountain-ranges touched by sunlight emerged into vision.

She struggled to explain to Farder Coram what it felt like.

"It's almost like talking to someone, only you can't quite hear them, and you feel kind of stupid because they're cleverer than you, only they don't get cross or anything . . . And they know such a lot, Farder Coram! As if they knew everything, almost! Mrs Coulter was clever, she knew ever such a lot, but this is a different kind of knowing . . . It's like understanding, I suppose . . ."

He would ask specific questions, and she would search for answers.

"What's Mrs Coulter doing now?" he'd say, and her hands would move at once, and he'd say, "Tell me what you're doing."

"Well, the Madonna is Mrs Coulter, and I think my *mother* when I put the hand there; and the ant is *busy* – that's easy, that's the top meaning; and the hourglass has got *time* in its meanings, and partway down there's *now*, and I just fix my mind on it."

"And how do you know where these meanings are?"

"I kind of see 'em. Or feel 'em rather, like climbing down a ladder at night, you put your foot down and there's another rung. Well, I put my mind down and there's another meaning, and I kind of sense what it is. Then I put 'em all together. There's a trick in it like focusing your eyes."

"Do that then, and see what it says."

Lyra did. The long needle began to swing at once, and stopped, moved on, stopped again in a precise series of sweeps and pauses. It was a sensation of such grace and power that Lyra, sharing it, felt like a young bird learning to fly. Farder Coram, watching from across the table, noted the places where the needle stopped, and watched the little girl holding her hair back from her face and biting her lower lip just a little, her eyes following the needle at first but then, when its path was settled, looking elsewhere on the dial. Not randomly, though. Farder Coram was a chess player, and he knew how chess players looked at a game in play. An expert player seemed to see lines of force and influence on the board, and looked along the important lines and ignored the weak ones; and Lyra's eyes moved the same way, according to some similar magnetic field that she could see and he couldn't.

The needle stopped at the thunderbolt, the infant, the serpent, the elephant, and at a creature Lyra couldn't find a name for: a sort of lizard with big eyes and a tail curled around the twig it stood on. It repeated the sequence time after time, while Lyra watched.

"What's that lizard mean?" said Farder Coram, breaking into her concentration.

"It don't make sense . . . I can see what it says, but I must be misreading it. The thunderbolt I think is anger, and the child . . . I think it's me . . . I was getting a meaning for that lizard thing, but you talked to me, Farder Coram, and I lost it. See, it's just floating any old where."

"Yes, I see that. I'm sorry, Lyra. You tired now? D'you want to stop?"

"No, I don't," she said, but her cheeks were flushed and her eyes bright. She had all the signs of fretful over-excitement, and it was made worse by her long confinement in this stuffy cabin.

He looked out of the window. It was nearly dark, and they were travelling along the last stretch of inland water before reaching the coast. Wide brown scummed expanses of an estuary extended under a dreary sky to a distant group of coal-spirit tanks, rusty and cobwebbed with pipework, beside a refinery where a thick smear of smoke ascended reluctantly to join the clouds.

"Where are we?" said Lyra. "Can I go outside just for a bit, Farder Coram?"

"This is Colby water," he said. "The estuary of the river Cole. When we reach the town we'll tie up by the Smokemarket and go on foot to the docks. We'll be there in an hour or two . . ."

But it was getting dark, and in the wide desolation of the creek nothing was moving but their own boat and a distant coal-barge labouring towards the refinery; and Lyra was so flushed and tired, and she'd been inside for so long; so Farder Coram went on:

"Well, I don't suppose it'll matter just for a few minutes in the open air. I wouldn't call it fresh; ten't fresh except when it's blowing off the sea; but you can sit out on top and look around till we get closer in."

Lyra leapt up, and Pantalaimon became a seagull at once, eager to stretch his wings in the open. It was cold outside and, although she was well wrapped up, Lyra was soon shivering. Pantalaimon, on the other hand, leapt into the air with a loud caw of delight, and wheeled and skimmed and darted now ahead of the boat, now behind the stern. Lyra exulted in it, feeling with him as he flew, and urging him mentally to provoke the old tillerman's cormorant-dæmon into a race. But she ignored him and settled down sleepily on the handle of the tiller near her man.

There was no life out on this bitter brown expanse, and only the steady chug of the engine and the subdued splashing of the water under the bows broke the wide silence. Heavy clouds hung low without offering rain; the air beneath was grimy with smoke. Only Pantalaimon's flashing elegance had anything in it of life and joy.

As he soared up out of a dive with wide wings white against the grey, something black hurtled at him and struck. He fell sideways in a flutter of shock and pain, and Lyra cried out, feeling it sharply. Another little black thing joined the first; they moved not like birds but like flying beetles, heavy and direct, and with a droning sound.

As Pantalaimon fell, trying to twist away and make for the boat and Lyra's desperate arms, the black things kept driving into him, droning, buzzing, and murderous. Lyra was nearly mad with Pantalaimon's fear and her own, but then something swept past her and upward.

It was the tillerman's dæmon, and clumsy and heavy as she looked, her flight was powerful and swift. Her head snapped this way and that – there was a flutter of black wings, a shiver of white – and a little black thing fell to the tarred roof of the cabin at Lyra's feet just as Pantalaimon landed on her outstretched hand.

Before she could comfort him, he changed into his wildcat-shape and sprang down on the creature, batting it back from the edge of the roof, where it was crawling swiftly to escape. Pantalaimon held it firmly down with a needle-filled paw and looked up at the darkening sky, where the black wing-flaps of the cormorant were circling higher as she cast around for the other.

Then the cormorant glided swiftly back and croaked something to the tillerman, who said, "It's gone. Don't let that other one escape. Here —" and he flung the dregs out of the tin mug he'd been drinking from, and tossed it to Lyra.

She clapped it over the creature at once. It buzzed and snarled like a little machine.

"Hold it still," said Farder Coram from behind her, and then he was kneeling to slip a piece of card under the mug.

"What is it, Farder Coram?" she said shakily.

"Let's go below and have a look. Take it careful, Lyra. Hold that tight."

She looked at the tillerman's dæmon as she passed, intending to thank her, but her old eyes were closed. She thanked the tiller-man instead.

"You oughter stayed below," was all he said.

She took the mug into the cabin, where Farder Coram had found a beer glass. He held the tin mug upside down over it and then slipped the card out from between them, so that the creature fell into the glass. He held it up so they could see the angry little thing clearly.

It was about as long as Lyra's thumb, and dark green, not black. Its wing cases were erect, like a ladybird's about to fly, and the wings inside were beating so furiously that they were only a blur. Its six clawed legs were scrabbling on the smooth glass.

"What is it?" she said.

Pantalaimon, a wildcat still, crouched on the table six inches away, his green eyes following it round and round inside the glass.

"If you was to crack it open," said Farder Coram, "you'd find no living thing in there. No animal nor insect, at any rate. I seen one of these things afore, and I never thought I'd see one again this far north. Afric things. There's a clockwork running in there, and pinned to the spring of it, there's a bad spirit with a spell through its heart."

"But who sent it?"

"You don't even need to read the symbols, Lyra; you can guess as easy as I can."

"Mrs Coulter?"

"Course. She en't only explored up North; there's strange things aplenty in the southern wild. It was Morocco where I saw one of these last. Deadly dangerous; while the spirit's in it, it won't never stop, and when you let the spirit free it's so monstrous angry it'll kill the first thing it gets at."

"But what was it after?"

"Spying. I was a cursed fool to let you up above. And I should have let you think your way through the symbols without interrupting."

"I see it now!" said Lyra, suddenly excited. "It means air, that lizard thing! I saw that, but I couldn't see why, so I tried to work it out and I lost it."

"Ah," said Farder Coram, "then I see it too. It en't a lizard, that's why; it's a chameleon. And it stands for air because they don't eat nor drink, they just live on air."

"And the elephant –"

"Africa," he said, and, "Aha."

They looked at each other. With every revelation of the alethiometer's power, they became more awed by it.

"It was telling us about these things all the time," said Lyra. "We oughter listened. But what can we do about this'un, Farder Coram? Can we kill it or something?"

"I don't know as we can do anything. We shall just have to keep him shut up tight in a box and never let him out. What worries me more is the other one, as got away. He'll be a-flying back to Mrs Coulter now, with the news that he's seen you. Damn me, Lyra, but I'm a fool."

He rattled about in a cupboard and found a smoke-leaf tin about three inches in diameter. It had been used for holding screws, but he tipped those out and wiped the inside with a rag before inverting the glass over it with the card still in place over the mouth.

After a tricky moment when one of the creature's legs escaped and thrust the tin away with surprising strength, they had it captured and the lid screwed down tight.

"As soon's we get about the ship I'll run some solder round the edge to make sure of it," Farder Coram said.

"But don't clockwork run down?"

"Ordinary clockwork, yes. But like I said, this'un's kept tight wound by the spirit pinned to the end. The more he struggles, the tighter it's wound, and the stronger the force is. Now let's put this feller out the way..."

He wrapped the tin in a flannel cloth to stifle the incessant buzzing and droning, and stowed it away under his bunk.

It was dark now, and Lyra watched through the window as the lights of Colby came closer. The heavy air was thickening into mist, and by the time they tied up at the wharves alongside the Smokemarket everything in sight was softened and blurred. The darkness shaded into pearly silver-grey veils laid over the warehouses and the cranes, the wooden market-stalls and the granite many-chimneyed building the market was named after, where day and night fish hung kippering in the fragrant oakwood smoke. The chimneys were contributing their thickness to the clammy air, and the pleasant reek of smoked herring and mackerel and haddock seemed to breathe out of the very cobbles.

Lyra, wrapped up in an oilskin and with a large hood hiding her revealing hair, walked along between Farder Coram and the tillerman. All three dæmons were alert, scouting around corners ahead, watching behind, listening for the slightest footfall.

But they were the only figures to be seen. The citizens of Colby were all indoors, probably sipping jenniver beside roaring stoves. They saw no one until they reached the dock, and the first man they saw there was Tony Costa, guarding the gates.

"Thank God you got here," he said quietly, letting them through. "We just heard as Jack Verhoeven's bin shot and his boat sunk, and no one'd heard where you was. John Faa's on board already and jumping to go."

The vessel looked immense to Lyra: a wheelhouse and funnel amidships, a high fo'c'sle and a stout derrick over a canvas-covered hatch; yellow light agleam in the portholes and the bridge, and white light at the masthead; and three or four men on deck, working urgently at things she couldn't see.

She hurried up the wooden gangway ahead of Farder Coram, and looked around with excitement. Pantalaimon became a monkey and clambered up the derrick at once, but she called him down again; Farder Coram wanted them indoors, or below, as you called it on board ship.

Down some stairs, or a companionway, there was a small saloon where John Faa was talking quietly with Nicholas Rokeby, the gyptian in charge of the vessel. John Faa did nothing hastily. Lyra was waiting for him to greet her, but he finished his remarks about the tide and pilotage before turning to the incomers.

"Good evening, friends," he said. "Poor Jack Verhoeven's dead, perhaps you've heard. And his boys captured."

"We have bad news too," said Farder Coram, and told of their encounter with the flying spirits.

John Faa shook his great head, but didn't reproach them.

"Where is the creature now?" he said.

Farder Coram took out the leaf-tin and laid it on the table. Such a furious buzzing came from it that the tin itself moved slowly over the wood.

"I've heard of them clockwork devils, but never seen one," John Faa said. "There en't no way of taming it and turning it back, I do know that much. Nor is it any use weighing it down with lead and dropping it in the ocean, because one day it'd rust through and out the devil would come and make for the child wherever she was. No, we'll have to keep it by, and exercise our vigilance."

Lyra being the only female on board (for John Faa had decided against taking women, after much thought), she had a cabin to herself. Not a grand cabin, to be sure; in fact little more than a closet with a bunk and a scuttle, which was the proper name for porthole. She stowed her few things in the drawer below the bunk and ran up excitedly to lean over the rail and watch England vanish behind, only to find that most of England had vanished in the mist before she got there.

But the rush of water below, the movement in the air, the ship's lights glowing bravely in the dark, the rumble of the engine, the smells of salt and fish and coal-spirit, were exciting enough by themselves. It wasn't long before another sensation joined them, as the vessel began to roll in the German Ocean swell. When someone called Lyra down for a bite of supper, she found she was less hungry than she'd thought, and presently she decided it would be a good idea to lie down, for Pantalaimon's sake, because the poor creature was feeling sadly ill at ease.

And so began her journey to the North.

PART TWO: BOLVANGAR

10

THE CONSUL AND THE BEAR

JOHN FAA AND the other leaders had decided that they would make for Trollesund, the main port of Lapland. The witches had a consulate in the town, and John Faa knew that without their help, or at least their friendly neutrality, it would be impossible to rescue the captive children.

He explained his idea to Lyra and Farder Coram next day, when Lyra's seasickness had abated slightly. The sun was shining brightly and the green waves were dashing against the bows, bearing white streams of foam as they curved away. Out on the deck, with the breeze blowing and the whole sea a-sparkle with light and movement, she felt little sickness at all; and now that Pantalaimon had discovered the delights of being a seagull and then a stormy petrel and skimming the wave-tops, Lyra was too absorbed by his glee to wallow in landlubberly misery.

John Faa, Farder Coram, and two or three others sat in the stern of the ship, with the sun full on them, talking about what to do next.

"Now Farder Coram knows these Lapland witches," John Faa said. "And if I en't mistaken there's an obligation there."

"That's right, John," said Farder Coram. "It were forty years back, but that's nothing to a witch. Some of 'em live to many times that."

"What happened to bring this obligation about, Farder Coram?" said Adam Stefanski, the man in charge of the fighting troop.

"I saved a witch's life," Farder Coram explained. "She fell out of the air, being pursued by a great red bird like to nothing I'd seen before. She fell injured in the marsh and I set out to find her. She was like to drowning, and I got her on board and shot that bird down, and it fell into a bog, to my regret, for it was as big as a bittern, and flame-red."

"Ah," the other men murmured, captured by Farder Coram's story.

"Now when I got her in the boat," he went on, "I had the most grim shock I'd ever known, because that young woman had no dæmon."

It was as if he'd said, "She had no head." The very thought was repugnant. The men shuddered, their dæmons bristled or shook themselves or cawed harshly, and the men soothed them. Pantalaimon crept into Lyra's breast, their hearts beating together.

"At least," Farder Coram said, "that's what it seemed. Being as she'd fell out of the air, I more than suspected she was a witch. She looked exactly like a young woman, thinner than some and prettier than most, but not seeing that dæmon gave me a hideous turn."

"En't they got dæmons then, the witches?" said the other man, Michael Canzona.

"Their dæmons is invisible, I expect," said Adam Stefanski. "He was there all the time, and Farder Coram never saw him."

"No, you're wrong, Adam," said Farder Coram. "He weren't there at all. The witches have the power to separate theirselves from their dæmons a mighty sight further'n what we can. If need be they can send their dæmons far abroad on the wind or the clouds, or down below the ocean. And this witch I found, she hadn't been resting above an hour when her dæmon came a-flying back, because he'd felt her fear and her injury, of course. And it's my belief, though she never admitted to this, that the great red bird I shot was another witch's dæmon, in pursuit. Lord! That made me shiver, when I thought of that. I'd have stayed my hand; I'd have taken any measures on sea or land; but there it was. Anyway, there was no doubt I'd saved her life, and she gave me a token of it, and said I was to call on her help if ever it was needed. And once she sent me help when the Skraelings shot me with a poison arrow. We had other connections, too . . . I haven't seen her for many years, but she'll remember."

"And does she live at Trollesund, this witch?"

"No, no. They live in forests and on the tundra, not in a sea-port among men and women. Their business is with the wild.

But they keep a consul there, and I shall get word to her, make no doubt about that."

Lyra was keen to know more about the witches, but the men had turned their talk to the matter of fuel and stores, and presently she grew impatient to see the rest of the ship. She wandered along the deck towards the bows, and soon made the acquaintance of an Able-Seaman by flicking at him the pips she'd saved from the apple she'd eaten at breakfast. He was a stout and placid man, and when he'd sworn at her and been sworn at in return, they became great friends. He was called Jerry. Under his guidance she found out that having something to do prevented you from feeling seasick, and that even a job like scrubbing a deck could be satisfying, if it was done in a seamanlike way. She was very taken with this notion, and later on she folded the blankets on her bunk in a seamanlike way, and put her possessions in the closet in a seamanlike way, and used "stow" instead of "tidy" for the process of doing so.

After two days at sea, Lyra decided that this was the life for her. She had the run of the ship, from the engine room to the bridge, and she was soon on first-name terms with all the crew. Captain Rokeby let her signal to a Hollands frigate by pulling the handle of the steam-whistle; the cook suffered her help in mixing plum-duff; and only a stern word from John Faa prevented her from climbing the foremast to inspect the horizon from the crow's nest.

All the time they were steaming north, and it grew colder daily. The ship's stores were searched for oilskins that could be cut down for her, and Jerry showed her how to sew, an art she learned willingly from him, though she had scorned it at Jordan and avoided instruction from Mrs Lonsdale. Together they made a waterproof bag for the alethiometer that she could wear around her waist, in case she fell in the sea, she said. With it safely in place she clung to the rail in her oilskins and sou'wester as the stinging spray broke over the bows and surged along the deck. She still felt seasick occasionally, especially when the wind got up and the ship plunged heavily over the crests of the grey-green waves, and then it was Pantalaimon's job to distract her from it by skimming the waves as a stormy petrel, because she could feel his boundless glee in the dash of wind and water, and forget her nausea. From time to time he even tried being a fish, and once joined a school of dolphins, to their surprise and pleasure. Lyra stood shivering in the fo'c'sle and laughed with delight as her beloved Pantalaimon, sleek and powerful, leapt from the water with half a dozen other swift grey shapes. It was pleasure, but not simple pleasure, for there was pain and fear in it too. Suppose he loved being a dolphin more than he loved her?

Her friend the Able-Seaman was nearby, and he paused as he adjusted the canvas cover of the forward hatch to look out at the little girl's dæmon skimming and leaping with the dolphins. His own dæmon, a seagull, had her head tucked under her wing on the capstan. He knew what Lyra was feeling.

"I remember when I first went to sea, my Belisaria hadn't settled on one form, I was that young, and she loved being a porpoise. I was afraid she'd settle like that. There was one old sailorman on my first vessel who could never go ashore at all, because his dæmon had settled as a dolphin, and he could never leave the water. He was a wonderful sailor; best navigator you ever knew; could have made a fortune at the fishing; but he wasn't happy like it. He was never quite happy till he died and he could be buried at sea."

"Why do dæmons have to settle?" Lyra said. "I want Pantalaimon to be able to change for ever. So does he."

"Ah, they always have settled, and they always will. That's part of growing up. There'll come a time when you'll be tired of his changing about, and you'll want a settled kind of form for him."

"I never will!"

"Oh, you will. You'll want to grow up like all the other girls. Anyway, there's compensations for a settled form."

"What are they?"

"Knowing what kind of person you are. Take old Belisaria. She's a seagull, and that means I'm a kind of seagull too. I'm not grand and splendid nor beautiful, but I'm a tough old thing and I can survive anywhere and always find a bit of food and company. That's worth knowing, that is. And when your dæmon settles, you'll know the sort of person you are."

"But suppose your dæmon settles in a shape you don't like?"

"Well, then, you're discontented, en't you? There's plenty of folk as'd like to have a lion as a dæmon and they end up with a poodle. And till they learn to be satisfied with what they are, they're going to be fretful about it. Waste of feeling, that is."

But it didn't seem to Lyra that she would ever grow up.

One morning there was a different smell in the air, and the ship was moving oddly, with a brisker rocking from side to side instead of the plunging and soaring. Lyra was on deck a minute after she woke up, gazing greedily at the land: such a strange sight, after all that water, for though they had only been at sea a few days, Lyra felt as if they'd been on the ocean for months. Directly ahead of the ship a mountain rose, green-flanked and snow-capped, and a little town and harbour lay below it: wooden houses with steep roofs, an oratory spire, cranes in the harbour, and clouds of gulls wheeling and crying. The smell was of fish, but mixed with it came land-smells too: pine-resin and earth and something animal and musky, and something else that was cold and blank and wild: it might have been snow. It was the smell of the North.

Seals frisked around the ship, showing their clown-faces above the water before sinking back without a splash. The wind that lifted spray off the white-capped waves was monstrously cold, and searched out every gap in Lyra's wolfskin, and her hands were soon aching and her face numb. Pantalaimon, in his ermine-shape, warmed her neck for her, but it was too cold to stay out-side for long without work to do, even to watch the seals, and Lyra went below to eat her breakfast porridge and look through the porthole in the saloon.

Inside the harbour the water was calm, and as they moved past the massive breakwater Lyra began to feel unsteady from the lack of motion. She and Pantalaimon avidly watched as the ship inched ponderously towards the quayside. During the next hour the sound of the engine died away to a quiet background rumble, voices shouted orders or queries, ropes were thrown, gangways lowered, hatches opened.

"Come on, Lyra," said Farder Coram. "Is everything packed?"

Lyra's possessions, such as they were, had been packed ever

since she'd woken up and seen the land. All she had to do was run to the cabin and pick up the shopping bag, and she was ready.

The first thing she and Farder Coram did ashore was to visit the house of the Witch-Consul. It didn't take long to find it; the little town was clustered around the harbour, with the oratory and the Governor's house the only buildings of any size. The Witch-Consul lived in a green-painted wooden house within sight of the sea, and when they rang the bell it jangled loudly in the quiet street.

A servant showed them into a little parlour and brought them coffee. Presently the Consul himself came in to greet them. He was a fat man with a florid face and a sober black suit, whose name was Martin Lanselius. His dæmon was a little serpent, the same intense and brilliant green as his eyes, which were the only witch-like thing about him; though Lyra was not sure what she had been expecting a witch to look like.

"How can I help you, Farder Coram?" he said.

"In two ways, Dr Lanselius. First, I'm anxious to get in touch with a witch-lady I met some years ago, in the Fen country of Eastern Anglia. Her name is Serafina Pekkala."

Dr Lanselius made a note with a silver pencil.

"How long ago was your meeting with her?" he said.

"Must be forty years. But I think she would remember."

"And what is the second way in which you seek my help?"

"I'm representing a number of gyptian families who've lost children. We've got reason to believe there's an organization capturing these children, ours and others, and bringing them to the North for some unknown purpose. I'd like to know whether you or your people have heard of anything like this a-going on."

Dr Lanselius sipped his coffee blandly.

"It's not impossible that notice of some such activity might have come our way," he said. "You realize, the relations between my people and the Northlanders are perfectly cordial. It would be difficult for me to justify disturbing them."

Farder Coram nodded as if he understood very well.

"To be sure," he said. "And it wouldn't be necessary for me to ask you if I could get the information any other way. That was why I asked about the witch-lady first."

Now Dr Lanselius nodded as if *he* understood. Lyra watched this game with puzzlement and respect. There were all kinds of things going on beneath it, and she saw that the Witch-Consul was coming to a decision.

"Very well," he said. "Of course, that's true, and you'll realize that your name is not unknown to us, Farder Coram. Serafina Pekkala is queen of a witch-clan in the region of Lake Enara. As for your other question, it is of course understood that this information is not reaching you through me."

"Quite so."

"Well, in this very town there is a branch of an organization called the Northern Progress Exploration Company, which pretends to be searching for minerals, but which is really controlled by something called the General Oblation Board of London. This organization, I happen to know, imports children. This is not generally known in the town; the Norroway government is not officially aware of it. The children don't remain here long. They are taken some distance inland."

"Do you know where, Dr Lanselius?"

"No. I would tell you if I did."

"And do you know what happens to them there?"

For the first time, Dr Lanselius glanced at Lyra. She looked stolidly back. The little green serpent-dæmon raised her head from the Consul's collar and whispered tongue-flickeringly in his ear.

The Consul said, "I have heard the phrase *the Maystadt Process* in connection with this matter. I think they use that in order to avoid calling what they do by its proper name. I have also heard the word *intercision*, but what it refers to I could not say."

"And are there any children in the town at the moment?" said Farder Coram.

He was stroking his dæmon's fur as she sat alert in his lap. Lyra noticed that she had stopped purring.

"No, I think not," said Dr Lanselius. "A group of about twelve arrived a week ago and moved out the day before yesterday."

"Ah! As recent as that? Then that gives us a bit of hope. How did they travel, Dr Lanselius?"

"By sledge."

"And you have no idea where they went?"

"Very little. It is not a subject we are interested in."

"Quite so. Now, you've answered all my questions very fairly, sir, and here's just one more. If you were me, what question would you ask of the Consul of the Witches?"

For the first time Dr Lanselius smiled.

"I would ask where I could obtain the services of an armoured bear," he said.

Lyra sat up, and felt Pantalaimon's heart leap in her hands.

"I understood the armoured bears to be in the service of the Oblation Board," said Farder Coram in surprise. "I mean, the Northern Progress Company, or whatever they're calling themselves."

"There is at least one who is not. You will find him at the sledge depot at the end of Langlokur Street. He earns a living there at the moment, but such is his temper and the fear he engenders in the dogs, his employment might not last for long."

"Is he a renegade, then?"

"It seems so. His name is Iorek Byrnison. You asked what I would ask, and I told you. Now here is what I would do: I would seize the chance to employ an armoured bear, even if it were far more remote than this."

Lyra could hardly sit still. Farder Coram, however, knew the etiquette for meetings such as this, and took another spiced honey-cake from the plate. While he ate it, Dr Lanselius turned to Lyra.

"I understand that you are in possession of an alethiometer," he said, to her great surprise; for how could he have known that?

"Yes," she said, and then, prompted by a nip from Pantalaimon, added, "Would you like to look at it?"

"I should like that very much."

She fished inelegantly in the oilskin pouch and handed him the velvet package. He unfolded it and held it up with great care, gazing at the face like a scholar gazing at a rare manuscript.

"How exquisite!" he said. "I have seen one other example, but it was not so fine as this. And do you possess the books of readings?"

"No," Lyra began, but before she could say any more, Farder Coram was speaking.

"No, the great pity is that although Lyra owns the alethiometer itself, there's no means of reading it whatsoever," he said. "It's just as much of a mystery as the pools of ink the Hindus use for reading the future. And the nearest book of readings I know of is in the Abbey of St Johann at Heidelberg."

Lyra could see why he was saying this: he didn't want Dr Lanselius to know of Lyra's power. But she could also see something Farder Coram couldn't, which was the agitation of Dr Lanselius's dæmon, and she knew at once that it was no good to pretend.

So she said, "Actually I *can* read it," speaking half to Dr Lanselius and half to Farder Coram, and it was the Consul who responded.

"That is wise of you," he said. "Where did you obtain this one?"

"The Master of Jordan College in Oxford gave it to me," she said. "Dr Lanselius, do you know who made them?"

"They are said to originate in the city of Prague," said the Consul. "The scholar who invented the first alethiometer was apparently trying to discover a way of measuring the influences of the planets, according to the ideas of astrology. He intended to make a device that would respond to the idea of Mars or Venus as a compass responds to the idea of North. In that he failed, but the mechanism he invented was clearly responding to something, even if no one knew what it was."

"And where did they get the symbols from?"

"Oh, this was in the seventeenth century. Symbols and emblems were everywhere. Buildings and pictures were designed to be read like books. Everything stood for something else; if you had the right dictionary you could read Nature itself. It was hardly surprising to find philosophers using the symbolism of their time to interpret knowledge that came from a mysterious source. But, you know, they haven't been used seriously for two centuries or so."

He handed the instrument back to Lyra, and added:

"May I ask a question? Without the books of symbols, how do you read it?"

"I just make my mind go clear and then it's sort of like looking down into water. You got to let your eyes find the right level, because that's the only one that's in focus. Something like that," she said.

"I wonder if I might ask to see you do it?" he said.

Lyra looked at Farder Coram, wanting to say yes but waiting for his approval. The old man nodded.

"What shall I ask?" said Lyra.

"What are the intentions of the Tartars with regard to Kamchatka?"

That wasn't hard. Lyra turned the hands to the camel, which meant Asia, which meant Tartars; to the cornucopia, for Kamchatka, where there were gold mines; and to the ant, which meant activity, which meant purpose and intention. Then she sat still, letting her mind hold the three levels of meaning together in focus, and relaxed for the answer, which came almost at once. The long needle trembled on the dolphin, the helmet, the baby and the anchor, dancing between them and on to the crucible in a complicated pattern that Lyra's eyes followed without hesitation, but which was incomprehensible to the two men.

When it had completed the movements several times Lyra looked up. She blinked once or twice as if she were coming out of a trance.

"They're going to pretend to attack it, but they're not really going to, because it's too far away and they'd be too stretched out," she said.

"Would you tell me how you read that?"

"The dolphin, one of its deep-down meanings is playing, sort of like being playful," she explained. "I know it's that one because it stopped that number of times and it just got clear at that level but nowhere else. And the helmet means war, and both together they mean pretend to go to war but not be serious. And the baby means – it means difficult – it'd be too hard for them to attack it, and the anchor says why, because they'd be stretched out as tight as an anchor rope. I just see it all like that, you see."

Dr Lanselius nodded.

"Remarkable," he said. "I am very grateful. I shall not forget that."

Then he looked strangely at Farder Coram, and back at Lyra.

"Could I ask you for one more demonstration?" he said. "In the yard behind this house, you will find several sprays of cloud-pine hanging on the wall. One of them has been used by Serafina Pekkala, and the others have not. Could you tell which is hers?"

"Yeah!" said Lyra, always ready to show off, and she took the alethiometer and hurried out. She was eager to see cloud-pine, because the witches used it for flying, and she'd never seen any before.

While she was gone, the Consul said, "Do you realize who this child is?"

"She's the daughter of Lord Asriel," said Farder Coram. "And her mother is Mrs Coulter, of the Oblation Board."

"And apart from that?"

The old gyptian had to shake his head. "No," he said, "I don't know any more. But she's a strange innocent creature, and I wouldn't have her harmed for the world. How she comes to read that instrument I couldn't guess, but I believe her when she talks of it. Why, Dr Lanselius? What do you know about her?"

"The witches have talked about this child for centuries past," said the Consul. "Because they live so close to the place where the veil between the worlds is thin, they hear immortal whispers from time to time, in the voices of those beings who pass between the worlds. And they have spoken of a child such as this, who has a great destiny that can only be fulfilled elsewhere – not in this world, but far beyond. Without this child, we shall all die. So the witches say. But she must fulfil this destiny in ignorance of what she is doing, because only in her ignorance can we be saved. Do you understand that, Farder Coram?"

"No," said Farder Coram, "I'm unable to say that I do."

"What it means is that she must be free to make mistakes. We must hope that she does not, but we can't guide her. I am glad to have seen this child before I die."

"But how did you recognize her as being that particular child? And what did you mean about the beings who pass between the worlds? I'm at a loss to understand you, Dr Lanselius, for all that I judge you're an honest man . . ."

But before the Consul could answer, the door opened and Lyra came in triumphantly bearing a small spray of pine.

"This is the one!" she said. "I tested 'em all, and this is it, I'm sure."

The Consul looked at it closely, and then nodded.

"Correct," he said. "Well, Lyra, that is remarkable. You are lucky to have an instrument like that, and I wish you well with it. I would like to give you something to take away with you . . ."

He took the spray and broke off a twig for her.

"Did she fly with this?" Lyra said, awed.

"Yes, she did. I can't give you all of it, because I need it to contact her, but this will be enough. Look after it."

"Yes, I will," she said. "Thank you."

And she tucked it into her purse beside the alethiometer. Farder Coram touched the spray of pine as if for luck, and on his face was an expression Lyra had never seen before: almost a longing. The Consul showed them to the door, where he shook hands with Farder Coram, and shook Lyra's hand too.

"I hope you find success," he said, and stood on his doorstep in the piercing cold to watch them up the little street.

"He knew the answer about the Tartars before I did," Lyra told Farder Coram. "The alethiometer told me, but I never said. It was the crucible."

"I expect he was testing you, child. But you done right to be polite, being as we can't be sure what he knows already. And that was a useful tip about the bear. I don't know how we would a heard otherwise."

They found their way to the depot, which was a couple of concrete warehouses in a scrubby area of waste ground where thin weeds grew between grey rocks and pools of icy mud. A surly man in an office told them that they could find the bear off duty at six, but they'd have to be quick, because he usually went straight to the yard behind Einarsson's Bar, where they gave him drink.

Then Farder Coram took Lyra to the best outfitter's in town and bought her some proper cold-weather clothing. They bought a parka made of reindeer skin, because reindeer hair is hollow and insulates well; and the hood was lined with wolverine fur, because that sheds the ice that forms when you breathe. They bought underclothing and boot liners of reindeer calf skin, and silk gloves to go inside big fur mittens. The boots and mittens were made of skin from the reindeer's forelegs, because that is extra tough, and the boots were soled with the skin of the bearded seal, which is as tough as walrus-hide, but lighter. Finally they bought a waterproof cape that enveloped her completely, made of semi-transparent seal intestine.

With all that on, and a silk muffler around her neck and a woollen cap over her ears and the big hood pulled forward, she was uncomfortably warm; but they were going to much colder regions than this.

John Faa had been supervising the unloading of the ship, and was keen to hear about the Witch-Consul's words, and even keener to learn of the bear.

"We'll go to him this very evening," he said. "Have you ever spoken to such a creature, Farder Coram?"

"Yes, I have; and fought one, too, though not by myself, thank God. We must be ready to treat with him, John. He'll ask a lot, I've no doubt, and be surly and difficult to manage; but we must have him."

"Oh, we must. And what of your witch?"

"Well, she's a long way off, and a clan-queen now," said Farder Coram. "I did hope it might be possible for a message to reach her, but it would take too long to wait for a reply."

"Ah, well. Now let me tell you what *I've* found, old friend."

For John Faa had been fidgeting with impatience to tell them something. He had met a prospector on the quayside, a New Dane by the name of Lee Scoresby, from the country of Texas, and this man had a balloon, of all things. The expedition he'd been hoping to join had failed for lack of funds even before it had left Amsterdam, so he was stranded.

"Think what we might do with the help of an aëronaut, Farder Coram!" said John Faa, rubbing his great hands together. "I've engaged him to sign up with us. Seems to me we struck lucky a-coming here."

"Luckier still if we had a clear idea of where we were going," said Farder Coram, but nothing could damp John Faa's pleasure in being on campaign once more.

After darkness had fallen, and when the stores and equipment had all been safely unloaded and stood in waiting on the quay, Farder Coram and Lyra walked along the waterfront and looked for Einarsson's Bar. They found it easily enough: a crude concrete shed with a red neon sign flashing irregularly over the door and the sound of loud voices through the condensation-frosted windows.

A pitted alley beside it led to a sheet-metal gate into a rear yard, where a lean-to shed stood crazily over a floor of frozen mud. Dim light through the rear window of the bar showed a vast pale form crouching upright and gnawing at a haunch of meat which it held in both hands. Lyra had an impression of blood-stained muzzle and face, small malevolent black eyes, and an immensity of dirty matted yellowish fur. As it gnawed, hideous growling, crunching, sucking noises came from it.

Farder Coram stood by the gate and called:

"Iorek Byrnison!"

The bear stopped eating. As far as they could tell, he was looking at them directly, but it was impossible to read any expression on his face.

"Iorek Byrnison," said Farder Coram again. "May I speak to you?"

Lyra's heart was thumping hard, because something in the bear's presence made her feel close to coldness, danger, brutal power, but a power controlled by intelligence; and not a human intelligence, nothing like a human, because of course bears had no dæmons. This strange hulking presence gnawing its meat was like nothing she had ever imagined, and she felt a profound admiration and pity for the lonely creature.

He dropped the reindeer leg in the dirt and slumped on all fours to the gate. Then he reared up massively, ten feet or more high, as if to show how mighty he was, to remind them how useless the gate would be as a barrier, and he spoke to them from that height.

"Well? Who are you?"

His voice was so deep it seemed to shake the earth. The rank smell that came from his body was almost overpowering.

"I'm Farder Coram, from the gyptian people of Eastern Anglia. And this little girl is Lyra Belacqua."

"What do you want?"

"We want to offer you employment, Iorek Byrnison."

"I am employed."

The bear dropped on all fours again. It was very hard to detect any expressive tones in his voice, whether of irony or anger, because it was so deep and so flat.

"What do you do at the sledge depot?" Farder Coram asked.

"I mend broken machinery and articles of iron. I lift heavy objects."

"What kind of work is that for a *panserbjørn*?"

"Paid work."

Behind the bear, the door of the bar opened a little way and a man put down a large earthenware jar before looking up to peer at them.

"Who's that?"

"Strangers," said the bear.

The bartender looked as if he was going to ask something more, but the bear lurched towards him suddenly and the man shut the door in alarm. The bear hooked a claw through the handle of the jar and lifted it to his mouth. Lyra could smell the tang of the raw spirits that splashed out.

After swallowing several times, the bear put the jar down and turned back to gnaw his haunch of meat, heedless of Farder Coram and Lyra, it seemed; but then he spoke again.

"What work are you offering?"

"Fighting, in all probability," said Farder Coram. "We're moving North until we find a place where they've taken some children captive. When we find it, we'll have to fight to get the children free; and then we'll bring them back."

"And what will you pay?"

"I don't know what to offer you, Iorek Byrnison. If gold is desirable to you, we have gold."

"No good."

"What do they pay you at the sledge depot?"

"My keep here in meat and spirits."

Silence from the bear; and then he dropped the ragged bone and lifted the jar to his muzzle again, drinking the powerful spirits like water.

"Forgive me for asking, Iorek Byrnison," said Farder Coram, "but you could live a free proud life on the ice hunting seals and walruses, or you could go to war and win great prizes. What ties you to Trollesund and Einarsson's Bar?"

Lyra felt her skin shiver all over. She would have thought a question like that, which was almost an insult, would enrage the great creature beyond reason, and she wondered at Farder Coram's courage in asking it. Iorek Byrnison put down his jar and came close to the gate to peer at the old man's face. Farder Coram didn't flinch.

"I know the people you are seeking, the child-cutters," the bear said. "They left town the day before yesterday to go North with more children. No one will tell you about them; they pretend not to see, because the child-cutters bring money and business. Now I don't like the child-cutters, so I shall answer you politely. I stay here and drink spirits because the men here took my armour away, and without that, I can hunt seals but I can't go to war; and I am an armoured bear: war is the sea I swim in and the air I breathe. The men of this town gave me spirits and let me drink till I was asleep, and then they took my armour away from me. If I knew where they keep it, I would tear down the town to get it back. If you want my service, the price is this: get me back my armour. Do that, and I shall serve you in your campaign, either until I am dead or until you have a victory. The price is my armour. I want it back, and then I shall never need spirits again."

11

ARMOUR

WHEN THEY RETURNED to the ship, Farder Coram and John Faa and the other leaders spent a long time in conference in the saloon, and Lyra went to her cabin to consult the alethiometer. Within five minutes she knew exactly where the bear's armour was, and why it would be difficult to get it back.

She wondered whether to go to the saloon and tell John Faa and the others, but decided that they'd ask her if they wanted to know. Perhaps they knew already.

She lay on her bunk thinking of that savage mighty bear, and the careless way he drank his fiery spirit, and the loneliness of him in his dirty lean-to. How different it was to be human, with one's dæmon always there to talk to! In the silence of the still ship, without the continual creak of metal and timber or the rumble of the engine or the rush of water along the side, Lyra gradually fell asleep, with Pantalaimon on her pillow sleeping too.

She was dreaming of her great imprisoned father when suddenly, for no reason at all, she woke up. She had no idea what time it was. There was a faint light in the cabin that she took for moonlight, and it showed her new cold-weather furs that lay stiffly in the corner of the cabin. No sooner did she see them than she longed to try them on again.

When they were on she had to go out on deck, and a minute later she opened the door at the top of the companionway and stepped out.

At once she saw that something strange was happening in the sky. She thought it was clouds, moving and trembling under a nervous agitation, but Pantalaimon whispered:

"The Aurora!"

Her wonder was so strong that she had to clutch the rail to keep from falling.

The sight filled the northern sky; the immensity of it was scarcely conceivable. As if from Heaven itself, great curtains of

delicate light hung and trembled. Pale green and rose-pink, and
as transparent as the most fragile fabric, and at the bottom edge
a profound and fiery crimson like the fires of Hell, they swung
and shimmered loosely with more grace than the most skilful
dancer. Lyra thought she could even hear them: a vast distant
whispering swish. In the evanescent delicacy she felt something
as profound as she'd felt close to the bear. She was moved by it:
it was so beautiful it was almost holy; she felt tears prick her eyes,
and the tears splintered the light even further into prismatic rainbows. It wasn't long before she found herself entering the same
kind of trance as when she consulted the alethiometer. Perhaps,
she thought calmly, whatever moves the alethiometer's needle is
making the Aurora glow too. It might even be Dust itself. She
thought that without noticing that she'd thought it, and she soon
forgot it, and only remembered it much later.

And as she gazed, the image of a city seemed to form itself
behind the veils and streams of translucent colour: towers and
domes, honey-coloured temples and colonnades, broad boulevards and sunlit parkland. Looking at it gave her a sense of vertigo,
as if she were looking not up but down, and across a gulf so wide
that nothing could ever pass over it. It was a whole universe away.

But something *was* moving across it, and as she tried to focus
her eyes on the movement, she felt faint and dizzy, because the
little thing moving wasn't part of the Aurora or of the other
universe behind it. It was in the sky over the roofs of the town.
When she could see it clearly, she had come fully awake and the
sky-city was gone.

The flying thing came closer and circled the ship on outspread
wings. Then it glided down and landed with brisk sweeps of its
powerful pinions, and came to a halt on the wooden deck a few
yards from Lyra.

In the Aurora's light she saw a great bird, a beautiful grey goose
whose head was crowned with a flash of pure white. And yet it
wasn't a bird: it was a dæmon, though there was no one in sight
but Lyra herself. The idea filled her with sickly fear.

The bird said:

"Where is Farder Coram?"

And suddenly Lyra realized who it must be. This was the

dæmon of Serafina Pekkala, the clan-queen, Farder Coram's witch-friend.

She stammered to reply:

"I – he's – I'll go and get him . . ."

She turned and scampered down the companionway to the cabin Farder Coram occupied, and opened the door to speak into the darkness:

"Farder Coram! The witch's dæmon's come! He's waiting on the deck! He flew here all by hisself – I seen him coming in the sky –"

The old man said, "Ask him to wait on the after-deck, child."

The goose made his stately way to the stern of the ship, where he looked around, elegant and wild simultaneously, and a cause of fascinated terror to Lyra, who felt as though she were entertaining a ghost.

Then Farder Coram came up, wrapped in his cold-weather gear, closely followed by John Faa. Both old men bowed respectfully, and their dæmons also acknowledged the visitor.

"Greetings," said Farder Coram. "And I'm happy and proud to see you again, Kaisa. Now, would you like to come inside, or would you prefer to stay out here in the open?"

"I would rather stay outside, thank you, Farder Coram. Are you warm enough for a while?"

Witches and their dæmons felt no cold, but they were aware that other humans did.

Farder Coram assured him that they were well wrapped up, and said "How is Serafina Pekkala?"

"She sends her greetings to you, Farder Coram, and she is well and strong. Who are these two people?"

Farder Coram introduced them both. The goose-dæmon looked hard at Lyra.

"I have heard of this child," he said. "She is talked about among witches. So you have come to make war?"

"Not war, Kaisa. We are going to free the children taken from us. And I hope the witches will help."

"Not all of them will. Some clans are working with the Dust-hunters."

"Is that what you call the Oblation Board?"

"I don't know what this Board may be. They are Dust-hunters. They came to our regions ten years ago with philosophical instruments. They paid us to allow them to set up stations in our lands, and they treated us with courtesy."

"What is this Dust?"

"It comes from the sky. Some say it has always been there, some say it is newly falling. What is certain is that when people become aware of it, a great fear comes over them, and they'll stop at nothing to discover what it is. But it is not of any concern to witches."

"And where are they now, these Dust-hunters?"

"Four days north-east of here, at a place called Bolvangar. Our clan made no agreement with them, and because of our ancient obligation to you, Farder Coram, I have come to show you how to find these Dust-hunters."

Farder Coram smiled, and John Faa clapped his great hands together in satisfaction.

"Thank you kindly, sir," he said to the goose. "But tell us this: do you know anything more about these Dust-hunters? What do they do at this Bolvangar?"

"They have put up buildings of metal and concrete, and some underground chambers. They burn coal-spirit, which they bring in at great expense. We don't know what they do, but there is an air of hatred and fear over the place and for miles around. Witches can see these things where other humans can't. Animals keep away too. No birds fly there; lemmings and foxes have fled. Hence the name Bolvangar: the fields of evil. They don't call it that. They call it The Station. But to everyone else it is Bolvangar."

"And how are they defended?"

"They have a company of Northern Tartars armed with rifles. They are good soldiers, but they lack practice, because no one has ever attacked the settlement since it was built. Then there is a wire fence around the compound, which is filled with anbaric force. There may be other means of defence that we don't know about, because as I say they have no interest for us."

Lyra was bursting to ask a question, and the goose-dæmon knew it and looked at her as if giving permission.

"Why do the witches talk about me?" she said.

"Because of your father, and his knowledge of the other worlds," the dæmon replied.

That surprised all three of them. Lyra looked at Farder Coram, who looked back in mild wonder, and at John Faa, whose expression was troubled.

"Other worlds?" he said. "Pardon me, sir, but what worlds would those be? Do you mean the stars?"

"Indeed, no."

"Perhaps the world of spirits?" said Farder Coram.

"Nor that."

"Is it the city in the lights?" said Lyra. "It is, en't it?"

The goose turned his stately head towards her. His eyes were black, surrounded by a thin line of pure sky-blue, and their gaze was intense.

"Yes," he said. "Witches have known of the other worlds for thousands of years. You can see them sometimes in the Northern Lights. They aren't part of this universe at all; even the furthest stars are part of this universe, but the lights show us a different universe entirely. Not further away, but interpenetrating with this one. Here, on this deck, millions of other universes exist, unaware of one another..."

He raised his wings and spread them wide before folding them again.

"There," he said, "I have just brushed ten million other worlds, and they knew nothing of it. We are as close as a heartbeat, but we can never touch or see or hear these other worlds except in the Northern Lights."

"And why there?" said Farder Coram.

"Because the charged particles in the Aurora have the property of making the matter of this world thin, so that we can see through it for a brief time. Witches have always known this, but we seldom speak of it."

"My father believes in it," Lyra said. "I know because I heard him talking and showing pictures of the Aurora."

"Is this anything to do with Dust?" said John Faa.

"Who can say?" said the goose-dæmon. "All I can tell you is that the Dust-hunters are as frightened of it as if it were deadly poison. That is why they imprisoned Lord Asriel."

"But why?" Lyra said.

"They think he intends to use Dust in some way in order to make a bridge between this world and the world beyond the Aurora."

There was a lightness in Lyra's head.

She heard Farder Coram say, "And does he?"

"Yes," said the goose-dæmon. "They don't believe he can, because they think he is mad to believe in the other worlds in the first place. But it is true: that is his intention. And he is so powerful a figure that they feared he would upset their own plans, so they made a pact with the armoured bears to capture him and keep him imprisoned in the fortress of Svalbard, out of the way. Some say they helped the new bear-king to gain his throne, as part of the bargain."

Lyra said, "Do the witches want him to make this bridge? Are they on his side or against him?"

"That is a question with too complicated an answer. Firstly, the witches are not united. There are differences of opinion among us. Secondly, Lord Asriel's bridge will have a bearing on a war being waged at the present between some witches and various other forces, some in the spirit world. Possession of the bridge, if it ever existed, would give a huge advantage to whoever held it. Thirdly, Serafina Pekkala's clan – my clan – is not yet part of any alliance, though great pressure is being put on us to declare for one side or another. You see, these are questions of high politics, and not easily answered."

"What about the bears?" said Lyra. "Whose side are they on?"

"On the side of anyone who pays them. They have no interest whatever in these questions; they have no dæmons; they are unconcerned about human problems. At least, that is how bears used to be, but we have heard that their new king is intent on changing their old ways ... At any rate, the Dust-hunters have paid them to imprison Lord Asriel, and they will hold him on Svalbard until the last drop of blood drains from the body of the last bear alive."

"But not all bears!" Lyra said. "There's one who en't on Svalbard at all. He's an outcast bear, and he's going to come with us."

The goose gave Lyra another of his piercing looks. This time she could feel his cold surprise.

Farder Coram shifted uncomfortably, and said, "The fact is, Lyra, I don't think he is. We heard he's serving out a term as an indentured labourer; he en't free, as we thought he might be, he's under sentence. Till he's discharged he won't be free to come, armour or no armour; and he won't never have that back, either."

"But he said they tricked him! They made him drunk and stole it away!"

"We heard a different story," said John Faa. "He's a dangerous rogue, is what we heard."

"If –" Lyra was passionate; she could hardly speak for indignation – "if the alethiometer says something, I know it's true. And I asked it, and it said that he was telling the truth, they did trick him, and they're telling lies and not him. I believe him, Lord Faa! Farder Coram – you saw him too, and you believe him, don't you?"

"I thought I did, child. I en't so certain of things as you are."

"But what are they afraid of? Do they think he's going to go round killing people as soon's he gets his armour on? He could kill dozens of 'em now!"

"He has done," said John Faa. "Well, if not dozens, then some. When they first took his armour away he went a-rampaging round looking for it. He tore open the police house and the bank and I don't know where else, and there's at least two men who died. The only reason they didn't shoot to kill him is because of his wondrous skill with metals; they wanted to use him like a labourer."

"Like a slave!" Lyra said hotly. "They hadn't got the right!"

"Be that as it may, they might have shot him for the killings he done, but they didn't. And they bound him over to labour in the town's interest until he's paid off the damage and the blood-money."

"John," said Farder Coram, "I don't know how you feel, but it's my belief they'll never let him have that armour back. The longer they keep him, the more angry he'll be when he gets it."

"But if *we* get his armour back he'll come with us and never bother 'em again," said Lyra. "I promise, Lord Faa."

"And how are we going to do that?"

"I know where it is!"

There was a silence, in which they all three became aware of the witch's dæmon and his fixed stare at Lyra. All three turned to him, and their own dæmons too, who had until then affected the extreme politeness of keeping their eyes modestly away from this singular creature, here without his body.

"You won't be surprised," said the goose, "to know that the alethiometer is one other reason the witches are interested in you, Lyra. Our consul told us about your visit this morning. I believe it was Dr Lanselius who told you about the bear."

"Yes, it was," said John Faa. "And she and Farder Coram went theirselves and talked to him. I daresay what Lyra says is true, but if we go breaking the law of these people we'll only get involved in a quarrel with them, and what we ought to be doing is pushing on towards this Bolvangar, bear or no bear."

"Ah, but you en't seen him, John," said Farder Coram. "And I do believe Lyra. We could promise on his behalf, maybe. He might make all the difference."

"What do you think, sir?" said John Faa to the witch's dæmon.

"We have few dealings with bears. Their desires are as strange to us as ours are to them. If this bear is an outcast, he might be less reliable than they are said to be. You must decide for yourselves."

"We will," said John Faa firmly. "But now, sir, can you tell us how to get to Bolvangar from here?"

The goose-dæmon began to explain. He spoke of valleys and hills, of the tree-line and the tundra, of star-sightings. Lyra listened a while, and then lay back in the deck-chair with Pantalaimon curled around her neck, and thought of the grand vision the goose-dæmon had brought with him. A bridge between two worlds ... This was far more splendid than anything she could have hoped for! And only her great father could have conceived it. As soon as they had rescued the children, she would go to Svalbard with the bear and take Lord Asriel the alethiometer, and use it to help set him free; and they'd build the bridge together, and be the first across ...

*   *   *

Sometime in the night John Faa must have carried Lyra to her bunk, because that was where she awoke. The dim sun was as high in the sky as it was going to get, only a hand's breadth above the horizon, so it must be nearly noon, she thought. Soon, when they moved further north, there would be no sun at all.

She dressed quickly and ran on deck to find nothing very much happening. All the stores had been unloaded, sledges and dog-teams had been hired and were waiting to go; everything was ready and nothing was moving. Most of the gyptians were sitting in a smoke-filled café facing the water, eating spice-cakes and drinking strong sweet coffee at the long wooden tables under the fizz and crackle of some ancient anbaric lights.

"Where's Lord Faa?" she said, sitting down with Tony Costa and his friends. "And Farder Coram? Are they getting the bear's armour for him?"

"They're a-talking to the Sysselman. That's their word for governor. You seen this bear, then, Lyra?"

"Yeah!" she said, and explained all about him. As she talked, someone else pulled a chair up and joined the group at the table.

"So you've spoken to old Iorek?" he said.

She looked at the newcomer with surprise. He was a tall, lean man with a thin black moustache and narrow blue eyes, and a perpetual expression of distant and sardonic amusement. She felt strongly about him at once, but she wasn't sure whether it was liking she felt, or dislike. His dæmon was a shabby hare as thin and tough-looking as he was.

He held out his hand and she shook it warily.

"Lee Scoresby," he said.

"The aëronaut!" she exclaimed. "Where's your balloon? Can I go up in it?"

"It's packed away right now, miss. You must be the famous Lyra. How did you get on with Iorek Byrnison?"

"You know him?"

"I fought beside him in the Tunguska campaign. Hell, I've known Iorek for years. Bears are difficult critters no matter what, but he's a problem, and no mistake. Say, are any of you gentlemen in the mood for a game of hazard?"

A pack of cards had appeared from nowhere in his hand. He riffled them with a snapping noise.

"Now I've heard of the card-power of your people," Lee Scoresby was saying, cutting and folding the cards over and over with one hand and fishing a cigar out of his breast pocket with the other, "and I thought you wouldn't object to giving a simple Texan traveller the chance to joust with your skill and daring on the field of pasteboard combat. What do you say, gentlemen?"

Gyptians prided themselves on their ability with cards, and several of the men looked interested and pulled their chairs up. While they were agreeing with Lee Scoresby what to play and for what stakes, his dæmon flicked her ears at Pantalaimon, who understood and leapt lightly to her side as a squirrel.

She was speaking for Lyra's ears too, of course, and Lyra heard her say quietly, "Go straight to the bear and tell him direct. As soon as they know what's going on they'll move his armour somewhere else."

Lyra got up, taking her spice-cake with her, and no one noticed; Lee Scoresby was already dealing the cards, and every suspicious eye was on his hands.

In the dull light, fading through an endless afternoon, she found her way to the sledge depot. It was something she knew she had to do, but she felt uneasy about it, and afraid, too.

Outside the largest of the concrete sheds the great bear was working, and Lyra stood by the open gate to watch. Iorek Byrnison was dismantling a gas-engined tractor that had crashed; the metal covering of the engine was twisted and buckled and one runner bent upwards. The bear lifted the metal off as if it were cardboard, and turned it this way and that in his great hands, seeming to test it for some quality or other, before setting a rear paw on one corner and then bending the whole sheet in such a way that the dents sprang out and the shape was restored. Leaning it against the wall, he lifted the massive weight of the tractor with one paw and laid it on its side before bending to examine the crumpled runner.

As he did so, he caught sight of Lyra. She felt a bolt of cold fear strike at her, because he was so massive and so alien. She was gazing through the chain-link fence about forty yards from him, and she thought how he could clear the distance in a bound or two and sweep the wire aside like a cobweb, and she almost turned and ran away; but Pantalaimon said, "Stop! Let me go and talk to him."

He was a tern, and before she could answer he'd flown off the fence and down to the icy ground beyond it. There was an open gate a little way along, and Lyra could have followed him, but she hung back unwillingly. Pantalaimon looked at her, and then became a badger.

She knew what he was doing. Dæmons could move no more than a few yards from their humans, and if she stood by the fence and he remained a bird, he wouldn't get near the bear; so he was going to pull.

She felt angry and miserable. His badger-claws dug into the earth and he walked forward. It was such a strange tormenting feeling when your dæmon was pulling at the link between you; part physical pain deep in the chest, part intense sadness and love. And she knew it was the same for him. Everyone tested it when they were growing up: seeing how far they could pull apart, coming back with intense relief.

He tugged a little harder.

"Don't, Pan!"

But he didn't stop. The bear watched, motionless. The pain in Lyra's heart grew more and more unbearable, and a sob of longing rose in her throat.

"Pan –"

Then she was through the gate, scrambling over the icy mud towards him, and he turned into a wildcat and sprang up into her arms, and then they were clinging together tightly with little shaky sounds of unhappiness coming from them both.

"I thought you really *would* –"

"No –"

"I couldn't *believe* how much it hurt –"

And then she brushed the tears away angrily and sniffed hard. He nestled in her arms, and she knew she would rather die than let them be parted and face that sadness again; it would send her mad with grief and terror. If she died they'd still be together, like the Scholars in the crypt at Jordan.

Then girl and dæmon looked up at the solitary bear. He had no dæmon. He was alone, always alone. She felt such a stir of pity and gentleness for him that she almost reached out to touch his matted pelt, and only a sense of courtesy towards those cold ferocious eyes prevented her.

"Iorek Byrnison," she said.

"Well?"

"Lord Faa and Farder Coram have gone to try and get your armour for you."

He didn't move or speak. It was clear what he thought of their chances.

"I know where it is, though," she said, "and if I told you, maybe you could get it by yourself, I don't know."

"How do you know where it is?"

"I got a symbol-reader. I think I ought to tell you, Iorek Byrnison, seeing as they tricked you out of it in the first place. I don't think that's right. They shouldn't've done that. Lord Faa's going to argue with the Sysselman, but probably they won't let you have it whatever he says. So if I tell you, will you come with us and help rescue the kids from Bolvangar?"

"Yes."

"I . . ." She didn't mean to be nosy, but she couldn't help being curious. She said, "Why don't you just make some more armour out of this metal here, Iorek Byrnison?"

"Because it's worthless. Look," he said and, lifting the engine-cover with one paw, he extended a claw on the other hand and ripped right through it like a tin-opener. "My armour is made of sky-iron, made for me. A bear's armour is his soul, just as your dæmon is your soul. You might as well take *him* away –" indicating Pantalaimon – "and replace him with a doll full of sawdust. That is the difference. Now, where is my armour?"

"Listen, you got to promise not to take vengeance. They done wrong taking it, but you just got to put up with that."

"All right. No vengeance afterwards. But no holding back as I take it, either. If they fight, they die."

"It's hidden in the cellar of the priest's house," she told him. "He thinks there's a spirit in it, and he's been a-trying to conjure it out. But that's where it is."

He stood high up on his hind legs, and looked west, so that the last of the sun coloured his face a creamy brilliant yellow-white amid the gloom. She could feel the power of the great creature coming off him like waves of heat.

"I must work till sunset," he said. "I gave my word this morning to the master here. I still owe a few minutes' work."

"The sun's set where I am," she pointed out, because from her point of view it had vanished behind the rocky headland to the south-west.

He dropped to all fours.

"It's true," he said, with his face now in shadow like hers. "What's your name, child?"

"Lyra Belacqua."

"Then I owe you a debt, Lyra Belacqua," he said.

Then he turned and lurched away, padding so swiftly across the freezing ground that Lyra couldn't keep up, even running. She did run, though, and Pantalaimon flew up as a seagull to watch where the bear went and called down to tell her where to follow.

Iorek Byrnison bounded out of the depot and along the narrow street before turning into the main street of the town, past the courtyard of the Sysselman's residence where a flag hung in the still air and a sentry marched stiffly up and down, down the hill past the end of the street where the Witch-Consul lived. The sentry by this time had realized what was happening, and was trying to gather his wits, but Iorek Byrnison was already turning a corner near the harbour.

People stopped to watch or scuttled out of his careering way. The sentry fired two shots in the air, and set off down the hill after the bear, spoiling the effect by skidding on the icy slope and only regaining his balance after seizing the nearest railings. Lyra was not far behind. As she passed the Sysselman's house she was aware of a number of figures coming out into the courtyard to see what was going on, and thought she saw Farder Coram among them; but then she was past, hurtling down the street towards the corner where the sentry was already turning to follow the bear.

The priest's house was older than most, and made of costly

bricks. Three steps led up to the front door, which was now hanging in matchwood splinters, and from inside the house came screams and the crashing and tearing of more wood. The sentry hesitated outside, his rifle at the ready; but then as passers-by began to gather and people looked out of windows from across the street, he realized that he had to act, and fired a shot into the air before running in.

A moment later, the whole house seemed to shake. Glass broke in three windows and a tile slid off the roof, and then a maid-servant ran out, terrified, her clucking hen of a dæmon flapping after her.

Another shot came from inside the house, and then a full-throated roar made the servant scream. As if fired from a cannon, the priest himself came hurtling out, with his pelican-dæmon in a wild flutter of feathers and injured pride. Lyra heard orders shouted, and turned to see a squad of armed policemen hurrying around the corner, some with pistols and some with rifles, and not far behind them came John Faa and the stout, fussy figure of the Sysselman.

A rending, splintering sound made them all look back at the house. A window at ground level, obviously opening on a cellar, was being wrenched apart with a crash of glass and a screech of tearing wood. The sentry who'd followed Iorek Byrnison into the house came running out and stood to face the cellar window, rifle at his shoulder; and then the window tore open completely, and out there climbed Iorek Byrnison, the bear in armour.

Without it he was formidable. With it, he was terrifying. It was rust-red, and crudely riveted together: great sheets and plates of dented discoloured metal that scraped and screeched as they rode over one another. The helmet was pointed like his muzzle, with slits for eyes, and it left the lower part of his jaw bare for tearing and biting.

The sentry fired several shots, and the policemen levelled their weapons too, but Iorek Byrnison merely shook the bullets off like raindrops, and lunged forward in a screech and clang of metal before the sentry could escape, and knocked him to the ground. His dæmon, a husky dog, darted at the bear's throat, but Iorek Byrnison took no more notice of him than he would of a fly and, dragging the sentry to him with one vast paw, he bent and enclosed his head in his jaws. Lyra could see exactly what would happen next: he'd crush the man's skull like an egg, and there would follow a bloody fight, more deaths, and more delay; and they would never get free, with or without the bear.

Without even thinking she darted forward and put her hand on the one vulnerable spot in the bear's armour, the gap that appeared between the helmet and the great plate over his shoulders when he bent his head, where she could see the yellow-white fur dimly between the rusty edges of metal. She dug her fingers in, and Pantalaimon instantly flew to the same spot and became a wildcat, crouched to defend her; but Iorek Byrnison was still, and the riflemen held their fire.

"Iorek!" she said in a fierce undertone. "Listen! You owe me a debt, right. Well now you can repay it. Do as I ask. Don't fight these men. Just turn around and walk away with me. We *want* you, Iorek, you can't stay here. Just come down the harbour with me and don't even look back. Farder Coram and Lord Faa, let them do the talking, they'll make it all right. Leave go this man and come away with me . . ."

The bear slowly opened his jaws. The sentry's head, bleeding and wet and ash-pale, fell to the ground as he fainted, and his dæmon set about calming and gentling him as the bear stepped away beside Lyra.

No one else moved. They watched as the bear turned away from his victim at the bidding of the little girl with the cat-dæmon, and then they shuffled aside to make room as Iorek Byrnison padded heavily through the midst of them at Lyra's side and made for the harbour.

Her mind was all on him, and she didn't see the confusion behind her, the fear and the anger that rose up safely when he was gone. She walked with him, and Pantalaimon padded ahead of them both as if to clear the way.

When they reached the harbour, Iorek Byrnison dipped his head and unfastened the helmet with a claw, letting it clang on the frozen ground. Gyptians came out of the café, having sensed that something was going on, and watched in the gleam of the anbaric lights on the ship's deck as Iorek Byrnison shrugged off the rest of his armour and left it in a heap on the quayside. Without a word to anyone he padded to the water and slipped into it without a ripple, and vanished.

"What's happened?" said Tony Costa, hearing the indignant voices from the streets above, as the townsfolk and the police made their way to the harbour.

Lyra told him, as clearly as she could.

"But where's he gone now?" he said. "He en't just left his armour on the ground? They'll have it back, as soon's they get here!"

Lyra was afraid they might, too, for around the corner came the first policemen, and then more, and then the Sysselman and the priest and twenty or thirty onlookers, with John Faa and Farder Coram trying to keep up.

But when they saw the group on the quayside they stopped, for someone else had appeared. Sitting on the bear's armour with one ankle resting on the opposite knee was the long-limbed form of Lee Scoresby, and in his hand was the longest pistol Lyra had ever seen, casually pointing at the ample stomach of the Sysselman.

"Seems to me you ain't taken very good care of my friend's armour," he said conversationally. "Why, look at the rust! And I wouldn't be surprised to find moths in it, too. Now you just stand where you are, still and easy, and don't anybody move till the bear comes back with some lubrication. Or I guess you could all go home and read the newspaper. 'S up to you."

"There he is!" said Tony, pointing to a ramp at the far end of the quay, where Iorek Byrnison was emerging from the water, dragging something dark with him. Once he was up on the quayside he shook himself, sending great sheets of water flying in all directions, till his fur was standing up thickly again. Then he bent to take the black object in his teeth once more and dragged it along to where his armour lay. It was a dead seal.

"Iorek," said the aëronaut, standing up lazily and keeping his pistol firmly fixed on the Sysselman. "Howdy."

The bear looked up and growled briefly, before ripping the seal open with one claw. Lyra watched fascinated as he laid the skin out flat and tore off strips of blubber, which he then rubbed all over his armour, packing it carefully into the places where the plates moved over one another.

"Are you with these people?" the bear said to Lee Scoresby as he worked.

"Sure. I guess we're both hired hands, Iorek."

"Where's your balloon?" said Lyra to the Texan.

"Packed away in two sledges," he said. "Here comes the boss."

John Faa and Farder Coram, together with the Sysselman, came down the quay with four armed policemen.

"Bear!" said the Sysselman, in a high, harsh voice. "For now, you are allowed to depart in the company of these people. But let me tell you that if you appear within the town limits again, you will be treated mercilessly."

Iorek Byrnison took not the slightest notice, but continued to rub the seal-blubber all over his armour; the care and attention he was paying the task reminding Lyra of her own devotion to Pantalaimon. Just as the bear had said: the armour was his soul. The Sysselman and the policemen withdrew, and slowly the other townspeople turned and drifted away, though a few remained to watch.

John Faa put his hands to his mouth and called, "Gyptians!"

They were all ready to move. They had been itching to get under way ever since they had disembarked; the sledges were packed, the dog-teams were in their traces.

John Faa said, "Time to move out, friends. We're all assembled now, and the road lies open. Mr Scoresby, you all a-loaded?"

"Ready to go, Lord Faa."

"And you, Iorek Byrnison?"

"When I am clad," said the bear.

He had finished oiling the armour. Not wanting to waste the seal-meat, he lifted the carcass in his teeth and flipped it on to the back of Lee Scoresby's larger sledge before donning the armour. It was astonishing to see how lightly he dealt with it: the sheets of metal were almost an inch thick in places, and yet he swung them round and into place as if they were silk robes. It took him less than a minute, and this time there was no harsh scream of rust.

So in less than half an hour, the expedition was on its way

northwards. Under a sky peopled with millions of stars and a glaring moon, the sledges bumped and clattered over the ruts and stones until they reached clear snow at the edge of town. Then the sound changed to a quiet crunch of snow and creak of timber; and the dogs began to step out eagerly, and the motion became swift and smooth.

Lyra, wrapped up so thickly in the back of Farder Coram's sledge that only her eyes were exposed, whispered to Pantalaimon:

"Can you see Iorek?"

"He's padding along beside Lee Scoresby's sledge," the dæmon replied, looking back in his ermine-form as he clung to her wolverine-fur hood.

Ahead of them, over the mountains to the north, the pale arcs and loops of the Northern Lights began to glow and tremble. Lyra saw them through half-closed eyes, and felt a sleepy thrill of perfect happiness, to be speeding north under the Aurora. Pantalaimon struggled against her sleepiness, but it was too strong; he curled up as a mouse inside her hood. He could tell her when they woke, and it was probably a marten, or a dream, or some kind of harmless local spirit; but something was following the train of sledges, swinging lightly from branch to branch of the close-clustering pine trees, and it put him uneasily in mind of a monkey.

12
THE LOST BOY

THEY TRAVELLED FOR several hours and then stopped to eat. While the men were lighting fires and melting snow for water, with Iorek Byrnison watching Lee Scoresby roast seal-meat close by, John Faa spoke to Lyra.

"Lyra, can you see that instrument to read it?" he said.

The moon itself had long set. The light from the Aurora was brighter than moonlight, but it was inconstant. However, Lyra's eyes were keen, and she fumbled inside her furs and tugged out the black velvet bag.

"Yes, I can see all right," she said. "But I know where most of the symbols are by now, anyway. What shall I ask it, Lord Faa?"

"I want to know more about how they're defending this place, Bolvangar," he said.

Without even having to think about it, she found her fingers moving the hands to point to the helmet, the griffin, and the crucible, and felt her mind settle into the right meanings like a complicated diagram in three dimensions. At once the needle began to swing round, back, round and on further, like a bee dancing its message to the hive. She watched it calmly, content not to know at first but to know that a meaning was coming, and then it began to clear. She let it dance on until it was certain.

"It's just like the witch's dæmon said, Lord Faa. There's a company of Tartars guarding the station, and they got wires all round it. They don't really expect to be attacked, that's what the symbol-reader says. But Lord Faa . . ."

"What, child?"

"It's a-telling me something else. In the next valley there's a village by a lake where the folk are troubled by a ghost."

John Faa shook his head impatiently, and said, "That don't matter now. There's bound to be spirits of all kinds among these forests. Tell me again about them Tartars. How many, for instance? What are they armed with?"

Lyra dutifully asked, and reported the answer:

"There's sixty men with rifles, and they got a couple of larger guns, sort of cannons. They got fire-throwers too. And . . . their dæmons are all wolves, that's what it says."

That caused a stir among the older gyptians, those who'd campaigned before.

"The Sibirsk regiments have wolf-dæmons," said one.

John Faa said, "I never met fiercer. We shall have to fight like tigers. And consult the bear; he's a shrewd warrior, that one."

Lyra was impatient, and said, "But Lord Faa, this ghost – I think it's the ghost of one of the kids!"

"Well, even if it is, Lyra, I don't know what anyone could do about it. Sixty Sibirsk riflemen, and fire-throwers . . . Mr Scoresby, step over here if you would, for a moment."

While the aëronaut came to the sledge, Lyra slipped away and spoke to the bear.

"Iorek, have you travelled this way before?"

"Once," he said in that deep flat voice.

"There's a village near, en't there?"

"Over the ridge," he said, looking up through the sparse trees.

"Is it far?"

"For you or for me?"

"For me," she said.

"Too far. Not at all far for me."

"How long would it take you to get there, then?"

"I could be there and back three times by next moonrise."

"Because Iorek, listen: I got this symbol-reader that tells me things, you see, and it's told me that there's something important I got to do over in that village, and Lord Faa won't let me go there. He just wants to get on quick, and I know that's important too. But unless I go and find out what it is, we might not know what the Gobblers are really doing."

The bear said nothing. He was sitting up like a human, his great paws folded in his lap, his dark eyes looking into hers down the length of his muzzle. He knew she wanted something.

Pantalaimon spoke: "Can you take us there and catch up with the sledges later on?"

"I could. But I have given my word to Lord Faa to obey him, not anyone else."

"If I got his permission?" said Lyra.

"Then yes."

She turned and ran back through the snow.

"Lord Faa! If Iorek Byrnison takes me over the ridge to the village, we can find out whatever it is, and then catch the sledges up further on. He knows the route," she urged. "And I wouldn't ask, except it's like what I did before, Farder Coram, you remember, with that chameleon? I didn't understand it then, but it was true, and we found out soon after. I got the same feeling now. I can't understand properly what it's saying, only I know it's important. And Iorek Byrnison knows the way, he says he could get there and back three times by next moonrise, and I couldn't be safer than I'd be with him, could I? But he won't go without he gets Lord Faa's permission."

There was a silence. Farder Coram sighed. John Faa was frowning, and his mouth inside the fur hood was set grimly.

But before he could speak, the aëronaut put in:

"Lord Faa, if Iorek Byrnison takes the little girl, she'll be as safe as if she was here with us. All bears are true, but I've known Iorek for years, and nothing under the sky will make him break his word. Give him the charge to take care of her and he'll do it, make no mistake. As for speed, he can lope for hours without tiring."

"But why should not some men go?" said John Faa.

"Well, they'd have to walk," Lyra pointed out, "because you couldn't run a sledge over that ridge. Iorek Byrnison can go faster than any man over that sort of country, and I'm light enough so's he won't be slowed down. And I promise, Lord Faa, I promise not to be any longer than I need, and not to give anything away about us, or to get in any danger."

"You're sure you need to do this? That symbol-reader en't playing the fool with you?"

"It never does, Lord Faa, and I don't think it could."

John Faa rubbed his chin.

"Well, if all comes out right, we'll have a piece more knowledge than we do now. Iorek Byrnison," he called, "are you willing to do as this child bids?"

"I do your bidding, Lord Faa. Tell me to take the child there, and I will."

"Very well. You are to take her where she wishes to go and do as she bids. Lyra, I'm a-commanding *you* now, you understand?"

"Yes, Lord Faa."

"You go and search for whatever it is, and when you've found it, you turn right round and come back. Iorek Byrnison, we'll be a-travelling on by that time, so you'll have to catch us up."

The bear nodded his great head.

"Are there any soldiers in the village?" he said to Lyra. "Will I need my armour? We shall be swifter without it."

"No," she said. "I'm certain of that, Iorek. Thank you, Lord Faa, and I promise I'll do just as you say."

Tony Costa gave her a strip of dried seal-meat to chew, and with Pantalaimon as a mouse inside her hood, Lyra clambered on to the great bear's back, gripping his fur with her mittens and his narrow muscular back between her knees. His fur was wondrously thick, and the sense of immense power she felt was overwhelming. As if she weighed nothing at all, he turned and loped away in a long swinging run up towards the ridge and into the low trees.

It took some time before she was used to the movement, and then she felt a wild exhilaration. She was riding a bear! And the Aurora was swaying above them in golden arcs and loops, and all around was the bitter Arctic cold and the immense silence of the North.

Iorek Byrnison's paws made hardly any sound as they padded forward through the snow. The trees were thin and stunted here, for they were on the edge of the tundra, but there were brambles and snagging bushes in the path. The bear ripped through them as if they were cobwebs.

They climbed the low ridge, among outcrops of black rock, and were soon out of sight of the party behind them. Lyra wanted to talk to the bear, and if he had been human she would already have been on familiar terms with him; but he was so strange and wild and cold that she was shy, almost for the first time in her life. So as he loped along, his great legs swinging tirelessly, she sat with the movement and said nothing. Perhaps he preferred that anyway, she thought; she must seem a little prattling cub, only just past babyhood, in the eyes of an armoured bear.

She had seldom considered herself before, and found the experience interesting but uncomfortable; very like riding the bear, in fact. Iorek Byrnison was pacing swiftly, moving both legs on one side of his body at the same time, and rocking from side to side in a steady powerful rhythm. She found she couldn't just sit: she had to ride actively.

They had been travelling for an hour or more, and Lyra was stiff and sore but deeply happy, when Iorek Byrnison slowed down and stopped.

"Look up," he said.

Lyra raised her eyes and had to wipe them with the inside of her wrist, for she was so cold that tears were blurring them. When she could see clearly she gasped at the sight of the sky. The Aurora had faded to a pallid trembling glimmer, but the stars were as bright as diamonds, and across the great dark diamond-scattered vault, hundreds upon hundreds of tiny black shapes were flying out of the east and south towards the north.

"Are they birds?" she said.

"They are witches," said the bear.

"Witches! What are they doing?"

"Flying to war, maybe. I have never seen so many at one time."

"Do you know any witches, Iorek?"

"I have served some. And fought some, too. This is a sight to frighten Lord Faa. If they are flying to the aid of your enemies, you should all be afraid."

"Lord Faa wouldn't be frightened. You en't afraid, are you?"

"Not yet. When I am, I shall master the fear. But we had better tell Lord Faa about the witches, because the men might not have seen them."

He moved on more slowly, and she kept watching the sky until her eyes splintered again with tears of cold, and she saw no end to the numberless witches flying north.

Finally Iorek Byrnison stopped and said, "There is the village."

They were looking down a broken, rugged slope towards a cluster of wooden buildings beside a wide stretch of snow as flat as could be, which Lyra took to be the frozen lake. A wooden jetty showed her she was right. They were no more than five minutes from the place.

"What do you want to do?" the bear asked.

Lyra slipped off his back, and found it hard to stand. Her face was stiff with cold and her legs were shaky, but she clung to his fur and stamped until she felt stronger.

"There's a child or a ghost or something down in that village," she said, "or maybe near it, I don't know for certain. I want to go and find him and bring him back to Lord Faa and the others if I can. I thought he was a ghost, but the symbol-reader might be telling me something I can't understand."

"If he is outside," said the bear, "he had better have some shelter."

"I don't think he's dead . . ." said Lyra, but she was far from sure. The alethiometer had indicated something uncanny and unnatural, which was alarming; but who was she? Lord Asriel's daughter. And who was under her command? A mighty bear. How could she possibly show any fear?

"Let's just go and look," she said.

She clambered on his back again, and he set off down the broken slope, walking steadily and not pacing any more. The dogs of the village smelled or heard or sensed them coming, and began to howl frightfully; and the reindeer in their enclosure moved about nervously, their antlers clashing like dry sticks. In the still air every movement could be heard for a long way.

As they reached the first of the houses, Lyra looked to right and left, peering hard into the dimness, for the Aurora was fading and the moon still far from rising. Here and there a light flickered under a snow-thick roof, and Lyra thought she saw pale faces behind some of the window-panes, and imagined their astonishment to see a child riding a great white bear.

At the centre of the little village there was an open space next to the jetty, where boats had been drawn up, mounds under the snow. The noise of the dogs was deafening, and just as Lyra thought it must have wakened everyone, a door opened and a man came out holding a rifle. His wolverine-dæmon leapt on to the woodstack beside the door, scattering snow.

Lyra slipped down at once and stood between him and Iorek Byrnison, conscious that she had told the bear there was no need for his armour.

The man spoke in words she couldn't understand. Iorek Byrnison replied in the same language, and the man gave a little moan of fear.

"He thinks we are devils," Iorek told Lyra. "What shall I say?"

"Tell him we're not devils, but we've got friends who are. And we're looking for ... Just a child. A strange child. Tell him that."

As soon as the bear had said that, the man pointed to the right, indicating some place further off, and spoke quickly.

Iorek Byrnison said, "He asks if we have come to take the child away. They are afraid of it. They have tried to drive it away, but it keeps coming back."

"Tell him we'll take it away with us, but they were very bad to treat it like that. Where is it?"

The man explained, gesticulating fearfully. Lyra was afraid he'd fire his rifle by mistake, but as soon as he'd spoken he hastened inside his house and shut the door. Lyra could see faces at every window.

"Where is the child?" she said.

"In the fish-house," the bear told her, and turned to pad down towards the jetty.

Lyra followed. She was horribly nervous. The bear was making for a narrow wooden shed, raising his head to sniff this way and that, and when he reached the door he stopped and said, "In there."

Lyra's heart was beating so fast she could hardly breathe. She raised her hand to knock at the door and then, feeling that that was ridiculous, took a deep breath to call out, but realized that she didn't know what to say. Oh, it was so dark now! She should have brought a lantern ...

There was no choice, and anyway, she didn't want the bear to see her being afraid. He had spoken of mastering his fear: that was what she'd have to do. She lifted the strap of reindeer hide

holding the latch in place, and tugged hard against the frost binding the door shut. It opened with a snap. She had to kick aside
the snow piled against the foot of the door before she could pull
it wide, and Pantalaimon was no help, running back and forth in
his ermine-shape, a white shadow over the white ground, uttering little frightened sounds.

"Pan, for God's sake!" she said. "Be a bat. Go and *look* for
me . . ."

But he wouldn't, and he wouldn't speak either. She had never
seen him like this except once, when she and Roger in the crypt
at Jordan had moved the dæmon-coins into the wrong skulls. He
was even more frightened than she was. As for Iorek Byrnison,
he was lying in the snow nearby, watching in silence.

"Come out," Lyra said as loud as she dared. "Come out!"

Not a sound came in answer. She pulled the door a little wider,
and Pantalaimon leapt up into her arms, pushing and pushing at
her in his cat-form, and said, "Go away! Don't stay here! Oh,
Lyra, go now! Turn back!"

Trying to hold him still, she was aware of Iorek Byrnison getting to his feet, and turned to see a figure hastening down the
track from the village, carrying a lantern. When he came close
enough to speak, he raised the lantern and held it to show his
face: an old man with a broad, lined face, and eyes nearly lost in
a thousand wrinkles. His dæmon was an Arctic fox.

He spoke, and Iorek Byrnison said:

"He says that it's not the only child of that kind. He's seen
others in the forest. Sometimes they die quickly, sometimes they
don't die. This one is tough, he thinks. But it would be better
for him if he died."

"Ask him if I can borrow his lantern," Lyra said.

The bear spoke, and the man handed it to her at once, nodding
vigorously. She realized that he'd come down in order to bring
it to her, and thanked him, and he nodded again and stood back,
away from her and the hut and away from the bear.

Lyra thought suddenly: what if the child is Roger? And she
prayed with all her force that it wouldn't be. Pantalaimon was
clinging to her, an ermine again, his little claws hooked deep into
her anorak.

She lifted the lantern high and took a step into the shed, and then she saw what it was that the Oblation Board was doing, and what was the nature of the sacrifice the children were having to make.

The little boy was huddled against the wood drying-rack where hung row upon row of gutted fish, all as stiff as boards. He was clutching a piece of fish to him as Lyra was clutching Pantalaimon, with both hands, hard, against her heart; but that was all he had, a piece of dried fish; because he had no dæmon at all. The Gobblers had cut it away. That was *intercision*, and this was a severed child.

13
FENCING

HER FIRST IMPULSE was to turn and run, or to be sick. A human being with no dæmon was like someone without a face, or with their ribs laid open and their heart torn out: something unnatural and uncanny that belonged to the world of night-ghasts, not the waking world of sense.

So Lyra clung to Pantalaimon and her head swam and her gorge rose, and cold as the night was, a sickly sweat moistened her flesh with something colder still.

"Ratter," said the boy. "You got my Ratter?"

Lyra was in no doubt what he meant.

"No," she said in a voice as frail and frightened as she felt. Then, "What's your name?"

"Tony Makarios," he said. "Where's Ratter?"

"I don't know . . ." she began, and swallowed hard to govern her nausea. "The Gobblers . . ." But she couldn't finish. She had to go out of the shed and sit down by herself in the snow, except that of course she wasn't by herself, she was never by herself, because Pantalaimon was always there. Oh, to be cut from him as this little boy had been parted from his Ratter! The worst thing in the world! She found herself sobbing, and Pantalaimon was whimpering too, and in both of them there was a passionate pity and sorrow for the half-boy.

Then she got to her feet again.

"Come on," she called in a trembling voice. "Tony, come out. We're going to take you somewhere safe."

There was a stir of movement in the fish-house, and he appeared at the door, still clutching his dried fish. He was dressed in warm enough garments, a thickly padded and quilted coal-silk anorak and fur boots, but they had a second-hand look and didn't fit well. In the wider light outside that came from the faint trails of the Aurora and the snow-covered ground he looked more lost and piteous even than he had at first, crouching in the lantern-light by the fish-racks.

The villager who'd brought the lantern had retreated a few yards, and called down to them.

Iorek Byrnison interpreted: "He says you must pay for that fish."

Lyra felt like telling the bear to kill him, but she said, "We're taking the child away for them. They can afford to give one fish to pay for that."

The bear spoke. The man muttered, but didn't argue. Lyra set his lantern down in the snow and took the half-boy's hand to guide him to the bear. He came helplessly, showing no surprise and no fear at the great white beast standing so close, and when Lyra helped him to sit on Iorek's back, all he said was:

"I dunno where my Ratter is."

"No, nor do we, Tony," she said. "But we'll . . . We'll punish the Gobblers. We'll do that, I promise. Iorek, is that all right if I sit up there too?"

"My armour weighs far more than children," he said.

So she scrambled up behind Tony and made him cling to the long stiff fur, and Pantalaimon sat inside her hood, warm and close and full of pity. Lyra knew that Pantalaimon's impulse was to reach out and cuddle the little half-child, to lick him and gentle him and warm him as his own dæmon would have done; but the great taboo prevented that, of course.

They rode through the village and up towards the ridge, and the villagers' faces were open with horror and a kind of fearful relief at seeing that hideously mutilated creature taken away by a little girl and a great white bear.

In Lyra's heart, revulsion struggled with compassion, and compassion won. She put her arms around the skinny little form to hold him safe. The journey back to the main party was colder, and harder, and darker, but it seemed to pass more quickly for all that. Iorek Byrnison was tireless, and Lyra's riding became automatic, so that she was never in danger of falling off. The cold body in her arms was so light that in one way he was easy to manage, but he was inert; he sat stiffly without moving as the bear moved, so in another way he was difficult too.

From time to time the half-boy spoke.

"What's that you said?" asked Lyra.

"I says is she gonna know where I am?"

"Yeah, she'll know, she'll find you and we'll find her. Hold on tight now, Tony. It en't far from here . . ."

The bear loped onwards. Lyra had no idea how tired she was until they caught up with the gyptians. The sledges had stopped to rest the dogs, and suddenly there they all were, Farder Coram, Lord Faa, Lee Scoresby, all lunging forward to help and then falling back silent as they saw the other figure with Lyra. She was so stiff that she couldn't even loosen her arms around his body, and John Faa himself had to pull them gently open and lift her off.

"Gracious God, what is this?" he said. "Lyra, child, what have you found?"

"He's called Tony," she mumbled through frozen lips. "And they cut his dæmon away. That's what the Gobblers do."

The men held back, fearful; but the bear spoke, to Lyra's weary amazement, chiding them.

"Shame on you! Think what this child has done! You might not have more courage, but you should be ashamed to show less."

"You're right, Iorek Byrnison," said John Faa, and turned to give orders. "Build that fire up and heat some soup for the child. For both children. Farder Coram, is your shelter rigged?"

"It is, John. Bring her over and we'll get her warm . . ."

"And the little boy," said someone else. "He can eat and get warm, even if . . ."

Lyra was trying to tell John Faa about the witches, but they were all so busy, and she was so tired. After a confusing few minutes full of lantern light, woodsmoke, figures hurrying to and fro, she felt a gentle nip on her ear from Pantalaimon's ermine-teeth, and woke to find the bear's face a few inches from hers.

"The witches," Pantalaimon whispered. "I called Iorek."

"Oh yeah," she mumbled. "Iorek, thank you for taking me there and back. I might not remember to tell Lord Faa about the witches, so you better do that instead of me."

She heard the bear agree, and then she fell asleep properly.

* * *

When she woke up, it was as close to daylight as it was ever going to get. The sky was pale in the south-east, and the air was suffused with a grey mist, through which the gyptians moved like bulky ghosts, loading sledges and harnessing dogs to the traces.

She saw it all from the shelter on Farder Coram's sledge, inside which she lay under a heap of furs. Pantalaimon was fully awake before she was, trying the shape of an Arctic fox before reverting to his favourite ermine.

Iorek Byrnison was asleep in the snow nearby, his head on his great paws; but Farder Coram was up and busy, and as soon as he saw Pantalaimon emerge, he limped across to wake Lyra properly.

She saw him coming, and sat up to speak.

"Farder Coram, I know what it was that I couldn't understand! The alethiometer kept saying *bird* and *not*, and that didn't make sense, because it meant *no dæmon* and I didn't see how it could be . . . What is it?"

"Lyra, I'm afraid to tell you this after what you done, but that little boy died an hour ago. He couldn't settle, he couldn't stay in one place; he kept asking after his dæmon, where she was, was she a-coming soon, and all; and he kept such a tight hold on that bare old piece of fish as if . . . Oh, I can't speak of it, child; but he closed his eyes finally and fell still, and that was the first time he looked peaceful, for he was like any other dead person then, with their dæmon gone in the course of nature. They've been a-trying to dig a grave for him, but the earth's bound like iron. So John Faa ordered a fire built, and they're a-going to cremate him, so as not to have him despoiled by carrion-eaters.

"Child, you did a brave thing and a good thing, and I'm proud of you. Now we know what terrible wickedness those people are capable of, we can see our duty plainer than ever. What you must do is rest and eat, because you fell asleep too soon to restore yourself last night, and you have to eat in these temperatures to stop yourself getting weak . . ."

He was fussing around, tucking the furs into place, tightening the tension-rope across the body of the sledge, running the traces through his hands to untangle them.

"Farder Coram, where is the little boy now? Have they burned him yet?"

"No, Lyra, he's a-lying back there."

"I want to go and see him."

He couldn't refuse her that, for she'd seen worse than a dead body, and it might calm her. So with Pantalaimon as a white hare bounding delicately at her side, she trudged along the line of sledges to where some men were piling brushwood.

The boy's body lay under a chequered blanket beside the path. She knelt and lifted the blanket in her mittened hands. One man was about to stop her, but the others shook their heads.

Pantalaimon crept close as Lyra looked down on the poor wasted face. She slipped her hand out of the mitten and touched his eyes. They were marble-cold, and Farder Coram had been right; poor little Tony Makarios was no different from any other human whose dæmon had departed in death. Oh, if they took Pantalaimon from her! She swept him up and hugged him as if she meant to press him right into her heart. And all little Tony had was his pitiful piece of fish . . .

Where was it?

She pulled the blanket down. It was gone.

She was on her feet in a moment, and her eyes flashed fury at the men nearby.

"Where's his fish?"

They stopped, puzzled, unsure what she meant; though some of their dæmons knew, and looked at one another. One of the men began to grin uncertainly.

"Don't you *dare* laugh! I'll tear your lungs out if you laugh at him! That's all he had to cling on to, just an old dried fish, that's all he had for a dæmon to love and be kind to! Who's took it from him? Where's it gone?"

Pantalaimon was a snarling snow leopard, just like Lord Asriel's dæmon, but she didn't see that; all she saw was right and wrong.

"Easy, Lyra," said one man. "Easy, child."

"Who's took it?" she flared again, and the gyptian took a step back from her passionate fury.

"I didn't know," said another man apologetically. "I thought it was just what he'd been eating. I took it out his hand because I thought it was more respectful. That's all, Lyra."

"Then where is it?"

The man said uneasily, "Not thinking he had a need for it, I gave it to my dogs. I do beg your pardon."

"It en't my pardon you need, it's his," she said, and turned at once to kneel again, and laid her hand on the dead child's icy cheek.

Then an idea came to her, and she fumbled inside her furs. The cold air struck through as she opened her anorak, but in a few seconds she had what she wanted, and took a gold coin from her purse before wrapping herself close again.

"I want to borrow your knife," she said to the man who'd taken the fish, and when he let her have it, she said to Pantalaimon: "What was her name?"

He understood, of course, and said, "Ratter."

She held the coin tight in her left mittened hand and, holding the knife like a pencil, scratched the lost dæmon's name deeply into the gold.

"I hope that'll do, if I provide for you like a Jordan Scholar," she whispered to the dead boy, and forced his teeth apart to slip the coin into his mouth. It was hard, but she managed it, and managed to close his jaw again.

Then she gave the man back his knife and turned in the morning twilight to go back to Farder Coram.

He gave her a mug of soup straight off the fire, and she sipped it greedily.

"What we going to do about them witches, Farder Coram?" she said. "I wonder if your witch was one of them."

"*My* witch? I wouldn't presume that far, Lyra. They might be going anywhere. There's all kinds of concerns that play on the life of witches; things invisible to us; mysterious sicknesses they fall prey to, which we'd shrug off; causes of war quite beyond our understanding; joys and sorrows bound up with the flowering of tiny plants up on the tundra . . . But I wish I'd seen them a-flying, Lyra. I wish I'd been able to see a sight like that. Now drink up all that soup. D'you want some more? There's some pan-bread a-cooking too. Eat up, child, because we're on our way soon."

The food revived Lyra, and presently the chill at her soul began to melt. With the others, she went to watch the little half-child laid on his funeral pyre, and bowed her head and closed her eyes for John Faa's prayers; and then the men sprinkled coal-spirit and set matches to it, and it was blazing in a moment.

Once they were sure he was safely burned, they set off to travel again. It was a ghostly journey. Snow began to fall early on, and soon the world was reduced to the grey shadows of the dogs ahead, the lurching and creaking of the sledge, the biting cold, and a swirling sea of big flakes only just darker than the sky and only just lighter than the ground.

Through it all the dogs continued to run, tails high, breath puffing steam. North and further north they ran, while the pallid noontide came and went and the twilight folded itself again around the world. They stopped to eat and drink and rest in a gap in the hills, and to get their bearings, and while John Faa talked to Lee Scoresby about the way they might best use the balloon, Lyra thought of the spy-fly; and she asked Farder Coram what had happened to the smoke-leaf tin he'd trapped it in.

"I've got it tucked away tight," he said. "It's down in the bottom of that kit-bag, but there's nothing to see; I soldered it shut on board ship, like I said I would. I don't know what we're a-going to do with it, to tell you the truth; maybe we could drop it down a fire-mine, maybe that would settle it. But you needn't worry, Lyra. While I've got it, you're safe."

The first chance she had, she plunged her arm down into the stiffly-frosted canvas of the kit-bag and brought up the little tin. She could feel the buzz it was making before she touched it.

While Farder Coram was talking to the other leaders, she took the tin to Iorek Byrnison and explained her idea. It had come to her when she remembered his slicing so easily through the metal of the engine-cover.

He listened, and then took the lid of a biscuit-tin and deftly folded it into a small flat cylinder. She marvelled at the skill of his hands: unlike most bears, he and his kin had opposable thumb-claws with which they could hold things still to work on them; and he had some innate sense of the strength and flexibility of metals which meant that he only had to lift it once or twice, flex it this way and that, and he could run a claw over it in a circle to score it for folding. He did this now, folding the sides in and in until they stood in a raised rim and then making a lid to fit it. At Lyra's bidding he made two: one the same size as the original smoke-leaf tin, and another just big enough to contain the tin itself and a quantity of hairs and bits of moss and lichen all packed down tight to smother the noise. When it was closed, it was the same size and shape as the alethiometer.

When that was done, she sat next to Iorek Byrnison as he gnawed a haunch of reindeer that was frozen as hard as wood.

"Iorek," she said, "is it hard not having a dæmon? Don't you get lonely?"

"Lonely?" he said. "I don't know. They tell me this is cold. I don't know what cold is, because I don't freeze. So I don't know what lonely means either. Bears are made to be solitary."

"What about the Svalbard bears?" she said. "There's thousands of them, en't there? That's what I heard."

He said nothing, but ripped the joint in half with a sound like a splitting log.

"Beg pardon, Iorek," she said. "I hope I en't offended you. It's just that I'm curious. See, I'm extra curious about the Svalbard bears because of my father."

"Who is your father?"

"Lord Asriel. And they got him captive on Svalbard, you see. I think the Gobblers betrayed him and paid the bears to keep him in prison."

"I don't know. I am not a Svalbard bear."

"I thought you was . . ."

"No. I was a Svalbard bear, but I am not now. I was sent away as a punishment because I killed another bear. So I was deprived of my rank and my wealth and my armour and sent out to live at the edge of the human world and fight when I could find employment at it, or work at brutal tasks and drown my memory in raw spirits."

"Why did you kill the other bear?"

"Anger. There are ways among bears of turning away our anger with each other, but I was out of my own control. So I killed him and I was justly punished."

"And you were wealthy and high-ranking," said Lyra, marvel-ling. "Just like my father, Iorek! That's just the same with him after I was born. He killed someone too and they took all his wealth away. That was long before he got made a prisoner on Svalbard, though. I don't know anything about Svalbard, except it's in the farthest North . . . Is it all covered in ice? Can you get there over the frozen sea?"

"Not from this coast. The sea is sometimes frozen south of it, sometimes not. You would need a boat."

"Or a balloon, maybe."

"Or a balloon, yes, but then you would need the right wind."

He gnawed the reindeer haunch, and a wild notion flew into Lyra's mind as she remembered all those witches in the night sky; but she said nothing about that. Instead she asked Iorek Byrnison about Svalbard, and listened eagerly as he told her of the slow-crawling glaciers; of the rocks and ice-floes where the bright-tusked walruses lay in groups of a hundred or more, of the seas teeming with seals, of narwhals clashing their long white tusks above the icy water; of the great grim iron-bound coast, the cliffs a thousand feet and more high, where the foul cliff-ghasts perched and swooped; of the coal-pits and the fire-mines where the bearsmiths hammered out mighty sheets of iron and riveted them into armour . . .

"If they took your armour away, Iorek, where did you get this set from?"

"I made it myself in Nova Zembla from sky-metal. Until I did that I was incomplete."

"So bears can make their own souls . . ." she said. There was a great deal in the world to know. "Who is the King of Svalbard?" she went on. "Do bears have a King?"

"He is called Iofur Raknison."

That name shook a little bell in Lyra's mind. She'd heard it before, but where? And not in a bear's voice, either, nor in a gyp-tian's. The voice that had spoken it was a Scholar's, precise and pedantic and lazily arrogant, very much a Jordan College voice. She tried it again in her mind. Oh, she knew it so well!

And then she had it: the Retiring Room. The Scholars listen-ing to Lord Asriel. It was the Palmerian Professor who had said something about Iofur Raknison. He'd used the word *pan-serbjørne*, which Lyra didn't know, and she hadn't known that Iofur Raknison was a bear; but what was it he'd said? The King of Svalbard was vain, and he could be flattered. There was something else, if only she could remember it, but so much had happened since then . . .

"If your father is a prisoner of the Svalbard bears," said Iorek Byrnison, "he will not escape. There is no wood there to make a boat. On the other hand, if he is a nobleman, he will be treated fairly. They will give him a house to live in and a servant to wait on him, and food and fuel."

"Could the bears ever be defeated, Iorek?"

"No."

"Or tricked, maybe?"

He stopped gnawing and looked at her directly. Then he said, "You will never defeat the armoured bears. You have seen my armour; now look at my weapons."

He dropped the meat and held out his paws, palm upward, for her to look at. Each black pad was covered in horny skin an inch or more thick, and each of the claws was as long as Lyra's hand at least, and as sharp as a knife. He let her run her hands over them wonderingly.

"One blow will crush a seal's skull," he said. "Or break a man's back, or tear off a limb. And I can bite. If you had not stopped me in Trollesund, I would have crushed that man's head like an egg. So much for strength; now for trickery. You cannot trick a bear. You want to see proof? Take a stick and fence with me."

Eager to try, she snapped a stick off a snow-laden bush, trimmed all the side-shoots off, and swished it from side to side like a rapier. Iorek Byrnison sat back on his haunches and waited, forepaws in his lap. When she was ready she faced him, but she didn't like to stab at him because he looked so peaceable. So she flourished it, feinting to right and left, not intending to hit him at all, and he didn't move. She did that several times, and not once did he move so much as an inch.

Finally she decided to thrust at him directly, not hard, but just to touch the stick to his stomach. Instantly his paw reached forward and flicked the stick aside.

Surprised, she tried again, with the same result. He moved far more quickly and surely than she did. She tried to hit him in earnest, wielding the stick like a fencer's foil, and not once did it land on his body. He seemed to know what she intended before she did, and when she lunged at his head, the great paw swept the stick aside harmlessly, and when she feinted, he didn't move at all.

She became exasperated, and threw herself into a furious attack, jabbing and lashing and thrusting and stabbing, and never once did she get past those paws. They moved everywhere, precisely in time to parry, precisely at the right spot to block.

Finally she was frightened, and stopped. She was sweating inside her furs, out of breath, exhausted, and the bear still sat impassive. If she had had a real sword with a murderous point, he would have been quite unharmed.

"I bet you could catch bullets," she said, and threw the stick away. "How do you *do* that?"

"By not being human," he said. "That's why you could never trick a bear. We see tricks and deceit as plain as arms and legs. We can see in a way humans have forgotten. But you know about this; you can understand the symbol-reader."

"That en't the same, is it?" she said. She was more nervous of the bear now than when she had seen his anger.

"It is the same," he said. "Adults can't read it, as I understand. As I am to human fighters, so you are to adults with the symbol-reader."

"Yes, I suppose," she said, puzzled and unwilling. "Does that mean I'll forget how to do it when I grow up?"

"Who knows? I have never seen a symbol-reader, nor anyone who could read them. Perhaps you are different from others."

He dropped to all fours again and went on gnawing his meat. Lyra had unfastened her furs, but now the cold was striking in again and she had to do them up. All in all, it was a disquieting episode. She wanted to consult the alethiometer there and then, but it was too cold, and besides, they were calling for her because it was time to move on. She took the tin boxes that Iorek Byrnison had made, put the empty one back into Farder Coram's kit-bag, and put the one with the spy-fly in it together

with the alethiometer in the pouch at her waist. She was glad
when they were moving again.

The leaders had agreed with Lee Scoresby that when they
reached the next stopping-place, they would inflate his balloon
and he would spy from the air. Naturally Lyra was eager to fly
with him, and naturally it was forbidden; but she rode with him
on the way there and pestered him with questions.

"Mr Scoresby, how would you fly to Svalbard?"

"You'd need a dirigible with a gas engine, something like a
zeppelin, or else a good south wind. But hell, I wouldn't dare.
Have you ever seen it? The bleakest barest most inhospitable
godforsaken dead-end of nowhere."

"I was just wondering, if Iorek Byrnison wanted to go
back . . ."

"He'd be killed. Iorek's in exile. As soon as he set foot there
they'd tear him to pieces."

"How do you inflate your balloon, Mr Scoresby?"

"Two ways. I can make hydrogen by pouring sulphuric acid
on to iron filings. You catch the gas it gives off and gradually fill
the balloon like that. The other way is to find a ground-gas vent
near a fire-mine. There's a lot of gas under the ground here, and
rock-oil besides. I can make gas from rock-oil, if I need to,
and from coal as well; it's not hard to make gas. But the quickest
way is to use ground-gas. A good vent will fill the balloon in an
hour."

"How many people can you carry?"

"Six, if I need to."

"Could you carry Iorek Byrnison in his armour?"

"I have done. I rescued him one time from the Tartars, when
he was cut off and they were starving him out – that was in the
Tunguska campaign; I flew in and took him off. Sounds easy, but
hell, I had to calculate the weight of that old boy by guesswork.
And then I had to bank on finding ground-gas under the ice-fort
he'd made. But I could see what kind of ground it was from the
air, and I reckoned we'd be safe in digging. See, to go down I have
to let gas out of the balloon, and I can't get airborne again without more. Anyway, we made it, armour and all."

"Mr Scoresby, you know the Tartars make holes in people's heads?"

"Oh, sure. They've been doing that for thousands of years. In the Tunguska campaign we captured five Tartars alive, and three of them had holes in their skulls. One of them had two."

"They do it to *each other*?"

"That's right. First they cut part-way around a circle of skin on the scalp, so they can lift up a flap and expose the bone. Then they cut a little circle of bone out of the skull, very carefully so they don't penetrate the brain, and then they sew the scalp back over."

"I thought they did it to their enemies!"

"Hell, no. It's a great privilege. They do it so the gods can talk to them."

"Did you ever hear of an explorer called Stanislaus Grumman?"

"Grumman? Sure. I met one of his team when I flew over the Yenisei River two years back. He was going to live among the Tartar tribes up that way. Matter of fact, I think *he* had that hole in the skull done. It was part of an initiation ceremony, but the man who told me didn't know much about it."

"So . . . If he was like an honorary Tartar, they wouldn't have killed him?"

"Killed him? Is he dead then?"

"Yeah. I saw his head," Lyra said proudly. "My father found it. I saw it when he showed it to the Scholars at Jordan College in Oxford. They'd scalped it, and all."

"Who'd scalped it?"

"Well, the Tartars, that's what the Scholars thought . . . But maybe it wasn't."

"It might not have been Grumman's head," said Lee Scoresby. "Your father might have been misleading the Scholars."

"I suppose he might," said Lyra thoughtfully. "He was asking them for money."

"And when they saw the head, they gave him the money?"

"Yeah."

"Good trick to play. People are shocked when they see a thing like that; they don't like to look too close."

"Especially Scholars," said Lyra.

"Well, you'd know better than I would. But if that was Grumman's head, I'll bet it wasn't the Tartars who scalped him. They scalp their enemies, not their own, and he was a Tartar by adoption."

Lyra turned that over in her mind as they drove on. There were wide currents full of meaning flowing fast around her: the Gobblers and their cruelty, their fear of Dust, the city in the Aurora, her father in Svalbard, her mother . . . And where was she? The alethiometer, the witches flying northwards. And poor little Tony Makarios; and the clockwork spy-fly; and Iorek Byrnison's uncanny fencing . . .

She fell asleep. And every hour they drew closer to Bolvangar.

14
BOLVANGAR LIGHTS

THE FACT THAT the gyptians had heard or seen nothing of Mrs Coulter worried Farder Coram and John Faa more than they let Lyra know; but they weren't to know that she was worried too. Lyra feared Mrs Coulter and thought about her often. And whereas Lord Asriel was now "father", Mrs Coulter was never "mother". The reason for that was Mrs Coulter's dæmon, the golden monkey, who had filled Pantalaimon with a powerful loathing and who, Lyra felt, had pried into her secrets, particularly that of the alethiometer.

And they were bound to be chasing her; it was silly to think otherwise. The spy-fly proved that, if nothing else.

But when an enemy did strike, it wasn't Mrs Coulter. The gyptians had planned to stop and rest their dogs, repair a couple of sledges, and get all their weapons into shape for the assault on Bolvangar. John Faa hoped that Lee Scoresby might find some ground-gas to fill his smaller balloon (for he had two, apparently) and go up to spy out the land. However, the aëronaut attended to the condition of the weather as closely as a sailor, and he said there was going to be a fog; and sure enough, as soon as they stopped, a thick mist descended. Lee Scoresby knew he'd see nothing from the sky, so he had to content himself with checking his equipment, though it was all in meticulous order. Then, with no warning at all, a volley of arrows flew out of the dark.

Three gyptian men went down at once, and died so silently that no one heard a thing. Only when they slumped clumsily across the dog-traces or lay unexpectedly still did the nearest men notice what was happening, and then it was already too late, because more arrows were flying at them. Some men looked up, puzzled by the fast irregular knocking sounds that came from up and down the line as arrows hurtled into wood or frozen canvas.

The first to come to his wits was John Faa, who shouted orders from the centre of the line. Cold hands and stiff limbs moved to obey as yet more arrows flew down like rain, straight rods of rain tipped with death.

Lyra was in the open, and the arrows were passing over her head. Pantalaimon heard before she did, and became a leopard and knocked her over, making her less of a target. Brushing snow out of her eyes, she rolled over to try and see what was happening, for the semi-darkness seemed to be overflowing with confusion and noise. She heard a mighty roar, and the clang and scrape of Iorek Byrnison's armour as he leapt fully clad over the sledges and into the fog, and that was followed by screams, snarling, crunching and tearing sounds, great smashing blows, cries of terror and roars of bearish fury as he laid them waste.

But who was *them*? Lyra had seen no enemy figures yet. The gyptians were swarming to defend the sledges, but that (as even Lyra could see) made them better targets; and their rifles were not easy to fire in gloves and mittens; she had only heard four or five shots, as against the ceaseless knocking rain of arrows. And more and more men fell every minute.

Oh, John Faa! she thought in anguish. You didn't foresee this, and I didn't help you!

But she had no more than a second to think that, for there was a mighty snarl from Pantalaimon, and something – another dæmon – hurtled at him and knocked him down, crushing all the breath out of Lyra herself; and then hands were hauling at her, lifting her, stifling her cry with foul-smelling mittens, tossing her through the air into another's arms, and then pushing her flat down into the snow again, so that she was dizzy and breathless and hurt all at once. Her arms were hauled behind till her shoulders cracked, and someone lashed her wrists together, and then a hood was crammed over her head to muffle her screams, for scream she did, and lustily:

"Iorek! Iorek Byrnison! Help me!"

But could he hear? She couldn't tell; she was hurled this way and that, crushed on to a hard surface which then began to lurch and bump like a sledge. The sounds that reached her were wild and confused. She might have heard Iorek Byrnison's roar, but it was a long way off, and then she was jolting over rough ground, arms twisted, mouth stifled, sobbing with rage and fear. And strange voices spoke around her.

"Pan!" she gasped.

"I'm here, ssh, I'll help you breathe. Keep still..."

His mouse-paws tugged at the hood until her mouth was freer, and she gulped at the frozen air.

"Who are they?" she whispered.

"They look like Tartars. I think they hit John Faa."

"No –"

"I saw him fall. But he should have been ready for this sort of attack. We know that."

"But we should have helped him! We should have been watching the alethiometer!"

"Hush. Pretend to be unconscious."

There was a whip cracking, and the howl of racing dogs. From the way she was being jerked and bounced about, Lyra could tell how fast they were going, and though she strained to hear the sounds of battle, all she made out was a forlorn volley of shots, muffled by the distance, and then the creak and rush and soft paw-thuds in the snow were all there was to hear.

"They'll take us to the Gobblers," she whispered.

The word *severed* came to their mind. Horrible fear filled Lyra's body, and Pantalaimon nestled close against her.

"I'll fight," he said.

"So will I. I'll *kill* them."

"So will Iorek when he finds out. He'll crush them to death."

"How far are we from Bolvangar?"

He didn't know, but they thought it was less than a day's ride. After they had been driving along for such a time that her body was in torment from cramp, the pace slackened a little, and someone roughly pulled off the hood.

She looked up at a broad Asiatic face, under a wolverine hood, lit by flickering lamplight. His black eyes showed a glint of satisfaction, especially when Pantalaimon slid out of Lyra's anorak to bare his white ermine-teeth in a hiss. The man's dæmon, a big heavy wolverine, snarled back, but Pantalaimon didn't flinch.

The man hauled Lyra up to a sitting position and propped her against the side of the sledge. She kept falling sideways because her hands were still tied behind her, and so he tied her feet together instead and released her hands.

Through the snow that was falling and the thick fog, she saw how powerful this man was, and the sledge-driver too, how balanced in the sledge, how much at home in this land in a way the gyptians weren't.

The man spoke, but of course she understood nothing. He tried a different language with the same result. Then he tried English.

"You name?"

Pantalaimon bristled warningly, and she knew what he meant at once. So these men didn't know who she was! They hadn't kidnapped her because of her connection with Mrs Coulter; so perhaps they weren't in the pay of the Gobblers after all.

"Lizzie Brooks," she said.

"Lissie Broogs," he said after her. "We take you nice place. Nice peoples."

"Who are you?"

"Samoyed peoples. Hunters."

"Where are you taking me?"

"Nice place. Nice peoples. You have *panserbjørn*?"

"For protection."

"No good! Ha, ha, bear no good! We got you anyway!"

He laughed loudly. Lyra controlled herself and said nothing.

"Who those peoples?" the man asked next, pointing back the way they had come.

"Traders."

"Traders . . . What they trade?"

"Fur, spirits," she said. "Smoke-leaf."

"They sell smoke-leaf, buy furs?"

"Yes."

He said something to his companion, who spoke back briefly. All the time the sledge was speeding onwards, and Lyra pulled herself up more comfortably to try and see where they were heading; but the snow was falling thickly, and the sky was dark, and presently she became too cold to peer out any longer, and lay down. She and Pantalaimon could feel each other's thoughts,

and tried to keep calm, but the thought of John Faa dead . . . And
what had happened to Farder Coram? And would Iorek manage
to kill the other Samoyeds? And would they ever manage to track
her down?

For the first time, she began to feel a little sorry for herself.

After a long time, the man shook her by the shoulder and
handed her a strip of dried reindeer-meat to chew. It was rank
and tough, but she was hungry, and there was nourishment in it.
After chewing it she felt a little better. She slipped her hand
slowly into her furs till she was sure the alethiometer was still
there, and then carefully withdrew the spy-fly tin and slipped it
down into her fur boot. Pantalaimon crept in as a mouse and
pushed it as far down as he could, tucking it under the bottom
of her reindeer-skin legging.

When that was done she closed her eyes. Fear had made her
exhausted, and soon she slipped uneasily into sleep.

She woke up when the motion of the sledge changed. It was
suddenly smoother, and when she opened her eyes there were
passing lights dazzling above her, so bright she had to pull the
hood further over her head before peering out again. She was
horribly stiff and cold, but she managed to pull herself upright
enough to see that the sledge was driving swiftly between a row
of high poles, each carrying a glaring anbaric light. As she got
her bearings, they passed through an open metal gate at the end
of the avenue of lights and into a wide open space like an empty
market-place or an arena for some game or sport. It was perfectly
flat and smooth and white, and about a hundred yards across.
Around the edge ran a high metal fence.

At the far end of this arena the sledge halted. They were outside a low building, or a range of low buildings over which the
snow lay deeply. It was hard to tell, but she had the impression
that tunnels connected one part of the buildings with another,
tunnels humped under the snow. At one side a stout metal mast
had a familiar look, though she couldn't say what it reminded
her of.

Before she could take much more in, the man in the sledge cut
through the cord around her ankles, and hauled her out roughly
while the driver shouted at the dogs to make them still. A door

opened in the building a few yards away, and an anbaric light came on overhead, swivelling to find them, like a searchlight.

Lyra's captor thrust her forward like a trophy, without letting go, and said something. The figure in the padded coal-silk anorak answered in the same language, and Lyra saw his features: he was not a Samoyed or a Tartar. He could have been a Jordan Scholar. He looked at her, and particularly at Pantalaimon.

The Samoyed spoke again, and the man from Bolvangar said to Lyra, "You speak English?"

"Yes," she said.

"Does your dæmon always take that form?"

Of all the unexpected questions! Lyra could only gape. But Pantalaimon answered it in his own fashion by becoming a falcon, and launching himself from her shoulder at the man's dæmon, a large marmot, which struck up at Pantalaimon with a swift movement and spat as he circled past on swift wings.

"I see," said the man in a tone of satisfaction, as Pantalaimon returned to Lyra's shoulder.

The Samoyed men were looking expectant, and the man from Bolvangar nodded and took off a mitten to reach into a pocket. He took out a draw-string purse and counted out a dozen heavy coins into the hunter's hand.

The two men checked the money, and then stowed it carefully, each man taking half. Without a backward glance they got in the sledge, and the driver cracked the whip and shouted to the dogs; and they sped away across the wide white arena and into the avenue of lights, gathering speed until they vanished into the dark beyond.

The man was opening the door again.

"Come in quickly," he said. "It's warm and comfortable. Don't stand out in the cold. What is your name?"

His voice was an English one, without any accent Lyra could name. He sounded like the sort of people she had met at Mrs Coulter's: smart and educated and important.

"Lizzie Brooks," she said.

"Come in, Lizzie. We'll look after you here, don't worry."

He was colder than she was, even though she'd been outside for far longer; he was impatient to be in the warm again. She decided to play slow and dim-witted and reluctant, and dragged her feet as she stepped over the high threshold into the building.

There were two doors, with a wide space between them so that not too much warm air escaped. Once they were through the inner doorway Lyra found herself sweltering in what seemed unbearable heat, and had to pull open her furs and push back her hood.

They were in a space about eight feet square, with corridors to the right and left and in front of her the sort of reception desk you might see in a hospital. Everything was brilliantly lit, with the glint of shiny white surfaces and stainless steel. There was the smell of food in the air, familiar food, bacon and coffee, and under it a faint perpetual hospital-medical smell; and coming from the walls all around was a slight humming sound, almost too low to hear, the sort of sound you had to get used to or go mad.

Pantalaimon at her ear, a goldfinch now, whispered, "Be stupid and dim. Be really slow and stupid."

Adults were looking down at her: the man who'd brought her in, another man wearing a white coat, a woman in a nurse's uniform.

"English," the first man was saying. "Traders, apparently."

"Usual hunters? Usual story?"

"Same tribe, as far as I could tell. Sister Clara, could you take little, umm, and see to her?"

"Certainly, Doctor. Come with me, dear," said the nurse, and Lyra obediently followed.

They went along a short corridor with doors on the right and a canteen on the left, from which came a clatter of knives and forks, and voices, and more cooking-smells. The nurse was about as old as Mrs Coulter, Lyra guessed, with a brisk, blank, sensible air; she would be able to stitch a wound or change a bandage, but never to tell a story. Her dæmon (and Lyra had a moment of strange chill when she noticed) was a little white trotting dog (and after a moment she had no idea why it had chilled her).

"What's your name, dear?" said the nurse, opening a heavy door.

"Lizzie."

"Just Lizzie?"

"Lizzie Brooks."

"And how old are you?"

"Eleven."

Lyra had been told that she was small for her age, whatever that meant. It had never affected her sense of her own importance, but she realized that she could use the fact now to make Lizzie shy and nervous and insignificant, and shrank a little as she went into the room.

She was half expecting questions about where she had come from and how she had arrived, and she was preparing answers; but it wasn't only imagination the nurse lacked, it was curiosity as well. Bolvangar might have been on the outskirts of London, and children might have been arriving all the time, for all the interest Sister Clara seemed to show. Her pert neat little dæmon trotted along at her heels just as brisk and blank as she was.

In the room they entered there was a couch and a table and two chairs and a filing cabinet, and a glass cupboard with medicines and bandages, and a wash-basin. As soon as they were inside, the nurse took Lyra's outer coat off and dropped it on the shiny floor.

"Off with the rest, dear," she said. "We'll have a quick little look to see you're nice and healthy, no frostbite or sniffles, and then we'll find some nice clean clothes. We'll pop you in the shower, too," she added, for Lyra had not changed or washed for days, and in the enveloping warmth, that was becoming more and more evident.

Pantalaimon fluttered in protest, but Lyra quelled him with a scowl. He settled on the couch as one by one all Lyra's clothes came off, to her resentment and shame; but she still had the presence of mind to conceal it and act dull-witted and compliant.

"And the money-belt, Lizzie," said the nurse, and untied it herself with strong fingers. She went to drop it on the pile with Lyra's other clothes, but stopped, feeling the edge of the alethiometer.

"What's this?" she said, and unbuttoned the oilcloth.

"Just a sort of toy," said Lyra. "It's mine."

"Yes, we won't take it away from you, dear," said Sister Clara, unfolding the black velvet. "That's pretty, isn't it, like a compass. Into the shower with you," she went on, putting the alethiometer down and whisking back a coal-silk curtain in the corner.

Lyra reluctantly slipped under the warm water and soaped herself while Pantalaimon perched on the curtain-rail. They were both conscious that he mustn't be too lively, for the dæmons of dull people were dull themselves. When she was washed and dry the nurse took her temperature and looked into her eyes and ears and throat, and then measured her height and put her on some scales before writing a note on a clipboard. Then she gave Lyra some pyjamas and a dressing-gown. They were clean, and of good quality, like Tony Makarios's anorak, but again there was a second-hand air about them. Lyra felt very uneasy.

"These en't mine," she said.

"No, dear. Your clothes need a good wash."

"Am I going to get my own ones back?"

"I expect so. Yes, of course."

"What is this place?"

"It's called the Experimental Station."

That wasn't an answer, and whereas Lyra would have pointed that out and asked for more information, she didn't think Lizzie Brooks would; so she assented dumbly in the dressing and said no more.

"I want my toy back," she said stubbornly when she was dressed.

"Take it, dear," said the nurse. "Wouldn't you rather have a nice woolly bear, though? Or a pretty doll?"

She opened a drawer where some soft toys lay like dead things. Lyra made herself stand and pretend to consider for several seconds before picking out a rag doll with big vacant eyes. She had never had a doll, but she knew what to do, and pressed it absently to her chest.

"What about my money-belt?" she said. "I like to keep my toy in there."

"Go on, then, dear," said Sister Clara, who was filling in a form on pink paper.

Lyra hitched up her unfamiliar pyjamas and tied the oilskin pouch around her waist.

"What about my coat and boots?" she said. "And my mittens and things?"

"We'll have them cleaned for you," said the nurse automatically.

Then a telephone buzzed, and while the nurse answered it, Lyra stooped quickly to recover the other tin, the one containing the spy-fly, and put it in the pouch with the alethiometer.

"Come along, Lizzie," said the nurse, putting the receiver down. "We'll go and find you something to eat. I expect you're hungry."

She followed Sister Clara to the canteen, where a dozen round white tables were covered in crumbs and the sticky rings where drinks had been carelessly put down. Dirty plates and cutlery were stacked on a steel trolley. There were no windows, so to give an illusion of light and space one wall was covered in a huge photogram showing a tropical beach, with bright blue sky and white sand and coconut palms.

The man who had brought her in was collecting a tray from a serving hatch.

"Eat up," he said.

There was no need to starve, so she ate the stew and mashed potatoes with relish. There was a bowl of tinned peaches and ice cream to follow. As she ate, the man and the nurse talked quietly at another table, and when she had finished, the nurse brought her a glass of warm milk and took the tray away.

The man came to sit down opposite. His dæmon, the marmot, was not blank and incurious as the nurse's dog had been, but sat politely on his shoulder watching and listening.

"Now, Lizzie," he said. "Have you eaten enough?"

"Yes, thank you."

"I'd like you to tell me where you come from. Can you do that?"

"London," she said.

"And what are you doing so far north?"

"With my father," she mumbled. She kept her eyes down,

avoiding the gaze of the marmot, and trying to look as if she was on the verge of tears.

"With your father? I see. And what's he doing in this part of the world?"

"Trading. We come with a load of New Danish smoke-leaf and we was buying furs."

"And was your father by himself?"

"No. There was my uncles and all, and some other men," she said vaguely, not knowing what the Samoyed hunter had told him.

"Why did he bring you on a journey like this, Lizzie?"

"'Cause two years ago he brung my brother and he says he'll bring me next, only he never. So I kept asking him, and then he did."

"And how old are you?"

"Eleven."

"Good, good. Well, Lizzie, you're a lucky little girl. Those huntsmen who found you brought you to the best place you could be."

"They never found me," she said doubtfully. "There was a fight. There was lots of 'em and they had arrows . . ."

"Oh, I don't think so. I think you must have wandered away from your father's party and got lost. Those huntsmen found you on your own and brought you straight here. That's what happened, Lizzie."

"I saw a fight," she said. "They was shooting arrows and that . . . I want my dad," she said more loudly, and felt herself beginning to cry.

"Well, you're quite safe here until he comes," said the doctor.

"But I saw them shooting arrows!"

"Ah, you thought you did. That often happens in the intense cold, Lizzie. You fall asleep and have bad dreams and you can't remember what's true and what isn't. That wasn't a fight, don't worry. Your father is safe and sound and he'll be looking for you now and soon he'll come here because this is the only place for hundreds of miles, you know, and what a surprise he'll have to find you safe and sound! Now Sister Clara will take you along to the dormitory where you'll meet some other little girls and boys who got lost in the wilderness just like you. Off you go. We'll have another little talk in the morning."

Lyra stood up, clutching her doll, and Pantalaimon hopped on to her shoulder as the nurse opened the door to lead them out.

More corridors, and Lyra was tired by now, so sleepy she kept yawning and could hardly lift her feet in the woolly slippers they'd given her. Pantalaimon was drooping, and he had to change to a mouse and settle inside her dressing-gown pocket. Lyra had the impression of a row of beds, children's faces, a pillow, and then she was asleep.

Someone was shaking her. The first thing she did was to feel at her waist, and both tins were still there, still safe; so she tried to open her eyes, but oh, it was hard; she had never felt so sleepy.

"Wake up! Wake up!"

It was a whisper in more than one voice. With a huge effort, as if she were pushing a boulder up a slope, Lyra forced herself to wake up.

In the dim light from a very low-powered anbaric bulb over the doorway she saw three other girls clustered around her. It wasn't easy to see, because her eyes were slow to focus, but they seemed about her own age, and they were speaking English.

"She's awake."

"They gave her sleeping pills. Must've . . ."

"What's your name?"

"Lizzie," Lyra mumbled.

"Is there a load more new kids coming?" demanded one of the girls.

"Dunno. Just me."

"Where'd they get you then?"

Lyra struggled to sit up. She didn't remember taking a sleeping pill, but there might well have been something in the drink she'd had. Her head felt full of eiderdown, and there was a faint pain throbbing behind her eyes.

"Where is this place?"

"Middle of nowhere. They don't tell us."

"They usually bring more'n one kid at a time . . ."

"What do they do?" Lyra managed to ask, gathering her doped wits as Pantalaimon stirred into wakefulness with her.

"We dunno," said the girl who was doing most of the talking. She was a tall, red-haired girl with quick twitchy movements and a strong London accent. "They sort of measure us and do these tests and that –"

"They measure Dust," said another girl, friendly and plump and dark-haired.

"*You* don't know," said the first girl.

"They do," said the third, a subdued-looking child cuddling her rabbit-dæmon. "I heard 'em talking."

"Then they take us away one by one and that's all we know. No one comes back," said the redhead.

"There's this boy, right," said the plump girl, "he reckons –"

"Don't tell her that!" said the redhead. "Not yet."

"Is there boys here as well?" said Lyra.

"Yeah. There's lots of us. There's about thirty, I reckon."

"More'n that," said the plump girl. "More like forty."

"Except they keep taking us away," said the redhead. "They usually start off with bringing a whole bunch here, and then there's a lot of us, and one by one they all disappear."

"They're Gobblers," said the plump girl. "You know Gobblers. We was all scared of 'em till we was caught..."

Lyra was gradually coming more and more awake. The other girls' dæmons, apart from the rabbit, were close by listening at the door, and no one spoke above a whisper. Lyra asked their names. The red-haired girl was Annie, the dark plump one Bella, the thin one Martha. They didn't know the names of the boys, because the two sexes were kept apart for most of the time. They weren't treated badly.

"It's all right here," said Bella, "there's not much to do, except they give us tests and make us do exercises and then they measure us and take our temperature and stuff. It's just boring really."

"Except when Mrs Coulter comes," said Annie.

Lyra had to stop herself crying out, and Pantalaimon fluttered his wings so sharply that the other girls noticed.

"He's nervous," said Lyra, soothing him. "They must've gave

us some sleeping pills, like you said, 'cause we're all dozy. Who's Mrs Coulter?"

"She's the one who trapped us, most of us, anyway," said Martha. "They all talk about her, the other kids. When she comes, you know there's going to be kids disappearing."

"She likes watching the kids, when they take us away, she likes seeing what they do to us. This boy Simon, he reckons they kill us, and Mrs Coulter watches."

"They *kill* us?" said Lyra, shuddering.

"Must do. 'Cause no one comes back."

"They're always going on about dæmons too," said Bella. "Weighing them and measuring them and all . . ."

"They *touch* your *dæmons*?"

"No! God! They put scales there and your dæmon has to get on them and change, and they make notes and take pictures. And they put you in this cabinet and measure Dust, all the time, they never stop measuring Dust."

"What dust?" said Lyra.

"We dunno," said Annie. "Just something from space. Not real dust. If you en't got any Dust, that's good. But everyone gets Dust in the end."

"You know what I heard Simon say?" said Bella. "He said that the Tartars make holes in their skulls to let the Dust in."

"Yeah, *he'd* know," said Annie scornfully. "I think I'll ask Mrs Coulter when she comes."

"You wouldn't dare!" said Martha admiringly.

"I would."

"When's she coming?" said Lyra.

"The day after tomorrow," said Annie.

A cold drench of terror went down Lyra's spine, and Pantalaimon crept very close. She had one day in which to find Roger and discover whatever she could about this place, and either escape or be rescued; and if all the gyptians had been killed, who would help the children stay alive in the icy wilderness?

The other girls went on talking, but Lyra and Pantalaimon nestled down deep in the bed and tried to get warm, knowing that for hundreds of miles all around her little bed there was nothing but fear.

15

THE DÆMON-CAGES

IT WASN'T LYRA'S way to brood; she was a sanguine and practical child, and besides, she wasn't imaginative. No one with much imagination would have thought seriously that it was possible to come all this way and rescue her friend Roger; or, having thought it, an imaginative child would immediately have come up with several ways in which it was impossible. Being a practised liar doesn't mean you have a powerful imagination. Many good liars have no imagination at all; it's that which gives their lies such wide-eyed conviction.

So now she was in the hands of the Oblation Board, Lyra didn't fret herself into terror about what had happened to the gyptians. They were all good fighters, and even though Pantalaimon said he'd seen John Faa shot, he might have been mistaken; or if he wasn't mistaken, John Faa might not have been seriously hurt. It had been bad luck that she'd fallen into the hands of the Samoyeds, but the gyptians would be along soon to rescue her, and if they couldn't manage it, nothing would stop Iorek Byrnison from getting her out; and then they'd fly to Svalbard in Lee Scoresby's balloon and rescue Lord Asriel.

In her mind, it was as easy as that.

So next morning, when she awoke in the dormitory, she was curious and ready to deal with whatever the day would bring. And eager to see Roger – in particular, eager to see him before he saw her.

She didn't have long to wait. The children in their different dormitories were woken at half-past seven by the nurses who looked after them. They washed and dressed and went with the others to the canteen for breakfast.

And there was Roger.

He was sitting with five other boys at a table just inside the door. The queue for the hatch went right past them, and she was able to pretend to drop a handkerchief and crouch to pick it up, bending low next to his chair, so that Pantalaimon could speak to Roger's dæmon Salcilia.

She was a chaffinch, and she fluttered so wildly that Pantalaimon had to be a cat and leap at her, pinning her down to whisper. Such brisk fights or scuffles between children's dæmons were common, luckily, and no one took much notice, but Roger went pale at once. Lyra had never seen anyone so white. He looked up at the blank haughty stare she gave him, and the colour flooded back into his cheeks as he brimmed over with hope, excitement, and joy; and only Pantalaimon, shaking Salcilia firmly, was able to keep Roger from shouting out and leaping up to greet his Jordan playmate.

Lyra looked away, acting as disdainfully as she could, and rolled her eyes at her new friends, leaving Pantalaimon to explain. The four girls collected their trays of cornflakes and toast and sat together, an instant gang, excluding everyone else in order to gossip about them.

You can't keep a large group of children in one place for long without giving them plenty to do, and in some ways Bolvangar was run like a school, with timetabled activities such as gymnastics and "art". Boys and girls were kept separate except for breaks and mealtimes, so it wasn't until mid-morning, after an hour and a half of sewing directed by one of the nurses, that Lyra had the chance to talk to Roger. But it had to look natural; that was the difficulty. All the children there were more or less at the same age, and it was the age when boys talk to boys and girls to girls, each making a conspicuous point of ignoring the opposite sex.

She found her chance in the canteen again, when the children came in for a drink and a biscuit. Lyra sent Pantalaimon, as a fly, to talk to Salcilia on the wall next to their table while she and Roger kept quietly in their separate groups. It was difficult to talk while your dæmon's attention was somewhere else, so Lyra pretended to look glum and rebellious as she sipped her milk with the other girls. Half her thoughts were with the tiny buzz of talk between the dæmons, and she wasn't really listening, but at one point she heard another girl with bright blonde hair say a name that made her sit up.

It was the name of Tony Makarios. As Lyra's attention snapped towards that, Pantalaimon had to slow down his whispered conversation with Roger's dæmon, and both children listened to what the girl was saying.

"No, I know why they took him," she said, as heads clustered close nearby. "It was because his dæmon didn't change. They thought he was older than he looked, or summing, and he weren't really a young kid. But really his dæmon never changed very often because Tony hisself never thought much about anything. I seen her change. She was called Ratter..."

"Why are they so interested in dæmons?" said Lyra.

"No one knows," said the blonde girl.

"I know," said one boy who'd been listening. "What they do is kill your dæmon and then see if you die."

"Well how come they do it over and over with different kids?" said someone. "They'd only need to do it once, wouldn't they?"

"I know what they do," said the first girl.

She had everyone's attention now. But because they didn't want to let the staff know what they were talking about, they had to adopt a strange, half-careless, indifferent manner, while listening with passionate curiosity.

"How?" said someone.

"'Cause I was with him when they came for him. We was in the linen room," she said.

She was blushing hotly. If she was expecting jeers and teasing, they didn't come. All the children were subdued, and no one even smiled.

The girl went on, "We was keeping quiet and then the nurse came in, the one with the soft voice. And she says, Come on, Tony, I know you're there, come on, we won't hurt you ... And he says, What's going to happen? And she says, We just put you to sleep, and then we do a little operation, and then you wake up safe and sound. But Tony didn't believe her. He says –"

"The holes!" said someone. "They make a hole in your head like the Tartars! I *bet*!"

"Shut up! What else did the nurse say?" someone else put in. By this time, a dozen or more children were clustered around her table, their dæmons as urgent to know as they were, all wide-eyed and tense.

The blonde girl went on, "Tony wanted to know what they was gonna do with Ratter, see. And the nurse says, Well, she's going to sleep too, just like when you do. And Tony says, You're gonna kill her, en't yer? I know you are. We all know that's what happens. And the nurse says, No, of course not. It's just a little operation. Just a little cut. It won't even hurt, but we put you to sleep to make sure."

All the room had gone quiet now. The nurse who'd been supervising had left for a moment, and the hatch to the kitchen was shut so no one could hear from there.

"What sort of cut?" said a boy, his voice quiet and frightened. "Did she say what sort of cut?"

"She just said, It's something to make you more grown up. She said everyone had to have it, that's why grown-ups' dæmons don't change like ours do. So they have a cut to make them one shape for ever, and that's how you get grown up."

"But —"

"Does that mean —"

"What, all grown-ups've had this cut?"

"What about —"

Suddenly all the voices stopped as if they themselves had been cut, and all eyes turned to the door. Sister Clara stood there, bland and mild and matter-of-fact, and beside her was a man in a white coat whom Lyra hadn't seen before.

"Bridget McGinn," he said.

The blonde girl stood up trembling. Her squirrel-dæmon clutched her breast.

"Yes, sir?" she said, her voice hardly audible.

"Finish your drink and come with Sister Clara," he said. "The rest of you run along and go to your classes."

Obediently the children stacked their mugs on the stainless-steel trolley before leaving in silence. No one looked at Bridget McGinn except Lyra, and she saw the blonde girl's face vivid with fear.

The rest of that morning was spent in exercise. There was a small gymnasium at the Station, because it was hard to exercise outside during the long Polar night, and each group of children took turns to play in there, under the supervision of a nurse. They had to form teams and throw balls around, and at first Lyra, who had never in her life played at anything like this, was at a loss what to do. But she was quick and athletic, and a natural leader, and soon found herself enjoying it. The shouts of the children, the shrieks and hoots of the dæmons, filled the little gymnasium and soon banished fearful thoughts; which of course was exactly what the exercise was intended to do.

At lunchtime, when the children were queueing once again in the canteen, Lyra felt Pantalaimon give a chirrup of recognition, and turned to find Billy Costa standing just behind her.

"Roger told me you was here," he muttered.

"Your brother's coming, and John Faa and a whole band of gyptians," she said. "They're going to take you home."

He nearly cried aloud with joy, but subdued the cry into a cough.

"And you got to call me Lizzie," Lyra said, "*never* Lyra. And you got to tell me everything you know, right."

They sat together, with Roger close by. It was easier to do this at lunchtime, when children spent more time coming and going between the tables and the hatch and the canteen was crowded. Under the clatter of knives and forks and plates Billy and Roger both told her as much as they knew. Billy had heard from a nurse that children who had had the operation were often taken to hostels further south, which might explain how Tony Makarios came to be wandering in the wild. But Roger had something even more interesting to tell her.

"I found a hiding-place," he said.

"What? Where?"

"See that picture..." He meant the big photogram of the tropical beach. "If you look in the top right corner, you see that ceiling panel?"

The ceiling consisted of large rectangular panels set in a framework of metal strips, and the corner of the panel above the picture had lifted slightly.

"I saw that," Roger said, "and I thought the others might be like it, so I lifted 'em, and they're all loose. They just lift up. Me and this boy tried it one night in our dormitory, before they took him away. There's a space up there and you can crawl inside . . ."

"How far can you crawl in the ceiling?"

"I dunno. We just went in a little way. We reckoned when it was time we could hide up there, but they'd probably find us."

Lyra saw it not as a hiding-place but as a highway. It was the best thing she'd heard since she'd arrived. But before they could talk any more, a doctor banged on a table with a spoon and began to speak.

"Listen, children," he said. "Listen carefully. Every so often we have to have a fire drill. It's very important that we all get dressed properly and make our way outside without any panic. So we're going to have a practice fire drill this afternoon. When the bell rings you must stop whatever you're doing and do what the nearest grown-up says. Remember where they take you. That's the place you must go to if there's a real fire."

Well, thought Lyra, there's an idea.

During the first part of the afternoon, Lyra and four other girls were tested for Dust. The doctors didn't say that was what they were doing, but it was easy to guess. They were taken one by one to a laboratory, and of course this made them all very frightened; how cruel it would be, Lyra thought, if she perished without striking a blow at them! But they were not going to do that operation just yet, it seemed.

"We want to make some measurements," the doctor explained. It was hard to tell the difference between these people: all the men looked similar in their white coats and with their clipboards and pencils, and the women resembled one another too, the uniforms and their strange bland calm manner making them all look like sisters.

"I was measured yesterday," Lyra said.

"Ah, we're making different measurements today. Stand on the metal plate – oh, slip your shoes off first. Hold your dæmon, if you like. Look forward, that's it, stare at the little green light. Good girl . . ."

Something flashed. The doctor made her face the other way and then to left and right, and each time something clicked and flashed.

"That's fine. Now come over to this machine and put your hand into the tube. Nothing to harm you, I promise. Straighten your fingers. That's it."

"What *are* you measuring?" she said. "Is it Dust?"

"Who told you about Dust?"

"One of the other girls, I don't know her name. She said we was all over Dust. I en't dusty, at least I don't think I am. I had a shower yesterday."

"Ah, it's a different sort of dust. You can't see it with your ordinary eyesight. It's a special dust. Now clench your fist – that's right. Good. Now if you feel around in there you'll find a sort of handle thing – got that? Take hold of that, there's a good girl. Now can you put your other hand over this way – rest it on this brass globe. Good. Fine. Now you'll feel a slight tingling, nothing to worry about, it's just a slight anbaric current . . ."

Pantalaimon, in his most tense and wary wildcat-form, prowled with lightning-eyed suspicion around the apparatus, continually returning to rub himself against Lyra.

She was sure by now that they weren't going to perform the operation on her yet, and sure too that her disguise as Lizzie Brooks was secure; so she risked a question.

"Why do you cut people's dæmons away?"

"What? Who's been talking to you about that?"

"This girl, I dunno her name. She said you cut people's dæmons away."

"Nonsense . . ."

He was agitated, though. She went on:

"'Cause you take people out one by one and they never come back. And some people reckon you just kill 'em, and other people say different, and this girl told me you cut –"

"It's not true at all. When we take children out, it's because it's time for them to move on to another place. They're growing up. I'm afraid your friend is alarming herself. Nothing of the sort! Don't even think about it. Who is your friend?"

"I only come here yesterday, I don't know anyone's name."

"What does she look like?"

"I forget. I think she had sort of brown hair ... light brown, maybe ... I dunno."

The doctor went to speak quietly to the nurse. As the two of them conferred, Lyra watched their dæmons. This nurse's was a pretty bird, just as neat and incurious as Sister Clara's dog, and the doctor's was a large heavy moth. Neither moved. They were awake, for the bird's eyes were bright and the moth's feelers waved languidly, but they weren't animated, as she would have expected them to be. Perhaps they weren't really anxious or curious at all.

Presently the doctor came back and they went on with the examination, weighing her and Pantalaimon separately, looking at her from behind a special screen, measuring her heartbeat, placing her under a little nozzle that hissed and gave off a smell like fresh air.

In the middle of one of the tests, a loud bell began to ring and kept ringing.

"The fire alarm," said the doctor, sighing. "Very well. Lizzie, follow Sister Betty."

"But all their outdoor clothes are down in the dormitory building, Doctor. She can't go outside like this. Should we go there first, do you think?"

He was annoyed at having his experiments interrupted, and snapped his fingers in irritation.

"I suppose this is just the sort of thing the practice is meant to show up," he said. "What a nuisance."

"When I came yesterday," Lyra said helpfully, "Sister Clara put my other clothes in a cupboard in that first room where she looked at me. The one next door. I could wear them."

"Good idea!" said the nurse. "Quick, then."

With a secret glee, Lyra hurried there behind the nurse and retrieved her proper furs and leggings and boots, and pulled them on quickly while the nurse dressed herself in coal-silk.

Then they hurried out. In the wide arena in front of the main group of buildings, a hundred or so people, adults and children, were milling about: some in excitement, some in irritation, many just bewildered.

"See?" one adult was saying. "It's worth doing this to find out what chaos we'd be in with a real fire."

Someone was blowing a whistle and waving their arms, but no one was taking much notice. Lyra saw Roger and beckoned. Roger tugged Billy Costa's arm and soon all three of them were together in a maelstrom of running children.

"No one'll notice if we take a look around," said Lyra. "It'll take 'em ages to count everyone, and we can say we just followed someone else and got lost."

They waited till most of the grown-ups were looking the other way, and then Lyra scooped up some snow and rammed it into a loose powdery snowball, and hurled it at random into the crowd. In a moment all the children were doing it, and the air was full of flying snow. Screams of laughter covered completely the shouts of the adults trying to regain control, and then the three children were around the corner and out of sight.

The snow was so thick that they couldn't move quickly, but it didn't seem to matter; no one was following. Lyra and the others scrambled over the curved roof of one of the tunnels, and found themselves in a strange moonscape of regular hummocks and hollows, all swathed in white under the black sky and lit by reflections from the lights around the arena.

"What we looking for?" said Billy.

"Dunno. Just looking," said Lyra, and led the way to a squat, square building a little apart from the rest, with a low-powered anbaric light at the corner.

The hubbub from behind was as loud as ever, but more distant. Clearly the children were making the most of their freedom, and Lyra hoped they'd keep it up for as long as they could. She moved around the edge of the square building, looking for a window. The roof was only seven feet or so off the ground, and unlike the other buildings, it had no roofed tunnel to connect it with the rest of the Station.

There was no window, but there was a door. A notice above it said ENTRY STRICTLY FORBIDDEN in red letters.

Lyra set her hand on it to try, but before she could turn the handle, Roger said:

"Look! A bird! Or –"

His *or* was an exclamation of doubt, because the creature swooping down from the black sky was no bird at all: it was someone Lyra had seen before.

"The witch's dæmon!"

The goose beat his great wings, raising a flurry of snow as he landed.

"Greetings, Lyra," he said. "I followed you here, though you didn't see me. I have been waiting for you to come out into the open. What is happening?"

She told him quickly.

"Where are the gyptians?" she said. "Is John Faa safe? Did they fight off the Samoyeds?"

"Most of them are safe. John Faa is wounded, though not severely. The men who took you were hunters and raiders who often prey on parties of travellers, and alone they can travel more quickly than a large party. The gyptians are still a day's journey away."

The two boys were staring in fear at the goose-dæmon and at Lyra's familiar manner with him, because of course they'd never seen a dæmon without his human before, and they knew little about witches.

Lyra said to them, "Listen, you better go and keep watch, right. Billy, you go that way, and Roger, watch out the way we just come. We en't got long."

They ran off to do as she said, and then Lyra turned back to the door.

"Why are you trying to get in there?" said the goose-dæmon.

"Because of what they do here. They cut –" she lowered her voice – "they cut people's dæmons away. Children's. And I think maybe they do it in here. At least, there's *something* here, and I was going to look. But it's locked . . ."

"I can open it," said the goose, and beat his wings once or twice, throwing snow up against the door; and as he did, Lyra heard something turn in the lock.

"Go in carefully," said the dæmon.

Lyra pulled opened the door against the snow and slipped inside. The goose-dæmon came with her. Pantalaimon was agitated and fearful, but he didn't want the witch's dæmon to see his fear, so he had flown to Lyra's breast and taken sanctuary inside her furs.

As soon as her eyes had adjusted to the light, Lyra saw why.

In a series of glass cases on shelves around the walls were all the dæmons of the severed children: ghost-like forms of cats, or birds, or rats, or other creatures, each bewildered and frightened and as pale as smoke.

The witch's dæmon gave a cry of anger, and Lyra clutched Pantalaimon to her and said, "Don't look! Don't look!"

"Where are the children of these dæmons?" said the goose-dæmon, shaking with rage.

Lyra explained fearfully about her encounter with little Tony Makarios, and looked over her shoulder at the poor caged dæmons, who were clustering forwards pressing their pale faces to the glass. Lyra could hear faint cries of pain and misery. In the dim light from a low-powered anbaric bulb she could see a name on a card at the front of each case, and yes, there was an empty one with *Tony Makarios* on it. There were four or five other empty ones with names on, too.

"I want to let these poor things go!" she said fiercely. "I'm going to smash the glass and let 'em out –"

And she looked around for something to do it with, but the place was bare. The goose-dæmon said, "Wait."

He was a witch's dæmon, and much older than she was, and stronger. She had to do as he said.

"We must make these people think someone forgot to lock the place and shut the cages," he explained. "If they see broken glass and footprints in the snow, how long do you think your disguise will last? And it must hold out till the gyptians come. Now do exactly as I say: take a handful of snow, and when I tell you, blow a little of it against each cage in turn."

She ran outside. Roger and Billy were still on guard, and there was still a noise of shrieking and laughter from the arena, because only a minute or so had gone by.

She grabbed a big double handful of the light powdery snow, and then came back to do as the goose-dæmon said. As she blew a little snow on each cage, the goose made a clicking sound in his throat, and the catch at the front of the cage came open.

When she had unlocked them all, she lifted the front of the first one, and the pale form of a sparrow fluttered out, but fell to the ground before she could fly. The goose tenderly bent and nudged her upright with his beak, and the sparrow became a mouse, staggering and confused. Pantalaimon leapt down to comfort her.

Lyra worked quickly, and within a few minutes every dæmon was free. Some were trying to speak, and they clustered around her feet and even tried to pluck at her leggings, though the taboo held them back. She could tell why, poor things; they missed the heavy solid warmth of their humans' bodies; just as Pantalaimon would have done, they longed to press themselves against a heartbeat.

"No quick," said the goose. "Lyra, you must run back and mingle with the other children. Be brave, child. The gyptians are coming as fast as they can. I must help these poor dæmons to find their people..." He came closer and said quietly, "But they'll never be one again. They're sundered for ever. This is the most wicked thing I have ever seen ... Leave the footprints you've made; I'll cover them up. Hurry now ..."

"Oh, please! Before you go! Witches ... They do fly don't they? I wasn't dreaming when I saw them flying the other night?"

"Yes, child; why?"

"Could they pull a balloon?"

"Undoubtedly, but –"

"Will Serafina Pekkala be coming?"

"There isn't time to explain the politics of witch-nations. There are vast powers involved here, and Serafina Pekkala must guard the interests of her clan. But it may be that what's happening here is part of all that's happening elsewhere. Lyra, you're needed inside. Run, run!"

She ran, and Roger, who was watching wide-eyed as the pale dæmons drifted out of the building, waded towards her through the thick snow.

"They're – it's like the crypt in Jordan – they're dæmons!"

"Yes, hush. Don't tell Billy, though. Don't tell anyone yet. Come on back."

Behind them, the goose was beating his wings powerfully,

throwing snow over the tracks they'd made; and near him, the lost dæmons were clustering or drifting away, crying little bleak cries of loss and longing. When the footprints were covered, the goose turned to herd the pale dæmons together. He spoke, and one by one they changed, though you could see the effort it cost them, until they were all birds; and like fledglings they followed the witch's dæmon, fluttering and falling and running through the snow after him, and finally, with great difficulty, taking off. They rose in a ragged line, pale and spectral against the deep black sky, slowly gaining height, feeble and erratic though some of them were, and though others lost their will and fluttered downwards; but the great grey goose wheeled round and nudged them back, herding them gently on until they were lost against the profound dark.

Roger was tugging at Lyra's arm.

"Quick," he said, "they're nearly ready."

They stumbled away to join Billy, who was beckoning from the corner of the main building. The children were tired now, or else the adults had regained some authority, because people were lining up raggedly by the main door, with much jostling and pushing. Lyra and the other two slipped out from the corner and mingled with them, but before they did, Lyra said:

"Pass the word around among all the kids – they got to be ready to escape. They got to know where the outdoor clothes are and be ready to get them and run out as soon as we give the signal. And they got to keep this a deadly secret, understand?"

Billy nodded, and Roger said, "What's the signal?"

"The fire bell," said Lyra. "When the time comes, I'll set it off."

They waited to be counted off. If anyone in the Oblation Board had had anything to do with a school, they would have arranged this better: because they had no regular group to go to, each child had to be ticked off against the complete list, and of course they weren't in alphabetical order; and none of the adults was used to keeping control. So there was a good deal of confusion, despite the fact that no one was running around any more.

Lyra watched and noticed. They weren't very good at this at all. They were slack in a lot of ways, these people; they grumbled about fire drills, they didn't know where the outdoor clothes should be kept, they couldn't get children to stand in line properly; and their slackness might be to her advantage.

They had almost finished when there came another distraction, though, and from Lyra's point of view, it was the worst possible.

She heard the sound as everyone else did. Heads began to turn and scan the dark sky for the zeppelin, whose gas-engine was throbbing clearly in the still air.

The one lucky thing was that it was coming from the direction opposite to the one in which the grey goose had flown. But that was the only comfort. Very soon it was visible, and a murmur of excitement went around the crowd. Its fat sleek silver form drifted over the avenue of lights, and its own lights blazed downwards from the nose and the cabin slung beneath the body.

The pilot cut the speed and began the complex business of adjusting the height. Lyra realized what the stout mast was for: of course, it was a mooring mast. As the adults ushered the children inside, with everyone staring back and pointing, the ground crew clambered up the ladders in the mast and prepared to attach the mooring cables. The engines were roaring, and snow was swirling up from the ground, and the faces of passengers showed in the cabin windows.

Lyra looked, and there was no mistake. Pantalaimon clutched at her, became a wildcat, hissed in hatred, because looking out with curiosity was the beautiful dark-haired head of Mrs Coulter, with her golden dæmon in her lap.

16

THE SILVER GUILLOTINE

LYRA DUCKED HER head at once under the shelter of her wolverine hood, and shuffled in through the double doors with the other children. Time enough later to worry about what she'd say when they came face to face: she had another problem to deal with first, and that was how to hide her furs where she could get at them without asking permission.

But luckily, there was such disorder inside, with the adults trying to hurry the children through so as to clear the way for the passengers from the zeppelin, that no one was watching very carefully. Lyra slipped out of the anorak, the leggings and the boots and bundled them up as small as she could before shoving through the crowded corridors to her dormitory.

Quickly she dragged a locker to the corner, stood on it, and pushed at the ceiling. The panel lifted, just as Roger had said, and into the space beyond she thrust the boots and leggings. As an afterthought, she took the alethiometer from her pouch and hid it in the inmost pocket of the anorak before shoving that through too.

She jumped down, pushed back the locker, and whispered to Pantalaimon, "We must just pretend to be stupid till she sees us, and then say we were kidnapped. And nothing about the gyptians or Iorek Byrnison especially."

Because Lyra now realized, if she hadn't done so before, that all the fear in her nature was drawn to Mrs Coulter as a compass needle is drawn to the Pole. All the other things she'd seen, and even the hideous cruelty of the intercision, she could cope with; she was strong enough; but the thought of that sweet face and gentle voice, the image of that golden playful monkey, was enough to melt her stomach and make her pale and nauseous.

But the gyptians were coming. Think of that. Think of Iorek Byrnison. And don't give yourself away, she said, and drifted back towards the canteen, where a lot of noise was coming from.

Children were lining up to get hot drinks, some of them still in their coal-silk anoraks. Their talk was all of the zeppelin and its passenger.

"It was *her* – with the monkey-dæmon –"

"Did she get you, too?"

"She said she'd write to my mum and dad and I bet she never . . ."

"She never told us about kids getting killed. She never said nothing about that."

"That monkey, he's the *worst* – he caught my Karossa and nearly killed her – I could feel all weak . . ."

They were as frightened as Lyra was. She found Annie and the others, and sat down.

"Listen," she said, "can you keep a secret?"

"Yeah!"

The three faces turned to her, vivid with expectation.

"There's a plan to escape," Lyra said quietly. "There's some people coming to take us away, right, and they'll be here in about a day. Maybe sooner. What we all got to do is be ready as soon as the signal goes and get our cold-weather clothes at once and run out. No waiting about. You just got to run. Only if you don't get your anoraks and boots and stuff you'll die of cold."

"What signal?" Annie demanded.

"The fire bell, like this afternoon. It's all organized. All the kids're going to know and none of the grown-ups. Especially not *her*."

Their eyes were gleaming with hope and excitement. And all through the canteen the message was being passed around. Lyra could tell that the atmosphere had changed. Outside, the children had been energetic and eager for play; then when they had seen Mrs Coulter they were bubbling with a suppressed hysterical fear; but now there was a control and purpose to their talkativeness. Lyra marvelled at the effect hope could have.

She watched through the open doorway, but carefully, ready to duck her head, because there were adult voices coming, and then Mrs Coulter herself was briefly visible, looking in and smiling at the happy children, with their hot drinks and their cake, so warm and well-fed. A little shiver ran almost instantaneously through the whole canteen, and every child was still and silent, staring at her.

Mrs Coulter smiled and passed on without a word. Little by little the talk started again.

Lyra said, "Where do they go to talk?"

"Probably the conference room," said Annie. "They took us there once," she added, meaning her and her dæmon. "There was about twenty grown-ups there and one of 'em was giving a lecture and I had to stand there and do what he told me, like seeing how far my Kyrillion could go away from me, and then he hypnotized me and did some other things . . . It's a big room with a lot of chairs and tables and a little platform. It's behind the front office. Hey, I bet *they're* going to pretend the fire drill went off all right. I bet they're scared of her, same as we are . . ."

For the rest of the day, Lyra stayed close to the other girls, watching, saying little, remaining inconspicuous. There was exercise, there was sewing, there was supper, there was playtime in the lounge: a big shabby room with board games and a few tattered books and a table-tennis table. At some point Lyra and the others became aware that there was some kind of subdued emergency going on, because the adults were hurrying to and fro or standing in anxious groups talking urgently. Lyra guessed they'd discovered the dæmons' escape, and were wondering how it had happened.

But she didn't see Mrs Coulter, which was a relief. When it was time for bed, she knew she had to let the other girls into her confidence.

"Listen," she said, "do they ever come round and see if we're asleep?"

"They just look in once," said Bella. "They just flash a lantern round, they don't really look."

"Good. 'Cause I'm going to go and look round. There's a way through the ceiling that this boy showed me . . ."

She explained, and before she'd even finished, Annie said, "I'll come with you!"

"No, you better not, 'cause it'll be easier if there's just one person missing. You can all say you fell asleep and you don't know where I've gone."

"But if I came with you –"

"More likely to get caught," said Lyra.

Their two dæmons were staring at each other, Pantalaimon as a wildcat, Annie's Kyrillion as a fox. They were quivering. Pantalaimon uttered the lowest, softest hiss and bared his teeth, and Kyrillion turned aside and began to groom himself unconcernedly.

"All right then," said Annie, resigned.

It was quite common for struggles between children to be settled by their dæmons in this way, with one accepting the dominance of the other. Their humans accepted the outcome without resentment, on the whole, so Lyra knew that Annie would do as she asked.

They all contributed items of clothing to bulk out Lyra's bed and make it look as if she was still there, and swore to say they knew nothing about it. Then Lyra listened at the door to make sure no one was coming, jumped up on the locker, pushed up the panel and hauled herself through.

"Just don't say anything," she whispered down to the three faces watching.

Then she dropped the panel gently back into place and looked around.

She was crouching in a narrow metal channel supported in a framework of girders and struts. The panels of the ceilings were slightly translucent, so some light came up from below, and in the faint gleam Lyra could see this narrow space (only two feet or so in height) extending in all directions around her. It was crowded with metal ducts and pipes, and it would be easy to get lost in, but provided she kept to the metal and avoided putting any weight on the panels, and as long as she made no noise, she should be able to go from one end of the Station to the other.

"It's just like back in Jordan, Pan," she whispered, "looking in the Retiring Room."

"If you hadn't done that, none of this would have happened," he whispered back.

"Then it's up to me to undo it, isn't it?"

She got her bearings, working out approximately which direction the conference room was in, and then set off. It was a far from easy journey. She had to move on hands and knees, because the space was too low to crouch in, and every so often she had to squeeze under a big square duct or lift herself over some heating pipes. The metal channels she crawled in followed the tops of internal walls, as far as she could tell, and as long as she stayed in them she felt a comforting solidity below her; but they were very narrow, and had sharp edges, so sharp that she cut her knuckles and her knee on them, and before long she was sore all over, and cramped, and dusty.

But she knew roughly where she was, and she could see the dark bulk of her furs crammed in above the dormitory to guide her back. She could tell where a room was empty because the panels were dark, and from time to time she heard voices from below, and stopped to listen, but it was only the cooks in the kitchen, or the nurses in what Lyra, in her Jordan way, thought of as their common room. They were saying nothing interesting, so she moved on.

At last she came to the area where the conference room should be, according to her calculations; and sure enough, there was an area free of any pipework, where air-conditioning and heating ducts led down at one end, and where all the panels in a wide rectangular space were lit evenly. She placed her ear to the panel, and heard a murmur of male adult voices, so she knew she had found the right place.

She listened carefully, and then inched her way along till she was as close as she could get to the speakers. Then she lay full-length in the metal channel and leaned her head sideways to hear as well as she could.

There was the occasional clink of cutlery, or the sound of glass on glass as drink was poured, so they were having dinner as they talked. There were four voices, she thought, including Mrs Coulter's. The other three were men. They seemed to be discussing the escaped dæmons.

"But who is in charge of supervising that section?" said Mrs Coulter's gentle musical voice.

"A research student called McKay," said one of the men. "But there are automatic mechanisms to prevent this sort of thing happening –"

"They didn't work," she said.

"With respect, they did, Mrs Coulter. McKay assures us that he locked all the cages when he left the building at eleven hundred hours today. The outer door of course would not have been open in any case, because he entered and left by the inner door, as he normally did. There's a code that has to be entered in the ordinator controlling the locks, and there's a record in its memory of his doing so. Unless that's done, an alarm goes off."

"But the alarm didn't go off," she said.

"It did. Unfortunately, it rang when everyone was outside, taking part in the fire drill."

"But when you went back inside —"

"Unfortunately both alarms are on the same circuit; that's a design fault that will have to be rectified. What it meant was that when the fire bell was turned off after the practice, the laboratory alarm was turned off as well. Even then it would still have been picked up, because of the normal checks that would have taken place after every disruption of routine; but by that time, Mrs Coulter, you had arrived unexpectedly, and if you recall, you asked specifically to meet the laboratory staff there and then, in your room. Consequently, no one returned to the laboratory until some time later."

"I see," said Mrs Coulter coldly. "In that case, the dæmons must have been released during the fire drill itself. And that widens the list of suspects to include every adult in the Station. Had you considered that?"

"Had you considered that it might have been done by a child?" said someone else.

She was silent, and the second man went on:

"Every adult had a task to do, and every task would have taken their full attention, and every task was done. There is no possibility that any of the staff here could have opened the door. None. So either someone came from outside altogether with the intention of doing that, or one of the children managed to find his way there, open the door and the cages, and return to the front of the main building."

"And what are you doing to investigate?" she said. "No; on second thoughts, don't tell me. Please understand, Dr Cooper,

I'm not criticizing out of malice. We have to be quite extraordinarily careful. It was an atrocious lapse to have allowed both alarms to be on the same circuit. That must be corrected at once. Possibly the Tartar officer in charge of the guard could help your investigation? I merely mention that as a possibility. Where were the Tartars during the fire drill, by the way? I suppose you have considered that?"

"Yes, we have," said the man wearily. "The guard was fully occupied on patrol, every man. They keep meticulous records."

"I'm sure you're doing your very best," she said. "Well, there we are. A great pity. But enough of that for now. Tell me about the new separator."

Lyra felt a thrill of fear. There was only one thing this could mean.

"Ah," said the doctor, relieved to find the conversation turning to another subject, "there's a real advance. With the first model we could never entirely overcome the risk of the patient dying of shock, but we've improved that no end."

"The Skraelings did it better by hand," said a man who hadn't spoken yet.

"Centuries of practice," said the other man.

"But simply *tearing* was the only option for some time," said the main speaker, "however distressing that was to the adult operators. If you remember, we had to discharge quite a number for reasons of stress-related anxiety. But the first big breakthrough was the use of anaesthesia combined with the Maystadt anbaric scalpel. We were able to reduce death from operative shock to below five per cent."

"And the new instrument?" said Mrs Coulter.

Lyra was trembling. The blood was pounding in her ears, and Pantalaimon was pressing his ermine-form against her side, and whispering, "Hush, Lyra, they won't do it – we won't let them do it –"

"Yes, it was a curious discovery by Lord Asriel himself that gave us the key to the new method. He discovered that an alloy of manganese and titanium has the property of insulating body from dæmon. By the way, what is happening with Lord Asriel?"

"Perhaps you haven't heard," said Mrs Coulter. "Lord Asriel

is under suspended sentence of death. One of the conditions of his exile in Svalbard was that he gave up his philosophical work entirely. Unfortunately, he managed to obtain books and materials, and he's pushed his heretical investigations to the point where it's positively dangerous to let him live. At any rate, it seems that the Consistorial Court of Discipline has begun to debate the question of the sentence of death, and the probability is that it'll be carried out. But your new instrument, Doctor. How does it work?"

"Ah – yes – sentence of death, you say? Gracious God . . . I'm sorry. The new instrument. We're investigating what happens when the intercision is made with the patient in a conscious state, and of course that couldn't be done with the Maystadt Process. So we've developed a kind of guillotine, I suppose you could say. The blade is made of manganese and titanium alloy, and the child is placed in a compartment – like a small cabin – of alloy mesh, with the dæmon in a similar compartment connecting with it. While there is a connection, of course, the link remains. Then the blade is brought down between them, severing the link at once. They are then separate entities."

"I should like to see it," she said. "Soon, I hope. But I'm tired now. I think I'll go to bed. I want to see all the children tomorrow. We shall find out who opened that door."

There was the sound of chairs being pushed back, polite expressions, a door closing. Then Lyra heard the others sit down again, and go on talking, but more quietly.

"What is Lord Asriel up to?"

"I think he's got an entirely different idea of the nature of Dust. That's the point. It's profoundly heretical, you see, and the Consistorial Court of Discipline can't allow any other interpretation than the authorized one. And besides, he wants to experiment –"

"To experiment? With Dust?"

"Hush! Not so loud . . ."

"Do you think she'll make an unfavourable report?"

"No, no. I think you dealt with her very well."

"Her *attitude* worries me . . ."

"Not philosophical, you mean?"

"Exactly. A *personal* interest. I don't like to use the word, but it's almost ghoulish."

"That's a bit strong."

"But do you remember the first experiments, when she was so keen to see them pulled apart —"

Lyra couldn't help it: a little cry escaped her, and at the same time she tensed and shivered, and her foot knocked against a stanchion.

"What was that?"

"In the ceiling —"

"Quick!"

The sound of chairs being thrown aside, feet running, a table pulled across the floor. Lyra tried to scramble away, but there was so little space, and before she could move more than a few yards the ceiling panel beside her was thrust up suddenly, and she was looking into the startled face of a man. She was close enough to see every hair in his moustache. He was as startled as she was, but with more freedom to move, he was able to thrust a hand into the gap and seize her arm.

"A child!"

"Don't let her go —"

Lyra sank her teeth into his large freckled hand. He cried out, but didn't let go, even when she drew blood. Pantalaimon was snarling and spitting, but it was no good, the man was much stronger than she was, and he pulled and pulled until her other hand, desperately clinging to the stanchion, had to loosen, and she half-fell through into the room.

Still she didn't utter a sound. She hooked her legs over the sharp edge of the metal above, and struggled upside down, scratching, biting, punching, spitting in passionate fury. The men were gasping and grunting with pain or exertion, but they pulled and pulled.

And suddenly all the strength went out of her.

It was as if an alien hand had reached right inside where no hand had a right to be, and wrenched at something deep and precious.

She felt faint, dizzy, sick, disgusted, limp with shock.

One of the men was *holding* Pantalaimon.

He had seized Lyra's dæmon in his human hands, and poor Pan was shaking, nearly out of his mind with horror and disgust. His wildcat shape, his fur now dull with weakness, now sparking glints of anbaric alarm ... He curved towards his Lyra as she reached with both hands for him ...

They fell still. They were captured.

She *felt* those hands ... It wasn't *allowed* ... Not *supposed* to touch ... *Wrong* ...

"Was she on her own?"

A man was peering into the ceiling space.

"Seems to be on her own ..."

"Who is she?"

"The new child."

"The one the Samoyed hunters ..."

"Yes."

"You don't suppose *she* ... the dæmons ..."

"Could well be. But not on her own, surely?"

"Should we tell −"

"I think that would put the seal on things, don't you?"

"I agree. Better she doesn't hear at all."

"But what can we do about this?"

"She can't go back with the other children."

"Impossible!"

"There's only one thing we *can* do, it seems to me."

"Now?"

"Have to. Can't leave it till the morning. She wants to watch."

"We could do it ourselves. No need to involve anyone else."

The man who seemed to be in charge, the man who wasn't holding either Lyra or Pantalaimon, tapped his teeth with a thumbnail. His eyes were never still; they flicked and slid and darted this way and that. Finally he nodded.

"Now. Do it now," he said. "Otherwise she'll talk. The shock will prevent that, at least. She won't remember who she is, what she saw, what she heard ... Come on."

Lyra couldn't speak. She could hardly breathe. She had to let herself be carried through the Station, along white empty corridors, past rooms humming with anbaric power, past the dormitories where children slept with their dæmons on the pillow beside them, sharing their dreams; and every second of the way she watched Pantalaimon, and he reached for her, and their eyes never left each other.

Then a door which opened by means of a large wheel; a hiss of air; and a brilliantly-lit chamber with dazzling white tiles and stainless steel. The fear she felt was almost a physical pain; it was a physical pain, as they pulled her and Pantalaimon over towards a large cage of pale silver mesh, above which a great pale silver blade hung poised to separate them for ever and ever.

She found a voice at last, and screamed. The sound echoed loudly off the shiny surfaces, but the heavy door had hissed shut; she could scream and scream for ever, and not a sound would escape.

But Pantalaimon, in answer, had twisted free of those hateful hands – he was a lion, an eagle; he tore at them with vicious talons, great wings beat wildly, and then he was a wolf, a bear, a polecat – darting, snarling, slashing, a succession of trans-formations too quick to register, and all the time leaping, flying, dodging from one spot to another as their clumsy hands flailed and snatched at the empty air.

But they had dæmons too, of course. It wasn't two against three, it was two against six. A badger, an owl and a baboon were all just as intent to pin Pantalaimon down, and Lyra was crying to them, "Why? Why are *you* doing this? Help us! You shouldn't be helping them!"

And she kicked and bit more passionately than ever, until the man holding her gasped and let go for a moment – and she was free, and Pantalaimon sprang towards her like a spark of lightning, and she clutched him to her fierce breast, and he dug his wildcat-claws into her flesh, and every stab of pain was dear to her.

"Never! Never! Never!" she cried, and backed against the wall to defend him to their death.

But they fell on her again, three big brutal men, and she was only a child, shocked and terrified; and they tore Pantalaimon away, and threw her into one side of the cage of mesh and carried him, struggling still, around to the other. There was a mesh bar-rier between them, but he was still part of her, they were still joined. For a second or so more, he was still her own dear soul.

Above the panting of the men, above her own sobs, above the high wild howl of her dæmon, Lyra heard a humming sound, and saw one man (bleeding from the nose) operate a bank of switches. The other two looked up, and her eyes followed theirs. The great pale silver blade was rising slowly, catching the brilliant light. The last moment in her complete life was going to be the worst by far.

"What is going on here?"

A light, musical voice: her voice. Everything stopped.

"What are you doing? And who is this child –"

She didn't complete the word *child*, because in that instant she recognized Lyra. Through tear-blurred eyes Lyra saw her totter and clutch at a bench; her face, so beautiful and composed, grew in a moment haggard and horror-struck.

"Lyra –" she whispered.

The golden monkey darted from her side in a flash, and tugged Pantalaimon out from the mesh cage as Lyra fell out herself. Pantalaimon pulled free of the monkey's solicitous paws and stumbled to Lyra's arms.

"Never, never," she breathed into his fur, and he pressed his beating heart to hers.

They clung together like survivors of a shipwreck, shivering on a desolate coast. Dimly she heard Mrs Coulter speaking to the men, but she couldn't even interpret her tone of voice. And then they were leaving that hateful room, and Mrs Coulter was half-carrying, half-supporting her along a corridor, and then there was a door, a bedroom, scent in the air, soft light.

Mrs Coulter laid her gently on the bed. Lyra's arm was so tight around Pantalaimon that she was trembling with the force of it. A tender hand stroked her head.

"My dear, dear child," said that sweet voice. "However did you come to be here?"

17

THE WITCHES

LYRA MOANED AND trembled uncontrollably, just as if she had been pulled out of water so cold that her heart had nearly frozen. Pantalaimon simply lay against her bare skin, inside her clothes, loving her back to herself, but aware all the time of Mrs Coulter, busy preparing a drink of something, and most of all of the golden monkey, whose hard little fingers had run swiftly over Lyra's body when only Pantalaimon could have noticed; and who had felt, around her waist, the oilskin pouch with its contents.

"Sit up, dear, and drink this," said Mrs Coulter, and her gentle arm slipped around Lyra's back and lifted her.

Lyra clenched herself, but relaxed almost at once as Pantalaimon thought to her: We're only safe as long as we pretend. She opened her eyes and found that they'd been containing tears, and to her surprise and shame she sobbed and sobbed.

Mrs Coulter made sympathetic sounds and put the drink into the monkey's hands while she mopped Lyra's eyes with a scented handkerchief.

"Cry as much as you need to, darling," said that soft voice, and Lyra determined to stop as soon as she possibly could. She struggled to hold back the tears, she pressed her lips together, she choked down the sobs that still shook her chest.

Pantalaimon played the same game: fool them, fool them. He became a mouse and crept away from Lyra's hand to sniff timidly at the drink in the monkey's clutch. It was innocuous: an infusion of camomile, nothing more. He crept back to Lyra's shoulder and whispered, "Drink it."

She sat up and took the hot cup in both hands, alternately sipping and blowing to cool it. She kept her eyes down. She must pretend harder than she'd ever done in her life.

"Lyra, darling," Mrs Coulter murmured, stroking her hair.

"I thought we'd lost you for ever! What happened? Did you get lost? Did someone take you out of the flat?"

"Yeah," Lyra whispered.

"Who was it, dear?"

"A man and a woman."

"Guests at the party?"

"I think so. They said you needed something that was downstairs and I went to get it and they grabbed hold of me and took me in a car somewhere. But when they stopped I ran out quick and dodged away and they never caught me. But I didn't know where I was . . ."

Another sob shook her briefly, but they were weaker now, and she could pretend this one was caused by her story.

"And I just wandered about trying to find my way back, only these Gobblers caught me . . . And they put me in a van with some other kids and took me somewhere, a big building, I dunno where it was."

With every second that went past, with every sentence she spoke, she felt a little strength flowing back. And now that she was doing something difficult and familiar and never quite predictable, namely lying, she felt a sort of mastery again, the same sense of complexity and control that the alethiometer gave her. She had to be careful not to say anything obviously impossible; she had to be vague in some places and invent plausible details in others; she had to be an artist, in short.

"How long did they keep you in this building?" said Mrs Coulter.

Lyra's journey along the canals and her time with the gyptians had taken weeks: she'd have to account for that time. She invented a voyage with the Gobblers to Trollesund, and then an escape, lavish with details from her observation of the town; and a time as maid-of-all-work at Einarsson's Bar, and then a spell working for a family of farmers inland, and then being caught by the Samoyeds and brought to Bolvangar.

"And they were going to – going to cut –"

"Hush, dear, hush. I'm going to find out what's been going on."

"But why were they going to do that? I never done anything

wrong! All the kids are afraid of what happens in there, and no one knows. But it's horrible. It's worse than anything . . . Why are they doing that, Mrs Coulter? Why are they so cruel?"

"There, there . . . You're safe, my dear. They won't ever do it to you. Now I know you're here, and you're safe, you'll never be in danger again. No one's going to harm you, Lyra darling; no one's ever going to hurt you . . ."

"But they do it to other children! Why?"

"Ah, my love –"

"It's Dust, isn't it?"

"Did they tell you that? Did the doctors say that?"

"The kids know it. All the kids talk about it, but no one knows! And they nearly done it to me – you got to tell me! You got no right to keep it secret, not any more!"

"Lyra . . . Lyra, Lyra. Darling, these are big difficult ideas, Dust and so on. It's not something for children to worry about. But the doctors do it for the children's own good, my love. Dust is something bad, something wrong, something evil and wicked. Grown-ups and their dæmons are infected with Dust so deeply that it's too late for them. They can't be helped . . . But a quick operation on children means they're safe from it. Dust just won't stick to them ever again. They're safe and happy and –"

Lyra thought of little Tony Makarios. She leaned forward suddenly and retched. Mrs Coulter moved back and let go.

"Are you all right, dear? Go to the bathroom –"

Lyra swallowed hard and brushed her eyes.

"You don't have to do that to us," she said. "You could just leave us. I bet Lord Asriel wouldn't let anyone do that if he knew what was going on. If he's got Dust and you've got Dust, and the Master of Jordan and every other grown-up's got Dust, it must be all right. When I get out I'm going to tell all the kids in the world about this. Anyway, if it was so good, why'd you stop them doing it to me? If it was good you should've let them do it. You should have been glad."

Mrs Coulter was shaking her head and smiling a sad wise smile.

"Darling," she said, "some of what's good has to hurt us a little, and naturally it's upsetting for others if *you're* upset . . . But it doesn't mean your dæmon is taken away from you. He's still there! Goodness me, a lot of the grown-ups here have had the operation. The nurses seem happy enough, don't they?"

Lyra blinked. Suddenly she understood their strange blank incuriosity, the way their little trotting dæmons seemed to be sleepwalking.

Say nothing, she thought, and shut her mouth hard.

"Darling, no one would ever dream of performing an operation on a child without testing it first. And no one in a thousand years would take a child's dæmon away altogether! All that happens is a little cut, and then everything's peaceful. For ever! You see, your dæmon's a wonderful friend and companion when you're young, but at the age we call puberty, the age you're coming to very soon, darling, dæmons bring all sorts of troublesome thoughts and feelings, and that's what lets Dust in. A quick little operation before that, and you're never troubled again. And your dæmon stays with you, only ... just not connected. Like a ... like a wonderful pet, if you like. The best pet in the world! Wouldn't you like that?"

Oh, the wicked liar, oh, the shameless untruths she was telling! And even if Lyra hadn't known them to be lies (Tony Makarios; those caged dæmons) she would have hated it with a furious passion. Her dear soul, the darling companion of her heart, to be cut away and reduced to a little trotting *pet*? Lyra nearly blazed with hatred, and Pantalaimon in her arms became a polecat, the most ugly and vicious of all his forms, and snarled.

But they said nothing. Lyra held Pantalaimon tight and let Mrs Coulter stroke her hair.

"Drink up your camomile," said Mrs Coulter softly. "We'll have them make up a bed for you in here. There's no need to go back and share a dormitory with other girls, not now I've got my little assistant back. My favourite! The best assistant in the world. D'you know, we searched all over London for you, darling? We had the police searching every town in the land. Oh, I missed you so much! I can't tell you how happy I am to find you again ..."

All the time, the golden monkey was prowling about restlessly, one minute perching on the table swinging his tail, the next clinging to Mrs Coulter and chittering softly in her ear, the next pacing the floor with tail erect. He was betraying Mrs Coulter's impatience, of course, and finally she couldn't hold it in.

"Lyra, dear," she said, "I think that the Master of Jordan gave you something before you left. Isn't that right? He gave you an alethiometer. The trouble is, it wasn't his to give. It was left in his care. It's really too valuable to be carried about – d'you know, it's one of only two or three in the world! I think the Master gave it to you in the hope that it would fall into Lord Asriel's hands. He told you not to tell me about it, didn't he?"

Lyra twisted her mouth.

"Yes, I can see. Well, never mind, darling, because you *didn't* tell me, did you? So you haven't broken any promises. But listen, dear, it really ought to be properly looked after. I'm afraid it's so rare and delicate that we can't let it be at risk any longer."

"Why shouldn't Lord Asriel have it?" Lyra said, not moving.

"Because of what he's doing. You know he's been sent away to exile, because he's got something dangerous and wicked in mind. He needs the alethiometer to finish his plan, but believe me, dear, the last thing anyone should do is let him have it. The Master of Jordan was sadly mistaken. But now that you know, it really would be better to let me have it, wouldn't it? It would save you the trouble of carrying it around, and all the worry of looking after it – and really it must have been such a puzzle, wondering what a silly old thing like that was any good for..."

Lyra wondered how she had ever, ever, ever found this woman to be so fascinating and clever.

"So if you've got it now, dear, you'd really better let me have it to look after. It's in that belt around your waist, isn't it? Yes, that was a clever thing to do, putting it away like this..."

Her hands were at Lyra's skirt, and then she was unfastening the stiff oilcloth. Lyra tensed herself. The golden monkey was crouching at the end of the bed, trembling with anticipation, little black hands to his mouth. Mrs Coulter pulled the belt away from Lyra's waist and unbuttoned the pouch. She was breathing fast. She took out the black velvet cloth and unfolded it, finding the tin box Iorek Byrnison had made.

Pantalaimon was a cat again, tensed to spring. Lyra drew her legs up away from Mrs Coulter, and swung them down to the floor so that she too could run when the time came.

"What's this?" said Mrs Coulter, as if amused. "What a funny old tin! Did you put it in here to keep it safe, dear? All this moss . . . You have been careful, haven't you? Another tin, inside the first one! And soldered! Who did this, dear?"

She was too intent on opening it to wait for an answer. She had a knife in her handbag with a lot of different attachments, and she pulled out a blade and dug it under the lid.

At once a furious buzzing filled the room.

Lyra and Pantalaimon held themselves still. Mrs Coulter, puzzled, curious, pulled at the lid, and the golden monkey bent close to look.

Then in a dazzling moment the black form of the spy-fly hurtled out of the tin and crashed hard into the monkey's face.

He screamed and flung himself backwards; and of course it was hurting Mrs Coulter too, and she cried out in pain and fright with the monkey, and then the little clockwork devil swarmed upwards at her, up her breast and throat towards her face.

Lyra didn't hesitate. Pantalaimon sprang for the door and she was after him at once, and she tore it open and raced away faster than she had ever run in her life.

"Fire alarm!" Pantalaimon shrieked, as he flew ahead of her.

She saw a button on the next corner, and smashed the glass with her desperate fist. She ran on, heading towards the dormitories, smashed another alarm and another, and then people began to come out into the corridor, looking up and down for the fire.

By this time she was near the kitchen, and Pantalaimon flashed a thought into her mind, and she darted in. A moment later she had turned on all the gas taps and flung a match at the nearest burner. Then she dragged a bag of flour from a shelf and hurled it at the edge of a table so it burst and filled the air with white, because she had heard that flour will explode if it's treated like that near a flame.

Then she ran out and on as fast as she could towards her own dormitory. The corridors were full now: children running this way and that, vivid with excitement, for the word *escape* had got around. The oldest were making for the store-rooms where the clothing was kept, and herding the younger ones with them. Adults were trying to control it all, and none of them knew what was happening. Shouting, pushing, crying, jostling people were everywhere.

Through it all Lyra and Pantalaimon darted like fish, making always for the dormitory, and just as they reached it, there was a dull explosion from behind that shook the building.

The other girls had fled: the room was empty. Lyra dragged the locker to the corner, jumped up, hauled the furs out of the ceiling, felt for the alethiometer. It was still there. She tugged the furs on quickly, pulling the hood forward, and then Pantalaimon, a sparrow at the door, called:

"Now!"

She ran out. By luck a group of children who'd already found some cold-weather clothing were racing down the corridor towards the main entrance, and she joined them, sweating, her heart thumping, knowing that she had to escape or die.

The way was blocked. The fire in the kitchen had taken quickly, and whether it was the flour or the gas, something had brought down part of the roof. People were clambering over twisted struts and girders to get up to the bitter cold air. The smell of gas was strong. Then came another explosion, louder than the first and closer. The blast knocked several people over, and cries of fear and pain filled the air.

Lyra struggled up, and with Pantalaimon calling, "This way! This way!" among the other dæmon-cries and flutterings, she hauled herself over the rubble. The air she was breathing was frozen, and she hoped that the children had managed to find their outdoor clothing; it would be a fine thing to escape from the Station only to die of cold.

There really was a blaze now. When she got out on to the roof under the night sky she could see flames licking at the edges of a great hole in the side of the building. There was a throng of children and adults by the main entrance, but this time the adults were more agitated and the children more fearful: much more fearful.

"Roger! Roger!" Lyra called, and Pantalaimon, keen-eyed as an owl, hooted that he'd seen him.

A moment later they found each other.

"Tell 'em all to come with me!" Lyra shouted into his ear.

"They won't – they're all panicky –"

"Tell 'em what they do to the kids that vanish! They cut their dæmons off with a big knife! Tell 'em what you saw this afternoon – all them dæmons we let out! Tell 'em that's going to happen to them too unless they get away!"

Roger gaped, horrified, but then collected his wits and ran to the nearest group of hesitating children. Lyra did the same, and as the message passed along, some children cried out and clutched their dæmons in fear.

"Come with me!" Lyra shouted. "There's a rescue a-coming! We got to get out the compound! Come on, run!"

The children heard her and followed, streaming across the enclosure towards the avenue of lights, their boots pattering and creaking in the hard-packed snow.

Behind them adults were shouting, and there was a rumble and crash as another part of the building fell in. Sparks gushed into the air, and flames billowed out with a sound like tearing cloth; but cutting through this came another sound, dreadfully close and violent. Lyra had never heard it before, but she knew it at once: it was the howl of the Tartar guards' wolf-dæmons. She felt weak from head to foot, and many children turned in fear and stumbled to a stop, for there running at a low swift tireless lope came the first of the Tartar guards, rifle at the ready, with the mighty leaping greyness of his dæmon beside him.

Then came another, and another. They were all in padded mail, and they had no eyes – or at least you couldn't see any eyes behind the snow-slits of their helmets. The only eyes you could see were the round black ends of the rifle-barrels and the blazing yellow eyes of the wolf-dæmons above the slaver dripping from their jaws.

Lyra faltered. She hadn't dreamed of how frightening those wolves were. And now that she knew how casually people at Bolvangar broke the great taboo, she shrank from the thought of those dripping teeth . . .

The Tartars ran to stand in a line across the entrance to the avenue of lights, their dæmons beside them as disciplined and drilled as they were. In another minute there'd be a second line, because more were coming, and more behind them. Lyra thought with despair: children can't fight soldiers. It wasn't like the battles in the Oxford Claybeds, hurling lumps of mud at the brick-burners' children.

Or perhaps it was! She remembered hurling a handful of clay in the broad face of a brick-burner boy bearing down on her. He'd stopped to claw the stuff out of his eyes, and then the townies leapt on him.

She'd been standing in the mud. She was standing in the snow.

Just as she'd done that afternoon, but in deadly earnest now, she scooped a handful together and hurled it at the nearest soldier.

"Get 'em in the eyes!" she yelled, and threw another.

Other children joined in, and then someone's dæmon had the notion of flying as a swift beside the snowball and nudging it directly at the eye-slits of the target – and then they all joined in, and in a few moments the Tartars were stumbling about spitting and cursing and trying to brush the packed snow out of the narrow gap in front of their eyes.

"Come on!" Lyra screamed, and flung herself at the gate into the avenue of lights.

The children streamed after her, every one, dodging the snapping jaws of the wolves and racing as hard as they could down the avenue towards the beckoning open dark beyond.

A harsh scream came from behind as an officer shouted an order, and then a score of rifle bolts worked at once, and then there was another scream and a tense silence, with only the fleeing children's pounding feet and gasping breath to be heard.

They were taking aim. They wouldn't miss.

But before they could fire, a choking gasp came from one of the Tartars, and a cry of surprise from another.

Lyra stopped and turned to see a man lying on the snow, with a grey-feathered arrow in his back. He was writhing and twitching and coughing out blood, and the other soldiers were looking around to left and right for whoever had fired it, but the archer was nowhere to be seen.

And then an arrow came flying straight down from the sky,

and struck another man behind the head. He fell at once. A shout from the officer, and everyone looked up at the dark sky.

"Witches!" said Pantalaimon.

And so they were: ragged elegant black shapes sweeping past high above, with a hiss and swish of air through the needles of the cloud-pine branches they flew on. As Lyra watched, one swooped low and loosed an arrow: another man fell.

And then all the Tartars turned their rifles up and blazed into the dark, firing at nothing, at shadows, at clouds, and more and more arrows rained down on them.

But the officer in charge, seeing the children almost away, ordered a squad to race after them. Some children screamed. And then more screamed, and they weren't moving forward any more, they were turning back in confusion, terrified by the monstrous shape hurtling towards them from the dark beyond the avenue of lights.

"Iorek Byrnison!" cried Lyra, her chest nearly bursting with joy.

The armoured bear at the charge seemed to be conscious of no weight except what gave him momentum. He bounded past Lyra almost in a blur and crashed into the Tartars, scattering soldiers, dæmons, rifles to all sides. Then he stopped and whirled round, with a lithe athletic power, and struck two massive blows, one to each side, at the guards closest to him.

A wolf-dæmon leapt at him: he slashed at her in mid-air, and bright fire spilled out of her as she fell to the snow, where she hissed and howled before vanishing. Her human died at once.

The Tartar officer, faced with this double attack, didn't hesitate. A long high scream of orders, and the force divided itself into two: one to keep off the witches, the bigger part to overcome the bear. His troops were magnificently brave. They dropped to one knee in groups of four and fired their rifles as if they were on the practice range, not budging an inch as Iorek's mighty bulk hurtled towards them. A moment later they were dead.

Iorek struck again, twisting to one side, slashing, snarling, crushing, while bullets flew about him like wasps or flies, doing no harm at all. Lyra urged the children on and out into the darkness beyond the lights. They must get away, because dangerous as the Tartars were, far more dangerous were the adults of Bolvangar.

So she called and beckoned and pushed to get the children moving. As the lights behind them threw long shadows on the snow, Lyra found her heart moving out towards the deep dark of the Arctic night and the clean coldness, leaping forward to love it as Pantalaimon was doing, a hare now delighting in his own propulsion.

"Where we going?" someone said.

"There's nothing out here but snow!"

"There's a rescue party coming," Lyra told them. "There's fifty gyptians or more. I bet there's some relations of yours, too. All the gyptian families that lost a kid, they all sent someone."

"I en't a gyptian," a boy said.

"Don't matter. They'll take you anyway."

"Where?" someone said querulously.

"Home," said Lyra. "That's what I come here for, to rescue you, and I brung the gyptians here to take you home again. We just got to go on a bit further and then we'll find 'em. The bear was with 'em, so they can't be far off."

"D'you see that bear!" one boy was saying. "When he slashed open that dæmon – the man died as if someone whipped his heart out, just like that!"

"I never knew dæmons could be killed," someone else said.

They were all talking now; the excitement and relief had loosened everyone's tongue. As long as they kept moving, it didn't matter if they talked.

"Is that true," said a girl, "about what they do back there?"

"Yeah," Lyra said. "I never thought I'd ever see anyone without their dæmon. But on the way here, we found this boy on his own without any dæmon. He kept asking for her, where she was, would she ever find him. He was called Tony Makarios."

"I know him!" said someone, and others joined in: "Yeah, they took him away about a week back . . ."

"Well, they cut his dæmon away," said Lyra, knowing how it would affect them. "And a little bit after we found him, he died. And all the dæmons they cut away, they kept them in cages in a square building back there."

"It's true," said Roger. "And Lyra let 'em out during the fire drill."

"Yeah, I seen 'em!" said Billy Costa. "I didn't know what they was at first, but I seen 'em fly away with that goose."

"But why do they do it?" demanded one boy. "Why do they cut people's dæmons away? That's torture! Why do they do it?"

"Dust," suggested someone doubtfully.

But the boy laughed in scorn. "Dust!" he said. "There en't no such thing! They just made that up! I don't believe in it."

"Here," said someone else, "look what's happening to the zeppelin!"

They all looked back. Beyond the dazzle of lights, where the fight was still continuing, the great length of the airship was not floating freely, at the mooring mast any longer; the free end was drooping downwards, and beyond it was rising a globe of –

"Lee Scoresby's balloon!" Lyra cried, and clapped her mittened hands with delight.

The other children were baffled. Lyra herded them onwards, wondering how the aëronaut had got his balloon that far. It was clear what he was doing, and what a good idea, to fill his balloon with the gas out of theirs, to escape by the same means that crippled their pursuit!

"Come on, keep moving, else you'll freeze," she said, for some of the children were shivering and moaning from the cold, and their dæmons were crying too in high thin voices.

Pantalaimon found this irritating, and as a wolverine he snapped at one girl's squirrel-dæmon who was just lying across her shoulder whimpering faintly.

"Get in her coat! Make yourself big and warm her up!" he snarled, and the girl's dæmon, frightened, crept inside her coal-silk anorak at once.

The trouble was that coal-silk wasn't as warm as proper fur, no matter how much it was padded out with hollow coal-silk fibres. Some of the children looked like walking puffballs, they were so bulky, but their gear had been made in factories and laboratories far away from the cold, and it couldn't really cope. Lyra's furs looked ragged and they stank, but they kept the warmth in.

"If we don't find the gyptians soon they en't going to last," she whispered to Pantalaimon.

"Keep 'em moving, then," he whispered back. "If they lie down they're finished. You know what Farder Coram said . . ."

Farder Coram had told her many tales of his own journeys in the North, and so had Mrs Coulter – always supposing that hers were true. But they were both quite clear about one point, which was that you must keep going.

"How far we gotta go?" said a little boy.

"She's just making us walk out here to kill us," said a girl.

"Rather be out here than back there," someone said.

"I wouldn't! It's warm back in the Station. There's food and hot drinks and everything."

"But it's all on fire!"

"What we going to do out here? I bet we starve to death . . ."

Lyra's mind was full of dark questions that flew around like witches, swift and untouchable, and somewhere, just beyond where she could reach, there was a glory and a thrill which she didn't understand at all.

But it gave her a surge of strength, and she hauled one girl up out of a snowdrift, and shoved at a boy who was dawdling, and called to them all: "Keep going! Follow the bear's tracks! He come up with the gyptians, so the track'll lead us to where they are! Just keep walking!"

Big flakes of snow were beginning to fall. Soon it would have covered Iorek Byrnison's tracks altogether. Now that they were out of sight of the lights of Bolvangar, and the blaze of the fire was only a faint glow, the only light came from the faint radiance of the snow-covered ground. Thick clouds obscured the sky, so there was neither moon nor Northern Lights; but by peering closely, the children could make out the deep trail Iorek Byrnison had ploughed in the snow. Lyra encouraged, bullied, hit, half-carried, swore at, pushed, dragged, lifted tenderly, wherever it was needed, and Pantalaimon (by the state of each child's dæmon) told her what was needed in each case.

I'll get 'em there, she kept saying to herself. I come here to get 'em and I'll bloody get 'em.

Roger was following her example, and Billy Costa was leading

the way, being sharper-eyed than most. Soon the snow was falling so thickly that they had to cling on to one another to keep
from getting lost, and Lyra thought, perhaps if we all lie close and
keep warm like that . . . Dig holes in the snow . . .

She was hearing things. There was the snarl of an engine somewhere, not the heavy thump of a zeppelin but something higher
like the drone of a hornet. It drifted in and out of hearing.

And howling . . . Dogs? Sledge dogs? That too was distant and
hard to be sure of, blanketed by millions of snowflakes and blown
this way and that by little puffing gusts of wind. It might have
been the gyptians' sledge dogs, or it might have been wild spirits
of the tundra, or even those freed dæmons crying for their lost
children.

She was seeing things . . . There weren't any lights in the snow,
were there? They must be ghosts as well . . . Unless they'd come
round in a circle, and were stumbling back into Bolvangar.

But these were little yellow lantern-beams, not the white glare
of anbaric lights. And they were moving, and the howling was
nearer, and before she knew for certain whether she'd fallen
asleep, Lyra was wandering among familiar figures, and men in
furs were holding her up: John Faa's mighty arm lifted her clear
of the ground, and Farder Coram was laughing with pleasure;
and as far through the blizzard as she could see, gyptians were
lifting children into sledges, covering them with furs, giving
them seal-meat to chew. And Tony Costa was there, hugging
Billy and then punching him softly only to hug him again and
shake him for joy. And Roger . . .

"Roger's coming with us," she said to Farder Coram. "It was
him I meant to get in the first place. We'll go back to Jordan in
the end. What's that noise – "

It was that snarl again, that engine, like a crazed spy-fly ten
thousand times the size.

Suddenly there came a blow that sent her sprawling, and
Pantalaimon couldn't defend her, because the golden monkey –
Mrs Coulter –

The golden monkey was wrestling, biting, scratching at
Pantalaimon, who was flickering through so many changes of
form it was hard to see him, and fighting back: stinging, lashing,

tearing. Mrs Coulter, meanwhile, her face in its furs a frozen glare of intense feeling, was dragging Lyra to the back of a motorized sledge, and Lyra struggled as hard as her dæmon. The snow was so thick that they seemed to be isolated in a little blizzard of their own, and the anbaric headlights of the sledge only showed up the thick swirling flakes a few inches ahead.

"Help!" Lyra cried, to the gyptians who were just *there* in the blinding snow and who could see nothing. "Help me! Farder Coram! Lord Faa! Oh God, help!"

Mrs Coulter shrieked a high command in the language of the northern Tartars. The snow swirled open, and there they were, a squad of them, armed with rifles, and the wolf-dæmons snarled beside them. The chief saw Mrs Coulter struggling, and picked up Lyra with one hand as if she were a doll and threw her into the sledge, where she lay stunned and dazed.

A rifle banged, and then another, as the gyptians realized what was happening. But firing at targets you can't see is dangerous when you can't see your own side either. The Tartars, in a tight group now around the sledge, were able to blaze at will into the snow, but the gyptians dared not shoot back for fear of hitting Lyra.

Oh, the bitterness she felt! The tiredness!

Still dazed, with her head ringing, she hauled herself up to find Pantalaimon desperately fighting the monkey still, with wolverine-jaws fastened tight in a golden arm, changing no more but grimly hanging on. And who was that?

Not Roger?

Yes, Roger, battering at Mrs Coulter with fists and feet, hurtling his head against hers, only to be struck down by a Tartar who swiped at him like someone brushing away a fly. It was all a phantasmagoria now: white, black, a swift green flutter across her vision, ragged shadows, racing light –

A great swirl lifted curtains of snow aside, and into the cleared area leapt Iorek Byrnison, with a clang and screech of iron on iron. A moment later and those great jaws snapped left, right, a paw ripped open a mailed chest, white teeth, black iron, red wet fur –

Then something was pulling her *up* powerfully, *up*, and she seized Roger too, tearing him out of the hands of Mrs Coulter and clinging tight, each child's dæmon a shrill bird fluttering in amazement as a greater fluttering swept all around them, and then Lyra saw in the air beside her a witch, one of those elegant ragged black shadows from the high air, but close enough to touch; and there was a bow in the witch's bare hands, and she exerted her bare pale arms (in this freezing air!) to pull the string and then loose an arrow into the eye-slit of a mailed and louring Tartar hood only three feet away –

And the arrow sped in and halfway out at the back, and the man's wolf-dæmon vanished in mid-leap even before he hit the ground.

Up! Into mid-air Lyra and Roger were caught and swept, and found themselves clinging with weakening fingers to a cloud-pine branch, where the young witch was sitting tense with balanced grace, and then she leant down and to the left and something huge was looming and there was the ground.

They tumbled into the snow beside the basket of Lee Scoresby's balloon.

"Skip inside," called the Texan, "and bring your friend, by all means. Have ye seen that bear?"

Lyra saw that three witches were holding a rope looped around a rock, anchoring the great buoyancy of the gas-bag to the earth.

"Get in!" she cried to Roger, and scrambled over the leather-bound rim of the basket to fall in a snowy heap inside. A moment later Roger fell on top of her, and then a mighty noise halfway between a roar and a growl made the very ground shake.

"C'mon, Iorek! On board, old feller!" yelled Lee Scoresby, and over the side came the bear in a hideous creak of wicker and bending wood.

Then a swirl of lighter air lifted the mist and snow aside for a moment, and in the sudden clearance Lyra saw everything that was happening around them. She saw a party of gyptian raiders under John Faa harrying the Tartar rearguard and sweeping them back towards the blazing ruins of Bolvangar; she saw the other gyptians helping child after child safe aboard their sledges, tucking them warmly down under the furs; she saw

Farder Coram casting around anxiously, leaning on his stick, his autumn-coloured dæmon leaping through the snow and looking this way and that.

"Farder Coram!" Lyra cried. "Over here!"

The old man heard, and turned to look in amazement at the balloon straining against the rope and the witches holding it down, at Lyra waving frantically from the basket.

"Lyra!" he cried. "You're safe, gal? You're safe?"

"As safe as I ever was!" she shouted back. "Goodbye, Farder Coram! Goodbye! Take all the kids back home!"

"We'll do that, sure as I live! Go well, my child – go well – go well, my dear –"

And at the same moment the aëronaut lowered his arm in a signal, and the witches let go of the rope.

The balloon lifted immediately and surged upwards into the snow-thick air at a rate Lyra could scarcely believe. After a moment the ground disappeared in the mist, and up they went, faster and faster, so that she thought no rocket could have left the earth more swiftly. She lay holding on to Roger on the floor of the basket, pressed down by the acceleration.

Lee Scoresby was cheering and laughing and uttering wild Texan yells of delight; Iorek Byrnison was calmly unfastening his armour, hooking a deft claw into all the linkages and undoing them with a twist before packing the separate pieces in a pile. Somewhere outside, the flap and swish of air through cloud-pine needles and witch-garments told that the witches were keeping them company into the upper airs.

Little by little Lyra recovered her breath, her balance and her heartbeat. She sat up and looked around.

The basket was much bigger than she'd thought. Ranged around the edges were racks of philosophical instruments, and there were piles of furs, and bottled air, and a variety of other things too small or confusing to make out in the thick mist they were ascending through.

"Is this a cloud?" she said.

"Sure is. Wrap your friend in some furs before he turns into an icicle. It's cold here but it's gonna get colder."

"How did you find us?"

"Witches. There's one witch-lady who wants to talk to you. When we get clear of the cloud we'll get our bearings and then we can sit and have a yarn."

"Iorek," said Lyra, "thank you for coming."

The bear grunted, and settled down to lick the blood off his fur. His weight meant that the basket was tilted to one side, but that didn't matter. Roger was wary, but Iorek Byrnison took no more notice of him than of a flake of snow. Lyra contented herself with clinging to the rim of the basket, just under her chin when she was standing, and peering wide-eyed into the swirling cloud.

Only a few seconds later the balloon passed out of the cloud altogether and, still rising rapidly, soared on into the heavens.

What a sight!

Directly above them the balloon swelled out in a huge curve. Above and ahead of them the Aurora was blazing, with more brilliance and grandeur than she had ever seen. It was all around, or nearly, and they were nearly part of it. Great swathes of incandescence trembled and parted like angels' wings beating; cascades of luminescent glory tumbled down invisible crags to lie in swirling pools or hang like vast waterfalls.

So Lyra gasped at that, and then she looked below, and saw a sight almost more wondrous.

As far as the eye could see, to the very horizon in all directions, a tumbled sea of white extended without a break. Soft peaks and vaporous chasms rose or opened here and there, but mostly it looked like a solid mass of ice.

And rising through it in ones and twos and larger groups as well came small black shadows, those ragged figures of such elegance, witches on their branches of cloud-pine.

They flew swiftly, without any effort, up and towards the balloon, leaning to one side or another to steer. And one of them, the archer who'd saved Lyra from Mrs Coulter, flew directly alongside the basket, and Lyra saw her clearly for the first time.

She was young – younger than Mrs Coulter; and fair, with bright green eyes; and clad like all the witches in strips of black silk, but wearing no furs, no hood or mittens. She seemed to feel no cold at all. Around her brow was a simple chain of little red flowers. She sat her cloud-pine branch as if it were a steed, and seemed to rein it in a yard from Lyra's wondering gaze.

"Lyra?"

"Yes! And are you Serafina Pekkala?"

"I am."

Lyra could see why Farder Coram loved her, and why it was breaking his heart, though she had known neither of those things a moment before. He was growing old; he was an old broken man; and she would be young for generations.

"Have you got the symbol-reader?" said the witch, in a voice so like the high wild singing of the Aurora itself that Lyra could hardly hear the sense for the sweet sound of it.

"Yes. I got it in my pocket, safe."

Great wing-beats told of another arrival, and then he was gliding beside her: the grey goose-dæmon. He spoke briefly and then wheeled away to glide in a wide circle around the balloon as it continued to rise.

"The gyptians have laid waste to Bolvangar," said Serafina Pekkala. "They have killed twenty-two guards and nine of the staff, and they've set light to every part of the buildings that still stood. They are going to destroy it completely."

"What about Mrs Coulter?"

"No sign of her."

She cried out in a wild yell, and other witches circled and flew in towards the balloon.

"Mr Scoresby," she said. "The rope, if you please."

"Ma'am, I'm very grateful. We're still rising. I guess we'll go on up a while yet. How many of you will it take to pull us north?"

"We are strong," was all she said.

Lee Scoresby was attaching a coil of stout rope to the leather-covered iron ring that gathered the ropes running over the gas-bag, and from which the basket itself was suspended. When it was securely fixed, he threw the free end out, and at once six witches darted towards it, caught hold, and began to pull, urging the cloud-pine branches towards the Polar Star.

As the balloon began to move in that direction, Pantalaimon came to perch on the edge of the basket as a tern. Roger's dæmon came out to look, but crept back again soon, for Roger was fast asleep, as was Iorek Byrnison. Only Lee Scoresby was awake, calmly chewing a thin cigar and watching his instruments.

"So, Lyra," said Serafina Pekkala. "Do you know why you're going to Lord Asriel?"

Lyra was astonished. "To take him the alethiometer, of course!" she said.

She had never considered the question; it was obvious. Then she recalled her first motive, from so long ago that she'd almost forgotten it.

"Or . . . To help him escape. That's it. We're going to help him get away."

But as she said that, it sounded absurd. Escape from Svalbard? Impossible!

"Try, anyway," she added stoutly. "Why?"

"I think there are things I need to tell you," said Serafina Pekkala.

"About Dust?"

It was the first thing Lyra wanted to know.

"Yes, among other things. But you are tired now, and it will be a long flight. We'll talk when you wake up."

Lyra yawned. It was a jaw-cracking, lung-bursting yawn that lasted almost a minute, or felt like it, and for all that Lyra struggled, she couldn't resist the onrush of sleep. Serafina Pekkala reached a hand over the rim of the basket and touched her eyes, and as Lyra sank to the floor, Pantalaimon fluttered down, changed to an ermine, and crawled to his sleeping-place by her neck.

The witch settled her branch into a steady speed beside the basket as they moved north towards Svalbard.

PART THREE: SVALBARD

18

FOG AND ICE

LEE SCORESBY ARRANGED some furs over Lyra. She curled up close to Roger and they lay together asleep as the balloon swept on towards the Pole. The aëronaut checked his instruments from time to time, chewed on the cigar he would never light with the inflammable hydrogen so close, and huddled deeper into his own furs.

"This little girl's pretty important, huh?" he said after several minutes.

"More than she will know," Serafina Pekkala said.

"Does that mean there's gonna be much in the way of armed pursuit? You understand, I'm speaking as a practical man with a living to earn. I can't afford to get busted up or shot to pieces without some kind of compensation agreed in advance. I ain't trying to lower the tone of this expedition, believe me, ma'am. But John Faa and the gyptians paid me a fee that's enough to cover my time and skill and the normal wear and tear on the balloon, and that's all. It didn't include acts-of-war insurance. And let me tell you, ma'am, when we land Iorek Byrnison on Svalbard, that will count as an act of war."

He spat a piece of smoke-leaf delicately overboard.

"So I'd like to know what we can expect in the way of may-hem and ructions," he finished.

"There may be fighting," said Serafina Pekkala. "But you have fought before."

"Sure, when I'm paid. But the fact is, I thought this was a straightforward transportation contract, and I charged according. And I'm a-wondering now, after that little dust-up down there, I'm a-wondering how far my transportation responsibility extends. Whether I'm bound to risk my life and my equipment in a war among the bears, for example. Or whether this little child has enemies on Svalbard as hot-tempered as the ones back at Bolvangar. I merely mention all this by way of making conversation."

"Mr Scoresby," said the witch, "I wish I could answer your question. All I can say is that all of us, humans, witches, bears, are engaged in a war already, although not all of us know it. Whether you find danger on Svalbard or whether you fly off unharmed, you are a recruit, under arms, a soldier."

"Well, that seems kinda precipitate. Seems to me a man should have a choice whether to take up arms or not."

"We have no more choice in that than in whether or not to be born."

"Oh, I like choice, though," he said. "I like choosing the jobs I take and the places I go and the food I eat and the companions I sit and yarn with. Don't you wish for a choice once in a while?"

Serafina Pekkala considered, and then said, "Perhaps we don't mean the same thing by *choice*, Mr Scoresby. Witches own nothing, so we're not interested in preserving value or making profits, and as for the choice between one thing and another, when you live for many hundreds of years you know that every opportunity will come again. We have different needs. You have to repair your balloon and keep it in good condition, and that takes time and trouble, I see that; but for us to fly, all we have to do is tear off a branch of cloud-pine; any will do, and there are plenty more. We don't feel cold, so we need no warm clothes. We have no means of exchange apart from mutual aid. If a witch needs something, another witch will give it to her. If there is a war to be fought, we don't consider cost one of the factors in deciding whether or not it is right to fight. Nor do we have any notion of honour, as bears do, for instance. An insult to a bear is a deadly thing. To us ... inconceivable. How could you insult a witch? What would it matter if you did?"

"Well, I'm kinda with you on that. Sticks and stones, I'll break yer bones, but names ain't worth a quarrel. But ma'am, you see my dilemma, I hope. I'm a simple aëronaut, and I'd like to end my days in comfort. Buy a little farm, a few head of cattle, some horses ... Nothing grand, you notice. No palace or slaves or heaps of gold. Just the evening wind over the sage, and a ceegar, and a glass of bourbon whiskey. Now the trouble is, that costs money. So I do my flying in exchange for cash, and after every job I send some gold back to the Wells Fargo Bank, and when I've got enough, ma'am, I'm gonna sell this balloon and book me a passage on a steamer to Port Galveston, and I'll never leave the ground again."

"There's another difference between us, Mr Scoresby. A witch would no sooner give up flying than give up breathing. To fly is to be perfectly ourselves."

"I see that, ma'am, and I envy you; but I ain't got your sources of satisfaction. Flying is just a job to me, and I'm just a technician. I might as well be adjusting valves in a gas-engine or wiring up anbaric circuits. But I chose it, you see. It was my own free choice. Which is why I find this notion of a war I ain't been told nothing about, kinda troubling."

"Iorek Byrnison's quarrel with his king is part of it too," said the witch. "This child is destined to play a part in that."

"You speak of destiny," he said, "as if it was fixed. And I ain't sure I like that any more than a war I'm enlisted in without knowing about it. Where's my free will, if you please? And this child seems to me to have more free will than anyone I ever met. Are you telling me that she's just some kind of clockwork toy wound up and set going on a course she can't change?"

"We are all subject to the fates. But we must all act as if we are not," said the witch, "or die of despair. There is a curious prophecy about this child: she is destined to bring about the end of destiny. But she must do so without knowing what she is doing, as if it were her nature and not her destiny to do it. If she's told what she must do, it will all fail; death will sweep through all the worlds; it will be the triumph of despair, for ever. The universes will all become nothing more than interlocking machines, blind and empty of thought, feeling, life . . ."

They looked down at Lyra, whose sleeping face (what little they could see inside her hood) wore a stubborn little frown.

"I guess part of her knows that," said the aëronaut. "Looks prepared for it, anyways. How about the little boy? You know she came all this way to save him from those fiends back there? They were playmates, back in Oxford or somewhere. Did you know that?"

"Yes, I did know that. Lyra is carrying something of immense value, and it seems that the fates are using her as a messenger to take it to her father. So she came all this way to find her friend, not knowing that her friend was brought to the North by the fates, in order that she might follow and bring something to her father."

"That's how you read it, huh?"

For the first time the witch seemed unsure.

"That is how it seems . . . But we can't read the darkness, Mr Scoresby. It is more than possible that I might be wrong."

"And what brought *you* into all this, if I can ask?"

"Whatever they were doing at Bolvangar, we felt it was wrong with all our hearts. Lyra is their enemy; so we are her friends. We don't see more clearly than that. But also there is my clan's friendship for the gyptian people, which goes back to the time when Farder Coram saved my life. We are doing this at their bidding. And they have ties of obligation with Lord Asriel."

"I see. So you're towing the balloon to Svalbard for the gyptians' sake. And does that friendship extend to towing us back again? Or will I have to wait for a kindly wind, and depend on the indulgence of the bears in the meantime? Once again, ma'am, I'm asking merely in a spirit of friendly enquiry."

"If we can help you back to Trollesund, Mr Scoresby, we shall do so. But we don't know what we shall meet on Svalbard. The bears' new king has made many changes; the old ways are out of favour; it might be a difficult landing. And I don't know how Lyra will find her way to her father. Nor do I know what Iorek Byrnison has it in mind to do, except that his fate is involved with hers."

"I don't know either, ma'am. I think he's attached himself to the little girl as a kind of protector. She helped him get his armour back, you see. Who knows what bears feel? But if a bear ever loved a human being, he loves her. As for landing on Svalbard, it's never been easy. Still, if I can call on you for a tug in the right direction, I'll feel kinda easier in my mind; and if there's anything I can do for you in return, you only have to say. But just so as I know, would you mind telling me whose side I'm on in this invisible war?"

"We are both on Lyra's side."

"Oh, no doubt about that."

They flew on. Because of the clouds below there was no way of telling how fast they were going. Normally, of course, a balloon remained still with respect to the wind, floating at whatever speed the air itself was moving; but now, pulled by the witches, the balloon was moving through the air instead of with it, and resisting the movement, too, because the unwieldy gas-bag had none of the streamlined smoothness of a zeppelin. As a result, the basket swung this way and that, rocking and bumping much more than on a normal flight.

Lee Scoresby wasn't concerned for his comfort so much as for his instruments, and he spent some time making sure they were securely lashed to the main struts. According to the altimeter, they were nearly ten thousand feet up. The temperature was minus twenty degrees. He had been colder than this, but not much, and he didn't want to get any colder now; so he unrolled the canvas sheet he used as an emergency bivouac, and spread it in front of the sleeping children to keep off the wind, before lying down back to back with his old comrade in arms, Iorek Byrnison, and falling asleep.

When Lyra woke up, the moon was high in the sky, and everything in sight was silver-plated, from the rolling surface of the clouds below to the frost-spears and icicles on the rigging of the balloon.

Roger was sleeping, and so were Lee Scoresby and the bear. Beside the basket, however, the witch-queen was flying steadily.

"How far are we from Svalbard?" Lyra said.

"If we meet no winds, we shall be over Svalbard in twelve hours or so."

"Where are we going to land?"

"It depends on the weather. We'll try to avoid the cliffs, though. There are creatures living there who prey on anything that moves. If we can, we'll set you down in the interior, away from Iofur Raknison's palace."

"What's going to happen when I find Lord Asriel? Will he want to come back to Oxford, or what? I don't know if I ought to tell him I know he's my father, neither. He might want to pretend he's still my uncle. I don't hardly know him at all."

"He won't want to go back to Oxford, Lyra. It seems that there is something to be done in another world, and Lord Asriel is the only one who can bridge the gulf between that world and this. But he needs something to help him."

"The alethiometer!" Lyra said. "The Master of Jordan gave it to me and I thought there was something he wanted to say about Lord Asriel, except he never had the chance. I knew he didn't *really* want to poison him. Is he going to read it and see how to make the bridge? I bet I could help him. I can probably read it as good as anyone now."

"I don't know," said Serafina Pekkala. "How he'll do it, and what his task will be, we can't tell. There are powers who speak to us, and there are powers above them; and there are secrets even from the most high."

"The alethiometer would tell me! I could read it now . . ."

But it was too cold; she would never have managed to hold it. She bundled herself up and pulled the hood tight against the chill of the wind, leaving only a slit to look through. Far ahead, and a little below, the long rope extended from the suspension-ring of the balloon, pulled by six or seven witches sitting on their cloud-pine branches. The stars shone as bright and cold and hard as diamonds.

"Why en't you cold, Serafina Pekkala?"

"We feel cold, but we don't mind it, because we will not come to harm. And if we wrapped up against the cold, we wouldn't feel other things, like the bright tingle of the stars, or the music of the Aurora, or best of all the silky feeling of moonlight on our skin. It's worth being cold for that."

"Could I feel them?"

"No. You would die if you took your furs off. Stay wrapped up."

"How long do witches live, Serafina Pekkala? Farder Coram says hundreds of years. But you don't look old at all."

"I am three hundred years or more. Our oldest witch-mother is nearly a thousand. One day, Yambe-Akka will come for her. One day she'll come for me. She is the goddess of the dead.

She comes to you smiling and kindly, and you know it is time to die."

"Are there men witches? Or only women?"

"There are men who serve us, like the Consul at Trollesund. And there are men we take for lovers or husbands. You are so young, Lyra, too young to understand this, but I shall tell you anyway and you'll understand it later: men pass in front of our eyes like butterflies, creatures of a brief season. We love them; they are brave, proud, beautiful, clever; and they die almost at once. They die so soon that our hearts are continually racked with pain. We bear their children, who are witches if they are female, human if not; and then in the blink of an eye they are gone, felled, slain, lost. Our sons, too. When a little boy is growing, he thinks he is immortal. His mother knows he isn't. Each time becomes more painful, until finally your heart is broken. Perhaps that is when Yambe-Akka comes for you. She is older than the tundra. Perhaps, for her, witches' lives are as brief as men's are to us."

"Did you love Farder Coram?"

"Yes. Does he know that?"

"I don't know, but I know he loves you."

"When he rescued me he was young and strong and full of pride and beauty. I loved him at once. I would have changed my nature, I would have forsaken the star-tingle and the music of the Aurora; I would never have flown again – I would have given all that up in a moment, without a thought, to be a gyptian boat-wife and cook for him and share his bed and bear his children. But you cannot change what you are, only what you do. I am a witch. He is a human. I stayed with him for long enough to bear him a child . . ."

"He never said! Was it a girl? A witch?"

"No. A boy, and he died in the great epidemic of forty years ago, the sickness that came out of the East. Poor little child; he flickered into life and out of it like a mayfly. And it tore pieces out of my heart, as it always does. It broke Coram's. And then the call came for me to return to my own people, because Yambe-Akka had taken my mother, and I was clan-queen. So I left, as I had to."

"Did you never see Farder Coram again?"

"Never. I heard of his deeds; I heard how he was wounded by the Skraelings, with a poisoned arrow, and I sent herbs and spells to help him recover, but I wasn't strong enough to see him. I heard how broken he was after that, and how his wisdom grew, how much he studied and read, and I was proud of him and his goodness. But I stayed away, for they were dangerous times for my clan, and witch-wars were threatening, and besides, I thought he would forget me and find a human wife..."

"He never would," said Lyra stoutly. "You oughter go and see him. He still loves you, I know he does."

"But he would be ashamed of his own age, and I wouldn't want to make him feel that."

"Perhaps he would. But you ought to send a message to him, at least. That's what I think."

Serafina Pekkala said nothing for a long time. Pantalaimon became a tern and flew to her branch for a second, to acknowledge that perhaps they had been insolent.

Then Lyra said, "Why do people have dæmons, Serafina Pekkala?"

"Everyone asks that, and no one knows the answer. As long as there have been human beings, there have been dæmons. It's what makes us different from animals."

"Yeah! We're different from them all right ... Like bears. They're strange, en't they, bears? You think they're like a person, and then suddenly they do something so strange or ferocious you think you'll never understand them ... But you know what Iorek said to me, he said that his armour for him was like what a dæmon is for a person. It's his soul, he said. But that's where they're different again, because he *made* this armour hisself. They took his first armour away when they sent him into exile, and he found some sky-iron and made some new armour, like making a new soul. We can't make our dæmons. Then the people at Trollesund, they got him drunk on spirits and stole it away, and I found out where it was and he got it back ... But what I wonder is, why's he coming to Svalbard? They'll fight him. They might kill him ... I love Iorek. I love him so much I wish he wasn't coming."

"Has he told you who he is?"

"Only his name. And it was the Consul at Trollesund who told us that."

"He is high-born. He is a prince. In fact, if he had not committed a great crime, he would be the king of the bears by now."

"He told me their king was called Iofur Raknison."

"Iofur Raknison became king when Iorek Byrnison was exiled. Iofur is a prince, of course, or he wouldn't be allowed to rule; but he is clever in a human way; he makes alliances and treaties; he lives not as bears do, in ice-forts, but in a new-built palace; he talks of exchanging ambassadors with human nations and developing the fire-mines with the help of human engineers . . . He is very skilful and subtle. Some say that he provoked Iorek into the deed for which he was exiled, and others say that even if he didn't, he encourages them to think he did, because it adds to his reputation for craft and subtlety."

"What *did* Iorek do? See, one reason I love Iorek, it's because of my father doing what *he* did and being punished. Seems to me they're like each other. Iorek told me he'd killed another bear, but he never said how it came about."

"The fight was over a she-bear. The male whom Iorek killed would not display the usual signals of surrender when it was clear that Iorek was stronger. For all their pride, bears never fail to recognize superior force in another bear and surrender to it, but for some reason this bear didn't do it. Some say that Iofur Raknison worked on his mind, or gave him confusing herbs to eat. At any rate, the young bear persisted, and Iorek Byrnison allowed his temper to master him. The case was not hard to judge; he should have wounded, not killed."

"So otherwise he'd be king," Lyra said. "And I heard something about Iofur Raknison from the Palmerian Professor at Jordan, 'cause he'd been to the North and met him. He said . . . I wish I could remember what it was . . . I think he'd tricked his way on to the throne or something . . . But you know, Iorek said to me once that bears couldn't be tricked, and showed me that I couldn't trick him. It sounds as if they was *both* tricked, him and the other bear. Maybe only bears can trick bears, maybe people can't. Except . . . The people at Trollesund, they tricked him, didn't they? When they got him drunk and stole his armour?"

"When bears act like people, perhaps they can be tricked," said Serafina Pekkala. "When bears act like bears, perhaps they can't. No bear would normally drink spirits. Iorek Byrnison drank to forget the shame of exile, and it was only that which let the Trollesund people trick him."

"Ah, yes," said Lyra, nodding. She was satisfied with that idea. She admired Iorek almost without limit, and she was glad to find confirmation of his nobility. "That's clever of you," she said. "I wouldn't have known that if you hadn't told me. I think you're probably cleverer than Mrs Coulter."

They flew on. Lyra chewed some of the seal-meat she found in her pocket.

"Serafina Pekkala," she said after some time, "what's Dust? 'Cause it seems to me that all this trouble's about Dust, only no one's told me what it is."

"I don't know," Serafina Pekkala told her. "Witches have never worried about Dust. All I can tell you is that where there are priests, there is fear of Dust. Mrs Coulter is not a priest, of course, but she is a powerful agent of the Magisterium, and it was she who set up the Oblation Board and persuaded the Church to pay for Bolvangar, because of her interest in Dust. We can't understand her feelings about it. But there are many things we have never understood. We see the Tartars making holes in their skulls, and we can only wonder at the strangeness of it. So Dust may be strange, and we wonder at it, but we don't fret and tear things apart to examine it. Leave that to the Church."

"The Church?" said Lyra. Something had come back to her: she remembered talking with Pantalaimon, in the Fens, about what it might be that was moving the needle of the alethiometer, and they had thought of the photo-mill on the high altar at Gabriel College, and how elementary particles pushed the little vanes around. The Intercessor there was clear about the link between elementary particles and religion. "Could be," she said, nodding. "Most Church things, they keep secret, after all. But most Church things are old, and Dust en't old, as far as I know. I wonder if Lord Asriel might tell me . . ."

She yawned again.

"I better lie down," she said to Serafina Pekkala, "else I'll probably freeze. I been cold down on the ground, but I never been this cold. I think I might die if I get any colder."

"Then lie down and wrap yourself in the furs."

"Yeah, I will. If I was going to die, I'd rather die up here than down there, any day. I thought when they put us under that blade thing, I thought that was it . . . We both did. Oh, that was cruel. But we'll lie down now. Wake us up when we get there," she said, and got down on the pile of furs, clumsy and aching in every part of her with the profound intensity of the cold, and lay as close as she could to the sleeping Roger.

And so the four travellers sailed on, sleeping in the ice-encrusted balloon, towards the rocks and glaciers, the fire-mines and the ice-forts of Svalbard.

Serafina Pekkala called to the aëronaut, and he woke at once, groggy with cold, but aware from the movement of the basket that something was wrong. It was swinging wildly as strong winds buffeted the gas-bag, and the witches pulling the rope were barely managing to hold it. If they let go, the balloon would be swept off course at once, and to judge by his glance at the compass, would be swept towards Nova Zembla at nearly a hundred miles an hour.

"Where are we?" Lyra heard him call. She was half-waking herself, uneasy because of the motion, and so cold that every part of her body was numb.

She couldn't hear the witch's reply, but through her half-closed hood she saw, in the light of an anbaric lantern, Lee Scoresby hold on to a strut and pull at a rope leading up into the gas-bag itself. He gave a sharp tug as if against some obstruction, and looked up into the buffeting dark before looping the rope around a cleat on the suspension-ring.

"I'm letting out some gas," he shouted to Serafina Pekkala. "We'll go down. We're way too high."

The witch called something in return, but again Lyra couldn't hear it. Roger was waking too; the creaking of the basket was enough to wake the deepest sleeper, never mind the rocking and bumping. Roger's dæmon and Pantalaimon clung together like marmosets, and Lyra concentrated on lying still and not leaping up in fear.

"'S all right," Roger said, sounding much more cheerful than she was. "Soon's we get down we can make a fire and get warm. I got some matches in me pocket. I pinched 'em out of the kitchen at Bolvangar."

The balloon was certainly descending, because they were enveloped a second later in the thick freezing cloud. Scraps and wisps of it flew through the basket, and then everything was obscured, all at once. It was like the thickest fog Lyra had ever known. After a moment or two there came another cry from Serafina Pekkala, and the aëronaut unlooped the rope from the cleat and let go. It sprang upwards through his hands, and even over the creak and the buffeting and the howl of the wind through the rigging, Lyra heard or felt a mighty thump from somewhere far above.

Lee Scoresby saw her wide eyes.

"That's the gas-valve," he shouted. "It works on a spring to hold the gas in. When I pull it down, some gas escapes outa the top, and we lose buoyancy and go down."

"Are we nearly —"

She didn't finish, because something hideous happened. A creature half the size of a man, with leathery wings and hooked claws, was crawling over the side of the basket towards Lee Scoresby. It had a flat head, with bulging eyes and a wide frog-mouth, and from it came wafts of abominable stink. Lyra had no time to scream, even, before Iorek Byrnison reached up and cuffed it away. It fell out of the basket and vanished with a shriek.

"Cliff-ghast," said Iorek briefly.

The next moment Serafina Pekkala appeared, and clung to the side of the basket, speaking urgently.

"The cliff-ghasts are attacking. We'll bring the balloon to the ground, and then we must defend ourselves. They're —"

But Lyra didn't hear the rest of what was said, because there was a rending, ripping sound, and everything tilted sideways. Then a terrific blow hurled the three humans against the side of the balloon where Iorek Byrnison's armour was stacked. Iorek put out a great paw to hold them in, because the basket was jolting so violently. Serafina Pekkala had vanished. The noise was appalling: over every other sound there came the shrieking of the cliff-ghasts, and Lyra saw them hurtling past, and smelt their foul stench.

Then there came another jerk, so sudden that it threw them all to the floor again, and the basket began to sink with frightening speed, spinning all the while. It felt as if they had torn loose from the balloon, and were dropping unchecked by anything; and then came another series of jerks and crashes, the basket being tossed rapidly from side to side as if they were bouncing between rock walls.

The last thing Lyra saw was Lee Scoresby firing his long-barrelled pistol directly in the face of a cliff-ghast; and then she shut her eyes tight, and clung to Iorek Byrnison's fur with passionate fear. Howls, shrieks, the lash and whistle of the wind, the creak of the basket like a tormented animal, all filled the wild air with hideous noise.

Then came the biggest jolt of all, and she found herself hurled out altogether. Her grip was torn loose, and all the breath was knocked out of her lungs as she landed in such a tangle that she couldn't tell which way was up; and her face in the tight-pulled hood was full of powder, dry, cold, crystals –

It was snow; she had landed in a snow-drift. She was so battered that she could hardly think. She lay quite still for several seconds before feebly spitting out the snow in her mouth, and then she blew just as feebly until there was a little space to breathe in.

Nothing seemed to be *hurting* in particular; she just felt utterly breathless. Cautiously she tried to move hands, feet, arms, legs, and to raise her head.

She could see very little, because her hood was still filled with snow. With an effort, as if her hands weighed a ton each, she brushed it off and peered out. She saw a world of grey, of pale greys and dark greys and blacks, where fog-drifts wandered like wraiths.

The only sounds she could hear were the distant cries of the cliff-ghasts, high above, and the crash of waves on rocks, some way off.

"Iorek!" she cried. Her voice was faint and shaky, and she tried again, but no one answered. "Roger!" she called, with the same result.

She might have been alone in the world, but of course she never was, and Pantalaimon crept out of her anorak as a mouse to keep her company.

"I've checked the alethiometer," he said, "and it's all right. Nothing's broken."

"We're lost, Pan!" she said. "Did you see those cliff-ghasts? And Mr Scoresby shooting 'em? God help us if they come down here . . ."

"We better try and find the basket," he said, "maybe."

"We better not call out," she said. "I did just now, but maybe I better not in case they hear us. I wish I knew where we were."

"We might not like it if we did," he pointed out. "We might be at the bottom of a cliff with no way up, and the cliff-ghasts at the top to see us when the fog clears."

She felt around, once she had rested a few more minutes, and found that she had landed in a gap between two ice-covered rocks. Freezing fog covered everything; to one side there was the crash of waves about fifty yards off, by the sound of it, and from high above there still came the shrieking of the cliff-ghasts, though that seemed to be abating a little. She could see no more than two or three yards in the murk, and even Pantalaimon's owl-eyes were helpless.

She made her way painfully, slipping and sliding on the rough rocks, away from the waves and up the beach a little, and found nothing but rocks and snow, and no sign of the balloon or any of the occupants.

"They *can't* have all just vanished," she whispered.

Pantalaimon prowled cat-formed a little further afield, and came across four heavy sand-bags broken open, with the scattered sand already freezing hard.

"Ballast," Lyra said. "He must've slung 'em off to fly up again . . ."

She swallowed hard to subdue the lump in her throat, or the fear in her breast, or both.

"Oh, God, I'm frightened," she said. "I hope they're safe."

He came to her arms and then, mouse-formed, crept into her hood where he couldn't be seen. She heard a noise, something scraping on rock, and turned to see what it was.

"Iorek!"

But she choked the word back unfinished, for it wasn't Iorek Byrnison at all. It was a strange bear, clad in polished armour with the dew on it frozen into frost, and with a plume in his helmet.

He stood still, about six feet away, and she thought she really was finished.

The bear opened his mouth and roared. An echo came back from the cliffs and stirred more shrieking from far above. Out of the fog came another bear, and another. Lyra stood still, clenching her little human fists.

The bears didn't move until the first one said, "Your name?"

"Lyra."

"Where have you come from?"

"The sky."

"In a balloon?"

"Yes."

"Come with us. You are a prisoner. Move, now. Quickly."

Weary and scared, Lyra began to stumble over the harsh and slippery rocks, following the bear, wondering how she could talk her way out of this.

19

CAPTIVITY

THE BEARS TOOK Lyra up a gully in the cliffs, where the fog lay even more thickly than on the shore. The cries of the cliff-ghasts and the crash of the waves grew fainter as they climbed, and presently the only sound was the ceaseless crying of seabirds. They clambered in silence over rocks and snowdrifts, and although Lyra peered wide-eyed into the enfolding greyness, and strained her ears for the sound of her friends, she might have been the only human on Svalbard; and Iorek might have been dead.

The bear-sergeant said nothing to her until they were on level ground. There they stopped. From the sound of the waves, Lyra judged them to have reached the top of the cliffs, and she dared not run away in case she fell over the edge.

"Look up," said the bear, as a waft of breeze moved aside the heavy curtain of the fog.

There was little daylight in any case, but Lyra did look, and found herself standing in front of a vast building of stone. It was as tall at least as the highest part of Jordan College, but much more massive, and carved all over with representations of warfare, showing bears victorious and Skraelings surrendering, showing Tartars chained and slaving in the fire-mines, showing zeppelins flying from all parts of the world bearing gifts and tributes to the king of the bears, Iofur Raknison.

At least, that was what the bear-sergeant told her the carvings showed. She had to take his word for it, because every projection and ledge on the deeply sculpted façade was occupied by gannets and skuas, which cawed and shrieked and wheeled constantly around overhead, and whose droppings had coated every part of the building with thick smears of dirty white.

The bears seemed not to see the mess, however, and they led the way in through the huge arch, over the icy ground that was filthy with the spatter of the birds. There was a courtyard, and high steps, and gateways, and at every point bears in armour challenged the incomers and were given a password. Their armour was polished and gleaming, and they all wore plumes in their helmets. Lyra couldn't help comparing every bear she saw with Iorek Byrnison, and always to his advantage; he was more powerful, more graceful, and his armour was real armour, rust-coloured, blood-stained, dented with combat, not elegant, enamelled and decorative like most of what she saw around her now.

As they went further in, the temperature rose, and so did something else. The smell in Iofur's palace was repulsive: rancid seal-fat, dung, blood, refuse of every sort. Lyra pushed back her hood to be cooler, but she couldn't help wrinkling her nose. She hoped bears couldn't read human expressions. There were iron brackets every few yards, holding blubber-lamps, and in their flaring shadows it wasn't always easy to see where she was treading, either.

Finally they stopped outside a heavy door of iron. A guard-bear pulled back a massive bolt, and the sergeant suddenly swung his head at Lyra, knocking her head over heels through the doorway. Before she could scramble up, she heard the door being bolted behind her.

It was profoundly dark, but Pantalaimon became a firefly, and shed a tiny glow around them. They were in a narrow cell where the walls dripped with damp, and there was one stone bench for furniture. In the furthest corner there was a heap of rags she took for bedding, and that was all she could see.

Lyra sat down, with Pantalaimon on her shoulder, and felt in her clothes for the alethiometer.

"It's certainly had a lot of banging about, Pan," she whispered. "I hope it still works."

Pantalaimon flew down to her wrist and sat there glowing, while Lyra composed her mind. With a part of her, she found it remarkable that she could sit here in terrible danger and yet sink into the calm she needed to read the alethiometer; and yet it was so much a part of her now that the most complicated questions sorted themselves out into their constituent symbols as naturally as her muscles moved her limbs: she hardly had to think about them.

She turned the hands and thought the question: "Where is Iorek?"

The answer came at once: "A day's journey away, carried there by the balloon after your crash; but hurrying this way."

"And Roger?"

"With Iorek."

"What will Iorek do?"

"He intends to break into the palace and rescue you, in the face of all the difficulties."

She put the alethiometer away, even more anxious than before.

"They won't let him, will they?" she said. "There's too many of 'em. I wish I was a witch, Pan, then you could go off and find him and take messages and all, and we could make a proper plan . . ."

Then she had the fright of her life.

A man's voice spoke in the darkness a few feet away, and said, "Who are you?"

She leapt up with a cry of alarm. Pantalaimon became a bat at once, shrieking, and flew around her head as she backed against the wall.

"Eh? Eh?" said the man again. "Who is that? Speak up! Speak up!"

"Be a firefly again, Pan," she said shakily. "But don't go too close."

The little wavering point of light danced through the air and fluttered around the head of the speaker. And it hadn't been a heap of rags after all: it was a grey-bearded man chained to the wall, whose eyes glittered in Pantalaimon's luminance, and whose tattered hair hung over his shoulders. His dæmon, a weary-looking serpent, lay in his lap, flicking out her tongue occasionally as Pantalaimon flew near.

"What's your name?" she said.

"Jotham Santelia," he replied. "I am the Regius Professor of Cosmology at the University of Gloucester. Who are you?"

"Lyra Belacqua. What have they locked you up for?"

"Malice and jealousy . . . Where do you come from? Eh?"

"From Jordan College," she said.

"What? Oxford?"

"Yes."

"Is that scoundrel Trelawney still there? Eh?"

"The Palmerian Professor? Yes," she said.

"Is he, by God! Eh? They should have forced his resignation long ago. Duplicitous plagiarist! Coxcomb!"

Lyra made a neutral sound.

"Has he published his paper on gamma-ray photons yet?" the Professor said, thrusting his face up towards Lyra's.

She moved back.

"I don't know," she said and then, making it up out of pure habit, "no," she went on. "I remember now. He said he still needed to check some figures. And . . . he said he was going to write about Dust as well. That's it."

"Scoundrel! Thief! Blackguard! Rogue!" shouted the old man, and he shook so violently that Lyra was afraid he'd have a fit. His dæmon slithered lethargically off his lap as the Professor beat his fists against his shanks. Drops of saliva flew out of his mouth.

"Yeah," said Lyra, "I always thought he was a thief. And a rogue and all that."

If it was unlikely for a scruffy little girl to turn up in his cell knowing the very man who figured in his obsessions, the Regius Professor didn't notice. He *was* mad, and no wonder, poor old man; but he might have some scraps of information that Lyra could use.

She sat carefully near him, not near enough for him to touch, but near enough for Pantalaimon's tiny light to show him clearly.

"One thing Professor Trelawney used to boast about," she said, "was how well he knew the king of the bears —"

"Boast! Eh? Eh? I should say he boasts! He's nothing but a popinjay! And a pirate! Not a scrap of original research to his name! Everything filched from better men!"

"Yeah, that's right," said Lyra earnestly. "And when he does do something of his own, he gets it wrong."

"Yes! Yes! Absolutely! No talent, no imagination, a fraud from top to bottom!"

"I mean, for example," said Lyra, "I bet you know more about the bears than he does, for a start."

"Bears," said the old man, "ha! I could write a treatise on them! That's why they shut me away, you know."

"Why's that?"

"I know too much about them, and they daren't kill me. They daren't do it, much as they'd like to. I know, you see. I have friends. Yes! Powerful friends."

"Yeah," said Lyra. "And I bet you'd be a wonderful teacher," she went on. "Being as you got so much knowledge and experience."

Even in the depths of his madness a little common sense still flickered, and he looked at her sharply, almost as if he suspected her of sarcasm. But she had been dealing with suspicious and cranky scholars all her life, and she gazed back with such bland admiration that he was soothed.

"Teacher," he said, "teacher . . . Yes, I could teach. Give me the right pupil, and I will light a fire in his mind!"

"Because your knowledge ought not to just vanish," Lyra said encouragingly. "It ought to be passed on so people remember you."

"Yes," he said, nodding seriously. "That's very perceptive of you, child. What is your name?"

"Lyra," she told him again. "Could you teach me about the bears?"

"The bears . . ." he said doubtfully.

"I'd really like to know about cosmology and Dust and all, but I'm not clever enough for that. You need really clever students for that. But I could learn about the bears. You could teach me about them all right. And we could sort of practise on that and work up to Dust, maybe."

He nodded again.

"Yes," he said, "yes, I believe you're right. There is a corres-pondence between the microcosm and the macrocosm! The stars are alive, child. Did you know that? Everything out there is alive, and there are grand purposes abroad! The universe is full of *intentions*, you know. Everything happens for a purpose. Your purpose is to remind me of that. Good, good – in my despair I had forgotten. Good! Excellent, my child!"

"So, have you seen the king? Iofur Raknison?"

"Yes. Oh, yes. I came here at his invitation, you know. He

intended to set up a university. He was going to make me Vice-Chancellor. That would be one in the eye for the Royal Arctic Society, eh! Eh? And that scoundrel Trelawney! Ha!"

"What happened?"

"I was betrayed by lesser men. Trelawney among them, of course. He was here, you know. On Svalbard. Spread lies and calumny about my qualifications. Calumny! Slander! Who was it discovered the final proof of the Barnard-Stokes hypothesis, eh? Eh? Yes, Santelia, that's who. Trelawney couldn't take it. Lied through his teeth. Iofur Raknison had me thrown in here. I'll be out one day, you'll see. I'll be Vice-Chancellor, oh yes. Let Trelawney come to me then begging for mercy! Let the Publications Committee of the Royal Arctic Society spurn my contributions then! Ha! I'll expose them all!"

"I expect Iorek Byrnison will believe you, when he comes back," Lyra said.

"Iorek Byrnison? No good waiting for that. *He'll* never come back."

"He's on his way now."

"Then they'll kill him. He's not a bear, you see. He's an out-cast. Like me. Degraded, you see. Not entitled to any of the privileges of a bear."

"Supposing Iorek Byrnison did come back, though," Lyra said. "Supposing he challenged Iofur Raknison to a fight . . ."

"Oh, they wouldn't allow it," said the Professor decisively. "Iofur would never lower himself to acknowledge Iorek Byrnison's right to fight him. Hasn't *got* a right. Iorek might as well be a seal now, or a walrus, not a bear. Or worse: Tartar or Skraeling. They wouldn't fight him honourably like a bear; they'd kill him with fire-hurlers before he got near. Not a hope. No mercy."

"Oh," said Lyra, with a heavy despair in her breast. "And what about the bears' other prisoners? Do you know where they keep them?"

"Other prisoners?"

"Like . . . Lord Asriel."

Suddenly the Professor's manner changed altogether. He cringed and shrank back against the wall, and shook his head warningly.

"Sssh! Quiet! They'll hear you!" he whispered.

"Why mustn't we mention Lord Asriel?"

"Forbidden! Very dangerous! Iofur Raknison will not allow him to be mentioned!"

"Why?" Lyra said, coming closer and whispering herself so as not to alarm him.

"Keeping Lord Asriel prisoner is a special charge laid on Iofur by the Oblation Board," the old man whispered back. "Mrs Coulter herself came here to see Iofur and offered him all kinds of rewards to keep Lord Asriel out of the way. I know about it, you see, because at the time I was in Iofur's favour myself. I met Mrs Coulter! Yes. Had a long conversation with her. Iofur was besotted with her. Couldn't stop talking about her. Would do anything for her. If she wants Lord Asriel kept a hundred miles away, that's what will happen. Anything for Mrs Coulter, anything. He's going to name his capital city after her, did you know that?"

"So he wouldn't let anyone go and see Lord Asriel?"

"No! Never! But he's afraid of Lord Asriel too, you know. Iofur's playing a difficult game. But he's clever. He's done what they both want. He's kept Lord Asriel isolated, to please Mrs Coulter; and he's let Lord Asriel have all the equipment he wants, to please *him*. Can't last, this equilibrium. Unstable. Pleasing both sides. Eh? The wave function of this situation is going to collapse quite soon. I have it on good authority."

"Really?" said Lyra, her mind elsewhere, furiously thinking about what he'd just said.

"Yes. My dæmon's tongue can taste probability, you know."

"Yeah. Mine too. When do they feed us, Professor?"

"Feed us?"

"They must put some food in sometime, else we'd starve. And there's bones on the floor. I expect they're seal bones, aren't they?"

"Seal ... I don't know. It might be."

Lyra got up and felt her way to the door. There was no handle, naturally, and no keyhole, and it fitted so closely at top and bottom that no light showed. She pressed her ear to it, but heard nothing. Behind her the old man was muttering to himself. She heard his chain rattle as he turned over wearily and lay the other way, and presently he began to snore.

She felt her way back to the bench. Pantalaimon, tired of putting out light, had become a bat, which was all very well for him; he fluttered around squeaking quietly while Lyra sat and chewed a fingernail.

Quite suddenly, with no warning at all, she remembered what it was that she'd heard the Palmerian Professor saying in the Retiring Room all that time ago. Something had been nagging at her ever since Iorek Byrnison had first mentioned Iofur's name, and now it came back: what Iofur Raknison wanted more than anything else, Professor Trelawney had said, was a dæmon.

Of course, she hadn't understood what he meant; he'd spoken of *panserbjørne* instead of using the English word, so she didn't know he was talking about bears, and she had no idea that Iofur Raknison wasn't a man. And a man would have had a dæmon anyway, so it hadn't made sense.

But now it was plain. Everything she'd heard about the bear-king added up: the mighty Iofur Raknison wanted nothing more than to be a human being, with a dæmon of his own.

And as she thought that, a plan came to her: a way of making Iofur Raknison do what he would normally never have done; a way of restoring Iorek Byrnison to his rightful throne; a way, finally, of getting to the place where they had put Lord Asriel, and taking him the alethiometer.

The idea hovered and shimmered delicately, like a soap bubble, and she dared not even look at it directly in case it burst. But she was familiar with the way of ideas, and she let it shimmer, looking away, thinking about something else.

She was nearly asleep when the bolts clattered and the door opened. Light spilled in, and she was on her feet at once, with Pantalaimon hidden swiftly in her pocket.

As soon as the bear-guard bent his head to lift the haunch of seal-meat and throw it in, she was at his side, saying:

"Take me to Iofur Raknison. You'll be in trouble if you don't. It's very urgent."

He dropped the meat from his jaws and looked up. It wasn't easy to read bears' expressions, but he looked angry.

"It's about Iorek Byrnison," she said quickly. "I know something about him, and the king needs to know."

"Tell me what it is, and I'll pass the message on," said the bear.

"That wouldn't be right, not for someone else to know before the king does," she said. "I'm sorry, I don't mean to be rude, but you see, it's the rule that the king has to know things first."

Perhaps he was slow-witted. At any rate, he paused, and then threw the meat into the cell before saying, "Very well. You come with me."

He led her out into the open air, for which she was grateful. The fog had lifted and there were stars glittering above the high-walled courtyard. The guard conferred with another bear, who came to speak to her.

"You cannot see Iofur Raknison when you please," he said. "You have to wait till he wants to see you."

"But this is urgent, what I've got to tell him," she said. "It's about Iorek Byrnison. I'm sure His Majesty would want to know it, but all the same I can't tell it to anyone else, don't you see? It wouldn't be polite. He'd be ever so cross if he knew we hadn't been polite."

That seemed to carry some weight, or else to mystify the bear sufficiently to make him pause. Lyra was sure her interpretation of things was right: Iofur Raknison was introducing so many new ways that none of the bears was certain yet how to behave, and she could exploit this uncertainty in order to get to Iofur.

So that bear retreated to consult the bear above him, and before long Lyra was ushered inside the Palace again, but into the State quarters this time. It was no cleaner here, and in fact the air was even harder to breathe than in the cell, because all the natural stinks had been overlaid by a heavy layer of cloying perfume. She was made to wait in the corridor, then in an ante-room, then outside a large door, while bears discussed and argued and scurried back and forth, and she had time to look around at the preposterous decoration: the walls were rich with gilt plaster-work, some of which was already peeling off or crumbling with damp, and the florid carpets were trodden with filth.

Finally the large door was opened from the inside. A blaze of light from half a dozen chandeliers, a crimson carpet, and more of that thick perfume hanging in the air; and the faces of a dozen or more bears, all gazing at her, none in armour but each with some kind of decoration: a golden necklace, a head-dress of purple feathers, a crimson sash. Curiously, the room was also occupied by birds; terns and skuas perched on the plaster cornice, and swooped low to snatch at bits of fish that had fallen out of one another's nests in the chandeliers.

And on a dais at the far end of the room, a mighty throne reared up high. It was made of granite for strength and massiveness, but like so many other things in Iofur's palace, it was decorated with over-elaborate swags and festoons of gilt that looked like tinsel on a mountainside.

Sitting on the throne was the biggest bear she had ever seen. Iofur Raknison was even taller and bulkier than Iorek, and his face was much more mobile and expressive, with a kind of humanness in it which she had never seen in Iorek's. When Iofur looked at her she seemed to see a man looking out of his eyes, the sort of man she had met at Mrs Coulter's, a subtle politician used to power. He was wearing a heavy gold chain around his neck, with a gaudy jewel hanging from it, and his claws – a good six inches long – were each covered in gold leaf. The effect was one of enormous strength and energy and craft; he was quite big enough to carry the absurd over-decoration; on him it didn't look preposterous, it looked barbaric and magnificent.

She quailed. Suddenly her idea seemed too feeble for words.

But she moved a little closer, because she had to, and then she saw that Iofur was holding something on his knee, as a human might let a cat sit there – or a dæmon.

It was a big stuffed doll, a manikin with a vacant stupid human face. It was dressed as Mrs Coulter would dress, and it had a sort of rough resemblance to her. He was pretending he had a dæmon. Then she knew she was safe.

She moved up close to the throne and bowed very low, with Pantalaimon keeping quiet and still in her pocket.

"Our greetings to you, great King," she said quietly. "Or I mean *my* greetings, not his."

"Not whose?" he said, and his voice was lighter than she had thought it would be, but full of expressive tones and subtleties. When he spoke, he waved a paw in front of his mouth to dislodge the flies that clustered there.

"Iorek Byrnison's, Your Majesty," she said. "I've got something very important and secret to tell you, and I think I ought to tell you in private, really."

"Something about Iorek Byrnison?"

She came close to him, stepping carefully over the bird-spattered floor, and brushed away the flies buzzing at her face.

"Something about dæmons," she said, so that only he could hear.

His expression changed. She couldn't read what it was saying, but there was no doubt that he was powerfully interested. Suddenly he lumbered forward off the throne, making her skip aside, and roared an order to the other bears. They all bowed their heads and backed out towards the door. The birds, which had risen in a flurry at his roar, squawked and swooped around overhead before settling again on their nests.

When the throne room was empty but for Iofur Raknison and Lyra, he turned to her eagerly.

"Well?" he said. "Tell me who you are. What is this about dæmons?"

"I *am* a dæmon, Your Majesty," she said.

He stopped still.

"Whose?" he said.

"Iorek Byrnison's," was her answer.

It was the most dangerous thing she had ever said. She could see quite clearly that only his astonishment prevented him from killing her on the spot. She went on at once:

"Please, Your Majesty, let me tell you all about it first before you harm me. I've come here at my own risk, as you can see, and there's nothing I've got that could hurt you. In fact I want to help you, that's why I've come. Iorek Byrnison was the first bear to get a dæmon, but it should have been you. I would much rather be your dæmon than his, that's why I came."

"How?" he said, breathlessly. "How has a bear got a dæmon? And why him? And how are you so far from him?"

The flies left his mouth like tiny words.

"That's easy. I can go far from him because I'm like a witch's dæmon. You know how they can go hundreds of miles from their humans? It's like that. And as for how he got me, it was at Bolvangar. You've heard of Bolvangar, because Mrs Coulter must have told you about it, but she probably didn't tell you everything they were doing there."

"Cutting . . ." he said.

"Yes, cutting, that's part of it, intercision. But they're doing all kinds of other things too, like making artificial dæmons. And experimenting on animals. When Iorek Byrnison heard about it he offered himself for an experiment to see if they could make a dæmon for him, and they did. It was me. My name is Lyra. Just like when people have dæmons, they're animal-formed, so when a bear has a dæmon, it'll be human. And I'm his dæmon. I can see into his mind and know exactly what he's doing and where he is and –"

"Where is he now?"

"On Svalbard. He's coming this way as fast as he can."

"Why? What does he want? He must be mad! We'll tear him to pieces!"

"He wants me. He's coming to get me back. But I don't want to be his dæmon, Iofur Raknison, I want to be yours. Because once they saw how powerful a bear was with a dæmon, the people at Bolvangar decided not to do that experiment ever again. Iorek Byrnison was going to be the only bear who ever had a dæmon. And with me helping him, he could lead all the bears against you. That's what he's come to Svalbard for."

The bear-king roared his anger. He roared so loudly that the crystal in the chandeliers tinkled, and every bird in the great room shrieked, and Lyra's ears rang.

But she was equal to it.

"That's why I love you best," she said to Iofur Raknison, "because you're passionate and strong as well as clever. And I just had to leave him and come and tell you, because I don't want him ruling the bears. It ought to be you. And there *is* a way of taking me away from him and making me your dæmon, but you wouldn't know what it was unless I told you, and you might do the usual thing about fighting bears like him that've been outcast; I mean, not fight him properly, but kill him with fire-hurlers or something. And if you did that, I'd just go out like a light and die with him."

"But you – how can –"

"I *can* become your dæmon," she said, "but only if you defeat Iorek Byrnison in single combat. Then his strength will flow into you, and my mind will flow into yours, and we'll be like one person, thinking each other's thoughts; and you can send me miles away to spy for you, or keep me here by your side, whichever you like. And I'd help you lead the bears to capture Bolvangar, if you like, and make them create more dæmons for your favourite bears; or if you'd rather be the only bear with a dæmon, we could destroy Bolvangar for ever. We could do anything, Iofur Raknison, you and me together!"

All the time she was holding Pantalaimon in her pocket with a trembling hand, and he was keeping as still as he could, in the smallest mouse-form he had ever assumed.

Iofur Raknison was pacing up and down with an air of explosive excitement.

"Single combat?" he was saying. "Me? I must fight Iorek Byrnison? Impossible! He is outcast! How can that be? How can I fight him? Is that the only way?"

"It's the only way," said Lyra, wishing it were not, because Iofur Raknison seemed bigger and more fierce every minute. Dearly as she loved Iorek, and strong as her faith was in him, she couldn't really believe that he would ever beat this giant among giant bears. But it was the only hope they had. Being mown down from a distance by fire-hurlers was no hope at all.

Suddenly Iofur Raknison turned.

"Prove it!" he said. "Prove that you are a dæmon!"

"All right," she said. "I can do that, easy. I can find out anything that you know and no one else does, something that only a dæmon would be able to find out."

"Then tell me what was the first creature I killed."

"I'll have to go into a room by myself to do this," she said. "When I'm your dæmon you'll be able to see how I do it, but until then it's got to be private."

"There is an ante-room behind this one. Go into that, and come out when you know the answer."

Lyra opened the door and found herself in a room lit by one torch, and empty but for a cabinet of mahogany containing some tarnished silver ornaments. She took out the alethiometer and asked: "Where is Iorek now?"

"Four hours away, and hurrying ever faster."

"How can I tell him what I've done?"

"You must trust him."

She thought anxiously of how tired he would be. But then she reflected that she was not doing what the alethiometer had just told her to do: she wasn't trusting him.

She put that thought aside and asked the question Iofur Raknison wanted. What was the first creature he had killed?

The answer came: Iofur's own father.

She asked further, and learned that Iofur had been alone on the ice as a young bear, on his first hunting expedition, and had come across a solitary bear. They had argued and fought, and Iofur had killed him. When he learned later that it was his own father (for bears were brought up by their mothers, and seldom saw their fathers) he concealed the truth of what he had done. No one knew about it but Iofur himself.

She put the alethiometer away, and wondered how to tell him about it.

"Flatter him!" whispered Pantalaimon. "That's all he wants."

So Lyra opened the door and found Iofur Raknison waiting for her, with an expression of triumph, slyness, apprehension, and greed.

"Well?"

She knelt down in front of him and bowed her head to touch his left forepaw, the stronger, for bears were left-handed.

"I beg your pardon, Iofur Raknison!" she said. "I didn't know you were so strong and great!"

"What's this? Answer my question!"

"The first creature you killed was your own father. I think you're a new god, Iofur Raknison. That's what you must be. Only a god would have the strength to do that."

"You know! You can see!"

"Yes, because I *am* a dæmon, like I said."

"Tell me one thing more. What did the Lady Coulter promise me when she was here?"

Once again Lyra went into the empty room and consulted the alethiometer before returning with the answer.

"She promised you that she'd get the Magisterium in Geneva to agree that you could be baptised as a Christian, even though you hadn't got a dæmon then. Well, I'm afraid that she hasn't done that, Iofur Raknison, and quite honestly I don't think they'd ever agree to that if you didn't have a dæmon. I think she knew that, and she wasn't telling you the truth. But in any case when you've got me as your dæmon you *could* be baptised if you wanted to, because no one could argue then. You could demand it and they wouldn't be able to turn you down."

"Yes ... True. That's what she said. True, every word. And she has deceived me? I trusted her, and she deceived me?"

"Yes, she did. But she doesn't matter any more. Excuse me, Iofur Raknison. I hope you won't mind me telling you, but Iorek Byrnison's only four hours away now, and maybe you better tell your guard bears not to attack him as they normally would. If you're going to fight him for me he'll have to be allowed to come to the Palace."

"Yes..."

"And maybe when he comes I better pretend I still belong to him, and say I got lost or something. He won't know. I'll pretend. Are you going to tell the other bears about me being Iorek's dæmon and then belonging to you when you beat him?"

"I don't know ... What should I do?"

"I don't think you better mention it yet. Once we're together, you and me, we can think what's best to do and decide then. What you need to do now is explain to all the other bears why you're going to let Iorek fight you like a proper bear, even though he's an outcast. Because they won't understand, and we got to find a reason for that. I mean, they'll do what you tell them anyway, but if they see the reason for it, they'll admire you even more."

"Yes. What should we tell them?"

"Tell them ... Tell them that to make your kingdom completely secure, you've called Iorek Byrnison here yourself to fight him, and the winner will rule over the bears for ever. See, if you make it look like *your* idea that he's coming, and not his, they'll be really impressed. They'll think you're able to call him here from far away. They'll think you can do anything."

"Yes ..."

The great bear was helpless. Lyra found her power over him almost intoxicating, and if Pantalaimon hadn't nipped her hand sharply to remind her of the danger they were all in, she might have lost all her sense of proportion.

But she came to herself and stepped modestly back to watch and wait as the bears, under Iofur's excited direction, prepared the combat-ground for Iorek Byrnison; and meanwhile Iorek, knowing nothing about it, was hurrying ever closer towards what she wished she could tell him was a fight for his life.

20

À OUTRANCE

FIGHTS BETWEEN BEARS were common, and the subject of much ritual. For a bear to kill another was rare, though, and when that happened it was usually by accident, or when one bear mistook the signals from another, as in the case of Iorek Byrnison. Cases of straightforward murder, like Iofur's killing of his own father, were rarer still.

But occasionally there came circumstances in which the only way of settling a dispute was a fight to the death. And for that, a whole ceremonial was prescribed.

As soon as Iofur announced that Iorek Byrnison was on his way, and a combat would take place, the combat-ground was swept and smoothed, and armourers came up from the fire-mines to check Iofur's armour. Every rivet was examined, every link tested, and the plates were burnished with the finest sand. Just as much attention was paid to his claws. The gold leaf was rubbed off, and each separate six-inch hook was sharpened and filed to a deadly point. Lyra watched with a growing sickness in the pit of her stomach, for Iorek Byrnison wouldn't be having this attention; he had been marching over the ice for nearly twenty-four hours already without rest or food; he might have been injured in the crash. And she had let him in for this fight without his knowledge. At one point, after Iofur Raknison had tested the sharpness of his claws on a fresh-killed walrus, slicing its skin open like paper, and the power of his crashing blows on the walrus's skull (two blows, and it was cracked like an egg), Lyra had to make an excuse to Iofur and go away by herself to weep with fear.

Even Pantalaimon, who could normally cheer her up, had little to say that was hopeful. All she could do was consult the alethiometer: he is an hour away, it told her, and again, she must trust him; and (this was harder to read) she even thought it was rebuking her for asking the same question twice.

By this time, word had spread among the bears, and every part of the combat-ground was crowded. Bears of high rank had the best places, and there was a special enclosure for the she-bears, including of course Iofur's wives. Lyra was profoundly curious about she-bears, because she knew so little about them, but this was no time to wander about asking questions. Instead she stayed close to Iofur Raknison and watched the courtiers around him assert their rank over the common bears from outside, and tried to guess the meaning of the various plumes and badges and tokens they all seemed to wear. Some of the highest-ranking, she saw, carried little manikins like Iofur's rag-doll dæmon, trying to curry favour, perhaps, by imitating the fashion he'd begun. She was sardonically pleased to notice that when they saw that Iofur had discarded his, they didn't know what to do with theirs. Should they throw them away? Were they out of favour now? How should they behave?

Because that was the prevailing mood in his court, she was beginning to see. They weren't sure what they were. They weren't like Iorek Byrnison, pure and certain and absolute; there was a constant pall of uncertainty hanging over them, as they watched one another and watched Iofur.

And they watched her, with open curiosity. She remained modestly close to Iofur and said nothing, lowering her eyes whenever a bear looked at her.

The fog had lifted by this time, and the air was clear; and as chance would have it, the brief lifting of darkness towards noon coincided with the time Lyra thought Iorek was going to arrive. As she stood shivering on a little rise of dense-packed snow at the edge of the combat-ground, she looked up towards the faint lightness in the sky, and longed with all her heart to see a flight of ragged elegant black shapes descending to bear her away; or to see the Aurora's hidden city, where she would be able to walk safely along those broad boulevards in the sunlight; or to see Ma Costa's broad arms, to smell the friendly smells of flesh and cooking that enfolded you in her presence . . .

She found herself crying, with tears which froze almost as soon as they formed, and which she had to brush away painfully. She was so frightened. Bears, who didn't cry, couldn't understand what was happening to her; it was some human process, meaningless. And of course Pantalaimon couldn't comfort her as he normally would, though she kept her hand in her pocket firmly around his warm little mouse-form, and he nuzzled at her fingers.

Beside her, the smiths were making the final adjustments to Iofur Raknison's armour. He reared like a great metal tower, shining in polished steel, the smooth plates inlaid with wires of gold; his helmet enclosed the upper part of his head in a glistening carapace of silver-grey, with deep eye-slits; and the underside of his body was protected by a close-fitting sark of chain-mail. It was when she saw this that Lyra realized that she had betrayed Iorek Byrnison, for Iorek had nothing like it. His armour protected only his back and sides. She looked at Iofur Raknison, so sleek and powerful, and felt a deep sickness in her, like guilt and fear combined.

She said, "Excuse me, Your Majesty, if you remember what I said to you before . . ."

Her shaking voice felt thin and weak in the air. Iofur Raknison turned his mighty head, distracted from the target three bears were holding up in front for him to slash at with his perfect claws.

"Yes? Yes?"

"Remember, I said I'd better go and speak to Iorek Byrnison first, and pretend –"

But before she could even finish her sentence, there was a roar from the bears on the watch-tower. The others all knew what it meant and took it up with a triumphant excitement. They had seen Iorek.

"Please?" Lyra said urgently. "I'll fool him, you'll see."

"Yes. Yes. Go now. Go and *encourage* him!"

Iofur Raknison was hardly able to speak for rage and excitement.

Lyra left his side and walked across the combat-ground, bare and clear as it was, leaving her little footprints in the snow, and the bears on the far side parted to let her through. As their great bodies lumbered aside, the horizon opened, gloomy in the pallor of the light. Where was Iorek Byrnison? She could see nothing; but then, the watch-tower was high, and they could see what was still hidden from her. All she could do was walk forward in the snow.

He saw her before she saw him. There was a bounding and a heavy clank of metal, and in a flurry of snow Iorek Byrnison stood beside her.

"Oh, Iorek! I've done a terrible thing! My dear, you're going to have to fight Iofur Raknison, and you en't ready – you're tired and hungry, and your armour's –"

"What terrible thing?"

"I told him you was coming, because I read it on the symbol-reader; and he's desperate to be like a person and have a dæmon, just desperate. So I tricked him into thinking that I was your dæmon, and I was going to desert you and be his instead, but he had to fight you to make it happen. Because otherwise, Iorek, dear, they'd never let you fight, they were going to just burn you up before you got close –"

"You tricked Iofur Raknison?"

"Yes. I made him agree that he'd fight you instead of just killing you straight off like an outcast, and the winner would be king of the bears. I had to do that, because –"

"Belacqua? No. You are Lyra Silvertongue," he said. "To fight him is all I want. Come, little dæmon."

She looked at Iorek Byrnison in his battered armour, lean and ferocious, and felt as if her heart would burst with pride.

They walked together towards the massive hulk of Iofur's palace, where the combat-ground lay flat and open at the foot of the walls. Bears clustered at the battlements, white faces filled every window, and their heavy forms stood like a dense wall of misty white ahead, marked with the black dots of eyes and noses. The nearest ones moved aside, making two lines for Iorek Byrnison and his dæmon to walk between. Every bear's eyes were fixed on them.

Iorek halted across the combat-ground from Iofur Raknison. The king came down from the rise of trodden snow, and the two bears faced each other several yards apart.

Lyra was so close to Iorek that she could feel a trembling in him like a great dynamo, generating mighty anbaric forces. She touched him briefly on the neck at the edge of his helmet and said, "Fight well, Iorek, my dear. You're the real king, and he en't. He's nothing."

Then she stood back.

"Bears!" Iorek Byrnison roared. An echo rang back from the palace walls, and startled birds out of their nests. He went on, "The terms of this combat are these. If Iofur Raknison kills me, then he will be king for ever, safe from challenge or dispute. If I kill Iofur Raknison, I shall be your king. My first order to you all will be to tear down that palace, that perfumed house of mockery and tinsel, and hurl the gold and marble into the sea. Iron is bear-metal. Gold is not. Iofur Raknison has polluted Svalbard. I have come to cleanse it. Iofur Raknison, I challenge you."

Then Iofur bounded forward a step or two, as if he could hardly hold himself back.

"Bears!" he roared in his turn. "Iorek Byrnison has come back at my invitation. I drew him here. It is for me to make the terms of this combat, and they are these: if I kill Iorek Byrnison, his flesh shall be torn apart and scattered to the cliff-ghasts. His head shall be displayed above my palace. His memory shall be obliterated. It shall be a capital crime to speak his name . . ."

He continued, and then each bear spoke again. It was a formula, a ritual faithfully followed. Lyra looked at the two of them, so utterly different: Iofur so glossy and powerful, immense in his strength and health, splendidly armoured, proud and kinglike; and Iorek smaller, though she had never thought he would look small, and poorly equipped, his armour rusty and dented. But his armour was his soul. He had made it and it fitted him. They were one. Iofur was not content with his armour; he wanted another soul as well. He was restless while Iorek was still.

And she was aware that all the other bears were making the comparison too. But Iorek and Iofur were more than just two bears. There were two kinds of beardom opposed here, two futures, two destinies. Iofur had begun to take them in one direction, and Iorek would take them in another, and in the same moment, one future would close for ever as the other began to unfold.

As their ritual combat moved towards the second phase, the two bears began to prowl restlessly on the snow, edging forward, swinging their heads. There was not a flicker of movement from the spectators, but all eyes followed them.

Finally the warriors were still and silent, watching each other face to face across the width of the combat-ground.

Then with a roar and a blur of snow both bears moved at the same moment. Like two great masses of rock balanced on adjoining peaks and shaken loose by an earthquake, that bound down the mountainsides gathering speed, leaping over crevasses and knocking trees into splinters, until they crash into each other so hard that both are smashed to powder and flying chips of stone: that was how the two bears came together. The crash as they met resounded in the still air and echoed back from the Palace wall. But they weren't destroyed, as rock would have been. They both fell aside, and the first to rise was Iorek. He twisted up in a lithe spring and grappled with Iofur, whose armour had been damaged by the collision and who couldn't easily raise his head. Iorek made at once for the vulnerable gap at his neck. He raked the white fur, and then hooked his claws beneath the edge of Iofur's helmet and wrenched it forward.

Sensing the danger, Iofur snarled and shook himself as Lyra had seen Iorek shake himself at the water's edge, sending sheets of water flying high into the air. And Iorek fell away, dislodged, and with a screech of twisting metal Iofur stood up tall, straightening the steel of his back-plates by sheer strength. Then like an avalanche he hurled himself down on Iorek, who was still trying to rise.

Lyra felt her own breath knocked out of her by the force of that crashing fall. Certainly the very ground shook beneath her. How could Iorek survive that? He was struggling to twist himself and gain a purchase on the ground, but his feet were uppermost, and Iofur had fixed his teeth somewhere near Iorek's throat. Drops of hot blood were flying through the air: one landed on Lyra's fur, and she pressed her hand to it like a token of love.

Then Iorek's rear claws dug into the links of Iofur's chain-mail sark and ripped downwards. The whole front came away, and Iofur lurched sideways to look at the damage, leaving Iorek to scramble upright again.

For a moment the two bears stood apart, getting their breath back. Iofur was hampered now by that chain-mail, because from a protection it had changed all at once into a hindrance: it was still fastened at the bottom, and trailed around his rear legs. However, Iorek was worse off. He was bleeding freely from a wound at his neck, and panting heavily.

But he leapt at Iofur before the king could disentangle himself from the clinging chain-mail, and knocked him head over heels, following up with a lunge at the bare part of Iofur's neck, where the edge of the helmet was bent. Iofur threw him off, and then the two bears were at each other again, throwing up fountains of snow that sprayed in all directions and sometimes made it hard to see who had the advantage.

Lyra watched, hardly daring to breathe, and squeezing her hands together so tight it hurt. She thought she saw Iofur tearing at a wound in Iorek's belly, but that couldn't be right, because a moment later, after another convulsive explosion of snow, both bears were standing upright like boxers, and Iorek was slashing with mighty claws at Iofur's face, with Iofur hitting back just as savagely.

Lyra trembled at the weight of those blows. As if a giant were swinging a sledgehammer, and that hammer were armed with five steel spikes . . .

Iron clanged on iron, teeth crashed on teeth, breath roared harshly, feet thundered on the hard-packed ground. The snow around was splashed with red and trodden down for yards into a crimson mud.

Iofur's armour was in a pitiful state by this time, the plates torn and distorted, the gold inlay torn out or smeared thickly with blood, and his helmet gone altogether. Iorek's was in much better condition, for all its ugliness: dented, but intact, standing up far better to the great sledgehammer-blows of the bear-king, and turning aside those brutal six-inch claws.

But against that, Iofur was bigger and stronger than Iorek, and Iorek was weary and hungry, and had lost more blood. He was wounded in the belly, on both arms, and at the neck, whereas Iofur was bleeding only from his lower jaw. Lyra longed to help her dear friend, but what could she do?

And it was going badly for Iorek now. He was limping; every

time he put his left forepaw on the ground, they could see that it hardly bore his weight. He never used it to strike with, and the blows from his right hand were feebler, too, almost little pats compared with the mighty crushing buffets he'd delivered only a few minutes before.

Iofur had noticed. He began to taunt Iorek, calling him broken-hand, whimpering cub, rust-eaten, soon-to-die, and other names, all the while swinging blows at him from right and left which Iorek could no longer parry. Iorek had to move backwards, a step at a time, and to crouch low under the rain of blows from the jeering bear-king.

Lyra was in tears. Her dear, her brave one, her fearless defender, was going to die, and she would not do him the treachery of looking away, for if he looked at her he must see her shining eyes and their love and belief, not a face hidden in cowardice or a shoulder fearfully turned away.

So she looked, but her tears kept her from seeing what was really happening, and perhaps it would not have been visible to her anyway. It certainly was not seen by Iofur.

Because Iorek was moving backwards only to find clean dry footing and a firm rock to leap up from, and the useless left arm was really fresh and strong. You could not trick a bear, but, as Lyra had showed him, Iofur did not want to be a bear, he wanted to be a man; and Iorek was tricking him.

At last he found what he wanted: a firm rock deep-anchored in the permafrost. He backed against it, tensing his legs and choosing his moment.

It came when Iofur reared high above, bellowing his triumph, and turning his head tauntingly towards Iorek's apparently weak left side.

That was when Iorek moved. Like a wave that has been building its strength over a thousand miles of ocean, and which makes little stir in the deep water, but which when it reaches the shallows rears itself up high into the sky, terrifying the shore-dwellers, before crashing down on the land with irresistible power – so Iorek Byrnison rose up against Iofur, exploding upwards from his firm footing on the dry rock and slashing with a ferocious left hand at the exposed jaw of Iofur Raknison.

It was a horrifying blow. It tore the lower part of his jaw clean off, so that it flew through the air scattering blood-drops in the snow many yards away.

Iofur's red tongue lolled down dripping over his open throat. The bear-king was suddenly voiceless, biteless, helpless. Iorek needed nothing more. He lunged, and then his teeth were in Iofur's throat, and he shook and shook this way, that way, lifting the huge body off the ground and battering it down as if Iofur were no more than a seal at the water's edge.

Then he ripped upwards, and Iofur Raknison's life came away in his teeth.

There was one ritual yet to perform. Iorek sliced open the dead king's unprotected chest, peeling the fur back to expose the narrow white and red ribs like the timbers of an upturned boat. Into the ribcage Iorek reached, and he plucked out Iofur's heart, red and steaming, and ate it there in front of Iofur's subjects.

Then there was acclamation, pandemonium, a crush of bears surging forward to pay homage to Iofur's conqueror.

Iorek Byrnison's voice rose above the clamour.

"Bears! Who is your king?"

And the cry came back, in a roar like that of all the shingle in the world in an ocean-battering storm:

"Iorek Byrnison!"

The bears knew what they must do. Every single badge and sash and coronet was thrown off at once and trampled contemptuously under-foot, to be forgotten in a moment. They were Iorek's bears now, and true bears, not uncertain semi-humans, conscious only of a torturing inferiority. They swarmed to the Palace and began to hurl great blocks of marble from the topmost towers, rocking the battlemented walls in their mighty fists until the stones came loose and then hurling them over the cliffs to crash on the jetty hundreds of feet below.

Iorek ignored them and unhooked his armour to attend to his wounds, but before he could begin, Lyra was beside him, stamping her foot on the frozen scarlet snow and shouting to the bears to stop smashing the Palace, because there were prisoners inside. They didn't hear, but Iorek did, and when he roared they stopped at once.

"Human prisoners?" Iorek said.

"Yes – Iofur Raknison put them in the dungeons – they ought to come out first and get shelter somewhere, else they'll be killed with all the falling rocks –"

Iorek gave swift orders, and some bears hurried into the Palace to release the prisoners. Lyra turned to Iorek.

"Let me help you – I want to make sure you en't too badly hurt, Iorek dear – oh, I wish there was some bandages or something! That's an awful cut on your belly –"

A bear laid a mouthful of some stiff green stuff, thickly frosted, on the ground at Iorek's feet.

"Bloodmoss," said Iorek. "Press it in the wounds for me, Lyra. Fold the flesh over it and then hold some snow there till it freezes."

He wouldn't let any bears attend to him, despite their eagerness. Besides, Lyra's hands were deft, and she was desperate to help; so the little child bent over the great bear-king, packing in the bloodmoss and freezing the raw flesh till it stopped bleeding. When she had finished, her mittens were sodden with Iorek's blood, but his wounds were staunched.

And by that time the prisoners – a dozen or so men, shivering and blinking and huddling together – had come out. There was no point in talking to the Professor, Lyra decided, because the poor man was mad; and she would have liked to know who the other men were, but there were many other urgent things to do. And she didn't want to distract Iorek, who was giving rapid orders and sending bears scurrying this way and that, but she was anxious about Roger, and about Lee Scoresby and the witches, and she was hungry and tired . . . She thought the best thing she could do just then was to keep out of the way.

So she curled up in a quiet corner of the combat-ground with Pantalaimon as a wolverine to keep her warm, and piled snow over herself as a bear would do, and went to sleep.

Something nudged her foot, and a strange bear voice said, "Lyra Silvertongue, the king wants you."

She woke up nearly dead with cold, and couldn't open her eyes, for they had frozen shut; but Pantalaimon licked them to melt the ice on her eyelashes, and soon she was able to see the young bear speaking to her in the moonlight.

She tried to stand, but fell over twice.

The bear said, "Ride on me," and crouched to offer his broad back, and half-clinging, half-falling, she managed to stay on while he took her to a steep hollow, where many bears were assembled.

And among them was a small figure who ran towards her, and whose dæmon leapt up to greet Pantalaimon.

"Roger!" she said.

"Iorek Byrnison made me stay out there in the snow while he came to fetch you away – we fell out the balloon, Lyra! After you fell out we got carried miles and miles, and then Mr Scoresby let some more gas out and we crashed into a mountain, and we fell down such a slope like you never seen! And I don't know where Mr Scoresby is now, nor the witches. There was just me and Iorek Byrnison. He come straight back this way to look for you. And they told me about his fight . . ."

Lyra looked around. Under the direction of an older bear, the human prisoners were building a shelter out of driftwood and scraps of canvas. They seemed pleased to have some work to do. One of them was striking a flint to light a fire.

"There is food," said the young bear who had woken Lyra.

A fresh seal lay on the snow. The bear sliced it open with a claw and showed Lyra where to find the kidneys. She ate one raw: it was warm and soft and delicious beyond imagining.

"Eat the blubber too," said the bear, and tore off a piece for her. It tasted of cream flavoured with hazelnuts. Roger hesitated, but followed her example. They ate greedily, and within a very few minutes Lyra was fully awake and beginning to be warm.

Wiping her mouth, she looked around, but Iorek was not in sight.

"Iorek Byrnison is speaking with his counsellors," said the young bear. "He wants to see you when you have eaten. Follow me."

He led them over a rise in the snow to a spot where bears were beginning to build a wall of ice-blocks. Iorek sat at the centre of a group of older bears, and he rose to greet her.

"Lyra Silvertongue," he said. "Come and hear what I am being told."

He didn't explain her presence to the other bears, or perhaps they had learned about her already; but they made room for her and treated her with immense courtesy, as if she were a queen. She felt proud beyond measure to sit beside her friend Iorek Byrnison under the Aurora as it flickered gracefully in the polar sky, and join the conversation of the bears.

It turned out that Iofur Raknison's dominance over them had been like a spell. Some of them put it down to the influence of Mrs Coulter, who had visited him before Iorek's exile, though Iorek had not known about it, and given Iofur various presents.

"She gave him a drug," said one bear, "which he fed secretly to Hjalmur Hjalmurson, and made him forget himself."

Hjalmur Hjalmurson, Lyra gathered, was the bear whom Iorek had killed, and whose death had brought about his exile. So Mrs Coulter was behind that! And there was more.

"There are human laws that prevent certain things that she was planning to do, but human laws don't apply on Svalbard. She wanted to set up another station here like Bolvangar, only worse, and Iofur was going to allow her to do it, against all the custom of the bears; because humans have visited, or been imprisoned, but never lived and worked here. Little by little she was going to increase her power over Iofur Raknison, and his over us, until we were her creatures running back and forth at her bidding, and our only duty to guard the abomination she was going to create . . ."

That was an old bear speaking. His name was Søren Eisarson, and he was a counsellor, one who had suffered under Iofur Raknison.

"What is she doing now, Lyra?" said Iorek Byrnison. "Once she hears of Iofur's death, what will her plans be?"

Lyra took out the alethiometer. There was not much light to see it by, and Iorek commanded that a torch be brought.

"What happened to Mr Scoresby?" Lyra said while they were waiting. "And the witches?"

"The witches were attacked by another witch-clan. I don't know if the others were allied to the child-cutters, but they were patrolling our skies in vast numbers, and they attacked in the storm. I didn't see what happened to Serafina Pekkala. As for Lee Scoresby, the balloon soared up again after I fell out with the boy, taking him with it. But your symbol-reader will tell you what their fate is."

A bear pulled up a sledge on which a cauldron of charcoal was smouldering, and thrust a resinous branch into the heart of it. The branch caught at once, and in its glare Lyra turned the hands of the alethiometer and asked about Lee Scoresby.

It turned out that he was still aloft, borne by the winds towards Nova Zembla, and that he had been unharmed by the cliff-ghasts and had fought off the other witch-clan.

Lyra told Iorek, and he nodded, satisfied.

"If he is in the air, he will be safe," he said. "What of Mrs Coulter?"

The answer was complicated, with the needle swinging from symbol to symbol in a sequence that made Lyra puzzle for a long time. The bears were curious, but restrained by their respect for Iorek Byrnison, and his for Lyra, and she put them out of her mind and sank again into the alethiometric trance.

The play of symbols, once she had discovered the pattern of it, was dismaying.

"It says she's ... She's heard about us flying this way, and she's got a transport zeppelin that's armed with machine-guns – I think that's it – and they're a-flying to Svalbard right now. She don't know yet about Iofur Raknison being beaten, of course, but she will soon because ... Oh yes, because some witches will tell her, and they'll learn it from the cliff-ghasts. So I reckon there are spies in the air all around, Iorek. She was a-coming to ... to pretend to help Iofur Raknison, but really she was going to take over power from him, with a regiment of Tartars that's a-coming by sea, and they'll be here in a couple of days.

"And as soon as she can she's a-going to where Lord Asriel is kept prisoner, and she's going to have him killed. Because ... It's coming clear now: something I never understood before, Iorek! It's why she wants to kill Lord Asriel: it's because she knows what he's going to do, and she fears it, and she wants to do it herself and gain control before he does ... It must be the city in the sky, it must be! She's trying to get to it first! And now it's telling me something else . . ."

She bent over the instrument, concentrating furiously as the needle darted this way and that. It moved almost too fast to follow: Roger, looking over her shoulder, couldn't even see it stop, and was conscious only of a swift flickering dialogue between Lyra's fingers turning the hands and the needle answering, as bewilderingly unlike language as the Aurora was.

"Yes," she said finally, putting the instrument down in her lap and blinking and sighing as she woke out of her profound concentration. "Yes, I see what it says. She's after me again. She wants something I've got, because Lord Asriel wants it too. They need it for this . . . For this experiment, whatever it is . . ."

She stopped there, to take a deep breath. Something was troubling her, and she didn't know what it was. She was sure that this *something* that was so important was the alethiometer itself, because after all, Mrs Coulter *had* wanted it, and what else could it be? And yet it wasn't, because the alethiometer had a different way of referring to itself, and this wasn't it.

"I suppose it's the alethiometer," she said unhappily. "It's what I thought all along. I've got to take it to Lord Asriel before she gets it. If *she* gets it, we'll all die."

As she said that, she felt so tired, so bone-deep weary and sad that to die would have been a relief. But the example of Iorek kept her from admitting it. She put the alethiometer away and sat up straight.

"How far away is she?" said Iorek.

"Just a few hours. I suppose I ought to take the alethiometer to Lord Asriel as soon as I can."

"I will go with you," said Iorek.

She didn't argue. While Iorek gave commands and organized an armed squad to accompany them on the final part of their journey north, Lyra sat still, conserving her energy. She felt that something had gone out of her during that last reading. She closed her eyes and slept, and presently they woke her and set off.

LORD ASRIEL'S WELCOME

LYRA RODE A strong young bear, and Roger rode another, while Iorek paced tirelessly ahead and a squad armed with a fire-hurler followed, guarding the rear.

The way was long and hard. The interior of Svalbard was mountainous, with jumbled peaks and sharp ridges deeply cut by ravines and steep-sided valleys, and the cold was intense. Lyra thought back to the smooth-running sledges of the gyptians on the way to Bolvangar; how swift and comfortable that progress now seemed to have been! The air here was more penetratingly chill than any she had experienced before; or it might have been that the bear she was riding wasn't as light-footed as Iorek; or it might have been that she was tired to her very soul. At all events, it was desperately hard going.

She knew little of where they were bound, or how far it was. All she knew was what the older bear Søren Eisarson had told her while they were preparing the fire-hurler. He had been involved in negotiating with Lord Asriel about the terms of his imprisonment, and he remembered it well.

At first, he'd said, the Svalbard bears regarded Lord Asriel as being no different from any of the other politicians, kings, or trouble-makers who had been exiled to their bleak island. The prisoners were important, or they would have been killed outright by their own people; they might be valuable to the bears one day, if their political fortunes changed and they returned to rule in their own countries; so it might pay the bears not to treat them with cruelty or disrespect.

So Lord Asriel had found conditions on Svalbard no better and no worse than hundreds of other exiles had done. But certain things had made his jailers more wary of him than of other prisoners they'd had. There was the air of mystery and spiritual peril surrounding anything that had to do with Dust; there was the clear panic on the part of those who'd brought him there; and there were Mrs Coulter's private communications with Iofur Raknison.

Besides, the bears had never met anything quite like Lord Asriel's own haughty and imperious nature. He dominated even Iofur Raknison, arguing forcefully and eloquently, and persuaded the bear-king to let him choose his own dwelling-place.

The first one he was allotted was too low down, he said. He needed a high spot, above the smoke and stir of the fire-mines and the smithies. He gave the bears a design of the accommodation he wanted, and told them where it should be; and he bribed them with gold, and he flattered and bullied Iofur Raknison, and with a bemused willingness the bears set to work. Before long a house had arisen on a headland facing north: a wide and solid place with fireplaces that burned great blocks of coal mined and hauled by bears, and with large windows of real glass. There he dwelt, a prisoner acting like a king.

And then he set about assembling the materials for a laboratory.

With furious concentration he sent for books, instruments, chemicals, all manner of tools and equipment. And somehow it had come, from this source or that; some openly, some smuggled in by the visitors he insisted he was entitled to have. By land, sea and air, Lord Asriel assembled his materials, and within six months of his committal, he had all the equipment he wanted.

And so he worked, thinking and planning and calculating, waiting for the one thing he needed to complete the task that so terrified the Oblation Board. It was drawing closer every minute.

Lyra's first glimpse of her father's prison came when Iorek Byrnison stopped at the foot of a ridge for the children to move and stretch themselves, because they had been getting dangerously cold and stiff.

"Look up there," he said.

A wide broken slope of tumbled rocks and ice, where a track had been laboriously cleared, led up to a crag outlined against the sky. There was no Aurora, but the stars were brilliant. The crag stood black and gaunt, but at its summit was a spacious building from which light spilled lavishly in all directions: not the smoky inconstant gleam of blubber-lamps, nor the harsh white of anbaric spotlights, but the warm creamy glow of naphtha.

The windows from which the light emerged also showed Lord Asriel's formidable power. Glass was expensive, and large sheets of it were prodigal of heat in these fierce latitudes; so to see them here was evidence of wealth and influence far greater than Iofur Raknison's vulgar palace.

They mounted their bears for the last time, and Iorek led the way up the slope towards the house. There was a courtyard that lay deep under snow, surrounded by a low wall, and as Iorek pushed open the gate they heard a bell ring somewhere in the building.

Lyra got down. She could hardly stand. She helped Roger down too and, supporting each other, the children stumbled through the thigh-deep snow towards the steps up to the door.

Oh, the warmth there would be inside that house! Oh, the peaceful rest!

She reached for the handle of the bell, but before she could reach it, the door opened. There was a small dimly-lit vestibule to keep the warm air in, and standing under the lamp was a figure she recognized: Lord Asriel's manservant Thorold, with his pinscher-dæmon Anfang.

Lyra wearily pushed back her hood.

"Who . . ." Thorold began, and then saw who it was, and went on, "Not Lyra? Little Lyra? Am I dreaming?"

He reached behind him to open the inner door.

A hall, with a coal fire blazing in a stone grate; warm naphtha light glowing on carpets, leather chairs, polished wood . . . It was like nothing Lyra had seen since leaving Jordan College, and it brought a choking gasp to her throat.

Lord Asriel's snow-leopard dæmon growled.

Lyra's father stood there, his powerful dark-eyed face at first fierce, triumphant, and eager; and then the colour faded from it. his eyes widened, in horror, as he recognized his daughter.

"No! No!"

He staggered back and clutched at the mantelpiece. Lyra couldn't move.

"Get out!" Lord Asriel cried. "Turn round, get out, go! *I did not send for you!*"

She couldn't speak. She opened her mouth twice, three times, and then managed to say:

"No, no, I came because –"

He seemed appalled; he kept shaking his head, he held up his hands as if to ward her off; she couldn't believe his distress.

She moved a step closer to reassure him, and Roger came to stand with her, anxious. Their dæmons fluttered out into the warmth, and after a moment Lord Asriel passed a hand across his brow and recovered slightly. The colour began to return to his cheeks as he looked down at the two children.

"Lyra," he said. "That is Lyra?"

"Yes, Uncle Asriel," she said, thinking that this wasn't the time to go into their true relationship. "I came to bring you the alethiometer from the Master of Jordan."

"Yes, of course you did," he said. "Who is this?"

"It's Roger Parslow," she said. "He's the Kitchen boy from Jordan College. But –"

"How did you get here?"

"I was just going to say, there's Iorek Byrnison outside, he's brought us here. He came with me all the way from Trollesund, and we tricked Iofur –"

"Who's Iorek Byrnison?"

"An armoured bear. He brought us here."

"Thorold," he called, "run a hot bath for these children, and prepare them some food. Then they will need to sleep. Their clothes are filthy; find them something to wear. Do it now, while I talk to this bear."

Lyra felt her head swim. Perhaps it was the heat, or perhaps it was relief. She watched the servant bow and leave the hall, and Lord Asriel go into the vestibule and close the door behind, and then she half-fell into the nearest chair.

Only a moment later, it seemed, Thorold was speaking to her.

"Follow me, miss," he was saying, and she hauled herself up and went with Roger to a warm bathroom, where soft towels hung on a heated rail, and where a tub of water steamed in the naphtha light.

"You go first," said Lyra. "I'll sit outside and we'll talk."

So Roger, wincing and gasping at the heat, got in and washed. They had swum naked together often enough, frolicking in the Isis or the Cherwell with other children, but this was different.

"I'm afraid of your uncle," said Roger through the open door. "I mean your father."

"Better keep calling him my uncle. I'm afraid of him too, sometimes."

"When we first come in he never saw me at all. He only saw you. And he was horrified, till he saw me. Then he calmed down all at once."

"He was just shocked," said Lyra. "Anyone would be, to see someone they didn't expect. He last saw me after that time in the Retiring Room. It's bound to be a shock."

"No," said Roger, "it's more than that. He was looking at me like a wolf, or summing."

"You're imagining it."

"I en't. I'm more scared of him than I was of Mrs Coulter, and that's the truth."

He splashed himself. Lyra took out the alethiometer.

"D'you want me to ask the symbol-reader about it?" Lyra said.

"Well, I dunno. There's things I'd rather not know. Seems to me everything I heard of since the Gobblers come to Oxford, everything's been bad. There en't been nothing good more than about five minutes ahead. Like I can see now, this bath's nice, and there's a nice warm towel there, about five minutes away. And once I'm dry maybe I'll think of summing nice to eat, but no further ahead than that. And when I've eaten maybe I'll look forward to a kip in a comfortable bed. But after that, I dunno, Lyra. There's been terrible things we seen, en't there? And more a-coming, more'n likely. So I think I'd rather not know what's in the future. I'll stick to the present."

"Yeah," said Lyra wearily. "There's times I feel like that too."

So although she held the alethiometer in her hands for a little longer, it was only for comfort; she didn't turn the wheels, and the swinging of the needle passed her by. Pantalaimon watched it in silence.

After they'd both washed, and eaten some bread and cheese

and drunk some wine and hot water, the servant Thorold said, "The boy is to go to bed. I'll show him where to go. His Lordship asks if you'd join him in the Library, Miss Lyra."

Lyra found Lord Asriel in a room whose wide windows overlooked the frozen sea far below. There was a coal fire under a wide chimney-piece, and a naphtha lamp turned down low, so there was little in the way of distracting reflections between the occupants of the room and the bleak starlit panorama outside. Lord Asriel, reclining in a large armchair on one side of the fire, beckoned her to come and sit in the other chair facing him.

"Your friend Iorek Byrnison is resting outside," he said. "He prefers the cold."

"Did he tell you about his fight with Iofur Raknison?"

"Not in detail. But I understand that he is now the king of Svalbard. Is that true?"

"Of course it's true. Iorek never lies."

"He seems to have appointed himself your guardian."

"No. John Faa told him to look after me, and he's doing it because of that. He's following John Faa's orders."

"How does John Faa come into this?"

"I'll tell you if you tell me something," she said. "You're my father, en't you?"

"Yes. So what?"

"So you should have told me before, that's what. You shouldn't hide things like that from people, because they feel stupid when they find out, and that's cruel. What difference would it make if I knew I was your daughter? You could have said it years ago. You could've told me and asked me to keep it secret, and I would, no matter how young I was, I'd have done that if you asked me. I'd have been so proud nothing would've torn it out of me, if you asked me to keep it secret. But you never. You let other people know, but you never told me."

"Who did tell you?"

"John Faa."

"Did he tell you about your mother?"

"Yes."

"Then there's not much left for me to tell. I don't think I want to be interrogated and condemned by an insolent child. I want to hear what you've seen and done on the way here."

"I brought you the bloody alethiometer, didn't I?" Lyra burst out. She was very near to tears. "I looked after it all the way from Jordan, I hid it and I treasured it, all through what's happened to us, and I learned about using it, and I carried it all this bloody way when I could've just given up and been safe, and you en't even said thank you, nor showed any sign that you're glad to see me. I don't know why I ever done it. But I did, and I kept on going, even in Iofur Raknison's stinking palace with all them bears around me I kept on going, all on me own, and I tricked him into fighting with Iorek so's I could come on here for your sake . . . And when you *did* see me you like to fainted, as if I was some horrible thing you never wanted to see again. You en't human, Lord Asriel. You en't my *father*. My *father* wouldn't treat me like that. Fathers are supposed to love their daughters, en't they? You don't love me, and I don't love you, and that's a fact. I love Farder Coram, and I love Iorek Byrnison; I love an armoured bear more'n I love my father. And I bet Iorek Byrnison loves me more'n you do."

"You told me yourself he's only following John Faa's orders. If you're going to be sentimental I shan't waste time talking to you."

"Take your bloody alethiometer, then, and I'm going back with Iorek."

"Where?"

"Back to the palace. He can fight with Mrs Coulter and the Oblation Board, when they turn up. If he loses then I'll die too, I don't care. If he wins we'll send for Lee Scoresby and I'll sail away in his balloon and —"

"Who's Lee Scoresby?"

"An aëronaut. He brought us here and then we crashed. Here you are, here's the alethiometer. It's all in good order."

He made no move to take it, and she laid it on the brass fender around the hearth.

"And I suppose I ought to tell you that Mrs Coulter's on her way to Svalbard, and as soon as she hears what's happened to Iofur Raknison, she'll be on her way here. In a zeppelin, with a whole lot of soldiers, and they're a-going to kill us all, by order of the Magisterium."

"They'll never reach us," he said calmly.

He was so quiet and relaxed that some of her ferocity dwindled.

"You don't know," she said uncertainly.

"Yes I do."

"Have you got another alethiometer, then?"

"I don't need an alethiometer for that. Now I want to hear about your journey here, Lyra. Start from the beginning. Tell me everything."

So she did. She began with her hiding in the Retiring Room, and went on to the Gobblers' taking Roger, and her time with Mrs Coulter, and everything else that had happened.

It was a long tale, and when she finished it she said, "So there's one thing I want to know, and I reckon I've got the right to know it, like I had the right to know who I really was. And if you didn't tell me that, you've got to tell me this, in recompense. So: what's Dust? And why's everyone so afraid of it?"

He looked at her as if trying to guess whether she would understand what he was about to say. He had never looked at her seriously before, she thought; until now he had always been like an adult indulging a child in a pretty trick. But he seemed to think she was ready.

"Dust is what makes the alethiometer work," he said.

"Ah . . . I thought it might! But what else? How did they find out about it?"

"In one way the Church has always been aware of it. They've been preaching about Dust for centuries, only they didn't call it by that name.

"But some years ago a Muscovite called Boris Mikhailovitch Rusakov discovered a new kind of elementary particle. You've heard of electrons, photons, neutrinos and the rest? They're called elementary particles because you can't break them down any further: there's nothing inside them but themselves. Well, this new kind of particle was elementary all right, but it was very hard to measure because it didn't react in any of the usual ways. The hardest thing for Rusakov to understand was why the new particle seemed to cluster where human beings were, as if it were attracted to us. And especially to adults. Children too, but not nearly so much until their dæmons have taken a fixed form. During the years of puberty they begin to attract Dust more strongly, and it settles on them as it settles on adults.

"Now all discoveries of this sort, because they have a bearing on the doctrines of the Church, have to be announced through the Magisterium in Geneva. And this discovery of Rusakov's was so unlikely and strange that the Inspector from the Consistorial Court of Discipline suspected Rusakov of diabolic possession. He performed an exorcism in the laboratory, he interrogated Rusakov under the rules of the Inquisition, but finally they had to accept the fact that Rusakov wasn't lying or deceiving them: Dust really existed.

"That left them with the problem of deciding what it was. And given the Church's nature, there was only one thing they could have chosen. The Magisterium decided that Dust was the physical evidence for original sin. Do you know what original sin is?"

She twisted her lips. It was like being back at Jordan, being quizzed on something she'd been half-taught. "Sort of," she said.

"No, you don't. Go to the shelf beside the desk and bring me the Bible."

Lyra did so, and handed the big black book to her father.

"You do remember the story of Adam and Eve?"

"Course," she said. "She wasn't supposed to eat the fruit and the serpent tempted her, and she did."

"And what happened then?"

"Umm ... They were thrown out. God threw them out of the garden."

"God had told them not to eat the fruit, because they would die. Remember, they were naked in the garden, they were like children, their dæmons took on any form they desired. But this is what happened."

He turned to Chapter Three of Genesis, and read:

"And the woman said unto the serpent, We may eat of the fruit of the trees of the garden:

"But of the fruit of the tree which is in the midst of the garden, God hath said, Ye shall not eat of it, neither shall ye touch it, lest ye die.

"And the serpent said unto the woman, Ye shall not surely die:

"For God doth know that in the day ye eat thereof, then your eyes shall be opened, and your dæmons shall assume their true forms, and ye shall be as gods, knowing good and evil.

"And when the woman saw that the tree was good for food, and that it was pleasant to the eyes, and a tree to be desired to reveal the true form of one's dæmon, she took of the fruit thereof, and did eat, and gave also unto her husband with her; and he did eat.

"And the eyes of them both were opened, and they saw the true form of their dæmons, and spoke with them.

"But when the man and the woman knew their own dæmons, they knew that a great change had come upon them, for until that moment it had seemed that they were at one with all the creatures of the earth and the air, and there was no difference between them:

"And they saw the difference, and they knew good and evil; and they were ashamed, and they sewed fig leaves together to cover their nakedness . . ."

He closed the book.

"And that was how sin came into the world," he said, "sin and shame and death. It came the moment their dæmons became fixed."

"But . . ." Lyra struggled to find the words she wanted: "but it en't *true*, is it? Not true like chemistry or engineering, not that kind of true? There wasn't *really* an Adam and Eve? The Cassington Scholar told me it was just a kind of fairy-tale."

"The Cassington Scholarship is traditionally given to a free-thinker; it's his function to challenge the faith of the Scholars. Naturally he'd say that. But think of Adam and Eve like an imaginary number, like the square root of minus one: you can never see any concrete proof that it exists, but if you include it in your equations, you can calculate all manner of things that couldn't be imagined without it.

"Anyway, it's what the Church has taught for thousands of years. And when Rusakov discovered Dust, at last there was a physical proof that something happened when innocence changed into experience.

"Incidentally, the Bible gave us the name Dust as well. At first they were called Rusakov Particles, but soon someone pointed out a curious verse toward the end of the Third Chapter of Genesis, where God's cursing Adam for eating the fruit."

He opened the Bible again and pointed it out to Lyra. She read:

"In the sweat of thy face shalt thou eat bread, till thou return unto the ground, for out of it wast thou taken: for dust thou art, and unto dust shalt thou return . . ."

Lord Asriel said, "Church scholars have always puzzled over the translation of that verse. Some say it should read not 'unto dust shalt thou return' but 'thou shalt be subject to dust', and others say the whole verse is a kind of pun on the words 'ground' and 'dust', and it really means that God's admitting his own nature to be partly sinful. No one agrees. No one can, because the text is corrupt. But it was too good a word to waste, and that's why the particles became known as Dust."

"And what about the Gobblers?" Lyra said.

"The General Oblation Board . . . Your mother's gang. Clever of her to spot the chance of setting up her own power base, but she's a clever woman, as I dare say you've noticed. It suits the Magisterium to allow all kinds of different agencies to flourish. They can play them off against one another; if one succeeds, they can pretend to have been supporting it all along, and if it fails, they can pretend it was a renegade outfit which had never been properly licensed.

"You see, your mother's always been ambitious for power. At first she tried to get it in the normal way, through marriage, but that didn't work, as I think you've heard. So she had to turn to the Church. Naturally she couldn't take the route a man could have taken – priesthood and so on – it had to be unorthodox;

she had to set up her own order, her own channels of influence, and work through that. It was a good move to specialize in Dust. Everyone was frightened of it; no one knew what to do; and when she offered to direct an investigation, the Magisterium was so relieved that they backed her with money and resources of all kinds."

"But they were *cutting* –" Lyra couldn't bring herself to say it; the words choked in her mouth. "You know what they were doing! Why did the Church let them do anything like that?"

"There was a precedent. Something like it had happened before. Do you know what the word *castration* means? It means removing the sexual organs of a boy so that he never develops the characteristics of a man. A *castrato* keeps his high treble voice all his life, which is why the Church allowed it: so useful in Church music. Some *castrati* became great singers, wonderful artists. Many just became fat spoiled half-men. Some died from the effects of the operation. But the Church wouldn't flinch at the idea of a little *cut*, you see. There was a precedent. And this would be so much more *hygienic* than the old methods, when they didn't have anaesthetics or sterile bandages or proper nursing care. It would be gentle by comparison."

"It isn't!" Lyra said fiercely. "It isn't!"

"No. Of course not. That's why they had to hide away in the far North, in darkness and obscurity. And why the Church was glad to have someone like your mother in charge. Who could doubt someone so charming, so well-connected, so sweet and reasonable? But because it was an obscure and unofficial kind of operation, she was someone the Magisterium could deny if they needed to, as well."

"But whose idea was it to do that *cutting* in the first place?"

"It was hers. She guessed that the two things that happen at adolescence might be connected: the change in one's dæmon and the fact that Dust began to settle. Perhaps if the dæmon were separated from the body, we might never be subject to Dust – to original sin. The question was whether it was possible to separate dæmon and body without killing the person. But she's travelled in many places, and seen all kinds of things. She's travelled in Africa, for instance. The Africans have a way of making a slave called a *zombi*. It has no will of its own; it will work day and night without ever running away or complaining. It looks like a corpse..."

"It's a person without their dæmon!"

"Exactly. So she found out that it was possible to separate them."

"And ... Tony Costa told me about the horrible phantoms they have in the Northern forests. I suppose they might be the same kind of thing."

"That's right. Anyway, the General Oblation Board grew out of ideas like that, and out of the Church's obsession with original sin."

Lord Asriel's dæmon twitched her ears, and he laid his hand on her beautiful head.

"There was something else that happened when they made the cut," he went on. "And they didn't see it. The energy that links body and dæmon is immensely powerful. When the cut is made, all that energy dissipates in a fraction of a second. They didn't notice, because they mistook it for shock, or disgust, or moral outrage, and they trained themselves to feel numb towards it. So they missed what it could do, and they never thought of harnessing it..."

Lyra couldn't sit still. She got up and walked to the window, and stared over the wide bleak darkness with unseeing eyes. They were too cruel. No matter how important it was to find out about original sin, it was too cruel to do what they'd done to Tony Makarios and all the others. Nothing justified that.

"And what were *you* doing?" she said. "Did you do any of that cutting?"

"I'm interested in something quite different. I don't think the Oblation Board goes far enough. I want to go to the source of Dust itself."

"The source? Where's it come from, then?"

"From the other universe we can see through the Aurora."

Lyra turned around again. Her father was lying back in his chair, lazy and powerful, his eyes as fierce as his dæmon's. She didn't love him, she couldn't trust him, but she had to admire him, and the extravagant luxury he'd assembled in this desolate wasteland, and the power of his ambition.

"What is that other universe?" she said.

"One of uncountable billions of parallel worlds. The witches have known about them for centuries, but the first theologians to prove their existence mathematically were excommunicated fifty or more years ago. However, it's true; there's no possible way of denying it.

"But no one thought it would ever be possible to cross from one universe to another. That would violate fundamental laws, we thought. Well, we were wrong; we learned to see the world up there. If light can cross, so can we. And we had to *learn* to see it, Lyra, just as you learned to use the alethiometer.

"Now that world, and every other universe, came about as a result of possibility. Take the example of tossing a coin: it can come down heads or tails, and we don't know before it lands which way it's going to fall. If it comes down heads, that means that the possibility of its coming down tails has collapsed. Until that moment the two possibilities were equal.

"But on another world, it does come down tails. And when that happens, the two worlds split apart. I'm using the example of tossing a coin to make it clearer. In fact, these possibility-collapses happen at the level of elementary particles, but they happen in just the same way: one moment several things are possible, the next moment only one happens, and the rest don't exist. Except that other worlds have sprung into being, on which they *did* happen.

"And I'm going to that world beyond the Aurora," he said, "because I think that's where all the Dust in this universe comes from. You saw those slides I showed the Scholars in the Retiring Room. You saw Dust pouring into this world from the Aurora. You've seen that city yourself. If light can cross the barrier between the universes, if Dust can, if we can see that city, then we can build a bridge and cross. It needs a phenomenal burst of energy. But I can do it. Somewhere out there is the origin of all the Dust, all the death, the sin, the misery, the destructiveness in the world. Human beings can't see anything without wanting to destroy it, Lyra. *That's* original sin. And I'm going to destroy it. Death is going to die."

"Is that why they put you here?"

"Yes. They are terrified. And with good reason."

He stood up, and so did his dæmon, proud and beautiful and deadly. Lyra sat still. She was afraid of her father, and she admired him profoundly, and she thought he was stark mad; but who was she to judge?

"Go to bed," he said. "Thorold will show you where to sleep."

He turned to go.

"You've left the alethiometer," she said.

"Ah, yes; I don't actually need that now," he said. "It would be no use to me without the books, anyway. D'you know, I think the Master of Jordan was giving it to *you*. Did he actually ask you to bring it to me?"

"Well, yes!" she said. But then she thought again, and realized that in fact the Master never had asked her to do that; she had assumed it all the time, because why else would he have given it to her? "No," she said. "I don't know. I thought –"

"Well, I don't want it. It's yours, Lyra."

"But –"

"Good night, child."

Speechless, too bewildered by this to voice any of the dozen urgent questions that pressed at her mind, she took up the alethiometer and wrapped it in its black velvet. Then she sat by the fire and watched him leave the room.

22

BETRAYAL

SHE WOKE TO find a stranger shaking her arm, and then as Pantalaimon sprang awake and growled, she recognized Thorold. He was holding a naphtha lamp, and his hand was trembling.

"Miss – miss – get up quickly. I don't know what to do. He's left no orders. I think he's mad, miss."

"What? What's happening?"

"Lord Asriel, miss. He's been almost in a delirium since you went to bed. I've never seen him so wild. He packed a lot of instruments and batteries in a sledge and he harnessed up the dogs and left. But he's got the boy, miss!"

"Roger? He's taken Roger?"

"He told me to wake him and dress him, and I didn't think to argue – I never have – the boy kept on asking for you, miss – but Lord Asriel wanted him alone – you know when you first came to the door, miss? And he saw you and couldn't believe his eyes, and wanted you gone?"

Lyra's head was in such a whirl of weariness and fear that she could hardly think but, "Yes? Yes?" she said.

"It was because he needed a child to finish his experiment, miss! And Lord Asriel has a way special to himself of bringing about what he wants, he just has to call for something and –"

Now Lyra's head was full of a roar, as if she were trying to stifle some knowledge from her own consciousness.

She had got out of bed, and was reaching for her clothes, and then she suddenly collapsed, and a fierce cry of despair enveloped her. She was uttering it, but it was bigger than she was; it felt as if the despair were uttering her. For she remembered his words: *the energy that links body and dæmon is immensely powerful*; and to bridge the gap between worlds needed *a phenomenal burst of energy . . .*

She had just realized what she'd done.

She had struggled all this way to bring something to Lord Asriel, thinking she knew what he wanted; and it wasn't the alethiometer at all. What he wanted was a child.

She had brought him Roger.

That was why he'd cried out, "I did not send for you!" when he saw her; he had sent for a child, and the fates had brought him his own daughter. Or so he'd thought, until she'd stepped aside and shown him Roger.

Oh, the bitter anguish! She had thought she was *saving* Roger, and all the time she'd been diligently working to betray him . . .

Lyra shook and sobbed in a frenzy of emotion. It couldn't be true.

Thorold tried to comfort her, but he didn't know the reason for her extremity of grief, and could only pat her shoulder nervously.

"Iorek —" she sobbed, pushing the servant aside. "Where's Iorek Byrnison? The bear? Is he still outside?"

The old man shrugged helplessly.

"Help me!" she said, trembling all over with weakness and fear. "Help me dress. I got to go. *Now!* Do it *quick!*"

He put the lamp down and did as she told him. When she commanded, in that imperious way, she was very like her father, for all that her face was wet with tears and her lips trembling. While Pantalaimon paced the floor lashing his tail, his fur almost sparking, Thorold hastened to bring her stiff, reeking furs and help her into them. As soon as all the buttons were done up and all the flaps secured, she made for the door, and felt the cold strike her throat like a sword and freeze the tears at once on her cheeks.

"Iorek!" she called. "Iorek Byrnison! Come, because I need you!"

There was a shake of snow, a clank of metal, and the bear was there. He had been sleeping calmly under the falling snow. In the light spilling from the lamp Thorold was holding at the window, Lyra saw the long faceless head, the dark eye holes, the gleam of white fur below red-black metal, and wanted to embrace him and seek some comfort from his iron helmet, his ice-tipped fur.

"Well?" he said.

"We got to catch Lord Asriel. He's taken Roger and he's a-going to – I daren't think – oh, Iorek, I beg you, go quick, my dear!"

"Come then," he said, and she leapt on his back.

There was no need to ask which way to go: the tracks of the sledge led straight out from the courtyard and over the plain, and Iorek leapt forward to follow them. His motion was now so much a part of Lyra's being that to sit balanced was entirely automatic. He ran over the thick snowy mantle on the rocky ground faster than he'd ever done, and the armour-plates shifted under her in a regular swinging rhythm.

Behind them, the other bears paced easily, pulling the fire-hurler with them. The way was clear, for the moon was high and the light it cast over the snowbound world was as bright as it had been in the balloon: a world of bright silver and profound black. The tracks of Lord Asriel's sledge ran straight towards a range of jagged hills, strange stark pointed shapes jutting up into a sky as black as the alethiometer's velvet cloth. There was no sign of the sledge itself – or was there a feather-touch of movement on the flank of the highest peak? Lyra peered ahead, straining her eyes, and Pantalaimon flew as high as he could and looked with an owl's clear vision.

"Yes," he said, on her wrist a moment later; "it's Lord Asriel, and he's lashing his dogs on furiously, and there's a child in the back…"

Lyra felt Iorek Byrnison change pace. Something had caught his attention. He was slowing and lifting his head to cast left and right.

"What is it?" Lyra said.

He didn't say. He was listening intently, but she could hear nothing. Then she did hear something: a mysterious, vastly distant rustling and crackling. It was a sound she had heard before: the sound of the Aurora. Out of nowhere a veil of radiance had fallen to hang shimmering in the northern sky. All those unseen billions and trillions of charged particles and possibly, she thought, of Dust, conjured a radiating glow out of the upper atmosphere. This was going to be a display more brilliant and extraordinary than any Lyra had yet seen, as if the Aurora knew

the drama that was taking place below, and wanted to light it with
the most awe-inspiring effects.

But none of the bears were looking up: their attention was
all on the earth. It wasn't the Aurora, after all, that had caught
Iorek's attention. He was standing stock still now, and Lyra
slipped off his back, knowing that his senses needed to cast
around freely. Something was troubling him.

Lyra looked around, back across the vast open plain leading to
Lord Asriel's house, back towards the tumbled mountains they'd
crossed earlier, and saw nothing. The Aurora grew more intense.
The first veils trembled and raced to one side, and jagged curtains
folded and unfolded above, increasing in size and brilliance every
minute; arcs and loops swirled across from horizon to horizon,
and touched the very zenith with bows of radiance. She could
hear more clearly than ever the immense singing hiss and swish
of vast intangible forces.

"Witches!" came a cry in a bear-voice, and Lyra turned in joy
and relief.

But a heavy muzzle knocked her forward, and with no breath
left to gasp she could only pant and shudder, for there in the place
where she had been standing was the plume of a green-feathered
arrow. The head and the shaft were buried in the snow.

Impossible! she thought weakly, but it was true, for another
arrow clattered off the armour of Iorek, standing above her. These
were not Serafina Pekkala's witches; they were from another clan.
They circled above, a dozen of them or more, swooping down
to shoot and soaring up again, and Lyra swore with every word
she knew.

Iorek Byrnison gave swift orders. It was clear that the bears
were practised at witch-fighting, for they had moved at once into
a defensive formation, and the witches moved just as smoothly
into attack. They could only shoot accurately from close range,
and in order not to waste arrows they would swoop down, fire
at the lowest part of their dive, and turn upwards at once. But
when they reached the lowest point, and their hands were busy
with bow and arrow, they were vulnerable, and the bears would
explode upwards with raking paws to drag them down. More
than one fell, and was quickly dispatched.

Lyra crouched low beside a rock, watching for a witch-dive. A few shot at her, but the arrows fell wide; and then Lyra, looking up at the sky, saw the greater part of the witch-flight peel off and turn back.

If she was relieved by that, her relief didn't last more than a few moments. Because from the direction in which they'd flown, she saw many others coming to join them; and in mid-air with them there was a group of gleaming lights; and across the broad expanse of the Svalbard plain, under the radiance of the Aurora, she heard a sound she dreaded. It was the harsh throb of a gas-engine. The zeppelin, with Mrs Coulter and her troops on board, was catching up.

Iorek growled an order and the bears moved at once into another formation. In the lurid flicker from the sky Lyra watched as they swiftly unloaded their fire-hurler. The advance-guard of the witch-flight had seen them too, and began to swoop downwards and rain arrows on them, but for the most part the bears trusted to their armour and worked swiftly to erect the apparatus: a long arm extending upwards at an angle, a cup or bowl a yard across; and a great iron tank wreathed in smoke and steam.

As she watched, a bright flame gushed out, and a team of bears swung into practised action. Two of them hauled the long arm of the fire-thrower down, another scooped shovelfuls of fire into the bowl, and at an order they released it, to hurl the flaming sulphur high into the dark sky.

The witches were swooping so thickly above them that three fell in flames at the first shot alone, but it was soon clear that the real target was the zeppelin. The pilot either had never seen a fire-hurler before, or was underestimating its power, for he flew straight on towards the bears without climbing or turning a fraction to either side.

Then it became clear that they had a powerful weapon in the zeppelin too: a machine-rifle mounted on the nose of the gondola. Lyra saw sparks flying up from some of the bears' armour, and saw them huddle over under its protection, before she heard the rattle of the bullets. She cried out in fear.

"They're safe," said Iorek Byrnison. "Can't pierce armour with little bullets."

The fire-thrower worked again: this time a mass of blazing sulphur hurtled directly upwards to strike the gondola and burst in a cascade of flaming fragments on all sides. The zeppelin banked to the left, and roared away in a wide arc before making again for the group of bears working swiftly beside the apparatus. As it neared, the arm of the fire-thrower creaked downwards; the machine-rifle coughed and spat, and two bears fell, to a low growl from Iorek Byrnison; and when the aircraft was nearly overhead, a bear shouted an order, and the springloaded arm shot upwards again.

This time the sulphur hurtled against the envelope of the zeppelin's gas-bag. The rigid frame held a skin of oiled silk in place to contain the hydrogen, and although this was tough enough to withstand minor scratches, a hundredweight of blazing rock was too much for it. The silk ripped straight through, and sulphur and hydrogen leapt to meet each other in a catastrophe of flame.

At once the silk became transparent; the entire skeleton of the zeppelin was visible, dark against an inferno of orange and red and yellow, hanging in the air for what seemed like an impossibly long time before drifting to the ground almost reluctantly. Little figures black against the snow and the fire came tottering or running from it, and witches flew down to help drag them away from the flames. Within a minute of the zeppelin's hitting the ground it was a mass of twisted metal, a pall of smoke, and a few scraps of fluttering fire.

But the soldiers on board, and the others too (though Lyra was too far away by now to spot Mrs Coulter, she knew she was there) wasted no time. With the help of the witches they dragged the machine-gun out and set it up, and began to fight in earnest on the ground.

"On," said Iorek. "They will hold out for a long time."

He roared, and a group of bears peeled away from the main group and attacked the Tartars' right flank. Lyra could feel his desire to be there among them, but all the time her nerves were screaming: On! On! and her mind was filled with pictures of Roger and Lord Asriel; and Iorek Byrnison knew, and turned up the mountain and away from the fight, leaving his bears to hold back the Tartars.

On they climbed. Lyra strained her eyes to look ahead, but not even Pantalaimon's owl-eyes could see any movement on the flank of the mountain they were climbing. Lord Asriel's sledge-tracks were clear, however, and Iorek followed them swiftly, loping through the snow and kicking it high behind them as he ran. Whatever happened behind now was simply that: behind. Lyra had left it. She felt she was leaving the world altogether, so remote and intent she was, so high they were climbing, so strange and uncanny was the light that bathed them.

"Iorek," she said, "will you find Lee Scoresby?"

"Alive or dead, I will find him."

"And if you see Serafina Pekkala . . ."

"I will tell her what you did."

"Thank you, Iorek," she said.

They spoke no more for some time. Lyra felt herself moving into a kind of trance beyond sleep and waking: a state of conscious dreaming, almost, in which she was dreaming that she was being carried by bears to a city in the stars.

She was going to say something about it to Iorek Byrnison, when he slowed down and came to a halt.

"The tracks go on," said Iorek Byrnison. "But I cannot."

Lyra jumped down and stood beside him to look. He was standing at the edge of a chasm. Whether it was a crevasse in the ice or a fissure in the rock was hard to say, and made little difference in any case; all that mattered was that it plunged downwards into unfathomable gloom.

And the tracks of Lord Asriel's sledge ran to the brink . . . and on, across a bridge of compacted snow.

This bridge had clearly felt the strain of the sledge's weight, for a crack ran across it close to the other edge of the chasm, and the surface on the near side of the crack had settled down a foot or so. It might support the weight of a child: it would certainly not stand under the weight of an armoured bear.

And Lord Asriel's tracks ran on beyond the bridge and further up the mountain. If she went on, it would have to be by herself.

Lyra turned to Iorek Byrnison.

"I got to go across," she said. "Thank you for all you done. I don't know what's going to happen when I get to him. We might all die, whether I get to him or not. But if I come back I'll come and see you to thank you properly, King Iorek Byrnison."

She laid a hand on his head. He let it lie there and nodded gently.

"Goodbye, Lyra Silvertongue," he said.

Her heart thumping painfully with love, she turned away and set her foot on the bridge. The snow creaked under her, and Pantalaimon flew up and over the bridge, to settle in the snow on the far side and encourage her onwards. Step after step she took, and wondered with every step whether it would be better to run swiftly and leap for the other side, or go slowly as she was doing and tread as lightly as possible. Halfway across there came another loud creak from the snow; a piece fell off near her feet and tumbled into the abyss, and the bridge settled down another few inches against the crack.

She stood perfectly still. Pantalaimon was crouched leopard-formed ready to leap down and reach for her.

The bridge held. She took another step, then another, and then she felt something settling down below her feet and leapt for the far side with all her strength. She landed belly-down in the snow as the entire length of the bridge fell into the crevasse with a soft *whoosh* behind her.

Pantalaimon's claws were in her furs, holding tight.

After a minute she opened her eyes and crawled up away from the edge. There was no way back. She stood and raised her hand to the watching bear. Iorek Byrnison stood on his hind legs to acknowledge her, and then turned and made off down the mountain in a swift run to help his subjects in the battle with Mrs Coulter and the soldiers from the zeppelin.

Lyra was alone.

23

THE BRIDGE TO THE STARS

ONCE IOREK BYRNISON was out of sight, Lyra felt a great weakness coming over her, and she turned blindly and felt for Pantalaimon.

"Oh, Pan, dear, I can't go on! I'm so frightened – and so tired – all this way, and I'm scared to death! I wish it was someone else instead of me, I do honestly!"

Her dæmon nuzzled at her neck in his cat-form, warm and comforting.

"I just don't know what we got to do," Lyra sobbed. "It's too much for us, Pan, we can't . . ."

She clung to him blindly, rocking back and forth and letting the sobs cry out wildly over the bare snow.

"And even if – if Mrs Coulter got to Roger first there'd be no saving him, because she'd take him back to Bolvangar, or worse, and they'd kill me out of vengeance . . . Why *do* they do these things to children, Pan? Do they all hate children so much, that they want to tear them apart like this? Why *do* they do it?"

But Pantalaimon had no answer; all he could do was hug her close. Little by little, as the storm of fear subsided, she came to a sense of herself again. She was Lyra, cold and frightened by all means, but herself.

"I wish . . ." she said, and stopped. There was nothing that could be gained by wishing for it. A final deep shaky breath, and she was ready to go on.

The moon had set by now, and the sky to the south was profoundly dark, though the billions of stars lay on it like diamonds on velvet. They were outshone, though, by the Aurora, outshone a hundred times. Never had Lyra seen it so brilliant and dramatic; with every twitch and shiver, new miracles of light danced across the sky. And behind the ever-changing gauze of light that other world, that sunlit city, was clear and solid.

The higher they climbed, the more the bleak land spread out below them. To the north lay the frozen sea, compacted here and there into ridges where two sheets of ice had pressed together, but otherwise flat and white and endless, reaching to the Pole itself and far beyond, featureless, lifeless, colourless, and bleak beyond Lyra's imagination. To the east and west were more mountains, great jagged peaks thrusting sharply upwards, their scarps piled high with snow and raked by the wind into blade-like edges as sharp as scimitars. To the south lay the way they had come, and Lyra looked most longingly back, to see if she could spy her dear friend Iorek Byrnison and his troops; but nothing stirred on the wide plain. She was not even sure if she could see the burned wreckage of the zeppelin, or the crimson-stained snow around the corpses of the warriors.

Pantalaimon flew high, and swooped back to her wrist in his owl-form.

"They're just beyond the peak!" he said. "Lord Asriel's laid out all his instruments, and Roger can't move away –"

And as he said that, the Aurora flickered and dimmed, like an anbaric bulb at the end of its life, and then *went out* altogether. In the gloom, though, Lyra sensed the presence of the Dust, for the air seemed to be full of dark intentions, like the forms of thoughts not yet born.

In the enfolding dark she heard a child's cry:

"Lyra! Lyra!"

"I'm a-coming!" she cried back, and stumbled upwards, clambering, sprawling, struggling, at the end of her strength; but hauling herself on and further on through the ghostly-gleaming snow.

"Lyra! Lyra!"

"I'm nearly there," she gasped. "Nearly there, Roger!"

Pantalaimon was changing rapidly, in his agitation: lion, ermine, eagle, wildcat, hare, salamander, owl, leopard, every form he'd ever taken, a kaleidoscope of forms among the Dust –

"*Lyra!*"

Then she reached the summit, and saw what was happening.

Fifty yards away in the starlight Lord Asriel was twisting

together two wires that led to his upturned sledge, on which stood a row of batteries and jars and pieces of apparatus, already frosted with crystals of cold. He was dressed in heavy furs, his face illuminated by the flame of a naphtha lamp. Crouching like the Sphinx beside him was his dæmon, her beautiful spotted coat glossy with power, her tail moving lazily in the snow.

In her mouth she held Roger's dæmon.

The little creature was struggling, flapping, fighting, one moment a bird, the next a dog, then a cat, a rat, a bird again, and calling every moment to Roger himself, who was a few yards off, straining, trying to pull away against the heart-deep tug, and crying out with the pain and the cold. He was calling his dæmon's name, and calling Lyra; he ran to Lord Asriel and plucked his arm, and Lord Asriel brushed him aside. He tried again, crying and pleading, begging, sobbing, and Lord Asriel took no notice except to knock him to the ground.

They were on the edge of a cliff. Beyond them was nothing but a huge illimitable dark. They were a thousand feet or more above the frozen sea.

All this Lyra saw by starlight alone; but then, as Lord Asriel connected his wires, the Aurora blazed all of a sudden into brilliant life. Like the long finger of blinding power that plays between two terminals, except that this was a thousand miles high and ten thousand miles long: dipping, soaring, undulating, glowing, a cataract of glory.

He was *controlling* it . . .

Or leading power down from it; for there was a wire running off a huge reel on the sledge, a wire that ran directly upwards to the sky. Down from the dark swooped a raven, and Lyra knew it for a witch-dæmon. A witch was helping Lord Asriel, and she had flown that wire into the heights.

And the Aurora was blazing again.

He was nearly ready.

He turned to Roger and beckoned, and Roger helplessly came, shaking his head, begging, crying, but helplessly going forward.

"No! Run!" Lyra cried, and hurled herself down the slope at him.

Pantalaimon leapt at the snow leopard and snatched Roger's dæmon from her jaws. In a moment the snow leopard had leapt after him, and Pantalaimon let the other dæmon go, and both young dæmons, changing flick-flick-flick, turned and battled with the great spotted beast.

She slashed left-right with needle-filled paws, and her snarling roar drowned even Lyra's cries. Both children were fighting her, too; or fighting the forms in the turbid air, those dark intentions, that came thick and crowding down the streams of Dust –

And the Aurora swayed above, its continual surging flicker picking out now this building, now that lake, now that row of palm trees, so close you'd think that you could step from this world to that.

Lyra leapt up and seized Roger's hand.

She pulled hard, and then they tore away from Lord Asriel and ran, hand in hand, but Roger cried and twisted, because the leopard had his dæmon again; and Lyra knew that heart-convulsing pain and tried to stop –

But they couldn't stop.

The cliff was sliding away beneath them.

An entire shelf of snow, sliding inexorably down –

The frozen sea, a thousand feet below –

"LYRA!"

Heart-beats –

Tight-clutching hands –

And high above, the greatest wonder.

The vault of heaven, star-studded, profound, was suddenly pierced as if by a spear.

A jet of light, a jet of pure energy released like an arrow from a great bow, shot upwards. The sheets of light and colour that were the Aurora tore apart; a great rending, grinding, crunching, tearing sound reached from one end of the universe to the other; there was dry land in the sky –

Sunlight!

Sunlight shining on the fur of a golden monkey . . .

For the fall of the snow-shelf had halted; perhaps an unseen ledge had broken its fall; and Lyra could see, over the trampled snow of the summit, the golden monkey spring out of the air to the side of the leopard, and she saw the two dæmons bristle, wary and powerful. The monkey's tail was erect, the snow leopard's swept powerfully from side to side. Then the monkey reached out a tentative paw, the leopard lowered her head with a graceful sensual acknowledgement, they touched –

And when Lyra looked up from them, Mrs Coulter herself stood there, clasped in Lord Asriel's arms. Light played around them like sparks and beams of intense anbaric power. Lyra, helpless, could only imagine what had happened: somehow Mrs Coulter must have crossed that chasm, and followed her up here . . .

Her own parents, together!

And embracing so passionately: an undreamt-of thing.

Her eyes were wide. Roger's body lay dead in her arms, still, quiet, at rest. She heard her parents talking:

Her mother said, "They'll never allow it –"

Her father said, "Allow it? We've gone beyond being *allowed*, as if we were children. I've made it possible for anyone to cross, if they wish."

"They'll forbid it! They'll seal it off and excommunicate anyone who tries!"

"Too many people will want to. They won't be able to prevent them. This will mean the end of the Church, Marisa, the end of the Magisterium, the end of all those centuries of darkness! Look at that light up there: that's the sun of another world! Feel the warmth of it on your skin, now!"

"They are stronger than anyone, Asriel! You don't know –"

"I don't know? I? No one in the world knows better than I how strong the Church is! But it isn't strong enough for this. The Dust will change everything, anyway. There's no stopping it now."

"Is that what you wanted? To choke us and kill us all with sin and darkness?"

"I wanted to break out, Marisa! And I have done. Look, look at the palm trees waving on the shore! Can you feel that wind? A wind from another world! Feel it on your hair, on your face . . ."

Lord Asriel pushed back Mrs Coulter's hood and turned her

head to the sky, running his hands through her hair. Lyra watched breathless, not daring to move a muscle.

The woman clung to Lord Asriel as if she were dizzy, and shook her head, distressed.

"No – no – they're coming, Asriel – they know where I've gone –"

"Then come with me, away and out of this world!"

"I daren't –"

"You? *Dare* not? Your child would come. Your child would dare anything, and shame her mother."

"Then take her and welcome. She's more yours than mine, Asriel."

"Not so. You took her in; you tried to mould her. You wanted her then."

"She was too coarse, too stubborn. I'd left it too late . . . But where is she now? I followed her footsteps up . . ."

"You want her, still? Twice you've tried to hold her, and twice she's got away. If I were her I'd run, and keep on running, sooner than give you a third chance."

His hands, still clasping her head, tensed suddenly and drew her towards him in a passionate kiss. Lyra thought it seemed more like cruelty than love, and looked at their dæmons, to see a strange sight: the snow leopard tense, crouching with her claws just pressing in the golden monkey's flesh, and the monkey relaxed, blissful, swooning on the snow.

Mrs Coulter pulled fiercely back from the kiss and said, "No, Asriel – my place is in this world, not that –"

"Come with me!" he said, urgent, powerful. "Come and work with me!"

"We couldn't work together, you and I."

"No? You and I could take the universe to pieces and put it together again, Marisa! We could find the source of Dust and stifle it for ever! And you'd like to be part of that great work; don't lie to me about it. Lie about everything else, lie about the Oblation Board, lie about your lovers – yes, I know about Boreal, and I care nothing – lie about the Church, lie about the child, even, but don't lie about what you truly want . . ."

And their mouths were fastened together with a powerful greed. Their dæmons were playing fiercely; the snow leopard rolled over on her back, and the monkey raked his claws in the soft fur of her neck, and she growled a deep rumble of pleasure.

"If I don't come, you'll try and destroy me," said Mrs Coulter, breaking away.

"Why should I want to destroy you?" he said, laughing, with the light of the other world shining around his head. "Come with me, work with me, and I'll care whether you live or die. Stay here, and you lose my interest at once. Don't flatter yourself that I'd give you a second's thought. Now stay and work your mischief in this world, or come with me."

Mrs Coulter hesitated; her eyes closed, she seemed to sway as if she were fainting; but she kept her balance and opened her eyes again, with an infinite beautiful sadness in them.

"No," she said. "No."

Their dæmons were apart again. Lord Asriel reached down and curled his strong fingers into the snow leopard's fur. Then he turned his back and walked up and away without another word. The golden monkey leapt into Mrs Coulter's arms, making little sounds of distress, reaching out to the snow leopard as she paced away, and Mrs Coulter's face was a mask of tears. Lyra could see them glinting; they were real.

Then her mother turned, shaking with silent sobs, and moved down the mountain and out of Lyra's sight.

Lyra watched her coldly, and then looked up towards the sky.

Such a vault of wonders she had never seen.

The city hanging there so empty and silent looked new-made, waiting to be occupied; or asleep, waiting to be woken. The sun of that world was shining into this, making Lyra's hands golden, melting the ice on Roger's wolfskin hood, making his pale cheeks transparent, glistening in his open sightless eyes.

She felt wrenched apart with unhappiness. And with anger, too; she could have killed her father: if she could have torn out his heart, she would have done so there and then, for what he'd done to Roger. And to her: tricking her – how *dare* he?

She was still holding Roger's body. Pantalaimon was saying

something, but her mind was ablaze, and she didn't hear until he pressed his wildcat-claws into the back of her hand to make her. She blinked.

"What? What?"

"Dust!" he said.

"What are you talking about?"

"Dust. He's going to find the source of Dust and destroy it, isn't he?"

"That's what he said."

"And the Oblation Board and the Church and Bolvangar and Mrs Coulter and all, they want to destroy it too, don't they?"

"Yeah . . . Or stop it affecting people . . . Why?"

"Because if *they* all think Dust is bad, it must be good."

She didn't speak. A little hiccup of excitement leapt in her chest.

Pantalaimon went on:

"We've heard them all talk about Dust, and they're so afraid of it, and you know what? We believed them, even though we could see that what they were doing was wicked and evil and wrong . . . We thought Dust must be bad too, because they were grown-up and they said so. But what if it isn't? What if it's –"

She said breathlessly, "Yeah! What if it's really *good* . . ."

She looked at him and saw his green wildcat-eyes ablaze with her own excitement. She felt dizzy, as if the whole world were turning beneath her.

If Dust were a *good* thing . . . If it were to be sought and welcomed and cherished . . .

"We could look for it too, Pan!" she said.

That was what he wanted to hear.

"We could get to it before he does," he went on, "and . . ."

The enormity of the task silenced them. Lyra looked up at the blazing sky. She was aware of how small they were, she and her dæmon, in comparison with the majesty and vastness of the universe; and of how little they knew, in comparison with the profound mysteries above them.

"We *could*," Pantalaimon insisted. "We came all this way, didn't we? We *could* do it."

"We'd be alone. Iorek Byrnison couldn't follow us and help.

Nor could Farder Coram or Serafina Pekkala, or Lee Scoresby or no one."

"Just us, then. Don't matter. We're not alone, anyway; not like . . ."

She knew he meant *not like Tony Makarios; not like those poor lost dæmons at Bolvangar; we're still one being; both of us are one.*

"And we've got the alethiometer," she said. "Yeah. I reckon we've got to do it, Pan. We'll go up there and we'll search for Dust, and when we've found it we'll know what to do."

Roger's body lay still in her arms. She let him down gently.

"And we'll do it," she said.

She turned away. Behind them lay pain and death and fear; ahead of them lay doubt, and danger, and fathomless mysteries. But they weren't alone.

So Lyra and her dæmon turned away from the world they were born in, and looked towards the sun, and walked into the sky.

LANTERN
SLIDES

SOMETIMES IT BECOMES possible for an author to revisit a story and play with it, not to adapt it into another medium (it's not always a good idea for the original author to do that), nor to revise or "improve" it (tempting though that is, it's too late: you should have done that before it was published, and your business now is with new books, not old ones). But simply to play.

And in every narrative there are gaps: places where, although things happened and the characters spoke and acted and lived their lives, the story says nothing about them. It was fun to visit a few of these gaps and speculate a little on what I might see there.

As for why I call these little pieces "lantern slides", it's because I remember the wooden boxes my grandfather used to have, each one packed neatly with painted glass slides showing scenes from Bible stories or fairy tales or ghost stories or comic little plays with absurd-looking figures. From time to time he would get out the heavy old magic lantern and project some of these pictures on to a screen, and we would sit in the darkened room with the smell of hot metal and watch one scene succeeding another, trying to make sense of the narrative and wondering what St Paul was doing in the story of Little Red Riding Hood; because they never came out of the box in quite the right order.

I think it was my grandfather's magic lantern that Lord Asriel used in the second chapter of this book. Here are some lantern slides, and it doesn't matter what order they come in.

Philip Pullman
Oxford
February 2007

JORDAN COLLEGE, like a great clockwork mechanism with every part connected ultimately to every other, and all slowly and heavily ticking despite the fur of dust on every cog, the curtains of cobweb draped in every corner, the mouse-dirt, the insect-husks, the leaf-skeletons blown in every time the wind was in the east . . . Rituals and habits whose origins no one could remember, but which no one wanted to disturb. The great wheels and the small, the pins and the levers all performing their functions despite the wheezing and the creaking and the groaning of ancient timber. Sometimes the individual parts (a servant or a Scholar) forgot precisely what their function was in relation to the whole, but never that the whole had a function; and it was enough to do again what you had done yesterday, and every day before that, and trust to custom.

LYRA hanging about the Castle Mill boatyard. Each gyptian family had their particular patterns for decorating their boats, based on simple floral designs but becoming more and more complex and fanciful. Lyra watching old Piet van Poppel touching up his boat one day and laboriously copying the rose-and-lily pattern he was using, and then back in her room trying to paint it on her second-best dress before realizing that it would be better embroidered. And very soon after, having pricked her fingers countless times and snapped the threads and lost all patience with the task, throwing it away in disgust, and having to explain its absence to Mrs Lonsdale.

LEE SCORESBY, attracted north by the money being made in the gold rush and making none, but acquiring a balloon by chance in a card game. He was the lover of a witch from the Karelia region, briefly, but she was killed in battle – "She spoiled me for women younger'n three hundred"; but he had plenty of lovers all the same.

ASRIEL among the bears: "Iofur Raknison, I'm going to be entirely frank with you," followed by a string of confident and overbearing lies – had he noticed the bear-king's doll-dæmon, the clue that he was unbearlike enough to be tricked? Or was it just luck? – but he knew the bears well enough. He was very like his daughter.

MRS COULTER selected her lovers for their power and influence, but it did no harm if they were good-looking. Did she ever become fond of a lover? Not once. She could not keep her servants, either.

LYRA had a crush on Dick Orchard, the older boy who could spit further than anyone else. She would hang about the Covered Market gazing at him hopelessly, and cover her pillow with clumsy kisses, just to see what it felt like.

EVERY YEAR the Domestic Bursar at Jordan would send for Lyra – or have her tracked down and caught – and have a photogram taken. Lyra submitted indifferently, and scowled at the camera; it was just one of the things that happened. It didn't occur to her to ask where the pictures went. As a matter of fact they all went to Lord Asriel, but he would never have let her know.

BENNY the pastry cook at Jordan, whose dæmon was male, sitting in the warm cabin with his cousins the Costa family and listening to the story of how Lyra hijacked their boat, and their demand that someone discipline the brat. Their indignation was too much to bear without laughing. In return he told them about how she rescued a starling from the Kitchen cat, only for it to die anyway, and of how she plucked and gutted it clumsily and smuggled it into the great ovens, hoping to retrieve it when it was cooked. But the chef sent her packing, and in the bustle the starling was sent to table with the rest of the Feast, and was eaten with relish by the Master. The truth came out when the doctor had to be summoned to deal with the poor man's suffering. Lyra was unrepentant. "It wasn't for him," she said. "He's obviously got a delicate stomach. I could have eaten it." She was banned from the Kitchens for a term. "Seems to me we got off lightly," said Tony Costa.

SERAFINA PEKKALA on her cloud-pine would find a still field of air at night and listen to the silence. Like the air itself, which was never quite still, the silence was full of little currents and turbulence, of patches of density and pockets of attenuation, all shot through with darts and drifts of whispering that were made of silence themselves. It was as different from the silence of a closed room as fresh spring water is from stale. Later, Serafina realized that she was listening to Dust.

THE SUBTLE
KNIFE

CONTENTS

I
THE CAT AND THE
HORNBEAM TREES

WILL TUGGED AT his mother's hand and said, "Come *on*, come *on* . . ."

But his mother hung back. She was still afraid. Will looked up and down the narrow street in the evening light, along the little terrace of houses, each behind its tiny garden and its box hedge, with the sun glaring off the windows of one side and leaving the other in shadow. There wasn't much time. People would be having their meal about now, and soon there would be other children around, to stare and comment and notice. It was dangerous to wait, but all he could do was persuade her, as usual.

"Mum, let's go in and see Mrs Cooper," he said. "Look, we're nearly there."

"Mrs Cooper?" she said doubtfully.

But he was already ringing the bell. He had to put down the bag to do it, because his other hand still held his mother's. It might have bothered him at twelve years of age to be seen holding his mother's hand, but he knew what would happen to her if he didn't.

The door opened, and there was the stooped elderly figure of the piano teacher, with the scent of lavender water about her as he remembered.

"Who's that? Is that William?" the old lady said. "I haven't seen you for over a year. What do you want, dear?"

"I want to come in, please, and bring my mother," he said firmly.

Mrs Cooper looked at the woman with the untidy hair and the distracted half-smile, and at the boy with the fierce unhappy glare in his eyes, the tight-set lips, the jutting jaw. And then she saw that Mrs Parry, Will's mother, had put make-up on one eye but not on the other. And she hadn't noticed. And neither had Will. Something was wrong.

"Well . . ." she said, and stepped aside to make room in the narrow hall.

Will looked up and down the road before closing the door, and Mrs Cooper saw how tightly Mrs Parry was clinging to her son's hand, and how tenderly he guided her into the sitting-room where the piano was (of course, that was the only room he knew); and she noticed that Mrs Parry's clothes smelt slightly musty, as if they'd been too long in the washing machine before drying; and how similar the two of them looked as they sat on the sofa with the evening sun full on their faces, their broad cheekbones, their wide eyes, their straight black brows.

"What is it, William?" the old lady said. "What's the matter?"

"My mother needs somewhere to stay for a few days," he said. "It's too difficult to look after her at home just now. I don't mean she's ill. She's just kind of confused and muddled and she gets a bit worried. She won't be hard to look after. She just needs someone to be kind to her and I think you could do that quite easily, probably."

The woman was looking at her son without seeming to understand, and Mrs Cooper saw a bruise on her cheek. Will hadn't taken his eyes off Mrs Cooper, and his expression was desperate.

"She won't be expensive," he went on. "I've brought some packets of food, enough to last, I should think. You could have some of it too. She won't mind sharing."

"But . . . I don't know if I should . . . Doesn't she need a doctor?"

"No! She's not ill."

"But there must be someone who can . . . I mean, isn't there a neighbour or someone in the family –"

"We haven't got any family. Only us. And the neighbours are too busy."

"What about the social services? I don't mean to put you off, dear, but –"

"No! No. She just needs a bit of help. I can't do it any more for a little while but I won't be long. I'm going to . . . I've got things to do. But I'll be back soon and I'll take her home again, I promise. You won't have to do it for long."

The mother was looking at her son with such trust, and he

turned and smiled at her with such love and reassurance that Mrs
Cooper couldn't say no.

"Well," she said, turning to Mrs Parry, "I'm sure it won't
matter for a day or so. You can have my daughter's room, dear;
she's in Australia; she won't be needing it again."

"Thank you," said Will, and stood up as if he were in a hurry
to leave.

"But where are you going to be?" said Mrs Cooper.

"I'm going to be staying with a friend," he said. "I'll phone
up as often as I can. I've got your number. It'll be all right."

His mother was looking at him, bewildered. He bent over and
kissed her clumsily.

"Don't worry," he said. "Mrs Cooper will look after you better
than me, honest. And I'll phone up and talk to you tomorrow."

They hugged tightly, and then Will kissed her again and gently
unfastened her arms from his neck before going to the front door.
Mrs Cooper could see he was upset, because his eyes were glistening, but he turned, remembering his manners, and held out
his hand.

"Goodbye," he said, "and thank you very much."

"William," she said, "I wish you'd tell me what the matter is —"

"It's a bit complicated," he said, "but she won't be any trouble,
honestly."

That wasn't what she meant, and they both knew it; but somehow Will was in charge of this business, whatever it was. The old
lady thought she'd never seen a child so implacable.

He turned away, already thinking about the empty house.

The close where Will and his mother lived was a loop of road in
a modern estate, with a dozen identical houses of which theirs
was by far the shabbiest. The front garden was just a patch of
weedy grass; his mother had planted some shrubs earlier in the
year, but they'd shrivelled and died for lack of watering. As Will
came round the corner, his cat Moxie rose up from her favourite
spot under the still-living hydrangea and stretched before greeting him with a soft miaow and butting her head against his leg.

He picked her up and whispered, "Have they come back,
Moxie? Have you seen them?"

The house was silent. In the last of the evening light the man across the road was washing his car, but he took no notice of Will, and Will didn't look at him. The less notice people took, the better.

Holding Moxie against his chest, he unlocked the door and went in quickly. Then he listened very carefully before putting her down. There was nothing to hear; the house was empty.

He opened a tin for her and left her to eat in the kitchen. How long before the man came back? There was no way of telling, so he'd better move quickly. He went upstairs and began to search.

He was looking for a battered green leather writing-case. There are a surprising number of places to hide something that size even in any ordinary modern house; you don't need secret panels and extensive cellars in order to make something hard to find. Will searched his mother's bedroom first, ashamed to be looking through the drawers where she kept her underclothes, and then he worked systematically through the rest of the rooms upstairs, even his own. Moxie came to see what he was doing and sat and cleaned herself nearby, for company.

But he didn't find it.

By that time it was dark, and he was hungry. He made himself baked beans on toast and sat at the kitchen table wondering about the best order to look through the downstairs rooms.

As he was finishing his meal, the phone rang.

He sat absolutely still, his heart thumping. He counted: twenty-six rings, and then it stopped. He put his plate in the sink and started to search again.

Four hours later he still hadn't found the green leather case. It was half-past one, and he was exhausted. He lay on his bed fully clothed and fell asleep at once, his dreams tense and crowded, his mother's unhappy frightened face always there just out of reach.

And almost at once, it seemed (though he'd been asleep for nearly three hours) he woke up knowing two things simultaneously.

First, he knew where the case was. And second, he knew that the men were downstairs, opening the kitchen door.

He lifted Moxie out of the way and softly hushed her sleepy

protest. Then he swung his legs over the side of the bed and put on his shoes, straining every nerve to hear the sounds from downstairs: very quiet sounds: a chair being lifted and replaced, a short whisper, the creak of a floorboard.

Moving more silently than they were, he left his bedroom and tiptoed to the spare room at the top of the stairs. It wasn't quite pitch dark, and in the ghostly grey pre-dawn light he could see the old treadle sewing machine. He'd been through the room thoroughly only hours before, but he'd forgotten the compartment at the side of the sewing machine, where all the patterns and bobbins were kept.

He felt for it delicately, listening all the while. The men were moving about downstairs, and Will could see a dim flicker of light at the edge of the door that might have been a torch.

Then he found the catch of the compartment and clicked it open, and there, just as he'd known it would be, was the leather writing-case.

And now what could he do?

Nothing, for the moment. He crouched in the dimness, heart pounding, listening hard.

The two men were in the hall. He heard one of them say quietly, "Come on. I can hear the milkman down the road."

"It's not here, though," said the other voice. "We'll have to look upstairs."

"Go on, then. Don't hang about."

Will braced himself as he heard the quiet creak of the top step. The man was making no noise at all, but he couldn't help the creak if he wasn't expecting it. Then there was a pause. A very thin beam of torchlight swept along the floor outside: Will saw it through the crack.

Then the door began to move. Will waited till the man was framed in the open doorway, and then exploded up out of the dark and crashed into the intruder's belly.

But neither of them saw the cat.

As the man had reached the top step, Moxie had come silently out of the bedroom and stood with raised tail just behind the man's legs, ready to rub herself against them. The man could have dealt with Will, because he was trained and fit and hard, but the cat was in the way, and as he tried to move back he tripped over her. With a sharp gasp he fell backwards down the stairs, crashing his head brutally against the hall table.

Will heard a hideous crack, and didn't stop to wonder about it: he swung himself down the banisters, leaping over the man's body that lay twitching and crumpled at the foot of the flight, seized the tattered shopping bag from the table, and was out of the front door and away before the other man could do more than come out of the living-room and stare.

Even in his fear and haste Will wondered why the other man didn't shout after him, or chase him. They'd be after him soon, though, with their cars and their cellphones. The only thing to do was run.

He saw the milkman turning into the close, the lights of his electric cart pallid in the dawn glimmer that was already filling the sky. Will jumped over the fence into next-door's garden, down the passage beside the house, over the next garden wall, across a dew-wet lawn, through the hedge, into the tangle of shrubs and trees between the housing estate and the main road, and there he crawled under a bush and lay panting and trembling. It was too early to be out on the road: wait till later, when the rush hour started.

He couldn't get out of his mind the crack as the man's head had struck the table, and the way his neck was bent so far and in such a wrong way, and the dreadful twitching of his limbs. The man was dead. He'd killed him.

He couldn't get it out of his mind, but he had to. There was quite enough to think about. His mother: would she really be safe where she was? Mrs Cooper wouldn't tell, would she? Even if Will didn't turn up as he'd said he would? Because he couldn't, now he'd killed someone.

And Moxie. Who'd feed Moxie? Would Moxie worry about where they both were? Would she try to follow them?

It was getting lighter by the minute. It was light enough already to check through the things in the shopping bag: his mother's purse, the latest letter from the lawyer, the road map of southern England, chocolate bars, toothpaste, spare socks and pants. And the green leather writing-case.

Everything was there. Everything was going to plan, really.
Except that he'd killed someone.

Will had first realized his mother was different from other people,
and that he had to look after her, when he was seven. They were
in a supermarket, and they were playing a game: they were only
allowed to put an item in the cart when no one was looking.
It was Will's job to look all around and whisper "Now," and she
would snatch a tin or a packet from the shelf and put it silently
in the cart. When things were in there they were safe, because
they became invisible.

It was a good game, and it went on for a long time, because
this was a Saturday morning and the shop was full, but they were
good at it and worked well together. They trusted each other.
Will loved his mother very much and often told her so, and she
told him the same.

So when they reached the checkout Will was excited and
happy because they'd nearly won. And when his mother couldn't
find her purse, that was part of the game too, even when she said
the enemies must have stolen it; but Will was getting tired by this
time, and hungry too, and Mummy wasn't so happy any more;
she was really frightened, and they went round and round putting
things back on the shelves, but this time they had to be extra
careful because the enemies were tracking them down by means
of her credit card numbers, which they knew because they had
her purse . . .

And Will got more and more frightened himself. He realized
how clever his mother had been to make this real danger into a
game so that he wouldn't be alarmed, and how, now that he
knew the truth, he had to pretend not to be frightened, so as to
reassure her.

So the little boy pretended it was a game still, so she didn't
have to worry that he was frightened, and they went home without any shopping, but safe from the enemies; and then Will
found the purse on the hall table anyway. On Monday they went
to the bank and closed her account, and opened another somewhere else, just to be sure. Thus the danger passed.

But some time during the next few months, Will realized

slowly and unwillingly that those enemies of his mother's were not in the world out there, but in her mind. That made them no less real, no less frightening and dangerous; it just meant he had to protect her even more carefully. And from the moment in the supermarket when he realized he had to pretend in order not to worry his mother, part of Will's mind was always alert to her anxieties. He loved her so much he would have died to protect her.

As for Will's father, he had vanished long before Will was able to remember him. Will was passionately curious about his father, and he used to plague his mother with questions, most of which she couldn't answer.

"Was he a rich man?"

"Where did he go?"

"Why did he go?"

"Is he dead?"

"Will he come back?"

"What was he like?"

The last question was the only one she could help him with. John Parry had been a handsome man, a brave and clever officer in the Royal Marines, who had left the army to become an explorer and lead expeditions to remote parts of the world. Will thrilled to hear about this. No father could be more exciting than an explorer. From then on, in all his games he had an invisible companion: he and his father were together hacking through the jungle, shading their eyes to gaze out across stormy seas from the deck of their schooner, holding up a torch to decipher mysterious inscriptions in a bat-infested cave . . . They were the best of friends, they saved each other's life countless times, they laughed and talked together over campfires long into the night.

But the older he got the more Will began to wonder. Why were there no pictures of his father in this part of the world or that, with frost-bearded men on Arctic sledges or examining creeper-covered ruins in the jungle? Had nothing survived of the trophies and curiosities he must have brought home? Was nothing written about him in a book?

His mother didn't know. But one thing she said stuck in his mind.

She said, "One day you'll follow in your father's footsteps. You're going to be a great man too. You'll take up his mantle . . ."

And though Will didn't know what that meant, he understood the sense of it, and felt uplifted with pride and purpose. All his games were going to come true. His father was alive, lost somewhere in the wild, and he was going to rescue him and take up his mantle . . . It was worth living a difficult life, if you had a great aim like that.

So he kept his mother's trouble secret. There were times when she was calmer and clearer than others, and he took care to learn from her then how to shop and cook and keep the house clean, so that he could do it when she was confused and frightened. And he learned how to conceal himself too, how to remain unnoticed at school, how not to attract attention from the neighbours, even when his mother was in such a state of fear and madness that she could barely speak. What Will himself feared more than anything was that the authorities would find out about her, and take her away, and put him in a home among strangers. Any difficulty was better than that. Because there came times when the darkness cleared from her mind, and she was happy again, and she laughed at her fears and blessed him for looking after her so well; and she was so full of love and sweetness then that he could think of no better companion, and wanted nothing more than to live with her alone for ever.

But then the men came.

They weren't police, and they weren't social services, and they weren't criminals – at least, as far as Will could judge. They wouldn't tell him what they wanted, in spite of his efforts to keep them away; they'd only speak to his mother. And her state was fragile just then.

But he listened outside the door, and heard them ask about his father, and felt his breath come more quickly.

The men wanted to know where John Parry had gone, and whether he'd sent anything back to her, and when she'd last heard from him, and whether he'd had contact with any foreign embassies. Will heard his mother getting more and more distressed, and finally he ran into the room and told them to go.

He looked so fierce that neither of the men laughed, though he was so young. They could easily have knocked him down, or held him off the floor with one hand, but he was fearless, and his anger was hot and deadly.

So they left. Naturally, this episode strengthened Will's conviction: his father was in trouble somewhere, and only he could help. His games weren't childish any more, and he didn't play so openly. It was coming true, and he had to be worthy of it.

And not long afterwards the men came back, insisting that Will's mother had something to tell them. They came when Will was at school, and one of them kept her talking downstairs while the other searched the bedrooms. She didn't realize what they were doing. But Will came home early and found them, and once again he blazed at them, and once again they left.

They seemed to know that he wouldn't go to the police, for fear of losing his mother to the authorities, and they got more and more persistent. Finally they broke into the house when Will had gone to fetch his mother home from the park: it was getting worse for her now, and she believed that she had to touch every separate slat in every separate bench beside the pond. Will would help her, to get it done quicker. When they got home they saw the back of the men's car disappearing out of the close, and he got inside to find that they'd been through the house and searched most of the drawers and cupboards.

He knew what they were after. The green leather case was his mother's most precious possession; he would never dream of looking through it, and he didn't even know where she kept it. But he knew it contained letters, and he knew she read them sometimes, and cried, and it was then that she talked about his father. So Will supposed that this was what the men were after, and knew he had to do something about it.

He decided first to find somewhere safe for his mother to stay. He thought and thought, but he had no friends to ask, and the neighbours were already suspicious, and the only person he thought he could trust was Mrs Cooper. Once his mother was safely there, he was going to find the green leather case, and look at what was in it, and then he was going to go to Oxford, where he'd find the answer to some of his questions. But the men came too soon.

And now he'd killed one of them.

So the police would be after him too.

Well, he was good at not being noticed. He'd have to *not be noticed* harder than he'd ever done in his life before, and keep it up as long as he could, till either he found his father or they found him. And if they found him first, he didn't care how many more of them he killed.

Later that day, towards midnight in fact, Will was walking out of the city of Oxford, forty miles away. He was tired to his very bones. He had hitch-hiked, and ridden on two buses, and walked, and reached Oxford at six in the evening, too late to do what he needed to do; and he'd eaten at a Burger King and gone to a cinema to hide (though what the film was, he forgot even as he was watching it) and now he was walking along an endless road through the suburbs, heading north.

No one had noticed him so far. But he was aware that he'd better find somewhere to sleep before long, because the later it got, the more noticeable he'd be. The trouble was that there was nowhere to hide in the gardens of the comfortable houses along this road, and there was still no sign of open country.

He came to a large roundabout where the road going north crossed the Oxford ring road going east and west. At this time of night there was very little traffic, and the road where he stood was quiet, with comfortable houses set back behind a wide expanse of grass on either side. Planted along the grass at the road's edge were two lines of hornbeam trees, odd-looking things with perfectly symmetrical close-leafed crowns, more like children's drawings than like real trees, and the street lights made the scene look artificial, like a stage set. Will was stupefied with exhaustion, and he might have gone on to the north, or he might have laid his head on the grass under one of those trees and slept; but as he stood trying to clear his head, he saw a cat.

She was a tabby, like Moxie. She padded out of a garden on the Oxford side of the road, where Will was standing. Will put down his shopping bag and held out his hand, and the cat came up to rub her head against his knuckles, just as Moxie did. Of course, every cat behaved like that, but all the same Will felt such a longing to turn for home that tears scalded his eyes.

Eventually this cat turned away. This was night, and there was a territory to patrol, there were mice to hunt. She padded across the road and towards the bushes just beyond the hornbeam trees, and there she stopped.

Will, still watching, saw the cat behave curiously.

She reached out a paw to pat something in the air in front of her, something quite invisible to Will. Then she leapt backwards, back arched and fur on end, tail held out stiffly. Will knew cat-behaviour. He watched more alertly as the cat approached the spot again, just an empty patch of grass between the hornbeams and the bushes of a garden hedge, and patted the air once more.

Again she leapt back, but less far and with less alarm this time. After another few seconds of sniffing, touching, whisker-twitching, curiosity overcame wariness.

The cat stepped forward, and vanished.

Will blinked. Then he stood still, close to the trunk of the nearest tree, as a truck came round the circle and swept its lights over him. When it had gone past he crossed the road, keeping his eyes on the spot where the cat had been investigating. It wasn't easy, because there was nothing to fix on, but when he came to the place and cast about to look closely, he saw it.

At least, he saw it from some angles. It looked as if someone had cut a patch out of the air, about two metres from the edge of the road, a patch roughly square in shape and less than a metre across. If you were level with the patch so that it was edge-on, it was nearly invisible, and it was completely invisible from behind. You could only see it from the side nearest the road, and you couldn't see it easily even from there, because all you could see through it was exactly the same kind of thing that lay in front of it on this side: a patch of grass lit by a street light.

But Will knew without the slightest doubt that that patch of grass on the other side was in a different world.

He couldn't possibly have said why. He knew it at once, as

strongly as he knew that fire burned and kindness was good. He was looking at something profoundly alien.

And for that reason alone, it enticed him to stoop and look further. What he saw made his head swim and his heart thump harder, but he didn't hesitate: he pushed his shopping bag through, and then scrambled through himself, through the hole in the fabric of this world and into another.

He found himself standing under a row of trees. But not hornbeam trees: these were tall palms, and they were growing, like the trees in Oxford, in a line along the grass. But this was the centre of a broad boulevard, and at the side of the boulevard was a line of cafés and small shops, all brightly lit, all open, and all utterly silent and empty beneath a sky thick with stars. The hot night was laden with the scent of flowers and with the salt smell of the sea.

Will looked around carefully. Behind him the full moon shone down over a distant prospect of great green hills, and on the slopes at the foot of the hills there were houses with rich gardens and an open parkland with groves of trees and the white gleam of a classical temple.

Just beside him was that bare patch in the air, as hard to see from this side as from the other, but definitely there. He bent to look through and saw the road in Oxford, his own world. He turned away with a shudder: whatever this new world was, it had to be better than what he'd just left. With a dawning lightheadedness, the feeling that he was dreaming but awake at the same time, he stood up and looked around for the cat, his guide.

She was nowhere in sight. No doubt she was already exploring those narrow streets and gardens beyond the cafés whose lights were so inviting. Will lifted up his tattered shopping bag and walked slowly across the road towards them, moving very carefully in case it all disappeared.

The air of the place had something Mediterranean or maybe Caribbean about it. Will had never been out of England, so he couldn't compare it with anywhere he knew, but it was the kind of place where people came out late at night to eat and drink, to dance and enjoy music. Except that there was no one here, and the silence was immense.

On the first corner he reached there stood a café, with little green tables on the pavement and a zinc-topped bar and an espresso machine. On some of the tables glasses stood half-empty; in one ashtray a cigarette had burned down to the butt; a plate of risotto stood next to a basket of stale rolls as hard as cardboard.

He took a bottle of lemonade from the cooler behind the bar and then thought for a moment before dropping a pound coin in the till. As soon as he'd shut it, he opened it again, realizing that the money in there might say what this place was called. The currency was called the corona, but he couldn't tell any more than that.

He put the money back and opened the bottle on the opener fixed to the counter before leaving the café and wandering down the street going away from the boulevard. Little grocers' shops and bakeries stood between jewellers and florists and bead-curtained doors opening into private houses, where wrought iron balconies thick with flowers overhung the narrow pavement, and where the silence, being enclosed, was even more profound.

The streets were leading downwards, and before very long they opened out on to a broad avenue where more palm trees reached high into the air, the underside of their leaves glowing in the street lights.

On the other side of the avenue was the sea.

Will found himself facing a harbour enclosed from the left by a stone breakwater and from the right by a headland on which a large building with stone columns and wide steps and ornate balconies stood floodlit among flowering trees and bushes. In the harbour one or two rowing boats lay still at anchor, and beyond the breakwater the starlight glittered on a calm sea.

By now, Will's exhaustion had been wiped out. He was wide awake and possessed by wonder. From time to time, on his way through the narrow streets, he'd put out a hand to touch a wall or a doorway or the flowers in a window-box, and found them solid and convincing. Now he wanted to touch the whole land-scape in front of him, because it was too wide to take in through his eyes alone. He stood still, breathing deeply, almost afraid.

He discovered that he was still holding the bottle he'd taken from the café. He drank from it, and it tasted like what it was, ice-cold lemonade; and welcome too, because the night air was hot.

He wandered along to the right, past hotels with awnings over brightly-lit entrances and bougainvillea flowering beside them, until he came to the gardens on the little headland. The building in the trees with its ornate façade lit by floodlights might have been a casino, or even an opera house. There were paths leading here and there among the lamp-hung oleander trees, but not a sound of life could be heard: no night-birds singing, no insects, nothing but the sound of Will's own footsteps.

The only sound he could hear came from the regular quiet breaking of delicate waves from the beach beyond the palm trees at the edge of the garden. Will made his way there. The tide was half-way in, or half-way out, and a row of pedal-boats was drawn up on the soft white sand above the high-water line. Every few seconds a tiny wave folded itself over at the sea's edge before sliding back neatly under the next. Fifty metres or so out on the calm water was a diving platform.

Will sat on the side of one of the pedal-boats and kicked off his shoes, his cheap trainers that were coming apart and cramping his hot feet. He dropped his socks beside them and pushed his toes deep into the sand. A few seconds later he had thrown off the rest of his clothes and was walking into the sea.

The water was deliciously between cool and warm. He splashed out to the diving platform and pulled himself out to sit on its weather-softened planking and look back at the city.

To his right the harbour lay enclosed by its breakwater. Beyond it a mile or so away stood a red and white striped light-house. And beyond the lighthouse, distant cliffs rose dimly, and beyond them, those great wide rolling hills he'd seen from the place he'd first come through.

Closer at hand were the light-bearing trees of the casino gardens, and the streets of the city, and the waterfront with its hotels and cafés and warm-lit shops, all silent, all empty.

And all safe. No one could follow him here; the man who'd searched the house would never know; the police would never find him. He had a whole world to hide in.

For the first time since he'd run out of his front door that morning, Will began to feel secure.

He was thirsty again, and hungry too, because he'd last eaten in another world, after all. He slipped back into the water and swam back more slowly to the beach, where he put on his under-pants and carried the rest of his clothes and the shopping bag. He dropped the empty bottle into the first rubbish bin he found and walked barefoot along the pavement towards the harbour.

When his skin had dried a little he pulled on his jeans and looked for somewhere he'd be likely to find food. The hotels were too grand. He looked inside the first hotel, but it was so large that he felt uncomfortable, and he kept moving down the waterfront until he found a little café that looked like the right place. He couldn't have said why; it was very similar to a dozen others, with its first-floor balcony laden with flower-pots and its tables and chairs on the pavement outside, but it welcomed him.

There was a bar with photographs of boxers on the wall, and a signed poster of a broadly smiling accordion player. There was a kitchen, and a door beside it that opened on to a narrow flight of stairs, carpeted in a bright floral pattern.

He climbed quietly up to the narrow landing and opened the first door he came to. It was the room at the front. The air was hot and stuffy, and Will opened the glass door on to the balcony to let in the night air. The room itself was small and furnished with things that were too big for it, and shabby, but it was clean and comfortable. Hospitable people lived here. There was a little shelf of books, a magazine on the table, a couple of photographs in frames.

Will left and looked in the other rooms: a little bathroom, a bedroom with a double bed.

Something made his skin prickle before he opened the last door. His heart raced. He wasn't sure if he'd heard a sound from inside, but something told him that the room wasn't empty. He thought how odd it was that this day had begun with someone outside a darkened room, and himself waiting inside; and now the positions were reversed –

And as he stood wondering, the door burst open and some-thing came hurtling at him like a wild beast.

But his memory had warned him, and he wasn't standing quite close enough to be knocked over. He fought hard: knee, head, fist, and the strength of his arms against it, him, her –

A girl about his own age, ferocious, snarling, with ragged dirty clothes and thin bare limbs.

She realized what he was at the same moment, and snatched herself away from his bare chest, to crouch in the corner of the dark landing like a cat at bay. And there was a cat beside her, to his astonishment: a large wildcat, as tall as his knee, fur on end, teeth bared, tail erect.

She put her hand on the cat's back and licked her dry lips, watching his every movement.

Will stood up slowly.

"Who are you?"

"Lyra Silvertongue," she said.

"Do you live here?"

"No," she said vehemently.

"Then what is this place? This city?"

"I don't know."

"Where do you come from?"

"From my world. It's joined on. Where's your dæmon?"

His eyes widened. Then he saw something extraordinary happen to the cat: it leapt into her arms, and when it got there, it had changed shape. Now it was a red-brown stoat with a cream throat and belly, and it glared at him as ferociously as the girl herself. But then another shift in things took place, because he realized that they were both, girl and stoat, profoundly afraid of him, as much as if he'd been a ghost.

"I haven't got a demon," he said. "I don't know what you mean." Then: "Oh! Is that your demon?"

She stood up slowly. The stoat curled himself around her neck and his dark eyes never left Will's face.

"But you're *alive*," she said, half-disbelievingly. "You en't . . . You en't been . . ."

"My name's Will Parry," he said. "I don't know what you mean about demons. In my world demon means . . . It means devil, something evil."

"In your world? You mean *this* en't your world?"

"No. I just found . . . a way in. Like your world, I suppose.
It must be joined on."

She relaxed a little, but she still watched him intensely, and he
stayed calm and quiet as if she were a strange cat he was making
friends with.

"Have you seen anyone else in this city?" he went on.

"No."

"How long have you been here?"

"Dunno. A few days. I can't remember."

"So why did you come here?"

"I'm looking for Dust," she said.

"Looking for dust? What, gold dust? What sort of dust?"

She narrowed her eyes and said nothing. He turned away to
go downstairs.

"I'm hungry," he said. "Is there any food in the kitchen?"

"I dunno . . ." she said, and followed, keeping her distance
from him.

In the kitchen Will found the ingredients for a casserole of
chicken and onions and peppers, but they hadn't been cooked,
and in the heat they were smelling bad. He swept them all into
the dustbin.

"Haven't you eaten anything?" he said, and opened the fridge.
Lyra came to look.

"I didn't know this was here," she said. "Oh! It's cold . . ."

Her dæmon had changed again, and become a huge brightly-
coloured butterfly, which fluttered into the fridge briefly and out
again at once to settle on her shoulder. The butterfly raised and
lowered his wings slowly. Will felt he shouldn't stare, though his
head was ringing with the strangeness of it.

"Haven't you seen a fridge before?" he said.

He found a can of cola and handed it to her before taking out a
tray of eggs. She pressed the can between her palms with pleasure.

"Drink it, then," he said.

She looked at it, frowning. She didn't know how to open it.
He snapped the lid for her, and the drink frothed out. She licked
it suspiciously and then her eyes opened wide.

"This is good?" she said, her voice half-hoping and half-
fearful.

"Yeah. They have Coke in this world, obviously. Look, I'll drink some to prove it isn't poison."

He opened another can. Once she saw him drink, she followed his example. She was obviously thirsty. She drank so quickly that the bubbles got up her nose, and she snorted and belched loudly, and scowled when he looked at her.

"I'm going to make an omelette," he said. "D'you want some?"

"I don't know what omelette is."

"Well, watch and you'll see. Or there's a can of baked beans if you like."

"I don't know baked beans."

He showed her the can. She looked for the snap-open top like the one on the cola can.

"No, you have to use a can-opener," he said. "Don't they have can-openers in your world?"

"In my world servants do the cooking," she said scornfully.

"Look in the drawer over there."

She rummaged through the kitchen cutlery while he broke six eggs into a bowl and whisked them with a fork.

"That's it," he said, watching. "With the red handle. Bring it here."

He pierced the tin and showed her how to open it.

"Now get that little saucepan off the hook and tip them in," he told her.

She sniffed the beans, and again an expression of pleasure and suspicion entered her eyes. She tipped the can into the saucepan and licked a finger, watching as Will shook salt and pepper into the eggs and cut a knob of butter from a package in the fridge into a cast-iron pan. He went into the bar to find some matches, and when he came back she was dipping her dirty finger in the bowl of beaten eggs and licking it greedily. Her dæmon, a cat again, was dipping his paw in it too, but he backed away when Will came near.

"It's not cooked yet," Will said, taking it away. "When did you last have a meal?"

"At my father's house on Svalbard," she said. "Days and days ago. I don't know. I found bread and stuff here and ate that."

He lit the gas, melted the butter, poured in the eggs and let them run all over the base of the pan. Her eyes followed everything greedily, watching him pull the eggs up into soft ridges in the centre as they cooked and tilt the pan to let raw egg flow into the space. She watched him, too, looked at his face and his working hands and his bare shoulders and his feet.

When the omelette was cooked he folded it over and cut it in half with the spatula.

"Find a couple of plates," he said, and Lyra obediently did so.

She seemed quite willing to take orders if she saw the sense of them, so he told her to go and clear a table in front of the café. He brought out the food and some knives and forks from a drawer, and they sat down together, a little awkwardly.

She ate hers in less than a minute, and then fidgeted, swinging back and forth on her chair and plucking at the plastic strips of the woven seat while he finished his omelette. Her dæmon changed yet again, and became a goldfinch, pecking at invisible crumbs on the table-top.

Will ate slowly. He'd given her most of the beans, but even so he took much longer than she did. The harbour in front of them, the lights along the empty boulevard, the stars in the dark sky above, all hung in the huge silence as if nothing else existed at all.

And all the time he was intensely aware of the girl. She was small and slight, but wiry, and she'd fought like a tiger; his fist had raised a bruise on her cheek, and she was ignoring it. Her expression was a mixture of the very young – when she first tasted the cola – and a kind of deep sad wariness. Her eyes were pale blue and her hair would be a darkish blonde once it was washed; because she was filthy, and she smelled as if she hadn't washed for days.

"Laura? Lara?" Will said.

"Lyra."

"Lyra . . . Silvertongue?"

"Yes."

"Where is your world? How did you get here?"

She shrugged. "I walked," she said. "It was all foggy. I didn't know where I was going. At least I knew I was going out of *my* world. But I couldn't see this one till the fog cleared. Then I found myself here."

"What did you say about dust?"

"Dust, yeah. I'm going to find out about it. But this world seems to be empty. There's no one here to ask. I've been here for . . . I dunno, three days, maybe four. And there's no one here."

"But why do you want to find out about dust?"

"Special Dust," she said shortly. "Not ordinary dust, obviously."

The dæmon changed again. He did so in the flick of an eye, and from a goldfinch he became a rat, a powerful pitch-black rat with red eyes. Will looked at him with wide wary eyes, and the girl saw his glance.

"You *have* got a dæmon," she said decisively. "Inside you."

He didn't know what to say.

"You have," she went on. "You wouldn't be human else. You'd be . . . half-dead. We seen a kid with his dæmon cut away. You en't like that. Even if you don't know you've got a dæmon, you have. We was scared at first when we saw you. Like you was a night-ghast or something. But then we saw you weren't like that at all."

"We?"

"Me and Pantalaimon. Us. Your dæmon en't *separate* from you. It's you. A part of you. You're part of each other. En't there *anyone* in your world like us? Are they all like you, with their dæmons all hidden away?"

Will looked at the two of them, the skinny, pale-eyed girl with her black rat-dæmon now sitting in her arms, and felt profoundly alone.

"I'm tired. I'm going to bed," he said. "Are you going to stay in this city?"

"Dunno. I've got to find out more about what I'm looking for. There must be some scholars in this world. There must be *someone* who knows about it."

"Maybe not in this world. But I came here out of a place called Oxford. There's plenty of scholars there, if that's what you want."

"Oxford?" she cried. "That's where I come from!"

"Is there an Oxford in your world, then? You never came from my world."

"No," she said decisively. "Different worlds. But in my world there's an Oxford too. We're both speaking English, en't we? Stands to reason there's other things the same. How did you get through? Is there a bridge, or what?"

"Just a kind of window in the air."

"Show me," she said.

It was a command, not a request. He shook his head.

"Not now," he said. "I want to sleep. Anyway it's the middle of the night."

"Then show me in the morning!"

"All right, I'll show you. But I've got my own things to do. You'll have to find your scholars by yourself."

"Easy," she said. "I know all about scholars."

He put the plates together and stood up.

"I cooked," he said, "so you can wash the dishes."

She looked incredulous. "Wash the dishes?" she scoffed. "There's millions of clean ones lying about! Anyway I'm not a servant. I'm not going to wash them."

"So I won't show you the way through."

"I'll find it by myself."

"You won't, it's hidden. You'd never find it. Listen. I don't know how long we can stay in this place. We've got to eat, so we'll eat what's here, but we'll tidy up afterwards and keep the place clean, because we ought to. You wash these dishes. We've got to treat this place *right*. Now I'm going to bed. I'll have the other room. I'll see you in the morning."

He went inside, cleaned his teeth with a finger and some toothpaste from his tattered bag, fell on the double bed and was asleep in a moment.

Lyra waited till she was sure he was asleep, and then took the dishes into the kitchen and ran them under the tap, rubbing hard with a cloth until they looked clean. She did the same with the knives and forks, but the procedure didn't work with the omelette pan, so she tried a bar of yellow soap on it, and picked at it stubbornly until it looked as clean as she thought it was going to. Then she dried everything on another cloth and stacked it neatly on the draining board.

Because she was still thirsty and because she wanted to try opening a tin again she snapped open another cola and took it upstairs. She listened outside Will's door and, hearing nothing, tiptoed into the other room and took out the alethiometer from under her pillow.

She didn't need to be close to Will to ask about him, but she wanted to look anyway, and she turned his door handle as quietly as she could before going in.

There was a light on the sea front outside shining straight up into the room, and in the glow reflected from the ceiling she looked down at the sleeping boy. He was frowning, and his face glistened with sweat. He was strong and stocky, not as formed as a grown man, of course, because he wasn't much older than she was, but he'd be powerful one day. How much easier if his dæmon had been visible! She wondered what its form might be, and whether it was fixed yet. Whatever its form was, it would express a nature that was savage, and courteous, and unhappy.

She tiptoed to the window. In the glow from the street lamp she carefully set the hands of the alethiometer, and relaxed her mind into the shape of a question. The needle began to sweep around the dial in a series of pauses and swings almost too fast to watch.

She had asked: *What is he? A friend or an enemy?*

The alethiometer answered: *He is a murderer.*

When she saw the answer, she relaxed at once. He could find food, and show her how to reach Oxford, and those were powers that were useful, but he might still have been untrustworthy or cowardly. A murderer was a worthy companion. She felt as safe with him as she'd done with Iorek Byrnison the armoured bear.

She swung the shutter across the open window so the morning sunlight wouldn't strike in on his face, and tiptoed out.

2
AMONG THE WITCHES

THE WITCH Serafina Pekkala, who had rescued Lyra and the other children from the experimental station at Bolvangar and flown with her to the island of Svalbard, was deeply troubled.

In the atmospheric disturbances that followed Lord Asriel's escape from his exile on Svalbard, she and her companions were blown far from the island and many miles out over the frozen sea. Some of them managed to stay with the damaged balloon of Lee Scoresby, the Texan aëronaut, but Serafina herself was tossed high into the banks of fog that soon came rolling in from the gap that Lord Asriel's experiment had torn in the sky.

When she found herself able to control her flight once more, her first thought was of Lyra; for she knew nothing of the fight between the false bear-king and the true one, Iorek Byrnison, nor of what had happened to Lyra after that.

So she began to search for her, flying through the cloudy gold-tinged air on her branch of cloud-pine, accompanied by her dæmon Kaisa the snow-goose. They moved back towards Svalbard and south a little, soaring for several hours under a sky turbulent with strange lights and shadows. Serafina Pekkala knew from the unsettling tingle of the light on her skin that it came from another world.

After some time had passed, Kaisa said, "Look! A witch's dæmon, lost . . ."

Serafina Pekkala looked through the fog-banks and saw a tern, circling and crying in the chasms of misty light. They wheeled and flew towards him. Seeing them come near, he darted up in alarm, but Serafina Pekkala signalled friendship, and he dropped down beside them.

Serafina Pekkala said, "What clan are you from?"

"Taymyr," he told her. "My witch is captured . . . Our companions have been driven away! I am lost . . ."

"Who has captured your witch?"

"The woman with the monkey-dæmon, from Bolvangar . . . Help me! Help us! I am so afraid!"

"Was your clan allied with the child-cutters?"

"Yes, until we found out what they were doing . . . After the fight at Bolvangar they drove us off, but my witch was taken prisoner . . . They have her on a ship . . . What can I do? She is calling to me and I can't find her! Oh, help, help me!"

"Quiet," said Kaisa the goose-dæmon. "Listen down below."

They glided lower, listening with keen ears, and Serafina Pekkala soon made out the beat of a gas-engine, muffled by the fog.

"They can't navigate a ship in fog like this," Kaisa said. "What are they doing?"

"It's a smaller engine than that," said Serafina Pekkala, and as she spoke there came a new sound from a different direction: a low brutal shuddering blast, like some immense sea creature calling from the depths. It roared for several seconds and then stopped abruptly.

"The ship's foghorn," said Serafina Pekkala.

They wheeled low over the water and cast about again for the sound of the engine. Suddenly they found it, for the fog seemed to have patches of different density, and the witch darted up out of sight just in time as a launch came chugging slowly through the swathes of damp air. The swell was slow and oily, as if the water was reluctant to rise.

They swung around and above, the tern-dæmon keeping close like a child to its mother, and watched the steersman adjust the course slightly as the foghorn boomed again. There was a light mounted on the bow, but all it lit up was the fog a few yards in front.

Serafina Pekkala said to the lost dæmon: "Did you say there are still some witches helping these people?"

"I think so – a few renegade witches from Volgorsk – unless they've fled too," he told her. "What are you going to do? Will you look for my witch?"

"Yes. But stay with Kaisa for now."

Serafina Pekkala flew down towards the launch, leaving the

dæmons out of sight above, and alighted on the counter just behind the steersman. His seagull-dæmon squawked, and the man turned to look.

"You taken your time, en't you?" he said. "Get up ahead and guide us in on the port side."

She took off again at once. It had worked: they still had some witches helping them, and he thought she was one. Port was left, she remembered, and the port light was red. She cast about in the fog until she caught its hazy glow no more than a hundred yards away. She darted back and hovered above the launch calling directions to the steersman, who slowed the craft down to a crawling pace and brought it in to the gangway-ladder that hung just above the water-line. The steersman called, and a sailor threw a line from above, and another hurried down the ladder to make it fast to the launch.

Serafina Pekkala flew up to the ship's rail, and retreated to the shadows by the lifeboats. She could see no other witches, but they were probably patrolling the skies; Kaisa would know what to do.

Below, a passenger was leaving the launch and climbing the ladder. The figure was fur-swathed, hooded, anonymous; but as it reached the deck, a golden monkey-dæmon swung himself lightly upon the rail and glared around, his black eyes radiating malevolence. Serafina caught her breath: the figure was Mrs Coulter.

A dark-clothed man hurried out on deck to greet her, and looked around as if he were expecting someone else as well.

"Lord Boreal –" he began.

But Mrs Coulter interrupted: "He has gone on elsewhere. Have they started the torture?"

"Yes, Mrs Coulter," was the reply, "but –"

"I ordered them to wait," she snapped. "Have they taken to disobeying me? Perhaps there should be more discipline on this ship."

She pushed her hood back. Serafina Pekkala saw her face clearly in the yellow light: proud, passionate, and to the witch, so young.

"Where are the other witches?" she demanded.

The man from the ship said, "All gone, ma'am. Fled to their homeland."

"But a witch guided the launch in," said Mrs Coulter. "Where has she gone?"

Serafina shrank back; obviously the sailor in the launch hadn't heard the latest state of things. The cleric looked around, bewildered, but Mrs Coulter was too impatient, and after a cursory glance above and along the deck, she shook her head and hurried in with her dæmon through the open door that cast a yellow nimbus on the air. The man followed.

Serafina Pekkala looked around to check her position. She was concealed behind a ventilator on the narrow area of decking between the rail and the central superstructure of the ship; and on this level, facing forward below the bridge and the funnel, was a saloon from which windows, not portholes, looked out on three sides. That was where the people had gone in. Light spilled thickly from the windows on to the fog-pearled railing, and dimly showed up the foremast and the canvas-covered hatch. Everything was wringing wet and beginning to freeze into stiffness. No one could see Serafina where she was; but if she wanted to see any more, she would have to leave her hiding-place.

That was too bad. With her pine branch she could escape, and with her knife and her bow she could fight. She hid the branch behind the ventilator and slipped along the deck until she reached the first window. It was fogged with condensation and impossible to see through, and Serafina could hear no voices, either. She withdrew to the shadows again.

There was one thing she could do; she was reluctant, because it was desperately risky, and it would leave her exhausted; but it seemed there was no choice. It was a kind of magic she could work to make herself unseen. True invisibility was impossible, of course: this was mental magic, a kind of fiercely-held modesty that could make the spell-worker not invisible but simply unnoticed. Holding it with the right degree of intensity she could pass through a crowded room, or walk beside a solitary traveller, without being seen.

So now she composed her mind and brought all her concentration to bear on the matter of altering the way she held herself so as to deflect attention completely. It took some minutes before she was confident. She tested it by stepping out of her hiding-place and into the path of a sailor coming along the deck with a bag of tools. He stepped aside to avoid her without looking at her once.

She was ready. She went to the door of the brightly-lit saloon and opened it, finding the room empty. She left the outer door ajar so that she could flee through it if she needed to, and saw a door at the far end of the room that opened on to a flight of stairs leading down into the bowels of the ship. She descended, and found herself in a narrow corridor hung with white-painted pipework, and illuminated with anbaric bulkhead lights, which led straight along the length of the hull, with doors opening off it on both sides.

She walked quietly along, listening, until she heard voices. It sounded as if some kind of council was in session.

She opened the door and walked in.

A dozen or so people were seated around a large table. One or two of them looked up for a moment, gazed at her absently, and forgot her at once. She stood quietly near the door and watched. The meeting was being chaired by an elderly man in the robes of a Cardinal, and the rest of them seemed clerics of one sort or another, apart from Mrs Coulter, who was the only woman pre-sent. Mrs Coulter had thrown her furs over the back of the chair, and her cheeks were flushed in the heat of the ship's interior.

Serafina Pekkala looked around carefully, and saw someone else in the room as well: a thin-faced man with a frog-dæmon, seated to one side at a table laden with leather-bound books and loose piles of yellowed paper. She thought at first that he was a clerk or a secretary, until she saw what he was doing: he was intently gazing at a golden instrument like a large watch or a compass, stopping every minute or so to note down what he found. Then he would open one of the books, search laboriously through the index, and look up a reference before writing that down too and turning back to the instrument.

Serafina looked back to the discussion at the table, because she heard the word *witch*.

"She knows something about the child," said one of the clerics. "She confessed that she knows something. All the witches know something about her."

"I am wondering what Mrs Coulter knows," said the Cardinal. "Is there something she should have told us before, I wonder?"

"You will have to speak more plainly than that," said Mrs Coulter icily. "You forget I am a woman, Your Eminence, and thus not so subtle as a prince of the Church. What is this truth that I should have known about the child?"

The Cardinal's expression was full of meaning, but he said nothing. There was a pause and then another cleric said almost apologetically:

"It seems that there is a prophecy. It concerns the child, you see, Mrs Coulter. All the signs have been fulfilled. The circumstances of her birth, to begin with. The gyptians know something about her too – they speak of her in terms of witch-oil and marsh-fire, uncanny, you see – hence her success in leading the gyptian men to Bolvangar. And then there's her astonishing feat of deposing the bear-king Iofur Raknison – this is no ordinary child. Fra Pavel can tell us more, perhaps . . ."

He glanced at the thin-faced man reading the alethiometer, who blinked, rubbed his eyes, and looked at Mrs Coulter.

"You may be aware that this is the only alethiometer left, apart from the one in the child's possession," he said. "All the others have been acquired and destroyed, by order of the Magisterium. I learn from this instrument that the child was given hers by the Master of Jordan College, and that she learned to read it by herself, and that she can use it without the books of readings. If it were possible to disbelieve the alethiometer, I would do so, because to use the instrument without the books is simply inconceivable to me. It takes decades of diligent study to reach any sort of understanding. She began to read it within a few weeks of acquiring it, and now she has an almost complete mastery. She is like no human scholar I can imagine."

"Where is she now, Fra Pavel?" said the Cardinal.

"In the other world," said Fra Pavel. "It is already late."

"The witch knows!" said another man, whose muskrat-dæmon gnawed unceasingly at a pencil. "It's all in place but for the witch's testimony! I say we should torture her again!"

"What is this prophecy?" demanded Mrs Coulter, who had been getting increasingly angry. "How dare you keep it from me?"

Her power over them was visible. The golden monkey glared round the table, and none of them could look him in the face.

Only the Cardinal did not flinch. His dæmon, a macaw, lifted a foot and scratched her head.

"The witch has hinted at something extraordinary," the Cardinal said. "I dare not believe what I think it means. If it's true, it places on us the most terrible responsibility men and women have ever faced. But I ask you again, Mrs Coulter – what do *you* know of the child and her father?"

Mrs Coulter's face was chalk-white with fury.

"How dare you interrogate me?" she spat. "And how dare you keep from me what you've learned from the witch? And finally, how dare you assume that I am keeping something from you? D'you think I'm on her side? Or perhaps you think I'm on her father's side? Perhaps you think I should be tortured like the witch. Well, we are all under your command, Your Eminence. You have only to snap your fingers and you could have me torn apart. But if you searched every scrap of flesh for an answer you wouldn't find one, because I know nothing of this prophecy, nothing whatever. And I demand that you tell me what *you* know. My child, my own child, conceived in sin and born in shame, but my child nonetheless, and you keep from me what I have every right to know!"

"Please," said another of the clerics nervously. "Please, Mrs Coulter; the witch hasn't spoken yet; we shall learn more from her. Cardinal Sturrock himself says that she's only hinted at it."

"And suppose the witch doesn't reveal it?" Mrs Coulter said. "What then? We guess, do we? We shiver and quail and guess?"

Fra Pavel said: "No, because that is the question I am now preparing to put to the alethiometer. We shall find the answer, whether from the witch or from the books of readings."

"And how long will that take?"

He raised his eyebrows wearily and said, "A considerable time. It is an immensely complex question."

"But the witch would tell us at once," said Mrs Coulter.

And she rose to her feet. As if in awe of her, most of the men did too. Only the Cardinal and Fra Pavel remained seated. Serafina Pekkala stood back, fiercely holding herself unseen. The golden monkey was gnashing his teeth, and all his shimmering fur was standing on end.

Mrs Coulter swung him up to her shoulder.

"So let us go and ask her," she said.

She turned and swept out into the corridor. The men hastened to follow her, jostling and shoving past Serafina Pekkala, who had only time to stand quickly aside, her mind in a turmoil. The last to go was the Cardinal.

Serafina took a few seconds to compose herself, because her agitation was beginning to make her visible. Then she followed the clerics down the corridor and into a smaller room, bare and white and hot, where they were all clustered around the dreadful figure in the centre: a witch bound tightly to a steel chair, with agony on her grey face and her legs twisted and broken.

Mrs Coulter stood over her. Serafina took up a position by the door, knowing that she could not stay unseen for long; this was too hard.

"Tell us about the child, witch," said Mrs Coulter.

"No!"

"You will suffer."

"I have suffered enough."

"Oh, there is more suffering to come. We have a thousand years of experience in this Church of ours. We can draw out your suffering endlessly. Tell us about the child," Mrs Coulter said, and reached down to break one of the witch's fingers. It snapped easily.

The witch cried out, and for a clear second Serafina Pekkala became visible to everyone, and one or two of the clerics looked at her, puzzled and fearful; but then she controlled herself again, and they turned back to the torture.

Mrs Coulter was saying, "If you don't answer I'll break

another finger, and then another. What do you know about the child? Tell me."

"All right! Please, please, no more!"

"Answer then."

There came another sickening crack, and this time a flood of sobbing broke from the witch. Serafina Pekkala could hardly hold herself back. Then came these words, in a shriek:

"No, no! I'll tell you! I beg you, no more! The child who was to come . . . The witches knew who she was before you did . . . We found out her name . . ."

"We know her name. What name do you mean?"

"Her true name! The name of her destiny!"

"What is this name? Tell me!" said Mrs Coulter.

"No . . . no . . ."

"And how? Found out how?"

"There was a test . . . If she was able to pick out one spray of cloud-pine from many others, she would be the child who would come, and it happened at our Consul's house at Trollesund, when the child came with the gyptian men . . . The child with the bear . . ."

Her voice gave out.

Mrs Coulter gave a little exclamation of impatience, and there came another loud slap, and a groan.

"But what was your prophecy about this child?" Mrs Coulter went on, and her voice was all bronze now, and ringing with passion. "And what is this name that will make her destiny clear?"

Serafina Pekkala moved closer, even among the tight throng of men around the witch, and none of them felt her presence at their very elbows. She must end this witch's suffering, and soon, but the strain of holding herself unseen was enormous. She trembled as she took the knife from her waist.

The witch was sobbing, "She is the one who came before, and you have hated and feared her ever since! Well, now she has come again, and you failed to find her . . . She was there on Svalbard – she was with Lord Asriel, and you lost her. She escaped, and she will be –"

But before she could finish, there came an interruption.

Through the open doorway there flew a tern, mad with terror, and it beat its wings brokenly as it crashed to the floor and struggled up and darted to the breast of the tortured witch, pressing itself against her, nuzzling, chirruping, crying, and the witch called in anguish: "Yambe-Akka! Come to me, come to me!"

No one but Serafina Pekkala understood. Yambe-Akka was the goddess who came to a witch when she was about to die.

And Serafina was ready. She became visible at once, and stepped forward smiling happily, because Yambe-Akka was merry and light-hearted and her visits were gifts of joy. The witch saw her and turned up her tear-stained face, and Serafina bent to kiss it, and slid her knife gently into the witch's heart. The tern-dæmon looked up with dim eyes and vanished.

And now Serafina Pekkala would have to fight her way out.

The men were still shocked, disbelieving, but Mrs Coulter recovered her wits almost at once.

"Seize her! Don't let her go!" she cried, but Serafina was already at the door, with an arrow nocked in her bowstring. She swung up the bow and loosed the arrow in less than a second, and the Cardinal fell choking and kicking to the floor.

Out, along the corridor to the stairs, turn, nock, loose; and another man fell, and already a loud jarring bell was filling the ship with its clangour.

Up the stairs and out on to the deck. Two sailors barred her way, and she said, "Down there! The prisoner has got loose! Get help!"

That was enough to puzzle them, and they stood undecided, which gave her time to dodge past and seize her cloud-pine from where she had hidden it behind the ventilator.

"Shoot her!" came a cry in Mrs Coulter's voice from behind, and at once three rifles fired, and the bullets struck metal and whined off into the fog, as Serafina leapt on the branch and urged it up like one of her own arrows. A few seconds later she was in the air, in the thick of the fog, safe, and then a great goose-shape glided out of the wraiths of grey to her side.

"Where to?" he said.

"Away, Kaisa, away," she said. "I want to get the stench of these people out of my nose."

In truth, she didn't know where to go or what to do next. But there was one thing she knew for certain: there was an arrow in her quiver that would find its mark in Mrs Coulter's throat.

They turned south, away from that troubling other-world gleam in the fog, and as they flew a question began to form more clearly in Serafina's mind. What was Lord Asriel doing?

Because all the events that had overturned the world had their origin in his mysterious activities.

The problem was that the usual sources of her knowledge were natural ones. She could track any animal, catch any fish, find the rarest berries; and she could read the signs in the pine marten's entrails, or decipher the wisdom in the scales of a perch, or interpret the warnings in the crocus-pollen; but these were children of nature, and they told her natural truths.

For knowledge about Lord Asriel, she had to go elsewhere. In the port of Trollesund, their consul Dr Lanselius maintained his contact with the world of men and women, and Serafina Pekkala sped there through the fog to see what he could tell her. Before she went to his house she circled over the harbour, where wisps and tendrils of mist drifted ghostlike on the icy water, and watched as the pilot guided in a large vessel with an African registration. There were several other ships riding at anchor outside the harbour. She had never seen so many.

As the short day faded, she flew down and landed in the back garden of the consul's house. She tapped on the window, and Dr Lanselius himself opened the door, a finger to his lips.

"Serafina Pekkala, greetings," he said. "Come in quickly, and welcome. But you had better not stay long." He offered her a chair at the fireside, having glanced through the curtains out of a window that fronted the street, and said, "You'll have some wine?"

She sipped the golden Tokay and told him of what she had seen and heard aboard the ship.

"Do you think they understood what she said about the child?" he asked.

"Not fully, I think. But they know she is important. As for that woman, I'm afraid of her, Dr Lanselius. I shall kill her, I think, but still I'm afraid of her."

"Yes," he said. "So am I."

And Serafina listened as he told her of the rumours that had swept the town. Amid the fog of rumour, a few facts had begun to emerge clearly.

"They say that the Magisterium is assembling the greatest army ever known, and this is an advance party. And there are unpleasant rumours about some of the soldiers, Serafina Pekkala. I've heard about Bolvangar, and what they were doing there – cutting children's dæmons away, the most evil work I've ever heard of – well, it seems there is a regiment of warriors who have been treated in the same way. Do you know the word *zombi*? They fear nothing, because they're mindless. There are some in this town now. The authorities keep them hidden, but word gets out, and the townspeople are terrified of them."

"What of the other witch-clans?" said Serafina Pekkala. "What news do you have of them?"

"Most have gone back to their homelands. All the witches are waiting, Serafina Pekkala, with fear in their hearts, for what will happen next."

"And what do you hear of the church?"

"They're in complete confusion. You see, they don't know what Lord Asriel intends to do."

"Nor do I," she said, "and I can't imagine what it might be. What do *you* think he's intending, Dr Lanselius?"

He gently rubbed the head of his serpent-dæmon with his thumb.

"He is a scholar," he said after a moment, "but scholarship is not his ruling passion. Nor is statesmanship. I met him once, and I thought he had an ardent and powerful nature, but not a despotic one. I don't think he wants to rule . . . I don't know, Serafina Pekkala. I suppose his servant might be able to tell you. He is a man called Thorold, and he was imprisoned with Lord Asriel in the house on Svalbard. It might be worth a visit there to see if he can tell you anything; but of course, he might have gone into the other world with his master."

"Thank you. That's a good idea . . . I'll do it. And I'll go at once."

She said farewell to the consul and flew up through the gathering dark to join Kaisa in the clouds.

* * *

Serafina's journey to the north was made harder by the confusion in the world around her. All the Arctic peoples had been thrown into panic, and so had the animals, not only by the fog and the magnetic variations but by unseasonal crackings of ice and stirrings in the soil. It was as if the earth itself, the permafrost, were slowly awakening from a long dream of being frozen.

In all this turmoil, where sudden shafts of uncanny brilliance lanced down through rents in towers of fog and then vanished as quickly, where herds of musk-ox were seized by the urge to gallop south and then wheeled immediately to the west or the north again, where tight-knit skeins of geese disintegrated into a honking chaos as the magnetic fields they flew by wavered and snapped this way and that, Serafina Pekkala set her cloud-pine and flew north, to the house on the headland in the wastes of Svalbard.

There she found Lord Asriel's servant Thorold fighting off a group of cliff-ghasts.

She saw the movement before she came close enough to see what was happening. A swirl of lunging leathery wings, and a malevolent *yowk-yowk-yowk* resounding in the snowy courtyard; and a single figure swathed in furs, firing a rifle into the midst of them with a gaunt dog-dæmon snarling and snapping beside him whenever one of the filthy things flew low enough.

She didn't know the man, but a cliff-ghast was an enemy always. She swung round above and loosed a dozen arrows into the mêlée. With shrieks and gibberings the gang – too loosely organized to be called a troop – circled, saw their new opponent, and fled in confusion. A minute later the skies were bare again, and their dismayed *yowk-yowk-yowk* echoed distantly off the mountains before dwindling into silence.

Serafina flew down to the courtyard and alighted on the trampled, blood-sprinkled snow. The man pushed his hood back, still holding his rifle warily, because a witch was an enemy sometimes, and she saw an elderly man, long-jawed and grizzled and steady-eyed.

"I am a friend of Lyra's," she said. "I hope we can talk. Look: I lay my bow down."

"Where is the child?" he said.

"In another world. I'm concerned for her safety. And I need to know what Lord Asriel is doing."

He lowered the rifle and said, "Step inside, then. Look: I lay my rifle down."

The formalities exchanged, they went indoors. Kaisa glided through the skies above, keeping watch, while Thorold brewed some coffee and Serafina told him of her involvement with Lyra.

"She was always a wilful child," he said when they were seated at the oaken table in the glow of a naphtha lamp. "I'd see her every year or so when his lordship visited his college. I was fond of her, mind, you couldn't help it. But what her place was in the wider scheme of things, I don't know."

"What was Lord Asriel planning to do?"

"You don't think he told me, do you, Serafina Pekkala? I'm his manservant, that's all. I clean his clothes and cook his meals and keep his house tidy. I may have learned a thing or two in the years I been with his lordship, but only by picking 'em up accidental. He wouldn't confide in me any more than in his shaving-mug."

"Then tell me the thing or two you've learned by accident," she insisted.

Thorold was an elderly man, but he was healthy and vigorous, and he felt flattered by the attention of this young witch and her beauty, as any man would. He was shrewd, though, too, and he knew the attention was not really on him, but on what he knew; and he was honest, so he did not draw out his telling for much longer than he needed.

"I can't tell you precisely what he's doing," he said, "because all the philosophical details are beyond my grasp. But I can tell you what drives his lordship, though he doesn't know I know. I've seen this in a hundred little signs. Correct me if I'm wrong, but the witch-people have different gods from ours, en't that right?"

"Yes, that's true."

"But you know about our God? The God of the church, the one they call the Authority?"

"Yes, I do."

"Well, Lord Asriel has never found hisself at ease in the doctrines of the church, so to speak. I've seen a spasm of disgust cross
his face when they talk of the sacraments, and atonement, and
redemption, and suchlike. It's death among our people, Serafina
Pekkala, to challenge the church, but Lord Asriel's been nursing
a rebellion in his heart for as long as I've served him, that's one
thing I do know."

"A rebellion against the church?"

"Partly, aye. There was a time when he thought of making it
an issue of force, but he turned away from that."

"Why? Was the church too strong?"

"No," said the old servant, "that wouldn't stop my master.
Now this might sound strange to you, Serafina Pekkala, but I
know the man better than any wife could know him, better than
a mother. He's been my master and my study for nigh on forty
years. I can't follow him to the height of his thought any more
than I can fly, but I can see where he's a-heading even if I can't
go after him. No, it's my belief he turned away from a rebellion
against the church not because the church was too strong, but
because it was too weak to be worth the fighting."

"So . . . what is he doing?"

"I think he's a-waging a higher war than that. I think he's
aiming a rebellion against the highest power of all. He's gone
a-searching for the dwelling place of the Authority Himself,
and he's a-going to destroy Him. That's what I think. It shakes
my heart to voice it, ma'am. I hardly dare think of it. But I can't
put together any other story that makes sense of what he's
doing."

Serafina sat quiet for a few moments, absorbing what Thorold
had said.

Before she could speak, he went on:

"Course, anyone setting out to do a grand thing like that
would be the target of the church's anger. Goes without saying.
It'd be the most gigantic blasphemy, that's what they'd say.
They'd have him before the Consistorial Court and sentenced to
death before you could blink. I've never spoke of it before and
I shan't again; I'd be afraid to speak it aloud to you if you weren't
a witch and beyond the power of the church; but that makes

sense, and nothing else does. He's a-going to find the Authority and kill Him."

"Is that possible?" said Serafina.

"Lord Asriel's life has been filled with things that were impossible. I wouldn't like to say there was anything he couldn't do. But on the face of it, Serafina Pekkala, yes, he's stark mad. If angels couldn't do it, how can a man dare to think about it?"

"Angels? What are angels?"

"Beings of pure spirit, the church says. The church teaches that some of the angels rebelled before the world was created, and got flung out of heaven and into hell. They failed, you see, that's the point. They couldn't do it. And they had the power of angels. Lord Asriel is just a man, with human power, no more than that. But his ambition is limitless. He dares to do what men and women don't even dare to think. And look what he's done already: he's torn open the sky, he's opened the way to another world. Who else has ever done that? Who else could think of it? So with one part of me, Serafina Pekkala, I say he's mad, wicked, deranged. Yet with another part I think, he's Lord Asriel, he's not like other men. Maybe . . . If it was ever going to be possible, it'd be done by him and by no one else."

"And what will you do, Thorold?"

"I'll stay here and wait. I'll guard this house till he comes back and tells me different, or till I die. And now I might ask you the same question, ma'am."

"I'm going to make sure the child is safe," she said. "It might be that I have to pass this way again, Thorold. I'm glad to know that you will still be here."

"I won't budge," he told her.

She refused Thorold's offer of food, and said goodbye.

A minute or so later she joined her goose-dæmon again, and the dæmon kept silence with her as they soared and wheeled above the foggy mountains. She was deeply troubled, and there was no need to explain: every strand of moss, every icy puddle, every midge in her homeland thrilled against her nerves and called her back. She felt fear for them, but fear for herself too, for she was having to change; these were human affairs she was inquiring into, this was a human matter; Lord Asriel's god was not hers. Was she becoming human? Was she losing her witch-hood?

If she were, she could not do it alone.

"Home now," she said. "We must talk to our sisters, Kaisa. These events are too big for us alone."

And they sped through the roiling banks of fog towards Lake Enara, and home.

In the forested caves beside the lake they found the others of their clan, and Lee Scoresby, too. The aëronaut had struggled to keep his balloon aloft after the crash of Svalbard, and the witches had guided him to their homeland, where he had begun to repair the damage to his basket and the gas-bag.

"Ma'am, I'm very glad to see you," he said. "Any news of the little girl?"

"None, Mr Scoresby. Will you join our council tonight and help us discuss what to do?"

The Texan blinked with surprise, for no man had ever been known to join a witch-council.

"I'd be greatly honoured," he said. "I may have a suggestion or two of my own."

All through that day the witches came, like flakes of black snow on the wings of a storm, filling the skies with the darting flutter of their silk and the swish of air through the needles of their cloud-pine branches. Men who hunted in the dripping forests or fished among melting ice-floes heard the sky-wide whisper through the fog, and if the sky was clear they would look up to see the witches flying, like scraps of darkness drifting on a secret tide.

By evening the pines around the lake were lit from below by a hundred fires, and the greatest fire of all was built in front of the gathering-cave. There, once they had eaten, the witches assembled. Serafina Pekkala sat in the centre, the crown of little scarlet flowers nestling among her fair hair. On her left sat Lee Scoresby, and on her right, a visitor: the queen of the Latvian witches, whose name was Ruta Skadi.

She had arrived only an hour before, to Serafina's surprise. Serafina had thought Mrs Coulter beautiful, for a short-life; but

Ruta Skadi was as lovely as Mrs Coulter, with an extra dimension of the mysterious, the uncanny. She had trafficked with spirits, and it showed. She was vivid and passionate, with large black eyes; it was said that Lord Asriel himself had been her lover. She wore heavy gold earrings and a crown on her black curly hair ringed with the fangs of snow-tigers. Serafina's dæmon Kaisa had learned from Ruta Skadi's dæmon that she had killed the tigers herself in order to punish the Tartar tribe who worshipped them, because the tribesmen had failed to do her honour when she had visited their territory. Without their tiger-gods the tribe declined into fear and melancholy, and begged her to allow them to worship her instead, only to be rejected with contempt; for what good would their worship do her, she asked? It had done nothing for the tigers. Such was Ruta Skadi: beautiful, proud and pitiless.

Serafina was not sure why she had come, but she made her welcome, and etiquette demanded that she should sit on Serafina's right. When they were all assembled, Serafina began to speak.

"Sisters! You know why we have come together: we must decide what to do about these new events. The universe is broken wide, and Lord Asriel has opened the way from this world to another. Should we concern ourselves with it, or live our lives as we have done until now, looking after our own affairs? Then there is the matter of the child Lyra Belacqua, now called Lyra Silvertongue by King Iorek Byrnison. She chose the right cloud-pine spray at the house of Dr Lanselius: she is the child we have always expected, and now she has vanished.

"We have two guests, who will tell us their thoughts. First we shall hear Queen Ruta Skadi."

Ruta Skadi stood. Her white arms gleamed in the firelight, her eyes glittered so brightly that even the furthest witch could see the play of expression on her vivid face.

"Sisters," she began, "let me tell you what is happening, and who it is that we must fight. For there is a war coming. I don't know who will join with us, but I know whom we must fight. It is the Magisterium, the church. For all its history – and that's not long by our lives, but it's many, many of theirs – it's tried to suppress and control every natural impulse. And when it can't control them, it cuts them out. Some of you have seen what they did at Bolvangar. And that was horrible, but it is not the only such place, not the only such practice. Sisters, you know only the north: I have travelled in the south lands. There are churches there, believe me, that cut their children too, as the people of Bolvangar did – not in the same way, but just as horribly – they cut their sexual organs, yes, both boys and girls – they cut them with knives so that they shan't feel. That is what the church does, and every church is the same: control, destroy, obliterate every good feeling. So if a war comes, and the church is on one side of it, we must be on the other, no matter what strange allies we find ourselves bound to.

"What I propose is that our clans join together and go north to explore this new world, and see what we can discover there. If the child is not to be found in our world, it's because she will have gone after Lord Asriel already. And Lord Asriel is the key to this, believe me. He was my lover once, and I would willingly join forces with him, because he hates the church and all it does.

"That is what I have to say."

Ruta Skadi spoke passionately, and Serafina admired her power and her beauty. When the Latvian queen sat down, Serafina turned to Lee Scoresby.

"Mr Scoresby is a friend of the child's, and thus a friend of ours," she said. "Would you tell us your thoughts, sir?"

The Texan got to his feet, whiplash-lean and courteous. He looked as if he were not conscious of the strangeness of the occasion, but he was. His hare-dæmon Hester crouched beside him, her ears flat along her back, her golden eyes half-closed.

"Ma'am," he said, "I have to thank you all first for the kindness you've shown to me, and the help you extended to an aëronaut battered by winds that came from another world. I won't trespass long on your patience.

"When I was travelling north to Bolvangar with the gyptians, the child Lyra told me about something that happened in the college she used to live in, back in Oxford. Lord Asriel had shown the other scholars the severed head of a man called Stanislaus Grumman, and that kinda persuaded them to give him some money to come north and find out what had happened.

"Now the child was so sure of what she'd seen that I didn't like to question her too much. But what she said made a kind of memory come to my mind, except that I couldn't reach it clearly. I knew something about this Dr Grumman. And it was only on the flight here from Svalbard that I remembered what it was. It was an old hunter from Tungusk who told me. It seems that Grumman knew the whereabouts of some kind of object that gives protection to whoever holds it. I don't want to belittle the magic that you witches can command, but this thing, whatever it is, has a kind of power that outclasses anything I've ever heard of.

"And I thought I might postpone my retirement to Texas, because of my concern for that child, and search for Dr Grumman. You see, I don't think he's dead. I think Lord Asriel was fooling those scholars.

"So I'm going to Nova Zembla, where I last heard of him alive, and I'm going to search for him. I cain't see the future, but I can see the present clear enough. And I'm with you in this war, for what my bullets are worth. But that's the task I'm going to take on, ma'am," he concluded, turning back to Serafina Pekkala: "I'm going to seek out Stanislaus Grumman, and find out what he knows, and if I can find that object he knows of, I'll take it to Lyra."

Serafina said, "Have you been married, Mr Scoresby? Have you any children?"

"No, ma'am, I have no child, though I would have liked to be a father. But I understand your question, and you're right: that little girl has had bad luck with her true parents, and maybe I can make it up to her. Someone has to do it, and I'm willing."

"Thank you, Mr Scoresby," she said.

And she took off her crown, and plucked from it one of the little scarlet flowers that, while she wore them, remained as fresh as if they had just been picked.

"Take this with you," she said, "and whenever you need my help, hold it in your hand and call to me. I shall hear you, wherever you are."

"Why, thank you, ma'am," he said, surprised. He took the little flower and tucked it carefully into his breast pocket.

"And we shall call up a wind to help you to Nova Zembla,"

Serafina Pekkala told him. "Now, sisters, who would like to speak?"

The council proper began. The witches were democratic, up to a point; every witch, even the youngest, had the right to speak, but only their queen had the power to decide. The talk lasted all night, with many passionate voices for open war at once, and some others urging caution, and a few, though those were the wisest, suggesting a mission to all the other witch-clans to urge them to join together for the first time.

Ruta Skadi agreed with that, and Serafina sent out messengers at once. As for what they should do immediately, Serafina picked out twenty of her finest fighters and ordered them to prepare to fly north with her, into the new world that Lord Asriel had opened, and search for Lyra.

"What of you, Queen Ruta Skadi?" Serafina said finally. "What are your plans?"

"I shall search for Lord Asriel, and learn what he's doing from his own lips. And it seems that the way he's gone is northwards too. May I come the first part of the journey with you, sister?"

"You may, and welcome," said Serafina, who was glad to have her company.

So they agreed.

But soon after the council had broken up, an elderly witch came to Serafina Pekkala and said, "You had better listen to what Juta Kamainen has to say, Queen. She's headstrong, but it might be important."

The young witch Juta Kamainen – young by witch standards, that is, she was only just over a hundred years old – was stubborn and embarrassed, and her robin-dæmon was agitated, flying from her shoulder to her hand and circling high above her before settling again briefly on her shoulder. The witch's cheeks were plump and red; she had a vivid and passionate nature. Serafina didn't know her very well.

"Queen," said the young witch, unable to stay silent under Serafina's gaze, "I know the man Stanislaus Grumman. I used to love him. But I hate him now with such a fervour that if I see him, I shall kill him. I would have said nothing, but my sister made me tell you."

She glanced with hatred at the elder witch, who returned her look with compassion: she knew about love.

"Well," said Serafina, "if he is still alive, he'll have to stay alive until Mr Scoresby finds him. You had better come with us into the new world, and then there'll be no danger of your killing him first. Forget him, Juta Kamainen. Love makes us suffer. But this task of ours is greater than revenge. Remember that."

"Yes, Queen," said the young witch humbly.

And Serafina Pekkala and her twenty-one companions and Queen Ruta Skadi of Latvia prepared to fly into the new world, where no witch had ever flown before.

3
A CHILDREN'S WORLD

LYRA WAS AWAKE EARLY. She'd had a horrible dream: she had been given the vacuum flask she'd seen her father Lord Asriel show to the Master and Scholars of Jordan College.

When that had really happened, Lyra had been hiding in the wardrobe, and she'd watched as Lord Asriel opened the flask to show the Scholars the severed head of Stanislaus Grumman the lost explorer; but in her dream, Lyra had to open the flask herself, and she didn't want to. In fact she was terrified. But she had to do it, whether she wanted to or not, and she felt her hands weakening with dread as she unclipped the lid, and heard the air rush into the frozen chamber. Then she lifted the lid away, nearly choking with fear, but knowing she had to, she had to do it. And there was nothing inside. The head had gone. There was nothing to be afraid of.

But she awoke all the same, crying and sweating, in the hot little bedroom facing the harbour, with the moonlight streaming through the window, and lay in someone else's bed clutching someone else's pillow, with the ermine-Pantalaimon nuzzling her and making soothing noises. Oh, she was so frightened! And how odd it was, that in real life she had been eager to see the head of Stanislaus Grumman, and begged Lord Asriel to open the flask again and let her look, and yet in her dream she was so terrified.

When morning came she asked the alethiometer what the dream meant, but all it said was *It was a dream about a head*.

She thought of waking the strange boy, but he was so deeply asleep that she decided not to. Instead she went down to the kitchen and tried to make an omelette, and twenty minutes later she sat down at a table on the pavement and ate the blackened, gritty thing with great pride while the sparrow-Pantalaimon pecked at the bits of shell.

She heard a sound behind her, and there was Will, heavy-eyed with sleep.

"I can make omelette," she said. "I'll make you some if you like."

He looked at her plate and said, "No, I'll have some cereal. There's still some milk in the fridge that's all right. They can't have been gone very long, the people who lived here."

She watched him shake corn flakes into a bowl and pour milk on them: something else she'd never seen before.

He carried the bowl outside and said, "If you don't come from this world, where's your world? How did you get here?"

"Over a bridge. My father made this bridge, and . . . I followed him across. But he's gone somewhere else, I don't know where. I don't care. But while I was walking across there was so much fog, and I got lost, I think. I walked around in the fog for days just eating berries and stuff I found. Then one day the fog cleared and we was up on that cliff back there –"

She gestured behind her. Will looked along the shore, past the lighthouse, and saw the coast rising in a great series of cliffs that disappeared into the haze of the distance.

"And we saw the town here, and came down, but there was no one here. At least there were things to eat and beds to sleep in. We didn't know what to do next."

"You sure this isn't another part of your world?"

"Course. This en't my world, I know that for certain."

Will remembered his own absolute certainty, on seeing the patch of grass through the window in the air, that it wasn't in his world, and he nodded.

"So there's three worlds at least that are joined on," he said.

"There's millions and millions," Lyra said. "This other dæmon told me. He was a witch's dæmon. No one can count how many worlds there are, all in the same space, but no one could get from one to another before my father made this bridge."

"What about the window I found?"

"I dunno about that. Maybe all the worlds are starting to move into one another."

"And why are you looking for dust?"

She looked at him coldly. "I might tell you some time," she said.

"All right. But how are you going to look for it?"

"I'm going to find a scholar who knows about it."

"What, any scholar?"

"No. An experimental theologian," she said. "In my Oxford, they were the ones who knew about it. Stands to reason it'll be the same in your Oxford. I'll go to Jordan College first, because Jordan had the best ones."

"I never heard of experimental theology," he said.

"They know all about elementary particles and fundamental forces," she explained. "And anbaromagnetism, stuff like that. Atomcraft."

"What-magnetism?"

"Anbaromagnetism. Like anbaric. Those lights," she said, pointing up at the ornamental street light, "they're anbaric."

"We call them electric."

"Electric ... That's like electrum. That's a kind of stone, a jewel, made out of gum from trees. There's insects in it, sometimes."

"You mean amber," he said, and they both said, "Anbar ..."

And each of them saw their own expression on the other's face. Will remembered that moment for a long time afterwards.

"Well, electromagnetism," he went on, looking away. "Sounds like what we call physics, your experimental theology. You want scientists, not theologians."

"Ah," she said warily. "I'll find 'em."

They sat in the wide clear morning, with the sun glittering placidly on the harbour, and each of them might have spoken next, because they were both burning with questions; but then they heard a voice from further along the harbour front, towards the casino gardens.

They both looked there, startled. It was a child's voice, but there was no one in sight.

Will said to Lyra quietly, "How long did you say you'd been here?"

"Three days, four, I lost count. I never seen anyone. There's no one here. I looked almost everywhere."

But there was. Two children, one a girl of Lyra's age and the other a younger boy, came out of one of the streets leading down to the harbour. They were carrying baskets, and they both had red hair. They were about a hundred yards away when they saw Will and Lyra at the café table.

Pantalaimon changed from a goldfinch to a mouse and ran up Lyra's arm to the pocket of her shirt. He'd seen that these new children were like Will: neither of them had a dæmon visible.

The two children wandered up and sat at a table nearby.

"You from Ci'gazze?" the girl said.

Will shook his head.

"From Sant'Elia?"

"No," said Lyra. "We're from somewhere else."

The girl nodded. This was a reasonable reply.

"What's happening?" said Will. "Where are the grown-ups?"

The girl's eyes narrowed. "Didn't the Spectres come to your city?" she said.

"No," Will said. "We just got here. We don't know about Spectres. What is this city called?"

"Ci'gazze," the girl said suspiciously. "Cittàgazze, all right."

"Cittàgazze," Lyra repeated. "Ci'gazze. Why do the grown-ups have to leave?"

"Because of the Spectres," the girl said with weary scorn. "What's your name?"

"Lyra. And he's Will. What's yours?"

"Angelica. My brother is Paolo."

"Where've you come from?"

"Up the hills. There was a big fog and storm and everyone was frightened, so we all run up in the hills. Then when the fog cleared the grown-ups could see with telescopes that the city was full of Spectres, so they couldn't come back. But the kids, we ain afraid of Spectres, all right. There's more kids coming down. They be here later, but we're first."

"Us and Tullio," said little Paolo proudly.

"Who's Tullio?"

Angelica was cross: Paolo shouldn't have mentioned him; but the secret was out now.

"Our big brother," she said. "He ain with us. He's hiding till he can . . . He's just hiding."

"He's gonna get —" Paolo began, but Angelica smacked him

hard, and he shut his mouth at once, pressing his quivering lips together.

"What did you say about the city?" said Will. "It's full of Spectres?"

"Yeah, Ci'gazze, Sant'Elia, all cities, the Spectres go where the people are. Where you from?"

"Winchester," said Will.

"I never heard of it. They ain got Spectres there?"

"No. I can't see any here either."

"Course not!" she crowed. "You ain grown up! When we grow up we see Spectres."

"I ain afraid of Spectres, all right," the little boy said, thrusting forward his grubby chin. "Kill the buggers."

"En't the grown-ups going to come back at all?" said Lyra.

"Yeah, in a few days," said Angelica. "When the Spectres go somewhere else. We like it when the Spectres come, 'cause we can run about in the city, do what we like, all right."

"But what do the grown-ups think the Spectres will do to them?" Will said.

"Well, when a Spectre catch a grown-up, that's bad to see. They eat the life out of them there and then, all right. I don't want to be grown-up, for sure. At first they know it's happening, and they're afraid, they cry and cry, they try and look away and pretend it ain happening, but it is. It's too late. And no one ain gonna go near them, they on they own. Then they get pale and they stop moving. They still alive, but it's like they been eaten out from inside. You look in they eyes, you see the back of they heads. Ain nothing there."

The girl turned to her brother and wiped his nose on the sleeve of his shirt.

"Me and Paolo's going to look for ice creams," she said. "You want to come and find some?"

"No," said Will, "we got something else to do."

"Goodbye, then," she said, and Paolo said, "Kill the Spectres!"

"Goodbye," said Lyra.

As soon as Angelica and the little boy had vanished, Pantalaimon appeared from Lyra's pocket, his mouse-head ruffled and bright-eyed.

He said to Will, "They don't know about this window you found."

It was the first time Will had heard him speak, and he was almost more startled by that than by anything else he'd seen so far. Lyra laughed at his astonishment.

"He – but he spoke – do all dæmons talk?" Will said.

"Course they do!" said Lyra. "Did you think he was just a *pet*?"

Will rubbed his hair and blinked. Then he shook his head. "No," he said, addressing Pantalaimon. "You're right, I think. They don't know about it."

"So we'd better be careful how we go through," Pantalaimon said.

It was only strange for a moment, talking to a mouse. Then it was no more strange than talking into a telephone, because he was really talking to Lyra. But the mouse was separate; there was something of Lyra in his expression, but something else too. It was too hard to work out, when there were so many strange things happening at once. Will tried to bring his thoughts together.

"You got to find some clothes first," he said to Lyra, "before you go into my Oxford."

"Why?" she said stubbornly.

"Because you can't go and talk to people in my world looking like that, they wouldn't let you near them. You got to look as if you fit in. You got to go about camouflaged. I *know*, see. I've been doing it for years. You better listen to me or you'll get caught, and if they find out where you come from, and the window, and everything . . . Well, this is a good hiding-place, this world. See, I'm . . . I got to hide from some men. This is the best hiding-place I could dream of, and I don't want it found out. So I don't want you giving it away by looking out of place or as if you don't belong. I got my own things to do in Oxford, and if you give me away, I'll kill you."

She swallowed. The alethiometer never lied: this boy was a murderer, and if he'd killed before, he could kill her too. She nodded seriously, and she meant it.

"All right," she said.

Pantalaimon had become a lemur, and was gazing at him with

disconcerting wide eyes. Will stared back, and the dæmon became a mouse once more and crept into her pocket.

"Good," he said. "Now while we're here, we'll pretend to these other kids that we just come from somewhere in their world. It's good there aren't any grown-ups about. We can just come and go and no one'll notice. But in my world, you got to do as I say. And the first thing is you better wash yourself. You need to look clean, or you'll stand out. We got to be camouflaged everywhere we go. We got to look as if we belong there so naturally that people don't even notice us. So go and wash your hair for a start. There's some shampoo in the bathroom. Then we'll go and find some different clothes."

"I dunno how," she said. "I never washed my hair. The housekeeper done it at Jordan, and then I never needed to after that."

"Well, you'll just have to work it out," he said. "Wash yourself all over. In my world people are clean."

"H'mm," said Lyra, and went upstairs. A ferocious rat-face glared at him over her shoulder, but he looked back coldly.

Part of him wanted to wander about this sunny silent morning exploring the city, and another part trembled with anxiety for his mother, and another part was still numb with shock at the death he'd caused. And overhanging them all there was the task he had to do. But it was good to keep busy, so while he waited for Lyra he cleaned the working surfaces in the kitchen, and washed the floor, and emptied the rubbish into the bin he found in the alley outside.

Then he took the green leather writing-case from his shopping bag and looked at it longingly. As soon as he'd shown Lyra how to get through the window into his Oxford, he'd come back and look at what was inside; but in the meanwhile, he tucked it under the mattress of the bed he'd slept in. In this world, it was safe.

When Lyra came down, clean and wet, they left to look for some clothes for her. They found a department store, shabby like everywhere else, with clothes in styles that looked a little old-fashioned to Will's eye, but they found Lyra a tartan skirt and a green sleeveless blouse with a pocket for Pantalaimon. She refused to wear jeans: refused even to believe Will when he told her that most girls did.

"They're trousers," she said. "I'm a girl. Don't be stupid."

He shrugged; the tartan skirt looked unremarkable, which was the main thing. Before they left, Will dropped some coins in the till behind the counter.

"What you doing?" she said.

"Paying. You have to pay for things. Don't they pay for things in your world?"

"They don't in this one! I bet those other kids en't paying for a thing."

"They might not, but I do."

"If you start behaving like a grown-up, the Spectres'll get you," she said, but she didn't know whether she could tease him yet, or whether she should be afraid of him.

In the daylight, Will could see how ancient the buildings in the heart of the city were, and how near to ruin some of them had come. Holes in the road had not been repaired; windows were broken, plaster was peeling. And yet there had once been a beauty and grandeur about this place: through carved archways they could see spacious courtyards filled with greenery, and there were great buildings that looked like palaces, for all that the steps were cracked and the door frames loose from the walls. It looked as if rather than knock a building down and build a new one, the citizens of Ci'gazze preferred to patch it up indefinitely.

At one point they came to a tower standing on its own in a little square. It was the oldest building they'd seen: a simple battle-mented tower four storeys high. Something about its stillness in the bright sun was intriguing, and both Will and Lyra felt drawn to the half-open door at the top of the broad steps; but they didn't speak of it, and they went half-reluctantly on.

When they reached the broad boulevard with the palm trees, he told her to look for a little café on a corner, with green-painted metal tables on the pavement outside. She found it within a minute. It looked smaller and shabbier by daylight, but it was the same place, with the zinc-topped bar, the espresso machine, the half-finished plate of risotto, now beginning to smell bad in the warm air.

"Is it in here?" she said.

"No. It's in the middle of the road. Make sure there's no other kids around . . ."

But they were alone. Will took her to the central reservation under the palm trees, and looked around to get his bearings.

"I think it was about here," he said. "When I came through I could just about see that big hill behind the white house up there, and looking this way there was the café there, and . . ."

"What's it look like? I can't see anything."

"You won't mistake it. It doesn't look like anything you've ever seen."

He cast up and down. Had it vanished? Had it closed? He couldn't see it anywhere.

And then suddenly he had it. He moved back and forth, watching the edge. Just as he'd found the night before, on the Oxford side of it, you could only see it at all from one side: when you moved behind it, it was invisible. And the sun on the grass beyond it was just like the sun on the grass on this side, except unaccountably different.

"Here it is," he said, when he was sure.

"Ah! I see it!"

She was agog: she looked as astounded as he'd looked himself to hear Pantalaimon talk. Her dæmon, unable to remain inside her pocket, had come out to be a wasp, and he buzzed up to the hole and back several times, while she rubbed her still slightly wet hair into spikes.

"Keep to one side," he told her. "If you stand in front of it people'd just see a pair of legs, and that *would* make 'em curious. I don't want anyone noticing."

"What's that noise?"

"Traffic. It's part of the Oxford ring road. It's bound to be busy. Get down and look at it from the side. It's the wrong time of day to go through, really, there's far too many people about. But it'd be hard to find somewhere to go if we went through in the middle of the night. At least once we're through we can blend in easy. You go through first. Just duck through quickly and then move away from the window."

She had a little blue rucksack that she'd been carrying since they left the café, and she unslung it and held it in her arms before crouching to look through.

"Ah –" she gasped. "And that's your world? That don't look like any part of Oxford. You sure you was in Oxford?"

"Course I'm sure. When you go through, you'll see a road right in front of you. Go to the left, and then a little further along you take the road that goes down to the right. That leads to the city centre. Make sure you can see where this window is, and remember, all right? It's the only way back."

"Right," she said. "I won't forget."

Taking her rucksack in her arms, she ducked through the window in the air and vanished. Will crouched down to see where she went.

And there she was, standing on the grass in his Oxford with Pan still as a wasp on her shoulder, and no one, as far as he could tell, had seen her appear. Cars and trucks raced past a few feet beyond, and no driver, at this busy junction, would have time to gaze sideways at an odd-looking bit of air, even if they could see it, and the traffic screened the window from anyone looking across from the far side.

There was a squeal of brakes, a shout, a bang. He flung himself down to look.

Lyra was lying on the grass. A car had braked so hard that a van had struck it from behind, and knocked the car forward anyway, and there was Lyra, lying still –

Will darted through after her. No one saw him come; all eyes were on the car, the crumpled bumper, the van driver getting out, and on the little girl.

"I couldn't help it – she ran out in front –" said the car driver, a middle-aged woman. "*You* were too close," she said, rounding on the van driver.

"Never mind that," he said, "how's the kid?"

The van driver was addressing Will, who was on his knees beside Lyra. Will looked up and around, but there was nothing for it; he was responsible. On the grass next to him, Lyra was moving her head about, blinking hard. Will saw the wasp-Pantalaimon crawling dazedly up a grass stem beside her.

"You all right?" Will said. "Move your legs and arms."

"Stupid!" said the woman from the car. "Just ran out in front. Didn't look once. What am I supposed to do?"

"You still there, love?" said the van driver.

"Yeah," muttered Lyra.

"Everything working?"

"Move your feet and hands," Will insisted.

She did. There was nothing broken.

"She's all right," said Will, "I'll look after her. She's fine."

"D'you know her?" said the truck driver.

"She's my sister," said Will. "It's all right. We just live round the corner. I'll take her home."

Lyra was sitting up now, and as she was obviously not badly hurt, the woman turned her attention back to the car. The rest of the traffic was moving around the two stationary vehicles, and as they went past the drivers looked curiously at the little scene, as people always do. Will helped Lyra up: the sooner they moved away the better. The woman and the van driver had realized that their argument ought to be handled by their insurance companies, and were exchanging addresses, when the woman saw Will helping Lyra to limp away.

"Wait!" she called. "You'll be witnesses. I need your name and address."

"I'm Mark Ransom," said Will, turning back, "and my sister's Lisa. We live at 26 Bourne Close."

"Postcode?"

"I can never remember," he said. "Look, I want to get her home."

"Hop in the cab," said the van driver, "and I'll take you round."

"No, it's no trouble, it'd be quicker to walk, honest."

Lyra wasn't limping badly. She walked away with Will, back along the grass under the hornbeam trees, and turned around the first corner they came to.

They sat on a low garden wall.

"You hurt?" Will said.

"Banged me leg. And when I fell down it shook me head," she said.

But she was more concerned about what was in the rucksack.

She felt inside it and brought out a heavy little bundle wrapped in black velvet and unfolded it. Will's eyes widened to see the alethiometer: the tiny symbols painted around the face, the golden hands, the questing needle, the heavy richness of the case took his breath away.

"What's that?" he said.

"It's my alethiometer. It's a truth-teller. A symbol-reader. I hope it en't broken . . ."

But it was unharmed. Even in her trembling hands the long needle swung steadily. She put it away and said, "I never seen so many carts and things . . . I never guessed they was going so fast."

"They don't have cars and vans in your Oxford?"

"Not so many. Not like these ones. I wasn't used to it. But I'm all right now."

"Well be careful from now on. If you go and walk under a bus or get lost or something, they'll realize you're not from this world, and start looking for the way through . . ."

He was far more angry than he needed to be. Finally he said:

"All right, look. If you pretend you're my sister, that'll be a disguise for me, because the person they're looking for hasn't got a sister. And if I'm with you I can show you how to cross roads without getting killed."

"All right," she said humbly.

"And money. I bet you haven't – well, how could you have any money? How are you going to get around and eat and so on?"

"I have got money," she said, and shook some gold coins out of her purse.

Will looked at them incredulously.

"Is that gold? It is, isn't it? Well, that would get people asking questions, and no mistake. You're just not safe. I'll give you some money. Put those coins away and keep them out of sight. And remember – you're my sister, and your name's Lisa Ransom."

"Lizzie. I pretended to call myself Lizzie before. I can remember that."

"All right, Lizzie then. And I'm Mark. Don't forget."

"All right," she said peaceably.

Her leg was going to be painful; already it was red and swollen where the car had struck it, and a dark massive bruise was forming. What with the bruise on her cheek where he'd struck her the night before, she looked as if she'd been badly treated, and that worried him too: suppose some police officer should become curious?

He tried to put it out of his mind, and they set off together, crossing at the traffic lights and casting just one glance back at the window under the hornbeam trees. They couldn't see it at all. It was quite invisible, and the traffic was flowing again.

In Summertown, ten minutes' walk down the Banbury Road, Will stopped in front of a bank.

"What are you doing?" said Lyra.

"I'm going to get some money. I probably better not do it too often, but they won't register it till the end of the working day, I shouldn't think."

He put his mother's bank card into the automatic dispenser and tapped out her PIN number. Nothing seemed to be going wrong, so he withdrew a hundred pounds, and the machine gave it up without a hitch. Lyra watched open-mouthed. He gave her a twenty-pound note.

"Use that later," he said. "Buy something and get some change. Let's find a bus into town."

Lyra let him deal with the bus, and sat very quiet, watching the houses and gardens of the city that was hers and not hers. It was like being in someone else's dream. They got off in the city centre next to an old stone church, which she did know, opposite a big department store which she didn't.

"It's all changed," she said. "Like ... That en't the Corn-market? And this is the Broad. There's Balliol. And Bodley's Library down there. But where's Jordan?"

Now she was trembling badly. It might have been delayed reaction from the accident, or present shock from finding an entirely different building in place of the Jordan College she knew as home.

"That en't right," she said. She spoke quietly, because Will had told her to stop pointing out so loudly the things that were wrong. "This is a different Oxford."

"Well, we knew that," he said.

He wasn't prepared for Lyra's wide-eyed helplessness. He couldn't know how much of her childhood had been spent running about streets almost identical with these, and how proud she'd been of belonging to Jordan College, whose scholars were the cleverest, whose coffers the richest, whose beauty the most splendid of all; and now it simply wasn't there, and she wasn't Lyra of Jordan any more; she was a lost little girl in a strange world, belonging nowhere.

"Well," she said shakily. "If it en't there . . ."

It was going to take longer than she'd thought, that was all.

4
TREPANNING

AS SOON AS LYRA had gone her way, Will found a phone box and dialled the number of the lawyer's office on the letter he held.

"Hello? I want to speak to Mr Perkins."

"Who's calling, please?"

"It's in connection with Mr John Parry. I'm his son."

"Just a moment, please . . ."

A minute went by and then a man's voice said, "Hello. This is Alan Perkins. Who am I speaking to?"

"William Parry. Excuse me for calling. It's about my father Mr John Parry. You send money every three months from my father to my mother's bank account."

"Yes . . ."

"Well, I want to know where my father is, please. Is he alive or dead?"

"How old are you, William?"

"Twelve. I want to know about him."

"Yes . . . Has your mother, is she, does she know you're phoning me?"

Will thought carefully.

"No," he said. "But she's not in very good health. She can't tell me very much and I want to know."

"Yes, I see. Where are you now? Are you at home?"

"No, I'm . . . I'm in Oxford."

"On your own?"

"Yes."

"And your mother's not well, you say?"

"No."

"Is she in hospital or something?"

"Something like that. Look, can you tell me or not?"

"Well, I can tell you something, but not much and not right now, and I'd rather not do it over the phone. I'm seeing a client in five minutes . . . Can you find your way to my office at about half-past two?"

"No," Will said. It would be too risky: the lawyer might have heard by then that he was wanted by the police. He thought quickly, and went on, "I've got to catch a bus to Nottingham and I don't want to miss it. But what I want to know, you can tell me over the phone, can't you? All I want to know is, is my father alive, and if he is, where I can find him. You can tell me that, can't you?"

"It's not quite as simple as that. I can't really give out private information about a client unless I'm sure the client would want me to. And I'd need some proof of who you were, anyway."

"Yes, I understand, but can you just tell me whether he's alive or dead?"

"Well . . . No, that wouldn't be confidential. Unfortunately I can't tell you anyway, because I don't know."

"What?"

"The money comes from a family trust. He left instructions to pay it until he told me to stop. I haven't heard from him from that day to this. What it boils down to is that he's . . . Well, I suppose he's vanished. That's why I can't answer your question."

"Vanished? Just . . . lost?"

"It's a matter of public record, actually. Look, why don't you come into the office and –"

"I can't. I'm going to Nottingham."

"Well, write to me or get your mother to write and I'll let you know what I can. But you must understand, I can't do very much over the phone."

"Yes, I suppose so. All right. But can you tell me where he disappeared?"

"As I say, it's a matter of public record. There were several newspaper stories at the time. You know he was an explorer?"

"My mother's told me some things, yes . . ."

"Well, he was leading an expedition and it just disappeared. About ten years ago."

"Where?"

"The far north. Alaska, I think. You can look it up in the public library. Why don't you –"

But at that point Will's money ran out, and he hadn't got any more change. The dialling tone purred in his ear. He put the phone down and looked around.

What he wanted above all was to speak to his mother. He had to stop himself dialling Mrs Cooper's number, because if he heard his mother's voice it would be very hard not to go back to her, and that would put them both in danger. But he could send her a postcard.

He chose a view of the city, and wrote, "Dear Mum, I am safe and well, and I will see you again soon. I hope everything is all right. I love you. Will." Then he addressed it and bought a stamp and held the card close to him for a minute before dropping it in the letter box.

It was mid-morning, and he was in the main shopping street, where buses shouldered their way through crowds of pedestrians. He began to realize how exposed he was; for it was a weekday, when a child of his age should have been in school. Where could he go?

It didn't take him long to hide. Will could vanish easily enough, because he was good at it; he was even proud of his skill. The way he did it was similar to the way Serafina Pekkala had made herself invisible on the ship: he made himself intensely inconspicuous. He made himself part of the background.

So now, knowing the sort of world he lived in, he went into a stationery shop and bought a ballpoint, a pad of paper, and a clipboard. Schools often sent groups of kids off to do a shopping survey, or something of the sort, and if he seemed to be on a project like that he wouldn't look as if he was at a loose end.

Then he wandered along, pretending to be making notes, and kept his eyes open for the public library.

Meanwhile, Lyra was looking for somewhere quiet to consult the alethiometer. In her own Oxford there would have been a dozen places within five minutes' walk, but this Oxford was so disconcertingly different, with patches of poignant familiarity right next to the downright outlandish: why had they painted those yellow lines on the road? What were those little white patches dotting every pavement? (In her own world, they had never heard of chewing gum.) What could those red and green lights mean at the corner of the road? It was all much harder to read than the alethiometer.

But here were St John's College gates, which she and Roger had once climbed after dark to plant fireworks in the flower-beds; and that particular worn stone at the corner of Catte Street – there were the initials SP that Simon Parslow had scratched, the very same ones! She'd seen him do it! Someone in this world with the same initials must have stood here idly and done exactly the same.

There might be a Simon Parslow in this world.

Perhaps there was a Lyra.

A chill ran down her back, and mouse-shaped Pantalaimon shivered in her pocket. She shook herself; there were mysteries enough without imagining more.

The other way in which this Oxford differed from hers was in the vast numbers of people swarming on every pavement, in and out of every building; people of every sort, women dressed like men, Africans, even a group of Tartars meekly following their leader, all neatly dressed and hung about with little black cases. She glared at them fearfully at first, because they had no dæmons, and in her world they would have been regarded as ghasts, or worse.

But (this was the strangest thing) they all looked fully alive. These creatures moved about cheerfully enough, for all the world as though they were human, and Lyra had to concede that human was what they probably were, and that their dæmons were inside them as Will's was.

After wandering about for an hour taking the measure of this mock-Oxford, she felt hungry and bought a bar of chocolatl with her twenty-pound note. The shopkeeper looked at her oddly, but he was from the Indies and didn't understand her accent, perhaps, although she asked very clearly. With the change she bought an apple from the Covered Market, which was much more like the proper Oxford, and walked up towards the park. There she found herself outside a grand building, a real Oxford-looking building that didn't exist in her world at all, though it wouldn't have looked out of place. She sat on the grass outside to eat, and regarded the building approvingly.

She discovered that it was a museum. The doors were open, and inside she found stuffed animals and fossil skeletons and cases of minerals, just like the Royal Geological Museum she'd visited with Mrs Coulter in her London. At the back of the great iron and glass hall was the entrance to another part of the museum, and because it was nearly deserted, she went through and looked around. The alethiometer was still the most urgent thing on her mind, but in this second chamber she found herself surrounded by things she knew well: there were showcases filled with Arctic clothing, just like her own furs – with sledges and walrus ivory carvings and seal-hunting harpoons – with a thousand and one jumbled trophies and relics and objects of magic and tools and weapons, and not only from the Arctic, as she saw, but from every part of this world.

Well, how strange. Those caribou-skin furs were *exactly* the same as hers, but they'd tied the traces on that sledge completely wrong. But here was a photogram showing some Samoyed hunters, the very doubles of the ones who'd caught Lyra and sold her to Bolvangar: look! They were the same men! And even that rope had frayed and been re-knotted in precisely the same spot, and she knew it intimately, having been tied up in that very sledge for several agonizing hours . . . What were these mysteries? Was there only one world after all, which spent its time dreaming of others?

And then she came across something that made her think of the alethiometer again. In an old glass case with a black-painted wooden frame there were a number of human skulls, and some of them had holes in them: some at the front, some on the side, some on the top. The one in the centre had two. This process, it said in spidery writing on a card, was called trepanning. The card also said that all the holes had been made during the owners' lifetimes, because the bone had healed and grown smooth around the edge. One, however, hadn't: the hole had been made by a bronze arrow-head which was still in it, and its edges were sharp and broken, so you could tell it was different.

This was just what the northern Tartars did. And what Stanis-laus Grumman had had done to himself, according to the Jordan scholars who'd known him. Lyra looked around quickly, saw no one nearby, and took out the alethiometer.

She focused her mind on the central skull and asked: What sort of person did this skull belong to, and why did he have those holes made in it?

As she stood concentrating in the dusty light that filtered through the glass roof and slanted down past the upper galleries, she didn't notice that she was being watched.

A powerful-looking man in his sixties, wearing a beautifully-tailored linen suit and holding a panama hat, stood on the gallery above and looked down over the iron railing.

His grey hair was brushed neatly back from his smooth, tanned, barely wrinkled forehead. His eyes were large, dark and long-lashed and intense, and every minute or so his sharp, dark-pointed tongue peeped out at the corner of his lips and flicked across them moistly. The snowy handkerchief in his breast pocket was scented with some heavy cologne like those hot-house plants so rich you can smell the decay at their roots.

He had been watching Lyra for some minutes. He had moved along the gallery above as she moved about below, and when she stood still by the case of skulls, he watched her closely, taking in all of her: her rough untidy hair, the bruise on her cheek, the new clothes, her bare neck arched over the alethiometer, her bare legs.

He shook out the breast pocket handkerchief and mopped his forehead, and then made for the stairs.

Lyra, absorbed, was learning strange things. These skulls were unimaginably old; the cards in the case said simply "Bronze Age", but the alethiometer, which never lied, said that the man whose skull it was had lived thirty-three thousand two hundred and fifty-four years before the present day, and that he had been a sorcerer, and that the hole had been made to let the gods into his head. And then the alethiometer, in the casual way it some-times had of answering a question Lyra hadn't asked, added that there was a good deal more Dust around the trepanned skulls than around the one with the arrow-head.

What in the world could that mean? Lyra came out of the focused calm she shared with the alethiometer and drifted back to the present moment, to find herself no longer alone. Gazing into the next case was an elderly man in a pale suit, who smelled sweetly. He reminded her of someone, but she couldn't think who.

He became aware of her staring at him, and looked up with a smile.

"You're looking at the trepanned skulls?" he said. "What strange things people do to themselves."

"Mm," she said expressionlessly.

"D'you know, people still do that?"

"Yeah," she said.

"Hippies, you know, people like that. Actually you're far too young to remember hippies. They say it's more effective than taking drugs."

Lyra had put the alethiometer in her rucksack, and was wondering how she could get away: she still hadn't asked it the main question, and now this old man was having a conversation with her. He seemed nice enough, and he certainly smelled nice. He was closer now. His hand brushed hers as he leaned across the case.

"Makes you wonder, doesn't it? No anaesthetic, no disinfectant, probably done with stone tools. They must have been tough, mustn't they? I don't think I've seen you here before. I come here quite a lot. What's your name?"

"Lizzie," she said comfortably.

"Lizzie. Hello, Lizzie. I'm Charles. Do you go to school in Oxford?"

She wasn't sure how to answer.

"No," she said.

"Just visiting? Well, you've chosen a wonderful place to look at. What are you specially interested in?"

She was more puzzled by this man than by anyone she'd met for a long time. On the one hand he was kind and friendly and very clean and smartly dressed, but on the other hand Pantalaimon, inside her pocket, was plucking at her attention and begging her to be careful, because he was half-remembering something too; and from somewhere she sensed, not a smell, but the idea of a smell, and it was the smell of dung, of putrefaction. She was reminded of Iofur Raknison's palace, where the air was perfumed but the floor was thick with filth.

"What am I interested in?" she said. "Oh, all sorts really. Those skulls I got interested in just now, when I saw them there. I shouldn't think anyone would want that done. It's horrible."

"No, I wouldn't enjoy it myself, but I promise you it does happen. I could take you to meet someone who's done it," he said, looking so friendly and helpful that she was very nearly tempted. But then out came that little dark tongue-point, as quick as a snake's, flick-moisten, and she shook her head.

"I got to go," she said. "Thank you for offering, but I better not. Anyway I got to go now because I'm meeting someone. My friend," she added. "Who I'm staying with."

"Yes, of course," he said kindly. "Well, it was nice talking to you. Bye-bye, Lizzie."

"Bye," she said.

"Oh – just in case – here's my name and address," he said, handing her a little slip of card, "just in case you want to know more about things like this."

"Thank you," she said blandly, and put it in the pocket on the back of her rucksack before leaving. She felt he was watching her all the way out.

Once she was outside the museum she turned into the park, which she knew as a field for cricket and other sports, and found a quiet spot under some trees and tried the alethiometer again.

This time she asked where she could find a scholar who knew about Dust. The answer she got was simple: it directed her to a certain room in the tall square building behind her. In fact the answer was so straightforward, and came so abruptly, that Lyra was sure the alethiometer had more to say: she was beginning to sense now that it had moods, like a person, and to know when it wanted to tell her more.

And it did now. What it said was: *You must concern yourself with the boy. Your task is to help him find his father. Put your mind to that.*

She blinked. She was genuinely startled. Will had appeared out of nowhere in order to help her: surely that was obvious. The idea that she had come all this way in order to help him took her breath away.

But the alethiometer still hadn't finished. The needle twitched again, and she read:

Do not lie to the scholar.

She folded the velvet around the alethiometer and thrust it into the rucksack out of sight. Then she stood and looked around for the building where her scholar would be found, and set off towards it, feeling awkward and defiant.

Will found the library easily enough. The reference librarian was perfectly prepared to believe that he was doing some research for a geography project, and helped him find the bound copies of *The Times* index for the year of his birth, which was when his father had disappeared. Will sat down to look through. Sure enough, there were several references to John Parry, in connection with an archaeological expedition.

Each month, he found, was on a separate roll of microfilm. He threaded each in turn into the projector, scrolled through to find the stories, and read them with fierce attention. The first story told of the departure of an expedition to the north of Alaska. The expedition was sponsored by the Institute of Archaeology at Oxford University, and it was going to survey an area in which they hoped to find evidence of early human settlements. It was accompanied by John Parry, late of the Royal Marines, a professional explorer.

The second story was dated six weeks later. It said briefly that the expedition had reached the North American Arctic Survey Station at Noatak in Alaska.

The third was dated two months after that. It said that there had been no reply to signals from the Survey Station, and that John Parry and his companions were presumed missing.

There was a brief series of articles following that, describing the parties that had set out fruitlessly to look for them, the search flights over the Bering Sea, the reaction of the Institute of Archaeology, interviews with relatives . . .

His heart thudded, because there was a picture of his own mother. Holding a baby. Him.

The reporter had written a standard tearful-wife-waiting-in-anguish-for-news story, which Will found disappointingly short of actual facts. There was a brief paragraph saying that John Parry had had a successful career in the Royal Marines and had left to specialize in organizing geographical and scientific expeditions, and that was all.

There was no other mention in the index, and Will got up from the microfilm reader baffled. There must be some more information somewhere else; but where could he go next? And if he took too long searching for it, he'd be traced . . .

He handed back the rolls of microfilm and asked the librarian, "Do you know the address of the Institute of Archaeology, please?"

"I could find out . . . What school are you from?"

"St Peter's," said Will.

"That's not in Oxford, is it?"

"No, it's in Hampshire. My class is doing a sort of residential field trip. Kind of environmental study research skills . . ."

"Oh, I see. What was it you wanted . . . Archaeology . . . Here we are."

Will copied down the address and phone number, and since it was safe to admit he didn't know Oxford, asked where to find it. It wasn't far away. He thanked the librarian and set off.

Inside the building Lyra found a wide desk at the foot of the stairs, with a porter behind it.

"Where are you going?" he said.

This was like home again. She felt Pan, in her pocket, enjoying it.

"I got a message for someone on the second floor," she said.

"Who?"

"Dr Lister," she said.

"Dr Lister's on the third floor. If you've got something for him, you can leave it here and I'll let him know."

"Yeah, but this is something he needs right now. He just

sent for it. It's not a *thing* actually, it's something I need to tell him."

He looked at her carefully, but he was no match for the bland and vacuous docility Lyra could command when she wanted to; and finally he nodded and went back to his newspaper.

The alethiometer didn't tell Lyra people's names, of course. She read the name Dr Lister off a pigeonhole on the wall behind him, because if you pretend you know someone, they're more likely to let you in. In some ways Lyra knew Will's world better than he did.

On the second floor she found a long corridor, where one door was open to an empty lecture theatre and another to a smaller room where two scholars stood discussing something at a blackboard. These rooms, the walls of this corridor, were all flat and bare and plain in a way Lyra thought belonged to poverty, not to the scholarship and splendour of Oxford; and yet the brick walls were smoothly painted, and the doors were of heavy wood and the banisters of polished steel, so they were costly. It was just another way in which this world was strange.

She soon found the door the alethiometer had told her about. The label pinned to it said "Dark Matter Research Unit", and under it someone had scribbled R.I.P. Another hand had added in pencil "Director: Lazarus".

Lyra made nothing of that. She knocked, and a woman's voice said, "Come in."

It was a small room, crowded with tottering piles of papers and books, and the whiteboards on the walls were covered in figures and equations. Pinned to the back of the door was a design that looked Chinese. Through an open doorway Lyra could see another room, where some kind of complicated anbaric machinery stood in silence.

For her part, Lyra was a little surprised to find that the scholar she sought was female, but the alethiometer hadn't said a man, and this was a strange world, after all. The woman was sitting at an engine that displayed figures and shapes on a small glass screen, in front of which all the letters of the alphabet had been laid out on grimy little blocks in an ivory tray. The scholar tapped one and the screen became blank.

"Who are you?" she said.

Lyra shut the door behind her. Mindful of what the alethio-meter had told her, she tried hard not to do what she normally would have done, and she told the truth.

"Lyra Silvertongue," she answered. "What's your name?"

The woman blinked. She was in her late thirties, Lyra supposed, perhaps a little older than Mrs Coulter, with short black hair and red cheeks. She wore a white coat open over a green shirt and those blue canvas trousers so many people wore in this world.

At Lyra's question the woman ran a hand through her hair and said, "Well, you're the second unexpected thing that's happened today. I'm Doctor Mary Malone. What do you want?"

"I want you to tell me about Dust," said Lyra, having looked around to make sure they were alone. "I know you know about it. I can prove it. You got to tell me."

"Dust? What are you talking about?"

"You might not call it that. It's elementary particles. In my world the scholars call it Rusakov Particles, but normally they call it Dust. They don't show up easily, but they come out of space and fix on people. Not children so much, though. Mostly on grown-ups. And something I only found out today – I was in that museum down the road and there was some old skulls with holes in their heads, like the Tartars make, and there was a lot more Dust round them than round this other one that hadn't got that sort of hole in. When's the Bronze Age?"

The woman was looking at her wide-eyed.

"The Bronze Age? Goodness, I don't know; about five thou-sand years ago," she said.

"Ah, well, they got it wrong then, when they wrote that label. That skull with the two holes in is thirty-three thousand years old."

She stopped then, because Dr Malone looked as if she was about to faint. The high colour left her cheeks completely, she put one hand to her breast while the other clutched the arm of her chair, and her jaw dropped.

Lyra stood, stubborn and puzzled, waiting for her to recover.

"Who are you?" the woman said at last.

"Lyra Silver –"

"No, where d'you come from? What are you? How do you know things like this?"

Wearily Lyra sighed; she had forgotten how roundabout scholars could be. It was difficult to tell them the truth when a lie would have been so much easier for them to understand.

"I come from another world," she began. "And in that world there's an Oxford like this, only different, and that's where I come from. And –"

"Wait, wait, wait. You come from where?"

"From somewhere else," said Lyra, more carefully. "Not here."

"Oh, somewhere else," the woman said. "I see. Well, I think I see."

"And I got to find out about Dust," Lyra explained. "Because the Church people in my world, right, they're frightened of Dust because they think it's original sin. So it's very important. And my father ... No," she said passionately, and even stamped, "that's not what I meant to say. I'm doing it all wrong."

Dr Malone looked at Lyra's desperate frown and clenched fists, at the bruises on her cheek and her leg, and said "Dear me, child, calm down ..."

She broke off and rubbed her eyes, which were red with tiredness.

"Why am I listening to you?" she went on. "I must be crazy. The fact is, this is the only place in the world where you'd get the answer you want, and they're about to close us down ... What you're talking about, your Dust, sounds like something we've been investigating for a while now, and what you say about the skulls in the museum gave me a turn, because ... Oh, no, this is just too much. I'm too tired. I want to listen to you, believe me, but not now, please. Did I say they were going to close us down? I've got a week to put together a proposal to the funding committee, but we haven't got a hope in hell ..."

She yawned widely.

"What was the first unexpected thing that happened today?" Lyra said.

"Oh. Yes. Someone I'd been relying on to back our funding application withdrew his support. I don't suppose it was *that* unexpected, anyway."

She yawned again.

"I'm going to make some coffee," she said. "If I don't I'll fall asleep. You'll have some too?"

She filled an electric kettle, and while she spooned instant coffee into two mugs Lyra stared at the Chinese pattern on the back of the door.

"What's that?" she said.

"It's Chinese. The symbols of the I Ching. D'you know what that is? Do they have that in your world?"

Lyra looked at her narrow-eyed, in case she was being sarcastic. She said: "There are some things the same and some that are different, that's all. I don't know everything about my world. Maybe they got this Ching thing there too."

"I'm sorry," said Dr Malone. "Yes, maybe they have."

"What's dark matter?" said Lyra. "That's what it says on the notice, isn't it?"

Dr Malone sat down again, and hooked another chair out with her ankle for Lyra.

She said, "Dark matter is what my research team is looking for. No one knows what it is. There's more stuff out there in the universe than we can see, that's the point. We can see the stars and the galaxies and the things that shine, but for it all to hang together and not fly apart, there needs to be a lot more of it – to make gravity work, you see. But no one can detect it. So there are lots of different research projects trying to find out what it is, and this is one of them."

Lyra was all focused attention. At last the woman was talking seriously.

"And what do you think it is?" she asked.

"Well, what *we* think it is . . ." she began, as the kettle boiled, so she got up and made the coffee as she continued: "We think it's some kind of elementary particle. Something quite different from anything discovered so far. But they're very hard to detect . . . Where do you go to school? Do you study physics?"

Lyra felt Pantalaimon nip her hand, warning her not to get cross. It was all very well the alethiometer telling her to be truthful, but she knew what would happen if she told the whole truth. She had to tread carefully, and just avoid direct lies.

"Yes," she said, "I know a little bit. But not about dark matter."

"Well, we're trying to detect this almost undetectable thing among the noise of all the other particles crashing about. Normally they put detectors hundreds of metres underground, but what we've done instead is to set up an electromagnetic field around the detector that shuts out the things we don't want and lets through the ones we do. Then we amplify the signal and put it through a computer."

She handed across a mug of coffee. There was no milk and no sugar, but she did find a couple of ginger biscuits in a drawer, and Lyra took one hungrily.

"And we found a particle that fits," Dr Malone went on. "We think it fits. But it's so strange ... Why am I telling you this? I shouldn't. It's not published, it's not refereed, it's not even written down. I'm a little crazy this afternoon.

"Well ..." she went on, and she yawned for so long that Lyra thought she'd never stop ... "our particles are strange little devils and no mistake. We call them shadow-particles, Shadows. You know what nearly knocked me off my chair just now? When you mentioned the skulls in the museum. Because one of our team, you see, is a bit of an amateur archaeologist. And he discovered something one day that we couldn't believe. But we couldn't ignore it, because it fitted in with the craziest thing of all about these Shadows. You know what? They're conscious. That's right. Shadows are particles of consciousness. You ever heard anything so stupid? No wonder we can't get our grant renewed."

She sipped her coffee. Lyra was drinking in every word like a thirsty flower.

"Yes," Dr Malone went on, "they know we're here. They answer back. And here goes the crazy part: you can't see them unless you expect to. Unless you put your mind in a certain state. You have to be confident and relaxed at the same time. You have to be capable – where's that quotation ..."

She reached into the muddle of papers on her desk, and found a scrap on which someone had written with a green pen. She read:

" '. . . capable of being in uncertainties, mysteries, doubts, without any irritable reaching after fact and reason –' You have to get into that state of mind. That's from the poet Keats, by the way. I found it the other day. So you get yourself in the right state of mind, and then you look at the Cave –"

"The cave?" said Lyra.

"Oh, sorry. The computer. We call it the Cave. Shadows on the walls of the Cave, you see, from Plato. That's our archaeologist again. He's an all-round intellectual. But he's gone off to Geneva for a job interview, and I don't suppose for a moment he'll be back . . . Where was I? OK, the Cave, that's right. Once you're linked up to it, if you *think*, the Shadows respond. There's no doubt about it. The Shadows flock to your thinking like birds . . ."

"What about the skulls?"

"I was coming to that. Oliver Payne, him, my colleague, was fooling about one day testing things with the Cave. And it was so odd. It didn't make any sense in the way a physicist would expect. He got a piece of ivory, just a lump, and there were no Shadows with that. It didn't react. But a carved ivory chess piece did. A big splinter of wood off a plank didn't, but a wooden ruler did. And a carved wooden statuette had more . . . I'm talking about elementary particles here, for goodness' sake. Little minute lumps of scarcely anything. *They knew what these objects were*. Anything that was associated with human workmanship and human thought was surrounded by Shadows . . .

"And then Oliver, Dr Payne, got some fossil skulls from a friend at the museum and tested them to see how far back in time the effect went. There was a cut-off point about thirty, forty thousand years ago. Before that, no Shadows. After that, plenty. And that's about the time, apparently, that modern human beings first appeared. I mean, you know, our remote ancestors, but people no different from us, really . . ."

"It's Dust," said Lyra authoritatively. "That's what it is."

"But you see, you can't say this sort of thing in a funding application if you want to be taken seriously. It does not make sense. It cannot exist. It's impossible, and if it isn't impossible it's irrelevant, and if it isn't either of those things it's embarrassing."

"I want to see the Cave," said Lyra.

She stood up.

Dr Malone was running her hands through her hair and blinking hard to keep her tired eyes clear.

"Well, I can't see why not," she said. "We might not have a
Cave tomorrow. Come along through."

She led Lyra into the other room. It was larger, and crowded
with electronic equipment.

"This is it. Over there," she said, pointing to a screen which
was glowing with an empty grey, "that's where the detector is,
behind all that wiring. To see the Shadows you have to be linked
up to some electrodes. Like for measuring brain waves."

"I want to try it," said Lyra.

"You won't see anything. Anyway I'm tired. It's too
complicated."

"Please! I know what I'm doing!"

"Do you, now. I wish I did. *No*, for heaven's sake. This is an
expensive, difficult scientific experiment. You can't come charging in here and expect to have a go as if it was a pinball machine
... Where *do* you come from, anyway? Shouldn't you be at
school? How did you find your way in here?"

And she rubbed her eyes again, as if she was only just waking up.

Lyra was trembling. *Tell the truth*, she thought. "I found my
way in with this," she said, and took out the alethiometer.

"What in the world is that? A compass?"

Lyra let her take it. Dr Malone's eyes widened as she felt the
weight.

"Dear Lord, it's made of gold. Where on earth – "

"I think it does what your Cave does. That's what I want to
find out. If I can answer a question truly," said Lyra desperately,
"something you know the answer to and I don't, can I try your
Cave then?"

"What, are we into fortune-telling now? What is this thing?"

"Please! Just ask me a question!"

Dr Malone shrugged. "Oh, all right," she said. "Tell me ...
Tell me what I was doing before I took up this business."

Eagerly Lyra took the alethiometer from her and turned the
winding-wheels. She could feel her mind reaching for the right

pictures even before the hands were pointing at them, and she sensed the longer needle twitching to respond. As it began to swing round the dial her eyes followed it, watching, calculating, seeing down the long chains of meaning to the level where the truth lay.

Then she blinked and sighed and came out of her temporary trance.

"You used to be a nun," she said. "I wouldn't have guessed that. Nuns are supposed to stay in their convents for ever. But you stopped believing in church things and they let you leave. This en't like my world at all, not a bit."

Dr Malone sat down in the only chair, staring.

Lyra said, "That's true, en't it?"

"Yes. And you found out from that . . ."

"From my alethiometer. It works by Dust, I think. I came all this way to find out more about Dust, and it told me to come to you. So I reckon your dark matter must be the same thing. *Now* can I try your Cave?"

Dr Malone shook her head, but not to say no, just out of helplessness. She spread her hands. "Very well," she said. "I think I'm dreaming. I might as well carry on."

She swung round in her chair and pressed several switches, bringing an electrical hum and the sound of a computer's cooling fan into the air; and at the sound of them, Lyra gave a little muffled gasp. It was because the sound in that room was the same sound she'd heard in that dreadful glittering chamber at Bolvangar, where the silver guillotine had nearly parted her and Pantalaimon. She felt him quiver in her pocket, and gently squeezed him for reassurance.

But Dr Malone hadn't noticed; she was too busy adjusting switches and tapping the letters in another of those ivory trays. As she did, the screen changed colour, and some small letters and figures appeared on it.

"Now you sit down," she said, and gave the chair to Lyra. Then she opened a small jar and said, "I need to put some gel on your skin to help the electrical contact. It washes off easily. Hold still, now."

Dr Malone took six wires, each ending in a flat pad, and

attached them to various places on Lyra's head. Lyra sat deter-
minedly still, but she was breathing quickly, and her heart was
beating hard.

"All right, you're all hooked up," said Dr Malone. "The
room's full of Shadows. The universe is full of Shadows, come
to that. But this is the only way we can see them, when you make
your mind empty and look at the screen. Off you go."

Lyra looked. The glass was dark and blank. She saw her own
reflection dimly, but that was all. As an experiment she pretended
that she was reading the alethiometer, and imagined herself asking: What does this woman know about Dust? What questions
is *she* asking?

She mentally moved the alethiometer's hands around the dial,
and as she did, the screen began to flicker. Astonished, she came
out of her concentration, and the flicker died. She didn't notice
the ripple of excitement that made Dr Malone sit up: she
frowned and sat forward and began to concentrate again.

This time the response came instantaneously. A stream of dancing lights, for all the world like the shimmering curtains of the
aurora, blazed across the screen. They took up patterns that were
held for a moment only to break apart and form again, in different
shapes, or different colours; they looped and swayed, they sprayed
apart, they burst into showers of radiance that suddenly swerved
this way or that like a flock of birds changing direction in the sky.
And as Lyra watched, she felt the same sense, as of trembling on
the brink of understanding, that she remembered from the time
when she was beginning to read the alethiometer.

She asked another question: Is *this* Dust? Is it the same thing
making these patterns and moving the needle of the alethiometer?

The answer came in more loops and swirls of light. She
guessed it meant yes. Then another thought occurred to her, and
she turned to speak to Dr Malone, and saw her open-mouthed,
hand to her head.

"What?" she said.

The screen faded. Dr Malone blinked.

"What is it?" Lyra said again.

"Oh – you've just put on the best display I've ever seen, that's all," said Dr Malone. "What were you doing? What were you thinking?"

"I was thinking you could get it clearer than this," Lyra said.

"Clearer? That's the clearest it's ever been!"

"But what does it mean? Can you read it?"

"Well," said Dr Malone, "you don't *read* it in the sense of reading a message, it doesn't work like that. What's happening is that the Shadows are responding to the attention that you pay them. That's revolutionary enough: it's our consciousness that they respond to, you see."

"No," Lyra explained, "what I mean is, those colours and shapes up there. They could do other things, those Shadows. They could make any shapes you wanted. They could make pictures if you wanted them to. Look."

And she turned back and focused her mind again, but this time she pretended to herself that the screen was the alethiometer, with all thirty-six symbols laid out round the edge. She knew them so well now that her fingers automatically twisted in her lap as she moved the imaginary hands to point at the candle (for understanding), the alpha and omega (for language), and the ant (for diligence), and framed the question: What would these people have to do in order to understand the language of the Shadows?

The screen responded as quickly as thought itself, and out of the welter of lines and flashes a series of pictures formed with perfect clarity: compasses, alpha and omega again, lightning, angel. Each picture flashed up a different number of times, and then came a different three: camel, garden, moon.

Lyra saw their meanings clearly, and unfocused her mind to explain. This time, when she turned around, she saw that Dr Malone was sitting back in her chair, white-faced, clutching the edge of the table.

"What it says," Lyra told her, "it's saying in my language, right, the language of pictures. Like the alethiometer. But what it says is that it could use ordinary language too, words, if you fixed it up like that. You could fix this so it put words on the screen. But you'd need a lot of careful figuring with numbers – that was the compasses, see – and the lightning meant anbaric,

I mean electric power, more of that. And the angel – that's all
about messages. There's things it wants to say. But when it went
on to that second bit . . . It meant Asia, almost the furthest east
but not quite. I dunno what country that would be – China,
maybe . . . And there's a way they have in that country of talking
to Dust, I mean Shadows, same as you got here and I got with
the – I got with pictures, only their way uses sticks. I think it
meant that picture on the door, but I didn't understand it really.
I thought when I first saw it there was something important
about it, only I didn't know what. So there must be lots of ways
of talking to Shadows."

Dr Malone was breathless.

"The I Ching," she said. "Yes, it's Chinese. A form of divination – fortune-telling, really . . . And yes, they use sticks. It's only
up there for decoration," she said, as if to reassure Lyra that she
didn't really believe in it. "You're telling me that when people
consult the I Ching, they're getting in touch with Shadow-
particles? With dark matter?"

"Yeah," said Lyra. "There's lots of ways, like I said. I hadn't
realized before. I thought there was only one."

"Those pictures on the screen . . ." Dr Malone began.

Lyra felt a flicker of a thought at the edge of her mind, and
turned back to the screen. She had hardly begun to formulate a
question when more pictures flashed up, succeeding each other
so quickly that Dr Malone could hardly follow them; but Lyra
knew what they were saying, and turned back to her.

"It says that *you're* important, too," she told the scientist.
"It says you got something important to do. I dunno what, but
it wouldn't say that unless it was true. So you probably ought to
get it using words, so you can understand what it says."

Dr Malone was silent. Then she said:

"All right, where *do* you come from?"

Lyra twisted her mouth. She realized that Dr Malone, who
until now had acted out of exhaustion and despair, would never
normally have shown her work to a strange child who turned up
from nowhere, and that she was beginning to regret it. But Lyra
had to tell the truth.

"I come from another world," she said. "It's true. I came

through to this one. I was ... I had to run away, because people in my world were chasing me, to kill me. And the alethiometer comes from ... from the same place. The Master of Jordan College gave it me. In *my* Oxford there's a Jordan College, but there en't one here. I looked. And I found out how to read the alethiometer by myself. I got a way of making my mind go blank, and I just see what they mean straight away. Just like you said about ... doubts and mysteries and that. So when I looked at the Cave I done the same thing and it works just the same way, so my Dust and your Shadows are the same, too. So ..."

Dr Malone was fully awake now. Lyra picked up the alethiometer and folded its velvet cloth over it, like a mother protecting her child, before putting it back in her rucksack.

"So anyway," she said, "you could make this screen so it could talk to you in words, if you wanted. Then you could talk to the Shadows like I talk to the alethiometer. But what I want to know is, why do the people in my world hate it? Dust, I mean, Shadows. Dark matter. They want to destroy it. They think it's evil. But I think what *they* do is evil. I seen them do it. So what is it, Shadows? Is it good or evil, or what?"

Dr Malone rubbed her face and made her cheeks even redder than they were.

"Everything about this is *embarrassing*," she said. "D'you know how embarrassing it is to mention good and evil in a scientific laboratory? Have you any idea? One of the reasons I became a scientist was not to have to think about that kind of thing."

"You *got* to think about it," said Lyra severely. "You can't investigate Shadows, Dust, whatever it is, without thinking about that kind of thing, good and evil and such. And it said you got to, remember. You can't refuse. When are they going to close this place down?"

'The funding committee decides at the end of the week ... Why?"

"'Cause you got tonight then," said Lyra. "You could fix this engine thing to put words on the screen instead of pictures like I made. You could do that easy. Then you could show 'em and they'd have to give you the money to carry on. And you could find out all about Dust, or Shadows, and tell me. You see," she went on a little haughtily, like a duchess describing an unsatisfactory housemaid, "the alethiometer won't exactly tell me what I need to know. But you could find out for me. Else I could probably do that Ching thing, with the sticks. But pictures are easier to work. I think so, anyway. I'm going to take this off now," she added, and pulled at the electrodes on her head.

Dr Malone gave her a tissue to wipe off the gel, and folded up the wires.

"So you're going?" she said. "Well, you've given me a strange hour, and no mistake."

"Are you going to make it do words?" Lyra said, gathering up her rucksack.

"It's about as much use as completing the funding application, I dare say," said Dr Malone. "No, listen. I want you to come back tomorrow. Can you do that? About the same time? I want you to show someone else."

Lyra narrowed her eyes. Was this a trap?

"Well, all right," she said. "But remember, there's things I need to know."

"Yes. Of course. You *will* come?"

"Yes," said Lyra. "If I say I will, I will. I could help you, I expect."

And she left. The porter at the desk looked up briefly and then went back to his paper.

"The Nuniatak dig," said the archaeologist, swinging his chair round. "You're the second person in a month to ask me about that."

"Who was the other one?" said Will, on his guard at once.

"I think he was a journalist, I'm not sure."

"Why did he want to know about it?" he said.

"In connection with one of the men who disappeared on that trip. It was the height of the cold war when the expedition vanished. Star Wars. You're probably too young to remember that. The Americans and the Russians were building enormous radar installations all across the Arctic . . . Anyway, what can I do for you?"

"Well," said Will, trying to keep calm, "I was just trying to find out about that expedition, really. For a school project about prehistoric people. And I read about this expedition that disappeared, and I got curious."

"Well, you're not the only one, as you see. There was a big to-do about it at the time. I looked it all up for the journalist. It was a preliminary survey, not a proper dig. You can't do a dig till you know whether it's worth spending time on it, so this group went out to look at a number of sites and make a report. Half a dozen blokes altogether. Sometimes on an expedition like this you combine forces with people from another discipline, you know, geologists or whatever, to split the cost. They look at their stuff and we look at ours. In this case there was a physicist on the team. I think he was looking at high-level atmospheric particles. The aurora, you know, the northern lights. He had balloons with radio transmitters, apparently.

"And there was another man with them. An ex-Marine, a sort of professional explorer. They were going up into some fairly wild territory, and polar bears are always a danger in the Arctic. Archaeologists can deal with some things, but we're not trained to shoot, and someone who can do that and navigate and make camp and do all the sort of survival stuff is very useful.

"But then they all vanished. They kept in radio contact with a local survey station, but one day the signal didn't come, and nothing more was heard. There'd been a blizzard, but that was nothing unusual. The search expedition found their last camp, more or less intact, though the bears had eaten their stores, but no sign of the people whatsoever.

"And that's all I can tell you, I'm afraid."

"Yes," said Will. "Thank you. Umm . . . that journalist," he went on, stopping at the door, "you said he was interested in one of the men. Which one was it?"

"The explorer type. A man called Parry."

"What did he look like? The journalist, I mean?"

"What d'you want to know that for?"

"Because . . ." Will couldn't think of a plausible reason. He shouldn't have asked. "No reason. I just wondered."

"As far as I can remember, he was a big blond man. Very pale hair."

"Right, thanks," Will said, and turned to go.

The man watched him leave the room, saying nothing, frowning a little. Will saw him reach for the phone, and left the building quickly.

He found he was shaking. The journalist, so called, was one of the men who'd come to his house: a tall man with such fair hair that he seemed to have no eyebrows or eyelashes. He wasn't the one Will had knocked down the stairs: he was the one who'd appeared at the door of the living-room as Will ran down and jumped over the body.

But he wasn't a journalist.

There was a large museum nearby. Will went in, holding his clipboard as if he were working, and sat down in a gallery hung with paintings. He was trembling hard and feeling sick, because pressing at him was the knowledge that he'd killed someone, he was a murderer. He'd kept it at bay till now, but it was closing in. He'd taken away the man's life.

He sat still for half an hour, and it was one of the worst half hours he'd ever spent. People came and went, looking at the paintings, talking in quiet voices, ignoring him; a gallery attendant stood in the doorway for a few minutes, hands behind his back, and then slowly moved away; and Will wrestled with the horror of what he'd done, and didn't move a muscle.

Gradually he grew calmer. He'd been defending his mother. They were frightening her: given the state she was in, they were persecuting her. He had a right to defend his home. His father would have wanted him to do that. He did it because it was the good thing to do. He did it to stop them stealing the green leather case. He did it so he could find his father; and didn't he have a right to do that? All his childish games came back to him, with himself and his father rescuing each other from avalanches or fighting pirates. Well, now it was real. "I'll find you," he said in his mind. "Just help me and I'll find you, and we'll look after Mum, and everything'll be all right . . ."

And after all he had somewhere to hide now, somewhere so safe no one would ever find him. And the papers from the case (which he still hadn't had time to read) were safe too, under the mattress in Cittàgazze.

Finally he noticed people moving more purposefully, and all in the same direction. They were leaving, because the attendant was telling them that the museum would shut in ten minutes. Will gathered himself and left. He found his way to the High Street, where the solicitor's office was, and wondered about going to see him, despite what he'd said earlier. The man had sounded friendly enough ...

But as he made up his mind to cross the street and go in, he stopped suddenly.

The tall man with the pale eyebrows was getting out of a car.

Will turned aside at once, casually, and looked in the window of the jeweller's shop beside him. He saw the man's reflection look around, settle the knot of his tie, and go in to the solicitor's office. As soon as he'd gone in, Will moved away, his heart thudding again. There wasn't anywhere safe. He drifted towards the university library, and waited for Lyra.

5

AIRMAIL PAPER

"WILL," SAID LYRA.

She spoke quietly, but he was startled all the same. She was sitting on the bench beside him and he hadn't even noticed.

"Where did you come from?"

"I found my scholar! She's called Dr Malone. And she's got an engine that can see Dust and she's going to make it talk . . ."

"I didn't see you coming."

"You weren't looking," she said. "You must've been thinking about something else. It's a good thing I found you. Look, it's easy to fool people. Watch . . ."

Two police officers were strolling towards them, a man and a woman on the beat, in their white summer shirtsleeves, with their radios and their batons and their suspicious eyes. Before they reached the bench, Lyra was on her feet and speaking to them.

"Please, could you tell me where the Museum is?" she said. "Me and my brother was supposed to meet our parents there and we got lost."

The policeman looked at Will, and Will, containing his anger, shrugged as if to say she's right, we're lost, isn't it silly. The man smiled. The woman said: "Which museum? The Ashmolean?"

"Yeah, that one," said Lyra, and pretended to listen carefully as the woman gave her instructions.

Will got up and said "Thanks," and he and Lyra moved away together. They didn't look back, but the police had already lost interest.

"See?" she said. "If they were looking for you, I put 'em off. 'Cause they won't be looking for someone with a sister. I better stay with you from now on," she went on scoldingly once they'd gone round the corner. "You en't safe on your own."

He said nothing. His heart was thumping with rage. They walked along towards a round building with a great leaden dome,

set in a square bounded by honey-coloured stone college buildings and a church and wide-crowned trees above high garden
walls. The afternoon sun drew the warmest tones out of it all,
and the air felt rich with it, almost the colour itself of heavy
golden wine. All the leaves were still, and in this little square even
the traffic noise was hushed.

She finally became aware of Will's feelings, and said, "What's
the matter?"

"If you speak to people you just attract their attention," he said,
with a shaking voice. "You should just keep quiet and still and
they overlook you. I've been doing it all my life. I know how to
do it. Your way, you just – you make yourself visible. You should-
n't do that. You shouldn't play at it. You're not being serious."

"You think so?" she said, and her anger flashed. "You think
I don't know about lying and that? I'm the best liar there ever
was. But I en't lying to you, and I never will, I swear it. You're in
danger, and if I hadn't done that just then, you'd've been caught.
Didn't you see 'em looking at you? 'Cause they were. You
en't careful enough. If you want my opinion, it's you that en't
serious."

"If I'm not serious, what am I doing hanging about waiting
for you when I could be miles away? Or hiding out of sight, safe
in that other city? I've got my own things to do, but I'm hanging
about here so I can help you. Don't tell me I'm not serious."

"You *had* to come through," she said, furious. No one should
speak to her like this: she was an aristocrat. She was Lyra. "You
had to, else you'd never find out anything about your father.
You done it for yourself, not for me."

They were quarrelling passionately, but in subdued voices,
because of the quiet in the square and the people who were
wandering past nearby. When she said this, though, Will stopped
altogether. He had to lean against the college wall beside him.
The colour had left his face.

"What do you know about my father?" he said very quietly.

She replied in the same tone. "I don't know anything. All
I know is you're looking for him. That's all I asked about."

"Asked *who*?"

"The alethiometer, of course."

It took a moment for him to remember what she meant. And then he looked so angry and suspicious that she took it out of her rucksack and said, "All right, I'll show you."

And she sat down on the stone kerb around the grass in the middle of the square and bent her head over the golden instrument and began to turn the hands, her fingers moving almost too quickly to see, and then pausing for several seconds while the slender needle whipped around the dial flicking to a stop here and there, and then turning the hands to new positions just as quickly. Will looked around carefully, but there was no one near to see; a group of tourists looked up at the domed building, an ice-cream vendor wheeled his cart along the pavement, but their attention was elsewhere.

Lyra blinked and sighed, as if she were waking after a sleep.

"Your mother's ill," she said quietly. "But she's safe. There's this lady looking after her. And you took some letters and ran away. And there was a man, I think he was a thief, and you killed him. And you're looking for your father, and –"

"All right, shut up," said Will. "That's enough. You've got no right to look into my life like that. Don't ever do that again. That's just spying."

"I know when to stop asking," she said. "See, the alethiometer's like a person, almost. I sort of know when it's going to be cross or when there's things it doesn't want me to know. I kind of feel it. But when you come out of nowhere yesterday, I had to ask it who you were or I might not have been safe. I had to. And it said . . ." She lowered her voice even more. "It said you was a murderer, and I thought good, that's all right, he's someone I can trust. But I didn't ask more than that till just now, and if you don't want me to ask any more, I promise I won't. This en't like a private peepshow. If I done nothing but spy on people it'd stop working. I know that as well as I know my own Oxford."

"You could have asked me instead of that thing. Did it say whether my father was alive or dead?"

"No, because I didn't ask."

They were both sitting by this time. Will put his head in his hands with weariness.

"Well," he said finally, "I suppose we'll have to trust each other."

"That's all right. I trust you."

Will nodded grimly. He was so tired, and there was not the slightest possibility of sleep in this world. Lyra wasn't usually so perceptive, but something in his manner made her think: he's afraid, but he's mastering his fear, like Iorek Byrnison said we had to do; like I did by the fish-house at the frozen lake.

"And Will," she added, "I won't give you away, not to anyone. I promise."

"Good."

"I done that before. I betrayed someone. And it was the worst thing I ever did. I thought I was saving his life actually, only I was taking him right to the most dangerous place there could be. I hated myself for that, for being so stupid. So I'll try very hard not to be careless or forget and betray you."

He said nothing. He rubbed his eyes and blinked hard to try and wake himself up.

"We can't go back through the window till much later," he said. "We shouldn't have come through in daylight anyway. We can't risk anyone seeing. And now we've got to hang around for hours . . ."

"I'm hungry," Lyra said.

Then he said, "I know! We can go to the cinema!"

"The what?"

"I'll show you. We can get some food there too."

There was a cinema near the city centre, ten minutes' walk away. Will paid for them both to get in, and bought hot dogs and popcorn and Coke, and they carried the food inside and sat down just as the film was beginning.

Lyra was entranced. She had seen projected photograms, but nothing in her world had prepared her for the cinema. She wolfed down the hot dog and the popcorn, gulped the Coca-Cola, and gasped and laughed with delight at the characters on the screen. Luckily it was a noisy audience, full of children, and her excitement wasn't conspicuous. Will closed his eyes at once and went to sleep.

He woke when he heard the clatter of seats as people moved

out, and blinked in the light. His watch showed a quarter past eight. Lyra came away reluctantly.

"That's the best thing I ever saw in my whole life," she said. "I dunno why they never invented this in my world. We got some things better than you, but this was better than *anything* we got."

Will couldn't even remember what the film had been. It was still light outside, and the streets were busy.

"D'you want to see another one?"

"Yeah!"

So they went to the next cinema, a few hundred yards away around the corner, and did it again. Lyra settled down with her feet on the seat, hugging her knees, and Will let his mind go blank. When they came out this time, it was nearly eleven o'clock: much better.

Lyra was hungry again, so they bought hamburgers from a mobile stall and ate them as they walked along, something else new to her.

"We always sit down to eat. I never seen people just walking along eating before," she told him. "There's so many ways this place is different. The traffic, for one. I don't like it. I like the cinema, though, and hamburgers. I like them a lot. And that scholar, Dr Malone, she's going to make that engine use words. I just know she is. I'll go back there tomorrow and see how she's getting on. I bet I could help her. I could probably get the scholars to give her the money she wants, too. You know how my father did it? Lord Asriel? He played a trick on them . . ."

As they walked up the Banbury Road, she told him about the night she hid in the wardrobe and watched Lord Asriel show the Jordan scholars the severed head of Stanislaus Grumman in the vacuum flask. And since Will was such a good audience, she went on and told him the rest of her story, from the time she escaped from Mrs Coulter's flat to the horrible moment when she realized she'd led Roger to his death on the icy cliffs of Svalbard. Will listened without comment, but attentively, with sympathy. Her account of a voyage in a balloon, of armoured bears and witches, of a vengeful arm of the Church, seemed all of a piece with his own fantastic dream of a beautiful city on the sea, empty and silent and safe: it couldn't be true, it was as simple as that.

But eventually they reached the ring road, and the hornbeam trees. There was very little traffic now: a car every minute or so, no more than that. And there was the window. Will felt himself smiling. It was going to be all right.

"Wait till there's no cars coming," he said. "I'm going through now."

And a moment later he was on the grass under the palm trees, and a second or two afterwards Lyra followed.

They felt as if they were home again. The wide warm night, and the scent of flowers and the sea, and the silence, bathed them like soothing water.

Lyra stretched and yawned, and Will felt a great weight lift off his shoulders. He had been carrying it all day, and he hadn't noticed how it had nearly pressed him into the ground; but now he felt light and free and at peace.

And then Lyra gripped his arm. In the same second he heard what had made her do it.

Somewhere in the little streets beyond the café, something was screaming.

Will set off at once towards the sound, and Lyra followed behind as he plunged down a narrow alley shadowed from the moonlight. After several twists and turns they came out into the square in front of the stone tower they'd seen that morning.

Twenty or so children were facing inwards in a semicircle at the base of the tower, and some of them had sticks in their hands, and some were throwing stones at whatever they had trapped against the wall. At first Lyra thought it was another child, but coming from inside the semicircle was a horrible high wailing that wasn't human at all. And the children were screaming too, in fear as well as hatred.

Will ran up to the children and pulled the first one back. It was a boy of about his own age, a boy in a striped T-shirt. As he turned Lyra saw the wild white rims around his pupils, and then the other children realized what was happening and stopped to look. Angelica and her little brother were there too, stones in hand, and all the children's eyes glittered fiercely in the moonlight.

They fell silent. Only the high wailing continued, and then both Will and Lyra saw what it was: a tabby cat, cowering against the wall of the tower, its ear torn and its tail bent. It was the cat Will had seen in Sunderland Avenue, the one like Moxie, the one that had led him to the window.

As soon as he saw her he flung the boy he was holding aside. The boy fell to the ground and was up in a moment, furious, but the others held him back. Will was already kneeling by the cat.

And then she was in his arms. She fled to his breast and he cradled her close and stood to face the children, and Lyra thought for a crazy second that his dæmon had appeared at last.

"What are you hurting this cat for?" he demanded, and they couldn't answer. They stood trembling at Will's anger, breathing heavily, clutching their sticks and their stones, and they couldn't speak.

But then Angelica's voice came clearly: "You ain from here! You ain from Ci'gazze! You didn' know about Spectres, you don' know about cats either. You ain like us!"

The boy in the striped T-shirt whom Will had thrown down was trembling to fight, and if it hadn't been for the cat in Will's arms he would have flown at Will with fists and teeth and feet, and Will would have gladly joined battle: there was a current of electric hatred between the two of them that only violence could earth. But the boy was afraid of the cat.

"Where you come from?" he said contemptuously.

"Doesn't matter where we come from. If you're scared of this cat I'll take her away from you. If she's bad luck to you she'll be good luck for us. Now get out of the way."

For a moment Will thought their hatred would overcome their fear, and he was preparing to put the cat down and fight, but then came a low thunderous growl from behind the children, and they turned to see Lyra standing with her hand on the shoulders of a great spotted leopard whose teeth shone white as he snarled. Even Will, who recognized Pantalaimon, was frightened for a second. Its effect on the children was dramatic: they turned and fled at once. A few seconds later the square was empty.

But before they left, Lyra looked up at the tower. A growl from

Pantalaimon prompted her, and just briefly she saw someone there on the very top, looking down over the battlemented rim, and not a child either, but a young man, with curly hair.

Half an hour later they were in the flat above the café. Will had found a tin of condensed milk, and the cat had lapped it hungrily and then begun to lick her wounds. Pantalaimon had become cat-formed out of curiosity, and at first the cat had bristled with suspicion, but she soon realized that whatever Pantalaimon was, he was neither a true cat nor a threat, and proceeded to ignore him.

Lyra watched Will tending this one with fascination. The only animals she had been close to in her world (apart from the armoured bears) were working animals of one sort or another: cats were for keeping Jordan College clear of mice, not for making pets of.

"I think her tail's broken," Will said. "I don't know what to do about that. Maybe it'll heal by itself. I'll put some honey on her ear. I read about that somewhere; it's antiseptic . . ."

It was messy, but at least it kept her occupied licking it off, and the wound was getting cleaner all the time.

"You sure this is the one you saw?" she said.

"Oh, yes. And if they're all so frightened of cats there wouldn't be any in this world anyway. She probably couldn't find her way back."

"They were just crazy," Lyra said. "They would have killed her. I never seen kids being like that."

"I have," said Will.

But his face had closed: he didn't want to talk about it, and she knew better than to ask. She knew she wouldn't even ask the alethiometer.

She was very tired, so presently she went to bed, and slept at once.

A little later, when the cat had curled up to sleep, Will took a cup of coffee and the green leather writing-case, and sat on the balcony. There was enough light coming through the window for him to read by, and he wanted to look at the papers.

There weren't many. As he'd thought, they were letters, written on airmail paper in black ink. These very marks were made by the hand of the man he wanted so much to find; he moved his fingers over and over them, and pressed them to his face, trying to get closer to the essence of his father. Then he started to read.

Fairbanks, Alaska
Wednesday 19 June 1985

My darling – the usual mixture of efficiency and chaos – all the stores are here but the physicist, a genial dimwit called Nelson, hasn't made any arrangements for carrying his damn balloons up into the mountains – having to twiddle our thumbs while he scrabbles around for transport. But it means I had a chance to talk to an old boy I met last time, a gold-miner called Jake Petersen – tracked him down to a dingy bar and under the sound of the baseball game on the TV I asked him about the anomaly. He wouldn't talk there – took me back to his apartment – with the help of a bottle of Jack Daniels he talked for a long time – hadn't seen it himself but he'd met an Eskimo who had – and this chap said it was a doorway into the spirit world – they'd known about it for centuries – part of the initiation of a medicine-man involved going through and bringing back a trophy of some kind – though some never came back – however, old Jake did have a map of the area, and he'd marked on it where his pal told him the thing was. (Just in case: it's at 69°02′11″N, 157°12′19″W, on a spur of Lookout Ridge a mile or two north of the Colville River.) We then got on to other Arctic legends – the Norwegian ship that's been drifting unmanned for sixty years – stuff like that. The archaeologists are a decent crew, keen to get to work, containing their impatience with Nelson and his balloons. None of them has ever heard of the anomaly, and believe me I'm going to keep it like that. My fondest love to you both. Johnny.

Umiat, Alaska
Saturday 22 June 1985

My darling – so much for what did I call him, a genial dimwit – the physicist Nelson is nothing of the sort, and if I'm not mistaken he's actually looking for the anomaly himself. The holdup in Fairbanks was orchestrated by him, would you believe – knowing that the rest of the team wouldn't want to wait for anything less than an unarguable reason like no transport, he personally sent ahead and cancelled the vehicles that had been ordered. I found this out by accident and I was going to ask him what the hell he was playing at when I overheard him talking on the radio to someone – describing the anomaly, no less, except he didn't know the location – later on I bought him a drink, played the bluff soldier, old Arctic hand, more things in heaven and earth line – pretended to tease him with the limitations of science – bet you can't explain Bigfoot, etc – watching him closely – then sprung the anomaly on him – Eskimo legend of a doorway into spirit world – invisible – somewhere near Lookout Ridge, would you believe, where we're heading for, fancy that. And you know he was jolted rigid. He knew exactly what I meant. I pretended not to notice and went on to witchcraft, told him the Zaire leopard story – so I hope he's got me down as a superstitious military blockhead. But I'm right, Elaine, he's looking for it too. The question is, do I tell him or not? Got to work out what his game is. Fondest love to both – Johnny.

Colville Bar, Alaska
24 June 1985

Darling – I won't get a chance to post another letter for a while – this is the last town before we take to the hills – the Brooks Range – the archaeologists are fizzing to get up there. One chap is convinced he'll find evidence of much earlier habitation than anyone suspected – I said how much earlier, and why was he convinced – he told me of some narwhal ivory carvings he'd found on a previous dig – Carbon 14 dated to some incredible age, way outside the range of what was previously assumed – anomalous, in fact. Wouldn't it be strange if they'd come through *my* anomaly, from some other world – talking of which, the physicist Nelson is my closest buddy now – kids me along, drops hints to imply that he knows that I know that he knows, etc – and I pretend to be bluff Major Parry, stout fellow in a crisis but not too much between the ears, what – but I know he's after it. For one thing, although he's a bona fide academic his funding actually comes from the Ministry of Defence – I know the financial codes they use – and for another his so-called weather balloons are nothing of the sort – I looked in the crate – a radiation suit if ever I've seen one. A rum do, my darling. I shall stick to my plan – take the archaeologists to their spot and go off by myself for a few days to look for the anomaly – if I bump into Nelson wandering about on Lookout Ridge I'll play it by ear.

Later – A real bit of luck. I met Jake Petersen's pal the Eskimo, Matt Kigalik. Jake had told me where to find him but I hadn't dared to hope he'd be there. He told me the Soviets had been looking for the anomaly too – he'd come across a man earlier this year high up in the range and watched him for a couple of days without being seen, because he guessed what he was doing, and he was right, and the man turned out to be Russian, a spy; he didn't tell me more than that. I got the impression he bumped him off. But he described the thing to me. It's like a gap in the air, a sort of window. You look through it and you see another world. But it's not easy to find because that part of the other world looks just like this – rocks and moss and so forth. It's on the north side of a small creek fifty paces or so to the west of a tall rock shaped like a standing bear, and the position Jake gave me is not quite right – it's nearer 12″N than 11.

Wish me luck my darling. I'll bring you back a trophy from the spirit world – I love you for ever – kiss the boy for me – Johnny.

Will found his head ringing.

His father was describing exactly what he himself had found under the hornbeam trees. He too had found a window – he even used the same word for it! So Will must be on the right track. And this knowledge was what the men had been searching for . . . So it was dangerous, too.

Will had been a year old when that letter was written. Six years after that had come the morning in the supermarket when he realized his mother was in terrible danger, and he had to protect her; and then slowly in the months that followed came his growing realization that the danger was in her mind, and he had to protect her all the more.

And then, brutally, the revelation that not all the danger had been in her mind after all. There really was someone after her. After these letters, this information.

He had no idea what it meant. But he felt deeply happy that he had something so important to share with his father; that John Parry and his son Will had each, separately, discovered this extraordinary thing. When they met they could talk about it, and his father would be proud that Will had followed in his footsteps.

The night was quiet and the sea was still. He folded the letters away and fell asleep.

6
LIGHTED FLIERS

"GRUMMAN?" SAID THE black-bearded fur-trader. "From the Berlin Academy? Reckless. I met him five years back over at the northern end of the Urals. I thought he was dead."

Sam Cansino, an old acquaintance and a Texan like Lee Scoresby, sat in the naphtha-laden, smoky bar of the Samirsky Hotel and tossed back a shot-glass of bitingly cold vodka. He nudged the plate of pickled fish and black bread towards Lee, who took a mouthful and nodded for Sam to tell him more.

"He'd walked into a trap that fool Yakovlev laid," the fur-trader went on, "and cut his leg open to the bone. Instead of using regular medicines, he insisted on using the stuff the bears use – bloodmoss – some kind of lichen, it ain't a true moss; anyway, he was lying on a sledge alternately roaring with pain and calling out instructions to his men – they were taking star-sights, and they had to get the measurements right or he'd lash them with his tongue, and boy, he had a tongue like barbed wire. A lean man, tough, powerful, curious about everything. You know he was a Tartar, by initiation?"

"You don't say," said Lee Scoresby, tipping more vodka into Sam's glass. His dæmon Hester crouched at his elbow on the bar, eyes half-closed as usual, ears flat along her back.

Lee had arrived that afternoon, borne to Nova Zembla by the wind the witches had called up, and once he'd stowed his equipment he'd made straight for the Samirsky Hotel, near the fish-packing station. This was a place where many Arctic drifters stopped to exchange news or look for employment or leave messages for one another, and Lee Scoresby had spent several days there in the past, waiting for a contract or a passenger or a fair wind, so there was nothing unusual in his conduct now.

And with the vast changes they sensed in the world around them, it was natural for people to gather and talk. With every day that passed came more news: the river Yenisei was free of ice, and at this time of year, too; part of the ocean had drained away, exposing strange regular formations of stone on the sea-bed; a squid a hundred feet long had snatched three fishermen out of their boat and torn them apart . . .

And the fog continued to roll in from the north, dense and cold and occasionally drenched with the strangest imaginable light, in which great forms could be vaguely seen, and mysterious voices heard.

Altogether it was a bad time to work, which was why the bar of the Samirsky Hotel was full.

"Did you say Grumman?" said the man sitting just along the bar, an elderly man in seal-hunter's rig, whose lemming-dæmon looked out solemnly from his pocket. "He was a Tartar all right. I was there when he joined that tribe. I saw him having his skull drilled. He had another name, too; a Tartar name; I'll think of it in a minute."

"Well, how about that," said Lee Scoresby. "Let me buy you a drink, my friend. I'm looking for news of this man. What tribe was it he joined?"

"The Yenisei Pakhtars. At the foot of the Semyonov range. Near a fork of the Yenisei and the, I forget what it's called, a river that comes down from the hills. There's a rock the size of a house at the landing stage."

"Ah, sure," said Lee. "I remember it now. I've flown over it. And Grumman had his skull drilled, you say? Why was that?"

"He was a shaman," said the old seal-hunter. "I think the tribe recognized him as a shaman before they adopted him. Some business, that drilling. It goes on for two nights and a day. They use a bow-drill, like for lighting a fire."

"Ah, that accounts for the way his team was obeying him," said Sam Cansino. "They were the roughest bunch of scoundrels I ever saw, but they ran round doing his bidding like nervous children. I thought it was his cursing that did it. If they thought he was a shaman it'd make even more sense. But you know, that man's curiosity was as powerful as a wolf's jaws; he would *not* let go. He made me tell him every scrap I knew about the land thereabouts, and the habits of wolverines and foxes. And he was in some pain from that damn trap of Yakovlev's; leg laid open, and he was writing the results of that bloodmoss, taking his temperature, watching the scar form, making notes on every damn thing . . . A strange man. There was a witch who wanted him for a lover, but he turned her down."

"Is that so?" said Lee, thinking of the beauty of Serafina Pekkala.

"He shouldn't have done that," said the seal-hunter. "A witch offers you her love, you should take it. If you don't, it's your own fault if bad things happen to you. It's like having to make a choice: a blessing or a curse. The one thing you can't do is choose neither."

"He might have had a reason," said Lee.

"If he had any sense, it will have been a good one."

"He was headstrong," said Sam Cansino.

"Maybe faithful to another woman," Lee guessed. "I heard some thing else about him; I heard he knew the whereabouts of some magic object, I don't know what it might be, that could protect anyone who held it. Did you ever hear that story?"

"Yes, I heard that," said the seal-hunter. "He didn't have it himself, but he knew where it was. There was a man who tried to make him tell, but Grumman killed him."

"His dæmon, now," said Sam Cansino, "that was curious. She was an eagle, a black eagle with a white head and breast, of a kind I'd never set eyes on, and I didn't know how she might be called."

"She was an osprey," said the barman, listening in. "You're talking about Stan Grumman? His dæmon was an osprey. A fish-eagle."

"What happened to him?" said Lee Scoresby.

"Oh, he got mixed up in the Skraeling wars over to Beringland. Last I heard he'd been shot," said the seal-hunter. "Killed outright."

"I heard they beheaded him," said Lee Scoresby.

"No, you're both wrong," said the barman, "and I know, because I heard it from an Inuit who was with him. Seems that they were camped out on Sakhalin somewhere and there was an avalanche. Grumman was buried under a hundred tons of rock. This Inuit saw it happen."

"What I can't understand," said Lee Scoresby, offering the

bottle round, "is what the man was doing. Was he prospecting for rock-oil, maybe? Or was he a military man? Or was it something philosophical? You said something about measurements, Sam. What would that be?"

"They were measuring the starlight. And the aurora. He had a passion for the aurora. I think his main interest was in ruins, though. Ancient things."

"I know who could tell you more," said the seal-hunter. "Up the mountain they have an observatory belonging to the Imperial Muscovite Academy. They'd be able to tell you. I know he went up there more than once."

"What d'you want to know for anyway, Lee?" said Sam Cansino.

"He owes me some money," said Lee Scoresby.

This explanation was so satisfying that it stopped their curiosity at once. The conversation turned to the topic on everyone's lips: the catastrophic changes taking place around them, which no one could see.

"The fishermen," said the seal-hunter, "they say you can sail right up into that new world."

"There's a new world?" said Lee.

"As soon as this damn fog clears we'll see right into it," the seal-hunter told them confidently. "When it first happened, I was out in my kayak and looking north, just by chance. I'll never forget what I saw. Instead of the earth curving down over the horizon it went straight on. I could see for ever, and as far as I could see, there was land and shoreline, mountains, harbours, green trees and fields of corn, for ever into the sky. I tell you, friends, that was something worth toiling fifty years to see, a sight like that. I would have paddled up the sky into that calm sea without a backward glance; but then came the fog . . ."

"Ain't never seen a fog like this," grumbled Sam Cansino. "Reckon it's set in for a month, maybe more. But you're out of luck if you want money from Stanislaus Grumman, Lee; the man's dead."

"Ah! I got his Tartar name!" said the seal-hunter. "I just remembered what they called him during the drilling. It sounded like Jopari."

"Jopari? That's no kind of name I've ever heard of," said Lee. "Might be Nipponese, I suppose. Well, if I want my money, maybe I can chase up his heirs and assigns. Or maybe the Berlin Academy can square the debt. I'll go ask at the observatory, see if they have an address I can apply to."

The observatory was some distance to the north, and Lee Scoresby hired a dog-sledge and driver. It wasn't easy to find someone willing to risk the journey in the fog, but Lee was persuasive, or his money was; and eventually an old Tartar from the Ob region agreed to take him there, after a lengthy bout of haggling.

The driver didn't rely on a compass, or he would have found it impossible. He navigated by other signs, his Arctic fox-dæmon for one, who sat at the front of the sledge keenly scenting the way. Lee, who carried his compass everywhere, had realized already that the earth's magnetic field was as disturbed as everything else.

The old driver said, as they stopped to brew coffee, "This happen before, this thing."

"What, the sky opening? That happened before?"

"Many thousand generation. My people remember. All long time ago, many thousand generation."

"What do they say about it?"

"Sky fall open, and spirits move between this world and that world. All the lands move. The ice melt, then freeze again. The spirits close up the hole after a while. Seal it up. But witches say the sky is thin there, behind the northern lights."

"What's going to happen, Umaq?"

"Same thing as before. Make all same again. But only after big trouble, big war. Spirit war."

The driver wouldn't tell him any more, and soon they moved on, tracking slowly over undulations and hollows and past outcrops of dim rock, dark through the pallid fog, until the old man said:

"Observatory up there. You walk now. Path too crooked for sledge. You want go back, I wait here."

"Yeah, I want to go back when I've finished, Umaq. You make

yourself a fire, my friend, and sit and rest a spell. I'll be three, four hours maybe."

Lee Scoresby set off, with Hester tucked into the breast of his coat, and after half an hour's stiff climb found a clump of buildings suddenly above him as if they'd just been placed there by a giant hand. But the effect was only due to a momentary lifting of the fog, and after a minute it closed in again. He saw the great dome of the main observatory, a smaller one a little way off, and between them a group of administration buildings and domestic quarters. No lights showed, because the windows were blacked out permanently so as not to spoil the darkness for their telescopes.

A few minutes after he arrived, Lee was talking to a group of astronomers eager to learn what news he could bring them, and there are few natural philosophers as frustrated as astronomers in a fog. He told them about everything he'd seen, and once that topic had been thoroughly dealt with, he asked about Stanislaus Grumman. The astronomers hadn't had a visitor in weeks, and they were keen to talk.

"Grumman? Yes, I'll tell you something about him," said the Director. "He was an Englishman, in spite of his name. I remember –"

"Surely not," said his deputy. "He was a member of the Imperial German Academy. I met him in Berlin. I was sure he was German."

"No, I think you'll find he was English. His command of that language was immaculate, anyway," said the Director. "But I agree, he was certainly a member of the Berlin Academy. He was a geologist –"

"No, no, you're wrong," said someone else. "He did look at the earth, but not as a geologist. I had a long talk with him once. I suppose you'd call him a palaeo-archaeologist."

They were sitting, five of them, around a table in the room that served as their common room, living- and dining-room, bar, recreation room and more or less everything else. Two of them were Muscovites, one was a Pole, one a Yoruba and one a Skrael-ing. Lee Scoresby sensed that the little community was glad to have a visitor, if only because he introduced a change of

conversation. The Pole had been the last to speak, and then the
Yoruba interrupted:

"What do you mean, a palaeo-archaeologist? Archaeologists
already study what's old; why do you need to put another word
meaning *old* in front of it?"

"His field of study went back much further than you'd expect,
that's all. He was looking for remains of civilizations from twenty,
thirty thousand years ago," the Pole replied.

"Nonsense!" said the Director. "Utter nonsense! The man
was pulling your leg. Civilizations thirty thousand years old? Ha!
Where is the evidence?"

"Under the ice," said the Pole. "That's the point. According
to Grumman, the earth's magnetic field changed dramatically at
various times in the past, and the earth's axis actually moved too,
so that temperate areas became ice-bound."

"How?" said the Yoruba.

"Oh, he had some complex theory. The point was, any evidence there might have been for very early civilizations was long
since buried under the ice. He claimed to have some photograms
of unusual rock formations . . ."

"Ha! Is that all?" said the Director.

"I'm only reporting, I'm not defending him," said the Pole.

"How long had you known Grumman, gentlemen?" Lee
Scoresby asked.

"Well, let me see," said the Director. "It was seven years ago
I met him for the first time."

"He made a name for himself a year or two before that, with
his paper on the variations in the magnetic pole," said the
Yoruba. "But he came out of nowhere. I mean no one had
known him as a student or seen any of his previous work . . ."

They talked on for a while, contributing reminiscences and
offering suggestions as to what might have become of Grumman,
though most of them thought he was probably dead. While the
Pole went to brew some more coffee, Lee's hare-dæmon Hester
said to him quietly:

"Check out the Skraeling, Lee."

The Skraeling had spoken very little. Lee had thought he was
naturally taciturn, but prompted by Hester he casually glanced

across during the next break in the conversation to see the man's dæmon, a snowy owl, glaring at him with bright orange eyes. Well, that was what owls looked like, and they did stare; but Hester was right, and there was a hostility and suspicion in the dæmon that the man's face showed nothing of.

And then Lee saw something else: the Skraeling was wearing a ring with the Church's symbol engraved on it. Suddenly he realized the reason for the man's silence. Every philosophical research establishment, so he'd heard, had to include on its staff a representative of the Magisterium, to act as a censor and suppress the news of any heretical discoveries.

So, realizing this, and remembering something he'd heard Lyra say, Lee asked:

"Tell me, gentlemen – do you happen to know if Grumman ever looked into the question of Dust?"

And instantly a silence fell in the stuffy little room, and everyone's attention focused on the Skraeling, though no one looked at him directly. Lee knew that Hester would remain inscrutable, with her eyes half-closed and her ears flat along her back, and he put on a cheerful innocence as he looked from face to face.

Finally he settled on the Skraeling, and said, "I beg your pardon – have I asked about something it's forbidden to know?"

The Skraeling said, "Where did you hear mention of this subject, Mr Scoresby?"

"From a passenger I flew across the sea a while back," Lee said easily. "They never said what it was, but from the way it was mentioned it seemed like the kind of thing Dr Grumman might have enquired into. I took it to be some kind of celestial thing, like the aurora. But it puzzled me, because as an aëronaut I know the skies pretty well, and I'd never come across this stuff. What is it, anyhow?"

"As you say, a celestial phenomenon," said the Skraeling. "It has no practical significance."

Presently Lee decided it was time to leave; he had learned no more, and he didn't want to keep Umaq waiting. He left the astronomers to their fog-bound observatory and set off down the track, feeling his way along by following his dæmon, whose eyes were closer to the ground.

And when they were only ten minutes down the path, something swept past his head in the fog and dived at Hester. It was the Skraeling's owl-dæmon.

But Hester sensed her coming and flattened herself in time, and the owl's claws just missed. Hester could fight: her claws were sharp, too, and she was tough and brave. Lee knew that the Skraeling himself must be close by, and reached for the revolver at his belt.

"Behind you, Lee," Hester said, and he whipped round, diving, as an arrow hissed over his shoulder.

He fired at once. The Skraeling fell, grunting, as the bullet thudded into his leg. A moment later the owl-dæmon, wheeling on silent wings, swooped with a clumsy fainting movement at his side, and half-lay on the snow, struggling to fold her wings.

Lee Scoresby cocked his pistol and held it to the man's head.

"Right, you damn fool," he said. "What did you try that for? Can't you see we're all in the same trouble now this thing's happened to the sky?"

"It's too late," said the Skraeling.

"Too late for what?"

"Too late to stop. I have already sent a messenger bird. The Magisterium will know of your enquiries, and they will be glad to know about Grumman –"

"What about him?"

"The fact that others are looking for him. It confirms what we thought. And that others know of Dust. You are an enemy of the church, Lee Scoresby. By their fruits shall ye know them. By their questions shall ye see the serpent gnawing at their heart . . ."

The owl was making soft hooting sounds, and raising and dropping her wings fitfully. Her bright orange eyes were filming over with pain. There was a gathering red stain in the snow around the Skraeling: even in the fog-thick dimness Lee could see that the man was going to die.

"Reckon my bullet must have hit an artery," he said. "Let go my sleeve and I'll make a tourniquet."

"No!" said the Skraeling harshly. "I am glad to die! I shall have the martyr's palm! You will not deprive me of that!"

"Then die if you want to. Just tell me this –"

But he never had the chance to complete his question, because with a bleak little shiver the owl-dæmon disappeared. The Skraeling's soul was gone. Lee had once seen a painting in which a saint of the church was shown being attacked by assassins. While they bludgeoned his dying body, the saint's dæmon was borne upwards by cherubs and offered a spray of palm, the badge of a martyr. The Skraeling's face now bore the same expression as the saint's in the picture: an ecstatic straining towards oblivion. Lee dropped him in distaste.

Hester clicked her tongue.

"Should a reckoned he'd send a message," she said. "Take his ring."

"What the hell for? We ain't thieves, are we?"

"No, we're renegades," she said. "Not by our choice, but by his malice. Once the church learns about this, we're done for anyway. Take every advantage we can in the meantime. Go on, take the ring and stow it away, and mebbe we can use it."

Lee saw the sense, and took the ring off the dead man's finger. Peering into the gloom, he saw that the path was edged by a steep drop into rocky darkness, and he rolled the Skraeling's body over. It fell for a long time before he heard any impact. Lee had never enjoyed violence, and he hated killing, although he'd had to do it three times before.

"No sense in thinking that," said Hester. "He didn't give us a choice, and we didn't shoot to kill. Damn it, Lee, he wanted to die. These people are insane."

"I guess you're right," he said, and put the pistol away.

At the foot of the path they found the driver, with the dogs harnessed and ready to move.

"Tell me, Umaq," Lee said as they set off back to the fish-packing station, "you ever hear of a man called Grumman?"

"Oh, sure," said the driver. "Everybody know Dr Grumman."

"Did you know he had a Tartar name?"

"Not Tartar. You mean Jopari? Not Tartar."

"What happened to him? Is he dead?"

"You ask me that, I have to say I don't know. So you never know the truth from me."

"I see. So who can I ask?"

"You better ask his tribe. Better go to Yenisei, ask them."

"His tribe . . . You mean the people who initiated him? Who drilled his skull?"

"Yes. You better ask them. Maybe he not dead, maybe he is. Maybe neither dead nor alive."

"How can he be neither dead nor alive?"

"In spirit world. Maybe he in spirit world. Already I say too much. Say no more now."

And he did not.

But when they returned to the station, Lee went at once to the docks and looked for a ship that could give him passage to the mouth of the Yenisei.

Meanwhile, the witches were searching too. The Latvian queen Ruta Skadi flew with Serafina Pekkala's company for many days and nights, through fog and whirlwind, over regions devastated by flood or landslide. It was certain that they were in a world none of them had known before, with strange winds, strange scents in the air, great unknown birds that attacked them on sight and had to be driven off with volleys of arrows; and when they found land to rest on, the very plants were strange.

Still, some of those plants were edible, and there were small creatures not unlike rabbits that made a tasty meal, and there was no shortage of water. It might have been a good land to live in, but for the spectral forms that drifted like mist over the grasslands and congregated near streams and low-lying water. In some lights they were hardly there at all, just visible as a drifting quality in the light, a rhythmic evanescence, like veils of transparency turning before a mirror. The witches had never seen anything like them before, and mistrusted them at once.

"Are they alive, do you think, Serafina Pekkala?" said Ruta Skadi, as they circled high above a group of the things that stood motionless at the edge of a tract of forest.

"Alive or dead, they're full of malice," Serafina replied. "I can feel that from here. And unless I knew what weapon could harm them, I wouldn't want to go closer than this."

The Spectres seemed to be earthbound, without the power of

flight, luckily for the witches. Later that day, they saw what the Spectres could do.

It happened at a river-crossing, where a dusty road went over a low stone bridge beside a stand of trees. The late afternoon sun slanted across the grassland, drawing an intense green out of the ground and a dusty gold out of the air, and in that rich oblique light the witches saw a band of travellers making for the bridge, some on foot, some in horse-drawn carts, two of them riding horses. They hadn't seen the witches, for they had no reason to look up, but they were the first people the witches had seen in this world, and Serafina was about to fly down to speak to them when they heard a cry of alarm.

It came from the rider on the leading horse. He was pointing at the trees, and as the witches looked down they saw a stream of those spectral forms pouring across the grass, seeming to flow with no effort towards the people, their prey.

The people scattered. Serafina was shocked to see the leading rider turn tail at once and gallop away, without staying to help his comrades, and the second rider did the same, escaping as fast as he could in another direction.

"Fly lower and watch, sisters," Serafina told her companions. "But don't interfere till I command."

They saw that the little band contained children as well, some riding in the carts, some walking beside them. And it was clear that the children couldn't see the Spectres, and the Spectres weren't interested in them: they made instead for the adults. One old woman seated on a cart held two little children on her lap, and Ruta Skadi was angered by her cowardice: because she tried to hide behind them, and thrust them out towards the Spectre that approached her, as if offering them up to save her own life.

The children pulled free of the old woman and jumped down from the cart, and now like the other children around them ran to and fro in fright, or stood and clung together weeping as the Spectres attacked the adults. The old woman in the cart was soon enveloped in a transparent shimmer that moved busily, working and feeding in some invisible way that made Ruta Skadi sick to watch. The same fate attacked every adult in the party apart from the two who had fled on their horses.

Fascinated and horrified, Serafina Pekkala flew down even closer. There was a father with his child who had tried to ford the river to get away, but a Spectre had caught up with them, and as the child clung to the father's back, crying, the man slowed down and stood waist-deep in the water, arrested and helpless.

What was happening to him? Serafina hovered above the water a few feet away, gazing horrified. She had heard from travellers in her own world of the legend of the vampyre, and she thought of that as she watched the Spectre busy gorging on – something, some quality the man had, his soul, his dæmon perhaps; for in this world, evidently, dæmons were inside, not outside. His arms slackened under the child's thighs, and the child fell into the water behind him and grabbed vainly at his hand, gasping, crying, but the man only turned his head slowly and looked down with perfect indifference at his little son drowning beside him.

That was too much for Serafina. She swooped lower and plucked the child from the water, and as she did so, Ruta Skadi cried out: "Be careful, sister! Behind you –"

And Serafina felt just for a moment a hideous dullness at the edge of her heart, and reached out and up for Ruta Skadi's hand, which pulled her away from the danger. They flew higher, the child screaming and clinging to her waist with sharp fingers, and Serafina saw the Spectre behind her, a drift of mist swirling on the water, casting about for its lost prey. Ruta Skadi shot an arrow into the heart of it, with no effect at all.

Serafina put the child down on the river bank, seeing that it was in no danger from the Spectres, and they retreated to the air again. The little band of travellers had halted for good now; the horses cropped the grass or shook their heads at flies, the children were howling or clutching one another and watching from a distance, and every adult had fallen still. Their eyes were open; some were standing, though most had sat down; and a terrible stillness hung over them. As the last of the Spectres drifted away, sated, Serafina flew down and alighted in front of a woman sitting on the grass, a strong healthy-looking woman whose cheeks were red and whose fair hair was glossy.

"Woman?" said Serafina. There was no response. "Can you hear me? Can you see me?"

She shook her shoulder. With an immense effort the woman looked up. She scarcely seemed to notice. Her eyes were vacant, and when Serafina pinched the skin of her forearm, she merely looked down slowly and then away again.

The other witches were moving through the scattered wagons, looking at the victims in dismay. The children, meanwhile, were gathering on a little knoll some way off, staring at the witches and whispering together fearfully.

"The horseman's watching," said a witch.

She pointed up to where the road led through a gap in the hills. The rider who'd fled had reined in his horse and turned round to look back, shading his eyes to see what was going on.

"We'll speak to him," said Serafina, and sprang into the air.

However the man had behaved when faced with the Spectres, he was no coward. As he saw the witches approach he unslung the rifle from his back and kicked the horse forward on to the grass, where he could wheel and fire and face them in the open; but Serafina Pekkala alighted slowly and held her bow out before laying it on the ground in front of her.

Whether or not they had that gesture here, its meaning was unmistakable. The man lowered the rifle from his shoulder and waited, looking from Serafina to the other witches, and up to their dæmons too, who circled in the skies above. Women, young and ferocious, dressed in scraps of black silk and riding pine-branches through the sky – there was nothing like that in his world, but he faced them with calm wariness. Serafina, coming closer, saw sorrow in his face as well, and strength. It was hard to reconcile with the memory of his turning tail and running while his companions perished.

"Who are you?" he said.

"My name is Serafina Pekkala. I am the queen of the witches of Lake Enara, which is in another world. What is your name?"

"Joachim Lorenz. Witches, you say? Do you treat with the devil then?"

"If we did, would that make us your enemy?"

He thought for a few moments, and settled his rifle across his thighs. "It might have done, once," he said, "but times have changed. Why have you come to this world?"

"Because the times have changed. What are those creatures who attacked your party?"

"Well, the Spectres ..." he said, shrugging, half astonished. "Don't you know the Spectres?"

"We've never seen them in our world. We saw you making your escape, and we didn't know what to think. Now I understand."

"There's no defence against them," said Joachim Lorenz. "Only the children are untouched. Every party of travellers has to include a man and a woman on horseback, by law, and they have to do what we did, or else the children will have no one to look after them. But times are bad now; the cities are thronged with Spectres, and there used to be no more than a dozen or so in each place."

Ruta Skadi was looking around. She saw the other rider moving back towards the wagons, and saw that it was, indeed, a woman. The children were running to meet her.

"But tell me what you're looking for," Joachim Lorenz went on. "You didn't answer me before. You wouldn't have come here for nothing. Answer me now."

"We're looking for a child," said Serafina, "a young girl from our world. Her name is Lyra Belacqua, called Lyra Silvertongue. But where she might be, in a whole world, we can't guess. You haven't seen a strange child, on her own?"

"No. But we saw angels the other night, making for the Pole."

"Angels?"

"Troops of them in the air, armed and shining. They haven't been so common in the last years, though in my grandfather's time they passed through this world often, or so he used to say."

He shaded his eyes and gazed down towards the scattered wagons, the halted travellers. The other rider had dismounted now, and was comforting some of the children.

Serafina followed his gaze and said, "If we camp with you tonight and keep guard against the Spectres, will you tell us more about this world, and these angels you saw?"

"Certainly I will. Come with me."

* * *

The witches helped to move the wagons further along the road, over the bridge and away from the trees where the Spectres had come from. The stricken adults had to stay where they were, though it was painful to see the little children clinging to a mother who no longer responded to them, or tugging the sleeve of a father who said nothing and gazed into nothing and had nothing in his eyes. The younger children couldn't understand why they had to leave their parents. The older ones, some of whom had already lost parents of their own and who had seen it before, simply looked bleak and stayed dumb. Serafina picked up the little boy who'd fallen in the river, and who was crying out for his daddy, reaching back over Serafina's shoulder to the silent figure still standing in the water, indifferent. Serafina felt his tears on her bare skin.

The horsewoman, who wore rough canvas breeches and rode like a man, said nothing to the witches. Her face was grim. She moved the children on, speaking sternly, ignoring their tears. The evening sun suffused the air with a golden light in which every detail was clear and nothing was dazzling, and the faces of the children and the man and woman too seemed immortal and strong and beautiful.

Later, as the embers of a fire glowed in a circle of ashy rocks and the great hills lay calm under the moon, Joachim Lorenz told Serafina and Ruta Skadi about the history of his world.

It had once been a happy one, he explained. The cities were spacious and elegant, the fields well-tilled and fertile. Merchant ships plied to and fro on the blue oceans, and fishermen hauled in brimming nets of cod and tunny, bass and mullet; the forests ran with game, and no children went hungry. In the courts and squares of the great cities ambassadors from Brasil and Benin, from Eireland and Corea mingled with tabaco-sellers, with commedia players from Bergamo, with dealers in fortune-bonds. At night masked lovers met under the rose-hung colonnades or in the lamp-lit gardens, and the air stirred with the scent of jasmine and throbbed to the music of the wire-strung mandarone.

The witches listened wide-eyed to this tale of a world so like theirs, and yet so different.

"But it went wrong," he said. "Three hundred years ago, it

all went wrong. Some people reckon the philosophers' Guild of the Torre degli Angeli, the Tower of the Angels, in the city we have just left, they're the ones to blame. Others say it was a judgment on us for some great sin, though I never heard any agreement about what that sin was. But suddenly out of nowhere there came the Spectres, and we've been haunted ever since. You've seen what they do. Now imagine what it is to live in a world with Spectres in it. How can we prosper, when we can't rely on anything continuing as it was? At any moment a father might be taken, or a mother, and the family fall apart; a merchant might be taken, and his enterprise fail, and all his clerks and factors lose their employment; and how can lovers trust their vows? All the trust and all the virtue fell out of our world when the Spectres came."

"Who are these philosophers?" said Serafina. "And where is this Tower you speak of?"

"In the city we left – Cittàgazze. The city of magpies. You know why it's called that? Because magpies steal, and that's all we can do now. We create nothing, we have built nothing for hundreds of years, all we can do is steal from other worlds. Oh yes, we know about other worlds. Those philosophers in the Torre degli Angeli discovered all we need to know about that subject. They have a spell which, if you say it, lets you walk through a door that isn't there, and find yourself in another world. Some say it's not a spell but a key that can open even where there isn't a lock. Who knows? Whatever it is, it let the Spectres in. And the philosophers use it still, I understand. They pass into other worlds and steal from them and bring back what they find. Gold and jewels, of course, but other things too, like ideas, or sacks of corn, or pencils. They are the source of all our wealth," he said bitterly, "that Guild of thieves."

"Why don't the Spectres harm children?" asked Ruta Skadi.

"That is the greatest mystery of all. In the innocence of children there's some power that repels the Spectres of Indifference. But it's more than that. Children simply don't see them, though we can't understand why. We never have. But Spectre-orphans are common, as you can imagine, children whose parents have been taken; they gather in bands and roam the country, and sometimes they hire themselves out to adults to look for food and supplies in a Spectre-ridden area, and sometimes they simply drift about and scavenge.

"So that is our world. Oh, we managed to live with this curse. They're true parasites: they won't kill their host, though they drain most of the life out of him. But there was a rough balance – till recently, till the great storm. Such a storm it was; it sounded as if the whole world was breaking and cracking apart; there hadn't been a storm like that in memory.

"And then there came a fog that lasted for days and covered every part of the world that I know of, and no one could travel; and when the fog cleared, the cities were full of the Spectres, hundreds and thousands of them. So we fled to the hills and out to sea, but there's no escaping them this time wherever we go. As you saw for yourselves.

"Now it's your turn. You tell me about your world, and why you've left it to come to this one."

Serafina told him truthfully as much as she knew. He was an honest man, and there was nothing that needed concealing from him. He listened closely, shaking his head with wonder, and when she had finished, he said:

"I told you about the power they say our philosophers have, of opening the way to other worlds. Well, some think that occasionally they leave a doorway open, out of forgetfulness; I wouldn't be surprised if travellers from other worlds found their way here from time to time. We know that angels pass through, after all."

"Angels?" said Serafina. "You mentioned them before. We have never heard of angels. What are they?"

"You want to know about angels?" said Joachim Lorenz. "Very well. Their name for themselves is *bene elim*, I'm told. Some call them Watchers, too. They're not beings of flesh like us, they're beings of spirit; or maybe their flesh is finer-drawn than ours, lighter and clearer, I wouldn't know; but they're not like us. They carry messages from heaven, that's their calling. We see them sometimes in the sky, passing through this world on the way to another, shining like fireflies way, way up high. On a still night you can even hear their wingbeats. They have concerns different from ours, though in the ancient days they came down and had dealings with men and women, and they bred with us, too, some say.

"And when the fog came, after the great storm, I was beset in the hills behind the city of Sant'Elia, on my way homewards. I took refuge in a shepherd's hut by a spring next to a birch wood, and all night long I heard voices above me in the fog, cries of alarm and anger, and wingbeats too, closer than I'd ever heard them before; and towards dawn there was the sound of a skirmish of arms, the whoosh of arrows, and the clang of swords. I daredn't go out and see, though I was powerfully curious, for I was afraid. I was stark terrified, if you want to know. When the sky was as light as it ever got during that fog, I ventured to look out, and I saw a great figure lying wounded by the spring. I felt as if I was seeing things I had no right to see – sacred things. I had to look away, and when I looked again the figure was gone.

"That's the closest I ever came to an angel. But as I told you, we saw them the other night, way high aloft among the stars, making for the Pole, like a fleet of mighty ships under sail ... Something is happening, and we don't know down here what it may be. There could be a war breaking out. There was a war in heaven once, oh, thousands of years ago, immense ages back, but I don't know what the outcome was. It wouldn't be impossible if there was another. But the devastation would be enormous, and the consequences for us ... I can't imagine it.

"Though," he went on, sitting up to stir the fire, "the end of it might be better than I fear. It might be that a war in heaven would sweep the Spectres from this world altogether, and back into the pit they come from. What a blessing that would be, eh! How fresh and happy we could live, free of that fearful blight!"

Though Joachim Lorenz looked anything but hopeful as he stared into the flames. The flickering light played over his face, but there was no play of expression in his strong features; he looked grim and sad.

Ruta Skadi said, "The Pole, sir. You said these angels were making for the Pole. Why would they do that, do you know? Is that where heaven lies?"

"I couldn't say. I'm not a learned man, you can see that plain enough. But the north of our world, well, that's the abode of spirits, they say. If angels were mustering, that's where they'd go, and if they were going to make an assault on heaven, I dare say that's where they'd build their fortress and sally out from."

He looked up, and the witches followed his eyes. The stars in this world were the same as theirs: the Milky Way blazed bright across the dome of the sky, and innumerable points of starlight dusted the dark, almost matching the moon for brightness . . .

"Sir," said Serafina, "did you ever hear of Dust?"

"Dust? I guess you mean it in some other sense than that dust on the roads. No, I never did. But look – there's a troop of angels now . . ."

He pointed to the constellation of Ophiucus. And sure enough, something was moving through it, a tiny cluster of lighted beings. And they didn't drift; they moved with the purposeful flight of geese or swans.

Ruta Skadi stood up.

"Sister, it's time I parted from you," she said to Serafina. "I'm going up to speak to these angels, whatever they may be. If they're going to Lord Asriel, I'll go with them. If not, I'll search on by myself. Thank you for your company, and go well."

They kissed, and Ruta Skadi took her cloud-pine branch and sprang into the air. Her dæmon Sergi, a bluethroat, sped out of the dark alongside her.

"We're going high?" he said.

"As high as those lighted fliers in Ophiucus. They're going swiftly, Sergi. Let's catch them!"

And she and her dæmon raced upwards, flying quicker than sparks from a fire, the air rushing through the twigs on her branch and making her black hair stream out behind. She didn't look back at the little fire in the wide darkness, at the sleeping children and her witch-companions. That part of her journey was over, and besides, those glowing creatures ahead of her were no larger yet, and unless she kept her eye on them they were easily lost against the great expanse of starlight.

So she flew on, never losing sight of the angels, and gradually as she came closer they took on a clearer shape.

They shone not as if they were burning but as if, wherever

they were and however dark the night, sunlight was shining on them. They were like humans, but winged, and much taller; and as they were naked, the witch could see that three of them were male, two female. Their wings sprang from their shoulder blades, and their backs and chests were deeply muscled. Ruta Skadi stayed behind them for some way, watching, measuring their strength in case she should need to fight them. They weren't armed, but on the other hand they were flying easily within their power, and might even outstrip her if it came to a chase.

Making her bow ready, just in case, she sped forward and flew alongside them, calling:

"Angels! Halt and listen to me! I am the witch Ruta Skadi, and I want to talk to you!"

They turned. Their great wings beat inwards, slowing them, and their bodies swung downwards till they were standing upright in the air, holding their position by the beating of their wings. They surrounded her, five huge forms glowing in the dark air, lit by an invisible sun.

She looked around, sitting her pine-branch proud and un-afraid, though her heart was beating with the strangeness of it, and her dæmon fluttered to sit close to the warmth of her body.

Each angel-being was distinctly an individual, and yet they had more in common with each other than with any human she had seen. What they shared was a shimmering, darting play of intelligence and feeling that seemed to sweep over them all simultaneously. They were naked, but she felt naked in front of their glance, it was so piercing and went so deep.

Still, she was unashamed of what she was, and she returned their gaze with head held high.

"So you are angels," she said, "or Watchers, or *bene elim*. Where are you going?"

"We are following a call," said one.

She was not sure which one had spoken. It might have been any or all of them at once.

"Whose call?" she said.

"A man's."

"Lord Asriel's?"

"It may be."

"Why are you following his call?"

"Because we are willing to," came the reply.

"Then wherever he is, you can guide me to him as well," she ordered them.

Ruta Skadi was four hundred and sixteen years old, with all the pride and knowledge of an adult witch-queen. She was wiser by far than any short-lived human, but she had not the slightest idea of how like a child she seemed beside these ancient beings. Nor did she know how far their awareness spread out beyond her like filamentary tentacles to the remotest corners of universes she had never dreamed of; nor that she saw them as human-formed only because her eyes expected to. If she were to perceive their true form, they would seem more like architecture than organism, like huge structures composed of intelligence and feeling.

But they expected nothing else: she was very young.

At once they beat their wings and surged forward, and she darted with them, surfing on the turbulence their pinions caused in the air and relishing the speed and power it added to her flight.

They flew throughout the night. The stars wheeled around them, and faded and vanished as the dawn seeped up from the east. The world burst into brilliance as the sun's rim appeared, and then they were flying through blue sky and clear air, fresh and sweet and moist.

In the daylight the angels were less visible, though to any eye their strangeness was clear. The light Ruta Skadi saw them by was still not that of the sun now climbing the sky, but some other light from somewhere else.

Tirelessly they flew on and on, and tirelessly she kept pace. She felt a fierce joy possessing her, that she could command these immortal presences. And she rejoiced in her blood and flesh, in the rough pine bark she felt next to her skin, in the beat of her heart and the life of all her senses, and in the hunger she was feeling now, and in the presence of her sweet-voiced blue-throat dæmon, and in the earth below her and the lives of every creature, plant and animal both; and she delighted in being of the same substance as them, and in knowing that when she died her flesh would nourish other lives as they had nourished her. And she rejoiced, too, that she was going to see Lord Asriel again.

Another night came, and still the angels flew on. And at some point the quality of the air changed, not for the worse or the better, but changed nonetheless, and Ruta Skadi knew that they'd passed out of that world and into another. How it had happened she couldn't guess.

"Angels!" she called, as she sensed the change. "How have we left the world I found you in? Where was the boundary?"

"There are invisible places in the air," came the answer, "gateways into other worlds. We can see them, but you cannot."

Ruta Skadi couldn't see the invisible gateway, but she didn't need to: witches could navigate better than birds. As soon as the angel spoke, she fixed her attention on three jagged peaks below her, and memorized their configuration exactly. Now she could find it again, if she needed to, despite what the angels might think.

They flew on further, and presently she heard an angel-voice:

"Lord Asriel is in this world, and there is the fortress he's building . . ."

They had slowed, and were circling like eagles in the middle airs. Ruta Skadi looked where one angel was pointing. The first faint glimmer of light was tinting the east, though all the stars above shone as brilliantly as ever against the profound velvet black of the high heavens. And on the very rim of the world, where the light was increasing moment by moment, a great mountain range reared its peaks – jagged spears of black rock, mighty broken slabs and sawtooth ridges piled in confusion like the wreckage of a universal catastrophe. But on the highest point, which as she looked was touched by the first rays of the morning sun and outlined in brilliance, stood a regular structure: a huge fortress whose battlements were formed of single slabs of basalt half a hill in height, and whose extent was to be measured in flying-time.

Beneath this colossal fortress, fires glared and furnaces smoked in the darkness of early dawn, and from many miles away Ruta Skadi heard the clang of hammers and the pounding of great mills. And from every direction, she could see more flights of angels winging towards it, and not only angels, but machines too: steel-winged craft gliding like albatrosses, glass cabins under flickering dragonfly-wings, droning zeppelins like huge bumble bees – all making for the fortress that Lord Asriel was building on the mountains at the edge of the world.

"And is Lord Asriel there?" she said.

"Yes, he is there," the angels replied.

"Then let's fly there to meet him. And you must be my guard of honour."

Obediently they spread their wings, and set their course towards the gold-rimmed fortress, with the eager witch flying before them.

7
THE ROLLS ROYCE

LYRA WOKE EARLY to find the morning quiet and warm, as if the city never had any other weather than this calm summer. She slipped out of bed and downstairs and, hearing some children's voices out on the water, went to see what they were doing.

Three boys and a girl were splashing across the sunlit harbour in a couple of pedal-boats, racing towards the steps. As they saw Lyra they slowed for a moment, but then the race took hold of them again. The winners crashed into the steps so hard that one of them fell into the water, and then he tried to climb into the other craft and tipped that over too, and then they all splashed about together as if the fear of the night before had never happened. They were younger than most of the children by the Tower, Lyra thought, and she joined them in the water, with Pantalaimon as a little silver fish glittering beside her. She never found it hard to talk to other children, and soon they were gathered round her, sitting in pools of water on the warm stone, their shirts drying quickly in the sun. Poor Pantalaimon had to creep into her pocket again, frog-shaped in the cool damp cotton.

"What you going to do with that cat?"

"Can you really take the bad luck away?"

"Where you come from?"

"Your friend, he ain afraid of Spectres?"

"Will en't afraid of anything," Lyra said. "Nor'm I. What you scared of cats for?"

"You don't know about cats?" the oldest boy said incredulously. "Cats, they got the devil in them, all right. You got to kill every cat you see. They bite you and put the devil in you too. And what was you doing with that big pard?"

She realized he meant Pantalaimon in his leopard-shape, and shook her head innocently.

"You must have been dreaming," she said. "There's all kinds

of things look different in the moonlight. But me and Will, we don't have Spectres where we come from, so we don't know much about 'em."

"If you can't see 'em, you're safe," said a boy. "You see 'em, you know they can get you. That's what my pa said, then they got him. He missed them that time."

"And they're here, all round us now?"

"Yeah," said the girl. She reached out a hand and grabbed a fistful of air, crowing, "I got one now!"

"They can't hurt you," one of the boys said. "So we can't hurt them, all right."

"And there's always been Spectres in this world?" said Lyra.

"Yeah," said one boy, but another said, "No, they came a long time ago. Hundreds of years."

"They came because of the Guild," said the third.

"The what?" said Lyra.

"They never!" said the girl. "My granny said they came because people were bad, and God sent them to punish us."

"Your granny don' know nothing," said a boy. "She got a beard, your granny. She's a goat, all right."

"What's the Guild?" Lyra persisted.

"You know the Torre degli Angeli," said a boy, "the stone tower, right, well it belongs to the Guild, and there's a secret place in there. The Guild, they're men who know all kind of things. Philosophy, alchemy, all kind of things they know. And they were the ones who let the Spectres in."

"That ain true," said another boy. "They came from the stars."

"It *is*! This is what happened, all right: this Guild man hundreds of years ago was taking some metal apart. Lead. He was going to make it into gold. And he cut it and cut it smaller and smaller till he came to the smallest piece he could get. There ain nothing smaller than that. So small you couldn't see it, even. But he cut that too, and inside the smallest little bit, there was all the Spectres packed in twisted over and folded up so tight they took up no space at all. But once he cut it, bam! They whooshed out, and they been here ever since. That's what my pappa said."

"Is there any Guild men in the tower now?" said Lyra.

"No! They run away like everyone else," said the girl.

"There ain no one in the tower. That's haunted, that place," said a boy. "That's why the cat came from there. We ain gonna go in there, all right. Ain no kids gonna go in there. That's scary."

"The Guild men ain afraid to go in there," said another.

"They got special magic, or something. They're greedy, they live off the poor people," said the girl. "The poor people do all the work, and the Guild men just live there for nothing."

"But there en't anyone in the tower now?" Lyra said. "No grown-ups?"

"No grown-ups in the city at all!"

"They wouldn't dare, all right."

But she had seen a young man up there. She was convinced of it. And there was something in the way these children spoke: as a practised liar, she knew liars when she met them, and they were lying about something.

And suddenly she remembered: little Paolo had mentioned that he and Angelica had an elder brother Tullio who was in the city too, and Angelica had hushed him . . . Could the young man she'd seen have been their brother?

She left them to rescue their boats and pedal back to the beach, and went inside to make some coffee and see if Will was awake. But he was still asleep, with the cat curled up at his feet, and Lyra was impatient to see her scholar again; so she wrote a note and left it on the floor by his bedside, and took her rucksack and went off to look for the window.

The way she took led her through the little square they'd come to the night before. But it was empty now, and the sunlight dusted the front of the ancient tower and showed up the blurred carvings beside the doorway: human-like figures with folded wings, their features eroded by centuries of weather, but some-how in their stillness expressing power and compassion and intellectual force.

"Angels," said Pantalaimon, a cricket on her shoulder.

"Maybe Spectres," Lyra said.

"No! They said this was something *angeli*," he insisted. "Bet that's angels."

"Shall we go in?"

They looked up at the great oak door on its ornate black

hinges. The half-dozen steps up to it were deeply worn, and the door itself stood slightly open. There was nothing to stop Lyra going in except her own fear.

She tiptoed to the top of the steps and looked through the opening. A dark stone-flagged hall was all she could see, and not much of that; but Pantalaimon was fluttering anxiously on her shoulder, just as he had when they'd played the trick on the skulls in the crypt at Jordan College, and she was a little wiser now. This was a bad place. She ran down the steps and out of the square, making for the bright sunlight of the palm-tree boulevard. And as soon as she was sure there was no one looking, she went straight across to the window and through into Will's Oxford.

Forty minutes later she was inside the physics building once more, arguing with the porter; but this time she had a trump card.

"You just ask Dr Malone," she said sweetly. "That's all you got to do, ask her. She'll tell you."

The porter turned to his telephone, and Lyra watched pityingly as he pressed the buttons and spoke into it. They didn't give him a proper lodge to sit in, like a real Oxford college, just a big wooden counter, as if it was a shop.

"All right," said the porter, turning back. "She says go on up. Mind you don't go anywhere else."

"No, I won't," she said demurely, a good little girl doing what she was told.

At the top of the stairs, though, she had a surprise, because just as she passed a door with a symbol indicating woman on it, it opened and there was Dr Malone silently beckoning her in.

She entered, puzzled. This wasn't the laboratory, it was a washroom, and Dr Malone was agitated.

She said, "Lyra – there's someone else in the lab – police officers or something – they know you came to see me yesterday – I don't know what they're after but I don't like it – what's going on?"

"How do they know I came to see you?"

"I don't know! They didn't know your name, but I knew who they meant –"

"Oh. Well, I can lie to them. That's easy."

"But *what is going on*?"

A woman's voice spoke from the corridor outside:

"Dr Malone? Have you seen the child?"

"Yes," Dr Malone called. "I was just showing her where the washroom is . . ."

There was no need for her to be so anxious, thought Lyra, but perhaps she wasn't used to danger.

The woman in the corridor was young and dressed very smartly, and she did try to smile when Lyra came out, but her eyes remained hard and suspicious.

"Hello," she said. "You're Lyra, are you?"

"Yeah. What's your name?"

"I'm Sergeant Clifford. Come along in."

Lyra thought this young woman had a nerve, acting as if it was her own laboratory, but she nodded meekly. That was the moment when she first felt a twinge of regret. She knew she shouldn't be here; she knew what the alethiometer wanted her to do, and it was not this. She stood doubtfully in the doorway.

In the room already there was a tall powerful man with white eyebrows. Lyra knew what scholars looked like, and neither of these two was a scholar.

"Come in, Lyra," said Sergeant Clifford again. "It's all right. This is Inspector Walters."

"Hello, Lyra," said the man. "I've been hearing all about you from Dr Malone here. I'd like to meet you, and ask you a few questions, if that's all right."

"What sort of questions?" she said.

"Nothing difficult," he said, smiling. "Come and sit down, Lyra."

He pushed a chair towards her. Lyra sat down carefully, and heard the door close itself. Dr Malone was standing nearby. Pantalaimon, cricket-formed in Lyra's breast pocket, was agitated: she could feel him against her breast, and hoped the tremor didn't show. She thought to him to keep still.

"Where d'you come from, Lyra?" said Inspector Walters.

If she said Oxford, they'd easily be able to check. But she couldn't say another world, either; these people were dangerous;

they'd want to know more at once. She thought of the only other name she knew of in this world: the place Will had come from.

"Winchester," she said.

"You've been in the wars, haven't you, Lyra?" said the inspector. "How did you get those bruises? There's a bruise on your cheek, and another on your leg – has someone been knocking you about?"

"No," said Lyra.

"Do you go to school, Lyra?"

"Yeah. Sometimes," she added.

"Shouldn't you be at school today?"

She said nothing. She was feeling more and more uneasy. She looked at Dr Malone, whose face was tight and unhappy.

"I just came here to see Dr Malone," Lyra said.

"Are you staying in Oxford, Lyra? Where are you staying?"

"With some people," she said. "Just friends."

"What's their address?"

"I don't know exactly what it's called. I can find it, easy, but I can't remember the name of the street."

"Who are these people?"

"Just friends of my father," she said.

"Oh, I see. How did you find Dr Malone?"

"'Cause my father's a physicist and he knows her."

It was going more easily now, she thought. She began to relax into it and lie more fluently.

"And she showed you what she was working on, did she?"

"Yeah. The engine with the screen . . . Yes, all that."

"You're interested in that sort of thing, are you? Science and so on?"

"Yeah. Physics, especially."

"You going to be a scientist when you grow up?"

That sort of question deserved a blank stare, which it got. He wasn't disconcerted. His pale eyes looked briefly at the young woman, and then back to Lyra.

"And were you surprised at what Dr Malone showed you?"

"Well, sort of, but I knew what to expect."

"Because of your father?"

"Yeah. 'Cause he's doing the same kind of work."

"Yes, quite. Do you understand it?"

"Some of it."

"Your father's looking into dark matter, then?"

"Yes."

"Has he got as far as Dr Malone?"

"Not in the same way. He can do some things better, but that engine with the words on the screen, he hasn't got one of those."

"Is Will staying with your friends as well?"

"Yes, he —"

And she stopped. She knew at once she'd made a horrible mistake.

So did they, and they were on their feet in a moment to stop her running out, but somehow Dr Malone was in the way, and the sergeant tripped and fell, blocking the way of the inspector. It gave Lyra time to dart out and slam the door shut behind her, and run full tilt for the stairs.

Two men in white coats came out of a door, and she bumped into them and suddenly Pantalaimon was a crow, shrieking and flapping, and he startled them so much they fell back and she pulled free of their hands and raced down the last flight of stairs into the lobby just as the porter put the phone down and lumbered along behind his counter calling out: "Oy! Stop there! You!"

But the flap he had to lift was at the other end, and she got to the revolving door before he could come out and catch her.

And behind her, the lift doors were opening, and the pale-haired man was running out, so fast, so strong —

And the door wouldn't turn! Pantalaimon shrieked at her: they were pushing the wrong side!

She cried out in fear and darted out and into the other compartment, hurling her little weight against the heavy glass, willing it to turn, and got it to move just in time to avoid the grasp of the porter, who then got in the way of the pale-haired man, so Lyra could dash out and away before they got through.

Across the road, ignoring the cars, the brakes, the squeal of tyres; into this gap between tall buildings, and then another road, with cars from both directions, but she was quick, dodging bicycles, always with the pale-haired man just behind her – oh, he was frightening!

Into a garden – over a fence – through some bushes – Pantalaimon skimming overhead, a swift, calling to her which way to go; crouching down behind a coal-bunker as the pale man's footsteps came racing past, and she couldn't hear him panting, he was so fast, and so fit; and Pantalaimon said "Back now – go back to the road –"

So she crept out of her hiding-place and ran back across the grass, out through the garden gate, into the open spaces of the Banbury Road again; and once again she dodged across, and once again tyres squealed on the road; and then she was running up Norham Gardens, a quiet tree-lined road of tall Victorian houses near the Park.

She stopped to gain her breath. There was a tall hedge in front of one of the gardens, with a low wall at its foot, and she sat there tucked closely in under the privet.

"She helped us!" Pantalaimon said. "Dr Malone got in their way. She's on our side, not theirs."

"Oh, Pan," she said, "I shouldn't have said that about Will – I should've been more careful –"

"Shouldn't have come," he said severely.

"I know. That too . . ."

But she hadn't got time to berate herself, because Pantalaimon fluttered to her shoulder, and then said, "Look out – behind –" and immediately changed to a cricket again and dived into her pocket.

She stood, ready to run, and saw a large dark-blue car gliding silently to the pavement beside her. She was braced to dart in either direction, but the car's rear window rolled down, and there looking out was a face she recognized.

"Lizzie," said the old man from the Museum. "How nice to see you again. Can I give you a lift anywhere?"

And he opened the door and moved up to make room beside him. Pantalaimon nipped her breast through the thin cotton, but she got in at once, clutching the rucksack, and the man leaned across her and pulled the door shut.

"You look as if you're in a hurry," he said. "Where d'you want to go?"

"Up Summertown," she said, "please."

The driver was wearing a peaked cap. Everything about the car was smooth and soft and powerful, and the smell of the old man's cologne was strong in the enclosed space. The car pulled out from the pavement and moved away with no noise at all.

"So what have you been up to, Lizzie?" the old man said. "Did you find out more about those skulls?"

"Yeah," she said, twisting to see out of the rear window. There was no sign of the pale-haired man. She'd got away! And he'd never find her now she was safe in a powerful car with a rich man like this. She felt a little hiccup of triumph.

"I made some enquiries too," he said. "An anthropologist friend of mine tells me that they've got several others in the collection, as well as the ones on display. Some of them are very old indeed. Neanderthal, you know."

"Yeah, that's what I heard too," Lyra said, with no idea what he was talking about.

"And how's your friend?"

"What friend?" said Lyra, alarmed: had she told him about Will too?

"The friend you're staying with."

"Oh. Yes. She's very well, thank you."

"What does she do? Is she an archaeologist?"

"Oh . . . She's a physicist. She studies dark matter," said Lyra, still not quite in control. This was a harder world to tell lies in than she'd thought. And something else was nagging at her: this old man was familiar in some long-lost way, and she just couldn't place it.

"Dark matter?" he was saying. "How fascinating! I saw something about that in the *Times* this morning. The universe is full of this mysterious stuff, and nobody knows what it is! And your friend is on the track of it, is she?"

"Yes. She knows a lot about it."

"And what are you going to do later on, Lizzie? Are you going in for physics too?"

"I might," said Lyra. "It depends."

The chauffeur coughed gently, and slowed the car down.

"Well, here we are in Summertown," said the old man. "Where would you like to be dropped?"

"Oh – just up past these shops – I can walk from there," said Lyra. "Thank you."

"Turn left into South Parade, and pull up on the right, could you, Allan," said the old man.

"Very good, sir," said the chauffeur.

A minute later the car came to a silent halt outside a public library. The old man held open the door on his side, so that Lyra had to climb past his knees to get out. There was a lot of space, but somehow it was awkward, and she didn't want to touch him, nice as he was.

"Don't forget your rucksack," he said, handing it to her.

"Thank you," she said.

"I'll see you again, I hope, Lizzie," he said. "Give my regards to your friend."

"Goodbye," she said, and lingered on the pavement till the car had turned the corner and gone out of sight before she set off towards the hornbeam trees. She had a feeling about that pale-haired man, and she wanted to ask the alethiometer.

Will was reading his father's letters again. He sat on the terrace hearing the distant shouts of children diving off the harbour mouth, and read the clear handwriting on the flimsy airmail sheets, trying to picture the man who'd penned it, and looking again and again at the reference to the baby, to himself.

He heard Lyra's running footsteps from some way off. He put the letters in his pocket and stood up, and almost at once Lyra was there, wild-eyed, with Pantalaimon a snarling savage wildcat, too distraught to hide. She who seldom cried was sobbing with rage; her chest was heaving, her teeth were grinding, and she flung herself at him, clutching his arms, and cried, "Kill him! Kill him! I want him dead! I wish Iorek was here – oh, Will, I done wrong, I'm so sorry –"

"What? What's the matter?"

"That old man – he en't nothing but a low thief – he *stole* it, Will! He stole my alethiometer! That stinky old man with his rich clothes and his servant driving the car – oh, I done such wrong things this morning – oh, I . . ."

And she sobbed so passionately he thought that hearts really did break, and hers was breaking now, for she fell to the ground wailing and shuddering, and Pantalaimon beside her became a wolf and howled with bitter grief.

Far off across the water, children stopped what they were doing and shaded their eyes to see. Will sat down beside Lyra and shook her shoulder.

"Stop! Stop crying!" he said. "Tell me from the beginning. What old man? What happened?"

"You're going to be so angry – I promised I wouldn't give you away, I *promised* it, and then . . ." she sobbed, and Pantalaimon became a young clumsy dog with lowered ears and wagging tail, squirming with self-abasement; and Will understood that Lyra had done something that she was too ashamed to tell him about, and he spoke to the dæmon.

"What *happened*? Just tell me," he said.

Pantalaimon said, "We went to the scholar, and there was someone else there, a man and a woman – and they tricked us – they asked a lot of questions and then they asked about you, and before we could stop we gave it away that we knew you, and then we ran away –"

Lyra was hiding her face in her hands, pressing her head down against the pavement. Pantalaimon was flickering from shape to shape in his agitation: dog, bird, cat, snow-white ermine.

"What did the man look like?" said Will.

"Big," said Lyra's muffled voice, "and ever so strong, and pale eyes . . ."

"Did he see you come back through the window?"

"No, but . . ."

"Well, he won't know where we are, then."

"But the alethiometer!" she cried, and she sat up fiercely, her face rigid with emotion, like a Greek mask.

"Yeah," said Will. "Tell me about that."

Between sobs and teeth-grindings she told him what had happened: how the old man had seen her using the alethiometer in the Museum the day before, and how he'd stopped the car today and she'd got in to escape from the pale man, and how the car had pulled up on that side of the road so she'd had to climb past him to get out, and how he must have swiftly taken the alethiometer as he'd passed her the rucksack . . .

He could see how devastated she was, but not why she should feel guilty. And then she said:

"And Will, please, I done something very bad. Because the alethiometer told me I had to stop looking for Dust, and I had to help you. I had to help you find your father. And I *could*, I could take you to wherever he is, if I had it. But I wouldn't listen. I just done what I wanted to do, and I shouldn't . . ."

He'd seen her use it, and he knew it could tell her the truth. He turned away. She seized his wrist, but he broke away from her and walked to the edge of the water. The children were playing again across the harbour. Lyra ran up to him and said, "Will, I'm so sorry –"

"What's the use of that? I don't care if you're sorry or not. You did it."

"But Will, we got to help each other, you and me, because there en't anyone else!"

"I can't see how."

"Nor can I, but . . ."

She stopped in mid-sentence, and a light came into her eyes. She turned and raced back to her rucksack, abandoned on the pavement, and rummaged through it feverishly.

"I know who he is! And where he lives! Look!" she said, and held up a little slip of white card. "He gave this to me in the Museum! We can go and get it back!"

Will took the card and read:

Sir Charles Latrom, CBE
Limefield House
Old Headington
Oxford

"He's a sir," he said. "A knight. That means people will automatically believe him and not us. What did you want me to do anyway? Go to the police? The police are after me! Or if they

weren't yesterday they will be by now. And if *you* go, they know
who you are now, and they know you know me, so that wouldn't
work either."

"We could steal it. We could go to his house and steal it.
I know where Headington is, there's a Headington in my Oxford
too. It en't far. We could walk there in an hour, easy."

"You're stupid."

"Iorek Byrnison would go there straight away and rip his head
off. I wish he was here. He'd —"

But she fell silent. Will was just looking at her, and she quailed.
She would have quailed in the same way if the armoured bear
had looked at her like that, because there was something not
unlike Iorek in Will's eyes, young as they were.

"I never heard anything so stupid in my life," he said. "You
think we can just go to his house and creep in and steal it?
You need to think. You need to use your bloody brain. He's
going to have all kinds of burglar alarms and stuff, if he's a rich
man, there'll be bells that go off and special locks and lights with
infra-red switches that come on automatically —"

"I never heard of those things," Lyra said. "We en't got 'em
in my world. I couldn't know that, Will."

"All right, then think of this: he's got a whole house to hide
it in, and how long would any burglar have to look through every
cupboard and drawer and hiding-place in a whole house? Those
men who came to my house had hours to look around, and they
never found what they were looking for, and I bet he's got a
whole lot bigger house than we have. And probably a safe, too.
So even if we did get into his house we'd never find it in time
before the police came."

She hung her head. It was all true.

"What we going to do then?" she said.

He didn't answer. But it was *we*, for certain. He was bound to
her now whether he liked it or not.

He walked to the water's edge, and back to the terrace, and
back to the water again. He beat his hands together, looking
for an answer, but no answer came, and he shook his head
angrily.

"Just . . . go there," he said. "Just go there and see him. It's no good asking your scholar to help us, either, not if the police have been to her. She's bound to believe them rather than us. At least if we get into his house we'll see where the main rooms are. That'll be a start."

Without another word he went inside and put the letters under the pillow in the room he'd slept in. Then, if he were caught, they'd never have them.

Lyra was waiting on the terrace, with Pantalaimon perched on her shoulder as a sparrow. She was looking more cheerful.

"We're going to get it back all right," she said. "I can feel it."

He said nothing. They set off for the window.

It took an hour and a half to walk to Headington. Lyra led the way, avoiding the city centre, and Will kept watch all around, saying nothing. It was much harder for Lyra now than it had been even in the Arctic, on the way to Bolvangar, for then she'd had the gyptians and Iorek Byrnison with her, and even if the tundra was full of danger, you knew the danger when you saw it. Here, in the city that was both hers and not hers, danger could look friendly, and treachery smiled and smelt sweet; and even if they weren't going to kill her or part her from Pantalaimon, they had robbed her of her only guide. Without the alethiometer, she was . . . just a little girl, lost.

Limefield House was the colour of warm honey, and half the front of it was covered in Virginia creeper. It stood in a large well-tended garden, with a shrubbery at one side and a gravel drive sweeping up to the front door. The Rolls Royce was parked in front of a double garage to the left. Everything Will could see spoke of wealth and power, the sort of informal settled superiority that some upper-class English people still took for granted. There was something about it that made him grit his teeth, and he didn't know why, until suddenly he remembered an occasion when he was very young – his mother had taken him to a house not unlike this – they'd dressed in their best clothes and he'd had to be on his best behaviour, and an old man and woman had made his mother cry and they'd left the house and she was still crying . . .

Lyra saw him breathing fast and clenching his fists, and was sensible enough not to ask why: it was something to do with him, not with her. Presently he took a deep breath.

"Well," he said, "might as well try."

He walked up the drive, and Lyra followed close behind. They felt very exposed.

The door had an old-fashioned bell-pull, like those in Lyra's world, and Will didn't know where to find it till Lyra showed him. When they pulled it, the bell jangled a long way off inside the house.

The man who opened the door was the servant who'd been driving the car, only now he didn't have his cap on. He looked at Will first, and then at Lyra, and his expression changed a little.

"We want to see Sir Charles Latrom," Will said.

His jaw was jutting as it had done last night facing the stone-throwing children by the tower. The servant nodded.

"Wait here," he said. "I'll tell Sir Charles."

He closed the door. It was solid oak, with two heavy locks, and bolts top and bottom, though Will thought that no sensible burglar would try the front door anyway. And there was a burglar alarm prominently fixed to the front of the house, and a large spotlight at each corner; they'd never be able to get near it, let alone break in.

Steady footsteps came to the door, and then it opened again. Will looked up at the face of this man who had so much that he wanted even more, and found him disconcertingly smooth and calm and powerful, not in the least guilty or ashamed.

Sensing Lyra beside him impatient and angry, Will said quickly:

"Excuse me, but Lyra thinks that when she had a lift in your car earlier on, she left something in it by mistake."

"Lyra? I don't know a Lyra. What an unusual name. I know a child called Lizzie. And who are you?"

Cursing himself for forgetting, Will said, "I'm her brother. Mark."

"I see. Hello, Lizzie, or Lyra. You'd better come in."

He stood aside. Neither Will nor Lyra was quite expecting this, and they stepped inside uncertainly. The hall was dim, and smelt of beeswax and flowers. Every surface was polished and clean, and a mahogany cabinet against the wall contained dainty porcelain figures. Will saw the servant standing in the background, as if he were waiting to be called.

"Come into my study," said Sir Charles, and held open another door off the hall.

He was being courteous, even welcoming, but there was an edge to his manner that put Will on guard. The study was large and comfortable in a cigar-smoke and leather-armchair sort of way, and seemed to be full of bookshelves, pictures, hunting trophies. There were three or four glass-fronted cabinets containing antique scientific instruments – brass microscopes, telescopes covered in green leather, sextants, compasses; it was clear why he wanted the alethiometer.

"Sit down," said Sir Charles, and indicated a leather sofa. He sat at the chair behind his desk, and went on, "Well? What have you got to say?"

"You stole –" began Lyra hotly, but Will looked at her, and she stopped.

"Lyra thinks she left something in your car," he said again. "We've come to get it back."

"Is this the object you mean?" he said, and took a velvet cloth from his drawer in the desk. Lyra stood up. He ignored her and unfolded the cloth, disclosing the golden splendour of the alethiometer resting in his palm.

"Yes!" Lyra burst out, and reached for it.

But he closed his hand. The desk was wide, and she couldn't reach; and before she could do anything else, he swung around and placed the alethiometer in a glass-fronted cabinet before locking it and dropping the key in his waistcoat pocket.

"But it isn't yours, Lizzie," he said. "Or Lyra, if that's your name."

"It is mine! It's my alethiometer!"

He shook his head, sadly and heavily, as if he were reproaching her and it was a sorrow to him, but he was doing it for her own good. "I think at the very least there's considerable doubt about the matter," he said.

"But it is hers!" said Will. "Honestly! She's shown it to me! I know it's hers!"

"You see, I think you'd have to prove that," he said. "I don't have to prove anything, because it's in my possession. It's assumed to be mine. Like all the other items in my collection. I must say, Lyra, I'm surprised to find you so dishonest –"

"I en't dishonest!" Lyra cried.

"Oh, but you are. You told me your name was Lizzie. Now I learn it's something else. Frankly, you haven't got a hope of convincing anyone that a precious piece like this belongs to you. I tell you what. Let's call the police."

He turned his head to call for the servant.

"No, wait –" said Will, before Sir Charles could speak, but Lyra ran round the desk, and from nowhere Pantalaimon was in her arms, a snarling wildcat baring his teeth and hissing at the old man. Sir Charles blinked at the sudden appearance of the dæmon, but hardly flinched.

"You don't even know what it is you stole," Lyra stormed. "You seen me using it and you thought you'd steal it, and you did. But you – you're worse than my mother – at least she knows it's important – you're just going to put it in a case and do nothing with it! You ought to die! If I can, I'll make someone kill you. You're not worth leaving alive. You're –"

She couldn't speak. All she could do was spit full in his face, so she did, with all her might.

Will sat still, watching, looking around, memorizing where everything was.

Sir Charles calmly shook out a silk handkerchief and mopped himself.

"Have you *any* control over yourself?" he said. "Go and sit down, you filthy brat."

Lyra felt tears shaken out of her eyes by the trembling of her body, and threw herself on to the sofa. Pantalaimon, his thick cat's tail erect, stood on her lap with his blazing eyes fixed on the old man.

Will sat silent and puzzled. Sir Charles could have thrown them out long before this. What was he playing at?

And then he saw something so bizarre he thought he had imagined it. Out of the sleeve of Sir Charles's linen jacket, past the snowy white shirt-cuff, came the emerald head of a snake.

Its black tongue flickered this way, that way, and its mailed head with its gold-rimmed black eyes moved from Lyra to Will and back again. She was too angry to see it at all, and Will saw it only for a moment before it retreated again up the old man's sleeve, but it made his eyes widen with shock.

Sir Charles moved to the window seat and calmly sat down, arranging the crease in his trousers.

"I think you'd better listen to me instead of behaving in this uncontrolled way," he said. "You really haven't any choice. The instrument is in my possession, and will stay there. I want it. I'm a collector. You can spit and stamp and scream all you like, but by the time you've persuaded anyone else to listen to you, I shall have plenty of documents to prove that I bought it. I can do that very easily. And then you'll never get it back."

They were both silent now. He hadn't finished. A great puzzlement was slowing Lyra's heartbeat, and making the room very still.

"However," he went on, "there's something I want even more. And I can't get it myself, so I'm prepared to make a deal with you. You fetch the object I want, and I'll give you back the – what did you call it?"

"Alethiometer," said Lyra hoarsely.

"Alethiometer. How interesting. Aletheia, truth – those emblems – yes, I see."

"What's this thing you want?" said Will. "And where is it?"

"It's somewhere I can't go, but you can. I'm perfectly well aware that you've found a doorway somewhere. I guess it's not too far from Summertown, where I dropped Lizzie, or Lyra, this morning. And that through the doorway is another world, one with no grown-ups in it. Right so far? Well, you see, the man who made that doorway has got a knife. He's hiding in that other world right now, and he's extremely afraid. He has reason to be. If he's where I think he is, he's in an old stone tower which has angels carved around the doorway. The Torre degli Angeli.

"So that's where you have to go, and I don't care how you do it, but I want that knife. Bring it to me, and you can have the alethiometer. I shall be sorry to lose it, but I'm a man of my word. That's what you have to do: bring me the knife."

8

THE TOWER OF THE ANGELS

WILL SAID, "Who is this man who's got the knife?"

They were in the Rolls Royce, driving up through Oxford. Sir Charles sat in the front, half turned round, and Will and Lyra sat in the back, with Pantalaimon a mouse now, soothed in Lyra's hands.

"Someone who has no more right to the knife than I have to the alethiometer," said Sir Charles. "Unfortunately for all of us, the alethiometer is in my possession, and the knife is in his."

"How do you know about that other world anyway?"

"I know many things that you don't. What else would you expect? I am a good deal older, and considerably better informed. There are a number of doorways between this world and that; those who know where they are can easily pass back and forth. In Cittàgazze there's a Guild of learned men, so-called, who used to do so all the time."

"You en't from this world at all!" said Lyra suddenly. "You're from there, en't you?"

And again came that strange nudge at her memory. She was almost certain she'd seen him before.

"No, I'm not," he said.

Will said, "If we've got to get the knife from that man, we need to know more about him. He's not going to just give it to us, is he?"

"Certainly not. It's the one thing keeping the Spectres away. It's not going to be easy by any means."

"The Spectres are afraid of the knife?"

"Very much so."

"Why do they only attack grown-ups?"

"You don't need to know that now. It doesn't matter. Lyra," Sir Charles said, turning to her, "tell me about your remarkable friend."

He meant Pantalaimon. And as soon as he said it, Will realized

that the snake he'd seen concealed in the man's sleeve was a
dæmon too, and that Sir Charles must come from Lyra's world.
He was asking about Pantalaimon to put them off the track: so
he didn't realize that Will had seen his own dæmon.

Lyra lifted Pantalaimon close to her breast, and he became a
black rat, whipping his tail round and round her wrist and glaring
at Sir Charles with red eyes.

"You weren't supposed to see him," she said. "He's my
dæmon. You think you en't got dæmons in this world, but you
have. Yours'd be a dung beetle."

He said, "If the Pharaohs of Egypt were content to be represented by a scarab, so am I. Well, you're from yet another world.
How interesting. Is that where the alethiometer comes from, or
did you steal it on your travels?"

"I was given it," said Lyra furiously. "The Master of Jordan
College in my Oxford gave it me. It's mine by right. And you
wouldn't know what to do with it, you stupid stinky old man,
you'd never read it in a hundred years. It's just a toy to you. But
I *need* it, and so does Will. We'll get it back, don't worry."

"We'll see," said Sir Charles. "This is where I dropped you
before. Shall we let you out here?"

"No," said Will, because he could see a police car further
down the road. "You can't come into Ci'gazze because of the
Spectres, so it doesn't matter if you know where the window is.
Take us further up towards the Ring Road."

"As you wish," said Sir Charles, and the car moved on.
"When, or if, you get the knife, call my number and Allan will
come to pick you up."

They said no more till the chauffeur drew the car to a halt.
As they got out, Sir Charles wound his window down and said
to Will:

"By the way, if you can't get the knife, don't bother to return.
Come to my house without it and I'll call the police. I imagine
they'll be there at once when I tell them your real name. It is
William Parry, isn't it? Yes, I thought so. There's a very good
photo of you in today's paper."

And the car pulled away. Will was speechless.

Lyra was shaking his arm. "It's all right," she said, "he won't tell anyone else. He would have done already if he was going to. Come on.''

Ten minutes later they stood in the little square at the foot of the Tower of the Angels. Will had told her about the snake-dæmon, and she had stopped still in the street, tormented again by the half-memory. Who was the old man? Where had she seen him? It was no good; the memory wouldn't come clear.

"I didn't want to tell *him*," Lyra said quietly, "but I saw a man up there last night. He looked down when the kids were making all that noise . . ."

"What did he look like?"

"Young, with curly hair. Not old at all. But I only saw him for a moment, at the very top, over those battlements. I thought he might be . . . You remember Angelica and Paolo, and he said they had an older brother, and he'd come into the city as well, and she made Paolo stop telling us, as if it was a secret? Well, I thought it might be him. He might be after this knife as well. And I reckon all the kids know about it. I think that's the real reason why they come back in the first place."

"Mmm," he said, looking up. "Maybe."

She remembered the children talking earlier that morning: no children would go in the tower, they'd said; there were scary things in there; and she remembered her own feeling of unease as she and Pantalaimon had looked through the open door before leaving the city. Maybe that was why they needed a grown man to go in there. Her dæmon was fluttering around her head now, moth-formed in the bright sunlight, whispering anxiously.

"Hush," she whispered back, "there en't any choice, Pan. It's our fault. We got to make it right, and this is the only way."

Will walked off to the right, following the wall of the tower. At the corner a narrow cobbled alley led between it and the next building, and Will went down there too, looking up, getting the measure of the place. Lyra followed. He stopped under a window at the second-storey level, and said to Pantalaimon:

"Can you fly up there? Can you look in?"

He became a sparrow at once and set off. He could only just reach it; Lyra gasped and gave a little cry when he was at the window sill, and he perched there for a second or two before diving down again. She sighed and took deep breaths like someone rescued from drowning. Will frowned, puzzled.

"It's hard," she explained; "when your dæmon goes away from you, it hurts . . ."

"Sorry. Did you see anything?" he said.

"Stairs," said Pantalaimon, "stairs and dark rooms. There were swords hung on the wall, and spears and shields, like a museum. And I saw the man. He was . . . dancing."

"Dancing?"

"Moving to and fro . . . waving his hand about. Or as if he was fighting something invisible . . . I just saw him through an open door. Not clearly."

"Fighting a Spectre?" Lyra guessed.

But they couldn't guess any better, so they moved on. Behind the tower a high stone wall, topped with broken glass, enclosed a small garden with formal beds of herbs around a fountain (once again Pantalaimon flew up to look); and then there was an alley on the other side, bringing them back to the square. The windows around the tower were small and deeply-set, like frowning eyes.

"We'll have to go in the front then," said Will.

He climbed the steps and pushed the door wide. Sunlight struck in, and the heavy hinges creaked. He took a step or two inside, and seeing no one, went in further. Lyra followed close behind. The floor was made of stone flags worn smooth over centuries, and the air inside was cool.

Will looked at a flight of steps going downwards, and went far enough down to see that it opened into a wide low-ceilinged room with an immense cold furnace at one end, where the plaster walls were black with soot; but there was no one there, and he went up to the entrance hall again, where he found Lyra with her finger to her lips, looking up.

"I can hear him," she whispered. "He's talking to himself, I reckon."

Will listened hard, and heard it too: a low crooning murmur interrupted occasionally by a harsh laugh or a short cry of anger. It sounded like the voice of a madman.

Will blew out his cheeks and set off to climb the staircase. It was made of blackened oak, immense and broad, with steps as worn as the flagstones: far too solid to creak underfoot. The light diminished as they climbed, because the only illumination was the small deep-set window on each landing. They climbed up one floor, stopped and listened, climbed the next, and the sound of the man's voice was now mixed with that of halting, rhythmic footsteps. It came from a room across the landing, whose door stood ajar.

Will tiptoed to it and pushed it open another few inches so he could see.

It was a large room with cobwebs thickly clustered on the ceiling. The walls were lined with bookshelves containing badly preserved volumes with the bindings crumbling and flaking, or distorted with damp. Several of them lay thrown out of the shelves, open on the floor or the wide dusty tables, and others had been thrust back higgledy-piggledy.

In the centre of the room, a young man was – dancing. Pantalaimon was right: it looked exactly like that. He had his back to the door, and he'd shuffle to one side, then to the other, and all the time his right hand moved in front of him as if he was clearing a way through some invisible obstacles. In that hand was a knife, not a special-looking knife, just a dull blade about eight inches long, and he'd thrust it forward, slice it sideways, feel forward with it, jab up and down, all in the empty air.

He moved as if to turn, and Will withdrew. He put a finger to his lips and beckoned to Lyra, and led her to the stairs and up to the next floor.

"What's he doing?" she whispered.

He described it as well as he could.

"He sounds mad," said Lyra. "Is he thin, with curly hair?"

"Yes. Red hair, like Angelica's. He certainly looks mad. I don't know, I think this is odder than Sir Charles said. Let's look further up before we speak to him."

She didn't question, but let him lead them up a further staircase to the top storey. It was much lighter up here, because a white-painted flight of steps led up to the roof – or rather, to a wood-and-glass structure like a little greenhouse. Even at the foot of the steps they could feel the heat it was absorbing.

And as they stood there, they heard a groan from above.

They jumped. They'd been sure there was only one man in the Tower. Pantalaimon was so startled that he changed at once from a cat to a bird, and flew to Lyra's breast. Will and Lyra realized as he did so that they'd seized each other's hand, and let go slowly.

"Better go and see," Will whispered. "I'll go first."

"I ought to go first," she whispered back, "seeing it's my fault."

"Seeing it's your fault, you got to do as I say."

She twisted her lip, but fell in behind him.

He climbed up into the sun. The light in the glass structure was blinding. It was as hot as a greenhouse, too, and Will could neither see nor breathe easily. He found a door handle and turned it and stepped out quickly, holding his hand up to keep the sun out of his eyes.

He found himself on a roof of lead, enclosed by the battlemented parapet. The glass structure was set in the centre, and the lead sloped slightly downwards all round towards a gutter inside the parapet, with square drainage holes in the stone for rainwater.

Lying on the lead, in the full sun, was an old man with white hair. His face was bruised and battered, and one eye was closed, and as they saw when they got closer, his hands were tied behind him.

He heard them coming, and groaned again, and tried to turn over to shield himself.

"It's all right," said Will quietly, "we aren't going to hurt you. Did the man with the knife do this?"

"Mmm," the old man grunted.

"Let's undo the rope. He hasn't tied it very well . . ."

It was clumsily and hastily knotted, and it fell away quickly once Will had seen how to work it. They helped the old man to get up and took him over to the shade of the parapet.

"Who are you?" Will said. "We didn't think there were two people here. We thought there was only one."

"Giacomo Paradisi," the old man muttered through broken teeth. "I am the bearer. No one else. That young man stole it from me. There are always fools who take risks like that for the sake of the knife. But this one is desperate. He is going to kill me . . ."

"No he en't," Lyra said. "What's the bearer? What's that mean?"

"I hold the subtle knife on behalf of the Guild. Where has he gone?"

"He's downstairs," said Will. "We came up past him. He didn't see us. He was waving it about in the air . . ."

"Trying to cut through. He won't succeed. When he —"

"Watch out," Lyra said.

Will turned. The young man was climbing up into the little wooden shelter. He hadn't seen them yet, but there was nowhere to hide, and as they stood up he saw the movement and whipped round to face them.

Immediately Pantalaimon became a bear, and reared up on his hind legs. Only Lyra knew that he wouldn't be able to touch the other man, and certainly the other blinked and stared for a second, but Will saw that he hadn't really registered it. The man was crazy. His curly red hair was matted, his chin was flecked with spit, and the whites of his eyes showed all round the pupils.

And he had the knife, and they had no weapons at all.

Will stepped up the lead, away from the old man, crouching, ready to jump or fight or leap out of the way.

The young man sprang forward and slashed at him with the knife, left — right — left, coming closer and closer, making Will back away till he was trapped in the angle where two sides of the tower met.

Lyra was scrambling towards the man from behind, with the loose rope in her hand. Will darted forward suddenly, just as he'd done to the man in his house, and with the same effect: his antagonist tumbled backwards unexpectedly, falling over Lyra to crash on to the lead. It was all happening too quickly for Will to be frightened. But he did have time to see the knife fly from the man's hand and sink at once into the lead some feet away, point first, with no more resistance than if it had fallen into butter. It plunged as far as the hilt and stopped suddenly.

And the young man twisted over and reached for it at once, but Will flung himself on his back and seized his hair. He had learned to fight at school: there had been plenty of occasion for it, once the other children had sensed that there was something the matter with his mother. And he'd learned that the object of a school fight was not to gain points for style but to force your enemy to give in, which meant hurting him more than he was hurting you. He knew that you had to be willing to hurt someone else, too, and he'd found out that not many people were, when it came to it; but he knew that he was.

So this wasn't unfamiliar to him, but he hadn't fought against a nearly-grown man armed with a knife before, and at all costs he must keep him away from picking it up now that he'd dropped it.

He twisted his fingers into the young man's thick damp hair and wrenched back as hard as he could. The man grunted and flung himself sideways, but Will hung on even tighter, and his opponent roared with pain and anger. He pushed up and then threw himself backwards, crushing Will between himself and the parapet, and that was too much: all the breath left Will's body, and in the shock his hands loosened. The man pulled free.

Will dropped to his knees in the gutter, winded badly, but he couldn't stay there. He pushed himself up to his knees, and then tried to stand – and in doing so, he thrust his foot through one of the drainage holes. For a horrible second he thought there was nothing there behind him. His fingers scraped desperately on the warm lead. But nothing happened; his left leg was thrust out into empty space, but the rest of him was safe.

He pulled his foot back inside the parapet and scrambled to his feet. The man had reached his knife again, but he didn't have time to pull it out of the lead before Lyra leapt on to his back, scratching, kicking, biting like a wildcat; but she missed the hold on his hair that she was trying for, and he threw her off. And when he got up, he had the knife in his hand.

Lyra had fallen to one side, with Pantalaimon a wildcat now, fur raised, teeth bared, beside her. Will faced the man directly, and saw him clearly for the first time. There was no doubt: he was Angelica's brother all right, and he was vicious. All his mind was focused on Will, and the knife was in his hand.

But Will wasn't harmless either.

He'd seized the rope when Lyra dropped it, and now he wrapped it around his left hand for protection against the knife. He moved sideways between the young man and the sun, so that his antagonist had to squint and blink. Even better, the glass structure threw brilliant reflections into his eyes, and Will could see that for a moment he was almost blinded.

He leapt to the man's left, away from the knife, holding his left hand high, and kicked hard at the man's knee. He'd taken care to aim, and his foot connected well. The man went down with a loud grunt, and twisted away awkwardly.

Will leapt after him, hitting with both hands and kicking again and again, kicking whatever parts he could reach, driving the man back and back towards the glass house. If he could get him to the top of the stairs . . .

This time the man fell more heavily, and his right hand with the knife in it came down on the lead at Will's feet. Will stamped on it at once, hard, crushing the man's fingers between the hilt and the lead, and then wrapped the rope more tightly around his hand and stamped a second time. The man yelled and let go of the knife. At once Will kicked it away, his shoe connecting with the hilt, luckily for him, and it spun across the lead and came to rest in the gutter just beside a drainage hole. The rope had come loose around his hand once more, and there seemed to be a surprising amount of blood from somewhere sprinkled on the lead and on his own shoes. The man was pulling himself up –

"Look out!" shouted Lyra, but Will was ready.

At the moment when the man was off balance he threw himself at him, crashing as hard as he could into the man's midriff. The man fell backwards into the glass, which shattered at once, and the flimsy wooden frame went too. He sprawled among the wreckage half over the stairwell, and grabbed the door frame, but it had nothing to support it any more, and it gave way. He fell downwards, and more glass fell all around him.

And Will darted back to the gutter, and picked up the knife, and the fight was over. The young man, cut and battered, clambered up the steps, and saw Will standing above him holding the knife, and stared with a sickly anger and then turned and fled.

"Ah," said Will, sitting down. "Ah."

Something was badly wrong, and he hadn't noticed it. He dropped the knife and hugged his left hand to himself. The tangle of rope was sodden with blood, and when he pulled it away –

"Your fingers!" Lyra breathed. "Oh, Will –"

His little finger and the finger next to it fell away with the rope.

His head swam. Blood was pulsing strongly from the stumps where his fingers had been, and his jeans and shoes were sodden already. He had to lie back and close his eyes for a moment. The pain wasn't that great, and a part of his mind registered that with a dull surprise: it was like a persistent deep hammer-thud more than the bright sharp clarity when you cut yourself superficially.

He'd never felt so weak. He supposed he had gone to sleep for a moment. Lyra was doing something to his arm. He sat up to look at the damage, and felt sick. The old man was somewhere close by, but Will couldn't see what he was doing, and meanwhile Lyra was talking to him.

"If only we had some bloodmoss," she was saying, "what the bears use, I could make it better, Will, I could – look, I'm going to tie this bit of rope round your arm, to stop the bleeding, 'cause I can't tie it round where your fingers were, there's nothing to tie it to – hold still –"

He let her do it, and looked around for his fingers. There they were, curled like a bloody quotation mark on the lead. He laughed.

"Hey," she said, "stop that. Get up now. Mr Paradisi's got some medicine, some salve, I dunno what it is. You got to come down-stairs. That other man's gone – we seen him run out the door. He's gone now. You beat him. Come on, Will – come on –"

Nagging and cajoling, she urged him down the steps, and they picked their way through the shattered glass and splintered wood and into a small cool room off the landing. The walls were lined with shelves of bottles, jars, pots, pestles and mortars and chem-ists' balances. Under the dirty window was a stone sink, where the old man was pouring something with a shaky hand from a large bottle into a smaller one.

"Sit down and drink this," he said, and filled a small glass with a dark liquid.

Will sat down and took the glass. The first mouthful hit the back of his throat like fire. Lyra took the glass to stop it falling as Will gasped.

"Drink it all," the old man commanded.

"What is it?"

"Plum brandy. Drink."

Will sipped it more cautiously. Now his hand was really beginning to hurt.

"Can you heal him?" said Lyra, her voice desperate.

"Oh, yes, we have medicines for everything. You, girl, open that drawer in the table and bring out a bandage."

Will saw the knife lying on the table in the centre of the room, but before he could pick it up the old man was limping towards him with a bowl of water.

"Drink again," the old man said.

Will held the glass tightly and closed his eyes while the old man did something to his hand. It stung horribly, but then he felt the rough friction of a towel on his wrist, and something mopping the wound more gently. Then there was a coolness for a moment, and it hurt again.

"This is precious ointment," the old man said. "Very difficult to obtain. Very good for wounds."

It was a dusty, battered tube of ordinary antiseptic cream, such as Will could have bought in any chemist's shop in his world. The old man was handling it as if it were made of myrrh. Will looked away.

And while the man was dressing the wound, Lyra felt Pantalaimon calling to her silently to come and look out of the window. He was a kestrel perching on the open window-frame, and his eyes had caught a movement below. She joined him, and saw a familiar figure: the girl Angelica was running towards her elder brother Tullio, who stood with his back against the wall on the other side of the narrow street, waving his arms in the air as if trying to keep a flock of bats from his face. Then he turned away and began to run his hands along the stones in the wall, looking closely at each one, counting them, feeling the edges, hunching up his shoulders as if warding off something behind him, shaking his head.

Angelica was desperate, and so was little Paolo behind her, and they reached their brother and seized his arms and tried to pull him away from whatever was troubling him.

And Lyra realized with a jolt of sickness what was happening: the man was being attacked by Spectres. Angelica knew it, though she couldn't see them, of course, and little Paolo was crying and striking at the empty air to try and drive them off, but it didn't help, and Tullio was lost. His movements became more and more lethargic, and presently they stopped altogether. Angelica clung to him, shaking and shaking his arm, but nothing woke him; and Paolo was crying his brother's name over and over as if that would bring him back.

Then Angelica seemed to feel Lyra watching her, and she looked up. For a moment their eyes met. Lyra felt a jolt as if the girl had struck her a physical blow, because the hatred in her eyes was so intense, and then Paolo saw her looking and looked up too, and his little boy's voice cried, "We'll kill you! You done this to Tullio! We gonna kill you, all right!"

The two children turned and ran, leaving their stricken brother, and Lyra, frightened and guilty, withdrew inside the room again and shut the window. The others hadn't heard. Giacomo Paradisi was dabbing more ointment on the wounds, and Lyra tried to put what she'd seen out of her mind, and focused on Will.

"You got to tie something round his arm," Lyra said, "to stop the bleeding. It won't stop otherwise."

"Yes, yes, I know," said the old man, but sadly.

Will kept his eyes averted while they did up a bandage, and drank the plum brandy sip by sip. Presently he felt soothed and distant, though his hand was hurting abominably.

"Now," said Giacomo Paradisi, "here you are, take the knife, it is yours."

"I don't want it," said Will. "I don't want anything to do with it."

"You haven't got the choice," said the old man. "You are the bearer now."

"I thought you said *you* was?" said Lyra.

"My time is over," he said. "The knife knows when to leave

one hand and settle in another, and I know how to tell. You don't
believe me? Look!"

He held up his own left hand. The little finger and the finger
next to it were missing, just like Will's.

"Yes," he said, "me too. I fought and lost the same fingers, the
badge of the bearer. And I did not know either, in advance."

Lyra sat down, wide-eyed. Will held on to the dusty table with
his good hand. He struggled to find words.

"But I – we only came here because – there was a man who
stole something of Lyra's, and he wanted the knife, and he said
if we brought him that, then he'd . . ."

"I know that man. He is a liar, a cheat. He wouldn't give you
anything, make no mistake. He wants the knife, and once he has
it he will betray you. He will never be bearer. The knife is yours
by right."

With a heavy reluctance, Will turned to the knife itself. He
pulled it towards him. It was an ordinary-looking dagger, with a
double-sided blade of dull metal about eight inches long, a short
cross-piece of the same metal, and a handle of rosewood. As he
looked at it more closely, he saw that the rosewood was inlaid
with golden wires, forming a design he didn't recognize till he
turned the knife around and saw an angel, with wings folded.
On the other side was a different angel, with wings upraised. The
wires stood out a little from the surface, giving a firm grip, and
as he picked it up he felt that it was light in his hand and strong
and beautifully balanced, and that the blade was not dull after all.
In fact, a swirl of cloudy colours seemed to live just under the
surface of the metal: bruise-purples, sea-blues, earth-browns,
cloud-greys, and the deep green under heavy-foliaged trees, the
clustering shades at the mouth of a tomb as evening falls over
a deserted graveyard – if there was such a thing as shadow-
coloured, it was the blade of the subtle knife.

But the edges were different. In fact the two edges differed
from each other. One was clear bright steel, merging a little way
back into those subtle shadow-colours, but steel of an incompar-
able sharpness. Will's eye shrank back from looking at it, so sharp
did it seem. The other edge was just as keen, but silvery in colour,
and Lyra, who was looking at it over Will's shoulder, said:

"I seen that colour before! That's the same as the blade they was going to cut me and Pan apart with – that's just the same!"

"This edge," said Giacomo Paradisi, touching the steel with the handle of a spoon, "will cut through any material in the world. Look."

And he pressed the silver spoon against the blade. Will, holding the knife, felt only the slightest resistance as the tip of the spoon's handle fell to the table, cut clean off.

"The other edge," the old man went on, "is more subtle still. With it you can cut an opening out of this world altogether. Try it now. Do as I say – you are the bearer. You have to know. No one can teach you but me, and I have not much time left. Stand up and listen."

Will pushed his chair back and stood, holding the knife loosely. He felt dizzy, sick, rebellious.

"I don't want –" he began, but Giacomo Paradisi shook his head.

"Be silent! You don't want – you don't want – you have no choice! Listen to me, because time is short. Now hold the knife out ahead of you – like that. It's not only the knife that has to cut, it's your own mind. You have to think it. So do this: put your mind out at the very tip of the knife. Concentrate, boy. Focus your mind. Don't think about your wound. It will heal. Think about the knife tip. That is where you are. Now feel with it, very gently. You're looking for a gap so small you could never see it with your eyes, but the knife tip will find it, if you put your mind there. Feel along the air till you sense the smallest little gap in the world . . ."

Will tried to do it. But his head was buzzing and his left hand throbbed horribly and he saw his two fingers again, lying on the roof, and then he thought of his mother, his poor mother . . . What would she say? How would she comfort him? How could he ever comfort her? And he put the knife down on the table and crouched low hugging his wounded hand, and cried. It was all too much to bear. The sobs racked his throat and his chest and the tears dazzled him, and he should be crying for her, the poor frightened unhappy dear beloved, he'd left her, he'd left her . . .

He was desolate. But then he felt the strangest thing, and

brushed the back of his right wrist across his eyes to find Pantalaimon's head on his knee. The dæmon, in the form of a wolf-hound, was gazing up at him with melting, sorrowing eyes, and then he gently licked Will's wounded hand again and again, and laid his head on Will's knee once more.

Will had no idea of the taboo in Lyra's world preventing one person from touching another's dæmon, and if he hadn't touched Pantalaimon before, it was politeness that had held him back and not knowledge. Lyra, in fact, was breathtaken. Her dæmon had done it on his own initiative, and now he withdrew, and fluttered to her shoulder as the smallest of moths. The old man was watching with interest but not incredulity. He'd seen dæmons before, somehow; he'd travelled to other worlds too.

Pantalaimon's gesture had worked. Will swallowed hard and stood up again, wiping the tears out of his eyes.

"All right," he said, "I'll try again. Tell me what to do."

This time he forced his mind to do what Giacomo Paradisi said, gritting his teeth, trembling with exertion, sweating. Lyra was bursting to interrupt, because she knew this process. So did Dr Malone, and so did the poet Keats, whoever he was, and all of them knew you couldn't get it by straining towards it. But she held her tongue and clasped her hands.

"Stop," said the old man gently. "Relax. Don't push. This is a subtle knife, not a heavy sword. You're gripping it too tight. Loosen your fingers. Let your mind wander down your arm to your wrist and then into the handle, and out along the blade, no hurry, go gently, don't force it. Just wander. Then along to the very tip, where the edge is sharpest of all. You become the tip of the knife. Just do that now. Go there and feel that, and then come back."

Will tried again. Lyra could see the intensity in his body, saw his jaw working, and then saw an authority descend over it, calming and relaxing and clarifying. The authority was Will's own – or his dæmon's, perhaps. How he must miss having a dæmon! The loneliness of it . . . No wonder he'd cried; and it was right of Pantalaimon to do what he'd done, though it had felt so strange to her. She reached up to her beloved dæmon, and, ermine-shaped, he flowed on to her lap.

They watched together as Will's body stopped trembling. No less intense, he was focused differently now, and the knife looked different too. Perhaps it was those cloudy colours along the blade, or perhaps it was the way it sat so naturally in Will's hand, but the little movement he was making with the tip now looked purposeful instead of random. He felt this way, then turned the knife over and felt the other, always feeling with the silvery edge; and then he seemed to find some little snag in the empty air.

"What's this? Is this it?" he said hoarsely.

"Yes. Don't force it. Come back now, come back to yourself."

Lyra imagined she could see Will's soul flowing back along the blade to his hand, and up his arm to his heart. He stood back, dropped his hand, blinked.

"I felt something there," he said to Giacomo Paradisi. "The knife was just slipping through the air at first and then I felt it . . ."

"Good. Now do it again. This time, when you feel it, slide the knife in and along. Make a cut. Don't hesitate. Don't be surprised. Don't drop the knife."

Will had to crouch and take two or three deep breaths and put his left hand under his other arm before he could go on. But he was intent on it; he stood up again after a couple of seconds, the knife held forward already.

This time it was easier. Having felt it once, he knew what to search for again, and he felt the curious little snag after less than a minute. It was like delicately searching out the gap between one stitch and the next with the point of a scalpel. He touched, withdrew, touched again to make sure, and then did as the old man had said, and cut sideways with the silver edge.

It was a good thing that Giacomo Paradisi had reminded him not to be surprised. He kept careful hold of the knife, and put it down on the table before giving in to his astonishment. Lyra was on her feet already, speechless, because there in the middle of the dusty little room was a window just like the one under the hornbeam trees: a gap in mid-air through which they could see another world.

And because they were high in the tower, they were high above north Oxford. Over a cemetery, in fact, looking back towards the city. There were the hornbeam trees a little way ahead of them; there were houses, trees, roads, and in the distance the towers and spires of the city.

If they hadn't already seen the first window, they would have thought this was some kind of optical trick. Except that it wasn't only optical; air was coming through it; they could smell the traffic fumes, which didn't exist in the world of Cittàgazze. Pantalaimon changed into a swallow and flew through, delighting in the open air, and then snapped up an insect before darting back through to Lyra's shoulder again.

Giacomo Paradisi was watching with a curious, sad smile. Then he said, "So much for opening. Now you must learn to close."

Lyra stood back to give Will room, and the old man came to stand beside him.

"For this you need your fingers," he said. "One hand will do. Feel for the edge as you felt with the knife to begin with. You won't find it unless you put your soul into your fingertips. Touch very delicately, feel again and again till you find the edge. Then you pinch it together. That's all. Try."

But Will was trembling. He couldn't get his mind back to the delicate balance he knew it needed, and he got more and more frustrated. Lyra could see what was happening.

She stood up and took his right arm and said, "Listen, Will, sit down, I'll tell you how to do it. Just sit down for a minute, 'cause your hand hurts and it's taking your mind off it. It's bound to. It'll ease off in a little while."

The old man raised both his hands and then changed his mind, shrugged, and sat down again.

Will sat down and looked at Lyra. "What am I doing wrong?" he said.

He was bloodstained, trembling, wild-eyed. He was living on the edge of his nerves: clenching his jaw, tapping his foot, breathing fast.

"It's your wound," she said. "*You* en't wrong at all. You're doing it right, but your hand won't let you concentrate on it. I don't know an easy way of getting round that, except maybe if you didn't try to shut it out . . ."

"What d'you mean?"

"Well, you're trying to do two things with your mind, both at once. You're trying to ignore the pain *and* close that window. I remember when I was reading the alethiometer once when I was frightened, and maybe I was used to it by that time, I don't know, but I was still frightened all the time I was reading it. Just sort of relax your mind and say yes, it does hurt, I know. Don't try and shut it out."

His eyes closed briefly. His breathing slowed a little.

"All right," he said. "I'll try that."

And this time it was much easier. He felt for the edge, found it within a minute, and did as Giacomo Paradisi had told him: pinched the edges together. It was the easiest thing in the world. He felt a brief, calm exhilaration, and then the window was gone. The other world was shut.

The old man handed him a leather sheath, backed with stiff horn, with buckles to hold the knife in place, because the slightest sideways movement of the blade would have cut through the thickest leather. Will slid the knife into it and buckled it as tight as he could with his clumsy hand.

"This should be a solemn occasion," Giacomo Paradisi said. "If we had days and weeks I could begin to tell you the story of the subtle knife, and the Guild of the Torre degli Angeli, and the whole sorry history of this corrupt and careless world. The Spectres are our fault, our fault alone. They came because my predecessors, alchemists, philosophers, men of learning, were making an enquiry into the deepest nature of things. They became curious about the bonds that held the smallest particles of matter together. You know what I mean by a bond? Something that binds?

"Well, this was a mercantile city. A city of traders and bankers. We thought we knew about bonds. We thought a bond was something negotiable, something that could be bought and sold and exchanged and converted ... But about these bonds, we were wrong. We undid them, and we let the Spectres in."

Will said, "Where do the Spectres come from? Why was the window left open under those trees, the one we first came in through? Are there other windows in the world?"

"Where the Spectres come from is a mystery. From another

world; from the darkness of space; who knows? What matters is that they are here, and they have destroyed us. Are there other windows into this world? Yes, a few, because sometimes a knife-bearer might be careless or forgetful, without time to stop and close as he should. And the window you came through, under the hornbeam trees . . . I left that open myself, in a moment of unforgivable foolishness. The man you spoke of – I thought to tempt him through and into the city where he would fall victim to the Spectres. But I think that he is too clever for a trick like that. He wants the knife. Please, never let him get it."

Will and Lyra shared a glance.

"Well," the old man finished, spreading his hands, "all I can do is hand the knife on to you and show you how to use it, which I have done, and tell you what the rules of the Guild used to be, before it decayed. First, never open without closing. Second, never let anyone else use the knife. It is yours alone. Third, never use it for a base purpose. Fourth, keep it secret. If there are other rules, I have forgotten them, and if I've forgotten them it is because they don't matter. You have the knife. You are the bearer. You should not be a child. But our world is crumbling, and the mark of the bearer is unmistakable. I don't even know your name. Now go. I shall die very soon, because I know where there are poisonous drugs, and I don't intend to wait for the Spectres to come in, as they will once the knife has left. Go."

"But, Mister Paradisi –" Lyra began, but he shook his head and went on:

"There is no time. You have come here for a purpose, and maybe you don't know what that purpose is, but the angels do who brought you here. Go. You are brave, and your friend is clever. And you have the knife. Go."

"You en't really going to poison yourself?" said Lyra, distressed.

"Come on," said Will.

"And what did you mean about angels?" she went on.

Will tugged her arm.

"Come on," he said again. "We got to go. Thank you, Mr Paradisi."

He held out his bloodstained dusty right hand, and the old man shook it gently. He shook Lyra's hand too, and nodded to Pantalaimon, who lowered his ermine-head in acknowledgement.

Clutching the knife in its leather sheath, Will led the way down the broad dark stairs and out of the tower. The sunlight was hot in the little square, and the silence was profound. Lyra looked all around, with immense caution, but the street was empty. And it would be better not to worry Will about what she'd seen; there was quite enough to worry about already. She led him away from the street where she'd seen the children, where the stricken Tullio was still standing, as still as death.

"I wish −" Lyra said when they had nearly left the square, stopping to look back up. "It's horrible, thinking of . . . and his poor teeth was all broken, and he could hardly see out his eye . . . He's just going to swallow some poison and die now, and I wish . . ."

She was on the verge of tears.

"Hush," said Will. "It won't hurt him. He'll just go to sleep. It's better than the Spectres, he said."

"Oh, what we going to do, Will?" she said. "What we going to do? You're hurt so bad, and that poor old man . . . I hate this place, I really do, I'd burn it to the ground. What we going to do now?"

"Well," he said, "that's easy. We've got to get the alethiometer back, so we'll have to steal it. That's what we're going to do."

9
THEFT

FIRST THEY WENT back to the café, to recover and rest and change their clothes. It was clear that Will couldn't go everywhere covered in blood, and the time of feeling guilty about taking things from shops was over; so he gathered a complete set of new clothes and shoes, and Lyra, demanding to help, and watching in every direction for the other children, carried them back to the café.

Lyra put some water on to boil, and Will took it up to the bathroom and stripped to wash from head to foot. The pain was dull and unrelenting, but at least the cuts were clean, and having seen what the knife could do, he knew that no cuts could be cleaner; but the stumps where his fingers had been were bleeding freely. When he looked at them he felt sick, and his heart beat faster, and that in turn seemed to make the bleeding even worse. He sat on the edge of the bath and closed his eyes and breathed deeply several times.

Presently he felt calmer and set himself to washing. He did the best he could, drying himself on the increasingly bloodied towels, and then dressed in his new clothes, trying not to make them bloody too.

"You're going to have to tie my bandage again," he said to Lyra. "I don't care how tight you make it as long as it stops the bleeding."

She tore up a sheet and wrapped it round and round, clamping it down over the wounds as tight as she could. He gritted his teeth, but he couldn't help tears. He brushed them away without a word, and she said nothing.

When she'd finished he said, "Thank you." Then he said, "Listen. I want you to take something in your rucksack for me, in case we can't come back here. It's only letters. You can read them if you want."

He took out the green leather writing-case and handed her the sheets of airmail paper.

"I won't read them unless –"

"I don't mind. Else I wouldn't have said."

She folded the letters up, and he lay on the bed, pushed the cat aside, and fell asleep.

Much later that night, Will and Lyra crouched in the lane that ran along beside the tree-shaded shrubbery in Sir Charles's garden. On the Cittàgazze side, they were in a grassy park surrounding a classical villa that gleamed white in the moonlight. They'd taken a long time to get to Sir Charles's house, moving mainly in Cittàgazze, with frequent stops to cut through and check their position in Will's world, closing the windows as soon as they knew where they were.

Not with them but not far behind came the tabby cat. She had slept since they'd rescued her from the stone-throwing children, and now she was awake again she was reluctant to leave them, as if she thought that wherever they were, she was safe. Will was far from sure about that, but he had enough on his mind without the cat, and he ignored her. All the time he was growing more familiar with the knife, more certain in his command of it; but his wound was hurting worse than before, with a deep unceasing throb, and the bandage Lyra had freshly tied after he woke up was already soaked.

He cut a window in the air not far from the white-gleaming villa, and they came through to the quiet lane in Headington to work out exactly how to get to the study where Sir Charles had put the alethiometer. There were two floodlights illuminating his garden, and lights were on in the front windows of the house, though not in the study. Only moonlight lit this side, and the study window was dark.

The lane ran down through trees to another road at the far end, and it wasn't lighted. It would have been easy for an ordinary burglar to get unobserved into the shrubbery and thus to the garden, except that there was a strong iron fence twice as high as Will, with spikes on the top, running the length of Sir Charles's property. However, it was no barrier to the subtle knife.

"Hold this bar while I cut it," Will whispered. "Catch it when it falls."

Lyra did as he said, and he cut through four bars altogether, enough for them to pass through without difficulty. Lyra laid them one by one on the grass, and then they were through, and moving among the bushes.

Once they had a clear sight of the side of the house, with the creeper-shaded window of the study facing them across the smooth lawn, Will said quietly:

"I'm going to cut through into Ci'gazze here, and leave the window open, and move in Ci'gazze to where I think the study is, and then cut back through to this world. Then I'll take the alethiometer out of that cabinet thing and I'll close that window and then I'll come back to this one. You stay here in this world and keep watch. As soon as you hear me call you, you come through this window into Ci'gazze and then I'll close it up again. All right?"

"Yeah," she whispered. "Me and Pan'll both look out."

Her dæmon was a small tawny owl, almost invisible in the dappled shadows under the trees. His wide pale eyes took in every movement.

Will stood back and held out the knife, searching, touching the air with the most delicate movements, until after a minute or so he found a point at which he could cut. He did it swiftly, opening a window through into the moon-drenched parkland of Ci'gazze, and then stood back, estimating how many steps it would take him in this world to reach the study, and memorizing the direction.

Then without a word he stepped through and vanished.

Lyra crouched down nearby. Pantalaimon was perched on a branch above her head, turning this way and that, silent. She could hear traffic from Headington behind her, and the quiet footsteps of someone going along the road at the end of the lane, and even the weightless movement of insects among the twigs and leaves at her feet.

A minute went by, and another. Where was Will now? She strained to look through the window of the study, but it was just a dark mullioned square overhung with creeper. Sir Charles had sat inside it on the window-seat only that morning, and crossed his legs, and arranged the creases in his trousers. Where was the cabinet in relation to the window? Would Will get inside without disturbing anyone in the house? Lyra could hear her heart beating, too.

Then Pantalaimon made a soft noise, and at the same moment a different sound came from the front of the house to Lyra's left. She couldn't see the front, but she could see a light sweeping across the trees, and heard a deep crunching sound: the sound of tyres on gravel. She hadn't heard the car's engine at all.

She looked for Pantalaimon, and he was already gliding ahead silently, as far as he could go from her. He turned in the darkness and swooped back to settle on her fist.

"Sir Charles is coming back," he whispered. "And there's someone with him."

He took off again, and this time Lyra followed, tiptoeing over the soft earth with the utmost care, crouching down behind the bushes, finally going on hands and knees to look between the leaves of a laurel.

The Rolls Royce stood in front of the house, and the chauffeur was moving around to the passenger side to open the door. Sir Charles stood waiting, smiling, offering his arm to the woman who was getting out, and as she came into view Lyra felt a blow at her heart, the worst blow since she'd escaped from Bolvangar, because Sir Charles's guest was her mother, Mrs Coulter.

Will stepped carefully across the moonlit grass in Cittàgazze, counting his paces, holding in his mind as clearly as he could a memory of where the study was and trying to locate it with reference to the villa, which stood nearby, stucco-white and columned in a formal garden with statues and a fountain. And he was aware of how exposed he was in this moon-drenched parkland.

When he thought he was in the right spot, he stopped and held out the knife again, feeling forward carefully. These little invisible gaps were anywhere, but not everywhere, or any slash of the knife would open a window.

He cut a small opening first, no bigger than his hand, and looked through. Nothing but darkness on the other side: he couldn't see where he was. He closed that one, turned through ninety degrees, and opened another. This time he found fabric in front of him – heavy green velvet: the curtains of the study. But where were they in relation to the cabinet? He had to close that one too, turn the other way, try again. Time was passing.

The third time was better: he found he could see the whole of the study in the dim light through the open door to the hall. There was the desk, the sofa, the cabinet! He could see a faint gleam along the side of a brass microscope. And there was no one in the room, and the house was silent. It couldn't be better.

He carefully estimated the distance, closed that window, stepped forward four paces, and held up the knife again. If he was right, he'd be in exactly the right spot to reach through, cut through the glass in the cabinet, take out the alethiometer and close the window behind him.

He cut a window at the right height. The glass of the cabinet door was only a hand's breadth in front of it. He put his face close, looking intently at this shelf and that, from top to bottom.

The alethiometer wasn't there.

At first Will thought he'd got the wrong cabinet. There were four of them in the room – he'd counted that morning, and memorized where they were – tall square cases made of dark wood, with glass sides and fronts and velvet-covered shelves, made for displaying valuable objects of porcelain or ivory or gold. Could he have simply opened a window in front of the wrong one? But on the top shelf was that bulky instrument with the brass rings: he'd made a point of noticing that. And on the shelf in the middle, where Sir Charles had placed the alethiometer, there was a space. This was the right cabinet, and the alethiometer wasn't there.

Will stepped back a moment and took a deep breath.

He'd have to go through properly and look around. Opening windows here and there at random would take all night. He closed the window in front of the cabinet, opened another to look at the rest of the room, and when he'd taken careful stock, he closed that one and opened a larger one behind the sofa through which he could easily get out in a hurry if he needed to.

His hand was throbbing brutally by this time, and the bandage was trailing loose. He wound it round as best he could and tucked the end in, and then went through into Sir Charles's house completely and crouched behind the leather sofa, the knife in his right hand, listening carefully.

Hearing nothing, he stood up slowly and looked around the room. The door to the hall was half-open, and the light that came through was quite enough to see by. The cabinets, the bookshelves, the pictures were all there, as they had been that morning, undisturbed.

He stepped out on the silent carpet and looked into each of the cabinets in turn. It wasn't there. Nor was it on the desk among the neatly piled books and papers, nor on the mantelpiece among the invitation cards to this opening or that reception, nor on the cushioned window-seat, nor on the octagonal table behind the door.

He moved back to the desk, intending to try the drawers, but with the heavy expectation of failure; and as he did so, he heard the faint crunch of tyres on gravel. It was so quiet that he half-thought he was imagining it, but he stood stock still, straining to listen. It stopped.

Then he heard the front door open.

He went at once to the sofa again, and crouched behind it, next to the window that opened on to the moon-silvered grass in Cittàgazze. And no sooner had he got there than he heard footsteps in that other world, lightly running over the grass, and looked through to see Lyra racing towards him. He was just in time to wave and put his finger to his lips, and she slowed, realizing that he was aware Sir Charles had returned.

"I haven't got it," he whispered when she came up. "It wasn't there. He's probably got it with him. I'm going to listen and see if he puts it back. Stay here."

"No! It's worse!" she said, and she was nearly in a genuine panic. "*She's* with him – Mrs Coulter – my mother – I dunno how she got here, but if she sees me I'm dead, Will, I'm lost – and I know who *he* is now! I remember where I seen him before!

Will, he's called Lord Boreal! I seen him at Mrs Coulter's cocktail
party, when I ran away! And he must have known who I was, all
the time . . ."

"Ssh. Don't stay here if you're going to make a noise."

She mastered herself, and swallowed hard, and shook her head.

"Sorry. I want to stay with you," she whispered. "I want to
hear what they say."

"Hush now . . ."

Because he could hear voices in the hall. The two of them
were close enough to touch, he in his world, she in Cittàgazze,
and seeing Will's trailing bandage, Lyra tapped him on the arm
and mimed tying it up again. He held out his hand for her to do
it, crouching meanwhile with his head cocked sideways, listening hard.

A light came on in the room. He heard Sir Charles speaking
to the servant, dismissing him, coming into the study, closing
the door.

"May I offer you a glass of Tokay?" he said.

A woman's voice, low and sweet, replied, "How kind of you,
Carlo. I haven't tasted Tokay for many years."

"Have the chair by the fireplace."

There was the faint glug of wine being poured, a tinkle of
decanter on glass-rim, a murmur of thanks, and then Sir Charles
seated himself on the sofa, inches away from Will.

"Your good health, Marisa," he said, sipping. "Now, suppose
you tell me what you want."

"I want to know where you got the alethiometer."

"Why?"

"Because Lyra had it, and I want to find her."

"I can't imagine why you would. She is a repellent brat."

"I'll remind you that she's my daughter."

"Then she is even more repellent, because she must have
resisted your charming influence on purpose. No one could do
it by accident."

"Where is she?"

"I'll tell you, I promise. But you must tell me something first."

"If I can," she said, in a different tone that Will thought
might be a warning. Her voice was intoxicating: soothing, sweet,

musical, and young, too. He longed to know what she looked like, because Lyra had never described her, and the face that went with this voice must be remarkable. "What do you want to know?"

"What is Asriel up to?"

There was a silence then, as if the woman were calculating what to say. Will looked back through the window at Lyra, and saw her face, moonlit and wide-eyed with fear, biting her lip to keep silent, and straining to hear, as he was.

Finally Mrs Coulter said, "Very well, I'll tell you. Lord Asriel is gathering an army, with the purpose of completing the war that was fought in heaven aeons ago."

"How medieval. However, he seems to have some very modern powers. What has he done to the magnetic pole?"

"He found a way of blasting open the barrier between our world and others. It caused profound disturbances to the earth's magnetic field, and that must resonate in this world too . . . But how do you know about that? Carlo, I think you should answer some questions of mine. What is this world? And how did you bring me here?"

"It is one of millions. There are openings between them, but they're not easily found. I know a dozen or so, but the places they open into have shifted, and that must be due to what Asriel's done. It seems that we can now pass directly from this world to our own, and probably to many others too. Previously, there was one world that acted as a sort of crossroads, and all the doorways opened into that. So you can imagine how surprised I was to see you, when I came through today, and how delighted that I could bring you here directly, without the risk of going through Cittàgazze."

"Cittàgazze? What is that?"

"The crossroads. A world in which I have an interest, my dear Marisa. But one too dangerous for us to visit at the moment."

"Why is it dangerous?"

"Dangerous for adults. Children can go there freely."

"What? I must know about this, Carlo," said the woman, and Will could hear her passionate impatience. "This is at the heart of everything, this difference between children and adults! It contains the whole mystery of Dust! This is why I must find the child.

And the witches have a name for her – I nearly had it, so nearly, from a witch in person, but she died too quickly. I must find the child. She has the answer, somehow, and I *must* have it . . ."

"And you shall. This instrument will bring her to me – never fear. And once she's given me what I want, you can have her. But tell me about your curious bodyguard, Marisa. I've never seen soldiers like that. Who are they?"

"Men, that's all. But . . . they've undergone intercision. They have no dæmons, so they have no fear and no imagination and no free will, and they'll fight till they're torn apart."

"No dæmons . . . Well, that's very interesting. I wonder if I might suggest a little experiment, if you can spare one of them? I'd like to see whether the Spectres are interested in them. If they're not, we might be able to travel in Cittàgazze after all."

"Spectres? What are they?"

"I'll explain later, my dear. They are the reason adults can't go into the world. Dust – children – Spectres – dæmons – intercision . . . Yes, it might very well work. Have some more wine."

"I want to know *everything*," she said, over the sound of wine being poured. "And I'll hold you to that. Now tell me: what are you doing in this world? Is this where you come when we thought you were in Brasil or the Indies?"

"I found my way here a long time ago. It was too good a secret to reveal, even to you, Marisa. I've made myself very comfortable, as you can see. Being part of the Council of State at home made it easy for me to see where the power lay here.

"As a matter of fact, I became a spy, though I never told my masters all I knew. The security services in this world were preoccupied for years with the Soviet Union – we know it as Muscovy. And although that threat has receded, there are still listening-posts and machines trained in that direction, and I'm still in touch with those who run the spies.

"And I heard recently about a profound disturbance in the earth's magnetic field. The security services are alarmed. Every nation that does research into fundamental physics – what we call experimental theology – is turning to its scientists urgently to discover what's going on. Because they know that *something* is happening. And they suspect it has to do with other worlds.

"They do have a few clues to this, as a matter of fact. There is some research being done into Dust. Oh, yes, they know it here as well. There is a team in this very city working on it. And another thing: there was a man who disappeared ten or twelve years ago, in the north, and the security services think he was in possession of some knowledge they badly need – specifically, the location of a doorway between the worlds, such as the one you came through earlier today. The one he found is the only one they know about: you can imagine I haven't told them what I know. When this new disturbance began, they set out to look for this man.

"And naturally, Marisa, I myself am curious. And I am keen to add to my knowledge."

Will sat frozen, with his heart thudding so hard he was afraid the adults would hear it. Sir Charles was talking about his own father! So that was who the men were, and what they were looking for!

But all the time, he was conscious of something else in the room as well as the voices of Sir Charles and the woman. There was a shadow moving across the floor, or that part of it he could see beyond the end of the sofa and past the legs of the little octagonal table. But neither Sir Charles nor the woman was moving. The shadow moved in a quick darting prowl, and it disturbed Will greatly. The only light in the room was a standard lamp beside the fireplace, so the shadow was clear and definite, but it never stopped long enough for Will to make out what it was.

Then two things happened. First, Sir Charles mentioned the alethiometer.

"For example," he said, continuing what he'd been saying, "I'm very curious about this instrument. Suppose you tell me how it works."

And he placed the alethiometer on the octagonal table at the end of the sofa. Will could see it clearly; he could almost reach it.

The second thing that happened was that the shadow fell still. The creature that was the source of it must have been perched on the back of Mrs Coulter's chair, because the light streaming over it threw its shadow clearly on the wall. And the moment it stopped, he realized it was the woman's dæmon: a crouching monkey, turning its head this way and that, searching for something.

Will heard an intake of breath from Lyra behind him as she saw it too. He turned silently and whispered:

"Go back to the other window, and come through into his garden. Find some stones and throw them at the study so they look away for a moment, and then I can get the alethiometer. Then run back to the other window and wait for me."

She nodded, and turned and ran away silently over the grass. Will turned back.

The woman was saying: ". . . the Master of Jordan College is a foolish old man. Why he gave it to her I can't imagine; you need several years of intensive study to make any sense of it at all. And now you owe me some information, Carlo. How did you find it? And where is the child?"

"I saw her using it in a museum in the city. I recognized her, of course, having seen her at your cocktail party all that time ago, and I realized she must have found a doorway. And then I realized that I could use it for a purpose of my own. So when I came across her a second time, I stole it."

"You're very frank."

"No need to be coy; we're both grown up."

"And where is she now? What did she do when she found it was missing?"

"She came to see me, which must have taken some nerve, I imagine."

"She doesn't lack nerve. And what are you going to do with it? What is this purpose of yours?"

"I told her that she could have it back, provided she got something for me – something I couldn't get myself."

"And what is that?"

"I don't know whether you –"

And that was the moment when the first stone smashed into the study window.

It broke with a satisfying crash of glass, and instantly the monkey-shadow leapt from the chair back as the adults gasped. There came another crash, and another, and Will felt the sofa move as Sir Charles got up.

Will leaned forward and snatched the alethiometer from the little table, thrust it into his pocket, and darted back through the window. As soon as he was on the grass in Cittàgazze he felt in the air for those elusive edges, calming his mind, breathing slowly, conscious all the time that only feet away there was horrible danger.

Then came a screech, not human, not animal, but worse than either, and he knew it was that loathsome monkey. By that time he'd got most of the window closed, but there was still a small gap at the level of his chest – and then he leapt back, because into that gap there came a small furry golden hand with black fingernails, and then a face: a nightmare face. The golden monkey's teeth were bared, his eyes glaring, and such a concentrated malevolence blazed from him that Will felt it almost like a spear.

Another second, and he would have been through, and that would have been the end; but Will was still holding the knife, and he brought it up at once and slashed left, right, across the monkey's face – or where the face would have been if the monkey hadn't withdrawn just in time. That gave Will the moment he needed to seize the edges of the window and press them shut.

His own world had vanished, and he was alone in the moonlit parkland in Cittàgazze, panting and trembling and horribly frightened.

But now there was Lyra to rescue. He ran back to the first window, the one he'd opened into the shrubbery, and looked through. The dark leaves of laurels and holly obscured the view, but he reached through and thrust them aside to see the side of the house clearly, with the broken study window sharp in the moonlight.

As he watched, he saw that monkey leaping around the corner of the house, scampering over the grass with the speed of a cat, and then saw Sir Charles and the woman following close behind. Sir Charles was carrying a pistol. The woman herself was beautiful – Will saw that with shock – lovely in the moonlight, her brilliant dark eyes wide with enchantment, her slender shape light and graceful; but as she snapped her fingers, the monkey stopped at once and leapt up into her arms, and he saw that the sweet-faced woman and the evil monkey were one being.

But where was Lyra?

The adults were looking around, and then the woman put the monkey down, and it began to cast this way and that on the grass as if it were scenting or looking for footprints. There was silence from all around. If Lyra were in the shrubbery already, she wouldn't be able to move without making a noise which would give her away at once.

Sir Charles adjusted something on his pistol with a soft click: the safety catch. He peered into the shrubbery, seeming to look directly at Will, and then his eyes travelled on past.

Then both of the adults looked to their left, for the monkey had heard something. And in a flash it leapt forward to where Lyra must be, and a moment later it would have found her –

And at that moment the tabby cat sprang out of the shrubbery and on to the grass, and hissed.

The monkey heard, and twisted in mid-air as if with astonishment; though he was hardly as astonished as Will himself. The monkey fell on his paws, facing the cat, and the cat arched her back, tail raised high, and stood sideways on, hissing, challenging, spitting.

And the monkey leapt for her. The cat reared up, slashing with needle-paws left and right too quick to see, and then Lyra was beside Will, tumbling through the window with Pantalaimon beside her. And the cat screamed and the monkey screamed too as the cat's claws raked his face; and then the monkey turned and leapt into Mrs Coulter's arms, and the cat shot away into the bushes of her own world, and vanished.

And Will and Lyra were through the window, and Will felt once again for the almost intangible edges in the air and pressed them swiftly together, closing the window all along its length as through the diminishing gap came the sound of feet among twigs and cracking branches –

And then there was only a hole the size of Will's hand, and then it was shut, and the whole world was silent. He fell to his knees on the dewy grass, and fumbled for the alethiometer.

"Here," he said to Lyra.

She took it. With shaking hands he slid the knife back into its sheath. Then he lay down trembling in all his limbs and closed his eyes, and felt the moonlight bathing him with silver, and felt Lyra undoing his bandage and tying it up again with delicate gentle movements.

"Oh, Will," he heard her say, "thank you for what you done, for all of it . . ."

"I hope the cat's all right," he muttered. "She's like my Moxie. She's probably gone home now. In her own world again. She'll be all right now."

"You know what I thought? I thought she was your dæmon, for a second. She done what a good dæmon would have done, anyway. We rescued her and she rescued us. Come on, Will, don't lie on the grass, it's wet. You got to come and lie down in a proper bed else you'll catch cold. We'll go in that big house over there. There's bound to be beds and food and stuff. Come on, I'll make a new bandage, I'll put some coffee on to cook, I'll make some omelette, whatever you want, and we'll sleep . . . We'll be safe now we've got the alethiometer back, you'll see. I'll do nothing now except help you find your father, I promise . . ."

She helped him up, and they walked slowly through the garden towards the great white-gleaming house under the moon.

10

THE SHAMAN

LEE SCORESBY DISEMBARKED at the port in the mouth of the Yenisei River, and found the place in chaos, with fishermen trying to sell their meagre catches of unknown kinds of fish to the canning factories, with ship-owners angry about the harbour charges the authorities had raised to cope with the floods, and with hunters and fur-trappers drifting into town unable to work because of the rapidly thawing forest and the disordered behaviour of the animals.

It was going to be hard to make his way into the interior along the road, that was certain; for in normal times the road was simply a cleared track of frozen earth, and now that even the permafrost was melting, the surface was a swamp of churned mud.

So Lee put his balloon and equipment into storage, and with his dwindling gold hired a boat with a gas-engine and bought several tanks of fuel and some stores, and set off up the swollen river.

He made slow progress at first. Not only was the current swift, but the waters were laden with all kinds of debris: tree trunks, brushwood, drowned animals, and once the bloated corpse of a man. He had to pilot carefully and keep the little engine beating hard to make any headway.

He was heading for the village of Grumman's tribe. For guidance he had only his memory of having flown over the country some years before, but that memory was good, and he had little difficulty in finding the right course among the swift-running streams, even though some of the banks had vanished under the milky-brown flood waters. The temperature had disturbed the insects, and a cloud of midges made every outline hazy. Lee smeared his face and hands with jimson-weed ointment and smoked a succession of pungent cigars, which kept the worst at bay.

As for Hester, she sat taciturn in the bow, her long ears flat against her skinny back and her eyes narrowed. He was used to her silence, and she to his. They spoke when they needed to.

On the morning of the third day, Lee steered the little craft up a creek that joined the main stream, flowing down from a line of low hills that should have been deep under snow, but now were patched and streaked with brown. Soon the stream was flowing between low pines and spruce, and after a few miles they came to a large round rock, the height of a house, where Lee drew in to the bank and tied up.

"There was a landing stage here," he said to Hester. "Remember the old seal-hunter in Nova Zembla who told us about it? It must be six feet under now."

"I hope they had sense enough to build the village high, then," she said, hopping ashore.

No more than half an hour later he laid his pack down beside the wooden house of the village headman and turned to salute the little crowd that had gathered. He used the gesture universal in the north to signify friendship, and laid his rifle down at his feet.

An old Siberian Tartar, his eyes almost lost in the wrinkles around them, laid his bow down beside it. His wolverine-dæmon twitched her nose at Hester, who flicked an ear in response, and then the headman spoke.

Lee replied, and they moved through half a dozen languages before finding one they could talk in.

"My respects to you and your tribe," Lee said. "I have some smoke-weed, which is not worthy, but I would be honoured to present it to you."

The headman nodded in appreciation, and one of his wives received the bundle Lee removed from his pack.

"I am seeking a man called Grumman," Lee said. "I heard tell he was a kinsman of yours by adoption. He may have acquired another name, but the man is European."

"Ah," said the headman, "we have been waiting for you."

The rest of the villagers, gathered in the thin steaming sunlight on the muddy ground in the middle of the houses, couldn't understand the words but they saw the headman's pleasure. Pleasure, and relief, Lee felt Hester think.

The headman nodded several times.

"We have been expecting you," he said again. "You have come to take Dr Grumman to the other world."

Lee's eyebrows rose, but he merely said, "As you say, sir. Is he here?"

"Follow me," said the headman.

The other villagers fell aside respectfully. Understanding Hester's distaste for the filthy mud she had to lope through, Lee scooped her up in his arms and shouldered his pack, following the headman along a forest path to a hut ten long bow-shots from the village, in a clearing in the larches.

The headman stopped outside the wood-framed, skin-covered hut. The place was decorated with boar-tusks and the antlers of elk and reindeer, but they weren't merely hunting trophies, for they had been hung with dried flowers and carefully plaited sprays of pine, as if for some ritualistic purpose.

"You must speak to him with respect," the headman said quietly. "He is a shaman. And his heart is sick."

Suddenly Lee felt a shiver go down his back, and Hester stiffened in his arms, for they saw that they had been watched all the time. From among the dried flowers and the pine-sprays a bright yellow eye looked out. It was a dæmon, and as Lee watched, she turned her head, and delicately took a spray of pine in her powerful beak and drew it across the space like a curtain.

The headman called out in his own tongue, addressing the man by the name the old seal-hunter had told him: Jopari. A moment later the door opened.

Standing in the doorway, gaunt, blazing-eyed, was a man dressed in skins and furs. His black hair was streaked with grey, his jaw jutted strongly, and his osprey-dæmon sat glaring on his fist.

The headman bowed three times and withdrew, leaving Lee alone with the shaman-academic he'd come to find.

"Dr Grumman," he said. "My name's Lee Scoresby. I'm from the country of Texas, and I'm an aëronaut by profession. If you'd let me sit and talk a spell, I'll tell you what brings me here. I am right, ain't I? You *are* Dr Stanislaus Grumman, of the Berlin Academy?"

"Yes," said the shaman. "And you're from Texas, you say. The

winds have blown you a long way from your homeland, Mr
Scoresby."

"Well, there are strange winds blowing through the world
now, sir."

"Indeed. The sun is warm, I think. You'll find a bench inside
my hut. If you help me bring it out we can sit in this agreeable
light, and talk out here. I have some coffee, if you would care to
share it."

"Most kind, sir," said Lee, and carried out the wooden bench
himself while Grumman went to the stove and poured the scalding drink into two tin cups. His accent was not German, to Lee's
ears, but English, of England. The Director of the Observatory
had been right.

When they were seated, Hester narrow-eyed and impassive
beside Lee and the great osprey-dæmon glaring into the full sun,
Lee began. He started with his meeting at Trollesund with John
Faa, Lord of the gyptians, and told how they recruited Iorek
Byrnison the bear and journeyed to Bolvangar, and rescued Lyra
and the other children; and then he spoke of what he'd learned
both from Lyra and from Serafina Pekkala in the balloon as they
flew towards Svalbard.

"You see, Dr Grumman, it seemed to me, from the way the
little girl described it, that Lord Asriel just brandished this
severed head packed in ice at the scholars there and frightened
them so much with it they didn't look closely. That's what made
me suspect you might still be alive. And clearly, sir, you have a
kind of specialist knowledge of this business. I've been hearing
about you all along the Arctic seaboard, about how you had your
skull pierced, about how your subject of study seems to vary
between digging on the ocean bed and gazing at the northern
lights, about how you suddenly appeared, like as it might be out
of nowhere, about ten – twelve years ago, and that's all mighty
interesting. But something's drawn me here, Dr Grumman,
beyond simple curiosity. I'm concerned about the child. I think
she's important, and so do the witches. If there's anything you
know about her and about what's going on, I'd like you to tell
me. As I said, something's given me the conviction that you can,
which is why I'm here.

"But unless I'm mistaken, sir, I heard the village headman say that I had come to take you to another world. Did I get it wrong, or is that truly what he said? And one more question for you, sir: what was that name he called you by? Was that some kind of tribal name, some magician's title?"

Grumman smiled briefly, and said, "The name he used is my own true name, John Parry. Yes, you have come to take me to the other world. And as for what brought you here, I think you'll find it was this."

And he opened his hand. In the palm lay something that Lee could see, but not understand. He saw a ring of silver and turquoise, a Navajo design, he saw it clearly and he recognized it as his own mother's, he knew its weight and the smoothness of the stone and the way the silversmith had folded the metal over more closely at the corner where the stone was chipped, and he knew how the chipped corner had worn smooth, because he had run his fingers over it many, many times, years and years ago in his boyhood in the sagelands of his native country.

He found himself standing. Hester was trembling, standing upright, ears pricked. The osprey had moved without Lee's noticing between him and Grumman, defending her man, but Lee wasn't going to attack; he felt undone; he felt like a child again, and his voice was tight and shaky as he said:

"Where did you get that?"

"Take it," said Grumman, or Parry. "Its work is done. It summoned you. Now I don't need it."

"But how – " said Lee, lifting the beloved thing from Grumman's palm. "I don't understand how you can have – did you – how did you get this? I ain't seen this thing for forty years."

"I am a shaman. I can do many things you don't understand. Sit down, Mr Scoresby. Be calm. I'll tell you what you need to know."

Lee sat again, holding the ring, running his fingers over it again and again.

"Well," he said, "I'm shaken, sir. I think I need to hear what you can tell me."

"Very well," said Grumman, "I'll begin. My name, as I told you, is Parry, and I was not born in this world. Lord Asriel is not the first by any means to travel between the worlds, though he's the first to open the way so spectacularly. In my own world I was a soldier and then an explorer. Twelve years ago I was accompanying an expedition to a place in my world that corresponds with your Beringland. My companions had other intentions, but I was looking for something I'd heard about from old legends: a rent in the fabric of the world, a hole that had appeared between our universe and another. Well, some of my companions got lost. In searching for them, I and two others walked through this hole, this doorway, without even seeing it, and left our world altogether. At first we didn't realize what had happened. We walked on till we found a town, and then there was no mistaking it: we were in a different world.

"Well, try as we might, we could not find that first doorway again. We'd come through it in a blizzard, and you are an old Arctic hand: you know what that means.

"So we had no choice but to stay in that new world. And we soon discovered what a dangerous place it was. It seemed that there was a strange kind of ghoul or apparition haunting it, something deadly and implacable. My two companions died soon afterwards, victims of the Spectres, as the things are called.

"The result was that I found their world an abominable place, and I couldn't wait to leave it. The way back to my own world was barred for ever. But there were other doorways into other worlds, and a little searching found the way into this.

"So here I came. And I discovered a marvel as soon as I did, Mr Scoresby, for worlds differ greatly, and in this world I saw my dæmon for the first time. Yes, I hadn't known of Sayan Kötör here till I entered yours. People here cannot conceive of worlds where dæmons are a silent voice in the mind and no more. Can you imagine my astonishment, in turn, at learning that part of my own nature was female, and bird-formed, and beautiful?

"So with Sayan Kötör beside me, I wandered through the northern lands, and I learned a good deal from the peoples of the Arctic, like my good friends in the village down there. What they told me of this world filled some gaps in the knowledge I'd acquired in mine, and I began to see the answer to many mysteries.

"I made my way to Berlin under the name of Grumman. I told no one about my origins; it was my secret. I presented a thesis to the Academy, and defended it in debate, which is their method. I was better informed than the Academicians, and I had no difficulty in gaining membership.

"So with my new credentials I could begin to work in this world, where I found myself, for the most part, greatly contented. I missed some things about my own world, to be sure. Are you a married man, Mr Scoresby? No? Well, I was; and I loved my wife dearly, as I loved my son, my only child, a little boy not yet one year old when I wandered out of my world. I missed them terribly. But I might search for a thousand years, and never find the way back. We were sundered for ever.

"However, my work absorbed me. I sought other forms of knowledge; I was initiated into the skull-cult; I became a shaman. And I have made some useful discoveries: I have found a way of making an ointment from bloodmoss, for example, that preserves all the virtues of the fresh plant.

"I know a great deal about this world now, Mr Scoresby. I know, for example, about Dust. I see from your expression that you have heard the term. It is frightening your theologians to death, but they are the ones who frighten me. I know what Lord Asriel is doing, and I know why, and that's why I summoned you here. I am going to help him, you see, because the task he's undertaken is the greatest in human history. The greatest in thirty-five thousand years of human history, Mr Scoresby.

"I can't do very much myself. My heart is diseased beyond the powers of anyone in this world to cure it. I have one great effort left in me, perhaps. But I know something Lord Asriel doesn't, something he needs to know if his effort is to succeed.

"You see, I was intrigued by that haunted world where the Spectres fed on human consciousness. I wanted to know what they were, how they had come into being. And as a shaman, I can discover things in the spirit where I cannot go in the body, and I spent much time in trance, exploring that world. I found that the philosophers there, centuries ago, had created a tool for their own undoing: an instrument they called the subtle knife. It had many powers – more than they'd guessed when they made it, far more than they know even now – and somehow, in using it, they had let the Spectres into their world.

"Well, I know about the subtle knife, and what it can do. And I know where it is, and I know how to recognize the one who must use it, and I know what he must do in Lord Asriel's cause. I hope he's equal to the task. So I have summoned you here, and you are to fly me northwards, into the world Asriel has opened, where I expect to find the bearer of the subtle knife.

"That is a dangerous world, mind. Those Spectres are worse than anything in your world or mine. We shall have to be careful and courageous. I shall not return, and if you want to see your country again, you'll need all your courage, all your craft, all your luck.

"That's your task, Mr Scoresby. That is why you sought me out."

And the shaman fell silent. His face was pallid, with a faint sheen of sweat.

"This is the craziest damn idea I ever heard in my life," said Lee.

He stood up in his agitation and walked a pace or two this way, a pace or two that, while Hester watched unblinking from the bench. Grumman's eyes were half-closed; his dæmon sat on his knee, watching Lee warily.

"Do you want money?" Grumman said after a few moments. "I can get you some gold. That's not hard to do."

"Damn, I didn't come here for gold," said Lee hotly. "I came here ... I came here to see if you were alive, like I thought you were. Well, my curiosity's kinda satisfied on that point."

"I'm glad to hear it."

"And there's another angle to this thing, too," Lee added, and told Grumman of the witch-council at Lake Enara, and the resolution the witches had sworn to. "You see," he finished, "that little girl Lyra ... Well, she's the reason I set out to help the witches in the first place. You say you brought me here with that Navajo ring. Maybe that's so and maybe it ain't. What I know is, I came here because I thought I'd be helping Lyra. I ain't never seen a child like that. If I had a daughter of my own, I hope she'd be half as strong and brave and good. Now I'd heard that you knew of some object, I didn't know what it might be, that confers a protection on anyone who holds it. And from what you say, I think it must be this subtle knife.

"So this is my price for taking you into the other world, Dr Grumman: not gold, but the subtle knife, and I don't want it for myself, I want it for Lyra. You have to swear you'll get her under the protection of that object, and then I'll take you wherever you want to go."

The shaman listened closely, and said, "Very well, Mr Scoresby; I swear. Do you trust my oath?"

"What will you swear by?"

"Name anything you like."

Lee thought, and then said, "Swear by whatever it was made you turn down the love of the witch. I guess that's the most important thing you know."

Grumman's eyes widened, and he said, "You guess well, Mr Scoresby. I'll gladly swear by that. I give you my word that I'll make certain the child Lyra Belacqua is under the protection of the subtle knife. But I warn you: the bearer of that knife has his own task to do, and it may be that his doing it will put her into even greater danger."

Lee nodded soberly. "Maybe so," he said, "but whatever little chance of safety there is, I want her to have it."

"You have my word. And now I must go into the new world, and you must take me."

"And the wind? You ain't been too sick to observe the weather, I guess?"

"Leave the wind to me.'

Lee nodded. He sat on the bench again and ran his fingers over and over the turquoise ring while Grumman gathered the few goods he needed into a deerskin bag, and then the two of them went back down the forest track to the village.

The headman spoke at some length. More and more of the villagers came out to touch Grumman's hand, to mutter a few words, and to receive what looked like a blessing in return. Lee, meanwhile, was looking at the weather. The sky was clear to the south, and a fresh-scented breeze was just lifting the twigs and stirring the pine-tops. To the north the fog still hung over the heavy river, but it was the first time for days that there seemed to be a promise of clearing it.

At the rock where the landing-stage had been he lifted Grumman's pack into the boat, and filled the little engine, which fired at once. He cast off, and with the shaman in the bow, the boat sped down with the current, darting under the trees and skimming out into the main river so fast that Lee was afraid for Hester, crouching just inside the gunwale; but she was a seasoned traveller, he should have known that; why was he so damn jumpy?

They reached the port at the river-mouth to find every hotel, every lodging-house, every private room commandeered by soldiers. Not just any soldiers, either: these were troops of the Imperial Guard of Muscovy, the most ferociously-trained and lavishly-equipped army in the world, and one sworn to uphold the power of the Magisterium.

Lee had intended to rest a night before setting off, because Grumman looked in need of it, but there was no chance of finding a room.

"What's going on?" he said to the boatman when he returned the hired boat.

"We don't know. The regiment arrived yesterday and commandeered every billet, every scrap of food, and every ship in the town. They'd have had this boat too if you hadn't taken it."

"D'you know where they're going?"

"North," said the boatman. "There's a war going to be fought, by all accounts, the greatest war ever known."

"North, into that new world?"

"That's right. And there's more troops coming – this is just the advance guard. There won't be a loaf of bread or a gallon of spirit left in a week's time. You did me a favour taking this boat – the price has already doubled . . ."

There was no sense in resting up now, even if they could find a place. Full of anxiety about his balloon, Lee went at once to the warehouse where he'd left it, with Grumman beside him. The man was keeping pace. He looked sick, but he was tough.

The warehouse-keeper, busy counting out some spare engine

parts to a requisitioning sergeant of the Guard, looked up briefly from his clip-board.

"Balloon – too bad – requisitioned yesterday," he said. "You can see how it is. I've got no choice."

Hester flicked her ears, and Lee understood what she meant.

"Have you delivered the balloon yet?" he said.

"They're going to collect it this afternoon."

"No they're not," said Lee, "because I have an authority that trumps the Guard."

And he showed the warehouseman the ring he'd taken from the finger of the dead Skraeling on Nova Zembla. The sergeant, beside him at the counter, stopped what he was doing and saluted at the sight of the Church's token, but for all his discipline he couldn't prevent a flicker of puzzlement passing over his face.

"So we'll have the balloon right now," said Lee, "and you can set some men to fill it. And I mean at once. And that includes food, and water, and ballast."

The warehouseman looked at the sergeant, who shrugged, and then hurried away to see to the balloon. Lee and Grumman withdrew to the wharf, where the gas-tanks were, to supervise the filling and talk quietly.

"Where did you get that ring?" said Grumman.

"Off a dead man's finger. Kinda risky using it, but I couldn't see another way of getting my balloon back. You reckon that sergeant suspected anything?"

"Of course he did. But he's a disciplined man. He won't question the Church. If he reports it at all, we'll be away by the time they can do anything about it. Well, I promised you a wind, Mr Scoresby; I hope you like it."

The sky was blue overhead now, and the sunlight was bright. To the north fog-banks still hung like a mountain range over the sea, but the breeze was pushing them back and back, and Lee was impatient for the air again.

As the balloon filled and began to swell up beyond the edge of the warehouse roof, Lee checked the basket, and stowed all his equipment with particular care; for in the other world, who knew what turbulence they'd meet? His instruments, too, he fixed to the framework with close attention, even the compass, whose needle was swinging around the dial quite uselessly. Finally he lashed a score of sandbags around the basket for ballast.

When the gas-bag was full and leaning northwards in the buffeting breeze, and the whole apparatus straining against the stout ropes anchoring it down, Lee paid the warehouseman with the last of his gold, and helped Grumman into the basket. Then he turned to the men at the ropes to give the order to let go.

But before they could do so, there was an interruption. From the alley at the side of the warehouse came the noise of pounding boots, moving at the double, and a shout of command:

"Halt!"

The men at the ropes paused, some looking that way, some looking to Lee, and he called sharply:

"Let go! Cast off!"

Two of the men obeyed, and the balloon lurched up, but the other two had their attention on the soldiers, who were moving at the double around the corner of the building. Those two men still held their ropes fast around the bollards, and the balloon lurched sickeningly sideways. Lee grabbed at the suspension-ring; Grumman was holding it too, and his dæmon had her claws tight around it.

Lee shouted, "Let go, you damn fools! She's going up!"

Because the buoyancy of the gas-bag was too great, and the men, haul as they might, couldn't hold it back. One let go, and his rope lashed itself loose from the bollard; but the other man, feeling the rope lift, instinctively clung on instead of letting go. Lee had seen this happen once before, and dreaded it. The poor man's dæmon, a heavy-set husky, howled with fear and pain from the ground as the balloon surged up towards the sky, and five endless seconds later it was over; the man's strength failed; he fell, half-dead, and crashed into the water.

But the soldiers had their rifles up already. A volley of bullets whistled past the basket, one striking a spark from the suspension-ring and making Lee's hands sting with the impact, but none of them did any damage. By the time they fired their second shot, the balloon was almost out of range, hurtling up into the blue and speeding out over the sea. Lee felt his heart lift with it. He'd said once to Serafina Pekkala that he didn't care for flying, that it was only a job, but he hadn't meant it. Soaring upwards, with a fair wind behind and a new world in front: what could be better in this life?

He let go the suspension-ring and saw that Hester was crouching in her usual corner, eyes half-closed. From far below and a long way back came another futile volley of rifle-fire. The town was receding fast, and the broad sweep of the river-mouth was glittering in the sunlight below them.

"Well, Dr Grumman," he said, "I don't know about you, but I feel better in the air. I wish that poor man had let go of the rope, though. It's so damned easy to do, and if you don't let go at once there's no hope for you."

"Thank you, Mr Scoresby," said the shaman. "You managed that very well. Now we settle down and fly. I would be grateful for those furs; the air is still cold."

IN THE GREAT white villa in the park Will slept uneasily, plagued with dreams that were filled with anxiety and with sweetness in equal measure, so that he struggled to wake up and yet longed for sleep again. When his eyes were fully open he felt so drowsy that he could scarcely move, and then he sat up to find his bandage loose and his bed crimson.

He struggled out of bed and made his way through the heavy dust-filled sunlight and silence of the great house down to the kitchen. He and Lyra had slept in servants' rooms under the attic, not feeling welcomed by the stately four-poster beds in the grand rooms further down, and it was a long unsteady walk.

"Will –" she said at once, her voice full of concern, and she turned from the stove to help him to a chair.

He felt dizzy. He supposed he'd lost a lot of blood; well, there was no need to suppose, with the evidence all over him. And the wounds were still bleeding.

"I was just making some coffee," she said. "Do you want that first, or shall I do another bandage? I can do whichever you want. And there's eggs in the cold cabinet, but I can't find any baked beans."

"This isn't a baked beans kind of house. Bandage first. Is there any hot water in the tap? I want to wash. I hate being covered in this . . ."

She ran some hot water and he stripped to his underpants. He was too faint and dizzy to feel embarrassed, but Lyra became embarrassed for him, and went out. He washed as best he could and then dried himself on the tea-towels that hung on a line by the stove.

When she came back she'd found some clothes for him, just a shirt and canvas trousers and a belt. He put them on and she tore a fresh tea-towel into strips and bandaged him tightly again. She was badly worried about his hand: not only were the wounds bleeding freely still, but the rest of the hand was swollen and red. But he said nothing about it, and neither did she.

Then she made the coffee and toasted some stale bread, and they took it into the grand room at the front of the house, over-looking the city. When he'd eaten and drunk he felt a little better.

"You better ask the alethiometer what to do next," he said. "Have you asked it anything yet?"

"No," she said. "I'm only going to do what you ask, from now on. I thought of doing it last night, but I never did. And I won't either unless you ask me to."

"Well, you better do it now," he said. "There's as much danger here as there is in my world, now. There's Angelica's brother for a start. And if—"

He stopped, because she began to say something, but she stopped as soon as he did. Then she collected herself and went on:

"Will, there was something that happened yesterday that I didn't tell you. I should've, but there was just so many other things going on. I'm sorry . . ."

And she told him everything she'd seen through the window of the Tower while Giacomo Paradisi was dressing his wound: Tullio being beset by the Spectres, Angelica seeing her at the window and her look of hatred, and Paolo's threat.

"And d'you remember," she went on, "when she first spoke to us? Her little brother said something about what they were all doing. He said 'He's gonna get—' and she wouldn't let him finish, she smacked him, remember? I bet he was going to say Tullio was after the knife, and that's why all the kids came here. 'Cause if they had the knife, they could do anything, they could even grow up without being afraid of Spectres."

"What did it look like, when he was attacked?" Will said. To her surprise he was sitting forward, his eyes demanding and urgent.

"He . . ." She tried to remember exactly: "He started counting the stones in the wall. He sort of felt all over them . . . But he couldn't keep it up. In the end he sort of lost interest and stopped. Then he was just still," she finished, and seeing Will's expression she said: "Why?"

"Because ... I think maybe they come from my world after all, the Spectres. If they make people behave like that, I wouldn't be surprised at all if they came from my world. And when the Guild men opened their first window, if it was into my world, the Spectres could have gone through then."

"But you don't have Spectres in your world! You never heard of them, did you?"

"Maybe they're not called Spectres. Maybe we call them something else."

Lyra wasn't sure what he meant, but she didn't want to press him. His cheeks were red and his eyes were hot.

"Anyway," she went on, turning away, "the important thing is that Angelica saw me in the window. And now she knows we've got the knife, she'll tell all of 'em. She'll think it's our fault that her brother was attacked by Spectres. I'm sorry, Will. I should've told you earlier. But there was just so many other things ..."

"Well," he said, "I don't suppose it would have made any difference. He was torturing the old man, and once he knew how to use the knife he'd have killed both of us if he could. We had to fight him."

"I just feel bad about it, Will. I mean, he was her brother. And I bet if we were them we'd have wanted the knife too."

"Yes," he said, "but we can't go back and change what happened. We had to get the knife to get the alethiometer back, and if we could have got it without fighting, we would."

"Yeah, we would," she said.

Like Iorek Byrnison, Will was a fighter truly enough, so she was prepared to agree with him when he said it would be better not to fight: she knew it wasn't cowardice that spoke, but strategy. He was calmer now, and his cheeks were pale again. He was looking into the middle distance and thinking.

Then he said, "It's probably more important now to think about Sir Charles and what he'll do, or Mrs Coulter. Maybe if she's got this special bodyguard they were talking about, these soldiers who'd had their dæmons cut away, maybe Sir Charles is right and they'll be able to ignore the Spectres. You know what I think? I think what they eat, the Spectres, is people's dæmons."

"But children have dæmons too. And they don't attack children. It can't be that."

"Then it must be the difference between children's dæmons and grown-ups'," Will said. "There *is* a difference, isn't there? You told me grown-ups' dæmons don't change shape. It must be something to do with that. If these soldiers of hers haven't got dæmons at all, maybe it has the same effect..."

"Yeah!" she said. "Could be. And *she* wouldn't be afraid of Spectres anyway. She en't afraid of anything. And she's so clever, Will, honest, and she's so ruthless and cruel, she could boss them, I bet she could. She could command them like she does people and they'd have to obey her, I bet. Lord Boreal is strong and clever, but she'll have him doing what she wants in no time. Oh, Will, I'm getting scared again, thinking what she might do ... I'm going to ask the alethiometer, like you said. Thank goodness we got that back, anyway."

She unfolded the velvet bundle and ran her hands lovingly over the heavy gold.

"I'm going to ask about your father," she said, "and how we can find him. See, I put the hands to point at –"

"No. Ask about my mother first. I want to know if she's all right."

Lyra nodded, and turned the hands before laying the alethiometer in her lap and tucking her hair behind her ears to look down and concentrate. Will watched the light needle swing purposefully round the dial, darting and stopping and darting on as swiftly as a swallow feeding, and he watched Lyra's eyes, so blue and fierce and full of clear understanding.

Then she blinked and looked up.

"She's safe still," she said. "This friend that's looking after her, she's ever so kind. No one knows where your mother is, and the friend won't give her away."

Will hadn't realized how worried he'd been. At this good news, he felt himself relax, and as a little tension left his body, he felt the pain of his wound more sharply.

"Thank you," he said. "All right, now ask about my father –"

But before she could even begin, they heard a shout from outside.

They looked out at once. At the lower edge of the park in front of the first houses of the city there was a belt of trees, and something was stirring there. Pantalaimon became a lynx at once and padded to the open door, gazing fiercely down.

"It's the children," he said.

They both stood up. The children were coming out of the trees, one by one, maybe forty or fifty of them. Many of them were carrying sticks. At their head was the boy in the striped T-shirt, and it wasn't a stick that he was carrying: it was a pistol.

"There's Angelica," Lyra whispered, pointing.

Angelica was beside the leading boy, tugging at his arm, urging him on. Just behind them her little brother Paolo was shrieking with excitement, and the other children, too, were yelling and waving their fists in the air. Two of them were lugging heavy rifles. Will had seen children in this mood before, but never so many of them, and the ones in his town didn't carry guns.

They were shouting, and Will managed to make out Angelica's voice high over them all: "You killed my brother and you stole the knife! You murderers! You made the Spectres get him! You killed him and we'll kill you! You ain gonna get away! We gonna kill you same as you killed him!"

"Will, you could cut a window!" Lyra said urgently, clutching his good arm. "We could get away, easy –"

"Yeah, and where would we be? In Oxford, a few yards from Sir Charles's house, in broad daylight. Probably in the main street in front of a bus. I can't just cut through anywhere and expect to be safe – I've got to look first and see where we are, and that'd take too long. There's a forest or woods or something behind this house. If we can get up there in the trees we'll be safer."

Lyra looked out of the window, furious. "I should have killed her yesterday!" she said. "She's as bad as her brother. I'd like to –"

"Stop talking and come on," said Will.

He checked that the knife was strapped to his belt, and Lyra put on her little rucksack with the alethiometer and the letters from Will's father. They ran through the echoing hall, along the corridor and into the kitchen, through the scullery and into a cobbled court beyond it. A gate in the wall led out into a kitchen garden, where beds of vegetables and herbs lay baking under the morning sun.

The edge of the wood was a few hundred yards away, up a slope of grass that was horribly exposed. On a knoll to the left, closer than the trees, stood a little building, a circular temple-like structure with an upper storey open like a balcony for viewing the city from.

"Let's run," said Will, though he felt less like running than like lying down and closing his eyes.

With Pantalaimon flying above to keep watch, they set off across the grass. But it was tussocky and ankle-high, and Will couldn't run more than a few steps before he felt too dizzy to carry on. He slowed to a walk.

Lyra looked back. The children hadn't seen them yet; they were still at the front of the house; maybe they'd take a while to look through all the rooms . . .

But Pantalaimon chirruped in alarm. There was a boy standing at an open window on the second floor of the villa, pointing at them. They heard a shout.

"Come *on*, Will," Lyra said.

She tugged at his good arm, helping him, lifting him. He tried to respond, but he didn't have the strength. He could only walk.

"All right," he said, "we can't get to the trees. Too far away. So we'll go to that temple place. If we shut the door maybe we can hold them out for long enough to cut through after all . . ."

Pantalaimon darted ahead, and Lyra gasped and called to him breathlessly, making him pause. Will could almost see the bond between them, the dæmon tugging and the girl responding. He stumbled through the thick grass with Lyra running ahead to see, and then back to help, and then ahead again, until they reached the stone pavement around the temple.

The door under the little portico was unlocked, and they ran inside to find themselves in a bare circular room with several statues of goddesses in niches around the wall. In the very centre a spiral staircase of wrought iron led up through an opening to the floor above. There was no key to lock the door, so they clambered up the staircase and on to the floorboards of an upper level that was really a viewing place, where people could come to take the air and look out over the city; for there were no windows or walls, simply a series of open arches all the way round supporting the roof. In each archway a window sill at waist height was broad enough to lean on, and below them the pantiled roof ran down in a gentle slope all around to the gutter.

As they looked out they could see the forest behind, tantaliz-ingly close; and the villa below them, and beyond that the open park and then the red-brown roofs of the city, with the Tower rising to the left. There were carrion crows wheeling in the air above the grey battlements, and Will felt a jolt of sickness as he realized what had drawn them there.

But there was no time to take in the view; first they had to deal with the children, who were racing up towards the temple, screaming with rage and excitement. The leading boy slowed down and held up his pistol, and fired two or three wild shots towards the temple, and then they came on again, yelling:

"Thiefs!"

"Murderers!'

"We gonna kill you!"

"You got our knife!"

"You don' come from here!"

"You gonna die!"

Will took no notice. He had the knife out already, and swiftly cut a small window to see where they were – only to recoil at once. Lyra looked too, and fell back in disappointment. They were fifty feet or so in the air, high above a main road busy with traffic.

"Of course," Will said bitterly, "we came up a slope . . . Well, we're stuck. We'll have to hold them off, that's all."

Another few seconds and the first children were crowding in through the door. The sound of their yelling echoed in the temple and reinforced their wildness; and then came a gunshot, enor-mously loud, and another, and the screaming took another tone, and then the stairs began to shake as the first ones climbed up.

Lyra was crouching paralysed against the wall, but Will still had the knife in his hand. He scrambled over to the opening in the floor and reached down and sliced through the iron of the top step as if it were paper. With nothing to hold it up, the staircase began to bend under the weight of the children crowding on it, and then it swung down and fell with a huge crash. More screams, more confusion; and again the gun went off, but this time by accident, it seemed, because someone had been hit, and the scream was of pain this time, and Will looked down to see a tangle of writhing bodies, covered in plaster and dust and blood.

They weren't individual children: they were a single mass, like a tide. They surged below him and leaped up in fury, snatching, threatening, screaming, spitting, but they couldn't reach.

Then someone called, and they looked to the door, and those who could move surged out towards it, leaving several pinned beneath the iron stairs or dazed and struggling to get up from the rubble-strewn floor.

Will soon realized why they'd run out. There was a scrabbling sound from the roof outside the arches, and he ran to the window sill to see the first pair of hands grasping the edge of the pantiles and pulling up. Someone was pushing from behind, and then came another head and another pair of hands, as they clambered over the shoulders and backs of those below and swarmed up on to the roof like ants.

But the pantiled ridges were hard to walk on, and the first ones scrambled up on hands and knees, their wild eyes never leaving Will's face. Lyra had joined him, and Pantalaimon was snarling as a leopard, paws on the sill, making the first children hesitate. But still they came on, more and more of them.

Someone was shouting "Kill! Kill! Kill!" and then others joined in, louder and louder, and those on the roof began to stamp and thump the tiles in rhythm, but they didn't quite dare come closer, faced by the snarling dæmon. Then a tile broke, and the boy standing on it slipped and fell, but the one beside him picked up the broken piece and hurled it at Lyra.

She ducked, and it shattered on the column beside her, showering her with broken pieces. Will had noticed the rail around the edge of the opening in the floor, and cut two sword-length pieces of it, and he handed one to Lyra now; and she swung it round as hard as she could and into the side of the first boy's head. He fell at once, but then came another, and it was Angelica, red-haired, white-faced, crazy-eyed; she scrambled up on to the sill, but Lyra jabbed the length of rail at her fiercely and she fell back again.

Will was doing the same. The knife was in its sheath at his waist, and he struck and swung and jabbed with the iron rail, and while several children fell back, others kept replacing them, and more and more were clambering up on to the roof from below.

Then the boy in the striped T-shirt appeared, but he'd lost the pistol, or perhaps it was empty. However, his eyes and Will's locked together, and each of them knew what was going to happen: they were going to fight, and it was going to be brutal and deadly.

"Come on," said Will, passionate for the battle, "come on then . . ."

Another second, and they would have fought.

But then the strangest thing appeared: a great white snow-goose swooping low, his wings spread wide, calling and calling so loud that even the children on the roof heard through their savagery and turned to see.

"Kaisa!" cried Lyra joyfully, for it was Serafina Pekkala's dæmon.

The snow-goose called again, a piercing whoop that filled the sky, and then wheeled and turned an inch away from the boy in the striped T-shirt. The boy fell back in fear and slid down and over the edge, and then others began to cry in alarm too, because there was something else in the sky, and as Lyra saw the little black shapes sweeping out of the blue she cheered and shouted with glee.

"Serafina Pekkala! Here! Help us! Here we are! In the temple –"

And with a hiss and rush of air a dozen arrows, and then another dozen swiftly after, and then another dozen loosed so quickly that they were all in the air at once, shot at the temple roof above the gallery and landed with a thunder of hammer-blows. Astonished and bewildered, the children on the roof felt all the aggression leave them in a moment, and horrible fear rushed in to take its place: what were these black-garbed women rushing at them in the air? How could it happen? Were they ghosts? Were they a new kind of Spectre?

And whimpering and crying they jumped off the roof, some of them falling clumsily and dragging themselves away limping and others rolling down the slope and dashing for safety, but a mob no longer; just a lot of frightened shame-faced children. A minute after the snow-goose had appeared, the last of the children left the temple and the only sound was the rush of air in the branches of the circling witches above.

Will looked up in wonder, too amazed to speak, but Lyra was leaping and calling with delight:

"Serafina Pekkala! How did you find us? Thank you, thank you! They was going to kill us! Come down and land..."

But Serafina and the others shook their heads, and flew up again, to circle high above. The snow-goose dæmon wheeled and flew down towards the roof, beating his great wings inwards to help him slow down, and landed with a clatter on the pantiles below the sill.

"Greetings, Lyra," he said. "Serafina Pekkala can't come to the ground, and nor can the others. The place is full of Spectres – a hundred or more surrounding the building, and more drifting up over the grass. Can't you see them?"

"No! We can't see 'em at all!"

"Already we've lost one witch. We can't risk any more. Can you get down from this building?"

"If we jump off the roof like they done. But how did you find us? And where –"

"Enough now. There's more trouble coming, and bigger. Get down as best you can and then make for the trees."

They climbed over the sill and moved sideways down through the broken tiles to the gutter. It wasn't high, and below it was grass, with a gentle slope away from the building. First Lyra jumped and then Will followed, rolling over and trying to protect his hand, which was bleeding freely again and hurting badly. His sling had come loose and trailed behind him, and as he tried to roll it up, the snow-goose landed on the grass at his side.

"Lyra, who is this?" Kaisa said.

"It's Will. He's coming with us –"

"Why are the Spectres avoiding you?" The goose-dæmon was speaking directly to Will.

By this time Will was hardly surprised by anything, and he said, "I don't know. We can't see them. No, wait!" And he stood up, struck by a thought. "Where are they now?" he said. "Where's the nearest one?"

"Ten paces away, down the slope," said the dæmon. "They don't want to come any closer, that's obvious."

Will took the knife out and looked in that direction, and he heard the dæmon hiss with surprise.

But Will couldn't do what he intended, because at the same moment a witch landed her branch on the grass beside him. He was taken aback not so much by her flying as by her astounding gracefulness, the fierce cold lovely clarity of her gaze, and by the pale bare limbs, so youthful, and yet so far from being young.

"Your name is Will?" she said.

"Yes, but –"

"Why are the Spectres afraid of you?"

"Because of the knife. Where's the nearest one? Tell me! I want to kill it!"

But Lyra came running before the witch could answer.

"Serafina Pekkala!" she cried, and she threw her arms around the witch and hugged her so tightly that the witch laughed out loud, and kissed the top of her head. "Oh, Serafina, where did you come from like that? We were – those kids – they were *kids*, and they were going to kill us – did you see them? We thought we were going to die, and – oh, I'm so glad you came! I thought I'd never see you again!"

Serafina Pekkala looked over Lyra's head to where the Spectres were obviously clustering a little way off, and then looked at Will.

"Now listen," she said, "there's a cave in these woods not far away. Head up the slope and then along the ridge to the left. We might be able to carry Lyra for a little way, but you're too big: you'll have to go on foot. The Spectres won't follow – they don't see us while we're in the air, and they're afraid of you. We'll meet you there – it's a half-hour walk."

And she leapt into the air again. Will shaded his eyes to watch her and the other ragged elegant figures wheel in the air and dart up over the trees.

"Oh, Will, we'll be safe now! It'll be all right now Serafina Pekkala's here!" said Lyra. "I never thought I'd see her again – she came just at the right time, didn't she? Just like before, at Bolvangar . . ."

Chattering happily, as if she'd already forgotten the fight, she led the way up the slope towards the forest. Will followed in silence. His hand was throbbing badly, and with each throb a little more blood was leaving him. He held it up across his chest and tried not to think about it.

It took not half an hour but an hour and three-quarters, because Will had to stop and rest several times. When they reached the cave they found a fire, a rabbit roasting, and Serafina Pekkala stirring something in a small iron pot.

"Let me see your wound," was the first thing she said to Will, and he dumbly held out his hand.

Pantalaimon, cat-formed, watched curiously, but Will looked away. He didn't like the sight of his mutilated fingers.

The witches spoke softly to each other, and then Serafina Pekkala said, "What weapon made this wound?"

Will reached for the knife and handed it to her silently. Her companions looked at it with wonder and suspicion, for they had never seen such a blade before, with such an edge on it.

"This will need more than herbs to heal. It will need a spell," said Serafina Pekkala. "Very well, we'll prepare one. It will be ready when the moon rises. In the meantime, you shall sleep."

She gave him a little horn cup, containing a hot potion whose bitterness was moderated by honey, and presently he lay back and fell deeply asleep. The witch covered him with leaves, and turned to Lyra, who was still gnawing the rabbit.

"Now, Lyra," she said, "tell me who this boy is, and what you know about this world, and about this knife of his."

So Lyra took a deep breath and began.

12

SCREEN LANGUAGE

"TELL ME AGAIN," said Dr Oliver Payne, in the little laboratory overlooking the park. "Either I didn't hear you or you're talking nonsense. A child from another world?"

"That's what she said. All right, it's nonsense, but *listen* to it, Oliver, will you?" said Dr Mary Malone. "She knew about Shadows. She calls them – it – she calls it Dust, but it's the same thing. It's our Shadow-particles. And I'm telling you, when she was wearing the electrodes linking her to the Cave, there was the most extraordinary display on the screen: pictures, symbols . . . She had an instrument too, a sort of compass thing made of gold, with different symbols all round the rim. And she said she could read that in the same way, and she knew about the state of mind, too, she knew it intimately."

It was mid-morning. Lyra's scholar Dr Malone was red-eyed from lack of sleep, and her colleague, who'd just returned from Geneva, was impatient to hear more, and sceptical, and preoccupied.

"And the point was, Oliver, she was communicating with them. They *are* conscious. And they can respond. And you remember your skulls? Well, she told me about some skulls in the Pitt-Rivers Museum – she'd found out with her compass thing that they were much older than the Museum said, and there were Shadows –"

"Wait a minute. Give me some sort of *structure* here. What are you saying? You saying she's confirmed what we know already, or that she's telling us something new?"

"Both. I don't know. But suppose something happened thirty, forty thousand years ago. There were Shadow-particles around before then, obviously – they've been around since the Big Bang – but there was no physical way of amplifying their effects at *our* level, the anthropic level. The level of human beings. And then something happened, I can't imagine what, but it involved evolution. Hence your skulls – remember? No Shadows before that time, lots afterwards? And the skulls the child found in the Museum, that she tested with her compass-thing. She told me the same thing. What I'm saying is that around that time, the human brain became the ideal vehicle for this amplification process. Suddenly we became conscious."

Dr Payne tilted his plastic mug and drank the last of his coffee.

"Why should it happen particularly at that time?" he said. "Why suddenly thirty-five thousand years ago?"

"Oh, who can say? We're not palaeontologists. I don't know, Oliver, I'm just speculating. Don't you think it's at least possible?"

"And this policeman. Tell me about him."

Dr Malone rubbed her eyes. "His name was Walters," she said. "He said he was from the Special Branch. I thought that was politics or something?"

"Terrorism, subversion, intelligence . . . All that. Go on. What did he want? Why did he come here?"

"Because of the girl. He said he was looking for a boy of about the same age, he didn't tell me why, and this boy had been seen in the company of the girl who came here. But he had something else in mind as well, Oliver, he *knew* about the research, he even asked –"

The telephone rang. She broke off, shrugging, and Dr Payne answered it. He spoke briefly and put it down, and said, "We've got a visitor."

"Who?"

"Not a name I know. Sir Somebody Something. Listen, Mary, I'm off, you realize that, don't you?"

"They offered you the job."

"Yes. I've got to take it. You must see that."

"Well, that's the end of this, then."

He spread his hands helplessly, and said, "To be frank . . . I can't see any point in the sort of stuff you've just been talking about. Children from another world and fossil Shadows . . . It's all too crazy. I just can't get involved. I've got a career, Mary."

"What about the skulls you tested? What about the Shadows around the ivory figurine?"

He shook his head and turned his back. Before he could answer, there came a tap at the door, and he opened it almost with relief.

Sir Charles said, "Good day to you. Dr Payne? Dr Malone? My name is Charles Latrom. It's very good of you to see me without any notice."

"Come in," said Dr Malone, weary, but puzzled. "Did Oliver say *Sir* Charles? What can we do for you?"

"It may be what I can do for you," he said. "I understand you're waiting for the results of your funding application."

"How do you know that?" said Dr Payne.

"I used to be a civil servant. As a matter of fact I was concerned with directing scientific policy. I still have a number of contacts in the field, and I heard . . . May I sit down?"

"Oh, please," said Dr Malone. She pulled out a chair, and he sat down as if he were in charge of a meeting.

"Thank you. I heard through a friend – I'd better not mention his name; the Official Secrets Act covers all sorts of silly things – I heard that your application was being considered, and what I heard about it intrigued me so much that I must confess I asked to see some of your work. I know I had no business to, except that I still act as a sort of unofficial adviser, so I used that as an excuse. And really, what I saw was quite fascinating."

"Does that mean you think we'll be successful?" said Dr Malone, leaning forward, eager to believe him.

"Unfortunately, no. I must be blunt. They're not minded to renew your grant."

Dr Malone's shoulders slumped. Dr Payne was watching the old man with cautious curiosity.

"Why have you come here now, then?" he said.

"Well, you see, they haven't officially made the decision yet. It doesn't look promising, and I'm being frank with you: they see no prospect of funding work of this sort in the future. However, it might be that if you had someone to argue the case for you, they would see it differently."

"An advocate? You mean yourself? I didn't think it worked

like that," said Dr Malone, sitting up. "I thought they went on peer review and so on . . ."

"It does in principle, of course," said Sir Charles, "but it also helps to know how these committees work in practice. And to know who's on them. Well, here I am. I'm intensely interested in your work, I think it might be very valuable, and it certainly ought to continue. Would you let me make informal representations on your behalf?"

Dr Malone felt like a drowning sailor being thrown a lifebelt. "Why . . . Well, yes! Good grief, of course! And thank you . . . I mean, do you really think it'll make a difference? I don't mean to suggest that . . . I don't know what I mean. Yes, of course!"

"What would we have to do?" said Dr Payne.

Dr Malone looked at him in surprise. Hadn't Oliver just said he was going to work in Geneva? But he seemed to be understanding Sir Charles better than she was, for a flicker of complicity was passing between them, and Oliver came to sit down too.

"I'm glad you take my point," said the old man. "You're quite right. There is a direction I'd be especially glad to see you taking. And provided we could agree, I might even be able to find you some extra money from another source altogether."

"Wait, wait," said Dr Malone, "wait a minute. The course of this research is a matter for us. I'm perfectly willing to discuss the results, but not the direction. Surely you see –"

Sir Charles spread his hands in a gesture of regret and got to his feet. Oliver Payne stood too, anxious.

"No, please, Sir Charles," he said, "I'm sure Dr Malone will hear you out. Mary, there's no harm in listening, for goodness' sake. And it might make all the difference."

"I thought you were going to Geneva?" she said.

"Geneva?" said Sir Charles. "Excellent place. Lot of scope there. Lot of money, too. Don't let me hold you back."

"No, no, it's not settled yet," said Dr Payne hastily. "There's a lot to discuss – it's all still very fluid. Sir Charles, please sit down. Can I get you some coffee?"

"That would be very kind," said Sir Charles, and sat again, with the air of a satisfied cat.

Dr Malone looked at him clearly for the first time. She saw a man in his late sixties, prosperous, confident, beautifully dressed, used to the very best of everything, used to moving among powerful people and whispering in important ears. Oliver was right: he did want something. And they wouldn't get his support unless they satisfied him.

She folded her arms.

Dr Payne handed him a mug, saying, "Sorry it's rather primitive . . ."

"Not at all. Shall I go on with what I was saying?"

"Do, please," said Dr Payne.

"Well, I understand that you've made some fascinating discoveries in the field of consciousness. Yes, I know, you haven't published anything yet, and it's a long way – seemingly – from the apparent subject of your research. Nevertheless, word gets around. And I'm especially interested in that. I would be very pleased if, for example, you were to concentrate your researches towards the manipulation of consciousness. Secondly, the many-worlds hypothesis – Everett, you remember, 1957 or thereabouts; I believe you're on the track of something that could take that theory a good deal further. And that line of research might even attract defence funding, which as you may know is still plentiful, even today, and certainly isn't subject to these wearisome application processes.

"Don't expect me to reveal my sources," he went on, holding up his hand as Dr Malone sat forward and tried to speak. "I mentioned the Official Secrets Act; a tedious piece of legislation, but we mustn't be naughty about it. I confidently expect some advances in the many-worlds area. I think you are the people to do it. And thirdly, there is a particular matter connected with an individual. A child."

He paused there, and sipped the coffee. Dr Malone couldn't speak. She'd gone pale, though she couldn't know that, but she did know that she felt faint.

"For various reasons," Sir Charles went on, "I am in contact with the intelligence services. They are interested in a child, a girl, who has an unusual piece of equipment, an antique scientific instrument, certainly stolen, which should be in safer hands than hers. There is also a boy of roughly the same age – twelve or so

– who is wanted in connection with a murder. It's a moot point whether a child of that age is capable of murder, of course, but he has certainly killed someone. And he has been seen with the girl.

"Now, Dr Malone, it may be that you have come across one or other of these children. And it may be that you are quite properly inclined to tell the police about what you know. But you would be doing a greater service if you were to let me know privately. I can make sure the proper authorities deal with it efficiently and quickly and with no stupid tabloid publicity. I know that Inspector Walters came to see you yesterday, and I know that the girl turned up – you see, I do know what I'm talking about. I would know, for instance, if you saw her again, and if you didn't tell me, I would know that too. You'd be very wise to think hard about that, and to clarify your recollections of what she said and did when she was here. This is a matter of national security. You understand me.

"Well, there I'll stop. Here's my card so you can get in touch. I shouldn't leave it too long; the funding committee meets tomorrow, as you know. But you can reach me on this number at any time."

He gave a card to Oliver Payne and, seeing Dr Malone with her arms still folded, laid one on the bench for her. Dr Payne held the door for him. Sir Charles set his Panama hat on his head, patted it gently, beamed at them both, and left.

When he'd shut the door again, Dr Payne said, "Mary, are you mad? Where's the sense in behaving like that?"

"I beg your pardon? You're not taken in by that old creep, are you?"

"You can't turn down offers like that! Do you want this project to survive or not?"

"It wasn't an offer," she said hotly, "it was an ultimatum. Do as he says, or close down. And Oliver, for God's sake, all those not-so-subtle threats and hints about national security and so on – can't you see where that would lead?"

"Well, I think I can see it more clearly than you can. If you said no, they wouldn't close this place down. They'd take it over. If they're as interested as he says, they'll want it to carry on. But only on their terms."

"But their terms would be . . . I mean, *defence* for God's sake – they want to find new ways of killing people. And you heard what he said about consciousness: he wants to *manipulate* it. I'm not going to get mixed up in that, Oliver, never."

"They'll do it anyway, and you'll be out of a job. If you stay, you might be able to influence it in a better direction. And you'd still have your hands on the work! You'd still be involved!"

"But what does it matter to you, anyway?" she said. "I thought Geneva was all settled?"

He ran his hands through his hair and said, "Well, not settled. Nothing's signed. And it would be a different angle altogether, and I'd be sorry to leave here now I think we're really on to something . . ."

"What are you saying?"

"I'm not saying –"

"You're hinting. What are you getting at?"

"Well . . ." He walked around the laboratory, spreading his hands, shrugging, shaking his head. "Well, if you don't get in touch with him, I will," he said finally.

She was silent. Then she said, "Oh, I see."

"Mary, I've got to think of –"

"Of course you have."

"It's not that –"

"No, no."

"You don't understand –"

"Yes I do. It's very simple. You promise to do as he says, you get the funding, I leave, you take over as Director. It's not hard to understand. You'd have a bigger budget. Lots of nice new machines. Half a dozen more Ph.D.s under you. Good idea. You do it, Oliver. You go ahead. But that's it for me, I'm off. It stinks."

"You haven't . . ."

But her expression silenced him. She took off her white coat and hung it on the door, gathered a few papers into a bag, and left without a word. As soon as she'd gone, he took Sir Charles's card and picked up the phone.

Several hours later, just before midnight in fact, Dr Malone parked her car outside the science building and let herself in at the side entrance. But just as she turned to climb the stairs, a man came out of another corridor, startling her so much she nearly dropped her briefcase. He was wearing uniform.

"Where are you going?" he said.

He stood in the way, bulky, his eyes hardly visible under the low brim of his cap.

"I'm going to my laboratory. I work here. Who are you?" she said, a little angry, a little frightened.

"Security. Have you got some ID?"

"What security? I left this building at three o'clock this afternoon and there was only a porter on duty, as usual. I should be asking you for identification. Who appointed you? And why?"

"Here's my ID," said the man, showing her a card, too quickly for her to read it. "Where's yours?"

She noticed he had a mobile phone in a holster at his hip. Or was it a gun? No, surely, she was being paranoid. And he hadn't answered her questions. But if she persisted she'd make him suspicious, and the important thing now was to get into the lab: soothe him like a dog, she thought. She fumbled through her bag and found her wallet.

"Will this do?" she said, showing him the card she used to operate the barrier in the car park.

He looked at it briefly.

"What are you doing here at this time of night?" he said.

"I've got an experiment running. I have to check the computer periodically."

He seemed to be searching for a reason to forbid her, or perhaps he was just exercising his power. Finally he nodded and stood aside. She went past, smiling at him, but his face remained blank.

When she reached the laboratory she was still trembling. There had never been any more "security" in this building than a lock on the door and an elderly porter, and she knew why the change had come about. But it meant that she had very little time: she'd have to get it right at once, because once they realized what she was doing, she wouldn't be able to come back again.

She locked the door behind her and lowered the blinds. She switched on the detector and then took a floppy disk from her pocket and slipped it into the computer that controlled the Cave, and within a minute she had begun to manipulate the numbers on the screen, going half by logic, half by guesswork, and half by the program she'd worked on all evening at home; and the complexity of her task was about as baffling as getting three halves to make one whole.

Finally she brushed the hair out of her eyes and put the electrodes on her head, and then flexed her fingers and began to type. She felt intensely self-conscious.

```
Hello. I'm not sure what I'm doing.
Maybe this is crazy.
```

The words arranged themselves on the left of the screen, which was the first surprise. She wasn't using a word-processing program of any kind – in fact she was by-passing much of the operating system – and whatever formatting was imposing itself on the words, it wasn't hers. She felt the hairs begin to stir on the back of her neck, and she became aware of the whole of the building around her, the corridors dark, the machines idling, various experiments running automatically, computers monitoring tests and recording the results, the air-conditioning sampling and adjusting the humidity and the temperature, all the ducts and pipework and cabling that were the arteries and the nerves of the building awake and alert . . . almost conscious, in fact.

She tried again.

```
I'm trying to do with words what I've done
before with a state of mind, but
```

Before she had even finished the sentence the cursor raced across to the right of the screen and printed:

```
                              Ask a question.
```

It was almost instantaneous.

She felt as if she had stepped on a space that wasn't there. Her whole being lurched with shock. It took several moments for her to calm down enough to try again. When she did, the answers lashed themselves across the right of the screen almost before she had finished.

Are you Shadows?	Yes.
Are you the same as Lyra's Dust?	Yes.
And is that dark matter?	Yes.
Dark matter is conscious?	Evidently.
What I said to Oliver this morning, my idea about human evolution, is it	Correct. But you need to ask more questions.

She stopped, took a deep breath, pushed her chair back, flexed her fingers. She could feel her heart racing. Every single thing about what was happening was impossible: all her education, all her habits of mind, all her sense of herself as a scientist were shrieking at her silently: this is wrong! It isn't happening! You're dreaming! And yet there they were on the screen: her questions, and answers from some other mind.

She gathered herself and typed again, and again the answers zipped into being with no discernible pause.

The mind that is answering these questions isn't human, is it?	No. But humans have always known us.
Us? There's more than one of you?	Uncountable billions.
But what are you?	Angels.

Mary Malone's head rang. She'd been brought up as a Catholic. More than that: as Lyra had discovered, she had once been a nun. None of her faith was left to her now, but she knew about angels. St Augustine had said, "Angel is the name of their office, not of their nature. If you seek the name of their nature, it is spirit; if you seek the name of their office, it is angel; from what they are, spirit, from what they do, angel."

Dizzy, trembling, she typed again:

Angels are creatures of Shadow-matter? Of Dust?	Structures. Complexifications. Yes.
And Shadow-matter is what we have called spirit?	From what we are, spirit; from what we do, matter. Matter and spirit are one.

She shivered. They'd been listening to her thoughts.

And did you intervene in human evolution?	Yes.
Why?	Vengeance.
Vengeance for — oh! Rebel angels! After the war in Heaven — Satan and the garden of Eden — but it isn't true, is it? Is that what you — but why?	Find the girl and the boy. Waste no more time. You must play the serpent.

She took her hands from the keyboard and rubbed her eyes. The words were still there when she looked again.

Where	Go to a road called Sunderland Avenue and find a tent. Deceive the guardian and go through. Take provisions for a long journey. You will be protected. The Spectres will not touch you.
But I	Before you go, destroy this equipment.

I don't understand — why me? And what's this journey? And	You have been preparing for this as long as you have lived. Your work here is finished. The last thing you must do in this world is prevent the enemies from taking control of it. Destroy the equipment. Do it now and go at once.

Mary Malone pushed back the chair and stood up, trembling. She pressed her fingers to her temples and discovered the electrodes still attached to her skin. She took them off absently. She might have doubted what she had done, and what she could still see on the screen, but she had passed in the last half-hour or so beyond doubt and belief altogether. Something had happened, and she was galvanized.

She switched off the detector and the amplifier. Then she bypassed all the safety codes and formatted the computer's hard disk, wiping it clean; and then she removed the interface between the detector and the amplifier, which was on a specially-adapted card, and put the card on the bench and smashed it with the heel of her shoe, there being nothing else heavy to hand. Next she disconnected the wiring between the electromagnetic shield and the detector, and found the wiring plan in a drawer of the filing cabinet and set light to it. Was there anything else she could do? She couldn't do much about Oliver Payne's knowledge of the program, but the special hardware was effectively demolished.

She crammed some papers from a drawer into her briefcase, and finally took down the poster with the I Ching hexagrams and folded it away in her pocket. Then she switched out the light and left.

The security guard was standing at the foot of the stairs, speaking into his telephone. He put it away as she came down and escorted her silently to the side entrance, watching through the glass door as she drove away.

* * *

An hour and a half later she drew up her car in a road near Sunderland Avenue. She had had to find it on a map of Oxford; she didn't know this part of town. Up till this moment she had been moving on pent-up excitement, but as she got out of her car in the dark of the small hours, and found the night cool and silent and still all round her, she felt a definite lurch of apprehension. Suppose she was dreaming? Suppose it was all some elaborate joke?

Well, it was too late to worry about that. She was committed. She lifted out the rucksack she'd often taken on camping journeys in Scotland and the Alps, and reflected that at least she knew how to survive out of doors; if the worst came to the worst, she could always run away, take to the hills . . .

Ridiculous.

But she swung the rucksack on to her back, and left the car and turned into the Banbury Road, and walked the two or three hundred yards up to where Sunderland Avenue ran left from the roundabout. She felt almost more foolish than she had ever felt in her life.

But as she turned the corner and saw those strange childlike trees that Will had seen, she knew that something at least was true about all this. Under the trees on the grass at the far side of the road there was a small square tent of red and white nylon, the sort that electricians put up to keep the rain off while they work, and parked close by was an unmarked white Transit van with darkened glass in the windows.

Better not hesitate. She walked straight across towards the tent. When she was nearly there, the back door of the van swung open, and a policeman stepped out. Without his helmet he looked very young, and the street lamp under the dense green of the leaves above shone full in his face.

"Could I ask where you're going, madam?" he said.

"Into the tent."

"I'm afraid you can't, madam. I've got orders not to let anyone near it."

"Good," she said, "I'm glad they've got the place protected. But I'm from the Department of Physical Sciences – Sir Charles Latrom asked us to make a preliminary survey and then report back before they look at it properly. It's important that it's done now while there aren't many people around – I'm sure you understand the reasons for that."

"Well, yes," he said. "But have you got anything to show who you are?"

"Oh, sure," she said, and swung the rucksack off her back to get at her purse. Among the items she had taken from the drawer in the laboratory was an expired library card of Oliver Payne's. Fifteen minutes' work at her kitchen table and the photograph from her own passport had produced something she hoped would pass for genuine. The policeman took the laminated card and looked at it closely.

"Dr Olive Payne," he read. "Do you happen to know a Dr Mary Malone?"

"Oh, yes. She's a colleague."

"Do you know where she is now?"

"At home in bed, if she's got any sense. Why?"

"Well, I understand her position in your organization's been terminated, and she wouldn't be allowed through here. In fact we've got orders to detain her if she tries. And seeing a woman, I naturally thought you might be her, if you see what I mean. Excuse me, Dr Payne."

"Ah, I see," said Mary Malone.

The policeman looked at the card once more.

"Still, this seems all right," he said, and handed it back. Nervous, wanting to talk, he went on: "Do you know what's in there under that tent?"

"Well, not at first hand," she said. "That's why I'm here now."

"I suppose it is. All right then, Dr Payne."

He stood back and let her unlace the flap of the tent. She hoped he wouldn't see the shaking of her hands. Clutching the rucksack to her breast, she stepped through. *Deceive the guardian* – well, she'd done that; but she had no idea what she would find inside the tent. She was prepared for some sort of archaeological dig; for a dead body; for a meteorite; but nothing in her life or her dreams had prepared her for that square metre or so in mid-air, or for the silent sleeping city by the sea that she found when she stepped through it.

13
ÆSAHÆTTR

AS THE MOON ROSE, the witches began their spell to heal Will's wound.

They woke him and asked him to lay the knife on the ground where it caught a glitter of starlight. Lyra sat nearby stirring some herbs in a pot of boiling water over a fire, and while her companions clapped and stamped and cried in rhythm, Serafina crouched over the knife and sang in a high fierce tone:

> "Little knife! They tore your iron
> out of mother earth's entrails,
> built a fire and boiled the ore,
> made it weep and bleed and flood,
> hammered it and tempered it,
> plunging it in icy water,
> heating it inside the forge
> till your blade was blood-red, scorching!
> Then they made you wound the water
> once again, and yet again,
> till the steam was boiling fog
> and the water cried for mercy.
> And when you sliced a single shade
> into thirty thousand shadows,
> then they knew that you were ready,
> then they called you subtle one.
> But little knife, what have you done?
> Unlocked blood-gates, left them wide!
> Little knife, your mother calls you,
> from the entrails of the earth,
> from her deepest mines and caverns,
> from her secret iron womb.
> Listen!"

And Serafina stamped again and clapped her hands with the other witches, and they shook their throats to make a wild ululation that tore at the air like claws. Will, seated in the middle of them, felt a chill at the core of his spine.

Then Serafina Pekkala turned to Will himself, and took his wounded hand in both of hers. When she sang this time he nearly flinched, so fierce was her high clear voice, so glittering her eyes; but he sat without moving, and let the spell go on.

> "Blood! Obey me! Turn around,
> be a lake and not a river.
> When you reach the open air,
> stop! And build a clotted wall,
> build it firm to hold the flood back.
> Blood, your sky is the skull-dome,
> your sun is the open eye,
> your wind the breath inside the lungs,
> blood, your world is bounded. Stay there!"

Will thought he could feel all the atoms of his body responding to her command, and he joined in, urging his leaking blood to listen and obey.

She put his hand down and turned to the little iron pot over the fire. A bitter steam was rising from it, and Will heard the liquid bubbling fiercely.

Serafina sang:

> "Oak bark, spider-silk,
> ground-moss, saltweed –
> grip close, bind tight,
> hold fast, close up,
> bar the door, lock the gate,
> stiffen the blood-wall,
> dry the gore-flood."

Then the witch took her own knife and split an alder sapling along its whole length. The wounded whiteness gleamed open in the moon. She daubed some of the steaming liquid into the split, and closed up the wood, easing it together from the root to the tip. And the sapling was whole again.

Will heard Lyra gasp, and turned to see another witch holding a squirming struggling hare in her tough hands. The animal was panting, wild-eyed, kicking furiously, but the witch's hands were merciless. In one she held its forelegs and with the other she grasped its hind legs and pulled the frenzied hare out straight, its heaving belly upwards.

Serafina's knife swept across it. Will felt himself grow dizzy, and Lyra was restraining Pantalaimon, hare-formed himself in sympathy, who was bucking and snapping in her arms. The real hare fell still, eyes bulging, breast heaving, entrails glistening.

But Serafina took some more of the decoction and trickled it into the gaping wound, and then closed the wound up with her fingers, smoothing the wet fur over it until there was no wound at all.

The witch holding the animal relaxed her grip and let it gently to the ground, where it shook itself, turned to lick its flank, flicked its ears, and nibbled a blade of grass as if it were completely alone. Suddenly it seemed to become aware of the circle of humans around it, and like an arrow it shot away, whole again, bounding swiftly off into the dark.

Lyra, soothing Pantalaimon, glanced at Will and saw that he knew what it meant: the medicine was ready. He held out his hand, and as Serafina daubed the steaming mixture on the bleeding stumps of his fingers he looked away and breathed in sharply several times, but he didn't flinch.

Once his open flesh was thoroughly soaked, the witch pressed some of the sodden herbs on to the wounds and tied them tight around with a strip of silk.

And that was it; the spell was done.

Will slept deeply through the rest of the night. It was cold, but the witches piled leaves over him, and Lyra slept huddled close behind his back. In the morning Serafina dressed his wound again, and he tried to see from her expression whether it was healing, but her face was calm and impassive.

Once they'd eaten, Serafina told the children that the witches had agreed that since they'd come into this world to find Lyra and be her guardian, they'd help Lyra do what she now knew her task to be: namely, to guide Will to his father.

So they set off; and it was quiet going for the most part. Lyra consulted the alethiometer to begin with, but warily, and learned that they should travel in the direction of the distant mountains they could see across the great bay. Never having been this high above the city, they weren't aware of how the coastline curved, and the mountains had been below the horizon; but now when the trees thinned, or when a slope fell away below them, they could look out to the empty blue sea and to the high blue mountains beyond which were their destination. It seemed a long way to go.

They spoke little. Lyra was busy looking at all the life in the forest, from woodpeckers to squirrels to little green moss-snakes with diamonds down their backs, and Will needed all his energy simply to keep going. Lyra and Pantalaimon discussed him endlessly.

"We *could* look at the alethiometer," Pantalaimon said at one point, when they'd dawdled on the path to see how close they could get to a browsing fawn before it saw them. "We never promised not to. And we could find out all kinds of things for him. We'd be doing it for him, not for us."

"Don't be stupid," Lyra said. "It *would* be us we'd be doing it for, 'cause he'd never ask. You're just greedy and nosy, Pan."

"That makes a change. It's normally you who's greedy and nosy and me who has to warn you not to do things. Like in the retiring room at Jordan. I never wanted to go in there."

"If we hadn't, Pan, d'you think all this would have happened?"

"No. 'Cause the Master would have poisoned Lord Asriel and that would've been the end of it."

"Yeah, I suppose . . . Who d'you think Will's father is, though? And why's he important?"

"That's what I mean! We could find out in a moment!"

And she looked wistful. "I might have done once," she said, "but I'm changing, I think, Pan."

"No you're not."

"*You* might not be ... Hey, Pan, when I change, you'll stop changing. What're you going to be?"

"A flea, I hope."

"No, but don't you get *any* feelings about what you might be?"

"No. I don't want to either."

"You're sulking because I won't do what you want."

He changed into a pig and grunted and squealed and snorted till she laughed at him, and then he changed into a squirrel and darted through the branches beside her.

"Who do *you* think his father is?" Pantalaimon said. "D'you think he could be anyone we've met?"

"Could be. But he's bound to be someone important, almost as important as Lord Asriel. Bound to be. We know what *we're* doing is important, after all."

"We don't know it," Pantalaimon pointed out. "We think it is, but we don't know. We just decided to look for Dust because Roger died."

"We *know* it's important!" Lyra said hotly, and she even stamped. "And so do the witches. They come all this way to look for us just to be my guardian and help me! And we got to help Will find his father. *That's* important. You know it is, too, else you wouldn't have licked him when he was wounded. Why'd you do that, anyway? You never asked me if you could. I couldn't believe it when you did that."

"I did it because he didn't have a dæmon, and he needed one. And if you were half as good at seeing things as you think you are, you'd've known that."

"I did know it really," she said.

They stopped then, because they caught up with Will, who was sitting on a rock beside the path. Pantalaimon became a fly-catcher, and as he flew among the branches, Lyra said, "Will, what d'you think those kids'll do now?"

"They won't be following us. They were too frightened of the witches. Maybe they'll just go back to drifting about."

"Yeah, probably ... They might want to use the knife, though. They might come after us for that."

"Let them. They're not having it, not now. I didn't want it at first. But if it can kill the Spectres ..."

"I never trusted Angelica, not from the beginning," Lyra said virtuously.

"Yes you did," he said.

"Yeah. I did really . . . I hated it in the end, that city."

"I thought it was heaven, when I first found it. I couldn't imagine anything better than that. And all the time it was full of Spectres, and we never knew . . ."

"Well, I won't trust kids again," said Lyra. "I thought back at Bolvangar that whatever grown-ups did, however bad it was, kids were different. They wouldn't do cruel things like that. But I en't sure now. I never seen kids like that before, and that's a fact."

"I have," said Will.

"When? In your world?"

"Yeah," he said, awkwardly. Lyra waited and sat still, and presently he went on: "It was when my mother was having one of her bad times. She and me, we lived on our own, see, because obviously my father wasn't there. And every so often she'd start thinking things that weren't true. And having to do things that didn't make sense, not to me, anyway. I mean she had to do them or else get so upset she used to be afraid of everything and so I used to help her. Like touching all the railings in the park, or counting the leaves on a bush, that kind of thing. She used to get better after a while. But I was afraid of anyone finding out she was like that, because I thought they'd take her away, so I used to look after her and hide it. I never told anyone.

"And once she got afraid when I wasn't there to help her. I was at school. And she went out and she wasn't wearing very much, only she didn't know. And some boys from my school, they found her, and they started . . ."

Will's face was hot. Without being able to help it he found himself walking up and down and looking away from Lyra because his voice was unsteady and his eyes were watering. He went on:

"They were tormenting her just like those kids were at the Tower with the cat . . . They thought she was mad and they wanted to hurt her, maybe kill her, I wouldn't be surprised. She was just different and they hated her. Anyway I found her and I got her home. And next day in school I fought the boy who was leading them. I fought him and I broke his arm and I think I broke some of his teeth, I don't know. And I was going to fight the rest of them too but I got in trouble and I realized I better stop because they'd find out, I mean the teachers and the authorities, they'd go to my mother and complain about me and then they'd find out about how she was and take her away. So I just pretended to be sorry and told the teachers I wouldn't do it again, and they punished me for fighting and I still said nothing. But I kept her safe, see. No one knew apart from those boys and they knew what I'd do if they said anything; they knew I'd kill them another time. Not just hurt them. And a bit later she got better again. No one knew, ever.

"But after that I never trusted children any more than grown-ups. They're just as keen to do bad things. So I wasn't surprised when those kids in Ci'gazze did that.

"But I was glad when the witches came."

He sat down again with his back to Lyra, and still not looking at her he wiped his hand across his eyes. She pretended not to see.

"Will," she said, "what you said about your mother . . . And Tullio, when the Spectres got him . . . And when you said yesterday that you thought the Spectres came from your world . . ."

"Yes. Because it doesn't make sense, what was happening to her. She's not mad. Those kids might think she was mad and laugh at her and try and hurt her but they were wrong; she wasn't mad. Except that she was afraid of things I couldn't see. And she had to do things that looked crazy, you couldn't see the point of them, but obviously she could. Like her counting all the leaves, or Tullio yesterday touching the stones in the wall. Maybe that was a way of trying to put the Spectres off. If they turned their back on something frightening behind them and tried to get really interested in the stones and how they fitted together, or the leaves on the bush, like if only they could make themselves find that really important, they'd be safe. I don't know. It looks like that. There were real things for her to be frightened of, like those men who came and robbed us, but there was something else as well as them. So maybe we do have the Spectres in my world, only we can't see them and we haven't got a name for them, but they're there, and they keep trying to attack my mother. So that's why I was glad yesterday when the alethiometer said she was all right."

He was breathing fast, and his right hand was gripping the handle of the knife in its sheath. Lyra said nothing, and Pantalaimon kept very still.

"When did you know you had to look for your father?" she said after a while.

"A long time ago," he told her. "I used to pretend he was a prisoner and I'd help him escape. I had long games by myself doing that, it used to go on for days. Or else he was on this desert island and I'd sail there and bring him home. And he'd know exactly what to do about everything, about my mother, especially, and she'd get better and he'd look after her and me and I could just go to school and have friends and I'd have a mother and a father too. So I always said to myself that when I grew up I'd go and look for my father ... And my mother used to tell me that I was going to take up, my father's mantle. She used to say that to make me feel good. I didn't know what it meant, but it sounded important."

"Didn't you have friends?"

"How could I have friends?" he said, simply puzzled. "Friends ... They come to your house and they know your parents and ... Sometimes a boy might ask me round to his house, and I might go or I might not, but I could never ask them back. So I never had friends, really. I would have liked ... I had my cat," he went on. "I hope she's all right now. I hope someone's looking after her ..."

"What about the man you killed?" Lyra said, her heart beating hard. "Who was he?"

"I don't know. If I killed him, I don't care. He deserved it. There were two of them. They kept coming to the house and pestering my mother till she was afraid again, and worse than ever. They wanted to know all about my father, and they wouldn't leave her alone. I'm not sure if they were police or what. I thought at first they were part of a gang or something, and they thought my father had robbed a bank maybe and hidden the money. But they didn't want money, they wanted papers. They wanted some letters that my father had sent. They broke into the house one day and then I saw it would be safer if my mother was somewhere else. See, I couldn't go to the police and ask them for help, because they'd take my mother away. I didn't know what to do.

"So in the end I asked this old lady who used to teach me the piano. She was the only person I could think of. I asked her if my mother could stay with her and I took her there. I think she'll look after her all right. Anyway I went back to the house to look for these letters, because I knew where she kept them, and I got them and the men came to look and broke into the house again. It was night-time, or early morning. And I was hiding at the top of the stairs and Moxie, my cat Moxie, she came out of the bedroom and I didn't see her and nor did the man, and when I knocked into him she tripped him up and he fell right to the bottom of the stairs . . .

"And I ran away. That's all that happened. So I didn't mean to kill him, but I don't care if I did. I ran away and came to Oxford and then I found that window. And that only happened because I saw the other cat and stopped to watch her, and she found the window first. If I hadn't seen her . . . Or if Moxie hadn't come out of the bedroom then . . ."

"Yeah," said Lyra, "that was lucky. And me and Pan were thinking just now, what if I'd never gone into the wardrobe in the retiring room at Jordan and seen the Master put poison in the wine? None of this would have happened either . . ."

They both sat silent on the moss-covered rock, in the slant of sunlight through the old pines, and thought how many tiny chances had conspired to bring them to this place. Each of those chances might have gone a different way. Perhaps in another world, another Will had not seen the window in Sunderland Avenue, and had wandered on tired and lost towards the Midlands until he was caught. And in another world another Pantalaimon had persuaded another Lyra not to stay in the retiring room, and another Lord Asriel had been poisoned, and another Roger had survived to play with that Lyra for ever on the roofs and in the alleys of another unchanging Oxford.

Presently Will was strong enough to go on, and they moved together along the path, with the great forest quiet around them.

*   *   *

They travelled on through the day, resting, moving, resting again, as the trees grew thinner and the land more rocky. Lyra checked the alethiometer: keep going, it said; this is the right direction. At noon they came to a village untroubled by Spectres: goats pastured on the hillside, a grove of lemon trees cast shade on the stony ground, and children playing in the stream called out and ran for their mothers at the sight of the girl in the tattered clothing and the white-faced fierce-eyed boy in the bloodstained shirt, and the elegant greyhound that walked beside them.

The grown-ups were wary, but willing to sell some bread and cheese and fruit for one of Lyra's gold coins. The witches kept out of the way, though both children knew they'd be there in a second if any danger threatened. After another round of Lyra's bargaining one old woman sold them two flasks of goatskin and a fine linen shirt, and Will renounced his filthy T-shirt with relief, washing himself in the icy stream and lying to dry in the hot sun afterwards.

Refreshed, they moved on. The land was harsher now; for shade they had to rest in the shadow of rocks, not under wide-spreading trees, and the ground underfoot was hot through the soles of their shoes. The sun pounded at their eyes. They moved more and more slowly as they climbed, and when the sun touched the mountain-rims, and they saw a little valley open below them, they decided to go no further.

They scrambled down the slope, nearly losing their footing more than once, and then had to shove their way through thickets of dwarf rhododendrons, dark glossy leaves and crimson flower-clusters heavy with the hum of bees, before they came out in the evening shade on a wild meadow bordering a stream. The grass was knee-high and thick with cornflowers, gentians, cinquefoil.

Will drank deeply in the stream and then lay down. He couldn't stay awake, and he couldn't sleep either; his head was spinning, a daze of strangeness hung over everything, and his hand was sore and throbbing.

And what was worse, it had begun to bleed again.

Serafina looked at it, and put more herbs on the wound, and

tied the silk tighter than ever, but this time her face was troubled. He didn't want to question her, for what would be the point? It was plain to him that the spell hadn't worked, and he could see she knew it too.

As darkness fell he heard Lyra come to lie down close by, and presently he heard a soft purring. Her dæmon, cat-formed, was dozing with folded paws only a foot or two away from him, and Will whispered:

"Pantalaimon?"

The dæmon's eyes opened. Lyra didn't stir. Pantalaimon whispered, "Yes?"

"Pan, am I going to die?"

"The witches won't let you die. Nor will Lyra."

"But the spell didn't work. I keep losing blood. I can't have much left to lose. And it's bleeding again, and it won't stop. I'm frightened . . ."

"Lyra doesn't think you are."

"Doesn't she?"

"She thinks you're the bravest fighter she ever saw, as brave as Iorek Byrnison."

"I suppose I better try not to seem frightened, then," Will said. He was quiet for a minute or so, and then he said, "I think Lyra's braver than me. I think she's the best friend I ever had."

"She thinks that about you as well," whispered the dæmon.

Presently Will closed his eyes.

Lyra lay unmoving, but her eyes were wide open in the dark, and her heart was beating hard.

When Will next became aware of things it was completely dark, and his hand was hurting more than ever. He sat up carefully and saw a fire burning not far away, where Lyra was trying to toast some bread on a forked stick. There were a couple of birds roasting on a spit as well, and as Will came to sit nearby, Serafina Pekkala flew down.

"Will," she said, "eat these leaves before you have any other food."

She gave him a handful of soft bitter-tasting leaves somewhat like sage, and he chewed them silently and forced them down.

They were astringent, but he felt more awake and less cold, and the better for it.

They ate the roasted birds, seasoning them with lemon juice, and then another witch brought some blueberries she'd found below the scree, and then the witches gathered around the fire. They talked quietly; some of them had flown high up to spy, and one had seen a balloon over the sea. Lyra sat up at once.

"Mr Scoresby's balloon?" she said.

"There were two men in it, but it was too far away to see who they were. A storm was gathering behind them."

Lyra clapped her hands. "If Mr Scoresby's coming," she said, "we'll be able to fly, Will! Oh, I hope it's him! I never said good-bye to him, and he was so kind . . . I wish I could see him again, I really do . . ."

The witch Juta Kamainen was listening, with her red-breasted robin-dæmon bright-eyed on her shoulder, because the mention of Lee Scoresby had reminded her of the quest he'd set out on. She was the witch who had loved Stanislaus Grumman and whose love he'd turned down, the witch Serafina Pekkala had brought into this world to prevent her from killing him in their own.

Serafina might have noticed, but something else happened: she held up her hand and lifted her head, as did all the other witches. Will and Lyra could hear very faintly to the north the cry of some night bird. But it wasn't a bird: the witches knew it at once for a dæmon. Serafina Pekkala stood up, gazing intently into the sky.

"I think it's Ruta Skadi," she said.

They kept still, tilting their heads to the wide silence, straining to hear.

And then came another cry, closer already, and then a third; and at that, all the witches seized their branches and leapt into the air. All but two, that is, who stood close by, arrows at their bowstrings, guarding Will and Lyra.

Somewhere in the dark above, a fight was taking place. And only seconds later, it seemed, they could hear the rush of flight, the whiz of arrows, and the grunt and scream of voices raised in pain or anger or command.

And then with a thud so sudden they had no time to jump, a creature fell from the sky at their feet – a beast of leathery skin and matted fur that Lyra recognized as a cliff-ghast, or something similar.

It was broken by the fall, and an arrow protruded from its side, but still it lurched up and lunged with a flopping malice at Lyra. The witches couldn't shoot, because she was in their line of fire, but Will was there first, and with the knife he slashed back-hand and the creature's head came off and rolled over once or twice. The air left its lungs with a gurgling sigh and it fell dead.

They turned their eyes upwards again, for the fight was coming lower, and the firelight glaring up showed a swift-rushing swirl of black silk, pale limbs, green pine-needles, grey-brown scabby leather. How the witches could keep their balance in the sudden turns and halts and forward darts, let alone aim and shoot, was beyond Will's understanding.

Another cliff-ghast and then a third fell in the stream or on the rocks nearby, stark dead; and then the rest fled skirling and chittering into the dark towards the north.

A few moments later Serafina Pekkala landed with her own witches, and with another: a beautiful witch, fierce-eyed and black-haired, whose cheeks were flushed with anger and excitement.

The new witch saw the headless cliff-ghast and spat.

"Not from our world," she said, "nor from this. Filthy abominations. There are thousands of them breeding like flies . . . Who is this? Is this the child Lyra? And who is the boy?"

Lyra returned her gaze stolidly, though she felt a quickening of her heart, for Ruta Skadi lived so brilliantly in her nerves that she set up a responding thrill in the nerves of anyone close by.

Then the witch turned to Will, and he felt the same tingle of intensity, but like Lyra he controlled his expression. He still had the knife in his hand, and she saw what he'd done with it and smiled. He thrust it into the earth to clean it of the foul thing's blood and then rinsed it in the stream.

Ruta Skadi was saying, "Serafina Pekkala, I am learning so much; all the old things are changing, or dying, or empty. I'm hungry . . ."

She ate like an animal, tearing at the remains of the roasted birds and cramming handfuls of bread into her mouth, washing it down with deep gulps from the stream. While she ate, some of the witches carried the dead cliff-ghast away and rebuilt the fire, and then set up a watch.

The rest came to sit near Ruta Skadi, and to hear what she could tell them. She told what had happened when she flew up to meet the angels, and then of her journey to Lord Asriel's fortress.

"Sisters, it is the greatest castle you can imagine – ramparts of basalt, rearing to the skies, with wide roads coming from every direction, and on them cargoes of gunpowder, of food, of armour-plate; how has he done this? I think he must have been preparing this for a long time, for aeons. He was preparing this before we were born, sisters, even though he is so much younger . . . But how can that be? I don't know. I can't understand. I think he commands time, he makes it run fast or slow according to his will.

"And coming to this fortress are warriors of every kind, from every world. Men and women, yes, and fighting spirits too, and armed creatures such as I had never seen – lizards and apes, great birds with poison spurs, creatures too outlandish to have a name I could guess at. And other worlds have witches, sisters: did you know that? I spoke to witches from a world like ours, but profoundly different, for those witches live no longer than our short-lives, and there are men among them too, men-witches who fly as we do . . ."

Her tale was causing the witches of Serafina Pekkala's clan to listen with awe and fear and disbelief. But Serafina believed her, and urged her on.

"Did you see Lord Asriel, Ruta Skadi? Did you find your way to him?"

"Yes, I did, and it was not easy, because he lives at the centre of so many circles of activity, and he directs them all. But I made myself invisible and found my way to his inmost chamber, when he was preparing to sleep."

Every witch there knew what had happened next, and neither Will nor Lyra dreamed of it. So Ruta Skadi had no need to tell, and she went on:

"And then I asked him why he was bringing all these forces together, and if it was true what we'd heard about his challenge to the Authority, and he laughed.

" 'Do they speak of it in Siberia, then?' he said, and I told him yes, and on Svalbard, and in every region of the north – our north; and I told him of our pact, and how I'd left our world to seek him and find out.

"And he invited us to join him, sisters. To join his army against the Authority. I wished with all my heart I could pledge us there and then; I would have thrown my clan into the war with a happy heart. He showed me that to rebel was right and just, when you considered what the agents of the Authority did in his name ... And I thought of the Bolvangar children, and the other terrible mutilations I have seen in our own south-lands; and he told me of many more hideous cruelties dealt out in the Authority's name – of how they capture witches, in some worlds, and burn them alive, sisters, yes, witches like ourselves ...

"He opened my eyes. He showed me things I never had seen, cruelties and horrors all committed in the name of the Authority, all designed to destroy the joys and the truthfulness of life.

"Oh, sisters, I longed to throw myself and my whole clan into the cause!

"But I knew I must consult you first, and then fly back to our world and talk to Ieva Kasku and Reina Miti and the other witch-queens.

"So I left his chamber invisibly and found my cloud-pine and flew away. But before I'd flown far, a great wind came up and hurled me high into the mountains, and I had to take refuge on a cliff-top. Knowing the sort of creatures who live on cliffs I made myself invisible again, and in the darkness I heard voices.

"It seemed that I'd stumbled on the nesting-place of the oldest of all cliff-ghasts. He was blind, and they were bringing him food: some stinking carrion from far below. And they were asking him for guidance.

" 'Grandfather,' they said, 'how far back does your memory go?'

" 'Way, way back. Back long before humans,' he said, and his voice was soft and cracked and frail.

" 'Is it true that the greatest battle ever known is coming soon, grandfather?'

" 'Yes, children,' he said. 'A greater battle than the last one, even. Fine feasting for all of us. These will be days of pleasure and plenty for every ghast in every world.'

" 'And who's going to win, grandfather? Is Lord Asriel going to defeat the Authority?'

" 'Lord Asriel's army numbers millions,' the old cliff-ghast told them, 'assembled from every world. It's a greater army than the one that fought the Authority before, and it's better led. As for the forces of the Authority, why, they number a hundred times as many. But the Authority is age-old, far older even than me, children, and his troops are frightened, and complacent where they're not frightened. It would be a close fight, but Lord Asriel would win, because he is passionate and daring and he believes his cause is just. Except for one thing, children. He hasn't got Æsahættr. Without Æsahættr, he and all his forces will go down to defeat. And then we shall feast for years, my children!'

"And he laughed and gnawed the stinking old bone they'd brought to him, and the others all shrieked with glee.

"Now you can imagine how I listened hard to hear more about this Æsahættr, but all I could hear over the howling of the wind was a young ghast asking, 'If Lord Asriel needs Æsahættr, why doesn't he call him?'

"And the old ghast said, 'Lord Asriel knows no more about Æsahættr than you do, child! That is the joke! Laugh long and loud –'

"But as I tried to get closer to the foul things to learn more, my power failed, sisters, I couldn't hold myself invisible any longer. The younger ones saw me and shrieked out, and I had to flee, back into this world through the invisible gateway in the air. A flock of them came after me, and those are the last of them, dead over there.

"But it's clear that Lord Asriel needs us, sisters. Whoever this Æsahættr is, Lord Asriel needs us! I wish I could go back to Lord Asriel now and say, Don't be anxious – we're coming – we the witches of the north, and we shall help you win ... Let's agree now, Serafina Pekkala, and call a great council of all the witches, every single clan, and make war!"

Serafina Pekkala looked at Will, and it seemed to him that she was asking his permission for something. But he could give no guidance, and she looked back at Ruta Skadi.

"Not us," she said. "Our task now is to help Lyra, and her task is to guide Will to his father. You should fly back, agreed, but we must stay with Lyra."

Ruta Skadi tossed her head impatiently.

"Well, if you must," she said.

Will lay down, because his wound was hurting him – much more now than when it was fresh. His whole hand was swollen. Lyra too lay down, with Pantalaimon curled at her neck, and watched the fire through half-closed lids, and listened sleepily to the murmur of the witches.

Ruta Skadi walked a little way upstream, and Serafina Pekkala went with her.

"Ah, Serafina Pekkala, you should see Lord Asriel," said the Latvian queen quietly. "He is the greatest commander there ever was. Every detail of his forces is clear in his mind. Imagine the daring of it, to make war on the creator! But who do you think this Æsahættr can be? How have we not heard of him? And how can we urge him to join Lord Asriel?"

"Maybe it's not a *him*, sister. We know as little as the young cliff-ghast. Maybe the old grandfather was laughing at his ignorance. The word sounds as if it means *god-destroyer*. Did you know that?"

"Then it might mean us after all, Serafina Pekkala! And if it does, then how much stronger his forces will be when we do join them. Ah, I long for my arrows to kill those fiends from Bolvangar, and every Bolvangar in every world! Sister, why do they do it? In every world, the agents of the Authority are sacrificing children to their cruel god! Why? Why?"

"They are afraid of Dust," said Serafina Pekkala, "though what that is, I don't know."

"And this boy you've found. Who is he? What world does he come from?"

Serafina Pekkala told her all she knew about Will. "I don't

know why he's important," she finished, "but we serve Lyra. And her instrument tells that that is her task. And sister, we tried to heal his wound, but we failed. We tried the holding spell, and it didn't work. Maybe the herbs in this world are less potent than ours. It's too hot here for bloodmoss to grow . . ."

"He's strange," said Ruta Skadi. "He is the same kind as Lord Asriel. Have you looked into his eyes?"

"To tell the truth," said Serafina Pekkala, "I haven't dared."

The two queens sat quietly by the stream. Time went past; stars set, and other stars rose; a little cry came from the sleepers, but it was only Lyra dreaming. The witches heard the rumbling of a storm, and they saw the lightning play over the sea and the foothills, but it was a long way off.

Later Ruta Skadi said, "The girl, Lyra. What of the part she was supposed to play? Is this it? She's important because she can lead the boy to his father? It was more than that, wasn't it?"

"That's what she has to do now. But as for later, yes, far more than that. What we witches have said about the child is that she would put an end to destiny. Well, we know the name that would make her meaningful to Mrs Coulter, and we know that the woman doesn't know it. The witch she was torturing on the ship near Svalbard nearly gave it away, but Yambe-Akka came to her in time.

"But I'm thinking now that Lyra might be what you heard those generals speak of, this Æsahættr. Not the witches, not those angel-beings, but that sleeping child: the final weapon in the war against the Authority. Why else would Mrs Coulter be so anxious to find her?"

"Mrs Coulter was a lover of Lord Asriel's," said Ruta Skadi. "Of course, and Lyra is their child . . . Serafina Pekkala, if I had borne his child, what a witch she would be! A queen of queens!"

"Hush, sister," said Serafina. "Listen . . . and what's that light?"

They stood, alarmed that something had slipped past their guard, and saw a gleam of light from the camping-place: not fire-light though, nothing remotely like firelight.

They ran back on silent feet, arrows already nocked to their bowstrings, and stopped suddenly.

All the witches were asleep on the grass, and so were Will and

Lyra. But surrounding the two children were a dozen or more angels, gazing down at them.

And then Serafina understood something for which the witches had no word: it was the idea of pilgrimage. She understood why these beings would wait for thousands of years and travel vast distances in order to be close to something important, and how they would feel differently for the rest of time, having been briefly in its presence. That was how these creatures looked now, these beautiful pilgrims of rarefied light, standing around the girl with the dirty face and the tartan skirt and the boy with the wounded hand who was frowning in his sleep.

There was a stir at Lyra's neck. Pantalaimon, a snow-white ermine, opened his black eyes sleepily and gazed around unafraid. Later, Lyra would remember it as a dream. Pantalaimon seemed to accept the attention as Lyra's due, and presently he curled up again and closed his eyes.

Finally one of the creatures spread his wings wide. The others, as close as they were, did so too, and their wings interpenetrated with no resistance, sweeping through one another like light through light, until there was a circle of radiance around the sleepers on the grass.

Then the watchers took to the air, one after another, rising like flames into the sky and increasing in size as they did so, until they were immense; but already they were far away, moving like shooting stars towards the north.

Serafina and Ruta Skadi sprang to their pine-branches and followed them upwards, but they were left far behind.

"Were they like the creatures you saw, Ruta Skadi?" said Serafina as they slowed down in the middle airs, watching the bright flames diminish towards the horizon.

"Bigger, I think, but the same kind. They have no flesh, did you see that? All they are is light. Their senses must be so different from ours ... Serafina Pekkala, I'm leaving you now, to call all the witches of our north together. When we meet again, it will be wartime. Go well, my dear ..."

They embraced in mid-air, and Ruta Skadi turned and sped southwards.

Serafina watched her go, and then turned to see the last of the gleaming angels disappear far away. She felt nothing but compassion for those great watchers. How much they must miss, never to feel the earth beneath their feet, or the wind in their hair, or the tingle of the starlight on their bare skin! And she snapped a little twig off the pine-branch she flew with, and sniffed the sharp resin smell with greedy pleasure, before flying slowly downwards to join the sleepers on the grass.

14

ALAMO GULCH

LEE SCORESBY LOOKED down at the placid ocean to his left, the green shore to his right, and shaded his eyes to search for human life. It was a day and a night since they had left the Yenisei.

"And this is a new world?" he said.

"New to those not born in it," said Stanislaus Grumman. "As old as yours or mine, otherwise. What Asriel's done has shaken everything up, Mr Scoresby, shaken it more profoundly than it's ever been shaken before. These doorways and windows that I spoke of – they open in unexpected places now. It's hard to navigate, but this wind is a fair one."

"New or old, that's a strange world down there," said Lee.

"Yes," said Stanislaus Grumman. "It is a strange world, though no doubt some feel at home there."

"It looks empty," said Lee.

"Not so. Beyond that headland you'll find a city that was once powerful and wealthy. And it's still inhabited by the descendants of the merchants and nobles who built it, though it's fallen on hard times in the past three hundred years . . ."

A few minutes later, as the balloon drifted on, Lee saw first a lighthouse, then the curve of a stone breakwater, then the towers and domes and red-brown roofs of a beautiful city around a harbour, with a sumptuous building like an opera house in lush gardens, and wide boulevards with elegant hotels and little streets where blossom-bearing trees hung over shaded balconies.

And Grumman was right: there were people there. But as they drifted closer, Lee was surprised to see that they were children. There was not an adult in sight. The children were playing on the beach, or running in and out of cafés, or eating and drinking, or gathering bags full of goods from houses and shops. And there was a group of boys fighting, and a red-haired girl urging them on, and a little boy throwing stones to smash all the windows of a nearby building. It was like a playground the size of a city, with not a teacher in sight; it was a world of children.

But they weren't the only presences there. Lee had to rub his eyes when he saw them first, but there was no doubt about it: columns of mist – or something more tenuous than mist – a thickening of the air . . . Whatever they were, the city was full of them; they drifted along the boulevards, they entered houses, they clustered in the squares and courtyards. The children moved among them unseeing.

But not unseen. The further they drifted over the city, the more Lee could observe the behaviour of these forms. And it was clear that some of the children were of interest to them, and they followed certain children around: the older children, those who (as far as Lee could see through his telescope) were on the verge of adolescence. There was one boy, a tall thin youth with a shock of black hair, who was so thickly surrounded by the transparent beings that his very outline seemed to shimmer in the air. They were like flies around meat. And the boy had no idea of it, though from time to time he would brush his eyes, or shake his head as if to clear his vision.

"What the hell are those things?" said Lee.

"The people call them Spectres."

"What do they do, exactly?"

"You've heard of vampyres?"

"Oh, in tales."

"The Spectres feast as vampyres feast on blood, but the Spectres' food is attention. A conscious and informed interest in the world. The immaturity of children is less attractive to them."

"They're the opposite of those devils at Bolvangar, then."

"On the contrary. The Oblation Board and the Spectres of Indifference are both bewitched by this truth about human beings: that innocence is different from experience. The Oblation Board fears and hates Dust, and the Spectres feast on it, but it's Dust they're both obsessed by."

"They're clustered around that kid down there . . ."

"He's growing up. They'll attack him soon, and then his life will become a blank indifferent misery. He's doomed."

"For Pete's sake! Can't we rescue him?"

"No. The Spectres would seize us at once. They can't touch us up here; all we can do is watch and fly on."

"But where are the adults? You don't tell me the whole world is full of children alone?"

"Those children are Spectre-orphans. There are many gangs of them in this world. They wander about living on what they can find when the adults flee. And there's plenty to find, as you can see. They don't starve. It looks as if a multitude of Spectres have invaded this city, and the adults have gone to safety. You notice how few boats there are in the harbour? The children will come to no harm."

"Except for the older ones. Like that poor kid down there . . ."

"Mr Scoresby, that is the way this world works. And if you want to put an end to cruelty and injustice you must take me further on. I have a job to do."

"Seems to me –" Lee said, feeling for the words – "seems to me the place you fight cruelty is where you find it, and the place you give help is where you see it needed. Or is that wrong, Dr Grumman? I'm only an ignorant aëronaut. I'm so damn ignorant I believed it when I was told that shamans had the gift of flight, for example. Yet here's a shaman who hasn't."

"Oh, but I have."

"How d'you make that out?"

The balloon was drifting lower, and the ground was rising. A square stone tower rose directly in their path, and Lee didn't seem to have noticed.

"I needed to fly," said Grumman, "so I summoned you, and here I am, flying."

He was fully aware of the peril they were in, but he held back from implying that the aëronaut wasn't. And in perfect time, Lee Scoresby leant over the side of the basket and pulled the cord on one of the bags of ballast. The sand flowed out, and the balloon lifted gently to clear the tower by six feet or so. A dozen or so crows, disturbed, rose cawing around them.

"I guess you are," said Lee. "You have a strange way about you, Dr Grumman. You ever spend any time among the witches?"

"Yes," said Grumman. "And among academicians, and among spirits. I found folly everywhere, but there were grains of wisdom in every stream of it. No doubt there was much more wisdom that I failed to recognize. Life is hard, Mr Scoresby, but we cling to it all the same."

"And this journey we're on? Is that folly or wisdom?"

"The greatest wisdom I know."

"Tell me again what your purpose is: you're going to find the bearer of this subtle knife, and what then?"

"Tell him what his task is."

"And that's a task that includes protecting Lyra," the aëronaut reminded him.

"It will protect all of us."

They flew on, and soon the city was out of sight behind them.

Lee checked his instruments. The compass was still gyrating loosely, but the altimeter was functioning accurately, as far as he could judge, and showed them to be floating about a thousand feet above the seashore and parallel with it. Some way ahead a line of high green hills rose into the haze, and Lee was glad he'd provided plenty of ballast.

But when he made his regular scan of the horizon, he felt a little check at his heart. Hester felt it too, and flicked up her ears, and turned her head so that one gold-hazel eye rested on his face. He picked her up and tucked her in the breast of his coat, and opened the telescope again.

No, he wasn't mistaken. Far to the south (if south it was, the direction they'd come from) another balloon was floating in the haze. The heat-shimmer and the distance made it impossible to see any details, but the other balloon was larger, and flying higher.

Grumman had seen it too.

"Enemies, Mr Scoresby?" he said, shading his eyes to peer into the pearly light.

"There can't be a doubt. I'm uncertain whether to lose ballast and go higher, to catch the quicker wind, or stay low and be less conspicuous. And I'm thankful that thing's not a zeppelin; they could overhaul us in a few hours. No, damn it, Dr Grumman, I'm going higher, because if I was in that balloon I'd have seen this one already; and I'll bet they have keen eyesight."

He set Hester down again, and leaned out to jettison three bags of ballast. The balloon rose at once, and Lee kept the telescope to his eye.

And a minute later he knew for certain they'd been sighted, for there was a stir of movement in the haze, which resolved itself into a line of smoke streaking up and away at an angle from the other balloon; and when it was some distance up, it burst into a flare. It blazed deep red for a moment and then dwindled into a patch of grey smoke, but it was a signal as clear as a tocsin in the night.

"Can you summon a stiffer breeze, Dr Grumman?" said Lee. "I'd like to make those hills by nightfall."

For they were leaving the shoreline now, and their course was taking them out over a wide bay thirty or forty miles across. A range of hills rose on the far side, and now that he'd gained some height Lee saw that they might more truthfully be called mountains.

He turned to Grumman, but found him deep in a trance. The shaman's eyes were closed, and beads of sweat stood out on his forehead as he rocked gently back and forth. A low rhythmic moaning came from his throat, and his dæmon gripped the edge of the basket, equally entranced.

And whether it was the result of gaining height or whether it was the shaman's spell, a breath did stir the air on Lee's face. He looked up to check the gas-bag and saw it sway a degree or two, leaning towards the hills.

But the breeze that moved them more swiftly was working on the other balloon, too. It was no closer, but nor had they left it behind. And as Lee turned the telescope on it again he saw darker, smaller shapes behind it in the shimmering distance. They were grouped purposefully, and becoming clearer and more solid every minute.

"Zeppelins," he said. "Well, there's no hiding out here."

He tried to make an estimate of their distance, and a similar calculation about the hills towards which they were flying. Their speed had certainly picked up now, and the breeze was flicking white tips off the waves far below.

Grumman sat resting in a corner of the basket while his dæmon groomed her feathers. His eyes were closed, but Lee knew he was awake.

"The situation's like this, Dr Grumman," he said. "I do not want to be caught aloft by those zeppelins. There ain't no defence; they'd have us down in a minute. Nor do I want to land in the water, by free choice or not; we could float for a while, but they could pick us off with grenades as easy as fishing.

"So I want to reach those hills, and make a landing. I can see some forest now; we can hide among the trees for a spell, maybe a long time.

"And meanwhile, the sun's going down. We have about three hours to sunset, by my calculation. And it's hard to say, but I think those zeppelins will have closed on us half-way by that time, and we should have got to the far shore of this bay.

"Now you understand what I'm saying. I'm going to take us up into those hills, and then land, because anything else is certain death. They'll have made a connection now between this ring I showed them and the Skraeling I killed on Nova Zembla, and they ain't chasing us this hard to say we left our wallet on the counter.

"So sometime tonight, Dr Grumman, this flight's gonna be over. You ever landed in a balloon?"

"No," said the shaman. "But I trust your skill."

"I'll try and get as high up that range as I can. It's a question of balance, because the further we go, the closer they'll be behind us. If I land when they're too close behind, they'll be able to see where we go, but if I take us down too early we won't find the shelter of those trees. Either way, there's going to be some shooting before long."

Grumman sat impassively, moving a magical token of feathers and beads from one hand to the other in a pattern that Lee could see had some purposeful meaning. His dæmon's eyes never left the pursuing zeppelins.

An hour went by, and another. Lee chewed an unlit cigar and sipped cold coffee from a tin flask. The sun settled lower in the sky behind them, and Lee could see the long shade of evening creep along the shore of the bay and up the lower flanks of the hills ahead while the balloon itself, and the mountain tops, were bathed in gold.

And behind them, almost lost in the sunset glare, the little dots of the zeppelins grew larger and firmer. They had already overtaken the other balloon, and could now be easily seen with the naked eye: four of them in line abreast. And across the wide silence of the bay came the sound of their engines, tiny but clear, an insistent mosquito-whine.

When they were still a few minutes from making the shore at the foot of the hills, Lee noticed something new in the sky behind the zeppelins. A bank of clouds had been building, and a massive thunderhead reared thousands of feet up into the still bright upper sky. How had he failed to notice? If a storm was coming, the sooner they landed the better.

And then a dark green curtain of rain drifted down and hung from the clouds, and the storm seemed to be chasing the zeppelins as they were chasing Lee's balloon, for the rain swept along towards them from the sea, and as the sun finally vanished, a mighty flash came from the clouds, and several seconds later a crash of thunder so loud it shook the very fabric of Lee's balloon, and echoed back for a long time from the mountains.

Then came another flash of lightning, and this time the jagged fork struck down direct from the thunderhead at one of the zeppelins. In a moment the gas was alight: a bright flower of flame blossomed against the bruise-dark clouds, and the craft drifted down slowly, ablaze like a beacon, and floated still blazing on the water.

Lee let out the breath he'd been holding. Grumman was standing beside him, one hand on the suspension-ring, with lines of exhaustion deep in his face.

"Did *you* bring that storm?" said Lee.

Grumman nodded.

The sky was now coloured like a tiger: bands of gold alternated with patches and stripes of deepest brown-black, and the pattern changed by the minute, for the gold was fading rapidly as the brown-black engulfed it. The sea behind was a patchwork of black water and phosphorescent foam, and the last of the burning zeppelin's flames were dwindling into nothing as it sank.

The remaining three, however, were flying on, buffeted hard but keeping to their course. More lightning flashed around them, and as the storm came closer Lee began to fear for the gas in his own balloon. One strike could have it tumbling to earth in flames, and he didn't suppose the shaman could control the storm so finely as to avoid that.

"Right, Dr Grumman," he said, "I'm going to ignore those zeppelins for now and concentrate on getting us safe into the mountains and on the ground. What I want you to do is sit tight and hold on, and be prepared to jump when I tell you. I'll give you warning, and I'll try to make it as gentle as I can, but landing in these conditions is a matter of luck as much as skill."

"I trust you, Mr Scoresby," said the shaman.

He sat back in a corner of the basket while his dæmon perched on the suspension-ring, her claws dug deep in the leather binding.

The wind was blowing them hard now, and the great gas-bag swelled and billowed in the gusts. The ropes creaked and strained, but Lee had no fear of their giving way. He let go some more ballast, and watched the altimeter closely. In a storm, when the air pressure sank, you had to offset that drop against the alti-metric reading, and very often it was a crude rule-of-thumb calculation. Lee ran through the figures, double-checked them, and then released the last of his ballast. The only control he had now was the gas-valve. He couldn't go higher; he could only descend.

He peered intently through the stormy air and made out the great bulk of the hills, dark against the dark sky. From below there came a roaring, rushing sound like the crash of surf on a stony beach, but he knew it for the wind tearing through the leaves on the trees. So far, already! They were moving faster than he'd thought.

And he shouldn't leave it too long before he brought them down. Lee was too cool by nature to rage at fate; his manner was to raise an eyebrow and greet it laconically; but he couldn't help a flicker of despair now, when the one thing he should do – namely fly before the storm and let it blow itself out – was the one thing guaranteed to get them shot down.

He scooped up Hester and tucked her securely into his breast, buttoning the canvas coat up close to keep her in. Grumman sat steady and quiet; his dæmon, wind-torn, clung firmly with her talons deep in the basket-rim and her feathers blown erect.

"I'm going to take us down, Dr Grumman," Lee shouted above the wind. "You should stand and be ready to jump clear. Hold the ring and swing yourself up when I call."

Grumman obeyed. Lee gazed down, ahead, down, ahead, checking each dim glimpse against the next, and blinking the rain out of his eyes; for a sudden squall had brought the heavy drops at them like handfuls of gravel, and the drumming they made on the gas-bag added to the wind-howl and the lash of the leaves below until Lee could hardly even hear the thunder.

"Here we go," he shouted. "You cooked up a fine storm, Mr Shaman."

He pulled at the gas-valve line and lashed it around a cleat to keep it open. As the gas streamed out of the top, invisible far above, the lower curve of the gas-bag withdrew into itself and a fold, and then another, appeared where there had been a bulging sphere only a minute before.

The basket was tossing and lurching so violently it was hard to tell if they were going down, and the gusts were so sudden and wayward that they might easily have been blown a long way sky-wards without knowing; but after a minute or so Lee felt a sudden snag and knew the grapnel had caught on a branch. It was only a temporary check, so the branch had broken, but it showed how close they were.

He shouted, "Fifty feet above the trees –"

The shaman nodded.

Then came another snag, more violent, and the two men were thrown hard against the rim of the basket. Lee was used to it, and found his balance at once, but the force took Grumman by surprise. However, he didn't lose his grip on the suspension-ring, and Lee could see him safely poised, ready to swing him-self clear.

A moment later came the most jolting shock of all as the grapnel found a branch that held it fast. The basket tilted at once and a second later was crashing into the tree-tops, and amid a lashing of wet leaves and the snapping of twigs and the creak of tormented branches it jolted to a precarious halt.

"Still there, Dr Grumman?" Lee called, for it was impossible to see anything.

"Still here, Mr Scoresby."

"Better keep still for a minute till we see the situation clearly," said Lee, for they were wildly swaying in the wind, and he could feel the basket settling with little jerks against whatever was holding them up.

There was still a strong sideways pull from the gas-bag, which was now nearly empty, but which as a result was catching the wind like a sail. It crossed Lee's mind to cut it loose, but if it didn't fly away altogether, it would hang in the tree-tops like a banner and give their position away; much better to take it in, if they could.

There came another lightning-flash, and a second later the thunder crashed. The storm was nearly overhead. The glare showed Lee an oak trunk, with a great white scar where a branch had been torn away, but torn only partially, for the basket was resting on it near the point where it was still attached to the trunk.

"I'm going to throw out a rope and climb down," he shouted. "As soon as our feet touch the ground we can make the next plan."

"I'll follow you, Mr Scoresby," said Grumman. "My dæmon tells me the ground is forty feet down."

And Lee was aware of a powerful flutter of wing-beats as the eagle-dæmon settled again on the basket-rim.

"She can go that far?" he said, surprised, but put that out of his mind and made the rope secure, first to the suspension-ring and then to the branch, so that even if the basket did fall, it wouldn't fall far.

Then, with Hester secure in his breast, he threw the rest of the rope over and clambered down till he felt solid ground beneath his feet. The branches grew thick around the trunk: this was a massive tree, a giant of an oak, and Lee muttered a thank you to it as he tugged on the rope to signal to Grumman that he could descend.

Was there another sound in the tumult? He listened hard. Yes, the engine of a zeppelin, maybe more than one, some way above

– it was impossible to tell how high, or which direction it was flying in; but the sound was there for a minute or so, and then it was gone.

The shaman reached the ground.

"Did you hear it?" said Lee.

"Yes. Going higher, into the mountains, I think. Congratulations on landing us safely, Mr Scoresby."

"We ain't finished yet. I want to git that gas-bag under the canopy before daybreak, or it'll show up our position from miles away. You up to some manual labour, Dr Grumman?"

"Tell me what to do."

"All right. I'm going back up the rope and I'll lower some things down to you. One of them's a tent. You can git that set up while I see what I can do up there to hide the balloon."

They laboured for a long time, and in peril at one point, when the branch that had been supporting the basket finally broke and pitched Lee down with it; but he didn't fall far, since the gas-bag still trailed among the tree-tops, and held the basket suspended.

The fall in fact made concealing it easier, since it pulled the lower part of the gas-bag down through the canopy; and working by flashes of lightning, tugging and wrenching and hacking, Lee managed to drag the whole body of the balloon down among the lower branches and out of sight.

The wind was still beating the tree-tops back and forth, but the worst of the rain had passed by the time he decided he could do no more. He clambered down and found that the shaman had not only pitched the tent but had conjured a fire into being, and was brewing some coffee.

"This done by magic?" said Lee, soaked and stiff, easing himself down into the tent and taking the mug Grumman handed him.

"No, you can thank the Boy Scouts for this," said Grumman. "Do they have Boy Scouts in your world? Be prepared. Of all the ways of starting a fire, the best is dry matches. I never travel without them. We could do worse than this as a campsite, Mr Scoresby."

"You heard those zeppelins again?"

Grumman held up his hand. Lee listened, and sure enough,

there was that engine-sound, easier to make out now the rain had eased a little.

"They've been over twice now," said Grumman. "They don't know where we are, but they know we're here somewhere."

And a minute later a flickering glow came from somewhere in the direction the zeppelin had flown. It was less bright than lightning, but it was persistent, and Lee knew it for a flare.

"Best put the fire out, Dr Grumman," he said, "sorry as I am to do without it. I think that canopy's thick, but you never know. I'm going to sleep now, wet through or not."

"You will be dry by the morning," said the shaman.

He took a handful of wet earth and pressed it down over the flames, and Lee struggled to lie down in the little tent and closed his eyes.

He had strange and powerful dreams. At one point he was convinced he had awoken to see the shaman sitting cross-legged, wreathed in flames, and the flames were rapidly consuming his flesh to leave only a white skeleton behind, still seated in a mound of glowing ash. Lee looked for Hester in alarm, and found her sleeping, which never happened, for when he was awake, so was she; so when he found her asleep, his laconic whip-tongued dæmon looking so gentle and vulnerable, he was moved by the strangeness of it, and he lay down uneasily beside her, awake in his dream, but really asleep, and he dreamt he lay awake for a long time.

Another dream focused on Grumman, too. Lee seemed to see the shaman shaking a feather-trimmed rattle, and commanding something to obey him. The something, Lee saw with a touch of nausea, was a Spectre like the ones they'd seen from the balloon. It was tall and nearly invisible, and it invoked such a gut-churning revulsion in Lee that he nearly woke in terror. But Grumman was directing it fearlessly, and coming to no harm either, because the thing listened closely to him and then drifted upwards like a soap bubble until it was lost in the canopy.

Then his exhausting night took another turn, for he was in the cockpit of a zeppelin, watching the pilot. In fact he was sitting in the co-pilot's seat, and they were cruising over the forest, looking down at the wildly tossing tree-tops, a wild sea of leaf and branch. Then that Spectre was in the cabin with them.

Pinioned in his dream, Lee could neither move nor cry out, and he suffered the terror of the pilot as the man became aware of what was happening to him.

The Spectre was leaning over the pilot and pressing what would be its face to his. His dæmon, a finch, fluttered and shrieked and tried to pull away, only to fall half-fainting on the instrument panel. The pilot turned his face to Lee and put out a hand, but Lee had no power of movement. The anguish in the man's eyes was wrenching. Something true and living was being drained from him, and his dæmon fluttered weakly and called in a wild high call, but she was dying.

Then she vanished. But the pilot was still alive. His eyes became filmy and dull, and his reaching hand fell back with a limp thud against the throttle. He was alive but not alive: he was indifferent to everything.

And Lee sat and watched helplessly as the zeppelin flew on directly into a scarp of the mountains that rose up before them. The pilot watched it rear up in the window, but nothing could interest him. Lee pushed back against the seat in horror, but nothing happened to stop it, and at the moment of impact he cried:

"Hester!"

And woke.

He was in the tent, safe, and Hester nibbled his chin. He was sweating. The shaman was sitting cross-legged, but a shiver passed over Lee as he saw that the eagle-dæmon was not there near him. Clearly this forest was a bad place, full of haunting phantasms.

Then he became aware of the light he was seeing the shaman by, because the fire was long out, and the darkness of the forest was profound. Some distant flicker picked out the tree-trunks and the underside of dripping leaves, and Lee knew at once what it was: his dream had been true, and a zeppelin pilot had flown into the hillside.

"Damn, Lee, you're twitching like an aspen leaf. What's the matter with you?" Hester grumbled, and flicked her long ears.

"Ain't you dreaming too, Hester?" he muttered.

"You ain't dreaming, Lee, you're seeing. If I'd a known you was a seer I'd a cured you a long while back. Now you cut it out, you hear?"

He rubbed her head with his thumb and she shook her ears.

And without the slightest transition he was floating in the air alongside the shaman's dæmon, Sayan Kötör the osprey. To be in the presence of another man's dæmon and away from his own affected Lee with a powerful throb of guilt and strange pleasure. They were gliding, as if he too were a bird, on the turbulent updraughts above the forest, and Lee looked round through the dark air, now suffused with a pallid glow from the full moon that occasionally glared through a brief rent in the cloud-cover and made the tree-tops ring with silver.

The eagle-dæmon uttered a harsh scream, and from below came in a thousand different voices the calls of a thousand birds: the too-whoo of owls, the alarm-shriek of little sparrows, the liquid music of the nightingale. Sayan Kötör was calling them. And in answer they came, every bird in the forest, whether they had been gliding in the hunt on silent wings or roosting asleep, they came fluttering upwards in their thousands through the tumbling air.

And Lee felt whatever bird-nature he was sharing respond with joy to the command of the eagle queen, and whatever human-ness he had left felt the strangest of pleasures: that of offering eager obedience to a stronger power that was wholly right. And he wheeled and turned with the rest of the mighty flock, a hundred different species all turning as one in the magnetic will of the eagle, and saw against the silver cloud-rack the hateful dark regularity of a zeppelin.

They all knew exactly what they must do. And they streamed towards the airship, the swiftest reaching it first, but none so swiftly as Sayan Kötör; the tiny wrens and finches, the darting swifts, the silent-winged owls – within a minute the craft was laden with them, their claws scrabbling for purchase on the oiled silk or puncturing it to gain a hold.

They avoided the engine, though some were drawn into it and dashed to pieces by the slicing propellers. Most of the birds simply perched on the body of the zeppelin, and those that came next seized on to them, until they covered not only the whole body of the craft (now venting hydrogen through a thousand tiny claw-holes) but the windows of the cabin too, and the struts and cables – every square inch of room had a bird, two birds, three or more, clinging to it.

The pilot was helpless. Under the weight of the birds the craft began to sink further and further down, and then another of those sudden cruel scarps appeared, shouldering up out of the night and of course quite invisible to the men inside the zeppelin, who were swinging their guns wildly and firing at random.

At the last moment Sayan Kötör screamed, and a thunder of wing-beats drowned even the roar of the engine as every bird took off and flew away. And the men in the cabin had four or five horrified seconds of knowledge before the zeppelin crashed and burst into flames.

Fire, heat, flames . . . Lee woke up again, his body as hot as if he'd been lying in the desert sun.

Outside the tent there was still the endless drip-drip of wet leaves on the canvas, but the storm was over. Pale grey light seeped in, and Lee propped himself up to find Hester blinking beside him and the shaman wrapped in a blanket so deeply asleep he might have been dead, had not Sayan Kötör been perched asleep on a fallen branch outside.

The only sound apart from the drip of water was the normal forest birdsong. No engines in the sky, no enemy voices; so Lee thought it might be safe to light the fire, and after a struggle he got it going and brewed some coffee.

"What now, Hester?" he said.

"Depends. There was four of those zeppelins, and he destroyed three."

"I mean, have we discharged our duty?"

She flicked her ears and said, "Don't remember no contract."

"It ain't a contractual thing. It's a moral thing."

"We got one more zeppelin to think about before you start fretting about morals, Lee. There's thirty, forty men with guns all coming for us. Imperial soldiers, what's more. Survival first, morals later."

She was right, of course, and as he sipped the scalding brew and smoked a cigar, with the daylight gradually growing stronger, he wondered what he would do if he were in charge of the one remaining zeppelin. Withdraw and wait for full daylight, no doubt, and fly high enough to scan the edge of the forest over a wide area, so they could see when Lee and Grumman broke cover.

The osprey-dæmon Sayan Kötör awoke, and stretched her great wings above where Lee was sitting. Hester looked up and turned her head this way and that, looking at the mighty dæmon with each golden eye in turn, and a moment later the shaman himself came out of the tent.

"Busy night," Lee remarked.

"A busy day to come. We must leave the forest at once, Mr Scoresby. They are going to burn it."

Lee looked around incredulously at the soaking vegetation and said, "How?"

"They have an engine that throws out a kind of naphtha blended with potash, which ignites when it touches water. The Imperial Navy developed it to use in their war with Nippon. If the forest is saturated, it will catch all the more quickly."

"You can see that, can you?"

"As clearly as you saw what happened to the zeppelins during the night. Pack what you want to carry, and come away now."

Lee rubbed his jaw. The most valuable things he owned were also the most portable, namely the instruments from the balloon, so he retrieved them from the basket, stowed them carefully in a knapsack, and made sure his rifle was loaded and dry; and left the basket, the rigging, and the gas-bag where they lay, tangled and twisted among the branches. From now on he was an aëronaut no more, unless by some miracle he escaped with his life and found enough money to buy another balloon. Now he had to move like an insect, along the surface of the earth.

They smelled the smoke before they heard the flames, because a breeze from the sea was lifting it inland. By the time they reached the edge of the trees they could hear the fire, a deep and greedy roar.

"Why didn't they do this last night?" said Lee. "They could have barbecued us in our sleep."

"I guess they want to catch us alive," Grumman replied, stripping a branch of its leaves so he could use it as a walking-stick, "and they're waiting to see where we leave the forest."

And sure enough the drone of the zeppelin soon became audible even over the sound of the flames and of their own laboured breathing, for they were hurrying now, clambering upwards over roots and rocks and fallen tree-trunks and stopping only to gather breath. Sayan Kötör, flying high, swooped down to tell them how much progress they were making, and how far behind the flames were; though it wasn't long before they could see smoke above the trees behind them, and then a streaming banner of flame.

Small creatures of the forest, squirrels, birds, wild boar, were fleeing with them and a chorus of squealings, shriekings, alarm calls of every sort rose around them. The two travellers struggled on towards the edge of the tree-line, which was not far ahead; and then they reached it, as wave after wave of heat rolled up at them from the roaring billows of flame that now reached fifty feet into the air. Trees blazed like torches; the sap in their veins boiled and split them asunder, the pitch in the conifers caught like naphtha, the twigs seemed to blossom with ferocious orange flowers all in a moment.

Gasping, Lee and Grumman forced themselves up the steep slope of rocks and scree. Half the sky was obscured by smoke and heat-shimmer, but high above there floated the squat shape of the one remaining zeppelin – too far away, Lee thought hopefully, to see them even through binoculars.

The mountainside rose sheer and impassable ahead of them. There was only one route out of the trap they were in, and that was a narrow defile ahead, where a dry river bed emerged from a fold in the cliffs.

Lee pointed, and Grumman said, "My thoughts exactly, Mr Scoresby."

His dæmon, gliding and circling above, tipped her wings and sped to the ravine on a billowing updraught. The men didn't pause, climbing on as quickly as they could, but Lee said:

"Excuse me for asking this if it's impertinent, but I never knew anyone whose dæmon could do that except witches. But you're no witch. Was that something you learned to do, or did it come natural?"

"For a human being, nothing comes naturally," said Grumman. "We have to learn everything we do. Sayan Kötör is telling me that the ravine leads to a pass. If we get there before they see us, we could escape yet."

The eagle swooped down again, and the men climbed on. Hester preferred to find her own way over the rocks, so Lee followed where she led, avoiding the loose stones and moving as swiftly as he could over the larger rocks, making all the time for the little gulch.

Lee was anxious about Grumman, because the other man was pale and drawn and breathing hard. His labours in the night had drained a lot of his energy. How far they could keep going was a question Lee didn't want to face; but when they were nearly at the entrance to the ravine, and actually on the edge of the dried river bed, he heard a change in the sound of the zeppelin.

"They've seen us," he said.

And it was like receiving a sentence of death. Hester stumbled, even sure-footed firm-hearted Hester stumbled and faltered. Grumman leant on the stick he carried and shaded his eyes to look back, and Lee turned to look too.

The zeppelin was descending fast, making for the slope directly below them. It was clear that the pursuers intended to capture them, not kill them, for a burst of gunfire just then would have finished them both in a second. Instead the pilot brought the airship skilfully to a hover just above the ground, at the highest point in the slope where he safely could, and from the cabin door a stream of blue-uniformed men jumped down, their wolf-dæmons beside them, and began to climb.

Lee and Grumman were six hundred yards above them, and not far from the entrance to the ravine. Once they reached it they could hold the soldiers off as long as their ammunition held out: but they had only one rifle.

"They're after me, Mr Scoresby," said Grumman, "not you.

If you give me the rifle and surrender yourself, you'll survive. They're disciplined troops. You'll be a prisoner of war."

Lee ignored that, and said, "Git moving. Make the gulch and I'll hold them off from the mouth while you find your way out the other end. I brought you this far, and I ain't going to sit back and let 'em catch you now."

The men below were moving up quickly, for they were fit and rested. Grumman nodded.

"I had no strength left to bring the fourth one down," was all he said, and they moved quickly into the shelter of the gulch.

"Just tell me before you go," said Lee, "because I won't be easy till I know. What side I'm fighting for I cain't tell, and I don't greatly care. Just tell me this: what I'm a-going to do now, is that going to help that little girl Lyra, or harm her?"

"It's going to help her," said Grumman.

"And your oath. You won't forget what you swore to me?"

"I won't forget."

"Because, Dr Grumman, or John Parry, or whatever name you take up in whatever world you end in, you be aware of this. I love that little child like a daughter. If I'd had a child of my own, I couldn't love her more. And if you break the oath, whatever remains of me will pursue whatever remains of you, and you'll spend the rest of eternity wishing you never existed. That's how important that oath is."

"I understand. And you have my word."

"Then that's all I need to know. Go well."

The shaman held out his hand, and Lee shook it. Then Grumman turned and made his way up the gulch, and Lee looked around for the best place to make his stand.

"Not the big boulder, Lee," said Hester. "You cain't see to the right from there, and they could rush us. Take the smaller one."

There was a roaring in Lee's ears that had nothing to do with the conflagration in the forest below, or with the labouring drone of the zeppelin trying to rise again. It had to do with his childhood, and the Alamo. How often he and his companions had played that heroic battle, in the ruins of the old fort, taking turns to be Danes and French! His childhood was coming back to him, with a vengeance. He took out the Navajo ring of his mother's and laid it on the rock beside him. In the old Alamo games, Hester had often been a cougar or a wolf, and once or twice a rattlesnake, but mostly a mockingbird. Now –

"Quit daydreaming and take a sight," she said. "This ain't play, Lee."

The men climbing the slope had fanned out, and were moving more slowly, because they saw the problem as well as he did. They knew they'd have to capture the gulch, and they knew that one man with a rifle could hold them off for a long time. Behind them, to Lee's surprise, the zeppelin was still labouring to rise. Maybe its buoyancy was going, or maybe the fuel was running low, but either way it hadn't taken off yet, and it gave him an idea.

He adjusted his position and sighted along the old Winchester until he had the port engine mounting plumb in view, and fired. The crack raised the soldiers' heads as they climbed towards him, but a second later the engine suddenly roared and then just as suddenly seized and died. The zeppelin lurched over to one side. Lee could hear the other engine howling, but the airship was grounded now.

The soldiers had halted and taken cover as well as they could. Lee could count them, and he did: twenty-five. He had thirty bullets.

Hester crept up close to his left shoulder.

"I'll watch this way," she said.

Crouched on the grey boulder, her ears flat along her back, she looked like a little stone herself, grey-brown and inconspicuous, except for her eyes. Hester was no beauty; she was about as plain and scrawny as a hare could be; but her eyes were marvellously coloured, gold-hazel flecked with rays of deepest peat-brown and forest-green. And now those eyes were looking down at the last landscape they'd ever see: a barren slope of brutal tumbled rocks, and beyond it a forest on fire. Not a blade of grass, not a speck of green to rest on.

Her ears flicked slightly.

"They're talking," she said. "I can hear, but I cain't understand."

"Russian," he said. "They're gonna come up all together and at a run. That would be hardest for us, so they'll do that."

"Aim straight," she said.

"I will. But hell, I don't like taking lives, Hester."

"Ours or theirs."

"No, it's more than that," he said. "It's theirs or Lyra's. I cain't see how, but we're connected to that child, and I'm glad of it."

"There's a man on the left about to shoot," said Hester, and as she spoke a crack came from his rifle, and chips of stone flew off the boulder a foot from where she crouched. The bullet whined off into the gulch, but she didn't move a muscle.

"Well, that makes me feel better about doing this," said Lee, and took careful aim.

He fired. There was only a small patch of blue to aim at, but he hit it. With a surprised cry the man fell back and died.

And then the fight began. Within a minute the crack of rifles, the whine of ricocheting bullets, the smash of pulverizing rock echoed and rang the length of the mountainside and along the hollow gulch behind. The smell of cordite, and the burning smell that came from the powdered rock where the bullets hit, were just variations on the smell of burning wood from the forest, until it seemed that the whole world was burning.

Lee's boulder was soon scarred and pitted, and he felt the thud of the bullets as they hit it. Once he saw the fur on Hester's back ripple as the wind of a bullet passed over it, but she didn't budge. Nor did he stop firing.

That first minute was fierce. And after it, in the pause that came, Lee found that he was wounded: there was blood on the rock under his cheek, and his right hand and the rifle bolt were red.

Hester moved round to look.

"Nothing big," she said. "A bullet clipped your scalp."

"Did you count how many fell, Hester?"

"No. Too busy ducking. Reload while you can, boy."

He rolled down behind the rock and worked the bolt back and forth. It was hot, and the blood that had flowed freely over it from the scalp wound was drying and making the mechanism stiff. He spat on it carefully and it loosened.

Then he hauled himself back into position, and even before he'd set his eye to the sight, he took a bullet.

It felt like an explosion in his left shoulder. For a few seconds he was dazed, and then he came to his senses, with his left arm numb and useless. There was a great deal of pain waiting to spring on him, but it hadn't raised the courage yet, and that thought gave him the strength to focus his mind on shooting again.

He propped the rifle on the dead and useless arm that had been so full of life a minute ago, and sighted with stolid concentration: one shot, two, three, and each found its man.

"How we doing?" he muttered.

"Good shooting," she whispered back, very close to his cheek. "Don't stop. Over by the black boulder . . ."

He looked, aimed, shot. The figure fell.

"Damn, these are men like me," he said.

"Makes no sense," she said. "Do it anyway."

"Do you believe him? Grumman?"

"Sure. Plumb ahead, Lee."

Crack: another man fell, and his dæmon went out like a candle.

Then there was a long silence. Lee fumbled in his pocket and found some more bullets. As he reloaded he felt something so rare his heart nearly failed; he felt Hester's face pressed to his own, and it was wet with tears.

"Lee, this is my fault," she said.

"Why?"

"The Skraeling. I told you to take his ring. Without that we'd never be in this trouble."

"You think I ever did what you told me? I took it because the witch —"

He didn't finish, because another bullet found him. This time it smashed into his left leg, and before he could even blink, a third one clipped his head again, like a red-hot poker laid along his skull.

"Not long now, Hester," he muttered, trying to hold still.

"The witch, Lee! You said the witch! Remember?"

Poor Hester, she was lying now, not crouching tense and watchful as she'd done all his adult life. And her beautiful gold-brown eyes were growing dull.

"Still beautiful," he said. "Oh, Hester, yeah, the witch. She gave me . . ."

"Sure she did. The flower . . ."

"In my breast pocket. Fetch it, Hester, I cain't move."

It was a hard struggle, but she tugged out the little scarlet flower with her strong teeth and laid it by his right hand. With a great effort he closed it in his fist and said, "Serafina Pekkala! Help me, I beg . . ."

A movement below: he let go the flower, sighted, fired. The movement died.

Hester was failing.

"Hester, don't you go before I do," Lee whispered.

"Lee, I couldn't abide to be anywhere away from you for a single second," she whispered back.

"You think the witch will come?"

"Sure she will. We should have called her before."

"We should have done a lot of things."

"Maybe so —"

Another crack, and this time the bullet went deep somewhere inside, seeking out the centre of his life. He thought: it won't find it there. Hester's my centre. And he saw a blue flicker down below, and strained to bring the barrel over to it.

"He's the one," Hester breathed.

Lee found it hard to pull the trigger. Everything was hard. He had to try three times, and finally he got it. The blue uniform tumbled away down the slope.

Another long silence. The pain nearby was losing its fear of him. It was like a pack of jackals, circling, sniffing, treading closer, and he knew they wouldn't leave him now till they'd eaten him bare.

"There's one man left," Hester muttered. "He's a-making for the zeppelin."

And Lee saw him mistily, one soldier of the Imperial Guard creeping away from his company's defeat.

"I cain't shoot a man in the back," Lee said.

"Shame to die with one bullet left, though."

So he took aim with his last bullet at the zeppelin itself, still roaring and straining to rise with its one engine, and the bullet must have been red-hot; or maybe a burning brand from the forest below was wafted to the airship on an updraught; for the gas suddenly billowed into an orange fireball, and the envelope and the metal skeleton rose a little way and then tumbled down very slowly, gently, but full of a fiery death.

And the man creeping away and the six or seven others who were the only remnant of the Guard, and who hadn't dared come closer to the man holding the ravine, were engulfed by the fire that fell on them.

Lee saw the fireball and heard through the roar in his ears Hester saying, "That's all of 'em, Lee."

He said, or thought, "Those poor men didn't have to come to this, and nor did we."

She said, "We held 'em off. We held out. We're a-helping Lyra."

Then she was pressing her little proud broken self against his face, as close as she could get, and then they died.

"ON," SAID THE alethiometer, "further, higher."

So on they climbed. The witches flew above to spy out the best routes, because the hilly land soon gave way to steeper slopes and rocky footing, and as the sun rose towards noon the travellers found themselves in a tangled land of dry gullies, cliffs, and boulder-strewn valleys where not a single green leaf grew, and where the stridulation of insects was the only sound.

They moved on, stopping only for sips of water from their goatskin flasks, and talking little. Pantalaimon flew above Lyra's head for a while until he tired of that, and then he became a little sure-footed mountain sheep, vain of his horns, leaping among rocks while Lyra scrambled laboriously alongside. Will moved on grimly, screwing up his eyes against the glare, ignoring the worsening pain from his hand, and finally reaching a state in which movement alone was good and stillness bad, so that he suffered more from resting than from toiling on. And since the failure of the witches' spell to stop his bleeding, he thought they were regarding him with fear, too, as if he was marked by some curse greater than their own powers.

At one point they came to a little lake, a patch of intense blue scarcely thirty yards across among the red rocks. They stopped there awhile to drink and refill their flasks, and to soak their aching feet in the icy water. They stayed a few minutes and moved on, and soon afterwards, when the sun was at its highest and hottest, Serafina Pekkala darted down to speak to them. She was agitated.

"I must leave you for a while," she said. "Lee Scoresby needs me. I don't know why. But he wouldn't call if he didn't need my help. Keep going, and I'll find you . . ."

"Mr Scoresby?" said Lyra, excited and anxious. "But where –"

But Serafina was gone, speeding out of sight before Lyra could finish the question. Lyra reached automatically for the alethiometer to ask what had happened to Lee Scoresby, but she let her hand drop, because she'd promised to do no more than guide Will.

She looked across to him. He was sitting nearby, his hand loosely on his knee still slowly dripping blood, his face scorched by the sun and pale under the burning.

"Will," she said, "do you know why you have to find your father?"

"It's what I've always known. My mother said I'd take up my father's mantle. That's all I know."

"What does that mean, taking up his mantle? What's a mantle?"

"A task, I suppose. Whatever he's been doing, I've got to carry on. It makes as much sense as anything else."

He wiped the sweat out of his eyes with his right hand. What he couldn't say was that he longed for his father as a lost child yearns for home. That comparison wouldn't have occurred to him, because home was the place he kept safe for his mother, not the place others kept safe for him; but it had been five years now since that Saturday morning in the supermarket when the pretend game of hiding from the enemies became desperately real, such a long time in his life, and his heart craved to hear the words, "Well done, well done, my child; no one on earth could have done better; I'm proud of you. Come and rest now . . ."

Will longed for that so much that he hardly knew he did. It was just part of what everything felt like. So he couldn't express that to Lyra now, though she could see it in his eyes, and that was new for her, too, to be quite so perceptive. The fact was that where Will was concerned, she was developing a new kind of sense, as if he were simply more in focus than anyone she'd known before. Everything about him was clear and close and immediate.

And she might have said that to him, but at that moment a witch flew down.

"I can see someone behind us," she said. "They're a long way back, but they're moving quickly. Shall I go closer and look?"

"Yes, do," said Lyra, "but fly low, and hide, and don't let them see you."

Will and Lyra got painfully to their feet again and clambered on.

"I been cold plenty of times," Lyra said, to take her mind off the pursuers, "but I en't been this hot, ever. Is it this hot in your world?"

"Not where I used to live. Not normally. But the climate's been changing. The summers are hotter than they used to be. They say that people have been interfering with the atmosphere by putting chemicals in it and the weather's going out of control."

"Yeah, well they have," said Lyra, "and it is. And we're here in the middle of it."

He was too hot and thirsty to reply, and they climbed on breathlessly in the throbbing air. Pantalaimon was a cricket now, and sat on Lyra's shoulder, too tired to leap or fly. From time to time the witches would see a spring high up, too high to climb to, and fly up to fill the children's flasks. They would soon have died without water and there was none where they were; any spring that made its way into the air was soon swallowed again among the rocks.

And so they moved on, towards evening.

The witch who flew back to spy was called Lena Feldt. She flew low, from crag to crag, and as the sun was setting and drawing a wild blood-red out of the rocks she came to the little blue lake, and found a troop of soldiers making camp.

But her first glimpse of them told her more than she wanted to know; these soldiers had no dæmons. And they weren't from Will's world, or the world of Cittàgazze, where people's dæmons were inside them, and where they still looked alive: these men were from her own world, and to see them without dæmons was a gross and sickening horror.

Then out of a tent by the lakeside came the explanation. Lena Feldt saw a woman, a short-life, graceful in her khaki hunting clothes and as full of life as the golden monkey who capered along the water's edge beside her.

Lena Feldt hid among the rocks above and watched as Mrs Coulter spoke to the officer in charge, and his men put up tents, made fires, boiled water.

The witch had been among Serafina Pekkala's troop who rescued the children at Bolvangar, and she longed to shoot Mrs Coulter on the spot; but some fortune was protecting the woman, for it was just too far for a bow-shot from where she was, and the witch could get no closer without making herself invisible. So she began to make the spell. It took ten minutes of deep concentration.

Confident at last, Lena Feldt went down the rocky slope towards the lake, and as she walked through the camp one or two blank-eyed soldiers glanced up briefly, but found what they saw too hard to remember, and looked away again. The witch stopped outside the tent Mrs Coulter had gone into, and fitted an arrow to her bowstring.

She listened to the low voice through the canvas, and then moved carefully to the open flap that overlooked the lake.

Inside the tent Mrs Coulter was talking to a man Lena Feldt hadn't seen before: an older man, grey-haired and powerful, with a serpent-dæmon twined around his wrist. He was sitting in a canvas chair beside hers, and she was leaning towards him, speaking softly.

"Of course, Carlo," she was saying, "I'll tell you anything you like. What do you want to know?"

"How do you command the Spectres?" the man said. "I didn't think it possible, but you have them following you like dogs . . . Are they afraid of your bodyguard? What is it?"

"Simple," she said. "They know I can give them more nourishment if they let me live than if they consume me. I can lead them to all the victims their phantom hearts desire. As soon as you described them to me I knew I could dominate them, and so it turns out. And a whole world trembles in the power of these pallid things! But Carlo," she whispered, "I can please you, too, you know. Would you like me to please you even more?"

"Marisa," he murmured, "it's enough of a pleasure to be close to you . . ."

"No, it isn't, Carlo; you know it isn't. You know I can please you more than this."

Her dæmon's little black horny hands were stroking the serpent-dæmon. Little by little the serpent loosened herself and began to flow along the man's arm towards the monkey. The man and the woman were both holding glasses of golden wine, and she sipped hers and leaned a little closer to him.

"Ah," said the man, as the dæmon slipped slowly off his arm and let her weight into the golden monkey's hands. The monkey raised her slowly to his face and ran his cheek softly along her emerald skin. Her tongue flicked blackly this way and that, and the man sighed.

"Carlo, tell me why you're pursuing the boy," Mrs Coulter whispered, and her voice was as soft as the monkey's caress. "Why do you need to find him?"

"He has something I want. Oh, Marisa –"

"What is it, Carlo? What's he got?"

He shook his head. But he was finding it hard to resist; his dæmon was twined gently around the monkey's breast, and running her head through and through the long lustrous fur as his hands moved along her fluid length.

Lena Feldt watched, standing invisibly just two paces from where they sat. Her bowstring was taut, the arrow nocked to it in readiness: she could have pulled and loosed in less than a second, and Mrs Coulter would have been dead before she finished drawing breath. But the witch was curious. She stood still and silent and wide-eyed.

But while she was watching Mrs Coulter, she didn't look behind her across the little blue lake. On the far side of it in the darkness a grove of ghostly trees seemed to have planted itself, a grove that shivered every so often with a tremor like a conscious intention. But they were not trees, of course; and while all the curiosity of Lena Feldt and her dæmon was directed at Mrs Coulter, one of the pallid forms detached itself from its fellows and drifted across the surface of the icy water, causing not a single ripple, until it paused a foot from the rock on which Lena Feldt's dæmon was perched.

"You could easily tell me, Carlo," Mrs Coulter was murmuring. "You could whisper it. You could pretend to be talking in your sleep, and who could blame you for that? Just tell me what the boy has, and why you want it. I could get it for you ... Wouldn't you like me to do that? Just tell me, Carlo. I don't want it. I want the girl. What is it? Just tell me, and you shall have it."

He gave a soft shudder. His eyes were closed. Then he said, "It's a knife. The subtle knife of Cittàgazze. You haven't heard of it, Marisa? Some people call it *teleutaia makhaira*, the last knife of all. Others call it Æsahættr . . ."

"What does it do, Carlo? Why is it special?"

"Ah . . . It's the knife that will cut anything . . . Not even its makers knew what it could do . . . Nothing, no one, matter, spirit, angel, air — nothing is invulnerable to the subtle knife. Marisa, it's mine, you understand?"

"Of course, Carlo. I promise. Let me fill your glass . . ."

And as the golden monkey slowly ran his hands along the emerald serpent again and again, squeezing just a little, lifting, stroking, as Sir Charles sighed with pleasure, Lena Feldt saw what was truly happening: because while the man's eyes were closed, Mrs Coulter secretly tilted a few drops from a small flask into the glass before filling it again with wine.

"Here, darling," she whispered. "Let's drink, to each other . . ."

He was already intoxicated. He took the glass and sipped greedily, once, again, and again.

And then without any warning Mrs Coulter stood up and turned and looked Lena Feldt full in the face.

"Well, witch," she said, "did you think I don't know how you make yourself invisible?"

Lena Feldt was too surprised to move.

Behind her, the man was struggling to breathe. His chest was heaving, his face was red, and his dæmon was limp and fainting in the monkey's hands. The monkey shook her off in contempt.

Lena Feldt tried to swing her bow up, but a fatal paralysis had touched her shoulder. She couldn't make herself do it. This had never happened before, and she uttered a little cry.

"Oh, it's too late for that," said Mrs Coulter. "Look at the lake, witch."

Lena Feldt turned, and saw her snow-bunting dæmon fluttering and shrieking as if he were in a glass chamber that was being emptied of air, fluttering and falling, slumping, failing, his beak opening widely, gasping in panic. The Spectre had enveloped him.

"No!" she cried, and tried to move towards it, but was driven back by a spasm of nausea. Even in her sickened distress, Lena Feldt could see that Mrs Coulter had more force in her soul than anyone she had ever seen. It didn't surprise her to see that the Spectre was under Mrs Coulter's power: no one could resist that authority. Lena Feldt turned back to the woman in anguish.

"Let him go! Please let him go!" she cried.

"We'll see. Is the child with you? The girl Lyra?"

"Yes!"

"And a boy, too? A boy with a knife?"

"Yes – I beg you –"

"And how many witches have you?"

"Twenty! Let him go, let him go!"

"All in the air? Or do some of you stay on the ground with the children?"

"Most in the air, three or four on the ground always – this is anguish – let him go or kill me now!"

"How far up the mountain are they? Are they moving on, or have they stopped to rest?"

Lena Feldt told her everything. She could have resisted any torture but what was happening to her dæmon now. When Mrs Coulter had learned all she wanted to know about where the witches were, and how they guarded Lyra and Will, she said:

"And now tell me this. You witches know something about the child Lyra. I nearly learned it from one of your sisters, but she died before I could complete the torture. Well, there is no one to save you now. Tell me the truth about my daughter."

Lena Feldt gasped: "She will be the mother – she will be life – mother – she will disobey – she will –"

"Name her! You are saying everything but the most important thing! Name her!" cried Mrs Coulter.

"Eve! Mother of all! Eve, again! Mother Eve!" stammered Lena Feldt, sobbing.

"Ah," said Mrs Coulter.

And she breathed a great sigh, as if the purpose of her life was clear to her at last.

Dimly the witch saw what she had done, and through the horror that was enveloping her she tried to cry out:

"What will you do to her? What will you do?"

"Why, I shall have to destroy her," said Mrs Coulter, "to prevent another Fall . . . Why didn't I see this before? It was too large to see . . ."

She clapped her hands together softly, like a child, wide-eyed. Lena Feldt, whimpering, heard her go on:

"Of course. Asriel will make war on the Authority, and then . . . Of course, of course . . . As before, so again. And Lyra is Eve. And this time she will not fall. I'll see to that. There will be no Fall . . ."

And Mrs Coulter drew herself up, and snapped her fingers to the Spectre feeding on the witch's dæmon. The little snow-bunting dæmon lay twitching on the rock as the Spectre moved towards the witch herself, and then whatever Lena Feldt had undergone before was doubled and trebled and multiplied a hundredfold. She felt a nausea of the soul, a hideous and sickening despair, a melancholy weariness so profound that she was going to die of it. Her last conscious thought was disgust at life: her senses had lied to her; the world was not made of energy and delight but of foulness, betrayal, and lassitude. Living was hateful and death was no better, and from end to end of the universe, this was the first and last and only truth.

Thus she stood, bow in hand, indifferent, dead in life.

So Lena Feldt failed to see or to care about what Mrs Coulter did next. Ignoring the grey-haired man slumped unconscious in the canvas chair and his dull-skinned dæmon coiled in the dust, she called the captain of the soldiers and ordered them to get ready for a night-march up the mountain.

Then she went to the edge of the water and called to the Spectres.

They came at her command, gliding like pillars of mist across the water. She raised her arms and made them forget they were earth bound, so that one by one they rose into the air and floated free like malignant thistledown, drifting up into the night and borne by the air-currents towards Will and Lyra and the other witches; but Lena Feldt saw nothing of it.

*   *   *

The temperature dropped quickly after dark, and when Will and Lyra had eaten the last of their dry bread they lay down under an overhanging rock to keep warm and try to sleep. At least, Lyra didn't have to try: she was unconscious in less than a minute, curled tightly around Pantalaimon, but Will couldn't find sleep, no matter how long he lay there. It was partly his hand, which was now throbbing right up to the elbow and uncomfortably swollen, and partly the hard ground, and partly the cold, and partly utter exhaustion, and partly his longing for his mother.

He was afraid for her, of course, and he knew she'd be safer if he was there to look after her; but he wanted her to look after him, too, as she'd done when he was very small; he wanted her to bandage him and tuck him into bed and sing to him and take away all the trouble and surround him with all the warmth and softness and mother-kindness he needed so badly; and it was never going to happen. Part of him was only a little boy still. So he cried, but he lay very still as he did, not wanting to wake Lyra.

But he still wasn't asleep. He was more awake than ever. Finally he uncurled his stiff limbs and got up quietly, shivering, and with the knife at his waist he set off higher up the mountain, to calm his restlessness.

Behind him the sentry-witch's robin-dæmon cocked his head, and she turned from the watch she was keeping to see Will clambering up the rocks. She reached for her pine-branch and silently took to the air, not to disturb him but to see he came to no harm.

He didn't notice. He felt such a need to move and keep moving that he hardly noticed the pain in his hand any more. He felt as if he should walk all night, all day, for ever, because nothing else would calm this fever in his breast. And as if in sympathy with him, a wind was rising. There were no leaves to stir in this wilderness, but the air buffeted his body and made his hair stream away from his face; it was wild outside him and wild within.

He climbed higher and higher, hardly once thinking of how he might find his way back down to Lyra, until he came out on a little plateau almost at the top of the world, it seemed. All around him, on every horizon, the mountains reached no higher. In the brilliant glare of the moon the only colours were stark black and dead white, and every edge was jagged and every surface bare.

The wild wind must have been bringing clouds overhead, because suddenly the moon was covered, and darkness swept over the whole landscape: thick clouds, too, for no gleam of moonlight shone through them. In less than a minute Will found himself in nearly total darkness.

And at the same moment Will felt a grip on his right arm.

He cried out with shock and twisted away at once, but the grip was tenacious. And Will was savage now. He felt he was at the very end of everything, and if it was the end of his life too, he was going to fight and fight till he fell.

So he twisted and kicked and twisted again, but that hand wouldn't let go; and since it was his right arm being held, he couldn't get at the knife. He tried with his left, but he was being jerked around so much, and his hand was so painful and swollen, that he couldn't reach: he had to fight with one bare wounded hand against a grown man.

He sank his teeth into the hand on his forearm, but all that happened was that the man landed a dizzying blow on the back of his head. Then Will kicked again and again, and some of the kicks connected and some didn't, and all the time he was pulling, jerking, twisting, shoving, and still the grip held him fast.

Dimly he heard his own panting and the man's grunts and harsh breathing; and then by chance he got his leg behind the man's and hurled himself against his chest, and the man fell with Will on top of him, heavily: but never for a moment did that grip slacken, and Will, rolling around violently on the stony ground, felt a heavy fear tighten round his heart: this man would never let him go, and even if he killed him, his corpse would still be holding fast.

But Will was weakening, and he was crying too now, sobbing bitterly as he kicked and tugged and beat at the man with his head and feet, and he knew his muscles would give up soon. And then he noticed the man had fallen still, though his hand still gripped as tight as ever. He was lying there letting Will batter at him with knees and head, and as soon as Will saw that, the last of his strength left him, and he fell helpless beside his opponent, every nerve in his body ringing and dizzy and throbbing.

Will hauled himself up painfully and peered through the deep darkness, and made out a blur of white on the ground beside the man. It was the white breast and head of a great bird, an osprey, a dæmon, and it was lying still. Will tried to pull away, and his feeble tug woke a response from the man, whose hand hadn't loosened.

But he was moving. He was feeling Will's right hand carefully with his free one. Will's hair stood on end.

Then the man said, "Give me your other hand."

"Be careful," said Will.

The man's free hand felt down Will's left arm, and his fingertips moved gently over the wrist and on to the swollen palm and with the utmost delicacy on to the stumps of Will's two lost fingers.

His other hand let go at once, and he sat up.

"You've got the knife," he said. "You're the knife-bearer."

His voice was resonant, harsh, but breathless. Will sensed that he was badly hurt. Had he wounded this dark opponent?

Will was still lying on the stones, utterly spent. All he could see was the man's shape, crouching above him, but he couldn't see his face. The man was reaching sideways for something, and after a few moments a marvellous soothing coolness spread into his hand from the stumps of his fingers, as the man massaged a salve into his skin.

"What are you doing?" Will said.

"Curing your wound. Keep still."

"Who are you?"

"I'm the only man who knows what the knife is for. Hold your hand up like that. Don't move."

The wind was beating more wildly than ever, and a drop or two of rain splashed into Will's face. He was trembling violently, but he propped up his left hand with his right while the man spread more ointment over the stumps and wound a strip of linen tightly around the hand.

And as soon as the dressing was secure, the man slumped sideways and lay down himself. Will, still bemused by the blessed cool numbness in his hand, tried to sit up and look at him. But it was darker than ever. He felt forward with his right hand and found himself touching the man's chest, where the heart was beating like a bird against the bars of a cage.

"Yes," the man said hoarsely. "Try and cure that, go on."

"Are you ill?"

"I'll be better soon. You have the knife, yes?"

"Yes."

"And you know how to use it?"

"Yes, yes. But are you from this world? How do you know about it?"

"Listen," said the man, sitting up with a struggle. "Don't interrupt. If you're the bearer of the knife, you have a task that's greater than you can imagine. A *child* . . . How could they let it happen? Well, so it must be . . . There is a war coming, boy. The greatest war there ever was. Something like it happened before, and this time the right side must win . . . We've had nothing but lies and propaganda and cruelty and deceit for all the thousands of years of human history. It's time we started again, but properly this time . . ."

He stopped to take in several rattling breaths.

"The knife," he went on after a minute; "they never knew what they were making, those old philosophers. They invented a device that could split open the very smallest particles of matter, and they used it to steal candy. They had no idea that they'd made the one weapon in all the universes that could defeat the tyrant. The Authority. God. The rebel angels fell because they didn't have anything like the knife; but now . . ."

"I didn't want it! I don't want it now!" Will cried. "If you want it, you can have it! I hate it and I hate what it does –"

"Too late. You haven't any choice: you're the bearer: it's picked you out. And what's more they know you've got it, and if you don't use it against them, they'll tear it from your hands and use it against the rest of us, for ever and ever."

"But why should I fight them? I've been fighting too much, I can't go on fighting, I want to –"

"Have you won your fights?"

Will was silent. Then he said, "Yes, I suppose."

"You fought for the knife?"

"Yes, but –"

"Then you're a warrior. That's what you are. Argue with anything else, but don't argue with your own nature."

Will knew that the man was speaking the truth. But it wasn't a welcome truth. It was heavy and painful. The man seemed to know that, because he let Will bow his head before he spoke again.

"There are two great powers," the man said, "and they've been fighting since time began. Every advance in human life, every scrap of knowledge and wisdom and decency we have has been torn by one side from the teeth of the other. Every little increase in human freedom has been fought over ferociously between those who want us to know more and be wiser and stronger, and those who want us to obey and be humble and submit.

"And now those two powers are lining up for battle. And each of them wants that knife of yours more than anything else. You have to choose, boy. We've been guided here, both of us: you with the knife and me to tell you about it."

"No! You're wrong!" cried Will. "I wasn't looking for anything like that! That's not what I was looking for at all!"

"You might not think so, but that's what you've found," said the man in the darkness.

"But what must I do?"

And then Stanislaus Grumman, Jopari, John Parry hesitated.

He was painfully aware of the oath he'd sworn to Lee Scoresby, and he hesitated before he broke it; but break it he did.

"You must go to Lord Asriel," he said, "and tell him that Stanislaus Grumman sent you, and that you have the one weapon he needs above all others. Like it or not, boy, you have a job to do. Ignore everything else, no matter how important it seems, and go and do this. Someone will appear to guide you: the night is full of angels. Your wound will heal now. Wait. Before you go, I want to look at you properly."

He felt for the pack he'd been carrying and took something out, unfolding layers of oilskin and then striking a match to light a little tin lantern. In its light, through the rain-dashed windy air, the two looked at each other.

Will saw blazing blue eyes in a haggard face with several days' growth of beard on the stubborn jaw, grey-haired, drawn with pain, a thin body hunched in a heavy cloak trimmed with feathers.

The shaman saw a boy even younger than he'd thought, his slim body shivering in a torn linen shirt and his expression exhausted and savage and wary, but alight with a wild curiosity, his eyes wide under the straight black brows, so like his mother's . . .

And there came just the first flicker of something else to both of them.

But in that same moment, as the lantern light flared over John Parry's face, something shot down from the turbid sky and he fell back dead before he could say a word, an arrow in his failing heart. The osprey-dæmon vanished in a moment.

Will could only sit stupefied.

A flicker crossed the corner of his vision, and his right hand darted up at once and he found he was clutching a robin, a dæmon, red-breasted, panicking.

"No! No!" cried the witch Juta Kamainen, and fell down after him, clutching at her own heart, crashing clumsily into the rocky ground and struggling up again.

But Will was there before she could find her feet, and the subtle knife was at her throat.

"Why did you do that?" he shouted. "Why did you kill him?"

"Because I loved him and he scorned me! I am a witch! I don't forgive!"

And because she was a witch she wouldn't have been afraid of a boy, normally. But she was afraid of Will. This young wounded figure held more force and danger than she'd ever met in a human before, and she quailed. She fell backwards, and he followed and gripped her hair with his left hand, feeling no pain, feeling only an immense and shattering despair.

"You don't know who he was," he cried. "He was my father!"

She shook her head and whispered, "No. No! That can't be true. Impossible!"

"You think things have to be *possible*? Things have to be *true*! He was my father, and neither of us knew it till the second you killed him! Witch, I wait all my life and come all this way and I find him at last, and you *kill* him . . ."

And he shook her head like a rag and threw her back against the ground, half-stunning her. Her astonishment was almost greater than her fear of him, which was real enough, and she pulled herself up dazed and seized his shirt in supplication. He knocked her hand away.

"What did he ever do that you needed to kill him?" he cried. "Tell me that, if you can!"

And she looked at the dead man. Then she looked back at Will and shook her head sadly.

"No, I can't explain," she said. "You're too young. It wouldn't make sense to you. I loved him. That's all. That's enough."

And before Will could stop her she fell softly sideways, her hand on the hilt of the knife she had just taken from her own belt and pushed between her ribs.

Will felt no horror, only desolation and bafflement.

He stood up slowly and looked down at the dead witch, at her rich black hair, her flushed cheeks, her smooth pale limbs wet with rain, her lips parted like a lover's.

"I don't understand," he said aloud. "It's too strange."

Will turned back to the dead man, his father.

A thousand things jostled at his throat, and only the dashing rain cooled the hotness in his eyes. The little lantern still flickered and flared as the draught through the ill-fitting window licked around the flame, and by its light Will knelt and put his hands on the man's body, touching his face, his shoulders, his chest, closing his eyes, pushing the wet grey hair off his forehead, pressing his hands to the rough cheeks, closing his father's mouth, squeezing his hands.

"Father," he said, "Dad, Daddy ... Father ... I don't understand why she did that. It's too strange for me. But whatever you wanted me to do, I promise, I swear I'll do it. I'll fight. I'll be a warrior, I will. This knife, I'll take it to Lord Asriel, wherever he is, and I'll help him fight that enemy. I'll do it. You can rest now. It's all right. You can sleep now."

Beside the dead man lay his deerskin pack with the oilskin and the lantern and the little horn box of bloodmoss ointment. Will picked them up, and then he noticed his father's feather-trimmed cloak trailing behind his body on the ground, heavy and sodden, but warm. His father had no more use for it, and Will was shaking with cold. He unfastened the bronze buckle at the dead man's throat and swung the canvas pack over his shoulder before wrapping the cloak around himself.

He blew out the lantern and looked back at the dim shapes of his father, of the witch, of his father again before turning to go down the mountain.

The stormy air was electric with whispers, and in the tearing of the wind Will could hear other sounds too: confused echoes of cries and chanting, the clash of metal on metal, pounding wingbeats that one moment sounded so close they might actually be inside his head, and the next so far away they might have been on another planet. The rocks underfoot were slippery and loose, and it was much harder going down than it had been climbing up; but he didn't falter.

And as he turned down the last little gully before they reached the place where Lyra was sleeping, he stopped suddenly. He could see two men simply standing there, in the dark, as if they were waiting. Will put his hand on the knife.

Then one of the men spoke.

"You're the boy with the knife?" he said, and his voice had the strange quality of those wingbeats. Whoever he was, he wasn't a human being.

"Who are you?" Will said. "Are you men, or –"

"Not men, no. We are Watchers. *Bene elim*. In your language, angels."

Will was silent. The speaker went on:

"Other angels have other functions, and other powers. Our task is simple: we need you. We have been following the shaman every inch of his way, hoping he would lead us to you, and so he has. And now we have come to guide you in turn to Lord Asriel."

"You were with my father all the time?"

"Every moment."

"Did he know?"

"He had no idea."

"Why didn't you stop the witch, then? Why did you let her kill him?"

"We would have done, earlier. But his task was over once he'd led us to you."

Will said nothing. His head was ringing; this was no less difficult to understand than anything else.

"All right," he said finally, "I'll come with you. But first I must wake Lyra."

They stood aside to let him pass, and he felt a tingle in the air as he went close to them, but he ignored it and concentrated on getting down the slope towards the little shelter where Lyra was sleeping.

But something made him stop.

In the dimness, he could see the witches who had been guarding Lyra all sitting or standing still. They looked like statues, except that they were breathing, but they were scarcely alive. There were several black-silk-clad bodies on the ground, too, and as he gazed in horror from one to another of them, Will saw what must have happened: they had been attacked in mid-air by the Spectres, and had fallen to their deaths, indifferently.

But –

"Where's Lyra?" he cried aloud.

The hollow under the rock was empty. Lyra was gone.

There was something under the overhang where she'd been lying. It was Lyra's little canvas rucksack, and from the weight of it he knew without looking that the alethiometer was still inside it.

Will was shaking his head. It couldn't be true, but it was: Lyra was gone, Lyra was captured, Lyra was lost.

The two dark figures of the *bene elim* had not moved. But they spoke:

"You must come with us now. Lord Asriel needs you at once. The enemy's power is growing every minute. The shaman has told you what your task is. Follow us and help us win. Come with us. Come this way. Come now."

And Will looked from them to Lyra's rucksack and back again, and he didn't hear a word they said.

LANTERN SLIDES

JOHN PARRY and the turquoise ring: how did he get hold of it? You could tell a story about the ring, and everything that had happened to it since it left Lee Scoresby's mother's finger; and you could tell a story about Lee himself, and recount his entire history from boyhood to the moment he sat beside the little hut on the flooded banks of the Yenisei, and saw the shaman's fist open to disclose the well-loved thing that he'd turned and turned round and round his mother's finger so long ago. The story-lines diverge, and move a very long way apart, and come together, and something happens when they touch. That something would lead Lee to his death, but what happened to the ring? It must still be around, somewhere.

A DÆMON is not an animal, of course; a dæmon is a person. A real cat, face to face with a dæmon in cat form, would not be puzzled for a moment. She would see a human being.

ALL THE TIME IN CITTÀGAZZE, the sense of how different a place this could have been if it hadn't been corrupted; how easy it would have been not to make the knife, if they'd seen the consequences. A world of teeming plenty, of beautiful seas and temperate weather, of prosperity and peace – and still they wanted more.

WILL AND HIS MOTHER, visiting an elderly-seeming couple in a large house, and getting a cold welcome. He was puzzled: he was too young to understand the conversation, the murmuring voices, his mother's tears. Later, all he remembered was the contempt on the older woman's face, the feeling that these two regarded his beloved mother as dirt, and his savage resolution never to let her be exposed to that brutality again. He was six. He would have killed them if he could. Very much later, he realized they were his father's parents.

LYRA lying awake on the cold rocks, pretending to be asleep, while Will whispered to her dæmon. How often did she think of that in the days that followed!

THE WINDOW IN ALASKA. Natural that the people of the area, if they knew about it at all, would regard it as a doorway to the spirit world; and natural that the other windows into our world should be hard to find, and often neglected. People don't like the uncanny, and rather than look fully at something disturbing, they'll avoid it altogether. That house that no one seems to live in for long, that corner of a field that the farmer never quite manages to plough, that broken wall that's always going to be repaired, but never is . . . There is such a place on Cader Idris in north Wales, and another in a hotel bedroom in Glasgow.

SIR CHARLES LATROM every morning applying two drops of a floral oil to the centre of a large silk handkerchief, which he then bundled and tucked as it were carelessly into his top pocket. He couldn't have named the oil: he'd stolen it from a bazaar in Damascus, but the Damascus of another world where the flowers were bred for the flesh-like exuberance of their scent. As it developed through the day, the fragrance of the oil rotted like a medlar; Sir Charles would lean his head to the left and sniff appreciatively, perhaps too frankly for the comfort of most companions.

CITTÀGAZZE under the moonlight, deserted and silent and open: the colonnades drenched in soft shadow, the Casino gardens so perfectly clipped and swept, the gravel paths . . . Every house lit, every door open to the warm night. It was the first place where Will had ever felt entirely safe and entirely welcome and entirely at home. Lonely, yes, at first, but he lived in that condition like a fish in water. He would never know how inconceivably strange he appeared, at first, to Lyra.

THE AMBER
SPYGLASS

O tell of his might, O sing of his grace,
Whose robe is the light, whose canopy space;
His chariots of wrath the deep thunder clouds form,
And dark is his path on the wings of the storm.

ROBERT GRANT,
From *Hymns Ancient and Modern*

O stars,
isn't it from you that the lover's desire for the face
of his beloved arises? Doesn't his secret insight
into her pure features come from the pure
constellations?

RAINER MARIA RILKE, *The Third Duino Elegy*
From *The Selected Poetry of Rainer Maria Rilke*
(transl. Stephen Mitchell)

Fine vapors escape from whatever is doing the living.
The night is cold and delicate and full of angels
Pounding down the living. The factories are all lit up,
The chime goes unheard.
We are together at last, though far apart.

JOHN ASHBERY, *The Ecclesiast*
From *River and Mountains*

CONTENTS

I

THE ENCHANTED SLEEPER

While the beasts of prey,
Come from caverns deep,
Viewed the maid asleep.

— WILLIAM BLAKE

IN A VALLEY shaded with rhododendrons, close to the snow line, where a stream milky with melt-water splashed and where doves and linnets flew among the immense pines, lay a cave, half-hidden by the crag above and the stiff heavy leaves that clustered below.

The woods were full of sound: the stream between the rocks, the wind among the needles of the pine branches, the chitter of insects and the cries of small arboreal mammals, as well as the bird-song; and from time to time a stronger gust of wind would make one of the branches of a cedar or a fir move against another and groan like a cello.

It was a place of brilliant sunlight, never undappled; shafts of lemon-gold brilliance lanced down to the forest floor between bars and pools of brown-green shade; and the light was never still, never constant, because drifting mist would often float among the tree-tops, filtering all the sunlight to a pearly sheen and brushing every pine-cone with moisture that glistened when the mist lifted. Sometimes the wetness in the clouds condensed into tiny drops half-mist and half-rain, that floated downwards rather than fell, making a soft rustling patter among the millions of needles.

There was a narrow path beside the stream, which led from a village – little more than a cluster of herdsmen's dwellings – at the foot of the valley, to a half-ruined shrine near the glacier at its head, a place where faded silken flags streamed out in the perpetual winds from the high mountains, and offerings of barley-cakes and dried tea were placed by pious villagers. An odd effect of the light, and the ice, and the vapour enveloped the head of the valley in perpetual rainbows.

The cave lay some way above the path. Many years before, a holy man had lived there, meditating and fasting and praying, and the place was venerated for the sake of his memory. It was thirty feet or so deep, with a dry floor: an ideal den for a bear or a wolf, but the only creatures living in it for years had been birds and bats.

But the form that was crouching inside the entrance, his black eyes watching this way and that, his sharp ears pricked, was neither bird nor bat. The sunlight lay heavy and rich on his lustrous golden fur, and his monkey-hands turned a pine-cone this way and that, snapping off the scales with sharp fingers and scratching out the sweet nuts.

Behind him, just beyond the point where the sunlight reached, Mrs Coulter was heating some water in a small pan over a naphtha stove. Her dæmon uttered a warning murmur, and Mrs Coulter looked up.

Coming along the forest path was a young village girl. Mrs Coulter knew who she was: Ama had been bringing her food for some days now. Mrs Coulter had let it be known when she first arrived that she was a holy woman engaged in meditation and prayer, and under a vow never to speak to a man. Ama was the only person whose visits she accepted.

This time, though, the girl wasn't alone. Her father was with her, and while Ama climbed up to the cave, he waited a little way off.

Ama came to the cave entrance and bowed.

"My father sends me with prayers for your goodwill," she said.

"Greetings, child," said Mrs Coulter.

The girl was carrying a bundle wrapped in faded cotton, which she laid at Mrs Coulter's feet. Then she held out a little bunch of flowers, a dozen or so anemones bound with a cotton thread, and began to speak in a rapid, nervous voice. Mrs Coulter understood some of the language of these mountain people, but it would never do to let them know how much. So she smiled and motioned to the girl to close her lips, and to watch their two dæmons. The golden monkey was holding out his little black hand, and Ama's butterfly-dæmon was fluttering closer and closer until he settled on a horny forefinger.

The monkey brought him slowly to his ear, and Mrs Coulter

felt a tiny stream of understanding flow into her mind, clarifying the girl's words. The villagers were happy for a holy woman, such as herself, to take refuge in the cave, but it was rumoured that she had a companion with her, who was in some way dangerous and powerful.

It was that which made the villagers afraid. Was this other being Mrs Coulter's master, or her servant? Did she mean harm? Why was she there in the first place? Were they going to stay long? Ama conveyed these questions with a thousand misgivings.

A novel answer occurred to Mrs Coulter as the dæmon's understanding filtered into hers. She could tell the truth. Not all of it, naturally, but some. She felt a little quiver of laughter at the idea, but kept it out of her voice as she explained:

"Yes, there is someone else with me. But there is nothing to be afraid of. She is my daughter, and she is under a spell that made her fall asleep. We have come here to hide from the enchanter who put the spell on her, while I try to cure her and keep her from harm. Come and see her, if you like."

Ama was half-soothed by Mrs Coulter's soft voice, and half-afraid still; and the talk of enchanters and spells added to the awe she felt. But the golden monkey was holding her dæmon so gently, and she was curious, besides, so she followed Mrs Coulter into the cave.

Her father on the path below took a step forward, and his crow-dæmon raised her wings once or twice, but he stayed where he was.

Mrs Coulter lit a candle, because the light was fading rapidly, and led Ama to the back of the cave. The little girl's eyes glittered widely in the gloom, and her hands were moving together in a repetitive gesture of finger on thumb, finger on thumb, to ward off danger by confusing the evil spirits.

"You see?" said Mrs Coulter. "She can do no harm. There's nothing to be afraid of."

Ama looked at the figure in the sleeping-bag. It was a girl older than she was, by three or four years, perhaps; and she had hair of a colour Ama had never seen before — a tawny fairness like a lion's. Her lips were pressed tightly together, and she was deeply asleep, there was no doubt about that, for her dæmon lay coiled and unconscious at her throat. He had the form of some creature like a mongoose, but red-gold in colour, and smaller. The golden monkey was tenderly smoothing the fur between the sleeping dæmon's ears, and as Ama looked, the mongoose-creature stirred uneasily and uttered a hoarse little mew. Ama's dæmon, mouse-formed, pressed himself close to Ama's neck and peered fearfully through her hair.

"So you can tell your father what you've seen," Mrs Coulter went on. "No evil spirit. Just my daughter, asleep under a spell, and in my care. But please, Ama, tell your father that this must be a secret. No one but you two must know Lyra is here. If the enchanter knew where she was, he would seek her out and destroy her, and me, and everything nearby. So hush! Tell your father, and no one else."

She knelt beside Lyra and smoothed the damp hair back from the sleeping face before bending low to kiss her daughter's cheek. Then she looked up with sad and loving eyes, and smiled at Ama with such brave compassion that the little girl felt tears fill her gaze.

Mrs Coulter took Ama's hand as they went back to the cave entrance, and saw the girl's father watching anxiously from below. The woman put her hands together and bowed to him, and he responded with relief as his daughter, having bowed both to Mrs Coulter and to the enchanted sleeper, turned and scampered down the slope in the twilight. Father and daughter bowed once more to the cave, and then set off, to vanish among the gloom of the heavy rhododendrons.

Mrs Coulter turned back to the water on her stove, which was nearly at the boil.

Crouching down, she crumbled some dried leaves into it, two pinches from this bag, one from that, and added three drops of a pale yellow oil. She stirred it briskly, counting in her head till five minutes had gone by. Then she took the pan off the stove, and sat down to wait for the liquid to cool.

Around her there lay some of the equipment from the camp by the blue lake where Sir Charles Latrom had died: a sleeping-bag, a rucksack with changes of clothes and washing equipment, and so on. There was also a case of canvas with a tough wooden frame, lined with kapok, containing various instruments; and there was a pistol in a holster.

The decoction cooled rapidly in the thin air, and as soon as it was at blood-heat she poured it carefully into a metal beaker and carried it to the rear of the cave. The monkey-dæmon dropped his pine-cone and came with her.

Mrs Coulter placed the beaker carefully on a low rock, and knelt beside the sleeping Lyra. The golden monkey crouched on her other side, ready to seize Pantalaimon if he woke up.

Lyra's hair was damp, and her eyes moved behind their closed lids. She was beginning to stir: Mrs Coulter had felt her eyelashes flutter when she'd kissed her, and knew she didn't have long before Lyra woke up altogether.

She slipped a hand under the girl's head, and with the other lifted the damp strands of hair off her forehead. Lyra's lips parted, and she moaned softly; Pantalaimon moved a little closer to her breast. The golden monkey's eyes never left Lyra's dæmon, and his little black fingers twitched at the edge of the sleeping-bag.

A look from Mrs Coulter, and he let go and moved back a hand's breadth. The woman gently lifted her daughter so that her shoulders were off the ground and her head lolled, and then Lyra caught her breath and her eyes half-opened, fluttering, heavy.

"Roger," she murmured. "Roger . . . where are you . . . I can't see . . ."

"Ssh," her mother whispered, "ssh, my darling, drink this."

Holding the beaker in Lyra's mouth, she tilted it to let a drop moisten the girl's lips. Lyra's tongue sensed it and moved to lick them, and then Mrs Coulter let a little more of the liquid trickle into her mouth, very carefully, letting her swallow each sip before allowing her more.

It took several minutes, but eventually the beaker was empty, and Mrs Coulter laid her daughter down again. As soon as Lyra's head lay on the ground, Pantalaimon moved back around her throat. His red-gold fur was as damp as her hair. They were deeply asleep again.

The golden monkey picked his way lightly to the mouth of the cave and sat once more watching the path. Mrs Coulter dipped a flannel in a basin of cold water and mopped Lyra's face, and then unfastened the sleeping-bag and washed her arms and neck and shoulders, because Lyra was hot. Then her mother took a comb and gently teased out the tangles in Lyra's hair, smoothing it back from her forehead, parting it neatly.

She left the sleeping-bag open so the girl could cool down, and unfolded the bundle that Ama had brought: some flat loaves of bread, a cake of compressed tea, some sticky rice wrapped in a large leaf. It was time to build the fire. The chill of the mountains was fierce at night. Working methodically, she shaved some dry tinder, set the fire and struck a match. That was something else to think of: the matches were running out, and so was the naphtha for the stove; she must keep the fire alight day and night from now on.

Her dæmon was discontented. He didn't like what she was doing here in the cave, and when he tried to express his concern she brushed him away. He turned his back, contempt in every line of his body as he flicked the scales from his pine-cone out into the dark. She took no notice, but worked steadily and skilfully to build up the fire and set the pan to heat some water for tea.

Nevertheless, his scepticism affected her, and as she crumbled the dark grey tea-brick into the water, she wondered what in the world she thought she was doing, and whether she had gone mad, and over and over again, what would happen when the church found out. The golden monkey was right. She wasn't only hiding Lyra: she was hiding her own eyes.

Out of the dark the little boy came, hopeful and frightened, whispering over and over:

"Lyra – Lyra – Lyra . . ."

Behind him there were other figures, even more shadowy than he was, even more silent. They seemed to be of the same company and of the same kind, but they had no faces that were visible and no voices that spoke; and his voice never rose above a whisper, and his face was shaded and blurred like something half-forgotten.

"Lyra . . . Lyra . . ."

Where were they?

On a great plain where no light shone from the iron-dark sky, and where a mist obscured the horizon on every side. The ground was bare earth, beaten flat by the pressure of millions of feet, even though those feet had less weight than feathers; so it must have been time that pressed it flat, even though time had been stilled in this place; so it must have been the way things were. This was the end of all places and the last of all worlds.

"Lyra . . ."

Why were they there?

They were imprisoned. Someone had committed a crime, though no one knew what it was, or who had done it, or what authority sat in judgment.

Why did the little boy keep calling Lyra's name?

Hope.

Who were they?

Ghosts.

And Lyra couldn't touch them, no matter how she tried. Her baffled hands moved through and through, and still the little boy stood there pleading.

"Roger," she said, but her voice came out in a whisper, "oh, Roger, where are you? What is this place?"

He said, "It's the world of the dead, Lyra — I dunno what to do — I dunno if I'm here for ever, and I dunno if I done bad things or what, because I tried to be good, but I hate it, I'm scared of it all, I hate it —"

And Lyra said, "I

2
BALTHAMOS AND BARUCH

Then a spirit passed before my face; the hair of my flesh stood up.

— THE BOOK OF JOB

"BE QUIET," said Will. "Just be quiet. Don't disturb me."

It was just after Lyra had been taken, just after Will had come down from the mountain-top, just after the witch had killed his father. Will lit the little tin lantern he'd taken from his father's pack, using the dry matches that he'd found with it, and crouched in the lee of the rock to open Lyra's rucksack.

He felt inside with his good hand, and found the heavy velvet-wrapped alethiometer. It glittered in the lantern-light, and he held it out to the two shapes that stood beside him, the shapes who called themselves angels.

"Can you read this?" he said.

"No," said a voice. "Come with us. You must come. Come now to Lord Asriel."

"Who made you follow my father? You said he didn't know you were following him. But he did," Will said fiercely. "He told me to expect you. He knew more than you thought. Who sent you?"

"No one sent us. Ourselves only," came the voice. "We want to serve Lord Asriel. And the dead man, what did *he* want you to do with the knife?"

Will had to hesitate.

"He said I should take it to Lord Asriel," he said.

"Then come with us."

"No. Not till I've found Lyra."

He folded the velvet over the alethiometer and put it into his rucksack. Securing it, he swung his father's heavy cloak around him against the rain and crouched where he was, looking steadily at the two shadows.

"Do you tell the truth?" he said.

"Yes."

"Then are you stronger than human beings, or weaker?"

"Weaker. You have true flesh, we have not. Still, you must come with us."

"No. If I'm stronger, you have to obey me. Besides, I have the knife. So I can command you: help me find Lyra. I don't care how long it takes, I'll find her first and *then* I'll go to Lord Asriel."

The two figures were silent for several seconds. Then they drifted away and spoke together, though Will could hear nothing of what they said.

Finally they came close again, and he heard:

"Very well. You are making a mistake, though you give us no choice. We shall help you find this child."

Will tried to pierce the darkness and see them more clearly, but the rain filled his eyes.

"Come closer so I can see you," he said.

They approached, but seemed to become even more obscure.

"Shall I see you better in daylight?"

"No, worse. We are not of a high order among angels."

"Well, if I can't see you, no one else will either, so you can stay hidden. Go and see if you can find out where Lyra's gone. She surely can't be far away. There was a woman – she'll be with her – the woman took her. Go and search, and come back and tell me what you see."

The angels rose up into the stormy air and vanished. Will felt a great sullen heaviness settle over him; he'd had little strength left before the fight with his father, and now he was nearly finished. All he wanted to do was close his eyes, which were so heavy and so sore with weeping.

He tugged the cloak over his head, clutched the rucksack to his breast, and fell asleep in a moment.

"Nowhere," said a voice.

Will heard it in the depths of sleep and struggled to wake. Eventually (and it took most of a minute, because he was so profoundly unconscious) he managed to open his eyes to the bright morning in front of him.

"Where are you?" he said.

"Beside you," said the angel. "This way."

The sun was newly risen, and the rocks and the lichens and

mosses on them shone crisp and brilliant in the morning light, but nowhere could he see a figure.

"I said we would be harder to see in daylight," the voice went on. "You will see us best at half-light, at dusk or dawn; next best in darkness; least of all in the sunshine. My companion and I searched further down the mountain, and found neither woman nor child. But there is a lake of blue water where she must have camped. There is a dead man there, and a witch eaten by a Spectre."

"A dead man? What does he look like?"

"He was in his sixties. Fleshy and smooth-skinned. Silver-grey hair. Dressed in expensive clothes, and with traces of a heavy scent around him."

"Sir Charles," said Will. "That's who it is. Mrs Coulter must have killed him. Well, that's something good, at least."

"She left traces. My companion has followed them, and he will return when he's found out where she went. I shall stay with you."

Will got to his feet and looked around. The storm had cleared the air, and the morning was fresh and clean, which only made the scene around him more distressing; for nearby lay the bodies of several of the witches who had escorted him and Lyra towards the meeting with his father. Already a brutal-beaked carrion crow was tearing at the face of one of them, and Will could see a bigger bird circling above, as if choosing the richest feast.

Will looked at each of the bodies in turn, but none of them was Serafina Pekkala, the queen of the witch-clan, Lyra's particular friend. Then he remembered: hadn't she left suddenly on another errand not long before the evening?

So she might still be alive. The thought cheered him, and he scanned the horizon for any sign of her, but found nothing but the blue air and the sharp rock in every direction he looked.

"Where are you?" he said to the angel.

"Beside you," came the voice, "as always."

Will looked to his left, where the voice was, but saw nothing.

"So no one can see you. Could anyone else hear you as well as me?"

"Not if I whisper," said the angel, tartly.

"What is your name? Do you have names?"

"Yes, we do. My name is Balthamos. My companion is Baruch."

Will considered what to do. When you choose one way out of many, all the ways you don't take are snuffed out like candles, as if they'd never existed. At the moment all Will's choices existed at once. But to keep them all in existence meant doing nothing. He had to choose, after all.

"We'll go back down the mountain," he said. "We'll go to that lake. There might be something there I can use. And I'm getting thirsty anyway. I'll take the way I think it is and you can guide me if I go wrong."

It was only when he'd been walking for several minutes down the pathless, rocky slope that Will realized his hand wasn't hurting. In fact he hadn't thought of his wound since he woke up.

He stopped and looked at the rough cloth that his father had bound around it after their fight. It was greasy with the ointment he'd spread on it, but there was not a sign of blood; and after the incessant bleeding he'd undergone since the fingers had been lost, this was so welcome that he felt his heart leap almost with joy.

He moved his fingers experimentally. True, the wounds still hurt, but with a different quality of pain: not the deep life-sapping ache of the day before, but a smaller, duller sensation. It felt as if it were healing. His father had done that. The witches' spell had failed, but his father had healed him.

He moved on down the slope, cheered.

It took three hours, and several words of guidance, before he came to the little blue lake. By the time he reached it he was parched with thirst, and in the baking sun the cloak was heavy and hot; though when he took it off he missed its cover, for his bare arms and neck were burning. He dropped cloak and ruck-sack and ran the last few yards to the water, to fall on his face and swallow mouthful after freezing mouthful. It was so cold that it made his teeth and skull ache.

Once he'd slaked the thirst he sat up and looked around. He'd been in no condition to notice things the day before, but now he saw more clearly the intense colour of the water, and heard the strident insect noises from all around.

"Balthamos?"

"Always here."

"Where is the dead man?"

"Beyond the high rock on your right."

"Are there any Spectres around?"

"No, none."

Will took up his rucksack and cloak and made his way along the edge of the lake and up on to the rock Balthamos had pointed out.

Beyond it a little camp had been set up, with five or six tents and the remains of cooking fires. Will moved down warily in case there was someone still alive and hiding.

But the silence was profound, with the insect-scrapings only scratching at the surface of it. The tents were still, the water was placid, with the ripples still drifting slowly out from where he'd been drinking. A flicker of green movement near his foot made him start briefly, but it was only a tiny lizard.

The tents were made of camouflage material, which only made them stand out more among the dull red rocks. He looked in the first and found it empty. So was the second, but in the third he found something valuable: a mess-tin and a box of matches. There was also a strip of some dark substance as long and as thick as his forearm. At first he thought it was leather, but in the sunlight he saw it clearly to be dried meat.

Well, he had a knife, after all. He cut a thin sliver and found it chewy and very slightly salty, but full of good flavour. He put the meat and the matches together with the mess-tin into his rucksack and searched the other tents, but found them empty.

He left the largest till last.

"Is that where the dead man is?" he said to the air.

"Yes," said Balthamos. "He has been poisoned."

Will walked carefully around to the entrance, which faced the lake. Sprawled beside an overturned canvas chair was the body of the man known in Will's world as Sir Charles Latrom, and in Lyra's as Lord Boreal, the man who stole her alethiometer, which theft in turn led Will to the subtle knife itself. Sir Charles had been smooth, dishonest, and powerful, and now he was dead. His face was distorted unpleasantly, and Will didn't want to look at it, but a glance inside the tent showed that there were plenty of things to steal, so he stepped over the body to look more closely.

His father, the soldier, the explorer, would have known exactly what to take. Will had to guess. He took a small magnifying glass in a steel case, because he could use it to light fires and save his matches; a reel of tough twine; an alloy canteen for water, much lighter than the goatskin flask he had been carrying, and a small tin cup; a small pair of binoculars; a roll of gold coins the size of a man's thumb, wrapped in paper; a first-aid kit; water purifying tablets; a packet of coffee; three packs of compressed dried fruit; a bag of oatmeal biscuits; six bars of Kendal Mint Cake; a packet of fish-hooks and nylon line; and finally, a notebook and a couple of pencils, and a small electric torch.

He packed it all in his rucksack, cut another sliver of meat, filled his belly and then his canteen from the lake, and said to Balthamos:

"Do you think I need anything else?"

"You could do with some sense," came the reply. "Some faculty to enable you to recognize wisdom and incline you to respect and obey it."

"Are you wise?"

"Much more so than you."

"Well, you see, I can't tell. Are you a man? You sound like a man."

"Baruch was a man. I was not. Now he is angelic."

"So –" Will stopped what he was doing, which was arranging his rucksack so the heaviest objects were in the bottom, and tried to see the angel. There was nothing there to see. "So he was a man," he went on, "and then . . . Do people become angels when they die? Is that what happens?"

"Not always. Not in the vast majority of cases . . . Very rarely."

"When was he alive, then?"

"Four thousand years ago, more or less. I am much older."

"And did he live in my world? Or Lyra's? Or this one?"

"In yours. But there are myriads of worlds. You know that."

"But how do people become angels?"

"What is the point of this metaphysical speculation?"

"I just want to know."

"Better to stick to your task. You have plundered this dead man's property, you have all the toys you need to keep you alive; now may we move on?"

"When I know which way to go."

"Whichever way we go, Baruch will find us."

"Then he'll still find us if we stay here. I've got a couple more things to do."

Will sat down where he couldn't see Sir Charles's body and ate three squares of the Kendal Mint Cake. It was wonderful how refreshed and strengthened he felt as the food began to nourish him. Then he looked at the alethiometer again. The thirty-six little pictures painted on ivory were each perfectly clear: there was no doubt that this was a baby, that a puppet, this a loaf of bread, and so on. It was what they meant that was obscure.

"How did Lyra read this?" he said to Balthamos.

"Quite possibly she made it up. Those who use these instruments have studied for many years, and even then they can only understand them with the help of many books of reference."

"She wasn't making it up. She read it truly. She told me things she could never have known otherwise."

"Then it is as much of a mystery to me, I assure you," said the angel.

Looking at the alethiometer, Will remembered something Lyra had said about reading it: something about the state of mind she had to be in to make it work. It had helped him, in turn, to feel the subtleties of the silver blade.

Feeling curious, he took out the knife and cut a small window in front of where he was sitting. Through it he saw nothing but blue air, but below, far below, was a landscape of trees and fields: his own world, without a doubt.

So mountains in this world didn't correspond to mountains in his. He closed the window, using his left hand for the first time. The joy of being able to use it again!

Then an idea came to him so suddenly it felt like an electric shock.

If there were myriads of worlds, why did the knife only open windows between this one and his own?

Surely it should cut into any of them.

He held it up again, letting his mind flow along to the very tip of the blade as Giacomo Paradisi had told him, until his consciousness nestled among the atoms themselves, and he felt every tiny snag and ripple in the air.

Instead of cutting as soon as he felt the first little halt, as he usually did, he let the knife move on to another and another. It was like tracing a row of stitches while pressing so softly that none of them was harmed.

"What are you doing?" said the voice from the air, bringing him back.

"Exploring," said Will. "Be quiet and keep out of the way. If you come near this you'll get cut, and if I can't see you, I can't avoid you."

Balthamos made a sound of muted discontent. Will held out the knife again and felt for those tiny halts and hesitations. There were far more of them than he'd thought. And as he felt them without the need to cut through at once, he found that they each had a different quality: this one was hard and definite, that one cloudy; a third was slippery, a fourth brittle and frail . . .

But among them all there were some he felt more easily than others, and, already knowing the answer, he cut one through to be sure: his own world again.

He closed it up and felt with the knife-tip for a snag with a different quality. He found one that was elastic and resistant, and let the knife feel its way through.

And yes! The world he saw through that window was not his own: the ground was closer here, and the landscape was not green fields and hedges but a desert of rolling dunes.

He closed it and opened another: the smoke-laden air over an industrial city, with a line of chained and sullen workers trudging into a factory.

He closed that one too and came back to himself. He felt a little dizzy. For the first time he understood some of the true power of the knife, and laid it very carefully on the rock in front of him.

"Are you going to stay here all day?" said Balthamos.

"I'm thinking. You can only move easily from one world to another if the ground's in the same place. And maybe there are places where it is, and maybe that's where a lot of cutting-through happens ... And you'd have to know what your own world felt like with the point or you might never get back. You'd be lost for ever."

"Indeed. But may we –"

"And you'd have to know which world had the ground in the same place or there wouldn't be any point in opening it," said Will, as much to himself as to the angel. "So it's not as easy as I thought. We were just lucky in Oxford and Cittàgazze, maybe. But I'll just ..."

He picked up the knife again. As well as the clear and obvious feeling he got when he touched a point that would open to his own world, there had been another kind of sensation he'd touched more than once: a quality of resonance, like the feeling of striking a heavy wooden drum, except of course that it came, like every other one, in the tiniest movement through the empty air.

There it was. He moved away and felt somewhere else: there it was again.

He cut through, and found that his guess was right. The resonance meant that the ground in the world he'd opened was in the same place as this one. He found himself looking at a grassy upland meadow under an overcast sky, in which a herd of placid beasts was grazing – animals such as he'd never seen before – creatures the size of bison, with wide horns and shaggy blue fur and a crest of stiff hair along their backs.

He stepped through. The nearest animal looked up incuriously and then turned back to the grass. Leaving the window open, Will, in the other-world meadow, felt with the knife-point for the familiar snags, and tried them.

Yes, he could open his own world from this one, and he was still high above the farms and hedges; and yes, he could easily find the solid resonance that meant the Cittàgazze-world he'd just left.

With a deep sense of relief, Will went back to the camp by the lake, closing everything behind him. Now he could find his way home; now he would not get lost; now he could hide when he needed to, and move about safely.

With every increase in his knowledge came a gain in strength. He sheathed the knife at his waist and swung the rucksack over his shoulder.

"Well, are you ready now?" said that sarcastic voice.

"Yes. I'll explain if you like, but you don't seem very interested."

"Oh, I find whatever you do a source of perpetual fascination. But never mind me. What are you going to say to these people who are coming?"

Will looked around, startled. Further down the trail – a long way down – there was a line of travellers with packhorses, making their way steadily up towards the lake. They hadn't seen him yet, but if he stayed where he was, they would soon.

Will gathered up his father's cloak, which he'd laid over a rock in the sun. It weighed much less now it was dry. He looked around: there was nothing else he could carry.

"Let's go further on," he said.

He would have liked to re-tie the bandage, but it could wait. He set off along the edge of the lake, away from the travellers, and the angel followed him, invisible in the bright air.

Much later that day they came down from the bare mountains on to a spur covered in grass and dwarf rhododendrons. Will was aching for rest, and soon, he decided, he'd stop.

He'd heard little from the angel. From time to time Balthamos had said, "Not that way," or, "There is an easier path to the left," and he'd accepted the advice; but really he was moving for the sake of moving, and to keep away from those travellers, because until the other angel came back with more news, he might as well have stayed where they were.

Now the sun was setting, he thought he could see his strange companion. The outline of a man seemed to quiver in the light, and the air was thicker inside it.

"Balthamos?" he said. "I want to find a stream. Is there one nearby?"

"There is a spring half-way down the slope," said the angel, "just above those trees."

"Thank you," said Will.

He found the spring and drank deeply, filling his canteen. But before he could go on down to the little wood, there came an exclamation from Balthamos, and Will turned to see his outline dart across the slope towards – what? The angel was visible only as a flicker of movement, and Will could see him better when he didn't look at him directly; but he seemed to pause, and listen, and then launch himself into the air to skim back swiftly to Will.

"Here!" he said, and his voice was free of disapproval and sarcasm for once. "Baruch came this way! And there is one of those windows, almost invisible. Come – come. Come now."

Will followed eagerly, his weariness forgotten. The window, he saw when he reached it, opened on to a dim tundra-like landscape that was flatter than the mountains in the Cittàgazze world, and colder, with an overcast sky. He went through, and Balthamos followed him at once.

"Which world is this?" Will said.

"The girl's own world. This is where they came through. Baruch has gone ahead to follow them."

"How do you know where he is? Do you read his mind?"

"Of course I read his mind. Wherever he goes, my heart goes with him; we feel as one, though we are two."

Will looked around. There was no sign of human life, and the chill in the air was increasing by the minute as the light failed.

"I don't want to sleep here," he said. "We'll stay in the Ci'gazze world for the night and come through in the morning. At least there's wood back there, and I can make a fire. And now I know what her world feels like, I can find it with the knife . . . Oh, Balthamos? Can you take any other shape?"

"Why would I wish to do that?"

"In this world, human beings have dæmons, and if I go about without one, they'll be suspicious. Lyra was frightened of me at first because of that. So if we're going to travel in her world, you'll have to pretend to be my dæmon, and take the shape of some animal. A bird, maybe. Then you could fly, at least."

"Oh, how tedious."

"Can you, though?"

"I *could* . . ."

"Do it now, then. Let me see."

The form of the angel seemed to condense and swirl into a little vortex in mid-air, and then a blackbird swooped down on to the grass at Will's feet.

"Fly to my shoulder," said Will.

The bird did so, and then spoke in the angel's familiar acid tone:

"I shall only do this when it's absolutely necessary. It's unspeakably humiliating."

"Too bad," said Will. "Whenever we see people, in this world, you become a bird. There's no point in fussing or arguing. Just do it."

The blackbird flew off his shoulder and vanished in mid-air, and there was the angel again, sulking in the half-light. Before they went back through, Will looked all around, sniffing the air, taking the measure of the world where Lyra was captive.

"Where is your companion now?" he said.

"Following the woman south."

"Then we shall go that way too, in the morning."

Next day, Will walked for hours, and saw no one. The country consisted for the most part of low hills covered in short dry grass, and whenever he found himself on any sort of high point he looked all round for signs of human habitation, but found none. The only variation in the dusty brown-green emptiness was a distant smudge of darker green, which he made for because Balthamos said it was a forest and there was a river there, which led south. When the sun was at its height, he tried and failed to sleep among some low bushes; and as the evening approached, he was footsore and weary.

"Slow progress," said Balthamos sourly.

"I can't help that," said Will. "If you can't say anything useful, don't speak at all."

By the time he reached the edge of the forest the sun was low and the air heavy with pollen, so much so that he sneezed several times, startling a bird that flew up shrieking from somewhere nearby.

"That was the first living thing I've seen today," Will said.

"Where are you going to camp?" said Balthamos.

The angel was occasionally visible now in the long shadows of the trees. What Will could see of his expression was petulant.

Will said, "I'll have to stop here somewhere. You could help look for a good spot. I can hear a stream – see if you can find it."

The angel disappeared. Will trudged on, through the low clumps of heather and bog myrtle, wishing there was such a thing as a path for his feet to follow, and eyeing the light with apprehension: he must choose where to stop soon, or the dark would force him to stop without a choice.

"Left," said Balthamos, an arm's length away. "A stream and a dead tree for firewood. This way . . ."

Will followed the angel's voice, and soon found the spot he described. A stream splashed swiftly between mossy rocks, and disappeared over a lip into a narrow little chasm, dark under the over-arching trees. Beside the stream, a grassy bank extended a little way back to bushes and undergrowth.

Before he let himself rest, he set about collecting wood, and soon came across a circle of charred stones in the grass, where someone else had made a fire long before. He gathered a pile of twigs and heavier branches and with the knife cut them to a useful length before trying to get them lit. He didn't know the best way to go about it, and wasted several matches before he managed to coax the flames into life.

The angel watched with a kind of weary patience.

Once the fire was going, Will ate two oatmeal biscuits, some dried meat, and some Kendal Mint Cake, washing it down with gulps of cold water. Balthamos sat nearby, silent, and finally Will said:

"Are you going to watch me all the time? I'm not going anywhere."

"I'm waiting for Baruch. He will come back soon, and then I shall ignore you, if you like."

"Would you like some food?"

Balthamos moved slightly: he was tempted.

"I mean, I don't know if you eat at all," Will said, "but if you'd like something, you're welcome."

"What is that . . ." said the angel fastidiously, indicating the Kendal Mint Cake.

"Mostly sugar, I think, and peppermint. Here."

Will broke off a square and held it out. Balthamos inclined his head and sniffed. Then he picked it up, his fingers light and cool against Will's palm.

"I think this will nourish me," he said. "One piece is quite enough, thank you."

He sat and nibbled quietly. Will found that if he looked at the fire, with the angel just at the edge of his vision, he had a much stronger impression of him.

"Where is Baruch?" he said. "Can he communicate with you?"

"I feel that he is close. He'll be here very soon. When he returns, we shall talk. Talking is best."

And barely ten minutes later the soft sound of wingbeats came to their ears, and Balthamos stood up eagerly. The next moment, the two angels were embracing, and Will, gazing into the flames, saw their mutual affection. More than affection: they loved each other with a passion.

Baruch sat down beside his companion, and Will stirred the fire, so that a cloud of smoke drifted past the two of them. It had the effect of outlining their bodies so that he could see them both clearly for the first time. Balthamos was slender; his narrow wings were folded elegantly behind his shoulders, and his face bore an expression that mingled haughty disdain with a tender, ardent sympathy, as if he would love all things if only his nature could let him forget their defects. But he saw no defects in Baruch, that was clear. Baruch seemed younger, as Balthamos had said he was, and was more powerfully built, his wings snow-white and massive. He had a simpler nature; he looked up to Balthamos as to the fount of all knowledge and joy. Will found himself intrigued and moved by their love for each other.

"Did you find out where Lyra is?" he said, impatient for news.

"Yes," said Baruch. "There is a Himalayan valley, very high up, near a glacier where the light is turned into rainbows by the ice. I shall draw you a map in the soil, so you don't mistake it. The girl is captive in a cave among the trees, kept asleep by the woman."

"Asleep? And the woman's alone? No soldiers with her?"

"Alone, yes. In hiding."

"And Lyra's not harmed?"

"No. Just asleep, and dreaming. Let me show you where they are."

With his pale finger, Baruch traced a map in the bare soil beside the fire. Will took his notebook and copied it exactly. It showed a glacier with a curious serpentine shape, flowing down between three almost identical mountain peaks.

"Now," said the angel, "we go closer. The valley with the cave runs down from the left side of the glacier, and a river of melt-water runs through it. The head of the valley is here . . ."

He drew another map, and Will copied that; and then a third, getting closer in each time, so that Will felt he could find his way there without difficulty – provided that he'd crossed the four or five thousand miles between the tundra and the mountains. The knife was good for cutting between worlds, but it couldn't abolish distance within them.

"There is a shrine near the glacier," Baruch ended by saying, "with red silk banners half-torn by the winds. And a young girl brings food to the cave. They think the woman is a saint who will bless them if they look after her needs."

"Do they," said Will. "And she's *hiding* . . . That's what I don't understand. Hiding from the church?"

"It seems so."

Will folded the maps carefully away. He had set the tin cup on the stones at the edge of the fire to heat some water, and now he trickled some powdered coffee into it, stirring it with a stick, and wrapped his hand in a handkerchief before picking it up to drink.

A burning stick settled in the fire; a night bird called.

Suddenly, for no reason Will could see, both angels looked up and in the same direction. He followed their gaze, but saw nothing. He had seen his cat do this once: look up alert from her half-sleep, and watch something or someone invisible come into the room and walk across. That had made his hair stand up, and so did this.

"Put out the fire," Balthamos whispered.

Will scooped up some earth with his good hand and doused the flames. At once the cold struck into his bones, and he began to shiver. He pulled the cloak around himself and looked up again.

And now there was something to see: above the clouds a shape was glowing, and it was not the moon.

He heard Baruch murmur, "The Chariot? Could it be?"

"What is it?" Will whispered.

Baruch leaned close and whispered back, "They know we're here. They've found us. Will, take your knife and –"

Before he could finish, something hurtled out of the sky and crashed into Balthamos. In a fraction of a second Baruch had leapt on it, and Balthamos was twisting to free his wings. The three beings fought this way and that in the dimness, like great wasps caught in a mighty spider's web, making no sound: all Will could hear was the breaking twigs and the brushing leaves as they struggled together.

He couldn't use the knife: they were all moving too quickly. Instead, he took the electric torch from the rucksack and switched it on.

None of them expected that. The attacker threw up his wings, Balthamos flung his arm across his eyes, and only Baruch had the presence of mind to hold on. But Will could see what it was, this enemy: another angel, much bigger and stronger than they were, and Baruch's hand was clamped over his mouth.

"Will!" cried Balthamos. "The knife – cut a way out –"

And at the same moment the attacker tore himself free of Baruch's hands, and cried:

"Lord Regent! I have them!"

His voice made Will's head ring; he had never heard such a cry. And a moment later the angel would have sprung into the air, but Will dropped his torch and leapt forward. He had killed a cliff-ghast, but using the knife on a being shaped like himself was much harder. Nevertheless, he gathered the great beating wings into his arms and slashed again and again at the feathers until the air was filled with whirling flakes of white, remembering even in the sweep of violent sensations the words of Balthamos: *You have true flesh, we have not.* Human beings were stronger than angels, and it was true: he was bearing the angel down to the ground.

The attacker was still shouting in that ear-splitting voice: "*Lord Regent! To me, to me!*"

Will managed to glance upwards, and saw the clouds stirring and swirling, and that gleam – something immense – growing more powerful, as if the clouds themselves were becoming luminous with energy, like plasma.

Balthamos cried, "Will – come away and cut through, before he comes –"

But the angel was struggling hard, and now he had one wing free and he was forcing himself up from the ground, and Will had to hang on or lose him entirely. Baruch sprang to help him, and forced the attacker's head back and back.

"No!" cried Balthamos again. "No! No!"

He hurled himself at Will, shaking his arm, his shoulder, his hands, and the attacker was trying to shout again but Baruch's hand was over his mouth. From above there came a deep tremor, like a mighty dynamo, almost too low to hear, though it shook the very atoms of the air and jolted the marrow in Will's bones.

"He's coming –" Balthamos said, almost sobbing, and now Will did catch some of his fear. "Please, please, Will –"

Will looked up.

The clouds were parting, and through the dark gap a figure was speeding down: small at first, but as it came closer second by second the form became bigger and more imposing. He was making straight for them, with unmistakable malevolence; Will was sure he could even see his eyes.

"Will, you must," said Baruch urgently.

Will stood up, meaning to say, "Hold him tight," but even as the words came to his mind, the angel sagged against the ground, dissolving and spreading out like mist, and then he was gone. Will looked around, feeling foolish and sick.

"Did I kill him?" he said shakily.

"You had to," said Baruch. "But now –"

"I hate this," said Will passionately, "truly, truly, I hate this killing! When will it stop?"

"We must go," said Balthamos faintly. "Quickly, Will – quickly please –"

They were both mortally afraid.

Will felt in the air with the tip of the knife: any world, out of this one. He cut swiftly, and looked up: that other angel from the sky was only seconds away, and his expression was terrifying. Even from that distance, and even in that urgent second or so, Will felt himself searched and scoured from one end of his being to the other by some vast, brutal, and merciless intellect.

And what was more, he had a spear — he was raising it to hurl —

And in the moment it took the angel to check his flight and turn upright and pull back his arm to fling the weapon, Will followed Baruch and Balthamos through and closed the window behind him. As his fingers pressed the last inch together, he felt a shock of air — but it was gone, he was safe: it was the spear that would have passed through him in that other world.

They were on a sandy beach under a brilliant moon. Giant fern-like trees grew some way inland; low dunes extended for miles along the shore. It was hot and humid.

"Who was that?" said Will, trembling, facing the two angels.

"That was Metatron," said Balthamos. "You should have —"

"Metatron? Who's he? Why did he attack? And don't lie to me."

"We must tell him," said Baruch to his companion. "You should have done already."

"Yes, I should," Balthamos agreed, "but I was cross with him, and anxious for you."

"Tell me now then," said Will. "And remember, it's no good telling me what I should do — none of it matters to me, none. Only Lyra matters, and my mother. And *that*," he added to Balthamos, "is the point of all this metaphysical speculation, as you called it."

Baruch said, "I think we should tell you our information. Will, this is why we two have been seeking you, and why we must take you to Lord Asriel. We discovered a secret of the kingdom — of the Authority's world — and we must share it with him. Are we safe here?" he added, looking around. "There is no way through?"

"This is a different world. A different universe."

The sand they stood on was soft, and the slope of the dune nearby was inviting. They could see for miles in the moonlight; they were utterly alone.

"Tell me, then," said Will. "Tell me about Metatron, and what this secret is. Why did that angel call him Regent? And what is the Authority? Is he God?"

He sat down, and the two angels, their forms clearer in the moonlight than he had ever seen them before, sat with him.

Balthamos said quietly, "The Authority, God, the Creator, the Lord, Yahweh, El, Adonai, the King, the Father, the Almighty – those were all names he gave himself. He was never the creator. He was an angel like ourselves – the first angel, true, the most powerful, but he was formed of Dust as we are, and Dust is only a name for what happens when matter begins to understand itself. Matter loves matter. It seeks to know more about itself, and Dust is formed. The first angels condensed out of Dust, and the Authority was the first of all. He told those who came after him that he had created them, but it was a lie. One of those who came later was wiser than he was, and she found out the truth, so he banished her. We serve her still. And the Authority still reigns in the kingdom, and Metatron is his Regent.

"But as for what we discovered in the Clouded Mountain, we can't tell you the heart of it. We swore to each other that the first to hear should be Lord Asriel himself."

"Then tell me what you can. Don't keep me in the dark."

"We found our way into the Clouded Mountain," said Baruch, and at once went on: "I'm sorry; we use these terms too easily. It's sometimes called the Chariot. It's not fixed, you see; it moves from place to place. Wherever it goes, there is the heart of the kingdom, his citadel, his palace. When the Authority was young, it wasn't surrounded by clouds, but as time passed, he gathered them around him more and more thickly. No one has seen the summit for thousands of years. So his citadel is known now as the Clouded Mountain."

"What did you find there?"

"The Authority himself dwells in a chamber at the heart of the mountain. We couldn't get close, although we saw him. His power –"

"He has delegated much of his power," Balthamos interrupted, "to Metatron, as I was saying. You've seen what he's like. We escaped from him before, and now he's seen us again, and what is more, he's seen you, and he's seen the knife. I did say –"

"Balthamos," said Baruch gently, "don't chide Will. We need his help, and he can't be blamed for not knowing what it took *us* so long to find out."

Balthamos looked away.

Will said, "So you're not going to tell me this secret of yours? All right. Tell me this instead: what happens when we die?"

Balthamos looked back, in surprise.

Baruch said, "Well, there is a world of the dead. Where it is, and what happens there, no one knows. My ghost, thanks to Balthamos, never went there; I am what was once the ghost of Baruch. The world of the dead is just dark to us."

"It is a prison camp," said Balthamos. "The Authority established it in the early ages. Why do you want to know? You will see it in time."

"My father has just died, that's why. He would have told me all he knew, if he hadn't been killed. You say it's a world – do you mean a world like this one, another universe?"

Balthamos looked at Baruch, who shrugged.

"And what happens in the world of the dead?" Will went on.

"It's impossible to say," said Baruch. "Everything about it is secret. Even the churches don't know; they tell their believers that they'll live in Heaven, but that's a lie. If people really knew . . ."

"And my father's ghost has gone there."

"Without a doubt, and so have the countless millions who died before him."

Will found his imagination trembling.

"And why didn't you go directly to Lord Asriel with your great secret, whatever it is," he said, "instead of looking for me?"

"We were not sure," said Balthamos, "that he would believe us, unless we brought him proof of our good intentions. Two angels of low rank, among all the powers he is dealing with – why should he take us seriously? But if we could bring him the knife and its bearer, he might listen. The knife is a potent weapon, and Lord Asriel would be glad to have you on his side."

"Well, I'm sorry," said Will, "but that sounds feeble to me. If you had any confidence in your secret, you wouldn't need an excuse to see Lord Asriel."

"There's another reason," said Baruch. "We knew that Meta-tron would be pursuing us, and we wanted to make sure the knife didn't fall into his hands. If we could persuade you to come to Lord Asriel first, then at least –"

"Oh, no, that's not going to happen," said Will. "You're making it *harder* for me to reach Lyra, not easier. She's the most important thing, and you're forgetting her completely. Well, I'm not. Why don't you just go to Lord Asriel and leave me alone? *Make* him listen. You could fly to him much more quickly than I can walk, and I'm going to find Lyra first, come what may. Just do that. Just go. Just leave me."

"But you need me," said Balthamos stiffly, "because I can pretend to be your dæmon, and in Lyra's world you'd stand out, otherwise."

Will was too angry to speak. He got up and walked twenty steps away through the soft deep sand, and then stopped, for the heat and humidity were stunning.

He turned around to see the two angels talking closely together, and then they came up to him, humble and awkward, but proud too.

Baruch said, "We are sorry. I shall go on my own to Lord Asriel, and give him our information, and ask him to send you help to find his daughter. It will be two days' flying time, if I navigate truly."

"And I shall stay with you, Will," said Balthamos.

"Well," said Will, "thank you."

The two angels embraced. Then Baruch folded his arms around Will and kissed him on both cheeks. The kiss was light and cool, like the hands of Balthamos.

"If we keep moving towards Lyra," Will said, "will you find us?"

"I shall never lose Balthamos," said Baruch, and stepped back. Then he leapt into the air, soared swiftly into the sky, and vanished among the scattered stars. Balthamos was looking after him with desperate longing.

"Shall we sleep here, or should we move on?" he said finally, turning to Will.

"Sleep here," said Will.

"Then sleep, and I'll watch out for danger. Will, I have been short with you, and it was wrong of me. You have the greatest burden, and I should help you, not chide you. I shall try to be kinder from now on."

So Will lay down on the warm sand, and somewhere nearby, he thought, the angel was keeping watch; but that was little comfort.

'll get us out of here, Roger, I promise. And Will's coming, I'm sure he is!"

He didn't understand. He spread his pale hands and shook his head.

"I dunno who that is, and he won't come here," he said, "and if he does he won't know me."

"He's coming to me," she said, "and me and Will, oh, I don't know how, Roger, but I swear we'll help. And don't forget there's others on our side. There's Serafina and there's Iorek, and

3
SCAVENGERS

The knight's bones are dust,
And his good sword rust; –
His soul is with the saints,
I trust.

— S. T. COLERIDGE

SERAFINA PEKKALA, the clan-queen of the witches of Lake Enara, wept as she flew through the turbid skies of the Arctic. She wept with rage and fear and remorse: rage against the woman Coulter, whom she had sworn to kill; fear of what was happening to her beloved land; and remorse ... She would face the remorse later.

Meanwhile, she looked down at the melting ice-cap, the flooded lowland forests, the swollen sea, and felt heartsick.

But she didn't stop to visit her homeland, or to comfort and encourage her sisters. Instead she flew north and further north, into the fogs and gales around Svalbard, the kingdom of Iorek Byrnison, the armoured bear.

She hardly recognized the main island. The mountains lay bare and black, and only a few hidden valleys facing away from the sun had retained a little snow in their shaded corners; but what was the sun doing here anyway, at this time of year? The whole of nature was overturned.

It took her most of a day to find the bear-king. She saw him among the rocks off the northern edge of the island, swimming fast after a walrus. It was harder for bears to kill in the water: when the land was covered in ice and the great sea-mammals had to come up to breathe, the bears had the advantage of camouflage and their prey was out of its element. That was how things should be.

But Iorek Byrnison was hungry, and even the stabbing tusks of the mighty walrus couldn't keep him at bay. Serafina watched as the creatures fought, turning the white sea-spray red, and saw Iorek haul the carcass out of the waves and on to a broad shelf of rock, watched at a respectful distance by three ragged-furred foxes, waiting for their turn at the feast.

When the bear-king had finished eating, Serafina flew down to speak to him. Now was the time to face her remorse.

"King Iorek Byrnison," she said, "please may I speak with you? I lay my weapons down."

She placed her bow and arrows on the wet rock between them. Iorek looked at them briefly, and she knew that if his face could register any emotion, it would be surprise.

"Speak, Serafina Pekkala," he growled. "We have never fought, have we?"

"King Iorek, I have failed your comrade, Lee Scoresby."

The bear's small black eyes and bloodstained muzzle were very still. She could see the wind ruffling the tips of the creamy-white hairs along his back. He said nothing.

"Mr Scoresby is dead," Serafina went on. "Before I parted from him, I gave him a flower to summon me with, if he should need me. I heard his call and flew to him, but I arrived too late. He died fighting a force of Muscovites, but I know nothing of what brought them there, or why he was holding them off when he could easily have escaped. King Iorek, I am wretched with remorse."

"Where did this happen?" said Iorek Byrnison.

"In another world. This will take me some time to tell."

"Then begin."

She told him what Lee Scoresby had set out to do: to find the man who had been known as Stanislaus Grumman. She told him about how the barrier between the worlds had been breached by Lord Asriel, and about some of the consequences – the melting of the ice, for example. She told of the witch Ruta Skadi's flight after the angels, and she tried to describe those flying beings to the bear-king as Ruta had described them to her: the light that shone on them, the crystalline clarity of their appearance, the richness of their wisdom.

Then she described what she had found when she answered Lee's call.

"I put a spell on his body to preserve it from corruption," she told him. "It will last until you see him, if you wish to do that.

But I am troubled by this, King Iorek. Troubled by everything, but mostly by this."

"Where is the child?"

"I left her with my sisters, because I had to answer Lee's call."

"In that same world?"

"Yes, the same."

"How can I get there from here?"

She explained. Iorek Byrnison listened expressionlessly, and then said, "I shall go to Lee Scoresby. And then I must go south."

"South?"

"The ice has gone from these lands. I have been thinking about this, Serafina Pekkala. I have chartered a ship."

The three little foxes had been waiting patiently. Two of them were lying down, heads on their paws, watching, and the other was still sitting up, following the conversation. The foxes of the Arctic, scavengers that they were, had picked up some language, but their brains were so formed that they could only understand statements in the present tense. Most of what Iorek and Serafina said was meaningless noise to them. Furthermore, when they spoke, much of what they said was lies, so it didn't matter if they repeated what they'd heard: no one could sort out which parts were true, though the credulous cliff-ghasts often believed most of it, and never learned from their disappointment. The bears and the witches alike were used to their conversations being scavenged, like the meat they'd finished with.

"And you, Serafina Pekkala?" Iorek went on. "What will you do now?"

"I'm going to find the gyptians," she said. "I think they will be needed."

"Lord Faa," said the bear, "yes. Good fighters. Go well."

He turned away and slipped into the water without a splash, and began to swim in his steady tireless paddle towards the new world.

And some time later, Iorek Byrnison stepped through the blackened undergrowth and the heat-split rocks at the edge of a burnt forest. The sun was glaring through the smoky haze, but he ignored the heat as he ignored the charcoal dust that blackened his white fur and the midges that searched in vain for skin to bite.

He had come a long way, and at one point in his journey, he had found himself swimming into that other world. He noticed the change in the taste of the water and the temperature of the air, but the air was still good to breathe, and the water still held his body up, so he swam on, and now he had left the sea behind, and he was nearly at the place Serafina Pekkala had described. He cast around, his black eyes gazing up at the sun-shimmering rocks of a wall of limestone crags above him.

Between the edge of the burnt forest and the mountains, a rocky slope of heavy boulders and scree was littered with scorched and twisted metal: girders and struts that had belonged to some complex machine. Iorek Byrnison looked at them as a smith as well as a warrior, but there was nothing in these fragments he could use. He scored a line with a mighty claw along a strut less damaged than most, and feeling a flimsiness in the quality of the metal, turned away at once and scanned the mountain wall again.

Then he saw what he was looking for: a narrow gully leading back between jagged walls, and at the entrance, a large low boulder.

He clambered steadily towards it. Beneath his huge feet, dry bones snapped loudly in the stillness, because many men had died here, to be picked clean by coyotes and vultures and lesser creatures; but the great bear ignored them and stepped up carefully towards the rock. The going was loose and he was heavy, and more than once the scree shifted under his feet and carried him down again in a scramble of dust and gravel. But as soon as he slid down he began to move up once more, relentlessly, patiently, until he reached the rock itself, where the footing was firmer.

The boulder was pitted and chipped with bullet-marks. Everything the witch had told him was true. And in confirmation, a little Arctic flower, a purple saxifrage, blossomed improbably where the witch had planted it as a signal in a cranny of the rock.

Iorek Byrnison moved around to the upper side. It was a good shelter from an enemy below, but not good enough; for among the hail of bullets that had chipped fragments off the rock had been a few that had found their target, and that lay where they had come to rest, in the body of the man lying stiff in the shadow.

He was a body, still, and not a skeleton, because the witch had laid a spell to preserve him from corruption. Iorek could see the face of his old comrade drawn and tight with the pain of his wounds, and see the jagged holes in his garments where the bullets had entered. The witch's spell did not cover the blood that must have spilled, and insects and the sun and the wind had dispersed it completely. Lee Scoresby looked not asleep, nor at peace; he looked as if he had died in battle; but he looked as if he knew that his fight had been successful.

And because the Texan aëronaut was one of the very few humans Iorek had ever esteemed, he accepted the man's last gift to him. With deft movements of his claws, he ripped aside the dead man's clothes, opened the body with one slash, and began to feast on the flesh and blood of his old friend. It was his first meal for days, and he was hungry.

But a complex web of thoughts was weaving itself in the bear-king's mind, with more strands in it than hunger and satisfaction. There was the memory of the little girl Lyra, whom he had named Silvertongue, and whom he had last seen crossing the fragile snow-bridge across a crevasse in his own island of Svalbard. Then there was the agitation among the witches, the rumours of pacts and alliances and war; and then there was the surpassingly strange fact of this new world itself, and the witch's insistence that there were many more such worlds, and that the fate of them all hung somehow on the fate of the child.

And then there was the melting of the ice. He and his people lived on the ice; ice was their home; ice was their citadel. Since the vast disturbances in the Arctic, the ice had begun to disappear, and Iorek knew that he had to find an ice-bound fastness for his kin, or they would perish. Lee had told him that there were mountains in the south so high that even his balloon could not fly over them, and they were crowned with snow and ice all year round. Exploring those mountains was his next task.

But for now, something simpler possessed his heart, something bright and hard and unshakeable: vengeance. Lee Scoresby, who had rescued Iorek from danger in his balloon and fought beside him in the Arctic of his own world, had died. Iorek would avenge him. The good man's flesh and bone would both nourish him and keep him restless until blood was spilled enough to still his heart.

The sun was setting as Iorek finished his meal, and the air was cooling down. After gathering the remaining fragments into a single heap, the bear lifted the flower in his mouth and dropped it in the centre of them, as humans liked to do. The witch's spell was broken now; the rest of Lee's body was free to all who came. Soon it would be nourishing a dozen different kinds of life.

Then Iorek set off down the slope towards the sea again, towards the south.

Cliff-ghasts were fond of fox, when they could get it. The little creatures were cunning and hard to catch, but their meat was tender and rank.

Before he killed this one, the cliff-ghast let it talk, and laughed at its silly babble.

"Bear must go south! Swear! Witch is troubled! True! Swear! Promise!"

"Bears don't go south, lying filth!"

"True! King bear must go south! Show you walrus – fine fat good –"

"King bear go south?"

"And flying things got treasure! Flying things – angels – crystal treasure!"

"Flying things – like cliff-ghasts? Treasure?"

"Like light, not like cliff-ghast. Rich! Crystal! And witch troubled – witch sorry – Scoresby dead –"

"Dead? Balloon man dead?" The cliff-ghast's laugh echoed around the dry cliffs.

"Witch kill him – Scoresby dead, king bear go south –"

"Scoresby dead! Ha, ha, Scoresby dead!"

The cliff-ghast wrenched off the fox's head, and fought his brothers for the entrails.

they will come, they will!''

"But where are you, Lyra?''

And that she couldn't answer. "I think I'm dreaming, Roger,'' was all she could find to say.

Behind the little boy she could see more ghosts, dozens, hundreds, their heads crowded together, peering close and listening to every word.

"And that woman?'' said Roger. "I hope she en't dead. I hope she stays alive as long as ever she can. Because if she comes down here, then there'll be nowhere to hide, she'll have us for ever then. That's the only good thing I can see about being dead, that she en't. *Except I know she will be one day . . .''*

Lyra was alarmed.

"I think I'm dreaming, and I don't know where she is!'' she said. "She's somewhere near, and I can't

4

AMA AND THE BATS

She lay as if at play
Her life had leaped away –
Intending to return –
But not so soon –

— EMILY DICKINSON

AMA, THE HERDSMAN'S daughter, carried the image of the sleeping girl in her memory: she could not stop thinking about her. She didn't question for a moment the truth of what Mrs Coulter had told her. Sorcerers existed, beyond a doubt, and it was only too likely that they would cast sleeping-spells, and that a mother would care for her daughter in that fierce and tender way. Ama conceived an admiration amounting almost to worship for the beautiful woman in the cave and her enchanted daughter.

She went as often as she could to the little valley, to run errands for the woman or simply to chatter and listen, for the woman had wonderful tales to tell. Again and again she hoped for a glimpse of the sleeper, but it had only happened once, and she accepted that it would probably never be allowed again.

And during the time she spent milking the sheep, or carding and spinning their wool, or grinding barley to make bread, she thought incessantly about the spell that must have been cast, and about why it had happened. Mrs Coulter had never told her, so Ama was free to imagine.

One day she took some flat bread sweetened with honey and walked the three-hour journey along the trail to Cho-Lung-Se, where there was a monastery. By wheedling and patience and by bribing the porter with some of the honey-bread, she managed to gain an audience with the great healer Pagdzin *tulku*, who had cured an outbreak of the white fever only the year before, and who was immensely wise.

Ama entered the great man's cell, bowing very low and offering her remaining honey-bread with all the humility she could muster. The monk's bat-dæmon swooped and darted around her, frightening her own dæmon Kulang, who crept into her hair to hide, but Ama tried to remain still and silent until Pagdzin *tulku* spoke.

"Yes, child? Be quick, be quick," he said, his long grey beard wagging with every word.

In the dimness, the beard and his brilliant eyes were most of what she could see of him. His dæmon settled on the beam above him, hanging still at last, so she said, "Please, Pagdzin *tulku*, I want to gain wisdom. I would like to know how to make spells and enchantments. Can you teach me?"

"No," he said.

She was expecting that. "Well, could you tell me just one remedy?" she asked humbly.

"Maybe. But I won't tell you what it is. I can give you the medicine, not tell you the secret."

"All right, thank you, that is a great blessing," she said, bowing several times.

"What is the disease, and who has it?" the old man said.

"It's a sleeping sickness," Ama explained. "It's come upon the son of my father's cousin."

She was being extra clever, she knew, changing the sex of the sufferer, just in case the healer had heard of the woman in the cave.

"And how old is this boy?"

"Three years older than me, Pagdzin *tulku*," she guessed, "so he is twelve years old. He sleeps and sleeps and can't wake up."

"Why haven't his parents come to me? Why did they send you?"

"Because they live far on the other side of my village and they are very poor, Pagdzin *tulku*. I only heard of my kinsman's illness yesterday and I came at once to seek your advice."

"I should see the patient and examine him thoroughly, and enquire into the positions of the planets at the hour when he fell asleep. These things can't be done in a hurry."

"Is there no medicine you can give me to take back?"

The bat-dæmon fell off her beam and fluttered blackly aside before she hit the floor, darting silently across the room again and again, too quickly for Ama to follow; but the bright eyes of the healer saw exactly where she went, and when she had hung once more upside down on her beam and folded her dark wings around herself, the old man got up and moved around from shelf to shelf and jar to jar and box to box, here tapping out a spoonful of powder, there adding a pinch of herbs, in the order in which the dæmon had visited them.

He tipped all the ingredients into a mortar and ground them up together, muttering a spell as he did so. Then he tapped the pestle on the ringing edge of the mortar, dislodging the final grains, and took a brush and ink and wrote some characters on a sheet of paper. When the ink had dried he tipped all the powder on to the inscription and folded the paper swiftly into a little square package.

"Let them brush this powder into the nostrils of the sleeping child a little at a time as he breathes in," he told her, "and he will wake up. It has to be done with great caution. Too much at once and he will choke. Use the softest of brushes."

"Thank you, Pagdzin *tulku*," said Ama, taking the package and placing it in the pocket of her innermost shirt. "I wish I had another honey-bread to give you."

"One is enough," said the healer. "Now go, and next time you come, tell me the whole truth, not part of it."

The girl was abashed, and bowed very low to hide her confusion. She hoped she hadn't given too much away.

Next evening she hurried to the valley as soon as she could, carrying some sweet rice wrapped in a heart-fruit leaf. She was bursting to tell the woman what she had done, and to give her the medicine and receive her praise and thanks, and eager most of all for the enchanted sleeper to wake and talk to her. They could be friends!

But as she turned the corner of the path and looked upwards, she saw no golden monkey, no patient woman seated at the cave-mouth. The place was empty. She ran the last few yards, afraid they had gone for ever – but there was the chair the woman sat in, and the cooking-equipment, and everything else.

Ama looked into the darkness further back in the cave, her heart beating fast. Surely the sleeper hadn't woken already: in the dimness Ama could make out the shape of the sleeping-bag, the lighter patch that was the girl's hair, and the white curve of her sleeping dæmon.

She crept a little closer. There was no doubt about it – they had gone out and left the enchanted girl alone.

A thought struck Ama like a musical note: suppose *she* woke her before the woman returned . . .

But she had hardly time to feel the thrill of that idea before she heard sounds on the path outside, and in a shiver of guilt she and her dæmon darted behind a ridge of rock at the side of the cave. She shouldn't be here. She was spying. It was wrong.

And now that golden monkey was squatting in the entrance, sniffing and turning his head this way and that. Ama saw him bare his sharp teeth, and felt her own dæmon burrow into her clothes, mouse-formed and trembling.

"What is it?" said the woman's voice, speaking to the monkey, and then the cave darkened as her form came into the entrance. "Has the girl been? Yes – there's the food she left. She shouldn't come in, though. We must arrange a spot on the path for her to leave the food at."

Without a glance at the sleeper, the woman stooped to bring the fire to life, and set a pan of water to heat while her dæmon crouched nearby watching over the path. From time to time he got up and looked around the cave, and Ama, getting cramped and uncomfortable in her narrow hiding-place, wished ardently that she'd waited outside and not gone in. How long was she going to be trapped?

The woman was mixing some herbs and powders into the heating water. Ama could smell the astringent flavours as they drifted out with the steam. Then came a sound from the back of the cave: the girl was murmuring and stirring. Ama turned her head: she could see the enchanted sleeper moving, tossing from side to side, throwing an arm across her eyes. She was waking!

And the woman took no notice!

She heard all right, because she looked up briefly, but she soon turned back to her herbs and the boiling water. She poured the decoction into a beaker and let it stand, and only then turned her full attention to the waking girl.

Ama could understand none of these words, but she heard them with increasing wonder and suspicion:

"Hush, dear," the woman said. "Don't worry yourself. You're safe."

"Roger –" the girl murmured, half-awake. "Serafina! Where's Roger gone . . . Where is he?"

"No one here but us," her mother said, in a sing-song voice, half-crooning. "Lift yourself and let Mama wash you . . . Up you come, my love . . ."

Ama watched as the girl, moaning, struggling into wake-fulness, tried to push her mother away; and the woman dipped a sponge into the bowl of water and mopped at her daughter's face and body before patting her dry.

By this time the girl was nearly awake, and the woman had to move more quickly.

"Where's Serafina? And Will? Help me, help me! I don't want to sleep – No, no! I won't! No!"

The woman was holding the beaker in one steely-firm hand while her other was trying to lift Lyra's head.

"Be still, dear – be calm – hush now – drink your tea –"

But the girl lashed out and nearly spilled the drink, and cried louder:

"Leave me alone! I want to go! Let me go! Will, Will, help me – oh, help me –"

The woman was gripping her hair tightly, forcing her head back, cramming the beaker against her mouth.

"I won't! You dare touch me and Iorek will tear your head off! Oh, Iorek, where are you? Iorek Byrnison! Help me, Iorek! I won't – I won't –"

Then, at a word from the woman, the golden monkey sprang on Lyra's dæmon, gripping him with hard black fingers. The dæmon flicked from shape to shape more quickly than Ama had ever seen a dæmon change before: cat-snake-rat-fox-bird-wolf-cheetah-lizard-polecat –

But the monkey's grip never slackened; and then Pantalaimon became a porcupine.

The monkey screeched and let go. Three long quills were stuck shivering in his paw. Mrs Coulter snarled and with her free hand slapped Lyra hard across the face, a vicious backhand crack that threw her flat; and before Lyra could gather her wits, the beaker was at her mouth and she had to swallow or choke.

Ama wished she could shut her ears: the gulping, crying, coughing, sobbing, pleading, retching was almost too much to bear. But little by little it died away, and only a shaky sob or two came from the girl, who was now sinking once more into sleep – enchanted sleep? Poisoned sleep! Drugged, deceitful sleep! Ama saw a streak of white materialize at the girl's throat as her dæmon effortfully changed into a long, sinuous, snowy-furred creature with brilliant black eyes and black-tipped tail, and laid himself alongside her neck.

And the woman was singing softly, crooning baby-songs, smoothing the hair off the girl's brow, patting her hot face dry, humming songs to which even Ama could tell she didn't know the words, because all she could sing was a string of nonsense-syllables, la-la-la, ba-ba-boo-boo, her sweet voice mouthing gibberish.

Eventually that stopped, and then the woman did a curious thing: she took a pair of scissors and trimmed the girl's hair, holding her sleeping head this way and that to see the best effect. She took one dark blonde curl and put it in a little gold locket she had around her own neck. Ama could tell why: she was going to work some further magic with it. But the woman held it to her lips first . . . Oh, this was strange.

The golden monkey drew out the last of the porcupine quills, and said something to the woman, who reached up to snatch a roosting bat from the cave ceiling. The little black thing flapped and squealed in a needle-thin voice that pierced Ama from one ear to the other, and then she saw the woman hand the bat to her dæmon, and she saw the dæmon pull one of the black wings out and out and out till it snapped and broke and hung from a white string of sinew, while the dying bat screamed and its fellows flapped around in anguished puzzlement. Crack – crack – snap – as the golden monkey pulled the little thing apart limb by limb, and the woman lay moodily on her sleeping-bag by the fire and slowly ate a bar of chocolatl.

Time passed. Light faded and the moon rose, and the woman and her dæmon fell asleep.

Ama, stiff and painful, crept up from her hiding-place and tip-toed out past the sleepers, and didn't make a sound till she was half-way down the path.

With fear to give her speed, she ran along the narrow trail, her dæmon as an owl on silent wings beside her. The clean cold air, the constant motion of the tree-tops, the brilliance of the moon-painted clouds in the dark sky and the millions of stars all calmed her a little.

She stopped in sight of the little huddle of stone houses and her dæmon perched on her fist.

"She lied!" Ama said. "She *lied* to us! What can we do, Kulang? Can we tell Dada? What can we *do*?"

"Don't tell," said her dæmon. "More trouble. We've got the medicine. We can wake her. We can go there when the woman's away again, and wake the girl up, and take her away."

The thought filled them both with fear. But it had been said, and the little paper package was safe in Ama's pocket, and they knew how to use it.

wake up, I can't see her – I think she's close by – she's hurt me –"

"Oh, Lyra, don't be frightened! If you're frightened too, I'll go mad –"

They tried to hold each other tight, but their arms passed through the empty air. Lyra tried to say what she meant, whispering close to his little pale face in the darkness:

"I'm just trying to wake up – I'm so afraid of sleeping all my life and then dying – I want to wake up first! I wouldn't care if it was just for an hour, as long as I was properly alive and awake – I don't know if this is real or not, even – but I will help you, Roger! I swear I will!"

"But if you're dreaming, Lyra, you might not believe it when you wake up. That's what I'd do, I'd just think it was only a dream."

"No!" she said fiercely, and

5
THE ADAMANT TOWER

With ambitious aim
Against the throne and monarchy of God
Rais'd impious war in heav'n and battel proud.

— JOHN MILTON

A LAKE OF MOLTEN sulphur extended the length of an immense canyon, releasing its mephitic vapours in sudden gusts and belches, and barring the way to the solitary winged figure who stood at its edge.

If he took to the sky, the enemy scouts who had spotted him, and lost him, would find him again at once; but if he stayed on the ground, it would take so long to get past this noxious pit that his message might arrive too late.

He would have to take the greater risk. He waited until a cloud of stinking smoke billowed off the yellow surface, and darted upwards into the thick of it.

Four pairs of eyes in different parts of the sky all saw the brief movement, and at once four pairs of wings beat hard against the smoke-fouled air, hurling the watchers forward to the cloud.

Then began a hunt in which the pursuers couldn't see the quarry, and the quarry could see nothing at all. The first to break out of the cloud on the far side of the lake would have the advantage, and that might mean survival, or it might mean a success-ful kill.

And unluckily for the single flier, he found the clear air a few seconds after one of his pursuers. At once they closed with each other, trailing streams of vapour, and dizzy, both of them, from the sickening fumes. The quarry had the best of it at first, but then another hunter flew free of the cloud, and in a swift and furious struggle all three of them, twisting in the air like scraps of flame, rose and fell and rose again, only to fall, finally, among the rocks on the far side. The other two hunters never emerged from the cloud.

* * *

At the western end of a range of saw-toothed mountains, on a peak that commanded wide views of the plain below and the valleys behind, a fortress of basalt seemed to grow out of the mountain as if some volcano had thrust it up a million years before.

In vast caverns beneath the rearing walls, provisions of every sort were stored and labelled; in the arsenals and magazines, engines of war were being calibrated, armed and tested; in the mills below the mountain, volcanic fires fed mighty forges where phosphor and titanium were being melted and combined in alloys never known or used before.

On the most exposed side of the fortress, at a point deep in the shadow of a buttress where the mighty walls rose sheer out of the ancient lava-flows, there was a small gate, a postern where a sentry watched day and night and challenged all who sought to enter.

While the watch was being changed on the ramparts above, the sentry stamped once or twice and slapped his gloved hands on his upper arms for warmth, for it was the coldest hour of the night, and the little naphtha flare in the bracket beside him gave no heat. His relief would come in another ten minutes, and he was looking forward to the mug of chocolatl, the smoke-leaf, and most of all his bed.

To hear a hammering at the little door was the last thing he expected.

However, he was alert, and he snapped open the spy-hole, at the same time opening the tap that allowed a flow of naphtha past the pilot-light in the buttress outside. In the glare it threw, he saw three hooded figures carrying between them a fourth whose shape was indistinct, and who seemed ill, or wounded.

The figure in front threw back his hood. He had a face the sentry knew, but he gave the password anyway, and said, "We found him at the sulphur lake. Says his name is Baruch. He's got an urgent message for Lord Asriel."

The sentry unbarred the door, and his terrier-dæmon quivered as the three figures manoeuvred their burden with difficulty through the narrow entrance. Then the dæmon gave a soft involuntary howl, quickly cut off, as the sentry saw that the figure being carried was an angel, wounded: an angel of low rank and little power, but an angel nevertheless.

"Lay him in the guardroom," the sentry told them, and as they did so he turned the crank of the telephone-bell, and reported what was happening to the officer of the watch.

On the highest rampart of the fortress was a tower of adamant: just one flight of steps up to a set of rooms whose windows looked out north, south, east and west. The largest room was furnished with a table and chairs and a map chest, another with a camp bed. A small bathroom completed the set.

Lord Asriel sat in the adamant tower facing his spy-captain across a mass of scattered papers. A naphtha lamp hung over the table, and a brazier held burning coals against the bitter chill of the night. Inside the door, a small blue hawk was perching on a bracket.

The spy-captain was called Lord Roke. He was striking to look at: he was no taller than Lord Asriel's hand-span, and as slender as a dragonfly, but the rest of Lord Asriel's captains treated him with profound respect, for he was armed with a poisonous sting in the spurs on his heels.

It was his custom to sit on the table, and his manner to repel anything but the greatest courtesy with a haughty and malevolent tongue. He and his kind, the Gallivespians, had few of the qualities of good spies except, of course, their exceptional smallness: they were so proud and touchy that they would never have remained inconspicuous if they had been of Lord Asriel's size.

"Yes," he said, his voice clear and sharp, his eyes glittering like droplets of ink, "your child, my Lord Asriel: I know about her. Evidently I know more than you do."

Lord Asriel looked at him directly, and the little man knew at once that he'd taken advantage of his commander's courtesy: the force of Lord Asriel's glance flicked him like a finger, so that he lost his balance and had to put out a hand to steady himself on Lord Asriel's wineglass. A moment later Lord Asriel's expression was bland and virtuous, just as his daughter's could be, and from then on Lord Roke was more careful.

"No doubt, Lord Roke," said Lord Asriel. "But for reasons

I don't understand, the girl is the focus of the church's attention, and I need to know why. What are they saying about her?"

"The Magisterium is alive with speculation; one branch says one thing, another is investigating something else, and each of them is trying to keep its discoveries secret from the rest. The most active branches are the Consistorial Court of Discipline and the Society of the Work of the Holy Spirit, and," said Lord Roke, "I have spies in both of them."

"Have you turned a member of the Society, then?" said Lord Asriel. "I congratulate you. They used to be impregnable."

"My spy in the Society is the Lady Salmakia," said Lord Roke, "a very skilful agent. There is a priest whose dæmon, a mouse, she approached in their sleep. My agent suggested that the man perform a forbidden ritual designed to invoke the presence of Wisdom. At the critical moment, the Lady Salmakia appeared in front of him. The priest now thinks he can communicate with Wisdom whenever he pleases, and that she has the form of a Gallivespian and lives in his bookcase."

Lord Asriel smiled, and said, "And what has she learned?"

"The Society thinks that your daughter is the most important child who has ever lived. They think that a great crisis will come before very long, and that the fate of everything will depend on how she behaves at that point. As for the Consistorial Court of Discipline, it's holding an inquiry at the moment, with witnesses from Bolvangar and elsewhere. My spy in the Court, the Chevalier Tialys, is in touch with me every day by means of the lodestone resonator, and he is letting me know what they discover. In short, I would say that the Society of the Work of the Holy Spirit will find out very soon where the child is, but they will do nothing about it. It will take the Consistorial Court a little longer, but when they do they will act decisively, and at once."

"Let me know the moment you hear any more."

Lord Roke bowed and snapped his fingers, and the small blue hawk perching on the bracket beside the door spread her wings and glided to the table. She had a bridle, a saddle, and stirrups. Lord Roke sprang on her back in a second, and they flew out of the window which Lord Asriel held wide for them.

He left it open for a minute, in spite of the bitter air, and leant on the window-seat, playing with the ears of his snow-leopard dæmon.

"She came to me on Svalbard and I ignored her," he said. "You remember the shock . . . I needed a sacrifice, and the first child to arrive was my own daughter . . . But when I realized that there was another child with her, so she was safe, I relaxed. Was that a fatal mistake? I didn't consider her after that, not for a moment, but she is important, Stelmaria!"

"Let's think clearly," his dæmon replied. "What can she do?"

"*Do* – not much. Does she *know* something?"

"She can read the alethiometer; she has access to knowledge."

"That's nothing special. So have others. And where in hell's name can she be?"

There was a knock at the door behind him, and he turned at once.

"My lord," said the officer who came in, "an angel has just arrived at the western gate – wounded – he insists on speaking to you."

And a minute later, Baruch was lying on the camp bed, which had been brought through to the main room. A medical orderly had been summoned, but it was clear that there was little hope for the angel: he was wounded sorely, his wings torn and his eyes dimmed.

Lord Asriel sat close by and threw a handful of herbs on to the coals in the brazier. As Will had found with the smoke of his fire, that had the effect of defining the angel's body so he could see it more clearly.

"Well, sir," he said, "what have you come to tell me?"

"Three things. Please let me say them all before you speak. My name is Baruch. My companion Balthamos and I are of the rebels' party, and so we were drawn to your standard as soon as you raised it. But we wanted to bring you something valuable, because our power is small, and not long ago we managed to find our way to the heart of the Clouded Mountain, the Authority's citadel in the kingdom. And there we learned . . ."

He had to stop for a moment to breathe in the smoke of the herbs, which seemed to steady him. He continued:

"We learned the truth about the Authority. We learned that he has retired to a chamber of crystal deep within the Clouded Mountain, and that he no longer runs the daily affairs of the kingdom. Instead he contemplates deeper mysteries. In his place, ruling on his behalf, there is an angel called Metatron. I have reason to know that angel well, though when I knew him . . ."

Baruch's voice faded. Lord Asriel's eyes were blazing, but he held his tongue and waited for Baruch to continue.

"Metatron is proud," Baruch went on when he had recovered a little strength, "and his ambition is limitless. The Authority chose him four thousand years ago to be his Regent, and they laid their plans together. They have a new plan, which my companion and I were able to discover. The Authority considers that conscious beings of every kind have become dangerously independent, so Metatron is going to intervene much more actively in human affairs. He intends to move the Authority secretly away from the Clouded Mountain, to a permanent citadel somewhere else, and turn the mountain into an engine of war. The churches in every world are corrupt and weak, he thinks, they compromise too readily . . . He wants to set up a permanent inquisition in every world, run directly from the kingdom. And his first campaign will be to destroy your republic . . ."

They were both trembling, the angel and the man, but one from weakness and the other from excitement.

Baruch gathered his remaining strength, and went on:

"The second thing is this. There is a knife which can cut openings between the worlds, as well as anything in them. Its power is unlimited, but only in the hands of the one who knows how to use it. And that person is a boy . . ."

Once again the angel had to stop and recover. He was frightened; he could feel himself drifting apart. Lord Asriel could see the effort he made to hold himself together, and sat tensely gripping the arms of his chair until Baruch found the strength to go on.

"My companion is with that boy now. We wanted to bring him directly to you, but he refused, because . . . This is the third thing I must tell you: he and your daughter are friends. And he will not agree to come to you until he has found her. She is –"

"Who is this boy?"

"He is the son of the shaman. Of Stanislaus Grumman."

Lord Asriel was so surprised he stood up involuntarily, sending billows of smoke swirling around the angel.

"Grumman had a *son*?" he said.

"Grumman was not born in your world. Nor was his real name Grumman. My companion and I were led to him by his own desire to find the knife. We followed him, knowing he would lead us to it and its bearer, intending to bring the bearer to you. But the boy refused to . . ."

Once again Baruch had to stop. Lord Asriel sat down again, cursing his own impatience, and sprinkled some more herbs on the fire. His dæmon lay nearby, her tail sweeping slowly across the oaken floor, her golden eyes never leaving the angel's pain-filled face. Baruch took several slow breaths, and Lord Asriel held his silence. The slap of the rope on the flagpole above was the only sound.

"Take your time, sir," Lord Asriel said gently. "Do you know where my daughter is?"

"Himalaya . . . in her own world," whispered Baruch. "Great mountains. A cave near a valley full of rainbows . . ."

"A long way from here in both worlds. You flew quickly."

"It is the only gift I have," said Baruch, "except the love of Balthamos, whom I shall never see again."

"And if *you* found her so easily –"

"Then any other angel may too."

Lord Asriel seized a great atlas from the map-chest and flung it open, looking for the pages that showed the Himalaya.

"Can you be precise?" he said. "Can you show me exactly where?"

"With the knife . . ." Baruch tried to say, and Lord Asriel realized his mind was wandering: "With the knife he can enter and leave any world at will . . . Will is his name. But they are in danger, he and Balthamos . . . Metatron knows we have his secret. They pursued us . . . They caught me alone on the borders of your world . . . I was his brother . . . That was how we found our way to him in the Clouded Mountain. Metatron was once Enoch, the son of Jared, the son of Mahalalel . . . Enoch had many wives. He was a lover of the flesh ... My brother Enoch cast me out, because I ... Oh, my dear Balthamos ..."

"Where is the girl?"

"Yes. Yes. A cave ... her mother ... valley full of winds and rainbows ... tattered flags on the shrine..."

He raised himself to look at the atlas.

Then the snow-leopard dæmon got to her feet in one swift movement, and leapt to the door, but it was too late: the orderly who knocked had opened without waiting. That was the way things were done; it was no one's fault; but seeing the expression on the soldier's face as he looked past him, Lord Asriel turned back to see Baruch straining and quivering to hold his wounded form together. The effort was too much. A draught from the open door sent an eddy of air across the bed, and the particles of the angel's form, loosened by the waning of his strength, swirled upwards into randomness, and vanished.

"Balthamos!" came a whisper from the air.

Lord Asriel put his hand on his dæmon's neck; she felt him tremble, and stilled him. He turned to the orderly.

"My lord, I beg your –"

"Not your fault. Take my compliments to King Ogunwe. I would be glad if he and my other commanders could step here at once. I would also like Mr Basilides to attend, with the alethiometer. Finally, I want No. 2 Squadron of gyropters armed and fuelled, and a tanker zeppelin to take off at once and head south-west. I shall send further orders in the air."

The orderly saluted, and with one more swift uneasy glance at the empty bed, went out and shut the door.

Lord Asriel tapped the desk with a pair of brass dividers, and crossed to open the southern window. Far below, the deathless fires put out their glow and smoke on the darkling air, and even at this great height the clang of hammers could be heard in the snapping wind.

"Well, we've learned a lot, Stelmaria," he said quietly.

"But not enough."

There came another knock at the door, and the alethiometrist came in. He was a pale, thin man in early middle age; his name was Teukros Basilides, and his dæmon was a nightingale.

"Mr Basilides, good evening to you," said Lord Asriel. "This is our problem, and I would like you to put everything else aside while you deal with it..."

He told the man what Baruch had said, and showed him the atlas.

"Pinpoint that cave," he said. "Get me the co-ordinates as precisely as you can. This is the most important task you have ever undertaken. Begin at once, if you please."

stamped her foot so hard it even hurt her in the dream. "You don't believe I'd do that, Roger, so don't say it. I will wake up and I won't forget, so there."

She looked around, but all she could see were wide eyes and hopeless faces, pale faces, dark faces, old faces, young faces, all the dead cramming and crowding close and silent and sorrowful.

Roger's face was different. His expression was the only one that contained hope.

She said, "Why d'you look like that? Why en't you miserable, like them? Why en't you at the end of your hope?"

And he said, "Because

6

PRE-EMPTIVE ABSOLUTION

Reliques, Beads,
Indulgences, Dispenses, Pardons, Bulls,
The sport of Winds

— JOHN MILTON

"NOW, FRA PAVEL," said the Inquirer of the Consistorial Court of Discipline: "I want you to recall exactly, if you can, the words you heard the witch speak on the ship."

The twelve members of the Court looked through the dim afternoon light at the cleric on the stand, their last witness. He was a scholarly-looking priest whose dæmon had the form of a frog. The Court had been hearing evidence in this case for eight days already, in the ancient high-towered College of St Jerome.

"I cannot call the witch's words exactly to mind," said Fra Pavel wearily. "I had not seen torture before, as I said to the court yesterday, and I found it made me feel faint and sick. So *exactly* what she said I cannot tell you, but I remember the meaning of it. The witch said that the child Lyra had been recognized by the clans of the north as the subject of a prophecy they had long known. She was to have the power to make a fateful choice, on which the future of all the worlds depended. And furthermore, there was a name that would bring to mind a parallel case, and which would make the church hate and fear her."

"And did the witch reveal that name?"

"No. Before she could utter it, another witch, who had been present under a spell of invisibility, managed to kill her and escape."

"So on that occasion, the woman Coulter will not have heard the name?"

"That is so."

"And shortly afterwards Mrs Coulter left?"

"Indeed."

"What did you discover after that?"

"I learned that the child had gone into another world through the rift opened by Lord Asriel, and that there she has acquired the help of a boy who owns, or has got the use of, a knife of extraordinary powers," said Fra Pavel. Then he cleared his throat nervously and went on: "I may speak entirely freely in this court?"

"With perfect freedom, Fra Pavel," came the harsh clear tones of the President. "You will not be punished for telling us what you in turn have been told. Please continue."

Reassured, the cleric went on:

"The knife in the possession of this boy is able to make openings between worlds. Furthermore, it has a power greater than that – please, once again, I am afraid of what I am saying . . . It is capable of killing the most high angels, and what is higher than them. There is nothing this knife cannot destroy."

He was sweating and trembling, and his frog-dæmon fell from the edge of the witness-stand to the floor in her agitation. Fra Pavel gasped in pain and scooped her up swiftly, letting her sip at the water in the glass in front of him.

"And did you ask further about the girl?" said the Inquirer. "Did you discover this name the witch spoke of?"

"Yes, I did. Once again I crave the assurance of the court that –"

"You have it," snapped the President. "Don't be afraid. You are not a heretic. Report what you have learned, and waste no more time."

"I beg your pardon, truly. The child, then, is in the position of Eve, the wife of Adam, the mother of us all, and the cause of all sin."

The stenographers taking down every word were nuns of the order of St Philomel, sworn to silence; but at Fra Pavel's words there came a smothered gasp from one of them, and there was a flurry of hands as they crossed themselves. Fra Pavel twitched, and went on:

"Please, remember – the alethiometer does not *forecast*; it says, '*If* certain things come about, *then* the consequences will be – ' and so on. And it says that if it comes about that the child is tempted, as Eve was, then she is likely to fall. On the outcome will depend . . . everything. And if this temptation does take place, and if the child gives in, then Dust and sin will triumph."

There was silence in the courtroom. The pale sunlight that filtered in through the great leaded windows held in its slanted beams a million golden motes, but these were dust, not Dust; though more than one member of the court had seen in them an image of that other invisible Dust that settled over every human being, no matter how dutifully they kept the laws.

"Finally, Fra Pavel," said the Inquirer, "tell us what you know of the child's present whereabouts."

"She is in the hands of Mrs Coulter," said Fra Pavel. "And they are in the Himalayas. So far, that is all I have been able to tell. I shall go at once and ask for a more precise location, and as soon as I have it I shall tell the court; but . . ."

He stopped, shrinking in fear, and held the glass to his lips with a trembling hand.

"Yes, Fra Pavel?" said Father MacPhail. "Hold nothing back."

"I believe, Father President, that the Society of the Work of the Holy Spirit knows more about this than I do."

Fra Pavel's voice was so faint it was almost a whisper.

"Is that so?" said the President, his eyes seeming to radiate his passion as they glared.

Fra Pavel's dæmon uttered a little frog-whimper. The cleric knew about the rivalry between the different branches of the Magisterium, and knew that to get caught in the crossfire between them would be very dangerous; but to hold back what he knew would be more dangerous still.

"I believe," he went on, trembling, "that they are much closer to finding out exactly where the child is. They have other sources of knowledge forbidden to me."

"Quite so," said the Inquirer. "And did the alethiometer tell you about this?"

"Yes, it did."

"Very well. Fra Pavel, you would do well to continue that line of investigation. Whatever you need in the way of clerical or secretarial help is yours to command. Please stand down."

Fra Pavel bowed, and with his frog-dæmon on his shoulder he gathered his notes and left the courtroom. The nuns flexed their fingers.

Father MacPhail tapped a pencil on the oak bench in front of him.

"Sister Agnes, Sister Monica," he said, "you may leave us now. Please have the transcription on my desk by the end of the day."

The two nuns bowed their heads and left.

"Gentlemen," said the President, for that was the mode of address in the Consistorial Court, "let's adjourn."

The twelve members, from the oldest (Father Makepwe, ancient and rheumy-eyed) to the youngest (Father Gomez, pale and trembling with zealotry), gathered their notes and followed the President through to the council chamber, where they could face one another across a table and talk in the utmost privacy.

The current President of the Consistorial Court was a Scot called Hugh MacPhail. He had been elected young: Presidents served for life, and he was only in his forties, so it was to be expected that Father MacPhail would mould the destiny of the Consistorial Court, and thus of the whole church, for many years to come. He was a dark-featured man, tall and imposing, with a shock of wiry grey hair, and he would have been fat were it not for the brutal discipline he imposed on his body: he drank only water and ate only bread and fruit, and he exercised for an hour daily under the supervision of a trainer of champion athletes. As a result, he was gaunt and lined and restless. His dæmon was a lizard.

Once they were seated, Father MacPhail said:

"This, then, is the state of things. There seem to be several points to bear in mind.

"Firstly, Lord Asriel. A witch friendly to the church reports that he is assembling a great army, including forces that may be angelic. His intentions, as far as the witch knows, are malevolent towards the church, and towards the Authority Himself.

"Secondly, the Oblation Board. Their actions in setting up the research programme at Bolvangar, and in funding Mrs Coulter's activities, suggest that they are hoping to replace the Consistorial Court of Discipline as the most powerful and effective arm of the Holy Church. We have been outpaced, gentlemen. They have acted ruthlessly and skilfully. We should be chastised for our laxity in letting it happen. I shall return to what we might do about it shortly.

"Thirdly, the boy in Fra Pavel's testimony, with the knife that can do these extraordinary things. Clearly we must find him and gain possession of it as soon as possible.

"Fourthly, Dust. I have taken steps to find out what the Oblation Board has discovered about it. One of the experimental theologians working at Bolvangar has been persuaded to tell us what exactly they discovered. I shall talk to him this afternoon downstairs."

One or two of the priests shifted uncomfortably, for "downstairs" meant the cellars below the building: white-tiled rooms with points for anbaric current, sound-proofed and well-drained.

"Whatever we do learn about Dust, though," the President went on, "we must bear our purpose firmly in mind. The Oblation Board sought to understand the effects of Dust: we must destroy it altogether. Nothing less than that. If in order to destroy Dust we also have to destroy the Oblation Board, the College of Bishops, every single agency by which the Holy Church does the work of the Authority – then so be it. It may be, gentlemen, that the Holy Church itself was brought into being to perform this very task and to perish in the doing of it. But better a world with no church and no Dust than a world where every day we have to struggle under the hideous burden of sin. Better a world purged of all that!"

Blazing-eyed Father Gomez nodded passionately.

"And finally," said Father MacPhail, "the child. Still just a child, I think. This Eve, who is going to be tempted and who, if precedent is any guide, will fall, and whose fall will involve us all in ruin. Gentlemen, of all the ways of dealing with the problem she sets us, I am going to propose the most radical, and I have confidence in your agreement.

"I propose to send a man to find her and kill her before she *can* be tempted."

"Father President," said Father Gomez at once, "I have done pre-emptive penance every day of my adult life. I have studied, I have trained –"

The President held up his hand. Pre-emptive penance and absolution were doctrines researched and developed by the Consistorial Court, but not known to the wider church. They involved doing penance for a sin not yet committed, intense and fervent penance accompanied by scourging and flagellation, so as to build up, as it were, a store of credit. When the penance had reached the appropriate level for a particular sin, the penitent was granted absolution in advance, though he might never be called on to commit the sin. It was sometimes necessary to kill people, for example: and it was so much less troubling for the assassin if he could do so in a state of grace.

"I had you in mind," said Father MacPhail kindly. "I have the agreement of the Court? Yes. When Father Gomez leaves, with our blessing, he will be on his own, unable to be reached or recalled. Whatever happens to anything else, he will make his way like the arrow of God, straight to the child, and strike her down. He will be invisible; he will come in the night, like the angel that blasted the Assyrians; he will be silent. How much better for us all if there had been a Father Gomez in the garden of Eden! We would never have left paradise."

The young priest was nearly weeping with pride. The Court gave its blessing.

And in the darkest corner of the ceiling, hidden among the dark oak beams, sat a man no larger than a hand-span. His heels were armed with spurs, and he heard every word they said.

In the cellars the man from Bolvangar, dressed only in a dirty white shirt and loose trousers with no belt, stood under the bare light bulb clutching the trousers with one hand and his rabbit-dæmon with the other. In front of him, in the only chair, sat Father MacPhail.

"Dr Cooper," the President began, "do sit down."

There was no furniture except the chair, the wooden bunk, and a bucket. The President's voice echoed unpleasantly off the white tiles that lined the wall and ceiling.

Dr Cooper sat on the bunk. He could not take his eyes off the gaunt and grey-haired President. He licked his dry lips and waited to see what new discomfort was coming.

"So you nearly succeeded in severing the child from her dæmon?" said Father MacPhail.

Dr Cooper said shakily, "We considered that it would serve

no purpose to wait, since the experiment was due to take place anyway, and we put the child in the experimental chamber, but then Mrs Coulter herself intervened and took the child to her own quarters."

The rabbit-dæmon opened her round eyes and gazed fearfully at the President, and then shut them again and hid her face.

"That must have been distressing," said Father MacPhail.

"The whole programme was intensely difficult," said Dr Cooper, hastening to agree.

"I am surprised you did not seek the aid of the Consistorial Court, where we have strong nerves."

"We – I – we understood that the programme was licensed by ... It was an Oblation Board matter, but we were told it had the approval of the Consistorial Court of Discipline. We would never have taken part, otherwise. Never!"

"No, of course not. And now for another matter. Did you have any idea," said Father MacPhail, turning to the real subject of his visit to the cellars, "of the subject of Lord Asriel's researches? Of what might have been the source of the colossal energy he managed to release on Svalbard?"

Dr Cooper swallowed. In the intense silence a drop of sweat fell from his chin to the concrete floor, and both men heard it distinctly.

"Well ..." he began, "there was one of our team who observed that in the process of severance there was a release of energy. Controlling it would involve enormous forces, but just as an atomic explosion is detonated by conventional explosives, this could be done by focusing a powerful anbaric current ... However, he wasn't taken seriously. I paid no attention to his ideas," he added earnestly, "knowing that without authority they might well be heretical."

"Very wise. And that colleague now? Where is he?"

"He was one of those who died in the attack."

The President smiled. It was so kindly an expression that Dr Cooper's dæmon shivered and swooned against his breast.

"Courage, Dr Cooper," said Father MacPhail. "We need you to be strong and brave! There is a great work to be done, a great battle to be fought. You must earn the forgiveness of the

Authority by co-operating fully with us, by holding nothing back, not even wild speculation, not even gossip. Now I want you to devote all your attention to what you remember your colleague saying. Did he make any experiments? Did he leave any notes? Did he take anyone else into his confidence? What equipment was he using? Think of *everything*, Dr Cooper. You'll have pen and paper and all the time you need.

"And this room is not very comfortable. We'll have you moved to somewhere more suitable. Is there anything you need in the way of furnishing, for example? Do you prefer to write at a table or a desk? Would you like a typewriting machine? Perhaps you would rather dictate to a stenographer?

"Let the guards know, and you shall have everything you need. But every moment, Dr Cooper, I want you to think back to your colleague and his theory. Your great task is to recall, and if necessary to rediscover, what he knew. Once you know what instruments you require, you shall have those as well. It is a great task, Dr Cooper! You are blessed to be entrusted with it! Give thanks to the Authority."

"I do, Father President! I do!"

Grasping the loose waistband of his trousers, the philosopher stood up and bowed almost without realizing it, again and again, as the President of the Consistorial Court of Discipline left his cell.

That evening, the Chevalier Tialys, the Gallivespian spy, made his way through the lanes and alleys of Geneva to meet his colleague, the Lady Salmakia. It was a dangerous journey for both of them: dangerous for anyone or anything that challenged them, too, but certainly full of peril for the small Gallivespians. More than one prowling cat had met its death at their spurs, but only the week before the chevalier had nearly lost an arm to the teeth of a mangy dog; only the lady's swift action had saved him.

They met at the seventh of their appointed meeting-places, among the roots of a plane tree in a shabby little square, and exchanged their news. The Lady Salmakia's contact in the Society had told her that earlier that evening, they had received a friendly invitation from the President of the Consistorial Court to come and discuss matters of mutual interest.

"Quick work," said the chevalier. "A hundred to one he doesn't tell them about his assassin, though."

He told her about the plan to kill Lyra. She was not surprised.

"It's the logical thing to do," she said. "Very logical people. Tialys, do you think we shall ever see this child?"

"I don't know, but I should like to. Go well, Salmakia. Tomorrow at the fountain."

Unspoken behind that brief exchange was the one thing they never spoke of: the shortness of their lives compared with those of humans. Gallivespians lived to nine years or ten, rarely more, and Tialys and Salmakia were both in their eighth year. They didn't fear old age; their people died in the full strength and vigour of their prime, suddenly, and their childhoods were very brief; but compared to them, the life of a child like Lyra would extend as far into the future as the lives of the witches extended past Lyra's own.

The chevalier returned to the College of St Jerome and began to compose the message he would send to Lord Roke on the lodestone resonator.

But while he was at the rendezvous talking to Salmakia, the President sent for Father Gomez. In his study, they prayed together for an hour, and then Father MacPhail granted the young priest the pre-emptive absolution which would make his murder of Lyra no murder at all. Father Gomez seemed transfigured; the certainty that ran through his veins seemed to make his very eyes incandescent.

They discussed practical arrangements, money, and so forth; and then the President said, "Once you leave here, Father Gomez, you will be completely cut off, for ever, from any help we can give. You can never come back; you will never hear from us. I can't offer you any better advice than this: *don't* look for the child. That would give you away. Instead, look for the tempter. Follow the tempter, and she will lead you to the child."

"She?" said Father Gomez, shocked.

"Yes, *she*," said Father MacPhail. "We have learned that much from the alethiometer. The world the tempter comes from is a strange one. You will see many things that will shock and startle you, Father Gomez. Don't let yourself be distracted by their oddness from the sacred task you have to do. I have faith," he added kindly, "in the power of *your* faith. This woman is travelling, guided by the powers of evil, to a place where she may, eventually, meet the child in time to tempt her. That is, of course, if we do not succeed in removing the girl from her present location. That remains our first plan. You, Father Gomez, are our ultimate guarantee that if that falls through, the infernal powers will still not prevail."

Father Gomez nodded. His dæmon, a large and iridescent green-backed beetle, clicked her wing-cases.

The President opened a drawer and handed the young priest a folded packet of papers.

"Here is all we know about the woman," he said, "and the world she comes from, and the place she was last seen. Read it well, my dear Luis, and go with my blessing."

He had never used the priest's given name before. Father Gomez felt tears of joy prick his eyes as he kissed the President farewell.

you're Lyra.''

Then she realized what that meant. She felt dizzy, even in her dream; she felt a great burden settle on her shoulders. And to make it even heavier, sleep was closing in again, and Roger's face receding into shadow.

"Well, I . . . I know . . . There's all kinds of people on our side, like Dr Malone . . . You know there's another Oxford, Roger, just like ours? Well, she . . . I found her in . . . She'd help . . . But there's only one person really who . . .''

It was almost impossible now to see the little boy, and her thoughts were spreading out and wandering away like sheep in a field.

"But we can trust him, Roger, I swear,'' she said with a final effort,

7

MARY, ALONE

Last
Rose as in Dance the stately Trees, and spred
Thir branches hung with copious Fruit

— JOHN MILTON

ALMOST AT THE same time, the tempter whom Father Gomez was setting out to follow was being tempted herself.

"Thank you, no, no, that's all I need, no more, honestly, thank you," said Dr Mary Malone to the old couple in the olive grove, as they tried to give her more food than she could carry.

They lived here isolated and childless, and they had been afraid of the Spectres they'd seen among the silver-grey trees; but when Mary Malone came up the road with her rucksack the Spectres had taken fright and drifted away. The old couple had welcomed Mary into their little vine-sheltered farmhouse, plied her with wine and cheese and bread and olives, and now didn't want to let her go.

"I must go on," said Mary again, "thank you, you've been very kind – I can't carry – oh, all right, another little cheese – thank you –"

Evidently they saw her as a talisman against the Spectres. She wished she could be. In her week in the world of Cittàgazze she had seen enough devastation, enough Spectre-eaten adults and wild scavenging children, to have a horror of those ethereal vampires. All she knew was that they did drift away when she approached; but she couldn't stay with everyone who wanted her to, because she had to move on.

She found room for the last little goat's cheese wrapped in its vine leaf, smiled and bowed again, and took a last drink from the spring that bubbled up among the grey rocks. Then she clapped her hands gently together as the old couple were doing, and turned firmly away and left.

She looked more decisive than she felt. The last communication with those entities she called Shadow-particles and Lyra called Dust had been on the screen of her computer, and at their instruction she had destroyed that. Now she was at a loss. They'd told her to go through the opening in the Oxford she had lived in, the Oxford of Will's world, which she'd done – to find herself dizzy and quaking with wonder in this extraordinary other world. Beyond that, her only task was to find the boy and the girl, and then play the serpent, whatever that meant.

So she'd walked and explored and enquired, and found nothing. But now, she thought, as she turned up the little track away from the olive grove, she would have to look for guidance.

Once she was far enough away from the little farmstead to be sure she wouldn't be disturbed, she sat under the pine trees and opened her rucksack. At the bottom, wrapped in a silk scarf, was a book she'd had for twenty years: a commentary on the Chinese method of divination, the I Ching.

She had taken it with her for two reasons. One was sentimental: her grandfather had given it to her, and she had used it a lot as a schoolgirl. The other was that when Lyra had first found her way to Mary's laboratory, she had asked: "What's that?" and pointed to the poster on the door that showed the symbols from the I Ching; and shortly afterwards, in her spectacular reading of the computer, Lyra had learned (she claimed) that Dust had many other ways of speaking to human beings, and one of them was the method from China that used those symbols.

So in her swift packing to leave her own world, Mary Malone had taken with her the *Book of Changes*, as it was called, and the little yarrow stalks with which she read it. And now the time had come to use them.

She spread the silk on the ground and began the process of dividing and counting, dividing and counting and setting aside, which she'd done so often as a passionate curious teenager, and hardly ever since. She had almost forgotten how to do it, but she soon found the ritual coming back, and with it a sense of that calm and concentrated attention that played such an important part in talking to the Shadows.

Eventually she came to the numbers which indicated the hexagram she was being given, the group of six broken or unbroken lines, and then she looked up the meaning. This was the difficult part, because the Book expressed itself in such an enigmatic style.

She read:

> Turning to the summit
> For provision of nourishment
> Brings good fortune.
> Spying about with sharp eyes
> Like a tiger with insatiable craving.

That seemed encouraging. She read on, following the commentary through the mazy paths it led her on, until she came to: *Keeping still is the mountain; it is a bypath; it means little stones, doors and openings.*

She had to guess. The mention of "openings" recalled the mysterious window in the air through which she had entered this world; and the first words seemed to say that she should go upwards.

Both puzzled and encouraged, she packed the book and the yarrow stalks away and set off up the path.

Four hours later she was very hot and tired. The sun was low over the horizon. The rough track she was following had petered out, and she was clambering with more and more discomfort among tumbled boulders and smaller stones. To her left the slope fell away towards a landscape of olive and lemon groves, of poorly-tended vineyards and abandoned windmills, lying hazy in the evening light. To her right a scree of small rocks and gravel sloped up to a cliff of crumbling limestone.

Wearily she hoisted her rucksack again and set her foot on the next flat stone – but before she even transferred her weight, she stopped. The light was catching something curious, and she shaded her eyes against the glare from the scree and tried to find it again.

And there it was: like a sheet of glass hanging unsupported in the air, but glass with no attention-catching reflections in it: just a square patch of difference. And then she remembered what the I Ching had said: *a bypath, little stones, doors and openings.*

It was a window like the one in Sunderland Avenue. She could only see it because of the light: with the sun any higher it probably wouldn't show up at all.

She approached the little patch of air with passionate curiosity, because she hadn't had time to look at the first one: she'd had to get away as quickly as possible. But she examined this one in detail, touching the edge, moving around to see how it became invisible from the other side, noting the absolute difference between *this* and *that*, and found her mind almost bursting with excitement that such things could be.

The knife-bearer who had made it, at about the time of the American Revolution, had been too careless to close it, but at least he'd cut through at a point very similar to the world on this side: next to a rockface. But the rock on the other side was different, not limestone but granite, and as Mary stepped through into the new world she found herself not at the foot of a towering cliff but almost at the top of a low outcrop overlooking a vast plain.

It was evening here, too, and she sat down to breathe the air and rest her limbs and taste the wonder without rushing.

Wide golden light, and an endless prairie or savannah, like nothing she had ever seen in her own world. To begin with, although most of it was covered in short grass in an infinite variety of buff-brown-green-ochre-yellow-golden shades, and undulating very gently in a way that the long evening light showed up clearly, the prairie seemed to be laced through and through with what looked like rivers of rock with a light grey surface.

And secondly, here and there on the plain were stands of the tallest trees Mary had ever seen. Attending a high-energy physics conference once in California she had taken time out to look at the great redwood trees, and marvelled: but whatever these trees were, they would have overtopped the redwoods by half again at least. Their foliage was dense and dark green, their vast trunks gold-red in the heavy evening light.

And finally, herds of creatures, too far off to see distinctly, grazed on the prairie. There was a strangeness about their movement which she couldn't quite work out.

She was desperately tired, and thirsty and hungry besides. Somewhere nearby, though, she heard the welcome trickle of a spring, and only a minute later she found it: just a seepage of clear water from a mossy fissure, and a tiny stream that led away down the slope. She drank long and gratefully, and filled her bottles, and then set about making herself comfortable, for night was falling rapidly.

Propped against the rock, wrapped in her sleeping-bag, she ate some of the rough bread and the goat's cheese, and then fell deeply asleep.

She awoke with the early sun full in her face. The air was cool, and the dew had settled in tiny beads on her hair and on the sleeping-bag. She lay for a few minutes lapped in freshness, feeling as if she were the first human being who had ever lived.

She sat up, yawned, stretched, shivered, and washed in the chilly spring before eating a couple of dried figs and taking stock of the place.

Behind the little rise she had found herself on, the land sloped gradually down and then up again; the fullest view lay in front, across that immense prairie. The long shadows of the trees lay towards her now, and she could see flocks of birds wheeling in front of them, so small against the towering green canopy that they looked like motes of dust.

Loading her rucksack again, she made her way down on to the coarse rich grass of the prairie, aiming for the nearest stand of trees, four or five miles away.

The grass was knee-high, and growing among it there were low-lying bushes, no higher than her ankles, of something like juniper; and there were flowers like poppies, like buttercups, like cornflowers, giving a haze of different tints to the landscape; and then she saw a large bee, the size of the top joint of her thumb, visiting a blue flower-head and making it bend and sway. But as it backed out of the petals and took to the air again, she saw that it was no insect, for a moment later it made for her hand and perched on her finger, dipping a long needle-like beak against her skin with the utmost delicacy and then taking flight again when it found no nectar. It was a minute hummingbird, its bronze-feathered wings moving too fast for her to see.

How every biologist on earth would envy her, if they could see what she was seeing!

She moved on, and found herself getting closer to a herd of those grazing creatures she had seen the previous evening, and whose movement had puzzled her without her knowing why. They were about the size of deer or antelopes, and similarly coloured, but what made her stop still and rub her eyes was the arrangement of their legs. They grew in a diamond formation: two in the centre, one at the front, and one under the tail, so that the animals moved with a curious rocking motion. Mary longed to examine a skeleton and see how the structure worked.

For their part, the grazing creatures regarded her with mild incurious eyes, showing no alarm. She would have loved to go closer and take time to look at them, but it was getting hot, and the shade of the great trees looked inviting; and there was plenty of time, after all.

Before long she found herself stepping out of the grass on to one of those rivers of stone she'd seen from the hill: something else to wonder at.

It might once have been some kind of lava-flow. The underlying colour was dark, almost black, but the surface was paler, as if it had been ground down or worn by crushing. It was as smooth as a stretch of well-laid road in Mary's own world, and certainly easier to walk on than the grass.

She followed the one she was on, which flowed in a wide curve towards the trees. The closer she got, the more astounded she was by the enormous size of the trunks, as wide, she estimated, as the house she lived in, and as tall – as tall as ... She couldn't even make a guess.

When she came to the first trunk she rested her hands on the deeply-ridged red-gold bark. The ground was covered ankle-deep in brown leaf-skeletons as long as her foot, soft and fragrant to walk on. She was soon surrounded by a cloud of midge-like flying things, as well as a little flock of the tiny hummingbirds, a yellow butterfly with a wingspread as broad as her hand, and too many crawling things for comfort. The air was full of humming and buzzing and scraping.

She walked along the floor of the grove feeling much as if she were in a cathedral: there was the same stillness, the same sense of upwardness in the structures, the same awe in herself.

It had taken her longer than she thought to walk here. It was getting on for midday, for the shafts of light coming down through the canopy were almost vertical. Drowsily, Mary wondered why the grazing creatures didn't move under the shade of the trees during this hottest part of the day.

She soon found out.

Feeling too hot to move any further, she lay down to rest between the roots of one of the giant trees, with her head on her rucksack, and fell into a doze.

Her eyes were closed for twenty minutes or so, and she was not quite asleep, when suddenly, from very close by, there came a resounding crash that shook the ground.

Then came another. Alarmed, Mary sat up and gathered her wits, and saw a movement which resolved itself into a round object, about a yard across, rolling along the ground, coming to a halt, and falling on its side.

And then another fell, further off; she saw the massive thing descend, and watched it crash into the buttress-like root of the nearest trunk and roll away.

The thought of one of those things falling on her was enough to make her take her rucksack and run out of the grove altogether. What were they? Seed-pods?

Watching carefully upwards, she ventured under the canopy again to look at the nearest of the fallen objects. She pulled it upright and rolled it out of the grove, and then laid it on the grass to look at it more closely.

It was perfectly circular, and as thick as the width of her palm. There was a depression in the centre, where it had been attached to the tree. It wasn't heavy, but it was immensely hard, and covered in fibrous hairs that lay along the circumference so that she could run her hand around it easily one way but not the other. She tried her knife on the surface: it made no impression at all.

Her fingers seemed smoother. She smelt them: there was a faint fragrance there, under the smell of dust. She looked at the seed-pod again. In the centre there was a slight glistening, and as she touched it again she felt it slide easily under her fingers. It was exuding a kind of oil.

Mary laid the thing down and thought about the way this world had evolved.

If her guess about these universes was right, and they were the multiple worlds predicted by quantum theory, then some of them would have split off from her own much earlier than others. And clearly in this world evolution had favoured enormous trees and large creatures with a diamond-framed skeleton.

She was beginning to see how narrow her scientific horizons were. No botany, no geology, no biology of any sort – she was as ignorant as a baby.

And then she heard a low thunder-like rumble, which was hard to locate until she saw a cloud of dust moving along one of the roads – towards the stand of trees, and towards her. It was about a mile away, but it wasn't moving slowly, and all of a sudden she felt afraid.

She darted back into the grove. She found a narrow space between two great roots and crammed herself into it, peering over the great buttress beside her and out towards the approaching dust-cloud.

What she saw made her head spin. At first it looked like a motorcycle gang. Then she thought it was a herd of *wheeled* animals. But that was impossible. No animal could have wheels. She wasn't seeing it. But she was.

There were a dozen or so. They were roughly the same size as the grazing creatures, but leaner and grey-coloured, with horned heads and short trunks like elephants'. They had the same diamond-shaped structure as the grazers, but somehow they had evolved, on their fore and rear single legs, a wheel.

But wheels did not exist in nature, her mind insisted; they couldn't; you needed an axle with a bearing that was completely separate from the rotating part, it couldn't happen, it was impossible –

Then, as they came to a halt not fifty yards away, and the dust settled, she suddenly made the connection, and she couldn't help laughing out loud with a little cough of delight.

The wheels were seed-pods. Perfectly round, immensely hard

and light – they couldn't have been designed better. The creatures hooked a claw through the centre of the pods with their front and rear legs, and used their two lateral legs to push against the ground and move along. While she marvelled at this, she was also a little anxious, for their horns looked formidably sharp, and even at this distance she could see intelligence and curiosity in their gaze.

And they were looking for her.

One of them had spotted the seed-pod she had taken out of the grove, and he trundled off the road towards it. When he reached it, he lifted it on to an edge with his trunk and rolled it over to his companions.

They gathered around the pod and touched it delicately with those powerful, flexible trunks, and she found herself interpreting the soft chirrups and clicks and hoots they were making as expressions of disapproval. Someone had tampered with this: it was wrong.

Then she thought: I came here for a purpose, although I don't understand it yet. Be bold. Take the initiative.

So she stood up and called, very self-consciously:

"Over here. This is where I am. I looked at your seed-pod. I'm sorry. Please don't harm me."

Instantly their heads snapped round to look at her, trunks held out, glittering eyes facing forward. Their ears had all flicked upright.

She stepped out of the shelter of the roots and faced them directly. She held out her hands, realizing that such a gesture might mean nothing to creatures with no hands themselves. Still, it was all she could do. Picking up her rucksack, she walked across the grass and stepped on to the road.

Close up – not five steps away – she could see much more about their appearance, but her attention was held by something lively and aware in their gaze, by an intelligence. These creatures were as different from the grazing animals nearby as a human was from a cow.

Mary pointed to herself and said, "Mary."

The nearest creature reached forward with its trunk. She moved closer, and it touched her on the breast, where she had pointed, and she heard her voice coming back to her from the creature's throat: "Merry."

"What are you?" she said, and, "Watahyu?" the creature responded.

All she could do was respond. "I am a human," she said.

"Ayama yuman," said the creature, and then something even odder happened: the creatures laughed.

Their eyes wrinkled, their trunks waved, they tossed their heads – and from their throats came the unmistakable sound of merriment. She couldn't help it: she laughed too.

Then another creature moved forward and touched her hand with its trunk. Mary offered her other hand as well to its soft, bristled, questing touch.

"Ah," she said, "you're smelling the oil from the seed-pod . . ."

"Seepot," said the creature.

"If you can make the sounds of my language, we might be able to communicate, one day. God knows how. *Mary*," she said, pointing to herself again.

Nothing. They watched. She did it again: "Mary."

The nearest creature touched its own breast with its trunk and spoke. Was it three syllables, or two? The creature spoke again, and this time Mary tried hard to make the same sounds: "Mulefa," she said tentatively.

Others repeated "Mulefa" in her voice, laughing, and even seemed to be teasing the creature who had spoken. "Mulefa!" they said again, as if it was a fine joke.

"Well, if you can laugh, I don't suppose you'll eat me," Mary said. And from that moment, there was an ease and friendliness between her and them, and she felt nervous no more.

And the group itself relaxed: they had things to do, they weren't roaming at random. Mary saw that one of them had a saddle or pack on its back, and two others lifted the seed-pod on to it, making secure by tying straps around it, with deft and intricate movements of their trunks. When they stood still, they balanced with their lateral legs, and when they moved, they turned both front and back legs to steer. Their movements were full of grace and power.

One of them wheeled to the edge of the road and raised its

trunk to utter a trumpeting call. The herd of grazers all looked up as one and began to trot towards them. When they arrived they stood patiently at the verge and let the wheeled creatures move slowly through them, checking, touching, counting.

Then Mary saw one reach beneath a grazer and milk it with her trunk; and then the wheeled one rolled over to her, and raised her trunk delicately to Mary's mouth.

At first she flinched, but there was an expectation in the creature's eye, so she came forward again and opened her lips. The creature expressed a little of the sweet thin milk into her mouth, watched her swallow, and gave her some more, again and again. The gesture was so clever and kindly that Mary impulsively put her arms around the creature's head and kissed her, smelling the hot dusty hide and feeling the hard bones underneath and the muscular power of the trunk.

Presently, the leader trumpeted softly and the grazers moved away. The *mulefa* were preparing to leave. She felt joy that they had welcomed her, and sadness that they were leaving; but then she felt surprise as well.

One of the creatures was lowering itself, kneeling down on the road, and gesturing with its trunk, and the others were beckoning and inviting her ... No doubt about it: they were offering to carry her, to take her with them.

Another took her rucksack and fastened it to the saddle of a third, and awkwardly Mary climbed on the back of the kneeling one, wondering where to put her legs – in front of the creature's, or behind? And what could she hold on to?

But before she could work it out, the creature had risen, and the group began to move away along the highway, with Mary riding among them.

because he's Will."

8

VODKA

I have been a stranger in a strange land.

— EXODUS

BALTHAMOS FELT THE death of Baruch the moment it happened. He cried aloud and soared into the night air over the tundra, flailing his wings and sobbing his anguish into the clouds; and it was some time before he could compose himself and go back to Will, who was wide awake, knife in hand, peering up into the damp and chilly murk. They were back in Lyra's world.

"What is it?" said Will, as the angel appeared trembling beside him. "Is it danger? Get behind me —"

"Baruch is dead," cried Balthamos, "my dear Baruch is dead —"

"When? Where?"

But Balthamos couldn't tell; he only knew that half his heart had been extinguished. He couldn't keep still: he flew up again, scouring the sky as if to seek out Baruch in this cloud or that, calling, crying, calling; and then he'd be overcome with guilt, and fly down to urge Will to hide and keep quiet, and promise to watch over him tirelessly; and then the pressure of his grief would crush him to the ground, and he'd remember every instance of kindness and courage that Baruch had ever shown, and there were thousands, and he'd forgotten none of them; and he'd cry that a nature so gracious could never be snuffed out, and he'd soar into the skies again, casting about in every direction, reckless and wild and stricken, cursing the very air, the clouds, the stars.

Finally Will said, "Balthamos, come here."

The angel came at his command, helpless. In the bitter cold gloom of the tundra, the boy shivering in his cloak said to him, "You must try to keep quiet now. You know there are things out there that'll attack if they hear a noise. I can protect you with the knife if you're nearby, but if they attack you up there, I won't be able to help. And if you die too, that'll be the end for me. Balthamos, I need you to help guide me to Lyra. Please don't forget that. Baruch was strong – be strong too. Be like him for me."

At first Balthamos didn't speak, but then he said, "Yes. Yes, of course I must. Sleep now, Will, and I shall stand guard, I shan't fail you."

Will trusted him; he had to. And presently he fell asleep again.

When he woke up, soaked with dew and cold to his bones, the angel was standing nearby. The sun was just rising, and the reeds and the marsh plants were all tipped with gold.

Before Will could move, Balthamos said, "I've decided what I must do. I shall stay with you day and night, and do it cheerfully and willingly, for the sake of Baruch. I shall guide you to Lyra, if I can, and then I shall guide you both to Lord Asriel. I have lived thousands of years, and unless I am killed I shall live many thousands of years more; but I never met a nature that made me so ardent to do good, or to be kind, as Baruch did. I failed so many times, but each time his goodness was there to redeem me. Now it's not, I shall have to try without it. Perhaps I shall fail from time to time, but I shall try all the same."

"Then Baruch would be proud of you," said Will, shivering.

"Shall I fly ahead now and see where we are?"

"Yes," said Will, "fly high, and tell me what the land's like further on. Walking on this marshland is going to take for ever."

Balthamos took to the air. He hadn't told Will everything he was anxious about, because he was trying to do his best and not worry him; but he knew that the angel Metatron, the Regent, from whom they'd escaped so narrowly, would have Will's face firmly imprinted on his mind. And not only his face, but every-thing about him which angels were able to see, including parts of which Will himself was not aware, such as that aspect of his nature Lyra would have called his dæmon. Will was in great danger from Metatron now, and at some time Balthamos would have to tell him; but not quite yet. It was too difficult.

Will, reckoning that it would be quicker to get warm by walk-ing than by gathering fuel and waiting for a fire to catch, simply slung the rucksack over his shoulders, wrapped the cloak around everything, and set off towards the south. There was a path, muddy and rutted and potholed, so people did sometimes come this way; but the flat horizon was so far away on every side that he had little sense of making progress.

Some time later, when the light was brighter, Balthamos's voice spoke beside him.

"About half a day's walk ahead, there is a wide river and a town, where there's a wharf for boats to tie up. I flew high enough to see that the river goes a long way directly south and north. If you could get a passage, then you could move much more quickly."

"Good," said Will fervently. "And does this path go to the town?"

"It goes through a village, with a church and farms and orchards, and then on to the town."

"I wonder what language they speak. I hope they don't lock me up if I can't speak theirs."

"As your dæmon," said Balthamos, "I shall translate for you. I have learned many human languages; I can certainly understand the one they speak in this country."

Will walked on. The toil was dull and mechanical, but at least he was moving, and at least every step took him closer to Lyra.

The village was a shabby place: a huddle of wooden buildings, with paddocks containing reindeer, and dogs that barked as he approached. Smoke crept out of the tin chimneys and hung low over the shingled roofs. The ground was heavy and dragged at his feet, and there had obviously been a recent flood: walls were marked with mud to half-way up the doors, and broken beams of wood and loose-hanging sheets of corrugated iron showed where sheds and verandas and outbuildings had been swept away.

But that was not the most curious feature of the place. At first he thought he was losing his balance; it even made him stumble once or twice; for the buildings were two or three degrees out of the vertical, all leaning the same way. The dome of the little church had cracked badly. Had there been an earthquake?

Dogs were barking with hysterical fury, but not daring to come close. Balthamos, being a dæmon, had taken the form of a large snow-white dog with black eyes, thick fur, and tight-curled tail, and he snarled so fiercely that the real dogs kept their distance. They were thin and mangy, and the few reindeer he could see were scabby-coated and listless.

Will paused in the centre of the little village and looked around, wondering where to go, and as he stood there, two or three men appeared ahead and stood staring at him. They were the first people he had ever seen in Lyra's world. They wore heavy felt coats, muddy boots, fur hats, and they didn't look friendly.

The white dog changed into a sparrow, and flew to Will's shoulder. No one blinked an eye at this: each of the men had a dæmon, Will saw, dogs, most of them, and that was how things happened in this world. On his shoulder, Balthamos whispered: "Keep moving. Don't look them in the eye. Keep your head down. That is the respectful thing to do."

Will kept walking. He could make himself inconspicuous; it was his greatest talent. By the time he got to them, the men had already lost interest in him. But then a door opened in the biggest house in the road, and a voice called something loudly.

Balthamos said softly, "The priest. You will have to be polite to him. Turn and bow."

Will did so. The priest was an immense, grey-bearded man, wearing a black cassock, with a crow-dæmon on his shoulder. His restless eyes moved over Will's face and body, taking everything in. He beckoned.

Will went to the doorway and bowed again.

The priest said something, and Balthamos murmured, "He's asking where you come from. Say whatever you like."

"I speak English," Will said slowly and clearly. "I don't know any other languages."

"Ah, English!" cried the priest gleefully in the same language. "My dear young man! Welcome to our village, our little no-longer-perpendicular Kholodnoye! What is your name, and where are you going?"

"My name is Will, and I'm going south. I have lost my family, and I'm trying to find them again."

"Then you must come inside and have some refreshment," said the priest, and put a heavy arm around Will's shoulders, pulling him in through the doorway.

The man's crow-dæmon was showing a vivid interest in

Balthamos. But the angel was equal to that: he became a mouse, and crept into Will's shirt as if he was shy.

The priest led him into a parlour heavy with tobacco-smoke, where a cast-iron samovar steamed quietly on a side-table.

"What was your name?" said the priest. "Tell me again."

"Will Parry. But I don't know what to call you."

"Otyets Semyon," said the priest, stroking Will's arm as he guided him to a chair. "Otyets means Father. I am a priest of the Holy Church. My given name is Semyon, and the name of my father was Boris, so I am Semyon Borisovitch. What is your father's name?"

"John Parry."

"John is Ivan. So you are Will Ivanovitch, and I am Father Semyon Borisovitch. Where have you come from, Will Ivanovitch, and where are you going?"

"I'm lost," Will said. "I was travelling with my family to the south. My father is a soldier, but he was exploring in the Arctic, and then something happened and we got lost. So I'm travelling south because I know that's where we were going next."

The priest spread his hands and said, "A soldier? An explorer from England? No one so interesting as that has trodden the dirty roads of Kholodnoye for centuries, but in this time of upheaval, how can we know that he will not appear tomorrow? You yourself are a welcome visitor, Will Ivanovitch. You must stay the night in my house and we will talk and eat together. Lydia Alexandrovna!" he called.

An elderly woman came in silently. He spoke to her in Russian, and she nodded and took a glass and filled it with hot tea from the samovar. She brought the glass of tea to Will, together with a little saucer of jam with a silver spoon.

"Thank you," said Will.

"The conserve is to sweeten the tea," said the priest. "Lydia Alexandrovna made it from bilberries."

The result was that the tea was sickly as well as bitter, but Will sipped it nonetheless. The priest kept leaning forward to look closely at him, and felt his hands to see whether he was cold, and stroked his knee. In order to distract him, Will asked why the buildings in the village sloped.

"There has been a convulsion in the earth," the priest said. "It is all foretold in the Apocalypse of St John. Rivers flow backwards . . . The great river only a short way from here used to flow north into the Arctic Ocean. All the way from the mountains of central Asia it flowed north for thousands and thousands of years, ever since the Authority of God the Almighty Father created the earth. But when the earth shook and the fog and the floods came, everything changed, and then the great river flowed south for a week or more before it turned again and went north. The world is turned upside down. Where were you when the great convulsion came?"

"A long way from here," Will said. "I didn't know what was happening. When the fog cleared I had lost my family and I don't know where I am now. You've told me the name of this place, but where is it? Where are we?"

"Bring me that large book on the bottom shelf," said Semyon Borisovitch. "I will show you."

The priest drew his chair up to the table and licked his fingers before turning the pages of the great atlas.

"Here," he said, pointing with a dirty fingernail at a spot in central Siberia, a long way east of the Urals. The river nearby flowed as the priest had said, from the northern part of the mountains in Tibet all the way to the Arctic. He looked closely at the Himalayas, but he could see nothing like the map Baruch had sketched.

Semyon Borisovitch talked and talked, pressing Will for details of his life, his family, his home, and Will, a practised dissembler, answered him fully enough. Presently the housekeeper brought in some beetroot soup and dark bread, and after the priest had said a long grace they ate.

"Well, how shall we pass our day, Will Ivanovitch?" said Semyon Borisovitch. "Shall we play at cards, or would you prefer to talk?"

He drew another glass of tea from the samovar, and Will took it doubtfully.

"I can't play cards," he said, "and I'm anxious to get on and keep travelling. If I went to the river, for example, do you think I could find a passage on a steamer going south?"

The priest's huge face darkened, and he crossed himself with a delicate flick of the wrist.

"There is trouble in the town," he said. "Lydia Alexandrovna has a sister who came here and told her there is a boat carrying bears up the river. Armoured bears. They come from the Arctic. You did not see armoured bears when you were in the north?"

The priest was suspicious, and Balthamos whispered so quietly that only Will could hear: "Be careful." And Will knew at once why he'd said it: his heart had begun to pound when Semyon Borisovitch mentioned the bears, because of what Lyra had told him about them. He must try to contain his feelings.

He said, "We were a long way from Svalbard, and the bears were occupied with their own affairs."

"Yes, that is what I heard," said the priest, to Will's relief. "But now they are leaving their homeland and coming south. They have a boat, and the people of the town will not let them refuel. They are afraid of the bears. And so they should be – they are children of the devil. All things from the north are devilish. Like the witches – daughters of evil! The church should have put them all to death many years ago. Witches – have nothing to do with them, Will Ivanovitch, you hear me? You know what they will do when you come to the right age? They will try to seduce you. They will use all the soft cunning deceitful ways they have, their flesh, their soft skin, their sweet voices, and they will take your seed – you know what I mean by that – they will drain you and leave you hollow! They will take your future, your children that are to come, and leave you nothing. They should be put to death, every one."

The priest reached across to the shelf beside his chair and took down a bottle and two small glasses.

"Now I am going to offer you a little drink, Will Ivanovitch," he said. "You are young, so not very many glasses. But you are growing, and so you need to know some things, like the taste of vodka. Lydia Alexandrovna collected the berries last year, and I distilled the liquor, and here in the bottle is the result, the only place where Otyets Semyon Borisovitch and Lydia Alexandrovna lie together!"

He laughed and uncorked the bottle, filling each glass to the rim. This kind of talk made Will hideously uneasy. What should he do? How could he refuse to drink without discourtesy?

"Otyets Semyon," he said, standing, "you have been very kind, and I wish I could stay longer to taste your drink and to hear you talk, because what you tell me has been very interesting. But you understand I am unhappy about my family, and very anxious to find them again, so I think I must move on, much as I would like to stay."

The priest pushed out his lips, in the thicket of his beard, and frowned; but then he shrugged, and said, "Well, you shall go if you must. But before you leave, you must drink your vodka. Stand with me now! Take it, and down all in one, like this!"

He threw back the glass, swallowing it all at once, and then hauled his massive body up and stood very close to Will. In his fat dirty fingers the glass he held out seemed tiny; but it was brimming with the clear spirit, and Will could smell the heady tang of the drink and the stale sweat and the food-stains on the man's cassock, and he felt sick before he began.

"Drink, Will Ivanovitch!" the priest cried, with a threatening heartiness.

Will lifted the glass and unhesitatingly swallowed the fiery, oily liquid in one gulp. Now he would have to fight hard to avoid being sick.

There was one more ordeal to come. Semyon Borisovitch leaned forward from his great height, and took Will by both shoulders.

"My boy," he said, and then closed his eyes and began to intone a prayer or a psalm. Vapours of tobacco and alcohol and sweat came powerfully from him, and he was close enough for his thick beard, wagging up and down, to brush Will's face. Will held his breath.

The priest's hands moved behind Will's shoulders, and then Semyon Borisovitch was hugging him tightly and kissing his cheeks, right, left, right again. Will felt Balthamos dig tiny claws into his shoulder, and kept still. His head was swimming, his stomach lurching, but he didn't move.

Finally it was over, and the priest stepped back and pushed him away.

"Go then," he said, "go south, Will Ivanovitch. Go."

Will gathered his cloak and the rucksack, and tried to walk straight as he left the priest's house and took the road out of the village.

He walked for two hours, feeling the nausea gradually subside and a slow, pounding headache take its place. Balthamos made him stop at one point, and laid his cool hands on Will's neck and forehead, and the ache eased a little; but Will made himself a promise that he would never drink vodka again.

And in the late afternoon, the path widened and came out of the reeds, and Will saw the town ahead of him, and beyond it an expanse of water so broad it might have been a sea.

Even from some way off, Will could see that there was trouble. Puffs of smoke were erupting from beyond the roofs, followed a few seconds later by the boom of a gun.

"Balthamos," he said, "you'll have to be a dæmon again. Just keep near me and watch out for danger."

He walked into the outskirts of the scruffy little town, where the buildings leant even more perilously than the village, and where the flooding had left its mud-stains on the walls high above Will's head. The edge of the town was deserted, but as he made his way towards the river, the noise of shouting, of screams, and of the crackle of rifle fire got louder.

And here at last there were people: some watching from upper floor windows, some craning anxiously around the corners of buildings to look ahead at the waterfront, where the metal fingers of cranes and derricks and the masts of big vessels rose above the rooftops.

An explosion shook the walls, and glass fell out of a nearby window. People drew back and then peered round again, and more cries rose into the smoky air.

Will reached the corner of the street, and looked along the waterfront. When the smoke and dust cleared a little, he saw one rusting vessel standing offshore, keeping its place against the flow of the river, and on the wharf a mob of people armed with rifles or pistols surrounding a great gun, which, as he watched, boomed again. A flash of fire, a lurching recoil, and near the vessel, a mighty splash.

Will shaded his eyes. There were figures in the boat, but – he rubbed his eyes, even though he knew what to expect: they weren't human. They were huge beings of metal, or creatures in heavy armour, and on the foredeck of the vessel a bright flower of flame suddenly bloomed, and the people cried out in alarm. The flame sped into the air, rising higher and coming closer and shedding sparks and smoke, and then fell with a great splash of fire near the gun. Men cried and scattered, and some ran in flames to the water's edge and plunged in, to be swept along and out of sight in the current.

Will found a man close by who looked like a teacher, and said:

"Do you speak English?"

"Yes, yes, indeed –"

"What is happening?"

"The bears, they are attacking, and we try to fight them, but is difficult, we have only one gun, and –"

The fire-thrower on the boat hurled another gout of blazing pitch, and this time it landed even closer to the gun. Three big explosions almost immediately afterwards showed that it had found the ammunition, and the gunners leapt away, letting the barrel swing down low.

"Ah," the man lamented, "it's no good, they can't fire –"

The commander of the boat brought its head round and moved in towards the shore. Many people cried out in alarm and despair, especially when another great bulb of flame burst into being on the foredeck, and some of those with rifles fired a shot or two and turned to flee; but this time the bears didn't launch the fire, and soon the vessel moved broadside on towards the wharf, engine beating hard to hold it against the current.

Two sailors (human, not bears) leapt down to throw ropes around the bollards, and a great hiss and cry of anger rose from the townsfolk at these human traitors. The sailors took no notice, but ran to lower a gangplank.

Then as they turned to go back on board, a shot was fired from somewhere near Will, and one of the sailors fell. His dæmon –

a seagull – vanished as if she'd been pinched out of existence like a candle flame.

The reaction from the bears was pure fury. At once the fire-thrower was re-lit and hauled around to face the shore, and the mass of flame shot upwards and then cascaded in a hundred spilling gouts over the rooftops. And at the top of the gangway appeared a bear larger than any of the others, an apparition of iron-clad might, and the bullets that rained on him whined and clanged and thudded uselessly, unable to make the slightest dent in his massive armour.

Will said to the man beside him, "Why are they attacking the town?"

"They want fuel. But we have no dealings with bears. Now they are leaving their kingdom and sailing up the river, who knows what they will do? So we must fight them. Pirates – robbers –"

The great bear had come down the gangway, and massed behind him were several others, so heavy that the ship listed; and Will saw that the men on the wharf had gone back to the gun, and were loading a shell into the breech.

An idea came, and he ran out on to the quayside, right into the empty space between the gunners and the bear.

"Stop!" he shouted. "Stop fighting. Let me speak to the bear!"

There was a sudden lull, and everyone stood still, astonished at this crazy behaviour. The bear himself, who had been gathering his strength to charge the gunners, stayed where he was, but every line of his body trembled with ferocity. His great claws dug into the ground, and his black eyes glowed with rage under the iron helmet.

"What are you? What do you want?" he roared in English, since Will had spoken in that language.

The people watching looked at one another in bewilderment, and those who could understand translated for the others.

"I'll fight you, in single combat," cried Will, "and if you give way, then the fighting has to stop."

The bear didn't move. As for the people, as soon as they understood what Will was saying, they shouted and jeered and hooted with mocking laughter. But not for long, because Will turned to face the crowd, and stood cold-eyed, contained, and perfectly still, until the laughter stopped. He could feel the blackbird-Balthamos trembling on his shoulder.

When the people were silent, he called out, "If I make the bear give way, you must agree to sell them fuel. Then they'll go on along the river and leave you alone. You must agree. If you don't, they'll destroy all of you."

He knew that the huge bear was only a few yards behind him, but he didn't turn; he watched the townspeople talking, gesticulating, arguing, and after a minute, a voice called, "Boy! Make the bear agree!"

Will turned back. He swallowed hard and took a deep breath and called:

"Bear! You must agree. If you give way to me, the fighting has to stop, and you can buy fuel and go peacefully up the river."

"Impossible," roared the bear. "It would be shameful to fight you. You are as weak as an oyster out of its shell. I cannot fight you."

"I agree," said Will, and every scrap of his attention was now focused on this great ferocious being in front of him. "It's not a fair contest at all. You have all that armour, and I have none. You could take off my head with one sweep of your paw. Make it fairer, then. Give me one piece of your armour, any one you like. Your helmet, for example. Then we'll be better matched, and it'll be no shame to fight me."

With a snarl that expressed hatred, rage, scorn, the bear reached up with a great claw and unhooked the chain that held his helmet in place.

And now there was a deep hush over the whole waterfront. No one spoke – no one moved. They could tell that something was happening such as they'd never seen before, and they couldn't tell what it was. The only sound now was the splashing of the river against the wooden pilings, the beat of the ship's engine, and the restless crying of seagulls overhead; and then the great clang as the bear hurled his helmet down at Will's feet.

Will put his rucksack down, and hoisted the helmet up on its end. He could barely lift it. It consisted of a single sheet of iron, dark and dented, with eye-holes on top and a massive chain underneath. It was as long as Will's forearm, and as thick as his thumb.

"So this is your armour," he said. "Well, it doesn't look very strong to me. I don't know if I can trust it. Let me see."

And he took the knife from the rucksack and rested the edge against the front of the helmet, and sliced off a corner as if he were cutting butter.

"That's what I thought," he said, and cut another and another, reducing the massive thing to a pile of fragments in less than a minute. He stood up and held out a handful.

"That was your armour," he said, and dropped the pieces with a clatter on to the rest at his feet, "and this is my knife. And since your helmet was no good to me, I'll have to fight without it. Are you ready, bear? I think we're well matched. I could take off your head with one sweep of my knife, after all."

Utter stillness. The bear's black eyes glowed like pitch, and Will felt a drop of sweat trickle down his spine.

Then the bear's head moved. He shook it and took a step backwards.

"Too strong a weapon," he said. "I can't fight that. Boy, you win."

Will knew that a second later the people would cheer and hoot and whistle, so even before the bear had finished saying the word "win", Will had begun to turn and call out, to keep them quiet:

"Now you must keep the bargain. Look after the wounded people and start repairing the buildings. Then let the boat tie up and refuel."

He knew that it would take a minute to translate that and let the message spread out among the watching townsfolk, and he knew too that the delay would prevent their relief and anger from bursting out, as a net of sandbanks baffles and breaks up the flow of a river. The bear watched and saw what he was doing and why, and understood more fully than Will himself did what the boy had achieved.

Will put the knife back in the rucksack, and he and the bear exchanged another glance, but a different kind this time. They approached, and behind them the bears began to dismantle their fire-thrower; the other two ships manoeuvred their way to the quayside.

On shore, some of the people set about clearing up, but several more came crowding to see Will, curious about this boy and the power he had to command the bear. It was time for Will to become inconspicuous again, so he performed the magic that had deflected all kinds of curiosity away from his mother and kept them safe for years. Of course, it wasn't magic, but simply a way of behaving. He made himself quiet and dull-eyed and slow, and in under a minute he became less interesting, less attractive to human attention. The people simply became bored with this dull child, and forgot him and turned away.

But the bear's attention was not human, and he could see what was happening, and he knew it was yet another extraordinary power at Will's command. He came close and spoke quietly, in his voice that seemed to throb as deeply as the ship's engines.

"What is your name?" he said.

"Will Parry. Can you make another helmet?"

"Yes. What do you seek?"

"You're going up the river. I want to come with you. I'm going to the mountains and this is the quickest way. Will you take me?"

"Yes. I want to see that knife."

"I will only show it to a bear I can trust. There is one bear I've heard of who's trustworthy. He is the king of the bears, a good friend of the girl I'm going to the mountains to find. Her name is Lyra Silvertongue. The bear is called Iorek Byrnison."

"I am Iorek Byrnison," said the bear.

"I know you are," said Will.

The boat was taking fuel on board; the rail trucks were hauled alongside and tilted sideways to let coal thunder down the chutes into the hold, and the black dust rose high above them. Un-noticed by the townspeople, who were busy sweeping up glass and haggling over the price of the fuel, Will followed the bear-king up the gangway and aboard the ship.

9
UP-RIVER

A shade upon the mind there passes
As when on Noon
A Cloud the mighty Sun encloses

— EMILY DICKINSON

"LET ME SEE the knife," said Iorek Byrnison. "I understand metal. Nothing made of iron or steel is a mystery to a bear. But I have never seen a knife like yours, and I would be glad to look at it closely."

Will and the bear-king were on the foredeck of the river steamer, in the warm rays of the setting sun, and the vessel was making swift progress up-stream; there was plenty of fuel on board, there was food that Will could eat, and he and Iorek Byrnison were taking their second measure of each other. They had taken the first already.

Will held out the knife towards Iorek, handle first, and the bear took it from him delicately. His thumb-claw opposed the four finger-claws, letting him manipulate objects as skilfully as a human, and now he turned the knife this way and that, bringing it closely to his eyes, holding it to catch the light, testing the edge – the steel edge – on a piece of scrap iron.

"This edge is the one you cut my armour with," he said. "The other is very strange. I cannot tell what it is, what it will do, how it was made. But I want to understand it. How did you come to possess it?"

Will told him most of what had happened, leaving out only what concerned him alone: his mother, the man he killed, his father.

"You fought for this, and lost two fingers?" the bear said. "Show me the wound."

Will held out his hand. Thanks to his father's ointment, the raw surfaces were healing well, but they were still very tender. The bear sniffed at them.

"Bloodmoss," he said. "And something else I cannot identify. Who gave you that?"

"A man who told me what I should do with the knife. Then he died. He had some ointment in a horn box, and it cured my wound. The witches tried, but their spell didn't work."

"And what did he tell you to do with the knife?" said Iorek Byrnison, handing it carefully back to Will.

"To use it in a war on the side of Lord Asriel," Will replied. "But first I must rescue Lyra Silvertongue."

"Then we shall help," said the bear, and Will's heart leapt with pleasure.

Over the next few days Will learned why the bears were making this voyage into Central Asia, so far from their homeland.

Since the catastrophe which had burst the worlds open, all the Arctic ice had begun to melt, and new and strange currents appeared in the water. Since the bears depended on ice and on the creatures who lived in the cold sea, they could see that they would soon starve if they stayed where they were; and being rational, they decided how they should respond. They would have to migrate to where there was snow and ice in plenty: they would go to the highest mountains, to the range that touched the sky, half a world away but unshakeable, eternal, and deep in snow. From bears of the sea they would become bears of the mountains, for as long as it took the world to settle itself again.

"So you're not making war?" Will said.

"Our old enemies vanished with the seals and the walruses. If we meet new ones, we know how to fight."

"I thought there was a great war coming that would involve everyone. Which side would you fight for in that case?"

"The side that gave advantage to the bears. What else? But I have some regard for a few who are not bears. One was a man who flew a balloon. He is dead. Another is the witch Serafina Pekkala. The third is the child Lyra Silvertongue. So first, I would do whatever serves the bears, and then whatever serves the child, or the witch, or avenges my dead comrade Lee Scoresby. That is why I will help you rescue Lyra Silvertongue from the abominable woman Coulter."

He told Will of how he and a few of his subjects had swum to
the rivermouth and paid for the charter of this vessel with gold,
and hired the crew, and turned the draining of the Arctic to their
own advantage by letting the river take them as far inland as it
could — and as it had its source in the northern foothills of the
very mountains they sought, and as Lyra was imprisoned there
too, things had fallen out well so far.

So time went past.

During the day Will dozed on deck, resting, gathering
strength, because he was exhausted in every part of his being. He
watched as the scenery began to change, and the rolling steppe
gave way to low grassy hills and then to higher land, with the
occasional gorge or cataract; and still the boat steamed south.

He talked to the captain and the crew, out of politeness, but
lacking Lyra's instant ease with strangers, he found it difficult to
think of much to say; and in any case they were little interested
in him. This was only a job, and when it was over they would leave
without a backward glance, and besides, they didn't much like the
bears, for all their gold. Will was a foreigner, and as long as he paid
for his food, they cared little what he did. Besides, there was that
strange dæmon of his, which seemed so like a witch's: sometimes
it was there, and sometimes it seemed to have vanished. Superstitious, like many sailors, they were happy to leave him alone.

Balthamos, for his part, kept quiet too. Sometimes his grief
would become too strong for him to put up with, and he'd leave
the boat and fly high among the clouds, searching for any patch
of light or taste of air, any shooting stars or pressure-ridges that
might remind him of experiences he had shared with Baruch.
When he talked, at night in the dark of the little cabin Will slept
in, it was only to report on how far they had gone, and how much
further ahead the cave and the valley lay. Perhaps he thought Will
had little sympathy, though if he'd sought it, he would have
found plenty. He became more and more curt and formal,
though never sarcastic; he kept that promise, at least.

As for Iorek, he examined the knife obsessively. He looked at
it for hours, testing both edges, flexing it, holding it up to the
light, touching it with his tongue, sniffing it, and even listening
to the sound the air made as it flowed over the surface. Will had

no fear for the knife, because Iorek was clearly a craftsman of the highest accomplishment; nor for Iorek himself, because of the delicacy of movement in those mighty paws.

Finally Iorek came to Will and said, "This other edge. It does something you have not told me about. What is it, and how does it work?"

"I can't show you here," said Will, "because the boat is moving. As soon as we stop I'll show you."

"I can think of it," said the bear, "but not understand what I am thinking. It is the strangest thing I have ever seen."

And he gave it back to Will, with a disconcerting long unreadable stare out of his deep black eyes.

The river by this time had changed colour, because it was meeting the remains of the first flood-waters that had swept down out of the Arctic. The convulsions had affected the earth differently in different places, Will saw; village after village stood up to its roofs in water and hundreds of dispossessed people tried to salvage what they could with rowing boats and canoes. The earth must have sunk a little here, because the river broadened and slowed, and it was hard for the skipper to trace his true course through the wide and turbid streams. The air was hotter here, and the sun higher in the sky, and the bears found it hard to keep cool; some of them swam alongside as the steamer made its way, tasting their native waters in this foreign land.

But eventually the river narrowed and deepened again, and soon ahead of them began to rise the mountains of the great central Asian plateau. Will saw a rim of white on the horizon one day and watched as it grew and grew, separating itself into different peaks and ridges and passes between them, and so high that it seemed that they must be close at hand – only a few miles – but they were far off still; it was just that the mountains were immense, and with every hour that they came closer, they seemed yet more inconceivably high.

Most of the bears had never seen mountains, apart from the cliffs on their own island of Svalbard, and fell silent as they looked up at the giant ramparts, still so far off.

"What will we hunt there, Iorek Byrnison?" said one. "Are there seals in the mountains? How shall we live?"

"There is snow and ice," was the king's reply. "We shall be comfortable. And there are wild creatures there in plenty. Our lives will be different for a while. But we shall survive, and when things return to what they should be, and the Arctic freezes once more, we shall still be alive to go back and claim it. If we had stayed there we would have starved. Be prepared for strangeness and for new ways, my bears."

Eventually the steamer could sail no further, because at this point the river-bed had narrowed and become shallow. The skipper brought the vessel to a halt in a valley bottom which normally would have been carpeted with grass and mountain flowers, where the river meandered over gravel beds; but the valley was now a lake, and the captain insisted that he dare not go past it, because beyond this point there would be not enough depth below the keel, even with the massive flood from the north.

So they drew up to the edge of the valley, where an outcrop of rock formed a sort of jetty, and disembarked.

"Where are we now?" said Will to the captain, whose English was limited.

The captain found a tattered old map and jabbed at it with his pipe, saying, "This valley here, we now. You take, go on."

"Thank you very much," Will said, and wondered if he ought to offer to pay; but the captain had turned away to supervise the unloading.

Before long all thirty or so bears and all their armour were on the narrow shore. The captain shouted an order, and the vessel began to turn ponderously against the current, manoeuvring out into mid-stream and giving a blast on the whistle that echoed for a long time around the valley.

Will sat on a rock, reading the map. If he was right, the valley where Lyra was captive, according to the angel, lay some way to the east and the south, and the best way there led through a pass called Sungchen.

"Bears, mark this place," said Iorek Byrnison to his subjects. "When the time comes for us to move back to the Arctic, we shall assemble here. Now go your ways, hunt, feed, and live. Do not make war. We are not here for war. If war threatens, I shall call for you."

The bears were solitary creatures for the most part, and they only came together in times of war or emergency. Now that they were at the edge of a land of snow, they were impatient to be off, each of them, exploring on their own.

"Come then, Will," said Iorek Byrnison, "and we shall find Lyra."

Will lifted his rucksack and they set off.

It was good walking for the first part of their journey. The sun was warm, but the pines and the rhododendrons kept the worst of the heat off their shoulders, and the air was fresh and clear. The ground was rock but the rocks were thick with moss and pine-needles, and the slopes they climbed were not precipitous. Will found himself relishing the exercise. The days he had spent on the boat, the enforced rest, had built up his strength. When he came across Iorek he had been at the very last of it. He didn't know that, but the bear did.

And as soon as they were alone, Will showed Iorek how the other edge of the knife worked. He opened a world where a tropical rainforest steamed and dripped, and where vapours laden with heavy scent drifted out into the thin mountain air. Iorek watched closely, and touched the edge of the window with his paw, and sniffed at it, and stepped through into the hot moist air to look around in silence. The monkey-shrieks and bird-calls, the insect-scrapings and frog-croakings and the incessant drip-drip of condensing moisture sounded very loud to Will, outside it.

Then Iorek came back and watched Will close the window, and asked to see the knife again, peering so closely at the silver edge that Will thought he was in danger of cutting his eye. He examined it for a long time, and handed it back without a word except to say, "I was right: I could not have fought this."

They moved on, speaking little, which suited them both. Iorek Byrnison caught a gazelle and ate most of it, leaving the tender meat for Will to cook; and once they came to a village, and while Iorek waited in the forest, Will exchanged one of his gold coins for some flat coarse bread and some dried fruit, and for boots of yak leather and a waistcoat of a kind of sheepskin, for it was becoming cold at night.

He also managed to ask about the valley with the rainbows. Balthamos helped by assuming the form of a crow, like the dæmon of the man Will was speaking to; he made the passage of understanding easier between them, and Will got directions which were helpful and clear.

It was another three days' walk. Well, they were getting there.

And so were others.

Lord Asriel's force, the squadron of gyropters and the zeppelin fuel tanker, had reached the opening between the worlds: the breach in the sky above Svalbard. They had a very long way to go still, but they flew without pause except for essential maintenance, and the commander, the African King Ogunwe, kept in twice-daily touch with the basalt fortress. He had a Gallivespian lodestone operator aboard his gyropter, and through him he was able to learn as quickly as Lord Asriel himself about what was going on elsewhere.

The news was disconcerting. The little spy, the Lady Salmakia, had watched from the shadows as the two powerful arms of the church, the Consistorial Court of Discipline and the Society of the Work of the Holy Spirit, agreed to put their differences aside and pool their knowledge. The Society had a swifter and more skilful alethiometrist than Fra Pavel, and thanks to him, the Consistorial Court now knew exactly where Lyra was, and more: they knew that Lord Asriel had sent a force to rescue her. Wasting no time, the Court commandeered a flight of zeppelins, and that same day a battalion of the Swiss Guard began to embark aboard the zeppelins waiting in the still air beside the lake of Geneva.

So each side was aware that the other was also making its way towards the cave in the mountains. And they both knew that whoever got there first would have the advantage, but there wasn't much in it: Lord Asriel's gyropters were faster than the zeppelins of the Consistorial Court, but they had further to fly, and they were limited by the speed of their own zeppelin tanker.

And there was another consideration: whoever seized Lyra first would have to fight their way out against the other force.

It would be easier for the Consistorial Court, because they didn't have to consider getting Lyra away safely. They were flying there to kill her.

The zeppelin carrying the President of the Consistorial Court was carrying other passengers as well, unknown to him. The Chevalier Tialys had received a message on his lodestone resonator, ordering him and the Lady Salmakia to smuggle themselves aboard. When the zeppelins arrived at the valley, he and the lady were to go ahead and make their way independently to the cave where Lyra was held, and protect her as well as they could until King Ogunwe's force arrived to rescue her. Her safety was to come above every other consideration.

Getting themselves aboard the zeppelin was hazardous for the spies, not least because of the equipment they had to carry. Apart from the lodestone resonator, the most important items were a pair of insect larvae, and their food. When the adult insects emerged, they would be more like dragonflies than anything else, but they were not like any kind of dragonfly that the humans of Will's world, or Lyra's, would have seen before. They were very much larger, for one thing. The Gallivespians bred these creatures carefully, and each clan's insects differed from the rest. The Chevalier Tialys's clan bred powerful red-and-yellow striped dragonflies with vigorous and brutal appetites, whereas the one the Lady Salmakia was nurturing would be a slender, fast-flying creature with an electric blue body and the power of glowing in the dark.

Every spy was equipped with a number of these larvae, which by feeding carefully regulated amounts of oil and honey they could either keep in suspended animation or bring rapidly to adulthood. Tialys and Salmakia had thirty-six hours, depending on the winds, to hatch these larvae now; because that was about the time the flight would take, and they needed the insects to emerge before the zeppelins landed.

The chevalier and his colleague found an overlooked space behind a bulkhead, and made themselves as safe as they could while the vessel was loaded and fuelled; and then the engines began to roar, shaking the light structure from end to end as the ground crew cast off and the eight zeppelins rose into the night sky.

Their kind would have regarded the comparison as a mortal insult, but they were able to conceal themselves at least as well as rats. From their hiding-place, the Gallivespians could overhear a good deal, and they kept in hourly touch with Lord Roke, who was aboard King Ogunwe's gyropter.

But there was one thing they couldn't learn any more about on the zeppelin, because the President never spoke of it: and that was the matter of the assassin, Father Gomez, who had been absolved already of the sin he was going to commit if the Consistorial Court failed in their mission. Father Gomez was somewhere else, and no one was tracking him at all.

There ariseth a little cloud out of the sea, like a man's hand.

— I KINGS

"YEAH," SAID THE red-haired girl, in the garden of the deserted Casino. "We seen her, me and Paolo both seen her. She come through here days ago."

Father Gomez said, "And do you remember what she looked like?"

"She look hot," said the little boy. "Sweaty in the face, all right."

"How old did she seem to be?"

"About..." said the girl, considering; "I suppose maybe forty or fifty. We didn't see her close. She could be thirty, maybe. But she was hot, like Paolo said, and she was carrying a big rucksack, much bigger than yours, *this* big..."

Paolo whispered something to her, screwing up his eyes to look at the priest as he did so. The sun was bright in his face.

"Yeah," said the girl impatiently, "I know. The Spectres," she said to Father Gomez, "she wasn' afraid of the Spectres at all. She just walked through the city and never worried a bit. I ain never seen a grown-up do that before, all right. She looked like she didn' know about them, even. Same as you," she added, looking at him with a challenge in her eyes.

"There's a lot I don't know," said Father Gomez mildly.

The little boy plucked at her sleeve and whispered again.

"Paolo says," she told the priest, "he thinks you're going to get the knife back."

Father Gomez felt his skin bristle. He remembered the testimony of Fra Pavel in the inquiry at the Consistorial Court: this must be the knife he meant.

"If I can," he said, "I shall. The knife comes from here, does it?"

"From the Torre degli Angeli," said the girl, pointing at the square stone tower over the red-brown rooftops. It shimmered in the midday glare. "And the boy who stole it, he kill our brother Tullio. The Spectres got him, all right. You want to kill that boy, that's OK. And the girl – she was a liar, she was as bad as him."

"There was a girl, too?" said the priest, trying not to seem too interested.

"Lying filth," spat the red-haired child. "We nearly killed them both, but then there came some women, flying women –"

"Witches," said Paolo.

"Witches, and we couldn' fight them. They took them away, the girl and boy. We don' know where they went. But the woman, she came later. We thought maybe *she* got some kind of knife, to keep the Spectres away, all right. And maybe *you* have, too," she added, lifting her chin to stare at him boldly.

"I have no knife," said Father Gomez. "But I have a sacred task. Maybe that is protecting me against these – Spectres."

"Yeah," said the girl, "maybe. Anyway, you want her, she went south, towards the mountains. We don' know where. But you ask anyone, they know if she go past, because there ain no one like her in Ci'gazze, not before and not now. She be *easy* to find."

"Thank you, Angelica," said the priest. "Bless you, my children."

He shouldered his pack, left the garden, and set off through the hot silent streets, satisfied.

After three days in the company of the wheeled creatures Mary Malone knew rather more about them, and they knew a great deal about her.

That first morning, they carried her for an hour or so along the basalt highway to a settlement by a river, and the journey was uncomfortable; she had nothing to hold on to, and the creature's back was hard. They sped along at a pace that frightened her, but the thunder of their wheels on the hard road and the beat of their scudding feet made her exhilarated enough to ignore the discomfort.

And in the course of the ride she became more aware of the creatures' physiology. Like the grazers, their skeletons had a diamond-shaped frame, with a limb at each of the corners. Some time in the distant past, a line of ancestral creatures must have developed this structure and found it worked, just as generations of long-ago crawling things in Mary's world had developed the central spine.

The basalt highway led gradually downwards, and after a while the slope increased, so the creatures could free-wheel. They tucked their side legs up and steered by leaning to one side or the other, and hurtled along at a speed Mary found terrifying; though she had to admit that the creature she was riding never gave her the slightest feeling of danger. If only she'd had something to hold on to, she would have enjoyed it.

At the foot of the mile-long slope there was a stand of the great trees, and nearby a river meandered on the level grassy ground. Some way off, Mary saw a gleam that looked like a wider expanse of water, but she didn't spend long looking at that, because the creatures were making for a settlement on the river bank, and she was burning with curiosity to see it.

There were twenty or thirty huts, roughly grouped in a circle, made of – she had to shade her eyes against the sun to see – wooden beams covered with a kind of wattle-and-daub mixture on the walls and thatch on the roofs. Other wheeled creatures were working: some repairing the roofs, others hauling a net out of the river, others bringing brushwood for a fire.

So they had language, and they had fire, and they had society. And about then she found an adjustment being made in her mind, as the word *creatures* became the word *people*. These beings weren't human, but they were *people*, she told herself; it's not *them*, they're *us*.

They were quite close now, and seeing what was coming, some of the villagers looked up and called to each other to look. The party from the road slowed to a halt, and Mary clambered stiffly down, knowing that she would ache later on.

"Thank you," she said to her ... her what? Her steed? Her cycle? Both ideas were absurdly wrong for the bright-eyed amiability that stood beside her. She settled for – friend.

He raised his trunk and imitated her words:

"Anku," he said, and again they laughed, in high spirits.

She took her rucksack from the other creature (anku! anku!)

and walked with them off the basalt and on to the hard-packed earth of the village.

And then her absorption truly began.

In the next few days she learned so much that she felt like a child again, bewildered by school. What was more, the wheeled people seemed to be just as wonderstruck by her. Her hands, to begin with. They couldn't get enough of them: their delicate trunks felt over every joint, searching out thumbs, knuckles and fingernails, flexing them gently, and they watched with amazement as she picked up her rucksack, conveyed food to her mouth, scratched, combed her hair, washed.

In return, they let her feel their trunks. They were infinitely flexible, and about as long as her arm, thicker where they joined the head, and quite powerful enough to crush her skull, she guessed. The two finger-like projections at the tip were capable of enormous force and great gentleness; the creatures seemed to be able to vary the tone of their skin on the inside, on their equivalent of fingertips, from a soft velvet to a solidity like wood. As a result, they could use them both for a delicate task like milking a grazer and for the rough business of tearing and shaping branches.

Little by little, Mary realized that their trunks were playing a part in communication, too. A movement of the trunk would modify the meaning of a sound, so the word that sounded like "chuh" meant water when it was accompanied by a sweep of the trunk from left to right, "rain" when the trunk curled up at the tip, "sadness" when it curled under, and "young shoots of grass" when it made a quick flick to the left. As soon as she saw this, Mary imitated it, moving her arm as best she could in the same way, and when the creatures realized that she was beginning to talk to them, their delight was radiant.

Once they had begun to talk (mostly in their language, although she managed to teach them a few words of English: they could say "anku" and "grass" and "tree" and "sky" and "river", and pronounce her name, with a little difficulty) they progressed much more quickly. Their word for themselves as a people was *mulefa*, but an individual was a *zalif*. Mary thought there was a difference between the sounds for *he-zalif* and *she-zalif*, but it was too subtle for her to make easily. She began to write it all down, and compile a dictionary.

But before she let herself become truly absorbed, she took out her battered paperback and the yarrow stalks, and asked the I Ching: should I be here doing this, or should I go on somewhere else and keep searching?

The reply came: *Keeping still, so that restlessness dissolves; then, beyond the tumult, one can perceive the great laws.*

It went on: *As a mountain keeps still within itself, thus a wise man does not permit his will to stray beyond his situation.*

That could hardly be clearer. She folded the stalks away and closed the book, and then realized that she'd drawn a circle of watching creatures around her.

One said, *Question? Permission? Curious.*

She said, *Please. Look.*

Very delicately their trunks moved, sorting through the stalks in the same counting movement she'd been making, or turning the pages of the book. One thing they were astonished by was the doubleness of her hands: by the fact that she could both hold the book and turn the pages at the same time. They loved to watch her lace her fingers together, or play the childhood game "This is the church, and this is the steeple," or make that over-and-over thumb-to-opposite-forefinger movement which was what Ama was using, at exactly the same moment in Lyra's world, as a charm to keep evil spirits away.

Once they had examined the yarrow stalks and the book, they folded the cloth over them carefully and put them with the book into her rucksack. She was happy and reassured by the message from ancient China, because it meant that what she wanted most to do was exactly, at that moment, what she should do.

So she set herself to learning more about the mulefa, with a cheerful heart.

She learnt that there were two sexes, and that they lived monogamously in couples. Their offspring had a long childhood: ten years at least, growing very slowly, as far as she could interpret their explanation. There were five young ones in this settlement, one almost grown and the others somewhere in between, and being smaller than the adults, they could not manage the seed-pod wheels. The children had to move as the grazers did, with all four feet on the ground, but for all their energy and adventurousness (skipping up to Mary and shying away, trying to clamber up tree-trunks, floundering in the shallow water, and so on) they seemed clumsy, as if they were in the wrong element. The speed and power and grace of the adults was startling by contrast, and Mary saw how much a growing youngster must long for the day when the wheels would fit. She watched the oldest child, one day, go quietly to the store-house where a number of seed-pods were kept, and try to fit his fore-claw into the central hole; but when he tried to stand up he fell over at once, trapping himself, and the sound attracted an adult. The child struggled to get free, squeaking with anxiety, and Mary couldn't help laughing at the sight, at the indignant parent and the guilty child, who pulled himself out at the last minute and scampered away.

The seed-pod wheels were clearly of the utmost importance, and soon Mary began to see just how valuable they were.

The mulefa spent much of their time, to begin with, in maintaining their wheels. By deftly lifting and twisting the claw they could slip it out of the hole, and then they used their trunks to examine the wheel all over, cleaning the rim, checking for cracks. The claw was formidably strong: a spur of horn or bone at right angles to the leg, and slightly curved so that the highest part, in the middle, bore the weight as it rested on the inside of the hole. Mary watched one day as a zalif examined the hole in her front wheel, touching here and there, lifting her trunk up in the air and back again, as if sampling the scent.

Mary remembered the oil she'd found on her fingers when she had examined the first seed-pod. With the zalif's permission she looked at her claw, and found the surface more smooth and slick than anything she'd felt on her world. Her fingers simply would not stay on the surface. The whole of the claw seemed impregnated with the faintly fragrant oil, and after she had seen a number of the villagers sampling, testing, checking the state of their wheels and their claws she began to wonder which had come first: wheel or claw? Rider or tree?

Although of course there was a third element as well, and that was geology. Creatures could only use wheels on a world which provided them with natural highways. There must be some feature of the mineral content of these lava-flows that made them run in ribbon-like lines over the vast savannah, and be so resistant to weathering or cracking. Little by little Mary came to see the way everything was linked together, and all of it, seemingly, managed by the mulefa. They knew the location of every herd of grazers, every stand of wheel-trees, every clump of sweet-grass, and they knew every individual within the herds, and every separate tree, and they discussed their well-being and their fate. On one occasion she saw the mulefa cull a herd of grazers, selecting some individuals and herding them away from the rest, to dispatch them by breaking their necks with a wrench of a powerful trunk. Nothing was wasted. Holding flakes of razor-sharp stone in their trunks, the mulefa skinned and gutted the animals within minutes, and then began a skilful butchery, separating out the offal and the tender meat and the tougher joints, trimming the fat, removing the horns and the hooves, and working so efficiently that Mary watched with the pleasure she felt at seeing anything done well.

Soon strips of meat were hanging to dry in the sun, and others were packed in salt and wrapped in leaves; the skins were scraped clear of fat, which was set by for later use, and then laid to soak in pits of water filled with oak-bark to tan; and the oldest child was playing with a set of horns, pretending to be a grazer, making the other children laugh. That evening there was fresh meat to eat, and Mary feasted well.

In a similar way the mulefa knew where the best fish were to be had, and exactly when and where to lay their nets. Looking for something she could do, Mary went to the net-makers and offered to help. When she saw how they worked, not on their own but two by two, working their trunks together to tie a knot, she realized how astonished they'd been by her hands, because of course she could tie knots on her own. At first she felt that this gave her an advantage – she needed no one else; and then she realized how it cut her off from others. Perhaps all human beings were like that. And from that time on, she used one hand to knot the fibres, sharing the task with a female zalif who had become her particular friend, fingers and trunk moving in and out together.

But of all the living things the wheeled people managed, it was the seed-pod trees that they took most care with.

There were half a dozen groves within the area looked after by this group. There were others further away, but they were the responsibility of other groups. Each day a party went out to check on the well-being of the mighty trees, and to harvest any fallen seed-pods. It was clear what the mulefa gained; but how did the trees benefit from this interchange? One day she saw. As she was riding along with the group, suddenly there was a loud *crack*, and everyone came to a halt, surrounding one individual whose wheel had split. Every group carried a spare or two with it, so the zalif with the broken wheel was soon remounted; but the broken wheel itself was carefully wrapped in a cloth and taken back to the settlement.

There they prised it open and took out all the seeds – flat pale ovals as big as Mary's little fingernail – and examined each one carefully. They explained that the seed-pods needed the constant pounding they got on the hard roads if they were to crack at all, and also that the seeds were difficult to germinate. Without the mulefa's attention, the trees would all die. Each species depended on the other, and furthermore, it was the oil that made it possible. It was hard to understand, but they seemed to be saying that the oil was the centre of their thinking and feeling; that young ones didn't have the wisdom of their elders because they couldn't use the wheels, and thus could absorb no oil through their claws.

And that was when Mary began to see the connection between the mulefa and the question which had occupied the past few years of her life.

But before she could examine it any further (and conversations with the mulefa were long and complex, because they loved qualifying and explaining and illustrating their arguments with dozens of examples, as if they had forgotten nothing, and everything they had ever known was available immediately for reference) the settlement was attacked.

* * *

Mary was the first to see the attackers coming, though she didn't know what they were.

It happened in mid-afternoon, when she was helping repair the roof of a hut. The mulefa only built one storey high, because they were not climbers; but Mary was happy to clamber above the ground, and she could lay thatch and knot it in place with her two hands, once they had shown her the technique, much more quickly than they could.

So she was braced against the rafters of a house, catching the bundles of reeds thrown up to her, and enjoying the cool breeze from the water that was tempering the heat of the sun, when her eye was caught by a flash of white.

It came from that distant glitter she thought was the sea. She shaded her eyes, and saw one – two – more – a fleet of tall white sails, emerging out of the heat-haze, some way off but making with a silent grace for the river-mouth.

Mary! called the zalif from below. *What are you seeing?*

She didn't know the word for sail, or boat, so she said *tall, white, many.*

At once the zalif gave a call of alarm, and everyone in earshot stopped work and sped to the centre of the settlement, calling the young ones. Within a minute all the mulefa were ready to flee.

Atal, her friend, called: *Mary! Mary! Come! Tualapi! Tualapi!*

It had all happened so quickly that Mary had hardly moved. The white sails by this time had already entered the river, easily making headway against the current. Mary was impressed by the discipline of the sailors: they tacked so swiftly, the sails moving together like a flock of starlings, all changing direction simultaneously. And they were so beautiful, those snow-white slender sails, bending and dipping and filling –

There were forty of them, at least, and they were coming up-river much more swiftly than she'd thought. But she saw no crew on board, and then she realized that they weren't boats at all: they were gigantic birds, and the sails were their wings, one fore and one aft, held upright and flexed and trimmed by the power of their own muscles.

There was no time to stop and study them, because they had already reached the bank, and were climbing out. They had necks like swans, and beaks as long as her forearm. Their wings were twice as tall as she was, and – glancing back, frightened now, over her shoulder as she fled – they had powerful legs: no wonder they had moved so fast on the water.

She ran hard after the mulefa, who were calling her name as they streamed out of the settlement and on to the highway. She reached them just in time: her friend Atal was waiting, and as Mary scrambled on her back she beat the road with her feet, speeding away up the slope after her companions.

The birds, who couldn't move as fast on land, soon gave up the chase and turned back to the settlement.

They tore open the food-stores, snarling and growling and tossing their great cruel beaks high as they swallowed the dried meat and all the preserved fruit and grain. Everything edible was gone in under a minute.

And then the tualapi found the wheel-store, and tried to smash open the great seed-pods, but that was beyond them. Mary felt her friends tense with alarm all around her as they watched from the crest of the low hill and saw pod after pod hurled to the ground, kicked, rasped by the claws on the mighty legs, but of course no harm came to them from that. What worried the mulefa was that several of them were pushed and shoved and nudged towards the water, where they floated heavily down-stream towards the sea.

Then the great snow-white birds set about demolishing every-thing they could see with brutal raking blows of their feet, and stabbing, smashing, shaking, tearing movements of their beaks. The mulefa around her were murmuring, almost crooning with sorrow.

I help, Mary said. *We make again.*

But the foul creatures hadn't finished yet; holding their beauti-ful wings high, they squatted among the devastation and voided their bowels. The smell drifted up the slope with the breeze; heaps and pools of green-black-brown-white dung lay among the broken beams, the scattered thatch. Then, their clumsy movement on land giving them a swaggering strut, the birds went back to the water, and sailed away down-stream towards the sea.

Only when the last white wing had vanished in the afternoon haze did the mulefa ride down the highway again. They were full of sorrow and anger, but mainly they were powerfully anxious about the seed-pod store.

Out of the fifteen pods that had been there, only two were left. The rest had been pushed into the water and lost. But there was a sandbank in the next bend of the river, and Mary thought she could spot a wheel that was caught there; so to the mulefa's surprise and alarm she took off her clothes, wound a length of cord around her waist, and swam across to it. On the sandbank she found not one but five of the precious wheels, and passing the cord through their softening centres she swam heavily back pulling them behind her.

The mulefa were full of gratitude. They never entered the water themselves, and only fished from the bank, taking care to keep their feet and wheels dry. Mary felt she had done something useful for them at last.

Later that night, after a scanty meal of sweet-roots, they told her why they had been so anxious about the wheels. There had once been a time when the seed-pods were plentiful, and when the world was rich and full of life, and the mulefa lived with their trees in perpetual joy. But something bad had happened many years ago; some virtue had gone out of the world; because despite every effort and all the love and attention the mulefa could give them, the wheel-pod trees were dying.

THE DRAGONFLIES

A truth that's told with bad intent
Beats all the lies you can invent.

— WILLIAM BLAKE

AMA CLIMBED THE path to the cave, bread and milk in the bag on her back, a heavy puzzlement in her heart. How in the world could she ever manage to reach the sleeping girl?

She came to the rock where the woman had told her to leave the food. She put it down, but she didn't go straight home; she climbed a little further, up past the cave and through the thick rhododendrons, and further up still to where the trees thinned out and the rainbows began.

There she and her dæmon played a game: they climbed up over the rock-shelves and around the little green-white cataracts, past the whirlpools and through the spectrum-tinted spray, until her hair and her eyelids and his squirrel-fur were beaded all over with a million tiny pearls of moisture. The game was to get to the top without wiping your eyes, despite the temptation, and soon the sunlight sparkled and fractured into red, yellow, green, blue, and all the colours in between, but she mustn't brush her hand across to see better until she got right to the top, or the game would be lost.

Kulang her dæmon sprang to the rock at the edge of the top-most little waterfall, and she knew he'd turn at once to make sure she didn't brush the moisture off her eyelashes – except that he didn't.

Instead he clung there, gazing forward.

Ama wiped her eyes, because the game was cancelled by the surprise her dæmon was feeling. As she pulled herself up to look over the edge, she gasped and fell still, because looking down at her was the face of a creature she had never seen before: a bear, but immense, terrifying, four times the size of the brown bears in the forest, and ivory-white, with a black nose and black eyes and claws the length of daggers. He was only an arm's length away. She could see every separate hair on his head.

"Who's that?" said the voice of a boy, and while Ama couldn't understand the words, she caught the sense easily enough.

After a moment the boy appeared next to the bear: fierce-looking, with frowning eyes and a jutting jaw. And was that a dæmon beside him, bird-shaped? But such a strange bird: unlike any she'd seen before. It flew to Kulang and spoke briefly: *Friends. We shan't hurt you.*

The great white bear hadn't moved at all.

"Come up," said the boy, and again her dæmon made sense of it for her.

Watching the bear with superstitious awe, Ama scrambled up beside the little waterfall and stood shyly on the rocks. Kulang became a butterfly, and settled for a moment on her cheek, but left it to flutter around the other dæmon, who sat still on the boy's hand.

"Will," said the boy, pointing to himself, and she responded, "Ama." Now she could see him properly, she was frightened of the boy almost more than the bear: he had a horrible wound: two of his fingers were missing. She felt dizzy when she saw it.

The bear turned away along the milky stream and lay down in the water as if to cool himself. The boy's dæmon took to the air, and fluttered with Kulang among the rainbows, and slowly they began to understand each other.

And what should they turn out to be looking for but a cave, with a girl asleep?

The words tumbled out of her in response: "I know where it is! And she's being kept asleep by a woman who says she is her mother, but no mother would be so cruel, would she? She makes her drink something to keep her asleep, but I have some herbs to make her wake up, if only I could get to her!"

Will could only shake his head and wait for Balthamos to translate. It took more than a minute.

"Iorek," he called, and the bear lumbered along the bed of the stream, licking his chops, for he had just swallowed a fish. "Iorek," Will said, "this girl is saying she knows where Lyra is. I'll go with her to look, while you stay here and watch."

Iorek Byrnison, foursquare in the stream, nodded silently. Will hid his rucksack and buckled on the knife before clambering down through the rainbows with Ama. He had to brush his eyes and peer through the dazzle to see where it was safe to put his feet, and the mist that filled the air was icy.

When they reached the foot of the falls, Ama indicated that they should go carefully and make no noise, and Will walked behind her down the slope, between mossy rocks and great gnarled pine-trunks where the dappled light danced intensely green, and a billion tiny insects scraped and sang. Down they went, and further down, and still the sunlight followed them, deep into the valley, while overhead the branches tossed unceasingly in the bright sky.

Then Ama halted. Will drew himself behind the massive bole of a cedar, and looked where she was pointing. Through a tangle of leaves and branches he saw the side of a cliff, rising up to the right, and part-way up –

"Mrs Coulter," he whispered, and his heart was beating fast.

The woman appeared from behind the rock and shook out a thick-leafed branch before dropping it and brushing her hands together. Had she been sweeping the floor? Her sleeves were rolled, and her hair was bound up with a scarf. Will could never have imagined her looking so domestic.

But then there was a flash of gold, and that vicious monkey appeared, leaping up to her shoulder. As if they suspected something, they looked all around, and suddenly Mrs Coulter didn't look domestic at all.

Ama was whispering urgently: she was afraid of the golden monkey-dæmon; he liked to tear the wings off bats while they were still alive.

"Is there anyone else with her?" Will said. "No soldiers, or anyone like that?"

Ama didn't know. She had never seen soldiers, but people did talk about strange and frightening men, or they might be ghosts, seen on the mountainsides at night . . . But there had always been ghosts in the mountains, everyone knew that. So they might not have anything to do with the woman.

Well, thought Will, if Lyra's in the cave and Mrs Coulter doesn't leave it, I'll have to go and pay a call.

He said, "What is this drug you have? What do you have to do with it to wake her up?"

Ama explained.

"And where is it now?"

In her home, she said. Hidden away.

"All right. Wait here and don't come near. When you see her, you mustn't say that you know me. You've never seen me, or the bear. When do you next bring her food?"

Half an hour before sunset, Ama's dæmon said.

"Bring the medicine with you then," said Will. "I'll meet you here."

She watched with great unease as he set off along the path. Surely she didn't believe what she had just told him about the monkey-dæmon, or he wouldn't walk so recklessly up to the cave.

Actually, Will felt very nervous. All his senses seemed to be clarified, so that he was aware of the tiniest insects drifting in the sun-shafts and the rustle of every leaf and the movement of the clouds above, even though his eyes never left the cave-mouth.

"Balthamos," he whispered, and the angel-dæmon flew to his shoulder as a bright-eyed small bird with red wings. "Keep close to me, and watch that monkey."

"Then look to your right," said Balthamos tersely.

And Will saw a patch of golden light at the cave-mouth that had a face and eyes, and was watching them. They were no more than twenty paces away. He stood still, and the golden monkey turned his head to look in the cave, said something, and turned back.

Will felt for the knife-handle, and walked on.

When he reached the cave, the woman was waiting for him.

She was sitting at her ease in the little canvas chair, with a book on her lap, watching him calmly. She was wearing traveller's clothes of khaki, but so well were they cut and so graceful was her figure that they looked like the highest of high fashion, and the little spray of red blossom she'd pinned to her shirt-front looked like the most elegant of jewels. Her hair shone and her dark eyes glittered, and her bare legs gleamed golden in the sunlight.

She smiled. Will very nearly smiled in response, because he was so unused to the sweetness and gentleness a woman could put into a smile, and it unsettled him.

"You're Will," she said, in that low, intoxicating voice.

"How do you know my name?" he said harshly.

"Lyra says it in her sleep."

"Where is she?"

"Safe."

"I want to see her."

"Come on then," she said, and got to her feet, dropping the book on the chair.

For the first time since coming into her presence Will looked at the monkey-dæmon. His fur was long and lustrous, each hair seeming to be made of pure gold, much finer than a human's, and his little face and hands were black. Will had last seen that face, contorted with hate, on the evening when he and Lyra stole the alethiometer back from Sir Charles Latrom in the house in Oxford. The monkey had tried to tear at him with his teeth until Will had slashed left-right with the knife, forcing the dæmon backwards, so he could close the window and shut them away in a different world. Will thought that nothing on earth would make him turn his back on that monkey now.

But the bird-shaped Balthamos was watching closely, and Will stepped carefully over the floor of the cave and followed Mrs Coulter to the little figure lying still in the shadows.

And there she was, his dearest friend, asleep. So small she looked! He was amazed at how all the force and fire that was Lyra awake could look so gentle and mild when she was sleeping. At her neck Pantalaimon lay in his polecat-shape, his fur glistening, and Lyra's hair lay damp across her forehead.

He knelt down beside her and lifted the hair away. Her face was hot. Out of the corner of his eye Will saw the golden monkey crouching to spring, and set his hand on the knife; but Mrs Coulter shook her head very slightly, and the monkey relaxed.

Without seeming to, Will was memorizing the exact layout

of the cave: the shape and size of every rock, the slope of the floor, the exact height of the ceiling above the sleeping girl. He would need to find his way through it in the dark, and this was the only chance he'd have to see it first.

"So you see, she's quite safe," said Mrs Coulter.

"Why are you keeping her here? And why don't you let her wake up?"

"Let's sit down."

She didn't take the chair, but sat with him on the moss-covered rocks at the entrance to the cave. She sounded so kindly, and there was such sad wisdom in her eyes, that Will's mistrust deepened. He felt that every word she said was a lie, every action concealed a threat, and every smile was a mask of deceit. Well, he would have to deceive her in turn: he'd have to make her think he was harmless. But he had successfully deceived every teacher and every police officer and every social worker and every neighbour who had ever taken an interest in him and his home; he'd been preparing for this all his life.

Right, he thought. I can deal with you.

"Would you like something to drink?" said Mrs Coulter. "I'll have some too ... It's quite safe. Look."

She cut open some brownish wrinkled fruit and pressed the cloudy juice into two small beakers. She sipped one and offered the other to Will, who sipped as well, and found it fresh and sweet.

"How did you find your way here?" she said.

"It wasn't hard to follow you."

"Evidently. Have you got Lyra's alethiometer?"

"Yes," he said, and let her work out for herself whether or not he could read it.

"And you've got a knife, I understand."

"Sir Charles told you that, did he?"

"Sir Charles? Oh – Carlo, of course. Yes, he did. It sounds fascinating. May I see it?"

"No, of course not," he said. "Why are you keeping Lyra here?"

"Because I love her," she said. "I'm her mother. She's in appalling danger and I won't let anything happen to her."

"Danger from what?" said Will.

"Well . . ." she said, and set her beaker down on the ground, leaning forward so that her hair swung down on either side of her face. When she sat up again she tucked it back behind her ears with both hands, and Will smelt the fragrance of some scent she was wearing combined with the fresh smell of her body, and he felt disturbed.

If Mrs Coulter saw his reaction, she didn't show it. She went on: "Look, Will, I don't know how you came to meet my daughter, and I don't know what you know already, and I certainly don't know if I can trust you; but equally, I'm tired of having to lie. So here it is: the truth.

"I found out that my daughter is in danger from the very people I used to belong to – from the church. Frankly, I think they want to kill her. So I found myself in a dilemma, you see: obey the church, or save my daughter. And I was a faithful servant of the church, too. There was no one more zealous; I gave my life to it; I served it with a passion.

"But I had this daughter . . .

"I know I didn't look after her well when she was young. She was taken away from me and brought up by strangers. Perhaps that made it hard for her to trust me. But when she was growing up, I saw the danger that she was in, and three times now I've tried to save her from it. I've had to become a renegade and hide in this remote place, and I thought we were safe; but now to learn that you found us so easily – well, you can understand, that worries me. The church won't be far behind. And they want to kill her, Will. They will not let her live."

"Why? Why do they hate her so much?"

"Because of what they think she's going to do. I don't know what that is; I wish I did, because then I could keep her even more safe. But all I know is that they hate her, and they have no mercy, none."

She leaned forward, talking urgently and quietly and closely.

"Why am I telling you this?" she went on. "Can I trust you? I think I have to. I can't escape any more, there's nowhere else to go. And if you're a friend of Lyra's, you might be my friend too. And I do need friends, I do need help. Everything's against me now. The church will destroy me too, as well as Lyra, if they find us. I'm alone, Will, just me in a cave with my daughter, and all the forces of all the worlds are trying to track us down. And here you are, to show how easy it is to find us, apparently. What are you going to do, Will? What do you want?"

"Why are you keeping her asleep?" he said, stubbornly avoiding her questions.

"Because what would happen if I let her wake? She'd run away at once. And she wouldn't last five days."

"But why don't you explain it to her and give her the choice?"

"Do you think she'd listen? Do you think even if she listened she'd believe me? She doesn't trust me. She hates me, Will. You must know that. She despises me. I, well . . . I don't know how to say it . . . I love her so much I've given up everything I had – a great career, great happiness, position and wealth – everything, to come to this cave in the mountains and live on dry bread and sour fruit, just so I can keep my daughter alive. And if to do that I have to keep her asleep, then so be it. But I *must* keep her alive. Wouldn't your mother do as much for you?"

Will felt a jolt of shock and rage that Mrs Coulter had dared to bring his own mother in to support her argument. Then the first shock was complicated by the thought that his mother, after all, had not protected him; he had had to protect her. Did Mrs Coulter love Lyra more than Elaine Parry loved him? But that was unfair: his mother wasn't well.

Either Mrs Coulter did not know the boil of feelings that her simple words had lanced, or she was monstrously clever. Her beautiful eyes watched mildly as Will reddened and shifted uncomfortably; and for a moment Mrs Coulter looked uncannily like her daughter.

"But what are *you* going to do?" she said.

"Well, I've seen Lyra now," Will said, "and she's alive, that's clear, and she's safe, I suppose. That's all I was going to do. So now I've done it I can go and help Lord Asriel like I was supposed to."

That did surprise her a little, but she mastered it.

"You don't mean – I thought you might help us," she said quite calmly, not pleading but questioning. "With the knife. I saw what you did at Sir Charles's house. You could make it safe for us, couldn't you? You could help us get away?"

"I'm going to go now," Will said, standing up.

She held out her hand. A rueful smile, a shrug, and a nod as if to a skilful opponent who'd made a good move at the chessboard: that was what her body said. He found himself liking her, because she was brave, and because she seemed like a more complicated and richer and deeper Lyra. He couldn't help but like her.

So he shook her hand, finding it firm and cool and soft. She turned to the golden monkey, who had been sitting behind her all the time, and a look passed between them that Will couldn't interpret.

Then she turned back with a smile.

"Goodbye," he said, and she said quietly, "Goodbye, Will."

He left the cave, knowing her eyes were following, and he didn't look back once. Ama was nowhere in sight. He walked back the way he'd come, keeping to the path until he heard the sound of the waterfall ahead.

"She's lying," he said to Iorek Byrnison thirty minutes later. "Of course she's lying. She'd lie even if it made things worse for herself, because she just loves lying too much to stop."

"What is your plan, then?" said the bear, who was basking in the sunlight, his belly flat down in a patch of snow among the rocks.

Will walked up and down, wondering whether he could use the trick that had worked in Headington: use the knife to move into another world and then go to a spot right next to where Lyra lay, cut back through into this world, pull her through into safety and then close up again. That was the obvious thing to do: why did he hesitate?

Balthamos knew. In his own angel-shape, shimmering like a heat-haze in the sunlight, he said, "You were foolish to go to her. All you want to do now is see her again."

Iorek uttered a deep quiet growl. At first Will thought he was warning Balthamos, but then with a little shock of embarrassment he realized that the bear was agreeing with the angel. The two of them had taken little notice of each other until now; their modes of being were so different; but they were of one mind about this, clearly.

And Will scowled, but it was true. He had been captivated by Mrs Coulter. All his thoughts referred to her: when he thought of Lyra, it was to wonder how like her mother she'd be when she grew up; if he thought of the church, it was to wonder how many of the priests and cardinals were under her spell; if he thought of his own dead father, it was to wonder whether he would have detested her or admired her; and if he thought of his own mother . . .

He felt his heart grimace. He walked away from the bear, and stood on a rock from which he could see across the whole valley. In the clear cold air he could hear the distant tok-tok of someone chopping wood, he could hear a dull iron bell around the neck of a sheep, he could hear the rustling of the tree-tops far below. The tiniest crevices in the mountains at the horizon were clear and sharp to his eyes, as were the vultures wheeling over some near-dead creature many miles away.

There was no doubt about it: Balthamos was right. The woman had cast a spell on him. It was pleasant and tempting to think about those beautiful eyes and the sweetness of that voice, and to recall the way her arms rose to push back that shining hair . . .

With an effort he came back to his senses and heard another sound altogether: a far-distant drone.

He turned this way and that to locate it, and found it in the north, the very direction he and Iorek had come from.

"Zeppelins," said the bear's voice, startling Will, for he hadn't heard the great creature come near. Iorek stood beside him looking in the same direction, and then reared up high, fully twice the height of Will, his gaze intent.

"How many?"

"Eight of them," said Iorek after a minute, and then Will saw them too: little specks in a line.

"Can you tell how long it will take them to get here?" Will said.

"They will be here not long after nightfall."

"So we won't have very much darkness. That's a pity."

"What is your plan?"

"To make an opening and take Lyra through into another

world, and close it again before her mother follows. The girl has a drug to wake Lyra up, but she couldn't explain very clearly how to use it, so she'll have to come into the cave as well. I don't want to put her in danger, though. Maybe you could distract Mrs Coulter while we do that."

The bear grunted and closed his eyes. Will looked around for the angel, and saw his shape outlined in droplets of mist in the late afternoon light.

"Balthamos," he said, "I'm going back into the forest now, to find a safe place to make the first opening. I need you to keep watch for me, and tell me the moment she comes near – her or that dæmon of hers."

Balthamos nodded, and raised his wings to shake off the moisture. Then he soared up into the cold air and glided out over the valley as Will began to search for a world where Lyra would be safe.

In the creaking, thrumming double bulkhead of the leading zeppelin, the dragonflies were hatching. The Lady Salmakia bent over the splitting cocoon of the electric-blue one, easing the damp filmy wings clear, taking care to let her face be the first thing that imprinted itself on the many-faceted eyes, soothing the fine-stretched nerves, whispering its name to the brilliant creature, teaching it who it was.

In a few minutes, the Chevalier Tialys would do the same to his. But for now, he was sending a message on the lodestone resonator, and his attention was fully occupied with the movement of the bow and his fingers.

He transmitted:

"To Lord Roke:

"We are three hours from the estimated time of arrival at the valley. The Consistorial Court of Discipline intends to send a squad to the cave as soon as they land.

It will divide into two units. The first unit will fight its way into the cave and kill the child, removing her head so as to prove her death. If possible they will also capture the woman, though if that is impossible they are to kill her.

"The second unit is to capture the boy alive.

"The remainder of the force will engage the gyropters of King Ogunwe. They estimate that the gyropters will arrive shortly after the zeppelins. In accordance with your orders, the Lady Salmakia and I will shortly leave the zeppelin and fly directly to the cave, where we shall try to defend the girl against the first unit and hold them at bay until reinforcements arrive.

"We await your response."

The answer came almost immediately.

"To the Chevalier Tialys:

"In the light of your report, here is a change of plan.

"In order to prevent the enemy from killing the child, which would be the worst possible outcome, you and the Lady Salmakia are to co-operate with the boy. While he has the knife, he has the initiative, so if he opens another world and takes the girl into it, let him do so, and follow them through. Stay by their side at all times."

The Chevalier Tialys replied:

"To Lord Roke:

"Your message is heard and understood. The lady and I shall leave at once."

The little spy closed the resonator and gathered his equipment together.

"Tialys," came a whisper from the dark, "it's hatching. You should come now."

He leapt up to the strut where his dragonfly had been struggling into the world, and eased it gently free of the broken cocoon. Stroking its great fierce head, he lifted the heavy antennae, still moist and curled, and let the creature taste the flavour of his skin until it was entirely under his command.

Salmakia was fitting her dragonfly with the harness she carried everywhere: spider-silk reins, stirrups of titanium, a saddle of hummingbird-skin. It was almost weightless. Tialys did the same with his, easing the straps around the insect's body, tightening, adjusting. It would wear the harness till it died.

Then he quickly slung the pack over his shoulder, and sliced through the oiled fabric of the zeppelin's skin. Beside him, the lady had mounted her dragonfly, and now she urged it through the narrow gap into the hammering gusts. The long frail wings trembled as she squeezed through, and then the joy of flight took over the creature, and it plunged into the wind. A few seconds later Tialys joined her in the wild air, his mount eager to fight the swift-gathering dusk itself.

The two of them whirled upwards in the icy currents, took a few moments to get their bearings, and set their course for the valley.

12

THE BREAK

Still as he fled, his eye was backward cast,
As if his fear still followed him behind.

— EDMUND SPENSER

AS DARKNESS FELL, this was how things stood.

In his adamant tower, Lord Asriel paced up and down. His attention was fixed on the little figure beside the lodestone resonator, and every other report had been diverted, every part of his mind was directed to the news that came to the small square block of stone under the lamplight.

King Ogunwe sat in the cabin of his gyropter, swiftly working out a plan to counter the intentions of the Consistorial Court, which he'd just learned about from the Gallivespian in his own aircraft. The navigator was scribbling some figures on a scrap of paper, which he handed to the pilot. The essential thing was speed: getting their troops on the ground first would make all the difference. The gyropters were faster than zeppelins, but they were still some way behind.

In the zeppelins of the Consistorial Court, the Swiss Guard were attending to their kit. Their cross-bows were deadly over five hundred yards, and an archer could load and fire fifteen bolts a minute. The spiral fins, made of horn, gave the bolt a spin and made the weapon as accurate as a rifle. It was also, of course, silent, which might be a great advantage.

Mrs Coulter lay awake in the entrance to the cave. The golden monkey was restless, and frustrated: the bats had left the cave with the coming of darkness, and there was nothing to torment. He prowled about by Mrs Coulter's sleeping-bag, scratching with a little horny finger at the occasional glow-flies that settled in the cave and smearing their luminescence over the rock.

Lyra lay hot and almost as restless, but deep, deep asleep, locked into oblivion by the draught her mother had forced down her only an hour before. There was a dream that had occupied her for a long time, and now it had returned, and little whimpers of pity and rage and Lyratic resolution shook her breast and her throat, making Pantalaimon grind his polecat-teeth in sympathy.

Not far away, under the wind-tossed pines on the forest path, Will and Ama were making their way towards the cave. Will had tried to explain to Ama what he was going to do, but her dæmon could make no sense of it, and when he cut a window and showed her, she was so terrified that she nearly fainted. He had to move calmly and speak quietly in order to keep her nearby, because she refused to let him take the powder from her, or even to tell him how it was to be used. In the end he had to say simply, "Keep very quiet and follow me," and hope that she would.

Iorek, in his armour, was somewhere close by, waiting to hold off the soldiers from the zeppelins so as to give Will enough time to work. What neither of them knew was that Lord Asriel's force was also closing in: the wind from time to time brought a far-distant clatter to Iorek's ears, but whereas he knew what zeppelin engines sounded like, he had never heard a gyropter, and he could make nothing of it.

Balthamos might have been able to tell them, but Will was troubled about him. Now that they'd found Lyra, the angel had begun to withdraw back into his grief: he was silent, distracted, and sullen. And that in turn made it harder to talk to Ama.

As they paused on the path, Will said to the air, "Balthamos? Are you there?"

"Yes," said the angel tonelessly.

"Balthamos, please stay with me. Stay close and warn me of any danger. I need you."

"I haven't abandoned you yet," said the angel.

That was the best Will could get out of him.

Far above in the buffeting mid-air, Tialys and Salmakia soared over the valley, trying to see down to the cave. The dragonflies would do exactly as they were told, but their bodies couldn't easily cope with cold, and besides, they were tossed about dangerously in the wild wind. Their riders guided them low, among the shelter of the trees, and then flew from branch to branch, taking their bearings in the gathering dark.

*   *   *

Will and Ama crept up in the windy moonlight to the closest point they could reach that was still out of sight of the cave-mouth. It happened to be behind a heavy-leafed bush just off the path, and there he cut a window in the air.

The only world he could find with the same conformation of ground was a bare rocky place, where the moon glared down from a starry sky on to a bleached bone-white ground where little insects crawled and uttered their scraping, chittering sounds over a wide silence.

Ama followed him through, fingers and thumbs moving furiously to protect her from the devils that must be haunting this ghastly place; and her dæmon, adapting at once, became a lizard and scampered over the rocks with quick feet.

Will saw a problem. It was simply that the brilliant moonlight on the bone-coloured rocks would shine like a lantern once he opened the window in Mrs Coulter's cave. He'd have to open it quickly, pull Lyra through, and close it again at once. They could wake her up in this world, where it was safer.

He stopped on the dazzling slope and said to Ama: "We must be very quick and completely silent. No noise, not even a whisper."

She understood, though she was frightened. The little packet of powder was in her breast pocket: she'd checked it a dozen times, and she and her dæmon had rehearsed the task so often that she was sure they could do it in total darkness.

They climbed on up the bone-white rocks, Will measuring the distance carefully until he estimated that they would be well inside the cave.

Then he took the knife and cut the smallest possible window he could see through, no larger than the circle he could make with thumb and forefinger.

He put his eye to it quickly to keep the moonlight out, and looked through. There it all was: he'd calculated well. He could see the cave-mouth ahead, the rocks dark against the night sky; he could see the shape of Mrs Coulter, asleep, with her golden dæmon beside her; he could even see the monkey's tail, trailing negligently over the sleeping-bag.

Changing his angle and looking closer, he saw the rock behind which Lyra was lying. He couldn't see her, though. Was he too close? He shut that window, moved back a step or two, and opened again.

She wasn't there.

"Listen," he said to Ama and her dæmon, "the woman has moved her and I can't see where she is. I'm going to have to go through and look around the cave to find her, and cut through as soon as I've done that. So stand back – keep out of the way so I don't accidentally cut you when I come back. If I get stuck there for any reason, go back and wait by the other window, where we came in."

"We should both go through," Ama said, "because I know how to wake her, and you don't, and I know the cave better than you do, too."

Her face was stubborn, her lips pressed together, her fists clenched. Her lizard-dæmon acquired a ruff and raised it slowly around his neck.

Will said, "Oh, very well. But we go through quickly and in complete silence, and you do exactly what I say, at once, you understand?"

She nodded, and patted her pocket yet again to check the medicine.

Will made a small opening, low down, looked through, and enlarged it swiftly, getting through in a moment on hands and knees. Ama was right behind him, and altogether the window was open for less than ten seconds.

They crouched on the cave floor behind a large rock, with the bird-formed Balthamos beside them, their eyes taking some moments to adjust from the moon-drenched brilliance of the other world. Inside the cave it was much darker, and much more full of sound: mostly the wind in the trees, but below that was another sound, too. It was the roar of a zeppelin's engine, and it wasn't far away.

With the knife in his right hand, Will balanced himself carefully and looked around.

Ama was doing the same, and her owl-eyed dæmon was peering this way and that; but Lyra was not at this end of the cave. There was no doubt about it.

Will raised his head over the rock and took a long steady look down towards the entrance, where Mrs Coulter and her dæmon lay deep in sleep.

And then his heart sank. There lay Lyra, stretched out in the depths of her sleep, right next to Mrs Coulter. Their outlines had merged in the darkness; no wonder he hadn't seen her.

Will touched Ama's hand and pointed.

"We'll just have to do it very carefully," he whispered.

Something was happening outside. The roar of the zeppelins was now much louder than the wind in the trees, and lights were moving about, too, shining down through the branches from above. The quicker they got Lyra out the better, and that meant darting down there *now* before Mrs Coulter woke up, cutting through, pulling her to safety and closing again.

He whispered that to Ama. She nodded.

Then, as he was about to move, Mrs Coulter woke up.

She stirred and said something, and instantly the golden monkey sprang to his feet. Will could see his silhouette in the cave-mouth, crouching, attentive, and then Mrs Coulter herself sat up, shading her eyes against the light outside.

Will's left hand was tight around Ama's wrist. Mrs Coulter got up, fully dressed, lithe, alert, not at all as if she'd just been asleep. Perhaps she'd been awake all the time. She and the golden monkey were crouching inside the cave-mouth, watching and listening, as the light from the zeppelins swung from side to side above the tree-tops and the engines roared, and shouts, male voices warning or calling orders, made it clear that they should move fast, very fast.

Will squeezed Ama's wrist and darted forward, watching the ground in case he stumbled, running fast and low.

Then he was at Lyra's side, and she was deep asleep, Pantalaimon around her neck; and then Will held up the knife and felt carefully, and a second later there would have been an opening to pull Lyra through into safety –

But he looked up. He looked at Mrs Coulter. She had turned around silently, and the glare from the sky, reflected off the damp cave wall, lit her face, and for a moment it wasn't her face at all; it was his own mother's face, reproaching him, and his heart quailed from sorrow; and then as he thrust with the knife, his mind left the point, and with a wrench and a crack, the knife fell in pieces to the ground.

It was broken.

Now he couldn't cut his way out at all.

He said to Ama, "Wake her up. Do it now."

Then he stood up, ready to fight. He'd strangle that monkey first. He was tensed to meet its leap, and he found he still had the hilt of the knife in his hand: at least he could use it to hit with.

But there was no attack either from the golden monkey or from Mrs Coulter. She simply moved a little to let the light from outside show the pistol in her hand. In doing so she let some of the light shine on what Ama was doing: she was sprinkling a powder on Lyra's upper lip, and watching as Lyra breathed in, helping it into her nostrils by using her own dæmon's tail as a brush.

Will heard a change in the sounds from outside: there was another note now as well as the roar of the zeppelin. It sounded familiar, like an intrusion from his own world, and then he recognized the clatter of a helicopter. Then there was another and another, and more lights swept across the ever-moving trees outside, in a brilliant green scatter of radiance.

Mrs Coulter turned briefly as the new sound came to her, but too briefly for Will to jump and seize the gun. As for the monkey-dæmon, he glared at Will without blinking, crouched ready to spring.

Lyra was moving and murmuring. Will bent down and squeezed her hand, and the other dæmon nudged Pantalaimon, lifting his heavy head, whispering to him.

Outside there was a shout, and a man fell out of the sky, to land with a sickening crash not five yards from the entrance to the cave. Mrs Coulter didn't flinch; she looked at him coolly and turned back to Will. A moment later there came a crack of rifle fire from above, and a second after that a storm of shooting broke out, and the sky was full of explosions, of the crackle of flame, of bursts of gunfire.

Lyra was struggling up into consciousness, gasping, sighing, moaning, pushing herself up only to fall back weakly, and

Pantalaimon was yawning, stretching, snapping at the other dæmon, flopping clumsily to one side as his muscles failed to act.

As for Will, he was searching the cave floor with the utmost care for the pieces of the broken knife. No time to wonder how it had happened, or whether it could be mended; but he was the knife-bearer, and he had to gather it up safely. As he found each piece he lifted it carefully, every nerve in his body aware of his missing fingers, and slipped it into the sheath. He could see the pieces quite easily, because the metal caught the gleam from outside: seven of them, the smallest being the point itself. He picked them all up, and then turned back to try and make sense of the fight outside.

Somewhere above the trees, the zeppelins were hovering, and men were sliding down ropes, but the wind made it difficult for the pilots to hold the aircraft steady. Meanwhile, the first gyropters had arrived above the cliff. There was only room for them to land one at a time, and then the African riflemen had to make their way down the rock face. It was one of them who had been picked off by a lucky shot from the swaying zeppelins.

By this time, both sides had landed some troops. Some had been killed between the sky and the ground; several more were wounded, and lay on the cliff or among the trees. But neither force had yet reached the cave, and still the power inside it lay with Mrs Coulter.

Will said above the noise:

"What are you going to do?"

"Hold you captive."

"What, as hostages? Why should they take any notice of that? They want to kill us all anyway."

"One force does, certainly," she said, "but I'm not sure about the other. We must hope the Africans win."

She sounded happy, and in the glare from outside, Will saw her face full of joy and life and energy.

"You broke the knife," he said.

"No, I didn't. I wanted it whole, so we could get away. You were the one who broke it."

Lyra's voice came urgently: "Will?" she muttered. "Is that Will?"

"Lyra!" he said, and knelt quickly beside her. Ama was helping her sit up.

"What's happening?" Lyra said. "Where are we? Oh, Will, I had this dream . . ."

"We're in a cave. Don't move too fast, you'll get dizzy. Just take it carefully. Find your strength. You've been asleep for days and days."

Her eyes were still heavy, and she was racked by deep yawns, but she was desperate to be awake, and he helped her up, putting her arm over his shoulder and taking much of her weight. Ama watched timidly, for now the strange girl was awake, she was nervous of her. Will breathed in the scent of Lyra's sleepy body with a happy satisfaction: she was here, she was real.

They sat on a rock. Lyra held his hand and rubbed her eyes.

"What's happening, Will?" she whispered.

"Ama here got some powder to wake you up," he said speaking very quietly, and Lyra turned to the girl, seeing her for the first time, and put her hand on Ama's shoulder in thanks. "I got here as soon as I could," Will went on, "but some soldiers did too. I don't know who they are. We'll get out as soon as we can."

Outside, the noise and confusion was reaching a height; one of the gyropters had taken a fusillade from a zeppelin's machine gun while the riflemen were jumping out on the clifftop, and it burst into flames, not only killing the crew but also preventing the remaining gyropters from landing.

Another zeppelin, meanwhile, had found a clear space further down the valley, and the crossbow-men who disembarked from it were now running up the path to reinforce those already in action. Mrs Coulter was following as much as she could see from the cave-mouth, and now she raised her pistol, supporting it with both hands, and took careful aim before firing. Will saw the flash from the muzzle, but heard nothing over the explosions and gunfire from outside.

If she does that again, he thought, I'll rush and knock her over, and he turned to whisper that to Balthamos; but the angel was nowhere near. Instead, Will saw with dismay, he was cowering against the wall of the cave, back in his angel form, trembling and whimpering.

"Balthamos!" Will said urgently. "Come on, they can't hurt you! And you have to help us! You can fight – you know that – you're not a coward – and we need you –"

But before the angel could reply, something else happened.

Mrs Coulter cried out and reached down to her ankle, and simultaneously the golden monkey snatched at something in mid-air, with a snarl of glee.

A voice – a woman's voice – but somehow *minute* – came from the thing in the monkey's paw:

"Tialys! Tialys!"

It was a tiny woman, no bigger than Lyra's hand, and the monkey was already pulling and pulling at one of her arms so that she cried out in pain. Ama knew he wouldn't stop till he'd torn it off, but Will leapt forward as he saw the pistol fall from Mrs Coulter's hand.

And he caught the gun – but then Mrs Coulter fell still, and Will became aware of a strange stalemate.

The golden monkey and Mrs Coulter were both utterly motionless. Her face was distorted with pain and fury, but she dared not move, because standing on her shoulder was a tiny man with his heel pressed against her neck, his hands entwined in her hair; and Will, through his astonishment, saw on that heel a glistening horny spur, and knew what had caused her to cry out a moment before. He must have stung her ankle.

But the little man couldn't hurt Mrs Coulter any more, because of the danger his partner was in at the hands of the monkey; and the monkey couldn't harm *her*, in case the little man dug his poison spur into Mrs Coulter's jugular vein. None of them could move.

Breathing deeply and swallowing hard to govern the pain, Mrs Coulter turned her tear-dashed eyes to Will and said calmly, "So, Master Will, what do you think we should do now?"

13

TIALYS AND SALMAKIA

Frowning, frowning night
O'er this desert bright
Let thy moon arise
While I close my eyes.

— WILLIAM BLAKE

HOLDING THE HEAVY GUN, Will swept his hand sideways and knocked the golden monkey off his perch, stunning him so that Mrs Coulter groaned aloud, and the monkey's paw relaxed enough to let the tiny woman struggle free.

In a moment she leapt up to the rocks, and the man sprang away from Mrs Coulter, both of them moving as quickly as grass-hoppers. The three children had no time to be astonished. The man was concerned: he felt his companion's shoulder and arm tenderly, and embraced her swiftly before calling to Will.

"You! Boy!" he said, and although his voice was small in volume, it was as deep as a grown man's. "Have you got the knife?"

"Of course I have," said Will. If they didn't know it was broken, he wasn't going to tell them.

"You and the girl will have to follow us. Who is the other child?"

"Ama, from the village," said Will.

"Tell her to return there. Move now, before the Swiss come."

Will didn't hesitate. Whatever these two intended, he and Lyra could still get away through the window he'd opened behind the bush on the path below.

So he helped her up, and watched curiously as the two small figures leapt on – what? Birds? No, dragonflies, almost as long as his forearm, which had been waiting in the darkness. They darted forward to the cave-mouth, where Mrs Coulter lay. She was half-stunned with pain and drowsy from the chevalier's sting, but she reached up as they went past her, and cried:

"Lyra! Lyra, my daughter, my dear one! Lyra, don't go! Don't go!"

Lyra looked down at her, anguished; but then she stepped over her mother's body and loosened Mrs Coulter's feeble clutch from her ankle. The woman was sobbing now; Will saw the tears glistening on her cheeks.

Crouching just beside the cave-mouth, the three children waited until there was a brief pause in the shooting, and then followed the dragonflies as they darted down the path. The light had changed: as well as the cold anbaric gleam from the zeppelins' flood-lights, there was the leaping orange of flames.

Will looked back once. In the glare Mrs Coulter's face was a mask of tragic passion, and her dæmon clung piteously to her as she knelt and held out her arms, crying:

"Lyra! Lyra my love! My heart's treasure, my little child, my only one! Oh Lyra, Lyra, don't go, don't leave me! My darling daughter – you're tearing my heart –"

And a great and furious sob shook Lyra herself, for after all Mrs Coulter was the only mother she would ever have, and Will saw a cascade of tears run down the girl's cheeks.

But he had to be ruthless. He pulled at Lyra's hand, and as the dragonfly-rider darted close to his head, urging them to hurry, he led her at a crouching run down the path and away from the cave. In Will's left hand, bleeding again from the blow he'd landed on the monkey, was Mrs Coulter's pistol.

"Make for the top of the cliff," said the dragonfly-rider, "and give yourself up to the Africans. They're your best hope."

Mindful of those sharp spurs, Will said nothing, though he hadn't the least intention of obeying. There was only one place he was making for, and that was the window behind the bush; so he kept his head low and ran fast, and Lyra and Ama ran behind him.

"Halt!"

There was a man, three men, blocking the path ahead – uniformed – white men with cross-bows and snarling wolf-dog dæmons – the Swiss Guard.

"Iorek!" cried Will at once. "Iorek Byrnison!" He could hear the bear crashing and snarling not far away, and hear the screams and cries of the soldiers unlucky enough to meet him.

But someone else came from nowhere to help them: Balthamos, in a blur of desperation, hurled himself between the children and the soldiers. The men fell back, amazed, as this apparition shimmered into being in front of them.

But they were trained warriors, and a moment later their dæmons leapt at the angel, savage teeth flashing white in the gloom – and Balthamos flinched: he cried out in fear and shame, and shrank back. Then he sprang upwards, beating his wings hard. Will watched in dismay as the figure of his guide and friend soared up to vanish out of sight among the tree-tops.

Lyra was following it all with still-dazed eyes. It had taken no more than two or three seconds, but it was enough for the Swiss to re-group, and now their leader was raising his cross-bow, and Will had no choice: he swung up the pistol and clamped his right hand to the butt and pulled the trigger, and the blast shook his bones, but the bullet found the man's heart.

The soldier fell back as if he'd been kicked by a horse. Simultaneously the two little spies launched themselves at the other two, leaping from the dragonflies at their victims before Will could blink. The woman found a neck, the man a wrist, and each made a quick backward stab with a heel. A choking anguished gasp, and the two Swiss died, their dæmons vanishing in mid-howl.

Will leapt over the bodies, and Lyra went with him, running hard and fast with Pantalaimon racing wildcat-formed at their heels. *Where's Ama?* Will thought, and he saw her in the same moment dodging down a different path. *Now she'll be safe*, he thought, and a second later he saw the pale gleam of the window deep behind the bushes. He seized Lyra's arm and pulled her towards it. Their faces were scratched, their clothes were snagged, their ankles twisted on roots and rocks, but they found the window and tumbled through, into the other world, on to the bone-white rocks under the glaring moon, where only the scraping of the insects broke the immense silence.

And the first thing Will did was to hold his stomach and retch, heaving and heaving with a mortal horror. That was two men now that he'd killed, not to mention the youth in the Tower of the Angels . . . Will *did not want* this. His body revolted at what his instinct had made him do, and the result was a dry, sour, agonizing spell of kneeling and vomiting until his stomach and his heart were empty.

Lyra watched helpless nearby, nursing Pan, rocking him against her breast.

Finally Will recovered a little and looked around. And at once he saw that they weren't alone in this world, because the little spies were there too, with their packs laid on the ground nearby. Their dragonflies were skimming over the rocks, snapping up moths. The man was massaging the shoulder of the woman, and both of them looked at the children sternly. Their eyes were so bright and their features so distinct that there was no doubt about their feelings, and Will knew they were a formidable pair, whoever they were.

He said to Lyra, "The alethiometer's in my rucksack, there."

"Oh, Will – I did so hope you'd find it – whatever *happened*? Did you find your father? And my *dream*, Will – it's too much to believe, what we got to do, oh, I daren't even think of it . . . And it's *safe*! You brung it all this way safe for me . . ."

The words tumbled out of her so urgently that even she didn't expect answers. She turned the alethiometer over and over, her fingers stroking the heavy gold and the smooth crystal and the knurled wheels they knew so well.

Will thought: *It'll tell us how to mend the knife!*

But he said first, "Are you all right? Are you hungry or thirsty?"

"I dunno . . . yeah. But not too much. Anyway –"

"We should move away from this window," Will said, "just in case they find it and come through."

"Yes, that's true," she said, and they moved up the slope, Will carrying his rucksack and Lyra happily carrying the little bag she kept the alethiometer in. Out of the corner of his eye Will saw the two small spies following, but they kept their distance and made no threat.

Over the brow of the rise there was a ledge of rock that offered a narrow shelter, and they sat beneath it, having carefully checked it for snakes, and shared some dried fruit and some water from Will's canteen.

Will said quietly, "The knife's broken. I don't know how it happened. Mrs Coulter did something, or said something, and I thought of my mother and that made the knife twist, or catch, or – I don't know what happened. But we're stuck till we can get it mended. I didn't want those two little people to know, because while they think I can still use it, I've got the upper hand. I thought you could ask the alethiometer, maybe, and –"

"Yeah!" she said at once. "Yeah, I will."

She had the golden instrument out in a moment, and moved into the moonlight so she could see the dial clearly. Looping back the hair behind her ears, just as Will had seen her mother do, she began to turn the wheels in the old familiar way, and Pantalaimon, mouse-formed now, sat on her knee. But it wasn't as easy to see as she'd thought; perhaps the moonlight was deceptive. She had to turn it around once or twice, and blink to clear her eyes, before the symbols became clear, and then she had it again.

She had hardly started before she gave a little gasp of excitement, and she looked up at Will with shining eyes as the needle swung. But it hadn't finished yet, and she looked back, frowning, until the instrument fell still.

She put it away, saying, "Iorek? Is he nearby, Will? I thought I heard you call him, but then I thought I was just wishing. Is he *really*?"

"Yes. Could he mend the knife? Is that what the alethiometer said?"

"Oh, he can do anything with metal, Will! Not only armour – he can make little delicate things as well ..." She told him about the small tin box Iorek had made for her to shut the spy-fly in. "But where is he?"

"Close by. He would have come when I called, but obviously he was fighting ... And Balthamos! Oh, he must have been so frightened ..."

"Who?"

He explained briefly, feeling his cheeks warm with the shame that the angel must be feeling.

"But I'll tell you more about him later," he said. "It's so

strange . . . He told me so many things, and I think I understand them, too . . ." He ran his hands through his hair and rubbed his eyes.

"You got to tell me *everything*," she said firmly. "Everything you did since she caught me. Oh, Will, you en't still bleeding? Your poor hand . . ."

"No. My father cured it. I just opened it up when I hit the golden monkey, but it's better now. He gave me some ointment that he'd made –"

"You *found* your father?"

"That's right, on the mountain, that night . . ."

He let her clean his wound and put on some fresh ointment from the little horn box while he told her some of what had happened: the fight with the stranger, the revelation that came to them both a second before the witch's arrow struck home, his meeting with the angels, his journey to the cave and his meeting with Iorek.

"All that happening, and I was asleep," she marvelled. "D'you know, I think she was kind to me, Will – I *think* she was – I don't think she ever wanted to hurt me . . . She did such bad things, but . . ."

She rubbed her eyes.

"Oh, but my *dream*, Will – I can't tell you how strange it was! It was like when I read the alethiometer, all that clearness and understanding going so deep you can't see the bottom, but clear all the way down.

"It was . . . Remember I told you about my friend Roger, and how the Gobblers caught him and I tried to rescue him, and it went wrong and Lord Asriel killed him?

"Well, I saw him. In my dream I saw him again, only he was dead, he was a ghost, and he was like beckoning to me, calling to me, only I couldn't hear. He didn't want me to be *dead*, it wasn't that. He wanted to speak to me.

"And . . . It was me that took him there, to Svalbard, where he got killed, it was my fault he was dead. And I thought back to when we used to play in Jordan College, Roger and me, on the roof, all through the town, in the markets and by the river and down the Claybeds . . . Me and Roger and all the others . . . And

I went to Bolvangar to fetch him safe home, only I made it worse, and if I don't say sorry it'll all be no good, just a huge waste of time. I got to do that, you see, Will. I got to go down into the land of the dead and find him, and . . . and say sorry. I don't care what happens after that. Then we can . . . I can . . . It doesn't matter after that."

Will said, "This place where the dead are. Is it a world like this one, like mine or yours or any of the others? Is it a world I could get to with the knife?"

She looked at him, struck by the idea.

"You could ask," he went on. "Do it now. Ask where it is, and how we get there."

She bent over the alethiometer, having to rub her eyes and peer closely again, and her fingers moved swiftly. A minute later she had the answer.

"Yes," she said, "but it's a strange place, Will . . . *So* strange . . . Could we really do that? Could we really go to the land of the dead? But – what part of us does that? Because dæmons fade away when we die – I've seen them – and our bodies, well, they just stay in the grave and decay, don't they?"

"Then there must be a third part. A different part."

"You know," she said, full of excitement, "I think that must be true! Because I can think about my body and I can think about my dæmon – so there *must* be another part, to do the thinking!"

"Yes. And that's the ghost."

Lyra's eyes blazed. She said, "Maybe we could get Roger's ghost out. Maybe we could rescue him."

"Maybe. We could try."

"Yeah, we'll do it!" she said at once. "We'll go together! That's *exactly* what we'll do!"

But if they didn't get the knife mended, Will thought, they'd be able to do nothing at all.

As soon as his head cleared and his stomach felt calmer, he sat up and called to the little spies. They were busy with some minute apparatus nearby.

"Who are you?" he said. "And whose side are you on?"

The man finished what he was doing and shut a wooden box, like a violin-case no longer than a walnut. The woman spoke first.

"We are Gallivespian," she said. "I am the Lady Salmakia, and my companion is the Chevalier Tialys. We are spies for Lord Asriel."

She was standing on a rock three or four paces away from Will and Lyra, distinct and brilliant in the moonlight. Her little voice was perfectly clear and low, her expression confident. She wore a loose skirt of some silver material and a sleeveless top of green, and her spurred feet were bare, like the man's. His costume was similarly coloured, but his sleeves were long and his wide trousers reached to mid-calf. Both of them looked strong, capable, ruthless and proud.

"What world do you come from?" said Lyra. "I never seen people like you before."

"Our world has the same problems as yours," said Tialys. "We are outlaws. Our leader Lord Roke heard of Lord Asriel's revolt, and pledged our support."

"And what did you want to do with me?"

"To take you to your father," said the Lady Salmakia. "Lord Asriel sent a force under King Ogunwe to rescue you and the boy and bring you both to his fortress. We are here to help."

"Ah, but suppose I don't want to go to my father? Suppose I don't trust him?"

"I'm sorry to hear that," she said, "but those are our orders: to take you to him."

Lyra couldn't help it: she laughed out loud at the notion of these tiny people making her do anything. But it was a mistake. Moving suddenly, the woman seized Pantalaimon, and holding his mouse-body in a fierce grip, she touched the tip of a spur to his leg. Lyra gasped: it was like the shock when the men at Bolvangar had seized him. No one should touch someone else's dæmon – it was a violation.

But then she saw that Will had swept up the man in his right hand, holding him tightly around the legs so he couldn't use his spurs, and was holding him high.

"Stalemate again," said the lady calmly. "Put the chevalier down, boy."

"Let go of Lyra's dæmon first," said Will. "I'm not in the mood to argue."

Lyra saw with a cold thrill that Will was perfectly ready to dash the Gallivespian's head against the rock. And both little people knew it.

Salmakia lifted her foot away from Pantalaimon's leg, and at once he fought free of her grasp and changed into a wildcat, hissing ferociously, fur on end, tail lashing. His bared teeth were a hand's breadth from the lady's face, and she gazed at him with perfect composure. After a moment he turned and fled to Lyra's breast, ermine-shaped, and Will carefully placed Tialys back on the rock beside his partner.

"You should show some respect," the chevalier said to Lyra. "You are a thoughtless insolent child, and several brave men have died this evening in order to make you safe. You'd do better to act politely."

"Yes," she said humbly, "I'm sorry, I will. Honest."

"As for you −" he went on, turning to Will.

But Will interrupted: "As for me, I'm not going to be spoken to like that, so don't try. Respect goes two ways. Now listen carefully. You are not in charge here; we are. If you want to stay and help, then you do as we say. Otherwise, go back to Lord Asriel now. There's no arguing about it."

Lyra could see the pair of them bristling, but Tialys was looking at Will's hand, which was on the sheath at his belt, and she knew he was thinking that while Will had the knife, he was stronger than they were. At all costs they mustn't know it was broken, then.

"Very well," said the chevalier. "We shall help you, because that's the task we've been given. But you must let us know what you intend to do."

"That's fair," said Will. "I'll tell you. We're going back into Lyra's world as soon as we've rested, and we're going to find a friend of ours, a bear. He's not far away."

"The bear with the armour? Very well," said Salmakia. "We saw him fight. We'll help you do that. But then you must come with us to Lord Asriel."

"Yes," said Lyra, lying earnestly, "oh yes, we'll do that then all right."

Pantalaimon was calmer now, and curious, so she let him climb to her shoulder and change. He became a dragonfly, as big as the two that were skimming through the air as they spoke, and darted up to join them.

"That poison," Lyra said, turning back to the Gallivespians, "in your spurs I mean, is it deadly? Because you stung my mother, Mrs Coulter, didn't you? Will she die?"

"It was only a light sting," said Tialys. "A full dose would have killed her, yes, but a small scratch will make her weak and drowsy for half a day or so."

And full of maddening pain, he knew, but he didn't tell her that.

"I need to talk to Lyra in private," said Will. "We're just going to move away for a minute."

"With that knife," said the chevalier, "you can cut through from one world to another, isn't that so?"

"Don't you trust me?"

"No."

"All right, I'll leave it here then. If I haven't got it, I can't use it."

He unbuckled the sheath and laid it on the rock, and then he and Lyra walked away and sat where they could see the Gallivespians. Tialys was looking closely at the knife handle, but he wasn't touching it.

"We'll just have to put up with them," Will said. "As soon as the knife's mended, we'll escape."

"They're so *quick*, Will," she said. "And they wouldn't care, they'd kill you."

"I just hope Iorek can mend it. I hadn't realized how much we need it."

"He will," she said confidently.

She was watching Pantalaimon as he skimmed and darted through the air, snapping up tiny moths like the other dragonflies. He couldn't go as far as they could, but he was just as fast, and even more brightly patterned. She raised her hand, and he settled on it, his long transparent wings vibrating.

"Do you think we can trust them while we sleep?" Will said.

"Yes. They're fierce, but I think they're honest."

They went back to the rock, and Will said to the Gallivespians, "I'm going to sleep now. We'll move on in the morning."

The chevalier nodded, and Will curled up at once and fell asleep.

Lyra sat down beside him, with Pantalaimon cat-formed and warm in her lap. How lucky Will was that she was awake now to look after him! He was truly fearless, and she admired that beyond measure; but he wasn't good at lying and betraying and cheating, which all came to her as naturally as breathing. When she thought of that she felt warm and virtuous, because she did it for Will, never for herself.

She had intended to look at the alethiometer again, but to her deep surprise she found herself as weary as if she'd been awake all that time instead of unconscious, and she lay down close by and closed her eyes, just for a brief nap, as she assured herself before she fell asleep.

14
KNOW WHAT IT IS

Labour without joy is base. Labour without sorrow is base.
Sorrow without labour is base. Joy without labour is base.

— JOHN RUSKIN

WILL AND LYRA slept through the night, and woke up when the sun struck their eyelids. They actually awoke within seconds of each other, with the same thought: but when they looked around, the Chevalier Tialys was calmly on guard close by.

"The force of the Consistorial Court has retreated," he told them. "Mrs Coulter is in the hands of King Ogunwe, and on her way to Lord Asriel."

"How do you know?" said Will, sitting up stiffly. "Have you been back through the window?"

"No. We talk through the lodestone resonator. I reported our conversation," Tialys said to Lyra, "to my commander Lord Roke, and he has agreed that we should go with you to the bear, and that once you have seen him, you will come with us. So we are allies, and we shall help you as much as we can."

"Good," said Will. "Then let's eat together. Do you eat our food?"

"Thank you, yes," said the lady.

Will took out his last few dried peaches and the stale flat loaf of rye bread which was all he had left, and shared it all out among them, though of course the spies did not take much.

"As for water, there doesn't seem to be any round here on this world," Will said. "We'll have to wait till we go back through before we can have a drink."

"Then we better do that soon," said Lyra.

First, though, she took out the alethiometer. She could see it clearly, unlike the night before, but her fingers were slow and stiff after her long sleep. She asked if there was still any danger in the valley. No, came the answer, all the soldiers have gone, and the villagers are in their homes; so they prepared to leave.

The window looked strange in the dazzling air of the desert, giving on to the deep-shaded bush, a square of thick green vegetation hanging in the air like a painting. The Gallivespians wanted to look at it, and were astounded to see how it was just not there from the back, and how it only sprang into being when you came round from the side.

"I'll have to close it once we're through," Will said.

Lyra tried to pinch the edges together, but her fingers couldn't find it at all; nor could the spies, despite the fineness of their hands. Only Will could feel exactly where the edges were, and he did it cleanly and quickly.

"How many worlds can you enter with the knife?" said Tialys.

"As many as there are," said Will. "No one would ever have time to find out."

He swung his rucksack up and led the way along the forest path. The dragonflies relished the fresh moist air, and darted like needles through the shafts of sunlight. The movement of the trees above was less violent, and the air was cool and tranquil; so it was all the more shocking to see the twisted wreckage of a gyropter suspended among the branches, with the body of its African pilot tangled in his seat-belt half out of the door, and to find the charred remains of the zeppelin a little further up – soot-black strips of cloth, blackened struts and pipework, broken glass, and then the bodies: three men burnt to cinders, their limbs contorted and drawn up as if they were still threatening to fight.

And they were only the ones who had fallen near the path. There were other bodies and more wreckage on the cliff above and among the trees further down. Shocked and silenced, the two children moved through the carnage, while the spies on their dragonflies looked around more coolly, accustomed to battle, noting how it had gone and who had lost most.

When they reached the top of the valley, where the trees thinned out and the rainbow-waterfalls began, they stopped to drink deeply of the ice-cold water.

"I hope that little girl's all right," said Will. "We'd never have got you away if she hadn't woken you up. She went to a holy man to get that powder specially."

"She is all right," said Lyra, "cause I asked the alethiometer, last night. She thinks we're devils though. She's afraid of us. She probably wishes she'd never got mixed up in it, but she's safe all right."

They climbed up beside the waterfalls, and refilled Will's canteen before striking off across the plateau towards the ridge where the alethiometer told Lyra that Iorek had gone.

And then there came a day of long, hard walking: no trouble for Will, but a torment to Lyra, whose limbs were weakened and softened after her long sleep. But she would sooner have her tongue torn out than confess how bad she felt: limping, tight-lipped, trembling, she kept pace with Will and said nothing. Only when they sat down at noon did she allow herself so much as a whimper, and then only when Will had gone apart to relieve himself.

The Lady Salmakia said, "Rest. There is no disgrace in being weary."

"But I don't want to let Will down! I don't want him to think I'm weak and holding him back."

"That's the last thing he thinks."

"You don't know," said Lyra rudely. "You don't know him any more than you know me."

"I know impertinence when I hear it," said the lady calmly. "Do as I tell you now and rest. Save your energy for the walking."

Lyra felt mutinous, but the lady's glittering spurs were very clear in the sunlight, so she said nothing.

Her companion the chevalier was opening the case of the lodestone resonator, and, curiosity overcoming resentment, Lyra watched to see what he did. The instrument looked like a short length of pencil made of dull grey-black stone, resting on a stand of wood, and the chevalier swept a tiny bow like a violinist's across the end while he pressed his fingers at various points along the surface. The places weren't marked, so he seemed to be touching it at random, but from the intensity of his expression and the certain fluency of his movements, Lyra knew it was as skilful and demanding a process as her own reading of the alethiometer.

After several minutes the spy put the bow away and took up a pair of headphones, the earpieces no larger than Lyra's little fingernail, and wrapped one end of the wire tightly around a peg in the end of the stone, leading the rest along to another peg at the other end and wrapping it around that. By manipulating the two pegs and the tension on the wire between them, he could obviously hear a response to his own message.

"How does that work?" she said when he'd finished.

Tialys looked at her as if to judge whether she was genuinely interested, and then said, "Your scientists, what do you call them, experimental theologians, would know of something called quantum entanglement. It means that two particles can exist that only have properties in common, so that whatever happens to one happens to the other at the same moment, no matter how far apart they are. Well, in our world there is a way of taking a common lodestone and entangling all its particles, and then splitting it in two so that both parts resonate together. The counterpart to this is with Lord Roke, our commander. When I play on this one with my bow, the other one reproduces the sounds exactly, and so we communicate."

He put everything away and said something to the lady. She joined him and they went a little apart, talking too quietly for Lyra to hear, though Pantalaimon became an owl and turned his great ears in their direction.

Presently Will came back and then they moved on, more slowly as the day went by, and the track got steeper and the snow line nearer. They rested once more at the head of a rocky valley, because even Will could tell that Lyra was nearly finished: she was limping badly and her face was grey.

"Let me see your feet," he said to her, "because if they're blistered, I'll put some ointment on."

They were, badly, and she let him rub in the bloodmoss salve, closing her eyes and gritting her teeth.

Meanwhile, the chevalier was busy, and after a few minutes he put his lodestone away and said, "I have told Lord Roke of our position, and they are sending a gyropter to bring us away as soon as you have spoken to your friend."

Will nodded. Lyra took no notice. Presently she sat up wearily and pulled on her socks and shoes, and they set off once more.

Another hour, and most of the valley was in shadow, and Will was wondering whether they would find any shelter before night fell; but then Lyra gave a cry of relief and joy.

"Iorek! Iorek!"

She had seen him before Will had. The bear-king was some way off still, his white coat indistinct against a patch of snow, but when Lyra's voice echoed out he turned his head, raised it to sniff, and bounded down the mountainside towards them.

Ignoring Will, he let Lyra clasp his neck and bury her face in his fur, growling so deep that Will felt it through his feet; but Lyra felt it as pleasure, and forgot her blisters and her weariness in a moment.

"Oh, Iorek, my dear, I'm so glad to see you! I never thought I'd ever see you again – after that time on Svalbard – and all the things that've happened – is Mr Scoresby safe? How's your kingdom? Are you all alone here?"

The little spies had vanished; at all events, there seemed to be only the three of them now on the darkening mountainside, the boy and the girl and the great white bear. As if she had never wanted to be anywhere else, Lyra climbed up as Iorek offered his back and rode proud and happy as her dear friend carried her up the last stretch of the way to his cave.

Will, preoccupied, didn't listen as Lyra talked to Iorek, though he did hear a cry of dismay at one point, and heard her say:

"Mr Scoresby – oh no! Oh, it's too cruel! *Really* dead? You're sure, Iorek?"

"The witch told me he set out to find the man called Grumman," said the bear.

Will listened more closely now, for Baruch and Balthamos had told him some of this.

"What happened? Who killed him?" said Lyra, her voice shaky.

"He died fighting. He kept a whole company of Muscovites at bay while the man escaped. I found his body. He died bravely. I shall avenge him."

Lyra was weeping freely, and Will didn't know what to say, for it was his father whom this unknown man had died to save; and Lyra and the bear had both known and loved Lee Scoresby, and he had not.

Soon Iorek turned aside, and made for the entrance to a cave, very dark against the snow. Will didn't know where the spies were, but he was perfectly sure they were nearby. He wanted to speak quietly to Lyra, but not till he could see the Gallivespians and know he wasn't being overheard.

He laid his rucksack in the cave-mouth and sat down wearily. Behind him the bear was kindling a fire, and Lyra watched, curious despite her sorrow. Iorek held a small rock of some sort of ironstone in his left forepaw and struck it no more than three or four times on a similar one on the floor. Each time a scatter of sparks burst out, and went exactly where Iorek directed them: into a heap of shredded twigs and dried grass. Very soon that was ablaze, and Iorek calmly placed one log and then another and another until the fire was burning strongly.

The children welcomed it, because the air was very cold now, and then came something even better: a haunch of something that might have been goat. Iorek ate his meat raw, of course, but he spitted this joint on a sharp stick and laid it to roast across the fire for the two of them.

"Is it easy, hunting up in these mountains, Iorek?" she said.

"No. My people can't live here. I was wrong, but luckily so, since I found you. What are your plans now?"

Will looked around the cave. They were sitting close to the fire, and the fire-light threw warm yellows and oranges on the bear-king's fur. Will could see no sign of the spies, but there was nothing for it: he had to ask.

"King Iorek," he began, "my knife is broken —" and then he looked past the bear and said, "No, wait." He was pointing at the wall. "If you're listening," he went on more loudly, "come out and do it honestly. Don't spy on us."

Lyra and Iorek Byrnison turned to see who he was talking to. The little man came out of the shadow and stood calmly in the light, on a ledge higher than the children's heads. Iorek growled.

"You haven't asked Iorek Byrnison for permission to enter his cave," Will said. "And he is a king, and you're just a spy. You should show more respect."

Lyra loved hearing that. She looked at Will with pleasure, and saw him fierce and contemptuous.

But the chevalier's expression, as he looked at Will, was displeased.

"We have been truthful with you," he said. "It was dishonourable to deceive us."

Will stood up. His dæmon, Lyra thought, would have the form of a tigress, and she shrank back from the anger she imagined the great animal to show.

"If we deceived you, it was necessary," he said. "Would you have agreed to come here if you knew the knife was broken? Of course you wouldn't. You'd have used your venom to make us unconscious, and then you'd call for help and have us kidnapped and taken to Lord Asriel. So we had to trick you, Tialys, and you'll just have to put up with it."

Iorek Byrnison said, "Who is this?"

"Spies," said Will. "Sent by Lord Asriel. They helped us escape yesterday, but if they're on our side they shouldn't hide and eavesdrop on us. And if they do, they're the last people who should talk about dishonour."

The spy's glare was so ferocious that he looked ready to take on Iorek himself, never mind the unarmed Will; but Tialys was in the wrong, and he knew it. All he could do was bow and apologize.

"Your Majesty," he said to Iorek, who growled at once.

The chevalier's eyes flashed hatred at Will, and defiance and warning at Lyra, and a cold and wary respect at Iorek. The clarity of his features made all these expressions vivid and bright, as if a light shone on him. Beside him the Lady Salmakia was emerging from the shadow, and, ignoring the children completely, she made a curtsey to the bear.

"Forgive us," she said to Iorek. "The habit of concealment is hard to break, and my companion the Chevalier Tialys and I, the Lady Salmakia, have been among our enemies for so long that out of pure habit we neglected to pay you the proper courtesy. We're accompanying this boy and girl to make sure they arrive safely in the care of Lord Asriel. We have no other aim, and certainly no harmful intentions towards you, King Iorek Byrnison."

If Iorek wondered how any such tiny beings could cause him harm, he didn't show it; not only was his expression naturally hard to read, but he had his courtesy too, and the lady had spoken graciously enough.

"Come down by the fire," he said. "There is food enough and plenty if you are hungry. Will, you began to speak about the knife."

"Yes," said Will, "and I thought it could never happen, but it's broken. And the alethiometer told Lyra that you'd be able to mend it. I was going to ask more politely, but there it is: can you mend it, Iorek?"

"Show me."

Will shook all the pieces out of the sheath and laid them on the rocky floor, pushing them about carefully until they were in their right places and he could see that they were all there. Lyra held a burning branch up, and in its light Iorek bent low to look closely at each piece, touching it delicately with his massive claws and lifting it up to turn it this way and that and examine the break. Will marvelled at the deftness in those huge black hooks.

Then Iorek sat up again, his head rearing high into the shadow.

"Yes," he said, answering exactly the question and no more.

Lyra said, knowing what he meant, "Ah, but *will* you, Iorek? You couldn't believe how important this is – if we can't get it mended then we're in desperate trouble, and not only us –"

"I don't like that knife," Iorek said. "I fear what it can do. I have never known anything so dangerous. The most deadly fighting machines are little toys compared to that knife; the harm it can do is unlimited. It would have been infinitely better if it had never been made."

"But with it –" began Will.

Iorek didn't let him finish, but went on, "With it you can do strange things. What you don't know is what the knife does on its own. Your intentions may be good. The knife has intentions too."

"How can that be?" said Will.

"The intentions of a tool are what it does. A hammer intends to strike, a vice intends to hold fast, a lever intends to lift. They are what it is made for. But sometimes a tool may have other uses that you don't know. Sometimes in doing what *you* intend, you also do what the knife intends, without knowing. Can you see the sharpest edge of that knife?"

"No," said Will, for it was true: the edge diminished to a thinness so fine that the eye could not reach it.

"Then how can you know everything it does?"

"I can't. But I must still use it, and do what I can to help good things come about. If I did nothing I'd be worse than useless. I'd be guilty."

Lyra was following this closely, and seeing Iorek still unwilling, she said:

"Iorek, you *know* how wicked those Bolvangar people were. If we can't win, then they're going to be able to carry on doing those kind of things for ever. And besides, if we don't have the knife, then they might get hold of it theirselves. We never knew about it when I first met you, Iorek, and nor did anyone, but now that we do, we *got* to use it ourselves – we can't just *not*. That'd be feeble, and it'd be wrong too, it'd be just like handing it over to 'em and saying go on, use it, we won't stop you. All right, we don't know what it does, but I can ask the alethiometer, can't I? Then we'd know. And we could think about it properly instead of just guessing and being afraid."

Will didn't want to mention his own most pressing reason: if the knife were not repaired, he'd never get home, never see his mother again; she would never know what had happened; she'd think he'd abandoned her as his father had done. The knife had been directly responsible for both their desertions. He *must* use it to return to her, or never forgive himself.

Iorek Byrnison said nothing for a long time, but turned his head to look out at the darkness. Then he slowly got to his feet and stalked to the cave-mouth, and looked up at the stars: some the same as those he knew, from the north, and some that were strange to him.

Behind him, Lyra turned the meat over on the fire, and Will looked at his wounds, to see how they were healing. Tialys and Salmakia sat silent on their ledge.

Then Iorek turned around.

"Very well, I shall do it on one condition," he said. "Though I feel it is a mistake. My people have no gods, no ghosts or dæmons. We live and die and that is that. Human affairs bring us nothing but sorrow and trouble, but we have language and we make war and we use tools; maybe we should take sides. But full knowledge is better than half-knowledge. Lyra, read your instrument. Know what it is that you're asking. If you still want it then, I shall mend the knife."

At once Lyra took out the alethiometer and edged nearer to the fire so that she could see the face. The inconstant flicker made it hard to see, or perhaps the smoke was getting in her eyes, and the reading took her longer than usual. When she blinked and sighed and came out of the trance her face was troubled.

"I never known it so confused," she said. "There was lots of things it said. I think I got it clear. I *think* so. It said about balance first. It said the knife could be harmful or it could do good, but it was so slight, such a delicate kind of a balance, that the faintest thought or wish could tip it one way or the other ... And it meant *you*, Will, it meant what you wished or thought, only it didn't say what would be a good thought or a bad one.

"Then ... it said yes," she said, her eyes flashing at the spies. "It said yes, do it, repair the knife."

Iorek looked at her steadily, and then nodded once.

Tialys and Salmakia climbed down to watch more closely, and Lyra said, "D'you need more fuel, Iorek? Me and Will could go and fetch some, I'm sure."

Will understood what she meant: away from the spies they could talk.

Iorek said, "Below the first spur on the track there is a bush with resinous wood. Bring as much of that as you can."

She jumped up at once, and Will went with her.

The moon was brilliant, the path a track of scumbled footprints in the snow, the air cutting and cold. Both of them felt brisk and hopeful and alive. They didn't talk till they were well away from the cave.

"What else did it say?" Will said.

"It said some things I didn't understand then and I still don't understand now. It said the knife would be the death of Dust, but then it said it was the only way to keep Dust alive. I didn't understand it, Will. But it said again it was dangerous, it kept saying that. It said if we – you know – what I thought –"

"If we go to the world of the dead –"

"Yeah – if we do that – it said that we might never come back, Will. We might not survive."

He said nothing, and they walked along more soberly now, watching out for the bush that Iorek had mentioned, and silenced by the thought of what they might be taking on.

"We've got to, though," he said, "haven't we?"

"I don't know."

"Now we *know*, I mean. You have to speak to Roger, and I have to speak to my father. We have to, now."

"I'm frightened," she said.

And he knew she'd never admit that to anyone else.

"Did it say what would happen if we *didn't*?" he asked.

"Just emptiness. Just blankness. I really didn't understand it, Will. But I *think* it meant that even if it *is* that dangerous, we should still try and rescue Roger. But it won't be like when I rescued him from Bolvangar; I didn't know what I was doing then, really, I just set off, and I was lucky. I mean there was all kinds of other people to help, like the gyptians and the witches. There won't be any help where we'd have to go. And I can see . . . In my dream I saw . . . The place was . . . It was worse than Bolvangar. That's why I'm afraid."

"What *I'm* afraid of," said Will after a minute, not looking at her at all, "is getting stuck somewhere and never seeing my mother again."

From nowhere, a memory came to him: he was very young, and it was before her troubles began, and he was ill. All night long, it seemed, his mother had sat on his bed in the dark, singing nursery rhymes, telling him stories, and as long as her dear voice was there, he knew he was safe. He *couldn't* abandon her now. He couldn't! He'd look after her all his life long if she needed it.

And as if Lyra had known what he was thinking, she said warmly:

"Yeah, that's true, that would be awful . . . You know, with my mother, I never realized . . . I just grew up on my own, really; I don't remember anyone ever holding me or cuddling me, it was just me and Pan as far back as I can go . . . I can't remember Mrs Lonsdale being like that to me; she was the housekeeper at Jordan College, all she did was make sure I was clean, that's all

she thought about, oh and manners ... But in the cave, Will,
I really felt – oh it's *strange*, I know she's done terrible things,
but I really felt she was loving me and looking after me ... She
must have thought I was going to die, being asleep all that time –
I suppose I must've caught some disease – but she never stopped
looking after me. And I remember waking up once or twice and
she was holding me in her arms ... I *do* remember that, I'm
sure ... That's what I'd do in her place, if I had a child."

So she didn't know why she'd been asleep all that time. Should
he tell her, and betray that memory, even if it was false? No, of
course he shouldn't.

"Is that the bush?" Lyra said.

The moonlight was brilliant enough to show every leaf. Will
snapped off a twig, and the piny resinous smell stayed strongly on
his fingers.

"And we en't going to say anything to those little spies," she
added.

They gathered armfuls of the bush, and carried them back up
towards the cave.

15
THE FORGE

As I was walking among the fires of hell, delighted with the enjoyments of Genius

— WILLIAM BLAKE

AT THAT MOMENT, the Gallivespians were talking about the knife. Having made a suspicious peace with Iorek Byrnison, they climbed back to their ledge to be out of the way, and as the crackle of flames rose and the snapping and roaring of the fire filled the air, Tialys said, "We must never leave his side. As soon as the knife is mended, we must keep closer than a shadow."

"He is too alert. He watches everywhere for us," said Salmakia. "The girl is more trusting. I think we could win her round. She's innocent, and she loves easily. We could work on her. I think we should do that, Tialys."

"But he has the knife. He is the one who can use it."

"He won't go anywhere without her."

"But she has to follow him, if he has the knife. And I think that as soon as the knife's intact again, they'll use it to slip into another world so as to get away from us. Did you see how he stopped her from speaking when she was going to say something more? They have some secret purpose, and it's very different from what we want them to do."

"We'll see. But you're right, Tialys, I think. We must stay close to the boy at all costs."

They both watched with some scepticism as Iorek Byrnison laid out the tools in his improvised workshop. The mighty workers in the ordnance factories under Lord Asriel's fortress, with their blast furnaces and rolling mills, their anbaric forges and hydraulic presses, would have laughed at the open fire, the stone hammer, the anvil consisting of a piece of Iorek's armour. Nevertheless, the bear had taken the measure of the task, and in the certainty of his movements the little spies began to see some quality that muffled their scorn.

When Lyra and Will came in with the bushes, Iorek directed

them in placing branches carefully on the fire. He looked at each branch, turning it from side to side, and then told Will or Lyra to place it at such-and-such an angle, or to break off part and place it separately at the edge. The result was a fire of extraordinary ferocity, with all its energy concentrated at one side.

By this time the heat in the cave was intense. Iorek continued to build the fire, and made the children take two more trips down the path to ensure that there was enough fuel for the whole operation.

Then the bear turned over a small stone on the floor, and told Lyra to find some more stones of the same kind. He said that those stones, when heated, gave off a gas which would surround the blade and keep the air from it, for if the hot metal came in contact with the air it would absorb some and be weakened by it.

Lyra set about searching, and with owl-eyed Pantalaimon's help soon had a dozen or more stones to hand. Iorek told her how to place them, and where, and showed her exactly the kind of draught she should get moving, with a leafy branch, to make sure the gas flowed evenly over the work piece.

Will was placed in charge of the fire, and Iorek spent several minutes directing him and making sure he understood the principles he was to use. So much depended on exact placement, and Iorek could not stop and correct each one: Will had to understand, and then he'd do it properly.

Furthermore, he mustn't expect the knife to look exactly the same when it was mended. It would be shorter, because each section of the blade would have to overlap the next by a little way, so they could be forged together; and the surface would have oxidized a little, despite the stone-gas, so some of the play of colour would be lost; and no doubt the handle would be charred. But the blade would be just as sharp, and it would work.

So Will watched as the flames roared along the resinous twigs, and with streaming eyes and scorched hands he adjusted each fresh branch till the heat was focused as Iorek wanted it.

Meanwhile Iorek himself was grinding and hammering a fist-sized stone, having rejected several until he found one of the right weight. With massive blows he shaped it and smoothed it, the cordite-smell of smashed rocks joining the smoke in the nostrils of the two spies, watching from high up. Even Pantalaimon was active, changing to a crow so he could flap his wings and make the fire burn faster.

Eventually the hammer was formed to Iorek's satisfaction, and he set the first two pieces of the blade of the subtle knife among the fierce-burning wood at the heart of the fire, and told Lyra to begin wafting the stone-gas over them. The bear watched, his long white face lurid in the glare, and Will saw the surface of the metal begin to glow red and then yellow and then white.

Iorek was watching closely, his paw held ready to snatch the pieces out. After a few moments the metal changed again, and the surface became shiny and glistening, and sparks just like those from a firework sprayed up from it.

Then Iorek moved. His right paw darted in and seized first one piece and then the other, holding them between the tips of his massive claws and placing them on the slab of iron that was the backplate of his armour. Will could smell the claws burning, but Iorek took no notice of that, and moving with extraordinary speed he adjusted the angle at which the pieces overlapped and then raised his left paw high and struck a blow with the rock hammer.

The knife-tip leaped on the rock under the massive blow. Will was thinking that the whole of the rest of his life depended on what happened in that tiny triangle of metal, that point that searched out the gaps inside the atoms, and all his nerves trembled, sensing every flicker of every flame and the loosening of every atom in the lattice of the metal. Before this began, he had supposed that only a full-scale furnace, with the finest tools and equipment, could work on that blade; but now he saw that these were the finest tools, and that Iorek's artistry had constructed the best furnace there could be.

Iorek roared above the clangour: "Hold it still in your mind! You have to forge it too! This is your task as much as mine!"

Will felt his whole being quiver under the blows of the stone hammer in the bear's fist. The second piece of the blade was heating too, and Lyra's leafy branch sent the hot gas along to bathe both pieces in its flow and keep out the iron-eating air. Will sensed it all, and felt the atoms of the metal linking each to each across the fracture, forming new crystals again, strengthening and straightening themselves in the invisible lattice as the join came good.

"The edge!" roared Iorek. "Hold the edge in line!"

He meant *with your mind*, and Will did it instantly, sensing the minute snags and then the minute easement as the edges lined up perfectly. Then that join was made, and Iorek turned to the next piece.

"A new stone," he called to Lyra, who knocked the first one aside and placed a second on the spot to heat.

Will checked the fuel and snapped a branch in two to direct the flames better, and Iorek began to work with the hammer once more. Will felt a new layer of complexity added to his task, because he had to hold the new piece in a precise relation with both the previous two, and he understood that only by doing that accurately could he help Iorek mend it.

So the work continued. He had no idea how long it took; Lyra, for her part, found her arms aching, her eyes streaming, her skin scorched and red, and every bone in her body aching with fatigue; but still she placed each stone as Iorek had told her, and still the weary Pantalaimon raised his wings readily and beat them over the flames.

When it came to the final joint, Will's head was ringing, and he was so exhausted by the intellectual effort he could barely lift the next branch on to the fire. He had to understand every connection, or the knife would not hold together; and when it came to the most complex one, the last, which would fix the nearly-finished blade on to the small part remaining at the handle – if he couldn't hold it in his full consciousness together with all the others, then the knife would simply fall apart as if Iorek had never begun.

The bear sensed this, too, and paused before he began heating the last piece. He looked at Will, and in his eyes Will could see nothing, no expression, just a bottomless black brilliance. Nevertheless, he understood: this was work, and it was hard, but they were equal to it, all of them.

That was enough for Will, so he turned back to the fire and

sent his imagination out to the broken end of the haft, and braced himself for the last and fiercest part of the task.

So he and Iorek and Lyra between them forged the knife, and how long the final joint took he had no idea; but when Iorek had struck the final blow, and Will had felt the final tiny settling as the atoms connected across the break, he sank down on to the floor of the cave and let exhaustion possess him. Lyra nearby was in the same state, her eyes glassy and red-rimmed, her hair full of soot and smoke; and Iorek himself stood heavy-headed, his fur singed in several places, dark streaks of ash marking its rich cream-white.

Tialys and Salmakia had slept in turns, one of them always alert. Now she was awake and he was sleeping, but as the blade cooled from red to grey and finally to silver, and as Will reached out for the handle, she woke her partner with a hand on his shoulder. He was alert at once.

But Will didn't touch the knife: he held his palm close by, and the heat was still too great for his hand. The spies relaxed on the rocky shelf as Iorek said to Will:

"Come outside."

Then he said to Lyra: "Stay here, and don't touch the knife."

Lyra sat close to the anvil, where the knife lay cooling, and Iorek told her to bank the fire up and not let it burn down: there was a final operation yet.

Will followed the great bear out on to the dark mountain-side. The cold was bitter and instantaneous, after the inferno in the cave.

"They should not have made that knife," said Iorek, after they had walked a little way. "Maybe I should not have mended it. I'm troubled, and I have never been troubled before, never in doubt. Now I am full of doubt. Doubt is a human thing, not a bear thing. If I am becoming human, something's wrong, something's bad. And I've made it worse."

"But when the first bear made the first piece of armour, wasn't that bad too, in the same way?"

Iorek was silent. They walked on till they came to a big drift of snow, and Iorek lay in it and rolled this way and that, sending flurries of snow up into the dark air so that it looked as if he himself were made of snow, he was the personification of all the snow in the world.

When he had finished he rolled over and stood up and shook himself vigorously, and then, seeing Will still waiting for an answer to his question, said:

"Yes, I think it might have been, too. But before that first armoured bear, there were no others. We know of nothing before that. That was when custom began. We know our customs, and they are firm and solid and we follow them without change. Bear-nature is weak without custom, as bear-flesh is unprotected without armour.

"But I think I have stepped outside bear-nature in mending this knife. I think I've been as foolish as Iofur Raknison. Time will tell. But I am uncertain and doubtful. Now you must tell me: why did the knife break?"

Will rubbed his aching head with both hands.

"The woman looked at me and I thought she had the face of my mother," he said, trying to recollect the experience with all the honesty he had. "And the knife came up against something it couldn't cut, and because my mind was pushing it through and forcing it back both at the same time, it snapped. That's what I think. The woman knew what she was doing, I'm sure. She's very clever."

"When you talk of the knife, you talk of your mother and father."

"Do I? Yes . . . I suppose I do."

"What are you going to do with it?"

"I don't know."

Suddenly Iorek lunged at Will and cuffed him hard with his left paw: so hard that Will fell half-stunned into the snow and tumbled over and over until he ended some way down the slope with his head ringing.

Iorek came down slowly to where Will was struggling up, and said, "Answer me truthfully."

Will was tempted to say, "You wouldn't have done that if I'd had the knife in my hand." But he knew that Iorek knew that, and knew that he knew it, and that it would be discourteous and stupid to say it; but he was tempted, all the same.

He held his tongue until he was standing upright, facing Iorek directly.

"I said I don't know," he said, trying hard to keep his voice calm, "because I haven't looked clearly at what it is that I'm going to do. At what it means. It frightens me. And it frightens Lyra too. Anyway, I agreed as soon as I heard what she said."

"And what was that?"

"We want to go down to the land of the dead and talk to the ghost of Lyra's friend Roger, the one who got killed on Svalbard. And if there really is a world of the dead, then my father will be there too, and if we can talk to ghosts, I want to talk to him.

"But I'm divided, I'm pulled apart, because also I want to go back and look after my mother, because I *could*, and also because my father and the angel Balthamos told me I should go to Lord Asriel and offer it to him, and I think maybe they were right as well . . ."

"The angel fled," said the bear.

"He wasn't a warrior. He did as much as he could, and then he couldn't do any more. He wasn't the only one to be afraid; I'm afraid, too. So I have to think it through. Maybe sometimes we don't do the right thing because the wrong thing looks more dangerous, and we don't want to look scared, so we go and do the wrong thing just *because* it's dangerous. We're more concerned with not looking scared than with judging right. It's very hard. That's why I didn't answer you."

"I see," said the bear.

They stood in silence for what felt like a long time, especially to Will, who had little protection from the bitter cold. But Iorek hadn't finished yet, and Will was still weak and dizzy from the blow, and didn't quite trust his feet, so they stayed where they were.

"Well, I have compromised myself in many ways," said the bear-king. "It may be that in helping you I have brought final destruction on my kingdom. And it may be that I have not, and that destruction was coming anyway; maybe I have held it off. So I am troubled, having to do unbearlike deeds and speculate and doubt like a human.

"And I shall tell you one thing. You know it already, but you don't want to, which is why I tell you openly, so that you don't mistake it. If you want to succeed in this task, you must no longer think about your mother. You must put her aside. If your mind is divided, the knife will break.

"Now I'm going to say farewell to Lyra. You must wait in the cave; those two spies will not let you out of their sight, and I do not want them listening when I speak to her."

Will had no words, though his breast and his throat were full. He managed to say, "Thank you, Iorek Byrnison," but that was all he could say.

He walked with Iorek up the slope towards the cave, where the fire-glow shone warmly still in the vast surrounding dark.

There Iorek carried out the last process in the mending of the subtle knife. He laid it among the brighter cinders until the blade was glowing, and Will and Lyra saw a hundred colours swirling in the smoky depths of the metal, and when he judged the moment was right, Iorek told Will to take it and plunge it directly into the snow that had drifted outside.

The rosewood handle was charred and scorched, but Will wrapped his hand in several folds of a shirt and did as Iorek told him. In the hiss and flare of steam he felt the atoms finally settle together, and he knew that the knife was as keen as before, the point as infinitely rare.

But it did look different. It was shorter, and much less elegant, and there was a dull silver surface over each of the joins. It looked ugly now; it looked like what it was, wounded.

When it was cool enough, he packed it away in the rucksack, and sat, ignoring the spies, to wait for Lyra to come back.

Iorek had taken her a little further up the slope, to a point out of sight of the cave, and there he had let her sit cradled in the shelter of his great arms, with Pantalaimon nestling mouse-formed at her breast. Iorek bent his head over her, and nuzzled at her scorched and smoky hands. Without a word he began to lick them clean; his tongue was soothing on the burns, and she felt as safe as she had ever felt in her life.

But when her hands were free of soot and dirt, Iorek spoke. She felt his voice vibrate against her back.

"Lyra Silvertongue, what is this plan to visit the dead?"

"It came to me in a dream, Iorek. I saw Roger's ghost, and I knew he was calling to me . . . You remember Roger; well, after we left you he was killed, and it was my fault, at least I felt it was. And I think I should just finish what I began, that's all: I should go and say sorry, and if I can, I should rescue him from there. If Will can open a way to the world of the dead, then we must do it."

"Can is not the same as must."

"But if you must and you can, then there's no excuse."

"While you are alive, your business is with life."

"No, Iorek," she said gently, "our business is to keep promises, no matter how difficult they are. You know, secretly, I'm deadly scared. And I wish I'd never had that dream, and I wish Will hadn't thought of using the knife to go there. But we did, so we can't get out of it."

Lyra felt Pantalaimon trembling, and stroked him with her sore hands.

"We don't know how to get there, though," she went on. "We won't know anything till we try. What are *you* going to do, Iorek?"

"I'm going back north, with my people. We can't live in the mountains. Even the snow is different. I thought we could live here, but we can live more easily in the sea, even if it is warm. That was worth learning. And besides, I think we will be needed. I can feel war, Lyra Silvertongue; I can smell it; I can hear it. I spoke to Serafina Pekkala before I came this way, and she told me she was going to Lord Faa and the gyptians. If there is war, we shall be needed."

Lyra sat up, excited at hearing the names of her old friends. But Iorek hadn't finished. He went on:

"If you do not find a way out of the world of the dead, we shall not meet again, because I have no ghost. My body will remain on the earth, and then become part of it. But if it turns out that you and I both survive, then you will always be a welcome and honoured visitor to Svalbard; and the same is true of Will. Has he told you what happened when we met?"

"No," said Lyra, "except that it was by a river."

"He outfaced me. I thought no one could ever do that, but

this half-grown boy was too daring for me, and too clever. I am not happy that you should do what you plan, but there is no one I would trust to go with you, except that boy. You are worthy of each other. Go well, Lyra Silvertongue, my dear friend."

She reached up and put her arms around his neck, and pressed her face into his fur, unable to speak.

After a minute he stood up gently and disengaged her arms, and then he turned and walked silently away into the dark. Lyra thought his outline was lost almost at once against the pallor of the snow-covered ground, but it might have been that her eyes were full of tears.

When Will heard her footsteps on the path, he looked at the spies and said, "Don't you move. Look – here's the knife – I'm not going to use it. Stay here."

He went outside and found Lyra standing still, weeping, with Pantalaimon as a wolf raising his face to the black sky. She was quite silent. The only light came from the pale reflection in the snow-bank of the remains of the fire, and that in turn was reflected from her wet cheeks, and her tears found their own reflection in Will's eyes, and so those photons wove the two together in a silent web.

"I love him so much, Will!" she managed to whisper shakily. "And he looked *old*! He looked hungry and old and sad . . . Is it all coming on to us now, Will? We can't rely on anyone else now, can we . . . It's just us. But we en't old enough yet. We're only young . . . We're *too* young . . . If poor Mr Scoresby's dead and Iorek's old . . . It's all coming on to us, what's got to be done."

"We can do it," he said. "I'm not going to look back any more. We can do it. But we've got to sleep now, and if we stay in this world those gyropter things might come, that the spies sent for . . . I'm going to cut through now and we'll find another world to sleep in, and if the spies come with us, that's too bad; we'll have to get rid of them another time."

"Yes," she said, and sniffed and wiped the back of her hand across her nose and rubbed her eyes with both palms. "Let's do that. You sure the knife will work? You tested it?"

"I know it'll work."

With Pantalaimon tiger-formed to deter the spies, they hoped, Will and Lyra went back and picked up their rucksacks.

"What are you doing?" said Salmakia.

"Going into another world," said Will, taking out the knife. It felt like being whole again; he hadn't realized how much he loved it.

"But you must wait for Lord Asriel's gyropters," said Tialys, his voice hard.

"We're not going to," said Will. "If you come near the knife I'll kill you. Come through with us if you must, but you can't make us stay here. We're leaving."

"You lied!"

"No," said Lyra, "I lied. Will doesn't lie. You didn't think of that."

"But where are you going?"

Will didn't answer. He felt forward in the dim air and cut an opening.

Salmakia said, "This is a mistake. You should realize that, and listen to us. You haven't thought –"

"Yes we have," said Will, "we've thought hard, and we'll tell you what we've thought tomorrow. You can come where we're going, or you can go back to Lord Asriel."

The window opened on to the world into which he had escaped with Baruch and Balthamos, and where he'd slept safely: the warm endless beach with the fern-like trees behind the dunes. He said:

"Here – we'll sleep here – this'll do."

He let them through, and closed it behind them at once. While he and Lyra lay down where they were, exhausted, the Lady Salmakia kept watch, and the chevalier opened his lodestone resonator and began to play a message into the dark.

16

THE INTENTION CRAFT

From the archèd roof
Pendant by suttle Magic many a row
Of Starry Lamps and blazing Cressets fed
With Naphtha and Asphaltus yeilded light

— JOHN MILTON

"MY *CHILD*! MY *DAUGHTER*! Where is she? What have you done? My Lyra — you'd do better to tear the fibres from my heart — she was safe with me, *safe*, and now where is she?"

Mrs Coulter's cry resounded through the little chamber at the top of the adamant tower. She was bound to a chair, her hair dishevelled, her clothing torn, her eyes wild; and her monkey-dæmon thrashed and struggled on the floor in the coils of a silver chain.

Lord Asriel sat nearby, scribbling on a piece of paper, taking no notice. An orderly stood beside him, glancing nervously at the woman. When Lord Asriel handed him the paper he saluted and hurried out, his terrier-dæmon close at his heels with her tail tucked low.

Lord Asriel turned to Mrs Coulter.

"Lyra? Frankly, I don't care," he said, his voice quiet and hoarse. "The wretched child should have stayed where she was put, and done what she was told. I can't waste any more time or resources on her; if she refuses to be helped, let her deal with the consequences."

"You don't mean that, Asriel, or you wouldn't have —"

"I mean every word of it. The fuss she's caused is out of all proportion to her merits. An ordinary English girl, not very clever —"

"She is!" said Mrs Coulter.

"All right; bright but not intellectual; impulsive, dishonest, greedy —"

"Brave, generous, loving."

"A perfectly ordinary child, distinguished by nothing —"

"Perfectly ordinary? Lyra? She's unique. Think of what she's done already. Dislike her if you will, Asriel, but don't you dare patronize your daughter. And she was safe with me, until –"

"You're right," he said, getting up. "She *is* unique. To have tamed and softened you – that's no everyday feat. She's drawn your poison, Marisa. She's taken your teeth out. Your fire's been quenched in a drizzle of sentimental piety. Who would have thought it? The pitiless agent of the church, the fanatical persecutor of children, the inventor of hideous machines to slice them apart and look in their terrified little beings for any evidence of *sin* – and along comes a foul-mouthed ignorant little brat with dirty fingernails, and you cluck and settle your feathers over her like a hen. Well, I admit: the child must have some gift I've never seen myself. But if all it does is turn you into a doting mother, it's a pretty thin, drab, puny little gift. And now you might as well be quiet. I've asked my chief commanders to come in for an urgent conference, and if you can't control your noise I'll have you gagged."

Mrs Coulter was more like her daughter than she knew. Her answer to this was to spit in Lord Asriel's face. He wiped it calmly away and said, "A gag would put an end to that kind of behaviour, too."

"Oh, do correct me, Asriel," she said; "someone who displays a captive to his under-officers tied to a chair is clearly a prince of politeness. Untie me, or I'll *force* you to gag me."

"As you wish," he said, and took a silk scarf from the drawer; but before he could tie it around her mouth, she shook her head.

"No, no," she said, "Asriel, don't, I beg you, please don't humiliate me."

Angry tears dashed from her eyes.

"Very well, I'll untie you, but he can stay in his chains," he said, and dropped the scarf back in the drawer before cutting her bonds with a clasp knife.

She rubbed her wrists, stood up, stretched, and only then noticed the condition of her clothes and her hair. She looked haggard and pale; the last of the Gallivespian venom still remained in her body, causing agonizing pains in her joints, but she was not going to show him that.

Lord Asriel said, "You can wash in there," indicating a small room hardly bigger than a closet.

She picked up her chained dæmon, whose baleful eyes glared at Lord Asriel over her shoulder, and went through to make herself tidier.

The orderly came in to announce:

"His Majesty King Ogunwe and the Lord Roke."

The African general and the Gallivespian came in: King Ogunwe in a clean uniform, with a wound on his temple freshly dressed, and Lord Roke gliding swiftly to the table astride his blue hawk.

Lord Asriel greeted them warmly and offered wine. The bird let his rider step off, and then flew to the bracket by the door as the orderly announced the third of Lord Asriel's high commanders, an angel by the name of Xaphania. She was of a much higher rank than Baruch or Balthamos, and visible by a shimmering, disconcerting light that seemed to come from somewhere else.

By this time Mrs Coulter had emerged, much tidied, and all three commanders bowed to her; and if she was surprised at their appearance, she gave no sign, but inclined her head and sat down peaceably, holding the pinioned monkey in her arms.

Without wasting time, Lord Asriel said, "Tell me what happened, King Ogunwe."

The African, powerful and deep-voiced, said, "We killed seventeen Swiss Guards and destroyed two zeppelins. We lost five men and one gyropter. The girl and the boy escaped. We captured the Lady Coulter, despite her courageous defence, and brought her here. I hope she feels we treated her courteously."

"I am quite content with the way you treated me, sir," she said, with the faintest possible stress on the *you*.

"Any damage to the other gyropters? Any wounded?" said Lord Asriel.

"Some damage and some wounds, but all minor."

"Good. Thank you, King; your force did well. My Lord Roke, what have you heard?"

The Gallivespian said, "My spies are with the boy and girl in another world. Both children are safe and well, though the girl has been kept in a drugged sleep for many days. The boy lost the use of his knife during the events in the cave: by some accident, it broke in pieces. But it is now whole again, thanks to a creature from the north of *your* world, Lord Asriel, a giant bear, very skilled at smith-work. As soon as the knife was mended, the boy cut through into another world, where they are now. My spies are with them, of course, but there is a difficulty: while the boy has the knife, he cannot be compelled to do anything; and yet if they were to kill him in his sleep, the knife would be useless to us. For the time being, the Chevalier Tialys and the Lady Salmakia will go with them wherever they go, so at least we can keep track of them. They seem to have a plan in mind; they are refusing to come here, at any rate. My two will not lose them."

"Are they safe in this other world they're in now?" said Lord Asriel.

"They're on a beach near a forest of tree-ferns. There is no sign of animal life nearby. As we speak, both boy and girl are asleep; I spoke to the Chevalier Tialys not five minutes ago."

"Thank you," said Lord Asriel. "Now that your two agents are following the children, of course, we have no eyes in the Magisterium any more. We shall have to rely on the alethiometer. At least —"

Then Mrs Coulter spoke, to their surprise.

"I don't know about the other branches," she said, "but as far as the Consistorial Court is concerned, the reader they rely on is Fra Pavel Rasek. And he's thorough, but slow. They won't know where Lyra is for another few hours."

Lord Asriel said, "Thank you, Marisa. Do *you* have any idea what Lyra and this boy intend to do next?"

"No," she said, "none. I've spoken to the boy, and he seemed to be a stubborn child, and one well used to keeping secrets. I can't guess what he would do. As for Lyra, she is quite impossible to read."

"My Lord," said King Ogunwe, "may we know whether the lady is now part of this commanding council? If so, what is her function? If not, should she not be taken elsewhere?"

"She is our captive and my guest, and as a distinguished former agent of the church, she may have information that would be useful."

"Will she reveal anything willingly? Or will she need to be tortured?" said Lord Roke, watching her directly as he spoke.

Mrs Coulter laughed.

"I would have thought Lord Asriel's commanders would know better than to expect truth to come out of torture," she said.

Lord Asriel couldn't help enjoying her barefaced insincerity.

"I will guarantee Mrs Coulter's behaviour," he said. "She knows what will happen if she betrays us; though she will not have the chance. However, if any of you has a doubt, express it now, fearlessly."

"I do," said King Ogunwe, "but I doubt you, not her."

"Why?" said Lord Asriel.

"If she tempted you, you would not resist. It was right to capture her, but wrong to invite her to this council. Treat her with every courtesy, give her the greatest comfort, but place her somewhere else, and stay away from her."

"Well, I invited you to speak," said Lord Asriel, "and I must accept your rebuke. I value your presence more than hers, King. I'll have her taken away."

He reached for the bell, but before he could ring, Mrs Coulter spoke.

"Please," she said urgently, "listen to me first. I can help. I've been closer to the heart of the Magisterium than anyone you're likely to find again. I know how they think, I can guess what they'll do. You wonder why you should trust me, what's made me leave them? It's simple: they're going to kill my daughter. They daren't let her live. The moment I found out who she is – what she is – what the witches prophesy about her – I knew I had to leave the church; I knew I was their enemy, and they were mine; I didn't know what *you* were, or what I was to you – that was a mystery; but I knew that I had to set myself against the church, against everything they believed in, and if need be, against the Authority himself. I . . ."

She stopped. All the commanders were listening intently. Now she looked Lord Asriel full in the face and seemed to speak to him alone, her voice low and passionate, her brilliant eyes glittering.

"I have been the worst mother in the world. I let my only child be taken away from me when she was a tiny infant, because I didn't care about her; I was concerned only with my own advancement. I didn't think of her for years, and if I did, it was only to regret the embarrassment of her birth.

"But then the church began to take an interest in Dust and in children, and something stirred in my heart, and I remembered that I was a mother and Lyra was . . . *my* child.

"And because there was a threat, I saved her from it. Three times now I've stepped in to pluck her out of danger. First when the Oblation Board began its work: I went to Jordan College and I took her to live with me, in London, where I could keep her safe from the Board . . . or so I hoped. But she ran away.

"The second time was at Bolvangar, when I found her just in time, under the – under the blade of the . . . My heart nearly stopped . . . It was what they – we – what I had done to other children, but when it was *mine* . . . Oh, you can't conceive the horror of that moment, I hope you never suffer as I did then . . . But I got her free; I took her out; I saved her a second time.

"But even as I did that, I still felt myself part of the church, a servant, a loyal and faithful and devoted servant, because I was doing the Authority's work.

"And then I learned the witches' prophecy. Lyra will some-how, sometime soon, be tempted, as Eve was – that's what they say. What form this temptation will take, I don't know, but she's growing up, after all. It's not hard to imagine. And now that the church knows that, too, they'll kill her. If it all depends on her, could they risk letting her live? Would they dare take the chance that she'd refuse this temptation, whatever it will be?

"No, they're bound to kill her. If they could, they'd go back to the garden of Eden and kill Eve before *she* was tempted. Killing is not difficult for them; Calvin himself ordered the deaths of children; they'd kill her with pomp and ceremonial and prayers and lamentations and psalms and hymns, but they would kill her. If she falls into their hands, she's dead already.

"So when I heard what the witch said, I saved my daughter

for the third time. I took her to a place where I kept her safe, and there I was going to stay."

"You drugged her," said King Ogunwe. "You kept her unconscious."

"I had to," said Mrs Coulter, "because she hated me," and here her voice, which had been full of emotion but under control, spilled over into a sob, and it trembled as she went on: "She feared me and hated me, and she would have fled from my presence like a bird from a cat if I hadn't drugged her into oblivion. Do you know what that means to a mother? But it was the only way to keep her safe! All that time in the cave ... asleep, her eyes closed, her body helpless, her dæmon curled up at her throat ... Oh, I felt such a love, such a tenderness, such a deep, deep ... My own child, the first time I had ever been able to do these things for her, my little ... I washed her and fed her and kept her safe and warm, I made sure her body was nourished as she slept ... I lay beside her at night, I cradled her in my arms, I wept into her hair, I kissed her sleeping eyes, my little one ..."

She was shameless. She spoke quietly; she didn't declaim or raise her voice; and when a sob shook her, it was muffled almost into a hiccup, as if she were stifling her emotions for the sake of courtesy. Which made her barefaced lies all the more effective, Lord Asriel thought with disgust; she lied in the very marrow of her bones.

She directed her words mainly at King Ogunwe, without seeming to, and Lord Asriel saw that too. Not only was the king her chief accuser; he was also human, unlike the angel, or Lord Roke, and she knew how to play on him.

In fact, though, it was on the Gallivespian that she made the greatest impression. Lord Roke sensed in her a nature as close to that of a scorpion as he had ever encountered, and he was well aware of the power in the sting he could detect under her gentle tone. Better to keep scorpions where you could see them, he thought.

So he supported King Ogunwe when the latter changed his mind and argued that she should stay, and Lord Asriel found himself out-flanked: for he now wanted her elsewhere, but he had already agreed to abide by his commanders' wishes.

Mrs Coulter looked at him with an expression of mild and virtuous concern. He was certain that no one else could see the glitter of sly triumph in the depths of her beautiful eyes.

"Stay then," he said. "But you've spoken enough. Stay quiet now. I want to consider this proposal for a garrison on the southern border. You've seen the report: is it workable? Is it desirable? Next I want to look at the armoury. And then I want to hear from Xaphania about the dispositions of the angelic forces. First, the garrison. King Ogunwe?"

The African leader began. They spoke for some time, and Mrs Coulter was impressed by their accurate knowledge of the church's defences, and their clear assessment of its leaders' strengths.

But now that Tialys and Salmakia were with the children, and Lord Asriel no longer had a spy in the Magisterium, their knowledge would soon be dangerously out of date. An idea came to Mrs Coulter's mind, and she and the monkey-dæmon exchanged a glance that felt like a powerful anbaric spark; but she said nothing, and stroked his golden fur as she listened to the commanders.

Then Lord Asriel said, "Enough. That is a problem we'll deal with later. Now for the armoury. I understand they're ready to test the intention craft. We'll go and look at it."

He took a silver key from his pocket and unlocked the chain around the golden monkey's feet and hands, and carefully avoided touching even the tip of one golden hair.

Lord Roke mounted his hawk, and followed with the others as Lord Asriel set off down the stairs of the tower and out on to the battlements.

A cold wind was blowing, snapping at their eyelids, and the dark-blue hawk soared up in a mighty draught, wheeling and screaming in the wild air. King Ogunwe drew his coat around him and rested his hand on his cheetah-dæmon's head.

Mrs Coulter said humbly to the angel:

"Excuse me, my lady: your name is Xaphania?"

"Yes," said the angel.

Her appearance impressed Mrs Coulter just as her fellows had impressed the witch Ruta Skadi when she found them in the sky: she was not shining, but shone on, though there was no source of light. She was tall, naked, winged, and her lined face was older than any living creature Mrs Coulter had ever seen.

"Are you one of the angels who rebelled so long ago?"

"Yes. And since then I have been wandering between many worlds. Now I have pledged my allegiance to Lord Asriel, because I see in his great enterprise the best hope of destroying the tyranny at last."

"But if you fail?"

"Then we shall all be destroyed, and cruelty will reign for ever."

As they spoke, they followed Lord Asriel's rapid strides along the wind-beaten battlements towards a mighty staircase going down so deep that even the flaring lights on sconces down the walls could not disclose the bottom. Past them swooped the blue hawk, gliding down and down into the gloom, with each flaring light making his feathers flicker as he passed it until he was merely a tiny spark, and then nothing.

The angel had moved on to Lord Asriel's side, and Mrs Coulter found herself descending next to the African king.

"Excuse my ignorance, sir," she said, "but I had never seen or heard of a being like the man on the blue hawk until the fight in the cave yesterday . . . Where does he come from? Can you tell me about his people? I wouldn't offend him for the world, but if I speak without knowing something about him, I might be unintentionally rude."

"You do well to ask," said King Ogunwe. "His people are proud. Their world developed unlike ours; there are two kinds of conscious being there, humans and Gallivespians. The humans are mostly servants of the Authority, and they have been trying to exterminate the small people since the earliest time anyone can remember. They regard them as diabolic. So the Gallivespians still cannot quite trust those who are our size. But they are fierce and proud warriors, and deadly enemies, and valuable spies."

"Are all his people with you, or are they divided as humans are?"

"There are some who are with the enemy, but most are with us."

"And the angels? You know, I thought until recently that

angels were an invention of the Middle Age; they were just imaginary . . . To find yourself speaking to one is disconcerting, isn't it . . . How many are with Lord Asriel?"

"Mrs Coulter," said the king, "these questions are just the sort of things a spy would want to find out."

"A fine sort of spy I'd be, to ask you so transparently," she replied. "I'm a captive, sir. I couldn't get away, even if I had a safe place to flee to. From now on, I'm harmless, you can take my word for that."

"If you say so, I am happy to believe you," said the king. "Angels are more difficult to understand than any human being. They're not all of one kind, to begin with; some have greater powers than others; and there are complicated alliances among them, and ancient enmities, that we know little about. The Authority has been suppressing them since he came into being."

She stopped. She was genuinely shocked. The African king halted beside her, thinking she was unwell, and indeed the light of the flaring sconce above her did throw ghastly shadows over her face.

"You say that so casually," she said, "as if it were something I should know too, but . . . How can it be? The Authority created the worlds, didn't he? He existed before everything. How can he have *come into being*?"

"This is angelic knowledge," said Ogunwe. "It shocked some of us too to learn that the Authority is not the creator. There may have been a creator, or there may not: we don't know. All we know is that at some point the Authority took charge, and since then, angels have rebelled, and human beings have struggled against him too. This is the last rebellion. Never before have humans and angels, and beings from all the worlds, made a common cause. This is the greatest force ever assembled. But it may still not be enough. We shall see."

"But what does Lord Asriel intend? What is this world, and why has he come here?"

"He led us here because this world is empty. Empty of conscious life, that is. We are not colonialists, Mrs Coulter. We haven't come to conquer, but to build."

"And is he going to attack the kingdom of heaven?"

Ogunwe looked at her levelly.

"We're not going to invade the kingdom," he said, "but if the kingdom invades us, they had better be ready for war, because we are prepared. Mrs Coulter, I am a king, but it's my proudest task to join Lord Asriel in setting up a world where there are no kingdoms at all. No kings, no bishops, no priests. The kingdom of heaven has been known by that name since the Authority first set himself above the rest of the angels. And we want no part of it. This world is different. We intend to be free citizens of the republic of heaven."

Mrs Coulter wanted to say more, to ask the dozen questions that rose to her lips, but the king had moved on, unwilling to keep his commander waiting, and she had to follow.

The staircase led so far down that by the time it reached a level floor the sky behind them at the head of the flight was quite invisible. Well before half-way she had little breath left, but she made no complaint, and moved on down till it opened out into a massive hall lit by glowing crystals in the pillars that supported the roof. Ladders, gantries, beams and walkways crossed the gloom above, with small figures moving about them purposefully.

Lord Asriel was speaking to his commanders when Mrs Coulter arrived, and without waiting to let her rest he moved on across the great hall, where occasionally a bright figure would sweep through the air or alight on the floor for a brief snatched word with him. The air was dense and warm. Mrs Coulter noticed that, presumably as a courtesy to Lord Roke, every pillar had an empty bracket at human head-height so that his hawk could perch there and allow the Gallivespian to be included in the discussion.

But they did not stay in the great hall for long. At the far side, an attendant hauled open a heavy double door to let them through, on to the platform of a railway. There waiting was a small closed carriage, drawn by an anbaric locomotive.

The engineer bowed, and his brown monkey-dæmon retreated behind his legs at the sight of the golden monkey. Lord Asriel spoke to the man briefly and showed the others into the carriage, which like the hall was lit by those glowing crystals, held on silver brackets against mirrored mahogany panels.

As soon as Lord Asriel had joined them the train began to move, gliding smoothly away from the platform and into a tunnel, accelerating briskly. Only the sound of the wheels on the smooth track gave any idea of their speed.

"Where are we going?" Mrs Coulter asked.

"To the armoury," Lord Asriel said shortly, and turned away to talk quietly with the angel.

Mrs Coulter said to Lord Roke, "My lord, are your spies always sent out in pairs?"

"Why do you ask?"

"Simple curiosity. My dæmon and I found ourselves at a stale-mate when we met them recently in that cave, and I was intrigued to see how well they fought."

"Why *intrigued*? Did you not expect people of our size to be good fighters?"

She looked at him coolly, aware of the ferocity of his pride.

"No," she said. "I thought we would beat you easily, and you very nearly beat us. I'm happy to admit my mistake. But do you always fight in pairs?"

"*You* are a pair, are you not, you and your dæmon? Did you expect us to concede the advantage?" he said, and his haughty stare, brilliantly clear even in the soft light of the crystals, dared her to ask more.

She looked down modestly and said nothing.

Several minutes went past, and Mrs Coulter felt the train taking them downwards, even deeper into the mountain's heart. She couldn't guess how far they went, but when at least fifteen minutes had gone by, the train begin to slow; and presently they drew up to a platform where the anbaric lights seemed brilliant after the darkness of the tunnel.

Lord Asriel opened the doors, and they got out into an atmosphere so hot and sulphur-laden that Mrs Coulter had to gasp. The air rang with the pounding of mighty hammers and the clangorous screech of iron on stone.

An attendant hauled open the doors leading off the platform, and instantly the noise redoubled and the heat swept over them like a breaking wave. A blaze of scorching light made them shade their eyes; only Xaphania seemed unaffected by the onslaught of sound and light and heat. When her senses had adjusted, Mrs Coulter looked around, alive with curiosity.

She had seen forges, iron-works, manufactories in her own world: the biggest seemed like a village smithy beside this. Hammers the size of houses were lifted in a moment to the distant ceiling and then hurled downwards to flatten baulks of iron the size of tree-trunks, pounding them flat in a fraction of a second with a blow that made the very mountain tremble; from a vent in the rocky wall, a river of sulphurous molten metal flowed until it was cut off by an adamant gate, and the brilliant seething flood rushed through channels and sluices and over weirs into row upon row of moulds, to settle and cool in a cloud of evil smoke; gigantic slicing machines and rollers cut and folded and pressed sheets of inch-thick iron as if it were tissue-paper, and then those monstrous hammers pounded it flat again, layering metal upon metal with such force that the different layers became one tougher one, over and over again.

If Iorek Byrnison could have seen this armoury, he might have admitted that these people knew something about working with metal. Mrs Coulter could only look and wonder. It was impossible to speak and be understood, and no one tried. And now Lord Asriel was gesturing to the small group to follow him along a grated walkway suspended over an even larger vault below, where miners toiled with picks and spades to hack the bright metals from the mother-rock.

They passed over the walkway and down a long rocky corridor, where stalactites hung gleaming with strange colours and where the pounding and grinding and hammering gradually faded. Mrs Coulter could feel a cool breeze on her heated face. The crystals that gave them light were neither mounted on sconces nor enclosed in glowing pillars, but scattered loosely on the floor, and there were no flaring torches to add to the heat, so little by little the party began to feel cold again; and presently they came out, quite suddenly, into the night air.

They were at a place where part of the mountain had been hacked away, making a space as wide and open as a parade-ground. Further along they could see, dimly lit, great iron doors in the mountainside, some open and some shut; and from out of one of the mighty doorways, men were hauling something draped in a tarpaulin.

"What is that?" Mrs Coulter said to the African king, and he replied:

"The intention craft."

Mrs Coulter had no idea what that could mean, and watched with intense curiosity as they prepared to take off the tarpaulin.

She stood close to King Ogunwe as if for shelter and said, "How does it work? What does it do?"

"We're about to see," said the king.

It looked like some kind of complex drilling apparatus, or the cockpit of a gyropter, or the cabin of a massive crane. It had a glass canopy over a seat with at least a dozen levers and handles banked in front of it. It stood on six legs, each jointed and sprung at a different angle to the body, so that it seemed both energetic and ungainly; and the body itself was a mass of pipework, cylinders, pistons, coiled cables, switchgear and valves and gauges. It was hard to tell what was structure and what was not, because it was only lit from behind, and most of it was hidden in gloom.

Lord Roke on his hawk had glided up to it directly, circling above, examining it from all sides. Lord Asriel and the angel were close in discussion with the engineers, and men were clambering down from the craft itself, one carrying a clipboard, another a length of cable.

Mrs Coulter's eyes gazed at the craft hungrily, memorizing every part of it, making sense of its complexity. And as she watched, Lord Asriel swung himself up into the seat, fastening a leather harness around his waist and shoulders and setting a helmet securely on his head. His dæmon, the snow leopard, sprang up to follow him, and he turned to adjust something beside her. The engineer called up, Lord Asriel replied, and the men withdrew to the doorway.

The intention craft moved, though Mrs Coulter was not sure how. It was almost as if it had quivered, though there it was, quite still, poised with a strange energy on those six insect-legs. As she looked it moved again, and then she saw what was happening: various parts of it were revolving, turning this way and that, scanning the dark sky overhead. Lord Asriel sat busily moving this

lever, checking that dial, adjusting that control; and then suddenly the intention craft vanished.

Somehow, it had sprung into the air. It was hovering above
them now, as high as a tree-top, turning slowly to the left. There
was no sound of an engine, no hint of how it was held against
gravity. It simply hung in the air.

"Listen," said King Ogunwe. "To the south."

She turned her head and strained to hear. There was a wind
that moaned around the edge of the mountain, and there were
the deep hammer-blows from the presses which she felt through
the soles of her feet, and there was the sound of voices from the
lighted doorway, but at some signal the voices stopped and the
lights were extinguished. And in the quiet Mrs Coulter could
hear, very faintly, the chop-chop-chop of gyropter engines on
the gusts of wind.

"Who are they?" she said quietly.

"Decoys," said the king. "My pilots, flying a mission to tempt
the enemy to follow. Watch."

She widened her eyes, trying to see anything against the heavy
dark with its few stars. Above them, the intention craft hung as
firmly as if it were anchored and bolted there; no gust of wind
had the slightest effect on it. No light came from the cockpit, so
it was very difficult to see, and the figure of Lord Asriel was out
of sight completely.

Then she caught the first sight of a group of lights low in the
sky, at the same moment as the engine-sound became loud
enough to hear steadily. Six gyropters, flying fast, one of them
seemingly in trouble, for smoke trailed from it, and it flew lower
than the others. They were making for the mountain, but on a
course to take them past it and beyond.

And behind them, in close pursuit, came a motley collection
of flyers. It was not easy to make out what they were, but Mrs
Coulter saw a heavy gyropter of a strange kind, two straight-
winged aircraft, one great bird that glided with effortless speed
carrying two armed riders, and three or four angels.

"A raiding party," said King Ogunwe.

They were closing on the gyropters. Then a line of light blazed
from one of the straight-winged aircraft, followed a second or

two later by the sound, a deep crack. But the shell never reached its target, the crippled gyropter, because in the same instant as they saw the light, and before they heard the crack, the watchers on the mountain saw a flash from the intention craft, and a shell exploded in mid-air.

Mrs Coulter had hardly time to understand that almost instantaneous sequence of light and sound before the battle was under way. Nor was it at all easy to follow, because the sky was so dark and the movement of every flier so quick; but a series of nearly silent flashes lit the mountainside, accompanied by short hisses like the escape of steam. Each flash struck somehow at a different raider: the aircraft caught fire or exploded, the giant bird uttered a scream like the tearing of a mountain-high curtain and plummeted on to the rocks far below; and as for the angels, each of them simply vanished in a drift of glowing air, a myriad particles twinkling and glowing dimmer until they flickered out like a dying firework.

Then there was silence. The wind carried away the sound of the decoy gyropters, which had now disappeared around the flank of the mountain, and no one watching spoke. Flames far below glared on the underside of the intention craft, still somehow hovering in the air and now turning slowly as if to look around. The destruction of the raiding party was so complete that Mrs Coulter, who had seen many things to be shocked by, was nevertheless shocked by this. As she looked up at the intention craft, it seemed to shimmer or dislodge itself and then there it was, solidly on the ground again.

King Ogunwe hurried forward, as did the other commanders and the engineers, who had thrown open the doors and let the light flood out over the proving-ground. Mrs Coulter stayed where she was, puzzling over the workings of the intention craft.

"Why is he showing it to us?" her dæmon said quietly.

"Surely he can't have read our mind," she replied in the same tone.

They were thinking of the moment in the adamant tower when that spark-like idea had flashed between them. They had thought of making Lord Asriel a proposition: of offering to go to the Consistorial Court of Discipline and spy for him. She knew every lever of power; she could manipulate them all. It would be hard at first to convince them of her good faith, but she could do it. And now that the Gallivespian spies had left to go with Will and Lyra, surely Asriel couldn't resist an offer like that.

But now, as they looked at that strange flying machine, another idea struck even more forcibly, and she hugged the golden monkey with glee.

"Asriel," she called innocently, "may I see how the machine works?"

He looked down, his expression distracted and impatient, but full of excited satisfaction too. He was delighted with the intention craft: she knew he wouldn't be able to resist showing it off.

King Ogunwe stood aside, and Lord Asriel reached down and pulled her up into the cockpit. He helped her into the seat, and watched as she looked around the controls.

"How does it work? What powers it?" she said.

"Your intentions," he said. "Hence the name. If you intend to go forward, it will go forward."

"That's no answer. Come on, tell me. What sort of engine is it? How does it fly? I couldn't see anything aerodynamic at all. But these controls . . . from inside, it's almost like a gyropter."

He was finding it hard not to tell her; and since she was in his power, he did. He held out a cable at the end of which was a leather grip, deeply marked by his dæmon's teeth.

"Your dæmon," he explained, "has to hold this handle – whether in teeth, or hands, it doesn't matter. And you have to wear that helmet. There's a current flowing between them, and a capacitor amplifies it – oh, it's more complicated than that, but the thing's simple to fly. We put in controls like a gyropter for the sake of familiarity, but eventually we won't need controls at all. Of course, only a human with a dæmon can fly it."

"I see," she said.

And she pushed him hard, so that he fell out of the machine.

In the same moment she slipped the helmet on her head, and the golden monkey snatched up the leather handle. She reached for the control which in a gyropter would tilt the aerofoil, and pushed the throttle forward, and at once the intention craft leapt into the air.

But she didn't quite have the measure of it yet. The craft hung still for some moments, slightly tilted, before she found the controls to move it forward, and in those few seconds, Lord Asriel did three things. He leapt to his feet; he put up his hand to stop King Ogunwe from ordering the soldiers to fire on the intention craft; and he said, "Lord Roke, go with her, if you would be so kind."

The Gallivespian urged his blue hawk upwards at once, and the bird flew straight to the still-open cabin door. The watchers below could see the woman's head looking this way and that, and the golden monkey likewise, and they could see that neither of them noticed the little figure of Lord Roke leaping from his hawk into the cabin behind them.

A moment later, the intention craft began to move, and the hawk wheeled away to skim down to Lord Asriel's wrist. No more than two seconds later, the aircraft was already vanishing from sight in the damp and starry air.

Lord Asriel watched with rueful admiration.

"Well, King, you were quite right," he said, "and I should have listened to you in the first place. She is Lyra's mother; I might have expected something like that."

"Aren't you going to pursue her?" said King Ogunwe.

"What, and destroy a perfectly good aircraft? Certainly not."

"Where d'you think she'll go? In search of the child?"

"Not at first. She doesn't know where to find her. I know exactly what she'll do: she'll go to the Consistorial Court, and give them the intention craft as an earnest of good faith, and then she'll spy. She'll spy on them for us. She's tried every other kind of duplicity: that one'll be a novel experience. And as soon as she finds out where the girl is, she'll go there, and we shall follow."

"And when will Lord Roke let her know he's come with her?"

"Oh, I think he'll keep that as a surprise, don't you?"

They laughed, and moved back into the workshops, where a later, more advanced model of the intention craft was awaiting their inspection.

17
OIL AND LACQUER

Now the serpent was more subtil than any beast of the field which the LORD God had made.

— GENESIS

MARY MALONE WAS constructing a mirror. Not out of vanity, for she had little of that, but because she wanted to test an idea she had. She wanted to try and catch Shadows, and without the instruments in her laboratory she had to improvise with the materials to hand. Mulefa technology had little use for metal. They did extraordinary things with stone and wood and cord and shell and horn, but what metals they had were hammered from native nuggets of copper and other metals which they found in the sand of the river, and they were never used for tool-making. They were ornamental. Mulefa couples, for example, on entering marriage, would exchange strips of bright copper, which were bent around the base of one of their horns with much the meaning of a wedding ring.

So they were fascinated by the Swiss Army knife which was Mary's most valuable possession.

The zalif who was her particular friend, Atal by name, exclaimed with astonishment one day when Mary unfolded the knife, and showed her all the parts and explained as well as she could, with her limited language, what they were for. One attachment was a miniature magnifying glass with which she began to burn a design on to a dry branch, and it was that which set her thinking about Shadows.

They were fishing at the time, but the river was low and the fish must have been elsewhere, so they let the net lie across the water and sat on the grassy bank and talked, until Mary saw the dry branch, which had a smooth white surface. She burned the design – a simple daisy – into the wood, and delighted Atal; but as the thin line of smoke wafted up from the spot where the focused sunlight touched the wood, Mary thought: If this became fossilized, and a scientist in ten million years found it, they could still find Shadows around it, because I've worked on it.

She drifted into a sun-doped reverie until Atal asked:

What are you dreaming?

Mary tried to explain about her work, her research, the laboratory, the discovery of Shadow-particles, the fantastical revelation that they were conscious, and found the whole tale gripping her again, so that she longed to be back among her equipment.

She didn't expect Atal to follow her explanation, partly because of her own imperfect command of their language, but partly because the *mulefa* seemed so practical, so strongly rooted in the physical everyday world, and much of what she was saying was mathematical; but Atal surprised her by saying, *Yes – we know what you mean – we call it . . .* and then she used a word that sounded like their word for *light*.

Mary said, *Light?* and Atal said, *Not light, but . . .* and said the word more slowly for Mary to catch, explaining: *like the light on water when it makes small ripples, at sunset, and the light comes off in bright flakes, we call it that, but it is a make-like.*

Make-like was their term for metaphor, Mary had discovered.

So she said, *It is not really light, but you see it and it looks like that light on water at sunset?*

Atal said, *Yes. All the mulefa have this. You have too. That is how we knew you were like us and not like the grazers, who don't have it. Even though you look so bizarre and horrible, you are like us, because you have –* and again came that word that Mary couldn't hear quite clearly enough to say: something like *sraf*, or *sarf*, accompanied by a leftward flick of the trunk.

Mary was excited. She had to keep herself calm enough to find the right words.

What do you know about it? Where does it come from?

From us, and from the oil, was Atal's reply, and Mary knew she meant the oil in the great seed-pod wheels.

From you?

When we are grown-up. But without the trees it would just vanish again. With the wheels and the oil, it stays among us.

When we are grown-up . . . Again Mary had to keep herself from becoming incoherent. One of the things she'd begun to suspect about Shadows was that children and adults reacted to them differently, or attracted different kinds of Shadow-activity. Hadn't Lyra said that the scientists in her world had discovered something like that about Dust, which was their name for Shadows? Here it was again.

And it was connected to what the Shadows had said to her on the computer screen just before she'd left her own world: whatever it was, this question, it had to do with the great change in human history symbolized in the story of Adam and Eve; with the Temptation, the Fall, Original Sin. In his investigations among fossil skulls, her colleague Oliver Payne had discovered that around thirty thousand years ago, a great increase had taken place in the number of Shadow-particles associated with human remains. Something had happened then, some development in evolution, to make the human brain an ideal channel for amplifying their effects.

She said to Atal:

How long have there been mulefa?

And Atal said:

Thirty-three thousand years.

She was able to read Mary's expressions by this time, or the most obvious of them at least, and she laughed at the way Mary's jaw dropped. Their laughter was free and joyful and so infectious that Mary usually had to join in, but now she remained serious and astounded and said:

How can you know so exactly? Do you have a history of all those years?

Oh, yes, said Atal. *Ever since we have had the sraf, we have had memory and wakefulness. Before that, we knew nothing.*

What happened to give you the sraf?

We discovered how to use the wheels. One day a creature with no name discovered a seed-pod and began to play, and as she played she —

She?

She, yes. She had no name before then. She saw a snake coiling itself through the hole in a seed-pod, and the snake said —

The snake spoke to her?

No! no! It is a make-like. The story tells that the snake said What do you know? What do you remember? What do you see ahead? And she said Nothing, nothing, nothing. So the snake said Put your foot through the hole in the seed-pod where I was playing, and you will become wise. So she put a foot in where the snake had been. And the oil entered her foot and made her see more clearly than before, and the first thing she saw was the sraf. *It was so strange and pleasant that she wanted to share it at once with all her kindred. So she and her mate took the first ones, and they discovered that they knew who they were, they knew they were mulefa and not grazers. They gave each other names. They named themselves mulefa. They named the seed-tree, and all the creatures and plants.*

Because they were different, said Mary.

Yes, they were. And so were their children, because as more seed-pods fell, they showed their children how to use them. And when the children were old enough, they began to generate the sraf *as well, and as they were big enough to ride on the wheels, the* sraf *came back with the oil and stayed with them. So they saw that they had to plant more seed-pod trees, for the sake of the oil, but the pods were so hard that they very seldom germinated. And the first mulefa saw what they must do to help the trees, which was to ride on the wheels and break them, so mulefa and seed-pod trees have always lived together.*

Mary directly understood about a quarter of what Atal was saying, but by questioning and guessing she found out the rest quite accurately; and her own command of the language was increasing all the time. The more she learned, though, the more difficult it became, as each new thing she found out suggested half a dozen questions, each leading in a different direction.

But she pulled her mind after the subject of *sraf*, because that was the biggest; and that was why she thought about the mirror.

It was the comparison of sraf to the sparkles on water that suggested it. Reflected light like the glare off the sea was polarized: it might be that the Shadow-particles, when they behaved like waves as light did, were capable of being polarized too.

I can't see sraf *as you can,* she said, *but I would like to make a mirror out of the sap-lacquer, because I think that might help me see it.*

Atal was excited by this idea, and they hauled in their net at once and began to gather what Mary needed. As a token of good luck there were three fine fish in the net.

The sap-lacquer was a product of another and much smaller

tree, which the mulefa cultivated for that purpose. By boiling the sap and dissolving it in the alcohol they made from distilled fruit juice, the mulefa made a substance like milk in consistency, and delicate amber in colour, which they used as a varnish. They would put up to twenty coats on a base of wood or shell, letting each one cure under wet cloth before applying the next, and gradually build up a surface of great hardness and brilliance. They would usually make it opaque with various oxides, but sometimes they left it transparent, and that was what had interested Mary: because the clear amber-coloured lacquer had the same curious property as the mineral known as Iceland Spar. It split light rays in two, so that when you looked through it you saw double.

She wasn't sure what she wanted to do, except that she knew that if she fooled around for long enough, without fretting, or nagging herself, she'd find out. She remembered quoting the words of the poet Keats to Lyra, and Lyra's understanding at once that that was her own state of mind when she read the alethiometer – that was what Mary had to find now.

So she began by finding herself a more or less flat piece of a wood like pine, and grinding at the surface with a piece of sandstone (no metal: no planes) until it was as flat as she could make it. That was the method the mulefa used, and it worked well enough, with time and effort.

Then she visited the lacquer-grove with Atal, having carefully explained what she was intending, and asked permission to take some sap. The mulefa were happy to let her, but too busy to be concerned. With Atal's help she drew off some of the sticky resinous sap, and then came the long process of boiling, dissolving, boiling again, until the varnish was ready to use.

The mulefa used pads of a cottony fibre from another plant to apply it, and following the instructions of a craftsman, she laboriously painted her mirror over and over again, seeing hardly any difference each time as the layer of lacquer was so thin, but letting them cure unhurriedly and finding gradually that the thickness was building up. She painted on over forty coats – she lost count – but by the time her lacquer had run out, the surface was at least five millimetres thick.

After the final layer came the polishing: a whole day of rubbing the surface gently, in smooth circular movements, until her arms ached and her head was throbbing and she could bear the labour no more.

Then she slept.

Next morning the group went to work in a coppice of what they called knot-wood, making sure the shoots were growing as they had been set, tightening the inter-weaving so that the grown sticks would be properly shaped. They valued Mary's help for this task, as she on her own could squeeze into narrower gaps than the mulefa, and, with her double hands, work in tighter spaces.

It was only when that work was done, and they had returned to the settlement, that Mary could begin to experiment – or rather to play, since she still didn't have a clear idea of what she was doing.

First she tried using the lacquer sheet simply as a mirror, but for lack of a silvered back, all she could see was a doubled reflection faintly in the wood.

Then she thought that what she really needed was the lacquer without the wood, but she quailed at the idea of making another sheet; how could she make it flat without a backing anyway?

The idea came of simply cutting the wood away to leave the lacquer. That would take time too, but at least she had the Swiss Army knife. And she began, splitting it very delicately from the edge, taking the greatest of care not to scratch the lacquer from behind, but eventually removing most of the pine and leaving a mess of torn and splintered wood stuck immovably to the pane of clear hard varnish.

She wondered what would happen if she soaked it in water. Did the lacquer soften if it got wet? *No*, said her master in the craft, *it will remain hard for ever; but why not do it like this?* – and he showed her a liquid kept in a stone bowl, which would eat through any wood in only a few hours. It looked and smelt to Mary like an acid.

That would hurt the lacquer hardly at all, he said, and she could repair any damage easily enough. He was intrigued by her project, and helped her to swab the acid delicately on to the wood, telling her how they made it by grinding and dissolving and distilling a mineral they found at the edge of some shallow lakes she had not yet visited. Gradually the wood softened and came free, and Mary was left with the single sheet of clear brown-yellow lacquer, about the size of a page from a paperback book.

She polished the reverse as highly as the top, until both were as flat and smooth as the finest mirror.

And when she looked through it . . .

Nothing in particular. It was perfectly clear, but it showed her a double image, the right one quite close to the left and about fifteen degrees upwards.

She wondered what would happen if she looked through two pieces, one on top of the other.

So she took the Swiss Army knife again and tried to score a line across the sheet so she could cut it in two. By working and re-working and by keeping the knife sharp on a smooth stone she managed to score a line deep enough for her to risk snapping the sheet. She laid a thin stick under the score line and pushed sharply down on the lacquer, as she'd seen a glazier cutting glass, and it worked: now she had two sheets.

She put them together and looked through. The amber colour was denser, and like a photographic filter it emphasized some colours and held back others, giving a slightly different cast to the landscape. The curious thing was that the double-ness had disappeared, and everything was single again; but there was no sign of Shadows.

She moved the two pieces apart, watching how the appearance of things changed as she did so. When they were about a hand-span apart, a curious thing happened: the amber colouring disappeared, and everything seemed its normal colour, but brighter and more vivid.

At that point Atal came along to see what she was doing.

Can you see sraf now? she said.

No, but I can see other things, Mary said, and tried to show her.

Atal was interested, but politely, not with the sense of discovery that was animating Mary, and presently the zalif tired of looking through the small pieces of lacquer and settled down on the grass to maintain her wheels. Sometimes the mulefa would groom each other's claws, out of pure sociability, and once or twice Atal had invited Mary to attend to hers. Mary in turn let Atal tidy her hair, enjoying how the soft trunk lifted it and let it fall, stroking and massaging her scalp.

She sensed that Atal wanted this now, so she put down the two pieces of lacquer and ran her hands over the astonishing smoothness of Atal's claws, that surface smoother and slicker than Teflon that rested on the lower rim of the central hole and served as a bearing when the wheel turned. The contours matched exactly, of course, and as Mary ran her hands around the inside of the wheel she could feel no difference in texture: it was as if the mulefa and the seed-pod really were one creature which by a miracle could disassemble itself and put itself together again.

Atal was soothed, and so was Mary, by this contact. Her friend was young and unmarried, and there were no young males in this group, so she would have to marry a zalif from outside; but contact wasn't easy, and sometimes Mary thought that Atal was anxious about her future. So she didn't grudge the time she spent with her, and now she was happy to clean the wheel-holes of all the dust and grime that accumulated there, and smooth the fragrant oil gently over her friend's claws while Atal's trunk lifted and straightened her hair.

When Atal had had enough, she set herself on the wheels again and moved away to help with the evening meal. Mary turned back to her lacquer, and almost at once she made her discovery.

She held the two plates a hand-span apart so that they showed that clear bright image she'd seen before, but something had happened.

As she looked through, she saw a swarm of golden sparkles surrounding the form of Atal. They were only visible through one small part of the lacquer, and then Mary realized why: at that point she had touched the surface of it with her oily fingers.

"Atal!" she called. "Quick! Come back!"

Atal turned and wheeled back.

"Let me take a little oil," Mary said, "just enough to put on the lacquer."

Atal willingly let her run her fingers around the wheel-holes again, and watched curiously as Mary coated one of the pieces with a film of the clear sweet substance.

Then she pressed the plates together and moved them around to spread the oil evenly, and held them a hand-span apart once more.

And when she looked through, everything was changed. She could see Shadows. If she'd been in the Jordan College Retiring Room when Lord Asriel had projected the photograms he'd made with the special emulsion, she would have recognized the effect. Everywhere she looked she could see gold, just as Atal had described it: sparkles of light, floating and drifting and sometimes moving in a current of purpose. Among it all was the world she could see with the naked eye, the grass, the river, the trees; but wherever she saw a conscious being, one of the mulefa, the light was thicker and more full of movement. It didn't obscure their shapes in any way; if anything it made them clearer.

I didn't know it was beautiful, Mary said to Atal.

Why, of course it is, her friend replied. *It is strange to think that you couldn't see it. Look at the little one . . .*

She indicated one of the small children playing in the long grass, leaping clumsily after grasshoppers, suddenly stopping to examine a leaf, falling over, scrambling up again to rush and tell his mother something, being distracted again by a piece of stick, trying to pick it up, finding ants on his trunk and hooting with agitation . . . There was a golden haze around him as there was around the shelters, the fishing-nets, the evening fire: stronger than theirs, though not by much. But unlike theirs it was full of little swirling currents of intention, that eddied and broke off and drifted about, to disappear as new ones were born.

Around his mother, on the other hand, the golden sparkles were much stronger, and the currents they moved in more settled and powerful. She was preparing food, spreading flour on a flat stone, making the thin bread like chapattis or tortillas, watching her child at the same time, and the Shadows or the sraf or the Dust that bathed her looked like the very image of responsibility and wise care.

So at last you can see, said Atal. *Well, now you must come with me.*
Mary looked at her friend in puzzlement. Atal's tone was

strange: it was as if she were saying *Finally you're ready; we've been waiting; now things must change.*

And others were appearing, from over the brow of the hill, from out of their shelters, from along the river: members of the group, but strangers too, mulefa who were new to her, and who looked curiously towards where she was standing. The sound of their wheels on the hard-packed earth was low and steady.

Where must I go? Mary said. *Why are they all coming here?*

Don't worry, said Atal, *come with me, we shall not hurt you.*

It seemed to have been long planned, this meeting, for they all knew where to go and what to expect. There was a low mound at the edge of the village that was regular in shape and packed with hard earth, with ramps at each end, and the crowd – fifty or so at least, Mary estimated – was moving towards it. The smoke of the cooking fires hung in the evening air, and the setting sun spread its own kind of hazy gold over everything; and Mary was aware of the smell of roasting corn, and the warm smell of the mulefa themselves – part oil, part warm flesh, a sweet horse-like smell.

Atal urged her towards the mound.

Mary said, *What is happening? Tell me!*

No, no . . . Not me. Sattamax will speak . . .

Mary didn't know the name Sattamax, and the zalif whom Atal indicated was a stranger to her. He was older than anyone she'd seen so far: at the base of his trunk was a scatter of white hairs, and he moved stiffly, as if he had arthritis. The others all moved with care around him, and when Mary stole a glance through the lacquer glass she saw why: the old zalif's Shadow-cloud was so rich and complex that Mary herself felt respect, even though she knew so little of what it meant.

When Sattamax was ready to speak, the rest of the crowd fell silent. Mary stood close to the mound, with Atal nearby for re-assurance; but she sensed all their eyes on her, and felt as if she were a new girl at school.

Sattamax began to speak. His voice was deep, the tones rich and varied, the gestures of his trunk low and graceful.

We have all come together to greet the stranger Mary. Those of us who know her have reason to be grateful for her activities since she arrived among us. We have waited until she had some command of our language.

With the help of many of us, but especially the zalif Atal, the stranger Mary can now understand us.

But there was another thing she had to understand, and that was sraf. She knew about it, but she could not see it as we can, until she made an instrument to look through.

And now she has succeeded, she is ready to learn more about what she must do to help us.

Mary, come here and join me.

She felt dizzy, self-conscious, bemused, but she did as she had to and stepped up beside the old zalif. She thought she had better speak, so she began:

You have all made me feel I am a friend. You are kind and hospitable. I came from a world where life is very different, but some of us are aware of sraf, as you are, and I'm grateful for your help in making this glass, through which I can see it. If there is any way in which I can help you, I will be glad to do it.

She spoke more awkwardly than she did with Atal, and she was afraid she hadn't made her meaning clear. It was hard to know where to face when you had to gesture as well as speak, but they seemed to understand.

Sattamax said: *It is good to hear you speak. We hope you will be able to help us. If not, I cannot see how we will survive. The tualapi will kill us all. There are more of them than there ever were, and their numbers are increasing every year. Something has gone wrong with the world. For most of the thirty-three thousand years that there have been mulefa, we have taken care of the earth. Everything balanced. The trees prospered, the grazers were healthy, and even if once in a while the tualapi came, our numbers and theirs remained constant.*

But three hundred years ago the trees began to sicken. We watched them anxiously and tended them with care and still we found them producing fewer seed-pods, and dropping their leaves out of season, and some of them died outright, which had never been known. All our memory could not find a cause for this.

To be sure, it was slow, but so is the rhythm of our lives. We did not know that until you came. We have seen butterflies and birds, but they have no sraf. You do, strange as you seem; but you are swift and immediate, like birds, like butterflies. You realize there is a need for something to help you see sraf and instantly, out of the materials we have known for thousands of years, you put together an instrument to do so. Beside us, you think and act with the speed of a bird. That is how it seems, which is how we know that our rhythm seems slow to you.

But that fact is our hope. You can see things that we cannot, you can see connections and possibilities and alternatives that are invisible to us, just as sraf was invisible to you. And while we cannot see a way to survive, we hope that you may. We hope that you will go swiftly to the cause of the trees' sickness and find a cure; we hope you will invent a means of dealing with the tualapi, who are so numerous and so powerful.

And we hope you can do so soon, or we shall all die.

There was a murmur of agreement and approval from the crowd. They were all looking at Mary, and she felt more than ever like the new pupil at a school where they had high expectations of her. She also felt a strange flattery: the idea of herself as swift and darting and bird-like was new and pleasant, because she had always thought of herself as dogged and plodding. But along with that came the feeling that they'd got it terribly wrong, if they saw her like that; they didn't understand at all; she couldn't possibly fulfil this desperate hope of theirs.

But equally, she must. They were waiting.

Sattamax, she said, *mulefa, you put your trust in me and I shall do my best. You have been kind and your life is good and beautiful and I will try very hard to help you, and now I have seen sraf, I know what it is that I am doing. Thank you for trusting me.*

They nodded and murmured and stroked her with their trunks as she stepped down. She was daunted by what she had agreed to do.

At that very moment in the world of Cittàgazze, the assassin-priest Father Gomez was making his way up a rough track in the mountains between the twisted trunks of olive trees. The evening light slanted through the silvery leaves and the air was full of the noise of crickets and cicadas.

Ahead of him he could see a little farmhouse sheltered among vines, where a goat bleated and a spring trickled down through the grey rocks. There was an old man attending to some task beside the house, and an old woman leading the goat towards a stool and a bucket.

In the village some way behind, they had told him that the woman he was following had passed this way, and that she'd talked of going up into the mountains; perhaps this old couple had seen her. At least there might be cheese and olives to buy, and spring water to drink. Father Gomez was quite used to living frugally, and there was plenty of time.

18

THE SUBURBS OF THE DEAD

O that it were possible we might
But hold some two days' conference with the dead

— JOHN WEBSTER

LYRA WAS AWAKE before dawn, with Pantalaimon shivering at her breast, and she got up to walk about and warm herself up as the grey light seeped into the sky. She had never known such silence, not even in the snow-blanketed Arctic; there was not a stir of wind, and the sea was so still that not the tiniest ripple broke on the sand; the world seemed suspended between breathing in and breathing out.

Will lay curled up fast asleep, with his head on the rucksack to protect the knife. The cloak had fallen off his shoulder, and she tucked it around him, pretending that she was taking care to avoid his dæmon, and that she had the form of a cat, curled up just as he was. *She must be here somewhere*, she thought.

Carrying the still sleepy Pantalaimon, she walked away from Will and sat down on the slope of a sand dune a little way off, so their voices wouldn't wake him.

"Those little people," Pantalaimon said.

"I don't like 'em," said Lyra decisively. "I think we should get away from 'em as soon as we can. I reckon if we trap 'em in a net or something Will can cut through and close up and that's it, we'll be free."

"We haven't got a net," he said, "or something. Anyway, I bet they're cleverer than that. *He's* watching us now."

Pantalaimon was a hawk as he said that, and his eyes were keener than hers. The darkness of the sky was turning minute by minute into the palest ethereal blue, and as she looked across the sand the first edge of the sun just cleared the rim of the sea, dazzling her. Because she was on the slope of the dune, the light reached her a few seconds before it touched the beach, and she watched it flow around her and along towards Will; and then she saw the hand-high figure of the Chevalier Tialys, standing by Will's head, clear and wide awake and watching them.

"The thing is," said Lyra, "they can't make us do what they want. They got to follow us. I bet they're fed up."

"If they got hold of us," said Pan, meaning him and Lyra, "and got their stings ready to stick in us, Will'd *have* to do what they said."

Lyra thought about it. She remembered vividly the horrible scream of pain from Mrs Coulter, the eye-rolling convulsions, the ghastly lolling drool of the golden monkey as the poison entered her bloodstream . . . And that was only a scratch, as her mother had recently been reminded elsewhere. Will would *have* to give in and do what they wanted.

"Suppose they thought he wouldn't, though," she said, "suppose they thought he was so cold-hearted he'd just watch us die. Maybe he better make 'em think that, if he can."

She had brought the alethiometer with her, and now it was light enough to see, she took the beloved instrument out and laid it on its black velvet cloth in her lap. Little by little she drifted into that trance in which the many layers of meaning were clear to her, and where she could sense intricate webs of connectedness between them all. As her fingers found the symbols, her mind found the words: how can we get rid of the spies?

Then the needle began to dart this way and that, faster than she had ever seen it move before – so fast, in fact, that she was afraid for the first time that she'd miss some of the swings and stops; but some part of her awareness was counting them, and saw at once the meaning of what the movement said.

It told her: *Do not try, because your lives depend on them.*

That was a surprise, and not a happy one. But she went on and asked: *How can we get to the land of the dead?*

The answer came: *Go down. Follow the knife. Go onwards. Follow the knife.*

And finally she asked hesitantly, half-ashamed: *Is this the right thing to do?*

Yes, said the alethiometer instantly. *Yes.*

She sighed, coming out of her trance, and tucked the hair behind her ears, feeling the first warmth of the sun on her face and shoulders. There were sounds in the world now too: insects were stirring, and a very slight breeze was rustling the dry grass-stems growing higher up the dune.

She put the alethiometer away and wandered back to Will, with Pantalaimon as large as he could make himself and lion-shaped, in the hope of daunting the Gallivespians.

The man was using his lodestone apparatus, and when he'd finished Lyra said:

"You been talking to Lord Asriel?"

"To his representative," said Tialys.

"We en't going."

"That's what I told him."

"What did he say?"

"That was for my ears, not yours."

"Suit yourself," she said. "Are you married to that lady?"

"No. We are colleagues."

"Have you got any children?"

"No."

Tialys continued to pack the lodestone resonator away, and as he did so the Lady Salmakia woke up nearby, sitting up graceful and slow from the little hollow she'd made in the soft sand. The dragonflies were still asleep, tethered with cobweb-thin cord, their wings damp with dew.

"Are there big people on your world, or are they all small like you?" Lyra said.

"We know how to deal with big people," Tialys replied, not very helpfully, and went to talk quietly to the lady. They spoke too softly for Lyra to hear, but she enjoyed watching them sip dew-drops from the marram grass to refresh themselves. Water must be different for them, she thought to Pantalaimon: imagine drops the size of your fist! They'd be hard to get into; they'd have a sort of elastic rind, like a balloon.

By this time Will was waking too, wearily. The first thing he did was to look for the Gallivespians, who looked back at once, fully focused on him.

He looked away and found Lyra.

"I want to tell you something," she said. "Come over here, away from . . ."

"If you go away from us," said Tialys's clear voice, "you must leave the knife. If you won't leave the knife, you must talk to each other here."

"Can't we be private?" Lyra said indignantly. "We don't want you listening to what we say!"

"Then go away, but leave the knife."

There was no one else nearby, after all, and certainly the Gallivespians wouldn't be able to use it. Will rummaged in the rucksack for the water-canteen and a couple of biscuits, and handing one to Lyra, he went with her up the slope of the dune.

"I asked the alethiometer," she told him, "and it said we shouldn't try and escape from the little people, because they were going to save our lives. So maybe we're stuck with 'em."

"Have you told them what we're going to do?"

"No! And I won't, either. Cause they'll only tell Lord Asriel on that speaking-fiddle and he'd go there and stop us – so we got to just go, and not talk about it in front of them."

"They are spies, though," Will pointed out. "They must be good at listening and hiding. So maybe we better not mention it at all. We know where we're going. So we'll just go and not talk about it, and they'll have to put up with it and come along."

"They can't hear us now. They're too far off. Will, I asked how we get there, too. It said to follow the knife, just that."

"Sounds easy," he said. "But I bet it isn't. D'you know what Iorek told me?"

"No. He said – when I went to say goodbye – he said it would be very difficult for you, but he thought you could do it. But he never told me why . . ."

"The knife broke because I thought of my mother," he explained. "So I've got to put her out of my mind. But . . . It's like when someone says don't think about a crocodile, you *do*, you can't help it . . ."

"Well, you cut through last night all right," she said.

"Yeah, because I was tired, I think. Well, we'll see. Just follow the knife?"

"That's all it said."

"Might as well go now, then. Except there's not much food

left. We ought to find something to take with us, bread and fruit or something. So first I'll find a world where we can get food, and then we'll start looking properly."

"All right," said Lyra, quite happy to be moving again, with Pan and Will, alive and awake.

They made their way back to the spies, who were sitting alertly by the knife, packs on their backs.

"We should like to know what you intend," said Salmakia.

"Well, we're not coming to Lord Asriel, anyway," said Will. "We've got something else to do first."

"And will you tell us what that is, since it's clear we can't stop you doing it?"

"No," said Lyra, "because you'd just go and tell them. You'll have to come along without knowing where we're going. Course, you could always give up and go back to them."

"Certainly not," said Tialys.

"We want some kind of guarantee," said Will. "You're spies, so you're bound to be dishonest, that's your trade. We need to know we can trust you. Last night we were all too tired and we couldn't think about it, but there'd be nothing to stop you waiting till we were asleep and then stinging us to make us helpless and calling up Lord Asriel on that lodestone thing. You could do that easily. So we need to have a proper guarantee that you won't. A promise isn't enough."

The two Gallivespians trembled with anger at this slur on their honour.

Tialys, controlling himself, said, "We don't accept one-sided demands. You must give something in exchange. You must tell us what your intentions are, and then I shall give the lodestone resonator into your care. You must let me have it when I want to send a message, but you will always know when that happens, and we shall not be able to use it without your agreement. That will be our guarantee. And now you tell us where you are going, and why."

Will and Lyra exchanged a glance to confirm it.

"All right," Lyra said, "that's fair. So here's where we're going: we're going to the world of the dead. We don't know where it is, but the knife'll find it. That's what we're going to do."

The two spies were looking at her with open-mouthed incredulity.

Then Salmakia blinked and said, "What you say doesn't make sense. The dead are dead, that's all. There is no world of the dead."

"I thought that was true, as well," said Will. "But now I'm not sure. At least with the knife we can find out."

"But *why*?"

Lyra looked at Will, and saw him nod.

"Well," she said, "before I met Will, long before I was asleep, I led this friend into danger, and he was killed. I thought I was rescuing him, only I was making things worse. And while I was asleep I dreamt of him and I thought maybe I could make amends if I went where he's gone and said I was sorry. And Will wants to find his father, who died just when he found him before. See, Lord Asriel wouldn't think of that. Nor would Mrs Coulter. If we went to him we'd have to do what *he* wants, and he wouldn't think of Roger at all – that's my friend who died – it wouldn't matter to him. But it matters to me. To us. So that's what we want to do."

"Child," said Tialys, "when we die, everything is over. There is no other life. You have seen death. You've seen dead bodies, and you've seen what happens to a dæmon when death comes. It vanishes. What else can there be to live on after that?"

"We're going to go and find out," said Lyra. "And now we've told you, I'll take your lodestone resonator."

She held out her hand, and leopard-Pantalaimon stood, tail swinging slowly, to reinforce her demand. Tialys unslung the pack from his back and laid it in her palm. It was surprisingly heavy; no burden for her, of course, but she marvelled at his strength.

"And how long do you think this expedition will take?" said the chevalier.

"We don't know," Lyra told him. "We don't know anything about it, any more than you do. We'll just go there and see."

"First thing," Will said, "we've got to get some water and some more food, something easy to carry. So I'm going to find a world where we can do that, and then we'll set off."

Tialys and Salmakia mounted their dragonflies, and held them quivering on the ground. The great insects were eager for flight, but the command of their riders was absolute, and Lyra, watching them in daylight for the first time, saw the extraordinary fineness of the grey silk reins, the silvery stirrups, the tiny saddles.

Will took the knife, and a powerful temptation made him feel for the touch of his own world: he had the credit card still; he could buy familiar food; he could even telephone Mrs Cooper and ask for news of his mother –

The knife jarred with a sound like a nail being drawn along rough stone, and his heart nearly stopped. If he broke the blade again, it would be the end.

After a few moments he tried again. Instead of trying not to think of his mother he said to himself: *Yes, I know she's there, but I'm just going to look away while I do this . . .*

And that time it worked. He found a new world and slid the knife along to make an opening, and a few moments later all of them were standing in what looked like a neat and prosperous farmyard in some northern country like Holland or Denmark, where the stone-flagged yard was swept and clean and a row of stable doors stood open. The sun shone down through a hazy sky, and there was the smell of burning in the air, as well as something less pleasant. There was no sound of human life, though a loud buzzing, so active and vigorous that it sounded like a machine, came from the stables.

Lyra went and looked, and came back at once, looking pale.

"There's four –" she gulped, hand to her throat, and recovered – "four dead horses in there. And millions of flies . . ."

"Look," said Will, swallowing, "or maybe better not."

He was pointing at the raspberry canes that edged the kitchen garden. He'd just seen a man's legs, one with a shoe on and one without, protruding from the thickest part of the bushes.

Lyra didn't want to look, but Will went to see if the man was still alive and needed help. He came back shaking his head, looking uneasy.

The two spies were already at the farmhouse door, which was ajar.

Tialys darted back and said, "It smells sweeter in there," and then he flew back over the threshold while Salmakia scouted further around the outbuildings.

Will followed the chevalier. He found himself in a big square kitchen, an old-fashioned place with white china on a wooden dresser, and a scrubbed pine table, and a hearth where a black kettle stood cold. Next door there was a pantry, with two shelves full of apples that filled the whole room with fragrance. The silence was oppressive.

Lyra said quietly, "Will, is *this* the world of the dead?"

The same thought had occurred to him. But he said, "No, I don't think so. It's one we haven't been in before. Look, we'll load up with as much as we can carry. There's sort of rye bread, that'll be good – it's light – and here's some cheese . . ."

When they had taken what they could carry, Will dropped a gold coin into the drawer in the big pine table.

"Well?" said Lyra, seeing Tialys raise his eyebrows. "You should always pay for what you take."

At that moment Salmakia came in through the back door, landing her dragonfly on the table in a shimmer of electric blue.

"There are men coming," she said, "on foot, with weapons. They're only a few minutes' walk away. And there is a village burning beyond the fields."

And as she spoke they could hear the sound of boots on gravel, and a voice issuing orders, and the jingle of metal.

"Then we should go," said Will.

He felt in the air with the knife-point. And at once he was aware of a new kind of sensation. The blade seemed to be sliding along a very smooth surface, like a mirror, and then it sank through slowly until he was able to cut. But it was resistant, like heavy cloth, and when he made an opening he blinked with surprise and alarm: because the world he was opening into was the same in every detail as the one they were already standing in.

"What's happening?" said Lyra.

The spies were looking through, puzzled. But it was more than puzzlement they felt. Just as the air had resisted the knife, so something in this opening resisted their going through. Will had to push against something invisible and then help pull Lyra after him, and the Gallivespians could hardly make any headway at all.

They had to perch the dragonflies on the children's hands, and even then it was like pulling them against a pressure in the air; their filmy wings bent and twisted, and the little riders had to stroke their heads and whisper to calm their fears.

But after a few seconds of struggle they were all through, and Will found the edge of the window (though it was impossible to see) and closed it, shutting the sound of the soldiers away in their own world.

"Will," said Lyra, and he turned to see that there was another figure in the kitchen with them.

His heart jolted. It was the man he'd seen not ten minutes before, stark dead in the bushes with his throat cut.

He was middle-aged, lean, with the look of a man who spent most of the time in the open air. But now he was looking almost crazed, or paralysed, with shock. His eyes were so wide that the white showed all around the iris, and he was clutching the edge of the table with a trembling hand. His throat, Will was glad to see, was intact.

He opened his mouth to speak, but no words came out. All he could do was point at Will and Lyra.

Lyra said, "Excuse us for being in your house, but we had to escape from the men who were coming. I'm sorry if we startled you. I'm Lyra, and this is Will, and these are our friends, the Chevalier Tialys and the Lady Salmakia. Could you tell us your name and where we are?"

This normal-sounding request seemed to bring the man to his senses, and a shudder passed over him as if he were waking from a dream.

"I'm dead," he said. "I'm lying out there, dead. I know I am. *You* ain't dead. What's happening? God help me, they cut my throat. What's happening?"

Lyra stepped closer to Will when the man said *I'm dead*, and Pantalaimon fled to her breast as a mouse. As for the Gallivespians, they were trying to control their dragonflies, because the great insects seemed to have an aversion for the man, and darted here and there in the kitchen, looking for a way out.

But the man didn't notice them. He was still trying to understand what had happened.

"Are you a ghost?" Will said cautiously.

The man reached out his hand, and Will tried to take it, but his fingers closed on the air. A tingle of cold was all he felt.

When he saw it happen, the man looked at his own hand, appalled. The numbness was beginning to wear off, and he could feel the pity of his state.

"Truly," he said, "I *am* dead . . . I'm dead, and I'm going to hell . . ."

"Hush," said Lyra, "we'll go together. What's your name?"

"Dirk Jansen I was," he said, "but already I . . . I don't know what to do . . . Don't know where to go . . ."

Will opened the door. The barnyard looked the same, the kitchen garden was unchanged, the same hazy sun shone down. And there was the man's body, untouched.

A little groan broke from Dirk Jansen's throat, as if there was no denying it any more. The dragonflies darted out of the door and skimmed over the ground and then shot up high, faster than birds. The man was looking around helplessly, raising his hands, lowering them again, uttering little cries.

"I can't stay here . . . Can't stay," he was saying. "But this ain't the farm I knew. This is wrong. I got to go . . ."

"Where are you going, Mr Jansen?" said Lyra.

"Down the road. Dunno. Got to go. Can't stay here . . ."

Salmakia flew down to perch on Lyra's hand. The dragonfly's little claws pricked as the lady said, "There are people walking from the village – people like this man – all walking in the same direction."

"Then we'll go with them," said Will, and swung his rucksack over his shoulder.

Dirk Jansen was already passing his own body, averting his eyes. He looked almost as if he were drunk, stopping, moving on, wandering to left and right, stumbling over little ruts and stones on the path his living feet had known so well.

Lyra came after Will, and Pantalaimon became a kestrel and flew up as high as he could, making Lyra gasp.

"They're right," he said when he came down. "There's lines of people all coming from the village. Dead people . . ."

And soon they saw them too: twenty or so men, women

and children, all moving as Dirk Jansen had done, uncertain and shocked. The village was half a mile away, and the people were coming towards them, close together in the middle of the road. When Dirk Jansen saw the other ghosts he broke into a stumbling run, and they held out their hands to greet him.

"Even if they don't know where they're going, they're all going there together," Lyra said. "We better just go with them."

"D'you think they had dæmons in this world?" said Will.

"Can't tell. If you saw one of 'em in your world, would you know he was a ghost?"

"It's hard to say. They don't look normal, exactly . . . There was a man I used to see in my town, and he used to walk about outside the shops always holding the same old plastic bag, and he never spoke to anyone or went inside. And no one ever looked at him. I used to pretend he was a ghost. They look a bit like him. Maybe my world's full of ghosts and I never knew."

"I don't think mine is," said Lyra doubtfully.

"Anyway, this must be the world of the dead. These people have just been killed – those soldiers must've done it – and here they are, and it's just like the world they were alive in. I thought it'd be a lot different . . ."

"Well, it's fading," she said. "Look!"

She was clutching his arm. He stopped and looked around, and she was right. Not long before he had found the window in Oxford and stepped through into the other world of Cittàgazze, there had been an eclipse of the sun, and like millions of others Will had stood outside at midday and watched as the bright day-light faded and dimmed until a sort of eerie twilight covered the houses, the trees, the park. Everything was just as clear as in full daylight, but there was less light to see it by, as if all the strength were draining out of a dying sun.

What was happening now was like that, but odder, because the edges of things were losing their definition as well and becoming blurred.

"It's not like going blind, even," said Lyra, frightened, "because it's not that we can't see things, it's like the things them-selves are fading . . ."

The colour was slowly seeping out of the world. A dim green-grey for the bright green of the trees and the grass, a dim sand-grey for the vivid yellow of a field of corn, a dim blood-grey for the red bricks of a neat farmhouse . . .

The people themselves, closer now, had begun to notice too, and were pointing and holding one another's arms for re-assurance.

The only bright things in the whole landscape were the brilliant red-and-yellow and electric blue of the dragonflies, and their little riders, and Will and Lyra, and Pantalaimon, who was hovering kestrel-shaped close above.

They were close to the first of the people now, and it was clear: they were all ghosts. Will and Lyra took a step towards each other, but there was nothing to fear, for the ghosts were far more afraid of them, and were hanging back, unwilling to approach.

Will called out, "Don't be afraid. We're not going to hurt you. Where are you going?"

They looked at the oldest man among them, as if he was their guide.

"We're going where all the others go," he said. "Seems as if I know, but I can't remember learning it. Seems as if it's along the road. We'll know it when we get there."

"Mamma," said a child, "why's it getting dark in the day-time?"

"Hush, dear, don't fret," the mother said. "Can't make anything better by fretting. We're dead, I expect."

"But where are we going?" the child said. "I don't want to be dead, mamma!"

"We're going to see Grandpa," the mother said desperately.

But the child wouldn't be consoled, and wept bitterly. Others in the group looked at the mother with sympathy or annoyance, but there was nothing they could do to help, and they all walked on disconsolately through the fading landscape as the child's thin cries went on, and on, and on.

The Chevalier Tialys had spoken to Salmakia before skimming away ahead, and Will and Lyra watched the dragonfly with eyes greedy for its brightness and vigour as it got smaller and smaller. The lady flew down and perched her insect on Will's hand.

"The chevalier has gone to see what's ahead," she said. "We think the landscape is fading because these people are forgetting it. The further they go away from their homes the darker it will get."

"But why d'you think they're moving?" Lyra said. "If I was a ghost I'd want to stay in the places I knew, not wander along and get lost."

"They feel unhappy there," Will said, guessing. "It's where they've just died. They're afraid of it."

"No, they're pulled onwards by something," said the lady. "Some instinct is drawing them down the road."

And indeed the ghosts were moving more purposefully now that they were out of sight of their own village. The sky was as dark as if a mighty storm were threatening, but there was none of the electric tension that comes ahead of a storm. The ghosts walked on steadily, and the road ran straight ahead across a landscape that was almost featureless.

From time to time one of them would glance at Will or Lyra, or at the brilliant dragonfly and its rider, as if they were curious. Finally the oldest man said:

"You, you boy and girl. You ain't dead. You ain't ghosts. What you coming along here for?"

"We came through by accident," Lyra told him before Will could speak. "I don't know how it happened. We were trying to escape from those men, and we just seemed to find ourselves here."

"How will you know when you've got to the place where you've got to go?" said Will.

"I expect we'll be told," said the ghost confidently. "They'll separate out the sinners and the righteous, I dare say. It's no good praying now. It's too late for that now. You should have done that when you were alive. No use now."

It was quite clear which group he expected to be in, and quite clear too that he thought it wouldn't be a big one. The other ghosts heard him uneasily, but he was all the guidance they had, so they followed without arguing.

And on they walked, trudging in silence under a sky that had finally darkened to a dull iron-grey and remained there without getting any darker. The living ones found themselves looking to left and right, above and below, for anything that was bright or lively or joyful, and they were always disappointed until a little spark appeared ahead and raced towards them through the air. It was the chevalier, and Salmakia urged her dragonfly ahead to meet him, with a cry of pleasure.

They conferred, and sped back to the children.

"There's a town ahead," said Tialys. "It looks like a refugee camp, but it's obviously been there for centuries or more. And I think there's a sea or a lake beyond it, but that's covered in mist. I could hear the cries of birds. And there are hundreds of people arriving every minute, from every direction, people like these – ghosts . . ."

The ghosts themselves listened as he spoke, though without much curiosity. They seemed to have settled into a dull trance, and Lyra wanted to shake them, to urge them to struggle and wake up and look around for a way out.

"How are we going to help these people, Will?" she said.

He couldn't even guess. As they moved on, they could see a movement on the horizon to left and right, and ahead of them a dirty-coloured smoke was rising slowly to add its darkness to the dismal air. The movement was people, or ghosts: in lines or pairs or groups or alone, but all empty-handed, hundreds and thousands of men and women and children were drifting over the plain towards the source of the smoke.

The ground was sloping downwards now, and becoming more and more like a rubbish dump. The air was heavy and full of smoke, and of other smells besides: acrid chemicals, decaying vegetable matter, sewage. And the further down they went, the worse it got. There was not a patch of clean soil in sight, and the only plants growing anywhere were rank weeds and coarse greyish grass.

Ahead of them, above the water, was the mist. It rose like a cliff to merge with the gloomy sky, and from somewhere inside it came those bird cries that Tialys had referred to.

Between the waste heaps and the mist, there lay the first town of the dead.

19
LYRA AND HER DEATH

I was angry with my friend:
I told my wrath, my wrath did end.

— WILLIAM BLAKE

HERE AND THERE, fires had been lit among the ruins. The town was a jumble, with no streets, no squares, and no open spaces except where a building had fallen. A few churches or public buildings still stood above the rest, though their roofs were holed or their walls cracked, and in one case a whole portico had crumpled on to its columns. Between the shells of the stone buildings, a mazy clutter of shacks and shanties had been put together out of lengths of roofing timber, beaten-out petrol cans or biscuit tins, torn sheets of polythene, scraps of plywood or hardboard.

The ghosts who had come with them were hurrying towards the town, and from every direction came more of them, so many that they looked like the grains of sand that trickle towards the hole of an hourglass. The ghosts walked straight into the squalid confusion of the town as if they knew exactly where they were going, and Lyra and Will were about to follow them; but then they were stopped.

A figure stepped out of a patched-up doorway and said, "Wait, wait."

A dim light was glowing behind him, and it wasn't easy to make out his features; but they knew he wasn't a ghost. He was like them, alive. He was a thin man who could have been any age, dressed in a drab and tattered business suit, and he was holding a pencil and a sheaf of papers held together with a bulldog clip. The building he'd stepped out of had the look of a customs post on a rarely-visited frontier.

"What is this place?" said Will. "And why can't we go in?"

"You're not dead," said the man wearily. "You have to wait in the holding area. Go further along the road to the left and give these papers to the official at the gate."

"But excuse me, sir," said Lyra, "I hope you don't mind me

asking, but how can we have come this far if we en't dead? Because this *is* the world of the dead, isn't it?"

"It's a suburb of the world of the dead. Sometimes the living come here by mistake, but they have to wait in the holding area before they can go on."

"Wait for how long?"

"Until they die."

Will felt his head swim. He could see Lyra was about to argue, and before she could speak he said, "Can you just explain what happens then? I mean, these ghosts who come here, do they stay in this town for ever?"

"No, no," said the official. "This is just a port of transit. They go on beyond here by boat."

"Where to?" said Will.

"That's not something I can tell you," said the man, and a bitter smile pulled his mouth down at the corners. "You must move along, please. You must go to the holding area."

Will took the papers the man was holding out, and then held Lyra's arm and urged her away.

The dragonflies were flying sluggishly now, and Tialys explained that they needed to rest; so they perched on Will's rucksack, and Lyra let the spies sit on her shoulders. Pantalaimon, leopard-shaped, looked up at them jealously, but he said nothing. They moved along the track, skirting the wretched shanties and the pools of sewage, and watching the never-ending stream of ghosts arriving and passing without hindrance into the town itself.

"We've got to get over the water, like the rest of them," said Will. "And maybe the people in this holding place will tell us how. They don't seem to be angry, anyway, or dangerous. It's strange. And these papers . . ."

They were simply scraps of paper torn from a notebook, with random words scribbled in pencil and crossed out. It was as if these people were playing a game, and waiting to see when the travellers would challenge them or give in and laugh. And yet it all looked so real.

It was getting darker and colder, and time was hard to keep track of. Lyra thought they walked for half an hour, or maybe it was twice as long; the look of the place didn't change. Finally, they reached a little wooden shack like the one they'd stopped at earlier, where a dim bulb glowed on a bare wire over the door.

As they approached, a man dressed much like the other one came out holding a piece of bread and butter in one hand, and without a word looked at their papers and nodded.

He handed them back and was about to go inside when Will said, "Excuse me, where do we go now?"

"Go and find somewhere to stay," said the man, not unkindly. "Just ask. Everybody's waiting, same as you."

He turned away and shut his door against the cold, and the travellers turned down into the heart of the shanty town where the living people had to stay.

It was very much like the main town: shabby little huts, repaired a dozen times, patched with scraps of plastic or corrugated iron, leaning crazily against each other over muddy alleyways. At some places, an electric cable looped down from a bracket and provided enough feeble current to power a naked light bulb or two, strung out over the nearby huts. Most of what light there was, however, came from the fires. Their smoky glow flickered redly over the scraps and tatters of building material, as if they were the last remaining flames of a great conflagration, staying alive out of pure malice.

But as Will and Lyra and the Gallivespians came closer and saw more detail, they picked out several – more – many figures, sitting in the darkness by themselves or leaning against the walls or gathered in small groups, talking quietly.

"Why aren't those people inside?" said Lyra. "It's cold."

"They're not people," said the Lady Salmakia. "They're not even ghosts. They're something else, but I don't know what."

The travellers came to the first group of shacks, which were lit by one of those big weak electric bulbs on a cable swinging slightly in the cold wind, and Will put his hand on the knife at his belt. There was a group of those people-shaped things outside, crouching on their heels and rolling dice, and when the children came near they stood up: five of them, all men, their faces in shadow and their clothes shabby, all silent.

"What is the name of this town?" said Will.

There was no reply. Some of them took a step backwards, and all five moved a little closer together, as if *they* were afraid. Lyra felt her skin crawling, and all the tiny hairs on her arms standing on end, though she couldn't have said why. Inside her shirt, Pantalaimon was shivering and whispering, "No, no, Lyra, no, go away, let's go back, please . . ."

The "people" made no move, and finally Will shrugged and said, "Well, good evening to you anyway," and moved on. They met a similar response from all the other figures they spoke to, and all the time their apprehension grew.

"Will, are they Spectres?" Lyra said quietly. "Are we grown up enough to see Spectres now?"

"I don't think so. If we were, they'd attack us, but they seem to be afraid themselves. I don't know what they are."

A door opened, and light spilled out on the muddy ground. A man – a real man, a human being – stood in the doorway, watching them approach. The little cluster of figures around the door moved back a step or two, as if out of respect, and they saw the man's face: stolid, harmless, and mild.

"Who are you?" he said.

"Travellers," said Will. "We don't know where we are. What is this town?"

"This is the holding area," said the man. "Have you travelled far?"

"A long way, yes, and we're tired," said Will. "Could we buy some food and pay for shelter?"

The man was looking past them, into the dark, and then he came out and looked around further, as if there was someone missing. Then he turned to the strange figures standing by and said:

"Did *you* see any death?"

They shook their heads, and the children heard a murmur of, "No, no, none."

The man turned back. Behind him, in the doorway, there were faces looking out: a woman, two young children, another man. They were all nervous and apprehensive.

"Death?" said Will. "We're not bringing any death."

But that seemed to be the very thing they were worried about, because when Will spoke, there was a soft gasp from the living people, and even the figures outside shrank away a little.

"Excuse me," said Lyra, stepping forward in her best polite way, as if the housekeeper of Jordan College were glaring at her. "I couldn't help noticing, but these gentlemen here, are they dead? I'm sorry for asking, if it's rude, but where we come from it's very unusual, and we never saw anyone like them before. If I'm being impolite I do beg your pardon. But you see, in my world, we have dæmons, everyone has a dæmon, and we'd be shocked if we saw someone without one, just like you're shocked to see us. And now we've been travelling, Will and me – this is Will, and I'm Lyra – I've learned there are some people who don't seem to have dæmons, like Will doesn't, and I was scared till I found out they were just ordinary like me really. So maybe that's why someone from your world might be just a bit sort of nervous when they see us, if you think we're different."

The man said, "Lyra? And Will?"

"Yes, sir," she said humbly.

"Are *those* your dæmons?" he said, pointing to the spies on her shoulder.

"No," said Lyra, and she was tempted to say, "They're our servants," but she felt Will would have thought that a bad idea; so she said, "They're our friends, the Chevalier Tialys and the Lady Salmakia, very distinguished and wise people who are travelling with us. Oh, and this is my dæmon," she said, taking mouse-Pantalaimon out of her pocket. "You see, we're harmless, we promise we won't hurt you. And we do need food and shelter. We'll move on tomorrow. Honest."

Everyone waited. The man's nervousness was soothed a little by her humble tone, and the spies had the good sense to look modest and harmless. After a pause the man said:

"Well, though it's strange, I suppose these are strange times . . . Come in then, be welcome . . ."

The figures outside nodded, one or two of them gave little bows, and they stood aside respectfully as Will and Lyra walked into the warmth and light. The man closed the door behind them and hooked a wire over a nail to keep it shut.

It was a single room, lit by a naphtha lamp on the table, and

clean but shabby. The plywood walls were decorated with pictures cut from film-star magazines, and with a pattern made with
fingerprints of soot. There was an iron stove against one wall,
with a clothes-horse in front of it where some dingy shirts were
steaming, and on a dressing-table, there was a shrine of plastic
flowers, sea-shells, coloured scent bottles, and other gaudy bits
and pieces, all surrounding the picture of a jaunty skeleton with
a top hat and dark glasses.

The shanty was crowded: as well as the man and a woman and
the two young children, there was a baby in a crib, an older man,
and in one corner, in a heap of blankets, a very old woman was
lying and watching everything with glittering eyes in a face as
wrinkled as the blankets. As Lyra looked at her, she had a shock:
the blankets stirred, and a very thin arm emerged, in a black
sleeve, and then another face, a man's, so ancient it was almost a
skeleton. In fact he looked more like the skeleton in the picture
than like a living human being; and then Will too noticed, and all
the travellers together realized that he was one of those shadowy
polite figures like the ones outside. And all of them felt as non-
plussed as the man had been when he'd first seen them.

In fact, all the people in the crowded little shack – all except
the baby, who was asleep – were at a loss for words. It was Lyra
who found her voice first.

"That's very kind of you," she said, "thank you, good evening, we're very pleased to be here. And like I said, we're sorry to
have arrived without any death, if that's the normal way of
things. But we won't disturb you any more than we have to. You
see, we're looking for the land of the dead, and that's how we
happened to come here. But we don't know where it is, or
whether this is part of it, or how to get there, or what. So if you
can tell us anything about it, we'll be very grateful."

The people in the shack were still staring, but Lyra's words
eased the atmosphere a little, and the woman invited them to sit
at the table, drawing out a bench. Will and Lyra lifted the sleeping dragonflies up to a shelf in a dark corner, where Tialys said
they would rest till daylight, and then the Gallivespians joined
them on the table.

The woman had been preparing a dish of stew, and she peeled

a couple of potatoes and cut them into it to make it go further, urging her husband to offer the travellers some other refreshment while it cooked. He brought out a bottle of clear and pungent spirit that smelt to Lyra like the gyptians' jenniver, and the two spies accepted a glass into which they dipped little vessels of their own.

Lyra would have expected the family to stare most at the Galli-vespians, but their curiosity was directed just as much, she thought, at her and Will. She didn't wait long to ask why.

"You're the first people we ever saw without a death," said the man, whose name, they'd learned, was Peter. "Since we come here, that is. We're like you, we come here before we was dead, by some chance or accident. We got to wait till our death tells us it's time."

"Your *death* tells you?" said Lyra.

"Yes. What we found out when we come here, oh, long ago for most of us, we found we all brought our deaths with us. This is where we found out. We had 'em all the time, and we never knew. See, everyone has a death. It goes everywhere with 'em, all their life long, right close by. Our deaths, they're outside, taking the air; they'll come in by and by. Granny's death, he's there with her, he's close to her, very close."

"Doesn't it scare you, having your death close by all the time?" said Lyra.

"Why ever would it? If he's there, you can keep an eye on him. I'd be a lot more nervous not knowing where he was."

"And everyone has their own death?" said Will, marvelling.

"Why yes, the moment you're born, your death comes into the world with you, and it's your death that takes you out."

"Ah," said Lyra, "that's what we need to know, because we're trying to find the land of the dead, and we don't know how to get there. Where do we go then, when we die?"

"Your death taps you on the shoulder, or takes your hand, and says, come along o' me, it's time. It might happen when you're sick with a fever, or when you choke on a piece of dry bread, or when you fall off a high building; in the middle of your pain and travail, your death comes to you kindly and says easy now, easy, child, you come along o' me, and you go with them in a boat out across the lake into the mist. What happens there, no one knows. No one's ever come back."

The woman told a child to call the deaths in, and he scampered to the door and spoke to them. Will and Lyra watched in wonder, and the Gallivespians drew closer together, as the deaths – one for each of the family – came in through the door: pale, unremarkable figures in shabby clothes, just drab and quiet and dull.

"These are your deaths?" said Tialys.

"Indeed, sir," said Peter.

"Do you know when they'll tell you it's time to go?"

"No. But you know they're close by, and that's a comfort."

Tialys said nothing, but it was clear that he felt it would be anything but a comfort. The deaths stood politely along the wall, and it was strange to see how little space they took up, and to find how little notice they attracted. Lyra and Will soon found themselves ignoring them altogether, though Will thought: those men I killed – their deaths were close beside them all the time – they didn't know, and I didn't know . . .

The woman, Martha, dished up the stew on to chipped enamel plates, and put some in a bowl for the deaths to pass about among themselves. They didn't eat, but the good smell kept them content. Presently all the family and their guests were eating hungrily, and Peter asked the children where they'd come from, and what their world was like.

"I'll tell you all about it," said Lyra.

As she said that, as she took charge, part of her felt a little stream of pleasure rising upwards in her breast like the bubbles in champagne. And she knew Will was watching, and she was happy that he could see her doing what she was best at, doing it for him and for all of them.

She started by telling about her parents. They were a duke and duchess, very important and wealthy, who had been cheated out of their estate by a political enemy and thrown into prison. But they managed to escape by climbing down a rope with the baby Lyra in her father's arms, and they regained the family fortune only to be attacked and murdered by outlaws. Lyra would have been killed as well, and roasted and eaten, had not Will rescued her just in time and taken her back to the wolves, in the forest where he was being brought up as one of them. He had fallen overboard as a baby from the side of his father's ship and been washed up on a desolate shore, where a female wolf had suckled him and kept him alive.

The people ate up this nonsense with placid credulity, and even the deaths crowded close to listen, perching on the bench or lying on the floor close by, gazing at her with their mild and courteous faces as she spun out the tale of her life with Will in the forest.

He and Lyra stayed with the wolves for a while, and then moved to Oxford to work in the kitchens of Jordan College. There they met Roger, and when Jordan was attacked by the brick-burners who lived in the Claybeds, they had to escape in a hurry; so she and Will and Roger captured a gyptian narrow-boat and sailed it all the way down the Thames, nearly getting caught at Abingdon Lock, and then they'd been sunk by the Wapping pirates and had to swim for safety to a three-masted clipper just setting off for Hang Chow in Cathay to trade for tea.

And on the clipper they'd met the Gallivespians, who were strangers from the Moon, blown down to the earth by a fierce gale out of the Milky Way. They'd taken refuge in the crow's nest, and she and Will and Roger used to take it in turns going up there to see them, only one day Roger lost his footing and plunged down into Davy Jones's Locker.

They tried to persuade the captain to turn the ship round and look for him, but he was a hard fierce man only interested in the profit he'd make by getting to Cathay quickly, and he clapped them in irons. But the Gallivespians brought them a file, and . . .

And so on. From time to time she'd turn to Will or the spies for confirmation, and Salmakia would add a detail or two, or Will would nod, and the story wound itself up to the point where the children and their friends from the Moon had to find their way to the land of the dead in order to learn, from her parents, the secret of where the family fortune had been buried.

"And if we knew our deaths, in our land," she said, "like you do here, it would be easier, probably; but I think we're really lucky to find our way here, so's we could get your advice. And thank you very much for being so kind and listening, and for giving us this meal, it was really nice.

"But what we need now, you see, or in the morning maybe, is we need to find a way out across the water where the dead people go, and see if we can get there too. Is there any boats we could sort of hire?"

They looked doubtful. The children, flushed with tiredness, looked with sleepy eyes from one grown-up to the other, but no one could suggest where they could find a boat.

Then came a voice that hadn't spoken before. From the depths of the bedclothes in the corner came a dry-cracked-nasal tone – not a woman's voice – not a living voice: it was the voice of the grandmother's death.

"The only way you'll cross the lake and go to the land of the dead," he said, and he was leaning up on his elbow, pointing with a skinny finger at Lyra, "is with your own deaths. You must call up your own deaths. I have heard of people like you, who keep their deaths at bay. You don't like them, and out of courtesy they stay out of sight. But they're not far off. Whenever you turn your head, your deaths dodge behind you. Wherever you look, they hide. They can hide in a teacup. Or in a dewdrop. Or in a breath of wind. Not like me and old Magda here," he said, and he pinched her withered cheek, and she pushed his hand away. "We live together in kindness and friendship. That's the answer, that's it, that's what you've got to do, say welcome, make friends, be kind, invite your deaths to come close to you, and see what you can get them to agree to."

His words fell into Lyra's mind like heavy stones, and Will, too, felt the deadly weight of them.

"How should we do that?" he said.

"You've only got to wish for it, and the thing is done."

"Wait," said Tialys.

Every eye turned to him, and those deaths lying on the floor sat up to turn their blank mild faces to his tiny passionate one. He was standing close by Salmakia, his hand on her shoulder. Lyra could see what he was thinking: he was going to say that this had gone too far, they must turn back, they were taking this foolishness to irresponsible lengths.

So she stepped in. "Excuse me," she said to the man Peter, "but me and our friend the chevalier, we've got to go outside for a minute, because he needs to talk to his friends in the Moon through my special instrument. We won't be long."

And she picked him up carefully, avoiding his spurs, and took him outside into the dark, where a loose piece of corrugated iron roofing was banging in the cold wind with a melancholy sound.

"You must stop," he said, as she set him on an upturned oil drum, in the feeble light of one of those electric bulbs that swung on its cable overhead. "This is far enough. No more."

"But we made an agreement," Lyra said.

"No, no. Not to these lengths."

"All right. Leave us. You fly on back. Will can cut a window into your world, or any world you like, and you can fly through and be safe, that's all right, we don't mind."

"Do you realize what you're doing?"

"Yes."

"You don't. You're a thoughtless irresponsible lying child. Fantasy comes so easily to you that your whole nature is riddled with dishonesty, and you don't even admit the truth when it stares you in the face. Well, if you can't see it, I'll tell you plainly: you cannot, you must not risk your death. You must come back with us now. I'll call Lord Asriel and we can be safe in the fortress in hours."

Lyra felt a great sob of rage building up in her chest, and stamped her foot, unable to keep still.

"You *don't know*," she cried, "you just don't know what I got in my head or my heart, do you? I don't know if you people ever have children, maybe you lay *eggs* or something, I wouldn't be surprised, because you're not kind, you're not generous, you're not considerate – you're not *cruel*, even – that would be *better*, if you were cruel, because it'd mean you took us serious, you didn't just go along with us when it suited you . . . Oh, I can't trust you at all now! You said you'd help and we'd do it together, and now you want to stop us – *you're* the dishonest one, Tialys!"

"I wouldn't let a child of my own speak to me in the insolent high-handed way you're speaking, Lyra – why I haven't punished you before –"

"Then go ahead! Punish me, since you *can*! Take your bloody spurs and dig 'em in hard, go on! Here's my hand – do it! You got no idea what's in my heart, you proud selfish creature – you got no notion how I feel sad and wicked and sorry about my friend Roger – you kill people just like *that*," snapping her finger, "they don't matter to you – but it's a torment and a sorrow to me that I never said goodbye to my friend Roger, and I want to say sorry and make it as good as I can – you'd never understand that, for all your pride, for all your grown-up cleverness – and if I have to *die* to do what's proper, then I *will*, and be happy while I do. I seen worse than that. So you want to kill me, you hard man, you strong man, you poison-bearer, you chevalier, you do it, go on, kill me. Then me and Roger can play in the land of the dead for ever, and laugh at you, you pitiful thing."

What Tialys might have done then wasn't hard to see, for he was ablaze from head to foot with a passionate anger, shaking with it; but he didn't have time to move before a voice spoke behind Lyra, and they both felt a chill fall over them. Lyra turned around, knowing what she'd see and dreading it despite her bravado.

The death stood very close, smiling kindly, his face exactly like those of all the others she'd seen; but this was hers, her very own death, and Pantalaimon at her breast howled and shivered, and his ermine-shape flowed up around her neck and tried to push her away from the death. But by doing that, he only pushed himself closer, and realizing it he shrank back towards her again, to her warm throat and the strong pulse of her heart.

Lyra clutched him to her and faced the death directly. She couldn't remember what he'd said, and out of the corner of her eye she could see Tialys quickly preparing the lodestone resonator, busy.

"You're my death, en't you?" she said.

"Yes, my dear," he said.

"You en't going to take me yet, are you?"

"You wanted me. I am always here."

"Yes, but . . . I *did*, yes, but . . . I want to go to the land of the dead, that's true. But not to die. I don't want to die. I love being alive, and I love my dæmon, and . . . Dæmons don't go down there, do they? I seen 'em vanish and just go out like candles when people die. Do they have dæmons in the land of the dead?"

"No," he said. "Your dæmon vanishes into the air, and you vanish under the ground."

"Then I want to take my dæmon with me when I go to the land of the dead," she said firmly. "And I want to come back again. Has it ever been known, for people to do that?"

"Not for many, many ages. Eventually, child, you will come to the land of the dead with no effort, no risk, a safe calm journey, in the company of your own death, your special devoted friend, who's been beside you every moment of your life, who knows you better than yourself –"

"But *Pantalaimon* is my special and devoted friend! I don't know you, Death, I know Pan and I love Pan and if he ever – if we ever –"

The death was nodding. He seemed interested and kindly, but she couldn't for a moment forget what he was: her very own death, and so close.

"*I know* it'll be an effort to go on now," she said more steadily, "and dangerous, but I want to, Death, I do truly. And so does Will. We both had people taken away too soon, and we need to make amends, at least I do."

"Everyone wishes they could speak again to those who've gone to the land of the dead. Why should there be an exception for you?"

"Because," she began, lying, "because there's something I've got to do there, not just seeing my friend Roger, something else. It was a task put on me by an angel, and no one else can do it, only me. It's too important to wait till I die in the natural way, it's got to be done now. See, the angel *commanded* me. That's why we came here, me and Will. We *got* to."

Behind her, Tialys put away his instrument, and sat watching the child plead with her own death to be taken where no one should go.

The death scratched his head and held up his hands, but nothing could stop Lyra's words, nothing could deflect her desire, not even fear: she'd seen worse than death, she claimed, and she had, too.

So eventually her death said:

"If nothing can put you off, then all I can say is, come with me, and I will take you there, into the land of the dead. I'll be your guide. I can show you the way in, but as for getting out again, you'll have to manage by yourself."

"And my friends," said Lyra. "My friend Will and the others."

"Lyra," said Tialys, "against every instinct, we'll go with you. I was angry with you a minute ago. But you make it hard . . ."

Lyra knew that this was a time to conciliate, and she was happy to do that, having got her way.

"Yes," she said, "I *am* sorry, Tialys, but if you hadn't got angry we'd never have found this gentleman to guide us. So I'm glad you were here, you and the lady, I'm really grateful to you for being with us."

So Lyra persuaded her own death to guide her and the others into the land where Roger had gone, and Will's father, and Tony Makarios, and so many others; and her death told her to go down to the jetty when the first light came to the sky, and prepare to leave.

But Pantalaimon was trembling and shivering, and nothing Lyra could do could soothe him into stillness, or quieten the soft little moan he couldn't help uttering. So her sleep was broken and shallow, on the floor of the shack with all the other sleepers, and her death sat watchfully beside her.

20

CLIMBING

I gained it so –
By Climbing slow –
By Catching at the Twigs that grow
Between the Bliss – and me –

– EMILY DICKINSON

THE MULEFA MADE many kinds of rope and cord, and Mary Malone spent a morning inspecting and testing the ones Atal's family had in their stores before choosing what she wanted. The principle of twisting and winding hadn't caught on in their world, so all the cords and ropes were braided; but they were strong and flexible, and Mary soon found exactly the sort she wanted.

What are you doing? said Atal.

The mulefa had no term for *climb*, so Mary had to do a lot of gesturing and roundabout explaining. Atal was horrified.

To go into the high part of the trees?

I must see what is happening, Mary explained. *Now you can help me prepare the rope.*

Once in California Mary had met a mathematician who spent every weekend climbing among the trees. Mary had done a little rock-climbing, and she'd listened avidly as he had talked about the techniques and equipment, and had decided to try it herself as soon as she had the chance. Of course, she'd never expected to be climbing trees in another universe, and climbing solo didn't greatly appeal either, but there was no choice about that. What she could do was make it as safe as possible beforehand.

She took a coil long enough to reach over one of the branches of a high tree and back down to the ground, and strong enough to bear several times her weight. Then she cut a large number of short pieces of a smaller but very tough cord and made slings with them: short loops tied with a fisherman's knot, which could make hand and footholds when she tied them to the main line.

Then there was the problem of getting the rope over the branch in the first place. An hour or two's experimenting with some fine tough cord and a length of springy branch produced a bow; the Swiss Army knife cut some arrows, with stiff leaves in place of feathers to stabilize them in flight; and finally, after a day's work, Mary was ready to begin. But the sun was setting, and her hands were tired, and she ate and slept, preoccupied, while the mulefa discussed her endlessly in their quiet musical whispers.

First thing in the morning, she set off to shoot the arrow over a branch. Some of the mulefa gathered to watch, anxious for her safety. Climbing was so alien to creatures with wheels that the very thought of it horrified them.

Privately, Mary knew how they felt. She swallowed her nervousness, and tied an end of the thinnest, lightest line to one of her arrows, and sent it flying upwards from the bow.

She lost the first arrow: it stuck in the bark part way up, and wouldn't come out. She lost the second because, although it did clear the branch, it didn't fall far enough to reach the ground on the other side, and pulling it back, she caught it and snapped it. The long line fell back attached to the broken shaft, and she tried again with the third and last, and this time it worked.

Pulling carefully and steadily so as not to snag the line and break it, she hauled the prepared rope up and over until both ends were on the ground. Then she tied them both securely to a massive buttress of one of the roots, as thick around as her own hips, so it should be fairly solid, she thought. It had better be. What she couldn't tell from the ground, of course, was what kind of branch the whole thing, including her, would be depending on. Unlike climbing on rock, where you could fasten the rope to pitons on the cliff-face every few metres so you never had far to fall, this business involved one very long free length of rope, and one very long fall if anything went wrong. To make herself a little more secure, she braided together three small ropes into a harness, and passed it around both hanging ends of the main rope with a loose knot that she could tighten the moment she began to slip.

Mary put her foot in the first sling, and began to climb.

* * *

She reached the canopy in less time than she'd anticipated. The climbing was straightforward, the rope was kindly on her hands, and although she hadn't wanted to think about the problem of getting on top of the first branch, she found that the deep fissures in the bark helped her to get a solid purchase and feel secure. In fact, only fifteen minutes after she'd left the ground, she was standing on the first branch and planning her route to the next.

She had brought two more coils of rope with her, intending to make a web of fixed lines to serve in place of the pitons and anchors and "friends" and other hardware she relied on when climbing a rock face. Tying them in place took her some minutes more, and once she'd secured herself, she chose what looked like the most promising branch, coiled her spare rope again, and set off.

After ten minutes' careful climbing she found herself right in the thickest part of the canopy. She could reach the long leaves and run them through her hands; she found flower after flower, off-white and absurdly small, each growing the little coin-sized thing that would later become one of those great iron-hard seed-pods.

She reached a comfortable spot where three branches forked, tied the rope securely, fastened her harness, and rested.

Through the gaps in the leaves she could see the blue sea, clear and sparkling as far as the horizon; and in the other direction over her right shoulder she could see the succession of low rises in the gold-brown prairie, laced across by the black highways.

There was a light breeze, which lifted a faint scent out of the flowers and rustled the stiff leaves, and Mary imagined a huge dim benevolence holding her up, like a pair of giant hands. As she lay in the fork of the great branches, she felt a kind of bliss she had only felt once before; and that was not when she made her vows as a nun.

Eventually she was brought back to her normal state of mind by cramp in her right ankle, which was resting awkwardly in the crook of the fork. She eased it away and turned her attention to the task, still dizzy from the sense of oceanic gladness that surrounded her.

She'd explained to the mulefa how she had to hold the sap-lacquer plates a hand-span apart in order to see the sraf; and at once they'd seen the problem and made a short tube of bamboo, fixing the amber-coloured plates at each end like a telescope. This spyglass was tucked in her breast pocket, and she took it out now. When she looked through it, she saw those drifting golden sparkles, the sraf, the Shadows, Lyra's Dust, like a vast cloud of tiny beings floating through the wind. For the most part they drifted randomly like dust motes in a shaft of sunlight, or molecules in a glass of water.

For the most part.

But the longer she looked, the more she began to see another kind of motion. Underlying the random drifting was a deeper, slower, universal movement, out from the land towards the sea.

Well, that was curious. Securing herself to one of her fixed ropes, she crawled out along a horizontal branch, looking closely at all the flowerheads she could find. And presently she began to see what was happening. She watched and waited till she was perfectly sure, and then began the careful, lengthy, strenuous process of climbing down.

Mary found the mulefa in a fearful state, having suffered a thousand anxieties for their friend so far off the ground.

Atal was especially relieved, and touched her nervously all over with her trunk, uttering gentle whinnies of pleasure to find her safe, and carrying her swiftly down to the settlement along with a dozen or so others.

As soon as they came over the brow of the hill, the call went out among those in the village, and by the time they reached the speaking ground, the throng was so thick that Mary guessed there were many visitors from elsewhere, come to hear what she said. She wished she had better news for them.

The old zalif, Sattamax, mounted the platform and welcomed her warmly, and she responded with all the mulefa-courtesy she could remember. As soon as the greetings were over, she began to speak.

Haltingly and with many roundabout phrasings, she said:

My good friends, I have been into the high canopy of your trees and looked closely at the growing leaves and the young flowers and the seed-pods.

I could see that there is a current of sraf high in the tree-tops, she went on, *and it moves against the wind. The air is moving inland off the sea, but the sraf is moving slowly against it. Can you see that from the ground? Because I could not.*

No, said Sattamax. *That is the first we ever heard about that.*

Well, she continued, *the trees are filtering the sraf as it moves through them, and some of it is attracted to the flowers. I could see it happening: the flowers are turned upwards, and if the sraf were falling straight down it would enter their petals and fertilize them like pollen from the stars.*

But the sraf isn't falling down, it's moving out towards the sea. When a flower happens to be facing the land, the sraf can enter it. That's why there are still some seed-pods growing. But most of them face upwards, and the sraf just drifts past without entering. The flowers must have evolved like that because in the past all the sraf fell straight down. Something has happened to the sraf, not to the trees. And you can only see that current from high up, which is why you never knew about it.

So if you want to save the trees, and mulefa life, we must find out why the sraf is doing that. I can't think of a way yet, but I will try.

She saw many of them craning to look upwards at this drift of Dust. But from the ground you couldn't see it: she looked herself through the spyglass, but the dense blue of the sky was all she could see.

They spoke for a long time, trying to recall any mention of the sraf-wind among their legends and histories, but there was none. All they had ever known was that sraf came from the stars, as it had always done.

Finally they asked if she had any more ideas, and she said:

I need to make more observations. I need to find out whether the wind goes always in that direction or whether it alters like the air-currents during the day and the night. So I need to spend more time in the tree-tops, and sleep up there and observe at night. I will need your help to build a platform of some kind so I can sleep safely. But we do need more observations.

The mulefa, practical and anxious to find out, offered at once to build her whatever she needed. They knew the techniques of using pulleys and tackle, and presently one suggested a way of lifting Mary easily into the canopy so as to save her the dangerous labour of climbing.

Glad to have something to do, they set about gathering materials at once, braiding and tying and lashing spars and ropes and lines under her guidance, and assembling everything she needed for a tree-top observation platform.

After speaking to the old couple by the olive grove, Father Gomez lost the track. He spent several days searching and enquiring in every direction round about, but the woman seemed to have vanished completely.

He would never have given up, although it was discouraging; the crucifix around his neck and the rifle at his back were twin tokens of his absolute determination to complete the task.

But it would have taken him much longer, if it hadn't been for a difference in the weather. In the world he was in, it was hot and dry, and he was increasingly thirsty; and seeing a wet patch of rock at the top of a scree, he climbed up to see if there was a spring there. There wasn't, but in the world of the wheel-pod trees, there had just been a shower of rain; and so it was that he discovered the window, and found where Mary had gone.

21

THE HARPIES

I hate things all fiction . . . There should always be
some foundation of fact

— BYRON

LYRA AND WILL each awoke with a heavy dread: it was like being a condemned prisoner on the morning fixed for the execution. Tialys and Salmakia were attending to their dragonflies, bringing them moths lassoed near the anbaric lamp over the oil-drum outside, flies cut from spider-webs, and water in a tin plate. When she saw the expression on Lyra's face and the way that Pantalaimon, mouse-formed, was pressing himself close to her breast, the Lady Salmakia left what she was doing to come and speak with her. Will, meanwhile, left the hut to walk about outside.

"You can still decide differently," said Salmakia.

"No, we can't. We decided already," said Lyra, stubborn and fearful at once.

"And if we don't come back?"

"*You* don't have to come," Lyra pointed out.

"We're not going to abandon you."

"Then what if *you* don't come back?"

"We shall have died doing something important."

Lyra was silent. She hadn't really looked at the lady before; but she could see her very clearly now, in the smoky light of the naphtha lamp, standing on the table just an arm's length away. Her face was calm and kindly, not beautiful, not pretty, but the very sort of face you would be glad to see if you were ill or unhappy or frightened. Her voice was low and expressive, with a current of laughter and happiness under the clear surface. In all the life she could remember Lyra had never been read to in bed; no one had told her stories or sung nursery rhymes with her before kissing her and putting out the light. But she suddenly thought now that if ever there was a voice that would lap you in safety and warm you with love, it would be a voice like the Lady

Salmakia's, and she felt a wish in her heart to have a child of her own, to lull and soothe and sing to, one day, in a voice like that.

"Well," Lyra said, and found her throat choked, so she swallowed and shrugged.

"We'll see," said the lady, and turned back.

Once they had eaten the thin dry bread and drunk the bitter tea which was all the people had to offer them, they thanked their hosts, took their rucksacks and set off through the shanty town for the lake shore. Lyra looked around for her death, and sure enough, there he was, walking politely a little way ahead; but he didn't want to come closer, though he kept looking back to see they were following.

The day was overhung with a gloomy mist. It was more like dusk than daylight, and wraiths and streamers of the fog rose dismally from puddles in the road, or clung like forlorn lovers to the anbaric cables overhead. They saw no people, and few deaths, but the dragonflies skimmed through the damp air as if they were sewing it all together with invisible threads, and it was a delight to the eyes to watch their bright colours flashing back and forth.

Before long they had reached the edge of the settlement, and made their way beside a sluggish stream through bare-twigged scrubby bushes. Occasionally they would hear a harsh croak or a splash as some amphibian was disturbed, but the only creature they saw was a toad as big as Will's foot, which could only flop in a pain-filled sideways heave as if it were horribly injured. It lay across the path, trying to move out of the way and looking at them as if it knew they meant to hurt it.

"It would be merciful to kill it," said Tialys.

"How do you know?" said Lyra. "It might still like being alive, in spite of everything."

"If we killed it, we'd be taking it with us," said Will. "It wants to stay here. I've killed enough living things. Even a filthy stagnant pool might be better than being dead."

"But if it's in pain?" said Tialys.

"If it could tell us, we'd know. But since it can't, I'm not going to kill it. That would be considering our feelings rather than the toad's."

They moved on. Before long the changing sound their foot-steps made told them that there was an openness nearby, although the mist was even thicker. Pantalaimon was a lemur, with the big-gest eyes he could manage, clinging to Lyra's shoulder, pressing himself into her fog-pearled hair, peering all round and seeing no more than she did. And still he was trembling and trembling.

Suddenly they all heard a little wave breaking. It was quiet, but it was very close by. The dragonflies returned with their riders to the children, and Pantalaimon crept into Lyra's breast as she and Will moved closer together, treading carefully along the slimy path.

And then they were at the shore. The oily, scummy water lay still in front of them, an occasional ripple breaking languidly on the pebbles.

The path turned to the left, and a little way along, more like a thickening of the mist than a solid object, a wooden jetty stood crazily out over the water. The piles were decayed and the planks were green with slime, and there was nothing else; nothing beyond it; the path ended where the jetty began, and where the jetty ended, the mist began. Lyra's death, having guided them there, bowed to her and stepped into the fog and vanished before she could ask him what to do next.

"Listen," said Will.

There was a slow sound out on the invisible water: a creak of wood and a quiet regular splash. Will put his hand on the knife at his belt, and moved forward carefully on to the rotting planks. Lyra followed close behind. The dragonflies perched on the two weed-covered mooring posts, looking like heraldic guardians, and the children stood at the end of the jetty, pressing their open eyes against the mist, and having to brush their lashes free of the drops that settled on them. The only sound was that slow creak and splash that was getting closer and closer.

"Don't let's go!" Pantalaimon whispered.

"Got to," Lyra whispered back.

She looked at Will. His face was set hard and grim and eager: he wouldn't turn aside. And the Gallivespians, Tialys on Will's shoulder, Salmakia on Lyra's, were calm and watchful. The dragonflies' wings were pearled with mist, like cobwebs, and from time to time they'd beat them quickly to clear them, because the drops must make them heavy, Lyra thought. She hoped there would be food for them in the land of the dead.

Then suddenly there was the boat.

It was an ancient rowing boat, battered, patched, rotting; and the figure rowing it was aged beyond age, huddled in a robe of sacking bound with string, crippled and bent, his bony hands crooked permanently around the oar-handles, and his moist pale eyes sunk deep among folds and wrinkles of grey skin.

He let go of an oar and reached his crooked hand up to the iron ring set in the post at the corner of the jetty. With the other hand he moved the oar to bring the boat right up against the planks.

There was no need to speak. Will got in first, and then Lyra came forward to step down too.

But the boatman held up his hand.

"Not him," he said, in a harsh whisper.

"Not who?"

"Not him."

He extended a yellow-grey finger, pointing directly at Pantalaimon, whose red-brown stoat-form immediately became ermine-white.

"But he *is* me!" Lyra said.

"If you come, he must stay."

"But we can't! We'd die!"

"Isn't that what you want?"

And then for the first time Lyra truly realized what she was doing. This was the real consequence. She stood aghast, trembling, and clutched her dear dæmon so tightly that he whimpered in pain.

"*They* . . ." said Lyra helplessly, then stopped: it wasn't fair to point out that the other three didn't have to give anything up.

Will was watching her anxiously. She looked all around, at the lake, at the jetty, at the rough path, the stagnant puddles, the dead and sodden bushes . . . Her Pan, alone here: how could he live without her? He was shaking inside her shirt, against her bare flesh, his fur needing her warmth. Impossible! Never!

"He must stay here if you are to come," the boatman said again.

The Lady Salmakia flicked the rein, and her dragonfly skimmed away from Lyra's shoulder to land on the gunwale of the boat, where Tialys joined her. They said something to the boatman. Lyra watched as a condemned prisoner watches the stir at the back of the courtroom that might be a messenger with a pardon.

The boatman bent to listen, and then shook his head.

"No," he said. "If she comes, he has to stay."

Will said, "That's not right. We don't have to leave part of ourselves behind. Why should Lyra?"

"Oh, but you do," said the boatman. "It's her misfortune that she can see and talk to the part she must leave. You will not know until you are on the water, and then it will be too late. But you all have to leave that part of yourselves here. There is no passage to the land of the dead for such as him."

No, Lyra thought, and Pantalaimon thought with her: *We didn't go through Bolvangar for this, no; how will we ever find each other again?*

And she looked back again at the foul and dismal shore, so bleak and blasted with disease and poison, and thought of her dear Pan waiting there alone, her heart's companion, watching her disappear into the mist, and she fell into a storm of weeping. Her passionate sobs didn't echo, because the mist muffled them, but all along the shore in innumerable ponds and shallows, in wretched broken tree stumps, the damaged creatures that lurked there heard her full-hearted cry and drew themselves a little closer to the ground, afraid of such passion.

"If he could come —" cried Will, desperate to end her grief, but the boatman shook his head.

"He can come in the boat, but if he does, the boat stays here," he said.

"But how will she find him again?"

"I don't know."

"When we leave, will we come back this way?"

"Leave?"

"We're going to come back. We're going to the land of the dead and we are going to come back."

"Not this way."

"Then some other way, but we will!"

"I have taken millions, and none came back."

"Then we shall be the first. We'll find our way out. And since we're going to do that, be kind, boatman, be compassionate, let her take her dæmon!"

"No," he said and shook his ancient head. "It's not a rule you can break. It's a law like this one . . ." He leant over the side and cupped a handful of water, and then tilted his hand so it ran out again. "The law that makes the water fall back into the lake, it's a law like that. I can't tilt my hand and make the water fly upwards. No more can I take her dæmon to the land of the dead. Whether or not *she* comes, he must stay."

Lyra could see nothing: her face was buried in Pantalaimon's cat-fur. But Will saw Tialys dismount from his dragonfly and prepare to spring at the boatman, and he half-agreed with the spy's intention: but the old man had seen him, and turned his ancient head to say:

"How many ages do you think I've been ferrying people to the land of the dead? D'you think if anything could hurt me, it wouldn't have happened already? D'you think the people I take come with me gladly? They struggle and cry, they try to bribe me, they threaten and fight; nothing works. You can't hurt me, sting as you will. Better comfort the child; she's coming; take no notice of me."

Will could hardly watch. Lyra was doing the cruellest thing she had ever done, hating herself, hating the deed, suffering for Pan and with Pan and because of Pan; trying to put him down on the cold path, disengaging his cat-claws from her clothes, weeping, weeping. Will closed his ears: the sound was too unhappy to bear. Time after time she pushed her dæmon away, and still he cried and tried to cling.

She *could* turn back.

She could say no, this is a bad idea, we mustn't do it.

She could be true to the heart-deep, life-deep bond linking her to Pantalaimon, she could put that first, she could push the rest out of her mind –

But she couldn't.

"Pan, no one's done this before," she whispered shiveringly, "but Will says we're coming back and I *swear*, Pan, I love you, I *swear* we're coming back – I will – take care, my dear – you'll be safe – we will come back, and if I have to spend every minute of my life finding you again I will, I won't stop, I won't rest, I won't – oh Pan – dear Pan – I've got to, I've got to . . ."

And she pushed him away, so that he crouched bitter and cold and frightened on the muddy ground.

What animal he was now, Will could hardly tell. He seemed to be so young, a cub, a puppy, something helpless and beaten, a creature so sunk in misery that it was more misery than creature. His eyes never left Lyra's face, and Will could see her making herself not look away, not avoid the guilt, and he admired her honesty and her courage at the same time as he was wrenched with the shock of their parting. There were so many vivid currents of feeling between them that the very air felt electric to him.

And Pantalaimon didn't say, "Why?", because he knew; and he didn't ask whether Lyra loved Roger more than him, because he knew the true answer to that, too. And he knew that if he spoke, she wouldn't be able to resist; so the dæmon held himself quiet so as not to distress the human who was abandoning him, and now they were both pretending that it wouldn't hurt, it wouldn't be long before they were together again, it was all for the best. But Will knew that the little girl was tearing her heart out of her breast.

Then she stepped down into the boat. She was so light that it barely rocked at all. She sat beside Will, and her eyes never left Pantalaimon, who stood trembling at the shore end of the jetty; but as the boatman let go of the iron ring and swung his oars out to pull the boat away, the little dog-dæmon trotted helplessly out to the very end, his claws clicking softly on the soft planks, and stood watching, just watching, as the boat drew away and the jetty faded and vanished in the mist.

Then Lyra gave a cry so passionate that even in that muffled mist-hung world it raised an echo, but of course it wasn't an echo, it was the other part of her crying in turn from the land of the living as Lyra moved away into the land of the dead.

"My *heart*, Will . . ." she groaned, and clung to him, her wet face contorted with pain.

And thus the prophecy that the Master of Jordan College had made to the Librarian, that Lyra would make a great betrayal and it would hurt her terribly, was fulfilled.

But Will too found an agony building inside him, and through the pain he saw that the two Gallivespians, clinging together just as he and Lyra were doing, were moved by the same anguish.

Part of it was physical. It felt as if an iron hand had gripped his heart and was pulling it out between his ribs, so that he pressed his hands to the place and vainly tried to hold it in. It was far deeper and far worse than the pain of losing his fingers. But it was mental, too: something secret and private was being dragged into the open where it had no wish to be, and Will was nearly overcome by a mixture of pain and shame and fear and self-reproach, because he himself had caused it.

And it was worse than that. It was as if he'd said, "No, don't kill me, I'm frightened; kill my mother instead; she doesn't matter, I don't love her," and as if she'd heard him say it, and pretended she hadn't so as to spare his feelings, and offered herself in his place anyway because of her love for him. He felt as bad as that. There was nothing worse to feel.

So Will knew that all those things were part of having a dæmon, and that whatever his dæmon was, she too was left behind, with Pantalaimon, on that poisoned and desolate shore. The thought came to Will and Lyra at the same moment, and they exchanged a tear-filled glance. And for the second time in their lives, but not the last, each of them saw their own expression on the other's face.

Only the boatman and the dragonflies seemed indifferent to the journey they were making. The great insects were fully alive and bright with beauty even in the clinging mist, shaking their filmy wings to dislodge the moisture; and the old man in his sacking robe leaned forward and back, forward and back, bracing his bare feet against the slime-puddled floor.

The journey lasted longer than Lyra wanted to measure. Though part of her was raw with anguish, imagining Pantalaimon abandoned on the shore, another part was adjusting to the pain, measuring her own strength, curious to see what would happen and where they would land.

Will's arm was strong around her, but he too was looking ahead, trying to peer through the wet grey gloom and to hear anything other than the dank splash of the oars. And presently something did change: a cliff or an island lay ahead of them. They heard the enclosing of the sound before they saw the mist darken.

The boatman pulled on one oar to turn the boat a little to the left.

"Where are we?" said the voice of the Chevalier Tialys, small but strong as ever, though there was a harsh edge to it as if he too had been suffering pain.

"Near the island," said the boatman. "Another five minutes, we'll be at the landing stage."

"What island?" said Will. He found his own voice strained too, so tight it hardly seemed his.

"The gate to the land of the dead is on this island," said the boatman. "Everyone comes here, kings, queens, murderers, poets, children; everyone comes this way, and none come back."

"*We* shall come back," whispered Lyra fiercely.

He said nothing, but his ancient eyes were full of pity.

As they moved closer, they could see branches of cypress and yew hanging down low over the water, dark green, dense and gloomy. The land rose steeply, and the trees grew so thickly that hardly a ferret could slip between them, and at that thought, Lyra gave a little half-hiccup-half-sob, for Pan would have shown her how well he could do it; but not now, maybe not ever again.

"Are we dead now?" Will said to the boatman.

"Makes no difference," he said. "There's some that came here never believing they were dead. They insisted all the way that they were alive, it was a mistake, someone would have to pay; made no difference. There's others who longed to be dead when they were alive, poor souls; lives full of pain or misery; killed themselves for a chance of a blessed rest, and found that nothing had changed except for the worse, and this time there was no escape; you can't make yourself alive again. And there's been others so frail and sickly, little infants, sometimes, that they're scarcely born into the living before they come down to the dead. I've rowed this boat with a little crying baby on my lap many, many times, that never knew the difference between up there and down here.

And old folk too, the rich ones are the worst, snarling and savage and cursing me, railing and screaming: what did I think I was? Hadn't they gathered and saved all the gold they could garner? Wouldn't I take some now, to put them back ashore? They'd have the law on me, they had powerful friends, they knew the Pope and the King of this and the Duke of that, they were in a position to see I was punished and chastised . . . But they knew what the truth was in the end: the only position they were in was in my boat going to the land of the dead, and as for those kings and popes, they'd be in here too, in their turn, sooner than they wanted. I let 'em cry and rave; they can't hurt me; they fall silent in the end.

"So if you don't know whether you're dead or not, and the little girl swears blind she'll come out again to the living, I say nothing to contradict you. What you are, you'll know soon enough."

All the time he had been steadily rowing along the shore, and now he shipped the oars, slipping the handles down inside the boat and reaching out to his right for the first wooden post that rose out of the lake.

He pulled the boat alongside the narrow wharf and held it still for them. Lyra didn't want to get out: as long as she was near the boat, then Pantalaimon would be able to think of her properly, because that was how he last saw her, but when she moved away from it, he wouldn't know how to picture her any more. So she hesitated, but the dragonflies flew up, and Will got out, pale and clutching his chest; so she had to as well.

"Thank you," she said to the boatman. "When you go back, if you see my dæmon, tell him I love him the best of everything in the land of the living or the dead, and I swear I'll come back to him, even if no one's ever done it before, I swear I will."

"Yes, I'll tell him that," said the old boatman.

He pushed off, and the sound of his slow oar strokes faded away in the mist.

The Gallivespians flew back, having gone a little way, and perched on the children's shoulders as before, she on Lyra, he on Will. So they stood, the travellers, at the edge of the land of the dead. Ahead of them there was nothing but mist, though they could see from the darkening of it that a great wall rose in front of them.

Lyra shivered. She felt as if her skin had turned into lace and the damp and bitter air could flow in and out of her ribs, scaldingly cold on the raw wound where Pantalaimon had been. Still, she thought, Roger must have felt like that as he plunged down the mountainside, trying to cling to her desperate fingers.

They stood still and listened. The only sound was an endless drip-drip-drip of water from the leaves, and as they looked up they felt one or two drops splash coldly on their cheeks.

"Can't stay here," said Lyra.

They moved off the wharf, keeping close together, and made their way to the wall. Gigantic stone blocks, green with ancient slime, rose higher into the mist than they could see. And now they were closer, they could hear the sound of cries behind it, though whether they were human voices crying was impossible to tell: high mournful shrieks and wails that hung in the air like the drifting filaments of a jellyfish, causing pain wherever they touched.

"There's a door," said Will, in a hoarse strained voice.

It was a battered wooden postern under a slab of stone. Before Will could lift his hand and open it, one of those high harsh cries sounded very close by, jarring their ears and frightening them horribly.

Immediately the Gallivespians darted into the air, the dragonflies like little war-horses eager for battle. But the thing that flew down swept them aside with a brutal blow from her wing, and then settled heavily on a ledge just above the children's heads. Tialys and Salmakia gathered themselves and soothed their shaken mounts.

The thing was a great bird the size of a vulture, with the face and breasts of a woman. Will had seen pictures of creatures like her, and the word *harpy* came to mind as soon as he saw her clearly. Her face was smooth and unwrinkled, but aged beyond even the age of the witches: she had seen thousands of years pass, and the cruelty and misery of all of them had formed the hateful expression on her features. But as the travellers saw her more clearly, she became even more repulsive. Her eye-sockets were clotted with filthy slime, and the redness of her lips was caked and crusted as if she had vomited ancient blood again and again. Her matted, filthy black hair hung down to her shoulders; her jagged claws gripped the stone fiercely; her powerful dark wings were folded along her back, and a drift of putrescent stink wafted from her every time she moved.

Will and Lyra, both of them sick and full of pain, tried to stand upright and face her.

"But you are alive!" the harpy said, her harsh voice mocking them.

Will found himself hating and fearing her more than any human being he had ever known.

"Who are you?" said Lyra, who was just as repelled as Will.

For answer the harpy screamed. She opened her mouth and directed a jet of noise right in their faces, so that their heads rang and they nearly fell backwards. Will clutched at Lyra and they both clung together as the scream turned into wild mocking peals of laughter, which were answered by other harpy-voices in the fog along the shore. The jeering hate-filled sound reminded Will of the merciless cruelty of children in a playground, but there were no teachers here to regulate things, no one to appeal to, nowhere to hide.

He set his hand on the knife at his belt and looked her in the eyes, though his head was ringing and the sheer power of her scream had made him dizzy.

"If you're trying to stop us," he said, "then you'd better be ready to fight as well as scream. Because we're going through that door."

The harpy's sickening red mouth moved again, but this time it was to purse her lips into a mock-kiss.

Then she said, "Your mother is alone. We shall send her nightmares. We shall scream at her in her sleep!"

Will didn't move, because out of the corner of his eye he could see the Lady Salmakia moving delicately along the branch where the harpy was perching. Her dragonfly, wings quivering, was being held by Tialys on the ground, and then two things happened: the lady leapt at the harpy and spun around to dig her spur deep into the creature's scaly leg, and Tialys launched the dragonfly upwards. In less than a second Salmakia had spun away and leapt off the branch, directly on to the back of her electric-blue steed and up into the air.

The effect on the harpy was immediate. Another scream shattered the silence, much louder than before, and she beat her dark wings so hard that Will and Lyra both felt the wind, and staggered. But she clung to the stone with her claws, and her face was suffused with dark-red anger, and her hair stood out from her head like a crest of serpents.

Will tugged at Lyra's hand, and they both tried to run towards the door, but the harpy launched herself at them in a fury and only pulled up from the dive when Will turned, thrusting Lyra behind him and holding up the knife.

The Gallivespians flew at the harpy at once, darting close at her face and then darting away again, unable to get in a blow but distracting her so that she beat her wings clumsily and half-fell on to the ground.

Lyra called out, "Tialys! Salmakia! Stop, stop!"

The spies reined back their dragonflies and skimmed high over the children's heads. Other dark forms were clustering in the fog, and the jeering screams of a hundred more harpies sounded from further along the shore. The first one was shaking her wings, shaking her hair, stretching each leg in turn and flexing her claws. She was unhurt, and that was what Lyra had noticed.

The Gallivespians hovered, and then dived back towards Lyra, who was holding out both hands for them to land on. Salmakia realized what Lyra had meant, and said to Tialys: "She's right. We can't hurt her, for some reason."

Lyra said, "Lady, what's your name?"

The harpy shook her wings wide, and the travellers nearly fainted in the hideous smells of corruption and decay that wafted from her.

"No-Name!" she cried.

"What do you want with us?" said Lyra.

"What can you give me?"

"We could tell you where we've been, and maybe you'd be interested, I don't know. We saw all kinds of strange things on the way here."

"Oh, and you're offering to tell me a story?"

"If you'd like."

"Maybe I would. And what then?"

"You might let us go in through that door and find the ghost we've come here to look for, I hope you would, anyway. If you'd be so kind."

"Try, then," said No-Name.

And even in her sickness and pain, Lyra felt that she'd just been dealt the ace of trumps.

"Oh, be careful," whispered Salmakia, but Lyra's mind was already racing ahead through the story she'd told the night before, shaping and cutting and improving and adding: *parents dead; family treasure; shipwreck; escape . . .*

"Well," she said, settling in to her story-telling frame of mind, "it began when I was a baby, really. My father and mother were the Duke and Duchess of Abingdon, you see, and they were as rich as anything. My father was one of the king's advisers, and the king himself used to come and stay, oh, all the time. They'd go hunting in our forest. The house there, where I was born, it was the biggest house in the whole south of England. It was called –"

Without even a cry of warning the harpy launched herself at Lyra, claws outstretched. Lyra just had time to duck, but still one of the claws caught her scalp and tore out a clump of hair.

"Liar! Liar!" the harpy was screaming. "Liar!"

She flew around again, aiming directly for Lyra's face; but Will took out the knife, and threw himself in the way. No-Name swerved out of reach just in time, and Will hustled Lyra over towards the door, because she was numb with shock and half-blinded by the blood running down her face. Where the Galli-vespians were, Will had no idea, but the harpy was flying at them again and screaming and screaming in rage and hatred:

"*Liar! Liar! Liar!*"

And it sounded as if her voice was coming from everywhere, and the word echoed back from the great wall in the fog, muffled and changed, so that she seemed to be screaming Lyra's name, so that *Lyra* and *liar* were one and the same thing.

Will had the girl pressed against his chest, with his shoulder curved over to protect her, and he felt her shaking and sobbing against him; but then he thrust the knife into the rotten wood of the door, and cut out the lock with a quick slash of the blade.

Then he and Lyra, with the spies beside them on their darting dragonflies, tumbled through into the realm of the ghosts as the harpy's cry was doubled and redoubled by others on the foggy shore behind them.

22

THE WHISPERERS

Thick as Autumnal Leaves that strow the Brooks
In Vallombrosa, where th'Etrurian shades
High overarch't imbowr

— JOHN MILTON

THE FIRST THING Will did was to make Lyra sit down, and then he took out the little pot of bloodmoss ointment and looked at the wound on her head. It was bleeding freely, as scalp wounds do, but it wasn't deep. He tore a strip off the edge of his shirt and mopped it clean, and spread some of the ointment over the gash, trying not to think of the filthy state of the claw that made it.

Lyra's eyes were glazed, and she was ash-pale.

"Lyra! Lyra!" he said, and shook her gently. "Come on now, we've got to move."

She gave a shudder and took a long shaky breath, and her eyes focused on him, full of a wild despair.

"Will — I can't do it any more — I can't do it! I can't tell lies! I thought it was so easy — but it didn't work — it's all I can do, and it doesn't work!"

"It's *not* all you can do. You can read the alethiometer, can't you? Come on, let's see where we are. Let's look for Roger."

He helped her up, and for the first time they looked around at the land where the ghosts were.

They found themselves on a great plain that extended far ahead into the mist. The light by which they saw was a dull self-luminescence that seemed to exist everywhere equally, so that there were no true shadows and no true light, and everything was the same dingy colour.

Standing on the floor of this huge space were adults and children — ghost-people — so many that Lyra couldn't guess their number. At least, most of them were standing, though some were sitting and some lying down listless or asleep. No one was moving about, or running or playing, though many of them turned to look at these new arrivals, with a fearful curiosity in their wide eyes.

"Ghosts," she whispered. "This is where they all are, everyone that's ever died . . ."

No doubt it was because she didn't have Pantalaimon any more, but she clung close to Will's arm, and he was glad she did. The Gallivespians had flown ahead, and he could see their bright little forms darting and skimming over the heads of the ghosts, who looked up and followed them with wonder; but the silence was immense and oppressive, and the grey light filled him with fear, and Lyra's warm presence beside him was the only thing that felt like life.

Behind them, outside the wall, the screams of the harpies were still echoing up and down the shore. Some of the ghost-people were looking up apprehensively, but more of them were staring at Will and Lyra, and then they began to crowd forward. Lyra shrank back; she didn't have the strength just yet to face them as she would have liked to do, and it was Will who had to speak first.

"Do you speak our language?" he said. "Can you speak at all?"

Shivering and frightened and full of pain as they were, he and Lyra had more authority than the whole mass of the dead put together. These poor ghosts had little power of their own, and hearing Will's voice, the first clear voice that had sounded there in all the memory of the dead, many of them came forward, eager to respond.

But they could only whisper. A faint pale sound, no more than a soft breath, was all they could utter. And as they thrust forward, jostling and desperate, the Gallivespians flew down and darted to and fro in front of them, to prevent them from crowding too close. The ghost-children looked up with a passionate longing, and Lyra knew at once why: they thought the dragonflies were dæmons; they were wishing with all their hearts that they could hold their own dæmons again.

"Oh, they *en't* dæmons," Lyra burst out, compassionately; "and if my own dæmon was here, you could all stroke him and touch him, I promise –"

And she held out her hands to the children. The adult ghosts hung back, listless or fearful, but the children all came thronging forward. They had as much substance as fog, poor things, and Lyra's hands passed through and through them, as did Will's. They crammed forward, light and lifeless, to warm themselves at the flowing blood and the strong-beating hearts of the two travellers, and both Will and Lyra felt a succession of cold delicate brushing sensations as the ghosts passed through their bodies, warming themselves on the way. The two living children felt that little by little they were becoming dead too; they hadn't got an infinite amount of life and warmth to give, and they were so cold already, and the endless crowds pressing forward looked as if they were never going to stop.

Finally Lyra had to plead with them to hold back.

She held up her hands and said, "Please – we wish we could touch you all, but we came down here to look for someone, and I need you to tell me where he is and how to find him. Oh, Will," she said, leaning her head to his, "I wish I knew what to do!"

The ghosts were fascinated by the blood on Lyra's forehead. It glowed as brightly as a holly berry in the dimness, and several of them had brushed through it, longing for the contact with something so vibrantly alive. One ghost-girl, who when she was alive must have been about nine or ten, reached up shyly to try and touch it, and then shrank back in fear; but Lyra said, "Don't be afraid – we en't come here to hurt you – speak to us, if you can!"

The ghost-girl spoke, but in her thin pale voice it was only a whisper.

"Did the harpies do that? Did they try and hurt you?"

"Yeah," said Lyra, "but if that's all they can do, I en't worried about them."

"Oh, it isn't – oh, they do worse –"

"What? What do they do?"

But they were reluctant to tell her. They shook their heads and kept silent, until one boy said, "It en't so bad for them that's been here hundreds of years, because you get tired after all that time, they can't 'fraid you up so much –"

"It's the new ones that they like talking to most," said the first girl. "It's just . . . Oh, it's just hateful. They . . . I can't tell you."

Their voices were no louder than dry leaves falling. And it

was only the children who spoke; the adults all seemed sunk in a lethargy so ancient that they might never move or speak again.

"Listen," said Lyra, "please listen. We came here, me and my friends, because we got to find a boy called Roger. He en't been here long, just a few weeks, so he won't know very many people, but if you know where he is . . ."

But even as she spoke she knew that they could stay here till they grew old, searching everywhere and looking at every face, and still they might never see more than a tiny fraction of the dead. She felt despair sit on her shoulders, as heavy as if the harpy herself were perching there.

However, she clenched her teeth and tried to hold her chin high. We got here, she thought; that's part of it, anyway.

The first ghost-girl was saying something in that lost little whisper.

"Why do we want to find him?" said Will. "Well, Lyra wants to speak to him. But there's someone I want to find as well. I want to find my father, John Parry. He's here too, somewhere, and I want to speak to him before I go back to the world. So please ask, if you can, ask for Roger and for John Parry to come and speak to Lyra and to Will. Ask them —"

But suddenly the ghosts all turned and fled, even the grown-ups, like dry leaves scattered by a sudden gust of wind. In a moment the space around the children was empty, and then they heard why: screams, cries, shrieks came from the air above, and then the harpies were on them, with gusts of rotten stink, batter-ing wings, and those raucous screams, jeering, mocking, cack-ling, deriding.

Lyra shrank to the ground at once, covering her ears, and Will, knife in hand, crouched over her. He could see Tialys and Salmakia skimming towards them, but they were some way off yet, and he had a moment or two to watch the harpies as they wheeled and dived. He saw their human faces snap at the air as if they were eating insects, and he heard the words they were shouting — scoffing words, filthy words, all about his mother, words that shook his heart; but part of his mind was quite cold and separate, thinking, calculating, observing. None of them wanted to come anywhere near the knife.

To see what would happen, he stood up. One of them –
it might have been No-Name herself – had to swerve heavily out
of the way, because she'd been diving low, intending to skim just
over his head. Her heavy wings beat clumsily, and she only just
made the turn. He could have reached out and slashed off her
head with the knife.

By this time, the Gallivespians had arrived, and the two of
them were about to attack, but Will called: "Tialys! Come here!
Salmakia, come to my hand!"

They landed on his shoulders, and he said, "Watch. See what
they do. They only come and scream. I think it was a mistake,
when she hit Lyra. I don't think they want to touch us at all.
We can ignore them."

Lyra looked up, wide-eyed. The creatures flew around Will's
head, sometimes only a foot or so away, but they always swerved
aside or upwards at the last moment. He could sense the two spies
eager for battle, and the dragonflies' wings were quivering with
desire to dart through the air with their deadly riders, but they
held themselves back: they could see he was right.

And it had an effect on the ghosts, too: seeing Will standing
unafraid and unharmed, they began to drift back towards the
travellers. They watched the harpies cautiously, but for all that,
the lure of the warm flesh and blood, those strong heartbeats, was
too much to resist.

Lyra stood up to join Will. Her wound had opened again, and
fresh blood was trickling down her cheek, but she wiped it aside.

"Will," she said, "I'm so glad we came down here together . . ."

He heard a tone in her voice, and he saw an expression on
her face, which he knew and liked more than anything he'd ever
known: it showed she was thinking of something daring, but she
wasn't ready to speak of it yet.

He nodded, to show he'd understood.

The ghost-girl said, "This way – come with us – we'll find
them!"

And both of them felt the strangest sensation, as if little ghost-
hands were reaching inside and tugging at their ribs to make
them follow.

So they set off across the floor of that great desolate plain, and the harpies wheeled higher and higher overhead, screaming and screaming. But they kept their distance, and the Gallivespians flew above, keeping watch.

As they walked along, the ghosts talked to them.

"Excuse me," said one ghost-girl, "but where's your dæmons? Excuse me for asking. But..."

Lyra was conscious every single second of her dear abandoned Pantalaimon. She couldn't speak easily, so Will answered instead.

"We left our dæmons outside," he said, "where it's safe for them. We'll collect them later. Did you have a dæmon?"

"Yes," said the ghost; "his name was Sandling ... oh, I loved him..."

"And had he settled?" said Lyra.

"No, not yet. He used to think he'd be a bird, and I hoped he wouldn't, because I liked him all furry in bed at night. But he was a bird more and more. What's your dæmon called?"

Lyra told her, and the ghosts pressed forward eagerly again. They all wanted to talk about their dæmons, every one.

"Mine was called Matapan –"

"We used to play hide-and-seek, she'd change like a chameleon and I couldn't see her at all, she was ever so good –"

"Once I hurt my eye and I couldn't see and he guided me all the way home –"

"He never wanted to settle, but I wanted to grow up, and we used to argue –"

"She used to curl up in my hand and go to sleep –"

"Are they still there, somewhere else? Will we see them again?"

"No. When you die your dæmon just goes out like a candle flame. I seen it happen. I never saw my Castor, though – I never said goodbye –"

"They en't *nowhere*! They must be *somewhere*! My dæmon's still there somewhere, I know he is!"

The jostling ghosts were animated and eager, their eyes shining and their cheeks warm as if they were borrowing life from the travellers.

Will said, "Is there anyone here from my world, where we don't have dæmons?"

A thin ghost-boy of his own age nodded, and Will turned to him.

"Oh yes," came the answer. "We didn't understand what dæmons were, but we knew what it felt like to be without them. There's people here from all kinds of worlds."

"I knew my death," said one girl, "I knew him all the while I was growing up. When I heard them talk about dæmons, I thought they meant something like our deaths. I miss him now. I won't never see him again. *I'm over and done with,* that's the last thing he said to me, and then he went for ever. When he was with me I always knew there was someone I could trust, someone who knew where we was going and what to do. But I ain't got him no more. I don't know what's going to happen ever again."

"There ain't *nothing* going to happen!" someone else said. "Nothing, for ever!"

"*You* don't know," said another. "*They* came, didn't they? No one ever knew *that* was going to happen."

She meant Will and Lyra.

"This is the first thing that ever happened here," said a ghost-boy. "Maybe it's all going to change now."

"What would you do, if you could?" said Lyra.

"Go up to the world again!"

"Even if it meant you could only see it once, would you still want to do that?"

"Yes! Yes! Yes!"

"Well, anyway, I've got to find Roger," said Lyra, burning with her new idea; but it was for Will to know first.

On the floor of the endless plain, there was a vast slow movement among the uncountable ghosts. The children couldn't see it, but Tialys and Salmakia, flying above, watched the little pale figures all moving with an effect that looked like the migration of immense flocks of birds or herds of reindeer. At the centre of the movement were the two children who were not ghosts, moving steadily on; not leading, and not following, but somehow focusing the movement into an intention of all the dead.

The spies, their thoughts moving even more quickly than their darting steeds, exchanged a glance and brought the dragonflies to rest side by side on a dry withered branch.

"Do *we* have dæmons, Tialys?" said the lady.

"Since we got into that boat I have felt as if my heart had been torn out and thrown still beating on the shore," he said. "But it wasn't; it's still working in my breast. So something of mine is out there with the little girl's dæmon, and something of yours too, Salmakia, because your face is drawn and your hands are pale and tight. Yes, we have dæmons, whatever they are. Maybe the people in Lyra's world are the only living beings to know they have. Maybe that's why it was one of them who started the revolt."

He slipped off the dragonfly's back and tethered it safely, and then took out the lodestone resonator. But he had hardly begun to touch it when he stopped.

"No response," he said sombrely.

"So we're beyond everything?"

"Beyond help, certainly. Well, we knew we were coming to the land of the dead."

"The boy would go with her to the end of the world."

"Will his knife open the way back, do you think?"

"I'm sure he thinks so. But oh, Tialys, I don't know."

"He's very young. Well, they are both young. You know, if she doesn't survive this, the question of whether she'll choose the right thing when she's tempted won't arise. It won't matter any more."

"Do you think she's chosen already? When she chose to leave her dæmon on the shore? Was that the choice she had to make?"

The chevalier looked down on the slow-moving millions on the floor of the land of the dead, all drifting after that bright and living spark Lyra Silvertongue. He could just make out her hair, the lightest thing in the gloom, and beside it the boy's head, black-haired and solid and strong.

"No," he said, "not yet. That's still to come, whatever it may be."

"Then we must bring her to it safely."

"Bring them both. They're bound together now."

The Lady Salmakia flicked the cobweb-light rein, and her dragonfly darted off the branch at once, and sped down towards the living children, with the chevalier close behind.

But they didn't stop with them; having skimmed low to make sure they were all right, they flew on ahead, partly because the dragonflies were restless, and partly because they wanted to find out how far this dismal place extended.

Lyra saw them flashing overhead and felt a pang of relief that there was still something that darted and glowed with beauty. Then, unable to keep her idea to herself any more, she turned to Will; but she had to whisper. She put her lips to his ear, and in a noisy rush of warmth he heard her say:

"Will, I want us to take *all* these poor dead ghost-kids outside – the grown-ups as well – we could set 'em free! We'll find Roger and your father, and then let's open the way to the world outside, and set 'em all free!"

He turned and gave her a true smile, so warm and happy she felt something stumble and falter inside her; at least, it felt like that, but without Pantalaimon she couldn't ask herself what it meant. It might have been a new way for her heart to beat. Deeply surprised, she told herself to walk straight and stop feeling giddy.

So they moved on. The whisper *Roger* was spreading out faster than they could move; the words "Roger – Lyra's come – Roger – Lyra's here –" passed from one ghost to another like the electric message that one cell in the body passes on to the next.

And Tialys and Salmakia, cruising above on their tireless dragonflies, and looking all around as they flew, eventually noticed a new kind of movement. Some way off there was a little gyration of activity. Skimming down closer they found themselves ignored, for the first time, because something more interesting was gripping the minds of all the ghosts. They were talking excitedly in their near-silent whispers, they were pointing, they were urging someone forward.

Salmakia flew down low, but couldn't land: the press was too great, and none of their hands or shoulders would support her, even if they dared to try. She saw a young ghost-boy with an honest unhappy face, dazed and puzzled by what he was being told, and she called out:

"Roger? Is that Roger?"

He looked up, bemused, nervous, and nodded.

Salmakia flew back up to her companion, and together they sped back to Lyra. It was a long way, and hard to navigate, but by watching the patterns of movement, they finally found her.

"There she is," said Tialys, and called: "Lyra! Lyra! Your friend is there!"

Lyra looked up and held out her hand for the dragonfly. The great insect landed at once, its red and yellow gleaming like enamel, and its filmy wings stiff and still on either side. Tialys kept his balance as she held him at eye-level.

"Where?" she said, breathless with excitement. "Is he far off?"

"An hour's walk," said the chevalier. "But he knows you're coming. The others have told him, and we made sure it was him. Just keep going, and soon you'll find him."

Tialys saw Will make the effort to stand up straight and force himself to find some more energy. Lyra was charged with it already, and plied the Gallivespians with questions: how did Roger seem? Had he spoken to them? Did he seem glad? Were the other children aware of what was happening, and were they helping, or were they just in the way?

And so on. Tialys tried to answer everything truthfully and patiently, and step by step the living girl drew closer to the boy she had brought to his death.

23

NO WAY OUT

And ye shall know the truth, and the truth shall make you free.

— ST JOHN'S GOSPEL

"WILL," SAID LYRA, "what d'you think the harpies will do when we let the ghosts out?"

Because the creatures were getting louder and flying closer, and there were more and more of them all the time, as if the gloom were gathering itself into little clots of malice and giving them wings. The ghosts kept looking up fearfully.

"Are we getting close?" Lyra called to the Lady Salmakia.

"Not far now," she called down, hovering above them. "You could see him, if you climbed that rock."

But Lyra didn't want to waste time. She was trying with all her heart to put on a cheerful face for Roger, but in front of her mind's eye every moment was that terrible image of the little dog-Pan abandoned on the jetty as the mist closed around him, and she could barely keep from howling. She must, though; she must be hopeful for Roger; she always had been.

When they did come face to face, it happened quite suddenly. In among the press of all the ghosts, there he was, his familiar features wan but his expression as full of delight as a ghost could be. He rushed to embrace her.

But he passed like cold smoke through her arms, and though she felt his little hand clutch at her heart, it had no strength to hold on. They could never truly touch again.

But he could whisper, and his voice said, "Lyra, I never thought I'd ever see you again — I thought even if you did come down here when you was dead, you'd be much older, you'd be grown up, and you wouldn't want to speak to me —"

"Why ever not?"

"Because I done the wrong thing when Pan got my dæmon away from Lord Asriel's! We should've run, we shouldn't have tried to fight her! We should've run to you! Then she wouldn't have been able to get my dæmon again and when the cliff fell away she'd've still been with me!"

"But that weren't *your* fault, stupid!" Lyra said. "It was me that brung you there in the first place, and I should've let you go back with the other kids and the gyptians. It was my fault. I'm so sorry, Roger, honest, it was *my* fault, you wouldn't've been here otherwise..."

"Well," he said, "I dunno. Maybe I would've got dead some other way. But it weren't your *fault*, Lyra, see."

She felt herself beginning to believe it; but all the same, it was heart-rending to see the poor little cold thing, so close and yet so out of reach. She tried to grasp his wrist, though her fingers closed in the empty air; but he understood, and sat down beside her.

The other ghosts withdrew a little, leaving them alone, and Will moved apart too, to sit down and nurse his hand. It was bleeding again, and while Tialys flew fiercely at the ghosts to force them away, Salmakia helped Will tend to the wound.

But Lyra and Roger were oblivious to that.

"And you en't dead," he said. "How'd you come here if you're still alive? And where's Pan?"

"Oh, Roger – I had to leave him on the shore – it was the worst thing I ever had to do, it hurt so much – you know how it hurts – and he just stood there, just looking, oh, I felt like a murderer, Roger – but I *had* to, or else I couldn't have come!"

"I been pretending to talk to you all the time since I died," he said. "I been wishing I could, and wishing so hard... Just wishing I could get out, me and all the other dead 'uns, cause this is a terrible place, Lyra, it's hopeless, there's no change when you're dead, and them bird-things... You know what they do? They wait till you're resting – you can't never sleep properly, you just sort of doze – and they come up quiet beside you and they whisper all the bad things you ever did when you was alive, so you can't forget 'em. They know all the worst things about you. They know how to make you feel horrible, just thinking of all the stupid things and bad things you ever did. And all the greedy and unkind thoughts you ever had, they know 'em all, and they shame you up and they make you feel sick with yourself... But you can't get away from 'em."

"Well," she said, "listen."

Dropping her voice and leaning closer to the little ghost, just as she used to do when they were planning mischief at Jordan, she went on:

"You probably don't know, but the witches – you remember Serafina Pekkala – the witches've got a prophecy about me. They don't know I know – no one does. I never spoke to anyone about it before. But when I was in Trollesund, and Farder Coram the gyptian took me to see the witches' consul, Dr Lanselius, he gave me like a kind of a test. He said I had to go outside and pick out the right piece of cloud-pine out of all the others to show I could really read the alethiometer.

"Well, I done that, and then I came in quickly, because it was cold and it only took a second, it was easy. The consul was talking to Farder Coram, and they didn't know I could hear 'em. He said the witches had this prophecy about me, I was going to do something great and important, and it was going to be in another world...

"Only I never spoke of it, and I reckon I must have even forgot it, there was so much else going on. So it sort of sunk out of my mind. I never even talked about it with Pan, 'cause he would have laughed, I reckon.

"But then later on Mrs Coulter caught me and she kept me in a trance, and I was dreaming and I dreamed of that, and I dreamed of you. And I remembered the gyptian boat-mother, Ma Costa – you remember – it was their boat we got on board of, in Jericho, with Simon and Hugh and them –"

"Yes! And we nearly sailed it to Abingdon! That was the best thing we ever done, Lyra! I won't never forget that, even if I'm down here dead for a thousand years –"

"Yes, but *listen* - when I ran away from Mrs Coulter the first time, right, I found the gyptians again and they looked after me and... Oh, Roger, there's so *much* I found out, you'd be amazed – but this is the important thing: Ma Costa said to me, she said I'd got witch-oil in my soul, she said the gyptians were water people but I was a fire person.

"And what I think that means is she was sort of preparing me for the witch-prophecy. I *know* I got something important to do, and Dr Lanselius the consul said it was vital I never found out what my destiny was till it happened, see – I must never *ask* about it . . . So I never did. I never even thought what it might be. I never asked the alethiometer, even.

"But *now* I think I know. And finding you again is just a sort of proof. What I got to do, Roger, what my destiny is, is I got to help all the ghosts out of the land of the dead for ever. Me and Will – we got to rescue you all. I'm sure it's that. It must be. And because Lord Asriel, because of something my father said . . . *Death is going to die*, he said. I dunno what'll happen, though. You mustn't tell 'em yet, promise. I mean you might not *last* up there. But –"

He was desperate to speak, so she stopped.

"That's *just* what I wanted to tell you!" he said. "I told 'em, all the other dead 'uns, I *told* them you'd come! Just like you came and rescued the kids from Bolvangar! I says, Lyra'll do it, if any-one can. They wished it'd be true, they wanted to believe me, but they never really did, I could tell.

"For one thing," he went on, "every kid that's ever come here, every single one, starts by saying I bet my dad'll come and get me, or I bet my mum, as soon as she knows where I am, she'll fetch me home again. If it en't their dad or mum it's their friends, or their grandpa, but *someone*'s going to come and rescue 'em. Only they never do. So no one believed me when I told 'em you'd come. Only I was right!"

"Yeah," she said, "well, I couldn't have done it without Will. That's Will over there, and that's the Chevalier Tialys and the Lady Salmakia. There's so *much* to tell you, Roger . . ."

"Who's Will? Where's he come from?"

Lyra began to explain, quite unaware of how her voice changed, how she sat up straighter, and how even her eyes looked different when she told the story of her meeting with Will and the fight for the subtle knife. How could she have known? But Roger noticed, with the sad voiceless envy of the unchanging dead.

Meanwhile, Will and the Gallivespians were a little way off, talking quietly.

"What are you going to do, you and the girl?" said Tialys.

"Open this world and let the ghosts out. That's what I've got the knife for."

He had never seen such astonishment on any faces, let alone those of people whose good opinion he valued. He'd acquired a great respect for these two. They sat silent for a few moments, and then Tialys said:

"This will undo everything. It's the greatest blow you could strike. The Authority will be powerless after this."

"How would they ever suspect it?" said the lady. "It'll come at them out of nowhere!"

"And what then?" Tialys asked Will.

"What then? Well, then we'll have to get out ourselves, and find our dæmons, I suppose. Don't think of *then*. It's enough to think of now. I haven't said anything to the ghosts, in case ... in case it doesn't work. So don't you say anything either. Now I'm going to find a world I can open, and those harpies are watching. So if you want to help, you can go and distract them while I do that."

Instantly the Gallivespians urged their dragonflies up into the murk overhead, where the harpies were as thick as blowflies. Will watched the great insects charging fearlessly up at them, for all the world as if the harpies were flies and they could snap them up in their jaws, big as they were. He thought how much the brilliant creatures would love it when the sky was open and they could skim about over bright water again.

Then he took up the knife. And instantly there came back the words the harpies had thrown at him – taunts about his mother – and he stopped. He put the knife down, trying to clear his mind.

He tried again, with the same result. He could hear them clamouring above, despite the ferocity of the Gallivespians; there were so many of them that two flyers alone could do little to stop them.

Well, this was what it was going to be like. It wasn't going to get any easier. So Will let his mind relax and become disengaged, and just sat there with the knife held loosely until he was ready again.

This time the knife cut straight into the air – and met rock. He had opened a window in this world into the underground of another. He closed it up, and tried again.

And the same thing happened, though he knew it was a different world. He'd opened windows before to find himself above the ground of another world, so he shouldn't have been surprised to find he was underground for a change, but it was disconcerting.

Next time he felt carefully in the way he'd learned, letting the tip search for the resonance that revealed a world where the ground was in the same place. But the touch was wrong wherever he felt. There was no world anywhere he could open into; everywhere he touched, it was solid rock.

Lyra had sensed that something was wrong, and she jumped up from her close conversation with Roger's ghost to hurry to Will's side.

"What is it?" she said quietly.

He told her, and added, "We're going to have to move somewhere else before I can find a world we can open into. And those harpies aren't going to let us. Have you told the ghosts what we were planning?"

"No. Only Roger, and I told him to keep it quiet. He'll do whatever I tell him. Oh, Will, I'm scared, I'm so scared. We might not ever get out. Suppose we get stuck here for ever?"

"The knife can cut through rock. If we need to, we'll just cut a tunnel. It'll take a long time and I hope we won't have to, but we could. Don't worry."

"Yeah. You're right. Course we could."

But she thought he looked so ill, with his face drawn in pain and with dark rings around his eyes, and his hand was shaking, and his fingers were bleeding again; he looked as sick as she felt. They couldn't go on much longer without their dæmons. She felt her own ghost quail in her body, and hugged her arms tightly, aching for Pan.

But meanwhile the ghosts were pressing close, poor things, and the children especially couldn't leave Lyra alone.

"Please," said one girl, "you won't forget us when you go back, will you?"

"No," said Lyra, "never."

"You'll tell them about us?"

"I promise. What's your name?"

But the poor girl was embarrassed and ashamed: she'd forgotten. She turned away, hiding her face, and a boy said:

"It's better to forget, I reckon. I've forgotten mine. Some en't been here long, and they still know who they are. There's some kids been here thousands of years. They're no older than us, and they've forgotten a whole lot. Except the sunshine. No one forgets that. And the wind."

"Yeah," said another, "tell us about that!"

And more and more of them clamoured for Lyra to tell them about the things they remembered, the sun and the wind and the sky, and the things they'd forgotten, such as how to play; and she turned to Will and whispered, "What should I do, Will?"

"Tell them."

"I'm scared. After what happened back there – the harpies –"

"Tell them the truth. We'll keep the harpies off."

She looked at him doubtfully. In fact, she felt sick with apprehension. She turned back to the ghosts, who were thronging closer and closer.

"Please!" they were whispering. "You've just come from the world! Tell us, tell us! Tell us about the world!"

There was a tree not far away – just a dead trunk with its bone-white branches thrusting into the chilly grey air – and because Lyra was feeling weak, and because she didn't think she could walk and talk at the same time, she made for that so as to have somewhere to sit. The crowd of ghosts jostled and shuffled aside to make room.

When they were nearly at the tree, Tialys landed on Will's hand and indicated that Will should bend his head to listen.

"They're coming back," he said quietly, "those harpies. More and more of them. Have your knife ready. The lady and I will hold them off as long as we can, but you might need to fight."

Without worrying Lyra, Will loosened the knife in its sheath and kept his hand close to it. Tialys took off again, and then Lyra reached the tree and sat down on one of the thick roots.

So many dead figures clustered around, pressing hopefully, wide-eyed, that Will had to make them keep back and leave room; but he let Roger stay close, because he was gazing at Lyra, listening with a passion.

And Lyra began to talk about the world she knew.

She told them the story of how she and Roger had climbed over Jordan College roof and found the rook with the broken leg, and how they had looked after it until it was ready to fly again; and how they had explored the wine cellars, all thick with dust and cobwebs, and drunk some canary, or it might have been Tokay, she couldn't tell, and how drunk they had been. And Roger's ghost listened, proud and desperate, nodding and whispering, "Yes, yes! That's just what happened, that's true, all right!"

Then she told them all about the great battle between the Oxford townies and the clay-burners.

First she described the Claybeds, making sure she got in everything she could remember, the wide ochre-coloured washing pits, the dragline, the kilns like great brick beehives. She told them about the willow trees along the river's edge, with their leaves all silvery underneath; and she told how when the sun shone for more than a couple of days, the clay began to split up into great handsome plates, with deep cracks between, and how it felt to squish your fingers into the cracks and slowly lever up a dried plate of mud, trying to keep it as big as you could without breaking it. Underneath it was still wet, ideal for throwing at people.

And she described the smells around the place: the smoke from the kilns, the rotten-leaf-mould smell of the river when the wind was in the south-west, the warm smell of the baking potatoes the clay-burners used to eat; and the sound of the water slipping slickly over the sluices and into the washing-pits; and the slow thick suck as you tried to pull your foot out of the ground; and the heavy wet slap of the gate-paddles in the clay-thick water.

As she spoke, playing on all their senses, the ghosts crowded closer, feeding on her words, remembering the time when they had flesh and skin and nerves and senses, and willing her never to stop.

Then she told how the clay-burners' children always made war on the townies, but how they were slow and dull, with clay in their brains, and how the townies were as sharp and quick as sparrows by contrast; and how one day all the townies had swallowed their differences and plotted and planned and attacked the Claybeds from three sides, pinning the clay-burners' children back against the river, hurling handfuls and handfuls of heavy claggy clay at one another, rushing their muddy castle and tearing it down, turning the fortifications into missiles until the air and the ground and the water were all mixed inextricably together, and every child looked exactly the same, mud from scalp to sole, and none of them had had a better day in all their lives.

When she'd finished, she looked at Will, exhausted. Then she had a shock.

As well as the ghosts, silent all around, and her companions, close and living, there was another audience too; because the branches of the tree were clustered with those dark bird-forms, their women's faces gazing down at her, solemn and spellbound.

She stood up in sudden fear, but they didn't move.

"You," she said, desperate, "you flew at me before, when I tried to tell you something. What's stopping you now? Go on, tear at me with your claws and make a ghost out of me!"

"That is the least we shall do," said the harpy in the centre, who was No-Name herself. "Listen to me. Thousands of years ago, when the first ghosts came down here, the Authority gave us the power to see the worst in every one, and we have fed on the worst ever since, till our blood is rank with it and our very hearts are sickened.

"But still, it was all we had to feed on. It was all we had. And now we learn that you are planning to open a way to the upper world and lead all the ghosts out into the air —"

And her harsh voice was drowned by a million whispers, as every ghost who could hear cried out in joy and hope; but all the harpies screamed and beat their wings until the ghosts fell silent again.

"Yes," cried No-Name, "to lead them out! What will we do now? I shall tell you what we will do: from now on, we shall hold nothing back. We shall hurt and defile and tear and rend every ghost that comes through, and we shall send them mad with fear and remorse and self-hatred. This is a wasteland now; we shall make it a hell!"

Every single harpy shrieked and jeered, and many of them flew up off the tree and straight at the ghosts, making them scatter in terror. Lyra clung to Will's arm and said, "They've given it away now, and we can't do it – they'll hate us – they'll think we betrayed them! We've made it worse, not better!"

"Quiet," said Tialys. "Don't despair. Call them back and make them listen to us."

So Will cried out, "Come back! Come back, every one of you! Come back and listen!"

One by one the harpies, their faces eager and hungry and suffused with the lust for misery, turned and flew back to the tree, and the ghosts drifted back as well. The chevalier left his dragonfly in the care of Salmakia, and his little tense figure, green-clad and dark-haired, leapt to a rock where they could all see him.

"Harpies," he said, "we can offer you something better than that. Answer my questions truly, and hear what I say, and then judge. When Lyra spoke to you outside the wall, you flew at her. Why did you do that?"

"Lies!" the harpies all cried. "Lies and fantasies!"

"Yet when she spoke just now, you all listened, every one of you, and you kept silent and still. Again, why was that?"

"Because it was true," said No-Name. "Because she spoke the truth. Because it was nourishing. Because it was feeding us. Because we couldn't help it. Because it was true. Because we had no idea that there was anything but wickedness. Because it brought us news of the world and the sun and the wind and the rain. Because it was true."

"Then," said Tialys, "let's make a bargain with you. Instead of seeing only the wickedness and cruelty and greed of the ghosts that come down here, from now on you will have the right to ask every ghost to tell you the story of their lives, and they will have to tell the truth about what they've seen and touched and heard and loved and known in the world. Every one of these ghosts has a story; every single one that comes down in the future will have true things to tell you about the world. And you'll have the right to hear them, and they will have to tell you."

Lyra marvelled at the nerve of the little spy. How did he dare speak to these creatures as if he had the power to give them rights? Any one of them could have snapped him up in a moment, wrenched him apart in her claws, or carried him high and then hurled him down to the ground to smash in pieces. And yet there he stood, proud and fearless, making a bargain with them! And they listened, and conferred, their faces turning to one another, their voices low.

All the ghosts watched, fearful and silent.

Then No-Name turned back.

"That's not enough," she said. "We want more than that. We had a *task* under the old dispensation. We had a place and a duty. We fulfilled the Authority's commands diligently, and for that we were honoured. Hated and feared, but honoured too. What will happen to our honour now? Why should the ghosts take any notice of us, if they can simply walk out into the world again? We have our pride, and you should not let that be dispensed with. We need an honourable place! We need a duty and a task to do, that will bring us the respect we deserve!"

They shifted on the branches, muttering and raising their wings. But a moment later Salmakia leapt up to join the chevalier, and called out:

"You are quite right. Everyone should have a task to do that's important, one that brings them honour, one they can perform with pride. So here is your task, and it's one that only you can do, because you are the guardians and the keepers of this place. Your task will be to guide the ghosts from the landing-place by the lake all the way through the land of the dead to the new opening out into the world. In exchange, they will tell you their stories as a fair and just payment for this guidance. Does that seem right to you?"

No-Name looked at her sisters, and they nodded. She said:

"And we have the right to refuse to guide them if they lie, or if they hold anything back, or if they have nothing to tell us. If they live in the world, they *should* see and touch and hear and love and learn things. We shall make an exception for infants who have not had time to learn anything, but otherwise, if they come down here bringing nothing, we shall not guide them out."

"That is fair," said Salmakia, and the other travellers agreed.

So they made a treaty. And in exchange for the story of Lyra's that they'd already heard, the harpies offered to take the travellers and their knife to a part of the land of the dead where the upper world was close. It was a long way off, through tunnels and caves, but they would guide them faithfully, and all the ghosts could follow.

But before they could begin, a voice cried out, as loudly as a whisper could cry. It was the ghost of a thin man with an angry, passionate face, and he cried:

"What will happen? When we leave the world of the dead, will we live again? Or will we vanish as our dæmons did? Brothers, sisters, we shouldn't follow this child anywhere till we know what's going to happen to us!"

Others took up the question: "Yes, tell us where we're going! Tell us what to expect! We won't go unless we know what'll happen to us!"

Lyra turned to Will in despair, but he said, "Tell them the truth. Ask the alethiometer, and tell them what it says."

"All right," she said.

She took out the golden instrument. The answer came at once. She put it away and stood up.

"This is what'll happen," she said, "and it's true, perfectly true. When you go out of here, all the particles that make you up will loosen and float apart, just like your dæmons did. If you've seen people dying, you know what that looks like. But your dæmons en't just *nothing* now; they're part of everything. All the atoms that were them, they've gone into the air and the wind and the trees and the earth and all the living things. They'll never vanish. They're just part of everything. And that's exactly what'll happen to you, I swear to you, I promise on my honour. You'll drift apart, it's true, but you'll be out in the open, part of everything alive again."

No one spoke. Those who had seen how dæmons dissolved were remembering it, and those who hadn't were imagining it, and no one spoke until a young woman came forward. She had died as a martyr centuries before. She looked around and said:

"When we were alive, they told us that when we died we'd go to heaven. And they said that heaven was a place of joy and glory and we would spend eternity in the company of saints and angels praising the Almighty, in a state of bliss. That's what they said. And that's what led some of us to give our lives, and others to spend years in solitary prayer, while all the joy of life was going to waste around us, and we never knew.

"Because the land of the dead isn't a place of reward or a place of punishment. It's a place of nothing. The good come here as well as the wicked, and all of us languish in this gloom for ever, with no hope of freedom, or joy, or sleep or rest or peace.

"But now this child has come offering us a way out and I'm going to follow her. Even if it means oblivion, friends, I'll welcome it, because it won't be nothing, we'll be alive again in a thousand blades of grass, and a million leaves, we'll be falling in the raindrops and blowing in the fresh breeze, we'll be glittering in the dew under the stars and the moon out there in the physical world which is our true home and always was.

"So I urge you: come with the child out to the sky!"

But her ghost was thrust aside by the ghost of a man who looked like a monk: thin, and pale even in his death, with dark zealous eyes. He crossed himself and murmured a prayer, and then he said:

"This is a bitter message, a sad and cruel joke. Can't you see the truth? This is not a child. This is an agent of the Evil One himself! The world we lived in was a vale of corruption and tears. Nothing there could satisfy us. But the Almighty has granted us this blessed place for all eternity, this paradise, which to the fallen soul seems bleak and barren, but which the eyes of faith see as it is, overflowing with milk and honey and resounding with the sweet hymns of the angels. *This* is heaven, truly! What this evil girl promises is nothing but lies. She wants to lead you to hell! Go with her at your peril. My companions and I of the true faith will remain here in our blessed paradise, and spend eternity singing the praises of the Almighty, who has given us the judgement to tell the false from the true."

Once again he crossed himself, and then he and his companions turned away in horror and loathing.

Lyra felt bewildered. Was she wrong? Was she making some great mistake? She looked around: gloom and desolation on every side. But she'd been wrong before about the appearance of things, trusting Mrs Coulter because of her beautiful smile and her sweet scented glamour. It was so easy to get things wrong; and without her dæmon to guide her, maybe she was wrong about this too.

But Will was shaking her arm. Then he put his hands to her face and held it roughly.

"You *know* that's not true," he said, "just as well as you can feel this. Take no notice! *They* can all see he's lying, too. And they're depending on us. Come on, let's make a start."

She nodded. She had to trust her body and the truth of what her senses told her; she knew Pan would have done.

So they set off, and the numberless millions of ghosts began to follow them. Behind them, too far back for the children to see, other inhabitants of the world of the dead had heard what was happening, and were coming to join the great march. Tialys and Salmakia flew back to look, and were overjoyed to see their own people there, and every other kind of conscious being who had ever been punished by the Authority with exile and death. Among them were beings who didn't look human at all, beings like the mulefa, whom Mary Malone would have recognized, and stranger ghosts as well.

But Will and Lyra had no strength to look back; all they could do was move on after the harpies, and hope.

"Have we almost done it, Will?" Lyra whispered. "Is it nearly over?"

He couldn't tell. But they were so weak and sick that he said, "Yes, it's nearly over, we've nearly done it. We'll be out soon."

24

MRS COULTER IN GENEVA

As is the mother, so is her daughter.

— EZEKIEL

MRS COULTER WAITED till nightfall before she approached the
College of St Jerome. After darkness had fallen, she brought the
intention craft down through the cloud and moved slowly along
the lakeshore at tree-top height. The College was a distinctive
shape among the other ancient buildings of Geneva, and she soon
found the spire, the dark hollow of the cloisters, the square tower
where the President of the Consistorial Court of Discipline had
his lodging. She had visited the College three times before; she
knew that the ridges and gables and chimneys of the roof concealed plenty of hiding-places, even for something as large as the
intention craft.

Flying slowly above the tiles, which glistened with the recent
rain, she edged the machine into a little gully between a steep
tiled roof and the sheer wall of the tower. The place was only
visible from the belfry of the Chapel of the Holy Penitence
nearby; it would do very well.

She lowered the aircraft delicately, letting its six feet find their
own purchase and adjust themselves to keep the cabin level. She
was beginning to love this machine: it sprang to her bidding as
fast as she could think, and it was so silent; it could hover above
someone's head closely enough for them to touch, and they'd
never know it was there. In the day or so since she'd stolen it,
Mrs Coulter had mastered the controls, but she still had no idea
how it was powered, and that was the only thing she worried
about: she had no way of telling when the fuel or the batteries
would run out.

Once she was sure it had settled, and that the roof was solid
enough to support it, she took off the helmet and climbed down.

Her dæmon was already prising up one of the heavy old tiles.
She joined him, and soon they had lifted half a dozen out of the

way, and then she snapped off the battens on which they'd been hung, making a gap big enough to get through.

"Go in and look around," she whispered, and the dæmon dropped through into the dark.

She could hear his claws as he moved carefully over the floor of the attic, and then his gold-fringed black face appeared in the opening. She understood at once, and followed him through, waiting to let her eyes adjust. In the dim light she gradually saw a long attic where the dark shapes of cupboards, tables, bookcases, furniture of all kinds had been put to store.

The first thing she did was to push a tall cupboard in front of the gap where the tiles had been. Then she tiptoed to the door in the wall at the far end, and tried the handle. It was locked, of course, but she had a hairpin, and the lock was simple. Three minutes later she and her dæmon were standing at one end of a long corridor, where a dusty skylight let them see a narrow staircase descending at the other.

And five minutes after that, they had opened a window in the pantry next to the kitchen two floors below, and climbed out into the alley. The gatehouse of the College was just around the corner, and as she said to the golden monkey, it was important to arrive in the orthodox way, no matter how they intended to leave.

"Take your hands off me," she said calmly to the guard, "and show me some courtesy, or I shall have you flayed. Tell the President that Mrs Coulter has arrived, and that she wishes to see him at once."

The man fell back, and his pinscher-dæmon, who had been baring her teeth at the mild-mannered golden monkey, instantly cowered and tucked her tail-stump as low as it would go.

The guard cranked the handle of a telephone, and under a minute later a fresh-faced young priest came hastening into the gatehouse, wiping his palms on his robe in case she wanted to shake hands. She didn't.

"Who are you?" she said.

"Brother Louis," said the man, soothing his rabbit-dæmon, "Convenor of the Secretariat of the Consistorial Court. If you would be so kind –"

"I haven't come here to parley with a scrivener," she told him. "Take me to Father MacPhail. And do it now."

The man bowed helplessly, and led her away. The guard behind her blew out his cheeks with relief.

Brother Louis, after trying two or three times to make conversation, gave up and led her in silence to the President's rooms in the tower. Father MacPhail was at his devotions, and poor Brother Louis's hand shook violently as he knocked. They heard a sigh and a groan, and then heavy footsteps crossed the floor.

The President's eyes widened as he saw who it was, and he smiled wolfishly.

"Mrs Coulter," he said, offering his hand. "I am very glad to see you. My study is cold, and our hospitality is plain, but come in, come in."

"Good evening," she said, following him inside the bleak stone-walled room, allowing him to make a little fuss and show her to a chair. "Thank you," she said to Brother Louis, who was still hovering, "I'll take a glass of chocolatl."

Nothing had been offered, and she knew how insulting it was to treat him like a servant, but his manner was so abject that he deserved it. The President nodded, and Brother Louis had to leave and deal with it, to his great annoyance.

"Of course, you are under arrest," said the President, taking the other chair and turning up the lamp.

"Oh, why spoil our talk before we've even begun?" said Mrs Coulter. "I came here voluntarily, as soon as I could escape from Asriel's fortress. The fact is, Father President, I have a great deal of information about his forces, and about the child, and I came here to give it to you."

"The child, then. Begin with the child."

"My daughter is now twelve years old. Very soon she will approach the cusp of adolescence, and then it will be too late for any of us to prevent the catastrophe; nature and opportunity will come together like spark and tinder. Thanks to your intervention, that is now far more likely. I hope you're satisfied."

"It was your duty to bring her here into our care. Instead you chose to skulk in a mountain cave – though how a woman of your intelligence hoped to remain hidden is a mystery to me."

"There's probably a great deal that's mysterious to you, my Lord President, starting with the relations between a mother and her child. If you thought for one moment that I would release my daughter into the care – the *care!* – of a body of men with a feverish obsession with sexuality, men with dirty finger-nails, reeking of ancient sweat, men whose furtive imaginations would crawl over her body like cockroaches – if you thought I would expose my child to *that*, my Lord President, you are more stupid than you take *me* for."

There was a knock on the door before he could reply, and Brother Louis came in with two glasses of chocolatl on a wooden tray. He laid the tray on the table with a nervous bow, smiling at the President in hopes of being asked to stay; but Father MacPhail nodded towards the door, and the young man left reluctantly.

"So what *were* you going to do?" said the President.

"I was going to keep her safe until the danger had passed."

"What danger would that be?" he said, handing her a glass.

"Oh, I think you know what I mean. Somewhere there is a tempter, a serpent, so to speak, and I had to keep them from meeting."

"There is a boy with her."

"Yes. And if you hadn't interfered, they would both be under my control. As it is, they could be anywhere. At least they're not with Lord Asriel."

"I have no doubt he will be looking for them. The boy has a knife of extraordinary power. They would be worth pursuing for that alone."

"I'm aware of that," said Mrs Coulter. "I managed to break it, and he managed to get it mended again."

She was smiling. Surely she didn't approve of this wretched boy?

"We know," he said shortly.

"Well, well," she said. "Fra Pavel must be getting quicker. When I knew him it would have taken him a month at least to read all that."

She sipped her chocolatl, which was thin and weak; how like these tedious priests, she thought, to take their self-righteous abstinence out on their visitors too.

"Tell me about Lord Asriel," said the President. "Tell me everything."

Mrs Coulter settled back comfortably and began to tell him – not everything, but he never thought for a moment that she would. She told him about the fortress, about the allies, about the angels, about the mines and the foundries.

Father MacPhail sat without moving a muscle, his lizard-dæmon absorbing and remembering every word.

"And how did you get here?" he asked.

"I stole a gyropter. It ran out of fuel and I had to abandon it in the countryside not far from here. The rest of the way I walked."

"Is Lord Asriel actively searching for the girl and the boy?"

"Of course."

"I assume he's after that knife. You know it has a name? The cliff-ghasts of the north call it the god-destroyer," he went on, crossing to the window and looking down over the cloisters. "That's what Asriel is aiming to do, isn't it? Destroy the Authority? There are some people who claim that God is dead already. Presumably Asriel is not one of those, if he retains the ambition to kill him."

"Well, where is God," said Mrs Coulter, "if he's alive? And why doesn't he speak any more? At the beginning of the world, God walked in the garden and spoke with Adam and Eve. Then he began to withdraw, and Moses only heard his voice. Later, in the time of Daniel, he was aged – he was the Ancient of Days. Where is he now? Is he still alive, at some inconceivable age, decrepit and demented, unable to think or act or speak and unable to die, a rotten hulk? And if that *is* his condition, wouldn't it be the most merciful thing, the truest proof of our love for God, to seek him out and give him the gift of death?"

Mrs Coulter felt a calm exhilaration as she spoke. She wondered if she'd ever get out alive; but it was intoxicating, to speak like that to this man.

"And Dust?" he said. "From the depths of heresy, what is your view of Dust?"

"I have no view of Dust," she said. "I don't know what it is. No one does."

"I see. Well, I began by reminding you that you are under

arrest. I think it's time we found you somewhere to sleep. You'll be quite comfortable; no one will hurt you; but you're not going to get away. And we shall talk more tomorrow."

He rang a bell, and Brother Louis came in almost at once.

"Show Mrs Coulter to the best guest room," said the President. "And lock her in."

The best guest room was shabby and the furniture was cheap, but at least it was clean. After the lock had turned behind her, Mrs Coulter looked around at once for the microphone, and found one in the elaborate light-fitting and another under the frame of the bed. She disconnected them both, and then had a horrible surprise.

Watching her from the top of the chest of drawers behind the door was Lord Roke.

She cried out and put a hand on the wall to steady herself. The Gallivespian was sitting cross-legged, entirely at his ease, and neither she nor the golden monkey had seen him. Once the pounding of her heart had subsided, and her breathing had slowed, she said, "And when would you have done me the courtesy of letting me know you were here, my lord? Before I undressed, or afterwards?"

"Before," he said. "Tell your dæmon to calm down, or I'll disable him."

The golden monkey's teeth were bared, and all his fur was standing on end. The scorching malice of his expression was enough to make any normal person quail, but Lord Roke merely smiled. His spurs glittered in the dim light.

The little spy stood up and stretched.

"I've just spoken to my agent in Lord Asriel's fortress," he went on. "Lord Asriel presents his compliments, and asks you to let him know as soon as you find out what these people's intentions are."

She felt winded, as if Lord Asriel had thrown her hard in wrestling. Her eyes widened, and she sat down slowly on the bed.

"Did you come here to spy on me, or to help?" she said.

"Both, and it's lucky for you I'm here. As soon as you arrived, they set some anbaric work in motion down in the cellars. I don't know what it is, but there's a team of scientists working on it right now. You seem to have galvanized them."

"I don't know whether to be flattered or alarmed. As a matter of fact, I'm exhausted, and I'm going to sleep. If you're here to help me, you can keep watch. You can begin by looking the other way."

He bowed, and faced the wall until she had washed in the chipped basin, dried herself on the thin towel, and undressed and got into bed. Her dæmon patrolled the room, checking the wardrobe, the picture rail, the curtains, the view of the dark cloisters out of the window. Lord Roke watched him every inch of the way. Finally the golden monkey joined Mrs Coulter, and they fell asleep at once.

Lord Roke hadn't told her everything that he'd learned from Lord Asriel. The allies had been tracking the flight of all kinds of beings in the air above the frontiers of the republic, and had noticed a concentration of what might have been angels, and might have been something else entirely, in the west. They had sent patrols out to investigate, but so far they had learned nothing: whatever it was that hung there had wrapped itself in impenetrable fog.

The spy thought it best not to trouble Mrs Coulter with that, though; she was exhausted. Let her sleep, he decided, and he moved silently about the room, listening at the door, watching out of the window, awake and alert.

An hour after she had first come into the room, he heard a quiet noise outside the door: a faint scratch and a whisper. At the same moment, a dim light outlined the door. Lord Roke moved to the furthest corner, and stood behind one of the legs of the chair on which Mrs Coulter had thrown her clothes.

A minute went by, and then the key turned very quietly in the lock. The door opened an inch, no more, and then the light went out.

Lord Roke could see well enough in the dim glow through the thin curtains, but the intruder was having to wait for his eyes to adjust. Finally the door opened further, very slowly, and the young priest, Brother Louis, stepped in.

He crossed himself, and tiptoed to the bed. Lord Roke prepared to spring, but the priest merely listened to Mrs Coulter's steady breathing, looked closely to see whether she was asleep, and then turned to the bedside table.

He covered the bulb of the battery-light with his hand and switched it on, letting a thin gleam escape through his fingers. He peered at the table so closely that his nose nearly touched the surface, but whatever he was looking for, he didn't find it. Mrs Coulter had put a few things there before she got into bed: a couple of coins, a ring, her watch; but Brother Louis wasn't interested in those.

He turned to her again, and then he saw what he was looking for, uttering a soft hiss between his teeth. Lord Roke could see his dismay: the object of his search was the locket on the gold chain around Mrs Coulter's neck.

Lord Roke moved silently along the skirting board towards the door.

The priest crossed himself again, for he was going to have to touch her. Holding his breath, he bent over the bed – and the golden monkey stirred.

The young man froze, hands outstretched. His rabbit-dæmon trembled at his feet, no use at all: she could at least have kept watch for the poor man, Lord Roke thought. The monkey turned over in his sleep, and fell still again.

After a minute poised like a waxwork, Brother Louis lowered his shaking hands to Mrs Coulter's neck. He fumbled for so long that Lord Roke thought the dawn would break before he got the catch undone, but finally he lifted the locket gently away and stood up.

Lord Roke, as quick and as quiet as a mouse, was out of the door before the priest had turned around. He waited in the dark corridor, and when the young man tiptoed out and turned the key, the Gallivespian began to follow him.

Brother Louis made for the tower, and when the President opened his door, Lord Roke darted through and made for the prie-dieu in the corner of the room. There he found a shadowy ledge where he crouched and listened.

Father MacPhail wasn't alone: the alethiometrist, Fra Pavel, was busy with his books, and another figure stood nervously by the window. This was Dr Cooper, the experimental theologian from Bolvangar. They both looked up.

"Well done, Brother Louis," said the President. "Bring it here, sit down, show me, show me. Well done!"

Fra Pavel moved some of his books, and the young priest laid the gold chain on the table. The others bent over to look as Father MacPhail fiddled with the catch. Dr Cooper offered him a pocket knife, and then there was a soft click.

"Ah!" sighed the President.

Lord Roke climbed to the top of the desk so that he could see. In the naphtha lamplight there was a gleam of dark gold: it was a lock of hair, and the President was twisting it between his fingers, turning it this way and that.

"Are we certain this is the child's?" he said.

"I am certain," came the weary voice of Fra Pavel.

"And is there enough of it, Dr Cooper?"

The pale-faced man bent low and took the lock from Father MacPhail's fingers. He held it up to the light.

"Oh, yes," he said. "One single hair would be enough. This is ample."

"I'm very pleased to hear it," said the President. "Now, Brother Louis, you must return the locket to the good lady's neck."

The priest sagged faintly: he had hoped his task was over. The President placed the curl of Lyra's hair in an envelope and shut the locket, looking up and around as he did so, and Lord Roke had to drop out of sight.

"Father President," said Brother Louis, "I shall of course do as you command, but may I know why you need the child's hair?"

"No, Brother Louis, because it would disturb you. Leave these matters to us. Off you go."

The young man took the locket and left, smothering his resentment. Lord Roke thought of going back with him, and waking Mrs Coulter just as he was trying to replace the chain, in order to see what she'd do; but it was more important to find out what these people were up to.

As the door closed, the Gallivespian went back into the shadows and listened.

"How did you know where she had it?" said the scientist.

"Every time she mentioned the child," the President said, "her hand went to the locket. Now then, how soon can it be ready?"

"A matter of hours," said Dr Cooper.

"And the hair? What do you do with that?"

"We place the hair in the resonating chamber. You understand, each individual is unique, and the arrangement of genetic particles quite distinct . . . Well, as soon as it's analysed, the information is coded in a series of anbaric pulses and transferred to the aiming device. That locates the, the origin of the material, the hair, wherever she may be. It's a process that actually makes use of the Barnard-Stokes heresy, the many-worlds idea . . ."

"Don't alarm yourself, Doctor. Fra Pavel has told me that the child is in another world. Please go on. The force of the bomb is directed by means of the hair?"

"Yes. To each of the hairs from which these ones were cut. That's right."

"So when it's detonated, the child will be destroyed, wherever she is?"

There was a heavy indrawn breath from the scientist, and then a reluctant "Yes". He swallowed, and went on, "The power needed is enormous. The anbaric power. Just as an atomic bomb needs a high-explosive to force the uranium together and set off the chain reaction, this device needs a colossal current to release the much greater power of the severance process. I was wondering –"

"It doesn't matter where it's detonated, does it?"

"No. That is the point. Anywhere will do."

"And it's completely ready?"

"Now we have the hair, yes. But the power, you see –"

"I have seen to that. The hydro-anbaric generating station at Saint-Jean-les-Eaux has been requisitioned for our use. They produce enough power there, wouldn't you say?"

"Yes," said the scientist.

"Then we shall set out at once. Please go and see to the apparatus, Dr Cooper. Have it ready for transportation as soon as you can. The weather changes quickly in the mountains, and there is a storm on the way."

The scientist took the little envelope containing Lyra's hair, and bowed nervously as he left. Lord Roke left with him, making no more noise than a shadow.

As soon as they were out of earshot of the President's room, the Gallivespian sprang. Dr Cooper, below him on the stairs, felt an agonizing stab in his shoulder, and grabbed for the banister: but his arm was strangely weak, and he slipped and tumbled down the whole flight, to land semi-conscious at the bottom.

Lord Roke hauled the envelope out of the man's twitching hand with some difficulty, for it was half as big as he was, and set off in the shadows towards the room where Mrs Coulter was asleep.

The gap at the foot of the door was wide enough for him to slip through. Brother Louis had come and gone, but he hadn't dared to try and fasten the chain around Mrs Coulter's neck: it lay beside her on the pillow.

Lord Roke pressed her hand to wake her up. She was profoundly exhausted, but she focused on him at once, and sat up, rubbing her eyes.

He explained what had happened, and gave her the envelope.

"You should destroy it at once," he told her; "one single hair would be enough, the man said."

She looked at the little curl of dark blonde hair, and shook her head.

"Too late for that," she said. "This is only half the lock I cut from Lyra. He must have kept back some of it."

Lord Roke hissed with anger.

"When he looked around!" he said. "Ach – I moved to be out of his sight – he must have set it aside then . . ."

"And there's no way of knowing where he'll have put it," said Mrs Coulter. "Still, if we can find the bomb –"

"Sssh!"

That was the golden monkey. He was crouching by the door, listening, and then they heard it too: heavy footsteps, hurrying towards the room.

Mrs Coulter thrust the envelope and the lock of hair at Lord Roke, who took it and leapt for the top of the wardrobe. Then she lay down next to her dæmon as the key turned noisily in the door.

"Where is it? What have you done with it? How did you attack Dr Cooper?" said the President's harsh voice, as the light fell across the bed.

Mrs Coulter threw up an arm to shade her eyes, and struggled to sit up.

"You do like to keep your guests entertained," she said drowsily. "Is this a new game? What do I have to do? And who is Dr Cooper?"

The guard from the gatehouse came in with Father MacPhail, and shone a torch into the corners of the room and under the bed. The President was slightly disconcerted: Mrs Coulter's eyes were heavy with sleep, and she could hardly see in the glare from the corridor light. It was obvious that she hadn't left her bed.

"You have an accomplice," he said. "Someone has attacked a guest of the college. Who is it? Who came here with you? Where is he?"

"I haven't the faintest idea what you're talking about. And what's this . . .?"

Her hand, which she'd put down to help herself sit up, had found the locket on the pillow. She stopped, picked it up, looked at the President with wide-open sleepy eyes, and Lord Roke saw a superb piece of acting as she said, puzzled, "But this is my . . . what's it doing here? Father MacPhail, who's been in here? Someone has taken this from around my neck. And – *where is Lyra's hair*? There was a lock of my child's hair in here. Who's taken it? Why? What's going on?"

And now she was standing, her hair disordered, passion in her voice – plainly just as bewildered as the President himself.

Father MacPhail took a step backwards, and put his hand to his head.

"Someone else must have come with you. There must be an accomplice," he said, his voice rasping at the air. "Where is he hiding?"

"I have no accomplice," she said angrily. "If there's an invisible assassin in this place, I can only imagine it's the Devil himself. I dare say he feels quite at home."

Father MacPhail said to the guard, "Take her to the cellars. Put her in chains. I know just what we can do with this woman; I should have thought of it as soon as she appeared."

She looked wildly around, and met Lord Roke's eyes for a fraction of a second, glittering in the darkness near the ceiling. He caught her expression at once, and understood exactly what she meant him to do.

25
SAINT-JEAN-LES-EAUX

A bracelet of bright hair about the bone

– JOHN DONNE

THE CATARACT OF Saint-Jean-les-Eaux plunged between pinnacles of rock at the eastern end of a spur of the Alps, and the generating station clung to the side of the mountain above it. It was a wild region, a bleak and battered wilderness, and no one would have built anything there at all had it not been for the promise of driving great anbaric generators with the power of the thousands of tons of water that roared through the gorge.

It was the night following Mrs Coulter's arrest, and the weather was stormy. Near the sheer stone front of the generating station, a zeppelin slowed to a hover in the buffeting wind. The search-lights below the craft made it look as if it was standing on several legs of light and gradually lowering itself to lie down.

But the pilot wasn't satisfied; the wind was swept into eddies and cross-gusts by the edges of the mountain. Besides, the cables, the pylons, the transformers were too close: to be swept in among them, with a zeppelin full of inflammable gas, would be instantly fatal. Sleet drummed slantwise at the great rigid envelope of the craft, making a noise that almost drowned the clatter and howl of the straining engines, and obscuring the view of the ground.

"Not here," the pilot shouted over the noise. "We'll go around the spur."

Father MacPhail watched fiercely as the pilot moved the throttle forward and adjusted the trim of the engines. The zeppelin rose with a lurch and moved over the rim of the mountain. Those legs of light suddenly lengthened, and seemed to feel their way down the ridge, their lower ends lost in the whirl of sleet and rain.

"You can't get closer to the station than this?" said the President, leaning forward to let his voice carry to the pilot.

"Not if you want to land," the pilot said.

"Yes, we want to land. Very well, put us down below the ridge."

The pilot gave orders for the crew to prepare to moor. As the equipment they were going to unload was heavy as well as delicate, it was important to make the craft secure. The President settled back, tapping his fingers on the arm of his seat, gnawing his lip, but saying nothing and letting the pilot work unflustered.

From his hiding-place in the transverse bulkheads at the rear of the cabin, Lord Roke watched. Several times during the flight, his little shadowy form had passed along behind the metal mesh, clearly visible to anyone who might have looked, if only they had turned their heads; but in order to hear what was happening, he had to come to a place where they could see him. The risk was unavoidable.

He edged forward, listening hard through the roar of the engines, the thunder of the hail and sleet, the high-pitched singing of the wind in the wires, and the clatter of booted feet on metal walkways. The flight engineer called some figures to the pilot, who confirmed them, and Lord Roke sank back into the shadows, holding tight to the struts and beams as the airship plunged and tilted.

Finally, sensing from the movement that the craft was nearly anchored, he made his way back through the skin of the cabin to the seats on the starboard side.

There were men passing through in both directions: crew members, technicians, priests. Many of their dæmons were dogs, too, brimming with curiosity. On the other side of the aisle, Mrs Coulter sat awake and silent, her golden dæmon watching everything from her lap and exuding malice.

Lord Roke waited for the chance and then darted across to Mrs Coulter's seat, and was up in the shadow of her shoulder in a moment.

"What are they doing?" she murmured.

"Landing. We're near the generating station."

"Are you going to stay with me, or work on your own?" she whispered.

"I'll stay with you. I'll have to hide under your coat."

She was wearing a heavy sheepskin coat, uncomfortably hot

in the heated cabin, but with her hands manacled she couldn't take it off.

"Go on, now," she said, looking around, and he darted inside the breast, finding a fur-lined pocket where he could sit securely. The golden monkey tucked Mrs Coulter's silk collar inside solicitously, for all the world like a fastidious couturier attending to his favourite model, while all the time making sure that Lord Roke was completely hidden in the folds of the coat.

He was just in time. Not a minute later, a soldier armed with a rifle came to order Mrs Coulter out of the airship.

"Must I have these handcuffs on?" she said.

"I haven't been told to remove them," he replied. "On your feet, please."

"But it's hard to move if I can't hold on to things. I'm stiff — I've been sitting here for the best part of a day without moving — and you know I haven't got any weapons, because you searched me. Go and ask the President if it's really necessary to manacle me. Am I going to try and run away in this wilderness?"

Lord Roke was impervious to her charm, but interested in its effect on others. The guard was a young man: they should have sent a grizzled old warrior.

"Well," said the guard, "I'm sure you won't, ma'am, but I can't do what I en't been ordered to do. You see that, I'm sure. Please to stand up, ma'am, and if you stumble I'll catch hold of your arm."

She stood up, and Lord Roke felt her move clumsily forwards. She was the most graceful human the Gallivespian had ever seen: this clumsiness was feigned. As they reached the head of the gangway Lord Roke felt her stumble, and cry out in alarm, and felt the jar as the guard's arm caught her. He heard the change in the sounds around them, too; the howl of the wind, the engines turning over steadily to generate power for the lights, voices from somewhere nearby giving orders.

They moved down the gangway, Mrs Coulter leaning heavily on the guard. She was speaking softly, and Lord Roke could just make out his reply.

"The sergeant, ma'am — over there by the large crate — he's got the keys. But I daren't ask him, ma'am, I'm sorry."

"Oh well," she said with a pretty sigh of regret. "Thank you anyway."

Lord Roke heard booted feet moving away over rock, and then she whispered: "You heard about the keys?"

"Tell me where the sergeant is. I need to know where and how far."

"About ten of my paces away. To the right. A big man. I can see the keys in a bunch at his waist."

"No good unless I know which one. Did you see them lock the manacles?"

"Yes. A short stubby key with black tape wound around it."

Lord Roke climbed down hand over hand in the thick fleece of her coat, until he reached the hem at the level of her knees. There he clung and looked around.

They had rigged a flood-light, which cast a glare over the wet rocks. But as he looked down, casting around for shadows, he saw the glare begin to swing sideways in a gust of wind. He heard a shout, and the light went out abruptly.

He dropped to the ground at once, and sprang through the dashing sleet towards the sergeant, who had lurched forward to try and catch the falling flood-light.

In the confusion, Lord Roke leapt at the big man's leg as it swung past him, seized the camouflage cotton of the trousers – heavy and sodden with rain already – and kicked a spur into the flesh just above the boot.

The sergeant gave a grunting cry and fell clumsily, grasping his leg, trying to breathe, trying to call out. Lord Roke let go and sprang away from the falling body.

No one had noticed: the noise of the wind and the engines and the pounding hail covered the man's cry, and in the darkness his body couldn't be seen. But there were others close by, and Lord Roke had to work quickly. He leapt to the fallen man's side, where the bunch of keys lay in a pool of icy water, and hauled aside the great shafts of steel, as big around as his arm and half as long as he was, till he found the one with the black tape. And then there was the clasp of the keyring to wrestle with, and the perpetual risk of the hail, which for a Gallivespian was deadly: blocks of ice as big as his two fists.

And then a voice above him said, "You all right, Sergeant?"

The soldier's dæmon was growling and nuzzling at the sergeant's, who had fallen into a semi-stupor. Lord Roke couldn't wait: a spring and a kick, and the other man fell beside the sergeant.

Hauling, wrestling, heaving, Lord Roke finally snapped open the key-ring, and then he had to lift six other keys out of the way before the black-taped one was free. Any second now they'd get the light back on, but even in the half-dark they could hardly miss two men lying unconscious –

And as he hoisted the key out, a shout went up. He hauled up the massive shaft with all the strength he had, tugging, heaving, lifting, crawling, dragging, and hid beside a small boulder just as pounding feet arrived and voices called for light.

"Shot?"

"Didn't hear a thing –"

"Are they breathing?"

Then the flood-light, secure again, snapped on once more. Lord Roke was caught in the open, as clear as a fox in the headlights of a car. He stood stock still, his eyes moving to left and right, and once he was sure that everyone's attention was on the two men who had fallen so mysteriously, he hauled the key to his shoulder and ran around the puddles and the boulders until he reached Mrs Coulter.

A second later she had unlocked the handcuffs and lowered them silently to the ground. Lord Roke leapt for the hem of her coat and ran up to her shoulder.

"Where's the bomb?" he said, close to her ear.

"They've just begun to unload it. It's the big crate on the ground over there. I can't do anything till they take it out, and even then –"

"All right," he said, "run. Hide yourself. I'll stay here and watch. Run!"

He leapt down to her sleeve, and sprang away. Without a sound she moved away from the light, slowly at first so as not to catch the eye of the guard, and then she crouched and ran into the rain-lashed darkness further up the slope, the golden monkey darting ahead to see the way.

Behind her she heard the continuing roar of the engines, the confused shouts, the powerful voice of the President trying to impose some order on the scene. She remembered the long horrible pain and hallucination that she'd suffered at the spur of the Chevalier Tialys, and didn't envy the two men their waking up.

But soon she was higher up, clambering over the wet rocks, and all she could see behind her was the wavering glow of the flood-light reflected back from the great curved belly of the zeppelin; and presently that went out again, and all she could hear was the engine-roar, straining vainly against the wind and the thunder of the cataract below.

The engineers from the hydro-anbaric station were struggling over the edge of the gorge to bring a power cable to the bomb.

The problem for Mrs Coulter was not how to get out of this situation alive: that was a secondary matter. The problem was how to get Lyra's hair out of the bomb before they set it off. Lord Roke had burned the hair from the envelope after her arrest, letting the wind take the ashes away into the night sky; and then he'd found his way to the laboratory, and watched as they placed the rest of the little dark-golden curl in the resonating chamber in preparation. He knew exactly where it was, and how to open the chamber, but the brilliant light and the glittering surfaces in the laboratory, not to mention the constant coming and going of technicians, made it impossible for him to do anything about it there.

So they'd have to remove the lock of hair after the bomb was set up.

And that was going to be even harder, because of what the President intended to do with Mrs Coulter. The energy of the bomb came from cutting the link between human and dæmon, and that meant the hideous process of intercision: the cages of mesh, the silver guillotine. He was going to sever the lifelong connection between her and the golden monkey, and use the power released by that to destroy her daughter. She and Lyra would perish by the means she herself had invented. It was neat, at least, she thought.

Her only hope was Lord Roke. But in their whispered exchanges in the zeppelin, he'd explained about the power of his poison spurs: he couldn't go on using them continually, because with each sting, the venom weakened. It took a day for the full potency to build up again. Before long his main weapon would lose its force, and then they'd only have their wits.

She found an overhanging rock next to the roots of a spruce tree which clung to the side of the gorge, and settled herself beneath it to look around.

Behind her and above, over the lip of the ravine and in the full force of the wind, stood the generating station. The engineers were rigging a series of lights to help them bring the cable to the bomb: she could hear their voices not far away, shouting commands, and see the lights wavering through the trees. The cable itself, as thick as a man's arm, was being hauled from a gigantic reel on a truck at the top of the slope, and at the rate they were edging their way down over the rocks, they'd reach the bomb in five minutes or less.

At the zeppelin, Father MacPhail had rallied the soldiers. Several men stood guard, looking out into the sleet-filled dark with rifles at the ready, while others opened the wooden crate containing the bomb and made it ready for the cable. Mrs Coulter could see it clearly in the wash of the flood-lights, streaming with rain, an ungainly mass of machinery and wiring slightly tilted on the rocky ground. She heard a high-tension crackle and hum from the lights, whose cables swung in the wind, scattering the rain and throwing shadows up over the rocks and down again, like a grotesque skipping-rope.

Mrs Coulter was horribly familiar with one part of the structure: the mesh cages, the silver blade above. They stood at one end of the apparatus. The rest of it was strange to her; she could see no principle behind the coils, the jars, the banks of insulators, the lattice of tubing. Nevertheless, somewhere in all that complexity was the little lock of hair on which everything depended.

To her left, the slope fell away into the dark, and far below was a glimmer of white and a thunder of water from the cataract of Saint-Jean-les-Eaux.

There came a cry. A soldier dropped his rifle and stumbled

forwards, to fall to the ground kicking and thrashing and groaning with pain. In response the President looked up to the sky, put his hands to his mouth, and uttered a piercing yell.

What was he doing?

A moment later Mrs Coulter found out. Of all unlikely things, a witch flew down and landed beside the President as he shouted above the wind:

"Search nearby! There is a creature of some kind helping the woman. It's attacked several of my men already. You can see through the dark. Find it and kill it!"

"There is something coming," said the witch, in a tone that carried clearly to Mrs Coulter's shelter. "I can see it in the north."

"Never mind that. Find the creature and destroy it," said the President. "It can't be far away. And look for the woman too. Go!"

The witch sprang into the air again.

Suddenly the monkey seized Mrs Coulter's hand, and pointed.

There was Lord Roke, lying in the open on a patch of moss. How could they not have seen him? But something had happened, for he wasn't moving.

"Go and bring him back," she said, and the monkey, crouching low, darted from one rock to another, making for the little patch of green among the rocks. His golden fur was soon darkened by the rain and plastered close to his body, making him smaller and less easy to see, but all the same he was horribly conspicuous.

Father MacPhail, meanwhile, had turned to the bomb again. The engineers from the generating station had brought their cable right down to it, and the technicians were busy securing the clamps and making ready the terminals.

Mrs Coulter wondered what he intended to do, now that his victim had escaped. Then the President turned to look over his shoulder, and she saw his expression. It was so fixed and intense that he looked more like a mask than a man. His lips were moving in prayer, his eyes were turned up wide open as the rain beat into them, and altogether he looked like some gloomy Spanish painting of a saint in the ecstasy of martyrdom. Mrs Coulter felt a sudden bolt of fear, because she knew exactly what he intended:

he was going to sacrifice himself. The bomb would work whether or not she was part of it.

Darting from rock to rock, the golden monkey reached Lord Roke.

"My left leg is broken," said the Gallivespian calmly. "The last man stepped on me. Listen carefully –"

As the monkey lifted him away from the lights, Lord Roke explained exactly where the resonating chamber was, and how to open it. They were practically under the eyes of the soldiers, but step by step, from shadow to shadow, the dæmon crept with his little burden.

Mrs Coulter, watching and biting her lip, heard a rush of air and felt a heavy knock – not to her body, but to the tree. An arrow stuck there quivering less than a hand's breadth from her left arm. At once she rolled away, before the witch could shoot another, and tumbled down the slope towards the monkey.

And then everything was happening at once, too quickly: there was a burst of gunfire, and a cloud of acrid smoke billowed across the slope, though she saw no flames. The golden monkey, seeing Mrs Coulter attacked, set Lord Roke down and sprang to her defence, just as the witch flew down, knife at the ready. Lord Roke pushed himself back against the nearest rock, and Mrs Coulter grappled directly with the witch. They wrestled furiously among the rocks, while the golden monkey set about tearing all the needles from the witch's cloud-pine branch.

Meanwhile, the President was thrusting his lizard-dæmon into the smaller of the silver mesh cages. She writhed and screamed and kicked and bit, but he struck her off his hand and slammed the door shut quickly. The technicians were making the final adjustments, checking their meters and gauges.

Out of nowhere a seagull flew down with a wild cry, and seized the Gallivespian in his claw. It was the witch's dæmon. Lord Roke fought hard, but the bird had him too tightly, and then the witch tore herself from Mrs Coulter's grasp, snatched the tattered pine branch, and leapt into the air to join her dæmon.

Mrs Coulter hurled herself towards the bomb, feeling the smoke attack her nose and throat like claws: tear-gas. The soldiers, most of them, had fallen or stumbled away choking (and where had the gas come from, she wondered?), but now, as the wind dispersed it, they were beginning to gather themselves again. The great ribbed belly of the zeppelin bulked over the bomb, straining at its cables in the wind, its silver sides running with moisture.

But then a sound from high above made Mrs Coulter's ears ring: a scream so high and horrified that even the golden monkey clutched her in fear. And a second later, pitching down in a swirl of white limbs, black silk, and green twigs, the witch fell right at the feet of Father MacPhail, her bones crunching audibly on the rock.

Mrs Coulter darted forward to see if Lord Roke had survived the fall. But the Gallivespian was dead. His right spur was deep in the witch's neck.

The witch herself was still just alive, and her mouth moved shudderingly, saying, "Something coming – something else – coming –"

It made no sense. The President was already stepping over her body to reach the larger cage. His dæmon was running up and down the sides of the other, her little claws making the silver mesh ring, her voice crying for pity.

The golden monkey leapt for Father MacPhail, but not to attack: he scrambled up and over the man's shoulders to reach the complex heart of the wires and the pipework, the resonating chamber. The President tried to grab him, but Mrs Coulter seized the man's arm and tried to pull him back. She couldn't see: the rain was driving into her eyes, and there was still gas in the air.

And all around there was gunfire: what was happening?

The flood-lights swung in the wind so that nothing seemed steady, not even the black rocks of the mountainside. The President and Mrs Coulter fought hand-to-hand, scratching, punching, tearing, pulling, biting, and she was tired and he was strong; but she was desperate too, and she might have pulled him away, but part of her was watching her dæmon as he manipulated the handles, his fierce black paws snapping the mechanism this way, that way, pulling, twisting, reaching in –

Then came a blow to her temple. She fell stunned, and the

President broke free and hauled himself bleeding into the cage, dragging the door shut after him.

And the monkey had the chamber open – a glass door on heavy hinges, and he was reaching inside – there was the lock of hair: held between rubber pads in a metal clasp! Still more to undo; and Mrs Coulter was hauling herself up with shaking hands. She shook the silvery mesh with all her might, looking up at the blade, the sparking terminals, the man inside. The monkey was unscrewing the clasp, and the President, his face a mask of grim exultation, was twisting wires together.

There was a flash of intense white, a lashing *crack*, and the monkey's form was flung high in the air. With him came a little cloud of gold: was it Lyra's hair? Was it his own fur? Whatever it was, it blew away at once in the dark. Mrs Coulter's right hand had convulsed so tightly that it clung to the mesh, leaving her half-lying, half-hanging, while her head rang and her heart pounded.

But something had happened to her sight. A terrible clarity had come over her eyes, the power to see the most tiny details, and they were focused on the one detail in the universe that mattered: stuck to one of the pads of the clasp in the resonating chamber, there was a single dark-gold hair.

She cried a great wail of anguish, and shook and shook the cage, trying to loosen the hair with the little strength she had left. The President passed his hands over his face, wiping it clear of the rain. His mouth moved as though he were speaking, but she couldn't hear a word. She tore at the mesh, helpless, and then hurled her whole weight against the machine as he brought two wires together with a spark. In utter silence the brilliant silver blade shot down.

Something exploded, somewhere, but Mrs Coulter was beyond feeling it.

There were hands lifting her up: Lord Asriel's hands. There was nothing to be surprised at any more; the intention craft stood behind him, poised on the slope and perfectly level. He lifted her in his arms and carried her to the craft, ignoring the gunfire, the billowing smoke, the cries of alarm and confusion.

"Is he dead? Did it go off?" she managed to say.

Lord Asriel climbed in beside her, and the snow leopard leapt in too, the half-stunned monkey in her mouth. Lord Asriel took the controls and the craft sprang at once into the air. Through pain-dazed eyes Mrs Coulter looked down at the mountain slope. Men were running here and there like ants; some lay dead, while others crawled brokenly over the rocks; the great cable from the generating station snaked down through the chaos, the only purposeful thing in sight, making its way to the glittering bomb where the President's body lay crumpled inside the cage.

"Lord Roke?" said Lord Asriel.

"Dead," she whispered.

He pressed a button, and a lance of flame jetted towards the tossing, swaying zeppelin. An instant later the whole airship bloomed into a rose of white fire, engulfing the intention craft, which hung motionless and unharmed in the middle of it. Lord Asriel moved the craft unhurriedly away, and they watched as the blazing zeppelin fell slowly, slowly down on top of the whole scene, bomb, cable, soldiers and all, and everything began to tumble in a welter of smoke and flames down the mountainside, gathering speed and incinerating the resinous trees as it went, until it plunged into the white waters of the cataract, which whirled it all away into the dark.

Lord Asriel touched the controls again, and the intention craft began to speed away northwards. But Mrs Coulter couldn't take her eyes off the scene; she watched behind them for a long time, gazing with tear-filled eyes at the fire, until it was no more than a vertical line of orange scratched on the dark and wreathed in smoke and steam, and then it was nothing.

26

THE ABYSS

The Sun has left his blackness & has found a fresher morning,
And the fair Moon rejoices in the clear & cloudless night

— WILLIAM BLAKE

IT WAS DARK, with an enfolding blackness that pressed on Lyra's eyes so heavily that she almost felt the weight of the thousands of tons of rock above them. The only light they had came from the luminous tail of the Lady Salmakia's dragonfly, and even that was fading; for the poor insects had found no food in the world of the dead, and the chevalier's had died not long before.

So while Tialys sat on Will's shoulder, Lyra held the lady's dragonfly in her hands as the lady soothed it and whispered to the trembling creature, feeding it first on crumbs of biscuit and then on her own blood. If Lyra had seen her do that, she would have offered hers, since there was more of it; but it was all she could do to concentrate on placing her feet safely and avoiding the lowest parts of the rock above.

No-Name the harpy had led them into a system of caves which would bring them, she said, to the nearest point in the world of the dead from which they could open a window to another world. Behind them came the endless column of ghosts. The tunnel was full of whispers, as the foremost encouraged those behind, as the brave urged on the faint-hearted, as the old gave hope to the young.

"Is it much further, No-Name?" said Lyra quietly. "Because this poor dragonfly's dying, and then his light'll go out."

The harpy stopped and turned to say:

"Just follow. If you can't see, listen. If you can't hear, feel."

Her eyes shone fierce in the gloom. Lyra nodded and said, "Yes, I will, but I'm not as strong as I used to be, and I'm not brave, not very anyway. Please don't stop. I'll follow you – we all will. Please keep going, No-Name."

The harpy turned back and moved on. The dragonfly-shine

was getting dimmer by the minute, and Lyra knew it would soon be completely gone.

But as she stumbled forward, a voice spoke just beside her – a familiar voice.

"Lyra – Lyra, child . . ."

And she turned in delight.

"Mr Scoresby! Oh, I'm so glad to hear you! And it *is* you – I can see, just – oh, I wish I could touch you!"

In the faint, faint light she made out the lean form and the sardonic smile of the Texan aëronaut, and her hand reached forward of its own accord, in vain.

"Me too, honey. But listen to me – they're working some trouble out there, and it's aimed at you – don't ask me how. Is this the boy with the knife?"

Will had been looking at him, eager to see this old companion of Lyra's; but now his eyes went right past Lee to look at the ghost beside him. Lyra saw at once who it was, and marvelled at this grown-up vision of Will – the same jutting jaw, the same way of holding his head.

Will was speechless, but his father said:

"Listen – there's no time to talk about this – just do exactly as I say. Take the knife now and find a place where a lock has been cut from Lyra's hair."

His tone was urgent, and Will didn't waste time asking why. Lyra, her eyes wide with alarm, held up the dragonfly with one hand and felt her hair with the other.

"No," said Will, "take your hand away – I can't see."

And in the faint gleam, he could see it: just above her left temple, there was a little patch of hair that was shorter than the rest.

"Who did that?" said Lyra. "And –"

"Hush," said Will, and asked his father's ghost, "What must I do?"

"Cut the short hair off right down to her scalp. Collect it carefully, every single hair. Don't miss even one. Then open another world – any will do – and put the hair through into it, and then close it again. Do it now, at once."

The harpy was watching; the ghosts behind were crowding

close. Lyra could see their faint faces in the dimness. Frightened and bewildered, she stood biting her lip while Will did as his father told him, his face close up to the knife-point in the pale dragonfly-light. He cut a little hollow space in the rock of another world, put all the tiny golden hairs into it, and replaced the rock before closing the window.

And then the ground began to shake. From somewhere very deep there came a growling, grinding noise, as if the whole centre of the earth were turning on itself like a vast millwheel, and little fragments of stone began to fall from the roof of the tunnel. The ground lurched suddenly to one side. Will seized Lyra's arm, and they clung together as the rock under their feet began to shift and slide, and loose pieces of stone came tumbling past and bruising their legs and feet –

The two children, sheltering the Gallivespians, crouched down with their arms over their heads; and then in a horrible sliding movement they found themselves being borne away down to the left, and they held each other fiercely, too breathless and shaken even to cry out. Their ears were filled with the roar of thousands of tons of rock tumbling and rolling down with them.

Finally their movement stopped, though all around them smaller rocks were still tumbling and bounding down a slope that hadn't been there a minute before. Lyra was lying on Will's left arm. With his right hand he felt for the knife: it was still there at his belt.

"Tialys? Salmakia?" said Will, shakily.

"Both here, both alive," said the chevalier's voice near his ear.

The air was full of dust, and of the cordite-smell of smashed rock. It was hard to breathe, and impossible to see: the dragonfly was dead.

"Mr Scoresby?" said Lyra. "We can't see anything . . . What happened?"

"I'm here," said Lee, close by. "I guess the bomb went off, and I guess it missed."

"Bomb?" said Lyra, frightened; but then she said, "Roger – are you there?"

"Yeah," came the little whisper. "Mr Parry, he saved me. I was going to fall, and he caught hold."

"Look," said the ghost of John Parry. "But hold still to the rock, and don't move."

The dust was clearing, and from somewhere there was light: a strange faint golden glimmer, like a luminous misty rain falling all around them. It was enough to strike their hearts ablaze with fear, for it lit up what lay to their left, the place into which it was all falling – or flowing, like a river over the edge of a waterfall.

It was a vast black emptiness, like a shaft into the deepest darkness. The golden light flowed into it and died. They could see the other side, but it was much further away than Will could have thrown a stone. To their right, a slope of rough stones, loose and precariously balanced, rose high into the dusty gloom.

The children and their companions were clinging to what was not even a ledge – just some lucky hand and footholds – on the edge of that abyss, and there was no way out except forwards, along the slope, among the shattered rocks and the teetering boulders which, it seemed, the slightest touch would send hurtling down below.

And behind them, as the dust cleared, more and more of the ghosts were gazing in horror at the abyss. They were crouching on the slope, too frightened to move. Only the harpies were unafraid; they took to their wings and soared above, scanning backwards and forwards, flying back to reassure those still in the tunnel, flying ahead to search for the way out.

Lyra checked: at least the alethiometer was safe. Suppressing her fear, she looked around, found Roger's little face, and said:

"Come on then, we're all still here, we en't been hurt. And we can see now, at least. So just keep going, just keep on moving. We can't go any other way than round the edge of this . . ." She gestured at the abyss. "So we just got to keep going ahead. I swear Will and me'll just keep on till we do. So don't be scared, don't give up, don't lag behind. Tell the others. I can't look back all the time because I got to watch where I'm going, so I got to trust you to come on steady after us, all right?"

The little ghost nodded. And so, in a shocked silence, the column of the dead began their journey along the edge of the abyss. How long it took, neither Lyra nor Will could guess; how fearful and dangerous it was, they were never able to forget. The darkness below was so profound that it seemed to pull the eye-sight down into it, and a ghastly dizziness swam over their minds when they looked. Whenever they could, they looked ahead of them fixedly, on this rock, that foothold, this projection, that loose slope of gravel, and kept their eyes from the gulf; but it pulled, it tempted, and they couldn't help glancing into it, only to feel their balance tilting and their eyesight swimming and a dreadful nausea gripping their throats.

From time to time the living ones looked back, and saw the infinite line of the dead winding out of the crack they'd come through: mothers pressing their infants' faces to their breasts, aged fathers clambering slowly, little children clutching the skirts of the person in front, young boys and girls of Roger's age keep-ing staunch and careful, so many of them ... And all following Will and Lyra, so they still hoped, towards the open air.

But some didn't trust them. They crowded close behind, and both children felt cold hands on their hearts and their entrails, and they heard vicious whispers:

"Where is the upper world? How much further?"

"We're frightened here!"

"We should never have come − at least back in the world of the dead we had a little light and a little company − this is far worse!"

"You did a wrong thing when you came to our land! You should have stayed in your own world and waited to die before you came down to disturb us!"

"By what right are you leading us? You are only children! Who gave you the authority?"

Will wanted to turn and denounce them, but Lyra held his arm; they were unhappy and frightened, she said.

Then the Lady Salmakia spoke, and her clear calm voice carried a long way in the great emptiness.

"Friends, be brave! Stay together and keep going! The way is hard, but Lyra can find it. Be patient and cheerful and we'll lead you out, don't fear!"

Lyra felt herself strengthened by hearing this, and that was really the lady's intention. And so they toiled on, with painful effort.

"Will," said Lyra after some minutes, "can you hear that wind?"

"Yes, I can," said Will. "But I can't *feel* it at all. And I tell you something about that hole down there. It's the same kind of thing as when I cut a window. The same kind of edge. There's something special about that kind of edge; once you've felt it you never forget it. And I can see it there, just where the rock falls away into the dark. But that big space down there, that's not another world like all the others. It's different. I don't like it. I wish I could close it up."

"You haven't closed every window you've made."

"No, because I couldn't, some of them. But I know I *should*. Things go wrong if they're left open. And one that big . . ." He gestured downwards, not wanting to look. "It's wrong. Something bad will happen."

While they were talking together, another conversation had been taking place a little way off: the Chevalier Tialys was talking quietly with the ghosts of Lee Scoresby and John Parry.

"So what are you saying, John?" said Lee. "You're saying we ought *not* to go out into the open air? Man, every single part of me is aching to join the rest of the living universe again!"

"Yes, and so am I," said Will's father. "But I believe that if those of us who are used to fighting could manage to hold ourselves back, we might be able to throw ourselves into the battle on Asriel's side. And if it came at the right moment, it might make all the difference."

"Ghosts?" said Tialys, trying to hold the scepticism from his voice, and failing. "How could you fight?"

"We couldn't hurt living creatures, that's quite true. But Asriel's army is going to contend with other kinds of being as well."

"Those Spectres," said Lee.

"Just what I was thinking. They make for the dæmon, don't they? And our dæmons are long gone. It's worth a try, Lee."

"Well, I'm with you, my friend."

"And you, sir," said John Parry's ghost to the chevalier: "I have spoken to the ghosts of your people. Will you live long enough to see the world again, before you die and come back as a ghost?"

"It's true, our lives are short compared to yours. I have a few days more to live," said Tialys, "and the Lady Salmakia a little longer, perhaps. But thanks to what those children are doing, our exile as ghosts will not be permanent. I have been proud to help them."

They moved on. And that abominable fall yawned all the time, and one little slip, one footstep on a loose rock, one careless handhold, would send you down for ever and ever, thought Lyra, so far down you'd die of starvation before you ever hit the bottom, and then your poor ghost would go on falling and falling into an infinite gulf, with no one to help, no hands to reach down and lift you out, for ever conscious and for ever falling . . .

Oh, that would be far worse than the grey silent world they were leaving, wouldn't it?

A strange thing happened to her mind then. The thought of falling induced a kind of vertigo in Lyra, and she swayed. Will was ahead of her, just too far to reach, or she might have taken his hand; but at that moment she was more conscious of Roger, and a little flicker of vanity blazed up for a moment in her heart. There'd been an occasion once on Jordan College roof, when just to frighten him she'd defied her vertigo and walked along the edge of the stone gutter.

She looked back to remind him of it now. She was Roger's Lyra, full of grace and daring; she didn't need to creep along like an insect.

But the little boy's whispering voice said, "Lyra, be *careful* – remember, you en't dead like us –"

And it seemed to happen so slowly, but there was nothing she could do: her weight shifted, the stones moved under her feet, and helplessly she began to slide. In the first moment it was annoying, and then it was comic: she thought *how silly!* But as she utterly failed to hold on to anything, as the stones rolled and tumbled beneath her, as she slid down towards the edge, gathering speed, the horror of it slammed into her. She was going to fall. There was nothing to stop her. It was already too late.

Her body convulsed with terror. She wasn't aware of the ghosts who flung themselves down to try and catch her, only to find her hurtling through them like a stone through mist; she didn't know that Will was yelling her name so loudly that the abyss resounded with it. Instead her whole being was a vortex of roaring fear. Faster and faster she tumbled, down and down, and some ghosts couldn't bear to watch: they hid their eyes and cried aloud.

Will felt electric with fear. He watched in anguish as Lyra slid further and further, knowing he could do nothing, and knowing he had to watch. He couldn't hear the desperate wail he was uttering any more than she could. Another two seconds – another second – she was at the edge, she couldn't stop, she was there, she was falling –

And out of the dark swooped that creature whose claws had raked her scalp not long before, No-Name the harpy, woman-faced, bird-winged; and those same claws closed tight around the girl's wrist. Together they plunged on down, the extra weight almost too much for the harpy's strong wings, but they beat and beat and beat, and her claws held firm, and slowly, heavily, slowly, heavily, the harpy carried the child up and up out of the gulf and brought her limp and fainting to Will's reaching arms.

He held her tight, pressing her to his chest, feeling the wild beat of her heart against his ribs. She wasn't Lyra just then, and he wasn't Will; she wasn't a girl, and he wasn't a boy. They were the only two human beings in that vast gulf of death. They clung together, and the ghosts clustered around, whispering comfort, blessing the harpy. Closest at hand were Will's father and Lee Scoresby, and how they longed to hold her too; and Tialys and Salmakia spoke to No-Name, praising her, calling her the saviour of them all, generous one, blessing her kindness.

As soon as Lyra could move, she reached out trembling for the harpy and put her arms around her neck, kissing and kissing her ravaged face. She couldn't speak. All the words, all the confidence, all the vanity had been shaken out of her.

They lay still for some minutes. Once the terror had begun to subside, they set off again, Will holding Lyra's hand tightly in his good one, and crept forward testing each spot before they put any weight on it, a process so slow and wearisome that they thought they might die of fatigue; but they couldn't rest, they couldn't stop. How could anyone rest, with that fearful gulf below them?

And after another hour of toil, he said to her:

"Look ahead. I think there's a way out..."

It was true: the slope was getting easier, and it was even possible to climb slightly, up and away from the edge. And ahead: wasn't that a fold in the wall of the cliff? Could that really be a way out?

Lyra looked into Will's brilliant strong eyes, and smiled.

They clambered on, up and further up, with every step moving further from the abyss. And as they climbed, they found the ground firmer, the handholds more secure, the footholds less liable to roll and twist their ankles.

"We must have climbed a fair way now," Will said. "I could try the knife and see what I find."

"Not yet," said the harpy. "Further to go yet. This is a bad place to open. Better place higher up."

They carried on quietly, hand, foot, weight, move, test, hand, foot ... Their fingers were raw, their knees and hips were trembling with the effort, their heads ached and rang with exhaustion. They climbed the last few feet up to the foot of the cliff, where a narrow defile led a little way into the shadow.

Lyra watched with aching eyes as Will took the knife and began to search the air, touching, withdrawing, searching, touching again.

"Ah," he said.

"You found an open space?"

"I think so..."

"Will," said his father's ghost, "stop a moment. Listen to me."

Will put down the knife and turned. In all the effort he hadn't been able to think of his father, but it was good to know he was there. Suddenly he realized that they were going to part for the last time.

"What will happen when you go outside?" Will said. "Will you just vanish?"

"Not yet. Mr Scoresby and I have an idea. Some of us will remain here for a little while, and we shall need you to let us into Lord Asriel's world, because he might need our help. What's more," he went on sombrely, looking at Lyra, "you'll need to travel there yourselves, if you want to find your dæmons again. Because that's where they've gone."

"But Mr Parry," said Lyra, "how do you know our dæmons have gone into my father's world?"

"I was a shaman when I was alive. I learned how to see things. Ask your alethiometer – it'll confirm what I say. But remember this about dæmons," he said, and his voice was intense and emphatic. "The man you knew as Sir Charles Latrom had to return to his own world periodically; he could not live permanently in mine. The philosophers of the Guild of the Torre degli Angeli, who travelled between worlds for three hundred years or more, found the same thing to be true, and gradually their world weakened and decayed as a result.

"And then there is what happened to me. I was a soldier; I was an officer in the Marines, and then I earned my living as an explorer; I was as fit and healthy as it's possible for a human to be. Then I walked out of my own world by accident, and couldn't find the way back. I did many things and learned a great deal in the world I found myself in, but ten years after I arrived there, I was mortally sick.

"And this is the reason for all those things: your dæmon can only live its full life in the world it was born in. Elsewhere it will eventually sicken and die. We can travel, if there are openings into other worlds, but we can only live in our own. Lord Asriel's great enterprise will fail in the end for the same reason: we have to build the republic of heaven where we are, because for us there is no elsewhere.

"Will, my boy, you and Lyra can go out now for a brief rest; you need that, and you deserve it; but then you must come back into the dark with me and Mr Scoresby for one last journey."

Will and Lyra exchanged a look. Then he cut a window, and it was the sweetest thing they had ever seen.

The night air filled their lungs, fresh and clean and cool; their eyes took in a canopy of dazzling stars, and the shine of water somewhere below, and here and there groves of great trees, as high as castles, dotting the wide savannah.

Will enlarged the window as wide as he could, moving across

the grass to left and right, making it big enough for six, seven, eight to walk through abreast, out of the land of the dead.

The first ghosts trembled with hope, and their excitement passed back like a ripple over the long line behind them, young children and aged parents alike looking up and ahead with delight and wonder as the first stars they had seen for centuries shone through into their poor starved eyes.

The first ghost to leave the world of the dead was Roger. He took a step forward, and turned to look back at Lyra, and laughed in surprise as he found himself turning into the night, the starlight, the air ... and then he was gone, leaving behind such a vivid little burst of happiness that Will was reminded of the bubbles in a glass of champagne.

The other ghosts followed him, and Will and Lyra fell exhausted on the dew-laden grass, every nerve in their bodies blessing the sweetness of the good soil, the night air, the stars.

27

THE PLATFORM

My Soul into the boughs does glide:
There like a Bird it sits, and sings,
Then whets, and combs its silver wings

— ANDREW MARVELL

ONCE THE MULEFA began to build the platform for Mary, they worked quickly and well. She enjoyed watching them, because they could discuss without quarrelling and co-operate without getting in each other's way, and because their techniques of splitting and cutting and joining wood were so elegant and effective.

Within two days, the observation platform was designed and built and lifted into place. It was firm and spacious and comfortable, and when she had climbed up to it she was as happy, in one way, as she had ever been. That one way was physically. In the dense green of the canopy, with the rich blue of the sky between the leaves; with a breeze keeping her skin cool, and the faint scent of the flowers delighting her whenever she sensed it; with the rustle of the leaves, the song of the hundreds of birds, and the distant murmur of the waves on the seashore, all her senses were lulled and nurtured, and if she could have stopped thinking, she would have been entirely lapped in bliss.

But of course thinking was what she was there for.

And when she looked through her spyglass and saw the relentless outward drift of the sraf, the Shadow-particles, it seemed to her as if happiness and life and hope were drifting away with them. She could find no explanation at all.

Three hundred years, the mulefa had said: that was how long the trees had been failing. Given that the Shadow-particles passed through all the worlds alike, presumably the same thing was happening in her universe too, and in every other one. Three hundred years ago, the Royal Society was set up: the first true scientific society in her world. Newton was making his discoveries about optics and gravitation.

Three hundred years ago in Lyra's world, someone invented the alethiometer.

At the same time in that strange world through which she'd come to get here, the subtle knife was invented.

She lay back on the planks, feeling the platform move in a very slight, very slow rhythm as the great tree swayed in the seabreeze. Holding the spyglass to her eye, she watched the myriad tiny sparkles drift through the leaves, past the open mouths of the blossoms, through the massive boughs, moving against the wind, in a slow deliberate current that looked all but conscious.

What had happened three hundred years ago? Was it the cause of the Dust-current, or was it the other way round? Or were they both the results of a different cause altogether? Or were they simply not connected at all?

The drift was mesmerizing. How easy it would be to fall into a trance, and let her mind drift away with the floating particles . . .

Before she knew what she was doing, and because her body was lulled, that was exactly what happened. She suddenly snapped awake to find herself outside her body, and she panicked.

She was a little way above the platform, and a few feet off among the branches. And something had happened to the Dust-wind: instead of that slow drift, it was racing like a river in flood. Had it speeded up, or was time moving differently for her, now she was outside her body? Either way, she was conscious of the most horrible danger, because the flood was threatening to sweep her loose completely, and it was immense. She flung out her arms to seize hold of anything solid – but she had no arms. Nothing connected. Now she was almost over that abominable drop, and her body was further and further from reach, sleeping so hoggishly below her. She tried to shout and wake herself up: not a sound. The body slumbered on, and the self that observed was being borne away out of the canopy of leaves altogether and into the open sky.

And no matter how she struggled she could make no headway. The force that carried her out was as smooth and powerful as water pouring over a weir: the particles of Dust were streaming along as if they too were pouring over some invisible edge.

And carrying her away from her body.

She flung a mental lifeline to that physical self, and tried to recall the feeling of being in it: all the sensations that made up being alive. The exact touch of her friend Atal's soft-tipped trunk caressing her neck. The taste of bacon and eggs. The triumphant strain in her muscles as she pulled herself up a rock face. The delicate dancing of her fingers on a computer keyboard. The smell of roasting coffee. The warmth of her bed on a winter night.

And gradually she stopped moving; the lifeline held fast, and she felt the weight and strength of the current pushing against her as she hung there in the sky.

And then a strange thing happened. Little by little (as she reinforced those sense-memories, adding others: tasting an iced Margarita in California, sitting under the lemon trees outside a restaurant in Lisbon, scraping the frost off the windscreen of her car) she felt the Dust-wind easing. The pressure was lessening.

But only on *her*: all around, above and below, the great flood was streaming as fast as ever. Somehow there was a little patch of stillness around her, where the particles were resisting the flow.

They *were* conscious! They felt her anxiety, and responded to it. And they began to carry her back to her deserted body, and when she was close enough to see it once more, so heavy, so warm, so safe, a silent sob convulsed her heart.

And then she sank back into her body, and awoke.

She took in a deep shuddering breath. She pressed her hands and her legs against the rough planks of the platform, and having a minute ago nearly gone mad with fear, she was now suffused with a deep slow ecstasy at being one with her body and the earth and everything that was matter.

Finally she sat up and tried to take stock. Her fingers found the spyglass, and she held it to her eye, supporting one trembling hand with the other. There was no doubt about it: that slow sky-wide drift had become a flood. There was nothing to hear and nothing to feel, and without the spyglass, nothing to see, but even when she took the glass from her eye, the sense of that swift silent inundation remained vividly, together with something she hadn't noticed in the terror of being outside her body: the profound, helpless regret that was abroad in the air.

The Shadow-particles knew what was happening, and were sorrowful.

And she herself was partly Shadow-matter. Part of her was subject to this tide that was moving through the cosmos. And so were the mulefa, and so were human beings in every world, and every kind of conscious creature, wherever they were.

And unless she found out what was happening, they might all find themselves drifting away to oblivion, every one.

Suddenly she longed for the earth again. She put the spyglass in her pocket and began the long climb down to the ground.

Father Gomez stepped through the window as the evening light lengthened and mellowed. He saw the great stands of wheel-trees and the roads lacing through the prairie, just as Mary had done from the same spot some time before. But the air was free of haze, for it had rained a little earlier, and he could see further than she had; in particular, he could see the glimmer of a distant sea, and some flickering white shapes that might be sails.

He lifted the rucksack higher on his shoulders, and turned towards them, to see what he could find. In the calm of the long evening it was pleasant to walk on this smooth road, with the sound of some cicada-like creatures in the long grass and the setting sun warm in his face. The air was fresh, too, clear and sweet and entirely free of the taint of naphtha-fumes, kerosene-fumes, whatever they were, which had lain so heavily on the air in one of the worlds he'd passed through: the world his target, the tempter herself, belonged to.

He came out at sunset on a little headland beside a shallow bay. If they had tides in this sea, the tide was high, because there was only a narrow fringe of soft white sand above the water.

And floating in the calm bay were a dozen or more ... Father Gomez had to stop and think carefully. A dozen or more enormous snow-white birds, each the size of a rowing-boat, with long straight wings which trailed on the water behind them: very long wings, six feet or more in length. *Were* they birds? They had feathers, and heads and beaks not unlike swans', but those wings were situated one in front of the other, surely ...

Suddenly they saw him. Heads turned with a snap, and at once all those wings were raised high, exactly like the sails of a yacht, and they all leaned in with the breeze, making for the shore.

Father Gomez was impressed by the beauty of those wing-sails, by how they were flexed and trimmed so perfectly, and by the speed of the birds. Then he saw that they were paddling, too: they had legs under the water, placed not fore-and-aft like the wings but side by side, and with the wings and the legs together, they had an extraordinary speed and grace in the water.

As the first one reached the shore it lumbered up through the dry sand, making directly for the priest. It was hissing with malice, stabbing its head forward as it waddled heavily up the shore, and the beak snapped and clacked. There were teeth in the beak, too, like a series of sharp incurved hooks.

Father Gomez was about a hundred yards from the edge of the water, on a low grassy promontory, and he had plenty of time to put down his rucksack, take out the rifle, load and aim and fire.

The bird's head exploded in a mist of red and white, and the dead creature blundered on clumsily for several steps before sinking on to its breast. It didn't die for a minute or more; the legs kicked, the wings rose and fell, and the great bird beat itself round and round in a bloody circle, kicking up the rough grass, until a long bubbling expiration from its lungs ended with a coughing spray of red, and it fell still.

The other birds had stopped as soon as the first one fell, and stood watching it, and watching the man, too. There was a quick, ferocious intelligence in their eyes. They looked from him to the dead bird, from that to the rifle, from the rifle to his face.

He raised the rifle to his shoulder again, and saw them react, shifting backwards clumsily, crowding together. They understood.

They were fine strong creatures, large and broad-backed; like living boats, in fact. If they knew what death was, thought Father Gomez, and if they could see the connection between death and himself, then there was the basis of a fruitful understanding between them. Once they had truly learned to fear him, they would do exactly as he said.

28

MIDNIGHT

For many a time
I have been half in love with easeful Death

— JOHN KEATS

LORD ASRIEL SAID, "Marisa, wake up. We're about to land."

A blustery dawn was breaking over the basalt fortress as the intention craft flew in from the south. Mrs Coulter, sore and heartsick, opened her eyes; she had not been asleep. She could see the angel Xaphania gliding above the landing ground, and then rising and wheeling up to the tower as the craft made for the ramparts.

As soon as the craft had landed, Lord Asriel leapt out and ran to join King Ogunwe on the western watch-tower, ignoring Mrs Coulter entirely. The technicians who came at once to attend to the flying machine took no notice of her, either; no one questioned her about the loss of the aircraft she'd stolen; it was as if she'd become invisible. She made her way sadly up to the room in the adamant tower, where the orderly offered to bring her some food and coffee.

"Whatever you have," she said. "And thank you. Oh, by the way," she went on as the man turned to go: "Lord Asriel's alethiometrist, Mr ..."

"Mr Basilides?"

"Yes. Is he free to come here for a moment?"

"He's working with his books at the moment, ma'am. I'll ask him to step up here when he can."

She washed, and changed into the one clean shirt she had left. The cold wind that shook the windows, and the grey morning light made her shiver. She put some more coals on the iron stove, hoping it would stop her trembling, but the cold was in her bones, not just her flesh.

Ten minutes later there was a knock on the door. The pale, dark-eyed alethiometrist, with his nightingale-dæmon on his shoulder, came in and bowed slightly. A moment later the orderly arrived with a tray of bread, cheese and coffee, and Mrs Coulter said:

"Thank you for coming, Mr Basilides. May I offer you some refreshment?"

"I will take some coffee, thank you."

"Please tell me," she said as soon as she'd poured the drink, "because I'm sure you've been following what's happened: is my daughter alive?"

He hesitated. The golden monkey clutched her arm.

"She is alive," said Basilides carefully, "but also . . ."

"Yes? Oh, please, what do you mean?"

"She is in the world of the dead. For some time I could not interpret what the instrument was telling me: it seemed impossible. But there is no doubt. She and the boy have gone into the world of the dead, and they have opened a way for the ghosts to come out. As soon as the dead reach the open they dissolve as their dæmons did, and it seems that this is the most sweet and desirable end for them. And the alethiometer tells me that the girl did this because she overheard a prophecy that there would come an end to death, and she thought that this was a task for her to accomplish. As a result, there is now a way out of the world of the dead."

Mrs Coulter couldn't speak. She had to turn away and go to the window to conceal the emotion on her face. Finally she said:

"And will she come out alive? But no, I know you can't predict. Is she – how is she – has she . . ."

"She is suffering, she is in pain, she is afraid. But she has the companionship of the boy, and of the two Gallivespian spies, and they are still all together."

"And the bomb?"

"The bomb did not hurt her."

Mrs Coulter felt suddenly exhausted. She wanted nothing more than to lie down and sleep for months, for years. Outside, the flag-rope snapped and clattered in the wind, and the rooks cawed as they wheeled around the ramparts.

"Thank you, sir," she said, turning back to the reader. "I'm very grateful. Please would you let me know if you discover anything more about her, or where she is, or what she's doing?"

The man bowed and left. Mrs Coulter went to lie down on the camp bed, but try as she would, she couldn't keep her eyes closed.

"What do you make of that, King?" said Lord Asriel.

He was looking through the watch-tower telescope at something in the western sky. It had the appearance of a mountain hanging in the sky a hand's breadth above the horizon, and covered in cloud. It was a very long way off; so far, in fact, that it was no bigger than a thumb-nail held out at arm's length. But it had not been there for long, and it hung there absolutely still.

The telescope brought it closer, but there was no more detail: cloud still looks like cloud, however much it's magnified.

"The Clouded Mountain," said Ogunwe. "Or – what do they call it? The Chariot?"

"With the Regent at the reins. He's concealed himself well, this Metatron. They speak of him in the apocryphal scriptures: he was a man once, a man called Enoch, the son of Jared – six generations away from Adam. And now he rules the kingdom. And he's intending to do more than that, if that angel they found by the sulphur lake was correct – the one who entered the Clouded Mountain to spy. If he wins this battle, he intends to intervene directly in human life. Imagine that, Ogunwe – a permanent Inquisition, worse than anything the Consistorial Court of Discipline could dream up, staffed by spies and traitors in every world and directed personally by the intelligence that's keeping that mountain aloft ... The old Authority at least had the grace to withdraw; the dirty work of burning heretics and hanging witches was left to his priests. This new one will be far, far worse."

"Well, he's begun by invading the republic," said Ogunwe. "Look – is that smoke?"

A drift of grey was leaving the Clouded Mountain, a slowly spreading smudge against the blue sky. But it couldn't have been smoke: it was drifting *against* the wind that tore at the clouds.

The king put his field-glasses to his eyes, and saw what it was.

"Angels," he said.

Lord Asriel came away from the telescope and stood up, hand

shading his eyes. In hundreds, and then thousands, and tens of thousands, until half that part of the sky was darkened, the minute figures flew and flew and kept on coming. Lord Asriel had seen the billion-strong flocks of blue starlings that wheeled at sunset around the palace of the Emperor K'ang-Po, but he had never seen so vast a multitude in all his life. The flying beings gathered themselves and then streamed away slowly, slowly, to the north and the south.

"Ah! And what's that?" said Lord Asriel, pointing. "That's not the wind."

The cloud was swirling on the southern flank of the mountain, and long tattered banners of vapour streamed out in the powerful winds. But Lord Asriel was right: the movement was coming from within, not from the air outside. The cloud roiled and tumbled, and then it parted for a second.

There was more than a mountain there, but they only saw it for a moment; and then the cloud swirled back, as if drawn across by an unseen hand, to conceal it again.

King Ogunwe put down his field-glasses.

"That's not a mountain," he said. "I saw gun emplacements . . ."

"So did I. A whole complexity of things. Can he see out through the cloud, I wonder? In some worlds, they have machines to do that. But as for his army, if those angels are all they've got –"

The king gave a brief exclamation, half of astonishment, half of despair. Lord Asriel turned and gripped his arm with fingers that all but bruised him to the bone.

"They haven't got *this*!" he said, and shook Ogunwe's arm violently. "They haven't got *flesh*!"

He laid his hand against his friend's rough cheek.

"Few as we are," he went on, "and short-lived as we are, and weak-sighted as we are – in comparison with them, we're still *stronger*. They *envy* us, Ogunwe! That's what fuels their hatred, I'm sure of it. They long to have our precious bodies, so solid and powerful, so well adapted to the good earth! And if we *drive* at them with force and determination, we can sweep aside those infinite numbers as you can sweep your hand through mist. They have no more power than that!"

"Asriel, they have allies from a thousand worlds, living beings like us."

"We shall win."

"And suppose he's sent those angels to look for your daughter?"

"My daughter!" cried Lord Asriel, exulting. "Isn't it something to bring a child like that into the world? You'd think it was enough to go alone to the king of the armoured bears and trick his kingdom out of his paws – but to go down into the world of the dead and calmly let them all out –! And that boy; I want to meet that boy; I want to shake his hand. Did we know what we were taking on when we started this rebellion? No. But did they know – the Authority and his Regent, this Metatron – did they know what they were taking on when my daughter got involved?"

"Lord Asriel," said the king, "do you understand her importance for the future?"

"Frankly, no. That's why I want to see Basilides. Where did he go?"

"To the lady Coulter. But the man is worn out; he can do no more until he's rested."

"He should have rested before. Send for him, would you? Oh, one more thing: please ask Madame Oxentiel to come to the tower as soon as it's convenient. I must give her my condolences."

Madame Oxentiel had been the Gallivespians' second-in-command. Now she would have to take over Lord Roke's responsibilities. King Ogunwe bowed, and left his commander scanning the grey horizon.

All through that day the army assembled. Angels of Lord Asriel's force flew high over the Clouded Mountain, looking for an opening, but without success. Nothing changed; no more angels flew out or inwards; the high winds tore at the clouds, and the clouds endlessly renewed themselves, not parting even for a second. The sun crossed the cold blue sky and then moved down to the south-west, gilding the clouds and tinting the vapour around the mountain every shade of cream and scarlet, of apricot and orange. When the sun sank, the clouds glowed faintly from within.

Warriors were now in place from every world where Lord Asriel's rebellion had supporters; mechanics and artificers were fuelling aircraft, loading weapons, and calibrating sights and measures. As the darkness came, some welcome reinforcements arrived: padding silently over the cold ground from the north, separately, singly, came a number of armoured bears – a large number, and among them was their king. Not long afterwards, there arrived the first of several witch-clans, the sound of the air through their pine-branches whispering in the dark sky for a long time.

Along the plain to the south of the fortress glimmered thousands of lights, marking the camps of those who had arrived from far off. Further away, in all four corners of the compass, flights of spy-angels cruised tirelessly, keeping watch.

At midnight in the adamant tower, Lord Asriel sat in discussion with King Ogunwe, the angel Xaphania, Madame Oxentiel the Gallivespian, and Teukros Basilides. The alethiometrist had just finished speaking, and Lord Asriel stood up, crossed to the window, and looked out at the distant glow of the Clouded Mountain hanging in the western sky. The others were silent; they had just heard something that had made Lord Asriel turn pale and tremble, and none of them quite knew how to respond.

Finally Lord Asriel spoke.

"Mr Basilides," he said, "you must be very fatigued. I am grateful for all your efforts. Please take some wine with us."

"Thank you, my lord," said the reader.

His hands were trembling. King Ogunwe poured the golden Tokay and handed him the glass.

"What will this mean, Lord Asriel?" said the clear voice of Madame Oxentiel.

Lord Asriel came back to the table.

"Well," he said, "it will mean that when we join battle, we

shall have a new objective. My daughter and this boy have become separated from their dæmons, somehow, and managed to survive; and their dæmons are somewhere in this world – correct me if I'm summarizing wrongly, Mr Basilides – their dæmons are in this world, and Metatron is intent on capturing them. If he captures their dæmons, the children will have to follow; and if he can control those two children, the future is his, for ever. Our task is clear: we have to find the dæmons before he does, and keep them safe till the girl and the boy rejoin them."

The Gallivespian leader said, "What form do they have, these two lost dæmons?"

"They are not yet fixed, madame," said Teukros Basilides. "They might be any shape."

"So," said Lord Asriel, "to sum it up: all of us, our republic, the future of every conscious being – we all depend on my daughter's remaining alive, and on keeping her dæmon and the boy's out of the hands of Metatron?"

"That is so."

Lord Asriel sighed, almost with satisfaction; it was as if he'd come to the end of a long and complex calculation, and reached an answer that made quite unexpected sense.

"Very well," he said, spreading his hands wide on the table. "Then this is what we shall do when the battle begins. King Ogunwe, you will assume command of all the armies defending the fortress. Madame Oxentiel, you are to send your people out at once to search in every direction for the girl and the boy, and the two dæmons. When you find them, guard them with your lives until they come together again. At that point, I understand, the boy will be able to escape to another world, and safety."

The lady nodded. Her stiff grey hair caught the lamplight, glinting like stainless steel, and the blue hawk she had inherited from Lord Roke spread his wings briefly on the bracket by the door.

"Now, Xaphania," said Lord Asriel. "What do you know of this Metatron? He was once a man: does he still have the physical strength of a human being?"

"He came to prominence long after I was exiled," the angel said. "I have never seen him close to. But he would not have been able to dominate the kingdom unless he was very strong indeed, strong in every way. Most angels would avoid fighting hand-to-hand. Metatron would relish the combat, and win."

Ogunwe could tell that Lord Asriel had been struck by an idea. His attention suddenly withdrew, his eyes lost focus for an instant, and then snapped back to the moment with an extra charge of intensity.

"I see," he said. "Finally, Xaphania, Mr Basilides tells us that their bomb not only opened an abyss below the worlds, but also fractured the structure of things so profoundly that there are fissures and cracks everywhere. Somewhere nearby there must be a way down to the edge of that abyss. I want you to look for it."

"What are you going to do?" said King Ogunwe harshly.

"I'm going to destroy Metatron. But my part is nearly over. It's my daughter who has to live, and it's our task to keep all the forces of the kingdom away from her so that she has a chance to find her way to a safer world – she and that boy, and their dæmons."

"And what about Mrs Coulter?" said the king.

Lord Asriel passed a hand over his forehead.

"I would not have her troubled," he said. "Leave her alone, and protect her if you can. Although . . . Maybe I'm doing her an injustice. Whatever else she's done, she's never failed to surprise me. But we all know what *we* must do, and why we must do it: we have to protect Lyra until she has found her dæmon and escaped. Our republic might have come into being for the sole purpose of helping her do that. Well, let us do it as well as we can."

Mrs Coulter lay in Lord Asriel's bed next door. Hearing voices in the other room, she stirred, for she wasn't deeply asleep. She came out of her troubled slumber uneasy and heavy with longing.

Her dæmon sat up beside her, but she didn't want to move closer to the door; it was simply the sound of Lord Asriel's voice she wanted to hear rather than any particular words. She thought they were both doomed. She thought they were all doomed.

Finally she heard the door closing in the other room, and roused herself to stand up.

"Asriel," she said, going through into the warm naphtha light.

His dæmon growled softly: the golden monkey dropped his head low to propitiate her. Lord Asriel was rolling up a large map, and did not turn.

"Asriel, what will happen to us all?" she said, taking a chair.

He pressed the heels of his hands into his eyes. His face was ravaged with fatigue. He sat down and rested an elbow on the table. Their dæmons were very still: the monkey crouching on the chair-back, the snow leopard sitting upright and alert at Lord Asriel's side, watching Mrs Coulter unblinkingly.

"You didn't hear?" he said.

"I heard a little. I couldn't sleep, but I wasn't listening. Where is Lyra, does anyone know?"

"No."

He still hadn't answered her first question, and he wasn't going to, and she knew it.

"We should have married," she said, "and brought her up ourselves."

It was such an unexpected remark that he blinked. His dæmon uttered the softest possible growl at the back of her throat, and settled down with her paws outstretched in the manner of the Sphinx. He said nothing.

"I can't bear the thought of oblivion, Asriel," she continued. "Sooner anything than that. I used to think pain would be worse – to be tortured for ever – I thought that must be worse . . . But as long as you were conscious, it would be better, wouldn't it? Better than feeling nothing, just going into the dark, everything going out for ever and ever?"

His part was simply to listen. His eyes were locked on hers, and he was paying profound attention; there was no need to respond. She said:

"The other day, when you spoke about her so bitterly, and about me . . . I thought you hated her. I could understand your hating me. I've never hated you, but I could understand . . . I could see why you might hate me. But I couldn't see why you hated Lyra."

He turned his head away slowly, and then looked back.

"I remember you said something strange, on Svalbard, on the

mountaintop, just before you left our world," she went on. "You said: come with me, and we'll destroy Dust for ever. You remember saying that? But you didn't mean it. You meant the very opposite, didn't you? I see now. Why didn't you tell me what you were really doing? Why didn't you tell me you were really trying to preserve Dust? You could have told me the truth."

"I wanted you to come and join me," he said, his voice hoarse and quiet, "and I thought you would prefer a lie."

"Yes," she whispered, "that's what I thought."

She couldn't sit still, but she didn't really have the strength to stand up. For a moment she felt faint, her head swam, sounds receded, the room darkened, but almost at once her senses came back even more pitilessly than before, and nothing in the situation had changed.

"Asriel . . ." she murmured.

The golden monkey put a tentative hand out to touch the paw of the snow leopard. The man watched without a word, and Stelmaria didn't move; her eyes were fixed on Mrs Coulter.

"Oh, Asriel, what will happen to us?" Mrs Coulter said again. "Is this the end of everything?"

He said nothing.

Moving like someone in a dream, she got to her feet, picked up the rucksack which lay in the corner of the room, and reached inside it for her pistol; and what she would have done next, no one knew, because at that moment there came the sound of footsteps running up the stairs.

Both man and woman, and both dæmons, turned to look at the orderly who came in and said breathlessly:

"Excuse me, my lord – the two dæmons – they've been seen, not far from the eastern gate – in the form of cats – the sentry tried to talk to them, bring them inside, but they wouldn't come near. It was only a minute or so ago . . ."

Lord Asriel sat up, transfigured. All the fatigue had been wiped off his face in a moment. He sprang to his feet and seized his greatcoat.

Ignoring Mrs Coulter, he flung the coat around his shoulders and said to the orderly:

"Tell Madame Oxentiel at once. Put this order out: the

dæmons are not to be threatened, or frightened, or coerced in any way. Anyone seeing them should first . . ."

Mrs Coulter heard no more of what he was saying, because he was already half-way down the stairs. When his running footsteps had faded too, the only sounds were the gentle hiss of the naphtha lamp, and the moan of the wild wind outside.

Her eyes found the eyes of her dæmon. The golden monkey's expression was as subtle and complex as it had ever been, in all their thirty-five years of life.

"Very well," she said. "I can't see any other way. I think . . . I think we'll . . ."

He knew at once what she meant. He leapt to her breast, and they embraced. Then she found her fur-lined coat, and they very quietly left the chamber and made their way down the dark stairs.

29
THE BATTLE ON THE PLAIN

Each Man is in his Spectre's power
Until the arrival of that hour
When his Humanity awake

— WILLIAM BLAKE

IT WAS DESPERATELY hard for Lyra and Will to leave that sweet world where they had slept the night before, but if they were ever going to find their dæmons, they knew they had to go into the dark once more. And now, after hours of weary crawling through the dim tunnel, Lyra bent over the alethiometer for the twentieth time, making little unconscious sounds of distress – whimpers and catches of breath that would have been sobs if they were any stronger. Will, too, felt the pain where his dæmon had been, a scalded place of acute tenderness which every breath tore at with cold hooks.

How wearily she turned the wheels; on what leaden feet her thoughts moved. The ladders of meaning that led from every one of the alethiometer's thirty-six symbols, down which she used to move so lightly and confidently, felt loose and shaky. And holding the connections between them in her mind ... It had once been like running, or singing, or telling a story: something natural. Now she had to do it laboriously, and her grip was failing, and she mustn't fail because otherwise everything would fail...

"It's not far," she said at last. "And there's all kinds of danger – there's a battle, there's ... But we're nearly in the right place now. Just at the end of this tunnel there's a big smooth rock running with water. You cut through there."

The ghosts who were going to fight pressed forward eagerly, and she felt Lee Scoresby close at her side.

He said, "Lyra, gal, it won't be long now. When you see that old bear, you tell him Lee went out fighting. And when the battle's over, there'll be all the time in the world to drift along the wind and find the atoms that used to be Hester, and my mother in the sagelands, and my sweethearts – all my sweethearts . . . Lyra, child, you rest when this is done, you hear? Life is good, and death is over . . ."

His voice faded. She wanted to put her arms around him, but of course that was impossible. So she just looked at his pale form instead, and the ghost saw the passion and brilliance in her eyes, and took strength from it.

And on Lyra's shoulder, and on Will's, rode the two Gallivespians. Their short lives were nearly over; each of them felt a stiffness in their limbs, a coldness around the heart. They would both return soon to the world of the dead, this time as ghosts, but they caught each other's eye, and vowed that they would stay with Will and Lyra for as long as they could, and not say a word about their dying.

Up and up the children clambered. They didn't speak. They heard each other's harsh breathing, they heard their footfalls, they heard the little stones their steps dislodged. Ahead of them all the way, the harpy scrambled heavily, her wings dragging, her claws scratching, silent and grim.

Then came a new sound: a regular drip-drip, echoing in the tunnel. And then a faster dripping, a trickle, a running of water.

"Here!" said Lyra, reaching forward to touch a sheet of rock that blocked the way, smooth and wet and cold. "Here it is."

She turned to the harpy.

"I been thinking," she said, "how you saved me, and how you promised to guide all the other ghosts that'll come through the world of the dead to that land we slept in last night. And I thought, if you en't got a name, that can't be right, not for the future. So I thought I'd give you a name, like King Iorek Byrnison gave me my name Silvertongue. I'm going to call you Gracious Wings. So that's your name now, and that's what you'll be for evermore: Gracious Wings."

"One day," said the harpy, "I will see you again, Lyra Silvertongue."

"And if I know you're here, I shan't be afraid," Lyra said. "Goodbye, Gracious Wings, till I die."

She embraced the harpy, hugging her tightly and kissing her on both cheeks.

Then the Chevalier Tialys said: "This is the world of Lord Asriel's republic?"

"Yes," she said, "that's what the alethiometer says. It's close to his fortress."

"Then let me speak to the ghosts."

She held him high, and he called, "Listen, because the Lady Salmakia and I are the only ones among us who have seen this world before. There is a fortress on a mountaintop: that is what Lord Asriel is defending. Who the enemy is I do not know. Lyra and Will have only one task now, which is to search for their dæmons. Our task is to help them. Let's be of good courage and fight well."

Lyra turned to Will.

"All right," he said, "I'm ready."

He took out the knife, and looked into the eyes of his father's ghost, who stood close by. They wouldn't know each other for much longer, and Will thought how glad he would have been to see his mother beside them as well, all three together –

"Will," said Lyra, alarmed.

He stopped. The knife was stuck in the air. He took his hand away, and there it hung, fastened in the substance of an invisible world. He let out a deep breath.

"I nearly . . ."

"I could see," she said. "Look at *me*, Will."

In the ghost-light he saw her bright hair, her firm-set mouth, her candid eyes: he felt the warmth of her breath; he caught the friendly scent of her flesh.

The knife came loose.

"I'll try again," he said.

He turned away. Focusing hard, he let his mind flow down to the knife-tip, touching, withdrawing, searching, and then he found it. In, along, down, and back: the ghosts crowded so close that Will's body and Lyra's felt little jolts of cold along every nerve.

And he made the final cut.

The first thing they sensed was *noise*. The light that struck in was dazzling, and they had to cover their eyes, ghosts and living alike, so they could see nothing for several seconds; but the pounding, the explosions, the rattle of gunfire, the shouts and screams were all instantly clear, and horribly frightening.

John Parry's ghost, and the ghost of Lee Scoresby, recovered their senses first. Because both had been soldiers, experienced in battle, they weren't so disoriented by the noise. Will and Lyra simply watched in fear and amazement.

Explosive rockets were bursting in the air above, showering fragments of rock and metal over the slopes of the mountain, which they saw a little way off; and in the skies, angels were fighting angels, and witches, too, swooped and soared screaming their clan-cries as they shot arrows at their enemies. They saw a Gallivespian, mounted on a dragonfly, diving to attack a flying machine whose human pilot tried to fight him off hand-to-hand. While the dragonfly darted and skimmed above, its rider leapt off to clamp his spurs deep in the pilot's neck; and then the insect returned, swooping low to let its rider leap on the brilliant green back as the flying machine droned straight into the rocks at the foot of the fortress.

"Open it wider," said Lee Scoresby. "Let us out!"

"Wait, Lee," said John Parry. "Something's happening – look over there."

Will cut another small window in the direction he indicated, and as they looked out, they could all see a change in the pattern of the fighting. The attacking force began to withdraw: a group of armed vehicles stopped moving forward, and under covering fire, turned laboriously and moved back. A squadron of flying machines, which had been getting the better of a ragged battle with Lord Asriel's gyropters, wheeled in the sky and made off to the west. The kingdom's forces on the ground – columns of riflemen, troops equipped with flame-throwers, with poison-spraying cannons, with weapons such as none of the watchers had ever seen – began to disengage and pull back.

"What's going on?" said Lee. "They're leaving the field – but why?"

There seemed to be no reason for it: Lord Asriel's allies were outnumbered, their weapons were less potent, and many more of them were lying wounded.

Then Will felt a sudden movement among the ghosts. They were pointing out at something drifting in the air.

"Spectres!" said John Parry. "That's the reason."

And for the first time, Will and Lyra thought they could see those things, like veils of shimmering gauze, falling from the sky like thistledown. But they were very faint, and when they reached the ground they were much harder to see.

"What are they doing?" said Lyra.

"They're making for that platoon of riflemen –"

And Will and Lyra knew what would happen, and they both called out in fear: "Run! Get away!"

Some of the soldiers, hearing children's voices crying out from close by, looked around startled. Others, seeing a Spectre making for them, so strange and blank and greedy, raised their guns and fired, but of course with no effect. And then it struck the first man it came to.

He was a soldier from Lyra's own world, an African. His dæmon was a long-legged tawny cat spotted with black, and she drew back her teeth and prepared to spring.

They all saw the man aiming his rifle, fearless, not giving an inch – and then they saw the dæmon in the toils of an invisible net, snarling, howling, helpless, and the man trying to reach to her, dropping his rifle, crying her name, and sinking and fainting himself with pain and brutal nausea.

"Right, Will," said John Parry. "Let us out now; we can fight those things."

So Will opened the window wide, and ran out at the head of the army of ghosts; and then began the strangest battle he could imagine.

The ghosts clambered out of the earth, pale forms paler still in the midday light. They had nothing to fear any more, and they threw themselves against the invisible Spectres, grappling and wrestling and tearing at things Will and Lyra couldn't see at all.

The riflemen and the other living allies were bemused: they could make nothing of this ghostly, spectral combat. Will made his way through the middle of it, brandishing the knife, remembering how the Spectres had fled from it before.

Wherever he went Lyra went too, wishing she had something

to fight with as Will was doing, but looking around, watching more widely. She thought she could see the Spectres from time to time, in an oily glistening of the air; and it was Lyra who felt the first shiver of danger.

With Salmakia on her shoulder, she found herself on a slight rise, just a bank of earth surmounted by hawthorn bushes, from which she could see the great sweep of country the invaders were laying waste.

The sun was above her. Ahead, on the western horizon, clouds lay heaped and brilliant, riven with chasms of darkness, their tops drawn out in the high-altitude winds. That way too, on the plain, the enemy's ground forces waited: machines glinting brightly, flags astir with colour, regiments drawn up, waiting.

Behind, and to her left, was the ridge of jagged hills leading up to the fortress. They shone bright grey in the lurid pre-storm light, and on the distant ramparts of black basalt, she could even see little figures moving about, repairing the damaged battlements, bringing more weapons to bear, or simply watching.

And it was about then that Lyra felt the first distant lurch of nausea, pain, and fear that was the unmistakable touch of the Spectres.

She knew what it was at once, though she'd never felt it before. And it told her two things: first, that she must have grown up enough now to become vulnerable to the Spectres; and secondly, that Pan must be somewhere close by.

"Will – Will –" she cried.

He heard her and turned, knife in hand and eyes ablaze.

But before he could speak, he gave a gasp, a choking lurch, and clutched his breast, and she knew the same thing was happening to him.

"Pan! Pan!" she cried, standing on tiptoe to look all around.

Will was bending over trying not to be sick. After a few moments the feeling passed away, as if their dæmons had escaped; but they were no nearer to finding them, and all around the air was full of gunshots, cries, voices crying in pain or terror, the distant *yowk-yowk-yowk* of cliff-ghasts circling overhead, the occasional *whiz* and *thock* of arrows, and then a new sound: the rising of the wind.

Lyra felt it first on her cheeks, and then she saw the grass bending under it, and then she heard it in the hawthorns. The sky ahead was huge with storm: all the whiteness had gone from the thunderheads, and they rolled and swirled with sulphur-yellow, sea-green, smoke-grey, oil-black, a queasy churning miles high and as wide as the horizon.

Behind her the sun was still shining, so that every grove and every single tree between her and the storm blazed ardent and vivid, little frail things defying the dark with leaf and twig and fruit and flower.

And through it all went the two no-longer-quite-children, seeing the Spectres almost clearly now. The wind was snapping at Will's eyes and lashing Lyra's hair across her face, and it should have been able to blow the Spectres away; but the things drifted straight down through it towards the ground. Boy and girl, hand in hand, picked their way over the dead and the wounded, Lyra calling for her dæmon, Will alert in every sense for his.

And now the sky was laced with lightning, and then the first almighty crack of thunder hit their eardrums like an axe. Lyra put her hands to her head, and Will nearly stumbled, as if driven downwards by the sound. They clung to each other and looked up, and saw a sight no one had ever seen before in any of the millions of worlds.

Witches, Ruta Skadi's clan, and Reina Miti's, and half-a-dozen others, every single witch carrying a torch of flaring pitch-pine dipped in bitumen, were streaming over the fortress from the east, from the last of the clear sky, and flying straight towards the storm.

Those on the ground could hear the roar and crackle as the volatile hydrocarbons flamed high above. A few Spectres still remained in the upper airs, and some witches flew into them unseeing, to cry out and tumble blazing to the ground; but most of the pallid things had reached the earth by this time, and the great flight of witches streamed like a river of fire into the heart of the storm.

A flight of angels, armed with spears and swords, had emerged from the Clouded Mountain to meet the witches head-on. They had the wind behind them, and they sped forward faster than arrows; but the witches were equal to that, and the first ones soared up high and then dived into the ranks of the angels, lashing to left and right with their flaring torches. Angel after angel, outlined in fire, their wings ablaze, tumbled screaming from the air.

And then the first great drops of rain came down. If the commander in the storm-clouds meant to douse the witch-fires, he was disappointed; the pitch-pine and the bitumen blazed defiance at it, spitting and hissing the louder the more rain splashed into them. The raindrops hit the ground as if they'd been hurled in malice, breaking and splashing up into the air. Within a minute Lyra and Will were both soaked to the skin and shaking with cold, and the rain stung their heads and arms like tiny stones.

Through it all they stumbled and struggled, wiping the water from their eyes, calling: "Pan! Pan!" in the tumult.

The thunder overhead was almost constant now, ripping and grinding and crashing as if the very atoms were being torn open. Between thunder-crash and pang of fear ran Will and Lyra, howling, both of them: "Pan! My Pantalaimon! Pan!" and a wordless cry from Will, who knew what he had lost, but not what she was named.

With them everywhere went the two Gallivespians, warning them to look this way, to go that way, watching out for the Spectres the children could still not fully see. But Lyra had to hold Salmakia in her hands, because the lady had little strength left to cling to Lyra's shoulder. Tialys was scanning the skies all around, searching for his kindred and calling out whenever he saw a needle-bright darting movement through the air above. But his voice had lost much of its power, and in any case the other Gallivespians were looking for the clan-colours of their two dragonflies, the electric blue and the red-and-yellow; and those colours had long since faded, and the bodies that had shone with them lay in the world of the dead.

And then came a movement in the sky that was different from the rest. As the children looked up, sheltering their eyes from the lashing raindrops, they saw an aircraft unlike any they'd seen before: ungainly, six-legged, dark, and totally silent. It was flying low, very low, from the fortress. It skimmed overhead, no higher than a rooftop above them, and then moved away into the heart of the storm.

But they had no time to wonder about it, because another head-wrenching throb of nausea told Lyra that Pan was in danger again, and then Will felt it too, and they stumbled blindly through the puddles and the mud and the chaos of wounded men and fighting ghosts, helpless, terrified, and sick.

30

THE CLOUDED MOUNTAIN

Farr off th'Empyreal Heav'n, extended wide
In circuit, undetermined square or round,
With opal Towrs and Battlements adorn'd
Of living Saphire

— JOHN MILTON

THE INTENTION CRAFT was being piloted by Mrs Coulter. She and her dæmon were alone in the cockpit.

The barometric altimeter was little use in the storm, but she could judge her altitude roughly by watching the fires on the ground that blazed where angels fell; despite the hurtling rain, they were still flaring high. As for the course, that wasn't difficult either: the lightning that flickered around the mountain served as a brilliant beacon. But she had to avoid the various flying beings who were still fighting in the air, and keep clear of the rising land below.

She didn't use the lights, because she wanted to get close and find somewhere to land before they saw her and shot her down. As she flew closer, the updraughts became more violent, the gusts more sudden and brutal. A gyropter would have had no chance: the savage air would have slammed it to the ground like a fly. In the intention craft she could move lightly with the wind, adjusting her balance like a wave-rider in the Peaceable Ocean.

Cautiously she began to climb, peering forward, ignoring the instruments and flying by sight and by instinct. Her dæmon leapt from one side of the little glass cabin to the other, looking ahead, above, to left and right, and calling to her constantly. The lightning, great sheets and lances of brilliance, flared and cracked above and around the machine. Through it all she flew in the little aircraft, gaining height little by little, and always moving on towards the cloud-hung palace.

And as Mrs Coulter approached, she found her attention dazzled and bewildered by the nature of the mountain itself.

It reminded her of a certain abominable heresy, whose author was now deservedly languishing in the dungeons of the Consistorial Court. He had suggested that there were more spatial dimensions than the three familiar ones; that on a very small scale, there were up to seven or eight other dimensions, but that they were impossible to examine directly. He had even constructed a model to show how they might work, and Mrs Coulter had seen the object before it was exorcised and burnt. Folds within folds, corners and edges both containing and being contained: its inside was everywhere and its outside was everywhere else. The Clouded Mountain affected her in a similar way: it was less like a rock than like a force-field, manipulating space itself to enfold and stretch and layer it into galleries and terraces, chambers and colonnades and watch-towers of air and light and vapour.

She felt a strange exultation welling slowly in her breast, and she saw at the same time how to bring the aircraft safely up to the clouded terrace on the southern flank. The little craft lurched and strained in the turbid air, but she held the course firm, and her dæmon guided her down to land on the terrace.

The light she'd seen by till now had come from the lightning, the occasional gashes in the cloud where the sun struck through, the fires from the burning angels, the beams of anbaric searchlights; but the light here was different. It came from the substance of the mountain itself, which glowed and faded in a slow breath-like rhythm, with a mother-of-pearl radiance.

Woman and dæmon got down from the craft, and looked around to see which way they should go.

She had the feeling that other beings were moving rapidly above and below, speeding through the substance of the mountain itself with messages, orders, information. She couldn't see them; all she could see was confusing infolded perspectives of colonnade, staircase, terrace and façade.

Before she could make up her mind which way to go, she heard voices, and withdrew behind a column. The voices were singing a psalm, and coming closer, and then she saw a procession of angels carrying a litter.

As they neared the place where she was hiding, they saw the intention craft and stopped. The singing faltered, and some of the bearers looked around in doubt and fear.

Mrs Coulter was close enough to see the being in the litter: an angel, she thought, and indescribably aged. He wasn't easy to see, because the litter was enclosed all round with crystal that glittered and threw back the enveloping light of the mountain, but she had the impression of terrifying decrepitude, of a face sunken in wrinkles, of trembling hands and a mumbling mouth and rheumy eyes.

The aged being gestured shakily at the intention craft, and cackled and muttered to himself, plucking incessantly at his beard, and then threw back his head and uttered a howl of such anguish that Mrs Coulter had to cover her ears.

But evidently the bearers had a task to do, for they gathered themselves and moved further along the terrace, ignoring the cries and mumbles from inside the litter. When they reached an open space they spread their wings wide, and at a word from their leader they began to fly, carrying the litter between them, until they were lost to Mrs Coulter's sight in the swirling vapours.

But there wasn't time to think about that. She and the golden monkey moved on quickly, climbing great staircases, crossing bridges, always moving upwards. The higher they went, the more they felt that sense of invisible activity all around them, until finally they turned a corner into a wide space like a mist-hung piazza, and found themselves confronted by an angel with a spear.

"Who are you? What is your business?" he said.

Mrs Coulter looked at him curiously. These were the beings who had fallen in love with human women, with the daughters of men, so long ago.

"No, no," she said gently, "please don't waste time. Take me to the Regent at once. He's waiting for me."

Disconcert them, she thought, keep them off balance; and this angel did not know what he should do, so he did as she told him. She followed him for some minutes, through those confusing perspectives of light, until they came to an antechamber. How they had entered she didn't know, but there they were, and after a brief pause, something in front of her opened like a door.

Her dæmon's sharp nails were pressing into the flesh of her upper arms, and she gripped his fur for reassurance.

Facing them was a being made of light. He was man-shaped, man-sized, she thought, but she was too dazzled to see. The golden monkey hid his face in her shoulder, and she threw up an arm to hide her eyes.

Metatron said, "Where is she? Where is your daughter?"

"I've come to tell you, my Lord Regent," she said.

"If she was in your power, you would have brought her."

"She is not, but her dæmon is."

"How can that be?"

"I swear, Metatron, her dæmon is in my power. Please, great Regent, hide yourself a little – my eyes are dazzled . . ."

He drew a veil of cloud in front of himself. Now it was like looking at the sun through smoked glass, and her eyes could see him more clearly, though she still pretended to be dazzled by his face. He was exactly like a man in early middle age, tall, powerful, and commanding. Was he clothed? Did he have wings? She couldn't tell, because of the force of his eyes. She could look at nothing else.

"Please, Metatron, hear me. I have just come from Lord Asriel. He has the child's dæmon, and he knows that the child will soon come to search for him."

"What does he want with the child?"

"To keep her from you until she comes of age. He doesn't know where I've gone, and I must go back to him soon. I'm telling you the truth. Look at me, great Regent, as I can't easily look at you. Look at me clearly, and tell me what you see."

The prince of the angels looked at her. It was the most searching examination Marisa Coulter had ever undergone. Every scrap of shelter and deceit was stripped away, and she stood naked, body and ghost and dæmon together, under the ferocity of Metatron's gaze.

And she knew that her nature would have to answer for her, and she was terrified that what he saw in her would be insufficient. Lyra had lied to Iofur Raknison with her words: her mother was lying with her whole life.

"Yes, I see," said Metatron.

"What do you see?"

"Corruption and envy and lust for power. Cruelty and

coldness. A vicious probing curiosity. Pure, poisonous, toxic malice. You have never from your earliest years shown a shred of compassion or sympathy or kindness without calculating how it would return to your advantage. You have tortured and killed without regret or hesitation; you have betrayed and intrigued and gloried in your treachery. You are a cess-pit of moral filth."

That voice, delivering that judgement, shook Mrs Coulter profoundly. She knew it was coming, and she dreaded it; and yet she hoped for it too, and now it had been said, she felt a little gush of triumph.

She moved closer to him.

"So you see," she said, "I can betray him easily. I can lead you to where he's taking my daughter's dæmon, and you can destroy Asriel, and the child will walk unsuspecting into your hands."

She felt the movement of vapour about her, and her senses became confused: his next words pierced her flesh like darts of scented ice.

"When I was a man," he said, "I had wives in plenty, but none was as lovely as you."

"When you were a man?"

"When I was a man I was known as Enoch, the son of Jared, the son of Mahalalel, the son of Kenan, the son of Enosh, the son of Seth, the son of Adam. I lived on earth for sixty-five years, and then the Authority took me to his kingdom."

"And you had many wives."

"I loved their flesh. And I understood it when the sons of heaven fell in love with the daughters of earth, and I pleaded their cause with the Authority. But his heart was fixed against them, and he made me prophesy their doom."

"And you have not known a wife for thousands of years . . ."

"I have been Regent of the kingdom."

"And is it not time you had a consort?"

That was the moment she felt most exposed and in most danger. But she trusted to her flesh, and to the strange truth she'd learned about angels, perhaps especially those angels who had once been human: lacking flesh, they coveted it and longed for contact with it. And Metatron was close now, close enough to smell the perfume of her hair and to gaze at the texture of her skin, close enough to touch her with scalding hands.

There was a strange sound, like the murmur and crackle you hear before you realize that what you're hearing is your house on fire.

"Tell me what Lord Asriel is doing, and where he is," he said.

"I can take you to him now," she said.

The angels carrying the litter left the Clouded Mountain and flew south. Metatron's orders had been to take the Authority to a place of safety away from the battlefield, because he wanted him kept alive for a while yet; but rather than give him a bodyguard of many regiments, which would only attract the enemy's attention, he had trusted to the obscurity of the storm, calculating that in these circumstances, a small party would be safer than a large one.

And so it might have been, if a certain cliff-ghast, busy feasting on a half-dead warrior, had not looked up just as a random search-light caught the side of the crystal litter.

Something stirred in the cliff-ghast's memory. He paused, one hand on the warm liver, and as his brother knocked him aside, the recollection of a babbling Arctic fox came to his mind.

At once he spread his leathery wings and bounded upwards, and a moment later the rest of the troop followed.

Xaphania and her angels had searched diligently all the night and some of the morning, and finally they had found a minute crack in the mountainside to the south of the fortress, which had not been there the day before. They had explored it and enlarged it, and now Lord Asriel was climbing down into a series of caverns and tunnels extending a long way below the fortress.

It wasn't totally dark, as he'd thought. There was a faint source of illumination, like a stream of billions of tiny particles, faintly glowing. They flowed steadily down the tunnel like a river of light.

"Dust," he said to his dæmon.

He had never seen it with the naked eye, but then he had never seen so much Dust together. He moved on, until quite suddenly the tunnel opened out, and he found himself at the top of a vast cavern: a vault immense enough to contain a dozen cathedrals. There was no floor; the sides sloped vertiginously down towards the edge of a great pit hundreds of feet below, and darker than darkness itself, and into the pit streamed the endless Dust-fall, pouring ceaselessly down. Its billions of particles were like the stars of every galaxy in the sky, and every one of them was a little fragment of conscious thought. It was a melancholy light to see by.

He climbed with his dæmon down towards the abyss, and as they went they gradually began to see what was happening along the far side of the gulf, hundreds of yards away in the gloom. He had thought there was a movement there, and the further down he climbed, the more clearly it resolved itself: a procession of dim pale figures picking their way along the perilous slope, men, women, children, beings of every kind he had seen and many he had not. Intent on keeping their balance, they ignored him altogether, and Lord Asriel felt the hair stir at the back of his neck when he realized that they were ghosts.

"Lyra came here," he said quietly to the snow leopard.

"Tread carefully," was all she said in reply.

By this time, Will and Lyra were soaked through, shivering, racked with pain, and stumbling blindly through mud and over rocks and into little gullies where storm-fed streams ran red with blood. Lyra was afraid that the Lady Salmakia was dying: she hadn't uttered a word for several minutes, and she lay faint and limp in Lyra's hand.

As they sheltered in one river-bed where the water was white, at least, and scooped up handfuls to their thirsty mouths, Will felt Tialys rouse himself and say:

"Will – I can hear horses coming – Lord Asriel has no cavalry. It must be the enemy. Get across the stream and hide – I saw some bushes that way . . ."

"Come on," said Will to Lyra, and they splashed through the icy bone-aching water and scrambled up the far side of the gully just in time. The riders who came over the slope and clattered down to drink didn't look like cavalry: they seemed to be of the same kind of close-haired flesh as their horses, and they had neither clothes nor harness. They carried weapons, though: tridents, nets, and scimitars.

Will and Lyra didn't stop to look: they stumbled over the rough ground at a crouch, intent only on getting away unseen.

But they had to keep their heads low, to see where they were treading and avoid twisting an ankle, or worse; and thunder exploded overhead as they ran, so they couldn't hear the screeching and snarling of the cliff-ghasts until they ran into them.

The creatures were surrounding something that lay glittering in the mud: something slightly taller than they were, which lay on its side, a large cage, perhaps, with walls of crystal. They were hammering at it with fists and rocks, shrieking and yelling.

And before Will and Lyra could stop and run the other way, they had stumbled right into the middle of the troop.

31
AUTHORITY'S END

For Empire is no more, and now the Lion & Wolf shall cease.

— WILLIAM BLAKE

MRS COULTER WHISPERED to the shadow beside her:

"Look how he hides, Metatron! He creeps through the dark like a rat..."

They stood on a ledge high up in the great cavern, watching Lord Asriel and the snow leopard make their careful way down, a long way below.

"I could strike him now," the shadow whispered.

"Yes, of course you could," she whispered back, leaning close; "but I want to see his face, dear Metatron; I want him to *know* I've betrayed him. Come, let's follow and catch him..."

The Dust-fall shone like a great pillar of faint light as it descended smoothly and never-endingly into the gulf. Mrs Coulter had no attention to spare for it, because the shadow beside her was trembling with desire, and she had to keep him by her side, under what control she could manage.

They moved down, silent, following Lord Asriel. The further down they climbed, the more she felt a great weariness fall over her.

"What? What?" whispered the shadow, feeling her emotions, and suspicious at once.

"I was thinking," she said with a sweet malice, "how glad I am that the child will never grow up to love and be loved. I thought I loved her when she was a baby; but now –"

"There was *regret*," the shadow said, "in your heart there was *regret* that you will not see her grow up."

"Oh, Metatron, how long it is since you were a man! Can you really not tell what it is I'm regretting? It's not *her* coming of age, but mine. How bitterly I regret that I didn't know of you in my own girlhood; how passionately I would have devoted myself to you..."

She leaned towards the shadow, as if she couldn't control the impulses of her own body, and the shadow hungrily sniffed and seemed to gulp at the scent of her flesh.

They were moving laboriously over the tumbled and broken rocks towards the foot of the slope. The further down they went, the more the Dust-light gave everything a nimbus of golden mist. Mrs Coulter kept reaching for where his hand might be, if the shadow had been a human companion, and then seemed to recollect herself, and whispered:

"Keep behind me, Metatron — wait here — Asriel is suspicious — let me lull him first. When he's off guard I'll call you. But come as a shadow, in this small form, so he doesn't see you — otherwise he'll just let the child's dæmon fly away."

The Regent was a being whose profound intellect had had thousands of years to deepen and strengthen itself, and whose knowledge extended over a million universes. Nevertheless, at that moment he was blinded by his twin obsessions: to destroy Lyra and to possess her mother. He nodded, and stayed where he was, while the woman and the monkey moved forward as quietly as they could.

Lord Asriel was waiting behind a great block of granite, out of sight of the Regent. The snow leopard heard them coming, and Lord Asriel stood up as Mrs Coulter came around the corner. Everything, every surface, every cubic centimetre of air, was permeated by the falling Dust, which gave a soft clarity to every tiny detail; and in the Dust-light Lord Asriel saw that her face was wet with tears, and that she was gritting her teeth so as not to sob.

He took her in his arms, and the golden monkey embraced the snow leopard's neck and buried his black face in her fur.

"Is Lyra safe? Has she found her dæmon?" she whispered.

"The ghost of the boy's father is protecting both of them."

"Dust is beautiful . . . I never knew."

"What did you tell him?"

"I lied and lied, Asriel . . . Let's not wait too long, I can't bear it . . . We won't live, will we? We won't survive like the ghosts?"

"Not if we fall into the abyss. We came here to give Lyra time to find her dæmon, and then time to live and grow up. If we take Metatron to extinction, Marisa, she'll have that time, and if we go with him, it doesn't matter."

"And Lyra *will* be safe?"

"Yes, yes," he said gently.

He kissed her. She felt as soft and light in his arms as she'd done when Lyra was conceived thirteen years before.

She was sobbing quietly. When she could speak she whispered:

"I told him I was going to betray you, and betray Lyra, and he believed me because I was corrupt and full of wickedness; he looked so deep I felt sure he'd see the truth. But I lied too well. I was lying with every nerve and fibre and everything I'd ever done . . . I wanted him to find no good in me, and he didn't. There is none. But I love Lyra. Where did this love come from? I don't know; it came to me like a thief in the night, and now I love her so much my heart is bursting with it. All I could hope was that my crimes were so monstrous that the love was no bigger than a mustard-seed in the shadow of them, and I wished I'd committed even greater ones to hide it more deeply still . . . But the mustard-seed had taken root and was growing, and the little green shoot was splitting my heart wide open, and I was so afraid he'd see . . ."

She had to stop to gather herself. He stroked her shining hair, all set about with golden Dust, and waited.

"Any moment now he'll lose patience," she whispered. "I told him to make himself small. But he's only an angel after all, even if he was once a man. And we can wrestle with him and bring him to the edge of the gulf, and we'll both go down with him . . ."

He kissed her, and said, "Yes. Lyra will be safe, and the kingdom will be powerless against her. Call him now, Marisa, my love."

She took a deep breath and let it out in a long shuddering sigh. Then she smoothed her skirt down over her thighs and tucked the hair back behind her ears.

"Metatron," she called softly. "It's time."

Metatron's shadow-cloaked form appeared out of the golden air, and took in at once what was happening: the two dæmons, crouching and watchful, the woman with the nimbus of Dust, and Lord Asriel –

Who leapt at him at once, seizing him around the waist, and tried to hurl him to the ground. The angel's arms were free, though, and with fists, palms, elbows, knuckles, forearms, he battered Lord Asriel's head and body: great pummelling blows that forced the breath from his lungs and rebounded from his ribs, that cracked against his skull and shook his senses.

However, his arms encircled the angel's wings, cramping them to his side. And a moment later, Mrs Coulter had leapt up between those pinioned wings and seized Metatron's hair. His strength was enormous: it was like holding the mane of a bolting horse. As he shook his head furiously, she was flung this way and that, and she felt the power in the great folded wings as they strained and heaved at the man's arms locked so tightly around them.

The dæmons had seized hold of him, too. Stelmaria had her teeth firmly in his leg, and the golden monkey was tearing at one of the edges of the nearest wing, snapping feathers, ripping at the vanes, and this only roused the angel to greater fury. With a sudden massive effort he flung himself sideways, freeing one wing and crushing Mrs Coulter against a rock.

Mrs Coulter was stunned for a second, and her hands came loose. At once the angel reared up again, beating his one free wing to fling off the golden monkey; but Lord Asriel's arms were firm around him still, and in fact the man had a better grip now there wasn't so much to enclose. Lord Asriel set himself to crushing the breath out of Metatron, grinding his ribs together, and trying to ignore the savage blows that were landing on his skull and his neck.

But those blows were beginning to tell. And as Lord Asriel tried to keep his footing on the broken rocks, something shattering happened to the back of his head. When he flung himself sideways, Metatron had seized a fist-sized rock, and now he brought it down with brutal force on the point of Lord Asriel's skull. The man felt the bones of his head move against each other, and he knew that another blow like that would kill him outright. Dizzy with pain – pain that was worse for the pressure of his head against the angel's side – he still clung fast, the fingers of his right hand crushing the bones of his left, and stumbled for a footing among the fractured rocks.

And as Metatron raised the bloody stone high, a golden-furred shape sprang up like a flame leaping to a tree-top, and the monkey sank his teeth into the angel's hand. The rock came loose and clattered down towards the edge, and Metatron swept his arm to left and right, trying to dislodge the dæmon; but the golden monkey clung with teeth, claws, and tail, and then Mrs Coulter gathered the great white beating wing to herself and smothered its movement.

Metatron was hampered, but he still wasn't hurt. Nor was he near the edge of the abyss.

And by now Lord Asriel was weakening. He was holding fast to his blood-soaked consciousness, but with every movement a little more was lost. He could feel the edges of the bones grinding together in his skull; he could hear them. His senses were disordered: all he knew was *hold tight and drag down*.

Then Mrs Coulter found the angel's face under her hand, and she dug her fingers deep into his eyes.

Metatron cried out. From far off across the great cavern, echoes answered, and his voice bounded from cliff to cliff, doubling and diminishing and causing those distant ghosts to pause in their endless procession and look up.

And Stelmaria the snow-leopard dæmon, her own consciousness dimming with Lord Asriel's, made one last effort and leapt for the angel's throat.

Metatron fell to his knees. Mrs Coulter, falling with him, saw the blood-filled eyes of Lord Asriel gaze at her. And she scrambled up, hand over hand, forcing the beating wing aside, and seized the angel's hair to wrench back his head and bare his throat for the snow-leopard's teeth.

And now Lord Asriel was dragging him, dragging him backwards, feet stumbling and rocks falling, and the golden monkey was leaping down with them, snapping and scratching and tearing, and they were almost there, almost at the edge; but Metatron forced himself up, and with a last effort spread both wings wide – a great white canopy that beat down and down and down, again and again and again, and then Mrs Coulter had fallen away, and Metatron was upright, and the wings beat harder and harder, and he was aloft – he was leaving the ground, with Lord Asriel still clinging tight, but weakening fast. The golden monkey's fingers were entwined in the angel's hair, and he would never let go

But they were over the edge of the abyss. They were rising. And if they flew higher, Lord Asriel would fall, and Metatron would escape.

"*Marisa! Marisa!*"

The cry was torn from Lord Asriel, and with the snow-leopard beside her, with a roaring in her ears, Lyra's mother stood and found her footing and leapt with all her heart, to hurl herself against the angel and her dæmon and her dying lover, and seize those beating wings, and bear them all down together into the abyss.

The cliff-ghasts heard Lyra's exclamation of dismay, and their flat heads all snapped round at once.

Will sprang forward and slashed the knife at the nearest of them. He felt a little kick on his shoulder as Tialys leapt off and landed on the cheek of the biggest, seizing her hair and kicking hard below the jaw before she could throw him off. The creature howled and thrashed as she fell into the mud, and the other looked stupidly at the stump of his arm, and then in horror at his own ankle, which his sliced-off hand had seized as it fell. A second later, the knife was in his breast: Will felt the handle jump three or four times with the dying heartbeats, and pulled it out before the cliff-ghast could twist it away in falling.

He heard the others cry and shriek in hatred as they fled, and he knew that Lyra was unhurt beside him; but he threw himself down in the mud with only one thing in his mind.

"Tialys! Tialys!" he cried, and avoiding the snapping teeth, he hauled the biggest cliff-ghast's head aside. Tialys was dead, his spurs deep in her neck. The creature was kicking and biting still, so he cut off her head and rolled it away before lifting the dead Gallivespian clear of the leathery neck.

"Will," said Lyra behind him, "Will, look at this . . ."

She was gazing into the crystal litter. It was unbroken, although the crystal was stained and smeared with mud and the blood from what the cliff-ghasts had been eating before they found it. It lay tilted crazily among the rocks, and inside it –

"Oh, Will, he's still alive! But – the poor thing..."

Will saw her hands pressing against the crystal, trying to reach to the angel and comfort him; because he was so old, and he was terrified, crying like a baby and cowering away into the lowest corner.

"He must be so old – I've never seen anyone suffering like that – oh, Will, can't we let him out?"

Will cut through the crystal in one movement and reached in to help the angel out. Demented and powerless, the aged being could only weep and mumble in fear and pain and misery, and he shrank away from what seemed like yet another threat.

"It's all right," Will said, "we can help you hide, at least. Come on, we won't hurt you."

The shaking hand seized his and feebly held on. The old one was uttering a wordless groaning whimper that went on and on, and grinding his teeth, and compulsively plucking at himself with his free hand; but as Lyra reached in too to help him out, he tried to smile, and to bow, and his ancient eyes deep in their wrinkles blinked at her with innocent wonder.

Between them they helped the ancient of days out of his crystal cell; it wasn't hard, for he was as light as paper, and he would have followed them anywhere, having no will of his own, and responding to simple kindness like a flower to the sun. But in the open air there was nothing to stop the wind from damaging him, and to their dismay his form began to loosen and dissolve. Only a few moments later he had vanished completely, and their last impression was of those eyes, blinking in wonder, and a sigh of the most profound and exhausted relief.

Then he was gone: a mystery dissolving in mystery. It had all taken less than a minute, and Will turned back at once to the fallen chevalier. He picked up the little body, cradling it in his palms, and found his tears flowing fast.

But Lyra was saying something urgently.

"Will – we've got to move – we've *got* to – the lady can hear those horses coming –"

Out of the indigo sky an indigo hawk swooped low, and Lyra cried out and ducked; but Salmakia cried with all her strength, "No, Lyra! No! Stand high, and hold out your fist!"

So Lyra held still, supporting one arm with the other, and the blue hawk wheeled and turned and swooped again, to seize her knuckles in sharp claws.

On the hawk's back sat a grey-haired lady, whose clear-eyed face looked first at Lyra, then at Salmakia clinging to her collar.

"Madame . . ." said Salmakia faintly, "we have done . . ."

"You have done all you need. Now we are here," said Madame Oxentiel, and twitched the reins.

At once the hawk screamed three times, so loud that Lyra's head rang. In response there darted from the sky first one, then two and three and more, then hundreds of brilliant warrior-bearing dragonflies, all skimming so fast it seemed they were bound to crash into one another; but the reflexes of the insects and the skills of their riders were so acute that instead, they seemed to weave a tapestry of swift and silent needle-bright colour over and around the children.

"Lyra," said the lady on the hawk, "and Will: follow us now, and we shall take you to your dæmons."

As the hawk spread its wings and lifted away from one hand, Lyra felt the little weight of Salmakia fall into the other, and knew in a moment that only the lady's strength of mind had kept her alive this long. She cradled her body close, and ran with Will under the cloud of dragonflies, stumbling and falling more than once, but holding the lady gently against her heart all the time.

"Left! Left!" cried the voice from the blue hawk, and in the lightning-riven murk they turned that way; and to their right Will saw a body of men in light grey armour, helmeted, masked, their grey wolf-dæmons padding in step beside them. A stream of dragonflies made for them at once, and the men faltered: their guns were no use, and the Gallivespians were among them in a moment, each warrior springing from his insect's back, finding a hand, an arm, a bare neck, and plunging his spur in before leaping back to the insect as it wheeled and skimmed past again. They were so quick it was almost impossible to follow. The soldiers turned and fled in panic, their discipline shattered.

But then came hoolbeats in a sudden thunder from behind, and the children turned in dismay: those horse-people were bearing down on them at a gallop, and already one or two had nets in their hands, whirling them around over their heads and entrapping the dragonflies, to snap the nets like whips and fling the broken insects aside.

"This way!" came the lady's voice, and then she said, "Duck, now – get down low!"

They did, and felt the earth shake under them. Could that be hoofbeats? Lyra raised her head and wiped the wet hair from her eyes, and saw something quite different from horses.

"Iorek!" she cried, joy leaping in her chest. "Oh, Iorek!"

Will pulled her down again at once, for not only Iorek Byrnison but a regiment of his bears were making directly for them. Just in time Lyra tucked her head down, and then Iorek bounded over them, roaring orders to his bears to go left, go right, and crush the enemy between them.

Lightly, as if his armour weighed no more than his fur, the bear-king spun to face Will and Lyra, who were struggling upright.

"Iorek – behind you – they've got nets!" Will cried, because the riders were almost on them.

Before the bear could move, the rider's net hissed through the air, and instantly Iorek was enveloped in steel-strong cobweb. He roared, rearing high, slashing with huge paws at the rider. But the net was strong, and although the horse whinnied and reared back in fear, Iorek couldn't fight free of the coils.

"Iorek!" Will shouted. "Keep still! Don't move!"

He scrambled forward through the puddles and over the tussocks as the rider tried to control the horse, and reached Iorek just at the moment when a second rider arrived and another net hissed through the air.

But Will kept his head: instead of slashing wildly and getting in more of a tangle, he watched the flow of the net and cut it through in a matter of moments. The second net fell useless to the ground, and then Will leapt at Iorek, feeling with his left hand, cutting with his right. The great bear stood motionless as the boy darted here and there over his vast body, cutting, freeing, clearing the way.

"Now go!" Will yelled, leaping clear, and Iorek seemed to explode upwards full into the chest of the nearest horse.

The rider had raised his scimitar to sweep down at the bear's neck, but Iorek Byrnison in his armour weighed nearly two tons, and nothing at that range could withstand him. Horse and rider, both of them smashed and shattered, fell harmlessly aside. Iorek gathered his balance, looked around to see how the land lay, and roared to the children:

"On my back! Now!"

Lyra leapt up, and Will followed. Pressing the cold iron between their legs, they felt the massive surge of power as Iorek began to move.

Behind them, the rest of the bears were engaging with the strange cavalry, helped by the Gallivespians, whose stings enraged the horses. The lady on the blue hawk skimmed low, and called: "Straight ahead now! Among the trees in the valley!"

Iorek reached the top of a little rise in the ground, and paused. Ahead of them the broken ground sloped down towards a grove about a quarter of a mile away. Somewhere beyond that, a battery of great guns was firing shell after shell howling high overhead, and someone was firing flares, too, that burst just under the clouds and drifted down towards the trees, making them blaze with cold green light as a fine target for the guns.

And fighting for control of the grove itself were a score or more Spectres, being held back by a ragged band of ghosts. As soon as they saw that little group of trees, Lyra and Will both knew that their dæmons were in there, and that if they didn't reach them soon, they would die. More Spectres were arriving there every minute, streaming over the ridge from the right. Will and Lyra could see them very clearly now.

An explosion just over the ridge shook the ground and flung stones and clods of earth high into the air. Lyra cried out, and Will had to clutch his chest.

"Hold on," Iorek growled, and began to charge.

A flare burst high above, and another and another, drifting slowly downwards with a magnesium-bright glare. Another shell burst, closer this time, and they felt the shock of the air and a second or two later the sting of earth and stones on their faces. Iorek didn't falter, but they found it hard to hold on: they couldn't dig their fingers into his fur – they had to grip the armour between their knees, and his back was so broad that both of them kept slipping.

"Look!" cried Lyra, pointing up as another shell burst nearby.

A dozen witches were making for the flares, carrying thick-leafed, bushy branches, and with them they brushed the glaring lights aside, sweeping them away into the sky beyond. Darkness fell over the grove again, hiding it from the guns.

And now the trees were only a few yards away. Will and Lyra both felt their missing selves close by – an excitement, a wild hope chilled with fear: because the Spectres were thick among the trees, and they would have to go in directly among them, and the very sight of them evoked that nauseating weakness at the heart.

"They're afraid of the knife," said a voice beside them, and the bear-king stopped so suddenly that Will and Lyra tumbled off his back.

"Lee!" said Iorek. "Lee, my comrade, I have never seen this before. You are dead – what am I speaking to?"

"Iorek, old feller, you don't know the half of it. We'll take over now – the Spectres aren't afraid of bears. Lyra, Will – come this way, and hold up that knife –"

The blue hawk swooped once more to Lyra's fist, and the grey-haired lady said, "Don't waste a second – go in and find your dæmons and escape! There's more danger coming."

"Thank you, lady! Thank you all!" said Lyra, and the hawk took wing.

Will could see Lee Scoresby's ghost dimly beside them, urging them into the grove, but they had to say farewell to Iorek Byrnison.

"Iorek, my dear, there en't words – bless you, bless you!"

"Thank you, King Iorek," said Will.

"No time. Go. Go!"

He pushed them away with his armoured head.

Will plunged after Lee Scoresby's ghost into the undergrowth, slashing to right and left with the knife. The light here was broken and muted, and the shadows were thick, tangled, confusing.

"Keep close," he called to Lyra, and then cried out as a bramble sliced across his cheek.

All around them there was movement, noise, and struggle. The shadows moved to and fro like branches in a high wind. They might have been ghosts; both children felt the little dashes of cold they knew so well, and then they heard voices all around:

"This way!"

"Over here!"

"Keep going – we're holding them off!"

"Not far now!"

And then came a cry in a voice that Lyra knew and loved better than any other:

"Oh, come quick! Quick, Lyra!"

"Pan, darling – I'm here –"

She hurled herself into the dark, sobbing and shaking, and Will tore down branches and ivy and slashed at brambles and nettles, while all around them the ghost-voices rose in a clamour of encouragement and warning.

But the Spectres had found their target too, and they pressed in through the snagging tangle of bush and briar and root and branch, meeting no more resistance than smoke. A dozen, a score of the pallid malignities seemed to pour in towards the centre of the grove, where John Parry's ghost marshalled his companions to fight them off.

Will and Lyra were both trembling and weak with fear, exhaustion, nausea, and pain, but giving up was inconceivable. Lyra tore at the brambles with her bare hands, Will slashed and hacked to left and right, as around them the combat of the shadowy beings became more and more savage.

"There!" cried Lee. "See 'em? By that big rock –"

A wildcat, two wildcats, spitting and hissing and slashing. Both were dæmons, and Will felt that if there were time he'd easily be able to tell which was Pantalaimon; but there wasn't time, because a Spectre eased horribly out of the nearest patch of shadow and glided towards them.

Will leapt over the last obstacle, a fallen tree trunk, and plunged the knife into the unresisting shimmer in the air. He felt his arm go numb, but he clenched his teeth as he was clenching his fingers around the hilt, and the pale form seemed to boil away and melt back into the darkness again.

Almost there; and the dæmons were mad with fear, because more Spectres and still more came pressing through the trees, and only the valiant ghosts were holding them back.

"Can you cut through?" said John Parry's ghost.

Will held up the knife, and had to stop as a racking bout of nausea shook him from head to toe. There was nothing left in his stomach, and the spasm hurt dreadfully. Lyra beside him was in the same state. Lee's ghost, seeing why, leapt for the dæmons and wrestled with the pale thing that was coming through the rock from behind them.

"Will – please –" said Lyra, gasping.

In went the knife, along, down, back. Lee Scoresby's ghost looked through, and saw a wide quiet prairie under a brilliant moon, so very like his own homeland that he thought he'd been blessed.

Will leapt across the clearing and seized the nearest dæmon while Lyra scooped up the other.

And even in that horrible urgency, even at that moment of utmost peril, each of them felt the same little shock of excitement: for Lyra was holding Will's dæmon, the nameless wildcat, and Will was carrying Pantalaimon.

They tore their glance away from each other's eyes.

"Goodbye, Mr Scoresby!" Lyra cried, looking around for him. "I wish – oh, thank you, thank you – goodbye!"

"Goodbye, my dear child – goodbye, Will – go well!"

Lyra scrambled through, but Will stood still and looked into the eyes of his father's ghost, brilliant in the shadows. Before he left him, there was something he had to say.

Will said to his father's ghost, "You said I was a warrior. You told me that was my nature, and I shouldn't argue with it. Father, you were wrong. I fought because I had to. I can't choose my nature, but I can choose what I do. And I *will* choose, because now I'm free."

His father's smile was full of pride and tenderness. "Well done, my boy. Well done indeed," he said.

Will couldn't see him any more. He turned and climbed through after Lyra.

And now that their purpose was achieved, now the children

had found their dæmons and escaped, the dead warriors allowed their atoms to relax and drift apart, at long long last.

Out of the little grove, away from the baffled Spectres, out of the valley, past the mighty form of his old companion the armour-clad bear, the last little scrap of the consciousness that had been the aëronaut Lee Scoresby floated upwards, just as his great balloon had done so many times. Untroubled by the flares and the bursting shells, deaf to the explosions and the shouts and cries of anger and warning and pain, conscious only of his movement upwards, the last of Lee Scoresby passed through the heavy clouds and came out under the brilliant stars, where the atoms of his beloved dæmon Hester were waiting for him.

32

MORNING

The morning comes, the night decays, the watchmen leave their stations

— WILLIAM BLAKE

THE WIDE GOLDEN prairie that Lee Scoresby's ghost had seen briefly through the window was lying quiet under the first sun of morning.

Golden, but also yellow, brown, green, and every one of the million shades between them; and black, in places, in lines and streaks of bright pitch; and silvery, too, where the sun caught the tops of a particular kind of grass just coming into flower; and blue, where a wide lake some way off and a small pond closer by reflected back the wide blue of the sky.

And quiet, but not silent, for a soft breeze rustled the billions of little stems, and a billion insects and other small creatures scraped and hummed and chirruped in the grass, and a bird too high in the blue to be seen sang little looping falls of bell-notes now close by, now far off, and never twice the same.

In all that wide landscape the only living things that were silent and still were the boy and the girl lying asleep, back to back, under the shade of an outcrop of rock at the top of a little bluff.

They were so still, so pale, that they might have been dead. Hunger had drawn the skin over their faces, pain had left lines around their eyes, and they were covered in dust and mud and not a little blood. And from the absolute passivity of their limbs, they seemed in the last stages of exhaustion.

Lyra was the first to wake. As the sun moved up the sky, it came past the rock above and touched her hair, and she began to stir, and when the sunlight reached her eyelids she found herself pulled up from the depths of sleep like a fish, slow and heavy and resistant.

But there was no arguing with the sun, and presently she moved her head and threw her arm across her eyes and murmured: "Pan – Pan . . ."

Under the shadow of her arm she opened her eyes and came

properly awake. She didn't move for some time, because her arms and legs were so sore, and every part of her body felt limp with weariness; but still she was awake, and she felt the little breeze and the sun's warmth and she heard the little insect-scrapings and the bell-song of that bird high above. It was all good. She had forgotten how good the world was.

Presently she rolled over and saw Will, still fast asleep. His hand had bled a lot; his shirt was ripped and filthy, his hair was stiff with dust and sweat. She looked at him for a long time, at the little pulse in his throat, at his chest rising and falling slowly, at the delicate shadows his eyelashes made when the sun finally reached them.

He murmured something and stirred. Not wanting to be caught looking at him, she looked the other way at the little grave they'd dug the night before, just a couple of hand-breadths wide, where the bodies of the Chevalier Tialys and the Lady Salmakia now lay at rest. There was a flat stone nearby: she got up and prised it loose from the soil, and set it upright at the head of the grave, and then sat up and shaded her eyes to gaze across the plain.

It seemed to stretch for ever and ever. It was nowhere entirely flat; gentle undulations and little ridges and gullies varied the surface wherever she looked, and here and there she saw a stand of trees so tall they seemed to be constructed rather than grown: their straight trunks and dark green canopy seemed to defy distance, being so clearly visible at what must have been many miles away.

Closer, though – in fact at the foot of the bluff, not more than a hundred yards away – there was a little pond fed by a spring coming out of the rock, and Lyra realized how thirsty she was.

She got up on shaky legs and walked slowly down towards it. The spring gurgled and trickled through mossy rocks, and she dipped her hands in it again and again, washing them clear of the mud and grime before lifting the water to her mouth. It was teeth-achingly cold, and she swallowed it with delight.

The pond was fringed with reeds, where a frog was croaking. It was shallow and warmer than the spring, as she discovered when she took off her shoes and waded into it. She stood for a long time with the sun on her head and her body and relishing the cool mud under her feet and the cold flow of spring water around her calves.

She bent down to dip her face under the water, and wet her hair thoroughly, letting it trail out and flicking it back again, stirring it with her fingers to lift all the dust and grime out.

When she felt a little cleaner and her thirst was satisfied, she looked up the slope again, to see that Will was awake. He was sitting with his knees drawn up and his arms across them, looking out across the plain as she'd done, and marvelling at the extent of it. And at the light, and at the warmth, and at the quiet.

She climbed slowly back to join him, and found him cutting the names of the Gallivespians on the little headstone, and setting it more firmly in the soil.

"Are they . . ." he said, and she knew he meant the dæmons.

"Don't know. I haven't seen Pan. I got the feeling he's not far away, but I don't know. D'you remember what happened?"

He rubbed his eyes and yawned so deeply she heard little cracking noises in his jaw. Then he blinked and shook his head.

"Not much," he said. "I picked up Pantalaimon and you picked up – the other one and we came through, and it was moon-light everywhere, and I put him down to close the window."

"And your – the other dæmon just jumped out of my arms," she said. "And I was trying to see Mr Scoresby through the win-dow, and Iorek, and to see where Pan had gone, and when I looked around they just weren't there."

"It doesn't feel like when we went into the world of the dead, though. Like when we were really separated."

"No," she agreed. "They're somewhere near all right. I remember when we were young we used to try and play hide-and-seek except it never really worked, because I was too big to hide from him and I always used to know exactly where he was, even if he was camouflaged as a moth or something. But this is strange," she said, passing her hands over her head involuntarily as if she were trying to dispel some enchantment; "he en't here, but I don't feel torn apart, I feel safe, and I know he is."

"They're together, I think," Will said.

"Yeah. They must be."

He stood up suddenly.

"Look," he said, "over there..."

He was shading his eyes and pointing. She followed his gaze, and saw a distant tremor of movement, quite different from the shimmer of the heat-haze.

"Animals?" she said doubtfully.

"And listen," he said, putting his hand behind his ear.

Now he'd pointed it out, she could hear a low persistent rumble, almost like thunder, a very long way off.

"They've disappeared," Will said, pointing.

The little patch of moving shadows had vanished, but the rumble went on for a few moments. Then it became suddenly quieter, though it had been very quiet already. The two of them were still gazing in the same direction, and shortly afterwards they saw the movement start up again. And a few moments later came the sound.

"They went behind a ridge or something," said Will. "Are they closer?"

"Can't really see. Yes, they're turning, look, they're coming this way."

"Well, if we have to fight them, I want a drink first," said Will, and he took the rucksack down to the stream, where he drank deep and washed off most of the dirt. His wound had bled a lot. He was a mess; he longed for a hot shower with plenty of soap, and for some clean clothes.

Lyra was watching the ... whatever they were; they were very strange.

"Will," she called, "they're riding on wheels..."

But she said it uncertainly. He climbed back a little way up the slope and shaded his eyes to look. It was possible to see individuals now. The group or herd or gang was about a dozen strong, and they were moving, as Lyra said, on wheels. They looked like a cross between antelopes and motorcycles, but they were stranger than that, even: they had trunks like small elephants.

And they were making for Will and Lyra, with an air of intention. Will took out the knife, but Lyra, sitting on the grass beside him, was already turning the hands of the alethiometer.

It responded quickly, while the creatures were still a few hundred yards away. The needle darted swiftly left and right and left and left, and Lyra watched it anxiously, for her last few readings had been so difficult, and her mind felt awkward and tentative as she stepped down through the branches of under-standing. Instead of darting like a bird from one foothold to the next, she moved hand over hand for security; but the meaning was there as solid as ever, and soon she understood what it was saying.

"They're friendly," she said, "it's all right, Will, they're look-ing for us, they knew we were here . . . And it's odd, I can't quite make it out . . . Dr Malone?"

She said the name half to herself, because she couldn't believe Dr Malone would be in this world. Still, the alethiometer indi-cated her clearly, although of course it couldn't give her name. Lyra put it away and stood up slowly beside Will.

"I think we should go down to them," she said. "They en't going to hurt us."

Some of them had stopped, waiting. The leader moved ahead a little, trunk raised, and they could see how he propelled him-self, with powerful backward strokes of his lateral limbs. Some of the creatures had gone to the pond to drink; the others waited, but not with the mild passive curiosity of cows gathering at a gate. These were individuals, lively with intelligence and pur-pose. They were people.

Will and Lyra moved down the slope until they were close enough to speak to them. In spite of what Lyra had said, Will kept his hand on the knife.

"I don't know if you understand me," Lyra said cautiously, "but I know you're friendly. I think we should –"

The leader moved his trunk and said, "Come see Mary. You ride. We carry. Come see Mary."

"Oh!" she said, and turned to Will, smiling with delight.

Two of the creatures were fitted with bridles and stirrups of braided cord. Not saddles; their diamond-shaped backs turned out to be comfortable enough without them. Lyra had ridden a bear, and Will had ridden a bicycle, but neither had ridden a horse, which was the closest comparison. However, riders of horses are usually in control, and the children soon found that they were not: the reins and the stirrups were there simply to give them something to hold on to and balance with. The creatures themselves made all the decisions.

"Where are –" Will began to say, but had to stop and regain his balance as the creature moved under him.

The group swung around and moved down the slight slope, going slowly through the grass. The movement was bumpy, but not uncomfortable, because the creatures had no spine: Will and Lyra felt that they were sitting on chairs with a well-sprung seat.

Soon they came to what they hadn't seen clearly from the bluff: one of those patches of black or dark-brown ground. And they were as surprised to find roads of smooth rock lacing through the prairie as Mary Malone had been some time before.

The creatures rolled on to the surface and set off, soon picking up speed. The road was more like a watercourse than a highway, because in places it broadened into wide areas like small lakes, and at others it split into narrow channels only to combine again unpredictably. It was quite unlike the brutal rational way roads in Will's world sliced through hillsides and leapt across valleys on bridges of concrete. This was part of the landscape, not an imposition on it.

They were going faster and faster. It took Will and Lyra a while to get used to the living impulse of the muscles and the shuddering thunder of the hard wheels on the hard stone. Lyra found it more difficult than Will at first, because she had never ridden a bicycle, and she didn't know the trick of leaning into the corner; but she saw how he was doing it, and soon she was finding the speed exhilarating.

The wheels made too much noise for them to speak. Instead they had to point: at the trees, in amazement at their size and splendour; at a flock of birds, the strangest they had ever seen, their fore-and-aft wings giving them a twisting, screwing motion through the air; at a fat blue lizard as long as a horse basking in the very middle of the road (the wheeled creatures divided to ride on either side of it, and it took no notice at all).

The sun was high in the sky when they began to slow down. And in the air, unmistakable, was the salt smell of the sea. The road was rising towards a bluff, and presently they were moving no faster than a walk.

Lyra, stiff and sore, said, "Can you stop? I want to get off and walk."

Her creature felt the tug at the bridle, and whether or not he understood her words, he came to a halt. Will's did too, and both children climbed down, finding themselves stiff and shaken after the continued jolting and tensing.

The creatures wheeled around to talk together, their trunks moving elegantly in time with the sounds they made. After a minute they moved on, and Will and Lyra were happy to walk among the hay-scented, grass-warm creatures who trundled beside them. One or two had gone on ahead to the top of the rise, and the children, now they no longer had to concentrate on hanging on, were able to watch how they moved, and admire the grace and power with which they propelled themselves forward and leaned and turned.

As they came to the top of the rise, they stopped, and Will and Lyra heard the leader say, "Mary close. Mary there."

They looked down. On the horizon there was the blue gleam of the sea. A broad slow-moving river wound through rich grassland in the middle distance, and at the foot of the long slope, among copses of small trees and rows of vegetables, stood a village of thatched houses. More creatures like these moved about among the houses, or tended crops, or worked among the trees.

"Now ride again," said the leader.

There wasn't far to go. Will and Lyra climbed up once more, and the other creatures looked closely at their balance and checked the stirrups with their trunks, as if to make sure they were safe.

Then they set off, beating the road with their lateral limbs, and urging themselves forward down the slope until they were moving at a terrific pace. Will and Lyra clung tight with hands and knees and felt the air whip past their faces and fling their hair back and press on their eyeballs. The thundering of the wheels, the rush of the grassland on either side, the sure and powerful lean into the broad curve ahead, the clear-headed rapture of speed – the creatures loved this, and Will and Lyra felt their joy and laughed in happy response.

They stopped in the centre of the village, and the others, who had seen them coming, gathered around raising their trunks and speaking words of welcome.

And then Lyra cried, "Dr Malone!"

Mary had come out of one of the huts, her faded blue shirt, her stocky figure, her warm ruddy cheeks both strange and familiar.

Lyra ran and embraced her, and the woman hugged her tight, and Will stood back, careful and doubtful.

Mary kissed Lyra warmly, and then came forward to welcome Will. And then came a curious little mental dance of sympathy and awkwardness, which took place in a second or less.

Moved by compassion for the state they were in, Mary first meant to embrace him as well as Lyra. But Mary was grown up, and Will was nearly grown, and she could see that that kind of response would have made a child of him, because while she might have embraced a child, she would never have done that to a man she didn't know; so she drew back mentally, wanting above all to honour this friend of Lyra's and not cause him to lose face.

So instead she held out her hand and he shook it, and a current of understanding and respect passed between them so powerful that it became liking at once, and each of them felt that they had made a life-long friend; as indeed they had.

"This is Will," said Lyra, "he's from your world – remember, I told you about him –"

"I'm Mary Malone," she said, "and you're hungry, the pair of you, you look half-starved."

She turned to the creature by her side and spoke some of those singing, hooting sounds, moving her arm as she did so.

At once the creatures moved away, and some of them brought cushions and rugs from the nearest house and laid them on the firm soil under a tree nearby, whose dense leaves and low-hanging branches gave a cool and fragrant shade.

And as soon as they were comfortable, their hosts brought smooth wooden bowls brimming with milk, which had a faint lemony astringency and was wonderfully refreshing; and small nuts like hazels, but with a richer buttery taste; and salad plucked fresh from the soil, sharp peppery leaves mingled with soft thick ones that oozed a creamy sap, and little cherry-sized roots tasting like sweet carrots.

But they couldn't eat much. It was too rich. Will wanted to do justice to their generosity, but the only thing he could easily swallow, apart from the drink, was some flat, slightly scorched floury bread like chapattis or tortillas. It was plain and nourishing, and that was all Will could cope with. Lyra tried some of every-thing, but like Will she soon found that a little was quite enough.

Mary managed to avoid asking any questions. These two had passed through an experience that had marked them deeply: they didn't want to talk about it yet.

So she answered their questions about the mulefa, and told them briefly how she had arrived in this world; and then she left them under the shade of the tree, because she could see their eyelids drooping and their heads nodding.

"You don't have to do anything now but sleep," she said.

The afternoon air was warm and still, and the shade of the tree was drowsy and murmurous with crickets. Less than five minutes after they'd swallowed the last of the drink, both Will and Lyra were fast asleep.

They are of two sexes? said Atal, surprised. *But how can you tell?*

It's easy, said Mary. *Their bodies are different shapes. They move differently.*

They are not much smaller than you. But they have less sraf. When will that come to them?

I don't know, Mary said. *I suppose some time soon. I don't know when it happens to us.*

No wheels, said Atal sympathetically.

They were weeding the vegetable garden. Mary had made a hoe to save having to bend down; Atal used her trunk, so their conversation was intermittent.

But you knew they were coming, said Atal.

Yes.

Was it the sticks that told you?

No, said Mary, blushing. She was a scientist; it was bad enough to have to admit to consulting the I Ching, but this was even more embarrassing. *It was a night-picture,* she confessed.

The mulefa had no single word for dream. They dreamed vividly, though, and took their dreams very seriously.

You don't like night-pictures, Atal said.

Yes, I do. But I didn't believe them until now. I saw the boy and the girl so clearly, and a voice told me to prepare for them.

What sort of voice? How did it speak if you couldn't see it?

It was hard for Atal to imagine speech without the trunk-movements that clarified and defined it. She'd stopped in the middle of a row of beans and faced Mary with fascinated curiosity.

Well, I did see it, said Mary. *It was a woman, or a female wise one, like us, like my people. But very old and yet not old at all.*

Wise one was what the mulefa called their leaders. She saw that Atal was looking intensely interested.

How could she be old and also not old? said Atal.

It is a make-like, said Mary.

Atal swung her trunk, reassured.

Mary went on as best she could: *She told me that I should expect the children, and when they would appear, and where. But not why. I must just look after them.*

They are hurt and tired, said Atal. *Will they stop the sraf leaving?*

Mary looked up uneasily. She knew without having to check through the spyglass that the Shadow-particles were streaming away faster than ever.

I hope so, she said. *But I don't know how.*

In the early evening, when the cooking-fires were lit and the first stars were coming out, a group of strangers arrived. Mary was washing; she heard the thunder of their wheels, and the agitated murmur of their talk, and hurried out of her house, drying herself.

Will and Lyra had been asleep all afternoon, and they were just stirring now, hearing the noise. Lyra sat up groggily to see Mary talking to five or six of the mulefa, who were surrounding her, clearly excited; but whether they were angry or joyful, she couldn't tell.

Mary saw her and broke away.

"Lyra," she said, "something's happened — they've found something they can't explain and it's . . . I don't know what it is . . . I've got to go and look. It's an hour or so away. I'll come back as soon as I can. Help yourself to anything you need from my house — I can't stop, they're too anxious —"

"All right," said Lyra, still dazed from her long sleep.

Mary looked under the tree. Will was rubbing his eyes.

"I really won't be too long," she said. "Atal will stay with you."

The leader was impatient. Mary swiftly threw her bridle and stirrups over his back, excusing herself for being clumsy, and mounted at once. They wheeled and turned and drove away into the dusk.

They set off in a new direction, along the ridge above the coast to the north. Mary had never ridden in the dark before, and she found the speed even more alarming than by day. As they climbed, Mary could see the glitter of the moon on the sea far off to the left, and its silver-sepia light seemed to envelop her in a cool sceptical wonder. The wonder was in her and the scepticism was in the world, and the coolness was in both.

She looked up from time to time and touched the spyglass in her pocket, but she couldn't use it till they'd stopped moving. And these mulefa were moving urgently, with the air of not wanting to stop for anything. After an hour's hard riding they swung inland, leaving the stone road and moving slowly along a trail of beaten earth that ran between knee-high grass past a stand of wheel-trees and up towards a ridge. The landscape glowed under the moon: wide bare hills with occasional little gullies where streams trickled down among the trees that clustered there.

It was towards one of these gullies that they led her. She had dismounted when they left the road, and she walked steadily at their pace over the brow of the hill and down into the gully.

She heard the trickling of the spring, and the night-wind in the grass. She heard the quiet sound of the wheels crunching over the hard-packed earth, and she heard the mulefa ahead of her murmuring to one another, and then they stopped.

In the side of the hill, just a few yards away, was one of those openings made by the subtle knife. It was like the mouth of a cave, because the moonlight shone into it a little way, just as if inside the opening there was the inside of the hill: but it wasn't. And out of it was coming a procession of ghosts.

Mary felt as if the ground had given way beneath her mind. She caught herself with a start, and seized the nearest branch for reassurance that there still was a physical world, and she was still part of it.

She moved closer. Old men and women, children, babes in arms, humans and other beings too, more and more thickly they came out of the dark into the world of solid moonlight – and vanished.

That was the strangest thing. They took a few steps in the world of grass and air and silver light, and looked around, their faces transformed with joy – Mary had never seen such joy – and held out their arms as if they were embracing the whole universe; and then, as if they were made of mist or smoke, they simply drifted away, becoming part of the earth and the dew and the night breeze.

Some of them came towards Mary as if they wanted to tell her something, and reached out their hands, and she felt their touch like little shocks of cold. One of the ghosts – an old woman – beckoned, urging her to come close.

Then she spoke, and Mary heard her say:

"Tell them stories. That's what we didn't know. All this time, and we never knew! But they need the truth. That's what nourishes them. You must tell them true stories, and everything will be well, everything. Just tell them stories."

That was all, and then she was gone. It was one of those moments when we suddenly recall a dream that we've unaccountably forgotten, and back in a flood comes all the emotion we felt in our sleep. It was the dream she'd tried to describe to Atal, the night-picture; but as Mary tried to find it again, it dissolved and drifted apart, just as these presences did in the open air. The dream was gone.

All that was left was the sweetness of that feeling, and the injunction to *tell them stories*.

She looked into the darkness. As far as she could see into that endless silence, more of these ghosts were coming, thousands upon thousands, like refugees returning to their homeland.

"Tell them stories," she said to herself.

33
MARZIPAN

Sweet spring, full of sweet days and roses,
A box where sweets compacted lie

— GEORGE HERBERT

NEXT MORNING LYRA woke up from a dream in which Pantalaimon had come back to her, and revealed his final shape; and she had loved it, but now she had no idea what it was.

The sun hadn't long risen, and the air had a fresh bloom. She could see the sunlight through the open door of the little thatched hut she slept in, Mary's house. She lay for a while listening. There were birds outside, and some kind of cricket, and Mary was breathing quietly in her sleep nearby.

Lyra sat up, and found herself naked. She was indignant for a moment, and then she saw some clean clothes folded beside her on the floor: a shirt of Mary's, a length of soft light patterned cloth that she could tie into a skirt. She put them on, feeling swamped in the shirt, but at least decent.

She left the hut. Pantalaimon was nearby: she was sure of it. She could almost hear him talking and laughing. It must mean that he was safe, and they were still connected somehow. And when he forgave her and came back – the hours they'd spend just talking, just telling each other everything . . .

Will was still asleep under the tree, the lazy thing. Lyra thought of waking him up, but if she was on her own, she could swim in the river. She happily used to swim naked in the river Cherwell, with all the other Oxford children, but it would be quite different with Will, and she blushed even to think of it.

So she went down to the water alone in the pearl-coloured morning. Among the reeds at the edge there was a tall slender bird like a heron, standing perfectly still on one leg. She walked quietly and slowly so as not to disturb it, but the bird took no more notice of her than if she'd been a twig on the water.

"Well," she said.

She left the clothes on the bank and slipped into the river. She swam hard to keep warm, and then came out and huddled on the bank, shivering. Pan would help dry her, normally: was he a fish, laughing at her from under the water? Or a beetle, creeping into the clothes to tickle her, or a bird? Or was he somewhere else entirely with the other dæmon, and with Lyra not on his mind at all?

The sun was warm now, and she was soon dry. She dressed in Mary's loose shirt again and, seeing some flat stones by the bank, went to fetch her own clothes to wash them. But she found that someone had already done that: hers, and Will's too, were laid over the springy twigs of a fragrant bush, nearly dry.

Will was stirring. She sat nearby and called him softly.

"Will! Wake up!"

"Where are we?" he said at once, and sat up, reaching for the knife.

"Safe," she said, looking away. "And they washed our clothes too, or Dr Malone did. I'll get yours. They're nearly dry . . ."

She passed them in and sat with her back to him till he was dressed.

"I swam in the river," she said. "I went to look for Pan, but I think he's hiding."

"That's a good idea. I mean a swim. I feel as if I've got years and years of dirt on me . . . I'll go down and wash."

While he was gone, Lyra wandered around the village, not looking too closely at anything in case she broke some code of politeness, but curious about everything she saw. Some of the houses were very old and some quite new, but they were all built in much the same way out of wood and clay and thatch. There was nothing crude about them; each door and window-frame and lintel was covered in subtle patterns, but patterns that weren't carved in the wood: it was as if they'd persuaded the wood to grow in that shape naturally.

The more she looked, the more she saw all kinds of order and carefulness in the village, like the layers of meaning in the alethiometer. Part of her mind was eager to puzzle it all out, to step lightly from similarity to similarity, from one meaning to another as she did with the instrument; but another part was wondering how long they'd be able to stay here before they had to move on.

Well, I'm not going anywhere till Pan comes back, she said to herself.

Presently Will came up from the river, and then Mary came out of her house and offered them breakfast; and soon Atal came along too, and the village came to life around them. The two young mulefa children, without wheels, kept peeping around the edge of their houses to stare, and Lyra would suddenly turn and look at them directly to make them jump and laugh with terror.

"Well now," Mary said when they'd eaten some bread and fruit and drunk a scalding infusion of something like mint. "Yesterday you were too tired and all you could do was rest. But you look a lot more lively today, both of you, and I think we need to tell each other everything we've found out. And it'll take us a good long time, and we might as well keep our hands busy while we're doing it, so we'll make ourselves useful and mend some nets."

They carried the pile of stiff, tarry netting to the river bank and spread it out on the grass, and Mary showed them how to knot a new piece of cord where it was worn. She was wary, because Atal had told her that the families further along the coast had seen large numbers of the tualapi, the white birds, gathering out at sea, and everyone was prepared for a warning to leave at once; but work had to go on in the meantime.

So they sat working in the sun by the placid river, and Lyra told her story, from the moment so long ago when she and Pan decided to look in the Retiring Room at Jordan College.

The tide came in and turned, and still there was no sign of the tualapi. In the late afternoon Mary took Will and Lyra along the river bank, past the fishing-posts where the nets were tied, and through the wide salt-marsh towards the sea. It was safe to go there when the tide was out, because the white birds only came inland when the water was high. Mary led the way along a hard path above the mud; like many things the mulefa had made, it was ancient and perfectly maintained, more like a part of nature than something imposed on it.

"Did they make the stone roads?" Will said.

"No. I think the roads made them, in a way," Mary said. "I mean they'd never have developed the use of the wheels if there hadn't been plenty of hard flat surfaces to use them on. I think they're lava flows from ancient volcanoes.

"So the roads made it possible for them to use the wheels. And other things came together as well. Like the wheel-trees themselves, and the way their bodies are formed – they're not vertebrates, they don't have a spine. Some lucky chance in our worlds long ago must have meant that creatures with backbones had it a bit easier, so all kinds of other shapes developed, all based on the central spine. In this world, chance went another way, and the diamond-frame was successful. There are vertebrates, to be sure, but not many. There are snakes, for example. Snakes are important here. The people look after them and try not to hurt them.

"Anyway, their shape, and the roads, and the wheel-trees coming together all made it possible. A lot of little chances, all coming together. When did your part of the story begin, Will?"

"Lots of little chances for me, too," he began, thinking of the cat under the hornbeam trees. If he'd arrived there thirty seconds earlier or later, he would never have seen the cat, never have found the window, never have discovered Cittàgazze and Lyra; none of this would have happened.

He started from the very beginning, and they listened as they walked. By the time they reached the mud-flats, he had reached the point where he and his father were fighting on the mountaintop.

"And then the witch killed him . . ."

He had never really understood that. He explained what she'd told him before she killed herself: she had loved John Parry, and he had scorned her.

"Witches are fierce, though," Lyra said.

"But if she loved him . . ."

"Well," said Mary, "love is ferocious too."

"But he loved my mother," said Will. "And I can tell her that he was never unfaithful."

Lyra, looking at Will, thought that if he fell in love, he would be like that.

All around them the quiet noises of the afternoon hung in the warm air: the endless trickling sucking of the marsh, the scraping of insects, the calling of gulls. The tide was fully out, so the whole extent of the beach was clear and glistening under the bright sun. A billion tiny mud-creatures lived and ate and died in the top layer of sand, and the little casts and breathing-holes and invisible movements showed that the whole landscape was aquiver with life.

Without telling the others why, Mary looked out to the distant sea, scanning the horizon for white sails. But there was only hazy glitter where the blue of the sky paled at the edge of the sea, and the sea took up the pallor and made it sparkle through the shimmering air.

She showed Will and Lyra how to gather a particular kind of mollusc by finding their breathing-tubes just above the sand. The mulefa loved them, but it was hard for them to move on the sand and gather them. Whenever Mary came to the shore she harvested as many as she could, and now with three pairs of hands and eyes at work there would be a feast.

She gave each of them a cloth bag, and they worked as they listened to the next part of the story. Steadily they filled their bags, and Mary led them unobtrusively back to the edge of the marsh, for the tide was turning.

The story was taking a long time; they wouldn't get to the world of the dead that day. As they neared the village, Will was telling Mary what he and Lyra had come to realize about the three-part nature of human beings.

"You know," Mary said, "the church – the Catholic Church that I used to belong to – wouldn't use the word dæmon, but St Paul talks about spirit *and* soul *and* body. So the idea of three parts in human nature isn't so strange."

"But the best part is the body," Will said. "That's what Baruch and Balthamos told me. Angels wish they had bodies. They told me that angels can't understand why *we* don't enjoy the world more. It would be sort of ecstasy for them to have our flesh and our senses. In the world of the dead –"

"Tell it when we get to it," said Lyra, and she smiled at him, a smile of such sweet knowledge and joy that his senses felt confused. He smiled back, and Mary thought his expression showed more perfect trust than she'd ever seen on a human face.

By this time they had reached the village, and there was the evening meal to prepare. So Mary left the other two by the river bank where they sat to watch the tide flooding in, and went to join Atal by the cooking fire. Her friend was overjoyed by the shellfish-harvest.

But Mary, she said, *the tualapi destroyed a village further up the coast, and then another and another. They've never done that before. They usually attack one and then go back to sea. And another tree fell today . . .*

No! Where?

Atal mentioned a grove not far from a hot spring. Mary had been there only three days before, and nothing had seemed wrong. She took the spyglass and looked at the sky; sure enough, the great stream of shadow-particles was flowing more strongly, and at incomparably greater speed and volume, than the tide now rising between the river banks.

What can you do? said Atal.

Mary felt the weight of responsibility like a heavy hand between her shoulder-blades, but made herself sit up lightly.

Tell them stories, she said.

When supper was over, the three humans and Atal sat on rugs outside Mary's house, under the warm stars. They lay back, well fed and comfortable in the flower-scented night, and listened to Mary tell her story.

She began just before she first met Lyra, telling them about the work she was doing at the Dark Matter Research group, and the funding crisis. How much time she'd had to spend asking for money, and how little time there'd been left for research!

But Lyra's coming had changed everything, and so quickly: within a matter of days she'd left her world altogether.

"I did as you told me," she said. "I made a program – that's a set of instructions – to let the Shadows talk to me through the computer. They told me what to do. They said they were angels, and – well . . ."

"If you were a scientist," said Will, "I don't suppose that was a good thing for them to say. You might not have believed in angels."

"Ah, but I knew about them. I used to be a nun, you see. I thought physics could be done to the glory of God, till I saw there wasn't any God at all and that physics was more interesting anyway. The Christian religion is a very powerful and convincing mistake, that's all."

"When did you stop being a nun?" said Lyra.

"I remember it exactly," Mary said, "even to the time of day. Because I was good at physics, they let me keep up my university career, you see, and I finished my doctorate and I was going to teach. It wasn't one of those orders where they shut you away from the world. In fact we didn't even wear the habit; we just had to dress soberly and wear a crucifix. So I was going into university to teach and do research into particle physics.

"And there was a conference on my subject and they asked me to come and read a paper. The conference was in Lisbon, and I'd never been there before; in fact I'd never been out of England. The whole business – the plane flight, the hotel, the bright sunlight, the foreign languages all around me, the well-known people who were going to speak, and the thought of my own paper and wondering whether anyone would turn up to listen and whether I'd be too nervous to get the words out . . . Oh, I was keyed up with excitement, I can't tell you.

"And I was so innocent – you have to remember that. I'd been such a good little girl, I'd gone to Mass regularly, I'd thought I had a vocation for the spiritual life. I wanted to serve God with all my heart. I wanted to take my whole life and offer it up like this," she said, holding up her hands together, "and place it in front of Jesus to do as he liked with. And I suppose I was pleased with myself. Too much. I was holy *and* I was clever. Ha! That lasted until, oh, half-past nine on the evening of August the tenth, seven years ago."

Lyra sat up and hugged her knees, listening closely.

"It was the evening after I'd given my paper," Mary went on, "and it had gone well, and there'd been some well-known people listening, and I'd dealt with the questions without making a mess of it, and altogether I was full of relief and pleasure . . . And pride too, no doubt.

"Anyway, some of my colleagues were going to a restaurant a little way down the coast, and they asked if I'd like to go. Normally I'd have made some excuse, but this time I thought well, I'm a grown woman, I've presented a paper on an important subject and it was well received and I'm among good friends . . . And it was so warm, and the talk was about all the things I was most interested in, and we were all in high spirits, I thought I'd loosen up a bit. I was discovering another side of myself, you know, one that liked the taste of wine and grilled sardines and the feeling of warm air on my skin and the beat of music in the background. I relished it.

"So we sat down to eat in the garden. I was at the end of a long table under a lemon tree, and there was a sort of bower next to me with passion flowers, and my neighbour was talking to the person on the other side, and . . . Well, sitting opposite was a man I'd seen once or twice around the conference. I didn't know him to speak to; he was Italian, and he'd done some work that people were talking about, and I thought it would be interesting to hear about it.

"Anyway. He was only a little older than me, and he had soft black hair and beautiful olive-coloured skin and dark, dark eyes. His hair kept falling across his forehead and he kept pushing it back like that, slowly . . ."

She showed them. Will thought she looked as if she remembered it very well.

"He wasn't handsome," she went on. "He wasn't a ladies' man or a charmer. If he had been, I'd have been shy, I wouldn't have known how to talk to him. But he was nice and clever and funny and it was the easiest thing in the world to sit there in the lantern light under the lemon tree with the scent of the flowers and the grilled food and the wine, and talk and laugh and feel myself hoping that he thought I was pretty. Sister Mary Malone, flirting! What about my vows? What about dedicating my life to Jesus and all that?

"Well, I don't know if it was the wine or my own silliness or the warm air or the lemon tree, or whatever ... But it gradually seemed to me that I'd made myself believe something that wasn't true. I'd made myself believe that I was fine and happy and fulfilled on my own without the love of anyone else. Being in love was like China: you knew it was there, and no doubt it was very interesting, and some people went there, but I never would. I'd spend all my life without ever going to China, but it wouldn't matter, because there was all the rest of the world to visit.

"And then someone passed me a bit of some sweet stuff and I suddenly realized I *had* been to China. So to speak. And I'd forgotten it. It was the taste of the sweet stuff that brought it back – I think it was marzipan – sweet almond paste," she explained to Lyra, who was looking puzzled.

Lyra said, "Ah! Marchpane!" and settled back comfortably to hear what happened next.

"Anyway –" Mary went on – "I remembered the taste, and all at once I was back tasting it for the first time as a young girl.

"I was twelve years old. I was at a party at the house of one of my friends, a birthday party, and there was a disco – that's where they play music on a kind of recording machine and people dance," she explained, seeing Lyra's puzzlement. "Usually girls dance together because the boys are too shy to ask them. But this boy – I didn't know him – he asked me to dance, and so we had the first dance and then the next and by that time we were talking ... And you know what it is when you like someone, you know it at once; well, I liked him such a lot. And we kept on talking and then there was a birthday cake. And he took a bit of marzipan and he just gently put it in my mouth – I remember trying to smile, and blushing, and feeling so foolish – and I fell in love with him just for that, for the gentle way he touched my lips with the marzipan."

As Mary said that, Lyra felt something strange happen to her body. She felt a stirring at the roots of her hair: she found herself breathing faster. She had never been on a roller-coaster, or anything like one, but if she had, she would have recognized the sensations in her breast: they were exciting and frightening at the same time, and she had not the slightest idea why. The sensation continued, and deepened, and changed, as more parts of her body found themselves affected too. She felt as if she had been handed the key to a great house she hadn't known was there, a house that was somehow inside her, and as she turned the key, deep in the darkness of the building she felt other doors opening too, and lights coming on. She sat trembling, hugging her knees, hardly daring to breathe, as Mary went on:

"And I think it was at that party, or it might have been at another one, that we kissed each other for the first time. It was in a garden, and there was the sound of music from inside, and the quiet and the cool among the trees, and I was *aching* – all my body was *aching* for him, and I could tell he felt the same – and we were both almost too shy to move. Almost. But one of us did and then without any interval between – it was like a quantum leap, *suddenly* – we were kissing each other and oh, it was more than China, it was paradise.

"We saw each other about half a dozen times, no more. And then his parents moved away and I never saw him again. It was such a sweet time, so short ... But there it was. I'd known it. I *had* been to China."

It was the strangest thing: Lyra knew exactly what she meant, and half an hour earlier she would have had no idea at all. And inside her, that rich house with all its doors open and all its rooms lit stood waiting, quiet, expectant.

"And at half-past nine in the evening at that restaurant table in Portugal," Mary continued, quite unaware of the silent drama going on in Lyra, "someone gave me a piece of marzipan and it all came back. And I thought: am I really going to spend the rest of my life without ever feeling that again? I thought: I *want* to go to China. It's full of treasures and strangeness and mystery and joy. I thought, will anyone be better off if I go straight back to the hotel and say my prayers and confess to the priest and promise never to fall into temptation again? Will anyone be the better for making me miserable?

"And the answer came back – no. No one will. There's no one to fret, no one to condemn, no one to bless me for being a good girl, no one to punish me for being wicked. Heaven was empty. I didn't know whether God had died, or whether there never had been a God at all. Either way, I felt free and lonely and I didn't know whether I was happy or unhappy, but something very strange had happened. And all that huge change came about as I had the marzipan in my mouth, before I'd even swallowed it. A taste – a memory – a landslide...

"When I did swallow it and looked at the man across the table I could tell he knew something had happened. I couldn't tell him there and then; it was still too strange and private almost for me. But later on we went for a walk along the beach in the dark, and the warm night breeze kept stirring my hair about, and the Atlantic was being very well-behaved – little quiet waves around our feet...

"And I took the crucifix from around my neck and I threw it in the sea. That was it. All over. Gone.

"So that was how I stopped being a nun," she said.

"Was that man the same one that found out about the skulls?" Lyra said, intent.

"Oh – no. The skull man was Dr Payne, Oliver Payne. He came along much later. No, the man at the conference was called Alfredo Montale. He was very different."

"Did you kiss him?"

"Well," said Mary, smiling, "yes, but not then."

"Was it hard to leave the church?" said Will.

"In one way it was, because everyone was so disappointed. Everyone, from the Mother Superior to the priests to my parents – they were so upset and reproachful ... I felt as if something *they* all passionately believed in depended on *me* carrying on with something I didn't.

"But in another way it was easy, because it made sense. For the first time ever I felt I was doing something with all of my nature and not only a part of it. So it was lonely for a while but then I got used to it."

"Did you marry him?" said Lyra.

"No. I didn't marry anyone. I lived with someone – not Alfredo, someone else. I lived with him for four years, nearly. My family was scandalized. But then we decided we'd be happier not living together. So I'm on my own. The man I lived with used to like mountain climbing, and he taught me to climb, and I walk in the mountains and . . . And I've got my work. Well, I *had* my work. So I'm solitary but happy, if you see what I mean."

"What was the boy called?" said Lyra. "At the party?"

"Tim."

"What did he look like?"

"Oh . . . Nice. That's all I remember."

"When I first saw you, in your Oxford," Lyra said, "you said one of the reasons you became a scientist was that you wouldn't have to think about good and evil. Did you think about them when you were a nun?"

"H'mm. No. But I knew what I *should* think: it was whatever the church taught me to think. And when I did science I had to think about other things altogether. So I never had to think about them for myself at all."

"But do you now?" said Will.

"I think I *have* to," Mary said, trying to be accurate.

"When you stopped believing in God," he went on, "did you stop believing in good and evil?"

"No. But I stopped believing there was a power of good and a power of evil that were outside us. And I came to believe that good and evil are names for what people do, not for what they are. All we can say is that this is a good deed, because it helps someone, or that's an evil one, because it hurts them. People are too complicated to have simple labels."

"Yes," said Lyra firmly.

"Did you miss God?" asked Will.

"Yes," Mary said, "terribly. And I still do. And what I miss most is the sense of being connected to the whole of the universe. I used to feel I was connected to God like that, and because he was there, I was connected to the whole of his creation. But if he's not there, then . . ."

Far out on the marshes, a bird called with a long melancholy series of falling tones. Embers settled in the fire; the grass was stirring faintly with the night breeze. Atal seemed to be dozing like a cat, her wheels flat on the grass beside her, her legs folded under her body, eyes half-closed, attention half-there and half-elsewhere. Will was lying on his back, eyes open to the stars.

As for Lyra, she hadn't moved a muscle since that strange thing had happened, and she held the memory of those sensations inside her like a fragile vessel brim-full of new knowledge, which she hardly dared touch for fear of spilling it. She didn't know what it was, or what it meant, or where it had come from: so she sat still, hugging her knees, and tried to stop herself trembling with excitement. *Soon*, she thought, *soon I'll know. I'll know very soon.*

Mary was tired: she had run out of stories. No doubt she'd think of more tomorrow.

34
THERE IS NOW

Shew you all alive
The world, where every particle of dust breathes forth its joy.

— WILLIAM BLAKE

MARY COULDN'T SLEEP. Every time she closed her eyes, something made her sway and lurch as if she were at the brink of a precipice, and she snapped awake, tense with fear.

This happened three, four, five times, until she realized that sleep was not going to come; so she got up and dressed quietly, and stepped out of the house and away from the tree with its tent-like branches under which Will and Lyra were sleeping.

The moon was bright and high in the sky. There was a lively wind, and the great landscape was mottled with cloud-shadows, moving, Mary thought, like the migration of some herd of unimaginable beasts. But animals migrated for a purpose; when you saw herds of reindeer moving across the tundra, or wilde-beest crossing the savannah, you knew they were going where the food was, or to places where it was good to mate and bear offspring. Their movement had a meaning. These clouds were moving as the result of pure chance, the effect of utterly random events at the level of atoms and molecules; their shadows speeding over the grassland had no meaning at all.

Nevertheless, they looked as if they did. They looked tense and driven with purpose. The whole night did. Mary felt it too, except that she didn't know what that purpose was. But unlike her, the clouds seemed to *know* what they were doing and why, and the wind knew, and the grass knew. The entire world was alive and conscious.

Mary climbed the slope and looked back across the marshes, where the incoming tide laced a brilliant silver through the glistening dark of the mud-flats and the reed-beds. The cloud-shadows were very clear down there: they looked as if they were fleeing something frightful behind them, or hastening to embrace something wonderful ahead. But what that was, Mary would never know.

She turned towards the grove where her climbing tree stood. It was twenty minutes' walk away; she could see it clearly, towering high and tossing its great head in a dialogue with the urgent wind. They had things to say, and she couldn't hear them.

She hurried towards it, moved by the excitement of the night, and desperate to join in. This was the very thing she'd told Will about when he asked if she missed God: it was the sense that the whole universe was alive, and that everything was connected to everything else by threads of meaning. When she'd been a Christian, she had felt connected too; but when she left the Church, she felt loose and free and light, in a universe without purpose.

And then had come the discovery of the Shadows and her journey into another world, and now this vivid night, and it was plain that everything was throbbing with purpose and meaning, but she was cut off from it. And it was impossible to find a connection, because there was no God.

Half in exultation and half in despair, she resolved to climb her tree and try once again to lose herself in the Dust.

But she hadn't got half-way towards the grove before she heard a different sound among the lashing of the leaves and the streaming of the wind through the grass. Something was groaning, a deep, sombre note like an organ. And above that, the sound of cracking – snapping and breaking, and the squeal and scream of wood on wood.

Surely it couldn't be *her* tree?

She stopped where she was, in the open grassland, with the wind lashing her face and the cloud-shadows racing past her and the tall grasses whipping her thighs, and watched the canopy of the grove. Boughs groaned, twigs snapped, great baulks of green wood snapped off like dry sticks and fell all the long way to the ground, and then the crown itself – the crown of the very tree she knew so well – leaned and leaned and slowly began to topple.

Every fibre in the trunk, the bark, the roots, seemed to cry out separately against this murder. But it fell and fell, all the great length of it smashed its way out of the grove and seemed to lean towards Mary before crashing into the ground like a wave against a break-water; and the colossal trunk rebounded up a little way, and settled down finally, with a groaning of torn wood.

She ran up to touch the tossing leaves. There was her rope; there were the splintered ruins of her platform. Her heart thudding painfully, she climbed in among the fallen branches, hauling herself through the familiar boughs at their unfamiliar angles, and balanced herself as high up as she could get.

She braced herself against a branch and took out the spyglass. Through it she saw two quite different movements in the sky.

One was that of the clouds, driven across the moon in one direction, and the other was that of the stream of Dust, seeming to cross it in quite another.

And of the two, the Dust was flowing more quickly and at much greater volume. In fact the whole sky seemed to be flowing with it, a great inexorable flood pouring out of the world, out of all the worlds, into some ultimate emptiness.

Slowly, as if they were moving themselves in her mind, things joined up.

Will and Lyra had said that the subtle knife was three hundred years old at least. So the old man in the tower had told them.

The mulefa had told her that the sraf, which had nurtured their lives and their world for thirty-three thousand years, had begun to fail just over three hundred years ago.

According to Will the Guild of the Torre degli Angeli, the owners of the subtle knife, had been careless; they hadn't always closed the windows they opened. Well, Mary had found one, after all, and there must be many others.

Suppose that all this time, little by little, Dust had been leaking out of the wounds the subtle knife had made in nature . . .

She felt dizzy, and it wasn't only the swaying and rising and falling of the branches she was wedged among. She put the spyglass carefully in her pocket and hooked her arms over the branch in front, gazing at the sky, the moon, the scudding clouds.

The subtle knife was responsible for the small-scale, low-level leakage. It was damaging, and the universe was suffering because of it, and she must talk to Will and Lyra and find a way to stop it.

But the vast flood in the sky was another matter entirely. That was new, and it was catastrophic. And if it wasn't stopped, all conscious life would come to an end. As the mulefa had shown her, Dust came into being when living things became conscious of themselves; but it needed some feedback system to reinforce it and make it safe, as the mulefa had their wheels and the oil from the trees. Without something like that, it would all vanish. Thought, imagination, feeling, would all wither and blow away, leaving nothing but a brutish automatism; and that brief period when life was conscious of itself would flicker out like a candle in every one of the billions of worlds where it had burned brightly.

Mary felt the burden of it keenly. It felt like age. She felt eighty years old, worn out and weary and longing to die.

She climbed heavily out of the branches of the great fallen tree, and with the wind still wild in the leaves and the grass and her hair, set off back to the village.

At the summit of the slope she looked for the last time at the Dust-stream, with the clouds and the wind blowing across it and the moon standing firm in the middle.

And then she saw what they were doing, at last: she saw what that great urgent purpose was.

They were trying to hold back the Dust-flood. They were striving to put some barriers up against the terrible stream: wind, moon, clouds, leaves, grass, all those lovely things were crying out and hurling themselves into the struggle to keep the Shadow-particles in this universe, which they so enriched.

Matter *loved* Dust. It didn't want to see it go. That was the meaning of this night, and it was Mary's meaning too.

Had she thought there was no meaning in life, no purpose, when God had gone? Yes, she had thought that.

"Well, there is now," she said aloud, and again, louder: "There is now!"

As she looked again at the clouds and the moon in the Dust-flow, they looked as frail and doomed as a dam of little twigs and tiny pebbles trying to hold back the Mississippi. But they were trying, all the same. They'd go on trying till the end of everything.

How long she stayed out, Mary didn't know. When the intensity of her feeling began to subside, and exhaustion took its place, she made her way slowly down the hill towards the village.

And when she was half-way down, near a little grove of knot-wood bushes, she saw something strange out on the mud-flats. There was a glow of white, a steady movement: something coming up with the tide.

She stood still, gazing intently. It couldn't be the tualapi, because they always moved in a flock, and this was on its own; but everything about it was the same – the sail-like wings, the long neck – it was one of the birds, no doubt about it. She had never heard of their moving about alone, and she hesitated before running down to warn the villagers, because the thing had stopped, in any case. It was floating on the water close to the path.

And it was coming apart . . . No, something was getting off its back.

The something was a man.

She could see him quite clearly, even at that distance; the moonlight was brilliant, and her eyes were adjusted to it. She looked through the spyglass, and put the matter beyond doubt: it was a human figure, radiating Dust.

He was carrying something: a long stick of some kind. He came along the path quickly and easily, not running, but moving like an athlete or a hunter. He was dressed in simple dark clothes that would normally conceal him well; but through the spyglass, he showed up as if he was under a spotlight.

And as he came closer to the village, she realized what that stick was. He was carrying a rifle.

She felt as if someone had poured icy water over her heart. Every separate hair on her flesh stirred.

She was too far away to do anything: even if she'd shouted, he wouldn't have heard. She had to watch as he stepped into the village, looking to left and right, stopping every so often to listen, moving from house to house.

Mary's mind felt like the moon and the clouds trying to hold back the Dust as she cried out silently: *Don't look under the tree – go away from the tree –*

But he moved closer and closer to it, finally stopping outside her own house. She couldn't bear it; she put the spyglass in her pocket and began to run down the slope. She was about to call out, anything, a wild cry, but just in time she realized that it might wake Will or Lyra and make them reveal themselves, and she choked it back.

Then, because she couldn't bear not knowing what the man was doing, she stopped and fumbled for the spyglass again, and had to stand still while she looked through it.

He was opening the door of her house. He was going inside it. He vanished from sight, although there was a stir in the Dust he left behind, like smoke when a hand is passed through it. Mary waited for an endless minute, and then he appeared again.

He stood in her doorway, looking around slowly from left to right, and his gaze swept past the tree.

Then he stepped off the threshold and stood still, almost at a loss. Mary was suddenly conscious of how exposed she was on the bare hillside, an easy rifle-shot away, but he was only interested in the village; and when another minute or so had gone by, he turned and walked quietly away.

She watched every step he took down the river path, and saw quite clearly how he stepped on to the bird's back and sat cross-legged as it turned to glide away. Five minutes later they were lost to sight.

35

OVER THE HILLS AND FAR AWAY

The birthday of my life
Is come, my love is come to me.

— CHRISTINA ROSSETTI

"DR MALONE," said Lyra in the morning, "Will and me have
got to look for our dæmons. When we've found them we'll
know what to do. But we can't be without them for much
longer. So we just want to go and look."

"Where will you go?" said Mary, heavy-eyed and headachy
after her disturbed night. She and Lyra were on the river bank,
Lyra to wash, and Mary to look, surreptitiously, for the man's
footprints. So far she hadn't found any.

"Don't know," said Lyra. "But they're out there somewhere.
As soon as we came through from the battle, they ran away as if
they didn't trust us any more. Can't say I blame them either. But
we know they're in this world, and we thought we saw them a
couple of times, so maybe we can find them."

"Listen," Mary said reluctantly, and told Lyra what she'd seen
the night before.

As she spoke, Will came to join them, and both he and Lyra
listened, wide-eyed and serious.

"He's probably just a traveller and he found a window and
wandered through from somewhere else," Lyra said when Mary
had finished. Privately, she had quite different things to think
about, and this man wasn't as interesting as they were. "Like
Will's father did," she went on. "There's bound to be all kinds
of openings now. Anyway, if he just turned around and left he
can't have meant to do anything bad, can he?"

"I don't know. I didn't like it. And I'm worried about you
going off on your own – or I would be if I didn't know you'd
already done far more dangerous things than that. Oh, I don't
know. But please be careful. Please look all around. At least out on
the prairie you can see someone coming from a long way off . . ."

"If we do, we can escape straight away into another world, so he won't be able to hurt us," Will said.

They were determined to go, and Mary was reluctant to argue.

"At least," she said, "promise that you won't go in among the trees. If that man is still around, he might be hiding in a wood or a grove and you wouldn't see him in time to escape."

"We promise," said Lyra.

"Well, I'll pack you some food in case you're out all day."

Mary took some flat bread and cheese and some sweet thirst-quenching red fruits, wrapped them in a cloth, and tied a cord around it for one of them to carry over a shoulder.

"Good hunting," she said as they left. "Please take care."

She was still anxious. She stood watching them all the way to the foot of the slope.

"I wonder why she's so sad," Will said, as he and Lyra climbed the road up to the ridge.

"She's probably wondering if she'll ever go home again," said Lyra. "And if her laboratory'll still be hers when she does. And maybe she's sad about the man she was in love with."

"Mmm," said Will. "D'you think *we'll* ever go home?"

"Dunno. I don't suppose I've got a home anyway. They probably couldn't have me back at Jordan College, and I can't live with the bears or the witches. Maybe I could live with the gyptians. I wouldn't mind that, if they'd have me."

"What about Lord Asriel's world? Wouldn't you want to live there?"

"It's going to fail, remember," she said.

"Why?"

"Because of what your father's ghost said, just before we came out. About dæmons, and how they can only live for a long time if they stay in their own world. But probably Lord Asriel, I mean my father, couldn't have thought about that, because no one knew enough about other worlds when he started . . . All that," she said wonderingly, "all that bravery and skill . . . All that, all wasted! All for nothing!"

They climbed on, finding the going easy on the rock road,

and when they reached the top of the ridge they stopped and looked back.

"Will," she said, "supposing we *don't* find them?"

"I'm sure we will. What I'm wondering is what my dæmon will be like."

"You saw her. And I picked her up," Lyra said, blushing, because of course it was a gross violation of manners to touch something so private as someone else's dæmon. It was forbidden not only by politeness, but by something deeper than that — something like shame. A quick glance at Will's warm cheeks showed that he knew that just as well as she did. She couldn't tell whether he also felt that half-frightened, half-excited feeling, as she did, the one that had come over her the night before: here it was again.

They walked on side by side, suddenly shy with each other. But Will, not put off by being shy, said, "When does your dæmon stop changing shape?"

"About . . . I suppose about our age, or a bit older. Maybe more sometimes. We used to talk about Pan settling, him and me. We used to wonder what he'd be — "

"Don't people have any idea?"

"Not when they're young. As you grow up you start thinking, well, they might be this or they might be that . . . And usually they end up something that fits. I mean something like your real nature. Like if your dæmon's a dog, that means you like doing what you're told, and knowing who's boss, and following orders, and pleasing people who are in charge. A lot of servants are people whose dæmons are dogs. So it helps to know what you're like and to find what you'd be good at. How do people in your world know what they're like?"

"I don't know. I don't know much about my world. All I know is keeping secret and quiet and hidden, so I don't know much about . . . grown-ups, and friends. Or lovers. I think it'd be difficult having a dæmon because everybody would know so much about you just by looking. I like to keep secret and stay out of sight."

"Then maybe your dæmon'd be an animal that's good at hiding. Or one of those animals that looks like another — a butter-fly that looks like a wasp, for disguise. They must have creatures like that in your world, because we have, and we're so much alike."

They walked on together in a friendly silence. All around them the wide clear morning lay limpid in the hollows and pearly-blue in the warm air above. As far as the eye could see the great savannah rolled, brown, gold, buff-green, shimmering towards the horizon, and empty. They might have been the only people in the world.

"But it's not empty really," Lyra said.

"You mean that man?"

"No. You know what I mean."

"Yes, I do. I can see shadows in the grass . . . maybe birds," Will said.

He was following the little darting movements here and there. He found it easier to see the shadows if he didn't look at them. They were more willing to show themselves to the corners of his eye, and when he said so to Lyra she said, "It's negative capability."

"What's that?"

"The poet Keats said it first. Dr Malone knows. It's how I read the alethiometer. It's how you use the knife, isn't it?"

"Yes, I suppose it is. But I was just thinking that they might be the dæmons."

"So was I, but . . ."

She put her finger to her lips. He nodded.

"Look," he said, "there's one of those fallen trees."

It was Mary's climbing tree. They went up to it carefully, keeping an eye on the grove in case another one should fall. In the calm morning, with only a faint breeze stirring the leaves, it seemed impossible that a mighty thing like this should ever topple, but here it was.

The vast trunk, supported in the grove by its torn-up roots and out on the grass by the mass of branches, was high above their heads. Some of those branches, crushed and broken, were themselves as big around as the biggest trees Will had ever seen; the crown of the tree, tight-packed with boughs that still looked sturdy, leaves that were still green, towered like a ruined palace into the mild air.

Suddenly Lyra gripped Will's arm.

"Ssh," she whispered. "Don't look. I'm sure they're up there. I saw something move and I *swear* it was Pan . . ."

Her hand was warm. He was more aware of that than of the great mass of leaves and branches above them. Pretending to gaze vacantly at the horizon, he let his attention wander upwards into the confused mass of green, brown and blue, and there – she was right! – there was a something that was *not* the tree. And beside it, another.

"Walk away," Will said under his breath. "We'll go somewhere else and see if they follow us."

"Suppose they don't . . . But yes, all right," Lyra whispered back.

They pretended to look all around; they set their hands on one of the branches resting on the ground, as if they were intending to climb; they pretended to change their minds, by shaking their heads and walking away.

"I wish we could look behind," Lyra said when they were a few hundred yards away.

"Just go on walking. They can see us, and they won't get lost. They'll come to us when they want to."

They stepped off the black road and into the knee-high grass, swishing their legs through the stems, watching the insects hovering, darting, fluttering, skimming, hearing the million-voiced chorus chirrup and scrape.

"What are you going to do, Will?" Lyra said quietly after they'd walked some way in silence.

"Well, I've got to go home," he said.

She thought he sounded unsure, though. She hoped he sounded unsure.

"But they might still be after you," she said. "Those men."

"We've seen worse than them, after all."

"Yes, I suppose . . . But I wanted to show you Jordan College, and the Fens. I wanted us to . . ."

"Yes," he said, "and I wanted . . . It would be good to go to Cittàgazze again, even. It was a beautiful place, and if the Spectres are all gone . . . But there's my mother. I've got to go back and look after her. I just left her with Mrs Cooper, and it's not fair on either of them."

"But it's not fair on *you* to have to do that."

"No," he said, "but that's a different sort of not fair. That's just like an earthquake or a rainstorm. It might not be fair, but no one's to blame. But if I just leave my mother with an old lady who isn't very well herself, then that's a different kind of not fair. That would be wrong. I've just got to go home. But probably it's going to be difficult to go back as we were. Probably the secret's out now. I don't suppose Mrs Cooper will have been able to look after her, not if my mother's in one of those times when she gets frightened of things. So she's probably had to get help, and when I go back I'll be made to go into some kind of institution."

"No! Like an orphanage?"

"I think that's what they do. I just don't know. I'll hate it."

"You could escape with the knife, Will! You could come to my world!"

"I still belong there where I can be with her. When I'm grown up I'll be able to look after her properly, in my own house. No one can interfere then."

"D'you think you'll get married?"

He was quiet for a long time. She knew he was thinking, though.

"I can't see that far ahead," he said. "It would have to be some-one who understands about . . . I don't think there's anyone like that in my world. Would *you* get married?"

"Me too," she said, and her voice wasn't quite steady. "Not to anyone in my world, I shouldn't think."

They walked on slowly, wandering towards the horizon. They had all the time in the world: all the time the world had.

After a while Lyra said, "You *will* keep the knife, won't you? So you could visit my world?"

"Of course. I certainly wouldn't give it to anyone else, ever."

"Don't look –" she said, not altering her pace. "There they are again. On the left."

"They *are* following us," said Will, delighted.

"Ssh!"

"I thought they would. OK, we'll just pretend now, we'll just wander along as if we're looking for them, and we'll look in all sorts of stupid places."

It became a game. They found a pond and searched among the reeds and in the mud, saying loudly that the dæmons were bound to be shaped like frogs or water-beetles or slugs; they peeled off the bark of a long-fallen tree at the edge of a string-wood grove, pretending to have seen the two dæmons creeping underneath it in the form of earwigs; Lyra made a great fuss of an ant she claimed to have trodden on, sympathizing with its bruises, saying its face was just like Pan's, asking in mock-sorrow why it was refusing to speak to her.

But when she thought they were genuinely out of earshot, she said earnestly to Will, leaning close to speak quietly:

"We *had* to leave them, didn't we? We didn't have a choice really?"

"Yes, we had to. It was worse for you than for me, but we didn't have any choice at all. Because you made a promise to Roger, and you had to keep it."

"And you had to speak to your father again . . ."

"And we had to let them all out."

"Yes, we did. I'm so glad we did. Pan will be glad one day too, when *I* die. We won't be split up. It was a *good* thing we did."

As the sun rose higher in the sky and the air became warmer, they began to look for shade. Towards noon they found themselves on the slope rising towards the summit of a ridge, and when they'd reached it, Lyra flopped down on the grass and said, "Well! If we don't find somewhere shady soon . . ."

There was a valley leading down on the other side, and it was thick with bushes, so they guessed there might be a stream as well. They traversed the slope of the ridge till it dipped into the head of the valley, and there sure enough, among ferns and reeds, a spring bubbled out of the rock.

They dipped their hot faces in the water and swallowed gratefully, and then they followed the stream downwards, seeing it gather in miniature whirlpools and pour over tiny ledges of stone, and all the time get fuller and wider.

"How does it do that?" Lyra marvelled. "There's no *more*

water coming into it from anywhere else, but there's so much more of it here than up there."

Will, watching the shadows out of the corner of his eye, saw them slip ahead, leaping over the ferns to disappear into the bushes further down. He pointed silently.

"It just goes slower," he said. "It doesn't flow as fast as the spring comes out, so it gathers in these pools . . . They've gone in there," he whispered, indicating a little group of trees at the foot of the slope.

Lyra's heart was beating so fast she felt the pulse in her throat. She and Will looked at each other, a curiously formal and serious look, before setting off to follow the stream. The undergrowth got thicker as they went down the valley; the stream went into tunnels of green and emerged in dappled clearings, only to tumble over a lip of stone and bury itself in the green again, and they had to follow it as much by hearing as by sight.

At the foot of the hill it ran into a little wood of silver-barked trees.

Father Gomez watched from the top of the ridge. It hadn't been hard to follow them; despite Mary's confidence in the open savannah, there was plenty of concealment in the grass and the occasional thickets of string-wood and sap-lacquer bushes. The two young people had spent a lot of time earlier looking all around as if they thought they were being followed, and he had had to keep some distance away, but as the morning passed they became more and more absorbed in each other, and paid less attention to the landscape.

The one thing he didn't want to do was hurt the boy. He had a horror of harming an innocent person. The only way to make sure of his target was to get close enough to see her clearly, which meant following them into the wood.

Quietly and cautiously he moved down the course of the stream. His dæmon the green-backed beetle flew overhead, tasting the air; her eyesight was less good than his, but her sense of smell was acute, and she caught the scent of the young people's flesh very clearly. She would go a little ahead, perch on a stem of grass and wait for him, then move on again; and as she caught the trail in the air that their bodies left behind, Father Gomez found himself praising God for his mission, because it was clearer than ever that the boy and the girl were walking into mortal sin.

And there it was: the dark-blonde movement that was the girl's hair. He moved a little closer, and took out the rifle. There was a telescopic sight: low-powered, but beautifully made, so that looking through it was to feel your vision clarified as well as enlarged. Yes, there she was, and she paused and looked back so that he saw the expression on her face, and he could not understand how anyone so steeped in evil could look so radiant with hope and happiness.

His bewilderment at that made him hesitate, and then the moment was gone, and both children had walked in among the trees and out of sight. Well, they wouldn't go far. He followed them down the stream, moving at a crouch, holding the rifle in one hand, balancing with the other.

He was so close to success now that for the first time he found himself speculating on what he would do afterwards, and whether he would please the kingdom of heaven more by going back to Geneva or staying to evangelize this world. The first thing to do here would be to convince the four-legged creatures, who seemed to have the rudiments of reason, that their habit of riding on wheels was abominable and Satanic, and contrary to the will of God. Break them of that, and salvation would follow.

He reached the foot of the slope, where the trees began, and laid the rifle down silently.

He gazed into the silver-green-gold shadows, and listened, with both hands behind his ears to catch and focus any quiet voices through the insect-chirping and the trickle of the stream. Yes: there they were. They'd stopped.

He bent to pick up the rifle –

And found himself uttering a hoarse and breathless gasp, as something clutched his dæmon and pulled her away from him.

But there was nothing there! Where was she? The pain was atrocious. He heard her crying, and cast about wildly to left and right, looking for her.

"Keep still," said a voice from the air, "and be quiet. I have your dæmon in my hand."

"But – where are you? Who are you?"

"My name is Balthamos," said the voice.

Will and Lyra followed the stream into the wood, walking carefully, saying little, until they were in the very centre.

There was a little clearing in the middle of the grove, which was floored with soft grass and moss-covered rocks. The branches laced across overhead, almost shutting out the sky and letting through little moving spangles and sequins of sunlight, so that everything was dappled with gold and silver.

And it was quiet. Only the trickle of the stream, and the occasional rustle of leaves high up in a little curl of breeze, broke the silence.

Will put down the package of food; Lyra put down her little rucksack. There was no sign of the dæmon-shadows anywhere. They were completely alone.

They took off their shoes and socks and sat down on the mossy rocks at the edge of the stream, dipping their feet in the cold water and feeling the shock of it invigorate their blood.

"I'm hungry," Will said.

"Me too," said Lyra, though she was also feeling more than that, something subdued and pressing and half-happy and half-painful, so that she wasn't quite sure what it was.

They unfolded the cloth and ate some bread and cheese. For some reason their hands were slow and clumsy, and they hardly tasted the food, although the bread was floury and crisp from the hot baking-stones, and the cheese was flaky and salty and very fresh.

Then Lyra took one of those little red fruits. With a fast-beating heart, she turned to him and said, "Will . . ."

And she lifted the fruit gently to his mouth.

She could see from his eyes that he knew at once what she meant, and that he was too joyful to speak. Her fingers were still at his lips, and he felt them tremble, and he put his own hand up to hold hers there, and then neither of them could look; they were confused; they were brimming with happiness.

Like two moths clumsily bumping together, with no more weight than that, their lips touched. Then before they knew how it happened, they were clinging together, blindly pressing their faces towards each other.

"Like Mary said –" he whispered – "you know straight away when you like someone – when you were asleep, on the mountain, before she took you away, I told Pan –"

"I heard," she whispered, "I was awake and I wanted to tell you the same and now I know what I must have felt all the time: I love you, Will, I love you –"

The word *love* set his nerves ablaze. All his body thrilled with it, and he answered her in the same words, kissing her hot face over and over again, drinking in with adoration the scent of her body and her warm honey-fragrant hair and her sweet moist mouth that tasted of the little red fruit.

Around them there was nothing but silence, as if all the world were holding its breath.

Balthamos was terrified.

He moved up the stream and away from the wood, holding the scratching, stinging, biting insect-dæmon, and trying to conceal himself as much as he could from the man who was stumbling after them.

He mustn't let him catch up. He knew that Father Gomez would kill him in a moment. An angel of his rank was no match for a man, even if that angel was strong and healthy, and Balthamos was neither of those; besides which, he was crippled by grief over Baruch and shame at having deserted Will before. He no longer even had the strength to fly.

"Stop, stop," said Father Gomez. "Please keep still. I can't see you – let's talk, please – don't hurt my dæmon, I beg you –"

In fact the dæmon was hurting Balthamos. The angel could see the little green thing dimly through the backs of his clasped hands, and she was sinking her powerful jaws again and again into his palms. If he opened his hands just for a moment, she would be gone. Balthamos kept them closed.

"This way," he said, "follow me. Come away from the wood. I want to talk to you, and this is the wrong place."

"But who are you? I can't see you. Come closer – how can I tell what you are till I see you? Keep still, don't move so quickly!"

But moving quickly was the only defence Balthamos had. Trying to ignore the stinging dæmon, he picked his way up the little gully where the stream ran, stepping from rock to rock.

Then he made a mistake: trying to look behind him, he slipped and put a foot into the water.

"Ah," came a whisper of satisfaction as Father Gomez saw the splash.

Balthamos withdrew his foot at once and hurried on – but now a wet print appeared on the dry rocks each time he put his foot down. The priest saw it, and leapt forward, and felt the brush of feathers on his hand.

He stopped in astonishment: the word *angel* reverberated in his mind. Balthamos seized the moment to stumble forward again, and the priest felt himself dragged after him, as another brutal pang wrenched his heart.

Balthamos said over his shoulder: "A little further, just to the top of the ridge, and we shall talk, I promise."

"Talk here! Stop where you are, and I swear I shan't touch you!"

The angel didn't reply: it was too hard to concentrate. He had to split his attention three ways: behind him to avoid the man, ahead to see where he was going, and on the furious dæmon tormenting his hands.

As for the priest, his mind was working quickly. A truly danger-ous opponent would have killed his dæmon at once, and ended the matter there and then: this antagonist was afraid to strike.

With that in mind, he let himself stumble, and uttered little moans of pain, and pleaded once or twice for the other to stop – all the time watching closely, moving nearer, estimating how big the other was, how quickly he could move, which way he was looking.

"Please," he said brokenly, "you don't know how much this hurts – I can't do you any harm – please can we stop and talk?"

He didn't want to move out of sight of the wood. They were now at the point where the stream began, and he could see the shape of Balthamos's feet very lightly pressing the grass. The priest had watched every inch of the way, and he was sure now where the angel was standing.

Balthamos turned round. The priest raised his eyes to the place where he thought the angel's face would be, and saw him for the first time: just a shimmer in the air, but there was no mistaking it.

He wasn't quite close enough to reach in one movement, though, and in truth the pull on his dæmon had been painful and weakening. Maybe he should take another step or two . . .

"Sit down," said Balthamos. "Sit down where you are. Not a step closer."

"What do you want?" said Father Gomez, not moving.

"What do I want? I want to kill you, but I haven't got the strength."

"But are you an angel?"

"What does it matter?"

"You might have made a mistake. We might be on the same side."

"No, we're not. I have been following you. I know whose side you're on – no, no, don't move. Stay there."

"It's not too late to repent. Even angels are allowed to do that. Let me hear your confession."

"Oh, Baruch, help me!" cried Balthamos in despair, turning away.

And as he cried out, Father Gomez leapt for him. His shoulder hit the angel's, and knocked Balthamos off balance; and in throwing out a hand to save himself, the angel let go of the insect-dæmon. The beetle flew free at once, and Father Gomez felt a surge of relief and strength. In fact, it was that which killed him, to his great surprise. He hurled himself so hard at the faint form of the angel, and he expected so much more resistance than he met, that he couldn't keep his balance. His foot slipped; his momentum carried him down towards the stream; and Balthamos, thinking of what Baruch would have done, kicked aside the priest's hand as he flung it out for support.

Father Gomez fell hard. His head cracked against a stone, and he fell stunned with his face in the water. The cold shock woke him at once, but as he choked and feebly tried to rise, Balthamos, desperate, ignored the dæmon stinging his face and his eyes and his mouth, and used all the little weight he had to hold the man's head down in the water, and he kept it there, and kept it there, and kept it there.

When the dæmon suddenly vanished, Balthamos let go. The man was dead. As soon as he was sure, Balthamos hauled the body out of the stream and laid it carefully on the grass, folding the priest's hands over his breast and closing his eyes.

Then Balthamos stood up, sick and weary and full of pain.

"Baruch," he said, "oh, Baruch, my dear, I can do no more. Will and the girl are safe, and everything will be well, but this is the end for me, though truly I died when you did, Baruch my beloved."

A moment later, he was gone.

In the beanfield, drowsy in the late afternoon heat, Mary heard Atal's voice, and she couldn't tell excitement from alarm: had another tree fallen? Had the man with the rifle appeared?

Look! Look! Atal was saying, nudging Mary's pocket with her trunk, so Mary took the spyglass and did as her friend said, pointing it up to the sky.

Tell me what it's doing! said Atal. *I can feel it is different, but I can't see.*

The terrible flood of Dust in the sky had stopped flowing. It wasn't still, by any means; Mary scanned the whole sky with the amber lens, seeing a current here, an eddy there, a vortex further off; it was in perpetual movement, but it wasn't flowing away any more. In fact, if anything, it was falling like snowflakes.

She thought of the wheel-trees: the flowers that opened upwards would be drinking in this golden rain. Mary could almost feel them welcoming it in their poor parched throats, which were so perfectly shaped for it, and which had been starved for so long.

The young ones, said Atal.

Mary turned, spyglass in hand, to see Will and Lyra returning. They were some way off; they weren't hurrying. They were holding hands, talking together, heads close, oblivious to everything else; she could see that even from a distance.

She nearly put the spyglass to her eye, but held back, and returned it to her pocket. There was no need for the glass; she knew what she would see; they would seem to be made of living gold. They would seem the true image of what human beings always could be, once they had come into their inheritance.

The Dust pouring down from the stars had found a living home again, and these children-no-longer-children, saturated with love, were the cause of it all.

36

THE BROKEN ARROW

But Fate does iron wedges drive,
And alwaies crouds it self betwixt.

— ANDREW MARVELL

THE TWO DÆMONS moved through the silent village, in and out of the shadows, padding cat-formed across the moonlit gathering-floor, pausing outside the open door of Mary's house.

Cautiously they looked inside, and saw only the sleeping woman; so they withdrew, and moved through the moonlight again, towards the shelter-tree.

Its long branches trailed their fragrant corkscrew leaves almost down to the ground. Very slowly, very careful not to rustle a leaf or snap a fallen twig, the two shapes slipped in through the leaf-curtain and saw what they were seeking: the boy and the girl, fast asleep in each other's arms.

They moved closer over the grass and touched the sleepers softly with nose, paw, whiskers, bathing in the life-giving warmth they gave off, but being infinitely careful not to wake them.

As they checked their people (gently cleaning Will's fast-healing wound, lifting the lock of hair off Lyra's face) there was a soft sound behind them.

Instantly, in total silence, both dæmons sprang round, becoming wolves: mad light eyes, bare white teeth, menace in every line.

A woman stood there, outlined by the moon. It was not Mary, and when she spoke they heard her clearly, though her voice made no sound.

"Come with me," she said.

Pantalaimon's dæmon-heart leapt within him, but he said nothing until he could greet her away from the sleepers under the tree.

"Serafina Pekkala!" he said, joyful. "Where have you been? Do you know what's happened?"

"Hush. Let's fly to a place where we can talk," she said, mindful of the sleeping villagers.

Her branch of cloud-pine lay by the door of Mary's house, and as she took it up, the two dæmons changed into birds – a nightingale, an owl – and flew with her over the thatched roofs, over the grasslands, over the ridge, and towards the nearest wheel-tree grove, as huge as a castle, its crown looking like curds of silver in the moonlight.

There Serafina Pekkala settled on the highest comfortable branch, among the open flowers drinking in the Dust, and the two birds perched nearby.

"You won't be birds for long," she said. "Very soon now your shapes will settle. Look around and take this sight into your memory."

"What will we be?" said Pantalaimon.

"You'll find out sooner than you think. Listen," said Serafina Pekkala, "and I'll tell you some witch-lore that none but witches know. The reason I can do that is that you are here with me, and your humans are down there, sleeping. Who are the only people for whom that is possible?"

"Witches," said Pantalaimon, "and shamans. So . . ."

"In leaving you both on the shores of the world of the dead, Lyra and Will did something, without knowing it, that witches have done since the first time there were witches. There's a region of our north-land, a desolate abominable place, where a great catastrophe happened in the childhood of the world, and where nothing has lived since. No dæmons can enter it. To become a witch, a girl must cross it alone and leave her dæmon behind. You know the suffering they must undergo. But having done it, they find that their dæmons were not severed, as in Bolvangar; they are still one whole being; but now they can roam free, and go to far places and see strange things and bring back knowledge.

"And you are not severed, are you?"

"No," said Pantalaimon. "We are still one. But it was so painful, and we were so frightened . . ."

"Well," said Serafina, "the two of them will not fly like witches, and they will not live as long as we do; but thanks to what they did, you and they are witch in all but that."

The two dæmons considered the strangeness of this knowledge.

"Does that mean we shall be birds, like witches' dæmons?" said Pantalaimon.

"Be patient."

"And how can Will be a witch? I thought all witches were female."

"Those two have changed many things. We are all learning new ways, even witches. But one thing hasn't changed: you must help your humans, not hinder them. You must help them and guide them and encourage them towards wisdom. That's what dæmons are for."

They were silent. Serafina turned to the nightingale and said, "What is your name?"

"I have no name. I didn't know I was born until I was torn away from his heart."

"Then I shall name you Kirjava."

"Kirjava," said Pantalaimon, trying the sound. "What does it mean?"

"Soon you will see what it means. But now," Serafina went on, "you must listen carefully, because I'm going to tell you what you should do."

"No," said Kirjava forcefully.

Serafina said gently, "I can hear from your tone that you know what I'm going to say."

"We don't want to hear it!" said Pantalaimon.

"It's too soon," said the nightingale. "It's much too soon."

Serafina was silent, because she agreed with them, and she felt sorrowful. But still she was the wisest one there, and she had to guide them to what was right; but she let their agitation subside before she went on.

"Where did you go, in your wanderings?" she said.

"Through many worlds," said Pantalaimon. "Everywhere we found a window, we went through. There are more windows than we thought."

"And you saw –"

"Yes," said Kirjava, "we looked closely, and we saw what was happening."

"We saw many other things," said Pantalaimon quickly. "We saw angels, and talked to them. We saw the world where the little people come from, the Gallivespians. There are big people there, too, who try and kill them."

They told the witch more of what they'd seen, and they were trying to distract her, and she knew it; but she let them talk, because of the love they felt for each other's voices.

But eventually they ran out of things to tell her, and they fell silent. The only sound was the gentle endless whisper of the leaves, until Serafina Pekkala said:

"You have been keeping away from Will and Lyra to punish them. I know why you're doing that; my Kaisa did just the same after I came through the desolate barrens. But he came to me eventually, because we loved each other still. And they will need you soon to help them do what has to be done next. Because you have to tell them what you know."

Pantalaimon cried aloud, a pure cold owl-cry, a sound never heard in that world before. In nests and burrows for a long way around, and wherever any small night creature was hunting or grazing or scavenging, a new and unforgettable fear came into being.

Serafina watched from close by, and felt nothing but compassion until she looked at Will's dæmon, Kirjava the nightingale. She remembered talking to the witch Ruta Skadi, who had asked, after seeing Will only once, if Serafina had looked into his eyes; and Serafina had replied that she had not dared to. This little brown bird was radiating an implacable ferocity as palpable as heat, and Serafina was afraid of it.

Finally Pantalaimon's wild screaming died away, and Kirjava said:

"And we have to tell them."

"Yes, you do," said the witch gently.

Gradually the ferocity left the gaze of the little brown bird, and Serafina could look at her again. She saw a desolate sadness in its place.

"There is a ship coming," Serafina said. "I left it to fly here and find you. I came with the gyptians, all the way from our world. They will be here in another day or so."

The two birds sat close, and in a moment they had changed their forms, becoming two doves.

Serafina went on:

"This may be the last time you fly. I can see a little ahead; I can see that you will both be able to climb this high as long as there are trees this size; but I think you will not be birds when your forms settle. Take in all that you can, and remember it well. I know that you and Lyra and Will are going to think hard and painfully, and I know you will make the best choice. But it is yours to make, and no one else's."

They didn't speak. She took her branch of cloud-pine and lifted away from the towering tree-tops, circling high above, feeling on her skin the coolness of the breeze and the tingle of the starlight and the benevolent sifting of that Dust she had never seen.

Serafina flew down to the village once more, and went silently into the woman's house. She knew nothing about Mary, except that she came from the same world as Will, and that her part in the events was crucial. Whether she was fierce or friendly, Serafina had no way of telling; but she had to wake Mary up without startling her, and there was a spell for that.

She sat on the floor at the woman's head and watched through half-closed eyes, breathing in and out in time with her. Presently her half-vision began to show her the pale forms that Mary was seeing in her dreams, and she adjusted her mind to resonate with them, as if she were tuning a string. Then with a further effort Serafina herself stepped in among them. Once she was there, she could speak to Mary, and she did so with the instant easy affection that we sometimes feel for people we meet in dreams.

A moment later they were talking together in a murmured rush of which Mary later remembered nothing, and walking through a silly landscape of reed-beds and electrical transformers. It was time for Serafina to take charge.

"In a few moments," she said, "you'll wake up. Don't be alarmed. You'll find me beside you. I'm waking you like this so you'll know it's quite safe and there's nothing to hurt you. And then we can talk properly."

She withdrew, taking the dream-Mary with her, until she found herself in the house again, cross-legged on the earthen floor, with Mary's eyes glittering as they looked at her.

"You must be the witch," Mary whispered.

"I am. My name is Serafina Pekkala. What are you called?"

"Mary Malone. I've never been woken so quietly. *Am* I awake?"

"Yes. We must talk together, and dream-talk is hard to control, and harder to remember. It's better to talk awake. Do you prefer to stay inside, or will you walk with me in the moonlight?"

"I'll come," said Mary, sitting up and stretching. "Where are Lyra and Will?"

"Asleep under the tree."

They moved out of the house and past the tree with its curtain of all-concealing leaves, and walked down to the river.

Mary watched Serafina Pekkala with a mixture of wariness and admiration: she had never seen a human form so slender and graceful. She seemed younger than Mary herself, though Lyra had said she was hundreds of years old; the only hint of age came in her expression, which was full of a complicated sadness.

They sat on the bank over the silver-black water, and Serafina told her that she had spoken to the children's dæmons.

"They went looking for them today," Mary said, "but something else happened. Will's never seen his dæmon properly, except when they escaped from the battle, and that was only for a second. He didn't know for certain that he had one."

"Well, he has. And so have you."

Mary stared at her.

"If you could see him," Serafina went on, "you would see a black bird with red legs and a bright yellow beak, slightly curved. A bird of the mountains."

"An Alpine chough . . . How can *you* see him?"

"With my eyes half-closed, I can see him. If we had time, I could teach you to see him too, and to see the dæmons of others in your world. It's strange for us to think you can't see them."

Then she told Mary what she had said to the dæmons, and what it meant.

"And the dæmons will have to tell them?" Mary said.

"I thought of waking them to tell them myself. I thought of telling you and letting you have the responsibility. But I saw their dæmons, and I knew that would be best."

"They're in love."

"I know."

"They've only just discovered it . . ."

Mary tried to take in all the implications of what Serafina had told her, but it was too hard.

After a minute or so, Mary said, "Can you see Dust?"

"No, I've never seen it. Until the wars began we had never heard of it."

Mary took the spyglass from her pocket and handed it to the witch. Serafina put it to her eye, and gasped.

"*That* is Dust . . . It's beautiful!"

"Turn to look back at the shelter-tree."

Serafina did, and exclaimed again. "*They* did this?" she said.

"Something happened today, or yesterday, if it's after midnight," Mary said, trying to find the words to explain, and remembering her vision of the Dust-flow as a great river like the Mississippi. "Something tiny but crucial . . . If you wanted to divert a mighty river into a different course, and all you had was a single pebble, you could do it, as long as you put the pebble in the right place to send the first trickle of water *that* way instead of *this*. Something like that happened yesterday. I don't know what it was. They saw each other differently, or something . . . Until then, they hadn't felt like that, but suddenly they did. And then the Dust was attracted to them, very powerfully, and it stopped flowing the other way."

"So that was how it was to happen!" said Serafina, marvelling. "And now it's safe, or it will be when the angels fill the great chasm in the underworld."

She told Mary about the abyss, and about how she herself had found out.

"I was flying high," she explained, "looking for a landfall, and I met an angel: a female angel. She was very strange; she was old and young together," she went on, forgetting that that was how she herself appeared to Mary. "Her name was Xaphania. She told me many things . . . She said that all the history of human life has been a struggle between wisdom and stupidity. She and the rebel angels, the followers of wisdom, have always tried to open minds; the Authority and his churches have always tried to keep them closed. She gave me many examples from my world."

"I can think of many from mine."

"And for most of that time, wisdom has had to work in secret, whispering her words, moving like a spy through the humble places of the world while the courts and palaces are occupied by her enemies."

"Yes," said Mary, "I recognize that too."

"And the struggle isn't over now, though the forces of the kingdom have met a setback. They'll regroup under a new commander and come back strongly, and we must be ready to resist."

"But what happened to Lord Asriel?" said Mary.

"He fought the Regent of heaven, the angel Metatron, and he wrestled him down into the abyss. Metatron is gone for ever. So is Lord Asriel."

Mary caught her breath. "And Mrs Coulter?" she said.

For answer the witch took an arrow from her quiver. She took her time selecting it: the best, the straightest, the most perfectly balanced.

And she broke it in two.

"Once in my world," she said, "I saw that woman torturing a witch, and I swore to myself that I would send that arrow into her throat. Now I shall never do that. She sacrificed herself with Lord Asriel to fight the angel, and make the world safe for Lyra. They could not have done it alone, but together they did it."

Mary, distressed, said, "How can we tell Lyra?"

"Wait until she asks," said Serafina. "And she might not. In any case, she has her symbol-reader; that will tell her anything she wants to know."

They sat in silence for a while, companionably, as the stars slowly wheeled in the sky.

"Can you see ahead, and guess what they'll choose to do?" said Mary.

"No, but if Lyra returns to her own world, then I will be her sister as long as she lives. What will you do?"

"I . . ." Mary began, and found she hadn't considered that for a moment. "I suppose I belong in my own world. Though I'll

be sorry to leave this one; I've been very happy here. The happi-
est I've ever been in my life, I think."

"Well, if you do return home, you shall have a sister in another
world," said Serafina, "and so shall I. We shall see each other
again in a day or so, when the ship arrives, and we'll talk more
on the voyage home; and then we'll part for ever. Embrace me
now, sister."

Mary did so, and Serafina Pekkala flew away on her cloud-
pine branch over the reeds, over the marshes, over the mud-flats
and the beach and over the sea, until Mary could see her no more.

At about the same time, one of the large blue lizards came across
the body of Father Gomez. Will and Lyra had returned to the
village that afternoon by a different route, and hadn't seen it; the
priest lay undisturbed where Balthamos had laid him. The lizards
were scavengers, but they were mild and harmless creatures, and
by an ancient understanding with the mulefa, they were entitled
to take any creature left dead after dark.

The lizard dragged the priest's body back to her nest, and her
children feasted very well. As for the rifle, it lay in the grass where
Father Gomez had laid it down, quietly turning to rust.

37
THE DUNES

My soul, do not seek eternal life, but exhaust the realm of the possible.

— PINDAR

NEXT DAY WILL and Lyra went out by themselves again, speaking little, eager to be alone with each other. They looked dazed, as if some happy accident had robbed them of their wits; they moved slowly; their eyes were not focused on what they looked at.

They spent all day on the wide hills, and in the heat of the afternoon they visited their gold-and-silver grove. They talked, they bathed, they ate, they kissed, they lay in a trance of happiness murmuring words whose sound was as confused as their sense, and they felt they were melting with love.

In the evening they shared the meal with Mary and Atal, saying little, and because the air was hot they thought they'd walk down to the sea, where they thought there might be a cool breeze. They wandered along the river until they came to the wide beach, bright under the moon, where the low tide was turning.

They lay down in the soft sand at the foot of the dunes, and then they heard the first bird calling.

They both turned their heads at once, because it was a bird that sounded like no creature that belonged to the world they were in. From somewhere above in the dark came a delicate trilling song, and then another answered it from a different direction. Delighted, Will and Lyra jumped up and tried to see the singers, but all they could make out was a pair of dark skimming shapes that flew low and then darted up again, all the time singing and singing in rich liquid bell-tones an endlessly varied song.

And then, with a flutter of wings that threw up a little fountain of sand in front of him, the first bird landed a few yards away.

Lyra said, "Pan – ?"

He was formed like a dove, but his colour was dark and hard to tell in the moonlight; at any rate, he showed up clearly on the white sand. The other bird still circled overhead, still singing, and then she flew down to join him: another dove, but pearl-white, and with a crest of dark red feathers.

And Will knew what it was to see his dæmon. As she flew down to the sand, he felt his heart tighten and release in a way he never forgot. Sixty years and more would go by, and as an old man he would still feel some sensations as bright and fresh as ever: Lyra's fingers putting the fruit between his lips under the gold-and-silver trees; her warm mouth pressing against his; his dæmon being torn from his unsuspecting breast as they entered the world of the dead; and the sweet rightfulness of her coming back to him at the edge of the moonlit dunes.

Lyra made to move towards them, but Pantalaimon spoke.

"Lyra," he said, "Serafina Pekkala came to us last night. She told us all kinds of things. She's gone back to guide the gyptians here. Farder Coram's coming, and Lord Faa, and they'll be here –"

"Pan," she said, distressed, "oh, Pan, you're not happy – what is it? What is it?"

Then he changed, and flowed over the sand to her as a snow-white ermine. The other dæmon changed too – Will felt it happen, like a little grip at his heart – and became a cat.

Before she moved to him, she spoke. She said, "The witch gave me a name. I had no need of one before. She called me Kirjava. But listen, listen to us now..."

"Yes, you must listen," said Pantalaimon. "This is hard to explain."

Between them, the dæmons managed to tell them everything Serafina had told them, beginning with the revelation about the children's own natures: about how without intending it, they had become like witches in their power to separate and yet still be one being.

"But that's not all," Kirjava said.

And Pantalaimon said, "Oh, Lyra, forgive us, but we have to tell you what we found out..."

Lyra was bewildered. When had Pan ever needed forgiving? She looked at Will, and saw his puzzlement as clear as her own.

"Tell us," he said. "Don't be afraid."

"It's about Dust," said the cat-dæmon, and Will marvelled to hear part of his own nature telling him something he didn't know. "It was all flowing away, all the Dust there was, down into the abyss that you saw. Something's stopped it flowing down there, but –"

"Will, it was that golden light!" Lyra said. "The light that all flowed into the abyss and vanished . . . And that was Dust? Was it really?"

"Yes. But there's more leaking out all the time," Pantalaimon went on. "And it mustn't. It's vital that it doesn't all leak away. It's got to stay in the world and not vanish, because otherwise everything good will fade away and die."

"But where's the rest leaving from?" said Lyra.

Both dæmons looked at Will, and at the knife.

"Every time we made an opening," said Kirjava, and again Will felt that little thrill: *She's me, and I'm her –* "every time anyone made an opening between the worlds, us or the old Guild men, anyone, the knife cut into the emptiness outside. The same emptiness there is down in the abyss. We never knew. No one knew, because the edge was too fine to see. But it was quite big enough for Dust to leak out of. If they closed it up again at once, there wasn't time for much to leak out, but there were thousands that they never closed up. So all this time, Dust has been leaking out of the worlds and into nothingness."

The understanding was beginning to dawn on Will and Lyra. They fought it, they pushed it away, but it was just like the grey light that seeps into the sky and extinguishes the stars: it crept past every barrier they could put up and under every blind and around the edges of every curtain they could draw against it.

"Every opening," Lyra said in a whisper.

"Every single one – they must all be closed?" said Will.

"Every single one," said Pantalaimon, whispering like Lyra.

"Oh, no," said Lyra. "No, it can't be true –"

"And so we must leave our world to stay in Lyra's," said Kirjava, "or Pan and Lyra must leave theirs and come to stay in ours. There's no other choice."

Then the full bleak daylight struck in.

And Lyra cried aloud. Pantalaimon's owl-cry the night before had frightened every small creature that heard it, but it was nothing to the passionate wail that Lyra uttered now. The dæmons were shocked, and Will, seeing their reaction, understood why: they didn't know the rest of the truth; they didn't know what Will and Lyra themselves had learnt.

Lyra was shaking with anger and grief, striding up and down with clenched fists and turning her tear-streaming face this way and that as if looking for an answer. Will jumped up and seized her shoulders, and felt her tense and trembling.

"Listen," he said, "Lyra, listen: what did my father say?"

"Oh," she cried, tossing her head this way and that, "he said – you know what he said – you were there, Will, you listened too!"

He thought she would die of her grief there and then. She flung herself into his arms and sobbed, clinging passionately to his shoulders, pressing her nails into his back and her face into his neck, and all he could hear was, "No – no – no . . ."

"Listen," he said again, "Lyra, let's try and remember it exactly. There might be a way through. There might be a loophole."

He disengaged her arms gently and made her sit down. At once Pantalaimon, frightened, flowed up on to her lap, and the cat-dæmon tentatively came close to Will. They hadn't touched yet, but now he put out a hand to her, and she moved her cat-face against his fingers and then stepped delicately on to his lap.

"He said –" Lyra began, gulping – "he said that people could spend a little time in other worlds without being affected. They could. And we have, haven't we? Apart from what we had to do to go into the world of the dead, we're still healthy, aren't we?"

"They can spend a little time, but not a long time," Will said. "My father had been away from his world, my world, for ten years. And he was nearly dying when I found him. Ten years, that's all."

"But what about Lord Boreal? Sir Charles? He was healthy enough, wasn't he?"

"Yes, but remember, he could go back to his own world whenever he liked and get healthy again. That's where you saw him first, after all, in your world. He must have found some secret window that no one else knew about."

"Well, we could do that!"

"We could, except that . . ."

"All the windows must be closed," said Pantalaimon. "All of them."

"But how do you *know*?" demanded Lyra.

"An angel told us," said Kirjava. "We met an angel. She told us all about that, and other things as well. It's true, Lyra."

"She?" said Lyra passionately, suspicious.

"It was a female angel," said Kirjava.

"I've never heard of one of them. Maybe she was lying."

Will was thinking through another possibility. "Suppose they closed all the other windows," he said, "and we just made one when we needed to, and went through as quickly as we could and closed it up immediately – that would be safe, surely? If we didn't leave much time for Dust to go out?"

"Yes!"

"We'd make it where no one could ever find it," he went on, "and only us two would know –"

"Oh, it would work! I'm sure it would!" she said.

"And we could go from one to the other, and stay healthy –"

But the dæmons were distressed, and Kirjava was murmuring, "No, no," and Pantalaimon said, "The Spectres . . . She told us about the Spectres, too."

"The Spectres?" said Will. "We saw them during the battle, for the first time. What about them?"

"Well, we found out where they come from," said Kirjava. "And this is the worst thing: they're like the children of the abyss. Every time we open a window with the knife, it makes a Spectre. It's like a little bit of the abyss that floats out and enters the world. That's why the Cittàgazze world was so full of them, because of all the windows they left open there."

"And they grow by feeding on Dust," said Pantalaimon. "And on dæmons. Because Dust and dæmons are sort of similar; grown-up dæmons anyway. And the Spectres get bigger and stronger as they do . . ."

Will felt a dull horror at his heart, and Kirjava pressed herself against his breast, feeling it too and trying to comfort him.

"So every time *I've* used the knife," he said, "every single time, I've made another Spectre come to life?"

He remembered Iorek Byrnison in the cave where he'd forged

the knife again, saying, *What you don't know is what the knife does on its own. Your intentions may be good. The knife has intentions too.*

Lyra's eyes were watching him, wide with anguish.

"Oh, we *can't*, Will!" she said. "We can't do that to people – not let other Spectres out, not now we've seen what they do!"

"All right," he said, getting to his feet, holding his dæmon close to his breast. "Then we'll have to – one of us will have to – I'll come to your world and . . ."

She knew what he was going to say, and she saw him holding the beautiful healthy dæmon he hadn't even begun to know; and she thought of his mother, and she knew that he was thinking of her too. To abandon her and live with Lyra, even for the few years they'd have together – could he do that? He might be living with Lyra, but she knew he wouldn't be able to live with himself.

"No," she cried, jumping up beside him, and Kirjava joined Pantalaimon on the sand as boy and girl clung together desperately: "*I'll* do it, Will! We'll come to your world and live there! It doesn't matter if we get ill, me and Pan – we're strong, I bet we last a good long time – and there are probably good doctors in your world – Dr Malone would know! Oh, let's do that!"

He was shaking his head, and she saw the brilliance of tears on his cheeks.

"D'you think I could bear that, Lyra?" he said. "D'you think I could live happily watching you get sick and ill and fade away and then die, while I was getting stronger and more grown-up day by day? Ten years . . . That's nothing. It'd pass in a flash. We'd be in our twenties. It's not that far ahead. Think of that, Lyra, you and me grown up, just preparing to do all the things we want to do – and then . . . it all comes to an end. Do you think I could bear to live on after you died? Oh, Lyra, I'd follow you down to the world of the dead without thinking twice about it, just like you followed Roger; and that would be two lives gone for nothing, my life wasted like yours. No, we should spend our whole lifetimes together, good long busy lives, and if we can't spend them together, we . . . we'll have to spend them apart."

Biting her lip, she watched him as he walked up and down in his distracted anguish.

He stopped and turned, and went on: "D'you remember

another thing he said, my father? He said we have to build the republic of heaven where we are. He said that for us there isn't any elsewhere. That's what he meant, I can see now. Oh, it's too bitter. I thought he just meant Lord Asriel and his new world, but he meant us, he meant you and me. We have to live in our own worlds . . ."

"I'm going to ask the alethiometer," Lyra said. "That'll know. I don't know why I didn't think of it before."

She sat down, wiping her cheeks with the palm of one hand, and reaching for the rucksack with the other. She carried it everywhere: when Will thought of her in later years, it was often with that little bag over her shoulder. She tucked the hair behind her ears in the swift movement he loved and took out the black velvet bundle.

"Can you see?" he said, for although the moon was bright, the symbols around the face were very small.

"I know where they all are," she said, "I got it off by heart. Hush now . . ."

She crossed her legs, pulling the skirt over them to make a lap. Will lay on one elbow and watched. The bright moonlight, reflected off the white sand, lit up her face with a radiance that seemed to draw out some other radiance from inside her; her eyes glittered, and her expression was so serious and absorbed that Will could have fallen in love with her again if love didn't already possess every fibre of his being.

Lyra took a deep breath and began to turn the wheels. But after only a few moments she stopped and turned the instrument around.

"Wrong place," she said briefly, and tried again.

Will, watching, saw her beloved face clearly. And because he knew it so well, and he'd studied her expression in happiness and despair and hope and sorrow, he could tell that something was wrong; for there was no sign of the clear concentration she used to sink into so quickly. Instead an unhappy bewilderment spread gradually over her: she bit her lower lip, she blinked more and more, and her eyes moved slowly from symbol to symbol, almost at random, instead of darting swiftly and certainly.

"I don't know," she said, shaking her head, "I don't know

what's happening . . . I know it so well, but I can't seem to see what it means . . ."

She took a deep shuddering breath and turned the instrument around. It looked strange and awkward in her hands. Pantalaimon, mouse-formed, crept into her lap and rested his black paws on the crystal, peering at one symbol after another. Lyra turned one wheel, turned another, turned the whole thing round, and then looked up at Will, stricken.

"Oh, Will," she cried, "I can't do it! It's left me!"

"Hush," he said, "don't fret. It's still there inside you, all that knowledge. Just be calm and let yourself find it. Don't force it. Just sort of float down to touch it . . ."

She gulped and nodded and angrily brushed her wrist across her eyes, and took several deep breaths; but he could see she was too tense, and he put his hands on her shoulders and then felt her trembling and hugged her tight. She pulled back and tried again. Once more she gazed at the symbols, once more she turned the wheels, but those invisible ladders of meaning down which she'd stepped with such ease and confidence just weren't there. She just didn't know what any of the symbols meant.

She turned away and clung to Will and said desperately:

"It's no good — I can tell — it's gone for ever — it just came when I needed it, for all the things I had to do — for rescuing Roger, and then for us two — and now it's over, now everything's finished, it's just left me . . . I was afraid of that, because it's been so difficult — I thought I couldn't see it properly, or my fingers were stiff or something, but it wasn't that at all; the power was just leaving me, it was just fading away . . . Oh, it's gone, Will! I've lost it! It'll never come back!"

She sobbed with desperate abandon. All he could do was hold her. He didn't know how to comfort her, because it was plain that she was right.

Then both the dæmons bristled, and looked up. Will and Lyra sensed it too, and followed their eyes to the sky. A light was moving towards them: a light with wings.

"It's the angel we saw," said Pantalaimon, guessing.

He guessed correctly. As the boy and the girl and the two dæmons watched her approach, Xaphania spread her wings wider, and glided down to the sand. Will, for all the time he'd spent in the company of Balthamos, wasn't prepared for the strangeness of this encounter. He and Lyra held each other's hands tightly as the angel came towards them, with the light of another world shining on her. She was unclothed, but that meant nothing: what clothes could an angel wear anyway, Lyra thought? It was impossible to tell if she was old or young, but her expression was austere and compassionate, and both Will and Lyra felt as if she knew them to their hearts.

"Will," she said, "I have come to ask your help."

"My help? How can I help you?"

"I want you to show me how to close the openings that the knife makes."

Will swallowed. "I'll show you," he said, "and in return, can you help us?"

"Not in the way you want. I can see what you've been talking about. Your sorrow has left traces in the air. This is no comfort, but believe me, every single being who knows of your dilemma wishes things could be otherwise: but there are fates that even the most powerful have to submit to. There is nothing I can do to help you change the way things are."

"Why –" Lyra began, and found her voice weak and trembling – "why can't I read the alethiometer any more? Why can't I even do that? That was the one thing I could do really well, and it's just not there any more – it just vanished as if it had never come . . ."

"You read it by grace," said Xaphania, looking at her, "and you can regain it by work."

"How long will that take?"

"A lifetime."

"That long . . ."

"But your reading will be even better then, after a lifetime of thought and effort, because it will come from conscious under-standing. Grace attained like that is deeper and fuller than grace that comes freely, and furthermore, once you've gained it, it will never leave you."

"You mean a *full* lifetime, don't you?" Lyra whispered. "A whole long life? Not . . . not just . . . a few years . . ."

"Yes, I do," said the angel.

"And *must* all the windows be closed?" said Will. "Every single one?"

"Understand this," said Xaphania: "Dust is not a constant. There's not a fixed quantity that has always been the same. Conscious beings make Dust – they renew it all the time, by thinking and feeling and reflecting, by gaining wisdom and passing it on.

"And if you help everyone else in your worlds to do that, by helping them to learn and understand about themselves and each other and the way everything works, and by showing them how to be kind instead of cruel, and patient instead of hasty, and cheerful instead of surly, and above all how to keep their minds open and free and curious ... Then they will renew enough to replace what is lost through one window. So there could be one left open."

Will trembled with excitement, and his mind leapt to a single point: to a new window in the air between his world and Lyra's. And it would be their secret, and they could go through whenever they chose, and live for a while in each other's worlds, not living fully in either, so their dæmons kept their health; and they could grow up together and maybe, much later on, they might have children who would be secret citizens of two worlds; and they could bring all the learning of one world into the other, they could do all kinds of good –

But Lyra was shaking her head.

"No," she said, in a quiet wail, "we can't, Will –"

And he suddenly knew her thought, and in the same anguished tone he said, "No, the dead –"

"We must leave it open for them! We must!"

"Yes, otherwise . . ."

"And we must make enough Dust for them, Will, and keep the window open –"

She was trembling. She felt very young as he held her to his side.

"And if we do," he said shakily, "if we live our lives properly and think about them as we do, then there'll be something to tell the harpies about, as well. We've got to tell people that, Lyra."

"For the true stories, yes," she said, "the true stories the harpies want to hear in exchange. Yes. So if people live their whole lives and they've got nothing to tell about it when they've finished, then they'll never leave the world of the dead. We've got to tell them that, Will."

"Alone, though . . ."

"Yes," she said, "alone."

And at the word *alone*, Will felt a great wave of rage and despair moving outwards from a place deep within him, as if his mind were an ocean that some profound convulsion had disturbed. All his life he'd been alone, and now he must be alone again, and this infinitely precious blessing that had come to him must be taken away almost at once. He felt the wave build higher and steeper to darken the sky, he felt the crest tremble and begin to spill, he felt the great mass crashing down with the whole weight of the ocean behind it against the iron-bound coast of what had to be. And he found himself gasping and shaking and crying aloud with more anger and pain than he had ever felt in his life, and he found Lyra just as helpless in his arms. But as the wave expended its force and the waters withdrew, the bleak rocks remained; there was no arguing with fate; neither his despair nor Lyra's had moved them a single inch.

How long his rage lasted, he had no idea. But eventually it had to subside, and the ocean was a little calmer after the convulsion. The waters were still agitated, and perhaps they would never be truly calm again, but the great force had gone.

They turned to the angel, and saw she had understood, and that she felt as sorrowful as they did. But she could see further than they could, and there was a calm hope in her expression too.

Will swallowed hard, and said, "All right. I'll show you how to close a window. But I'll have to open one first, and make another Spectre. I never knew about them, or else I'd have been more careful."

"We shall take care of the Spectres," said Xaphania.

Will took the knife, and faced the sea. To his surprise, his hands were quite steady. He cut a window into his own world, and they found themselves looking at a great factory or chemical plant, where complicated pipework ran between buildings and storage tanks, where lights glowed at every corner, where wisps of steam rose into the air.

"It's strange to think that angels don't know the way to do this," Will said.

"The knife was a human invention."

"And you're going to close them all except one," Will said. "All except the one from the world of the dead."

"Yes, that is a promise. But it is conditional, and you know the condition."

"Yes, we do. Are there many windows to close?"

"Thousands. There is the terrible abyss made by the bomb, and there is the great opening Lord Asriel made out of his own world. They must both be closed, and they will. But there are many smaller openings too, some deep under the earth, some high in the air, which came about in other ways."

"Baruch and Balthamos told me that they used openings like that to travel between the worlds. Will angels no longer be able to do that? Will you be confined to one world as we are?"

"No; we have other ways of travelling."

"The way you have," Lyra said, "is it possible for us to learn?"

"Yes. You could learn to do it, as Will's father did. It uses the faculty of what you call imagination. But that does not mean *making things up*. It is a form of seeing."

"Not *real* travelling, then," said Lyra. "Just pretend . . ."

"No," said Xaphania, "nothing like pretend. Pretending is easy. This way is hard, but much truer."

"And is it like the alethiometer?" said Will. "Does it take a whole lifetime to learn?"

"It takes long practice, yes. You have to work. Did you think you could snap your fingers, and have it as a gift? What is worth having is worth working for. But you have a friend who has already taken the first steps, and who could help you."

Will had no idea who that could be, and at that moment he wasn't in the mood to ask.

"I see," he said, sighing. "And will we see you again? Will we ever speak to an angel once we go back to our own worlds?"

"I don't know," said Xaphania. "But you should not spend your time waiting."

"And I should break the knife," said Will.

"Yes."

While they had been speaking, the window had been open beside them. The lights were glowing in the factory, the work was going on; machines were turning, chemicals were combining, people were producing goods and earning their livings. That was the world where Will belonged.

"Well, I'll show you what to do," he said.

So he taught the angel how to feel for the edges of the window, just as Giacomo Paradisi had shown him, sensing them at his fingers' ends and pinching them together. Little by little the window closed, and the factory disappeared.

"The openings that *weren't* made by the subtle knife," Will said. "Is it really necessary to close them all? Because surely Dust only escapes through the openings the knife made. The other ones must have been there for thousands of years, and still Dust exists."

The angel said, "We shall close them all, because if you thought that any still remained, you would spend your life searching for one, and that would be a waste of the time you have. You have other work than that to do, much more important and valuable, in your own world. There will be no travel outside it any more."

"What work have I got to do, then?" said Will, but went on at once, "No, on second thoughts, don't tell me. *I* shall decide what I do. If you say my work is fighting, or healing, or exploring, or whatever you might say, I'll always be thinking about it, and if I do end up doing that I'll be resentful because it'll feel as if I didn't have a choice, and if I don't do it, I'll feel guilty because I should. Whatever I do, I will choose it, no one else."

"Then you have already taken the first steps towards wisdom," said Xaphania.

"There's a light out at sea," said Lyra.

"That is the ship bringing your friends to take you home. They will be here tomorrow."

The word *tomorrow* fell like a heavy blow. Lyra had never thought she would be reluctant to see Farder Coram, and John Faa, and Serafina Pekkala.

"I shall go now," said the angel. "I have learned what I needed to know."

She embraced each of them in her light, cool arms, and kissed their foreheads. Then she bent to kiss the dæmons, and they became birds and flew up with her as she spread her wings and rose swiftly into the air. Only a few seconds later, she had vanished.

A few moments after she had gone, Lyra gave a little gasp.

"What is it?" said Will.

"I never asked her about my father and mother – and I can't ask the alethiometer, either, now . . . I wonder if I'll ever know?"

She sat down slowly, and he sat down beside her.

"Oh, Will," she said, "what can we do? Whatever can we do? I want to live with you for ever. I want to kiss you and lie down with you and wake up with you every day of my life till I die, years and years and years away. I don't want a memory, just a memory . . ."

"No," he said, "memory's a poor thing to have. It's your own real hair and mouth and arms and eyes and hands I want. I didn't know I could ever love anything so much. Oh, Lyra, I wish this night would never end! If only we could stay here like this, and the world could stop turning, and everyone else could fall into a sleep . . ."

"Everyone except us! And you and I could live here for ever and just love each other."

"I *will* love you for ever, whatever happens. Till I die and after I die, and when I find my way out of the land of the dead I'll drift about for ever, all my atoms, till I find you again . . ."

"I'll be looking for you, Will, every moment, every single moment. And when we do find each other again we'll cling together so tight that nothing and no one'll ever tear us apart. Every atom of me and every atom of you . . . We'll live in birds and flowers and dragonflies and pine trees and in clouds and in those little specks of light you see floating in sunbeams . . . And when they use our atoms to make new lives, they won't just be able to take *one*, they'll have to take two, one of you and one of me, we'll be joined so tight . . ."

They lay side by side, hand in hand, looking at the sky.

"Do you remember," she whispered, "when you first came into that café in Ci'gazze, and you'd never seen a dæmon?"

"I couldn't understand what he was. But when I saw you I liked you straight away because you were brave."

"No, I liked you first."

"You didn't! You fought me!"

"Well," she said, "yes. But you attacked me."

"I did not! You came charging out and attacked *me*."

"Yes, but I soon stopped."

"Yes, but," he mocked softly.

He felt her tremble, and then under his hands the delicate bones of her back began to rise and fall and he heard her sob quietly. He stroked her warm hair, her tender shoulders, and then he kissed her face again and again, and presently she gave a deep shuddering sigh and fell still.

The dæmons flew back down now, and changed again, and came towards them over the soft sand. Lyra sat up to greet them, and Will marvelled at the way he could instantly tell which dæmon was which, never mind what form they had. Pantalaimon was now an animal whose name he couldn't quite find: like a large and powerful ferret, red-gold in colour, lithe and sinuous and full of grace. Kirjava was a cat again. But she was a cat of no ordinary size, and her fur was lustrous and rich, with a thousand different glints and shades of ink-black, shadow-grey, the blue of a deep lake under a noon sky, mist-lavender-moonlight-fog . . . To see the meaning of the word *subtlety* you had only to look at her fur.

"A marten," he said, finding the name for Pantalaimon, "a pine-marten."

"Pan," Lyra said as he flowed up on to her lap, "you're not going to change a lot any more, are you?"

"No," he said.

"It's funny," she said, "you remember when we were younger and I didn't want you to stop changing at all . . . Well, I wouldn't mind so much now. Not if you stay like this."

Will put his hand on hers. A new mood had taken hold of him, and he felt resolute and peaceful. Knowing exactly what he was doing and exactly what it would mean, he moved his hand from Lyra's wrist and stroked the red-gold fur of her dæmon.

Lyra gasped. But her surprise was mixed with a pleasure so like the joy that flooded through her when she had put the fruit to his lips that she couldn't protest, because she was breathless. With a racing heart she responded in the same way: she put her hand on the silky warmth of Will's dæmon, and as her fingers tightened in the fur she knew that Will was feeling exactly what she was.

And she knew too that neither dæmon would change now, having felt a lover's hands on them. These were their shapes for life: they would want no other.

So, wondering whether any lovers before them had made this blissful discovery, they lay together as the earth turned slowly and the moon and stars blazed above them.

38

THE BOTANIC GARDEN

THE GYPTIANS ARRIVED on the afternoon of the following day. There was no harbour, of course, so they had to anchor the ship some way out, and John Faa, Farder Coram, and the captain came ashore in a launch with Serafina Pekkala as their guide.

Mary had told the mulefa everything she knew, and by the time the gyptians were stepping ashore on to the wide beach, there was a curious crowd waiting to greet them. Each side, of course, was on fire with curiosity about the other, but John Faa had learned plenty of courtesy and patience in his long life, and he was determined that these strangest of all people should receive nothing but grace and friendship from the Lord of the western gyptians.

So he stood in the hot sun for some time while the old zalif, Sattamax, made a speech of welcome, which Mary translated as best she could; and John Faa replied, bringing them greetings from the Fens and the waterways of his homeland.

When they began to move up through the marshes to the village, the mulefa saw how hard it was for Farder Coram to walk, and at once they offered to carry him. He accepted gratefully, and so it was that they came to the gathering-ground, where Will and Lyra came to meet them.

Such an age had gone past since Lyra had seen these dear men! They'd last spoken together in the snows of the Arctic, on their way to rescue the children from the Gobblers. She was almost shy, and she offered her hand to shake, uncertainly; but John Faa caught her up in a tight embrace and kissed both her cheeks, and Farder Coram did the same, gazing at her before folding her tight to his chest.

"She's growed up, John," he said. "Remember that little girl we took to the north-lands? Look at her now, eh! Lyra, my dear, if I had the tongue of an angel, I couldn't tell you how glad I am to set eyes on you again."

But she looks so hurt, he thought, she looks so frail and weary. And neither he nor John Faa could miss the way she stayed close to Will, and how the boy with the straight black eyebrows was aware every second of where she was, and made sure he never strayed far from her.

The old men greeted him respectfully, because Serafina Pekkala had told them something of what Will had done. For Will's part, he admired the massive power of Lord Faa's presence, power tempered by courtesy, and he thought that that would be a good way to behave when he himself was old; John Faa was a shelter and a strong refuge.

"Dr Malone," said John Faa, "we need to take on fresh water, and whatever in the way of food your friends can sell us. Besides, our men have been on board ship for a fair while, and we've had some fighting to do, and it would be a blessing if they could all have a run ashore so they can breathe the air of this land and tell their families at home about the world they voyaged to."

"Lord Faa," said Mary, "the mulefa have asked me to say they will supply everything you need, and that they would be honoured if you could all join them this evening to share their meal."

"It'll be our great pleasure to accept," said John Faa.

So that evening the people of three worlds sat down together and shared bread and meat and fruit and wine. The gyptians presented their hosts with gifts from all the corners of their world: with crocks of genniver, carvings of walrus ivory, silken tapestries from Turkestan, cups of silver from the mines of Sveden, enamelled dishes from Corea.

The mulefa received them with delight, and in return offered objects of their own workmanship: rare vessels of ancient knot-wood, lengths of the finest rope and cord, lacquered bowls, and fishing nets so strong and light that even the Fen-dwelling gyptians had never seen the like.

Having shared the feast, the captain thanked his hosts and left to supervise the crew as they took on board the stores and water that they needed, because they meant to sail as soon as morning came. While they were doing that, the old zalif said to his guests:

A great change has come over everything. And as a token, we have been granted a responsibility. We would like to show you what this means.

So John Faa, Farder Coram, Mary and Serafina went with them to the place where the land of the dead opened, and where the ghosts were coming out, still in their endless procession. The mulefa were planting a grove around it, because it was a holy place, they said; they would maintain it for ever; it was a source of joy.

"Well, this is a mystery," said Farder Coram, "and I'm glad I lived long enough to see it. To go into the dark of death is a thing we all fear, say what we like, we fear it. But if there's a way out for that part of us that has to go down there, then it makes my heart lighter."

"You're right, Coram," said John Faa. "I've seen a good many folk die; I've sent more than a few men down into the dark myself, though it was always in the anger of battle. To know that after a spell in the dark we'll come out again to a sweet land like this, to be free of the sky like the birds, well, that's the greatest promise anyone could wish for."

"We must talk to Lyra about this," said Farder Coram, "and learn how it came about, and what it means."

Mary found it very hard to say goodbye to Atal and the other mulefa. Before she boarded the ship, they gave her a gift: a lacquer phial containing some of the wheel-tree oil, and most precious of all, a little bag of seeds.

They might not grow in your world, Atal said, *but if not, you have the oil. Don't forget us, Mary.*

Never, Mary said. *Never. If I live as long as the witches and forget everything else, I'll never forget you and the kindness of your people, Atal.*

So the journey home began. The wind was light, the seas were calm, and although they saw the glitter of those great snow-white wings more than once, the birds were wary, and stayed well clear. Will and Lyra spent every hour together, and for them the two weeks of the voyage passed like the blink of an eyelid.

Xaphania had told Serafina Pekkala that when all the openings were closed, then the worlds would all be restored to their proper relations with one another, and Lyra's Oxford and Will's would lie over each other again, like transparent images on two sheets of film being moved closer and closer until they merged; although they would never truly touch.

At the moment, however, they were a long way apart – as far as Lyra had had to travel from her Oxford to Cittàgazze. Will's Oxford was here now, just a knife-cut away. It was evening when they arrived, and as the anchor splashed into the water, the late sun lay warmly on the green hills, the terracotta roofs, that elegant crumbling waterfront and Will and Lyra's little café. A long search through the captain's telescope had shown no signs of life whatsoever, but John Faa planned to take half a dozen armed men ashore just in case. They wouldn't get in the way, but they were there if they were needed.

They ate a last meal together, watching the darkness fall. Will said goodbye to the captain and his officers, and to John Faa and Farder Coram. He had hardly seemed to be aware of them, and they saw him more clearly than he saw them: they saw someone young, but very strong, and deeply stricken.

Finally Will and Lyra and their dæmons, and Mary and Serafina Pekkala, set off through the empty city. And it was empty; the only footfalls and the only shadows were their own. Lyra and Will went ahead, hand in hand, to the place where they had to part, and the women stayed some way behind, talking like sisters.

"Lyra wants to come a little way into my Oxford," Mary said. "She's got something in mind. She'll come straight back afterwards."

"What will you do, Mary?"

"Me – go with Will, of course. We'll go to my flat – my house – tonight, and then tomorrow we'll go and find out where his mother is, and see what we can do to help her get better. There are so many rules and regulations in my world, Serafina; you have to satisfy the authorities and answer a thousand questions; I'll help him with all the legal side of things and the social services and housing and all that, and let him concentrate on his mother.

He's a strong boy ... But I'll help him. Besides, I *need* him. I haven't got a job any more, and not much money in the bank, and I wouldn't be surprised if the police are after me ... He'll be the only person in my whole world that I can talk to about all this."

They walked on through the silent streets, past a square tower with a doorway opening into darkness, past a little café where tables stood on the pavement, and out on to a broad boulevard with a line of palm trees in the centre.

"This is where I came through," said Mary.

The window Will had first seen in the quiet suburban road in Oxford opened here, and on the Oxford side it was guarded by police – or had been when Mary tricked them into letting her through. She saw Will reach the spot and move his hands deftly in the air, and the window vanished.

"That'll surprise them next time they look," she said.

It was Lyra's intention to go into Mary's Oxford and show Will something before returning with Serafina, and obviously they had to be careful where they cut through; so the women followed on behind, through the moonlit streets of Cittàgazze. On their right a wide and graceful parkland led up to a great house with a classical portico as brilliant as icing-sugar under the moon.

"When you told me the shape of my dæmon," Mary said, "you said you could teach me how to see him, if we had time ... I wish we had."

"Well, we have had time," Serafina said, "and haven't we been talking? I've taught you some witch-lore, which would be forbidden under the old ways in my world. But you are going back to your world, and the old ways have changed. And I too have learned much from you. Now then: when you spoke to the Shadows on your computer, you had to hold a special state of mind, didn't you?"

"Yes ... just as Lyra did with the alethiometer. Do you mean if I try that?"

"Not only that, but ordinary seeing at the same time. Try it now."

In Mary's world they had a kind of picture which looked at

first like random dots of colour, but which, when you looked at it in a certain way, seemed to advance into three dimensions: and there in front of the paper would be a tree, or a face, or something else surprisingly solid that simply wasn't there before.

What Serafina taught Mary to do now was similar to that. She had to hold on to her normal way of looking while simultaneously slipping into the trance-like open dreaming in which she could see the Shadows. But now she had to hold both ways together, the everyday and the trance, just as you have to look in two directions at once to see the 3D pictures among the dots.

And just as it happens with the dot-pictures, she suddenly got it.

"Ah!" she cried, and reached for Serafina's arm to steady herself, for there on the iron fence around the parkland sat a bird: glossy-black, with red legs and a curved yellow bill: an Alpine chough, just as Serafina had described. It – he – was only a foot or two away, watching her with his head slightly cocked, for all the world as though he was amused.

But she was so surprised that her concentration slipped, and he vanished.

"You've done it once, and next time it will be easier," Serafina said. "When you are in your world, you will learn to see the dæmons of other people too, in the same way. They won't see yours or Will's, though, unless you teach them as I've taught you."

"Yes . . . Oh, this is extraordinary. Yes!"

Mary thought: Lyra talked to her dæmon, didn't she? Would she hear this bird as well as see him? She walked on, glowing with anticipation.

Ahead of them, Will was cutting a window, and he and Lyra waited for the women so that he could close it again.

"D'you know where we are?" Will said.

Mary looked around. The road they were in now, in her world, was quiet and tree-lined, with big Victorian houses in shrub-filled gardens.

"Somewhere in north Oxford," Mary said. "Not far from my flat, as a matter of fact, though I don't know exactly which road this is."

"I want to go to the Botanic Garden," Lyra said.

"All right. I suppose that's about fifteen minutes' walk. This way . . ."

Mary tried the double-seeing again. She found it easier this time, and there was the chough, with her in her own world, perching on a branch that hung low over the pavement. To see what would happen, she held out her hand, and he stepped on to it without hesitation. She felt the slight weight, the tight grip of the claws on her finger, and gently moved him on to her shoulder. He settled into place as if he'd been there all her life.

Well, he has, she thought, and moved on.

There was not much traffic in the High Street, and when they turned down the steps opposite Magdalen College towards the gate of the Botanic Garden they were completely alone. There was an ornate gateway, with stone seats inside it, and while Mary and Serafina sat there, Will and Lyra climbed over the iron fence into the garden itself. Their dæmons slipped through the bars, and flowed ahead of them into the garden.

"It's this way," said Lyra, tugging at Will's hand.

She led him past a pool with a fountain under a wide-spreading tree, and then struck off to the left between beds of plants towards a huge many-trunked pine. There was a massive stone wall with a doorway in it, and in the further part of the garden the trees were younger and the planting less formal. Lyra led him almost to the end of the garden, over a little bridge, to a wooden seat under a spreading low-branched tree.

"Yes!" she said. "I hoped so much, and here it is, just the same . . . Will, I used to come here in *my* Oxford and sit on this exact same bench whenever I wanted to be alone, just me and Pan. What I thought was that if you – maybe just once a year – if we could come here at the same time, just for an hour or something, then we could pretend we were close again – because we *would* be close, if you sat here and I sat just *here* in my world –"

"Yes," he said, "as long as I live, I'll come back. Wherever I am in the world I'll come back here –"

"On Midsummer's Day," she said. "At midday. As long as I live. As long as I live . . ."

He found himself unable to see, but he let the hot tears flow and just held her close.

"And if we – later on –" she was whispering shakily – "if we meet someone that we like, and if we marry them, then we must be good to them, and not make comparisons all the time and wish we were married to each other instead ... But just keep up this coming here once a year, just for an hour, just to be together..."

They held each other tightly. Minutes passed; a water-bird on the river beside them stirred and called; the occasional car moved over Magdalen Bridge.

Finally they drew apart.

"Well," said Lyra softly.

Everything about her in that moment was soft; and that was one of his favourite memories later on – her tense grace made tender by the dimness, her eyes and hands and especially her lips, infinitely soft. He kissed her again and again, and each kiss was nearer to the last one of all.

Heavy and soft with love, they walked back to the gate. Mary and Serafina were waiting.

"Lyra –" Will said, and she said, "Will."

He cut a window into Cittàgazze. They were deep in the parkland around the great house, not far from the edge of the forest. They stepped through for the last time, and looked down over the silent city, the tiled roofs gleaming in the moonlight, the tower above them, the lighted ship waiting out on the still sea.

Will turned to Serafina and said as steadily as he could, "Thank you, Serafina Pekkala, for rescuing us at the belvedere, and for everything else. Please be kind to Lyra for as long as she lives. I love her more than anyone has ever been loved."

In answer the witch-queen kissed him on both cheeks. Lyra had been whispering to Mary, and then they too embraced, and first Mary and then Will stepped through the last window, back into their own world, in the shade of the trees of the Botanic Garden.

Being cheerful starts *now*, Will thought as hard as he could, but it was like trying to hold a fighting wolf still in his arms when it wanted to claw at his face and tear out his throat; nevertheless he did it, and he thought no one could see the effort it cost him.

And he knew that Lyra was doing the same, and that the tightness and strain in her smile were the sign of it.

Nevertheless, she smiled.

One last kiss, rushed and clumsy so that they banged cheek-bones, and a tear from her eye was transferred to his face; their two dæmons kissed farewell, and Pantalaimon flowed over the threshold and up into Lyra's arms; and then Will began to close the window, and then it was done, the way was closed, Lyra was gone.

"Now —" he said, trying to sound matter-of-fact, but having to turn away from Mary all the same — "I've got to break the knife."

He searched the air in the familiar way until he found a gap, and tried to bring to mind just what had happened before. He had been about to cut a way out of the cave, and Mrs Coulter had suddenly and unaccountably reminded him of his mother, and the knife had broken because, he thought, it had at last met something it couldn't cut, and that was his love for her.

So he tried it now, summoning an image of his mother's face as he'd last seen her, fearful and distracted in Mrs Cooper's little hallway.

But it didn't work. The knife cut easily through the air, and opened into a world where they were having a rainstorm: heavy drops hurtled through, startling them both. He closed it again quickly, and stood puzzled for a moment.

His dæmon knew what he should do, and said simply, "Lyra."

Of course. He nodded, and with the knife in his right hand, he pressed with his left the spot where her tear still lay on his cheek.

And this time, with a wrenching crack, the knife shattered and the blade fell in pieces to the ground, to glitter on the stones that were still wet with the rain of another universe.

Will knelt to pick them up carefully, Kirjava with her cat-eyes helping to find them all.

Mary was shouldering her rucksack.

"Well," she said, "well, listen now, Will. We've hardly spoken, you and I . . . So we're still strangers, largely. But Serafina Pekkala and I made a promise to each other, and I made a promise to Lyra just now, and even if I hadn't made any other promises I'd make a promise to you about the same thing, which is that if you'll let me, I'll be your friend for the rest of our lives. We're both on our own, and I reckon we could both do with that sort of . . . What I mean to say is, there isn't anyone else we can talk to about all this, except each other . . . And we've both got to get used to living with our dæmons, too . . . And we're both in trouble, and if *that* doesn't give us something in common I don't know what will."

"You're in trouble?" said Will, looking at her. Her open, friendly, clever face looked back directly.

"Well, I smashed up some property in the lab before I left, and I forged an identity card, and . . . It's nothing we can't deal with. And your trouble – we can deal with that too. We can find your mother and get her some proper treatment. And if you need somewhere to live, well, if you wouldn't mind living with me, if we can arrange that, then you won't have to go into, whatever they call it, into care. I mean, we'll have to decide on a story and stick to it, but we could do that, couldn't we?"

Mary was a friend. He had a friend. It was true. He'd never thought of that.

"Yes!" he said.

"Well, let's do it. My flat's about half a mile away, and you know what I'd like most of all in the world? I'd like a cup of tea. Come on, let's go and put the kettle on."

Three weeks after the moment Lyra had watched Will's hand closing his world away for ever, she found herself seated once more at that dinner table in Jordan College where she had first fallen under the spell of Mrs Coulter.

This time it was a smaller party: just herself and the Master and Dame Hannah Relf, the head of St Sophia's, one of the women's colleges. Dame Hannah had been at that first dinner, too, and if Lyra was surprised to see her here now, she greeted her politely, and found that her memory was at fault: for this Dame Hannah was much cleverer, and more interesting, and kindlier by far than the dim and frumpy person she remembered.

All kinds of things had happened while Lyra was away – to Jordan College, to England, to the whole world. It seemed that the power of the Church had increased greatly, and that many brutal laws had been passed, but that the power had waned as quickly as it had grown: upheavals in the Magisterium had toppled the zealots and brought more liberal factions into power. The General Oblation Board had been dissolved; the Consistorial Court of Discipline was confused and leaderless.

And the colleges of Oxford, after a brief and turbulent interlude, were settling back into the calm of scholarship and ritual. Some things had gone: the Master's valuable collection of silver had been looted; some college servants had vanished. The Master's manservant, Cousins, was still in place, however, and Lyra had been ready to meet his hostility with defiance, for they had been enemies as long as she could remember. She was quite taken aback when he greeted her so warmly and shook her hand with both of his: was that affection in his voice? Well, he *had* changed.

During dinner the Master and Dame Hannah talked of what had happened in Lyra's absence, and she listened in dismay, or sorrow, or wonder. When they withdrew to his sitting-room for coffee, the Master said:

"Now, Lyra, we've hardly heard from you. But I know you've seen many things. Are you able to tell us something of what you've experienced?"

"Yes," she said. "But not all at once. I don't understand some of it, and some makes me shudder and cry still; but I will tell you, I promise, as much as I can. Only you have to promise something too."

The Master looked at the grey-haired lady with the marmoset-dæmon in her lap, and a flicker of amusement passed between them.

"What's that?" said Dame Hannah.

"You have to promise to believe me," Lyra said seriously. "I know I haven't always told the truth, and I could only *survive* in some places by telling lies and making up stories. So I know that's what I've been like, and I know you know it, but my true story's too important for me to tell if you're only going to believe half of it. So I promise to tell the truth, if you promise to believe it."

"Well, I promise," said Dame Hannah, and the Master said, "And so do I."

"But you know the thing I wish," Lyra said, "almost – *almost* more than anything else? I wish I hadn't lost the way of reading the alethiometer. Oh, it was so strange, Master, how it came in the first place and then just left! One day I knew it so well – I could move up and down the symbol-meanings and step from one to another and make all the connections – it was like ..." She smiled, and went on, "Well, I was like a monkey in the trees, it was so quick. Then suddenly – nothing. None of it made sense; I couldn't even remember anything except just basic meanings like the anchor means hope and the skull means death. All those thousands of meanings ... Gone."

"They're not gone, though, Lyra," said Dame Hannah. "The books are still in Bodley's Library. The scholarship to study them is alive and well."

Dame Hannah was sitting opposite the Master in one of the two armchairs beside the fireplace, Lyra on the sofa between them. The lamp by the Master's chair was all the light there was, but it showed the expressions of the two old people clearly. And it was Dame Hannah's face that Lyra found herself studying. Kindly, Lyra thought, and sharp, and wise; but she could no more read what it meant than she could read the alethiometer.

"Well now," the Master went on. "We must think about your future, Lyra."

His words made her shiver. She gathered herself and sat up.

"All the time I was away," Lyra said, "I never thought about that. All I thought about was just the time I was in, just the present. There were plenty of times when I thought I didn't have a future at all. And now ... Well, suddenly finding I've got a whole life to live, but no ... but no idea what to do with it, well, it's like having the alethiometer but no idea how to read it. I suppose I'll have to work, but I don't know at what. My parents are probably rich but I bet they never thought of putting any money aside for me, and anyway I think they must have used all their money up one way or another by now, so even if I did have a claim on it, there wouldn't be any left. I don't know, Master. I came back to Jordan because this used to be my home, and I didn't have anywhere else to go. I think King Iorek Byrnison would let me live on Svalbard, and I think Serafina Pekkala would let me live with her witch-clan; but I'm not a bear and I'm not a witch, so I wouldn't really fit in there, much as I love them. Maybe the gyptians would take me in … But really I don't know what to do any more. I'm lost, really, now."

They looked at her: her eyes were glittering more than usual, her chin was held high with a look she'd learned from Will without knowing it. She looked defiant as well as lost, Dame Hannah thought, and admired her for it; and the Master saw something else – he saw how the child's unconscious grace had gone, and how she was awkward in her growing body. But he loved the girl dearly, and he felt half proud and half in awe of the beautiful adult she would be, so soon.

He said, "You will never be lost while this college is standing, Lyra. This is your home for as long as you need it. As for money – your father made over an endowment to care for all your needs, and appointed me executor; so you needn't worry about that."

In fact Lord Asriel had done nothing of the sort, but Jordan College was rich, and the Master had money of his own, even after the recent upheavals.

"No," he went on, "I was thinking about learning. You're still very young, and your education until now has depended on … Well, quite frankly, on which of our scholars you intimidated least," he said, but he was smiling. "It's been haphazard. Now it may turn out that in due course your talents will take you in a direction we can't foresee at all. But if you were to make the alethiometer the subject of your life's work, and set out to learn consciously what you could once do by intuition –"

"Yes," said Lyra, definitely.

"– then you could hardly do better than put yourself in the hands of my good friend Dame Hannah. Her scholarship in that field is unmatched."

"Let me make a suggestion," said the lady, "and you needn't respond now. Think about it for a while. Now my college is not as old as Jordan, and you're too young yet to become an undergraduate in any case, but a few years ago we acquired a large house in north Oxford, and we decided to set up a boarding school. I'd like you to come and meet the Headmistress and see whether you'd care to become one of our pupils. You see, one thing you'll need soon, Lyra, is the friendship of other girls of your age. There are things that we learn from one another when we're young, and I don't think that Jordan can provide quite all of them. The Headmistress is a clever young woman, energetic, imaginative, kindly. We're lucky to have her. You can talk to her, and if you like the idea, come and make St Sophia's your school, as Jordan is your home. And if you'd like to begin studying the alethiometer systematically, you and I could meet for some private lessons. But there's time, my dear, there's plenty of time. Don't answer me now. Leave it until you're ready."

"Thank you," said Lyra, "thank you, Dame Hannah, I will."

The Master had given Lyra her own key to the garden door, so she could come and go as she pleased. Later that night, just as the porter was locking the lodge, she and Pantalaimon slipped out and made their way through the dark streets, hearing all the bells of Oxford chiming midnight.

Once they were in the Botanic Garden, Pan ran away over the grass chasing a mouse towards the wall, and then let it go and sprang up into the huge pine tree nearby. It was delightful to see him leaping through the branches so far from her, but they had to be careful not to do it when anyone was looking; their painfully-acquired witch-power of separating had to stay a secret. Once, she would have revelled in showing it off to all her urchin friends, and making them goggle with fear, but Will had taught her the value of silence and discretion.

She sat on the bench and waited for Pan to come to her. He liked to surprise her, but she usually managed to see him before he reached her, and there was his shadowy form, flowing along beside the river bank. She looked the other way and pretended she hadn't seen him, and then seized him suddenly when he leapt on to the bench.

"I nearly did it," he said.

"You'll have to get better than that. I heard you coming all the way from the gate."

He sat on the back of the bench with his forepaws resting on her shoulder.

"What are we going to tell her?" he said.

"We'll say yes," she said. "It's only to meet this Headmistress, anyway. It's not to go to the school."

"But we will go, won't we?"

"Yes," she said, "probably."

"It might be good."

Lyra wondered about the other pupils. They might be cleverer than she was, or more sophisticated, and they were sure to know a lot more than she did about all the things that were important to girls of their age. And she wouldn't be able to tell them a hundredth of the things that she knew. They'd be bound to think she was simple and ignorant.

"D'you think Dame Hannah can really do the alethiometer?" said Pantalaimon.

"With the books, I'm sure she can. I wonder how many books there are? I bet we could learn them all, and do without. Imagine having to carry a pile of books everywhere ... Pan?"

"What?"

"Will you ever tell me what you and Will's dæmon did, when we were apart?"

"One day," he said. "And she'll tell Will, one day. We agreed that we'd know when the time had come, but we wouldn't tell either of you till then."

"All right," she said peaceably.

She had told Pantalaimon everything, but it was right that he should have some secrets from her, after the way she'd abandoned him.

And it was comforting to think that she and Will had another thing in common. She wondered whether there would ever come an hour in her life when she didn't think of him; didn't speak to him in her head, didn't relive every moment they'd been together, didn't long for his voice and his hands and his love. She had never dreamed of what it would feel like to love someone so much; of all the things that had astonished her in her adventures, that was what astonished her the most. She thought the tenderness it left in her heart was like a bruise that would never go away, but she would cherish it for ever.

Pan slipped down to the bench and curled up on her lap. They were safe together in the dark, she and her dæmon and their secrets. Somewhere in this sleeping city were the books that would tell her how to read the alethiometer again, and the kindly and learned woman who was going to teach her, and the girls at the school, who knew so much more than she did.

She thought: they don't know it yet, but they're going to be my friends.

Pantalaimon murmured, "That thing that Will said . . ."

"When?"

"On the beach, just before you tried the alethiometer. He said there wasn't any elsewhere. It was what his father had told you. But there was something else."

"I remember. He meant the kingdom was over, the kingdom of heaven, it was all finished. We shouldn't live as if it mattered more than this life in this world, because where we are is always the most important place."

"He said we had to build something . . ."

"That's why we needed our full life, Pan. We *would* have gone with Will and Kirjava, wouldn't we?"

"Yes. Of course! And they would have come with us. But –"

"But then we wouldn't have been able to build it. No one could, if they put themselves first. We have to be all those difficult things like cheerful and kind and curious and brave and patient, and we've got to study and think, and work hard, all of us, in all our different worlds, and then we'll build . . ."

Her hands were resting on his glossy fur. Somewhere in the garden a nightingale was singing, and a little breeze touched her hair and stirred the leaves overhead. All the different bells of the city chimed, once each, this one high, that one low, some close by, others further off, one cracked and peevish, another grave and sonorous, but agreeing in all their different voices on what the time was, even if some of them got to it a little more slowly than others. In that other Oxford where she and Will had kissed goodbye, the bells would be chiming too, and a nightingale would be singing, and a little breeze would be stirring the leaves in the Botanic Garden.

"And then what?" said her dæmon sleepily. "Build what?"

"The republic of heaven," said Lyra.

LANTERN
SLIDES

MARY thought the mulefa had no history, but that was because the history she'd been taught in school was about politics, the clash of nation states, the rise and fall of empires. In her time among the mulefa she learned about a different kind of history. They had forgotten nothing they'd ever known, and such things as the story of the great storm of fifteen thousand years before, or the discovery of the cord-fibre plant, or the week-long ride of the one survivor of the south shore earthquake nursing his broken wheel as he had to cross country to keep out of the floods, were all the subject of lengthy and complex recital, embroidered and counterpointed by the teller and the listeners jointly. Mary was not with them for long enough to discover whether they had any concept of fiction – or whether, indeed, those tales were remembered or invented.

KENDAL MINT CAKE, and the delicate fastidious curiosity of Balthamos as he nibbled the edge of it. For the rest of his life, the taste of sugared peppermint brought that picture back to Will's mind, and he was there again beside the smoky little fire with the stream splashing in the darkness nearby.

IN LYRA'S WORLD dæmons, in the world of the mulefa the oil-bearing wheels – both ways of making the workings of Dust apparent. In our world, what?

AGAIN, WILL, LATER: the sense his hand and mind had learned together as the point of the knife searched among the tiniest particles of the air, the sense of feeling without touching, of knowing without spoiling, of apprehending without calculating. He never lost it. When he was a medical student, he had to pretend to make a wrong diagnosis occasionally: his success was in danger of looking supernatural. Once he was qualified, it became safer to go straight to the right answer. And then began the lifelong process of learning to explain it.

MARY, absorbed and happy as she fooled around with the lacquer to make her spyglass; fooling around was something she'd never been able to explain to her colleague Oliver Payne, who needed to know where he was going before he got there. Back in Oxford, she gave three of her precious wheel-tree seeds to a scientist at the Botanic Garden, a nice man who understood the importance of fooling around. The seedlings are growing well, but she refuses to tell him where they came from.

ON THE BEACH, the alethiometer suddenly inert in Lyra's hands, as if it had abandoned her.

AN INFINITY of silvery greens and gold-sand-browns, the whispering of grass in the warm wind. Safety, sunlight.

MRS COULTER in the cave, watching Will, speculating; Will watching her, speculating. Their words like chess pieces, placed with great care, each carrying an invisible nimbus of implication and possibility and threat. Both afterwards felt as if they had barely escaped with their life.